THOMAS HARDY

LIBRARY OF ESSENTIAL WRITERS

THOMAS
HARDY

◆

FIVE NOVELS

◆

COMPLETE AND UNABRIDGED

Far from the Madding Crowd • The Return of
the Native • The Mayor of Casterbridge •
Tess of the d'Urbervilles • Jude the Obscure

BARNES & NOBLE
NEW YORK

Contents

INTRODUCTION

THOMAS HARDY, POET AND NOVELIST, IS ONE OF THE MOST FAMOUS WRITERS IN ENglish literature. His work was popular in his time and continues to be widely read and studied. Although his novels fall neatly into the Victorian era, his status as a Victorian writer is an uneasy one, not owing to historical chronology, but to the tension between what he wrote and the Victorian culture in which he flourished. His fiction anticipates the work of James Joyce, Virginia Woolf, and other stylistically innovative modernists who represent the end of Victorian culture's grip on artistic ideals. At the same time, it captures the tensions beneath the surface of Victorian society. Victorian England placed high value on decorum and restraint, maintaining a public *façade* that covered up any corruption and passion. Hardy's work went deep into the makeup of his world, exemplifying a thinly veiled criticism within the public framework.

Thomas Hardy was born in rural Dorset on June 2, 1840. Both his father and his grandfather were stonemasons. Hardy was given a classical education early at school in Dorchester, and at sixteen he was apprenticed to an architect. At twenty-one he found work in London with the architect Arthur Blomfield, primarily restoring churches. A prosperous career path stretched before him, but Hardy was also restless. He became intrigued by art and literature in London and during this time he began to write poetry, his first love in literature. He also gradually began to lose faith in organized religion, a crisis that would resonate through much of his future writing. When he was twenty-seven, he left London and returned to Dorset to work for the architect John Hicks. He also started to write fiction, producing a novel that was rejected by publishers. Receiving some encouragement, however, Hardy went to work on his next novel, *Desperate Remedies,* which was published anonymously in 1871, but did not do well. Hardy contemplated abandoning writing, but he married Emma Gifford in 1874, and ironically, given the coldness of their marriage, Emma's encouragement kept him writing. He published *Under the Greenwood Tree* in 1872 and *A Pair of Blue Eyes* serially between 1872 and 1873. *Far from the Madding Crowd,* published in 1874, earned him critical acclaim and with the publication of subsequent novels he became one of the most popular writers of his generation.

Much of Hardy's fiction is set in Wessex, a world that is just as sure and tangible as Joyce's Dublin, Woolf's London, and Faulkner's Yoknapatawpha County. Based on the Dorset countryside he knew so well, it is a place at once comfortable because of its verisimilitude. One can draw Hardy's Wessex on a map, trace the lines of travel of his main characters, and pinpoint the rolling hills and green countryside. Like many modernists, Hardy examined the universal by focusing on the individual and his or her role in a particular setting. Dickens, that other great critic of Victorian values, went to the front lines of industrialization—the manufacturing cities and the ghettos it spawned.

Dickens painted his scenes on a broad canvas, using exaggeration to pose the proposition that 'if we continue, this will be the result." His characters were often allegorical, recognizable types whose hyperbolic mannerisms caused them to be spotted easily for what they were. Hardy worked in more subtle ways, placing his rural setting under a microscope and deftly dissecting his characters to explore modernization, fate, and class and how these joined to erode the dignified lives of rural peoples. His wariness of rampant modernization is clear in his Wessex novels as his characters are continually oppressed by the rapidly evolving world around them. Despite their struggles, however, their lives are honorable, something that cannot be said for those of a higher social class. Hardy attacks the notion that upper class equals greater nobility. The Wessex novels are portraits of a fading life, threatened on various fronts, and Hardy's characters are reminders of values being lost.

The struggles of Hardy's heroes and heroines are the emotional centers of his stories. His people feel, and they feel deeply. Fate, whether expressed by the untimely disaster Gabriel Oak experiences in *Far From the Madding Crowd*, or by the cruelty society inflicts on Jude in *Jude the Obscure* and on Tess in *Tess of the d'Urbervilles*, is a force that flings Hardy's characters about mercilessly. Yet they endure and often are ennobled by their unshakeable resolve to simply go on. Shaped by the landscape, they are living, breathing, characters who make us care about them, and whose perseverance sparks our empathy.

In *Far from the Madding Crowd* (1874), fate, a power that cannot be tamed, manifests itself when Gabriel Oak's rural life is upset by the bizarre killing of his sheep. This tragedy is a wonderful metaphor for the havoc caused by rampant modernization. The old ways are dying, and Oak can either endure or fade away. The past, always with a strong hold on Wessex, is becoming obsolete as the "new" world imposes new ways of life. Oak ultimately adapts and even eventually prospers. His plight is intensified in the woman he loves, Bathsheba Everdene. Two men of higher "class" fall in love with her, both with secrets that betray their dignified exteriors. This sudden foray into the new world of "status" upsets her life, and she makes some ultimately tragic choices. In the end, Gabriel, the man of simple integrity who survives the ravages of a changing culture, gains Bathsheba's hand.

In *The Return of the Native* (1878), Clym Yeobright's desire to better his native country by starting a school for rural children is dashed by romantic entanglements. His motives are noble, yet he cannot escape from the upwardly mobile ambitions of those around him. Eustacia Vye, the woman whom Clym loves and marries, cannot accept his wishes for the school; it is simply not enough for her. She, like others, needs more, a more defined by status. Although Clym cannot escape tragedy at the need, just as his beloved home cannot hide from the destruction of Victorian modernization, he is able to maintain his own integrity.

Hardy called Michael Henchard in *The Mayor of Casterbridge* (1886) a "man of character." This description appears odd on first consideration. Can a man who sells his wife and daughter, who shuns his daughter after being reunited with her two decades later, who destroys his business because of jealousy, and whose dying wish is not to be remembered be singled out as a man of character? In Hardy's Wessex, however, Henchard's nobility stems from his will to keep living despite the retribution fate brings down on him. He will not allow himself to be crushed completely. He accepts that he has sinned and deserves punishment, but he does not let the punishment keep him from enduring.

Henchard has an uneasy relationship with his society. Like many manufacturers of the day, he succeeds in business, but money cannot soothe his soul. Status and economic power do not bring meaning to his life. The ever-changing modern world is especially cruel to Henchard, yet he continues to love and feel and live. He learns from his mistakes and finds what is truly meaningful in his relationships with others. He may request not to be remembered after death, but Hardy clearly intends for his readers to take special note of Henchard's "character." For Hardy, real fortitude is not found in simple purity; rather, it arises out of great struggle. In *The Mayor of Casterbridge*, a "man of value" is not one who always does the right thing; he is one who acknowledges fault, accepts punishment, and still has the will power to continue.

Tess of the d'Urbervilles (1891), perhaps Hardy's most controversial book at the time of publication, scathingly attacks the unfair class strictures that shackled society. Hardy called Tess "a pure woman," a description that outraged many Victorian readers. Class casts a large and suffocating shadow over the story of Tess Durbeyfield. When her father learns that his family name once carried the weight of nobility, his ambition is immediately set aflame and he dreams that the Durbeyfields can once again occupy a revered place in the county. It is striking how much a name and a history can alter one's perceptions. The nobility John Durbeyfield perceives is not tied to any actions or deeds—it is merely a quirk of genealogy.

Class betrays Tess, however, ultimately proving to be corrupt and hollow, and in her story Hardy constructs an almost perfect critique of a society that values name over behavior. Alec d'Urberville's rape of Tess shatters false notions of nobility, but Hardy takes this critique further through his incredible powers of characterization. Tess, pregnant after the rape, refuses to seek help from Alec. She will not lower herself to his lack of true class and thus remains pure, through character and resolve. Her last name may mean little to people of wealth, but her actions expose a will of unsurpassed dignity.

Tess's spirit remains strong despite prevailing religious attitudes. Class and religion worked hand in hand in shaping Victorian social order, but just as class cannot diminish Tess, religion cannot break her spirit. She presents a powerful contrast to the ostensibly pious Angel Clare. The son of a minister, Angel falls in love with Tess, viewing her as his own ideal image of the perfect domestic partner. A representative Victorian male, Angel cannot accept a woman unless she conforms to this image of female character. Hardy exposes the hypocrisy inherent in a male-constructed ideal of women that is legitimized through organized religion. Angel cannot forgive Tess for being raped, even though he admits he has committed his own transgression with a stranger. Decorum, not forgiveness, is the true foundation of Angel's Christianity, even when it calls for him to be a hypocrite. But his view cannot sully Tess's purity, her determination to endure. Her subsequent liaison with Alec d'Urberville appears at first to be her acceptance of her guilt as determined by society's norms. However, it is not a diminution of her character; rather, it exemplifies her resolve to survive. That she has to become the mistress of the man who raped her is an indictment of Victorian culture, not of Tess herself.

Tracing Hardy's own life in his novels can lead to some specious conclusions. However, certain facts do stand out in light of the thematic obsessions in his fiction. Love is a dangerous emotion in these works, often unfulfilled or bordering on the violent. Hardy's marriage to Emma devolved into a loveless union complete with petty backbiting by both parties. Early in adulthood, Hardy had become disillusioned with organized religion, which may have contributed to some of the problems with his wife. It is not difficult to see these real-life events being mirrored in the novels, especially in *Tess* and in Hardy's last major novel, *Jude the Obscure* (1895).

Jude, Hardy's penultimate published novel, is particularly concerned with the institution of marriage and its status in Victorian society. Jude's failed ambitions continue Hardy's examination of the suffocation of class barriers, but the portrayal of love and especially sex without marriage raised Victorian readers' ire. Hardy had the temerity to write of a love that valued togetherness more than marriage. Once again, his fully realized characters, for whom we feel for so deeply, lead us into territory that was uncomfortable for the Victorian public. Particularly remarkable is the portrait of Jude himself. His character is incorruptible. Despite his status as "sinner" in the eyes of an unforgiving public, Jude is a loving father and companion. In fact, he is a positive contrast to other parents or parent figures in the novel. As an early example, Jude's aunt is seen by the townsfolk as a saint for taking in the poor orphaned boy, yet she continually destroys the boy's dreams. Her narrow perspective on life is cruelly limiting for Jude, but he grows to understand the power of a nurturing relationship between adult and child.

Hardy himself knew the pain of a marriage without love and how that pain festered because of the "holy" status of marriage. In the story of Jude and Sue, Hardy again attacks the shallowness of decorum. Two people not married, no matter how strong their union, simply had to be thrust out of respectable society. Although the horrific end might be interpreted as punishment for Jude and Sue's "sin," closer inspection places the blame on Victorian society. Hypocritical Victorian mores, not God's, doom the relationship.

The public outcry over what was seen as decadence in *Tess* and *Jude* contributed significantly to Hardy's decision to return to his first love, poetry. He published one more novel, not considered a major work, and then poured himself into his verse. That Hardy earned distinction as a poet in this second stage of his literary career, after his success as a novelist, marks him as one of the more remarkable figures in English literature. In 1912 Emma died, and in 1914 Hardy married Florence Emily Dugdale. This marriage proved to be a great joy and help to Hardy, giving him peace he had not known for some time. Hardy died in 1928 and is buried in the "Poet's Corner" in Westminster Abbey.

Hardy's novels bridge the old with the new, the Victorian with the modern. He effectively critiqued the society of his time through the reaction of the rural community Wessex. It became such a popular literary landscape that tours of "Hardy country" began late in the nineteenth century. Its popularity grew not only because of Hardy's incredible powers of description, but because it mapped the rugged and imaginative terrain within the human heart. He peopled his fiction with characters as real as a neighbor, and through them he dissected his culture with the precision of a surgeon.

TOMMY JENKINS

Tommy Jenkins is a published author and has taught creative writing for several years. He studied at the University of North Carolina as an undergraduate and holds a master's degree from Columbia University. He is currently studying and teaching creative writing at North Carolina State University.

FAR FROM THE MADDING CROWD

PREFACE

I N REPRINTING THIS STORY FOR A NEW EDITION I AM REMINDED THAT IT WAS IN THE chapters of "Far from the Madding Crowd," as they appeared month by month in a popular magazine, that I first ventured to adopt the word "Wessex" from the pages of early English history, and give it a fictitious significance as the existing name of the district once included in that extinct kingdom. The series of novels I projected being mainly of the kind called local, they seemed to require a territorial definition of some sort to lend unity to their scene. Finding that the area of a single county did not afford a canvas large enough for this purpose, and that there were objections to an invented name, I disinterred the old one. The region designated was known but vaguely, and I was often asked even by educated people where it lay. However, the press and the public were kind enough to welcome the fanciful plan, and willingly joined me in the anachronism of imagining a Wessex population living under Queen Victoria;—a modern Wessex of railways, the penny post, mowing and reaping machines, union workhouses, lucifer matches, labourers who could read and write, and National school children. But I believe I am correct in stating that, until the existence of this contemporaneous Wessex in place of the usual counties was announced in the present story, in 1874, it had never been heard of in fiction and current speech, if at all, and that the expression, "a Wessex peasant," or "a Wessex custom," would theretofore have been taken to refer to nothing later in date than the Norman Conquest.

I did not anticipate that this application of the word to a modern use would extend outside the chapters of these particular chronicles. But it was soon taken up elsewhere, the first to adopt it being the now defunct *Examiner,* which, in the impression bearing date July 15, 1876, entitled one of its articles "The Wessex Labourer," the article turning out to be no dissertation on farming during the Heptarchy, but on the modern peasant of the south-west counties.

Since then the appellation which I had thought to reserve to the horizons and landscapes of a partly real, partly dream-country, has become more and more popular as a practical definition; and the dream-country has, by degrees, solidified into a utilitarian region which people can go to, take a house in, and write to the papers from. But I ask all good and idealistic readers to forget this, and to refuse steadfastly to believe that there are any inhabitants of a Victorian Wessex outside these volumes in which their lives and conversations are detailed.

Moreover, the village called Weatherbury, wherein the scenes of the present story of the series are for the most part laid, would perhaps be hardly discernible by the explorer, without help, in any existing place now-a-days; though at the time, comparatively recent, at which the tale was written, a sufficient reality to meet the descriptions, both of backgrounds and personages, might have been traced easily enough. The church remains, by great good fortune, unrestored and intact[1] and a few of the old houses; but the ancient malt-house, which was formerly so characteristic of the parish, has been pulled down these twenty years; also most of the thatched and dormered cottages that were once lifeholds. The heroine's fine old Jacobian house would be found in the story to have taken a witch's ride of a mile or more from its actual position; though with that difference its features are described as they still show themselves to the sun and moonlight. The game of prisoner's-base, which not so long ago seemed to enjoy a perennial vitality in front of the worn-out stocks, may, so far as I can say, be entirely unknown to the rising generation of schoolboys there. The practice of divination by Bible and key, the regarding of valentines as things of serious import, the shearing-supper, the long smock-frocks, and the harvest-home, have, too, nearly disappeared in the wake of the old houses; and with them has gone, it is said, much of that love of fuddling to which the village at one time was notoriously prone. The change at the root of this has been the recent supplanting of the class of stationary cottagers, who carried on the local traditions and humours, by a population of more or less migratory labourers, which has led to a break of continuity in local history, more fatal than any other thing to the preservation of legend, folk-lore, close inter-social relations, and eccentric individualities. For these the indispensable conditions of existence are attachment to the soil of one particular spot by generation after generation.

T. H.
1895–1902

1. This is no longer the case (1912).

Contents

I

Description of Farmer Oak—An Incident

WHEN FARMER OAK SMILED, THE CORNERS OF HIS MOUTH SPREAD TILL THEY were within an unimportant distance of his ears, his eyes were reduced to chinks, and diverging wrinkles appeared round them, extending upon his countenance like the rays in a rudimentary sketch of the rising sun.

His Christian name was Gabriel, and on working days he was a young man of sound judgment, easy motions, proper dress, and general good character. On Sundays he was a man of misty views, rather given to postponing, and hampered by his best clothes and umbrella: upon the whole, one who felt himself to occupy morally that vast middle space of Laodicean neutrality which lay between the Communion people of the parish and the drunken section—that is, he went to church, but yawned privately by the time the congregation reached the Nicene creed, and thought of what there would be for dinner when he meant to be listening to the sermon. Or, to state his character as it stood in the scale of public opinion, when his friends and critics were in tantrums, he was considered rather a bad man; when they were pleased, he was rather a good man; when they were neither, he was a man whose moral colour was a kind of pepper-and-salt mixture.

Since he lived six times as many working-days as Sundays, Oak's appearance in his old clothes was most peculiarly his own—the mental picture formed by his neighbours in imagining him being always dressed in that way. He wore a low-crowned felt hat, spread out at the base by tight jamming upon the head for security in high winds, and a coat like Dr. Johnson's; his lower extremities being encased in ordinary leather leggings and boots emphatically large, affording to each foot a roomy apartment so constructed that any wearer might stand in a river all day long and know nothing of damp—their maker being a conscientious man who endeavoured to compensate for any weakness in his cut by unstinted dimension and solidity.

Mr. Oak carried about him, by way of watch, what may be called a small silver clock; in other words, it was a watch as to shape and intention, and a small clock as to size. This instrument being several years older than Oak's grand-father, had the peculiarity of going either too fast or not at all. The smaller of its hands, too, occasionally slipped round on the pivot, and thus, though the minutes were told with precision, nobody could be quite certain of the hour they belonged to. The stopping peculiarity of his watch Oak remedied by thumps and shakes, and he escaped any evil consequences from the other two defects by constant comparisons with and observations of the sun and stars, and by pressing his face close to the glass of his neighbours' windows, till he could discern the hour marked by the green-faced timekeepers within. It may be mentioned that Oak's fob being difficult of access, by reason of its somewhat high situation in the waistband of his trousers (which also lay at a remote height under his waistcoat), the watch was as a necessity pulled out by throwing the body to one side, compressing the mouth and face to a mere mass of ruddy flesh on account of the exertion, and drawing up the watch by its chain, like a bucket from a well.

But some thoughtful persons, who had seen him walking across one of his fields on a certain December morning—sunny and exceedingly mild—might have regarded Gabriel Oak in other aspects than these. In his face one might notice that many of the hues and curves of youth had tarried on to manhood: there even remained in his remoter crannies some relics of the boy. His height and breadth would have been sufficient to make his presence imposing, had they been exhibited with due consideration. But there is a way some men have, rural and urban alike, for which the mind is more responsible than flesh and sinew: it is a way of curtailing their dimensions by their manner of showing them. And from a quiet modesty that would have become a vestal, which seemed continually to impress upon him that he had no great claim on the world's room, Oak walked unassumingly, and with a faintly perceptible bend, yet distinct from a bowing of the shoulders. This may be said to be a defect in an individual if he depends for his valuation more upon his appearance than upon his capacity to wear well, which Oak did not.

He had just reached the time of life at which "young" is ceasing to be the prefix of "man" in speaking of one. He was at the brightest period of masculine growth, for his intellect and his emotions were clearly separated: he had passed the time during which the influence of youth indiscriminately mingles them in the character of impulse, and he had not yet arrived at the stage wherein they become united again, in the character of prejudice, by the influence of a wife and family. In short, he was twenty-eight, and a bachelor.

The field he was in this morning sloped to a ridge called Norcombe Hill. Through a spur of this hill ran the highway between Emminster and Chalk-Newton. Casually glancing over the hedge, Oak saw coming down the incline before him an ornamental spring waggon, painted yellow and gaily marked, drawn by two horses, a waggoner walking alongside bearing a whip perpendicularly. The waggon was laden with household goods and window plants, and on the apex of the whole sat a woman, young and attractive. Gabriel had not beheld the sight for more than half a minute, when the vehicle was brought to a standstill just beneath his eyes.

"The tailboard of the waggon is gone, Miss," said the waggoner.

"Then I heard it fall," said the girl, in a soft, though not particularly low voice. "I heard a noise I could not account for when we were coming up the hill."

"I'll run back."

"Do," she answered.

The sensible horses stood perfectly still, and the waggoner's steps sank fainter and fainter in the distance.

The girl on the summit of the load sat motionless, surrounded by tables and chairs with their legs upwards, backed by an oak settle, and ornamented in front by pots of geraniums, myrtles, and cactuses, together with a caged canary—all probably from the windows of the house just vacated. There was also a cat in a willow basket, from the partly-opened lid of which she gazed with half-closed eyes, and affectionately surveyed the small birds around.

The handsome girl waited for some time idly in her place, and the only sound heard in the stillness was the hopping of the canary up and down the perches of its prison. Then she looked attentively downwards. It was not at the bird, nor at the cat; it was at an oblong package tied in paper, and lying between them. She turned her head to learn if the waggoner were coming. He was not yet in sight; and her eyes crept back to the package, her thoughts seeming to run upon what was inside it. At length she drew the article into her lap, and untied the paper covering; a small swing looking-glass was disclosed, in which she proceeded to survey herself attentively. She parted her lips and smiled.

It was a fine morning, and the sun lighted up to a scarlet glow the crimson jacket she wore, and painted a soft lustre upon her bright face and dark hair. The myrtles, geraniums, and cactuses packed around her were fresh and green, and at such a leafless season they invested the whole concern of horses, waggon, furniture, and girl with a peculiar vernal charm. What possessed her to indulge in such a performance in the sight of the sparrows, blackbirds, and unperceived farmer who were alone its spectators—whether the smile began as a factitious one, to test her capacity in that art—nobody knows; it ended certainly in a real smile. She blushed at herself, and seeing her reflection blush, blushed the more.

The change from the customary spot and necessary occasion of such an act—from the dressing hour in a bedroom to a time of travelling out of doors—lent to the idle deed a novelty it did not intrinsically possess. The picture was a delicate one. Woman's prescriptive infirmity had stalked into the sunlight, which had clothed it in the freshness of an originality. A cynical inference was irresistible by Gabriel Oak as he regarded the scene, generous though he fain would have been. There was no necessity whatever for her looking in the glass. She did not adjust her hat, or pat her hair, or press a dimple into shape, or do one thing to signify that any such intention had been her motive in taking up the glass. She simply observed herself as a fair product of Nature in the feminine kind, her thoughts seeming to glide into far-off though likely dramas in which men would play a part—vistas of probable triumphs—the smiles being of a phase suggesting that hearts were imagined as lost and won. Still, this was but conjecture, and the whole series of actions was so idly put forth as to make it rash to assert that intention had any part in them at all.

The waggoner's steps were heard returning. She put the glass in the paper, and the whole again into its place.

When the waggon had passed on, Gabriel withdrew from his point of espial, and descending into the road, followed the vehicle to the turnpike gate some way beyond the bottom of the hill, where the object of his contemplation now halted for the payment of toll. About twenty steps still remained between him and the gate, when he heard a dispute. It was a difference concerning twopence between the persons with the waggon and the man at the toll-bar.

"Mis'ess's niece is upon the top of the things, and she says that's enough that I've offered ye, you great miser, and she won't pay any more." These were the waggoner's words.

"Very well; then mis'ess's niece can't pass," said the turnpike-keeper, closing the gate.

Oak looked from one to the other of the disputants, and fell into a reverie. There was something in the tone of twopence remarkably insignificant. Threepence had a definite value as money—it was an appreciable infringement on a day's wages, and, as such, a higgling matter; but twopence—"Here," he said, stepping forward and handing twopence to the gatekeeper; "let the young woman pass." He looked up at her then; she heard his words, and looked down.

Gabriel's features adhered throughout their form so exactly to the middle line between the beauty of St. John and the ugliness of Judas Iscariot, as represented in a window of the church he attended, that not a single lineament could be selected and called worthy either of distinction or notoriety. The red-jacketed and dark-haired maiden seemed to think so too, for she carelessly glanced over him, and told her man to drive on. She might have looked her thanks to Gabriel on a minute scale, but she did not speak them; more probably she felt none, for in gaining her a passage he had lost her her point, and we know how women take a favour of that kind.

The gatekeeper surveyed the retreating vehicle. "That's a handsome maid," he said to Oak.

"But she has her faults," said Gabriel.

"True, farmer."

"And the greatest of them is—well, what it is always."

"Beating people down? ay, 'tis so."

"O no."

"What, then?"

Gabriel, perhaps a little piqued by the comely traveller's indifference, glanced back to where he had witnessed her performance over the hedge, and said, "Vanity."

II

NIGHT—THE FLOCK—AN INTERIOR—ANOTHER INTERIOR

IT WAS NEARLY MIDNIGHT ON THE EVE OF ST. THOMAS'S, THE SHORTEST DAY IN THE YEAR. A desolating wind wandered from the north over the hill whereon Oak had watched the yellow waggon and its occupant in the sunshine of a few days earlier.

Norcombe Hill—not far from lonely Toller-Down—was one of the spots which suggest to a passer-by that he is in the presence of a shape approaching the indestructible as nearly as any to be found on earth. It was a featureless convexity of chalk and soil—an ordinary specimen of those smoothly-outlined protuberances of the globe which may remain undisturbed on some great day of confusion, when far grander heights and dizzy granite precipices topple down.

The hill was covered on its northern side by an ancient and decaying plantation of beeches, whose upper verge formed a line over the crest, fringing its arched curve against the sky, like a mane. To-night these trees sheltered the southern slope from the keenest blasts, which smote the wood and floundered through it with a sound as of grumbling, or gushed over its crowning boughs in a weakened moan. The dry leaves in the ditch simmered and boiled in the same breezes, a tongue of air occasionally ferreting out a few, and sending them spinning across the grass. A group or two of the latest in date amongst the dead multitude had remained till this very mid-winter-time on the twigs which bore them, and in falling rattled against the trunks with smart taps.

Between this half-wooded half-naked hill, and the vague still horizon that its summit indistinctly commanded, was a mysterious sheet of fathomless shade—the sounds from which suggested that what it concealed bore some reduced resemblance to features here. The thin grasses, more or less coating the hill, were touched by the wind in breezes of differing powers, and almost of differing natures—one rubbing the blades heavily, another raking them piercingly, another brushing them like a soft broom. The instinctive act of humankind was to stand and listen, and learn how the trees on the right and the trees on the left wailed or chaunted to each other in the regular antiphonies of a cathedral choir; how hedges and other shapes to leeward then caught the note, lowering it to the tenderest sob; and how the hurrying gust then plunged into the south, to be heard no more.

The sky was clear—remarkably clear—and the twinkling of all the stars seemed to be but throbs of one body, timed by a common pulse. The North Star was directly in the wind's eye, and since evening the Bear had swung round it outwardly to the east, till he was now at a right angle with the meridian. A difference of colour in the stars—oftener read of than seen in England—was really perceptible here. The sovereign brilliancy of Sirius pierced the eye with a steely glitter, the star called Capella was yellow, Aldebaran and Betelgueux shone with a fiery red.

To persons standing alone on a hill during a clear midnight such as this, the roll of the world eastward is almost a palpable movement. The sensation may be caused by the panoramic glide of the stars past earthly objects, which is perceptible in a few minutes of stillness, or by the better outlook upon space that a hill affords, or by the wind, or by the solitude; but whatever be its origin the impression of riding along is vivid and abiding. The poetry of motion is a phrase much in use, and to enjoy the epic form of that gratification it is necessary to stand on a hill at a small hour of the night, and, having first expanded with a sense of difference from the mass of civilised mankind, who are dreamwrapt and disregardful of all such proceedings at this time, long and quietly watch your stately progress through the stars. After such a nocturnal reconnoitre it is hard to get back to earth, and to believe that the consciousness of such majestic speeding is derived from a tiny human frame.

Suddenly an unexpected series of sounds began to be heard in this place up against the sky. They had a clearness which was to be found nowhere in the wind, and a sequence which was to be found nowhere in nature. They were the notes of Farmer Oak's flute.

The tune was not floating unhindered into the open air: it seemed muffled in some way, and was altogether too curtailed in power to spread high or wide. It came from the direction of a small dark object under the plantation hedge—a shepherd's hut—now presenting an outline to which an uninitiated person might have been puzzled to attach either meaning or use.

The image as a whole was that of a small Noah's Ark on a small Ararat, allowing the traditional outlines and general form of the Ark which are followed by toy-makers—and by these means are established in men's imaginations among their firmest, because earliest impressions—to pass as an approximate pattern. The hut stood on little wheels, which raised its floor about a foot from the ground. Such shepherds' huts are dragged into the fields when the lambing season comes on, to shelter the shepherd in his enforced nightly attendance.

It was only latterly that people had begun to call Gabriel "Farmer" Oak. During the twelvemonth preceding this time he had been enabled by sustained efforts of industry and chronic good spirits to lease the small sheep-farm of which Norcombe Hill was a portion, and stock it with two hundred sheep. Previously he had been a bailiff for a short time, and earlier still a shepherd only, having from his childhood assisted his father in tending the flocks of large proprietors, till old Gabriel sank to rest.

This venture, unaided and alone, into the paths of farming as master and not as man, with an advance of sheep not yet paid for, was a critical juncture with Gabriel Oak, and he recognised his position clearly. The first movement in his new progress was the lambing of his ewes, and sheep having been his speciality from his youth, he wisely refrained from deputing the task of tending them at this season to a hireling or a novice.

The wind continued to beat about the corners of the hut, but the flute-playing ceased. A rectangular space of light appeared in the side of the hut, and in the opening the outline of Farmer Oak's figure. He carried a lantern in his hand, and closing the door behind him came forward and busied himself about this nook of the field for nearly twenty minutes, the lantern light appearing and disappearing here and there, and brightening him or darkening him as he stood before or behind it.

Oak's motions, though they had a quiet energy, were slow, and their deliberateness accorded well with his occupation. Fitness being the basis of beauty, nobody could have denied that his steady swings and turns in and about the flock had elements of grace. Yet, although if occasion demanded he could do or think a thing with as mercurial a dash as can the men of towns who are more to the manner born, his special power, morally, physically, and mentally, was static, owing little or nothing to momentum as a rule.

A close examination of the ground hereabout, even by the wan starlight only, revealed how a portion of what would have been casually called a wild slope had been appropriated by Farmer Oak for his great purpose this winter. Detached hurdles thatched with straw were stuck into the ground at various scattered points, amid and under which the whitish forms of his meek ewes moved and rustled. The ring of the sheep-bell, which had been silent during his absence, recommenced, in tones that had more mellowness than clearness, owing to an increasing growth of surrounding wool. This continued till Oak withdrew again from the flock. He returned to the hut, bringing in his arms a new-born lamb, consisting of four legs large enough for a full-grown sheep, united by a seemingly inconsiderable membrane about half the substance of the legs collectively, which constituted the animal's entire body just at present.

The little speck of life he placed on a wisp of hay before the small stove, where a can of milk was simmering. Oak extinguished the lantern by blowing into it and then pinching the snuff, the cot being lighted by a candle suspended by a twisted wire. A rather hard couch, formed of a few corn sacks thrown carelessly down, covered half the floor of this little habitation, and here the young man stretched himself along, loosened his woollen cravat, and closed his eyes. In about the time a person unaccustomed to bodily labour would have decided upon which side to lie, Farmer Oak was asleep.

The inside of the hut, as it now presented itself, was cosy and alluring, and the scarlet handful of fire in addition to the candle, reflecting its own genial colour upon whatever it could reach, flung associations of enjoyment even over utensils and tools. In the corner stood the sheep-crook, and along a shelf at one side were ranged bottles and canisters of the simple preparations pertaining to ovine surgery and physic; spirits of wine, turpentine, tar, magnesia, ginger, and castor-oil being the chief. On a triangular shelf across the corner stood bread, bacon, cheese, and a cup for ale or cider, which was supplied from a flagon beneath. Beside the provisions lay the flute, whose notes had lately been called forth by the lonely watcher to beguile a tedious hour. The house was ventilated by two round holes, like the lights of a ship's cabin, with wood slides.

The lamb, revived by the warmth, began to bleat, and the sound entered Gabriel's ears and brain with an instant meaning, as expected sounds will. Passing from the profoundest sleep to the most alert wakefulness with the same ease that had accompanied the reverse operation, he looked at his watch, found that the hour-hand had shifted again, put on his hat, took the lamb in his arms, and carried it into the darkness. After placing the little creature with its mother he stood and carefully examined the sky, to ascertain the time of night from the altitudes of the stars.

The Dog-star and Aldebaran, pointing to the restless Pleiades, were half-way up the Southern sky, and between them hung Orion, which gorgeous constellation never burnt more vividly than now, as it soared forth above the rim of the landscape. Castor and Pollux with their quiet shine were almost on the meridian: the barren and gloomy Square of Pegasus was creeping round to the north-west; far away through the plantation Vega sparkled like a lamp suspended amid the leafless trees, and Cassiopeia's chair stood daintily poised on the uppermost boughs.

"One o'clock," said Gabriel.

Being a man not without a frequent consciousness that there was some charm in this life he led, he stood still after looking at the sky as a useful instrument, and regarded it in an appreciative spirit, as a work of art superlatively beautiful. For a moment he seemed impressed with the speaking loneliness of the scene, or rather with the complete abstraction from all its compass of the sights and sounds of man. Human shapes, interferences, troubles, and joys were all as if they were not, and there seemed to be on the shaded hemisphere of the globe no sentient being save himself; he could fancy them all gone round to the sunny side.

Occupied thus, with eyes stretched afar, Oak gradually perceived that what he had previously taken to be a star low down behind the outskirts of the plantation was in reality no such thing. It was an artificial light, almost close at hand.

To find themselves utterly alone at night where company is desirable and expected makes some people fearful; but a case more trying by far to the nerves is to discover some mysterious companionship when intuition, sensation, memory, analogy, testimony, probability, induction—every kind of evidence in the logician's list—have united to persuade consciousness that it is quite in isolation.

Farmer Oak went towards the plantation and pushed through its lower boughs to the windy side. A dim mass under the slope reminded him that a shed occupied a place here, the site being a cutting into the slope of the hill, so that at its back part the roof was almost level with the ground. In front it was formed of boards nailed to posts and covered with tar as a preservative. Through crevices in the roof and side spread streaks and dots of light, a combination of which made the radiance that had attracted him. Oak stepped up behind, where, leaning down upon the roof and putting his eye close to a hole, he could see into the interior clearly.

The place contained two women and two cows. By the side of the latter a steaming bran-mash stood in a bucket. One of the women was past middle age. Her companion was apparently young and graceful; he could form no decided opinion upon her looks, her position being almost beneath his eye, so that he saw her in a bird's-eye view, as Milton's Satan first saw Paradise. She wore no bonnet or hat, but had enveloped herself in a large cloak, which was carelessly flung over her head as a covering.

"There, now we'll go home," said the elder of the two, resting her knuckles upon her hips, and looking at their goings-on as a whole. "I do hope Daisy will fetch round again now. I have never been more frightened in my life, but I don't mind breaking my rest if she recovers."

The young woman, whose eyelids were apparently inclined to fall together on the smallest provocation of silence, yawned without parting her lips to any inconvenient extent, whereupon Gabriel caught the infection and slightly yawned in sympathy.

"I wish we were rich enough to pay a man to do these things," she said.

"As we are not, we must do them ourselves," said the other; "for you must help me if you stay."

"Well, my hat is gone, however," continued the younger. "It went over the hedge, I think. The idea of such a slight wind catching it."

The cow standing erect was of the Devon breed, and was encased in a tight warm hide of rich Indian red, as absolutely uniform from eyes to tail as if the animal had been dipped in a dye of that colour, her long back being mathematically level. The other was spotted, grey and white. Beside her Oak now noticed a little calf about a day old, looking idiotically at the two women, which showed that it had not long been accustomed to the phenomenon of eyesight, and often turning to the lantern, which it apparently mistook for the moon, inherited instinct having as yet had little time for correction by experience. Between the sheep and the cows Lucina had been busy on Norcombe Hill lately.

"I think we had better send for some oatmeal," said the elder woman; "there's no more bran."

"Yes, aunt; and I'll ride over for it as soon as it is light."

"But there's no side-saddle."

"I can ride on the other: trust me."

Oak, upon hearing these remarks, became more curious to observe her features, but this prospect being denied him by the hooding effect of the cloak, and by his aërial position, he felt himself drawing upon his fancy for their details. In making even horizontal and clear inspections we colour and mould according to the wants within us whatever our eyes bring in. Had Gabriel been able from the first to get a distinct view of her countenance, his estimate of it as very handsome or slightly so would have been as his soul required a divinity at the moment or was ready supplied with one. Having for some time known the want of a satisfactory form to fill an increasing void within him, his position moreover affording the widest scope for his fancy, he painted her a beauty.

By one of those whimsical coincidences in which Nature, like a busy mother, seems to spare a moment from her unremitting labours to turn and make her children smile, the girl now dropped the cloak, and forth tumbled ropes of black hair over a red jacket. Oak knew her instantly as the heroine of the yellow waggon, myrtles, and looking-glass: prosily, as the woman who owed him twopence.

They placed the calf beside its mother again, took up the lantern, and went out, the light sinking down the hill till it was no more than a nebula. Gabriel Oak returned to his flock.

III

A GIRL ON HORSEBACK—CONVERSATION

THE SLUGGISH DAY BEGAN TO BREAK. EVEN ITS POSITION TERRESTRIALLY IS ONE OF THE elements of a new interest, and for no particular reason save that the incident of the night had occurred there Oak went again into the plantation. Lingering and musing here he heard the steps of a horse at the foot of the hill, and soon there appeared in view an auburn pony with a girl on its back, ascending by the path leading past the cattle-shed. She was the young woman of the night before. Gabriel instantly thought of the hat she had mentioned as having lost in the wind; possibly she had come to look for it. He hastily scanned the ditch, and after walking about ten yards along it found the hat among the leaves. Gabriel took it in his hand and returned to his hut. Here he ensconced himself, and peeped through the loophole in the direction of the rider's approach.

She came up and looked around—then on the other side of the hedge. Gabriel was about to advance and restore the missing article, when an unexpected performance induced him to suspend the action for the present. The path, after passing the cowshed, bisected the plantation. It was not a bridle-path—merely a pedestrian's track, and the boughs spread horizontally at a height not greater than seven feet above the ground, which made it impossible to ride erect beneath them. The girl, who wore no riding-habit, looked around for a moment, as if to assure herself that all humanity was out of view, then dexterously dropped backwards flat upon the pony's back, her head over its tail, her feet against its shoulders, and her eyes to the sky. The rapidity of her glide into this position was that of a kingfisher—its noiselessness that of a hawk. Gabriel's eyes had scarcely been able to follow her. The tall lank pony seemed used to such doings, and ambled along unconcerned. Thus she passed under the level boughs.

The performer seemed quite at home anywhere between a horse's head and its tail, and the necessity for this abnormal attitude having ceased with the passage of the plantation, she began to adopt another, even more obviously convenient than the first. She had no side-saddle, and it was very apparent that a firm seat upon the smooth leather beneath her was unattainable sideways. Springing to her accustomed perpendicular like a bowed sapling, and satisfying herself that nobody was in sight, she seated herself in the manner demanded by the saddle, though hardly expected of the woman, and trotted off in the direction of Tewnell Mill.

Oak was amused, perhaps a little astonished, and hanging up the hat in his hut went again among his ewes. An hour passed, the girl returned, properly seated now, with a bag of bran in front of her. On nearing the cattle-shed she was met by a boy bringing a milking-pail, who held the reins of the pony whilst she slid off. The boy led away the horse, leaving the pail with the young woman.

Soon soft spirts alternating with loud spirts came in regular succession from within the shed, the obvious sounds of a person milking a cow. Gabriel took the lost hat in his hand, and waited beside the path she would follow in leaving the hill.

She came, the pail in one hand, hanging against her knee. The left arm was extended as a balance, enough of it being shown bare to make Oak wish that the event had happened in the summer, when the whole would have been revealed. There was a bright air and manner about her now, by which she seemed to imply that the desirability of her existence could not be questioned; and this rather saucy assumption failed in being offensive because a beholder felt it to be, upon the whole, true. Like exceptional emphasis in the tone of a genius, that which would have made mediocrity ridiculous was an addition to recognised power. It was with some surprise that she saw Gabriel's face rising like the moon behind the hedge.

The adjustment of the farmer's hazy conceptions of her charms to the portrait of herself she now presented him with was less a diminution than a difference. The starting-point selected by the judgment was her height. She seemed tall, but the pail was a small one, and the hedge diminutive; hence, making allowance for error by comparison with these, she could have been not above the height to be chosen by women as best. All features of consequence were severe and regular. It may have been observed by persons who go about the shires with eyes for beauty that in Englishwomen a classically-formed face is seldom found to be united with a figure of the same pattern, the highly-finished features being generally too large for the remainder of the frame; that a graceful and proportionate figure of eight heads usually goes off into random facial curves. Without throwing a Nymphean tissue over a milkmaid, let it be said that here criticism checked itself as out of place, and looked at her proportions with a long consciousness of pleasure. From the contours of her figure in its upper part she must have had a beautiful neck and shoulders; but since her infancy nobody had ever seen them. Had she been put into a low dress she would have run and thrust her head into a bush. Yet she was not a shy girl by any means; it was merely her instinct to draw the line dividing the seen from the unseen higher than they do it in towns.

That the girl's thoughts hovered about her face and form as soon as she caught Oak's eyes conning the same page was natural, and almost certain. The self-consciousness shown would have been vanity if a little more pronounced, dignity if a little less. Rays of male vision seem to have a tickling effect upon virgin faces in rural districts; she brushed hers with her hand, as if Gabriel had been irritating its pink surface by actual touch, and the free air of her previous movements was reduced at the same time to a chastened phase of itself. Yet it was the man who blushed, the maid not at all.

"I found a hat," said Oak.

"It is mine," said she, and, from a sense of proportion, kept down to a small smile an inclination to laugh distinctly: "it flew away last night."

"One o'clock this morning?"

"Well—it was." She was surprised. "How did you know?" she said.

"I was here."

"You are Farmer Oak, are you not?"

"That or thereabouts. I'm lately come to this place."

"A large farm?" she enquired, casting her eyes round, and swinging back her hair, which was black in the shaded hollows of its mass; but it being now an hour past sunrise the rays touched its prominent curves with a colour of their own.

"No; not large. About a hundred." (In speaking of farms the word "acres" is omitted by the natives, by analogy to such old expressions as "a stag of ten.")

"I wanted my hat this morning," she went on. "I had to ride to Tewnell Mill."

"Yes you had."

"How do you know?"

"I saw you."

"Where?" she enquired, a misgiving bringing every muscle of her lineaments and frame to a standstill.

"Here—going through the plantation, and all down the hill," said Farmer Oak, with an aspect excessively knowing with regard to some matter in his mind, as he gazed at a remote point in the direction named, and then turned back to meet his colloquist's eyes.

A perception caused him to withdraw his own eyes from hers as suddenly as if he had been caught in a theft. Recollection of the strange antics she had indulged in when passing through the trees was succeeded in the girl by a nettled palpitation, and that by a hot face. It was a time to see a woman redden who was not given to reddening as a rule; not a point in the milkmaid but was of the deepest rose-colour. From the Maiden's Blush, through all varieties of the Provence down to the Crimson Tuscany the countenance of Oak's acquaintance quickly graduated; whereupon he, in considerateness, turned away his head.

The sympathetic man still looked the other way, and wondered when she would recover coolness sufficient to justify him in facing her again. He heard what seemed to be the flitting of a dead leaf upon the breeze, and looked. She had gone away.

With an air between that of Tragedy and Comedy Gabriel returned to his work.

Five mornings and evenings passed. The young woman came regularly to milk the healthy cow or to attend to the sick one, but never allowed her vision to stray in the direction of Oak's person. His want of tact had deeply offended her—not by seeing what he could not help, but by letting her know that he had seen it. For, as without law there is no sin, without eyes there is no indecorum; and she appeared to feel that Gabriel's espial had made her an indecorous woman without her own connivance. It was food for great regret with him; it was also a *contretemps* which touched into life a latent heat he had experienced in that direction.

The acquaintanceship might, however, have ended in a slow forgetting, but for an incident which occurred at the end of the same week. One afternoon it began to freeze, and the frost increased with evening, which drew on like a stealthy tightening of bonds. It was a time when in cottages the breath of the sleepers freezes to the sheets; when round the drawing-room fire of a thick-walled mansion the sitters' backs are cold, even whilst their faces are all aglow. Many a small bird went to bed supperless that night among the bare boughs.

As the milking-hour drew near Oak kept his usual watch upon the cowshed. At last he felt cold, and shaking an extra quantity of bedding round the yeaning ewes he entered the hut and heaped more fuel upon the stove. The wind came in at the bottom of the door, and to prevent it Oak laid a sack there and wheeled the cot round a little more to the south. Then the wind spouted in at a ventilating hole—of which there was one on each side of the hut.

Gabriel had always known that when the fire was lighted and the door closed one of these must be kept open—that chosen being always on the side away from the wind. Closing the slide to windward he turned to open the other; on second thoughts the farmer considered that he would first sit down, leaving both closed for a minute or two, till the temperature of the hut was a little raised. He sat down.

His head began to ache in an unwonted manner, and, fancying himself weary by reason of the broken rests of the preceding nights, Oak decided to get up, open the slide, and
then allow himself to fall asleep. He fell asleep, however, without having performed the
necessary preliminary.

How long he remained unconscious Gabriel never knew. During the first stages of his
return to perception peculiar deeds seemed to be in course of enactment. His dog was
howling, his head was aching fearfully—somebody was pulling him about, hands were
loosening his neckerchief.

On opening his eyes he found that evening had sunk to dusk in a strange manner of
unexpectedness. The young girl with the remarkably pleasant lips and white teeth was beside him. More than this—astonishingly more—his head was upon her lap, his face and
neck were disagreeably wet, and her fingers were unbuttoning his collar.

"Whatever is the matter?" said Oak vacantly.

She seemed to experience mirth, but of too insignificant a kind to start enjoyment.

"Nothing now," she answered, "since you are not dead. It is a wonder you were not
suffocated in this hut of yours."

"Ah, the hut!" murmured Gabriel. "I gave ten pounds for that hut. But I'll sell it, and
sit under thatched hurdles as they did in old times, and curl up to sleep in a lock of straw!
It played me nearly the same trick the other day!" Gabriel, by way of emphasis, brought
down his fist upon the floor.

"It was not exactly the fault of the hut," she observed in a tone which showed her to
be that novelty among women—one who finished a thought before beginning the sentence which was to convey it. "You should, I think, have considered, and not have been so
foolish as to leave the slides closed."

"Yes, I suppose I should," said Oak absently. He was endeavouring to catch and appreciate the sensation of being thus with her, his head upon her dress, before the event
passed on into the heap of bygone things. He wished she knew his impressions; but he
would as soon have thought of carrying an odour in a net as of attempting to convey the
intangibilities of his feeling in the coarse meshes of language. So he remained silent.

She made him sit up, and then Oak began wiping his face and shaking himself like a
Samson. "How can I thank 'ee?" he said at last gratefully, some of the natural rusty red
having returned to his face.

"Oh, never mind that," said the girl, smiling, and allowing her smile to hold good for
Gabriel's next remark, whatever that might prove to be.

"How did you find me?"

"I heard your dog howling and scratching at the door of the hut when I came to the
milking (it was so lucky, Daisy's milking is almost over for the season, and I shall not come
here after this week or the next). The dog saw me, and jumped over to me, and laid hold
of my skirt. I came across and looked round the hut the very first thing to see if the slides
were closed. My uncle has a hut like this one, and I have heard him tell his shepherd not to
go to sleep without leaving a slide open. I opened the door, and there you were like dead.
I threw the milk over you, as there was no water, forgetting it was warm, and no use."

"I wonder if I should have died?" Gabriel said in a low voice, which was rather meant
to travel back to himself than to her.

"O no!" the girl replied. She seemed to prefer a less tragic probability; to have saved a man from death involved talk that should harmonise with the dignity of such a deed—and she shunned it.

"I believe you saved my life, Miss—I don't know your name. I know your aunt's, but not yours."

"I would just as soon not tell it—rather not. There is no reason either why I should, as you probably will never have much to do with me."

"Still I should like to know."

"You can enquire at my aunt's—she will tell you."

"My name is Gabriel Oak."

"And mine isn't. You seem fond of yours in speaking it so decisively, Gabriel Oak."

"You see, it is the only one I shall ever have, and I must make the most of it."

"I always think mine sounds odd and disagreeable."

"I should think you might soon get a new one."

"Mercy!—how many opinions you keep about you concerning other people, Gabriel Oak."

"Well, Miss—excuse the words—I thought you would like them. But I can't match you, I know, in mapping out my mind upon my tongue. I never was very clever in my inside. But I thank you. Come, give me your hand!"

She hesitated, somewhat disconcerted at Oak's old-fashioned earnest conclusion to a dialogue lightly carried on. "Very well," she said, and gave him her hand, compressing her lips to a demure impassivity. He held it but an instant, and in his fear of being too demonstrative, swerved to the opposite extreme, touching her fingers with the lightness of a small-hearted person.

"I am sorry," he said the instant after.

"What for?"

"Letting your hand go so quick."

"You may have it again if you like; there it is." She gave him her hand again.

Oak held it longer this time—indeed, curiously long. "How soft it is—being wintertime, too—not chapped or rough, or anything!" he said.

"There—that's long enough," said she, though without pulling it away. "But I suppose you are thinking you would like to kiss it? You may if you want to."

"I wasn't thinking of any such thing," said Gabriel simply; "but I will—"

"That you won't!" She snatched back her hand.

Gabriel felt himself guilty of another want of tact.

"Now find out my name," she said, teasingly; and withdrew.

IV

GABRIEL'S RESOLVE—THE VISIT—THE MISTAKE

THE ONLY SUPERIORITY IN WOMEN THAT IS TOLERABLE TO THE RIVAL SEX IS, AS A RULE, that of the unconscious kind; but a superiority which recognises itself may sometimes please by suggesting possibilities of capture to the subordinated man.

This well-favoured and comely girl soon made appreciable inroads upon the emotional constitution of young Farmer Oak.

Love being an extremely exacting usurer (a sense of exorbitant profit, spiritually, by an exchange of hearts, being at the bottom of pure passions, as that of exorbitant profit, bodily or materially, is at the bottom of those of lower atmosphere), every morning Oak's feelings were as sensitive as the money-market in calculations upon his chances. His dog waited for his meals in a way so like that in which Oak waited for the girl's presence that the farmer was quite struck with the resemblance, felt it lowering, and would not look at the dog. However, he continued to watch through the hedge for her regular coming, and thus his sentiments towards her were deepened without any corresponding effect being produced upon herself. Oak had nothing finished and ready to say as yet, and not being able to frame love phrases which end where they begin; passionate tales—

—*Full of sound and fury*
—*Signifying nothing*—

he said no word at all.

By making enquiries he found that the girl's name was Bathsheba Everdene, and that the cow would go dry in about seven days. He dreaded the eighth day.

At last the eighth day came. The cow had ceased to give milk for that year, and Bathsheba Everdene came up the hill no more. Gabriel had reached a pitch of existence he never could have anticipated a short time before. He liked saying "Bathsheba" as a private enjoyment instead of whistling; turned over his taste to black hair, though he had sworn by brown ever since he was a boy, isolated himself till the space he filled in the public eye was contemptibly small. Love is a possible strength in an actual weakness. Marriage transforms a distraction into a support, the power of which should be, and happily often is, in direct proportion to the degree of imbecility it supplants. Oak began now to see light in this direction, and said to himself, "I'll make her my wife, or upon my soul I shall be good for nothing!"

All this while he was perplexing himself about an errand on which he might consistently visit the cottage of Bathsheba's aunt.

He found his opportunity in the death of a ewe, mother of a living lamb. On a day which had a summer face and a winter constitution—a fine January morning, when there was just enough blue sky visible to make cheerfully-disposed people wish for more, and an occasional gleam of silvery sunshine, Oak put the lamb into a respectable Sunday basket, and stalked across the fields to the house of Mrs. Hurst, the aunt—George, the dog, walking behind, with a countenance of great concern at the serious turn pastoral affairs seemed to be taking.

Gabriel had watched the blue wood-smoke curling from the chimney with strange meditation. At evening he had fancifully traced it down the chimney to the spot of its origin—seen the hearth and Bathsheba beside it—beside it in her out-door dress; for the clothes she had worn on the hill were by association equally with her person included in the compass of his affection; they seemed at this early time of his love a necessary ingredient of the sweet mixture called Bathsheba Everdene.

He had made a toilet of a nicely-adjusted kind—of a nature between the carefully neat and the carelessly ornate—of a degree between fine-market-day and wet-Sunday selection. He thoroughly cleaned his silver watch-chain with whiting, put new lacing straps to his boots, looked to the brass eyelet-holes, went to the inmost heart of the plantation for a new walking-stick, and trimmed it vigorously on his way back; took a new handkerchief from the bottom of his clothes-box, put on the light waistcoat patterned all over with sprigs of an elegant flower uniting the beauties of both rose and lily without the defects of either, and used all the hair-oil he possessed upon his usually dry, sandy, and inextricably curly hair, till he had deepened it to a splendidly novel colour, between that of guano and Roman cement, making it stick to his head like mace round a nutmeg, or wet seaweed round a boulder after the ebb.

Nothing disturbed the stillness of the cottage save the chatter of a knot of sparrows on the eaves; one might fancy scandal and rumour to be no less the staple topic of these little coteries on roofs than of those under them. It seemed that the omen was an unpropitious one, for, as the rather untoward commencement of Oak's overtures, just as he arrived by the garden gate, he saw a cat inside, going into various arched shapes and fiendish convulsions at the sight of his dog George. The dog took no notice, for he had arrived at an age at which all superfluous barking was cynically avoided as a waste of breath—in fact, he never barked even at the sheep except to order, when it was done with an absolutely neutral countenance, as a sort of Commination-service which, though offensive, had to be gone through once now and then to frighten the flock for their own good.

A voice came from behind some laurel-bushes into which the cat had run:

"Poor dear! Did a nasty brute of a dog want to kill it;—did he, poor dear!"

"I beg your pardon," said Oak to the voice, "but George was walking on behind me with a temper as mild as milk."

Almost before he had ceased speaking Oak was seized with a misgiving as to whose ear was the recipient of his answer. Nobody appeared, and he heard the person retreat among the bushes.

Gabriel meditated, and so deeply that he brought small furrows into his forehead by sheer force of reverie. Where the issue of an interview is as likely to be a vast change for the worse as for the better, any initial difference from expectation causes nipping sensations of failure. Oak went up to the door a little abashed: his mental rehearsal and the reality had had no common grounds of opening.

Bathsheba's aunt was indoors. "Will you tell Miss Everdene that somebody would be glad to speak to her?" said Mr. Oak. (Calling one's self merely Somebody, without giving a name, is not to be taken as an example of the ill-breeding of the rural world: it springs from a refined modesty of which townspeople, with their cards and announcements, have no notion whatever.)

Bathsheba was out. The voice had evidently been hers.

"Will you come in, Mr. Oak?"

"Oh, thank 'ee," said Gabriel, following her to the fireplace. "I've brought a lamb for Miss Everdene. I thought she might like one to rear; girls do."

"She might," said Mrs. Hurst musingly; "though she's only a visitor here. If you will wait a minute Bathsheba will be in."

"Yes, I will wait," said Gabriel, sitting down. "The lamb isn't really the business I came about, Mrs. Hurst. In short, I was going to ask her if she'd like to be married."

"And were you indeed?"

"Yes. Because if she would I should be very glad to marry her. D'ye know if she's got any other young man hanging about her at all?"

"Let me think," said Mrs. Hurst, poking the fire superfluously. . . . "Yes—bless you, ever so many young men. You see, Farmer Oak, she's so good-looking, and an excellent scholar besides—she was going to be a governess once, you know, only she was too wild. Not that her young men ever come here—but, Lord, in the nature of women, she must have a dozen!"

"That's unfortunate," said Farmer Oak, contemplating a crack in the stone floor with sorrow. "I'm only an everyday sort of man, and my only chance was in being the first comer . . . Well, there's no use in my waiting, for that was all I came about: so I'll take myself off home-along, Mrs. Hurst."

When Gabriel had gone about two hundred yards along the down, he heard a "hoi-hoi!" uttered behind him, in a piping note of more treble quality than that in which the exclamation usually embodies itself when shouted across a field. He looked round, and saw a girl racing after him, waving a white handkerchief.

Oak stood still—and the runner drew nearer. It was Bathsheba Everdene. Gabriel's colour deepened: hers was already deep, not, as it appeared, from emotion, but from running.

"Farmer Oak—I—" she said, pausing for want of breath, pulling up in front of him with a slanted face, and putting her hand to her side.

"I have just called to see you," said Gabriel pending her further speech.

"Yes—I know that," she said, panting like a robin, her face red and moist from her exertions, like a peony petal before the sun dries off the dew. "I didn't know you had come to ask to have me, or I should have come in from the garden instantly. I ran after you to say—that my aunt made a mistake in sending you away from courting me."

Gabriel expanded. "I'm sorry to have made you run so fast, my dear," he said, with a grateful sense of favours to come. "Wait a bit till you've found your breath."

"—It was quite a mistake—aunt's telling you I had a young man already," Bathsheba went on. "I haven't a sweetheart at all—and I never had one, and I thought that, as times go with women, it was *such* a pity to send you away thinking that I had several."

"Really and truly I am glad to hear that!" said Farmer Oak, smiling one of his long special smiles, and blushing with gladness. He held out his hand to take hers, which, when she had eased her side by pressing it there, was prettily extended upon her bosom to still her loud-beating heart. Directly he seized it she put it behind her, so that it slipped through his fingers like an eel.

"I have a nice snug little farm," said Gabriel, with half a degree less assurance than when he had seized her hand.

"Yes; you have."

"A man has advanced me money to begin with, but still, it will soon be paid off, and though I am only an everyday sort of man I have got on a little since I was a boy." Gabriel uttered "a little" in a tone to show her that it was the complacent form of "a great deal." He continued: "When we be married, I am quite sure I can work twice as hard as I do now."

He went forward and stretched out his arm again. Bathsheba had overtaken him at a point beside which stood a low stunted holly bush, now laden with red berries. Seeing his advance take the form of an attitude threatening a possible enclosure, if not compression, of her person, she edged off round the bush.

"Why, Farmer Oak," she said over the top, looking at him with rounded eyes, "I never said I was going to marry you."

"Well—that *is* a tale!" said Oak with dismay. "To run after anybody like this, and then say you don't want him!"

"What I meant to tell you was only this," she said eagerly, and yet half conscious of the absurdity of the position she had made for herself—"that nobody has got me yet as a sweetheart, instead of my having a dozen, as my aunt said; I *hate* to be thought men's property in that way, though possibly I shall be had some day. Why, if I'd wanted you I shouldn't have run after you like this; 'twould have been the *forwardest* thing! But there was no harm in hurrying to correct a piece of false news that had been told you."

"Oh, no—no harm at all." But there is such a thing as being too generous in expressing a judgment impulsively, and Oak added with a more appreciative sense of all the circumstances—"Well, I am not quite certain it was no harm."

"Indeed, I hadn't time to think before starting whether I wanted to marry or not, for you'd have been gone over the hill."

"Come," said Gabriel, freshening again; "think a minute or two. I'll wait a while, Miss Everdene. Will you marry me? Do, Bathsheba. I love you far more than common!"

"I'll try to think," she observed rather more timorously; "if I can think out of doors; my mind spreads away so."

"But you can give a guess."

"Then give me time." Bathsheba looked thoughtfully into the distance, away from the direction in which Gabriel stood.

"I can make you happy," said he to the back of her head, across the bush. "You shall have a piano in a year or two—farmers' wives are getting to have pianos now—and I'll practise up the flute right well to play with you in the evenings."

"Yes; I should like that."

"And have one of those little ten-pound gigs for market—and nice flowers, and birds—cocks and hens I mean, because they be useful," continued Gabriel, feeling balanced between poetry and practicality.

"I should like it very much."

"And a frame for cucumbers—like a gentleman and lady."

"Yes."

"And when the wedding was over, we'd have it put in the newspaper list of marriages."

"Dearly I should like that!"

"And the babies in the births—every man jack of 'em! And at home by the fire, whenever you look up, there I shall be—and whenever I look up, there will be you."

"Wait, wait, and don't be improper!"

Her countenance fell, and she was silent awhile. He regarded the red berries between them over and over again, to such an extent, that holly seemed in his after life to be a cypher signifying a proposal of marriage. Bathsheba decisively turned to him.

"No; 'tis no use," she said. "I don't want to marry you."

"Try."

"I have tried hard all the time I've been thinking; for a marriage would be very nice in one sense. People would talk about me and think I had won my battle, and I should feel triumphant, and all that. But a husband—"

"Well!"

"Why, he'd always be there, as you say; whenever I looked up, there he'd be."

"Of course he would—I, that is."

"Well, what I mean is that I shouldn't mind being a bride at a wedding, if I could be one without having a husband. But since a woman can't show off in that way by herself, I shan't marry—at least yet."

"That's a terrible wooden story!"

At this criticism of her statement Bathsheba made an addition to her dignity by a slight sweep away from him.

"Upon my heart and soul I don't know what a maid can say stupider than that," said Oak. "But dearest," he continued in a palliative voice, "don't be like it!" Oak sighed a deep honest sigh—none the less so in that, being like the sigh of a pine plantation, it was rather noticeable as a disturbance of the atmosphere. "Why won't you have me?" he appealed, creeping round the holly to reach her side.

"I cannot," she said, retreating.

"But why?" he persisted, standing still at last in despair of ever reaching her, and facing over the bush.

"Because I don't love you."

"Yes, but—"

She contracted a yawn to an inoffensive smallness, so that it was hardly ill-mannered at all. "I don't love you," she said.

"But I love you—and, as for myself, I am content to be liked."

"O Mr. Oak—that's very fine! You'd get to despise me."

"Never," said Mr Oak, so earnestly that he seemed to be coming, by the force of his words, straight through the bush and into her arms. "I shall do one thing in this life—one thing certain—that is, love you, and long for you, and *keep wanting you* till I die." His voice had a genuine pathos now, and his large brown hands perceptibly trembled.

"It seems dreadfully wrong not to have you when you feel so much!" she said with a little distress, and looking hopelessly around for some means of escape from her moral dilemma. "How I wish I hadn't run after you!" However, she seemed to have a short cut for getting back to cheerfulness and set her face to signify archness. "It wouldn't do, Mr Oak. I want somebody to tame me; I am too independent; and you would never be able to, I know."

Oak cast his eyes down the field in a way implying that it was useless to attempt argument.

"Mr. Oak," she said, with luminous distinctness and common sense, "you are better off than I. I have hardly a penny in the world—I am staying with my aunt for my bare sustenance. I am better educated than you—and I don't love you a bit: that's my side of the case. Now yours: you are a farmer just beginning, and you ought in common prudence, if you marry at all (which you should certainly not think of doing at present) to marry a woman with money, who would stock a larger farm for you than you have now."

Gabriel looked at her with a little surprise and much admiration.

"That's the very thing I had been thinking myself!" he naïvely said.

Farmer Oak had one-and-a-half Christian characteristics too many to succeed with Bathsheba: his humility, and a superfluous moiety of honesty. Bathsheba was decidedly disconcerted.

"Well, then, why did you come and disturb me?" she said, almost angrily, if not quite, an enlarging red spot rising in each cheek.

"I can't do what I think would be—would be—"

"Right?"

"No: wise."

"You have made an admission *now,* Mr. Oak," she exclaimed with even more hauteur, and rocking her head disdainfully. "After that, do you think I could marry you? Not if I know it."

He broke in passionately. "But don't mistake me like that! Because I am open enough to own what every man in my shoes would have thought of, you make your colours come up your face and get crabbed with me. That about your not being good enough for me is nonsense. You speak like a lady—all the parish notice it, and your uncle at Weatherbury is, I've heerd, a large farmer—much larger than ever I shall be. May I call in the evening, or will you walk along with me o' Sundays? I don't want you to make up your mind at once, if you'd rather not."

"No—no—I cannot. Don't press me any more—don't. I don't love you—so 'twould be ridiculous," she said, with a laugh.

No man likes to see his emotions the sport of a merry-go-round of skittishness. "Very well," said Oak firmly, with the bearing of one who was going to give his days and nights to Ecclesiastes forever. "Then I'll ask you no more."

V

DEPARTURE OF BATHSHEBA—A PASTORAL TRAGEDY

THE NEWS WHICH ONE DAY REACHED GABRIEL THAT BATHSHEBA EVERDENE HAD LEFT the neighbourhood, had an influence upon him which might have surprised any who never suspected that the more emphatic the renunciation the less absolute its character.

It may have been observed that there is no regular path for getting out of love as there is for getting in. Some people look upon marriage as a short cut that way, but it has been known to fail. Separation, which was the means that chance offered to Gabriel Oak by Bathsheba's disappearance, though effectual with people of certain humours, is apt to ide- alise the removed object with others—notably those whose affection, placid and regular as it may be, flows deep and long. Oak belonged to the even-tempered order of humanity, and felt the secret fusion of himself in Bathsheba to be burning with a finer flame now that she was gone—that was all.

His incipient friendship with her aunt had been nipped by the failure of his suit, and all that Oak learnt of Bathsheba's movements was done indirectly. It appeared that she had gone to a place called Weatherbury, more than twenty miles off, but in what capacity— whether as a visitor or permanently, he could not discover.

Gabriel had two dogs. George, the elder, exhibited an ebony-tipped nose, surrounded by a narrow margin of pink flesh, and a coat marked in random splotches approximating in colour to white and slaty grey; but the grey, after years of sun and rain, had been scorched and washed out of the more prominent locks, leaving them of a reddish-brown, as if the blue component of the grey had faded, like the indigo from the same kind of colour in Turner's pictures. In substance it had originally been hair, but long contact with sheep seemed to be turning it by degrees into wool of a poor quality and staple. .

This dog had originally belonged to a shepherd of inferior morals and dreadful tem- per, and the result was that George knew the exact degrees of condemnation signified by cursing and swearing of all descriptions better than the wickedest old man in the neigh- bourhood. Long experience had so precisely taught the animal the difference between such exclamations as "Come in!" and "D— ye, come in!" that he knew to a hair's breadth the rate of trotting back from the ewes' tails that each call involved, if a staggerer with the sheep-crook was to be escaped. Though old, he was clever and trustworthy still.

The young dog, George's son, might possibly have been the image of his mother, for there was not much resemblance between him and George. He was learning the sheep- keeping business, so as to follow on at the flock when the other should die, but had got no further than the rudiments as yet—still finding an insuperable difficulty in distinguishing between doing a thing well enough and doing it too well. So earnest and yet so wrong- headed was this young dog (he had no name in particular, and answered with perfect readi- ness to any pleasant interjection) that if sent behind the flock to help them on he did it so thoroughly that he would have chased them across the whole county with the greatest pleasure if not called off, or reminded when to stop by the example of old George.

Thus much for the dogs. On the further side of Norcombe Hill was a chalk-pit, from which chalk had been drawn for generations, and spread over adjacent farms. Two hedges converged upon it in the form of a V, but without quite meeting. The narrow opening left, which was immediately over the brow of the pit, was protected by a rough railing.

One night, when Farmer Oak had returned to his house, believing there would be no further necessity for his attendance on the down, he called as usual to the dogs, previously to shutting them up in the outhouse till next morning. Only one responded—old George; the other could not be found, either in the house, lane, or garden. Gabriel then remem- bered that he had left the two dogs on the hill eating a dead lamb (a kind of meat he usu- ally kept from them, except when other food ran short), and concluding that the young one had not finished his meal, he went indoors to the luxury of a bed, which latterly he had only enjoyed on Sundays.

It was a still, moist night. Just before dawn he was assisted in waking by the abnormal reverberation of familiar music. To the shepherd, the note of the sheep-bell, like the ticking of the clock to other people, is a chronic sound that only makes itself noticed by ceasing or altering in some unusual manner from the well-known idle twinkle which signifies to the accustomed ear, however distant, that all is well in the fold. In the solemn calm of the awakening morn that note was heard by Gabriel, beating with unusual violence and rapidity. This exceptional ringing may be caused in two ways—by the rapid feeding of the sheep bearing the bell, as when the flock breaks into new pasture, which gives it an intermittent rapidity, or by the sheep starting off in a run, when the sound has a regular palpitation. The experienced ear of Oak knew the sound he now heard to be caused by the running of the flock with great velocity.

He jumped out of bed, dressed, tore down the lane through a foggy dawn, and ascended the hill. The forward ewes were kept apart from those among which the fall of lambs would be later, there being two hundred of the latter class in Gabriel's flock. These two hundred seemed to have absolutely vanished from the hill. There were the fifty with their lambs, enclosed at the other end as he had left them, but the rest, forming the bulk of the flock, were nowhere. Gabriel called at the top of his voice the shepherd's call:

"Ovey, ovey, ovey!"

Not a single bleat. He went to the hedge; a gap had been broken through it, and in the gap were the footprints of the sheep. Rather surprised to find them break fence at this season, yet putting it down instantly to their great fondness for ivy in winter-time, of which a great deal grew in the plantation, he followed through the hedge. They were not in the plantation. He called again: the valleys and farthest hills resounded as when the sailors invoked the lost Hylas on the Mysian shore; but no sheep. He passed through the trees and along the ridge of the hill. On the extreme summit, where the ends of the two converging hedges of which we have spoken were stopped short by meeting the brow of the chalk-pit, he saw the younger dog standing against the sky—dark and motionless as Napoleon at St. Helena.

A horrible conviction darted through Oak. With a sensation of bodily faintness he advanced: at one point the rails were broken through, and there he saw the footprints of his ewes. The dog came up, licked his hand, and made signs implying that he expected some great reward for signal services rendered. Oak looked over the precipice. The ewes lay dead and dying at its foot—a heap of two hundred mangled carcases, representing in their condition just now at least two hundred more.

Oak was an intensely humane man: indeed, his humanity often tore in pieces any politic intentions of his which bordered on strategy, and carried him on as by gravitation. A shadow in his life had always been that his flock ended in mutton—that a day came and found every shepherd an arrant traitor to his defenseless sheep. His first feeling now was one of pity for the untimely fate of these gentle ewes and their unborn lambs.

It was a second to remember another phase of the matter. The sheep were not insured. All the savings of a frugal life had been dispersed at a blow; his hopes of being an independent farmer were laid low—possibly forever. Gabriel's energies, patience, and industry had been so severely taxed during the years of his life between eighteen and eight-and-twenty, to reach his present stage of progress, that no more seemed to be left in him. He leant down upon a rail, and covered his face with his hands.

Stupors, however, do not last forever, and Farmer Oak recovered from his. It was as remarkable as it was characteristic that the one sentence he uttered was in thankfulness:—

"Thank God I am not married: what would *she* have done in the poverty now coming upon me!"

Oak raised his head, and wondering what he could do, listlessly surveyed the scene. By the outer margin of the pit was an oval pond, and over it hung the attenuated skeleton of a chrome-yellow moon which had only a few days to last—the morning star dogging her on the left hand. The pool glittered like a dead man's eye, and as the world awoke a breeze blew, shaking and elongating the reflection of the moon without breaking it, and turning the image of the star to a phosphoric streak upon the water. All this Oak saw and remembered.

As far as could be learnt it appeared that the poor young dog, still under the impression that since he was kept for running after sheep, the more he ran after them the better, had at the end of his meal off the dead lamb, which may have given him additional energy and spirits, collected all the ewes into a corner, driven the timid creatures through the hedge, across the upper field, and by main force of worrying had given them momentum enough to break down a portion of the rotten railing, and so hurled them over the edge.

George's son had done his work so thoroughly that he was considered too good a workman to live, and was, in fact, taken and tragically shot at twelve o'clock that same day—another instance of the untoward fate which so often attends dogs and other philosophers who follow out a train of reasoning to its logical conclusion and attempt perfectly consistent conduct in a world made up so largely of compromise.

Gabriel's farm had been stocked by a dealer—on the strength of Oak's promising look and character—who was receiving a percentage from the farmer till such time as the advance should be cleared off. Oak found that the value of stock, plant, and implements which were really his own would be about sufficient to pay his debts, leaving himself a free man with the clothes he stood up in, and nothing more.

VI

THE FAIR—THE JOURNEY—THE FIRE

TWO MONTHS PASSED AWAY. WE ARE BROUGHT ON TO A DAY IN FEBRUARY, ON WHICH was held the yearly statute or hiring fair in the county-town of Casterbridge.

At one end of the street stood from two to three hundred blithe and hearty labourers waiting upon Chance—all men of the stamp to whom labour suggests nothing worse than a wrestle with gravitation, and pleasure nothing better than a renunciation of the same. Among these, carters and waggoners were distinguished by having a piece of whip-cord twisted round their hats; thatchers wore a fragment of woven straw; shepherds held their sheep-crooks in their hands; and thus the situation required was known to the hirers at a glance.

In the crowd was an athletic young fellow of somewhat superior appearance to the rest—in fact, his superiority was marked enough to lead several ruddy peasants standing by to speak to him enquiringly, as to a farmer, and to use "Sir" as a finishing word. His answer always was—

"I am looking for a place myself—a bailiff's. Do ye know of anybody who wants one?"

Gabriel was paler now. His eyes were more meditative, and his expression was more sad. He had passed through an ordeal of wretchedness which had given him more than it had taken away. He had sunk from his modest elevation as pastoral king into the very slime-pits of Siddim; but there was left to him a dignified calm he had never before known, and that indifference to fate which, though it often makes a villain of a man, is the basis of his sublimity when it does not. And thus the abasement had been exaltation, and the loss gain.

In the morning a regiment of cavalry had left the town, and a sergeant and his party had been beating up for recruits through the four streets. As the end of the day drew on, and he found himself not hired, Gabriel almost wished that he had joined them, and gone off to serve his country. Weary of standing in the market-place, and not much minding the kind of work he turned his hand to, he decided to offer himself in some other capacity than that of bailiff.

All the farmers seemed to be wanting shepherds. Sheep-tending was Gabriel's speciality. Turning down an obscure street and entering an obscurer lane, he went up to a smith's shop.

"How long would it take you to make a shepherd's crook?"

"Twenty minutes."

"How much?"

"Two shillings."

He sat on a bench and the crook was made, a stem being given him into the bargain.

He then went to a ready-made clothes shop, the owner of which had a large rural connection. As the crook had absorbed most of Gabriel's money, he attempted, and carried out, an exchange of his overcoat for a shepherd's regulation smock-frock.

This transaction having been completed he again hurried off to the centre of the town, and stood on the kerb of the pavement, as a shepherd, crook in hand.

Now that Oak had turned himself into a shepherd, it seemed that bailiffs were most in demand. However, two or three farmers noticed him and drew near. Dialogues followed, more or less in the subjoined form:—

"Where do you come from?"

"Norcombe."

"That's a long way."

"Fifteen miles."

"Whose farm were you upon last?"

"My own."

This reply invariably operated like a rumour of cholera. The enquiring farmer would edge away and shake his head dubiously. Gabriel, like his dog, was too good to be trustworthy, and he never made advance beyond this point.

It is safer to accept any chance that offers itself, and extemporise a procedure to fit it, than to get a good plan matured, and wait for a chance of using it. Gabriel wished he had not nailed up his colours as a shepherd, but had laid himself out for anything in the whole cycle of labour that was required in the fair. It grew dusk. Some merry men were whistling and singing by the corn-exchange. Gabriel's hand, which had lain for some time idle in his smock-frock pocket, touched his flute, which he carried there. Here was an opportunity for putting his dearly bought wisdom into practice.

He drew out his flute and began to play "Jockey to the Fair" in the style of a man who had never known moment's sorrow. Oak could pipe with Arcadian sweetness, and the sound of the well-known notes cheered his own heart as well as those of the loungers. He played on with spirit, and in half an hour had earned in pence what was a small fortune to a destitute man.

By making enquiries he learnt that there was another fair at Shottsford the next day. "How far is Shottsford?"

"Ten miles t'other side of Weatherbury."

Weatherbury! It was where Bathsheba had gone two months before. This information was like coming from night into noon.

"How far is it to Weatherbury?"

"Five or six miles."

Bathsheba had probably left Weatherbury long before this time, but the place had enough interest attaching to it to lead Oak to choose Shottsford fair as his next field of enquiry, because it lay in the Weatherbury quarter. Moreover, the Weatherbury folk were by no means uninteresting intrinsically. If report spoke truly they were as hardy, merry, thriving, wicked a set as any in the whole county. Oak resolved to sleep at Weatherbury that night on his way to Shottsford, and struck out at once into the high-road which had been recommended as the direct route to the village in question.

The road stretched through water-meadows traversed by little brooks, whose quivering surfaces were braided along their centres, and folded into creases at the sides; or, where the flow was more rapid, the stream was pied with spots of white froth, which rode on in undisturbed serenity. On the higher levels the dead and dry carcases of leaves tapped the ground as they bowled along helter-skelter upon the shoulders of the wind, and little birds in the hedges were rustling their feathers and tucking themselves in comfortably for the night, retaining their places if Oak kept moving, but flying away if he stopped to look at them. He passed by Yalbury Wood where the game-birds were rising to their roosts, and heard the crack-voiced cock-pheasants "cu-uck, cuck," and the wheezy whistle of the hens.

By the time he had walked three or four miles every shape in the landscape had assumed a uniform hue of blackness. He descended Yalbury Hill and could just discern ahead of him a waggon, drawn up under a great over-hanging tree by the roadside.

On coming close, he found there were no horses attached to it, the spot being apparently quite deserted. The waggon, from its position, seemed to have been left there for the night, for beyond about half a truss of hay which was heaped in the bottom, it was quite empty. Gabriel sat down on the shafts of the vehicle and considered his position. He calculated that he had walked a very fair proportion of the journey; and having been on foot since daybreak, he felt tempted to lie down upon the hay in the waggon instead of pushing on to the village of Weatherbury, and having to pay for a lodging.

Eating his last slices of bread and ham, and drinking from the bottle of cider he had taken the precaution to bring with him, he got into the lonely waggon. Here he spread half of the hay as a bed, and, as well as he could in the darkness, pulled the other half over him by way of bed-clothes, covering himself entirely, and feeling, physically, as comfortable as ever he had been in his life. Inward melancholy it was impossible for a man like Oak, introspective far beyond his neighbours, to banish quite, whilst conning the present untoward page of his history. So, thinking of his misfortunes, amorous and pastoral, he fell asleep, shepherds enjoying, in common with sailors, the privilege of being able to summon the god instead of having to wait for him.

On somewhat suddenly awaking, after a sleep of whose length he had no idea, Oak found that the waggon was in motion. He was being carried along the road at a rate rather considerable for a vehicle without springs, and under circumstances of physical uneasiness, his head being dandled up and down on the bed of the waggon like a kettledrumstick. He then distinguished voices in conversation, coming from the forepart of the waggon. His concern at this dilemma (which would have been alarm, had he been a thriving man; but misfortune is a fine opiate to personal terror) led him to peer cautiously from the hay, and the first sight he beheld was the stars above him. Charles's Wain was getting towards a right angle with the Pole star, and Gabriel concluded that it must be about nine o'clock—in other words, that he had slept two hours. This small astronomical calculation was made without any positive effort, and whilst he was stealthily turning to discover, if possible, into whose hands he had fallen.

Two figures were dimly visible in front, sitting with their legs outside the waggon, one of whom was driving. Gabriel soon found that this was the waggoner, and it appeared they had come from Casterbridge fair, like himself.

A conversation was in progress, which continued thus:—

"Be as 'twill, she's a fine handsome body as far's looks be concerned. But that's only the skin of the woman, and these dandy cattle be as proud as a lucifer in their insides."

"Ay—so 'a do seem, Billy Smallbury—so 'a do seem." This utterance was very shaky by nature, and more so by circumstance, the jolting of the waggon not being without its effect upon the speaker's larynx. It came from the man who held the reins.

"She's a very vain feymell—so 'tis said here and there."

"Ah, now. If so be 'tis like that, I can't look her in the face. Lord, no: not I—heh-heh-heh! Such a shy man as I be!"

"Yes—she's very vain. 'Tis said that every night at going to bed she looks in the glass to put on her nightcap properly."

"And not a married woman. Oh, the world!"

"And 'a can play the peanner, so 'tis said. Can play so clever that 'a can make a psalm tune sound as well as the merriest loose song a man can wish for."

"D'ye tell o't! A happy time for us, and I feel quite a new man! And how do she pay?"

"That I don't know, Master Poorgrass."

On hearing these and other similar remarks, a wild thought flashed into Gabriel's mind that they might be speaking of Bathsheba. There were, however, no grounds for retaining such a supposition, for the waggon, though going in the direction of Weatherbury, might be going beyond it, and the woman alluded to seemed to be the mistress of some estate. They were now apparently close upon Weatherbury, and not to alarm the speakers unnecessarily Gabriel slipped out of the waggon unseen.

He turned to an opening in the hedge, which he found to be a gate, and mounting thereon he sat meditating whether to seek a cheap lodging in the village, or to ensure a cheaper one by lying under some hay or corn-stack. The crunching jangle of the waggon died upon his ear. He was about to walk on, when he noticed on his left hand an unusual light—appearing about half a mile distant. Oak watched it, and the glow increased. Something was on fire.

Gabriel again mounted the gate, and, leaping down on the other side upon what he found to be ploughed soil, made across the field in the exact direction of the fire. The blaze, enlarging in a double ratio by his approach and its own increase, showed him as he drew nearer the outlines of ricks beside it, lighted up to great distinctness. A rick-yard was the source of the fire. His weary face now began to be painted over with a rich orange glow, and the whole front of his smock-frock and gaiters was covered with a dancing shadow pattern of thorn-twigs—the light reaching him through a leafless intervening hedge—and the metallic curve of his sheep-crook shone silver-bright in the same abounding rays. He came up to the boundary fence, and stood to regain breath. It seemed as if the spot was unoccupied by a living soul.

The fire was issuing from a long straw-stack, which was so far gone as to preclude a possibility of saving it. A rick burns differently from a house. As the wind blows the fire inwards, the portion in flames completely disappears like melting sugar, and the outline is lost to the eye. However, a hay or a wheat-rick, well put together, will resist combustion for a length of time if it begins on the outside.

This before Gabriel's eyes was a rick of straw, loosely put together, and the flames darted into it with lightning swiftness. It glowed on the windward side, rising and falling in intensity like the coal of a cigar. Then a superincumbent bundle rolled down with a whisking noise; flames elongated, and bent themselves about with a quiet roar, but no crackle. Banks of smoke went off horizontally at the back like passing clouds, and behind these burned hidden pyres, illuminating the semi-transparent sheet of smoke to a lustrous yellow uniformity. Individual straws in the foreground were consumed in a creeping movement of ruddy heat, as if they were knots of red worms, and above shone imaginary fiery faces, tongues hanging from lips, glaring eyes, and other impish forms, from which at intervals sparks flew in clusters like birds from a nest.

Oak suddenly ceased from being a mere spectator by discovering the case to be more serious than he had at first imagined. A scroll of smoke blew aside and revealed to him a wheat-rick in startling juxtaposition with the decaying one, and behind this a series of others, composing the main corn produce of the farm; so that instead of the straw-stack standing, as he had imagined comparatively isolated, there was a regular connection between it and the remaining stacks of the group.

Gabriel leapt over the hedge, and saw that he was not alone. The first man he came to was running about in a great hurry, as if his thoughts were several yards in advance of his body, which they could never drag on fast enough.

"O, man—fire, fire! A good master and a bad servant is fire, fire!—I mane a bad servant and a good master. O Mark Clark—come! And you, Billy Smallbury—and you, Maryann Money—and you, Jan Coggan, and Matthew there!" Other figures now appeared behind this shouting man and among the smoke, and Gabriel found that, far from being alone, he was in a great company—whose shadows danced merrily up and down, timed by the jigging of the flames, and not at all by their owners' movements. The assemblage—

belonging to that class of society which casts its thoughts into the form of feeling, and its feelings into the form of commotion—set to work with a remarkable confusion of purpose.

"Stop the draught under the wheat-rick!" cried Gabriel to those nearest to him. The corn stood on stone staddles, and between these, tongues of yellow hue from the burning straw licked and darted playfully. If the fire once got *under* this stack, all would be lost.

"Get a tarpaulin—quick!" said Gabriel.

A rick-cloth was brought, and they hung it like a curtain across the channel. The flames immediately ceased to go under the bottom of the corn-stack, and stood up vertical.

"Stand here with a bucket of water and keep the cloth wet," said Gabriel again.

The flames, now driven upwards, began to attack the angles of the huge roof covering the wheat-stack.

"A ladder," cried Gabriel.

"The ladder was against the straw-rick and is burnt to a cinder," said a spectrelike form in the smoke.

Oak seized the cut ends of the sheaves, as if he were going to engage in the operation of "reed-drawing," and digging in his feet, and occasionally sticking in the stem of his sheep-crook, he clambered up the beetling face. He at once sat astride the very apex, and began with his crook to beat off the fiery fragments which had lodged thereon, shouting to the others to get him a bough and a ladder, and some water.

Billy Smallbury—one of the men who had been on the waggon—by this time had found a ladder, which Mark Clark ascended, holding on beside Oak upon the thatch. The smoke at this corner was stifling, and Clark, a nimble fellow, having been handed a bucket of water, bathed Oak's face and sprinkled him generally, whilst Gabriel, now with a long beech-bough in one hand, in addition to his crook in the other, kept sweeping the stack and dislodging all fiery particles.

On the ground the groups of villagers were still occupied in doing all they could to keep down the conflagration, which was not much. They were all tinged orange, and backed up by shadows of varying pattern. Round the corner of the largest stack, out of the direct rays of the fire, stood a pony, bearing a young woman on its back. By her side was another woman, on foot. These two seemed to keep at a distance from the fire, that the horse might not become restive.

"He's a shepherd," said the woman on foot. "Yes—he is. See how his crook shines as he beats the rick with it. And his smock-frock is burnt in two holes, I declare! A fine young shepherd he is too, ma'am."

"Whose shepherd is he?" said the equestrian in a clear voice.

"Don't know, ma'am."

"Don't any of the others know?"

"Nobody at all—I've asked 'em. Quite a stranger, they say."

The young woman on the pony rode out from the shade and looked anxiously around.

"Do you think the barn is safe?" she said.

"D'ye think the barn is safe, Jan Coggan?" said the second woman, passing on the question to the nearest man in that direction.

"Safe-now—leastwise I think so. If this rick had gone the barn would have followed. 'Tis that bold shepherd up there that have done the most good—he sitting on the top o' rick, whizzing his great long arms about like a windmill."

"He does work hard," said the young woman on horseback, looking up at Gabriel through her thick woollen veil. "I wish he was shepherd here. Don't any of you know his name?"

"Never heard the man's name in my life, or seed his form afore."

The fire began to get worsted, and Gabriel's elevated position being no longer required of him, he made as if to descend.

"Maryann," said the girl on horseback, "go to him as he comes down, and say that the farmer wishes to thank him for the great service he has done."

Maryann stalked off towards the rick and met Oak at the foot of the ladder. She delivered her message.

"Where is your master the farmer?" asked Gabriel, kindling with the idea of getting employment that seemed to strike him now.

" 'Tisn't a master; 'tis a mistress, shepherd."

"A woman farmer?"

"Ay, 'a b'lieve, and a rich one too!" said a bystander. "Lately 'a came here from a distance. Took on her uncle's farm, who died suddenly. Used to measure his money in half-pint cups. They say now that she've business in every bank in Casterbridge, and thinks no more of playing pitch-and-toss sovereign than you and I do pitch-halfpenny—not a bit in the world, shepherd."

"That's she, back there upon the pony," said Maryann; "wi' her face a-covered up in that black cloth with holes in it."

Oak, his features smudged, grimy, and undiscoverable from the smoke and heat, his smock-frock burnt into holes and dripping with water, the ash stem of his sheep-crook charred six inches shorter, advanced with the humility stern adversity had thrust upon him up to the slight female form in the saddle. He lifted his hat with respect, and not without gallantry: stepping close to her hanging feet he said in a hesitating voice—

"Do you happen to want a shepherd, ma'am?"

She lifted the wool veil tied round her face, and looked all astonishment. Gabriel and his cold-hearted darling, Bathsheba Everdene, were face to face.

Bathsheba did not speak, and he mechanically repeated in an abashed and sad voice—

"Do you want a shepherd, ma'am?"

VII

RECOGNITION—A TIMID GIRL

BATHSHEBA WITHDREW INTO THE SHADE. SHE SCARCELY KNEW WHETHER MOST TO BE amused at the singularity of the meeting, or to be concerned at its awkwardness. There was room for a little pity, also for a very little exultation: the former at his position, the latter at her own. Embarrassed she was not, and she remembered Gabriel's declaration of love to her at Norcombe only to think she had nearly forgotten it.

"Yes," she murmured, putting on an air of dignity, and turning again to him with a little warmth of cheek; "I do want a shepherd. But—"

"He's the very man, ma'am," said one of the villagers, quietly.

Conviction breeds conviction. "Ay, that 'a is," said a second, decisively.

"The man, truly!" said a third, with heartiness.

"He's all there!" said number four, fervidly.

"Then will you tell him to speak to the bailiff," said Bathsheba.

All was practical again now. A summer eve and loneliness would have been necessary to give the meeting its proper fulness of romance.

The bailiff was pointed out to Gabriel, who, checking the palpitation within his breast at discovering that this Ashtoreth of strange report was only a modification of Venus the well-known and admired, retired with him to talk over the necessary preliminaries of hiring.

The fire before them wasted away. "Men," said Bathsheba, "you shall take a little refreshment after this extra work. Will you come to the house?"

"We could knock in a bit and a drop a good deal freer, Miss, if so be ye'd send it to Warren's Malthouse," replied the spokesman.

Bathsheba then rode off into the darkness, and the men straggled on to the village in twos and threes—Oak and the bailiff being left by the rick alone.

"And now," said the bailiff, finally, "all is settled, I think, about your coming, and I am going home-along. Good-night to ye, shepherd."

"Can you get me a lodging?" enquired Gabriel.

"That I can't, indeed," he said, moving past Oak as a Christian edges past an offertory-plate when he does not mean to contribute. "If you follow on the road till you come to Warren's Malthouse, where they are all gone to have their snap of victuals, I daresay some of 'em will tell you of a place. Good-night to ye, shepherd."

The bailiff who showed this nervous dread of loving his neighbour as himself, went up the hill, and Oak walked on to the village, still astonished at the re-encounter with Bathsheba, glad of his nearness to her, and perplexed at the rapidity with which the unpracticed girl of Norcombe had developed into the supervising and cool woman here. But some women only require an emergency to make them fit for one.

Obliged to some extent to forego dreaming in order to find the way, he reached the churchyard, and passed round it under the wall where several ancient trees grew. There was a wide margin of grass along here, and Gabriel's footsteps were deadened by its softness, even at this indurating period of the year. When abreast of a trunk which appeared to be the oldest of the old, he became aware that a figure was standing behind it. Gabriel did not pause in his walk, and in another moment he accidentally kicked a loose stone. The noise was enough to disturb the motionless stranger, who started and assumed a careless position.

It was a slim girl, rather thinly clad.

"Good-night to you," said Gabriel heartily.

"Good-night," said the girl to Gabriel.

The voice was unexpectedly attractive; it was the low and dulcet note suggestive of romance; common in descriptions, rare in experience.

"I'll thank you to tell me if I'm in the way for Warren's Malthouse?" Gabriel resumed, primarily to gain the information, indirectly to get more of the music.

"Quite right. It's at the bottom of the hill. And do you know—" The girl hesitated and then went on again. "Do you know how late they keep open the Buck's Head Inn?" She seemed to be won by Gabriel's heartiness, as Gabriel had been won by her modulations.

"I don't know where the Buck's Head is, or anything about it. Do you think of going there to-night?"

"Yes—" The woman again paused. There was no necessity for any continuance of speech, and the fact that she did add more seemed to proceed from an unconscious desire to show unconcern by making a remark, which is noticeable in the ingenuous when they are acting by stealth. "You are not a Weatherbury man?" she said timorously.

"I am not. I am the new shepherd—just arrived."

"Only a shepherd—and you seem almost a farmer by your ways."

"Only a shepherd," Gabriel repeated, in a dull cadence of finality. His thoughts were directed to the past, his eyes to the feet of the girl; and for the first time he saw lying there a bundle of some sort. She may have perceived the direction of his face, for she said coaxingly—

"You won't say anything in the parish about having seen me here, will you—at least, not for a day or two?"

"I won't if you wish me not to," said Oak.

"Thank you, indeed," the other replied. "I am rather poor, and I don't want people to know anything about me." Then she was silent and shivered.

"You ought to have a cloak on such a cold night," Gabriel observed. "I would advise 'ee to get indoors."

"O no! Would you mind going on and leaving me? I thank you much for what you have told me."

"I will go on," he said; adding hesitatingly—"Since you are not very well off, perhaps you would accept this trifle from me. It is only a shilling, but it is all I have to spare."

"Yes, I will take it," said the stranger gratefully.

She extended her hand; Gabriel his. In feeling for each other's palm in the gloom before the money could be passed, a minute incident occurred which told much. Gabriel's fingers alighted on the young woman's wrist. It was beating with a throb of tragic intensity. He had frequently felt the same quick, hard beat in the femoral artery of his lambs when overdriven. It suggested a consumption too great of a vitality which, to judge from her figure and stature, was already too little.

"What is the matter?"

"Nothing."

"But there is?"

"No, no, no! Let your having seen me be a secret!"

"Very well; I will. Good-night, again."

"Good-night."

The young girl remained motionless by the tree, and Gabriel descended into the village of Weatherbury, or Lower Longpuddle as it was sometimes called. He fancied that he had felt himself in the penumbra of a very deep sadness when touching that slight and fragile creature. But wisdom lies in moderating mere impressions, and Gabriel endeavoured to think little of this.

VIII

The Malthouse—The Chat—News

WARREN'S MALTHOUSE WAS ENCLOSED BY AN OLD WALL INWRAPPED WITH IVY, AND though not much of the exterior was visible at this hour, the character and purposes of the building were clearly enough shown by its outline upon the sky. From the walls an overhanging thatched roof sloped up to a point in the centre, upon which rose a small wooden lantern, fitted with louvre-boards on all the four sides, and from these openings a mist was dimly perceived to be escaping into the night air. There was no window in front; but a square hole in the door was glazed with a single pane, through which red, comfortable rays now stretched out upon the ivied wall in front. Voices were to be heard inside.

Oak's hand skimmed the surface of the door with fingers extended to an Elymas-the-Sorcerer pattern, till he found a leathern strap, which he pulled. This lifted a wooden latch, and the door swung open.

The room inside was lighted only by the ruddy glow from the kiln mouth, which shone over the floor with the streaming horizontality of the setting sun, and threw upwards the shadows of all facial irregularities in those assembled around. The stone-flag floor was worn into a path from the doorway to the kiln, and into undulations everywhere. A curved settle of unplaned oak stretched along one side, and in a remote corner was a small bed and bedstead, the owner and frequent occupier of which was the maltster.

This aged man was now sitting opposite the fire, his frosty white hair and beard overgrowing his gnarled figure like the grey moss and lichen upon a leafless apple-tree. He wore breeches and the laced-up shoes called ankle-jacks; he kept his eyes fixed upon the fire.

Gabriel's nose was greeted by an atmosphere laden with the sweet smell of new malt. The conversation (which seemed to have been concerning the origin of the fire) immediately ceased, and everyone ocularly criticised him to the degree expressed by contracting the flesh of their foreheads and looking at him with narrowed eyelids, as if he had been a light too strong for their sight. Several exclaimed meditatively, after this operation had been completed:—

"Oh, 'tis the new shepherd, 'a b'lieve."

"We thought we heard a hand pawing about the door for the bobbin, but weren't sure 'twere not a dead leaf blowed across," said another. "Come in, shepherd; sure ye be welcome, though we don't know yer name."

"Gabriel Oak, that's my name, neighbours."

The ancient maltster sitting in the midst turned at this—his turning being as the turning of a rusty crane.

"That's never Gable Oak's grand-son over at Norcombe—never!" he said, as a formula expressive of surprise, which nobody was supposed for a moment to take literally.

"My father and my grand-father were old men of the name of Gabriel," said the shepherd placidly.

"Thought I knowed the man's face as I seed him on the rick!—thought I did! And where be ye trading o't to now, shepherd?"

"I'm thinking of biding here," said Mr. Oak.

"Knowed yer grand-father for years and years!" continued the maltster, the words coming forth of their own accord as if the momentum previously imparted had been sufficient.

"Ah—and did you!"

"Knowed yer grand-mother."

"And her too!"

"Likewise knowed yer father when he was a child. Why, my boy Jacob there and your father were sworn brothers—that they were sure—weren't ye, Jacob?"

"Ay, sure," said his son, a young man about sixty-five, with a semi-bald head and one tooth in the left centre of his upper jaw, which made much of itself by standing prominent, like a milestone in a bank. "But 'twas Joe had most to do with him. However, my son William must have knowed the very man afore us—didn't ye, Billy, afore ye left Norcombe?"

"No, 'twas Andrew," said Jacob's son Billy, a child of forty, or thereabouts, who manifested the peculiarity of possessing a cheerful soul in a gloomy body, and whose whiskers were assuming a chinchilla shade here and there.

"I can mind Andrew," said Oak, "as being a man in the place when I was quite a child."

"Ay—the other day I and my youngest daughter, Liddy, were over at my grand-son's christening," continued Billy. "We were talking about this very family, and 'twas only last Purification Day in this very world, when the use-money is gied away to the second-best poor folk, you know, shepherd, and I can mind the day because they all had to traypse up to the vestry—yes, this very man's family."

"Come, shepherd, and drink. 'Tis gape and swaller with us—a drap of sommit, but not of much account," said the maltster, removing from the fire his eyes, which were vermilion-red and bleared by gazing into it for so many years. "Take up the God-forgive-me, Jacob. See if 'tis warm, Jacob."

Jacob stooped to the God-forgive-me, which was a two-handled tall mug standing in the ashes, cracked and charred with heat: it was rather furred with extraneous matter about the outside, especially in the crevices of the handles, the innermost curves of which may not have seen daylight for several years by reason of this encrustation thereon—formed of ashes accidentally wetted with cider and baked hard; but to the mind of any sensible drinker the cup was no worse for that, being incontestably clean on the inside and about the rim. It may be observed that such a class of mug is called a God-forgive-me in Weatherbury and its vicinity for uncertain reasons; probably because its size makes any given toper feel ashamed of himself when he sees its bottom in drinking it empty.

Jacob, on receiving the order to see if the liquor was warm enough, placidly dipped his forefinger into it by way of thermometer, and having pronounced it nearly of the proper degree, raised the cup and very civilly attempted to dust some of the ashes from the bottom with the skirt of his smock-frock, because Shepherd Oak was a stranger.

"A clane cup for the shepherd," said the maltster commandingly.

"No—not at all," said Gabriel, in a reproving tone of considerateness. "I never fuss about dirt in its pure state, and when I know what sort it is." Taking the mug he drank an inch or more from the depth of its contents, and duly passed it to the next man. "I wouldn't think of giving such trouble to neighbours in washing up when there's so much work to be done in the world already," continued Oak in a moister tone, after recovering from the stoppage of breath which is occasioned by pulls at large mugs.

"A right sensible man," said Jacob.

"True, true; it can't be gainsaidl" observed a brisk young man—Mark Clark by name, a genial and pleasant gentleman, whom to meet anywhere in your travels was to know, to know was to drink with, and to drink with was, unfortunately, to pay for.

"And here's a mouthful of bread and bacon that mis'ess have sent, shepherd. The cider will go down better with a bit of victuals. Don't ye chaw quite close, shepherd, for I let the bacon fall in the road outside as I was bringing it along, and may be 'tis rather gritty. There, 'tis clane dirt; and we all know what that is, as you say, and you bain't a particular man we see, shepherd."

"True, true—not at all," said the friendly Oak.

"Don't let your teeth quite meet, and you won't feel the sandiness at all. Ah! 'tis wonderful what can be done by contrivance!"

"My own mind exactly, neighbour."

"Ah, he's his grandfer's own grand-son!—his grandfer were just such a nice unparticular man!" said the maltster.

"Drink, Henry Fray—drink," magnanimously said Jan Coggan, a person who held Saint-Simonian notions of share and share alike where liquor was concerned, as the vessel showed signs of approaching him in its gradual revolution among them.

Having at this moment reached the end of a wistful gaze into mid-air, Henry did not refuse. He was a man of more than middle age, with eyebrows high up in his forehead, who laid it down that the law of the world was bad, with a long-suffering look through his listeners at the world alluded to, as it presented itself to his imagination. He always signed his name "Henery"—strenuously insisting upon that spelling, and if any passing schoolmaster ventured to remark that the second "e" was superfluous and old-fashioned, he received the reply that "H-e-n-e-r-y" was the name he was christened and the name he would stick to—in the tone of one to whom orthographical differences were matters which had a great deal to do with personal character.

Mr. Jan Coggan, who had passed the cup to Henery, was a crimson man with a spacious countenance and private glimmer in his eye, whose name had appeared on the marriage register of Weatherbury and neighbouring parishes as best man and chief witness in countless unions of the previous twenty years; he also very frequently filled the post of head godfather in baptisms of the subtly-jovial kind.

"Come, Mark Clark—come. Ther's plenty more in the barrel," said Jan.

"Ay—that I will, 'tis my only doctor," replied Mr. Clark, who, twenty years younger than Jan Coggan, revolved in the same orbit. He secreted mirth on all occasions for special discharge at popular parties.

"Why, Joseph Poorgrass, ye han't had a drop!" said Mr. Coggan to a self-conscious man in the background, thrusting the cup towards him.

"Such a modest man as he is!" said Jacob Smallbury. "Why, ye've hardly had strength of eye enough to look in our young mis'ess's face, so I hear, Joseph?"

All looked at Joseph Poorgrass with pitying reproach.

"No—I've hardly looked at her at all," simpered Joseph, reducing his body smaller whilst talking, apparently from a meek sense of undue prominence. "And when I seed her, 'twas nothing but blushes with me!"

"Poor feller," said Mr. Clark.

" 'Tis a curious nature for a man," said Jan Coggan.

"Yes," continued Joseph Poorgrass—his shyness, which was so painful as a defect, filling him with a mild complacency now that it was regarded as an interesting study. " 'Twere blush, blush, blush with me every minute of the time, when she was speaking to me."

"I believe ye, Joseph Poorgrass, for we all know ye to be a very bashful man."

" 'Tis a' awkward gift for a man, poor soul," said the maltster. "And ye have suffered from it a long time, we know."

"Ay, ever since I was a boy. Yes—mother was concerned to her heart about it—yes. But 'twas all nought."

"Did ye ever go into the world to try and stop it, Joseph Poorgrass?"

"Oh ay, tried all sorts o' company. They took me to Greenhill Fair, and into a great gay jerry-go-nimble show, where there were women-folk riding round—standing upon horses, with hardly anything on but their smocks; but it didn't cure me a morsel. And then I was put errand-man at the Women's Skittle Alley at the back of the Tailor's Arms in Casterbridge. 'Twas a horrible sinful situation, and a very curious place for a good man. I had to stand and look ba'dy people in the face from morning till night; but 'twas no use—I was just as bad as ever after all. Blushes hev been in the family for generations. There, 'tis a happy providence that I be no worse."

"True," said Jacob Smallbury, deepening his thoughts to a profounder view of the subject. " 'Tis a thought to look at, that ye might have been worse; but even as you be, 'tis a very bad affliction for 'ee, Joseph. For ye see, shepherd, though 'tis very well for a woman, dang it all, 'tis awkward for a man like him, poor feller?"

" 'Tis—'tis," said Gabriel, recovering from a meditation. "Yes, very awkward for the man."

"Ay, and he's very timid, too," observed Jan Coggan. "Once he had been working late at Yalbury Bottom, and had had a drap of drink, and lost his way as he was coming home-along through Yalbury Wood, didn't ye, Master Poorgrass?"

"No, no, no; not that story!" expostulated the modest man, forcing a laugh to bury his concern.

"—And so 'a lost himself quite," continued Mr. Coggan, with an impassive face, implying that a true narrative, like time and tide, must run its course and would respect no man. "And as he was coming along in the middle of the night, much afeared, and not able to find his way out of the trees nohow, 'a cried out, 'Man-a-lost! man-a-lost!' A owl in a tree happened to be crying 'Whoo-whoo-whoo!' as owls do, you know, shepherd" (Gabriel nodded), "and Joseph, all in a tremble, said, 'Joseph Poorgrass, of Weatherbury, sir!' "

"No, no, now—that's too much!" said the timid man, becoming a man of brazen courage all of a sudden. "I didn't say *sir*. I'll take my oath I didn't say 'Joseph Poorgrass o' Weatherbury, sir.' No, no; what's right is right, and I never said sir to the bird, knowing very well that no man of a gentleman's rank would be hollering there at that time o' night. 'Joseph Poorgrass of Weatherbury'—that's every word I said, and I shouldn't ha' said that if 't hadn't been for Keeper Day's metheglin. . . . There, 'twas a merciful thing it ended where it did."

The question of which was right being tacitly waived by the company, Jan went on meditatively:—

"And he's the fearfullest man, bain't ye, Joseph? Ay, another time ye were lost by Lambing-Down Gate, weren't ye, Joseph?"

"I was," replied Poorgrass, as if there were some conditions too serious even for modesty to remember itself under, this being one.

"Yes; that were the middle of the night, too. The gate would not open, try how he would, and knowing there was the Devil's hand in it, he kneeled down."

"Ay," said Joseph, acquiring confidence from the warmth of the fire, the cider, and a perception of the narrative capabilities of the experience alluded to. "My heart died within me, that time; but I kneeled down and said the Lord's Prayer, and then the Belief right through, and then the Ten Commandments, in earnest prayer. But no, the gate wouldn't open; and then I went on with Dearly Beloved Brethren, and, thinks I, this makes four, and 'tis all I know out of book, and if this don't do it nothing will, and I'm a lost man. Well, when I got to Saying After Me, I rose from my knees and found the gate would open— yes, neighbours, the gate opened the same as ever."

A meditation on the obvious inference was indulged in by all, and during its continuance each directed his vision into the ashpit, which glowed like a desert in the tropics under a vertical sun, shaping their eyes long and liny, partly because of the light, partly from the depth of the subject discussed.

Gabriel broke the silence. "What sort of a place is this to live at, and what sort of a mis'ess is she to work under?" Gabriel's bosom thrilled gently as he thus slipped under the notice of the assembly the innermost subject of his heart.

"We d' know little of her—nothing. She only showed herself a few days ago. Her uncle was took bad, and the doctor was called with his world-wide skill; but he couldn't save the man. As I take it, she's going to keep on the farm."

"That's about the shape o't, 'a b'lieve," said Jan Coggan. "Ay, 'tis a very good family. I'd as soon be under 'em as under one here and there. Her uncle was a very fair sort of man. Did ye know en, shepherd—a bachelor-man?"

"Not at all."

"I used to go to his house a-courting my first wife, Charlotte, who was his dairymaid. Well, a very good-hearted man were Farmer Everdene, and I being a respectable young fellow was allowed to call and see her and drink as much ale as I liked, but not to carry away any—outside my skin I mane, of course."

"Ay, ay, Jan Coggan; we know yer maning."

"And so you see 'twas beautiful ale, and I wished to value his kindness as much as I could, and not to be so ill-mannered as to drink only a thimbleful, which would have been insulting the man's generosity—"

"True, Master Coggan, 'twould so," corroborated Mark Clark.

"—And so I used to eat a lot of salt fish afore going, and then by the time I got there I were as dry as a lime-basket—so thorough dry that that ale would slip down—ah, 'twould slip down sweet! Happy times! heavenly times! Such lovely drunks as I used to have at that house! You can mind, Jacob? You used to go wi' me sometimes."

"I can—I can," said Jacob. "That one, too, that we had at Buck's Head on a White Monday was a pretty tipple."

" 'Twas. But for a wet of the better class, that brought you no nearer to the horned man than you were afore you begun, there was none like those in Farmer Everdene's kitchen. Not a single damn allowed; no, not a bare poor one, even at the most cheerful moment when all were blindest, though the good old word of sin thrown in here and there at such times is a great relief to a merry soul."

"True," said the maltster. "Nater requires her swearing at the regular times, or she's not herself; and unholy exclamations is a necessity of life."

"But Charlotte," continued Coggan—"not a word of the sort would Charlotte allow, nor the smallest item of taking in vain. . . . Ay, poor Charlotte, I wonder if she had the good fortune to get into Heaven when 'a died! But 'a was never much in luck's way, and perhaps 'a went downwards after all, poor soul."

"And did any of you know Miss Everdene's father and mother?" enquired the shepherd, who found some difficulty in keeping the conversation in the desired channel.

"I knew them a little," said Jacob Smallbury; "but they were townsfolk, and didn't live here. They've been dead for years. Father, what sort of people were mis'ess' father and mother?"

"Well," said the maltster, "he wasn't much to look at; but she was a lovely woman. He was fond enough of her as his sweetheart."

"Used to kiss her scores and long-hundreds o' times, so 'twas said," observed Coggan.

"He was very proud of her, too, when they were married, as I've been told," said the maltster.

"Ay," said Coggan. "He admired her so much that he used to light the candle three times a night to look at her."

"Boundless love; I shouldn't have supposed it in the universe!" murmured Joseph Poorgrass, who habitually spoke on a large scale in his moral reflections.

"Well, to be sure," said Gabriel.

"Oh, 'tis true enough. I knowed the man and woman both well. Levi Everdene—that was the man's name, sure. 'Man,' saith I in my hurry, but he were of a higher circle of life than that—'a was a gentleman-tailor really, worth scores of pounds. And he became a very celebrated bankrupt two or three times."

"Oh, I thought he was quite a common man!" said Joseph.

"O no, no! That man failed for heaps of money; hundreds in gold and silver."

The maltster being rather short of breath, Mr. Coggan, after absently scrutinising a coal which had fallen among the ashes, took up the narrative, with a private twirl of his eye:—

"Well, now, you'd hardly believe it, but that man—our Miss Everdene's father—was one of the ficklest husbands alive, after a while. Understand, 'a didn't want to be fickle, but he couldn't help it. The pore feller were faithful and true enough to her in his wish, but his heart would rove, do what he would. He spoke to me in real tribulation about it once. 'Coggan,' he said, 'I could never wish for a handsomer woman than I've got, but feeling she's ticketed as my lawful wife, I can't help my wicked heart wandering, do what I will.' But at last I believe he cured it by making her take off her wedding-ring and calling her by her maiden name as they sat together after the shop was shut, and so 'a would get to fancy she was only his sweetheart, and not married to him at all. And as soon as he could thoroughly fancy he was doing wrong and committing the seventh, 'a got to like her as well as ever, and they lived on a perfect picture of mutel love."

"Well, 'twas a most ungodly remedy," murmured Joseph Poorgrass; "but we ought to feel deep cheerfulness that a happy Providence kept it from being any worse. You see, he might have gone the bad road and given his eyes to unlawfulness entirely—yes, gross unlawfulness, so to say it."

"You see," said Billy Smallbury, "the man's will was to do right, sure enough, but his heart didn't chime in."

"He got so much better that he was quite godly in his later years, wasn't he, Jan?" said Joseph Poorgrass. "He got himself confirmed over again in a more serious way, and took to saying 'Amen' almost as loud as the clerk, and he liked to copy comforting verses from the tombstones. He used, too, to hold the money-plate at Let Your Light so Shine, and stand godfather to poor little come-by-chance children; and he kept a missionary box upon his table to nab folks unawares when they called; yes, and he would box the charity-boys' ears, if they laughed in church, till they could hardly stand upright, and do other deeds of piety natural to the saintly inclined."

"Ay, at that time he thought of nothing but high things," added Billy Smallbury. "One day Parson Thirdly met him and said, 'Good-morning, Mister Everdene; 'tis a fine day!' 'Amen' said Everdene, quite absentlike, thinking only of religion when he seed a parson. Yes, he was a very Christian man."

"Their daughter was not at all a pretty chiel at that time," said Henery Fray. "Never should have thought she'd have growed up such a handsome body as she is."

" 'Tis to be hoped her temper is as good as her face."

"Well, yes; but the baily will have most to do with the business and ourselves. Ah!" Henery gazed into the ashpit, and smiled volumes of ironical knowledge.

"A queer Christian, like the Devil's head in a cowl,[1] as the saying is," volunteered Mark Clark.

"He is," said Henery, implying that irony must cease at a certain point. "Between we two, man and man, I believe that man would as soon tell a lie Sundays as working-days—that I do so."

"Good faith, you do talk!" said Gabriel.

"True enough," said the man of bitter moods, looking round upon the company with the antithetic laughter that comes from a keener appreciation of the miseries of life than ordinary men are capable of. "Ah, there's people of one sort, and people of another, but that man—bless your souls!"

Gabriel thought fit to change the subject. "You must be a very aged man, malter, to have sons growed up so old and ancient," he remarked.

"Father's so old that 'a can't mind his age, can ye, father?" interposed Jacob. "And he's growed terrible crooked, too, lately," Jacob continued, surveying his father's figure, which was rather more bowed than his own. "Really, one may say that father there is three-double."

1. This phrase is a conjectural emendation of the unintelligible expression, "as the Devil said to the Owl," used by the natives.

"Crooked folk will last a long while," said the maltster, grimly, and not in the best humour.

"Shepherd would like to hear the pedigree of yer life, father—wouldn't ye, shepherd?"

"Ay, that I should," said Gabriel, with the heartiness of a man who had longed to hear it for several months. "What may your age be, malter?"

The maltster cleared his throat in an exaggerated form for emphasis, and elongating his gaze to the remotest point of the ashpit, said, in the slow speech justifiable when the importance of a subject is so generally felt that any mannerism must be tolerated in getting at it, "Well, I don't mind the year I were born in, but perhaps I can reckon up the places I've lived at, and so get it that way. I bode at Upper Longpuddle across there" (nodding to the north) "till I were eleven. I bode seven at Kingsbere" (nodding to the east) "where I took to malting. I went therefrom to Norcombe, and malted there two-and-twenty years, and two-and-twenty years I was there turnip-hoeing and harvesting. Ah, I knowed that old place, Norcombe, years afore you were thought of, Master Oak" (Oak smiled sincere belief in the fact). "Then I malted at Durnover four year, and four year turnip-hoeing; and I was fourteen times eleven months at Millpond St. Jude's" (nodding north-west-by-north). "Old Twills wouldn't hire me for more than eleven months at a time, to keep me from being chargeable to the parish if so be I was disabled. Then I was three year at Mellstock, and I've been here one-and-thirty year come Candlemas. How much is that?"

"Hundred and seventeen," chuckled another old gentleman, given to mental arithmetic and little conversation, who had hitherto sat unobserved in a corner.

"Well, then, that's my age," said the maltster emphatically.

"O no, father!" said Jacob. "Your turnip-hoeing were in the summer and your malting in the winter of the same years, and ye don't ought to count both halves, father."

"Chok' it all! I lived through the summers, didn't I? That's my question. I suppose ye'll say next I be no age at all to speak of?"

"Sure we shan't," said Gabriel soothingly.

"Ye be a very old aged person, malter," attested Jan Coggan, also soothingly. "We all know that, and ye must have a wonderful talented constitution to be able to live so long, mustn't he, neighbours?"

"True, true; ye must, malter, wonderful," said the meeting unanimously.

The maltster, being now pacified, was even generous enough to voluntarily disparage in a slight degree the virtue of having lived a great many years, by mentioning that the cup they were drinking out of was three years older than he.

While the cup was being examined, the end of Gabriel Oak's flute became visible over his smock-frock pocket, and Henery Fray exclaimed, "Surely, shepherd, I seed you blowing into a great flute by now at Casterbridge?"

"You did," said Gabriel, blushing faintly. "I've been in great trouble, neighbours, and was driven to it. I used not to be so poor as I be now."

"Never mind, heart!" said Mark Clark. "You should take it carelesslike, shepherd, and your time will come. But we could thank ye for a tune, if ye bain't too tired?"

"Neither drum nor trumpet have I heard since Christmas," said Jan Coggan. "Come, raise a tune, Master Oak!"

"That I will," said Gabriel, pulling out his flute and putting it together. "A poor tool, neighbours; but such as I can do ye shall have and welcome."

Oak then struck up "Jockey to the Fair," and played that sparkling melody three times through, accenting the notes in the third round in a most artistic and lively manner by bending his body in small jerks and tapping with his foot to beat time.

"He can blow the flute very well—that 'a can," said a young married man, who having no individuality worth mentioning was known as "Susan Tall's husband." He continued, "I'd as lief as not be able to blow into a flute as well as that."

"He's a clever man, and 'tis a true comfort for us to have such a shepherd," murmured Joseph Poorgrass, in a soft cadence. "We ought to feel full o' thanksgiving that he's not a player of ba'dy songs instead of these merry tunes; for 'twould have been just as easy for God to have made the shepherd a loose low man—a man of iniquity, so to speak it—as what he is. Yes, for our wives' and daughters' sakes we should feel real thanksgiving."

"True, true—real thanksgiving!" dashed in Mark Clark conclusively, not feeling it to be of any consequence to his opinion that he had only heard about a word and three-quarters of what Joseph had said.

"Yes," added Joseph, beginning to feel like a man in the Bible; "for evil do thrive so in these times that ye may be as much deceived in the clanest shaved and whitest shirted man as in the raggedest tramp upon the turnpike, if I may term it so."

"Ay, I can mind yer face now, shepherd," said Henery Fray, criticising Gabriel with misty eyes as he entered upon his second tune. "Yes—now I see 'ee blowing into the flute I know 'ee to be the same man I see play at Casterbridge, for yer mouth were scrimped up and yer eyes a-staring out like a strangled man's—just as they be now."

" 'Tis a pity that playing the flute should make a man look such a scarecrow," observed Mr. Mark Clark, with additional criticism of Gabriel's countenance, the latter person jerking out, with the ghastly grimace required by the instrument, the chorus of "Dame Durden":—

> 'Twas Moll' and Bet', and Doll' and Kate',
> And Dor'-othy Drag'-gle Tail'.

"I hope you don't mind that young man's bad manners in naming your features?" whispered Joseph to Gabriel.

"Not at all," said Mr. Oak.

"For by nature ye be a very handsome man, shepherd," continued Joseph Poorgrass with winning suavity.

"Ay, that ye be, shepherd," said the company.

"Thank you very much," said Oak, in the modest tone good manners demanded, thinking, however, that he would never let Bathsheba see him playing the flute; in this resolve showing a discretion equal to that related to its sagacious inventress, the divine Minerva herself.

"Ah, when I and my wife were married at Norcombe Church," said the old maltster, not pleased at finding himself left out of the subject, "we were called the handsomest couple in the neighbourhood—everybody said so."

"Danged if ye bain't altered now, malter," said a voice with the vigour natural to the enunciation of a remarkably evident truism. It came from the old man in the background, whose offensiveness and spiteful ways were barely atoned for by the occasional chuckle he contributed to general laughs.

"O no, no," said Gabriel.

"Don't ye play no more, shepherd" said Susan Tall's husband, the young married man who had spoken once before. "I must be moving and when there's tunes going on I seem as if hung in wires. If I thought after I'd left that music was still playing, and I not there, I should be quite melancholylike."

"What's yer hurry then, Laban?" enquired Coggan. "You used to bide as late as the latest."

"Well, ye see, neighbours, I was lately married to a woman, and she's my vocation now, and so ye see——" The young man halted lamely.

"New lords new laws, as the saying is, I suppose," remarked Coggan.

"Ay, 'a b'lieve—ha, ha!" said Susan Tall's husband, in a tone intended to imply his habitual reception of jokes without minding them at all. The young man then wished them good-night and withdrew.

Henery Fray was the first to follow. Then Gabriel arose and went off with Jan Coggan, who had offered him a lodging. A few minutes later, when the remaining ones were on their legs and about to depart, Fray came back again in a hurry. Flourishing his finger ominously he threw a gaze teeming with tidings just where his eye alighted by accident, which happened to be in Joseph Poorgrass's face.

"O—what's the matter, what's the matter, Henery?" said Joseph, starting back.

"What's a-brewing, Henery?" asked Jacob and Mark Clark.

"Baily Pennyways—Baily Pennyways—I said so; yes, I said so!"

"What, found out stealing anything?"

"Stealing it is. The news is, that after Miss Everdene got home she went out again to see all was safe, as she usually do, and coming in found Baily Pennyways creeping down the granary steps with half a bushel of barley. She fleed at him like a cat—never such a tomboy as she is—of course I speak with closed doors?"

"You do—you do, Henery."

"She fleed at him, and, to cut a long story short, he owned to having carried off five sack altogether, upon her promising not to persecute him. Well, he's turned out neck and crop, and my question is, who's going to be baily now?"

The question was such a profound one that Henery was obliged to drink there and then from the large cup till the bottom was distinctly visible inside. Before he had replaced it on the table, in came the young man, Susan Tall's husband, in a still greater hurry.

"Have ye heard the news that's all over parish?"

"About Baily Pennyways?"

"But besides that?"

"No—not a morsel of it!" they replied, looking into the very midst of Laban Tall as if to meet his words half-way down his throat.

"What a night of horrors!" murmured Joseph Poorgrass, waving his hands spasmodically. "I've had the news-bell ringing in my left ear quite bad enough for a murder, and I've seen a magpie all alone!"

"Fanny Robin—Miss Everdene's youngest servant—can't be found. They've been wanting to lock up the door these two hours, but she isn't come in. And they don't know what to do about going to bed for fear of locking her out. They wouldn't be so concerned if she hadn't been noticed in such low spirits these last few days, and Maryann d' think the beginning of a crowner's inquest has happened to the poor girl."

"Oh—'tis burned—'tis burned!" came from Joseph Poorgrass's dry lips.

"No—'tis drowned!" said Tall.

"Or 'tis her father's razor!" suggested Billy Smallbury with a vivid sense of detail.

"Well—Miss Everdene wants to speak to one or two of us before we go to bed. What with this trouble about the baily, and now about the girl, mis'ess is almost wild."

They all hastened up the lane to the farmhouse, excepting the old maltster, whom neither news, fire, rain, nor thunder could draw from his hole. There, as the others' footsteps died away, he sat down again and continued gazing as usual into the furnace with his red, bleared eyes.

From the bedroom window above their heads Bathsheba's head and shoulders, robed in mystic white, were dimly seen extended into the air.

"Are any of my men among you?" she said anxiously.

"Yes, ma'am, several," said Susan Tall's husband.

"To-morrow morning I wish two or three of you to make enquiries in the villages round if they have seen such a person as Fanny Robin. Do it quietly; there is no reason for alarm as yet. She must have left whilst we were all at the fire."

"I beg yer pardon, but had she any young man courting her in the parish, ma'am?" asked Jacob Smallbury.

"I don't know," said Bathsheba.

"I've never heard of any such thing, ma'am," said two or three.

"It is hardly likely, either," continued Bathsheba. "For any lover of hers might have come to the house if he had been a respectable lad. The most mysterious matter connected with her absence—indeed, the only thing which gives me serious alarm—is that she was seen to go out of the house by Maryann with only her indoor working gown on—not even a bonnet."

"And you mean, ma'am, excusing my words, that a young woman would hardly go to see her young man without dressing up," said Jacob, turning his mental vision upon past experiences. "That's true—she would not, ma'am."

"She had, I think, a bundle, though I couldn't see very well," said a female voice from another window, which seemed that of Maryann. "But she had no young man about here. Hers lives in Casterbridge, and I believe he's a soldier."

"Do you know his name?" Bathsheba said.

"No, mistress; she was very close about it."

"Perhaps I might be able to find out if I went to Casterbridge barracks," said William Smallbury.

"Very well; if she doesn't return to-morrow, mind you go there and try to discover which man it is, and see him. I feel more responsible than I should if she had had any friends or relations alive. I do hope she has come to no harm through a man of that kind. . . . And then there's this disgraceful affair of the bailiff—but I can't speak of him now."

Bathsheba had so many reasons for uneasiness that it seemed she did not think it worthwhile to dwell upon any particular one. "Do as I told you, then," she said in conclusion, closing the casement.

"Ay, ay, mistress; we will," they replied, and moved away.

That night at Coggan's Gabriel Oak, beneath the screen of closed eyelids, was busy with fancies, and full of movement, like a river flowing rapidly under its ice. Night had always been the time at which he saw Bathsheba most vividly, and through the slow hours of shadow he tenderly regarded her image now. It is rarely that the pleasures of the imagination will compensate for the pain of sleeplessness, but they possibly did with Oak tonight, for the delight of merely seeing her effaced for the time his perception of the great difference between seeing and possessing.

He also thought of plans for fetching his few utensils and books from Norcombe. *The Young Man's Best Companion*, *The Farrier's Sure Guide*, *The Veterinary Surgeon*, *Paradise Lost*, *The Pilgrim's Progress*, *Robinson Crusoe*, Ash's *Dictionary*, and Walkingame's *Arithmetic*, constituted his library; and though a limited series, it was one from which he had acquired more sound information by diligent perusal than many a man of opportunities has done from a furlong of laden shelves.

IX

THE HOMESTEAD—A VISITOR—HALF-CONFIDENCES

BY DAYLIGHT, THE BOWER OF OAK'S NEW-FOUND MISTRESS, BATHSHEBA EVERDENE, PRE-sented itself as a hoary building, of the early stage of Classic Renaissance as regards its architecture, and of a proportion which told at a glance that, as is so frequently the case, it had once been the memorial hall upon a small estate around it, now altogether effaced as a distinct property, and merged in the vast tract of a non-resident landlord, which comprised several such modest demesnes.

Fluted pilasters, worked from the solid stone, decorated its front, and above the roof the chimneys were panelled or columnar, some coped gables with finials and like features still retaining traces of their Gothic extraction. Soft brown mosses, like faded velveteen, formed cushions upon the stone tiling, and tufts of the houseleek or sengreen sprouted from the eaves of the low surrounding buildings. A gravel walk leading from the door to the road in front was encrusted at the sides with more moss—here it was a silver-green variety, the nut-brown of the gravel being visible to the width of only a foot or two in the centre. This circumstance, and the generally sleepy air of the whole prospect here, together with the animated and contrasting state of the reverse façade, suggested to the imagination that on the adaptation of the building for farming purposes the vital principle of the house had turned round inside its body to face the other way. Reversals of this kind, strange deformities, tremendous paralyses, are often seen to be inflicted by trade upon edifices—either individual or in the aggregate as streets and towns—which were originally planned for pleasure alone.

Lively voices were heard this morning in the upper rooms, the main staircase to which was of hard oak, the balusters, heavy as bed-posts, being turned and moulded in the quaint fashion of their century, the handrail as stout as a parapet-top, and the stairs themselves continually twisting round like a person trying to look over his shoulder. Going up, the floors above were found to have a very irregular surface, rising to ridges, sinking into valleys; and being just then uncarpeted, the face of the boards was seen to be eaten into innumerable vermiculations. Every window replied by a clang to the opening and shutting of every door, a tremble followed every bustling movement, and a creak accompanied a walker about the house, like a spirit, wherever he went.

In the room from which the conversation proceeded Bathsheba and her servant-companion, Liddy Smallbury, were to be discovered sitting upon the floor, and sorting a complication of papers, books, bottles, and rubbish spread out thereon—remnants from the household stores of the late occupier. Liddy, the maltster's great-grand-daughter, was about Bathsheba's equal in age, and her face was a prominent advertisement of the light-hearted English country girl. The beauty her features might have lacked in form was amply made up for by perfection of hue, which at this winter-time was the softened ruddiness on a surface of high rotundity that we meet with in a Terburg or a Gerard Douw; and, like the presentations of those great colourists, it was a face which kept well back from the boundary between comeliness and the ideal. Though elastic in nature she was less daring than Bathsheba, and occasionally showed some earnestness, which consisted half of genuine feeling, and half of mannerliness superadded by way of duty.

Through a partly-opened door the noise of a scrubbing-brush led up to the char-woman, Maryann Money, a person who for a face had a circular disc, furrowed less by age than by long gazes of perplexity at distant objects. To think of her was to get good-humoured; to speak of her was to raise the image of a dried Normandy pippin.

"Stop your scrubbing a moment," said Bathsheba through the door to her. "I hear something."

Maryann suspended the brush.

The tramp of a horse was apparent, approaching the front of the building. The paces slackened, turned in at the wicket, and, what was most unusual, came up the mossy path close to the door. The door was tapped with the end of a crop or stick.

"What impertinence!" said Liddy, in a low voice. "To ride up the footpath like that! Why didn't he stop at the gate? Lord! 'tis a gentleman! I see the top of his hat."

"Be quiet!" said Bathsheba.

The further expression of Liddy's concern was continued by aspect instead of narrative.

"Why doesn't Mrs. Coggan go to the door?" Bathsheba continued.

Rat-tat-tat-tat resounded more decisively from Bathsheba's oak.

"Maryann, you go!" said she, fluttering under the onset of a crowd of romantic possibilities.

"O ma'am—see, here's a mess!"

The argument was unanswerable after a glance at Maryann.

"Liddy—you must," said Bathsheba.

Liddy held up her hands and arms, coated with dust from the rubbish they were sorting, and looked imploringly at her mistress.

"There—Mrs. Coggan is going!" said Bathsheba, exhaling her relief in the form of a long breath which had lain in her bosom a minute or more.

The door opened, and a deep voice said—

"Is Miss Everdene at home?"

"I'll see, sir," said Mrs. Coggan, and in a minute appeared in the room.

"Dear, what a thirtover place this world is!" continued Mrs. Coggan (a wholesome-looking lady who had a voice for each class of remark according to the emotion involved; who could toss a pancake or twirl a mop with the accuracy of pure mathematics, and who at this moment showed hands shaggy with fragments of dough and arms encrusted with flour). "I am never up to my elbows, Miss, in making a pudding but one of two things do happen—either my nose must needs begin tickling, and I can't live without scratching it, or somebody knocks at the door. Here's Mr. Boldwood wanting to see you, Miss Everdene."

A woman's dress being a part of her countenance, and any disorder in the one being of the same nature with a malformation or wound in the other, Bathsheba said at once—

"I can't see him in this state. Whatever shall I do?"

Not-at-homes were hardly naturalised in Weatherbury farmhouses, so Liddy suggested—"Say you're a fright with dust, and can't come down."

"Yes—that sounds very well," said Mrs. Coggan critically.

"Say I can't see him—that will do."

Mrs. Coggan went downstairs, and returned the answer as requested, adding, however, on her own responsibility, "Miss is dusting bottles, sir, and is quite a object—that's why 'tis."

"Oh, very well," said the deep voice indifferently. "All I wanted to ask was, if anything had been heard of Fanny Robin?"

"Nothing, sir—but we may know to-night. William Smallbury is gone to Casterbridge, where her young man lives, as is supposed, and the other men be enquiring about everywhere."

The horse's tramp then recommenced and retreated, and the door closed.

"Who is Mr. Boldwood?" said Bathsheba.

"A gentleman-farmer at Little Weatherbury."

"Married?"

"No, miss."

"How old is he?"

"Forty, I should say—very handsome—rather stern-looking—and rich."

"What a bother this dusting is! I am always in some unfortunate plight or other," Bathsheba said complainingly. "Why should he enquire about Fanny?"

"Oh, because, as she had no friends in her childhood, he took her and put her to school, and got her her place here under your uncle. He's a very kind man that way, but Lord—there!"

"What?"

"Never was such a hopeless man for a woman! He's been courted by sixes and sevens—all the girls, gentle and simple, for miles round, have tried him. Jane Perkins worked at him for two months like a slave, and the two Miss Taylors spent a year upon him, and he cost Farmer Ives's daughter nights of tears and twenty pounds' worth of new clothes; but Lord—the money might as well have been thrown out of the window."

A little boy came up at this moment and looked in upon them. This child was one of the Coggans, who, with the Smallburys, were as common among the families of this district as the Avons and Derwents among our rivers. He always had a loosened tooth or a cut finger to show to particular friends, which he did with an air of being thereby elevated above the common herd of afflictionless humanity—to which exhibition people were expected to say "Poor child!" with a dash of congratulation as well as pity.

"I've got a pen-nee!" said Master Coggan in a scanning measure.

"Well—who gave it you, Teddy?" said Liddy.

"Mis-terr Bold-wood! He gave it to me for opening the gate."

"What did he say?"

"He said, 'Where are you going, my little man?' and I said, 'To Miss Everdene's please'; and he said, 'She is a staid woman, isn't she, my little man?' and I said, 'Yes.' "

"You naughty child! What did you say that for?"

" 'Cause he gave me the penny!"

"What a pucker everything is in!" said Bathsheba discontentedly, when the child had gone. "Get away, Maryann, or go on with your scrubbing, or do something! You ought to be married by this time, and not here troubling me!"

"Ay, mistress—so I did. But what between the poor men I won't have, and the rich men who won't have me, I stand as a pelican in the wilderness!"

"Did anybody ever want to marry you, miss?" Liddy ventured to ask when they were again alone. "Lots of 'em, I daresay?"

Bathsheba paused, as if about to refuse a reply, but the temptation to say yes, since it was really in her power, was irresistible by aspiring virginity, in spite of her spleen at having been published as old.

"A man wanted to once," she said, in a highly experienced tone, and the image of Gabriel Oak, as the farmer, rose before her.

"How nice it must seem!" said Liddy, with the fixed features of mental realization. "And you wouldn't have him?"

"He wasn't quite good enough for me."

"How sweet to be able to disdain, when most of us are glad to say, 'Thank you!' I seem I hear it. 'No, sir—I'm your better.' or 'Kiss my foot, sir; my face is for mouths of consequence.' And did you love him, miss?"

"Oh, no. But I rather liked him."

"Do you now?"

"Of course not—what footsteps are those I hear?"

Liddy looked from a back window into the courtyard behind, which was now getting low-toned and dim with the earliest films of night. A crooked file of men was approaching the back door. The whole string of trailing individuals advanced in the completest balance of intention, like the remarkable creatures known as Chain Salpæ, which, distinctly organised in other respects, have one will common to a whole family. Some were, as usual, in snow-white smock-frocks of Russia duck, and some in whitey-brown ones of drabbet—marked on the wrists, breasts, backs, and sleeves with honeycomb-work. Two or three women in pattens brought up the rear.

"The Philistines be upon us," said Liddy, making her nose white against the glass.

"Oh, very well. Maryann, go down and keep them in the kitchen till I am dressed, and then show them in to me in the hall."

X

MISTRESS AND MEN

HALF AN HOUR LATER BATHSHEBA, IN FINISHED DRESS, AND FOLLOWED BY LIDDY, ENtered the upper end of the old hall to find that her men had all deposited themselves on a long form and a settle at the lower extremity. She sat down at a table and opened the time-book, pen in her hand, with a canvas money-bag beside her. From this she poured a small heap of coin. Liddy chose a position at her elbow and began to sew, sometimes pausing and looking round, or, with the air of a privileged person, taking up one of the half-sovereigns lying before her, and surveying it merely as a work of art, while strictly preventing her countenance from expressing any wish to possess it as money.

"Now, before I begin, men," said Bathsheba, "I have two matters to speak of. The first is that the bailiff is dismissed for thieving, and that I have formed a resolution to have no bailiff at all, but to manage everything with my own head and hands."

The men breathed an audible breath of amazement.

"The next matter is, have you heard anything of Fanny?"

"Nothing, ma'am."

"Have you done anything?"

"I met Farmer Boldwood," said Jacob Smallbury, "and I went with him and two of his men, and dragged Newmill Pond, but we found nothing."

"And the new shepherd have been to Buck's Head, by Yalbury, thinking she had gone there, but nobody had seed her," said Laban Tall.

"Hasn't William Smallbury been to Casterbridge?"

"Yes, ma'am, but he's not yet come home. He promised to be back by six."

"It wants a quarter to six at present," said Bathsheba, looking at her watch. "I daresay he'll be in directly. Well, now then"—she looked into the book—"Joseph Poorgrass, are you there?"

"Yes, sir—ma'am I mane," said the person addressed. "I be the personal name of Poorgrass."

"And what are you?"

"Nothing in my own eye. In the eye of other people—well, I don't say it; though public thought will out."

"What do you do on the farm?"

"I do do carting things all the year, and in seed time I shoots the rooks and sparrows, and helps at pig-killing, sir."

"How much to you?"

"Please nine and ninepence and a good halfpenny where 'twas a bad one, sir—ma'am I mane."

"Quite correct. Now here are ten shillings in addition as a small present, as I am a new-comer."

Bathsheba blushed slightly at the sense of being generous in public, and Henery Fray, who had drawn up towards her chair, lifted his eyebrows and fingers to express amazement on a small scale.

"How much do I owe you—that man in the corner—what's your name?" continued Bathsheba.

"Matthew Moon, ma'am," said a singular frame-work of clothes with nothing of any consequence inside them, which advanced with the toes in no definite direction forwards, but turned in or out as they chanced to swing.

"Matthew Mark, did you say?—speak out—I shall not hurt you," enquired the young farmer kindly.

"Matthew Moon, mem," said Henery Fray, correctingly, from behind her chair, to which point he had edged himself.

"Matthew Moon," murmured Bathsheba, turning her bright eyes to the book. "Ten and twopence halfpenny is the sum put down to you, I see?"

"Yes, mis'ess," said Matthew, as the rustle of wind among dead leaves.

"Here it is, and ten shillings. Now the next—Andrew Randle, you are a new man, I hear. How come you to leave your last farm?"

"P-p-p-p-p-pl-pl-pl-pl-l-l-l-l-ease, ma'am, p-p-p-p-pl-pl-pl-pl-please, ma'am-please'm-please'm—"

" 'A's a stammering man, mem," said Henery Fray in an undertone, "and they turned him away because the only time he ever did speak plain he said his soul was his own, and other iniquities, to the squire. 'A can cuss, mem, as well as you or I, but 'a can't speak a common speech to save his life."

"Andrew Randle, here's yours—finish thanking me in a day or two. Temperance Miller—oh, here's another, Soberness—both women, I suppose?"

"Yes'm. Here we be, 'a b'lieve," was echoed in shrill unison.

"What have you been doing?"

"Tending thrashing-machine, and wimbling haybonds, and saying 'Hoosh!' to the cocks and hens when they go upon your seeds, and planting Early Flourballs and Thompson's Wonderfuls with a dibble."

"Yes—I see. Are they satisfactory women?" she enquired softly of Henery Fray.

"O mem—don't ask me! Yielding women—as scarlet a pair as ever was!" groaned Henery under his breath.

"Sit down."

"Who, mem?"

"Sit down."

Joseph Poorgrass, in the background, twitched, and his lips became dry with fear of some terrible consequences, as he saw Bathsheba summarily speaking, and Henery slinking off to a corner.

"Now the next. Laban Tall, you'll stay on working for me?"

"For you or anybody that pays me well, ma'am," replied the young married man.

"True—the man must live!" said a woman in the back quarter, who had just entered with clicking pattens.

"What woman is that?" Bathsheba asked.

"I be his lawful wife!" continued the voice with greater prominence of manner and tone. This lady called herself five-and-twenty, looked thirty, passed as thirty-five, and was forty. She was a woman who never, like some newly married, showed conjugal tenderness in public, perhaps because she had none to show.

"Oh, you are," said Bathsheba. "Well, Laban, will you stay on?"

"Yes, he'll stay, ma'am!" said again the shrill tongue of Laban's lawful wife.

"Well, he can speak for himself, I suppose."

"O Lord, not he, ma'am! A simple tool. Well enough, but a poor gawkhammer mortal," the wife replied.

"Heh-heh-heh!" laughed the married man, with a hideous effort of appreciation, for he was as irrepressibly good-humoured under ghastly snubs as a parliamentary candidate on the hustings.

The names remaining were called in the same manner.

"Now I think I have done with you," said Bathsheba, closing the book and shaking back a stray twine of hair. "Has William Smallbury returned?"

"No, ma'am."

"The new shepherd will want a man under him," suggested Henery Fray, trying to make himself official again by a sideway approach towards her chair.

"Oh—he will. Who can he have?"

"Young Cain Ball is a very good lad," Henery said, "and Shepherd Oak don't mind his youth?" he added, turning with an apologetic smile to the shepherd, who had just appeared on the scene, and was now leaning against the doorpost with his arms folded.

"No, I don't mind that," said Gabriel.

"How did Cain come by such a name?" asked Bathsheba.

"Oh you see, mem, his pore mother, not being a Scripture-read woman, made a mistake at his christening, thinking 'twas Abel killed Cain, and called en Cain, meaning Abel all the time. The parson put it right, but 'twas too late, for the name could never be got rid of in the parish. 'Tis very unfortunate for the boy."

"It is rather unfortunate."

"Yes. However, we soften it down as much as we can, and call him Cainy. Ah, pore widow-woman! she cried her heart out about it almost. She was brought up by a very heathen father and mother, who never sent her to church or school, and it shows how the sins of the parents are visited upon the children, mem."

Mr. Fray here drew up his features to the mild degree of melancholy required when the persons involved in the given misfortune do not belong to your own family.

"Very well then, Cainy Ball to be under-shepherd. And you quite understand your duties?—you I mean, Gabriel Oak?"

"Quite well, I thank you, Miss Everdene," said Shepherd Oak from the doorpost. "If I don't, I'll enquire." Gabriel was rather staggered by the remarkable coolness of her manner. Certainly nobody without previous information would have dreamt that Oak and the handsome woman before whom he stood had ever been other than strangers. But perhaps her air was the inevitable result of the social rise which had advanced her from a cottage to a large house and fields. The case is not unexampled in high places. When, in the writings of the later poets, Jove and his family are found to have moved from their cramped quarters on the peak of Olympus into the wide sky above it, their words show a proportionate increase of arrogance and reserve.

Footsteps were heard in the passage, combining in their character the qualities both of weight and measure, rather at the expense of velocity.

(All.) "Here's Billy Smallbury come from Casterbridge."

"And what's the news?" said Bathsheba, as William, after marching to the middle of the hall, took a handkerchief from his hat and wiped his forehead from its centre to its remoter boundaries.

"I should have been sooner, miss," he said, "if it hadn't been for the weather." He then stamped with each foot severely, and on looking down his boots were perceived to be clogged with snow.

"Come at last, is it?" said Henery.

"Well, what about Fanny?" said Bathsheba.

"Well, ma'am, in round numbers, she's run away with the soldiers," said William.

"No; not a steady girl like Fanny!"

"I'll tell ye all particulars. When I got to Casterbridge Barracks, they said, 'The Eleventh Dragoon Guards be gone away, and new troops have come.' The Eleventh left last week for Melchester and onwards. The Route came from Government like a thief in the night, as is his nature to, and afore the Eleventh knew it almost, they were on the march. They passed near here."

Gabriel had listened with interest. "I saw them go," he said.

"Yes," continued William, "they pranced down the street playing 'The Girl I Left Behind Me,' so 'tis said, in glorious notes of triumph. Every looker-on's inside shook with the blows of the great drum to his deepest vitals, and there was not a dry eye throughout the town among the public-house people and the nameless women!"

"But they're not gone to any war?"

"No, ma'am; but they be gone to take the places of them who may, which is very close connected. And so I said to myself, Fanny's young man was one of the regiment, and she's gone after him. There, ma'am, that's it in black and white."

"Did you find out his name?"

"No; nobody knew it. I believe he was higher in rank than a private."

Gabriel remained musing and said nothing, for he was in doubt.

"Well, we are not likely to know more to-night, at any rate," said Bathsheba. "But one of you had better run across to Farmer Boldwood's and tell him that much."

She then rose; but before retiring, addressed a few words to them with a pretty dignity, to which her mourning dress added a soberness that was hardly to be found in the words themselves:

"Now mind, you have a mistress instead of a master. I don't yet know my powers or my talents in farming; but I shall do my best, and if you serve me well, so shall I serve you. Don't any unfair ones among you (if there are any such, but I hope not) suppose that because I'm a woman I don't understand the difference between bad goings-on and good."

(All.) "No'm!"

(Liddy.) "Excellent well said."

"I shall be up before you are awake; I shall be afield before you are up; and I shall have breakfasted before you are afield. In short, I shall astonish you all."

(All.) "Yes'm!"

"And so good-night."

(All.) "Good-night, ma'am."

Then this small thesmothete stepped from the table, and surged out of the hall, her black silk dress licking up a few straws and dragging them along with a scratching noise upon the floor. Liddy, elevating her feelings to the occasion from a sense of grandeur, floated off behind Bathsheba with a milder dignity not entirely free from travesty, and the door was closed.

XI

OUTSIDE THE BARRACKS—SNOW—A MEETING

FOR DREARINESS NOTHING COULD SURPASS A PROSPECT IN THE OUTSKIRTS OF A CERTAIN town and military station, many miles north of Weatherbury, at a later hour on this same snowy evening—if that may be called a prospect of which the chief constituent was darkness.

It was a night when sorrow may come to the brightest without causing any great sense of incongruity: when, with impressible persons, love becomes solicitousness, hope sinks to misgiving, and faith to hope: when the exercise of memory does not stir feelings of regret at opportunities for ambition that have been passed by, and anticipation does not prompt to enterprise.

The scene was a public path, bordered on the left hand by a river, behind which rose a high wall. On the right was a tract of land, partly meadow and partly moor, reaching, at its remote verge, to a wide undulating upland.

The changes of the seasons are less obtrusive on spots of this kind than amid wood-land scenery. Still, to a close observer, they are just as perceptible; the difference is that their media of manifestation are less trite and familiar than such well-known ones as the bursting of the buds or the fall of the leaf. Many are not so stealthy and gradual as we may be apt to imagine in considering the general torpidity of a moor or waste. Winter, in com-ing to the country hereabout, advanced in well-marked stages, wherein might have been successively observed the retreat of the snakes, the transformation of the ferns, the filling of the pools, a rising of fogs, the embrowning by frost, the collapse of the fungi, and an obliteration by snow.

This climax of the series had been reached to-night on the aforesaid moor, and for the first time in the season its irregularities were forms without features; suggestive of any-thing, proclaiming nothing, and without more character than that of being the limit of something else—the lowest layer of a firmament of snow. From this chaotic skyful of crowding flakes the mead and moor momentarily received additional clothing, only to ap-pear momentarily more naked thereby. The vast arch of cloud above was strangely low, and formed as it were the roof of a large dark cavern, gradually sinking in upon its floor; for the instinctive thought was that the snow lining the heavens and that encrusting the earth would soon unite into one mass without any intervening stratum of air at all.

We turn our attention to the left-hand characteristics; which were flatness in respect of the river, verticality in respect of the wall behind it, and darkness as to both. These features made up the mass. If anything could be darker than the sky, it was the wall, and if anything could be gloomier than the wall it was the river beneath. The indistinct summit of the façade was notched and pronged by chimneys here and there, and upon its face were faintly signified the oblong shapes of windows, though only in the upper part. Below, down to the water's edge, the flat was unbroken by hole or projection.

An indescribable succession of dull blows, perplexing in their regularity, sent their sound with difficulty through the fluffy atmosphere. It was a neighbouring clock striking ten. The bell was in the open air, and being overlaid with several inches of muffling snow, had lost its voice for the time.

About this hour the snow abated: ten flakes fell where twenty had fallen, then one had the room of ten. Not long after a form moved by the brink of the river.

By its outline upon the colourless background a close observer might have seen that it was small. This was all that was positively discoverable, though it seemed human.

The shape went slowly along, but without much exertion, for the snow, though sudden, was not as yet more than two inches deep. At this time some words were spoken aloud:—

"One. Two. Three. Four. Five."

Between each utterance the little shape advanced about half-a-dozen yards. It was evident now that the windows high in the wall were being counted. The word "Five" represented the fifth window from the end of the wall.

Here the spot stopped, and dwindled smaller. The figure was stooping. Then a morsel of snow flew across the river towards the fifth window. It smacked against the wall at a point several yards from its mark. The throw was the idea of a man conjoined with the execution of a woman. No man who had ever seen bird, rabbit, or squirrel in his childhood, could possibly have thrown with such utter imbecility as was shown here.

Another attempt, and another; till by degrees the wall must have become pimpled with the adhering lumps of snow. At last one fragment struck the fifth window.

The river would have been seen by day to be of that deep smooth sort which races middle and sides with the same gliding precision, any irregularities of speed being immediately corrected by a small whirlpool. Nothing was heard in reply to the signal but the gurgle and cluck of one of these invisible wheels—together with a few small sounds which a sad man would have called moans, and a happy man laughter—caused by the flapping of the waters against trifling objects in other parts of the stream.

The window was struck again in the same manner.

Then a noise was heard, apparently produced by the opening of the window. This was followed by a voice from the same quarter:

"Who's there?"

The tones were masculine, and not those of surprise. The high wall being that of a barrack, and marriage being looked upon with disfavour in the army, assignations and communications had probably been made across the river before to-night.

"Is it Sergeant Troy?" said the blurred spot in the snow, tremulously.

This person was so much like a mere shade upon the earth, and the other speaker so much a part of the building, that one would have said the wall was holding a conversation with the snow.

"Yes," came suspiciously from the shadow. "What girl are you?"

"O, Frank—don't you know me?" said the spot. "Your wife, Fanny Robin."

"Fanny!" said the wall, in utter astonishment.

"Yes," said the girl, with a half-suppressed gasp of emotion.

There was something in the woman's tone which is not that of the wife, and there was a manner in the man which is rarely a husband's. The dialogue went on:

"How did you come here?"

"I asked which was your window. Forgive me!"

"I did not expect you to-night. Indeed, I did not think you would come at all. It was a wonder you found me here. I am orderly to-morrow."

"You said I was to come."

"Well—I said that you might."

"Yes, I mean that I might. You are glad to see me, Frank?"

"O yes—of course."

"Can you—come to me?"

My dear Fan, no! The bugle has sounded, the barrack gates are closed, and I have no leave. We are all of us as good as in the county gaol till to-morrow morning."

"Then I shan't see you till then!" The words were in a faltering tone of disappointment.

"How did you get here from Weatherbury?"

"I walked—some part of the way—the rest by the carriers."

"I am surprised."

"Yes—so am I. And Frank, when will it be?"

"What?"

"That you promised."

"I don't quite recollect."

"O you do! Don't speak like that. It weighs me to the earth. It makes me say what ought to be said first by you."

"Never mind—say it."

"O, must I?—it is, when shall we be married, Frank?"

"Oh, I see. Well—you have to get proper clothes."

"I have money. Will it be by banns or license?"

"Banns, I should think."

"And we live in two parishes."

"Do we? What then?"

"My lodgings are in St. Mary's, and this is not. So they will have to be published in both."

"Is that the law?"

"Yes. O Frank—you think me forward, I am afraid! Don't, dear Frank—will you—for I love you so. And you said lots of times you would marry me, and—and—I—I—I—"

"Don't cry, now! It is foolish. If I said so, of course I will."

"And shall I put up the banns in my parish, and will you in yours?"

"Yes."

"To-morrow?"

"Not to-morrow. We'll settle in a few days."

"You have the permission of the officers?"

"No—not yet."

"O—how is it? You said you almost had before you left Casterbridge."

"The fact is, I forgot to ask. Your coming like this is so sudden and unexpected."

"Yes—yes—it is. It was wrong of me to worry you. I'll go away now. Will you come and see me to-morrow, at Mrs. Twills's, in North Street? I don't like to come to the Barracks. There are bad women about, and they think me one."

"Quite, so. I'll come to you, my dear. Good-night."

"Good-night, Frank—good-night!"

And the noise was again heard of a window closing. The little spot moved away. When she passed the corner a subdued exclamation was heard inside the wall.

"Ho—ho—Sergeant—ho—ho!" An expostulation followed, but it was indistinct; and it became lost amid a low peal of laughter, which was hardly distinguishable from the gurgle of the tiny whirlpools outside.

XII

FARMERS—A RULE—AN EXCEPTION

THE FIRST PUBLIC EVIDENCE OF BATHSHEBA'S DECISION TO BE A FARMER IN HER OWN person and by proxy no more was her appearance the following market-day in the cornmarket at Casterbridge.

The low though extensive hall, supported by beams and pillars, and latterly dignified by the name of Corn Exchange, was thronged with hot men who talked among each other in twos and threes, the speaker of the minute looking sideways into his auditor's face and concentrating his argument by a contraction of one eyelid during delivery. The greater number carried in their hands ground-ash saplings, using them partly as walking-sticks and partly for poking up pigs, sheep, neighbours with their backs turned, and restful things in general, which seemed to require such treatment in the course of their peregrinations. During conversations each subjected his sapling to great varieties of usage—bending it round his back, forming an arch of it between his two hands, overweighting it on the ground till it reached nearly a semicircle; or perhaps it was hastily tucked under the arm whilst the sample-bag was pulled forth and a handful of corn poured into the palm, which, after criticism, was flung upon the floor, an issue of events perfectly well known to half-a-dozen acute town-bred fowls which had as usual crept into the building unobserved, and waited the fulfilment of their anticipations with a high-stretched neck and oblique eye.

Among these heavy yeomen a feminine figure glided, the single one of her sex that the room contained. She was prettily and even daintily dressed. She moved between them as a chaise between carts, was heard after them as a romance after sermons, was felt among them like a breeze among furnaces. It had required a little determination—far more than she had at first imagined—to take up a position here, for at her first entry the lumbering dialogues had ceased, nearly every face had been turned towards her, and those that were already turned rigidly fixed there.

Two or three only of the farmers were personally known to Bathsheba, and to these she had made her way. But if she was to be the practical woman she had intended to show herself, business must be carried on, introductions or none, and she ultimately acquired confidence enough to speak and reply boldly to men merely known to her by hearsay. Bathsheba too had her sample-bags, and by degrees adopted the professional pour into the hand—holding up the grains in her narrow palm for inspection, in perfect Casterbridge manner.

Something in the exact arch of her upper unbroken row of teeth, and in the keenly pointed corners of her red mouth when, with parted lips, she somewhat defiantly turned up her face to argue a point with a tall man, suggested that there was potentiality enough in that lithe slip of humanity for alarming exploits of sex, and daring enough to carry them out. But her eyes had a softness—invariably a softness—which, had they not been dark, would have seemed mistiness; as they were, it lowered an expression that might have been piercing to simple clearness.

Strange to say of a woman in full bloom and vigor, she always allowed her interlocutors to finish their statements before rejoining with hers. In arguing on prices she held to her own firmly, as was natural in a dealer, and reduced theirs persistently, as was inevitable in a woman. But there was an elasticity in her firmness which removed it from obstinacy, as there was a *naïveté* in her cheapening which saved it from meanness.

Those of the farmers with whom she had no dealings (by far the greater part) were continually asking each other, "Who is she?" The reply would be—

"Farmer Everdene's niece; took on Weatherbury Upper Farm; turned away the baily, and swears she'll do everything herself."

The other man would then shake his head.

"Yes, 'tis a pity she's so headstrong," the first would say. "But we ought to be proud of her here—she lightens up the old place. 'Tis such a shapely maid, however, that she'll soon get picked up."

It would be ungallant to suggest that the novelty of her engagement in such an occupation had almost as much to do with the magnetism as had the beauty of her face and movements. However, the interest was general, and this Saturday's *début* in the forum, whatever it may have been to Bathsheba as the buying and selling farmer, was unquestionably a triumph to her as the maiden. Indeed, the sensation was so pronounced that her instinct on two or three occasions was merely to walk as a queen among these gods of the fallow, like a little sister of a little Jove, and to neglect closing prices altogether.

The numerous evidences of her power to attract were only thrown into greater relief by a marked exception. Women seem to have eyes in their ribbons for such matters as these. Bathsheba, without looking within a right angle of him, was conscious of a black sheep among the flock.

It perplexed her first. If there had been a respectable minority on either side, the case would have been most natural. If nobody had regarded her, she would have taken the matter indifferently—such cases had occurred. If everybody, this man included, she would have taken it as a matter of course—people had done so before. But the smallness of the exception made the mystery.

She soon knew thus much of the recusant's appearance. He was a gentlemanly man, with full and distinctly outlined Roman features, the prominences of which glowed in the sun with a bronzelike richness of tone. He was erect in attitude, and quiet in demeanour. One characteristic pre-eminently marked him—dignity.

Apparently he had some time ago reached that entrance to middle age at which a man's aspect naturally ceases to alter for the term of a dozen years or so; and, artificially, a woman's does likewise. Thirty-five and fifty were his limits of variation—he might have been either, or anywhere between the two.

It may be said that married men of forty are usually ready and generous enough to fling passing glances at any specimen of moderate beauty they may discern by the way. Probably, as with persons playing whist for love, the consciousness of a certain immunity under any circumstances from that worst possible ultimate, the having to pay, makes them unduly speculative. Bathsheba was convinced that this unmoved person was not a married man.

When marketing was over, she rushed off to Liddy, who was waiting for her beside the yellow gig in which they had driven to town. The horse was put in, and on they trotted—Bathsheba's sugar, tea, and drapery parcels being packed behind, and expressing in some indescribable manner, by their colour, shape, and general lineaments, that they were that young lady-farmer's property, and the grocer's and draper's no more.

"I've been through it, Liddy, and it is over. I shan't mind it again, for they will all have grown accustomed to seeing me there; but this morning it was as bad as being married—eyes everywhere!"

"I knowed it would be," Liddy said. "Men be such a terrible class of society to look at a body."

"But there was one man who had more sense than to waste his time upon me." The information was put in this form that Liddy might not for a moment suppose her mistress was at all piqued. "A very good-looking man," she continued, "upright; about forty, I should think. Do you know at all who he could be?"

Liddy couldn't think.

"Can't you guess at all?" said Bathsheba with some disappointment.

"I haven't a notion; besides, 'tis no difference, since he took less notice of you than any of the rest. Now, if he'd taken more, it would have mattered a great deal."

Bathsheba was suffering from the reverse feeling just then, and they bowled along in silence. A low carriage, bowling along still more rapidly behind a horse of unimpeachable breed, overtook and passed them.

"Why, there he is!" she said.

Liddy looked. "That! That's Farmer Boldwood—of course 'tis—the man you couldn't see the other day when he called."

"Oh, Farmer Boldwood," murmured Bathsheba, and looked at him as he outstripped them. The farmer had never turned his head once, but with eyes fixed on the most advanced point along the road, passed as unconsciously and abstractedly as if Bathsheba and her charms were thin air.

"He's an interesting man—don't you think so?" she remarked.

"O yes, very. Everybody owns it," replied Liddy.

"I wonder why he is so wrapt up and indifferent, and seemingly so far away from all he sees around him."

"It is said—but not known for certain—that he met with some bitter disappointment when he was a young man and merry. A woman jilted him, they say."

"People always say that—and we know very well women scarcely ever jilt men; 'tis the men who jilt us. I expect it is simply his nature to be so reserved."

"Simply his nature—I expect so, miss—nothing else in the world."

"Still, 'tis more romantic to think he has been served cruelly, poor thing! Perhaps, after all, he has."

"Depend upon it he has. O yes, miss, he has! I feel he must have."

"However, we are very apt to think extremes of people. I shouldn't wonder after all if it wasn't a little of both—just between the two—rather cruelly used and rather reserved."

"O dear no, miss—I can't think it between the two!"

"That's most likely."

"Well, yes, so it is. I am convinced it is most likely. You may take my word, miss, that that's what's the matter with him."

XIII

SORTES SANCTORUM—THE VALENTINE

IT WAS SUNDAY AFTERNOON IN THE FARMHOUSE, ON THE THIRTEENTH OF FEBRUARY. DIN-ner being over Bathsheba, for want of a better companion, had asked Liddy to come and sit with her. The mouldy pile was dreary in winter-time before the candles were lighted and the shutters closed; the atmosphere of the place seemed as old as the walls; every nook behind the furniture had a temperature of its own, for the fire was not kindled in this part of the house early in the day; and Bathsheba's new piano, which was an old one in other annals, looked particularly sloping and out of level on the warped floor before night threw a shade over its less prominent angles and hid the unpleasantness. Liddy, like a little brook, though shallow, was always rippling; her presence had not so much weight as to task thought, and yet enough to exercise it.

On the table lay an old quarto Bible, bound in leather. Liddy looking at it said—

"Did you ever find out, miss, who you are going to marry by means of the Bible and key?"

"Don't be so foolish, Liddy. As if such things could be."

"Well, there's a good deal in it, all the same."

"Nonsense, child."

"And it makes your heart beat fearful. Some believe in it; some don't; I do."

"Very well, let's try it," said Bathsheba, bounding from her seat with that total disre-gard of consistency which can be indulged in towards a dependent, and entering into the spirit of divination at once. "Go and get the front door-key."

Liddy fetched it. "I wish it wasn't Sunday," she said, on returning. "Perhaps 'tis wrong."

"What's right week-days is right Sundays," replied her mistress in a tone which was a proof in itself.

The book was opened—the leaves, drab with age, being quite worn away at much-read verses by the forefingers of unpracticed readers in former days, where they were moved along under the line as an aid to the vision. The special verse in the Book of Ruth was sought out by Bathsheba, and the sublime words met her eye. They slightly thrilled and abashed her. It was Wisdom in the abstract facing Folly in the concrete. Folly in the concrete blushed, persisted in her intention, and placed the key on the book. A rusty patch immediately upon the verse, caused by previous pressure of an iron substance thereon, told that this was not the first time the old volume had been used for the purpose.

"Now keep steady, and be silent," said Bathsheba.

The verse was repeated; the book turned round; Bathsheba blushed guiltily.

"Who did you try?" said Liddy curiously.

"I shall not tell you."

"Did you notice Mr. Boldwood's doings in church this morning, miss?" Liddy continued, adumbrating by the remark the track her thoughts had taken.

"No, indeed," said Bathsheba, with serene indifference.

"His pew is exactly opposite yours, miss."

"I know it."

"And you did not see his goings on!"

"Certainly I did not, I tell you."

Liddy assumed a smaller physiognomy, and shut her lips decisively.

This move was unexpected, and proportionately disconcerting. "What did he do?" Bathsheba said perforce.

"Didn't turn his head to look at you once all the service."

"Why should he?" again demanded her mistress, wearing a nettled look. "I didn't ask him to."

"Oh, no. But everybody else was noticing you; and it was odd he didn't. There, 'tis like him. Rich and gentlemanly, what does he care?"

Bathsheba dropped into a silence intended to express that she had opinions on the matter too abstruse for Liddy's comprehension, rather than that she had nothing to say.

"Dear me—I had nearly forgotten the valentine I bought yesterday," she exclaimed at length.

"Valentine! who for, miss?" said Liddy. "Farmer Boldwood?"

It was the single name among all possible wrong ones that just at this moment seemed to Bathsheba more pertinent than the right.

"Well, no. It is only for little Teddy Coggan. I have promised him something, and this will be a pretty surprise for him. Liddy, you may as well bring me my desk and I'll direct it at once."

Bathsheba took from her desk a gorgeously illuminated and embossed design in post-octavo, which had been bought on the previous market-day at the chief stationer's in Casterbridge. In the centre was a small oval enclosure; this was left blank, that the sender might insert tender words more appropriate to the special occasion than any generalities by a printer could possibly be.

"Here's a place for writing," said Bathsheba. "What shall I put?"

"Something of this sort, I should think," returned Liddy promptly:—

> *"The rose is red,*
> *The violet blue,*
> *Carnation's sweet,*
> *And so are you."*

"Yes, that shall be it. It just suits itself to a chubby-faced child like him," said Bathsheba. She inserted the words in a small though legible handwriting; enclosed the sheet in an envelope, and dipped her pen for the direction.

"What fun it would be to send it to the stupid old Boldwood, and how he would wonder!" said the irrepressible Liddy, lifting her eyebrows, and indulging in an awful mirth on the verge of fear as she thought of the moral and social magnitude of the man contemplated.

Bathsheba paused to regard the idea at full length. Boldwood's had begun to be a troublesome image—a species of Daniel in her kingdom who persisted in kneeling eastward when reason and common sense said that he might just as well follow suit with the rest, and afford her the official glance of admiration which cost nothing at all. She was far from being seriously concerned about his nonconformity. Still, it was faintly depressing that the most dignified and valuable man in the parish should withhold his eyes, and that a girl like Liddy should talk about it. So Liddy's idea was at first rather harassing than piquant.

"No, I won't do that. He wouldn't see any humour in it."

"He'd worry to death," said the persistent Liddy.

"Really, I don't care particularly to send it to Teddy," remarked her mistress. "He's rather a naughty child sometimes."

"Yes—that he is."

"Let's toss, as men do," said Bathsheba idly. "Now then, head, Boldwood; tail, Teddy. No, we won't toss money on a Sunday, that would be tempting the devil indeed."

"Toss this hymn-book; there can't be no sinfulness in that, miss."

"Very well. Open, Boldwood—shut, Teddy. No; it's more likely to fall open. Open, Teddy—shut, Boldwood."

The book went fluttering in the air and came down shut.

Bathsheba, a small yawn upon her mouth, took the pen, and with offhand serenity directed the missive to Boldwood.

"Now light a candle, Liddy. Which seal shall we use? Here's a unicorn's head—there's nothing in that. What's this?—two doves—no. It ought to be something extraordinary, ought it not, Liddy? Here's one with a motto—I remember it is some funny one, but I can't read it. We'll try this, and if it doesn't do we'll have another."

A large red seal was duly affixed. Bathsheba looked closely at the hot wax to discover the words.

"Capital!" she exclaimed, throwing down the letter frolicsomely. " 'Twould upset the solemnity of a parson and clerk too."

Liddy looked at the words of the seal, and read—

MARRY ME.

The same evening the letter was sent, and was duly sorted in Casterbridge post-office that night, to be returned to Weatherbury again in the morning.

So very idly and unreflectingly was this deed done. Of love as a spectacle Bathsheba had a fair knowledge; but of love subjectively she knew nothing.

XIV

Effect of the Letter—Sunrise

At dusk on the evening of St. Valentine's day Boldwood sat down to supper as usual, by a beaming fire of aged logs. Upon the mantel-shelf before him was a time-piece, surmounted by a spread eagle, and upon the eagle's wings was the letter Bathsheba had sent. Here the bachelor's gaze was continually fastening itself, till the large red seal became as a blot of blood on the retina of his eye; and as he ate and drank he still read in fancy the words thereon, although they were too remote for his sight—

Marry Me.

The pert injunction was like those crystal substances, which, colourless themselves, assume the tone of objects about them. Here, in the quiet of Boldwood's parlour, where everything that was not grave was extraneous, and where the atmosphere was that of a Puritan Sunday lasting all the week, the letter and its dictum changed their tenor from the thoughtlessness of their origin to a deep solemnity, imbibed from their accessories now.

Since the receipt of the missive in the morning, Boldwood had felt the symmetry of his existence to be slowly getting distorted in the direction of an ideal passion. The disturbance was as the first floating weed to Columbus—the contemptibly little suggesting possibilities of the infinitely great.

The letter must have had an origin and a motive. That the latter was of the smallest magnitude compatible with its existence at all, Boldwood, of course, did not know. And such an explanation did not strike him as a possibility even. It is foreign to a mystified condition of mind to realise of the mystifier that the processes of approving a course suggested by circumstance, and of striking out a course from inner impulse, would look the same in the result. The vast difference between starting a train of events, and directing into a particular groove a series already started, is rarely apparent to the person confounded by the issue.

When Boldwood went to bed he placed the valentine in the corner of the looking-glass. He was conscious of its presence, even when his back was turned upon it. It was the first time in Boldwood's life that such an event had occurred. The same fascination that caused him to think it an act which had a deliberate motive prevented him from regarding it as an impertinence. He looked again at the direction. The mysterious influences of night invested the writing with the presence of the unknown writer. Somebody's—some *woman's*—hand had travelled softly over the paper bearing his name; her unrevealed eyes had watched every curve as she formed it; her brain had seen him in imagination the while. Why should she have imagined him? Her mouth—were the lips red or pale, plump or creased?—had curved itself to a certain expression as the pen went on—the corners had moved with all their natural tremulousness: what had been the expression?

The vision of the woman writing, as a supplement to the words written, had no individuality. She was a misty shape, and well she might be, considering that her original was at that moment sound asleep and oblivious of all love and letter-writing under the sky. Whenever Boldwood dozed she took a form, and comparatively ceased to be a vision: when he awoke there was the letter justifying the dream.

The moon shone to-night, and its light was not of a customary kind. His window admitted only a reflection of its rays, and the pale sheen had that reversed direction which snow gives, coming upward and lighting up his ceiling in an unnatural way, casting shadows in strange places, and putting lights where shadows had used to be.

The substance of the epistle had occupied him but little in comparison with the fact of its arrival. He suddenly wondered if anything more might be found in the envelope than what he had withdrawn. He jumped out of bed in the weird light, took the letter, pulled out the flimsy sheet, shook the envelope—searched it. Nothing more was there. Boldwood looked, as he had a hundred times the preceding day, at the insistent red seal: "Marry me," he said aloud.

The solemn and reserved yeoman again closed the letter, and stuck it in the frame of the glass. In doing so he caught sight of his reflected features, wan in expression, and insubstantial in form. He saw how closely compressed was his mouth, and that his eyes were wide-spread and vacant. Feeling uneasy and dissatisfied with himself for this nervous excitability, he returned to bed.

Then the dawn drew on. The full power of the clear heaven was not equal to that of a cloudy sky at noon, when Boldwood arose and dressed himself. He descended the stairs and went out towards the gate of a field to the east, leaning over which he paused and looked around.

It was one of the usual slow sunrises of this time of the year, and the sky, pure violet in the zenith, was leaden to the northward, and murky to the east, where, over the snowy down or ewe-lease on Weatherbury Upper Farm, and apparently resting upon the ridge, the only half of the sun yet visible burnt rayless, like a red and flameless fire shining over a white hearthstone. The whole effect resembled a sunset as childhood resembles age.

In other directions the fields and sky were so much of one colour by the snow that it was difficult in a hasty glance to tell whereabouts the horizon occurred; and in general there was here, too, that before-mentioned preternatural inversion of light and shade which attends the prospect when the garish brightness commonly in the sky is found on the earth, and the shades of earth are in the sky. Over the west hung the wasting moon, now dull and greenish-yellow, like tarnished brass.

Boldwood was listlessly noting how the frost had hardened and glazed the surface of the snow, till it shone in the red eastern light with the polish of marble; how, in some portions of the slope, withered grass-bents, encased in icicles, bristled through the smooth wan coverlet in the twisted and curved shapes of old Venetian glass; and how the footprints of a few birds, which had hopped over the snow whilst it lay in the state of a soft fleece, were now frozen to a short permanency. A half-muffled noise of light wheels interrupted

him. Boldwood turned back into the road. It was the mail-cart—a crazy two-wheeled vehicle, hardly heavy enough to resist a puff of wind. The driver held out a letter. Boldwood
seized it and opened it, expecting another anonymous one—so greatly are people's ideas
of probability a mere sense that precedent will repeat itself.

"I don't think it is for you, sir," said the man, when he saw Boldwood's action.
"Though there is no name, I think it is for your shepherd."

Boldwood looked then at the address—

> *To the New Shepherd,*
> *Weatherbury Farm,*
> *Near Casterbridge.*

"Oh—what a mistake!—it is not mine. Nor is it for my shepherd. It is for Miss Everdene's. You had better take it on to him—Gabriel Oak—and say I opened it in mistake."

At this moment on the ridge, up against the blazing sky, a figure was visible, like the
black snuff in the midst of a candle-flame. Then it moved and began to bustle about vigorously from place to place, carrying square skeleton masses, which were riddled by the
same rays. A small figure on all fours followed behind. The tall form was that of Gabriel
Oak; the small one that of George; the articles in course of transit were hurdles.

"Wait," said Boldwood. "That's the man on the hill. I'll take the letter to him myself."

To Boldwood it was now no longer merely a letter to another man. It was an opportunity. Exhibiting a face pregnant with intention, he entered the snowy field.

Gabriel, at that minute, descended the hill towards the right. The glow stretched down
in this direction now, and touched the distant roof of Warren's Malthouse—whither the
shepherd was apparently bent. Boldwood followed at a distance.

XV

A MORNING MEETING—THE LETTER AGAIN

THE SCARLET AND ORANGE LIGHT OUTSIDE THE MALTHOUSE DID NOT PENETRATE TO
its interior, which was, as usual, lighted by a rival glow of similar hue, radiating from
the hearth.

The maltster, after having lain down in his clothes for a few hours, was now sitting beside a three-legged table, breakfasting off bread and bacon. This was eaten on the plate-
less system, which is performed by placing a slice of bread upon the table, the meat flat
upon the bread, a mustard plaster upon the meat, and a pinch of salt upon the whole, then
cutting them vertically downwards with a large pocket-knife till wood is reached, when the
severed lump is impaled on the knife, elevated, and sent the proper way of food.

The maltster's lack of teeth appeared not to sensibly diminish his powers as a mill. He
had been without them for so many years that toothlessness was felt less to be a defect than
hard gums an acquisition. Indeed, he seemed to approach the grave as a hyperbolic curve

approaches a straight line—less directly as he got nearer, till it was doubtful if he would ever reach it at all.

In the ashpit was a heap of potatoes roasting, and a boiling pipkin of charred bread, called "coffee," for the benefit of whomsoever should call, for Warren's was a sort of club-house, used as an alternative to the inn.

"I say, says I, we get a fine day, and then down comes a snapper at night," was a remark now suddenly heard spreading into the malthouse from the door, which had been opened the previous moment. The form of Henery Fray advanced to the fire, stamping the snow from his boots when about half-way there. The speech and entry had not seemed to be at all an abrupt beginning to the maltster, introductory matter being often omitted in this neighbourhood, both from word and deed, and the maltster having the same latitude allowed him, did not hurry to reply. He picked up a fragment of cheese by pecking upon it with his knife, as a butcher picks up skewers.

Henery appeared in a drab kerseymere great-coat, buttoned over his smock-frock, the white skirts of the latter being visible to the distance of about a foot below the coat-tails, which, when you got used to the style of dress, looked natural enough, and even ornamental— it certainly was comfortable.

Matthew Moon, Joseph Poorgrass, and other carters and waggoners followed at his heels, with great lanterns dangling from their hands, which showed that they had just come from the cart-horse stables, where they had been busily engaged since four o'clock that morning.

"And how is she getting on without a baily?" the maltster enquired.

Henery shook his head, and smiled one of the bitter smiles, dragging all the flesh of his forehead into a corrugated heap in the centre.

"She'll rue it—surely, surely!" he said. "Benjy Pennyways were not a true man or an honest baily—as big a betrayer as Joey Iscariot himself. But to think she can carr' on alone!" He allowed his head to swing laterally three or four times in silence. "Never in all my creeping up—never!"

This was recognised by all as the conclusion of some gloomy speech which had been expressed in thought alone during the shake of the head; Henery meanwhile retained several marks of despair upon his face, to imply that they would be required for use again directly he should go on speaking.

"All will be ruined, and ourselves too, or there's no meat in gentlemen's houses!" said Mark Clark.

"A headstrong maid, that's what she is—and won't listen to no advice at all. Pride and vanity have ruined many a cobbler's dog. Dear, dear, when I think o' it, I sorrows like a man in travel!"

"True, Henery, you do, I've heard ye," said Joseph Poorgrass, in a voice of thorough attestation, and with a wire-drawn smile of misery.

"'Twould do a martel man no harm to have what's under her bonnet," said Billy Smallbury, who had just entered, bearing his one tooth before him. "She can spaik real language, and must have some sense somewhere. Do ye foller me?"

"I do; but no baily—I deserved that place," wailed Henery, signifying wasted genius by gazing blankly at visions of a high destiny apparently visible to him on Billy Smallbury's smock-frock. "There, 'twas to be, I suppose. Your lot is your lot, and Scripture is nothing; for if you do good you don't get rewarded according to your works, but be cheated in some mean way out of your recompense."

"No, no; I don't agree with'ee there," said Mark Clark. "God's a perfect gentleman in that respect."

"Good works good pay, so to speak it," attested Joseph Poorgrass.

A short pause ensued, and as a sort of *entr'acte* Henery turned and blew out the lanterns, which the increase of daylight rendered no longer necessary even in the malt-house, with its one pane of glass.

"I wonder what a farmer-woman can want with a harpsichord, dulcimer, pianner, or whatever 'tis they d'call it?" said the maltster. "Liddy saith she've a new one."

"Got a pianner?"

"Ay. Seems her old uncle's things were not good enough for her. She've bought all but everything new. There's heavy chairs for the stout, weak and wiry ones for the slender; great watches, getting on to the size of clocks, to stand upon the chimbley-piece."

"Pictures, for the most part wonderful frames."

"And long horse-hair settles for the drunk, with horse-hair pillows at each end," said Mr. Clark. "Likewise looking-glasses for the pretty, and lying books for the wicked."

A firm loud tread was now heard stamping outside; the door was opened about six inches, and somebody on the other side exclaimed—

"Neighbours, have ye got room for a few new-born lambs?"

"Ay, sure, shepherd," said the conclave.

The door was flung back till it kicked the wall and trembled from top to bottom with the blow. Mr. Oak appeared in the entry with a steaming face, hay-bands wound about his ankles to keep out the snow, a leather strap round his waist outside the smock-frock, and looking altogether an epitome of the world's health and vigour. Four lambs hung in various embarrassing attitudes over his shoulders, and the dog George, whom Gabriel had contrived to fetch from Norcombe, stalked solemnly behind.

"Well, Shepherd Oak, and how's lambing this year, if I mid say it?" enquired Joseph Poorgrass.

"Terrible trying," said Oak. "I've been wet through twice a-day, either in snow or rain, this last fortnight. Cainy and I haven't tined our eyes to-night."

"A good few twins, too, I hear?"

"Too many by half. Yes; 'tis a very queer lambing this year. We shan't have done by Lady Day."

"And last year 'twer all over by Sexajessamine Sunday," Joseph remarked.

"Bring on the rest, Cain," said Gabriel, "and then run back to the ewes. I'll follow you soon."

Cainy Ball—a cheery-faced young lad, with a small circular orifice by way of mouth, advanced and deposited two others, and retired as he was bidden. Oak lowered the lambs from their unnatural elevation, wrapped them in hay, and placed them round the fire.

"We've no lambing-hut here, as I used to have at Norcombe," said Gabriel, "and 'tis such a plague to bring the weakly ones to a house. If 'twasn't for your place here, malter, I don't know what I should do, this keen weather. And how is it with you to-day, malter?"

"Oh, neither sick nor sorry, shepherd; but no younger."

"Ay—I understand."

"Sit down, Shepherd Oak," continued the ancient man of malt. "And how was the old place at Norcombe, when ye went for your dog? I should like to see the old familiar spot; but faith, I shouldn't know a soul there now."

"I suppose you wouldn't. 'Tis altered very much."

"Is it true that Dicky Hill's wooden cider-house is pulled down?"

"O yes—years ago, and Dicky's cottage just above it."

"Well, to be sure!"

"Yes; and Tompkins's old apple-tree is rooted that used to bear two hogsheads of cider, and no help from other trees."

"Rooted?—you don't say it! Ah! stirring times we live in—stirring times."

"And you can mind the old well that used to be in the middle of the place? That's turned into a solid iron pump with a large stone trough, and all complete."

"Dear, dear—how the face of nations alter, and what we live to see now-a-days! Yes—and 'tis the same here. They've been talking but now of the mis'ess's strange doings."

"What have you been saying about her?" enquired Oak, sharply turning to the rest, and getting very warm.

"These middle-aged men have been pulling her over the coals for pride and vanity," said Mark Clark; "but I say, let her have rope enough. Bless her pretty face—shouldn't I like to do so—upon her cherry lips!" The gallant Mark Clark here made a peculiar and well-known sound with his own.

"Mark," said Gabriel sternly, "now you mind this: none of that dalliance-talk—that smack-and-coddle style of yours—about Miss Everdene. I don't allow it. Do you hear?"

"With all my heart, as I've got no chance," replied Mr. Clark cordially.

"I suppose you've been speaking against her?" said Oak, turning to Joseph Poorgrass with a very grim look.

"No, no—not a word I—'tis a real joyful thing that she's no worse, that's what I say," said Joseph, trembling and blushing with terror. "Matthew just said—"

"Matthew Moon, what have you been saying?" asked Oak.

"I? Why ye know I wouldn't harm a worm—no, not one underground worm?" said Matthew Moon, looking very uneasy.

"Well, somebody has—and look here, neighbours." Gabriel, though one of the quietest and most gentle men on earth, rose to the occasion, with martial promptness and vigour. "That's my fist." Here he placed his fist, rather smaller in size than a common loaf, in the mathematical centre of the maltster's little table, and with it gave a bump or two thereon, as if to ensure that their eyes all thoroughly took in the idea of fistiness before he went further. "Now—the first man in the parish that I hear prophesying bad of our mistress, why" (here the fist was raised and let fall, as Thor might have done with his hammer in assaying it)—"he'll smell and taste that—or I'm a Dutchman."

All earnestly expressed by their features that their minds did not wander to Holland for a moment on account of this statement, but were deploring the difference which gave rise to the figure; and Mark Clark cried, "Hear, hear; just what I should ha' said." The dog George looked up at the same time after the shepherd's menace, and though he understood English but imperfectly, began to growl.

"Now, don't ye take on so, shepherd, and sit down!" said Henery, with a deprecating peacefulness equal to anything of the kind in Christianity.

"We hear that ye be a extraordinary good and clever man, shepherd," said Joseph Poorgrass with considerable anxiety from behind the maltster's bedstead, whither he had retired for safety. " 'Tis a great thing to be clever, I'm sure," he added, making movements associated with states of mind rather than body; "we wish we were, don't we, neighbours?"

"Ay, that we do, sure," said Matthew Moon, with a small anxious laugh towards Oak, to show how very friendly disposed he was likewise.

"Who's been telling you I'm clever?" said Oak.

" 'Tis blowed about from pillar to post quite common," said Matthew. "We hear that ye can tell the time as well by the stars as we can by the sun and moon, shepherd."

"Yes, I can do a little that way," said Gabriel, as a man of medium sentiments on the subject.

"And that ye can make sun-dials, and prent folks' names upon their waggons almost like copper-plate, with beautiful flourishes, and great long tails. A excellent fine thing for ye to be such a clever man, shepherd. Joseph Poorgrass used to prent to Farmer James Everdene's waggons before you came, and 'a could never mind which way to turn the J's and E's—could ye, Joseph?" Joseph shook his head to express how absolute was the fact that he couldn't. "And so you used to do 'em the wrong way, like this, didn't ye, Joseph?" Matthew marked on the dusty floor with his whip-handle

⌐A M Ǝ S

"And how Farmer James would cuss, and call thee a fool, wouldn't he, Joseph, when 'a seed his name looking so inside-out-like?" continued Matthew Moon, with feeling.

"Ay—'a would," said Joseph meekly. "But, you see, I wasn't so much to blame, for them J's and E's be such trying sons o' witches for the memory to mind whether they face backward or forward; and I always had such a forgetful memory, too."

" 'Tis a very bad afiction for ye, being such a man of calamities in other ways."

"Well, 'tis; but a happy Providence ordered that it should be no worse, and I feel my thanks. As to shepherd, there, I'm sure mis'ess ought to have made ye her baily—such a fitting man for't as you be."

"I don't mind owning that I expected it," said Oak frankly. "Indeed, I hoped for the place. At the same time, Miss Everdene has a right to be her own baily if she choose—and to keep me down to be a common shepherd only." Oak drew a slow breath, looked sadly into the bright ashpit, and seemed lost in thoughts not of the most hopeful hue.

The genial warmth of the fire now began to stimulate the nearly lifeless lambs to bleat and move their limbs briskly upon the hay, and to recognise for the first time the fact that they were born. Their noise increased to a chorus of baas, upon which Oak pulled the milk-can from before the fire, and taking a small tea-pot from the pocket of his smock-frock, filled it with milk, and taught those of the helpless creatures which were not to be restored to their dams how to drink from the spout—a trick they acquired with astonishing aptitude.

"And she don't even let ye have the skins of the dead lambs, I hear?" resumed Joseph Poorgrass, his eyes lingering on the operations of Oak with the necessary melancholy.

"I don't have them," said Gabriel.

"Ye be very badly used, shepherd," hazarded Joseph again, in the hope of getting Oak as an ally in lamentation after all. "I think she's took against ye—that I do."

"O no—not at all," replied Gabriel hastily, and a sigh escaped him, which the deprivation of lamb skins could hardly have caused.

Before any further remark had been added a shade darkened the door, and Boldwood entered the malthouse, bestowing upon each a nod of a quality between friendliness and condescension.

"Ah! Oak, I thought you were here," he said. "I met the mail-cart ten minutes ago, and a letter was put into my hand, which I opened without reading the address. I believe it is yours. You must excuse the accident, please."

"O yes—not a bit of difference, Mr. Boldwood—not a bit," said Gabriel readily. He had not a correspondent on earth, nor was there a possible letter coming to him whose contents the whole parish would not have been welcome to peruse.

Oak stepped aside, and read the following in an unknown hand:—

DEAR FRIEND—I do not know your name, but I think these few lines will reach you, which I write to thank you for your kindness to me the night I left Weatherbury in a reckless way. I also return the money I owe you, which you will excuse my not keeping as a gift. All has ended well, and I am happy to say I am going to be married to the young man who has courted me for some time—Sergeant Troy, of the 11th Dragoon Guards, now quartered in this town. He would, I know, object to my having received anything except as a loan, being a man of great respectability and high honour—indeed, a nobleman by blood.

I should be much obliged to you if you would keep the contents of this letter a secret for the present, dear friend. We mean to surprise Weatherbury by coming there soon as husband and wife, though I blush to state it to one nearly a stranger. The sergeant grew up in Weatherbury. Thanking you again for your kindness,

I am, your sincere well-wisher,
FANNY ROBIN

"Have you read it, Mr. Boldwood?" said Gabriel; "if not, you had better do so. I know you are interested in Fanny Robin."

Boldwood read the letter and looked grieved.

"Fanny—poor Fanny! the end she is so confident of has not yet come, she should remember—and may never come. I see she gives no address."

"What sort of a man is this Sergeant Troy?" said Gabriel.

"H'm—I'm afraid not one to build much hope upon in such a case as this," the farmer murmured, "though he's a clever fellow, and up to everything. A slight romance attaches to him, too. His mother was a French governess, and it seems that a secret attachment existed between her and the late Lord Severn. She was married to a poor medical man, and soon after an infant was born; and while money was forthcoming all went on well. Unfortunately for her boy, his best friends died; and he got then a situation as second clerk at a lawyer's in Casterbridge. He stayed there for some time, and might have worked himself into a dignified position of some sort had he not indulged in the wild freak of enlisting. I have much doubt if ever little Fanny will surprise us in the way she mentions—very much doubt. A silly girl—silly girl!"

The door was hurriedly burst open again, and in came running Cainy Ball out of breath, his mouth red and open, like the bell of a penny trumpet, from which he coughed with noisy vigour and great distension of face.

"Now, Cain Ball," said Oak sternly, "why will you run so fast and lose your breath so? I'm always telling you of it."

"Oh—I—a puff of mee breath—went—the—wrong way, please, Mister Oak, and made me cough—hok—hok!"

"Well—what have you come for?"

"I've run to tell ye," said the junior shepherd, supporting his exhausted youthful frame against the doorpost, "that you must come directly. Two more ewes have twinned—that's what's the matter, Shepherd Oak."

"Oh, that's it," said Oak, jumping up, and dimissing for the present his thoughts on poor Fanny. "You are a good boy to run and tell me, Cain, and you shall smell a large plum pudding some day as a treat. But, before we go, Cainy, bring the tarpot, and we'll mark this lot and have done with 'em."

Oak took from his illimitable pockets a marking iron, dipped it into the pot, and imprinted on the buttocks of the infant sheep the initials of her he delighted to muse on—"B. E.," which signified to all the region round that henceforth the lambs belonged to Farmer Bathsheba Everdene, and to no one else.

"Now, Cainy, shoulder your two, and off. Good-morning, Mr. Boldwood." The shepherd lifted the sixteen large legs and four small bodies he had himself brought, and vanished with them in the direction of the lambing field hard by—their frames being now in a sleek and hopeful state, pleasantly contrasting with their death's-door plight of half an hour before.

Boldwood followed him a little way up the field, hesitated, and turned back. He followed him again with a last resolve, annihilating return. On approaching the nook in which the fold was constructed, the farmer drew out his pocket-book, unfastened it, and allowed it to lie open on his hand. A letter was revealed—Bathsheba's.

"I was going to ask you, Oak," he said, with unreal carelessness, "if you know whose writing this is?"

Oak glanced into the book, and replied instantly, with a flushed face, "Miss Everdene's."

Oak had coloured simply at the consciousness of sounding her name. He now felt a strangely distressing qualm from a new thought. The letter could of course be no other than anonymous, or the enquiry would not have been necessary.

Boldwood mistook his confusion: sensitive persons are always ready with their "Is it I?" in preference to objective reasoning.

"The question was perfectly fair," he returned—and there was something incongruous in the serious earnestness with which he applied himself to an argument on a valentine. "You know it is always expected that privy enquiries will be made: that's where the—fun lies." If the word "fun" had been "torture," it could not have been uttered with a more constrained and restless countenance than was Boldwood's then.

Soon parting from Gabriel, the lonely and reserved man returned to his house to breakfast—feeling twinges of shame and regret at having so far exposed his mood by those fevered questions to a stranger. He again placed the letter on the mantelpiece, and sat down to think of the circumstances attending it by the light of Gabriel's information.

XVI

ALL SAINTS' AND ALL SOULS'

O N A WEEK-DAY MORNING A SMALL CONGREGATION, CONSISTING MAINLY OF WOMEN and girls, rose from its knees in the mouldy nave of a church called All Saints', in the distant barrack-town before-mentioned, at the end of a service without a sermon. They were about to disperse, when a smart footstep, entering the porch and coming up the central passage, arrested their attention. The step echoed with a ring unusual in a church; it was the clink of spurs. Everybody looked. A young cavalry soldier in a red uniform, with the three chevrons of a sergeant upon his sleeve, strode up the aisle, with an embarrassment which was only the more marked by the intense vigour of his step, and by the determination upon his face to show none. A slight flush had mounted his cheek by the time he had run the gauntlet between these women; but, passing on through the chancel arch, he never paused till he came close to the altar railing. Here for a moment he stood alone.

The officiating curate, who had not yet doffed his surplice, perceived the new-comer, and followed him to the communion-space. He whispered to the soldier, and then beckoned to the clerk, who in his turn whispered to an elderly woman, apparently his wife, and they also went up the chancel steps.

" 'Tis a wedding!" murmured some of the women, brightening. "Let's wait!"

The majority again sat down.

There was a creaking of machinery behind, and some of the young ones turned their heads. From the interior face of the west wall of the tower projected a little canopy with a quarter-jack and small bell beneath it, the automaton being driven by the same clock machinery that struck the large bell in the tower. Between the tower and the church was a close screen, the door of which was kept shut during services, hiding this grotesque clockwork from sight. At present, however, the door was open, and the egress of the jack, the blows on the bell, and the mannikin's retreat into the nook again, were visible to many, and audible throughout the church.

The jack had struck half-past eleven.

"Where's the woman?" whispered some of the spectators.

The young sergeant stood still with the abnormal rigidity of the old pillars around. He faced the south-east, and was as silent as he was still.

The silence grew to be a noticeable thing as the minutes went on, and nobody else appeared, and not a soul moved. The rattle of the quarter-jack again from its niche, its blows for three-quarters, its fussy retreat, were almost painfully abrupt, and caused many of the congregation to start palpably.

"I wonder where the woman is!" a voice whispered again.

There began now that slight shifting of feet, that artificial coughing among several, which betrays a nervous suspense. At length there was a titter. But the soldier never moved. There he stood, his face to the south-east, upright as a column, his cap in his hand.

The clock ticked on. The women threw off their nervousness, and titters and giggling became more frequent. Then came a dead silence. Everyone was waiting for the end. Some persons may have noticed how extraordinarily the striking of quarters seems to quicken the flight of time. It was hardly credible that the jack had not got wrong with the minutes when the rattle began again, the puppet emerged, and the four quarters were struck fitfully as before. One could almost be positive that there was a malicious leer upon the hideous creature's face, and a mischievous delight in its twitchings. Then followed the dull and remote resonance of the twelve heavy strokes in the tower above. The women were impressed, and there was no giggle this time.

The clergyman glided into the vestry, and the clerk vanished. The sergeant had not yet turned; every woman in the church was waiting to see his face, and he appeared to know it. At last he did turn, and stalked resolutely down the nave, braving them all, with a compressed lip. Two bowed and toothless old almsmen then looked at each other and chuckled, innocently enough; but the sound had a strange weird effect in that place.

Opposite to the church was a paved square, around which several overhanging wood buildings of old time cast a picturesque shade. The young man on leaving the door went to cross the square, when, in the middle, he met a little woman. The expression of her face, which had been one of intense anxiety, sank at the sight of his nearly to terror.

"Well?" he said, in a suppressed passion, fixedly looking at her.

"O Frank—I made a mistake!—I thought that church with the spire was All Saints', and I was at the door at half-past eleven to a minute as you said. I waited till a quarter to twelve, and found then that I was in All Souls'. But I wasn't much frightened, for I thought it could be to-morrow as well."

"You fool, for so fooling me! But say no more."

"Shall it be to-morrow, Frank?" she asked blankly.

"To-morrow!" and he gave vent to a hoarse laugh. "I don't go through that experience again for some time, I warrant you!"

"But after all," she expostulated in a trembling voice, "the mistake was not such a terrible thing! Now, dear Frank, when shall it be?"

"Ah, when? God knows!" he said, with a light irony, and turning from her walked rapidly away.

XVII

IN THE MARKET-PLACE

ON SATURDAY BOLDWOOD WAS IN CASTERBRIDGE MARKET-HOUSE AS USUAL, WHEN THE disturber of his dreams entered, and became visible to him. Adam had awakened from his deep sleep, and behold! there was Eve. The farmer took courage, and for the first time really looked at her.

Material causes and emotional effects are not to be arranged in regular equation. The result from capital employed in the production of any movement of a mental nature is sometimes as tremendous as the cause itself is absurdly minute. When women are in a freakish mood their usual intuition, either from carelessness or inherent defect,

seemingly fails to teach them this, and hence it was that Bathsheba was fated to be astonished to-day.

Boldwood looked at her—not slily, critically, or understandingly, but blankly at gaze,
in the way a reaper looks up at a passing train—as something foreign to his element, and
but dimly understood. To Boldwood women had been remote phenomena rather than
necessary complements—comets of such uncertain aspect, movement, and permanence,
that whether their orbits were as geometrical, unchangeable, and as subject to laws as his
own, or as absolutely erratic as they superficially appeared, he had not deemed it his duty
to consider.

He saw her black hair, her correct facial curves and profile, and the roundness of her
chin and throat. He saw then the side of her eyelids, eyes, and lashes, and the shape of her
ear. Next he noticed her figure, her skirt, and the very soles of her shoes.

Boldwood thought her beautiful, but wondered whether he was right in his thought,
for it seemed impossible that this romance in the flesh, if so sweet as he imagined, could
have been going on long without creating a commotion of delight among men, and provoking more enquiry than Bathsheba had done, even though that was not a little. To the
best of his judgment neither nature nor art could improve this perfect one of an imperfect
many. His heart began to move within him. Boldwood, it must be remembered, though
forty years of age, had never before inspected a woman with the very centre and force of
his glance; they had struck upon all his senses at wide angles.

Was she really beautiful? He could not assure himself that his opinion was true even
now. He furtively said to a neighbour, "Is Miss Everdene considered handsome?"

"O yes; she was a good deal noticed the first time she came, if you remember. A very
handsome girl indeed."

A man is never more credulous than in receiving favourable opinions on the beauty of
a woman he is half, or quite, in love with; a mere child's word on the point has the weight
of an R.A.'s. Boldwood was satisfied now.

And this charming woman had in effect said to him, "Marry me." Why should she
have done that strange thing? Boldwood's blindness to the difference between approving
of what circumstances suggest, and originating what they do not suggest, was well
matched by Bathsheba's insensibility to the possibly great issues of little beginnings.

She was at this moment coolly dealing with a dashing young farmer, adding up accounts with him as indifferently as if his face had been the pages of a ledger. It was evident that such a nature as his had no attraction for a woman of Bathsheba's taste. But
Boldwood grew hot down to his hands with an incipient jealousy; he trod for the first time
the threshold of "the injured lover's hell." His first impulse was to go and thrust himself
between them. This could be done, but only in one way—by asking to see a sample of her
corn. Boldwood renounced the idea. He could not make the request; it was debasing loveliness to ask it to buy and sell, and jarred with his conceptions of her.

All this time Bathsheba was conscious of having broken into that dignified stronghold
at last. His eyes, she knew, were following her everywhere. This was a triumph; and had
it come naturally, such a triumph would have been the sweeter to her for this piquing delay.
But it had been brought about by misdirected ingenuity, and she valued it only as she valued an artificial flower or a wax fruit.

Being a woman with some good sense in reasoning on subjects wherein her heart was not involved, Bathsheba genuinely repented that a freak which had owed its existence as much to Liddy as to herself, should ever have been undertaken, to disturb the placidity of a man she respected too highly to deliberately tease.

She that day nearly formed the intention of begging his pardon on the very next occasion of their meeting. The worst features of this arrangement were that, if he thought she ridiculed him, an apology would increase the offence by being disbelieved; and if he thought she wanted him to woo her, it would read like additional evidence of her forwardness.

XVIII

Boldwood in Meditation—Regret

BOLDWOOD WAS TENANT OF WHAT WAS CALLED LITTLE WEATHERBURY FARM, AND HIS person was the nearest approach to aristocracy that this remoter quarter of the parish could boast of. Genteel strangers, whose god was their town, who might happen to be compelled to linger about this nook for a day, heard the sound of light wheels, and prayed to see good society, to the degree of a solitary lord, or squire at the very least, but it was only Mr. Boldwood going out for the day. They heard the sound of wheels yet once more, and were reanimated to expectancy: it was only Mr. Boldwood coming home again.

His house stood recessed from the road, and the stables, which are to a farm what a fireplace is to a room, were behind, their lower portions being lost amid bushes of laurel. Inside the blue door, open half-way down, were to be seen at this time the backs and tails of half-a-dozen warm and contented horses standing in their stalls; and as thus viewed, they presented alternations of roan and bay, in shapes like a Moorish arch, the tail being a streak down the midst of each. Over these, and lost to the eye gazing in from the outer light, the mouths of the same animals could be heard busily sustaining the above-named warmth and plumpness by quantities of oats and hay. The restless and shadowy figure of a colt wandered about a loose-box at the end, whilst the steady grind of all the eaters was occasionally diversified by the rattle of a rope or the stamp of a foot.

Pacing up and down at the heels of the animals was Farmer Boldwood himself. This place was his almonry and cloister in one: here, after looking to the feeding of his four-footed dependants, the celibate would walk and meditate of an evening till the moon's rays streamed in through the cobwebbed windows, or total darkness enveloped the scene.

His square-framed perpendicularity showed more fully now than in the crowd and bustle of the market-house. In this meditative walk his foot met the floor with heel and toe simultaneously, and his fine reddish-fleshed face was bent downwards just enough to render obscure the still mouth and the well-rounded though rather prominent and broad chin. A few clear and threadlike horizontal lines were the only interruption to the otherwise smooth surface of his large forehead.

The phases of Boldwood's life were ordinary enough, but his was not an ordinary nature. That stillness, which struck casual observers more than anything else in his character and habit, and seemed so precisely like the rest of inanition, may have been the perfect balance of enormous antagonistic forces—positives and negatives in fine adjustment. His equilibrium disturbed, he was in extremity at once. If an emotion possessed him at all, it ruled him; a feeling not mastering him was entirely latent. Stagnant or rapid, it was never slow. He was always hit mortally, or he was missed.

He had no light and careless touches in his constitution, either for good or for evil. Stern in the outlines of action, mild in the details, he was serious throughout all. He saw no absurd sides to the follies of life, and thus, though not quite companionable in the eyes of merry men and scoffers, and those to whom all things show life as a jest, he was not intolerable to the earnest and those acquainted with grief. Being a man who read all the dramas of life seriously, if he failed to please when they were comedies, there was no frivolous treatment to reproach him for when they chanced to end tragically.

Bathsheba was far from dreaming that the dark and silent shape upon which she had so carelessly thrown a seed was a hotbed of tropic intensity. Had she known Boldwood's moods her blame would have been fearful, and the stain upon her heart ineradicable. Moreover, had she known her present power for good or evil over this man, she would have trembled at her responsibility. Luckily for her present, unluckily for her future tranquillity, her understanding had not yet told her what Boldwood was. Nobody knew entirely; for though it was possible to form guesses concerning his wild capabilities from old floodmarks faintly visible, he had never been seen at the high tides which caused them.

Farmer Boldwood came to the stable-door and looked forth across the level fields. Beyond the first enclosure was a hedge, and on the other side of this a meadow belonging to Bathsheba's farm.

It was now early spring—the time of going to grass with the sheep, when they have the first feed of the meadows, before these are laid up for mowing. The wind, which had been blowing east for several weeks, had veered to the southward, and the middle of spring had come abruptly—almost without a beginning. It was that period in the vernal quarter when we may suppose the Dryads to be waking for the season. The vegetable world begins to move and swell and the saps to rise, till in the completest silence of lone gardens and trackless plantations, where everything seems helpless and still after the bond and slavery of frost, there are bustlings, strainings, united thrusts, and pulls-all-together, in comparison with which the powerful tugs of cranes and pulleys in a noisy city are but pigmy efforts.

Boldwood, looking into the distant meadows, saw there three figures. They were those of Miss Everdene, Shepherd Oak, and Cainy Ball.

When Bathsheba's figure shone upon the farmer's eyes it lighted him up as the moon lights up a great tower. A man's body is as the shell, or the tablet, of his soul, as he is reserved or ingenuous, overflowing or self-contained. There was a change in Boldwood's exterior from its former impassibleness; and his face showed that he was now living outside his defences for the first time, and with a fearful sense of exposure. It is the usual experience of strong natures when they love.

At last he arrived at a conclusion. It was to go across and enquire boldly of her.

The insulation of his heart by reserve during these many years, without a channel of any kind for disposable emotion, had worked its effect. It has been observed more than once that the causes of love are chiefly subjective, and Boldwood was a living testimony to the truth of the proposition. No mother existed to absorb his devotion, no sister for his tenderness, no idle ties for sense. He became surcharged with the compound, which was genuine lover's love.

He approached the gate of the meadow. Beyond it the ground was melodious with ripples, and the sky with larks; the low bleating of the flock mingling with both. Mistress and man were engaged in the operation of making a lamb "take," which is performed whenever an ewe has lost her own offspring, one of the twins of another ewe being given her as a substitute. Gabriel had skinned the dead lamb, and was tying the skin over the body of the live lamb in the customary manner, whilst Bathsheba was holding open a little pen of four hurdles, into which the mother and foisted lamb were driven, where they would remain till the old sheep conceived an affection for the young one.

Bathsheba looked up at the completion of the manoeuvre and saw the farmer by the gate, where he was overhung by a willow-tree in full bloom. Gabriel, to whom her face was as the uncertain glory of an April day, was ever regardful of its faintest changes, and instantly discerned thereon the mark of some influence from without, in the form of a keenly self-conscious reddening. He also turned and beheld Boldwood.

At once connecting these signs with the letter Boldwood had shown him, Gabriel suspected her of some coquettish procedure begun by that means, and carried on since, he knew not how.

Farmer Boldwood had read the pantomime denoting that they were aware of his presence, and the perception was as too much light turned upon his new sensibility. He was still in the road, and by moving on he hoped that neither would recognise that he had originally intended to enter the field. He passed by with an utter and overwhelming sensation of ignorance, shyness, and doubt. Perhaps in her manner there were signs that she wished to see him—perhaps not—he could not read a woman. The cabala of this erotic philosophy seemed to consist of the subtlest meanings expressed in misleading ways. Every turn, look, word, and accent contained a mystery quite distinct from its obvious import, and not one had ever been pondered by him until now.

As for Bathsheba, she was not deceived into the belief that Farmer Boldwood had walked by on business or in idleness. She collected the probabilities of the case, and concluded that she was herself responsible for Boldwood's appearance there. It troubled her much to see what a great flame a little wildfire was likely to kindle. Bathsheba was no schemer for marriage, nor was she deliberately a trifler with the affections of men, and a censor's experience on seeing an actual flirt after observing her would have been a feeling of surprise that Bathsheba could be so different from such a one, and yet so like what a flirt is supposed to be.

She resolved never again, by look or by sign, to interrupt the steady flow of this man's life. But a resolution to avoid an evil is seldom framed till the evil is so far advanced as to make avoidance impossible.

XIX

THE SHEEP-WASHING—THE OFFER

BOLDWOOD DID EVENTUALLY CALL UPON HER. SHE WAS NOT AT HOME. "OF COURSE not," he murmured. In contemplating Bathsheba as a woman, he had forgotten the accidents of her position as an agriculturist—that being as much of a farmer, and as extensive a farmer, as himself, her probable whereabouts was out-of-doors at this time of the year. This, and the other oversights Boldwood was guilty of, were natural to the mood, and still more natural to the circumstances. The great aids to idealization in love were present here: occasional observation of her from a distance, and the absence of social intercourse with her—visual familiarity, oral strangeness. The smaller human elements were kept out of sight; the pettinesses that enter so largely into all earthly living and doing were disguised by the accident of lover and loved-one not being on visiting terms; and there was hardly awakened a thought in Boldwood that sorry household realities appertained to her, or that she, like all others, had moments of commonplace, when to be least plainly seen was to be most prettily remembered. Thus a mild sort of apotheosis took place in his fancy, whilst she still lived and breathed within his own horizon, a troubled creature like himself.

It was the end of May when the farmer determined to be no longer repulsed by trivialities or distracted by suspense. He had by this time grown used to being in love; the passion now startled him less even when it tortured him more, and he felt himself adequate to the situation. On enquiring for her at her house they had told him she was at the sheep-washing, and he went off to seek her there.

The sheep-washing pool was a perfectly circular basin of brickwork in the meadows, full of the clearest water. To birds on the wing its glassy surface, reflecting the light sky, must have been visible for miles around as a glistening Cyclops' eye in a green face. The grass about the margin at this season was a sight to remember long—in a minor sort of way. Its activity in sucking the moisture from the rich damp sod was almost a process observable by the eye. The outskirts of this level water-meadow were diversified by rounded and hollow pastures, where just now every flower that was not a buttercup was a daisy. The river slid along noiselessly as a shade, the swelling reeds and sedge forming a flexible palisade upon its moist brink. To the north of the mead were trees, the leaves of which were new, soft, and moist, not yet having stiffened and darkened under summer sun and drought, their colour being yellow beside a green—green beside a yellow. From the recesses of this knot of foliage the loud notes of three cuckoos were resounding through the still air.

Boldwood went meditating down the slopes with his eyes on his boots, which the yellow pollen from the buttercups had bronzed in artistic gradations. A tributary of the main stream flowed through the basin of the pool by an inlet and outlet at opposite points of its diameter. Shepherd Oak, Jan Coggan, Moon, Poorgrass, Cain Ball, and several others were assembled here, all dripping wet to the very roots of their hair, and Bathsheba was standing by in a new riding-habit—the most elegant she had ever worn—the reins of her horse being looped over her arm. Flagons of cider were rolling about upon the green. The meek sheep were pushed into the pool by Coggan and Matthew Moon, who stood by the lower hatch, immersed to their waists; then Gabriel, who stood on the brink, thrust them under as they swam along, with an instrument like a crutch, formed for the purpose, and also for assisting the exhausted animals when the wool became saturated and they began to sink. They were let out against the stream, and through the upper opening, all impurities flowing away below. Cainy Ball and Joseph, who performed this latter operation, were if possible wetter than the rest; they resembled dolphins under a fountain, every protuberance and angle of their clothes dribbling forth a small rill.

Boldwood came close and bade her good-morning with such constraint that she could not but think he had stepped across to the washing for its own sake, hoping not to find her there; more, she fancied his brow severe and his eye slighting. Bathsheba immediately contrived to withdraw, and glided along by the river till she was a stone's throw off. She heard footsteps brushing the grass, and had a consciousness that love was encircling her like a perfume. Instead of turning or waiting, Bathsheba went further among the high sedges, but Boldwood seemed determined, and pressed on till they were completely past the bend of the river. Here, without being seen, they could hear the splashing and shouts of the washers above.

"Miss Everdene!" said the farmer.

She trembled, turned, and said "Good-morning." His tone was so utterly removed from all she had expected as a beginning. It was lowness and quiet accentuated: an emphasis of deep meanings, their form, at the same time, being scarcely expressed. Silence has sometimes a remarkable power of showing itself as the disembodied soul of feeling wandering without its carcase, and it is then more impressive than speech. In the same way, to say a little is often to tell more than to say a great deal. Boldwood told everything in that word.

As the consciousness expands on learning that what was fancied to be the rumble of wheels is the reverberation of thunder, so did Bathsheba's at her intuitive conviction.

"I feel—almost too much—to think," he said, with a solemn simplicity. "I have come to speak to you without preface. My life is not my own since I have beheld you clearly, Miss Everdene—I come to make you an offer of marriage."

Bathsheba tried to preserve an absolutely neutral countenance, and all the motion she made was that of closing lips which had previously been a little parted.

"I am now forty-one years old," he went on. "I may have been called a confirmed bachelor, and I was a confirmed bachelor. I had never any views of myself as a husband in my earlier days, nor have I made any calculation on the subject since I have been older. But we all change, and my change, in this matter, came with seeing you. I have felt lately, more and more, that my present way of living is bad in every respect. Beyond all things, I want you as my wife."

"I feel, Mr. Boldwood, that though I respect you much, I do not feel—what would justify me to—in accepting your offer," she stammered.

This giving back of dignity for dignity seemed to open the sluices of feeling that Boldwood had as yet kept closed.

"My life is a burden without you," he exclaimed, in a low voice. "I want you—I want you to let me say I love you again and again!"

Bathsheba answered nothing, and the mare upon her arm seemed so impressed that instead of cropping the herbage she looked up.

"I think and hope you care enough for me to listen to what I have to tell!"

Bathsheba's momentary impulse at hearing this was to ask why he thought that, till she remembered that, far from being a conceited assumption on Boldwood's part, it was but the natural conclusion of serious reflection based on deceptive premises of her own offering.

"I wish I could say courteous flatteries to you," the farmer continued in an easier tone, "and put my rugged feeling into a graceful shape: but I have neither power nor patience to learn such things. I want you for my wife—so wildly that no other feeling can abide in me; but I should not have spoken out had I not been led to hope."

"The valentine again! O that valentine!" she said to herself, but not a word to him.

"If you can love me say so, Miss Everdene. If not—don't say no!"

"Mr. Boldwood, it is painful to have to say I am surprised, so that I don't know how to answer you with propriety and respect—but am only just able to speak out my feeling—I mean my meaning; that I am afraid I can't marry you, much as I respect you. You are too dignified for me to suit you, sir."

"But, Miss Everdene!"

"I—I didn't—I know I ought never to have dreamt of sending that valentine—forgive me, sir—it was a wanton thing which no woman with any self-respect should have done. If you will only pardon my thoughtlessness, I promise never to—"

"No, no, no. Don't say thoughtlessness! Make me think it was something more—that it was a sort of prophetic instinct—the beginning of a feeling that you would like me. You torture me to say it was done in thoughtlessness—I never thought of it in that light, and I can't endure it. Ah! I wish I knew how to win you! but that I can't do—I can only ask if I have already got you. If I have not, and it is not true that you have come unwittingly to me as I have to you, I can say no more."

"I have not fallen in love with you, Mr. Boldwood—certainly I must say that." She allowed a very small smile to creep for the first time over her serious face in saying this, and the white row of upper teeth, and keenly-cut lips already noticed, suggested an idea of heartlessness, which was immediately contradicted by the pleasant eyes.

"But you will just think—in kindness and condescension think—if you cannot bear with me as a husband! I fear I am too old for you, but believe me I will take more care of you than would many a man of your own age. I will protect and cherish you with all my strength—I will indeed! You shall have no cares—be worried by no household affairs, and live quite at ease, Miss Everdene. The dairy superintendence shall be done by a man—I can afford it well—you shall never have so much as to look out of doors at haymaking time, or to think of weather in the harvest. I rather cling to the chaise, because it is the same my poor father and mother drove, but if you don't like it I will sell it, and you shall have a pony-carriage of your own. I cannot say how far above every other idea and object on earth you seem to me—nobody knows—God only knows—how much you are to me!"

Bathsheba's heart was young, and it swelled with sympathy for the deep-natured man who spoke so simply.

"Don't say it: don't! I cannot bear you to feel so much, and me to feel nothing. And I am afraid they will notice us, Mr. Boldwood. Will you let the matter rest now? I cannot think collectedly. I did not know you were going to say this to me. O, I am wicked to have made you suffer so!" She was frightened as well as agitated at his vehemence.

"Say then, that you don't absolutely refuse. Do not quite refuse?"

"I can do nothing. I cannot answer."

"I may speak to you again on the subject?"

"Yes."

"I may think of you?"

"Yes, I suppose you may think of me."

"And hope to obtain you?"

"No—do not hope! Let us go on."

"I will call upon you again to-morrow."

"No—please not. Give me time."

"Yes—I will give you any time," he said earnestly and gratefully. "I am happier now."

"No—I beg you! Don't be happier if happiness only comes from my agreeing. Be neutral, Mr. Boldwood! I must think."

"I will wait," he said.

And then she turned away. Boldwood dropped his gaze to the ground, and stood long like a man who did not know where he was. Realities then returned upon him like the pain of a wound received in an excitement which eclipses it, and he, too, then went on.

XX

Perplexity—Grinding the Shears—A Quarrel

"HE IS SO DISINTERESTED AND KIND TO OFFER ME ALL THAT I CAN DESIRE," BATHSHEBA mused.

Yet Farmer Boldwood, whether by nature kind or the reverse to kind, did not exercise kindness here. The rarest offerings of the purest loves are but a self-indulgence, and no generosity at all.

Bathsheba, not being the least in love with him, was eventually able to look calmly at his offer. It was one which many women of her own station in the neighbourhood, and not a few of higher rank, would have been wild to accept and proud to publish. In every point of view, ranging from politic to passionate, it was desirable that she, a lonely girl, should marry, and marry this earnest, well-to-do, and respected man. He was close to her doors: his standing was sufficient: his qualities were even supererogatory. Had she felt, which she did not, any wish whatever for the married state in the abstract, she could not reasonably have rejected him, being a woman who frequently appealed to her understanding for deliverance from her whims. Boldwood as a means to marriage was unexceptionable: she esteemed and liked him, yet she did not want him. It appears that ordinary men take wives because possession is not possible without marriage, and that ordinary women accept husbands because marriage is not possible without possession; with totally differing aims the method is the same on both sides. But the understood incentive on the woman's part was wanting here. Besides, Bathsheba's position as absolute mistress of a farm and house was a novel one, and the novelty had not yet begun to wear off.

But a disquiet filled her which was somewhat to her credit, for it would have affected few. Beyond the mentioned reasons with which she combated her objections, she had a strong feeling that, having been the one who began the game, she ought in honesty to accept the consequences. Still the reluctance remained. She said in the same breath that it would be ungenerous not to marry Boldwood, and that she couldn't do it to save her life.

Bathsheba's was an impulsive nature under a deliberative aspect. An Elizabeth in brain and a Mary Stuart in spirit, she often performed actions of the greatest temerity with a manner of extreme discretion. Many of her thoughts were perfect syllogisms; unluckily they always remained thoughts. Only a few were irrational assumptions; but, unfortunately, they were the ones which most frequently grew into deeds.

The next day to that of the declaration she found Gabriel Oak at the bottom of her garden, grinding his shears for the sheep-shearing. All the surrounding cottages were more or less scenes of the same operation; the scurr of whetting spread into the sky from all parts of the village as from an armoury previous to a campaign. Peace and war kiss each other at their hours of preparation—sickles, scythes, shears, and pruning-hooks, ranking with swords, bayonets, and lances, in their common necessity for point and edge.

Cainy Ball turned the handle of Gabriel's grindstone, his head performing a melancholy see-saw up and down with each turn of the wheel. Oak stood somewhat as Eros is represented when in the act of sharpening his arrows: his figure slightly bent, the weight of his body thrown over on the shears, and his head balanced sideways, with a critical compression of the lips and contraction of the eyelids to crown the attitude.

His mistress came up and looked upon them in silence for a minute or two; then she said—

"Cain, go to the lower mead and catch the bay mare. I'll turn the winch of the grindstone. I want to speak to you, Gabriel."

Cain departed, and Bathsheba took the handle. Gabriel had glanced up in intense surprise, quelled its expression, and looked down again. Bathsheba turned the winch, and Gabriel applied the shears.

The peculiar motion involved in turning a wheel has a wonderful tendency to benumb the mind. It is a sort of attenuated variety of Ixion's punishment, and contributes a dismal chapter to the history of gaols. The brain gets muddled, the head grows heavy, and the body's centre of gravity seems to settle by degrees in a leaden lump somewhere between the eyebrows and the crown. Bathsheba felt the unpleasant symptoms after two or three dozen turns.

"Will you turn, Gabriel, and let me hold the shears?" she said. "My head is in a whirl, and I can't talk."

Gabriel turned. Bathsheba then began, with some awkwardness, allowing her thoughts to stray occasionally from her story to attend to the shears, which required a little nicety in sharpening.

"I wanted to ask you if the men made any observations on my going behind the sedge with Mr. Boldwood yesterday?"

"Yes, they did," said Gabriel. "You don't hold the shears right, miss—I knew you wouldn't know the way—hold like this."

He relinquished the winch, and enclosing her two hands completely in his own (taking each as we sometimes slap a child's hand in teaching him to write), grasped the shears with her. "Incline the edge so," he said.

Hands and shears were inclined to suit the words, and held thus for a peculiarly long time by the instructor as he spoke.

"That will do," exclaimed Bathsheba. "Loose my hands. I won't have them held! Turn the winch."

Gabriel freed her hands quietly, retired to his handle, and the grinding went on.

"Did the men think it odd?" she said again.

"Odd was not the idea, miss."

"What did they say?"

"That Farmer Boldwood's name and your own were likely to be flung over pulpit together before the year was out."

"I thought so by the look of them! Why, there's nothing in it. A more foolish remark was never made, and I want you to contradict it: that's what I came for."

Gabriel looked incredulous and sad, but between his moments of incredulity, relieved.

"They must have heard our conversation," she continued.

"Well, then, Bathsheba!" said Oak, stopping the handle, and gazing into her face with astonishment.

"Miss Everdene, you mean," she said, with dignity.

"I mean this, that if Mr. Boldwood really spoke of marriage, I bain't going to tell a story and say he didn't to please you. I have already tried to please you too much for my own good!"

Bathsheba regarded him with round-eyed perplexity. She did not know whether to pity him for disappointed love of her, or to be angry with him for having got over it—his tone being ambiguous.

"I said I wanted you just to mention that it was not true I was going to be married to him," she murmured, with a slight decline in her assurance.

"I can say that to them if you wish, Miss Everdene. And I could likewise give an opinion to 'ee on what you have done."

"I daresay. But I don't want your opinion."

"I suppose not," said Gabriel bitterly, and going on with his turning; his words rising and falling in a regular swell and cadence as he stooped or rose with the winch, which directed them, according to his position, perpendicularly into the earth, or horizontally along the garden, his eyes being fixed on a leaf upon the ground.

With Bathsheba a hastened act was a rash act; but, as does not always happen, time gained was prudence ensured. It must be added, however, that time was very seldom gained. At this period the single opinion in the parish on herself and her doings that she valued as sounder than her own was Gabriel Oak's. And the outspoken honesty of his character was such that on any subject, even that of her love for, or marriage with, another man, the same disinterestedness of opinion might be calculated on, and be had for the asking. Thoroughly convinced of the impossibility of his own suit, a high resolve constrained him not to injure that of another. This is a lover's most stoical virtue, as the lack of it is a lover's most venial sin. Knowing he would reply truly she asked the question, painful as she must have known the subject would be. Such is the selfishness of some charming women. Perhaps it was some excuse for her thus torturing honesty to her own advantage, that she had absolutely no other sound judgment within easy reach.

"Well, what is your opinion of my conduct," she said quietly.

"That it is unworthy of any thoughtful, and meek, and comely woman."

In an instant Bathsheba's face coloured with the angry crimson of a Danby sunset. But she forbore to utter this feeling, and the reticence of her tongue only made the loquacity of her face the more noticeable.

The next thing Gabriel did was to make a mistake.

"Perhaps you don't like the rudeness of my reprimanding you, for I know it is rudeness; but I thought it would do good."

She instantly replied sarcastically—

"On the contrary, my opinion of you is so low, that I see in your abuse the praise of discerning people!"

"I am glad you don't mind it, for I said it honestly and with every serious meaning."

"I see. But, unfortunately, when you try not to speak in jest you are amusing—just as when you wish to avoid seriousness you sometimes say a sensible word."

It was a hard hit, but Bathsheba had unmistakably lost her temper, and on that account Gabriel had never in his life kept his own better. He said nothing. She then broke out—

"I may ask, I suppose, where in particular my unworthiness lies? In my not marrying you, perhaps!"

"Not by any means," said Gabriel quietly. "I have long given up thinking of that matter."

"Or wishing it, I suppose," she said; and it was apparent that she expected an unhesitating denial of this supposition.

Whatever Gabriel felt, he coolly echoed her words—

"Or wishing it either."

A woman may be treated with a bitterness which is sweet to her, and with a rudeness which is not offensive. Bathsheba would have submitted to an indignant chastisement for her levity had Gabriel protested that he was loving her at the same time; the impetuosity of passion unrequited is bearable, even if it stings and anathematises—there is a triumph in the humiliation, and a tenderness in the strife. This was what she had been expecting, and what she had not got. To be lectured because the lecturer saw her in the cold morning light of open-shuttered disillusion was exasperating. He had not finished, either. He continued in a more agitated voice:—

"My opinion is (since you ask it) that you are greatly to blame for playing pranks upon a man like Mr. Boldwood, merely as a pastime. Leading on a man you don't care for is not a praiseworthy action. And even, Miss Everdene, if you seriously inclined towards him, you might have let him find it out in some way of true loving-kindness, and not by sending him a valentine's letter."

Bathsheba laid down the shears.

"I cannot allow any man to—to criticise my private conduct!" she exclaimed. "Nor will I for a minute. So you'll please leave the farm at the end of the week!"

It may have been a peculiarity—at any rate it was a fact—that when Bathsheba was swayed by an emotion of an earthly sort her lower lip trembled: when by a refined emotion, her upper or heavenward one. Her nether lip quivered now.

"Very well, so I will," said Gabriel calmly. He had been held to her by a beautiful thread which it pained him to spoil by breaking, rather than by a chain he could not break. "I should be even better pleased to go at once," he added.

"Go at once then, in Heaven's name!" said she, her eyes flashing at his, though never meeting them. "Don't let me see your face any more."

"Very well, Miss Everdene—so it shall be."

And he took his shears and went away from her in placid dignity, as Moses left the presence of Pharaoh.

XXI

TROUBLES IN THE FOLD—A MESSAGE

GABRIEL OAK HAD CEASED TO FEED THE WEATHERBURY FLOCK FOR ABOUT FOUR-AND-twenty hours, when on Sunday afternoon the elderly gentlemen Joseph Poorgrass, Matthew Moon, Fray, and half-a-dozen others, came running up to the house of the mistress of the Upper Farm.

"Whatever *is* the matter, men?" she said, meeting them at the door just as she was coming out on her way to church, and ceasing in a moment from the close compression of her two red lips, with which she had accompanied the exertion of pulling on a tight glove.

"Sixty!" said Joseph Poorgrass.

"Seventy!" said Moon.

"Fifty-nine!" said Susan Tall's husband.

"—Sheep have broke fence," said Fray.

"—And got into a field of young clover," said Tall.

"—Young clover!" said Moon.

"—Clover!" said Joseph Poorgrass.

"And they be getting blasted," said Henery Fray.

"That they be," said Joseph.

"And will all die as dead as nits, if they bain't got out and cured!" said Tall.

Joseph's countenance was drawn into lines and puckers by his concern. Fray's forehead was wrinkled both perpendicularly and crosswise, after the pattern of a portcullis, expressive of a double despair. Laban Tall's lips were thin, and his face was rigid. Matthew's jaws sank, and his eyes turned whichever way the strongest muscle happened to pull them.

"Yes," said Joseph, "and I was sitting at home looking for Ephesians, and says I to myself, ' 'Tis nothing but Corinthians and Thessalonians in this danged Testament,' when who should come in but Henery there: 'Joseph,' he said, 'the sheep have blasted theirselves—' "

With Bathsheba it was a moment when thought was speech and speech exclamation. Moreover, she had hardly recovered her equanimity since the disturbance which she had suffered from Oak's remarks.

"That's enough—that's enough!—O you fools!" she cried, throwing the parasol and Prayer-book into the passage, and running out-of-doors in the direction signified. "To come to me, and not go and get them out directly! O, the stupid numskulls!"

Her eyes were at their darkest and brightest now. Bathsheba's beauty belonging rather to the demonian than to the angelic school, she never looked so well as when she was angry—and particularly when the effect was heightened by a rather dashing velvet dress, carefully put on before a glass.

All the ancient men ran in a jumbled throng after her to the clover-field, Joseph sinking down in the midst when about half-way, like an individual withering in a world which was more and more insupportable. Having once received the stimulus that her presence always gave them they went round among the sheep with a will. The majority of the afflicted animals were lying down, and could not be stirred. These were bodily lifted out, and the others driven into the adjoining field. Here, after the lapse of a few minutes, several more fell down, and lay helpless and livid as the rest.

Bathsheba, with a sad, bursting heart, looked at these primest specimens of her prime flock as they rolled there—

> *Swoln with wind and the rank mist they drew.*

Many of them foamed at the mouth, their breathing being quick and short, whilst the bodies of all were fearfully distended.

"O, what can I do, what can I do!" said Bathsheba, helplessly. "Sheep are such unfortunate animals!—there's always something happening to them! I never knew a flock pass a year without getting into some scrape or other."

"There's only one way of saving them," said Tall.

"What way? Tell me quick!"

"They must be pierced in the side with a thing made on purpose."

"Can you do it? Can I?"

"No, ma'am. We can't, nor you neither. It must be done in a particular spot. If ye go to the right or left but an inch you stab the ewe and kill her. Not even a shepherd can do it, as a rule."

"Then they must die," she said, in a resigned tone.

"Only one man in the neighbourhood knows the way," said Joseph, now just come up. "He could cure 'em all if he were here."

"Who is he? Let's get him!"

"Shepherd Oak," said Matthew. "Ah, he's a clever man in talents!"

"Ah, that he is so!" said Joseph Poorgrass.

"True—he's the man," said Laban Tall.

"How dare you name that man in my presence!" she said excitedly. "I told you never to allude to him, nor shall you if you stay with me. Ah!" she added, brightening, "Farmer Boldwood knows!"

"O no, ma'am," said Matthew. "Two of his store ewes got into some vetches t'other day, and were just like these. He sent a man on horseback here post-haste for Gable, and Gable went and saved 'em. Farmer Boldwood hev got the thing they do it with. 'Tis a holler pipe, with a sharp pricker inside. Isn't it, Joseph?"

"Ay—a holler pipe," echoed Joseph. "That's what 'tis."

"Ay, sure—that's the machine," chimed in Henery Fray reflectively, with an Oriental indifference to the flight of time.

"Well," burst out Bathsheba, "don't stand there with your 'ayes' and your 'sures' talking at me! Get somebody to cure the sheep instantly!"

All then stalked off in consternation, to get somebody as directed, without any idea of who it was to be. In a minute they had vanished through the gate, and she stood alone with the dying flock.

"Never will I send for him—never!" she said firmly.

One of the ewes here contracted its muscles horribly, extended itself, and jumped high into the air. The leap was an astonishing one. The ewe fell heavily, and lay still.

Bathsheba went up to it. The sheep was dead.

"O, what shall I do—what shall I do!" she again exclaimed, wringing her hands. "I won't send for him. No, I won't!"

The most vigorous expression of a resolution does not always coincide with the greatest vigour of the resolution itself. It is often flung out as a sort of prop to support a decaying conviction which, whilst strong, required no enunciation to prove it so. The "No, I won't" of Bathsheba meant virtually, "I think I must."

She followed her assistants through the gate, and lifted her hand to one of them. Laban answered to her signal.

"Where is Oak staying?"

"Across the valley at Nest Cottage."

"Jump on the bay mare, and ride across, and say he must return instantly—that I say so."

Tall scrambled off to the field, and in two minutes was on Poll, the bay, bare-backed, and with only a halter by way of rein. He diminished down the hill.

Bathsheba watched. So did all the rest. Tall cantered along the bridle-path through Sixteen Acres, Sheeplands, Middle Field, The Flats, Cappel's Piece, shrank almost to a point, crossed the bridge, and ascended from the valley through Springmead and Whitepits on the other side. The cottage to which Gabriel had retired before taking his final departure from the locality was visible as a white spot on the opposite hill, backed by blue firs. Bathsheba walked up and down. The men entered the field and endeavoured to ease the anguish of the dumb creatures by rubbing them. Nothing availed.

Bathsheba continued walking. The horse was seen descending the hill, and the wearisome series had to be repeated in reverse order: Whitepits, Springmead, Cappel's Piece, The Flats, Middle Field, Sheeplands, Sixteen Acres. She hoped Tall had had presence of mind enough to give the mare up to Gabriel, and return himself on foot. The rider neared them. It was Tall.

"O, what folly!" said Bathsheba.

Gabriel was not visible anywhere.

"Perhaps he is already gone!" she said.

Tall came into the enclosure, and leapt off, his face tragic as Morton's after the battle of Shrewsbury.

"Well?" said Bathsheba, unwilling to believe that her verbal *lettre-de-cachet* could possibly have miscarried.

"He says *beggars mustn't be choosers*," replied Laban.

"What!" said the young farmer, opening her eyes and drawing in her breath for an outburst. Joseph Poorgrass retired a few steps behind a hurdle.

"He says he shall not come unless you request en to come civilly and in a proper manner, as becomes any 'ooman begging a favour."

"Oh, oh, that's his answer! Where does he get his airs? Who am I, then, to be treated like that? Shall I beg to a man who has begged to me?"

Another of the flock sprang into the air, and fell dead.

The men looked grave, as if they suppressed opinion.

Bathsheba turned aside, her eyes full of tears. The strait she was in through pride and shrewishness could not be disguised longer: she burst out crying bitterly; they all saw it; and she attempted no further concealment.

"I wouldn't cry about it, miss," said William Smallbury compassionately. "Why not ask him softer like? I'm sure he'd come then. Gable is a true man in that way."

Bathsheba checked her grief and wiped her eyes. "O, it is a wicked cruelty to me—it is—it is!" she murmured. "And he drives me to do what I wouldn't; yes, he does!—Tall, come indoors."

After this collapse, not very dignified for the head of an establishment, she went into the house, Tall at her heels. Here she sat down and hastily scribbled a note between the small convulsive sobs of convalescence which follow a fit of crying as a ground-swell follows a storm. The note was none the less polite for being written in a hurry. She held it at a distance, was about to fold it, then added these words at the bottom:—

"Do not desert me, Gabriel!"

She looked a little redder in refolding it, and closed her lips, as if thereby to suspend till too late the action of conscience in examining whether such strategy were justifiable. The note was despatched as the message had been, and Bathsheba waited indoors for the result.

It was an anxious quarter of an hour that intervened between the messenger's departure and the sound of the horse's tramp again outside. She could not watch this time, but, leaning over the old bureau at which she had written the letter, closed her eyes, as if to keep out both hope and fear.

The case, however, was a promising one. Gabriel was not angry: he was simply neutral, although her first command had been so haughty. Such imperiousness would have damned a little less beauty; and on the other hand, such beauty would have redeemed a little less imperiousness.

She went out when the horse was heard, and looked up. A mounted figure passed between her and the sky, and drew on towards the field of sheep, the rider turning his face in receding. Gabriel looked at her. It was a moment when a woman's eyes and tongue tell distinctly opposite tales. Bathsheba looked full of gratitude, and she said:—

"O, Gabriel, how could you serve me so unkindly!"

Such a tenderly-shaped reproach for his previous delay was the one speech in the language that he could pardon for not being commendation of his readiness now.

Gabriel murmured a confused reply, and hastened on. She knew from the look which sentence in her note had brought him. Bathsheba followed to the field.

Gabriel was already among the turgid, prostrate forms. He had flung off his coat, rolled up his shirt-sleeves, and taken from his pocket the instrument of salvation. It was a small tube or trochar, with a lance passing down the inside; and Gabriel began to use it with a dexterity that would have graced a hospital-surgeon. Passing his hand over the sheep's left flank, and selecting the proper point, he punctured the skin and rumen with the lance as it stood in the tube; then he suddenly withdrew the lance, retaining the tube in its place. A current of air rushed up the tube, forcible enough to have extinguished a candle held at the orifice.

It has been said that mere ease after torment is delight for a time; and the countenances of these poor creatures expressed it now. Forty-nine operations were successfully performed. Owing to the great hurry necessitated by the far-gone state of some of the flock, Gabriel missed his aim in one case, and in one only—striking wide of the mark, and inflicting a mortal blow at once upon the suffering ewe. Four had died; three recovered without an operation. The total number of sheep which had thus strayed and injured themselves so dangerously was fifty-seven.

When the love-led man had ceased from his labours Bathsheba came and looked him in the face.

"Gabriel, will you stay on with me?" she said, smiling winningly, and not troubling to bring her lips quite together again at the end, because there was going to be another smile soon.

"I will," said Gabriel.

And she smiled on him again.

XXII

THE GREAT BARN AND THE SHEEP-SHEARERS

MEN THIN AWAY TO INSIGNIFICANCE AND OBLIVION QUITE AS OFTEN BY NOT MAKING the most of good spirits when they have them as by lacking good spirits when they are indispensable. Gabriel lately, for the first time since his prostration by misfortune, had been independent in thought and vigorous in action to a marked extent—conditions which, powerless without an opportunity as an opportunity without them is barren, would have given him a sure lift upwards when the favourable conjunction should have occurred. But this incurable loitering beside Bathsheba Everdene stole his time ruinously. The spring tides were going by without floating him off, and the neap might soon come which could not.

It was the first day of June, and the sheep-shearing season culminated, the landscape, even to the leanest pasture, being all health and colour. Every green was young, every pore was open, and every stalk was swollen with racing currents of juice. God was palpably present in the country, and the devil had gone with the world to town. Flossy catkins of the later kinds, fern-sprouts like bishops' croziers, the square-headed moschatel, the odd cuckoo-pint—like an apoplectic saint in a niche of malachite—snow-white ladies'-smocks, the toothwort, approximating to human flesh, the enchanter's night-shade, and the black-petaled doleful-bells, were among the quainter objects of the vegetable world in and about Weatherbury at this teeming time; and of the animal, the metamorphosed figures of Mr. Jan Coggan, the master-shearer; the second and third shearers, who travelled in the exercise of their calling, and do not require definition by name; Henery Fray the fourth shearer, Susan Tall's husband the fifth, Joseph Poorgrass the sixth, young Cain Ball as assistant-shearer, and Gabriel Oak as general supervisor. None of these were clothed to any extent worth mentioning, each appearing to have hit in the matter of raiment the decent mean between a high and low caste Hindoo. An angularity of lineament, and a fixity of facial machinery in general, proclaimed that serious work was the order of the day.

They sheared in the great barn, called for the nonce the Shearing-barn, which on ground-plan resembled a church with transepts. It not only emulated the form of the neighbouring church of the parish, but vied with it in antiquity. Whether the barn had ever formed one of a group of conventual buildings nobody seemed to be aware; no trace of such surroundings remained. The vast porches at the sides, lofty enough to admit a waggon laden to its highest with corn in the sheaf, were spanned by heavy-pointed arches of stone, broadly and boldly cut, whose very simplicity was the origin of a grandeur not apparent in erections where more ornament has been attempted. The dusky, filmed, chestnut roof, braced and tied in by huge collars, curves, and diagonals, was far nobler in design, because more wealthy in material, than nine-tenths of those in our modern churches. Along each side wall was a range of striding buttresses, throwing deep shadows on the spaces between them, which were perforated by lancet openings, combining in their proportions the precise requirements both of beauty and ventilation.

One could say about this barn, what could hardly be said of either the church or the castle, akin to it in age and style, that the purpose which had dictated its original erection was the same with that to which it was still applied. Unlike and superior to either of those two typical remnants of mediaevalism, the old barn embodied practices which had suffered no mutilation at the hands of time. Here at least the spirit of the ancient builders was at one with the spirit of the modern beholder. Standing before this abraded pile, the eye regarded its present usage, the mind dwelt upon its past history, with a satisfied sense of functional continuity throughout—a feeling almost of gratitude, and quite of pride, at the permanence of the idea which had heaped it up. The fact that four centuries had neither proved it to be founded on a mistake, inspired any hatred of its purpose, nor given rise to any reaction that had battered it down, invested this simple grey effort of old minds with a repose, if not a grandeur, which a too curious reflection was apt to disturb in its ecclesiastical and military compeers. For once mediaevalism and modernism had a common stand-point. The lanceolate windows, the time-eaten archstones and chamfers, the orientation of the axis, the misty chestnut work of the rafters, referred to no exploded fortifying art or worn-out religious creed. The defence and salvation of the body by daily bread is still a study, a religion, and a desire.

To-day the large side doors were thrown open towards the sun to admit a bountiful light to the immediate spot of the shearers' operations, which was the wood threshing-floor in the centre, formed of thick oak, black with age and polished by the beating of flails for many generations, till it had grown as slippery and as rich in hue as the state-room floors of an Elizabethan mansion. Here the shearers knelt, the sun slanting in upon their bleached shirts, tanned arms, and the polished shears they flourished, causing these to bristle with a thousand rays strong enough to blind a weak-eyed man. Beneath them a captive sheep lay panting, quickening its pants as misgiving merged in terror, till it quivered like the hot landscape outside.

This picture of to-day in its frame of four hundred years ago did not produce that marked contrast between ancient and modern which is implied by the contrast of date. In comparison with cities, Weatherbury was immutable. The citizen's *Then* is the rustic's *Now*. In London, twenty or thirty years ago are old times; in Paris ten years, or five; in Weatherbury three or four score years were included in the mere present, and nothing less than a century set a mark on its face or tone. Five decades hardly modified the cut of a gaiter, the embroidery of a smock-frock, by the breadth of a hair. Ten generations failed to alter the turn of a single phrase. In these Wessex nooks the busy outsider's ancient times are only old; his old times are still new; his present is futurity.

So the barn was natural to the shearers, and the shearers were in harmony with the barn.

The spacious ends of the building, answering ecclesiastically to nave and chancel extremities, were fenced off with hurdles, the sheep being all collected in a crowd within these two enclosures; and in one angle a catching-pen was formed, in which three or four sheep were continuously kept ready for the shearers to seize without loss of time. In the background, mellowed by tawny shade, were the three women, Maryann Money, and Temperance and Soberness Miller, gathering up the fleeces and twisting ropes of wool with a wimble for tying them round. They were indifferently well assisted by the old maltster, who, when the malting season from October to April had passed, made himself useful upon any of the bordering farmsteads.

Behind all was Bathsheba, carefully watching the men to see that there was no cutting or wounding through carelessness, and that the animals were shorn close. Gabriel, who flitted and hovered under her bright eyes like a moth, did not shear continuously, half his time being spent in attending to the others and selecting the sheep for them. At the present moment he was engaged in handing round a mug of mild liquor, supplied from a barrel in the corner, and cut pieces of bread and cheese.

Bathsheba, after throwing a glance here, a caution there, and lecturing one of the younger operators who had allowed his last finished sheep to go off among the flock without restamping it with her initials, came again to Gabriel, as he put down the luncheon to drag a frightened ewe to his shear-station, flinging it over upon its back with a dexterous twist of the arm. He lopped off the tresses about its head, and opened up the neck and collar, his mistress quietly looking on.

"She blushes at the insult," murmured Bathsheba, watching the pink flush which arose and overspread the neck and shoulders of the ewe where they were left bare by the clicking shears—a flush which was enviable, for its delicacy, by many queens of coteries, and would have been creditable, for its promptness, to any woman in the world.

Poor Gabriel's soul was fed with a luxury of content by having her over him, her eyes critically regarding his skilful shears, which apparently were going to gather up a piece of the flesh at every close, and yet never did so. Like Guildenstern, Oak was happy in that he was not over happy. He had no wish to converse with her: that his bright lady and himself formed one group, exclusively their own, and containing no others in the world, was enough.

So the chatter was all on her side. There is a loquacity that tells nothing, which was Bathsheba's; and there is a silence which says much: that was Gabriel's. Full of this dim and temperate bliss he went on to fling the ewe over upon her other side, covering her head with his knee, gradually running the shears line after line round her dewlap; thence about her flank and back, and finishing over the tail.

"Well done, and done quickly!" said Bathsheba looking at her watch as the last snip resounded.

"How long, miss?" said Gabriel, wiping his brow.

"Three-and-twenty minutes and a half since you took the first lock from its forehead. It is the first time that I have ever seen one done in less than half an hour."

The clean, sleek creature arose from its fleece—how perfectly like Aphrodite rising from the foam should have been seen to be realised—looking startled and shy at the loss of its garment, which lay on the floor in one soft cloud, united throughout, the portion visible being the inner surface only, which, never before exposed, was white as snow, and without flaw or blemish of the minutest kind.

"Cain Ball!"

"Yes, Mister Oak; here I be!"

Cainy now runs forward with the tar-pot. "B. E." is newly stamped upon the shorn skin, and away the simple dam leaps, panting, over the board into the shirtless flock outside. Then up comes Maryann; throws the loose locks into the middle of the fleece, rolls it up, and carries it into the background as three-and-a-half pounds of unadulterated warmth for the winter enjoyment of persons unknown and far away, who will, however, never experience the superlative comfort derivable from the wool as it here exists, new and pure—before the unctuousness of its nature whilst in a living state has dried, stiffened, and been washed out—rendering it just now as superior to anything *woollen* as cream is superior to milk-and-water.

But heartless circumstance could not leave entire Gabriel's happiness of this morning. The rams, old ewes, and two-shear ewes had duly undergone their stripping, and the men were proceeding with the shearlings and hogs, when Oak's belief that she was going to stand pleasantly by and time him through another performance was painfully interrupted by Farmer Boldwood's appearance in the extremest corner of the barn. Nobody seemed to have perceived his entry, but there he certainly was. Boldwood always carried with him a social atmosphere of his own, which everybody felt who came near him; and the talk, which Bathsheba's presence had somewhat suppressed, was now totally suspended.

He crossed over towards Bathsheba, who turned to greet him with a carriage of perfect ease. He spoke to her in low tones, and she instinctively modulated her own to the same pitch, and her voice ultimately even caught the inflection of his. She was far from having a wish to appear mysteriously connected with him; but woman at the impressionable age gravitates to the larger body not only in her choice of words, which is apparent everyday, but even in her shades of tone and humour when the influence is great.

What they conversed about was not audible to Gabriel, who was too independent to get near, though too concerned to disregard. The issue of their dialogue was the taking of her hand by the courteous farmer to help her over the spreading-board into the bright June sunlight outside. Standing beside the sheep already shorn, they went on talking again. Concerning the flock? Apparently not. Gabriel theorised, not without truth, that in quiet discussion of any matter within reach of the speakers' eyes, these are usually fixed upon it. Bathsheba demurely regarded a contemptible straw lying upon the ground, in a way which suggested less ovine criticism than womanly embarrassment. She became more or less red in the cheek, the blood wavering in uncertain flux and reflux over the sensitive space between ebb and flood. Gabriel sheared on, constrained and sad.

She left Boldwood's side, and he walked up and down alone for nearly a quarter of an hour. Then she reappeared in her new riding-habit of myrtle-green, which fitted her to the waist as a rind fits its fruit; and young Bob Coggan led on her mare, Boldwood fetching his own horse from the tree under which it had been tied.

Oak's eyes could not forsake them; and in endeavouring to continue his shearing at the same time that he watched Boldwood's manner, he snipped the sheep in the groin. The animal plunged; Bathsheba instantly gazed towards it, and saw the blood.

"O Gabriel!" she exclaimed, with severe remonstrance, "you who are so strict with the other men—see what you are doing yourself!"

To an outsider there was not much to complain of in this remark; but to Oak, who knew Bathsheba to be well aware that she herself was the cause of the poor ewe's wound, because she had wounded the ewe's shearer in a still more vital part, it had a sting which the abiding sense of his inferiority to both herself and Boldwood was not calculated to heal. But a manly resolve to recognise boldly that he had no longer a lover's interest in her, helped him occasionally to conceal a feeling.

"Bottle!" he shouted, in an unmoved voice of routine. Cainy Ball ran up, the wound was anointed, and the shearing continued.

Boldwood gently tossed Bathsheba into the saddle, and before they turned away she again spoke out to Oak with the same dominative and tantalising graciousness.

"I am going now to see Mr. Boldwood's Leicesters. Take my place in the barn, Gabriel, and keep the men carefully to their work."

The horses' heads were put about, and they trotted away.

Boldwood's deep attachment was a matter of great interest among all around him; but, after having been pointed out for so many years as the perfect exemplar of thriving bachelorship, his lapse was an anticlimax somewhat resembling that of St. John Long's death by consumption in the midst of his proofs that it was not a fatal disease.

"That means matrimony," said Temperance Miller, following them out of sight with her eyes.

"I reckon that's the size o't," said Coggan, working along without looking up.

"Well, better wed over the mixen than over the moor," said Laban Tall, turning his sheep.

Henery Fray spoke, exhibiting miserable eyes at the same time: "I don't see why a maid should take a husband when she's bold enough to fight her own battles, and don't want a home; for 'tis keeping another woman out. But let it be, for 'tis a pity he and she should trouble two houses."

As usual with decided characters, Bathsheba invariably provoked the criticism of individuals like Henery Fray. Her emblazoned fault was to be too pronounced in her objections, and not sufficiently overt in her likings. We learn that it is not the rays which bodies absorb, but those which they reject, that give them the colours they are known by; and in the same way people are specialised by their dislikes and antagonisms, whilst their good-will is looked upon as no attribute at all.

Henery continued in a more complaisant mood: "I once hinted my mind to her on a few things, as nearly as a battered frame dared to do so to such a froward piece. You all know, neighbours, what a man I be, and how I come down with my powerful words when my pride is boiling wi' scarn?"

"We do, we do, Henery."

"So I said, 'Mistress Everdene, there's places empty, and there's gifted men willing; but the spite'—no, not the spite—I didn't say spite—'but the villainy of the contrarikind,' I said (meaning womankind), 'keeps 'em out.' That wasn't too strong for her, say?"

"Passably well put."

"Yes; and I would have said it, had death and salvation overtook me for it. Such is my spirit when I have a mind."

"A true man, and proud as a lucifer."

"You see the artfulness? Why, 'twas about being baily really; but I didn't put it so plain that she could understand my meaning, so I could lay it on all the stronger. That was my depth! . . . However, let her marry an she will. Perhaps 'tis high time. I believe Farmer Boldwood kissed her behind the spear-bed at the sheep-washing t'other day—that I do."

"What a lie!" said Gabriel.

"Ah, neighbour Oak—how'st know?" said Henery mildly.

"Because she told me all that passed," said Oak, with a pharisaical sense that he was not as other shearers in this matter.

"Ye have a right to believe it," said Henery, with dudgeon; "a very true right. But I mid see a little distance into things! To be long-headed enough for a baily's place is a poor mere trifle—yet a trifle more than nothing. However, I look round upon life quite cool. Do you heed me, neighbours? My words, though made as simple as I can, mid be rather deep for some heads."

"O yes, Henery, we quite heed ye."

"A strange old piece, goodmen—whirled about from here to yonder, as if I were nothing! A little warped, too. But I have my depths; ha, and even my great depths! I might gird at a certain shepherd, brain to brain. But no—O no!"

"A strange old piece, ye say!" interposed the maltster, in a querulous voice. "At the same time ye be no old man worth naming—no old man at all. Yer teeth bain't half gone yet; and what's a old man's standing if so be his teeth bain't gone? Weren't I stale in wedlock afore ye were out of arms? 'Tis a poor thing to be sixty, when there's people far past four-score—a boast weak as water."

It was the unvarying custom in Weatherbury to sink minor differences when the maltster had to be pacified.

"Weak as water! yes," said Jan Coggan. "Malter, we feel ye to be a wonderful veteran man, and nobody can gainsay it."

"Nobody," said Joseph Poorgrass. "Ye be a very rare old spectacle, malter, and we all admire ye for that gift."

"Ay, and as a young man, when my senses were in prosperity, I was likewise liked by a good-few who knowed me," said the maltster.

" 'Ithout doubt you was—'ithout doubt."

The bent and hoary man was satisfied, and so apparently was Henery Fray. That matters should continue pleasant Maryann spoke, who, what with her brown complexion, and the working wrapper of rusty linsey, had at present the mellow hue of an old sketch in oils—notably some of Nicholas Poussin's:—

"Do anybody know of a crooked man, or a lame, or any second-hand fellow at all that would do for poor me?" said Maryann. "A perfect one I don't expect to get at my time of life. If I could hear of such a thing 'twould do me more good than toast and ale."

Coggan furnished a suitable reply. Oak went on with his shearing, and said not another word. Pestilent moods had come, and teased away his quiet. Bathsheba had shown indications of anointing him above his fellows by installing him as the bailiff that the farm imperatively required. He did not covet the post relatively to the farm: in relation to herself, as beloved by him and unmarried to another, he had coveted it. His readings of her seemed now to be vapoury and indistinct. His lecture to her was, he thought, one of the absurdest mistakes. Far from coquetting with Boldwood, she had trifled with himself in thus feigning that she had trifled with another. He was inwardly convinced that, in accordance with the anticipations of his easy-going and worse-educated comrades, that day would see Boldwood the accepted husband of Miss Everdene. Gabriel at this time of his life had out-grown the instinctive dislike which every Christian boy has for reading the Bible, perusing it now quite frequently, and he inwardly said, " 'I find more bitter than death the woman whose heart is snares and nets!' " This was mere exclamation—the froth of the storm. He adored Bathsheba just the same.

"We work-folk shall have some lordly junketing to-night," said Cainy Ball, casting forth his thoughts in a new direction. "This morning I see 'em making the great puddens in the milking-pails—lumps of fat as big as yer thumb, Mister Oak! I've never seed such splendid large knobs of fat before in the days of my life—they never used to be bigger then a horse-bean. And there was a great black crock upon the brandish with his legs a-sticking out, but I don't know what was in within."

"And there's two bushels of biffins for apple-pies," said Maryann.

"Well, I hope to do my duty by it all," said Joseph Poorgrass, in a pleasant, masticating manner of anticipation. "Yes; victuals and drink is a cheerful thing, and gives nerves to the nerveless, if the form of words may be used. 'Tis the gospel of the body, without which we perish, so to speak it."

XXIII

EVENTIDE—A SECOND DECLARATION

FOR THE SHEARING-SUPPER A LONG TABLE WAS PLACED ON THE GRASS-PLOT BESIDE THE house, the end of the table being thrust over the sill of the wide parlour-window and a foot or two into the room. Miss Everdene sat inside the window, facing down the table. She was thus at the head without mingling with the men.

This evening Bathsheba was unusually excited, her red cheeks and lips contrasting lustrously with the mazy skeins of her shadowy hair. She seemed to expect assistance, and the seat at the bottom of the table was at her request left vacant until after they had begun the meal. She then asked Gabriel to take the place and the duties appertaining to that end, which he did with great readiness.

At this moment Mr. Boldwood came in at the gate, and crossed the green to Bathsheba at the window. He apologised for his lateness: his arrival was evidently by arrangement.

"Gabriel," said she, "will you move again, please, and let Mr. Boldwood come there?"

Oak moved in silence back to his original seat.

The gentleman-farmer was dressed in cheerful style, in a new coat and white waist-coat, quite contrasting with his usual sober suits of grey. Inwardly, too, he was blithe, and consequently chatty to an exceptional degree. So also was Bathsheba now that he had come, though the uninvited presence of Pennyways, the bailiff who had been dismissed for theft, disturbed her equanimity for a while.

Supper being ended, Coggan began on his own private account, without reference to listeners:—

> *I've lost my love, and I care not,*
> *I've lost my love, and I care not;*
> *I shall soon have another*
> *That's better than t'other;*
> *I've lost my love, and I care not.*

This lyric, when concluded, was received with a silently appreciative gaze at the table, implying that the performance, like a work by those established authors who are independent of notices in the papers, was a well-known delight which required no applause.

"Now, Master Poorgrass, your song!" said Coggan.

"I be all but in liquor, and the gift is wanting in me," said Joseph, diminishing himself.

"Nonsense; wou'st never be so ungrateful, Joseph—never!" said Coggan, expressing hurt feelings by an inflection of voice. "And mistress is looking hard at ye, as much as to say, 'Sing at once, Joseph Poorgrass.' "

"Faith, so she is; well, I must suffer it! . . . Just eye my features, and see if the tell-tale blood overheats me much, neighbours?"

"No, yer blushes be quite reasonable," said Coggan.

"I always tries to keep my colours from rising when a beauty's eyes get fixed on me," said Joseph differently; "but if so be 'tis willed they do, they must."

"Now, Joseph, your song, please," said Bathsheba from the window.

"Well, really, ma'am," he replied, in a yielding tone, "I don't know what to say. It would be a poor plain ballet of my own composure."

"Hear, hear!" said the supper-party.

Poorgrass, thus assured, trilled forth a flickering yet commendable piece of sentiment, the tune of which consisted of the key-note and another, the latter being the sound chiefly dwelt upon. This was so successful that he rashly plunged into a second in the same breath, after a few false starts:—

> *I sow'-ed th'-e . . . . .*
> *I sow'-ed . . . . .*
> *I sow'-ed the'-e seeds' of' love',*
> *I-it was' all' i'-in the'-e spring',*
> *I-in A'-pril', Ma'-ay, a'-nd sun'-ny' June',*
> *When sma'-all bi'-irds they' do' sing.*

"Well put out of hand," said Coggan, at the end of the verse. " 'They do sing' was a very taking paragraph."

"Ay; and there was a pretty place at 'seeds of love,' and 'twas well heaved out. Though 'love' is a nasty high corner when a man's voice is getting crazed. Next verse, Master Poor-grass."

But during this rendering young Bob Coggan exhibited one of those anomalies which will afflict little people when other persons are particularly serious: in trying to check his laughter, he pushed down his throat as much of the table cloth as he could get hold of, when, after continuing hermetically sealed for a short time, his mirth burst out through his nose. Joseph perceived it, and with hectic cheeks of indignation instantly ceased singing. Coggan boxed Bob's ears immediately.

"Go on, Joseph—go on, and never mind the young scamp," said Coggan. " 'Tis a very catching ballet. Now then again—the next bar; I'll help ye to flourish up the shrill notes where yer wind is rather wheezy:—

> *'O the wi'-il-lo'-ow tree' will' twist',*
> *And the wil'-low' tre'-ee wi'-ill twine'.' "*

But the singer could not be set going again. Bob Coggan was sent home for his ill manners, and tranquility was restored by Jacob Smallbury, who volunteered a ballad as inclusive and interminable as that with which the worthy toper old Silenus amused on a similar occasion the swains Chromis and Mnasylus, and other jolly dogs of his day.

It was still the beaming time of evening, though night was stealthily making itself visible low down upon the ground, the western lines of light raking the earth without alighting upon it to any extent, or illuminating the dead levels at all. The sun had crept round the tree as a last effort before death, and then began to sink, the shearers' lower parts becoming steeped in embrowning twilight, whilst their heads and shoulders were still enjoying day, touched with a yellow of self-sustained brilliancy that seemed inherent rather than acquired.

The sun went down in an ochreous mist; but they sat, and talked on, and grew as merry as the gods in Homer's heaven. Bathsheba still remained enthroned inside the window, and occupied herself in knitting, from which she sometimes looked up to view the fading scene outside. The slow twilight expanded and enveloped them completely before the signs of moving were shown.

Gabriel suddenly missed Farmer Boldwood from his place at the bottom of the table. How long he had been gone Oak did not know; but he had apparently withdrawn into the encircling dusk. Whilst he was thinking of this, Liddy brought candles into the back part of the room overlooking the shearers, and their lively new flames shone down the table and over the men, and dispersed among the green shadows behind. Bathsheba's form, still in its original position, was now again distinct between their eyes and the light, which revealed that Boldwood had gone inside the room, and was sitting near her.

Next came the question of the evening. Would Miss Everdene sing to them the song she always sang so charmingly—*The Banks of Allan Water*—before they went home?

After a moment's consideration Bathsheba assented, beckoning to Gabriel, who hastened up into the coveted atmosphere.

"Have you brought your flute?" she whispered.

"Yes, miss."

"Play to my singing, then."

She stood up in the window-opening, facing the men, the candles behind her, Gabriel on her right hand, immediately outside the sash-frame. Boldwood had drawn up on her left, within the room. Her singing was soft and rather tremulous at first, but it soon swelled to a steady clearness. Subsequent events caused one of the verses to be remembered for many months, and even years, by more than one of those who were gathered there:—

> For his bride a soldier sought her,
>   And a winning tongue had he:
> On the banks of Allan Water
>   None was gay as she!

In addition to the dulcet piping of Gabriel's flute Boldwood supplied a bass in his customary profound voice, uttering his notes so softly, however, as to abstain entirely from making anything like an ordinary duet of the song; they rather formed a rich unexplored shadow, which threw her tones into relief. The shearers reclined against each other as at suppers in the early ages of the world, and so silent and absorbed were they that her breathing could almost be heard between the bars; and at the end of the ballad, when the last tone loitered on to an inexpressible close, there arose that buzz of pleasure which is the attar of applause.

It is scarcely necessary to state that Gabriel could not avoid noting the farmer's bearing to-night towards their entertainer. Yet there was nothing exceptional in his actions beyond what appertained to his time of performing them. It was when the rest were all looking away that Boldwood observed her; when they regarded her he turned aside; when they thanked or praised he was silent; when they were inattentive he murmured his thanks. The meaning lay in the difference between actions none of which had any meaning of itself; and the necessity of being jealous, which lovers are troubled with, did not lead Oak to underestimate these signs.

Bathsheba then wished them good-night, withdrew from the window, and retired to the back part of the room, Boldwood thereupon closing the sash and the shutters, and remaining inside with her. Oak wandered away under the quiet and scented trees. Recovering from the softer impressions produced by Bathsheba's voice, the shearers rose to leave, Coggan turning to Pennyways as he pushed back the bench to pass out:—

"I like to give praise where praise is due, and the man deserves it—that 'a do so," he remarked, looking at the worthy thief as if he were the masterpiece of some world-renowned artist.

"I'm sure I should never have believed it if we hadn't proved it, so to allude," hiccupped Joseph Poorgrass, "that every cup, every one of the best knives and forks, and every empty bottle be in their place as perfect now as at the beginning, and not one stole at all."

"I'm sure I don't deserve half the praise you give me," said the virtuous thief grimly.

"Well, I'll say this for Pennyways," added Coggan, "that whenever he do really make up his mind to do a noble thing in the shape of a good action, as I could see by his face he did to-night afore sitting down, he's generally able to carry it out. Yes, I'm proud to say, neighbours, that he's stole nothing at all."

"Well, 'tis an honest deed, and we thank ye for it, Pennyways," said Joseph; to which opinion the remainder of the company subscribed unanimously.

At this time of departure, when nothing more was visible of the inside of the parlour than a thin and still chink of light between the shutters, a passionate scene was in course of enactment there.

Miss Everdene and Boldwood were alone. Her cheeks had lost a great deal of their healthful fire from the very seriousness of her position; but her eye was bright with the excitement of a triumph—though it was a triumph which had rather been contemplated than desired.

She was standing behind a low arm-chair from which she had just risen, and he was kneeling in it—inclining himself over its back towards her, and holding her hand in both his own. His body moved restlessly, and it was with what Keats daintily calls a too happy happiness. This unwonted abstraction by love of all dignity from a man of whom it had ever seemed the chief component, was, in its distressing incongruity, a pain to her which quenched much of the pleasure she derived from the proof that she was idolised.

"I will try to love you," she was saying, in a trembling voice quite unlike her usual self-confidence. "And if I can believe in any way that I shall make you a good wife I shall indeed be willing to marry you. But, Mr. Boldwood, hesitation on so high a matter is honourable in any woman, and I don't want to give a solemn promise to-night. I would rather ask you to wait a few weeks till I can see my situation better."

"But you have every reason to believe that *then*—"

"I have every reason to hope that at the end of the five or six weeks, between this time and harvest, that you say you are going to be away from home, I shall be able to promise to be your wife," she said, firmly. "But remember this distinctly, I don't promise yet."

"It is enough; I don't ask more. I can wait on those dear words. And now, Miss Everdene, good-night!"

"Good-night," she said, graciously—almost tenderly; and Boldwood withdrew with a serene smile.

Bathsheba knew more of him now; he had entirely bared his heart before her, even until he had almost worn in her eyes the sorry look of a grand bird without the feathers that make it grand. She had been awe-struck at her past temerity, and was struggling to make amends without thinking whether the sin quite deserved the penalty she was schooling herself to pay. To have brought all this about her ears was terrible; but after a while the situation was not without a fearful joy. The facility with which even the most timid women sometimes acquire a relish for the dreadful when that is amalgamated with a little triumph, is marvellous.

XXIV

THE SAME NIGHT—THE FIR PLANTATION

AMONG THE MULTIFARIOUS DUTIES WHICH BATHSHEBA HAD VOLUNTARILY IMPOSED UPON herself by dispensing with the services of a bailiff, was the particular one of looking round the homestead before going to bed, to see that all was right and safe for the night. Gabriel had almost constantly preceded her in this tour every evening, watching her affairs as carefully as any specially appointed officer of surveillance could have done; but this tender devotion was to a great extent unknown to his mistress, and as much as was known was somewhat thanklessly received. Women are never tired of bewailing man's fickleness in love, but they only seem to snub his constancy.

As watching is best done invisibly, she usually carried a dark lantern in her hand, and every now and then turned on the light to examine nooks and corners with the coolness of a metropolitan policeman. This coolness may have owed its existence not so much to her fearlessness of expected danger as to her freedom from the suspicion of any; her worst anticipated discovery being that a horse might not be well bedded, the fowls not all in, or a door not closed.

This night the buildings were inspected as usual, and she went round to the farm paddock. Here the only sounds disturbing the stillness were steady munchings of many mouths, and stentorian breathings from all but invisible noses, ending in snores and puffs like the blowing of bellows slowly. Then the munching would recommence, when the lively imagination might assist the eye to discern a group of pink-white nostrils, shaped as caverns, and very clammy and humid on their surfaces, not exactly pleasant to the touch until one got used to them; the mouths beneath having a great partiality for closing upon any loose end of Bathsheba's apparel which came within reach of their tongues. Above each of these a still keener vision suggested a brown forehead and two staring though not unfriendly eyes, and above all a pair of whitish crescent-shaped horns like two particularly new moons, an occasional stolid "moo!" proclaiming beyond the shade of a doubt that these phenomena were the features and persons of Daisy, Whitefoot, Bonny-lass, Jolly-O, Spot, Twinkle-eye, etc., etc.—the respectable dairy of Devon cows belonging to Bathsheba aforesaid.

Her way back to the house was by a path through a young plantation of tapering firs, which had been planted some years earlier to shelter the premises from the north wind. By reason of the density of the interwoven foliage overhead, it was gloomy there at cloudless noontide, twilight in the evening, dark as midnight at dusk, and black as the ninth plague of Egypt at midnight. To describe the spot is to call it a vast, low, naturally formed hall, the plumy ceiling of which was supported by slender pillars of living wood, the floor being covered with a soft dun carpet of dead spikelets and mildewed cones, with a tuft of grass-blades here and there.

This bit of the path was always the crux of the night's ramble, though, before starting, her apprehensions of danger were not vivid enough to lead her to take a companion. Slipping along here covertly as Time, Bathsheba fancied she could hear footsteps entering the track at the opposite end. It was certainly a rustle of footsteps. Her own instantly fell as gently as snowflakes. She reassured herself by a remembrance that the path was public, and that the traveller was probably some villager returning home; regretting, at the same time, that the meeting should be about to occur in the darkest point of her route, even though only just outside her own door.

The noise approached, came close, and a figure was apparently on the point of gliding past her when something tugged at her skirt and pinned it forcibly to the ground. The instantaneous check nearly threw Bathsheba off her balance. In recovering she struck against warm clothes and buttons.

"A rum start, upon my soul!" said a masculine voice, a foot or so above her head. "Have I hurt you, mate?"

"No," said Bathsheba, attempting to shrink away.

"We have got hitched together somehow, I think."

"Yes."

"Are you a woman?"

"Yes."

"A lady, I should have said."

"It doesn't matter."

"I am a man."

"Oh!"

Bathsheba softly tugged again, but to no purpose.

"Is that a dark lantern you have? I fancy so," said the man.

"Yes."

"If you'll allow me I'll open it, and set you free."

A hand seized the lantern, the door was opened, the rays burst out from their prison, and Bathsheba beheld her position with astonishment.

The man to whom she was hooked was brilliant in brass and scarlet. He was a soldier. His sudden appearance was to darkness what the sound of a trumpet is to silence. Gloom, the *genius loci* at all times hitherto, was now totally overthrown, less by the lantern-light than by what the lantern lighted. The contrast of this revelation with her anticipations of some sinister figure in sombre garb was so great that it had upon her the effect of a fairy transformation.

It was immediately apparent that the military man's spur had become entangled in the gimp which decorated the skirt of her dress. He caught a view of her face.

"I'll unfasten you in one moment, miss," he said, with new-born gallantry.

"O no—I can do it, thank you," she hastily replied, and stooped for the performance.

The unfastening was not such a trifling affair. The rowel of the spur had so wound itself among the gimp cords in those few moments, that separation was likely to be a matter of time.

He too stooped, and the lantern standing on the ground betwixt them threw the gleam from its open side among the fir-tree needles and the blades of long damp grass with the effect of a large glowworm. It radiated upwards into their faces, and sent over half the plantation gigantic shadows of both man and woman, each dusky shape becoming distorted and mangled upon the tree-trunks till it wasted to nothing.

He looked hard into her eyes when she raised them for a moment; Bathsheba looked down again, for his gaze was too strong to be received point-blank with her own. But she had obliquely noticed that he was young and slim, and that he wore three chevrons upon his sleeve.

Bathsheba pulled again.

"You are a prisoner, miss; it is no use blinking the matter," said the soldier drily. "I must cut your dress if you are in such a hurry."

"Yes—please do!" she exclaimed helplessly.

"It wouldn't be necessary if you could wait a moment"; and he unwound a cord from the little wheel. She withdrew her own hand, but, whether by accident or design, he touched it. Bathsheba was vexed; she hardly knew why.

His unravelling went on, but it nevertheless seemed coming to no end. She looked at him again.

"Thank you for the sight of such a beautiful face!" said the young sergeant, without ceremony.

She coloured with embarrassment. " 'Twas unwillingly shown," she replied stiffly, and with as much dignity—which was very little—as she could infuse into a position of captivity.

"I like you the better for that incivility, miss," he said.

"I should have liked—I wish—you had never shown yourself to me by intruding here!" She pulled again, and the gathers of her dress began to give way like liliputian musketry.

"I deserve the chastisement your words give me. But why should such a fair and dutiful girl have such an aversion to her father's sex?"

"Go on your way, please."

"What, Beauty, and drag you after me? Do but look; I never saw such a tangle!"

"O, 'tis shameful of you; you have been making it worse on purpose to keep me here—you have!"

"Indeed, I don't think so," said the sergeant, with a merry twinkle.

"I tell you you have!" she exclaimed, in high temper. "I insist upon undoing it. Now, allow me!"

"Certainly, miss; I am not of steel." He added a sigh which had as much archness in it as a sigh could possess without losing its nature altogether. "I am thankful for beauty, even when 'tis thrown to me like a bone to a dog. These moments will be over too soon!"

She closed her lips in a determined silence.

Bathsheba was revolving in her mind whether by a bold and desperate rush she could free herself at the risk of leaving her skirt bodily behind her. The thought was too dreadful. The dress—which she had put on to appear stately at the supper—was the head and front of her wardrobe; not another in her stock became her so well. What woman in Bathsheba's position, not naturally timid, and within call of her retainers, would have bought escape from a dashing soldier at so dear a price?

"All in good time; it will soon be done, I perceive," said her cool friend.

"This trifling provokes, and—and—"

"Not too cruel!"

"—Insults me!"

"It is done in order that I may have the pleasure of apologising to so charming a woman, which I straightway do most humbly, madam," he said, bowing low.

Bathsheba really knew not what to say.

"I've seen a good many women in my time," continued the young man in a murmur, and more thoughtfully than hitherto, critically regarding her bent head at the same time; "but I've never seen a woman so beautiful as you. Take it or leave it—be offended or like it—I don't care."

"Who are you, then, who can so well afford to despise opinion?"

"No stranger. Sergeant Troy. I am staying in this place.—There! it is undone at last, you see. Your light fingers were more eager than mine. I wish it had been the knot of knots, which there's no untying!"

This was worse and worse. She started up, and so did he. How to decently get away from him—that was her difficulty now. She sidled off inch by inch, the lantern in her hand, till she could see the redness of his coat no longer.

"Ah, Beauty; good-bye!" he said.

She made no reply, and, reaching a distance of twenty or thirty yards, turned about, and ran indoors.

Liddy had just retired to rest. In ascending to her own chamber, Bathsheba opened the girl's door an inch or two, and, panting, said—

"Liddy, is any soldier staying in the village—sergeant somebody—rather gentlemanly for a sergeant, and good-looking—a red coat with blue facings?"

"No, miss . . . No, I say; but really it might be Sergeant Troy home on furlough, though I have not seen him. He was here once in that way when the regiment was at Casterbridge."

"Yes; that's the name. Had he a moustache—no whiskers or beard?"

"He had."

"What kind of a person is he?"

"O! miss—I blush to name it—a gay man! But I know him to be very quick and trim, who might have made his thousands, like a squire. Such a clever young dand as he is! He's a doctor's son by name, which is a great deal; and he's an earl's son by nature!"

"Which is a great deal more. Fancy! Is it true?"

"Yes. And he was brought up so well, and sent to Casterbridge Grammar School for years and years. Learnt all languages while he was there; and it was said he got on so far that he could take down Chinese in shorthand; but that I don't answer for, as it was only reported. However, he wasted his gifted lot, and listed a soldier; but even then he rose to be a sergeant without trying at all. Ah! such a blessing it is to be high-born; nobility of blood will shine out even in the ranks and files. And is he really come home, miss?"

"I believe so. Good-night, Liddy."

After all, how could a cheerful wearer of skirts be permanently offended with the man? There are occasions when girls like Bathsheba will put up with a great deal of unconventional behaviour. When they want to be praised, which is often, when they want to be mastered, which is sometimes; and when they want no nonsense, which is seldom. Just now the first feeling was in the ascendant with Bathsheba, with a dash of the second. Moreover, by chance or by devilry, the ministrant was antecedently made interesting by being a handsome stranger who had evidently seen better days.

So she could not clearly decide whether it was her opinion that he had insulted her or not.

"Was ever anything so odd!" she at last exclaimed to herself, in her own room. "And was ever anything so meanly done as what I did—to skulk away like that from a man who was only civil and kind!" Clearly she did not think his barefaced praise of her person an insult now.

It was a fatal omission of Boldwood's that he had never once told her she was beautiful.

XXV

THE NEW ACQUAINTANCE DESCRIBED

IDIOSYNCRASY AND VICISSITUDE HAD COMBINED TO STAMP SERGEANT TROY AS AN EXceptional being.

He was a man to whom memories were an incumbrance, and anticipations a superfluity. Simply feeling, considering, and caring for what was before his eyes, he was vulnerable only in the present. His outlook upon time was as a transient flash of the eye now and then: that projection of consciousness into days gone by and to come, which makes the past a synonym for the pathetic and the future a word for circumspection, was foreign to Troy. With him the past was yesterday; the future, to-morrow; never, the day after.

On this account he might, in certain lights, have been regarded as one of the most fortunate of his order. For it may be argued with great plausibility that reminiscence is less an endowment than a disease, and that expectation in its only comfortable form—that of absolute faith—is practically an impossibility; whilst in the form of hope and the secondary compounds, patience, impatience, resolve, curiosity, it is a constant fluctuation between pleasure and pain.

Sergeant Troy, being entirely innocent of the practice of expectation, was never disappointed. To set against this negative gain there may have been some positive losses from a certain narrowing of the higher tastes and sensations which it entailed. But limitation of the capacity is never recognised as a loss by the loser therefrom: in this attribute moral or aesthetic poverty contrasts plausibly with material, since those who suffer do not mind it, whilst those who mind it soon cease to suffer. It is not a denial of anything to have been always without it, and what Troy had never enjoyed he did not miss; but, being fully conscious that what sober people missed he enjoyed, his capacity, though really less, seemed greater than theirs.

He was moderately truthful towards men, but to women lied like a Cretan—a system of ethics above all others calculated to win popularity at the first flush of admission into lively society; and the possibility of the favour gained being transitory had reference only to the future.

He never passed the line which divides the spruce vices from the ugly; and hence, though his morals had hardly been applauded, disapproval of them had frequently been tempered with a smile. This treatment had led to his becoming a sort of regrater of other men's gallantries, to his own aggrandisement as a Corinthian, rather than to the moral profit of his hearers.

His reason and his propensities had seldom any reciprocating influence, having separated by mutual consent long ago: thence it sometimes happened that, while his intentions were as honourable as could be wished, any particular deed formed a dark background which threw them into fine relief. The sergeant's vicious phases being the offspring of impulse, and his virtuous phases of cool meditation, the latter had a modest tendency to be oftener heard of than seen.

Troy was full of activity, but his activities were less of a locomotive than a vegetative nature; and, never being based upon any original choice of foundation or direction, they were exercised on whatever object chance might place in their way. Hence, whilst he sometimes reached the brilliant in speech because that was spontaneous, he fell below the commonplace in action, from inability to guide incipient effort. He had a quick comprehension and considerable force of character; but, being without the power to combine them, the comprehension became engaged with trivialities whilst waiting for the will to direct it, and the force wasted itself in useless grooves through unheeding the comprehension.

He was a fairly well-educated man for one of middle class—exceptionally well educated for a common soldier. He spoke fluently and unceasingly. He could in this way be one thing and seem another: for instance, he could speak of love and think of dinner; call on the husband to look at the wife; be eager to pay and intend to owe.

The wondrous power of flattery in *passados* at woman is a perception so universal as to be remarked upon by many people almost as automatically as they repeat a proverb, or say that they are Christians and the like, without thinking much of the enormous corollaries which spring from the proposition. Still less is it acted upon for the good of the complemental being alluded to. With the majority such an opinion is shelved with all those trite aphorisms which require some catastrophe to bring their tremendous meanings thoroughly home. When expressed with some amount of reflectiveness it seems co-ordinate with a belief that this flattery must be reasonable to be effective. It is to the credit of men that few attempt to settle the question by experiment, and it is for their happiness, perhaps, that accident has never settled it for them. Nevertheless, that a male dissembler who by deluging her with untenable fictions charms the female wisely, may acquire powers reaching to the extremity of perdition, is a truth taught to many by unsought and wringing occurrences. And some profess to have attained to the same knowledge by experiment as aforesaid, and jauntily continue their indulgence in such experiments with terrible effect. Sergeant Troy was one.

He had been known to observe casually that in dealing with womankind the only alternative to flattery was cursing and swearing. There was no third method. "Treat them fairly, and you are a lost man," he would say.

This philosopher's public appearance in Weatherbury promptly followed his arrival there. A week or two after the shearing, Bathsheba, feeling a nameless relief of spirits on account of Boldwood's absence, approached her hay-fields and looked over the hedge towards the haymakers. They consisted in about equal proportions of gnarled and flexuous forms, the former being the men, the latter the women, who wore tilt bonnets covered with nankeen, which hung in a curtain upon their shoulders. Coggan and Mark Clark were mowing in a less forward meadow, Clark humming a tune to the strokes of his scythe, to which Jan made no attempt to keep time with his. In the first mead they were already loading hay, the women raking it into cocks and windrows, and the men tossing it upon the waggon.

From behind the waggon a bright scarlet spot emerged, and went on loading unconcernedly with the rest. It was the gallant sergeant, who had come haymaking for pleasure; and nobody could deny that he was doing the mistress of the farm real knight-service by this voluntary contribution of his labour at a busy time.

As soon as she had entered the field Troy saw her, and sticking his pitchfork into the ground and picking up his crop or cane, he came forward. Bathsheba blushed with half-angry embarrassment, and adjusted her eyes as well as her feet to the direct line of her path.

XXVI

Scene on the Verge of the Hay-Mead

A H, MISS EVERDENE!" SAID THE SERGEANT, TOUCHING HIS DIMINUTIVE CAP. "LITTLE did I think it was you I was speaking to the other night. And yet, if I had reflected, the 'Queen of the Corn-market' (truth is truth at any hour of the day or night, and I heard you so named in Casterbridge yesterday), the 'Queen of the Corn-market,' I say, could be no other woman. I step across now to beg your forgiveness a thousand times for having been led by my feelings to express myself too strongly for a stranger. To be sure I am no stranger to the place—I am Sergeant Troy, as I told you, and I have assisted your uncle in these fields no end of times when I was a lad. I have been doing the same for you to-day."

"I suppose I must thank you for that, Sergeant Troy," said the Queen of the Corn-market in an indifferently grateful tone.

The sergeant looked hurt and sad. "Indeed you must not, Miss Everdene," he said. "Why could you think such a thing necessary?"

"I am glad it is not."

"Why? if I may ask without offence."

"Because I don't much want to thank you for anything."

"I am afraid I have made a hole with my tongue that my heart will never mend. O these intolerable times: that ill-luck should follow a man for honestly telling a woman she is beautiful! 'Twas the most I said—you must own that; and the least I could say—that I own myself."

"There is some talk I could do without more easily than money."

"Indeed. That remark is a sort of digression."

"No. It means that I would rather have your room than your company."

"And I would rather have curses from you than kisses from any other woman; so I'll stay here."

Bathsheba was absolutely speechless. And yet she could not help feeling that the assistance he was rendering forbade a harsh repulse.

"Well," continued Troy, "I suppose there is a praise which is rudeness, and that may be mine. At the same time there is a treatment which is injustice, and that may be yours. Because a plain blunt man, who has never been taught concealment, speaks out his mind without exactly intending it, he's to be snapped off like the son of a sinner."

"Indeed there's no such case between us," she said, turning away. "I don't allow strangers to be bold and impudent—even in praise of me."

"Ah—it is not the fact but the method which offends you," he said, carelessly. "But I have the sad satisfaction of knowing that my words, whether pleasing or offensive, are unmistakably true. Would you have had me look at you, and tell my acquaintance that you are quite a commonplace woman, to save you the embarrassment of being stared at if they come near you? Not I. I couldn't tell any such ridiculous lie about a beauty to encourage a single woman in England in too excessive a modesty."

"It is all pretence—what you are saying!" exclaimed Bathsheba, laughing in spite of herself at the sergeant's sly method. "You have a rare invention, Sergeant Troy. Why couldn't you have passed by me that night, and said nothing?—that was all I meant to reproach you for."

"Because I wasn't going to. Half the pleasure of a feeling lies in being able to express it on the spur of the moment, and I let out mine. It would have been just the same if you had been the reverse person—ugly and old—I should have exclaimed about it in the same way."

"How long is it since you have been so afflicted with strong feeling, then?"

"Oh, ever since I was big enough to know loveliness from deformity."

" 'Tis to be hoped your sense of the difference you speak of doesn't stop at faces, but extends to morals as well."

"I won't speak of morals or religion—my own or anybody else's. Though perhaps I should have been a very good Christian if you pretty women hadn't made me an idolater."

Bathsheba moved on to hide the irrepressible dimplings of merriment. Troy followed, whirling his crop.

"But—Miss Everdene—you do forgive me?"

"Hardly."

"Why?"

"You say such things."

"I said you were beautiful, and I'll say so still; for, by —— so you are! The most beautiful ever I saw, or may I fall dead this instant! Why, upon my—"

"Don't—don't! I won't listen to you—you are so profane!" she said, in a restless state between distress at hearing him and a *penchant* to hear more.

"I again say you are a most fascinating woman. There's nothing remarkable in my saying so, is there? I'm sure the fact is evident enough. Miss Everdene, my opinion may be too forcibly let out to please you, and, for the matter of that, too insignificant to convince you, but surely it is honest, and why can't it be excused?"

"Because it—it isn't a correct one," she femininely murmured.

"O, fie—fie! Am I any worse for breaking the third of that Terrible Ten than you for breaking the ninth?"

"Well, it doesn't seem *quite* true to me that I am fascinating," she replied evasively.

"Not so to you: then I say with all respect that, if so, it is owing to your modesty, Miss Everdene. But surely you must have been told by everybody of what everybody notices? And you should take their words for it."

"They don't say so exactly."

"O yes, they must!"

"Well, I mean to my face, as you do," she went on, allowing herself to be further lured into a conversation that intention had rigorously forbidden.

"But you know they think so?"

"No—that is—I certainly have heard Liddy say they do, but—" She paused.

Capitulation—that was the purport of the simple reply, guarded as it was—capitulation, unknown to herself. Never did a fragile tailless sentence convey a more perfect meaning. The careless sergeant smiled within himself, and probably too the devil smiled from a loop-hole in Tophet, for the moment was the turning-point of a career. Her tone and mien signified beyond mistake that the seed which was to lift the foundation had taken root in the chink: the remainder was a mere question of time and natural changes.

"There the truth comes out!" said the soldier, in reply. "Never tell me that a young lady can live in a buzz of admiration without knowing something about it. Ah, well, Miss Everdene, you are—pardon my blunt way—you are rather an injury to our race than otherwise."

"How—indeed?" she said, opening her eyes.

"O, it is true enough. I may as well be hung for a sheep as a lamb (an old country saying, not of much account, but it will do for a rough soldier), and so I will speak my mind, regardless of your pleasure, and without hoping or intending to get your pardon. Why, Miss Everdene, it is in this manner that your good looks may do more harm than good in the world." The sergeant looked down the mead in critical abstraction. "Probably some one man on an average falls in love with each ordinary woman. She can marry him: he is content, and leads a useful life. Such women as you a hundred men always covet—your eyes will bewitch scores on scores into an unavailing fancy for you—you can only marry one of that many. Out of these say twenty will endeavour to drown the bitterness of despised love in drink; twenty more will mope away their lives without a wish or attempt to make a mark in the world, because they have no ambition apart from their attachment to you; twenty more—the susceptible person myself possibly among them—will be always draggling after you, getting where they may just see you, doing desperate things. Men are such constant fools! The rest may try to get over their passion with more or less success. But all these men will be saddened. And not only those ninety-nine men, but the ninety-nine women they might have married are saddened with them. There's my tale. That's why I say that a woman so charming as yourself, Miss Everdene, is hardly a blessing to her race."

The handsome sergeant's features were during this speech as rigid and stern as John Knox's in addressing his gay young queen.

Seeing she made no reply, he said, "Do you read French?"

"No; I began, but when I got to the verbs, father died," she said simply.

"I do—when I have an opportunity, which latterly has not been often (my mother was a Parisienne)—and there's a proverb they have, *Qui aime bien châtie bien*—'He chastens who loves well.' Do you understand me?"

"Ah!" she replied, and there was even a little tremulousness in the usually cool girl's voice; "if you can only fight half as winningly as you can talk, you are able to make a pleasure of a bayonet wound!" And then poor Bathsheba instantly perceived her slip in making this admission: in hastily trying to retrieve it, she went from bad to worse. "Don't, however, suppose that *I* derive any pleasure from what you tell me."

"I know you do not—I know it perfectly," said Troy, with much hearty conviction on the exterior of his face: and altering the expression to moodiness; "when a dozen men are ready to speak tenderly to you, and give the admiration you deserve without adding the warning you need, it stands to reason that my poor rough-and-ready mixture of praise and blame cannot convey much pleasure. Fool as I may be, I am not so conceited as to suppose that!"

"I think you—are conceited, nevertheless," said Bathsheba, looking askance at a reed she was fitfully pulling with one hand, having lately grown feverish under the soldier's system of procedure—not because the nature of his cajolery was entirely unperceived, but because its vigour was overwhelming.

"I would not own it to anybody else—nor do I exactly to you. Still, there might have been some self-conceit in my foolish supposition the other night. I knew that what I said in admiration might be an opinion too often forced upon you to give any pleasure, but I certainly did think that the kindness of your nature might prevent you judging an uncontrolled tongue harshly—which you have done—and thinking badly of me and wounding me this morning, when I am working hard to save your hay."

"Well, you need not think more of that: perhaps you did not mean to be rude to me by speaking out your mind: indeed, I believe you did not," said the shrewd woman, in painfully innocent earnest. "And I thank you for giving help here. But—but mind you don't speak to me again in that way, or in any other, unless I speak to you."

"O Miss Bathsheba! That is too hard!"

"No, it isn't. Why is it?"

"You will never speak to me; for I shall not be here long. I am soon going back again to the miserable monotony of drill—and perhaps our regiment will be ordered out soon. And yet you take away the one little ewe-lamb of pleasure that I have in this dull life of mine. Well, perhaps generosity is not a woman's most marked characteristic."

"When are you going from here?" she asked with some interest.

"In a month."

"But how can it give you pleasure to speak to me?"

"Can you ask, Miss Everdene—knowing as you do—what my offence is based on?"

"If you do care so much for a silly trifle of that kind, then, I don't mind doing it," she uncertainly and doubtingly answered. "But you can't really care for a word from me? you only say so—I think you only say so."

"That's unjust—but I won't repeat the remark. I am too gratified to get such a mark of your friendship at any price to cavil at the tone. I *do*, Miss Everdene, care for it. You may think a man foolish to want a mere word—just a good-morning. Perhaps he is—I don't know. But you have never been a man looking upon a woman, and that woman yourself."

"Well."

"Then you know nothing of what such an experience is like—and Heaven forbid that you ever should!"

"Nonsense, flatterer! What is it like? I am interested in knowing."

"Put shortly, it is not being able to think, hear, or look in any direction except one without wretchedness, nor there without torture."

"Ah, sergeant, it won't do—you are pretending!" she said, shaking her head. "Your words are too dashing to be true."

"I am not, upon the honour of a soldier."

"But *why* is it so?—Of course I ask for mere pastime."

"Because you are so distracting—and I am so distracted."

"You look like it."

"I am indeed."

"Why, you only saw me the other night!"

"That makes no difference. The lightning works instantaneously. I loved you then, at once—as I do now."

Bathsheba surveyed him curiously, from the feet upward, as high as she liked to venture her glance, which was not quite so high as his eyes.

"You cannot and you don't," she said demurely. "There is no such sudden feeling in people. I won't listen to you any longer. Dear me, I wish I knew what o'clock it is—I am going—I have wasted too much time here already!"

The sergeant looked at his watch and told her. "What, haven't you a watch, miss?" he enquired.

"I have not just at present—I am about to get a new one."

"No. You shall be given one. Yes—you shall. A gift, Miss Everdene—a gift."

And before she knew what the young man was intending, a heavy gold watch was in her hand.

"It is an unusually good one for a man like me to possess," he quietly said. "That watch has a history. Press the spring and open the back."

She did so.

"What do you see?"

"A crest and a motto."

"A coronet with five points, and beneath, *Cedit amor rebus*—'Love yields to circumstance.' It's the motto of the Earls of Severn. That watch belonged to the last lord, and was given to my mother's husband, a medical man, for his use till I came of age, when it was to be given to me. It was all the fortune that ever I inherited. That watch has regulated imperial interests in its time—the stately ceremonial, the courtly assignation, pompous travels, and lordly sleeps. Now it is yours."

"But, Sergeant Troy, I cannot take this—I cannot!" she exclaimed with round-eyed wonder. "A gold watch! What are you doing? Don't be such a dissembler!"

The sergeant retreated to avoid receiving back his gift, which she held out persistently towards him. Bathsheba followed as he retired.

"Keep it—do, Miss Everdene—keep it!" said the erratic child of impulse. "The fact of your possessing it makes it worth ten times as much to me. A more plebeian one will answer my purpose just as well, and the pleasure of knowing whose heart my old one beats against—well, I won't speak of that. It is in far worthier hands than ever it has been in before."

"But indeed I can't have it!" she said, in a perfect simmer of distress. "O, how can you do such a thing; that is if you really mean it! Give me your dead father's watch, and such a valuable one! You should not be so reckless, indeed, Sergeant Troy!"

"I loved my father: good; but better, I love you more. That's how I can do it," said the sergeant with an intonation of such exquisite fidelity to nature that it was evidently not all acted now. Her beauty, which, whilst it had been quiescent, he had praised in jest, had in its animated phases moved him to earnest; and though his seriousness was less than she imagined, it was probably more than he imagined himself.

Bathsheba was brimming with agitated bewilderment, and she said, in half-suspicious accents of feeling, "Can it be! O, how can it be, that you care for me, and so suddenly! You have seen so little of me: I may not be really so—so nice-looking as I seem to you. Please, do take it; O, do! I cannot and will not have it. Believe me, your generosity is too great. I have never done you a single kindness, and why should you be so kind to me?"

A factitious reply had been again upon his lips, but it was again suspended, and he looked at her with an arrested eye. The truth was, that as she now stood—excited, wild, and honest as the day—her alluring beauty bore out so fully the epithets he had bestowed upon it that he was quite startled at his temerity in advancing them as false. He said mechanically, "Ah, why?" and continued to look at her.

"And my work-folk see me following you about the field, and are wondering. O, this is dreadful!" she went on, unconscious of the transmutation she was effecting.

"I did not quite mean you to accept it at first, for it was my one poor patent of nobility," he broke out bluntly; "but, upon my soul, I wish you would now. Without any shamming, come! Don't deny me the happiness of wearing it for my sake? But you are too lovely even to care to be kind as others are."

"No, no; don't say so! I have reasons for reserve which I cannot explain."

"Let it be, then, let it be," he said, receiving back the watch at last; "I must be leaving you now. And will you speak to me for these few weeks of my stay?"

"Indeed I will. Yet, I don't know if I will! O, why did you come and disturb me so!"

"Perhaps in setting a gin, I have caught myself. Such things have happened. Well, will you let me work in your fields?" he coaxed.

"Yes, I suppose so; if it is any pleasure to you."

"Miss Everdene, I thank you."

"No, no."

"Good-bye!"

The sergeant brought his hand to the cap on the slope of his head, saluted, and returned to the distant group of haymakers.

Bathsheba could not face the haymakers now. Her heart erratically flitting hither and thither from perplexed excitement, hot, and almost tearful, she retreated homeward, murmuring, "Oh, what have I done! What does it mean! I wish I knew how much of it was true!"

XXVII

HIVING THE BEES

THE WEATHERBURY BEES WERE LATE IN THEIR SWARMING THIS YEAR. IT WAS IN THE LAT-ter part of June, and the day after the interview with Troy in the hayfield, that Bathsheba was standing in her garden, watching a swarm in the air and guessing their probable settling place. Not only were they late this year, but unruly. Sometimes throughout a whole season all the swarms would alight on the lowest attainable bough—such as part of a currant-bush or espalier apple-tree; next year they would, with just the same unanimity, make straight off to the uppermost member of some tall, gaunt costard, or quarrenden, and there defy all invaders who did not come armed with ladders and staves to take them.

This was the case at present. Bathsheba's eyes, shaded by one hand, were following the ascending multitude against the unexplorable stretch of blue till they ultimately halted by one of the unwieldy trees spoken of. A process somewhat analogous to that of alleged formations of the universe, time and times ago, was observable. The bustling swarm had swept the sky in a scattered and uniform haze, which now thickened to a nebulous centre: this glided on to a bough and grew still denser, till it formed a solid black spot upon the light.

The men and women being all busily engaged in saving the hay—even Liddy had left the house for the purpose of lending a hand—Bathsheba resolved to hive the bees herself, if possible. She had dressed the hive with herbs and honey, fetched a ladder, brush, and crook, made herself impregnable with armour of leather gloves, straw hat, and large gauze veil—once green but now faded to snuff colour—and ascended a dozen rungs of the ladder. At once she heard, not ten yards off, a voice that was beginning to have a strange power in agitating her.

"Miss Everdene, let me assist you; you should not attempt such a thing alone."

Troy was just opening the garden gate.

Bathsheba flung down the brush, crook, and empty hive, pulled the skirt of her dress tightly round her ankles in a tremendous flurry, and as well as she could slid down the ladder. By the time she reached the bottom Troy was there also, and he stooped to pick up the hive.

"How fortunate I am to have dropped in at this moment!" exclaimed the sergeant.

She found her voice in a minute. "What! and will you shake them in for me?" she asked, in what, for a defiant girl, was a faltering way; though, for a timid girl, it would have seemed a brave way enough.

"Will I!" said Troy. "Why, of course I will. How blooming you are to-day!" Troy flung down his cane and put his foot on the ladder to ascend.

"But you must have on the veil and gloves, or you'll be stung fearfully!"

"Ah, yes. I must put on the veil and gloves. Will you kindly show me how to fix them properly?"

"And you must have the broad-brimmed hat, too; for your cap has no brim to keep the veil off, and they'd reach your face."

"The broad-brimmed hat, too, by all means."

So a whimsical fate ordered that her hat should be taken off—veil and all attached—

and placed upon his head, Troy tossing his own into a gooseberry bush. Then the veil had to be tied at its lower edge round his collar and the gloves put on him.

He looked such an extraordinary object in this guise that, flurried as she was, she could not avoid laughing outright. It was the removal of yet another stake from the palisade of cold manners which had kept him off.

Bathsheba looked on from the ground whilst he was busy sweeping and shaking the bees from the tree, holding up the hive with the other hand for them to fall into. She made use of an unobserved minute whilst his attention was absorbed in the operation to arrange her plumes a little. He came down holding the hive at arm's length, behind which trailed a cloud of bees.

"Upon my life," said Troy, through the veil, "holding up this hive makes one's arm ache worse than a week of sword-exercise." When the manoeuvre was complete he approached her. "Would you be good enough to untie me and let me out? I am nearly stifled inside this silk cage."

To hide her embarrassment during the unwonted process of untying the string about his neck, she said:—

"I have never seen that you spoke of."

"What?"

"The sword-exercise."

"Ah! would you like to?" said Troy.

Bathsheba hesitated. She had heard wondrous reports from time to time by dwellers in Weatherbury, who had by chance sojourned awhile in Casterbridge, near the barracks, of this strange and glorious performance, the sword-exercise. Men and boys who had peeped through chinks or over walls into the barrack-yard returned with accounts of its being the most flashing affair conceivable; accoutrements and weapons glistening like stars—here, there, around—yet all by rule and compass. So she said mildly what she felt strongly:

"Yes; I should like to see it very much."

"And so you shall; you shall see me go through it."

"No! How?"

"Let me consider."

"Not with a walking-stick—I don't care to see that. It must be a real sword."

"Yes, I know; and I have no sword here; but I think I could get one by the evening. Now, will you do this?"

Troy bent over her and murmured some suggestion in a low voice.

"O no, indeed!" said Bathsheba, blushing. "Thank you very much, but I couldn't on any account."

"Surely you might? Nobody would know."

She shook her head, but with a weakened negation. "If I were to," she said, "I must bring Liddy too. Might I not?"

Troy looked far away. "I don't see why you want to bring her," he said coldly.

An unconscious look of assent in Bathsheba's eyes betrayed that something more than his coldness had made her also feel that Liddy would be superfluous in the suggested scene. She had felt it, even whilst making the proposal.

"Well, I won't bring Liddy—and I'll come. But only for a very short time," she added; "a very short time."

"It will not take five minutes," said Troy.

XXVIII

THE HOLLOW AMID THE FERNS

THE HILL OPPOSITE BATHSHEBA'S DWELLING EXTENDED, A MILE OFF, INTO AN UNCULTI-vated tract of land, dotted at this season with tall thickets of brake fern, plump and diaphanous from recent rapid growth, and radiant in hues of clear and untainted green.

At eight o'clock this midsummer evening, whilst the bristling ball of gold in the west still swept the tips of the ferns with its long, luxuriant rays, a soft brushing-by of garments might have been heard among them, and Bathsheba appeared in their midst, their soft, feathery arms caressing her up to her shoulders. She paused, turned, went back over the hill and half-way to her own door, whence she cast a farewell glance upon the spot she had just left, having resolved not to remain near the place after all.

She saw a dim spot of artificial red moving round the shoulder of the rise. It disappeared on the other side.

She waited one minute—two minutes—thought of Troy's disappointment at her non-fulfilment of a promised engagement, till she again ran along the field, clambered over the bank, and followed the original direction. She was now literally trembling and panting at this her temerity in such an errant undertaking; her breath came and went quickly, and her eyes shone with an infrequent light. Yet go she must. She reached the verge of a pit in the middle of the ferns. Troy stood in the bottom, looking up towards her.

"I heard you rustling through the fern before I saw you," he said, coming up and giving her his hand to help her down the slope.

The pit was a saucer-shaped concave, naturally formed, with a top diameter of about thirty feet, and shallow enough to allow the sunshine to reach their heads. Standing in the centre, the sky overhead was met by a circular horizon of fern: this grew nearly to the bottom of the slope and then abruptly ceased. The middle within the belt of verdure was floored with a thick flossy carpet of moss and grass intermingled, so yielding that the foot was half-buried within it.

"Now," said Troy, producing the sword, which, as he raised it into the sunlight, gleamed a sort of greeting, like a living thing; "first, we have four right and four left cuts; four right and four left thrusts. Infantry cuts and guards are more interesting than ours, to my mind; but they are not so swashing. They have seven cuts and three thrusts. So much as a preliminary. Well, next, our cut one is as if you were sowing your corn—so." Bathsheba saw a sort of rainbow, upside-down in the air, and Troy's arm was still again. "Cut two, as if you were hedging—so. Three, as if you were reaping—so. Four, as if you were threshing—in that way. Then the same on the left. The thrusts are these: one, two, three, four, right; one, two, three, four, left." He repeated them. "Have 'em again?" he said. "One, two—"

She hurriedly interrupted: "I'd rather not; though I don't mind your twos and fours; but your ones and threes are terrible!"

"Very well. I'll let you off the ones and threes. Next, cuts, points and guards altogether." Troy duly exhibited them. "Then there's pursuing practice, in this way." He gave the movements as before. "There, those are the stereotyped forms. The infantry have two most diabolical upward cuts, which we are too humane to use. Like this—three, four."

"How murderous and bloodthirsty!"

"They are rather deathly. Now I'll be more interesting, and let you see some loose play—giving all the cuts and points, infantry and cavalry, quicker than lightning, and as promiscuously—with just enough rule to regulate instinct and yet not to fetter it. You are my antagonist, with this difference from real warfare, that I shall miss you every time by one hair's breadth, or perhaps two. Mind you don't flinch, whatever you do."

"I'll be sure not to!" she said invincibly.

He pointed to about a yard in front of him.

Bathsheba's adventurous spirit was beginning to find some grains of relish in these highly novel proceedings. She took up her position as directed, facing Troy.

"Now just to learn whether you have pluck enough to let me do what I wish, I'll give you a preliminary test."

He flourished the sword by way of introduction number two, and the next thing of which she was conscious was that the point and blade of the sword were darting with a gleam towards her left side, just above her hip; then of their reappearance on her right side, emerging as it were from between her ribs, having apparently passed through her body. The third item of consciousness was that of seeing the same sword, perfectly clean and free from blood held vertically in Troy's hand (in the position technically called "recover swords"). All was as quick as electricity.

"Oh!" she cried out in affright, pressing her hand to her side. "Have you run me through?—no, you have not! Whatever have you done!"

"I have not touched you," said Troy, quietly. "It was mere sleight of hand. The sword passed behind you. Now you are not afraid, are you? Because if you are I can't perform. I give my word that I will not only not hurt you, but not once touch you."

"I don't think I am afraid. You are quite sure you will not hurt me?"

"Quite sure."

"Is the sword very sharp?"

"O no—only stand as still as a statue. Now!"

In an instant the atmosphere was transformed to Bathsheba's eyes. Beams of light caught from the low sun's rays, above, around, in front of her, well-nigh shut out earth and heaven—all emitted in the marvellous evolutions of Troy's reflecting blade, which seemed everywhere at once, and yet nowhere specially. These circling gleams were accompanied by a keen rush that was almost a whistling—also springing from all sides of her at once. In short, she was enclosed in a firmament of light, and of sharp hisses, resembling a sky full of meteors close at hand.

Never since the broadsword became the national weapon had there been more dexterity shown in its management than by the hands of Sergeant Troy, and never had he been in such splendid temper for the performance as now in the evening sunshine among the ferns with Bathsheba. It may safely be asserted with respect to the closeness of his cuts, that had it been possible for the edge of the sword to leave in the air a permanent substance wherever it flew past, the space left untouched would have been almost a mould of Bathsheba's figure.

Behind the luminous streams of this *aurora militaris*, she could see the hue of Troy's sword arm, spread in a scarlet haze over the space covered by its motions, like a twanged harpstring, and behind all Troy himself, mostly facing her; sometimes, to show the rear cuts, half turned away, his eye nevertheless always keenly measuring her breadth and outline, and his lips tightly closed in sustained effort. Next, his movements lapsed slower, and she could see them individually. The hissing of the sword had ceased, and he stopped entirely.

"That outer loose lock of hair wants tidying," he said, before she had moved or spoken. "Wait: I'll do it for you."

An arc of silver shone on her right side: the sword had descended. The lock dropped to the ground.

"Bravely borne!" said Troy. "You didn't flinch a shade's thickness. Wonderful in a woman!"

"It was because I didn't expect it. O, you have spoilt my hair!"

"Only once more."

"No—no! I am afraid of you—indeed I am!" she cried.

"I won't touch you at all—not even your hair. I am only going to kill that caterpillar settling on you. Now: still!"

It appeared that a caterpillar had come from the fern and chosen the front of her bodice as his resting place. She saw the point glisten towards her bosom, and seemingly enter it. Bathsheba closed her eyes in the full persuasion that she was killed at last. However, feeling just as usual, she opened them again.

"There it is, look," said the sergeant, holding his sword before her eyes.

The caterpillar was spitted upon its point.

"Why, it is magic!" said Bathsheba, amazed.

"O no—dexterity. I merely gave point to your bosom where the caterpillar was, and instead of running you through checked the extension a thousandth of an inch short of your surface."

"But how could you chop off a curl of my hair with a sword that has no edge?"

"No edge! This sword will shave like a razor. Look here."

He touched the palm of his hand with the blade, and then, lifting it, showed her a thin shaving of scarf-skin dangling therefrom.

"But you said before beginning that it was blunt and couldn't cut me!"

"That was to get you to stand still, and so make sure of your safety. The risk of injuring you through your moving was too great not to force me to tell you a fib to escape it."

She shuddered. "I have been within an inch of my life, and didn't know it!"

"More precisely speaking, you have been within half an inch of being pared alive two hundred and ninety-five times."

"Cruel, cruel, 'tis of you!"

"You have been perfectly safe, nevertheless. My sword never errs." And Troy returned the weapon to the scabbard.

Bathsheba, overcome by a hundred tumultuous feelings resulting from the scene, abstractedly sat down on a tuft of heather.

"I must leave you now," said Troy, softly. "And I'll venture to take and keep this in remembrance of you."

She saw him stoop to the grass, pick up the winding lock which he had severed from her manifold tresses, twist it round his fingers, unfasten a button in the breast of his coat, and carefully put it inside. She felt powerless to withstand or deny him. He was altogether too much for her, and Bathsheba seemed as one who, facing a reviving wind, finds it blow so strongly that it stops the breath.

He drew near and said, "I must be leaving you." He drew nearer still. A minute later and she saw his scarlet form disappear amid the ferny thicket, almost in a flash, like a brand swiftly waved.

That minute's interval had brought the blood beating into her face, set her stinging as if aflame to the very hollows of her feet, and enlarged emotion to a compass which quite swamped thought. It had brought upon her a stroke resulting, as did that of Moses in Horeb, in a liquid stream—here a stream of tears. She felt like one who has sinned a great sin.

The circumstance had been the gentle dip of Troy's mouth downwards upon her own. He had kissed her.

XXIX

PARTICULARS OF A TWILIGHT WALK

W E NOW SEE THE ELEMENT OF FOLLY DISTINCTLY MINGLING WITH THE MANY VARYing particulars which made up the character of Bathsheba Everdene. It was almost foreign to her intrinsic nature. Introduced as lymph on the dart of Eros it eventually permeated and coloured her whole constitution. Bathsheba, though she had too much understanding to be entirely governed by her womanliness, had too much womanliness to use her understanding to the best advantage. Perhaps in no minor point does woman astonish her helpmate more than in the strange power she possesses of believing cajoleries that she knows to be false—except, indeed, in that of being utterly sceptical on strictures that she knows to be true.

Bathsheba loved Troy in the way that only self-reliant women love when they abandon their self-reliance. When a strong woman recklessly throws away her strength she is worse than a weak woman who has never had any strength to throw away. One source of her inadequacy is the novelty of the occasion. She has never had practice in making the best of such a condition. Weakness is doubly weak by being new.

Bathsheba was not conscious of guile in this matter. Though in one sense a woman of the world, it was, after all, that world of daylight coteries and green carpets wherein cattle form the passing crowd and winds the busy hum; where a quiet family of rabbits or hares lives on the other side of your party-wall, where your neighbour is everybody in the tything, and where calculation is confined to market-days. Of the fabricated tastes of good fashionable society she knew but little, and of the formulated self-indulgence of bad, nothing at all. Had her utmost thoughts in this direction been distinctly worded (and by herself they never were), they would only have amounted to such a matter as that she felt her impulses to be pleasanter guides than her discretion. Her love was entire as a child's, and though warm as summer it was fresh as spring. Her culpability lay in her making no attempt to control feeling by subtle and careful enquiry into consequences. She could show others the steep and thorny way, but "reck'd not her own rede."

And Troy's deformities lay deep down from a woman's vision, whilst his embellishments were upon the very surface; thus contrasting with homely Oak, whose defects were patent to the blindest, and whose virtues were as metals in a mine.

The difference between love and respect was markedly shown in her conduct. Bathsheba had spoken of her interest in Boldwood with the greatest freedom to Liddy, but she had only communed with her own heart concerning Troy.

All this infatuation Gabriel saw, and was troubled thereby from the time of his daily journey a-field to the time of his return, and on to the small hours of many a night. That he was not beloved had hitherto been his great sorrow; that Bathsheba was getting into the toils was now a sorrow greater than the first, and one which nearly obscured it. It was a result which paralleled the oft-quoted observation of Hippocrates concerning physical pains.

That is a noble though perhaps an unpromising love which not even the fear of breeding aversion in the bosom of the one beloved can deter from combating his or her errors. Oak determined to speak to his mistress. He would base his appeal on what he considered her unfair treatment of Farmer Boldwood, now absent from home.

An opportunity occurred one evening when she had gone for a short walk by a path through the neighbouring cornfields. It was dusk when Oak, who had not been far a-field that day, took the same path and met her returning, quite pensively, as he thought.

The wheat was now tall, and the path was narrow; thus the way was quite a sunken groove between the embowing thicket on either side. Two persons could not walk abreast without damaging the crop, and Oak stood aside to let her pass.

"Oh, is it Gabriel?" she said. "You are taking a walk too. Good-night."

"I thought I would come to meet you, as it is rather late," said Oak, turning and following at her heels when she had brushed somewhat quickly by him.

"Thank you, indeed, but I am not very fearful."

"O no; but there are bad characters about."

"I never meet them."

Now Oak, with marvellous ingenuity, had been going to introduce the gallant sergeant through the channel of "bad characters." But all at once the scheme broke down, it suddenly occurring to him that this was rather a clumsy way, and too barefaced to begin with. He tried another preamble.

"And as the man who would naturally come to meet you is away from home, too—I mean Farmer Boldwood—why, thinks I, I'll go," he said.

"Ah, yes." She walked on without turning her head, and for many steps nothing further was heard from her quarter than the rustle of her dress against the heavy corn-ears. Then she resumed rather tartly—

"I don't quite understand what you meant by saying that Mr. Boldwood would naturally come to meet me."

I meant on account of the wedding which they say is likely to take place between you and him, miss. Forgive my speaking plainly."

"They say what is not true," she returned quickly. "No marriage is likely to take place between us."

Gabriel now put forth his unobscured opinion, for the moment had come. "Well, Miss Everdene," he said, "putting aside what people say, I never in my life saw any courting if his is not a courting of you."

Bathsheba would probably have terminated the conversation there and then by flatly forbidding the subject, had not her conscious weakness of position allured her to palter and argue in endeavours to better it.

"Since this subject has been mentioned," she said very emphatically, "I am glad of the opportunity of clearing up a mistake which is very common and very provoking. I didn't definitely promise Mr. Boldwood anything. I have never cared for him. I respect him, and he has urged me to marry him. But I have given him no distinct answer. As soon as he returns I shall do so; and the answer will be that I cannot think of marrying him."

"People are full of mistakes, seemingly."

"They are."

"The other day they said you were trifling with him, and you almost proved that you were not; lately they have said that you be not, and you straightway begin to show——"

"That I am, I suppose you mean."

"Well, I hope they speak the truth."

"They do, but wrongly applied. I don't trifle with him; but then, I have nothing to do with him."

Oak was unfortunately led on to speak of Boldwood's rival in a wrong tone to her after all. "I wish you had never met that young Sergeant Troy, miss," he sighed.

Bathsheba's steps became faintly spasmodic. "Why?" she asked.

"He is not good enough for 'ee."

"Did anyone tell you to speak to me like this?"

"Nobody at all."

"Then it appears to me that Sergeant Troy does not concern us here," she said intractably. "Yet I must say that Sergeant Troy is an educated man, and quite worthy of any woman. He is well born."

"His being higher in learning and birth than the ruck o' soldiers is anything but a proof of his worth. It shows his course to be down'ard."

"I cannot see what this has to do with our conversation. Mr. Troy's course is not by any means downward; and his superiority *is* a proof of his worth!"

"I believe him to have no conscience at all. And I cannot help begging you, miss, to have nothing to do with him. Listen to me this once—only this once! I don't say he's such a bad man as I have fancied—I pray to God he is not. But since we don't exactly know what he is, why not behave as if he *might* be bad, simply for your own safety? Don't trust him, mistress; I ask you not to trust him so."

"Why, pray?"

"I like soldiers, but this one I do not like," he said sturdily. "His cleverness in his calling may have tempted him astray, and what is mirth to the neighbours is ruin to the woman. When he tries to talk to 'ee again, why not turn away with a short 'Good-day'; and when you see him coming one way, turn the other. When he says anything laughable, fail to see the point and don't smile, and speak of him before those who will report your talk as 'that fantastical man,' or 'that Sergeant What's-his-name.' 'That man of a family that has come to the dogs.' Don't be unmannerly towards en, but harmless-uncivil, and so get rid of the man."

No Christmas robin detained by a window-pane ever pulsed as did Bathsheba now.

"I say—I say again—that it doesn't become you to talk about him. Why he should be mentioned passes me quite!" she exclaimed desperately. "I know this, th-th-that he is a thoroughly conscientious man—blunt sometimes even to rudeness—but always speaking his mind about you plain to your face!"

"Oh."

"He is as good as anybody in this parish! He is very particular, too, about going to church—yes, he is!"

"I am afeard nobody saw him there. I never did, certainly."

"The reason of that is," she said eagerly, "that he goes in privately by the old tower door, just when the service commences, and sits at the back of the gallery. He told me so."

This supreme instance of Troy's goodness fell upon Gabriel's ears like the thirteenth stroke of a crazy clock. It was not only received with utter incredulity as regarded itself, but threw a doubt on all the assurances that had preceded it.

Oak was grieved to find how entirely she trusted him. He brimmed with deep feeling as he replied in a steady voice, the steadiness of which was spoilt by the palpableness of his great effort to keep it so:—

"You know, mistress, that I love you, and shall love you always. I only mention this to bring to your mind that at any rate I would wish to do you no harm: beyond that I put it aside. I have lost in the race for money and good things, and I am not such a fool as to pretend to 'ee now I am poor, and you have got altogether above me. But Bathsheba, dear mistress, this I beg you to consider—that, both to keep yourself well honoured among the work-folk, and in common generosity to an honourable man who loves you as well as I, you should be more discreet in your bearing towards this soldier."

"Don't, don't, don't!" she exclaimed, in a choking voice.

"Are ye not more to me than my own affairs, and even life!" he went on. "Come, listen to me! I am six years older than you, and Mr. Boldwood is ten years older than I, and consider—I do beg of 'ee to consider before it is too late—how safe you would be in his hands!"

Oak's allusion to his own love for her lessened, to some extent, her anger at his interference; but she could not really forgive him for letting his wish to marry her be eclipsed by his wish to do her good, any more than for his slighting treatment of Troy.

"I wish you to go elsewhere," she commanded, a paleness of face invisible to the eye being suggested by the trembling words. "Do not remain on this farm any longer. I don't want you—I beg you to go!"

"That's nonsense," said Oak calmly. "This is the second time you have pretended to dismiss me; and what's the use o' it?"

"Pretended! You shall go, sir—your lecturing I will not hear! I am mistress here."

"Go, indeed—what folly will you say next? Treating me like Dick, Tom and Harry when you know that a short time ago my position was as good as yours! Upon my life, Bathsheba, it is too barefaced. You know, too, that I can't go without putting things in such a strait as you wouldn't get out of I can't tell when. Unless, indeed, you'll promise to have an understanding man as bailiff, or manager, or something. I'll go at once if you'll promise that."

"I shall have no bailiff; I shall continue to be my own manager," she said decisively.

"Very well, then; you should be thankful to me for biding. How would the farm go on with nobody to mind it but a woman? But mind this, I don't wish 'ee to feel you owe me anything. Not I. What I do, I do. Sometimes I say I should be as glad as a bird to leave the place—for don't suppose I'm content to be a nobody. I was made for better things. However, I don't like to see your concerns going to ruin, as they must if you keep in this mind. . . . I hate taking my own measure so plain, but, upon my life, your provoking ways make a man say what he wouldn't dream of at other times! I own to being rather interfering. But you know well enough how it is, and who she is that I like too well, and feel too much like a fool about to be civil to her!"

It is more than probable that she privately and unconsciously respected him a little for this grim fidelity, which had been shown in his tone even more than in his words. At any rate she murmured something to the effect that he might stay if he wished. She said more distinctly, "Will you leave me alone now? I don't order it as a mistress—I ask it as a woman, and I expect you not to be so uncourteous as to refuse."

"Certainly I will, Miss Everdene," said Gabriel gently. He wondered that the request should have come at this moment, for the strife was over, and they were on a most desolate hill, far from every human habitation, and the hour was getting late. He stood still and allowed her to get far ahead of him till he could only see her form upon the sky.

A distressing explanation of this anxiety to be rid of him at that point now ensued. A figure apparently rose from the earth beside her. The shape beyond all doubt was Troy's. Oak would not be even a possible listener, and at once turned back till a good two hundred yards were between the lovers and himself.

Gabriel went home by way of the churchyard. In passing the tower he thought of what she had said about the sergeant's virtuous habit of entering the church unperceived at the beginning of service. Believing that the little gallery-door alluded to was quite disused, he ascended the external flight of steps at the top of which it stood, and examined it. The pale lustre yet hanging in the north-western heaven was sufficient to show that a sprig of ivy had grown from the wall across the door to a length of more than a foot, delicately tying the panel to the stone jamb. It was a decisive proof that the door had not been opened at least since Troy came back to Weatherbury.

XXX

Hot Cheeks and Tearful Eyes

HALF AN HOUR LATER BATHSHEBA ENTERED HER OWN HOUSE. THERE BURNT UPON HER face when she met the light of the candles the flush and excitement which were little less than chronic with her now. The farewell words of Troy, who had accompanied her to the very door, still lingered in her ears. He had bidden her adieu for two days, which were, so he stated, to be spent at Bath in visiting some friends. He had also kissed her a second time.

It is only fair to Bathsheba to explain here a little fact which did not come to light till a long time afterwards: that Troy's presentation of himself so aptly at the roadside this evening was not by any distinctly preconcerted arrangement. He had hinted—she had forbidden; and it was only on the chance of his still coming that she had dismissed Oak, fearing a meeting between them just then.

She now sank down into a chair, wild and perturbed by all these new and fevering sequences. Then she jumped up with a manner of decision, and fetched her desk from a side-table.

In three minutes, without pause or modification, she had written a letter to Boldwood, at his address beyond Casterbridge, saying mildly but firmly that she had well considered the whole subject he had brought before her and kindly given her time to decide upon; that her final decision was that she could not marry him. She had expressed to Oak an intention to wait till Boldwood came home before communicating to him her conclusive reply. But Bathsheba found that she could not wait.

It was impossible to send this letter till the next day; yet to quell her uneasiness by getting it out of her hands, and so, as it were, setting the act in motion at once, she arose to take it to any one of the women who might be in the kitchen.

She paused in the passage. A dialogue was going on in the kitchen, and Bathsheba and Troy were the subject of it.

"If he marry her, she'll gie up farming."

" 'Twill be a gallant life, but may bring some trouble between the mirth—so say I."

"Well, I wish I had half such a husband."

Bathsheba had too much sense to mind seriously what her servitors said about her; but too much womanly redundance of speech to leave alone what was said till it died the natural death of unminded things. She burst in upon them.

"Who are you speaking of?" she asked.

There was a pause before anybody replied. At last Liddy said frankly, "What was passing was a bit of a word about yourself, miss."

"I thought so! Maryann and Liddy and Temperance—now I forbid you to suppose such things. You know I don't care the least for Mr. Troy—not I. Everybody knows how much I hate him.—Yes," repeated the froward young person, "*hate* him!"

"We know you do, miss," said Liddy; "and so do we all."

"I hate him too," said Maryann.

"Maryann—O you perjured woman! How can you speak that wicked story!" said Bathsheba excitedly. "You admired him from your heart only this morning in the very world, you did. Yes, Maryann, you know it!"

"Yes, miss, but so did you. He is a wild scamp now, and you are right to hate him."

"He's *not* a wild scamp! How dare you to my face! I have no right to hate him, nor you, nor anybody. But I am a silly woman! What is it to me what he is? You know it is nothing. I don't care for him; I don't mean to defend his good name, not I. Mind this, if any of you say a word against him you'll be dismissed instantly!"

She flung down the letter and surged back into the parlour, with a big heart and tearful eyes, Liddy following her.

"O miss!" said mild Liddy, looking pitifully into Bathsheba's face. "I am sorry we mistook you so! I did think you cared for him; but I see you don't now."

"Shut the door, Liddy."

Liddy closed the door, and went on: "People always say such foolery, miss. I'll make answer hencefor'ard, 'Of course a lady like Miss Everdene can't love him'; I'll say it out in plain black and white."

Bathsheba burst out: "O Liddy, are you such a simpleton? Can't you read riddles? Can't you see? Are you a woman yourself?"

Liddy's clear eyes rounded with wonderment.

"Yes; you must be a blind thing, Liddy!" she said in reckless abandonment and grief. "O, I love him to very distraction and misery and agony! Don't be frightened at me, though perhaps I am enough to frighten any innocent woman. Come closer—closer." She put her arms round Liddy's neck. "I must let it out to somebody; it is wearing me away! Don't you yet know enough of me to see through that miserable denial of mine? O God, what a lie it was! Heaven and my Love forgive me. And don't you know that a woman who loves at all thinks nothing of perjury when it is balanced against her love? There, go out of the room; I want to be quite alone."

Liddy went towards the door.

"Liddy, come here. Solemnly swear to me that he's not a fast man; that it is all lies they say about him!"

"But, miss, how can I say he is not if—"

"You graceless girl! How can you have the cruel heart to repeat what they say? Unfeeling thing that you are. . . . But *I'll* see if you or anybody else in the village, or town either, dare do such a thing!" She started off, pacing from fireplace to door, and back again.

"No, miss. I don't—I know it is not true!" said Liddy, frightened at Bathsheba's unwonted vehemence.

"I suppose you only agree with me like that to please me. But, Liddy, he *cannot be* bad, as is said. Do you hear?"

"Yes, miss, yes."

"And you don't believe he is?"

"I don't know what to say, miss," said Liddy, beginning to cry. "If I say No, you don't believe me; and if I say Yes, you rage at me!"

"Say you don't believe it—say you don't!"

"I don't believe him to be so bad as they make out."

"He is not bad at all. . . . My poor life and heart, how weak I am!" she moaned, in a relaxed, desultory way, heedless of Liddy's presence. "O, how I wish I had never seen him! Loving is misery for women always. I shall never forgive God for making me a woman, and dearly am I beginning to pay for the honour of owning a pretty face." She freshened and turned to Liddy suddenly. "Mind this, Lydia Smallbury, if you repeat anywhere a single word of what I have said to you inside this closed door, I'll never trust you, or love you, or have you with me a moment longer—not a moment!"

"I don't want to repeat anything," said Liddy, with womanly dignity of a diminutive order; "but I don't wish to stay with you. And, if you please, I'll go at the end of the harvest, or this week, or to-day. . . . I don't see that I deserve to be put upon and stormed at for nothing!" concluded the small woman, bigly.

"No, no, Liddy; you must stay!" said Bathsheba, dropping from haughtiness to entreaty with capricious inconsequence. "You must not notice my being in a taking just now. You are not as a servant—you are a companion to me. Dear, dear—I don't know what I am doing since this miserable ache o' my heart has weighted and worn upon me so! What shall I come to! I suppose I shall get further and further into troubles. I wonder sometimes if I am doomed to die in the Union. I am friendless enough, God knows!"

"I won't notice anything, nor will I leave you!" sobbed Liddy, impulsively putting up her lips to Bathsheba's, and kissing her.

Then Bathsheba kissed Liddy, and all was smooth again.

"I don't often cry, do I, Lidd? but you have made tears come into my eyes," she said, a smile shining through the moisture. "Try to think him a good man, won't you, dear Liddy?"

"I will, miss, indeed."

"He is a sort of steady man in a wild way, you know. That's better than to be as some are, wild in a steady way. I am afraid that's how I am. And promise me to keep my secret—do, Liddy! And do not let them know that I have been crying about him, because it will be dreadful for me, and no good to him, poor thing!"

"Death's head himself shan't wring it from me, mistress, if I've a mind to keep anything; and I'll always be your friend," replied Liddy emphatically, at the same time bringing a few more tears into her own eyes, not from any particular necessity, but from an artistic sense of making herself in keeping with the remainder of the picture, which seems to influence women at such times. "I think God likes us to be good friends, don't you?"

"Indeed I do."

"And, dear miss, you won't harry me and storm at me, will you? because you seem to swell so tall as a lion then, and it frightens me! Do you know, I fancy you would be a match for any man when you are in one o' your takings."

"Never! do you?" said Bathsheba, slightly laughing, though somewhat seriously alarmed by this Amazonian picture of herself. "I hope I am not a bold sort of maid—mannish?" she continued with some anxiety.

"O no, not mannish; but so almighty womanish that 'tis getting on that way sometimes. Ah! miss," she said, after having drawn her breath very sadly in and sent it very sadly out, "I wish I had half your failing that way. 'Tis a great protection to a poor maid in these illegit'mate days!"

XXXI

BLAME—FURY

THE NEXT EVENING BATHSHEBA, WITH THE IDEA OF GETTING OUT OF THE WAY OF MR. Boldwood in the event of his returning to answer her note in person, proceeded to fulfil an engagement made with Liddy some few hours earlier. Bathsheba's companion, as a gauge of their reconciliation, had been granted a week's holiday to visit her sister, who was married to a thriving hurdler and cattle-crib-maker living in a delightful labyrinth of hazel copse not far beyond Yalbury. The arrangement was that Miss Everdene should honour them by coming there for a day or two to inspect some ingenious contrivances which this man of the woods had introduced into his wares.

Leaving her instructions with Gabriel and Maryann, that they were to see everything carefully locked up for the night, she went out of the house just at the close of a timely thunder-shower, which had refined the air, and daintily bathed the coat of the land, though all beneath was dry as ever. Freshness was exhaled in an essence from the varied contours of bank and hollow, as if the earth breathed maiden breath; and the pleased birds were hymning to the scene. Before her, among the clouds, there was a contrast in the shape of lairs of fierce light which showed themselves in the neighbourhood of a hidden sun, lingering on to the farthest north-west corner of the heavens that this midsummer season allowed.

She had walked nearly two miles of her journey, watching how the day was retreating, and thinking how the time of deeds was quietly melting into the time of thought, to give place in its turn to the time of prayer and sleep, when she beheld advancing over Yalbury hill the very man she sought so anxiously to elude. Boldwood was stepping on, not with that quiet tread of reserved strength which was his customary gait, in which he always seemed to be balancing two thoughts. His manner was stunned and sluggish now.

Boldwood had for the first time been awakened to woman's privileges in tergiversation even when it involves another person's possible blight. That Bathsheba was a firm and positive girl, far less inconsequent than her fellows, had been the very lung of his hope; for he had held that these qualities would lead her to adhere to a straight course for consistency's sake, and accept him, though her fancy might not flood him with the iridescent hues of uncritical love. But the argument now came back as sorry gleams from a broken mirror. The discovery was no less a scourge than a surprise.

He came on looking upon the ground, and did not see Bathsheba till they were less than a stone's throw apart. He looked up at the sound of her pit-pat, and his changed appearance sufficiently denoted to her the depth and strength of the feelings paralyzed by her letter.

"Oh; is it you, Mr. Boldwood?" she faltered, a guilty warmth pulsing in her face.

Those who have the power of reproaching in silence may find it a means more effective than words. There are accents in the eye which are not on the tongue, and more tales come from pale lips than can enter an ear. It is both the grandeur and the pain of the remoter moods that they avoid the pathway of sound. Boldwood's look was unanswerable.

Seeing she turned a little aside, he said, "What, are you afraid of me?"

"Why should you say that?" said Bathsheba.

"I fancied you looked so," said he. "And it is most strange, because of its contrast with my feeling for you."

She regained self-possession, fixed her eyes calmly, and waited.

"You know what that feeling is," continued Boldwood deliberately. "A thing strong as death. No dismissal by a hasty letter affects that."

"I wish you did not feel so strongly about me," she murmured. "It is generous of you, and more than I deserve, but I must not hear it now."

"Hear it? What do you think I have to say, then? I am not to marry you, and that's enough. Your letter was excellently plain. I want you to hear nothing—not I."

Bathsheba was unable to direct her will into any definite groove for freeing herself from this fearfully awkward position. She confusedly said, "Good-evening," and was moving on. Boldwood walked up to her heavily and dully.

"Bathsheba—darling—is it final indeed?"

"Indeed it is."

"O, Bathsheba—have pity upon me!" Boldwood burst out. "God's sake, yes—I am come to that low, lowest stage—to ask a woman for pity! Still, she is you—she is you."

Bathsheba commanded herself well. But she could hardly get a clear voice for what came instinctively to her lips: "There is little honour to the woman in that speech." It was only whispered, for something unutterably mournful no less than distressing in this spectacle of a man showing himself to be so entirely the vane of a passion enervated the feminine instinct for punctilios.

"I am beyond myself about this, and am mad," he said. "I am no stoic at all to be supplicating here; but I do supplicate to you. I wish you knew what is in me of devotion to you; but it is impossible, that. In bare human mercy to a lonely man, don't throw me off now!"

"I don't throw you off—indeed, how can I? I never had you." In her noon-clear sense that she had never loved him she forgot for a moment her thoughtless angle on that day in February.

"But there was a time when you turned to me, before I thought of you! I don't reproach you, for even now I feel that the ignorant and cold darkness that I should have lived in if you had not attracted me by that letter—valentine you call it—would have been worse than my knowledge of you, though it has brought this misery. But, I say, there was a time when I knew nothing of you, and cared nothing for you, and yet you drew me on. And if you say you gave me no encouragement, I cannot but contradict you."

"What you call encouragement was the childish game of an idle minute. I have bitterly repented of it—ay, bitterly, and in tears. Can you still go on reminding me?"

"I don't accuse you of it—I deplore it. I took for earnest what you insist was jest, and now this that I pray to be jest you say is awful, wretched earnest. Our moods meet at wrong places. I wish your feeling was more like mine, or my feeling more like yours! O, could I but have foreseen the torture that trifling trick was going to lead me into, how I should have cursed you; but only having been able to see it since, I cannot do that, for I love you too well! But it is weak, idle drivelling to go on like this. . . . Bathsheba, you are the first woman of any shade or nature that I have ever looked at to love, and it is the having been so near claiming you for my own that makes this denial so hard to bear. How nearly you promised me! But I don't speak now to move your heart, and make you grieve because of my pain; it is no use, that. I must bear it; my pain would get no less by paining you."

"But I do pity you—deeply—O, so deeply!" she earnestly said.

"Do no such thing—do no such thing. Your dear love, Bathsheba, is such a vast thing beside your pity, that the loss of your pity as well as your love is no great addition to my sorrow, nor does the gain of your pity make it sensibly less. O sweet—how dearly you spoke to me behind the spear-bed at the washing-pool, and in the barn at the shearing, and that dearest last time in the evening at your home! Where are your pleasant words all gone—your earnest hope to be able to love me? Where is your firm conviction that you would get to care for me very much? Really forgotten?—really?"

She checked emotion, looked him quietly and clearly in the face, and said in her low, firm voice, "Mr. Boldwood, I promised you nothing. Would you have had me a woman of clay when you paid me that furthest, highest compliment a man can pay a woman—telling her he loves her? I was bound to show some feeling, if I would not be a graceless shrew. Yet each of those pleasures was just for the day—the day just for the pleasure. How was I to know that what is a pastime to all other men was death to you? Have reason, do, and think more kindly of me!"

"Well, never mind arguing—never mind. One thing is sure: you were all but mine, and now you are not nearly mine. Everything is changed, and that by you alone, remember. You were nothing to me once, and I was contented; you are now nothing to me again, and how different the second nothing is from the first! Would to God you had never taken me up, since it was only to throw me down!"

Bathsheba, in spite of her mettle, began to feel unmistakable signs that she was inherently the weaker vessel. She strove miserably against this femininity which would insist upon supplying unbidden emotions in stronger and stronger current. She had tried to elude agitation by fixing her mind on the trees, sky, any trivial object before her eyes, whilst his reproaches fell, but ingenuity could not save her now.

"I did not take you up—surely I did not!" she answered as heroically as she could. "But don't be in this mood with me. I can endure being told I am in the wrong, if you will only tell it me gently! O sir, will you not kindly forgive me, and look at it cheerfully?"

"Cheerfully! Can a man fooled to utter heart-burning find a reason for being merry? If I have lost, how can I be as if I had won? Heavens you must be heartless quite! Had I known what a fearfully bitter sweet this was to be, how I would have avoided you, and never seen you, and been deaf of you. I tell you all this, but what do you care! You don't care."

She returned silent and weak denials to his charges, and swayed her head desperately, as if to thrust away the words as they came showering about her ears from the lips of the trembling man in the climax of life, with his bronzed Roman face and fine frame.

"Dearest, dearest, I am wavering even now between the two opposites of recklessly renouncing you, and labouring humbly for you again. Forget that you have said No, and let it be as it was! Say, Bathsheba, that you only wrote that refusal to me in fun—come, say it to me!"

"It would be untrue, and painful to both of us. You overrate my capacity for love. I don't possess half the warmth of nature you believe me to have. An unprotected childhood in a cold world has beaten gentleness out of me."

He immediately said with more resentment: "That may be true, somewhat; but ah, Miss Everdene, it won't do as a reason! You are not the cold woman you would have me believe. No, no! It isn't because you have no feeling in you that you don't love me. You naturally would have me think so—you would hide from me that you have a burning heart like mine. You have love enough, but it is turned into a new channel. I know where."

The swift music of her heart became hubbub now, and she throbbed to extremity. He was coming to Troy. He did then know what had occurred! And the name fell from his lips the next moment.

"Why did Troy not leave my treasure alone?" he asked fiercely. "When I had no thought of injuring him, why did he force himself upon your notice! Before he worried you your inclination was to have me; when next I should have come to you your answer would have been Yes. Can you deny it—I ask, can you deny it?"

She delayed the reply, but was too honest to withhold it. "I cannot," she whispered.

"I know you cannot. But he stole in in my absence and robbed me. Why didn't he win you away before, when nobody would have been grieved?—when nobody would have been set tale-bearing. Now the people sneer at me—the very hills and sky seem to laugh at me till I blush shamefully for my folly. I have lost my respect, my good name, my standing—lost it, never to get it again. Go and marry your man—go on!"

"O sir—Mr. Boldwood!"

"You may as well. I have no further claim upon you. As for me, I had better go somewhere alone, and hide—and pray. I loved a woman once. I am now ashamed. When I am dead they'll say, Miserable love-sick man that he was. Heaven—heaven—if I had got jilted secretly, and the dishonour not known, and my position kept! But no matter, it is gone, and the woman not gained. Shame upon him—shame!"

His unreasonable anger terrified her, and she glided from him, without obviously moving, as she said, "I am only a girl—do not speak to me so!"

"All the time you knew—how very well you knew—that your new freak was my misery. Dazzled by brass and scarlet—O, Bathsheba—this is woman's folly indeed!"

She fired up at once. "You are taking too much upon yourself!" she said vehemently. "Everybody is upon me—everybody. It is unmanly to attack a woman so! I have nobody in the world to fight my battles for me; but no mercy is shown. Yet if a thousand of you sneer and say things against me, I *will not* be put down!"

"You'll chatter with him doubtless about me. Say to him, 'Boldwood would have died for me.' Yes, and you have given way to him, knowing him to be not the man for you. He has kissed you—claimed you as his. Do you hear—he has kissed you. Deny it!"

The most tragic woman is cowed by a tragic man, and although Boldwood was, in vehemence and glow, nearly her own self rendered into another sex, Bathsheba's cheek quivered. She gasped, "Leave me, sir—leave me! I am nothing to you. Let me go on!"

"Deny that he has kissed you."

"I shall not."

"Ha—then he has!" came hoarsely from the farmer.

"He has," she said slowly, and, in spite of her fear, defiantly. "I am not ashamed to speak the truth."

"Then curse him; and curse him!" said Boldwood, breaking into a whispered fury. "Whilst I would have given worlds to touch your hand, you have let a rake come in without right or ceremony and—kiss you! Heaven's mercy—kiss you! . . . Ah, a time of his life shall come when he will have to repent, and think wretchedly of the pain he has caused another man; and then may he ache, and wish, and curse, and yearn—as I do now!"

"Don't, don't, O don't pray down evil upon him!" she implored in a miserable cry. "Anything but that—anything. O, be kind to him, sir, for I love him true!"

Boldwood's ideas had reached that point of fusion at which outline and consistency entirely disappear. The impending night appeared to concentrate in his eye. He did not hear her at all now.

"I'll punish him—by my soul, that will I! I'll meet him, soldier or no, and I'll horsewhip the untimely stripling for this reckless theft of my one delight. If he were a hundred men I'd horsewhip him—" He dropped his voice suddenly and unnaturally. "Bathsheba, sweet, lost coquette, pardon me! I've been blaming you, threatening you, behaving like a churl to you, when he's the greatest sinner. He stole your dear heart away with his unfathomable lies! . . . It is a fortunate thing for him that he's gone back to his regiment—that he's away up the country, and not here! I hope he may not return here just yet. I pray God he may not come into my sight, for I may be tempted beyond myself. O, Bathsheba, keep him away—yes, keep him away from me!"

For a moment Boldwood stood so inertly after this that his soul seemed to have been entirely exhaled with the breath of his passionate words. He turned his face away, and withdrew, and his form was soon covered over by the twilight as his footsteps mixed in with the low hiss of the leafy trees.

Bathsheba, who had been standing motionless as a model all this latter time, flung her hands to her face, and wildly attempted to ponder on the exhibition which had just passed away. Such astounding wells of fevered feeling in a still man like Mr. Boldwood were incomprehensible, dreadful. Instead of being a man trained to repression he was—what she had seen him.

The force of the farmer's threats lay in their relation to a circumstance known at present only to herself: her lover was coming back to Weatherbury in the course of the very next day or two. Troy had not returned to his distant barracks as Boldwood and others supposed, but had merely gone to visit some acquaintance in Bath, and had yet a week or more remaining to his furlough.

She felt wretchedly certain that if he revisited her just at this nick of time, and came into contact with Boldwood, a fierce quarrel would be the consequence. She panted with solicitude when she thought of possible injury to Troy. The least spark would kindle the farmer's swift feelings of rage and jealousy; he would lose his self-mastery as he had this evening; Troy's blitheness might become aggressive; it might take the direction of derision, and Boldwood's anger might then take the direction of revenge.

With almost a morbid dread of being thought a gushing girl, this guileless woman too well concealed from the world under a manner of carelessness the warm depths of her strong emotions. But now there was no reserve. In her distraction, instead of advancing further she walked up and down, beating the air with her fingers, pressing on her brow, and sobbing brokenly to herself. Then she sat down on a heap of stones by the wayside to think. There she remained long. Above the dark margin of the earth appeared foreshores and promontories of coppery cloud, bounding a green and pellucid expanse in the western sky. Amaranthine glosses came over them then, and the unresting world wheeled her round to a contrasting prospect eastward, in the shape of indecisive and palpitating stars. She gazed upon their silent throes amid the shades of space, but realised none at all. Her troubled spirit was far away with Troy.

XXXII

NIGHT—HORSES TRAMPING

THE VILLAGE OF WEATHERBURY WAS QUIET AS THE GRAVEYARD IN ITS MIDST, AND THE living were lying well-nigh as still as the dead. The church clock struck eleven. The air was so empty of other sounds that the whirr of the clock-work immediately before the strokes was distinct, and so was also the click of the same at their close. The notes flew forth with the usual blind obtuseness of inanimate things—flapping and rebounding among walls, undulating against the scattered clouds, spreading through their interstices into unexplored miles of space.

Bathsheba's crannied and mouldy halls were to-night occupied only by Maryann, Liddy being, as was stated, with her sister, whom Bathsheba had set out to visit. A few minutes after eleven had struck, Maryann turned in her bed with a sense of being disturbed. She was totally unconscious of the nature of the interruption to her sleep. It led to a dream, and the dream to an awakening, with an uneasy sensation that something had happened. She left her bed and looked out of the window. The paddock abutted on this end of the building, and in the paddock she could just discern by the uncertain grey a moving figure approaching the horse that was feeding there. The figure seized the horse by the forelock, and led it to the corner of the field. Here she could see some object which circumstances proved to be a vehicle, for after a few minutes spent apparently in harnessing, she heard the trot of the horse down the road, mingled with the sound of light wheels.

Two varieties only of humanity could have entered the paddock with the ghostlike glide of that mysterious figure. They were a woman and a gipsy man. A woman was out of the question in such an occupation at this hour, and the comer could be no less than a thief, who might probably have known the weakness of the household on this particular night, and have chosen it on that account for his daring attempt. Moreover, to raise suspicion to conviction itself, there were gipsies in Weatherbury Bottom.

Maryann, who had been afraid to shout in the robber's presence, having seen him depart had no fear. She hastily slipped on her clothes, stumped down the disjointed staircase with its hundred creaks, ran to Coggan's, the nearest house, and raised an alarm. Coggan called Gabriel, who now again lodged in his house as at first, and together they went to the paddock. Beyond all doubt the horse was gone.

"Hark!" said Gabriel.

They listened. Distinct upon the stagnant air came the sounds of a trotting horse passing up Longpuddle Lane—just beyond the gipsies' encampment in Weatherbury Bottom.

"That's our Dainty—I'll swear to her step," said Jan.

"Mighty me! Won't mis'ess storm and call us stupids when she comes back!" moaned Maryann. "How I wish it had happened when she was at home, and none of us had been answerable!"

"We must ride after," said Gabriel decisively. "I'll be responsible to Miss Everdene for what we do. Yes, we'll follow."

"Faith, I don't see how," said Coggan. "All our horses are too heavy for that trick except little Poppet, and what's she between two of us?—If we only had that pair over the hedge we might do something."

"Which pair?"

"Mr. Boldwood's Tidy and Moll."

"Then wait here till I come hither again," said Gabriel. He ran down the hill towards Farmer Boldwood's.

"Farmer Boldwood is not at home," said Maryann.

"All the better," said Coggan. "I know what he's gone for."

Less than five minutes brought up Oak again, running at the same pace, with two halters dangling from his hand.

"Where did you find 'em?" said Coggan, turning round and leaping upon the hedge without waiting for an answer.

"Under the eaves. I knew where they were kept," said Gabriel, following him. "Coggan, you can ride bare-backed? there's no time to look for saddles."

"Like a hero!" said Jan.

"Maryann, you go to bed," Gabriel shouted to her from the top of the hedge.

Springing down into Boldwood's pastures, each pocketed his halter to hide it from the horses, who, seeing the men empty-handed, docilely allowed themselves to be seized by the mane, when the halters were dexterously slipped on. Having neither bit nor bridle, Oak and Coggan extemporised the former by passing the rope in each case through the animal's mouth and looping it on the other side. Oak vaulted astride, and Coggan clambered up by aid of the bank, when they ascended to the gate and galloped off in the direction taken by Bathsheba's horse and the robber. Whose vehicle the horse had been harnessed to was a matter of some uncertainty.

Weatherbury Bottom was reached in three or four minutes. They scanned the shady green patch by the roadside. The gipsies were gone.

"The villains!" said Gabriel. "Which way have they gone, I wonder?"

"Straight on, as sure as God made little apples," said Jan.

"Very well; we are better mounted, and must overtake em," said Oak. "Now, on at full speed!"

No sound of the rider in their van could now be discovered. The road-metal grew softer and more clayey as Weatherbury was left behind, and the late rain had wetted its surface to a somewhat plastic, but not muddy state. They came to cross-roads. Coggan suddenly pulled up Moll and slipped off.

"What's the matter?" said Gabriel.

"We must try to track 'em, since we can't hear 'em," said Jan, fumbling in his pockets. He struck a light, and held the match to the ground. The rain had been heavier here, and all foot and horse tracks made previous to the storm had been abraded and blurred by the drops, and they were now so many little scoops of water, which reflected the flame of the match like eyes. One set of tracks was fresh and had no water in them; one pair of ruts was also empty, and not small canals, like the others. The footprints forming this recent impression were full of information as to pace; they were in equidistant pairs, three or four feet apart, the right and left foot of each pair being exactly opposite one another.

"Straight on!" Jan exclaimed. "Tracks like that mean a stiff gallop. No wonder we don't hear him. And the horse is harnessed—look at the ruts. Ay, that's our mare, sure enough!"

"How do you know?"

"Old Jimmy Harris only shoed her last week, and I'd swear to his make among ten thousand."

"The rest of the gipsies must ha' gone on earlier or some other way," said Oak. "You saw there were no other tracks?"

"True." They rode along silently for a long weary time. Coggan carried an old pinch-beck repeater which he had inherited from some genius in his family; and it now struck one. He lighted another match, and examined the ground again.

" 'Tis a canter now," he said, throwing away the light. "A twisty, rickety pace for a gig. The fact is, they overdrove her at starting; we shall catch 'em yet."

Again they hastened on, and entered Blackmore Vale. Coggan's watch struck one. When they looked again the hoof-marks were so spaced as to form a sort of zigzag if united, like the lamps along a street.

"That's a trot, I know," said Gabriel.

"Only a trot now," said Coggan cheerfully. "We shall overtake him in time."

They pushed rapidly on for yet two or three miles. "Ah! a moment," said Jan. "Let's see how she was driven up this hill. 'Twill help us." A light was promptly struck upon his gaiters as before, and the examination made.

"Hurrah!" said Coggan. "She walked up here—and well she might. We shall get them in two miles, for a crown."

They rode three, and listened. No sound was to be heard save a mill-pond trickling hoarsely through a hatch, and suggesting gloomy possibilities of drowning by jumping in. Gabriel dismounted when they came to a turning. The tracks were absolutely the only guide as to the direction that they now had, and great caution was necessary to avoid confusing them with some others which had made their appearance lately.

"What does this mean?—though I guess," said Gabriel, looking up at Coggan as he moved the match over the ground about the turning. Coggan, who, no less than the panting horses, had latterly shown signs of weariness, again scrutinised the mystic characters. This time only three were of the regular horseshoe shape. Every fourth was a dot.

He screwed up his face and emitted a long "whew-w-w!"

"Lame," said Oak.

"Yes. Dainty is lamed; the near-foot-afore," said Coggan slowly, staring still at the footprints.

"We'll push on," said Gabriel, remounting his humid steed.

Although the road along its greater part had been as good as any turnpike road in the country, it was nominally only a byway. The last turning had brought them into the high-road leading to Bath. Coggan recollected himself.

"We shall have him now!" he exclaimed.

"Where?"

"Sherton Turnpike. The keeper of that gate is the sleepiest man between here and London—Dan Randall, that's his name—knowed en for years, when he was at Caster-bridge gate. Between the lameness and the gate 'tis a done job."

They now advanced with extreme caution. Nothing was said until, against a shady background of foliage, five white bars were visible, crossing their route a little way ahead.

"Hush—we are almost close!" said Gabriel.

"Amble on upon the grass," said Coggan.

The white bars were blotted out in the midst by a dark shape in front of them. The silence of this lonely time was pierced by an exclamation from that quarter.

"Hoy-a-hoy! Gate!"

It appeared that there had been a previous call which they had not noticed, for on their close approach the door of the turnpike-house opened, and the keeper came out half-dressed, with a candle in his hand. The rays illumined the whole group.

"Keep the gate close!" shouted Gabriel. "He has stolen the horse!"

"Who?" said the turnpike-man.

Gabriel looked at the driver of the gig, and saw a woman—Bathsheba, his mistress.

On hearing his voice she had turned her face away from the light. Coggan had, however, caught sight of her in the meanwhile.

"Why, 'tis mistress—I'll take my oath!" he said, amazed.

Bathsheba it certainly was, and she had by this time done the trick she could do so well in crises not of love, namely, mask a surprise by coolness of manner.

"Well, Gabriel," she enquired quietly, "where are you going?"

"We thought—" began Gabriel.

"I am driving to Bath," she said, taking for her own use the assurance that Gabriel lacked. "An important matter made it necessary for me to give up my visit to Liddy, and go off at once. What, then, were you following me?"

"We thought the horse was stole."

"Well—what a thing! How very foolish of you not to know that I had taken the trap and horse. I could neither wake Maryann nor get into the house, though I hammered for ten minutes against her window-sill. Fortunately, I could get the key of the coach-house, so I troubled no one further. Didn't you think it might be me?"

"Why should we, miss?"

"Perhaps not. Why, those are never Farmer Boldwood's horses! Goodness mercy! what have you been doing—bringing trouble upon me in this way? What! mustn't a lady move an inch from her door without being dogged like a thief?"

"But how was we to know, if you left no account of your doings?" expostulated Coggan, "and ladies don't drive at these hours, miss, as a jineral rule of society."

"I did leave an account—and you would have seen it in the morning. I wrote in chalk on the coach-house doors that I had come back for the horse and gig, and driven off; that I could arouse nobody, and should return soon."

"But you'll consider, ma'am, that we couldn't see that till it got daylight."

"True," she said, and though vexed at first she had too much sense to blame them long or seriously for a devotion to her that was as valuable as it was rare. She added with a very pretty grace, "Well, I really thank you heartily for taking all this trouble; but I wish you had borrowed anybody's horses but Mr. Boldwood's."

"Dainty is lame, miss," said Coggan. "Can ye go on?"

"It was only a stone in her shoe. I got down and pulled it out a hundred yards back. I can manage very well, thank you. I shall be in Bath by daylight. Will you now return, please?"

She turned her head—the gateman's candle shimmering upon her quick, clear eyes as she did so—passed through the gate, and was soon wrapped in the embowering shades of mysterious summer boughs. Coggan and Gabriel put about their horses, and, fanned by the velvety air of this July night, retraced the road by which they had come.

"A strange vagary, this of hers, isn't it, Oak?" said Coggan curiously.

"Yes," said Gabriel shortly.

"She won't be in Bath by no daylight!"

"Coggan, suppose we keep this night's work as quiet as we can?"

"I am of one and the same mind."

"Very well. We shall be home by three o'clock or so, and can creep into the parish like lambs."

Bathsheba's perturbed meditations by the roadside had ultimately evolved a conclusion that there were only two remedies for the present desperate state of affairs. The first was merely to keep Troy away from Weatherbury till Boldwood's indignation had cooled; the second to listen to Oak's entreaties, and Boldwood's denunciations, and give up Troy altogether.

Alas! Could she give up this new love—induce him to renounce her by saying she did not like him—could no more speak to him, and beg him, for her good, to end his furlough in Bath, and see her and Weatherbury no more?

It was a picture full of misery, but for a while she contemplated it firmly, allowing herself, nevertheless, as girls will, to dwell upon the happy life she would have enjoyed had Troy been Boldwood, and the path of love the path of duty—inflicting upon herself gratuitous tortures by imagining him the lover of another woman after forgetting her; for she had penetrated Troy's nature so far as to estimate his tendencies pretty accurately, but unfortunately loved him no less in thinking that he might soon cease to love her—indeed, considerably more.

She jumped to her feet. She would see him at once. Yes, she would implore him by word of mouth to assist her in this dilemma. A letter to keep him away could not reach him in time, even if he should be disposed to listen to it.

Was Bathsheba altogether blind to the obvious fact that the support of a lover's arms is not of a kind best calculated to assist a resolve to renounce him? Or was she sophistically sensible, with a thrill of pleasure, that by adopting this course for getting rid of him she was ensuring a meeting with him, at any rate, once more?

It was now dark, and the hour must have been nearly ten. The only way to accomplish her purpose was to give up her idea of visiting Liddy at Yalbury, return to Weatherbury Farm, put the horse into the gig, and drive at once to Bath. The scheme seemed at first impossible: the journey was a fearfully heavy one, even for a strong horse, at her own estimate; and she much underrated the distance. It was most venturesome for a woman, at night, and alone.

But could she go on to Liddy's and leave things to take their course? No, no; anything but that. Bathsheba was full of a stimulating turbulence, beside which caution vainly prayed for a hearing. She turned back towards the village.

Her walk was slow, for she wished not to enter Weatherbury till the cottagers were in bed, and, particularly, till Boldwood was secure. Her plan was now to drive to Bath during the night, see Sergeant Troy in the morning before he set out to come to her, bid him farewell, and dismiss him: then to rest the horse thoroughly (herself to weep the while, she thought), starting early the next morning on her return journey. By this arrangement she could trot Dainty gently all the day, reach Liddy at Yalbury in the evening, and come home to Weatherbury with her whenever they chose—so nobody would know she had been to Bath at all.

Such was Bathsheba's scheme. But in her topographical ignorance as a late comer to the place, she misreckoned the distance of her journey as not much more than half what it really was. Her idea, however, she proceeded to carry out, with what initial success we have already seen.

XXXIII

IN THE SUN—A HARBINGER

A WEEK PASSED, AND THERE WERE NO TIDINGS OF BATHSHEBA; NOR WAS THERE ANY EXplanation of her Gilpin's rig.

Then a note came for Maryann, stating that the business which had called her mistress to Bath still detained her there; but that she hoped to return in the course of another week.

Another week passed. The oat-harvest began, and all the men were a-field under a monochromatic Lammas sky, amid the trembling air and short shadows of noon. Indoors nothing was to be heard save the droning of blue-bottle flies; out-of-doors the whetting of scythes and the hiss of tressy oat-ears rubbing together as their perpendicular stalks of amber-yellow fell heavily to each swath. Every drop of moisture not in the men's bottles and flagons in the form of cider was raining as perspiration from their foreheads and cheeks. Drought was everywhere else.

They were about to withdraw for a while into the charitable shade of a tree in the fence, when Coggan saw a figure in a blue coat and brass buttons running to them across the field.

"I wonder who that is?" he said.

"I hope nothing is wrong about mistress," said Maryann, who with some other women was tying the bundles (oats being always sheafed on this farm), "but an unlucky token came to me indoors this morning. I went to unlock the door and dropped the key, and it fell upon the stone floor and broke into two pieces. Breaking a key is a dreadful bodement. I wish mis'ess was home."

" 'Tis Cain Ball," said Gabriel, pausing from whetting his reaphook.

Oak was not bound by his agreement to assist in the corn-field; but the harvest month is an anxious time for a farmer, and the corn was Bathsheba's, so he lent a hand.

"He's dressed up in his best clothes," said Matthew Moon. "He hev been away from home for a few days, since he's had that felon upon his finger; for 'a said, since I can't work I'll have a hollerday."

"A good time for one—a' excellent time," said Joseph Poorgrass, straightening his back; for he, like some of the others, had a way of resting a while from his labour on such hot days for reasons preternaturally small; of which Cain Ball's advent on a week-day in his Sunday-clothes was one of the first magnitude. " 'Twas a bad leg allowed me to read the *Pilgrim's Progress*, and Mark Clark learnt All-Fours in a whitlow."

"Ay, and my father put his arm out of joint to have time to go courting," said Jan Coggan, in an eclipsing tone, wiping his face with his shirt-sleeve and thrusting back his hat upon the nape of his neck.

By this time Cainy was nearing the group of harvesters, and was perceived to be carrying a large slice of bread and ham in one hand, from which he took mouthfuls as he ran, the other being wrapped in a bandage. When he came close, his mouth assumed the bell shape, and he began to cough violently.

"Now, Cainy!" said Gabriel, sternly. "How many more times must I tell you to keep from running so fast when you be eating? You'll choke yourself some day, that's what you'll do, Cain Ball."

"Hok-hok-hok!" replied Cain. "A crumb of my victuals went the wrong way—hok-hok! That's what 'tis, Mister Oak! And I've been visiting to Bath because I had a felon on my thumb; yes, and I've seen—ahok-hok!"

Directly Cain mentioned Bath, they all threw down their hooks and forks and drew round him. Unfortunately the erratic crumb did not improve his narrative powers, and a supplementary hindrance was that of a sneeze, jerking from his pocket his rather large watch, which dangled in front of the young man pendulum-wise.

"Yes," he continued, directing his thoughts to Bath and letting his eyes follow, "I've seed the world at last—yes—and I've seed our mis'ess—ahok-hok-hok!"

"Bother the boy!" said Gabriel. "Something is always going the wrong way down your throat, so that you can't tell what's necessary to be told."

"Ahok! there! Please, Mister Oak, a gnat have just fleed into my stomach and brought the cough on again!"

"Yes, that's just it. Your mouth is always open, you young rascal!"

" 'Tis terrible bad to have a gnat fly down yer throat, pore boy!" said Matthew Moon.

"Well, at Bath you saw—" prompted Gabriel.

"I saw our mistress," continued the junior shepherd, "and a sojer, walking along. And bymeby they got closer and closer, and then they went arm-in-crook, like courting complete—hok-hok! like courting complete—hok!—courting complete—" Losing the thread of his narrative at this point simultaneously with his loss of breath, their informant looked up and down the field apparently for some clue to it. "Well, I see our mis'ess and a soldier—a-ha-a-wk!"

"Damn the boy!" said Gabriel.

" 'Tis only my manner, Mister Oak, if ye'll excuse it," said Cain Ball, looking reproachfully at Oak, with eyes drenched in their own dew.

"Here's some cider for him—that'll cure his throat," said Jan Coggan, lifting a flagon of cider, pulling out the cork, and applying the hole to Cainy's mouth; Joseph Poorgrass in the meantime beginning to think apprehensively of the serious consequences that would follow Cain Ball's strangulation in his cough, and the history of his Bath adventures dying with him.

"For my poor self, I always say 'please God' afore I do anything," said Joseph, in an unboastful voice; "and so should you, Cain Ball. 'Tis a great safeguard, and might perhaps save you from being choked to death some day."

Mr. Coggan poured the liquor with unstinted liberality at the suffering Cain's circular mouth; half of it running down the side of the flagon, and half of what reached his mouth running down outside his throat, and half of what ran in going the wrong way, and being coughed and sneezed around the persons of the gathered reapers in the form of a cider fog, which for a moment hung in the sunny air like a small exhalation.

"There's a great clumsy sneeze! Why can't ye have better manners, you young dog!" said Coggan, withdrawing the flagon.

"The cider went up my nose!" cried Cainy, as soon as he could speak; "and now 'tis gone down my neck, and into my poor dumb felon, and over my shiny buttons and all my best cloze!"

"The poor lad's cough is terrible onfortunate," said Matthew Moon. "And a great history on hand, too. Bump his back, shepherd."

" 'Tis my nater," mourned Cain. "Mother says I always was so excitable when my feelings were worked up to a point!"

"True, true," said Joseph Poorgrass. "The Balls were always a very excitable family. I knowed the boy's grand-father—a truly nervous and modest man, even to genteel refinery. 'Twas blush, blush with him, almost as much as 'tis with me—not but that 'tis a fault in me!"

"Not at all, Master Poorgrass," said Coggan. " 'Tis a very noble quality in ye."

"Heh-heh! well, I wish to noise nothing abroad—nothing at all," murmured Poorgrass diffidently. "But we be born to things—that's true. Yet I would rather my trifle were hid; though, perhaps, a high nater is a little high, and at my birth all things were possible to my Maker, and he may have begrudged no gifts. . . . But under your bushel, Joseph! under your bushel with 'ee! A strange desire, neighbours, this desire to hide, and no praise due. Yet there is a Sermon on the Mount with a calendar of the blessed at the head, and certain meek men may be named therein."

"Cainy's grand-father was a very clever man," said Matthew Moon. "Invented a' apple-tree out of his own head, which is called by his name to this day—the Early Ball. You know 'em, Jan? A Quarrenden grafted on a Tom Putt, and a Rathe-ripe upon top o' that again. 'Tis trew 'a used to bide about in a public-house wi' a 'ooman in a way he had no business to by rights, but there—'a were a clever man in the sense of the term."

"Now then," said Gabriel impatiently, "what did you see, Cain?"

"I seed our mis'ess go into a sort of a park place, where there's seats, and shrubs and flowers, arm-in-crook with a sojer," continued Cainy firmly, and with a dim sense that his words were very effective as regarded Gabriel's emotions. "And I think the sojer was Sergeant Troy. And they sat there together for more than half an hour, talking moving things, and she once was crying a'most to death. And when they came out her eyes were shining and she was as white as a lily; and they looked into one another's faces, as far gone friendly as a man and woman can be."

Gabriel's features seemed to get thinner. "Well, what did you see besides?"

"Oh, all sorts."

"White as a lily? You are sure 'twas she?"

"Yes."

"Well, what besides?"

"Great glass windows to the shops, and great clouds in the sky, full of rain, and old wooden trees in the country round."

"You stun-poll! What will ye say next?" said Coggan.

"Let en alone," interposed Joseph Poorgrass. "The boy's maning is that the sky and the earth in the kingdom of Bath is not altogether different from ours here. 'Tis for our good to gain knowledge of strange cities, and as such the boy's words should be suffered, so to speak it."

"And the people of Bath," continued Cain, "never need to light their fires except as a luxury, for the water springs up out of the earth ready boiled for use."

" 'Tis true as the light," testified Matthew Moon. "I've heard other navigators say the same thing."

"They drink nothing else there," said Cain, "and seem to enjoy it, to see how they swaller it down."

"Well, it seems a barbarian practice enough to us, but I daresay the natives think nothing o' it," said Matthew.

"And don't victuals spring up as well as drink?" asked Coggan, twirling his eye.

"No—I own to a blot there in Bath—a true blot. God didn't provide 'em with victuals as well as drink, and 'twas a drawback I couldn't get over at all."

"Well, 'tis a curious place, to say the least," observed Moon; "and it must be a curious people that live therein."

"Miss Everdene and the soldier were walking about together, you say?" said Gabriel, returning to the group.

"Ay, and she wore a beautiful gold-colour silk gown, trimmed with black lace, that would have stood alone 'ithout legs inside if required. 'Twas a very winsome sight; and her hair was brushed splendid. And when the sun shone upon the bright gown and his red coat—my! how handsome they looked. You could see 'em all the length of the street."

"And what then?" murmured Gabriel.

"And then I went into Griffin's to hae my boots hobbed, and then I went to Riggs's batty-cake shop, and asked 'em for a penneth of the cheapest and nicest stales, that were all but blue-mouldy, but not quite. And whilst I was chawing 'em down I walked on and seed a clock with a face as big as a baking trendle—"

"But that's nothing to do with mistress!"

"I'm coming to that, if you'll leave me alone, Mister Oak!" remonstrated Cainy. "If you excites me, perhaps you'll bring on my cough, and then I shan't be able to tell ye nothing."

"Yes—let him tell it his own way," said Coggan.

Gabriel settled into a despairing attitude of patience, and Cainy went on:—

"And there were great large houses, and more people all the week long than at Weatherbury club-walking on White Tuesdays. And I went to grand churches and chapels. And how the parson would pray! Yes; he would kneel down and put up his hands together, and make the holy gold rings on his fingers gleam and twinkle in yer eyes, that he'd earned by praying so excellent well!—Ah yes, I wish I lived there."

"Our poor Parson Thirdly can't get no money to buy such rings," said Matthew Moon thoughtfully. "And as good a man as ever walked. I don't believe poor Thirdly have a single one, even of humblest tin or copper. Such a great ornament as they'd be to him on a dull afternoon, when he's up in the pulpit lighted by the wax candles! But 'tis impossible, poor man. Ah, to think how unequal things be."

"Perhaps he's made of different stuff than to wear 'em," said Gabriel grimly. "Well, that's enough of this. Go on, Cainy—quick."

"Oh—and the new style of pa'sons wear moustaches and long beards," continued the illustrious traveller, "and look like Moses and Aaron complete, and make we fokes in the congregation feel all over like the children of Israel."

"A very right feeling—very," said Joseph Poorgrass.

"And there's two religions going on in the nation now—High Church and High Chapel. And, thinks I, I'll play fair; so I went to High Church in the morning, and High Chapel in the afternoon."

"A right and proper boy," said Joseph Poorgrass.

"Well, at High Church they pray singing, and worship all the colours of the rainbow; and at High Chapel they pray preaching, and worship drab and whitewash only. And then—I didn't see no more of Miss Everdene at all."

"Why didn't you say so afore, then?" exclaimed Oak, with much disappointment.

"Ah," said Matthew Moon, "she'll wish her cake dough if so be she's over intimate with that man."

"She's not over intimate with him," said Gabriel indignantly.

"She would know better," said Coggan. "Our mis'ess has too much sense under they knots of black hair to do such a mad thing."

"You see, he's not a coarse, ignorant man, for he was well brought up," said Matthew dubiously. " 'Twas only wildness that made him a soldier, and maids rather like your man of sin."

"Now, Cain Ball," said Gabriel restlessly, "can you swear in the most awful form that the woman you saw was Miss Everdene?"

"Cain Ball, you be no longer a babe and suckling," said Joseph in the sepulchral tone the circumstances demanded, "and you know what taking an oath is. 'Tis a horrible testament mind ye, which you say and seal with your blood-stone, and the prophet Matthew tells us that on whomsoever it shall fall it will grind him to powder. Now, before all the work-folk here assembled, can you swear to your words as the shepherd asks ye?"

"Please no, Mister Oak!" said Cainy, looking from one to the other with great uneasiness at the spiritual magnitude of the position. "I don't mind saying 'tis true, but I don't like to say 'tis damn true, if that's what you mane."

"Cain, Cain, how can you!" asked Joseph sternly. "You be asked to swear in a holy manner, and you swear like wicked Shimei, the son of Gera, who cursed as he came. Young man, fie!"

"No, I don't! 'Tis you want to squander a pore boy's soul, Joseph Poorgrass—that's what 'tis!" said Cain, beginning to cry. "All I mane is that in common truth 'twas Miss Everdene and Sergeant Troy, but in the horrible so-help-me truth that ye want to make of it perhaps 'twas somebody else!"

"There's no getting at the rights of it," said Gabriel, turning to his work.

"Cain Ball, you'll come to a bit of bread!" groaned Joseph Poorgrass.

Then the reapers' hooks were flourished again, and the old sounds went on. Gabriel, without making any pretence of being lively, did nothing to show that he was particularly dull. However, Coggan knew pretty nearly how the land lay, and when they were in a nook together he said—

"Don't take on about her, Gabriel. What difference does it make whose sweetheart she is, since she can't be yours?"

"That's the very thing I say to myself," said Gabriel.

XXXIV

Home Again—A Trickster

THAT SAME EVENING AT DUSK GABRIEL WAS LEANING OVER COGGAN'S GARDEN GATE, taking an up-and-down survey before retiring to rest.

A vehicle of some kind was softly creeping along the grassy margin of the lane. From it spread the tones of two women talking. The tones were natural and not at all suppressed. Oak instantly knew the voices to be those of Bathsheba and Liddy.

The carriage came opposite and passed by. It was Miss Everdene's gig, and Liddy and her mistress were the only occupants of the seat. Liddy was asking questions about the city of Bath, and her companion was answering them listlessly and unconcernedly. Both Bathsheba and the horse seemed weary.

The exquisite relief of finding that she was here again, safe and sound, overpowered all reflection, and Oak could only luxuriate in the sense of it. All grave reports were forgotten.

He lingered and lingered on, till there was no difference between the eastern and western expanses of sky, and the timid hares began to limp courageously round the dim hillocks. Gabriel might have been there an additional half-hour when a dark form walked slowly by. "Good-night, Gabriel," the passer said.

It was Boldwood. "Good-night, sir," said Gabriel.

Boldwood likewise vanished up the road, and Oak shortly afterwards turned indoors to bed.

Farmer Boldwood went on towards Miss Everdene's house. He reached the front, and approaching the entrance, saw a light in the parlour. The blind was not drawn down, and inside the room was Bathsheba, looking over some papers or letters. Her back was towards Boldwood. He went to the door, knocked, and waited with tense muscles and an aching brow.

Boldwood had not been outside his garden since his meeting with Bathsheba in the road to Yalbury. Silent and alone, he had remained in moody meditation on woman's ways, deeming as essentials of the whole sex the accidents of the single one of their number he had ever closely beheld. By degrees a more charitable temper had pervaded him, and this was the reason of his sally to-night. He had come to apologise and beg forgiveness of Bathsheba with something like a sense of shame at his violence, having but just now learnt that she had returned—only from a visit to Liddy, as he supposed, the Bath escapade being quite unknown to him.

He enquired for Miss Everdene. Liddy's manner was odd, but he did not notice it. She went in, leaving him standing there, and in her absence the blind of the room containing Bathsheba was pulled down. Boldwood augured ill from that sign. Liddy came out.

"My mistress cannot see you, sir," she said.

The farmer instantly went out by the gate. He was unforgiven—that was the issue of it all. He had seen her who was to him simultaneously a delight and a torture, sitting in the room he had shared with her as a peculiarly privileged guest only a little earlier in the summer, and she had denied him an entrance there now.

Boldwood did not hurry homeward. It was ten o'clock at least, when, walking deliberately through the lower part of Weatherbury, he heard the carrier's spring van entering the village. The van ran to and from a town in a northern direction, and it was owned and driven by a Weatherbury man, at the door of whose house it now pulled up. The lamp fixed to the head of the hood illuminated a scarlet and gilded form, who was the first to alight.

"Ah!" said Boldwood to himself, "come to see her again."

Troy entered the carrier's house, which had been the place of his lodging on his last visit to his native place. Boldwood was moved by a sudden determination. He hastened home. In ten minutes he was back again, and made as if he were going to call upon Troy at the carrier's. But as he approached, someone opened the door and came out. He heard this person say "Good-night" to the inmates, and the voice was Troy's. This was strange, coming so immediately after his arrival. Boldwood, however, hastened up to him. Troy had what appeared to be a carpet-bag in his hand—the same that he had brought with him. It seemed as if he were going to leave again this very night.

Troy turned up the hill and quickened his pace. Boldwood stepped forward.

"Sergeant Troy?"

"Yes—I'm Sergeant Troy."

"Just arrived from up the country, I think?"

"Just arrived from Bath."

"I am William Boldwood."

"Indeed."

The tone in which this word was uttered was all that had been wanted to bring Boldwood to the point.

"I wish to speak a word with you," he said.

"What about?"

"About her who lives just ahead there—and about a woman you have wronged."

"I wonder at your impertinence," said Troy, moving on.

"Now look here," said Boldwood, standing in front of him, "wonder or not, you are going to hold a conversation with me."

Troy heard the dull determination in Boldwood's voice, looked at his stalwart frame, then at the thick cudgel he carried in his hand. He remembered it was past ten o'clock. It seemed worthwhile to be civil to Boldwood.

"Very well, I'll listen with pleasure," said Troy, placing his bag on the ground, "only speak low, for somebody or other may overhear us in the farmhouse there."

"Well then—I know a good deal concerning your—Fanny Robin's attachment to you. I may say, too, that I believe I am the only person in the village, excepting Gabriel Oak, who does know it. You ought to marry her."

"I suppose I ought. Indeed, I wish to, but I cannot."

"Why?"

Troy was about to utter something hastily; he then checked himself and said, "I am too poor." His voice was changed. Previously it had had a devil-may-care tone. It was the voice of a trickster now.

Boldwood's present mood was not critical enough to notice tones. He continued, "I may as well speak plainly; and understand, I don't wish to enter into the questions of right or wrong, woman's honour and shame, or to express any opinion on your conduct. I intend a business transaction with you."

"I see," said Troy. "Suppose we sit down here."

An old tree trunk lay under the hedge immediately opposite, and they sat down.

"I was engaged to be married to Miss Everdene," said Boldwood, "but you came and—"

"Not engaged," said Troy.

"As good as engaged."

"If I had not turned up she might have become engaged to you."

"Hang might!"

"Would, then."

"If you had not come I should certainly—yes, *certainly*—have been accepted by this time. If you had not seen her you might have been married to Fanny. Well, there's too much difference between Miss Everdene's station and your own for this flirtation with her ever to benefit you by ending in marriage. So all I ask is, don't molest her any more. Marry Fanny. I'll make it worth your while."

"How will you?"

"I'll pay you well now, I'll settle a sum of money upon her, and I'll see that you don't suffer from poverty in the future. I'll put it clearly. Bathsheba is only playing with you: you are too poor for her as I said; so give up wasting your time about a great match you'll never make for a moderate and rightful match you may make to-morrow; take up your carpet-bag, turn about, leave Weatherbury now, this night, and you shall take fifty pounds with you. Fanny shall have fifty to enable her to prepare for the wedding, when you have told me where she is living, and she shall have five hundred paid down on her wedding-day."

In making this statement Boldwood's voice revealed only too clearly a consciousness of the weakness of his position, his aims, and his method. His manner had lapsed quite from that of the firm and dignified Boldwood of former times; and such a scheme as he had now engaged in he would have condemned as childishly imbecile only a few months ago. We discern a grand force in the lover which he lacks whilst a free man; but there is a breadth of vision in the free man which in the lover we vainly seek. Where there is much bias there must be some narrowness, and love, though added emotion, is subtracted capacity. Boldwood exemplified this to an abnormal degree: he knew nothing of Fanny Robin's circumstances or whereabouts, he knew nothing of Troy's possibilities, yet that was what he said.

"I like Fanny best," said Troy; "and if, as you say, Miss Everdene is out of my reach, why I have all to gain by accepting your money, and marrying Fan. But she's only a servant."

"Never mind—do you agree to my arrangement?"

"I do."

"Ah!" said Boldwood, in a more elastic voice. "O, Troy, if you like her best, why then did you step in here and injure my happiness?"

"I love Fanny best now," said Troy. "But Bathsh—Miss Everdene inflamed me, and displaced Fanny for a time. It is over now."

"Why should it be over so soon? And why then did you come here again?"

"There are weighty reasons. Fifty pounds at once, you said!"

"I did," said Boldwood, "and here they are—fifty sovereigns." He handed Troy a small packet.

"You have everything ready—it seems that you calculated on my accepting them," said the sergeant, taking the packet.

"I thought you might accept them," said Boldwood.

"You've only my word that the programme shall be adhered to, whilst I at any rate have fifty pounds."

"I had thought of that, and I have considered that if I can't appeal to your honour I can trust to your—well, shrewdness we'll call it—not to lose five hundred pounds in prospect, and also make a bitter enemy of a man who is willing to be an extremely useful friend."

"Stop, listen!" said Troy in a whisper.

A light pit-pat was audible upon the road just above them.

"By George—'tis she," he continued. "I must go on and meet her."

"She—who?"

"Bathsheba."

"Bathsheba—out alone at this time o' night!" said Boldwood in amazement, and starting up. "Why must you meet her?"

"She was expecting me to-night—and I must now speak to her, and wish her good-bye, according to your wish."

"I don't see the necessity of speaking."

"It can do no harm—and she'll be wandering about looking for me if I don't. You shall hear all I say to her. It will help you in your love-making when I am gone."

"Your tone is mocking."

"O no. And remember this, if she does not know what has become of me, she will think more about me than if I tell her flatly I have come to give her up."

"Will you confine your words to that one point?—Shall I hear every word you say?"

"Every word. Now sit still there, and hold my carpet-bag for me, and mark what you hear."

The light footstep came closer, halting occasionally, as if the walker listened for a sound. Troy whistled a double note in a soft, fluty tone.

"Come to that, is it!" murmured Boldwood uneasily.

"You promised silence," said Troy.

"I promise again."

Troy stepped forward.

"Frank, dearest, is that you?" The tones were Bathsheba's.

"O God!" said Boldwood.

"Yes," said Troy to her.

"How late you are," she continued tenderly. "Did you come by the carrier? I listened and heard his wheels entering the village, but it was some time ago, and I had almost given you up, Frank."

"I was sure to come," said Frank. "You knew I should, did you not?"

"Well, I thought you would," she said playfully; "and, Frank, it is so lucky! There's not a soul in my house but me to-night. I've packed them all off, so nobody on earth will know of your visit to your lady's bower. Liddy wanted to go to her grand-father's to tell him about her holiday, and I said she might stay with them till to-morrow—when you'll be gone again."

"Capital," said Troy. "But, dear me, I had better go back for my bag, because my slippers and brush and comb are in it; you run home whilst I fetch it, and I'll promise to be in your parlour in ten minutes."

"Yes." She turned and tripped up the hill again.

During the progress of this dialogue there was a nervous twitching of Boldwood's tightly closed lips, and his face became bathed in a clammy dew. He now started forward towards Troy. Troy turned to him and took up the bag.

"Shall I tell her I have come to give her up and cannot marry her?" said the soldier mockingly.

"No, no; wait a minute. I want to say more to you—more to you!" said Boldwood, in a hoarse whisper.

"Now," said Troy, "you see my dilemma. Perhaps I am a bad man—the victim of my impulses—led away to do what I ought to leave undone. I can't, however, marry them both. And I have two reasons for choosing Fanny. First, I like her best upon the whole, and second, you make it worth my while."

At the same instant Boldwood sprang upon him, and held him by the neck. Troy felt Boldwood's grasp slowly tightening. The move was absolutely unexpected.

"A moment," he gasped. "You are injuring her you love!"

"Well, what do you mean?" said the farmer.

"Give me breath," said Troy.

Boldwood loosened his hand, saying, "By Heaven, I've a mind to kill you!"

"And ruin her."

"Save her."

"Oh, how can she be saved now, unless I marry her?"

Boldwood groaned. He reluctantly released the soldier, and flung him back against the hedge. "Devil, you torture me!" said he.

Troy rebounded like a ball, and was about to make a dash at the farmer; but he checked himself, saying lightly—

"It is not worthwhile to measure my strength with you. Indeed it is a barbarous way of settling a quarrel. I shall shortly leave the army because of the same conviction. Now after that revelation of how the land lies with Bathsheba, 'twould be a mistake to kill me, would it not?"

" 'Twould be a mistake to kill you," repeated Boldwood, mechanically, with a bowed head.

"Better kill yourself."

"Far better."

"I'm glad you see it."

"Troy, make her your wife, and don't act upon what I arranged just now. The alternative is dreadful, but take Bathsheba; I give her up! She must love you indeed to sell soul and body to you so utterly as she has done. Wretched woman—deluded woman—you are, Bathsheba!"

"But about Fanny?"

"Bathsheba is a woman well-to-do," continued Boldwood, in nervous anxiety, "and, Troy, she will make a good wife; and, indeed, she is worth your hastening on your marriage with her!"

"But she has a will—not to say a temper, and I shall be a mere slave to her. I could do anything with poor Fanny Robin."

"Troy," said Boldwood imploringly, "I'll do anything for you, only don't desert her; pray don't desert her, Troy."

"Which, poor Fanny?"

"No; Bathsheba Everdene. Love her best! Love her tenderly! How shall I get you to see how advantageous it will be to you to secure her at once?"

"I don't wish to secure her in any new way."

Boldwood's arm moved spasmodically towards Troy's person again. He repressed the instinct, and his form drooped as with pain.

Troy went on—

"I shall soon purchase my discharge, and then—"

"But I wish you to hasten on this marriage! It will be better for you both. You love each other, and you must let me help you to do it."

"How?"

"Why, by settling the five hundred on Bathsheba instead of Fanny, to enable you to marry at once. No; she wouldn't have it of me. I'll pay it down to you on the wedding-day."

Troy paused in secret amazement at Boldwood's wild infatuation. He carelessly said, "And am I to have anything now?"

"Yes, if you wish to. But I have not much additional money with me. I did not expect this; but all I have is yours."

Boldwood, more like a somnambulist than a wakeful man, pulled out the large canvas bag he carried by way of a purse, and searched it.

"I have twenty-one pounds more with me," he said. "Two notes and a sovereign. But before I leave you I must have a paper signed—"

"Pay me the money, and we'll go straight to her parlour, and make any arrangement you please to secure my compliance with your wishes. But she must know nothing of this cash business."

"Nothing, nothing," said Boldwood, hastily. "Here is the sum, and if you'll come to my house we'll write out the agreement for the remainder, and the terms also."

"First we'll call upon her."

"But why? Come with me to-night, and go with me to-morrow to the surrogate's."

"But she must be consulted; at any rate informed."

"Very well; go on."

They went up the hill to Bathsheba's house. When they stood at the entrance, Troy said, "Wait here a moment." Opening the door, he glided inside, leaving the door ajar.

Boldwood waited. In two minutes a light appeared in the passage. Boldwood then saw that the chain had been fastened across the door. Troy appeared inside carrying a bedroom candlestick.

"What, did you think I should break in?" said Boldwood contemptuously.

"Oh, no; it is merely my humour to secure things. Will you read this a moment? I'll hold the light."

Troy handed a folded newspaper through the slit between door and doorpost, and put the candle close. "That's the paragraph," he said, placing his finger on a line.

Boldwood looked and read—

MARRIAGES

On the 17th inst., at St. Ambrose's Church, Bath, by the Rev. G. Minc-ing, B.A., Francis Troy, only son of the late Edward Troy, Esq., M.D., of Weatherbury, and sergeant 11th Dragoon Guards, to Bathsheba, only surviving daughter of the late Mr. John Everdene, of Casterbridge.

"This may be called Fort meeting Feeble, hey, Boldwood?" said Troy. A low gurgle of derisive laughter followed the words.

The paper fell from Boldwood's hands. Troy continued—

"Fifty pounds to marry Fanny. Good. Twenty-one pounds not to marry Fanny, but Bath'sheba. Good. Finale: already Bathsheba's husband. Now, Boldwood, yours is the ridiculous fate which always attends interference between a man and his wife. And another word. Bad as I am, I am not such a villain as to make the marriage or misery of any woman a matter of huckster and sale. Fanny has long ago left me. I don't know where she is. I have searched everywhere. Another word yet. You say you love Bathsheba; yet on the merest apparent evidence you instantly believe in her dishonour. A fig for such love! Now that I've taught you a lesson, take your money back again."

"I will not; I will not!" said Boldwood, in a hiss.

"Anyhow I won't have it," said Troy contemptuously. He wrapped the packet of gold in the notes, and threw the whole into the road.

Boldwood shook his clenched fist at him. "You juggler of Satan! You black hound! But I'll punish you yet; mark me, I'll punish you yet!"

Another peal of laughter. Troy then closed the door, and locked himself in.

Throughout the whole of that night Boldwood's dark form might have been seen walking about the hills and downs of Weatherbury like an unhappy Shade in the Mourn-ful Fields by Acheron.

XXXV

AT AN UPPER WINDOW

IT WAS VERY EARLY THE NEXT MORNING—A TIME OF SUN AND DEW. THE CONFUSED BE-ginnings of many birds' songs spread into the healthy air, and the wan blue of the heaven was here and there coated with thin webs of incorporeal cloud which were of no effect in obscuring day. All the lights in the scene were yellow as to colour, and all the shadows were attenuated as to form. The creeping plants about the old manor-house were bowed with rows of heavy water drops, which had upon objects behind them the effect of minute lenses of high magnifying power.

Just before the clock struck five Gabriel Oak and Coggan passed the village cross, and went on together to the fields. They were yet barely in view of their mistress's house, when Oak fancied he saw the opening of a casement in one of the upper windows. The two men were at this moment partially screened by an elder bush, now beginning to be enriched with black bunches of fruit, and they paused before emerging from its shade.

A handsome man leaned idly from the lattice. He looked east and then west, in the manner of one who makes a first morning survey. The man was Sergeant Troy. His red jacket was loosely thrown on, but not buttoned, and he had altogether the relaxed bearing of a soldier taking his ease.

Coggan spoke first, looking quietly at the window.

"She has married him!" he said.

Gabriel had previously beheld the sight, and he now stood with his back turned, making no reply.

"I fancied we should know something to-day," continued Coggan. "I heard wheels pass my door just after dark—you were out somewhere." He glanced round upon Gabriel. "Good heavens above us, Oak, how white your face is; you look like a corpse!"

"Do I?" said Oak, with a faint smile.

"Lean on the gate: I'll wait a bit."

"All right, all right."

They stood by the gate a while, Gabriel listlessly staring at the ground. His mind sped into the future, and saw there enacted in years of leisure the scenes of repentance that would ensue from this work of haste. That they were married he had instantly decided. Why had it been so mysteriously managed? It had become known that she had had a fearful journey to Bath, owing to her miscalculating the distance: that the horse had broken down, and that she had been more than two days getting there. It was not Bathsheba's way to do things furtively. With all her faults she was candour itself. Could she have been entrapped? The union was not only an unutterable grief to him: it amazed him, notwithstanding that he had passed the preceding week in a suspicion that such might be the issue of Troy's meeting her away from home. Her quiet return with Liddy had to some extent dispersed the dread. Just as that imperceptible motion which appears like stillness is infinitely divided in its properties from stillness itself, so had his hope undistinguishable from despair differed from despair indeed.

In a few minutes they moved on again towards the house. The sergeant still looked from the window.

"Morning, comrades!" he shouted, in a cheery voice, when they came up.

Coggan replied to the greeting. "Bain't ye going to answer the man?" he then said to Gabriel. "I'd say good-morning—you needn't spend a hapeth of meaning upon it, and yet keep the man civil."

Gabriel soon decided too that, since the deed was done, to put the best face upon the matter would be the greatest kindness to her he loved.

"Good-morning, Sergeant Troy," he returned, in a ghastly voice.

"A rambling, gloomy house this," said Troy, smiling.

"Why—they *may* not be married!" suggested Coggan. "Perhaps she's not there."

Gabriel shook his head. The soldier turned a little towards the east, and the sun kindled his scarlet coat to an orange glow.

"But it is a nice old house," responded Gabriel.

"Yes—I suppose so; but I feel like new wine in an old bottle here. My notion is that sash-windows should be put throughout, and these old wainscoted walls brightened up a bit; or the oak cleared quite away, and the walls papered."

"It would be a pity, I think."

"Well, no. A philosopher once said in my hearing that the old builders, who worked when art was a living thing, had no respect for the work of builders who went before them, but pulled down and altered as they thought fit; and why shouldn't we? 'Creation and preservation don't do well together,' says he, 'and a million of antiquarians can't invent a style.' My mind exactly. I am for making this place more modern, that we may be cheerful whilst we can."

The military man turned and surveyed the interior of the room, to assist his ideas of improvement in this direction. Gabriel and Coggan began to move on.

"Oh, Coggan," said Troy, as if inspired by a recollection, "do you know if insanity has ever appeared in Mr. Boldwood's family?"

Jan reflected for a moment.

"I once heard that an uncle of his was queer in his head, but I don't know the rights o't," he said.

"It is of no importance," said Troy lightly. "Well, I shall be down in the fields with you some time this week; but I have a few matters to attend to first. So good-day to you. We shall, of course, keep on just as friendly terms as usual. I'm not a proud man: nobody is ever able to say that of Sergeant Troy. However, what is must be, and here's half-a-crown to drink my health, men."

Troy threw the coin dexterously across the front plot and over the fence towards Gabriel, who shunned it in its fall, his face turning to an angry red. Coggan twirled his eye, edged forward, and caught the money in its ricochet upon the road.

"Very well—you keep it, Coggan," said Gabriel with disdain, and almost fiercely. "As for me, I'll do without gifts from him!"

"Don't show it too much," said Coggan musingly. "For if he's married to her, mark my words, he'll buy his discharge and be our master here. Therefore 'tis well to say 'Friend' outwardly, though you say 'Troublehouse' within."

"Well—perhaps it is best to be silent; but I can't go further than that. I can't flatter, and if my place here is only to be kept by smoothing him down, my place must be lost."

A horseman, whom they had for some time seen in the distance, now appeared close beside them.

"There's Mr. Boldwood," said Oak. "I wonder what Troy meant by his question."

Coggan and Oak nodded respectfully to the farmer, just checked their paces to discover if they were wanted, and finding they were not, stood back to let him pass on.

The only signs of the terrible sorrow Boldwood had been combating through the night, and was combating now, were the want of colour in his well-defined face, the enlarged appearance of the veins in his forehead and temples, and the sharper lines about his mouth. The horse bore him away, and the very step of the animal seemed significant of dogged despair. Gabriel, for a minute, rose above his own grief in noticing Boldwood's. He saw the square figure sitting erect upon the horse, the head turned to neither side, the elbows steady by the hips, the brim of the hat level and undisturbed in its onward glide, until the keen edges of Boldwood's shape sank by degrees over the hill. To one who knew the man and his story there was something more striking in this immobility than in a collapse. The clash of discord between mood and matter here was forced painfully home to the heart; and, as in laughter there are more dreadful phases than in tears, so was there in the steadiness of this agonised man an expression deeper than a cry.

XXXVI

WEALTH IN JEOPARDY—THE REVEL

ONE NIGHT, AT THE END OF AUGUST, WHEN BATHSHEBA'S EXPERIENCES AS A MARRIED woman were still new, and when the weather was yet dry and sultry, a man stood motionless in the stackyard of Weatherbury Upper Farm, looking at the moon and sky.

The night had a sinister aspect. A heated breeze from the south slowly fanned the summits of lofty objects, and in the sky dashes of buoyant cloud were sailing in a course at right angles to that of another stratum, neither of them in the direction of the breeze below. The moon, as seen through these films, had a lurid metallic look. The fields were sallow with the impure light, and all were tinged in monochrome, as if beheld through stained glass. The same evening the sheep had trailed homeward head to tail, the behaviour of the rooks had been confused, and the horses had moved with timidity and caution.

Thunder was imminent, and, taking some secondary appearances into consideration, it was likely to be followed by one of the lengthened rains which mark the close of dry weather for the season. Before twelve hours had passed a harvest atmosphere would be a bygone thing.

Oak gazed with misgiving at eight naked and unprotected ricks, massive and heavy with the rich produce of one-half the farm for that year. He went on to the barn.

This was the night which had been selected by Sergeant Troy—ruling now in the room of his wife—for giving the harvest supper and dance. As Oak approached the building the sound of violins and a tambourine, and the regular jigging of many feet, grew more distinct. He came close to the large doors, one of which stood slightly ajar, and looked in.

The central space, together with the recess at one end, was emptied of all incumbrances, and this area, covering about two-thirds of the whole, was appropriated for the gathering, the remaining end, which was piled to the ceiling with oats, being screened off with sail-cloth. Tufts and garlands of green foliage decorated the walls, beams, and extemporised chandeliers, and immediately opposite to Oak a rostrum had been erected, bearing a table and chairs. Here sat three fiddlers, and beside them stood a frantic man with his hair on end, perspiration streaming down his cheeks, and a tambourine quivering in his hand.

The dance ended, and on the black oak floor in the midst a new row of couples formed for another.

"Now, ma'am, and no offence I hope, I ask what dance you would like next?" said the first violin.

"Really, it makes no difference," said the clear voice of Bathsheba, who stood at the inner end of the building, observing the scene from behind a table covered with cups and viands. Troy was lolling beside her.

"Then," said the fiddler, "I'll venture to name that the right and proper thing is 'The Soldier's Joy'—there being a gallant soldier married into the farm—hey, my sonnies, and gentlemen all?"

"It shall be 'The Soldier's Joy,' " exclaimed a chorus.

"Thanks for the compliment," said the sergeant gaily, taking Bathsheba by the hand and leading her to the top of the dance. "For though I have purchased my discharge from Her Most Gracious Majesty's regiment of cavalry the 11th Dragoon Guards, to attend to the new duties awaiting me here, I shall continue a soldier in spirit and feeling as long as I live."

So the dance began. As to the merits of "The Soldier's Joy," there cannot be, and never were, two opinions. It has been observed in the musical circles of Weatherbury and its vicinity that this melody, at the end of three-quarters of an hour of thunderous footing, still possesses more stimulative properties for the heel and toe than the majority of other dances at their first opening. "The Soldier's Joy" has, too, an additional charm, in being so admirably adapted to the tambourine aforesaid—no mean instrument in the hands of a performer who understands the proper convulsions, spasms, St. Vitus's dances, and fearful frenzies necessary when exhibiting its tones in their highest perfection.

The immortal tune ended, a fine DD rolling forth from the bass-viol with the sonorousness of a cannonade, and Gabriel delayed his entry no longer. He avoided Bathsheba, and got as near as possible to the platform, where Sergeant Troy was now seated, drinking brandy-and-water, though the others drank without exception cider and ale. Gabriel could not easily thrust himself within speaking distance of the sergeant, and he sent a message, asking him to come down for a moment. The sergeant said he could not attend.

"Will you tell him, then," said Gabriel, "that I only stepped ath'art to say that a heavy rain is sure to fall soon, and that something should be done to protect the ricks?"

"Mr. Troy says it will not rain," returned the messenger, "and he cannot stop to talk to you about such fidgets."

In juxtaposition with Troy, Oak had a melancholy tendency to look like a candle beside gas, and ill at ease he went out again, thinking he would go home; for, under the circumstances, he had no heart for the scene in the barn. At the door he paused for a moment: Troy was speaking.

"Friends, it is not only the harvest home that we are celebrating to-night; but this is also a Wedding Feast. A short time ago I had the happiness to lead to the altar this lady, your mistress, and not until now have we been able to give any public flourish to the event in Weatherbury. That it may be thoroughly well done, and that every man may go happy to bed, I have ordered to be brought here some bottles of brandy and kettles of hot water. A treble-strong goblet will be handed round to each guest."

Bathsheba put her hand upon his arm, and, with upturned pale face, said imploringly, "No—don't give it to them—pray don't, Frank! It will only do them harm: they have had enough of everything."

"True—we don't wish for no more, thank ye," said one or two.

"Pooh!" said the sergeant contemptuously, and raised his voice as if lighted up by a new idea. "Friends," he said, "we'll send the women-folk home! 'Tis time they were in bed. Then we cockbirds will have a jolly carouse to ourselves! If any of the men show the white feather, let them look elsewhere for a winter's work."

Bathsheba indignantly left the barn, followed by all the women and children. The musicians, not looking upon themselves as "company," slipped quietly away to their spring-waggon and put in the horse. Thus Troy and the men on the farm were left sole occupants of the place. Oak, not to appear unnecessarily disagreeable, stayed a little while; then he, too, arose and quietly took his departure, followed by a friendly oath from the sergeant for not staying to a second round of grog.

Gabriel proceeded towards his home. In approaching the door, his toe kicked something which felt and sounded soft, leathery, and distended, like a boxing-glove. It was a large toad humbly travelling across the path. Oak took it up, thinking it might be better to kill the creature to save it from pain; but finding it uninjured, he placed it again among the grass. He knew what this direct message from the Great Mother meant. And soon came another.

When he struck a light indoors there appeared upon the table a thin glistening streak, as if a brush of varnish had been lightly dragged across it. Oak's eyes followed the serpentine sheen to the other side, where it led up to a huge brown garden-slug, which had come indoors to-night for reasons of its own. It was Nature's second way of hinting to him that he was to prepare for foul weather.

Oak sat down meditating for nearly an hour. During this time two black spiders, of the kind common in thatched houses, promenaded the ceiling, ultimately dropping to the floor. This reminded him that if there was one class of manifestation on this matter that he thoroughly understood, it was the instincts of sheep. He left the room, ran across two or three fields towards the flock, got upon a hedge, and looked over among them.

They were crowded close together on the other side around some furze-bushes, and the first peculiarity observable was that, on the sudden appearance of Oak's head over the fence, they did not stir or run away. They had now a terror of something greater than their terror of man. But this was not the most noteworthy feature: they were all grouped in such a way that their tails, without a single exception, were towards that half of the horizon from which the storm threatened. There was an inner circle closely huddled, and outside these they radiated wider apart, the pattern formed by the flock as a whole not being unlike a vandyked lace collar, to which the clump of furze-bushes stood in the position of a wearer's neck.

This was enough to re-establish him in his original opinion. He knew now that he was right, and that Troy was wrong. Every voice in nature was unanimous in bespeaking change. But two distinct translations attached to these dumb expressions. Apparently there was to be a thunder-storm, and afterwards a cold continuous rain. The creeping things seemed to know all about the later rain, but little of the interpolated thunder-storm; whilst the sheep knew all about the thunder-storm and nothing of the later rain.

This complication of weathers being uncommon, was all the more to be feared. Oak returned to the stack-yard. All was silent here, and the conical tips of the ricks jutted darkly into the sky. There were five wheat-ricks in this yard, and three stacks of barley. The wheat when threshed would average about thirty quarters to each stack; the barley, at least forty. Their value to Bathsheba, and indeed to anybody, Oak mentally estimated by the following simple calculation:—

$$5 \times 30 = 150 \text{ quarters} = 500l.$$
$$3 \times 40 = 120 \text{ quarters} = 250l.$$
$$\text{Total . . } 750l.$$

Seven hundred and fifty pounds in the divinest form that money can wear—that of necessary food for man and beast: should the risk be run of deteriorating this bulk of corn to less than half its value, because of the instability of a woman? "Never, if I can prevent it!" said Gabriel.

Such was the argument that Oak set outwardly before him. But man, even to himself, is a palimpsest, having an ostensible writing, and another beneath the lines. It is possible that there was this golden legend under the utilitarian one: "I will help to my last effort the woman I have loved so dearly."

He went back to the barn to endeavour to obtain assistance for covering the ricks that very night. All was silent within, and he would have passed on in the belief that the party had broken up, had not a dim light, yellow as saffron by contrast with the greenish whiteness outside, streamed through a knot-hole in the folding doors.

Gabriel looked in. An unusual picture met his eye.

The candles suspended among the evergreens had burnt down to their sockets, and in some cases the leaves tied about them were scorched. Many of the lights had quite gone out, others smoked and stank, grease dropping from them upon the floor. Here, under the table, and leaning against forms and chairs in every conceivable attitude except the perpendicular, were the wretched persons of all the work-folk, the hair of their heads at such low levels being suggestive of mops and brooms. In the midst of these shone red and distinct the figure of Sergeant Troy, leaning back in a chair. Coggan was on his back, with his mouth open, huzzing forth snores, as were several others; the united breathings of the horizonal assemblage forming a subdued roar like London from a distance. Joseph Poorgrass was curled round in the fashion of a hedge-hog, apparently in attempts to present the least possible portion of his surface to the air; and behind him was dimly visible an unimportant remnant of William Smallbury. The glasses and cups still stood upon the table, a water-jug being overturned, from which a small rill, after tracing its course with marvellous precision down the centre of the long table, fell into the neck of the unconscious Mark Clark, in a steady, monotonous drip, like the dripping of a stalactite in a cave.

Gabriel glanced hopelessly at the group, which, with one or two exceptions, composed all the able-bodied men upon the farm. He saw at once that if the ricks were to be saved that night, or even the next morning, he must save them with his own hands.

A faint "ting-ting" resounded from under Coggan's waistcoat. It was Coggan's watch striking the hour of two.

Oak went to the recumbent form of Matthew Moon, who usually undertook the rough thatching of the homestead, and shook him. The shaking was without effect.

Gabriel shouted in his ear, "Where's your thatching-beetle and rick-stick and spars?"

"Under the staddles," said Moon mechanically, with the unconscious promptness of a medium.

Gabriel let go his head, and it dropped upon the floor like a bowl. He then went to Susan Tall's husband.

"Where's the key of the granary?"

No answer. The question was repeated, with the same result. To be shouted to at night was evidently less of a novelty to Susan Tall's husband than to Matthew Moon. Oak flung down Tall's head into the corner again and turned away.

To be just, the men were not greatly to blame for this painful and demoralising termination to the evening's entertainment. Sergeant Troy had so strenuously insisted, glass in hand, that drinking should be the bond of their union, that those who wished to refuse hardly liked to be so unmannerly under the circumstances. Having from their youth up been entirely unaccustomed to any liquor stronger than cider or mild ale, it was no wonder that they had succumbed, one and all, with extraordinary uniformity, after the lapse of about an hour.

Gabriel was greatly depressed. This debauch boded ill for that wilful and fascinating mistress whom the faithful man even now felt within him as the embodiment of all that was sweet and bright and hopeless.

He put out the expiring lights, that the barn might not be endangered, closed the door upon the men in their deep and oblivious sleep, and went again into the lone night. A hot breeze, as if breathed from the parted lips of some dragon about to swallow the globe, fanned him from the south, while directly opposite in the north rose a grim misshapen body of cloud, in the very teeth of the wind. So unnaturally did it rise that one could fancy it to be lifted by machinery from below. Meanwhile the faint cloudlets had flown back into the south-east corner of the sky, as if in terror of the large cloud, like a young brood gazed in upon by some monster.

Going on to the village, Oak flung a small stone against the window of Laban Tall's bedroom, expecting Susan to open it; but nobody stirred. He went round to the back door, which had been left unfastened for Laban's entry, and passed in to the foot of the staircase.

"Mrs. Tall, I've come for the key of the granary, to get at the rick-cloths," said Oak, in a stentorian voice.

"Is that you?" said Mrs. Susan Tall, half awake.

"Yes," said Gabriel.

"Come along to bed, do, you draw-latching rogue—keeping a body awake like this!"

"It isn't Laban—'tis Gabriel Oak. I want the key of the granary."

"Gabriel! What in the name of fortune did you pretend to be Laban for?"

"I didn't. I thought you meant—"

"Yes you did! What do you want here?"

"The key of the granary."

"Take it then. 'Tis on the nail. People coming disturbing women at this time of night ought—"

Gabriel took the key, without waiting to hear the conclusion of the tirade. Ten minutes later his lonely figure might have been seen dragging four large waterproof coverings across the yard, and soon two of these heaps of treasure in grain were covered snug—two cloths to each. Two hundred pounds were secured. Three wheat-stacks remained open, and there were no more cloths. Oak looked under the staddles and found a fork. He mounted the third pile of wealth and began operating, adopting the plan of sloping the upper sheaves one over the other; and, in addition, filling the interstices with the material of some untied sheaves.

So far all was well. By this hurried contrivance Bathsheba's property in wheat was safe for at any rate a week or two, provided always that there was not much wind.

Next came the barley. This it was only possible to protect by systematic thatching. Time went on, and the moon vanished not to reappear. It was the farewell of the ambassador previous to war. The night had a haggard look, like a sick thing; and there came finally an utter expiration of air from the whole heaven in the form of a slow breeze, which might have been likened to a death. And now nothing was heard in the yard but the dull thuds of the beetle which drove in the spars, and the rustle of thatch in the intervals.

XXXVII

THE STORM—THE TWO TOGETHER

A LIGHT FLAPPED OVER THE SCENE, AS IF REFLECTED FROM PHOSPHORESCENT WINGS crossing the sky, and a rumble filled the air. It was the first move of the approaching storm.

The second peal was noisy, with comparatively little visible lightning. Gabriel saw a candle shining in Bathsheba's bedroom, and soon a shadow swept to and fro upon the blind.

Then there came a third flash. Manoeuvres of a most extraordinary kind were going on in the vast firmamental hollows overhead. The lightning now was the colour of silver, and gleamed in the heavens like a mailed army. Rumbles became rattles. Gabriel from his elevated position could see over the landscape at least half-a-dozen miles in front. Every hedge, bush, and tree was distinct as in a line engraving. In a paddock in the same direction was a herd of heifers, and the forms of these were visible at this moment in the act of galloping about in the wildest and maddest confusion, flinging their heels and tails high into the air, their heads to earth. A poplar in the immediate foreground was like an ink stroke on burnished tin. Then the picture vanished, leaving the darkness so intense that Gabriel worked entirely by feeling with his hands.

He had stuck his ricking-rod, or poniard, as it was indifferently called—a long iron lance, polished by handling—into the stack, used to support the sheaves instead of the support called a groom used on houses. A blue light appeared in the zenith, and in some indescribable manner flickered down near the top of the rod. It was the fourth of the larger flashes. A moment later and there was a smack—smart, clear, and short. Gabriel felt his position to be anything but a safe one, and he resolved to descend.

Not a drop of rain had fallen as yet. He wiped his weary brow, and looked again at the black forms of the unprotected stacks. Was his life so valuable to him after all? What were his prospects that he should be so chary of running risk, when important and urgent labour could not be carried on without such risk? He resolved to stick to the stack. However, he took a precaution. Under the staddles was a long tethering chain, used to prevent the escape of errant horses. This he carried up the ladder, and sticking his rod through the clog at one end, allowed the other end of the chain to trail upon the ground. The spike attached to it he drove in. Under the shadow of this extemporised lightning-conductor he felt himself comparatively safe.

Before Oak had laid his hands upon his tools again out leapt the fifth flash, with the spring of a serpent and the shout of a fiend. It was green as an emerald, and the reverberation was stunning. What was this the light revealed to him? In the open ground before him, as he looked over the ridge of the rick, was a dark and apparently female form. Could it be that of the only venturesome woman in the parish—Bathsheba? The form moved on a step: then he could see no more.

"Is that you, ma'am?" said Gabriel to the darkness.

"Who is there?" said the voice of Bathsheba.

"Gabriel. I am on the rick, thatching."

"O, Gabriel!—and are you? I have come about them. The weather awoke me, and I thought of the corn. I am so distressed about it—can we save it anyhow? I cannot find my husband. Is he with you?"

"He is not here."

"Do you know where he is?"

"Asleep in the barn."

"He promised that the stacks should be seen to, and now they are all neglected! Can I do anything to help? Liddy is afraid to come out. Fancy finding you here at such an hour! Surely I can do something?"

"You can bring up some reed-sheaves to me, one by one, ma'am; if you are not afraid to come up the ladder in the dark," said Gabriel. "Every moment is precious now, and that would save a good deal of time. It is not very dark when the lightning has been gone a bit."

"I'll do anything!" she said resolutely. She instantly took a sheaf upon her shoulder, clambered up close to his heels, placed it behind the rod, and descended for another. At her third ascent the rick suddenly brightened with the brazen glare of shining majolica— every knot in every straw was visible. On the slope in front of him appeared two human shapes, black as jet. The rick lost its sheen—the shapes vanished. Gabriel turned his head. It had been the sixth flash which had come from the east behind him, and the two dark forms on the slope had been the shadows of himself and Bathsheba.

Then came the peal. It hardly was credible that such a heavenly light could be the parent of such a diabolical sound.

"How terrible!" she exclaimed, and clutched him by the sleeve. Gabriel turned, and steadied her on her aërial perch by holding her arm. At the same moment, while he was still reversed in his attitude, there was more light, and he saw, as it were, a copy of the tall poplar-tree on the hill drawn in black on the wall of the barn. It was the shadow of that tree, thrown across by a secondary flash in the west.

The next flare came. Bathsheba was on the ground now, shouldering another sheaf, and she bore its dazzle without flinching—thunder and all—and again ascended with the load. There was then a silence everywhere for four or five minutes, and the crunch of the spars, as Gabriel hastily drove them in, could again be distinctly heard. He thought the crisis of the storm had passed. But there came a burst of light.

"Hold on!" said Gabriel, taking the sheaf from her shoulder, and grasping her arm again.

Heaven opened then, indeed. The flash was almost too novel for its inexpressibly dangerous nature to be at once realised, and they could only comprehend the magnificence of its beauty. It sprang from east, west, north, south, and was a perfect dance of death. The forms of skeletons appeared in the air, shaped with blue fire for bones—dancing, leaping, striding, racing around, and mingling altogether in unparalleled confusion. With these were intertwined undulating snakes of green, and behind these was a broad mass of lesser light. Simultaneously from every part of the tumbling sky what may be called a shout; since, though no shout ever came near it, it was more of the nature of a shout than of anything else earthly. In the meantime one of the grisly forms had alighted upon the point of Gabriel's rod, to run invisibly down it, down the chain, and into the earth. Gabriel was almost blinded, and he could feel Bathsheba's warm arm tremble in his hand—a sensation novel and thrilling enough; but love, life, everything human, seemed small and trifling in such close juxtaposition with an infuriated universe.

Oak had hardly time to gather up these impressions into a thought, and to see how strangely the red feather of her hat shone in this light, when the tall tree on the hill before mentioned seemed on fire to a white heat, and a new one among these terrible voices mingled with the last crash of those preceding. It was a stupefying blast, harsh and pitiless, and it fell upon their ears in a dead, flat blow, without that reverberation which lends the tones of a drum to more distant thunder. By the lustre reflected from every part of the earth and from the wide domical scoop above it, he saw that the tree·was sliced down the whole length of its tall, straight stem, a huge riband of bark being apparently flung off. The other portion remained erect, and revealed the bared surface as a strip of white down the front. The lightning had struck the tree. A sulphurous smell filled the air; then all was silent, and black as a cave in Hinnom.

"We had a narrow escape!" said Gabriel hurriedly. "You had better go down."

Bathsheba said nothing; but he could distinctly hear her rhythmical pants, and the recurrent rustle of the sheaf beside her in response to her frightened pulsations. She descended the ladder, and, on second thoughts, he followed her. The darkness was now impenetrable by the sharpest vision. They both stood still at the bottom, side by side. Bathsheba appeared to think only of the weather—Oak thought only of her just then. At last he said—

"The storm seems to have passed now, at any rate."

"I think so too," said Bathsheba. "Though there are multitudes of gleams, look!"

The sky was now filled with an incessant light, frequent repetition melting into complete continuity, as an unbroken sound results from the successive strokes on a gong.

"Nothing serious," said he. "I cannot understand no rain falling. But Heaven be praised, it is all the better for us. I am now going up again."

"Gabriel, you are kinder than I deserve! I will stay and help you yet. O, why are not some of the others here!"

"They would have been here if they could," said Oak, in a hesitating way.

"O, I know it all—all," she said, adding slowly: "They are all asleep in the barn, in a drunken sleep, and my husband among them. That's it, is it not? Don't think I am a timid woman and can't endure things."

"I am not certain," said Gabriel. "I will go and see."

He crossed to the barn, leaving her there alone. He looked through the chinks of the door. All was in total darkness, as he had left it, and there still arose, as at the former time, the steady buzz of many snores.

He felt a zephyr curling about his cheek, and turned. It was Bathsheba's breath—she had followed him, and was looking into the same chink.

He endeavoured to put off the immediate and painful subject of their thoughts by remarking gently, "If you'll come back again, miss—ma'am, and hand up a few more; it would save much time."

Then Oak went back again, ascended to the top, stepped off the ladder for greater expedition, and went on thatching. She followed, but without a sheaf.

"Gabriel," she said, in a strange and impressive voice.

Oak looked up at her. She had not spoken since he left the barn. The soft and continual shimmer of the dying lightning showed a marble face high against the black sky of the opposite quarter. Bathsheba was sitting almost on the apex of the stack, her feet gathered up beneath her, and resting on the top round of the ladder.

"Yes, mistress," he said.

"I suppose you thought that when I galloped away to Bath that night it was on purpose to be married?"

"I did at last—not at first," he answered, somewhat surprised at the abruptness with which this new subject was broached.

"And others thought so, too?"

"Yes."

"And you blamed me for it?"

"Well—a little."

"I thought so. Now, I care a little for your good opinion, and I want to explain something—I have longed to do it ever since I returned, and you looked so gravely at me. For if I were to die—and I may die soon—it would be dreadful that you should always think mistakenly of me. Now, listen."

Gabriel ceased his rustling.

"I went to Bath that night in the full intention of breaking off my engagement to Mr. Troy. It was owing to circumstances which occurred after I got there that—that we were married. Now, do you see the matter in a new light?"

"I do—somewhat."

"I must, I suppose, say more, now that I have begun. And perhaps it's no harm, for you are certainly under no delusion that I ever loved you, or that I can have any object in speaking, more than that object I have mentioned. Well, I was alone in a strange city, and the horse was lame. And at last I didn't know what to do. I saw, when it was too late, that scandal might seize hold of me for meeting him alone in that way. But I was coming away, when he suddenly said he had that day seen a woman more beautiful than I, and that his constancy could not be counted on unless I at once became his. . . . And I was grieved and troubled—" She cleared her voice, and waited a moment, as if to gather breath. "And then, between jealousy and distraction, I married him!" she whispered with desperate impetuosity.

Gabriel made no reply.

"He was not to blame, for it was perfectly true about—about his seeing somebody else," she quickly added. "And now I don't wish for a single remark from you upon the subject—indeed, I forbid it. I only wanted you to know that misunderstood bit of my history before a time comes when you could never know it.—You want some more sheaves?"

She went down the ladder, and the work proceeded. Gabriel soon perceived a languor in the movements of his mistress up and down, and he said to her, gently as a mother—

"I think you had better go indoors now, you are tired. I can finish the rest alone. If the wind does not change the rain is likely to keep off."

"If I am useless I will go," said Bathsheba, in a flagging cadence. "But O, if your life should be lost!"

"You are not useless; but I would rather not tire you longer. You have done well."

"And you better!" she said gratefully. "Thank you for your devotion, a thousand times, Gabriel! Good-night—I know you are doing your very best for me."

She diminished in the gloom, and vanished, and he heard the latch of the gate fall as she passed through. He worked in a reverie now, musing upon her story, and upon the contradictoriness of that feminine heart which had caused her to speak more warmly to him to-night than she ever had done whilst unmarried and free to speak as warmly as she chose.

He was disturbed in his meditation by a grating noise from the coach-house. It was the vane on the roof turning round, and this change in the wind was the signal for a disastrous rain.

XXXVIII

RAIN—ONE SOLITARY MEETS ANOTHER

IT WAS NOW FIVE O'CLOCK, AND THE DAWN WAS PROMISING TO BREAK IN HUES OF DRAB and ash.

The air changed its temperature and stirred itself more vigorously. Cool breezes coursed in transparent eddies round Oak's face. The wind shifted yet a point or two and blew stronger. In ten minutes every wind of heaven seemed to be roaming at large. Some of the thatching on the wheat-stacks was now whirled fantastically aloft, and had to be replaced and weighted with some rails that lay near at hand. This done, Oak slaved away again at the barley. A huge drop of rain smote his face, the wind snarled round every corner, the trees rocked to the bases of their trunks, and the twigs clashed in strife. Driving in spars at any point and on any system, inch by inch he covered more and more safely from ruin this distracting impersonation of seven hundred pounds. The rain came on in earnest, and Oak soon felt the water to be tracking cold and clammy routes down his back. Ultimately he was reduced well-nigh to a homogeneous sop, and the dyes of his clothes trickled down and stood in a pool at the foot of the ladder. The rain stretched obliquely through the dull atmosphere in liquid spines, unbroken in continuity between their beginnings in the clouds and their points in him.

Oak suddenly remembered that eight months before this time he had been fighting against fire in the same spot as desperately as he was fighting against water now—and for a futile love of the same woman. As for her—But Oak was generous and true, and dismissed his reflections.

It was about seven o'clock in the dark leaden morning when Gabriel came down from the last stack, and thankfully exclaimed, "It is done!" He was drenched, weary, and sad, and yet not so sad as drenched and weary, for he was cheered by a sense of success in a good cause.

Faint sounds came from the barn, and he looked that way. Figures stepped singly and in pairs through the doors—all walking awkwardly, and abashed, save the foremost, who wore a red jacket, and advanced with his hands in his pockets, whistling. The others shambled after with a conscience-stricken air: the whole procession was not unlike Flaxman's group of the suitors tottering on towards the infernal regions under the conduct of Mercury. The gnarled shapes passed into the village, Troy, their leader, entering the farmhouse. Not a single one of them had turned his face to the ricks, or apparently bestowed one thought upon their condition.

Soon Oak too went homeward, by a different route from theirs. In front of him against the wet glazed surface of the lane he saw a person walking yet more slowly than himself under an umbrella. The man turned and plainly started; he was Boldwood.

"How are you this morning, sir?" said Oak.

"Yes, it is a wet day.—Oh, I am well, very well, I thank you; quite well."

"I am glad to hear it, sir."

Boldwood seemed to awake to the present by degrees. "You look tired and ill, Oak," he said then, desultorily regarding his companion.

"I am tired. You look strangely altered, sir."

"I? Not a bit of it: I am well enough. What put that into your head?"

"I thought you didn't look quite so topping as you used to, that was all."

"Indeed, then you are mistaken," said Boldwood shortly. "Nothing hurts me. My constitution is an iron one."

"I've been working hard to get our ricks covered, and was barely in time. Never had such a struggle in my life. . . . Yours of course are safe, sir."

"O yes." Boldwood added, after an interval of silence: "What did you ask, Oak?"

"Your ricks are all covered before this time?"

"No."

"At any rate, the large ones upon the stone staddles?"

"They are not."

"Them under the hedge?"

"No. I forgot to tell the thatcher to set about it."

"Nor the little one by the stile?"

"Nor the little one by the stile. I overlooked the ricks this year."

"Then not a tenth of your corn will come to measure, sir."

"Possibly not."

"Overlooked them," repeated Gabriel slowly to himself. It is difficult to describe the intensely dramatic effect that announcement had upon Oak at such a moment. All the night he had been feeling that the neglect he was labouring to repair was abnormal and iso-lated—the only instance of the kind within the circuit of the county. Yet at this very time, within the same parish, a greater waste had been going on, uncomplained of and disre-garded. A few months earlier Boldwood's forgetting his husbandry would have been as preposterous an idea as a sailor forgetting he was in a ship. Oak was just thinking that whatever he himself might have suffered from Bathsheba's marriage, here was a man who had suffered more, when Boldwood spoke in a changed voice—that of one who yearned to make a confidence and relieve his heart by an outpouring.

"Oak, you know as well as I that things have gone wrong with me lately. I may as well own it. I was going to get a little settled in life; but in some way my plan has come to nothing."

"I thought my mistress would have married you," said Gabriel, not knowing enough of the full depths of Boldwood's love to keep silence on the farmer's account, and deter-mined not to evade discipline by doing so on his own. "However, it is so sometimes, and nothing happens that we expect," he added, with the repose of a man whom misfortune had inured rather than subdued.

"I daresay I am a joke about the parish," said Boldwood, as if the subject came irre-sistibly to his tongue, and with a miserable lightness meant to express his indifference.

"O no—I don't think that."

"—But the real truth of the matter is that there was not, as some fancy, any jilting on—her part. No engagement ever existed between me and Miss Everdene. People say so, but it is untrue: she never promised me!" Boldwood stood still now and turned his wild face to Oak. "O, Gabriel," he continued, "I am weak and foolish, and I don't know what, and I can't fend off my miserable grief! . . . I had some faint belief in the mercy of God till I lost that woman. Yes, He prepared a gourd to shade me, and like the prophet I thanked Him and was glad. But the next day He prepared a worm to smite the gourd and wither it; and I feel it is better to die than to live!"

A silence followed. Boldwood aroused himself from the momentary mood of confi-dence into which he had drifted, and walked on again, resuming his usual reserve.

"No, Gabriel," he resumed, with a carelessness which was like the smile on the coun-tenance of a skull: "it was made more of by other people than ever it was by us. I do feel a little regret occasionally, but no woman ever had power over me for any length of time. Well, good-morning; I can trust you not to mention to others what has passed between us two here."

XXXIX

COMING HOME—A CRY

O N THE TURNPIKE ROAD, BETWEEN CASTERBRIDGE AND WEATHERBURY, AND ABOUT three miles from the former place, is Yalbury Hill, one of those steep long ascents which pervade the highways of this undulating part of South Wessex. In returning from market it is usual for the farmers and other gig-gentry to alight at the bottom and walk up.

One Saturday evening in the month of October Bathsheba's vehicle was duly creeping up this incline. She was sitting listlessly in the second seat of the gig, whilst walking beside her in a farmer's marketing suit of unusually fashionable cut was an erect, well-made young man. Though on foot, he held the reins and whip, and occasionally aimed light cuts at the horse's ear with the end of the lash, as a recreation. This man was her husband, formerly Sergeant Troy, who, having bought his discharge with Bathsheba's money, was gradually transforming himself into a farmer of a spirited and very modern school. People of unalterable ideas still insisted upon calling him "Sergeant" when they met him, which was in some degree owing to his having still retained the well-shaped moustache of his military days, and the soldierly bearing inseparable from his form and training.

"Yes, if it hadn't been for that wretched rain I should have cleared two hundred as easy as looking, my love," he was saying. "Don't you see, it altered all the chances? To speak like a book I once read, wet weather is the narrative, and fine days are the episodes, of our country's history; now, isn't that true?"

"But the time of year is come for changeable weather."

"Well, yes. The fact is, these autumn races are the ruin of everybody. Never did I see such a day as 'twas! 'Tis a wild open place, just out of Budmouth, and a drab sea rolled in towards us like liquid misery. Wind and rain—good Lord! Dark? Why, 'twas as black as my hat before the last race was run. 'Twas five o'clock, and you couldn't see the horses till they were almost in, leave alone colours. The ground was as heavy as lead, and all judgment from a fellow's experience went for nothing. Horses, riders, people, were all blown about like ships at sea. Three booths were blown over, and the wretched folk inside crawled out upon their hands and knees; and in the next field were as many as a dozen hats at one time. Ay, Pimpernel regularly stuck fast, when about sixty yards off, and when I saw Policy stepping on, it did knock my heart against the lining of my ribs, I assure you, my love!"

"And you mean, Frank," said Bathsheba sadly—her voice was painfully lowered from the fulness and vivacity of the previous summer—"that you have lost more than a hundred pounds in a month by this dreadful horse-racing? O, Frank, it is cruel; it is foolish of you to take away my money so. We shall have to leave the farm; that will be the end of it!"

"Humbug about cruel. Now, there 'tis again—turn on the waterworks; that's just like you."

"But you'll promise me not to go to Budmouth second meeting, won't you?" she implored. Bathsheba was at the full depth for tears, but she maintained a dry eye.

"I don't see why I should; in fact, if it turns out to be a fine day, I was thinking of taking you."

"Never, never! I'll go a hundred miles the other way first. I hate the sound of the very word!"

"But the question of going to see the race or staying at home has very little to do with the matter. Bets are all booked safely enough before the race begins, you may depend. Whether it is a bad race for me or a good one, will have very little to do with our going there next Monday."

"But you don't mean to say that you have risked anything on this one too!" she exclaimed, with an agonised look.

"There now, don't you be a little fool. Wait till you are told. Why, Bathsheba, you have lost all the pluck and sauciness you formerly had, and upon my life if I had known what a chicken-hearted creature you were under all your boldness, I'd never have—I know what."

A flash of indignation might have been seen in Bathsheba's dark eyes as she looked resolutely ahead after this reply. They moved on without further speech, some early-withered leaves from the trees which hooded the road at this spot occasionally spinning downward across their path to the earth.

A woman appeared on the brow of the hill. The ridge was in a cutting, so that she was very near the husband and wife before she became visible. Troy had turned towards the gig to remount, and whilst putting his foot on the step the woman passed behind him.

Though the overshadowing trees and the approach of eventide enveloped them in gloom, Bathsheba could see plainly enough to discern the extreme poverty of the woman's garb, and the sadness of her face.

"Please, sir, do you know at what time Casterbridge Union-house closes at night?"

The woman said these words to Troy over his shoulder.

Troy started visibly at the sound of the voice; yet he seemed to recover presence of mind sufficient to prevent himself from giving way to his impulse to suddenly turn and face her. He said, slowly—

"I don't know."

The woman, on hearing him speak, quickly looked up, examined the side of his face, and recognised the soldier under the yeoman's garb. Her face was drawn into an expression which had gladness and agony both among its elements. She uttered an hysterical cry, and fell down.

"O, poor thing!" exclaimed Bathsheba, instantly preparing to alight.

"Stay where you are, and attend to the horse!" said Troy peremptorily, throwing her the reins and the whip. "Walk the horse to the top: I'll see to the woman."

"But I—"

"Do you hear? Clk—Poppet!"

The horse, gig, and Bathsheba moved on.

"How on earth did you come here? I thought you were miles away, or dead! Why didn't you write to me?" said Troy to the woman, in a strangely gentle, yet hurried voice, as he lifted her up.

"I feared to."

"Have you any money?"

"None."

"Good Heaven—I wish I had more to give you! Here's—wretched—the merest trifle. It is every farthing I have left. I have none but what my wife gives me, you know, and I can't ask her now."

The woman made no answer.

"I have only another moment," continued Troy; "and now listen. Where are you going to-night? Casterbridge Union?"

"Yes; I thought to go there."

"You shan't go there; yet, wait. Yes, perhaps for to-night; I can do nothing better—worse luck! Sleep there to-night, and stay there to-morrow. Monday is the first free day I have; and on Monday morning, at ten exactly, meet me on Grey's Bridge just out of the town. I'll bring all the money I can muster. You shan't want—I'll see that, Fanny; then I'll get you a lodging somewhere. Good-bye till then. I am a brute—but good-bye!"

After advancing the distance which completed the ascent of the hill, Bathsheba turned her head. The woman was upon her feet, and Bathsheba saw her withdrawing from Troy, and going feebly down the hill by the third milestone from Casterbridge. Troy then came on towards his wife, stepped into the gig, took the reins from her hand, and without making any observation whipped the horse into a trot. He was rather agitated.

"Do you know who that woman was?" said Bathsheba, looking searchingly into his face.

"I do," he said, looking boldly back into hers.

"I thought you did," said she, with angry hauteur, and still regarding him. "Who is she?"

He suddenly seemed to think that frankness would benefit neither of the women.

"Nothing to either of us," he said. "I know her by sight."

"What is her name?"

"How should I know her name?"

"I think you do."

"Think if you will, and be—" The sentence was completed by a smart cut of the whip round Poppet's flank, which caused the animal to start forward at a wild pace. No more was said.

XL

ON CASTERBRIDGE HIGHWAY

FOR A CONSIDERABLE TIME THE WOMAN WALKED ON. HER STEPS BECAME FEEBLER, AND she strained her eyes to look afar upon the naked road, now indistinct amid the penumbrae of night. At length her onward walk dwindled to the merest totter, and she opened a gate within which was a haystack. Underneath this she sat down and presently slept.

When the woman awoke it was to find herself in the depths of a moonless and starless night. A heavy unbroken crust of cloud stretched across the sky, shutting out every speck of heaven; and a distant halo which hung over the town of Casterbridge was visible against the black concave, the luminosity appearing the brighter by its great contrast with the circumscribing darkness. Towards this weak, soft glow the woman turned her eyes.

"If I could only get there!" she said. "Meet him the day after to-morrow: God help me! Perhaps I shall be in my grave before then."

A manor-house clock from the far depths of shadow struck the hour, one, in a small, attenuated tone. After midnight the voice of a clock seems to lose in breadth as much as in length, and to diminish its sonorousness to a thin falsetto.

Afterwards a light—two lights—arose from the remote shade, and grew larger. A carriage rolled along the road, and passed the gate. It probably contained some late diners-out. The beams from one lamp shone for a moment upon the crouching woman, and threw her face into vivid relief. The face was young in the groundwork, old in the finish; the general contours were flexuous and childlike, but the finer lineaments had begun to be sharp and thin.

The pedestrian stood up, apparently with revived determination, and looked around. The road appeared to be familiar to her, and she carefully scanned the fence as she slowly walked along. Presently there became visible a dim white shape; it was another milestone. She drew her fingers across its face to feel the marks.

"Two more!" she said.

She leant against the stone as a means of rest for a short interval, then bestirred herself, and again pursued her way. For a slight distance she bore up bravely, afterwards flagging as before. This was beside a lone copsewood, wherein heaps of white chips strewn upon the leafy ground showed that woodmen had been faggoting and making hurdles during the day. Now there was not a rustle, not a breeze, not the faintest clash of twigs to keep her company. The woman looked over the gate, opened it, and went in. Close to the entrance stood a row of faggots, bound and unbound, together with stakes of all sizes.

For a few seconds the wayfarer stood with that tense stillness which signifies itself to be not the end, but merely the suspension, of a previous motion. Her attitude was that of a person who listens, either to the external world of sound, or to the imagined discourse of thought. A close criticism might have detected signs proving that she was intent on the latter alternative. Moreover, as was shown by what followed, she was oddly exercising the faculty of invention upon the speciality of the clever Jacquet Droz, the designer of automatic substitutes for human limbs.

By the aid of the Casterbridge aurora, and by feeling with her hands, the woman selected two sticks from the heaps. These sticks were nearly straight to the height of three or four feet, where each branched into a fork like the letter Y. She sat down, snapped off the small upper twigs, and carried the remainder with her into the road. She placed one of these forks under each arm as a crutch, tested them, timidly threw her whole weight upon them—so little that it was—and swung herself forward. The girl had made for herself a material aid.

The crutches answered well. The pat of her feet, and the tap of her sticks upon the highway, were all the sounds that came from the traveller now. She had passed the last milestone by a good long distance, and began to look wistfully towards the bank as if calculating upon another milestone soon. The crutches, though so very useful, had their limits of power. Mechanism only transfers labour, being powerless to supersede it, and the original amount of exertion was not cleared away; it was thrown into the body and arms.

She was exhausted, and each swing forward became fainter. At last she swayed sideways, and fell.

Here she lay, a shapeless heap, for ten minutes and more. The morning wind began to boom dully over the flats, and to move afresh dead leaves which had lain still since yesterday. The woman desperately turned round upon her knees, and next rose to her feet. Steadying herself by the help of one crutch, she essayed a step, then another, then a third, using the crutches now as walking-sticks only. Thus she progressed till descending Mellstock Hill another milestone appeared, and soon the beginning of an iron-railed fence came into view. She staggered across to the first post, clung to it, and looked around.

The Casterbridge lights were now individually visible. It was getting towards morning, and vehicles might be hoped for, if not expected soon. She listened. There was not a sound of life save that acme and sublimation of all dismal sounds, the bark of a fox, its three hollow notes being rendered at intervals of a minute with the precision of a funeral bell.

"Less than a mile!" the woman murmured. "No; more," she added, after a pause. "The mile is to the county-hall, and my resting-place is on the other side Casterbridge. A little over a mile, and there I am!" After an interval she again spoke. "Five or six steps to a yard—six perhaps. I have to go seventeen hundred yards. A hundred times six, six hundred. Seventeen times that. O pity me, Lord!"

Holding to the rails, she advanced, thrusting one hand forward upon the rail, then the other, then leaning over it whilst she dragged her feet on beneath.

This woman was not given to soliloquy; but extremity of feeling lessens the individuality of the weak, as it increases that of the strong. She said again in the same tone, "I'll believe that the end lies five posts forward, and no further, and so get strength to pass them."

This was a practical application of the principle that a half-feigned and fictitious faith is better than no faith at all.

She passed five posts and held on to the fifth.

"I'll pass five more by believing my longed-for spot is at the next fifth. I can do it."

She passed five more.

"It lies only five further."

She passed five more.

"But it is five further."

She passed them.

"That stone bridge is the end of my journey," she said, when the bridge over the Froom was in view.

She crawled to the bridge. During the effort each breath of the woman went into the air as if never to return again.

"Now for the truth of the matter," she said, sitting down. "The truth is, that I have less than half a mile." Self-beguilement with what she had known all the time to be false had given her strength to come over half a mile that she would have been powerless to face in the lump. The artifice showed that the woman, by some mysterious intuition, had grasped the paradoxical truth that blindness may operate more vigorously than prescience, and the short-sighted effect more than the far-seeing; that limitation, and not comprehensiveness, is needed for striking a blow.

The half-mile stood now before the sick and weary woman like a stolid Juggernaut. It was an impassive King of her world. The road here ran across Durnover Moor, open to the road on either side. She surveyed the wide space, the lights, herself, sighed, and lay down against a guard-stone of the bridge.

Never was ingenuity exercised so sorely as the traveller here exercised hers. Every conceivable aid, method, stratagem, mechanism, by which these last desperate eight hundred yards could be overpassed by a human being unperceived, was revolved in her busy brain, and dismissed as impracticable. She thought of sticks, wheels, crawling—she even thought of rolling. But the exertion demanded by either of these latter two was greater than to walk erect. The faculty of contrivance was worn out. Hopelessness had come at last.

"No further!" she whispered, and closed her eyes.

From the stripe of shadow on the opposite side of the bridge a portion of shade seemed to detach itself and move into isolation upon the pale white of the road. It glided noiselessly towards the recumbent woman.

She became conscious of something touching her hand; it was softness and it was warmth. She opened her eye's, and the substance touched her face. A dog was licking her cheek.

He was a huge, heavy, and quiet creature, standing darkly against the low horizon, and at least two feet higher than the present position of her eyes. Whether Newfoundland, mastiff, bloodhound, or what not, it was impossible to say. He seemed to be of too strange and mysterious a nature to belong to any variety among those of popular nomenclature. Being thus assignable to no breed, he was the ideal embodiment of canine greatness—a generalization from what was common to all. Night, in its sad, solemn, and benevolent aspect, apart from its stealthy and cruel side, was personified in this form. Darkness endows the small and ordinary ones among mankind with poetical power, and even the suffering woman threw her idea into figure.

In her reclining position she looked up to him just as in earlier times she had, when standing, looked up to a man. The animal, who was as homeless as she, respectfully withdrew a step or two when the woman moved, and, seeing that she did not repulse him, he licked her hand again.

A thought moved within her like lightning. "Perhaps I can make use of him—I might do it then!"

She pointed in the direction of Casterbridge, and the dog seemed to misunderstand: he trotted on. Then, finding she could not follow, he came back and whined.

The ultimate and saddest singularity of woman's effort and invention was reached when, with a quickened breathing, she rose to a stooping posture, and, resting her two little arms upon the shoulders of the dog, leant firmly thereon, and murmured stimulating words. Whilst she sorrowed in her heart she cheered with her voice, and what was stranger than that the strong should need encouragement from the weak was that cheerfulness should be so well stimulated by such utter dejection. Her friend moved forward slowly, and she with small mincing steps moved forward beside him, half her weight being thrown upon the animal. Sometimes she sank as she had sunk from walking erect, from the crutches, from the rails. The dog, who now thoroughly understood her desire and her incapacity, was frantic in his distress on these occasions; he would tug at her dress and run forward. She always called him back, and it was now to be observed that the woman listened for human sounds only to avoid them. It was evident that she had an object in keeping her presence on the road and her forlorn state unknown.

Their progress was necessarily very slow. They reached the bottom of the town, and the Casterbridge lamps lay before them like fallen Pleiads as they turned to the left into the dense shade of a deserted avenue of chestnuts, and so skirted the borough. Thus the town was passed, and the goal was reached.

On this much-desired spot outside the town rose a picturesque building. Originally it had been a mere case to hold people. The shell had been so thin, so devoid of excrescence, and so closely drawn over the accommodation granted, that the grim character of what was beneath showed through it, as the shape of a body is visible under a winding-sheet.

Then Nature, as if offended, lent a hand. Masses of ivy grew up, completely covering the walls, till the place looked like an abbey; and it was discovered that the view from the front, over the Casterbridge chimneys, was one of the most magnificent in the county. A neighbouring earl once said that he would give up a year's rental to have at his own door the view enjoyed by the inmates from theirs—and very probably the inmates would have given up the view for his year's rental.

This stone edifice consisted of a central mass and two wings, whereon stood as sentinels a few slim chimneys, now gurgling sorrowfully to the slow wind. In the wall was a gate, and by the gate a bell-pull formed of a hanging wire. The woman raised herself as high as possible upon her knees, and could just reach the handle. She moved it and fell forwards in a bowed attitude, her face upon her bosom.

It was getting on towards six o'clock, and sounds of movement were to be heard inside the building which was the haven of rest to this wearied soul. A little door by the large one was opened, and a man appeared inside. He discerned the panting heap of clothes, went back for a light, and came again. He entered a second time, and returned with two women.

These lifted the prostrate figure and assisted her in through the doorway. The man then closed the door.

"How did she get here?" said one of the women.

"The Lord knows," said the other.

"There is a dog outside," murmured the overcome traveller. "Where is he gone? He helped me."

"I stoned him away," said the man.

The little procession then moved forward—the man in front bearing the light, the two bony women next, supporting between them the small and supple one. Thus they entered the house and disappeared.

XLI

SUSPICION—FANNY IS SENT FOR

BATHSHEBA SAID VERY LITTLE TO HER HUSBAND ALL THAT EVENING OF THEIR RETURN from market, and he was not disposed to say much to her. He exhibited the unpleasant combination of a restless condition with a silent tongue. The next day, which was Sunday, passed nearly in the same manner as regarded their taciturnity, Bathsheba going to church both morning and afternoon. This was the day before the Budmouth races. In the evening Troy said, suddenly—

"Bathsheba, could you let me have twenty pounds?"

Her countenance instantly sank. "Twenty pounds?" she said.

"The fact is, I want it badly." The anxiety upon Troy's face was unusual and very marked. It was a culmination of the mood he had been in all the day.

"Ah! for those races to-morrow."

Troy for the moment made no reply. Her mistake had its advantages to a man who shrank from having his mind inspected as he did now. "Well, suppose I do want it for races?" he said, at last.

"O, Frank!" Bathsheba replied, and there was such a volume of entreaty in the words. "Only such a few weeks ago you said that I was far sweeter than all your other pleasures put together, and that you would give them all up for me; and now, won't you give up this one, which is more a worry than a pleasure? Do, Frank. Come, let me fascinate you by all I can do—by pretty words and pretty looks, and everything I can think of—to stay at home. Say yes to your wife—say yes!"

The tenderest and softest phases of Bathsheba's nature were prominent now—advanced impulsively for his acceptance, without any of the disguises and defences which the wariness of her character when she was cool too frequently threw over them. Few men could have resisted the arch yet dignified entreaty of the beautiful face, thrown a little back and sideways in the well-known attitude that expresses more than the words it accompanies, and which seems to have been designed for these special occasions. Had the woman not been his wife, Troy would have succumbed instantly; as it was, he thought he would not deceive her longer.

"The money is not wanted for racing debts at all," he said.

"What is it for?" she asked. "You worry me a great deal by these mysterious responsibilities, Frank."

Troy hesitated. He did not now love her enough to allow himself to be carried too far by her ways. Yet it was necessary to be civil. "You wrong me by such a suspicious manner," he said. "Such strait-waistcoating as you treat me to is not becoming in you at so early a date."

"I think that I have a right to grumble a little if I pay," she said, with features between a smile and a pout.

"Exactly; and, the former being done, suppose we proceed to the latter. Bathsheba, fun is all very well, but don't go too far, or you may have cause to regret something."

She reddened. "I do that already," she said, quickly.

"What do you regret?"

"That my romance has come to an end."

"All romances end at marriage."

"I wish you wouldn't talk like that. You grieve me to my soul by being smart at my expense."

"You are dull enough at mine. I believe you hate me."

"Not you—only your faults. I do hate them."

" 'Twould be much more becoming if you set yourself to cure them. Come, let's strike a balance with the twenty pounds, and be friends."

She gave a sigh of resignation. "I have about that sum here for household expenses. If you must have it, take it."

"Very good. Thank you. I expect I shall have gone away before you are in to breakfast to-morrow."

"And must you go? Ah! there was a time, Frank, when it would have taken a good many promises to other people to drag you away from me. You used to call me darling, then. But it doesn't matter to you how my days are passed now."

"I must go, in spite of sentiment." Troy, as he spoke, looked at his watch, and, apparently actuated by *non lucendo* principles, opened the case at the back, revealing, snugly stowed within it, a small coil of hair.

Bathsheba's eyes had been accidentally lifted at that moment, and she saw the action and saw the hair. She flushed in pain and surprise, and some words escaped her before she had thought whether or not it was wise to utter them. "A woman's curl of hair!" she said. "O, Frank, whose is that?"

Troy had instantly closed his watch. He carelessly replied, as one who cloaked some feelings that the sight had stirred: "Why, yours, of course. Whose should it be? I had quite forgotten that I had it."

"What a dreadful fib, Frank!"

"I tell you I had forgotten it!" he said loudly.

"I don't mean that—it was yellow hair."

"Nonsense."

"That's insulting me. I know it was yellow. Now whose was it? I want to know."

"Very well—I'll tell you, so make no more ado. It is the hair of a young woman I was going to marry before I knew you."

"You ought to tell me her name, then."

"I cannot do that."

"Is she married yet?"

"No."

"Is she alive?"

"Yes."

"Is she pretty?"

"Yes."

"It is wonderful how she can be, poor thing, under such an awful affliction!"

"Affliction—what affliction?" he enquired quickly.

"Having hair of that dreadful colour."

"Oh—ho—I like that!" said Troy, recovering himself. "Why, her hair has been admired by everybody who has seen her since she has worn it loose, which has not been long. It is beautiful hair. People used to turn their heads to look at it, poor girl!"

"Pooh! that's nothing—that's nothing!" she exclaimed, in incipient accents of pique. "If I cared for your love as much as I used to I could say people had turned to look at mine."

"Bathsheba, don't be so fitful and jealous. You knew what married life would be like, and shouldn't have entered it if you feared these contingencies."

Troy had by this time driven her to bitterness: her heart was big in her throat, and the ducts to her eyes were painfully full. Ashamed as she was to show emotion, at last she burst out:—

"This is all I get for loving you so well! Ah! when I married you your life was dearer to me than my own. I would have died for you—how truly I can say that I would have died for you! And now you sneer at my foolishness in marrying you. O! is it kind to me to throw my mistake in my face? Whatever opinion you may have of my wisdom, you should not tell me of it so mercilessly, now that I am in your power."

"I can't help how things fall out," said Troy; "upon my heart, women will be the death of me!"

"Well you shouldn't keep people's hair. You'll burn it, won't you, Frank?"

Frank went on as if he had not heard her. "There are considerations even before my consideration for you; reparations to be made—ties you know nothing of. If you repent of marrying, so do I."

Trembling now, she put her hand upon his arm, saying, in mingled tones of wretchedness and coaxing, "I only repent it if you don't love me better than any woman in the world! I don't otherwise, Frank. You don't repent because you already love somebody better than you love me, do you?"

"I don't know. Why do you say that?"

"You won't burn that curl. You like the woman who owns that pretty hair—yes; it is pretty—more beautiful than my miserable black mane! Well, it is no use; I can't help being ugly. You must like her best, if you will!"

"Until to-day, when I took it from a drawer, I have never looked upon that bit of hair for several months—that I am ready to swear."

"But just now you said 'ties'; and then—that woman we met?"

" 'Twas the meeting with her that reminded me of the hair."

"Is it hers, then?"

"Yes. There, now that you have wormed it out of me, I hope you are content."

"And what are the ties?"

"Oh! that meant nothing—a mere jest."

"A mere jest!" she said, in mournful astonishment. "Can you jest when I am so wretchedly in earnest? Tell me the truth, Frank. I am not a fool, you know, although I am a woman, and have my woman's moments. Come! treat me fairly," she said, looking honestly and fearlessly into his face. "I don't want much; bare justice—that's all! Ah! once I felt I could be content with nothing less than the highest homage from the husband I should choose. Now, anything short of cruelty will content me. Yes! the independent and spirited Bathsheba is come to this!"

"For Heaven's sake don't be so desperate!" Troy said snappishly, rising as he did so, and leaving the room.

Directly he had gone, Bathsheba burst into great sobs—dry-eyed sobs, which cut as they came, without any softening by tears. But she determined to repress all evidences of feeling. She was conquered; but she would never own it as long as she lived. Her pride was indeed brought low by despairing discoveries of her spoliation by marriage with a less pure nature than her own. She chafed to and fro in rebelliousness, like a caged leopard; her whole soul was in arms, and the blood fired her face. Until she had met Troy, Bathsheba had been proud of her position as a woman; it had been a glory to her to know that her lips had been touched by no man's on earth—that her waist had never been encircled by a lover's arm. She hated herself now. In those earlier days she had always nourished a secret contempt for girls who were the slaves of the first good-looking young fellow who should choose to salute them. She had never taken kindly to the idea of marriage in the abstract as did the majority of women she saw about her. In the turmoil of her anxiety for her lover she had agreed to marry him; but the perception that had accompanied her happiest hours on this account was rather that of self-sacrifice than of promotion and honour. Although she scarcely knew the divinity's name, Diana was the goddess whom Bathsheba instinctively adored. That she had never, by look, word, or sign, encouraged a man to approach her—that she had felt herself sufficient to herself, and had in the independence of her girlish heart fancied there was a certain degradation in renouncing the simplicity of a maiden existence to become the humbler half of an indifferent matrimonial whole—were facts now bitterly remembered. O, if she had never stooped to folly of this kind, respectable as it was, and could only stand again, as she had stood on the hill at Norcombe, and dare Troy or any other man to pollute a hair of her head by his interference!

The next morning she rose earlier than usual, and had the horse saddled for her ride round the farm in the customary way. When she came in at half-past eight—their usual hour for breakfasting—she was informed that her husband had risen, taken his breakfast, and driven off to Casterbridge with the gig and Poppet.

After breakfast she was cool and collected—quite herself in fact—and she rambled to the gate, intending to walk to another quarter of the farm, which she still personally superintended as well as her duties in the house would permit, continually, however, finding herself preceded in forethought by Gabriel Oak, for whom she began to entertain the genuine friendship of a sister. Of course, she sometimes thought of him in the light of an old lover, and had momentary imaginings of what life with him as a husband would have been like; also of life with Boldwood under the same conditions. But Bathsheba, though she could feel, was not much given to futile dreaming, and her musings under this head were short and entirely confined to the times when Troy's neglect was more than ordinarily evident.

She saw coming up the road a man like Mr. Boldwood. It was Mr. Boldwood. Bathsheba blushed painfully, and watched. The farmer stopped when still a long way off, and held up his hand to Gabriel Oak, who was in a footpath across the field. The two men then approached each other and seemed to engage in earnest conversation.

Thus they continued for a long time. Joseph Poorgrass now passed near them, wheeling a barrow of apples up the hill to Bathsheba's residence. Boldwood and Gabriel called to him, spoke to him for a few minutes, and then all three parted, Joseph immediately coming up the hill with his barrow.

Bathsheba, who had seen this pantomime with some surprise, experienced great relief when Boldwood turned back again. "Well, what's the message, Joseph?" she said.

He set down his barrow, and, putting upon himself the refined aspect that a conversation with a lady required, spoke to Bathsheba over the gate.

"You'll never see Fanny Robin no more—use nor principal—ma'am."

"Why?"

"Because she's dead in the Union."

"Fanny dead—never!"

"Yes, ma'am."

"What did she die from?"

"I don't know for certain; but I should be inclined to think it was from general neshness of constitution. She was such a limber maid that 'a could stand no hardship, even when I knowed her, and 'a went like a candle-snoff, so 'tis said. She was took bad in the morning, and, being quite feeble and worn out, she died in the evening. She belongs by law to our parish; and Mr. Boldwood is going to send a waggon at three this afternoon to fetch her home here and bury her."

"Indeed I shall not let Mr. Boldwood do any such thing—I shall do it! Fanny was my uncle's servant, and, although I only knew her for a couple of days, she belongs to me. How very, very sad this is!—the idea of Fanny being in a workhouse." Bathsheba had begun to know what suffering was, and she spoke with real feeling. . . . "Send across to Mr. Boldwood's, and say that Mrs. Troy will take upon herself the duty of fetching an old servant of the family. . . . We ought not to put her in a waggon; we'll get a hearse."

"There will hardly be time, ma'am, will there?"

"Perhaps not," she said, musingly. "When did you say we must be at the door—three o'clock?"

"Three o'clock this afternoon, ma'am, so to speak it."

"Very well—you go with it. A pretty waggon is better than an ugly hearse, after all. Joseph, have the new spring waggon with the blue body and red wheels, and wash it very clean. And, Joseph—"

"Yes, ma'am."

"Carry with you some evergreens and flowers to put upon her coffin—indeed, gather a great many, and completely bury her in them. Get some boughs of laurustinus, and variegated box, and yew, and boy's-love; ay, and some bunches of chrysanthemum. And let old Pleasant draw her, because she knew him so well."

"I will, ma'am. I ought to have said that the Union, in the form of four labouring men, will meet me when I gets to our churchyard gate, and take her and bury her according to the rites of the Board of Guardians, as by law ordained."

"Dear me—Casterbridge Union—and is Fanny come to this?" said Bathsheba, musing. "I wish I had known of it sooner. I thought she was far away. How long has she lived there?"

"On'y been there a day or two."

"Oh!—then she has not been staying there as a regular inmate?"

"No. She first went to live in a garrison-town t'other side o' Wessex, and since then she's been picking up a living at seampstering in Melchester for several months, at the house of a very respectable widow-woman who takes in work of that sort. She only got handy the Union-house on Sunday morning 'a b'lieve, and 'tis supposed here and there that she had traipsed every step of the way from Melchester. Why she left her place I can't say, for I don't know; and as to a lie, why, I wouldn't tell it. That's the short of the story, ma'am."

"Ah-h!"

No gem ever flashed from a rosy ray to a white one more rapidly than changed the young wife's countenance whilst this word came from her in a long-drawn breath. "Did she walk along our turnpike road?" she said, in a suddenly restless and eager voice.

"I believe she did. . . . Ma'am, shall I call Liddy? You bain't well, ma'am, surely? You look like a lily—so pale and fainty!"

"No; don't call her; it is nothing. When did she pass Weatherbury?"

"Last Saturday night."

"That will do, Joseph; now you may go."

"Certainly, ma'am."

"Joseph, come hither a moment. What was the colour of Fanny Robin's hair?"

"Really, mistress, now that 'tis put to me so judge-and-jury like, I can't call to mind, if ye'll believe me!"

"Never mind; go on and do what I told you. Stop—well no, go on."

She turned herself away from him, that he might no longer notice the mood which had set its sign so visibly upon her, and went indoors with a distressing sense of faintness and a beating brow. About an hour after, she heard the noise of the waggon and went out, still with a painful consciousness of her bewildered and troubled look. Joseph, dressed in his best suit of clothes, was putting in the horse to start. The shrubs and flowers were all piled in the waggon, as she had directed. Bathsheba hardly saw them now.

"Whose sweetheart did you say, Joseph?"

"I don't know, ma'am."

"Are you quite sure?"

"Yes, ma'am, quite sure."

"Sure of what?"

"I'm sure that all I know is that she arrived in the morning and died in the evening without further parley. What Oak and Mr. Boldwood told me was only these few words. 'Little Fanny Robin is dead, Joseph,' Gabriel said, looking in my face in his steady old way. I was very sorry, and I said, 'Ah!—and how did she come to die?' 'Well, she's dead in Casterbridge Union,' he said; 'and perhaps 'tisn't much matter about how she came to die. She reached the Union early Sunday morning, and died in the afternoon—that's clear enough.' Then I asked what she'd been doing lately, and Mr. Boldwood turned round to me then, and left off spitting a thistle with the end of his stick. He told me about her having lived by seampstering in Melchester, as I mentioned to you, and that she walked therefrom at the end of last week, passing near here Saturday night in the dusk. They then said I had better just name a hent of her death to you, and away they went. Her death might have been brought on by biding in the night wind, you know, ma'am; for people used to say she'd go off in a decline: she used to cough a good deal in winter-time. However, 'tisn't much odds to us about that now, for 'tis all over."

"Have you heard a different story at all?" She looked at him so intently that Joseph's eyes quailed.

"Not a word, mistress, I assure 'ee!" he said. "Hardly anybody in the parish knows the news yet."

"I wonder why Gabriel didn't bring the message to me himself. He mostly makes a point of seeing me upon the most trifling errand." These words were merely murmured, and she was looking upon the ground.

"Perhaps he was busy, ma'am," Joseph suggested. "And sometimes he seems to suffer from things upon his mind, connected with the time when he was better off than 'a is now. 'A's rather a curious item, but a very understanding shepherd, and learned in books."

"Did anything seem upon his mind whilst he was speaking to you about this?"

"I cannot but say that there did, ma'am. He was terrible down, and so was Farmer Boldwood."

"Thank you, Joseph. That will do. Go on now, or you'll be late."

Bathsheba, still unhappy, went indoors again. In the course of the afternoon she said to Liddy, who had been informed of the occurrence, "What was the colour of poor Fanny Robin's hair? Do you know? I cannot recollect—I only saw her for a day or two."

"It was light, ma'am; but she wore it rather short, and packed away under her cap, so that you would hardly notice it. But I have seen her let it down when she was going to bed, and it looked beautiful then. Real golden hair."

"Her young man was a soldier, was he not?"

"Yes. In the same regiment as Mr. Troy. He says he knew him very well."

"What, Mr. Troy says so? How came he to say that?"

"One day I just named it to him, and asked him if he knew Fanny's young man. He said, 'O yes, he knew the young man as well as he knew himself, and that there wasn't a man in the regiment he liked better.'"

"Ah! Said that, did he?"

"Yes; and he said there was a strong likeness between himself and the other young man, so that sometimes people mistook them—"

"Liddy, for Heaven's sake stop your talking!" said Bathsheba, with the nervous petulance that comes from worrying perceptions.

XLII

Joseph and His Burden—Buck's Head

A WALL BOUNDED THE SITE OF CASTERBRIDGE UNION-HOUSE, EXCEPT ALONG A PORTION of the end. Here a high gable stood prominent, and it was covered like the front with a mat of ivy. In this gable was no window, chimney, ornament, or protuberance of any kind. The single feature appertaining to it, beyond the expanse of dark green leaves, was a small door.

The situation of the door was peculiar. The sill was three or four feet above the ground, and for a moment one was at a loss for an explanation of this exceptional altitude, till ruts immediately beneath suggested that the door was used solely for the passage of articles and persons to and from the level of a vehicle standing on the outside. Upon the whole, the door seemed to advertise itself as a species of Traitor's Gate translated to another sphere. That entry and exit hereby was only at rare intervals became apparent on noting that tufts of grass were allowed to flourish undisturbed in the chinks of the sill.

As the clock over the South-street Alms-house pointed to five minutes to three, a blue spring waggon, picked out with red, and containing boughs and flowers, passed the end of the street, and up towards this side of the building. Whilst the chimes were yet stammering out a shattered form of "Malbrook," Joseph Poorgrass rang the bell, and received directions to back his waggon against the high door under the gable. The door then opened, and a plain elm coffin was slowly thrust forth, and laid by two men in fustian along the middle of the vehicle.

One of the men then stepped up beside it, took from his pocket a lump of chalk, and wrote upon the cover the name and a few other words in a large scrawling hand. (We believe that they do these things more tenderly now, and provide a plate.) He covered the whole with a black cloth, threadbare, but decent, the tail-board of the waggon was returned to its place, one of the men handed a certificate of registry to Poorgrass, and both entered the door, closing it behind them. Their connection with her, short as it had been, was over forever.

Joseph then placed the flowers as enjoined, and the evergreens around the flowers, till it was difficult to divine what the waggon contained; he smacked his whip, and the rather pleasing funeral car crept down the hill, and along the road to Weatherbury.

The afternoon drew on apace, and, looking to the right towards the sea as he walked beside the horse, Poorgrass saw strange clouds and scrolls of mist rolling over the long ridges which girt the landscape in that quarter. They came in yet greater volumes, and indolently crept across the intervening valleys, and around the withered papery flags of the moor and river brinks. Then their dank spongy forms closed in upon the sky. It was a sudden overgrowth of atmospheric fungi which had their roots in the neighbouring sea, and by the time that horse, man, and corpse entered Yalbury Great Wood, these silent workings of an invisible hand had reached them, and they were completely enveloped, this being the first arrival of the autumn fogs, and the first fog of the series.

The air was as an eye suddenly struck blind. The waggon and its load rolled no longer on the horizontal division between clearness and opacity, but were imbedded in an elastic body of a monotonous pallor throughout. There was no perceptible motion in the air, not a visible drop of water fell upon a leaf of the beeches, birches, and firs composing the wood on either side. The trees stood in an attitude of intentness, as if they waited longingly for a wind to come and rock them. A startling quiet overhung all surrounding things—so completely, that the crunching of the waggon-wheels was as a great noise, and small rustles, which had never obtained a hearing except by night, were distinctly individualised.

Joseph Poorgrass looked round upon his sad burden as it loomed faintly through the flowering laurustinus, then at the unfathomable gloom amid the high trees on each hand, indistinct, shadowless, and spectrelike in their monochrome of grey. He felt anything but cheerful, and wished he had the company even of a child or dog. Stopping the horse, he listened. Not a footstep or wheel was audible anywhere around, and the dead silence was broken only by a heavy particle falling from a tree through the evergreens and alighting with a smart rap upon the coffin of poor Fanny. The fog had by this time saturated the trees, and this was the first dropping of water from the overbrimming leaves. The hollow echo of its fall reminded the waggoner painfully of the grim Leveller. Then hard by came down another drop, then two or three. Presently there was a continual tapping of these heavy drops upon the dead leaves, the road, and the travellers. The nearer boughs were beaded with the mist to the greyness of aged men, and the rusty-red leaves of the beeches were hung with similar drops, like diamonds on auburn hair.

At the roadside hamlet called Roy-Town, just beyond this wood, was the old inn Buck's Head. It was about a mile and a half from Weatherbury, and in the meridian times of stage-coach travelling had been the place where many coaches changed and kept their relays of horses. All the old stabling was now pulled down, and little remained besides the habitable inn itself, which, standing a little way back from the road, signified its existence to people far up and down the highway by a sign hanging from the horizontal bough of an elm on the opposite side of the way.

Travellers—for the variety *tourist* had hardly developed into a distinct species at this date—sometimes said in passing, when they cast their eyes up to the sign-bearing tree, that artists were fond of representing the signboard hanging thus, but that they themselves had never before noticed so perfect an instance in actual working order. It was near this tree that the waggon was standing into which Gabriel Oak crept on his first journey to Weatherbury; but, owing to the darkness, the sign and the inn had been unobserved.

The manners of the inn were of the old-established type. Indeed, in the minds of its frequenters they existed as unalterable formulae: *e.g.*—

> Rap with the bottom of your pint for more liquor.
> For tobacco, shout.
> In calling for the girl in waiting, say, "Maid!"
> Ditto for the landlady, "Old Soul!" etc., etc.

It was a relief to Joseph's heart when the friendly signboard came in view, and, stopping his horse immediately beneath it, he proceeded to fulfil an intention made a long time before. His spirits were oozing out of him quite. He turned the horse's head to the green bank, and entered the hostel for a mug of ale.

Going down into the kitchen of the inn, the floor of which was a step below the passage, which in its turn was a step below the road outside, what should Joseph see to gladden his eyes but two copper-coloured discs, in the form of the countenances of Mr. Jan Coggan and Mr. Mark Clark. These owners of the two most appreciative throats in the neighbourhood, within the pale of respectability, were now sitting face to face over a three-legged circular table, having an iron rim to keep cups and pots from being accidentally elbowed off; they might have been said to resemble the setting sun and the full moon shining *vis-à-vis* across the globe.

"Why, 'tis neighbour Poorgrass!" said Mark Clark. "I'm sure your face don't praise your mistress's table, Joseph."

"I've had a very pale companion for the last four miles," said Joseph, indulging in a shudder toned down by resignation. "And to speak the truth, 'twas beginning to tell upon me. I assure ye, I ha'n't seed the colour of victuals or drink since breakfast-time this morning, and that was no more than a dew-bit a-field."

"Then drink, Joseph, and don't restrain yourself!" said Coggan, handing him a hooped mug three-quarters full.

Joseph drank for a moderately long time, then for a longer time, saying, as he lowered the jug, " 'Tis pretty drinking—very pretty drinking, and is more than cheerful on my melancholy errand, so to speak it."

"True, drink is a pleasant delight," said Jan, as one who repeated a truism so familiar to his brain that he hardly noticed its passage over his tongue; and, lifting the cup, Coggan tilted his head gradually backwards, with closed eyes, that his expectant soul might not be diverted for one instant from its bliss by irrelevant surroundings.

"Well, I must be on again," said Poorgrass. "Not but that I should like another nip with ye; but the parish might lose confidence in me if I was seed here."

"Where be ye trading o't to to-day, then, Joseph?"

"Back to Weatherbury. I've got poor little Fanny Robin in my waggon outside, and I must be at the churchyard gates at a quarter to five with her."

"Ay—I've heard of it. And so she's nailed up in parish boards after all, and nobody to pay the bell shilling and the grave half-crown."

"The parish pays the grave half-crown, but not the bell shilling, because the bell's a luxery: but 'a can hardly do without the grave, poor body. However, I expect our mistress will pay all."

"A pretty maid as ever I see! But what's yer hurry, Joseph? The poor woman's dead, and you can't bring her to life, and you may as well sit down comfortable, and finish another with us."

"I don't mind taking just the least thimbleful ye can dream of more with ye, sonnies. But only a few minutes, because 'tis as 'tis."

"Of course, you'll have another drop. A man's twice the man afterwards. You feel so warm and glorious, and you whop and slap at your work without any trouble, and everything goes on like sticks a-breaking. Too much liquor is bad, and leads us to that horned man in the smoky house; but after all, many people haven't the gift of enjoying a wet, and since we be highly favoured with a power that way, we should make the most o't."

"True," said Mark Clark. " 'Tis a talent the Lord has mercifully bestowed upon us, and we ought not to neglect it. But, what with the parsons and clerks and school-people and serious tea-parties, the merry old ways of good life have gone to the dogs—upon my carcase, they have!"

"Well, really, I must be onward again now," said Joseph.

"Now, now, Joseph; nonsense! The poor woman is dead, isn't she, and what's your hurry?"

"Well, I hope Providence won't be in a way with me for my doings," said Joseph, again sitting down. "I've been troubled with weak moments lately, 'tis true. I've been drinky once this month already, and I did not go to church a-Sunday, and I dropped a curse or two yesterday; so I don't want to go too far for my safety. Your next world is your next world, and not to be squandered offhand."

"I believe ye to be a chapel-member, Joseph. That I do."

"Oh, no, no! I don't go so far as that."

"For my part," said Coggan, "I'm staunch Church of England."

"Ay, and faith, so be I," said Mark Clark.

"I won't say much for myself; I don't wish to," Coggan continued, with that tendency to talk on principles which is characteristic of the barley-corn. "But I've never changed a single doctrine: I've stuck like a plaster to the old faith I was born in. Yes; there's this to be said for the Church, a man can belong to the Church and bide in his cheerful old inn, and never trouble or worry his mind about doctrines at all. But to be a meetinger, you must go to chapel in all winds and weathers, and make yerself as frantic as a skit. Not but that chapel-members be clever chaps enough in their way. They can lift up beautiful prayers out of their own heads, all about their families and shipwrecks in the newspaper."

"They can—they can," said Mark Clark, with corroborative feeling; "but we Church-men, you see, must have it all printed aforehand, or, dang it all, we should no more know what to say to a great gaffer like the Lord than babes unborn."

"Chapel-folk be more hand-in-glove with them above than we," said Joseph thoughtfully.

"Yes," said Coggan. "We know very well that if anybody do go to heaven, they will. They've worked hard for it, and they deserve to have it, such as 'tis. I bain't such a fool as to pretend that we who stick to the Church have the same chance as they, because we know we have not. But I hate a feller who'll change his old ancient doctrines for the sake of get-ting to heaven. I'd as soon turn king's-evidence for the few pounds you get. Why, neigh-bours, when every one of my taties were frosted, our Pa'son Thirdly were the man who gave me a sack for seed, though he hardly had one for his own use, and no money to buy 'em. If it hadn't been for him, I shouldn't hae had a tatie to put in my garden. D'ye think I'd turn after that? No, I'll stick to my side; and if we be in the wrong, so be it: I'll fall with the fallen!"

"Well said—very well said," observed Joseph.—"However, folks, I must be moving now: upon my life I must. Pa'son Thirdly will be waiting at the church gates, and there's the woman a-biding outside in the waggon."

"Joseph Poorgrass, don't be so miserable! Pa'son Thirdly won't mind. He's a gener-ous man; he's found me in tracts for years, and I've consumed a good many in the course of a long and shady life; but he's never been the man to cry out at the expense. Sit down."

The longer Joseph Poorgrass remained, the less his spirit was troubled by the duties which devolved upon him this afternoon. The minutes glided by uncounted, until the evening shades began perceptibly to deepen, and the eyes of the three were but sparkling points on the surface of darkness. Coggan's repeater struck six from his pocket in the usual still small tones.

At that moment hasty steps were heard in the entry, and the door opened to admit the figure of Gabriel Oak, followed by the maid of the inn bearing a candle. He stared sternly at the one lengthy and two round faces of the sitters, which confronted him with the ex-pressions of a fiddle and a couple of warming-pans. Joseph Poorgrass blinked, and shrank several inches into the background.

"Upon my soul, I'm ashamed of you; 'tis disgraceful, Joseph, disgraceful!" said Gabriel indignantly. "Coggan, you call yourself a man, and don't know better than this."

Coggan looked up indefinitely at Oak, one or other of his eyes occasionally opening and closing of its own accord, as if it were not a member, but a dozy individual with a dis-tinct personality.

"Don't take on so, shepherd!" said Mark Clark, looking reproachfully at the candle, which appeared to possess special features of interest for his eyes.

"Nobody can hurt a dead woman," at length said Coggan, with the precision of a machine. "All that could be done for her is done—she's beyond us: and why should a man put himself in a tearing hurry for lifeless clay that can neither feel nor see, and don't know what you do with her at all? If she'd been alive, I would have been the first to help her. If she now wanted victuals and drink, I'd pay for it, money down. But she's dead, and no speed of ours will bring her to life. The woman's past us—time spent upon her is throwed away: why should we hurry to do what's not required? Drink, shepherd, and be friends, for to-morrow we may be like her."

"We may," added Mark Clark emphatically, at once drinking himself, to run no further risk of losing his chance by the event alluded to, Jan meanwhile merging his additional thoughts of to-morrow in a song:—

> *To-mor-row, to-mor-row!*
> *And while peace and plen-ty I find at my board,*
> *With a heart free from sick-ness and sor-row,*
> *With my friends will I share what to-day may af-ford,*
> *And let them spread the ta-ble to-mor-row.*
> *To-mor-row', to-mor—*

"Do hold thy horning, Jan!" said Oak; and turning upon Poorgrass, "as for you, Joseph, who do your wicked deeds in such confoundedly holy ways, you are as drunk as you can stand."

"No, Shepherd Oak, no! Listen to reason, shepherd. All that's the matter with me is the affliction called a multiplying eye, and that's how it is I look double to you—I mean, you look double to me."

"A multiplying eye is a very bad thing," said Mark Clark.

"It always comes on when I have been in a public-house a little time," said Joseph Poorgrass meekly. "Yes; I see two of every sort, as if I were some holy man living in the times of King Noah and entering into the ark. . . . Y-y-y-yes," he added, becoming much affected by the picture of himself as a person thrown away, and shedding tears; "I feel too good for England: I ought to have lived in Genesis by rights, like the other men of sacrifice, and then I shouldn't have b-b-been called a d-d-drunkard in such a way!"

"I wish you'd show yourself a man of spirit, and not sit whining there!"

"Show myself a man of spirit? . . . Ah, well! let me take the name of drunkard humbly—let me be a man of contrite knees—let it be! I know that I always do say 'Please God' afore I do anything, from my getting up to my going down of the same, and I be willing to take as much disgrace as there is in that holy act. Hah, yes! . . . But not a man of spirit? Have I ever allowed the toe of pride to be lifted against my hinder parts without groaning manfully that I question the right to do so? I enquire that query boldly?"

"We can't say that you have, Hero Poorgrass," admitted Jan.

"Never have I allowed such treatment to pass unquestioned! Yet the shepherd says in the face of that rich testimony that I be not a man of spirit! Well, let it pass by, and death is a kind friend!"

Gabriel, seeing that neither of the three was in a fit state to take charge of the waggon for the remainder of the journey, made no reply, but, closing the door again upon them, went across to where the vehicle stood, now getting indistinct in the fog and gloom of this mildewy time. He pulled the horse's head from the large patch of turf it had eaten bare, readjusted the boughs over the coffin, and drove along through the unwholesome night.

It had gradually become rumoured in the village that the body to be brought and buried that day was all that was left of the unfortunate Fanny Robin who had followed the Eleventh from Casterbridge through Melchester and onwards. But, thanks to Boldwood's reticence and Oak's generosity, the lover she had followed had never been individualised as Troy. Gabriel hoped that the whole truth of the matter might not be published till at any rate the girl had been in her grave for a few days, when the interposing barriers of earth and time, and a sense that the events had been somewhat shut into oblivion, would deaden the sting that revelation and invidious remark would have for Bathsheba just now.

By the time that Gabriel reached the old manor-house, her residence, which lay in his way to the church, it was quite dark. A man came from the gate and said through the fog, which hung between them like blown flour—

"Is that Poorgrass with the corpse?"

Gabriel recognised the voice as that of the parson.

"The corpse is here, sir," said Gabriel.

"I have just been to enquire of Mrs. Troy if she could tell me the reason of the delay. I am afraid it is too late now for the funeral to be performed with proper decency. Have you the registrar's certificate?"

"No," said Gabriel. "I expect Poorgrass has that; and he's at the Buck's Head. I forgot to ask him for it."

"Then that settles the matter. We'll put off the funeral till to-morrow morning. The body may be brought on to the church, or it may be left here at the farm and fetched by the bearers in the morning. They waited more than an hour, and have now gone home."

Gabriel had his reasons for thinking the latter a most objectionable plan, notwithstanding that Fanny had been an inmate of the farmhouse for several years in the lifetime of Bathsheba's uncle. Visions of several unhappy contingencies which might arise from this delay flitted before him. But his will was not law, and he went indoors to enquire of his mistress what were her wishes on the subject. He found her in an unusual mood: her eyes as she looked up to him were suspicious and perplexed as with some antecedent thought. Troy had not yet returned. At first Bathsheba assented with a mien of indifference to his proposition that they should go on to the church at once with their burden; but immediately afterwards, following Gabriel to the gate, she swerved to the extreme of solicitousness on Fanny's account, and desired that the girl might be brought into the house. Oak argued upon the convenience of leaving her in the waggon, just as she lay now, with her flowers and green leaves about her, merely wheeling the vehicle into the coach-house till the morning, but to no purpose. "It is unkind and unchristian," she said, "to leave the poor thing in a coach-house all night."

"Very well, then," said the parson. "And I will arrange that the funeral shall take place early to-morrow. Perhaps Mrs. Troy is right in feeling that we cannot treat a dead fellow-creature too thoughtfully. We must remember that though she may have erred grievously in leaving her home, she is still our sister; and it is to be believed that God's uncovenanted mercies are extended towards her, and that she is a member of the flock of Christ."

The parson's words spread into the heavy air with a sad yet unperturbed cadence, and

Gabriel shed an honest tear. Bathsheba seemed unmoved. Mr. Thirdly then left them, and Gabriel lighted a lantern. Fetching three other men to assist him, they bore the unconscious truant indoors, placing the coffin on two benches in the middle of a little sitting-room next the hall, as Bathsheba directed.

Everyone except Gabriel Oak then left the room. He still indecisively lingered beside the body. He was deeply troubled at the wretchedly ironical aspect that circumstances were putting on with regard to Troy's wife, and at his own powerlessness to counteract them. In spite of his careful manoeuvring all this day, the very worst event that could in any way have happened in connection with the burial had happened now. Oak imagined a terrible discovery resulting from this afternoon's work that might cast over Bathsheba's life a shade which the interposition of many lapsing years might but indifferently lighten, and which nothing at all might altogether remove.

Suddenly, as in a last attempt to save Bathsheba from, at any rate, immediate anguish, he looked again, as he had looked before, at the chalk writing upon the coffin-lid. The scrawl was this simple one, *"Fanny Robin and child."* Gabriel took his handkerchief and carefully rubbed out the two latter words, leaving visible the inscription *"Fanny Robin"* only. He then left the room, and went out quietly by the front-door.

XLIII

FANNY'S REVENGE

DO YOU WANT ME ANY LONGER, MA'AM?" ENQUIRED LIDDY, AT A LATER HOUR THE same evening, standing by the door with a chamber candlestick in her hand, and addressing Bathsheba, who sat cheerless and alone in the large parlour beside the first fire of the season.

"No more to-night, Liddy."

"I'll sit up for master if you like, ma'am. I am not at all afraid of Fanny, if I may sit in my own room and have a candle. She was such a childlike, nesh young thing that her spirit couldn't appear to anybody if it tried, I'm quite sure."

"O no, no! You go to bed. I'll sit up for him myself till twelve o'clock, and if he has not arrived by that time, I shall give him up and go to bed too."

"It is half-past ten now."

"Oh: is it?"

"Why don't you sit upstairs, ma'am?"

"Why don't I?" said Bathsheba desultorily. "It isn't worthwhile—there's a fire here, Liddy." She suddenly exclaimed in an impulsive and excited whisper, "Have you heard anything strange said of Fanny?" The words had no sooner escaped her than an expression of unutterable regret crossed her face, and she burst into tears.

"No—not a word!" said Liddy, looking at the weeping woman with astonishment. "What is it makes you cry so, ma'am; has anything hurt you?" She came to Bathsheba's side with a face full of sympathy.

"No, Liddy—I don't want you any more. I can hardly say why I have taken to crying lately: I never used to cry. Good-night."

Liddy then left the parlour and closed the door.

Bathsheba was lonely and miserable now; not lonelier actually than she had been before her marriage; but her loneliness then was to that of the present time as the solitude of a mountain is to the solitude of a cave. And within the last day or two had come these disquieting thoughts about her husband's past. Her wayward sentiment that evening concerning Fanny's temporary resting-place had been the result of a strange complication of impulses in Bathsheba's bosom. Perhaps it would be more accurately described as a determined rebellion against her prejudices, a revulsion from a lower instinct of uncharitableness, which would have withheld all sympathy from the dead woman, because in life she had preceded Bathsheba in the attentions of a man whom Bathsheba had by no means ceased from loving, though her love was sick to death just now with the gravity of a further misgiving.

In five or ten minutes there was another tap at the door. Liddy reappeared, and coming in a little way stood hesitating, until at length she said, "Maryann has just heard something very strange, but I know it isn't true. And we shall be sure to know the rights of it in a day or two."

"What is it?"

"Oh, nothing connected with you or us, ma'am. It is about Fanny. That same thing you have heard."

"I have heard nothing."

"I mean that a wicked story is got to Weatherbury within this last hour—that—" Liddy came close to her mistress and whispered the remainder of the sentence slowly into her ear, inclining her head as she spoke in the direction of the room where Fanny lay.

Bathsheba trembled from head to foot.

"I don't believe it!" she said, excitedly. "And there's only one name written on the coffin-cover."

"Nor I, ma'am. And a good many others don't; for we should surely have been told more about it if it had been true—don't you think so, ma'am?"

"We might or we might not."

Bathsheba turned and looked into the fire, that Liddy might not see her face. Finding that her mistress was going to say no more, Liddy glided out, closed the door softly, and went to bed.

Bathsheba's face, as she continued looking into the fire that evening, might have excited solicitousness on her account even among those who loved her least. The sadness of Fanny Robin's fate did not make Bathsheba's glorious, although she was the Esther to this poor Vashti, and their fates might be supposed to stand in some respects as contrasts to each other. When Liddy came into the room a second time the beautiful eyes which met hers had worn a listless, weary look. When she went out after telling the story they had expressed wretchedness in full activity. Her simple country nature, fed on old-fashioned principles, was troubled by that which would have troubled a woman of the world very little, both Fanny and her child, if she had one, being dead.

Bathsheba had grounds for conjecturing a connection between her own history and the dimly suspected tragedy of Fanny's end which Oak and Boldwood never for a moment credited her with possessing. The meeting with the lonely woman on the previous Saturday night had been unwitnessed and unspoken of. Oak may have had the best of intentions in withholding for as many days as possible the details of what had happened to Fanny; but had he known that Bathsheba's perceptions had already been exercised in the matter, he would have done nothing to lengthen the minutes of suspense she was now undergoing, when the certainty which must terminate it would be the worst fact suspected after all.

She suddenly felt a longing desire to speak to someone stronger than herself, and so get strength to sustain her surmised position with dignity and her lurking doubts with stoicism. Where could she find such a friend? nowhere in the house. She was by far the coolest of the women under her roof. Patience and suspension of judgment for a few hours were what she wanted to learn, and there was nobody to teach her. Might she but go to Gabriel Oak!—but that could not be. What a way Oak had, she thought, of enduring things. Boldwood, who seemed so much deeper and higher and stronger in feeling than Gabriel, had not yet learnt, any more than she herself, the simple lesson which Oak showed a mastery of by every turn and look he gave—that among the multitude of interests by which he was surrounded, those which affected his personal well-being were not the most absorbing and important in his eyes. Oak meditatively looked upon the horizon of circumstances without any special regard to his own standpoint in the midst. That was how she would wish to be. But then Oak was not racked by incertitude upon the inmost matter of his bosom, as she was at this moment. Oak knew all about Fanny that he wished to know—she felt convinced of that. If she were to go to him now at once and say no more than these few words, "What is the truth of the story?" he would feel bound in honour to tell her. It would be an inexpressible relief. No further speech would need to be uttered. He knew her so well that no eccentricity of behaviour in her would alarm him.

She flung a cloak round her, went to the door and opened it. Every blade, every twig was still. The air was yet thick with moisture, though somewhat less dense than during the afternoon, and a steady smack of drops upon the fallen leaves under the boughs was almost musical in its soothing regularity. It seemed better to be out of the house than within it, and Bathsheba closed the door, and walked slowly down the lane till she came opposite to Gabriel's cottage, where he now lived alone, having left Coggan's house through being pinched for room. There was a light in one window only, and that was downstairs. The shutters were not closed, nor was any blind or curtain drawn over the window, neither robbery nor observation being a contingency which could do much injury to the occupant of the domicile. Yes, it was Gabriel himself who was sitting up: he was reading. From her standing-place in the road she could see him plainly, sitting quite still, his light curly head upon his hand, and only occasionally looking up to snuff the candle which stood beside him. At length he looked at the clock, seemed surprised at the lateness of the hour, closed his book, and arose. He was going to bed, she knew, and if she tapped it must be done at once.

Alas for her resolve! She felt she could not do it. Not for worlds now could she give a hint about her misery to him, much less ask him plainly for information on the cause of Fanny's death. She must suspect, and guess, and chafe, and bear it all alone.

Like a homeless wanderer she lingered by the bank, as if lulled and fascinated by the atmosphere of content which seemed to spread from that little dwelling, and was so sadly lacking in her own. Gabriel appeared in an upper room, placed his light in the window-bench, and then—knelt down to pray. The contrast of the picture with her rebellious and agitated existence at this same time was too much for her to bear to look upon longer. It was not for her to make a truce with trouble by any such means. She must tread her giddy distracting measure to its last note, as she had begun it. With a swollen heart she went again up the lane, and entered her own door.

More fevered now by a reaction from the first feelings which Oak's example had raised in her, she paused in the hall, looking at the door of the room wherein Fanny lay. She locked her fingers, threw back her head, and strained her hot hands rigidly across her forehead, saying, with a hysterical sob, "Would to God you would speak and tell me your secret, Fanny! . . . O, I hope, hope it is not true that there are two of you! . . . If I could only look in upon you for one little minute, I should know all!"

A few moments passed, and she added, slowly, *"And I will."*

Bathsheba in after times could never gauge the mood which carried her through the actions following this murmured resolution on this memorable evening of her life. She went to the lumber-closet for a screw-driver. At the end of a short though undefined time she found herself in the small room, quivering with emotion, a mist before her eyes, and an excruciating pulsation in her brain, standing beside the uncovered coffin of the girl whose conjectured end had so entirely engrossed her, and saying to herself in a husky voice as she gazed within—

"It was best to know the worst, and I know it now!"

She was conscious of having brought about this situation by a series of actions done as by one in an extravagant dream; of following that idea as to method, which had burst upon her in the hall with glaring obviousness, by gliding to the top of the stairs, assuring herself by listening to the heavy breathing of her maids that they were asleep, gliding down again, turning the handle of the door within which the young girl lay, and deliber-ately setting herself to do what, if she had anticipated any such undertaking at night and alone, would have horrified her, but which, when done, was not so dreadful as was the conclusive proof of her husband's conduct which came with knowing beyond doubt the last chapter of Fanny's story.

Bathsheba's head sank upon her bosom, and the breath which had been bated in sus-pense, curiosity, and interest, was exhaled now in the form of a whispered wail: "Oh-h-h!" she said, and the silent room added length to her moan.

Her tears fell fast beside the unconscious pair in the coffin: tears of a complicated ori-gin, of a nature indescribable, almost indefinable except as other than those of simple sor-row. Assuredly their wonted fires must have lived in Fanny's ashes when events were so shaped as to chariot her hither in this natural, unobtrusive, yet effectual manner. The one feat alone—that of dying—by which a mean condition could be resolved into a grand one, Fanny had achieved. And to that had destiny subjoined this re-encounter to-night, which had, in Bathsheba's wild imagining, turned her companion's failure to success, her humil-iation to triumph, her lucklessness to ascendency; it had thrown over herself a garish light of mockery, and set upon all things about her an ironical smile.

Fanny's face was framed in by that yellow hair of hers; and there was no longer much room for doubt as to the origin of the curl owned by Troy. In Bathsheba's heated fancy the innocent white countenance expressed a dim triumphant consciousness of the pain she was retaliating for her pain with all the merciless rigour of the Mosaic law: "Burning for burning; wound for wound; strife for strife."

Bathsheba indulged in contemplations of escape from her position by immediate death, which, thought she, though it was an inconvenient and awful way, had limits to its inconvenience and awfulness that could not be overpassed; whilst the shames of life were measureless. Yet even this scheme of extinction by death was but tamely copying her rival's method without the reasons which had glorified it in her rival's case. She glided rapidly up and down the room, as was mostly her habit when excited, her hands hanging clasped in front of her, as she thought and in part expressed in broken words: "O, I hate her, yet I don't mean that I hate her, for it is grievous and wicked; and yet I hate her a little! Yes, my flesh insists upon hating her, whether my spirit is willing or no! . . . If she had only lived, I could have been angry and cruel towards her with some justification; but to be vindictive towards a poor dead woman recoils upon myself. O God, have mercy! I am miserable at all this!"

Bathsheba became at this moment so terrified at her own state of mind that she looked around for some sort of refuge from herself. The vision of Oak kneeling down that night recurred to her, and with the imitative instinct which animates women she seized upon the idea, resolved to kneel, and, if possible, pray. Gabriel had prayed; so would she.

She knelt beside the coffin, covered her face with her hands, and for a time the room was silent as a tomb. Whether from a purely mechanical, or from any other cause, when Bathsheba arose it was with a quieted spirit, and a regret for the antagonistic instincts which had seized upon her just before.

In her desire to make atonement she took flowers from a vase by the window, and began laying them around the dead girl's head. Bathsheba knew no other way of showing kindness to persons departed than by giving them flowers. She knew not how long she remained engaged thus. She forgot time, life, where she was, what she was doing. A slamming together of the coach-house doors in the yard brought her to herself again. An instant after, the front door opened and closed, steps crossed the hall, and her husband appeared at the entrance to the room, looking in upon her.

He beheld it all by degrees, stared in stupefaction at the scene, as if he thought it an illusion raised by some fiendish incantation. Bathsheba, pallid as a corpse on end, gazed back at him in the same wild way.

So little are instinctive guesses the fruit of a legitimate induction that, at this moment, as he stood with the door in his hand, Troy never once thought of Fanny in connection with what he saw. His first confused idea was that somebody in the house had died.

"Well—what?" said Troy blankly.

"I must go! I must go!" said Bathsheba, to herself more than to him. She came with a dilated eye towards the door, to push past him.

"What's the matter, in God's name? who's dead?" said Troy.

"I cannot say; let me go out. I want air!" she continued.

"But no; stay, I insist!" He seized her hand, and then volition seemed to leave her, and she went off into a state of passivity. He, still holding her, came up the room, and thus, hand in hand, Troy and Bathsheba approached the coffin's side.

The candle was standing on a bureau close by them, and the light slanted down, distinctly enkindling the cold features of both mother and babe. Troy looked in, dropped his wife's hand, knowledge of it all came over him in a lurid sheen, and he stood still.

So still he remained that he could be imagined to have left in him no motive power whatever. The clashes of feeling in all directions confounded one another, produced a neutrality, and there was motion in none.

"Do you know her?" said Bathsheba, in a small enclosed echo, as from the interior of a cell.

"I do," said Troy.

"Is it she?"

"It is."

He had originally stood perfectly erect. And now, in the well-nigh congealed immobility of his frame could be discerned an incipient movement, as in the darkest night may be discerned light after a while. He was gradually sinking forwards. The lines of his features softened, and dismay modulated to illimitable sadness. Bathsheba was regarding him from the other side, still with parted lips and distracted eyes. Capacity for intense feeling is proportionate to the general intensity of the nature, and perhaps in all Fanny's sufferings, much greater relatively to her strength, there never was a time she suffered in an absolute sense what Bathsheba suffered now.

What Troy did was to sink upon his knees with an indefinable union of remorse and reverence upon his face, and, bending over Fanny Robin, gently kissed her, as one would kiss an infant asleep to avoid awakening it.

At the sight and sound of that, to her, unendurable act, Bathsheba sprang towards him. All the strong feelings which had been scattered over her existence since she knew what feeling was, seemed gathered together into one pulsation now. The revulsion from her indignant mood a little earlier, when she had meditated upon compromised honour, forestalment, eclipse in maternity by another, was violent and entire. All that was forgotten in the simple and still strong attachment of wife to husband. She had sighed for her self-completeness then, and now she cried aloud against the severance of the union she had deplored. She flung her arms round Troy's neck, exclaiming wildly from the deepest deep of her heart—

"Don't—don't kiss them! O, Frank, I can't bear it—I can't! I love you better than she did: kiss me too, Frank—kiss me! *You will, Frank, kiss me too!*"

There was something so abnormal and startling in the childlike pain and simplicity of this appeal from a woman of Bathsheba's calibre and independence, that Troy, loosening her tightly clasped arms from his neck, looked at her in bewilderment. It was such an unexpected revelation of all women being alike at heart, even those so different in their accessories as Fanny and this one beside him, that Troy could hardly seem to believe her to be his proud wife Bathsheba. Fanny's own spirit seemed to be animating her frame. But this was the mood of a few instants only. When the momentary surprise had passed, his expression changed to a silencing imperious gaze.

"I will not kiss you!" he said, pushing her away.

Had the wife now but gone no further. Yet, perhaps, under the harrowing circumstances, to speak out was the one wrong act which can be better understood, if not forgiven in her, than the right and politic one, her rival being now but a corpse. All the feeling she had been betrayed into showing she drew back to herself again by a strenuous effort of self-command.

"What have you to say as your reason?" she asked, her bitter voice being strangely low—quite that of another woman now.

"I have to say that I have been a bad, black-hearted man," he answered.

"And that this woman is your victim; and I not less than she."

"Ah! don't taunt me, madam. This woman is more to me, dead as she is, than ever you were, or are, or can be. If Satan had not tempted me with that face of yours, and those cursed coquetries, I should have married her. I never had another thought till you came in my way. Would to God that I had; but it is all too late! I deserve to live in torment for this!" He turned to Fanny then. "But never mind, darling," he said; "in the sight of Heaven you are my very, very wife!"

At these words there arose from Bathsheba's lips a long, low cry of measureless despair and indignation, such a wail of anguish as had never before been heard within those old-inhabited walls. It was the Τετέλεσται of her union with Troy.

"If she's—that—what—am I?" she added, as a continuation of the same cry, and sobbing pitifully: and the rarity with her of such abandonment only made the condition more dire.

"You are nothing to me—nothing," said Troy heartlessly. "A ceremony before a priest doesn't make a marriage. I am not morally yours."

A vehement impulse to flee from him, to run from this place, hide, and escape his words at any price, not stopping short of death itself, mastered Bathsheba now. She waited not an instant, but turned to the door and ran out.

XLIV

Under a Tree—Reaction

Bathsheba went along the dark road, neither knowing nor caring about the direction or issue of her flight. The first time that she definitely noticed her position was when she reached a gate leading into a thicket overhung by some large oak and beech trees. On looking into the place, it occurred to her that she had seen it by daylight on some previous occasion, and that what appeared like an impassable thicket was in reality a brake of fern now withering fast. She could think of nothing better to do with her palpitating self than to go in here and hide; and entering, she lighted on a spot sheltered from the damp fog by a reclining trunk, where she sank down upon a tangled couch of fronds and stems. She mechanically pulled some armfuls round her to keep off the breezes, and closed her eyes.

Whether she slept or not that night Bathsheba was not clearly aware. But it was with a freshened existence and a cooler brain that, a long time afterwards, she became conscious of some interesting proceedings which were going on in the trees above her head and around.

A coarse-throated chatter was the first sound.

It was a sparrow just waking.

Next: "Chee-weeze-weeze-weeze!" from another retreat.

It was a finch.

Third: "Tink-tink-tink-tink-a-chink!" from the hedge.

It was a robin.

"Chuck-chuck-chuck!" overhead.

A squirrel.

Then, from the road, "With my ra-ta-ta, and my rum-tum-tum!"

It was a ploughboy. Presently he came opposite, and she believed from his voice that he was one of the boys on her own farm. He was followed by a shambling tramp of heavy feet, and looking through the ferns Bathsheba could just discern in the wan light of daybreak a team of her own horses. They stopped to drink at a pond on the other side of the way. She watched them flouncing into the pool, drinking, tossing up their heads, drinking again, the water dribbling from their lips in silver threads. There was another flounce, and they came out of the pond, and turned back again towards the farm.

She looked further around. Day was just dawning, and beside its cool air and colours her heated actions and resolves of the night stood out in lurid contrast. She perceived that in her lap, and clinging to her hair, were red and yellow leaves which had come down from the tree and settled silently upon her during her partial sleep. Bathsheba shook her dress to get rid of them, when multitudes of the same family lying round about her rose and fluttered away in the breeze thus created, "like ghosts from an enchanter fleeing."

There was an opening towards the east, and the glow from the as yet unrisen sun attracted her eyes thither. From her feet, and between the beautiful yellowing ferns with their feathery arms, the ground sloped downwards to a hollow, in which was a species of swamp, dotted with fungi. A morning mist hung over it now—a fulsome yet magnificent silvery veil, full of light from the sun, yet semi-opaque—the hedge behind it being in some measure hidden by its hazy luminousness. Up the sides of this depression grew sheaves of the common rush, and here and there a peculiar species of flag, the blades of which glistened in the emerging sun, like scythes. But the general aspect of the swamp was malignant. From its moist and poisonous coat seemed to be exhaled the essences of evil things in the earth, and in the waters under the earth. The fungi grew in all manner of positions from rotting leaves and tree stumps, some exhibiting to her listless gaze their clammy tops, others their oozing gills. Some were marked with great splotches, red as arterial blood, others were saffron yellow, and others tall and attenuated, with stems like macaroni. Some were leathery and of richest browns. The hollow seemed a nursery of pestilences small and great, in the immediate neighbourhood of comfort and health, and Bathsheba arose with a tremor at the thought of having passed the night on the brink of so dismal a place.

There were now other footsteps to be heard along the road. Bathsheba's nerves were still unstrung: she crouched down out of sight again, and the pedestrian came into view. He was a schoolboy, with a bag slung over his shoulder containing his dinner, and a book in his hand. He paused by the gate, and, without looking up, continued murmuring words in tones quite loud enough to reach her ears.

" 'O Lord, O Lord, O Lord, O Lord, O Lord':—that I know out o' book. 'Give us, give us, give us, give us, give us':—that I know. 'Grace that, grace that, grace that, grace that':—that I know." Other words followed to the same effect. The boy was of the dunce class apparently; the book was a psalter, and this was his way of learning the collect. In the worst attacks of trouble there appears to be always a superficial film of consciousness which is left disengaged and open to the notice of trifles, and Bathsheba was faintly amused at the boy's method, till he too passed on.

By this time stupor had given place to anxiety, and anxiety began to make room for hunger and thirst. A form now appeared upon the rise on the other side of the swamp, half-hidden by the mist, and came towards Bathsheba. The woman—for it was a woman—approached with her face askance, as if looking earnestly on all sides of her. When she got a little further round to the left, and drew nearer, Bathsheba could see the new-comer's profile against the sunny sky, and knew the wavy sweep from forehead to chin, with neither angle nor decisive line anywhere about it, to be the familiar contour of Liddy Smallbury.

Bathsheba's heart bounded with gratitude in the thought that she was not altogether deserted, and she jumped up. "O, Liddy!" she said, or attempted to say; but the words had only been framed by her lips; there came no sound. She had lost her voice by exposure to the clogged atmosphere all these hours of night.

"O, ma'am! I am so glad I have found you," said the girl, as soon as she saw Bathsheba.

"You can't come across," Bathsheba said in a whisper, which she vainly endeavoured to make loud enough to reach Liddy's ears. Liddy, not knowing this, stepped down upon the swamp, saying, as she did so, "It will bear me up, I think."

Bathsheba never forgot that transient little picture of Liddy crossing the swamp to her there in the morning light. Iridescent bubbles of dank subterranean breath rose from the sweating sod beside the waiting-maid's feet as she trod, hissing as they burst and ex-panded away to join the vapoury firmament above. Liddy did not sink, as Bathsheba had anticipated.

She landed safely on the other side, and looked up at the beautiful though pale and weary face of her young mistress.

"Poor thing!" said Liddy, with tears in her eyes. "Do hearten yourself up a little, ma'am. However did—"

"I can't speak above a whisper—my voice is gone for the present," said Bathsheba hurriedly. "I suppose the damp air from that hollow has taken it away. Liddy, don't ques-tion me, mind. Who sent you—anybody?"

"Nobody. I thought, when I found you were not at home, that something cruel had happened. I fancy I heard his voice late last night; and so, knowing something was wrong—"

"Is he at home?"

"No; he left just before I came out."

"Is Fanny taken away?"

"Not yet. She will soon be—at nine o'clock."

"We won't go home at present, then. Suppose we walk about in this wood?"

Liddy, without exactly understanding everything, or anything, in this episode, as-sented, and they walked together further among the trees.

"But you had better come in, ma'am, and have something to eat. You will die of a chill!"

"I shall not come indoors yet—perhaps never."

"Shall I get you something to eat, and something else to put over your head besides that little shawl?"

"If you will, Liddy."

Liddy vanished, and at the end of twenty minutes returned with a cloak, hat, some slices of bread and butter, a tea-cup, and some hot tea in a little china jug.

"Is Fanny gone?" said Bathsheba.

"No," said her companion, pouring out the tea.

Bathsheba wrapped herself up and ate and drank sparingly. Her voice was then a little clearer, and trifling colour returned to her face. "Now we'll walk about again," she said.

They wandered about the wood for nearly two hours, Bathsheba replying in monosyllables to Liddy's prattle, for her mind ran on one subject, and one only. She interrupted with—

"I wonder if Fanny is gone by this time?"

"I will go and see."

She came back with the information that the men were just taking away the corpse; that Bathsheba had been enquired for; that she had replied to the effect that her mistress was unwell and could not be seen.

"Then they think I am in my bedroom?"

"Yes." Liddy then ventured to add: "You said when I first found you that you might never go home again—you didn't mean it, ma'am?"

"No; I've altered my mind. It is only women with no pride in them who run away from their husbands. There is one position worse than that of being found dead in your husband's house from his ill-usage, and that is, to be found alive through having gone away to the house of somebody else. I've thought of it all this morning, and I've chosen my course. A runaway wife is an incumbrance to everybody, a burden to herself and a byword—all of which make up a heap of misery greater than any that comes by staying at home—though this may include the trifling items of insult, beating, and starvation. Liddy, if ever you marry—God forbid that you ever should!—you'll find yourself in a fearful situation; but mind this, don't you flinch. Stand your ground, and be cut to pieces. That's what I'm going to do."

"O, mistress, don't talk so!" said Liddy, taking her hand; "but I knew you had too much sense to bide away. May I ask what dreadful thing it is that has happened between you and him?"

"You may ask; but I may not tell."

In about ten minutes they returned to the house by a circuitous route, entering at the rear. Bathsheba glided up the back stairs to a disused attic, and her companion followed.

"Liddy," she said, with a lighter heart, for youth and hope had begun to reassert themselves; "you are to be my confidante for the present—somebody must be—and I choose you. Well, I shall take up my abode here for a while. Will you get a fire lighted, put down a piece of carpet, and help me to make the place comfortable? Afterwards, I want you and Maryann to bring up that little stump bedstead in the small room, and the bed belonging to it, and a table, and some other things. . . . What shall I do to pass the heavy time away?"

"Hemming handkerchiefs is a very good thing," said Liddy.

"O no, no! I hate needlework—I always did."

"Knitting?"

"And that, too."

"You might finish your sampler. Only the carnations and peacocks want filling in; and then it could be framed and glazed, and hung beside your aunt's ma'am."

"Samplers are out of date—horribly countrified. No, Liddy, I'll read. Bring up some books—not new ones. I haven't heart to read anything new."

"Some of your uncle's old ones, ma'am?"

"Yes. Some of those we stowed away in boxes." A faint gleam of humour passed over her face as she said: "Bring Beaumont and Fletcher's *Maid's Tragedy*; and the *Mourning Bride*; and—let me see—*Night Thoughts*, and the *Vanity of Human Wishes.*"

"And that story of the black man, who murdered his wife Desdemona? It is a nice dismal one that would suit you excellent just now."

"Now, Liddy, you've been looking into my books without telling me; and I said you were not to! How do you know it would suit me? It wouldn't suit me at all."

"But if the others do—"

"No, they don't; and I won't read dismal books. Why should I read dismal books, indeed? Bring me *Love in a Village*, and *Maid of the Mill*, and *Doctor Syntax*, and some volumes of the *Spectator.*"

All that day Bathsheba and Liddy lived in the attic in a state of barricade; a precaution which proved to be needless as against Troy, for he did not appear in the neighbourhood or trouble them at all. Bathsheba sat at the window till sunset, sometimes attempting to read, at other times watching every movement outside without much purpose, and listening without much interest to every sound.

The sun went down almost blood-red that night, and a livid cloud received its rays in the east. Up against this dark background the west front of the church-tower—the only part of the edifice visible from the farmhouse windows—rose distinct and lustrous, the vane upon the summit bristling with rays. Hereabouts, at six o'clock, the young men of the village gathered, as was their custom, for a game of Prisoners' base. The spot had been consecrated to this ancient diversion from time immemorial, the old stocks conveniently forming a base facing the boundary of the churchyard, in front of which the ground was trodden hard and bare as a pavement by the players. She could see the brown and black heads of the young lads darting about right and left, their white shirt-sleeves gleaming in the sun; whilst occasionally a shout and a peal of hearty laughter varied the stillness of the evening air. They continued playing for a quarter of an hour or so, when the game concluded abruptly, and the players leapt over the wall and vanished round to the other side behind a yew-tree, which was also half behind a beech, now spreading in one mass of golden foliage, on which the branches traced black lines.

"Why did the base-players finish their game so suddenly?" Bathsheba enquired, the next time that Liddy entered the room.

"I think 'twas because two men came just then from Casterbridge and began putting up a grand carved tombstone," said Liddy. "The lads went to see whose it was."

"Do you know?" Bathsheba asked.

"I don't," said Liddy.

XLV

TROY'S ROMANTICISM

WHEN TROY'S WIFE HAD LEFT THE HOUSE AT THE PREVIOUS MIDNIGHT HIS FIRST ACT was to cover the dead from sight. This done he ascended the stairs, and throwing himself down upon the bed dressed as he was, he waited miserably for the morning.

Fate·had dealt grimly with him through the last four-and-twenty hours. His day had been spent in a way which varied very materially from his intentions regarding it. There is always an inertia to be overcome in striking out a new line of conduct—not more in ourselves, it seems, than in circumscribing events, which appear as if leagued together to allow no novelties in the way of amelioration.

Twenty pounds having been secured from Bathsheba, he had managed to add to the sum every farthing he could muster on his own account, which had been seven pounds ten. With this money, twenty-seven pounds ten in all, he had hastily driven from the gate that morning to keep his appointment with Fanny Robin.

On reaching Casterbridge he left the horse and trap at an inn, and at five minutes before ten came back to the bridge at the lower end of the town, and sat himself upon the parapet. The clocks struck the hour, and no Fanny appeared. In fact, at that moment she was being robed in her grave-clothes by two attendants at the Union poorhouse—the first and last tiring-women the gentle creature had ever been honoured with. The quarter went, the half-hour. A rush of recollection came upon Troy as he waited: this was the second time she had broken a serious engagement with him. In anger he vowed it should be the last, and at eleven o'clock, when he had lingered and watched the stone of the bridge till he knew every lichen upon their faces, and heard the chink of the ripples underneath till they oppressed him, he jumped from his seat, went to the inn for his gig, and in a bitter mood of indifference concerning the past, and recklessness about the future, drove on to Budmouth races.

He reached the race-course at two o'clock, and remained either there or in the town till nine. But Fanny's image, as it had appeared to him in the sombre shadows of that Saturday evening, returned to his mind, backed up by Bathsheba's reproaches. He vowed he would not bet, and he kept his vow, for on leaving the town at nine o'clock in the evening he had diminished his cash only to the extent of a few shillings.

He trotted slowly homeward, and it was now that he was struck for the first time with a thought that Fanny had been really prevented by illness from keeping her promise. This time she could have made no mistake. He regretted that he had not remained in Casterbridge and made enquiries. Reaching home he quietly unharnessed the horse and came indoors, as we have seen, to the fearful shock that awaited him.

As soon as it grew light enough to distinguish objects, Troy arose from the coverlet of the bed, and in a mood of absolute indifference to Bathsheba's whereabouts, and almost oblivious of her existence, he stalked downstairs and left the house by the back-door. His walk was towards the churchyard, entering which he searched around till he found a newly dug unoccupied grave—the grave dug the day before for Fanny. The position of this having been marked, he hastened on to Casterbridge, only pausing and musing for a while at the hill whereon he had last seen Fanny alive.

Reaching the town, Troy descended into a side street and entered a pair of gates surmounted by a board bearing the words, "Lester, stone and marble mason." Within were lying about stones of all sizes and designs, inscribed as being sacred to the memory of unnamed persons who had not yet died.

Troy was so unlike himself now in look, word, and deed, that the want of likeness was perceptible even to his own consciousness. His method of engaging himself in this business of purchasing a tomb was that of an absolutely unpracticed man. He could not bring himself to consider, calculate, or economise. He waywardly wished for something, and he set about obtaining it like a child in a nursery. "I want a good tomb," he said to the man who stood in a little office within the yard. "I want as good a one as you can give me for twenty-seven pounds."

It was all the money he possessed.

"That sum to include everything?"

"Everything. Cutting the name, carriage to Weatherbury, and erection. And I want it now, at once."

"We could not get anything special worked this week."

"I must have it now."

"If you would like one of these in stock it could be got ready immediately."

"Very well," said Troy, impatiently. "Let's see what you have."

"The best I have in stock is this one," said the stone-cutter, going into a shed. "Here's a marble head-stone beautifully crocketed, with medallions beneath of typical subjects; here's the foot-stone after the same pattern, and here's the coping to enclose the grave. The polishing alone of the set cost me eleven pounds—the slabs are the best of their kind, and I can warrant them to resist rain and frost for a hundred years without flying."

"And how much?"

"Well, I could add the name, and put it up at Weatherbury for the sum you mention."

"Get it done to-day, and I'll pay the money now."

The man agreed, and wondered at such a mood in a visitor who wore not a shred of mourning. Troy then wrote the words which were to form the inscription, settled the account and went away. In the afternoon he came back again, and found that the lettering was almost done. He waited in the yard till the tomb was packed, and saw it placed in the cart and starting on its way to Weatherbury, giving directions to the two men who were to accompany it to enquire of the sexton for the grave of the person named in the inscription.

It was quite dark when Troy came out of Casterbridge. He carried rather a heavy basket upon his arm, with which he strode moodily along the road, resting occasionally at bridges and gates, whereon he deposited his burden for a time. Midway on his journey he met, returning in the darkness, the men and the waggon which had conveyed the tomb. He merely enquired if the work was done, and, on being assured that it was, passed on again.

Troy entered Weatherbury churchyard about ten o'clock, and went immediately to the corner where he had marked the vacant grave early in the morning. It was on the obscure side of the tower, screened to a great extent from the view of passers along the road—a spot which until lately had been abandoned to heaps of stones and bushes of

alder, but now it was cleared and made orderly for interments, by reason of the rapid filling of the ground elsewhere.

Here now stood the tomb as the men had stated, snow-white and shapely in the gloom,
consisting of head- and foot-stone, and enclosing border of marble-work uniting them. In
the midst was mould, suitable for plants.

Troy deposited his basket beside the tomb, and vanished for a few minutes. When he
returned he carried a spade and a lantern, the light of which he directed for a few moments
upon the marble, whilst he read the inscription. He hung his lantern on the lowest bough
of the yew-tree, and took from his basket flower-roots of several varieties. There were
bundles of snowdrop, hyacinth and crocus bulbs, violets and double daisies, which were to
bloom in early spring, and of carnations, pinks, picotees, lilies of the valley, forget-me-
not, summer's farewell, meadow-saffron and others, for the later seasons of the year.

Troy laid these out upon the grass, and with an impassive face set to work to plant
them. The snowdrops were arranged in a line on the outside of the coping, the remainder
within the enclosure of the grave. The crocuses and hyacinths were to grow in rows; some
of the summer flowers he placed over her head and feet, the lilies and forget-me-nots over
her heart. The remainder were dispersed in the spaces between these.

Troy, in his prostration at this time, had no perception that in the futility of these
romantic doings, dictated by a remorseful reaction from previous indifference, there was
any element of absurdity. Deriving his idiosyncrasies from both sides of the Channel,
he showed at such junctures as the present the inelasticity of the Englishman, together
with that blindness to the line where sentiment verges on mawkishness, characteristic of
the French.

It was a cloudy, muggy, and very dark night, and the rays from Troy's lantern spread
into the two old yews with a strange illuminating power, flickering, as it seemed, up to the
black ceiling of cloud above. He felt a large drop of rain upon the back of his hand, and
presently one came and entered one of the holes of the lantern, whereupon the candle
sputtered and went out. Troy was weary, and it being now not far from midnight, and the
rain threatening to increase, he resolved to leave the finishing touches of his labour until
the day should break. He groped along the wall and over the graves in the dark till he
found himself round at the north side. Here he entered the porch, and, reclining upon the
bench within, fell asleep.

XLVI

The Gurgoyle: Its Doings

THE TOWER OF WEATHERBURY CHURCH WAS A SQUARE ERECTION OF FOURTEENTH-
century date, having two stone gurgoyles on each of the four faces of its parapet.
Of these eight carved protuberances only two at this time continued to serve the purpose
of their erection—that of spouting the water from the lead roof within. One mouth in
each front had been closed by bygone churchwardens as superfluous, and two others were

broken away and choked—a matter not of much consequence to the well-being of the tower, for the two mouths which still remained open and active were gaping enough to do all the work.

It has been sometimes argued that there is no truer criterion of the vitality of any given art-period than the power of the master-spirits of that time in grotesque; and certainly in the instance of Gothic art there is no disputing the proposition. Weatherbury tower was a somewhat early instance of the use of an ornamental parapet in parish as distinct from cathedral churches, and the gurgoyles, which are the necessary correlatives of a parapet, were exceptionally prominent—of the boldest cut that the hand could shape, and of the most original design that a human brain could conceive. There was, so to speak, that symmetry in their distortion which is less the characteristic of British than of Continental grotesques of the period. All the eight were different from each other. A beholder was convinced that nothing on earth could be more hideous than those he saw on the north side until he went round to the south. Of the two on this latter face, only that at the south-eastern corner concerns the story. It was too human to be called like a dragon, too impish to be like a man, too animal to be like a fiend, and not enough like a bird to be called a griffin. This horrible stone entity was fashioned as if covered with a wrinkled hide; it had short, erect ears, eyes starting from their sockets, and its fingers and hands were seizing the corners of its mouth, which they thus seemed to pull open to give free passage to the water it vomited. The lower row of teeth was quite washed away, though the upper still remained. Here and thus, jutting a couple of feet from the wall against which its feet rested as a support, the creature had for four hundred years laughed at the surrounding landscape, voicelessly in dry weather, and in wet with a gurgling and snorting sound.

Troy slept on in the porch, and the rain increased outside. Presently the gurgoyle spat. In due time a small stream began to trickle through the seventy feet of aërial space between its mouth and the ground, which the water-drops smote like duckshot in their accelerated velocity. The stream thickened in substance, and increased in power, gradually spouting further and yet further from the side of the tower. When the rain fell in a steady and ceaseless torrent the stream dashed downward in volumes.

We follow its course to the ground at this point of time. The end of the liquid parabola has come forward from the wall, has advanced over the plinth mouldings, over a heap of stones, over the marble border, into the midst of Fanny Robin's grave.

The force of the stream had, until very lately, been received upon some loose stones spread thereabout, which had acted as a shield to the soil under the onset. These during the summer had been cleared from the ground, and there was now nothing to resist the downfall but the bare earth. For several years the stream had not spouted so far from the tower as it was doing on this night, and such a contingency had been overlooked. Sometimes this obscure corner received no inhabitant for the space of two or three years, and then it was usually but a pauper, a poacher, or other sinner of undignified sins.

The persistent torrent from the gurgoyle's jaws directed all its vengeance into the grave. The rich tawny mould was stirred into motion, and boiled like chocolate. The water accumulated and washed deeper down, and the roar of the pool thus formed spread into the night as the head and chief among other noises of the kind created by the deluging rain. The flowers so carefully planted by Fanny's repentant lover began to move and writhe in their bed. The winter-violets turned slowly upside-down, and became a mere mat of mud. Soon the snowdrop and other bulbs danced in the boiling mass like ingredients in a cauldron. Plants of the tufted species were loosened, rose to the surface, and floated off.

Troy did not awake from his comfortless sleep till it was broad day. Not having been in bed for two nights his shoulders felt stiff, his feet tender, and his head heavy. He remembered his position, arose, shivered, took the spade, and again went out.

The rain had quite ceased, and the sun was shining through the green, brown, and yellow leaves, now sparkling and varnished by the raindrops to the brightness of similar effects in the landscapes of Ruysdael and Hobbema, and full of all those infinite beauties that arise from the union of water and colour with high lights. The air was rendered so transparent by the heavy fall of rain that the autumn hues of the middle distance were as rich as those near at hand, and the remote fields intercepted by the angle of the tower appeared in the same plane as the tower itself.

He entered the gravel path which would take him behind the tower. The path, instead of being stony as it had been the night before, was browned over with a thin coating of mud. At one place in the path he saw a tuft of stringy roots washed white and clean as a bundle of tendons. He picked it up—surely it could not be one of the primroses he had planted? He saw a bulb, another, and another as he advanced. Beyond doubt they were the crocuses. With a face of perplexed dismay Troy turned the corner and then beheld the wreck the stream had made.

The pool upon the grave had soaked away into the ground, and in its place was a hollow. The disturbed earth was washed over the grass and pathway in the guise of the brown mud he had already seen, and it spotted the marble tombstone with the same stains. Nearly all the flowers were washed clean out of the ground, and they lay, roots upwards, on the spots whither they had been splashed by the stream.

Troy's brow became heavily contracted. He set his teeth closely, and his compressed lips moved as those of one in great pain. This singular accident, by a strange confluence of emotions in him, was felt as the sharpest sting of all. Troy's face was very expressive, and any observer who had seen him now would hardly have believed him to be a man who had laughed, and sung, and poured love-trifles into a woman's ear. To curse his miserable lot was at first his impulse, but even that lowest stage of rebellion needed an activity whose absence was necessarily antecedent to the existence of the morbid misery which wrung him. The sight, coming as it did, superimposed upon the other dark scenery of the previous days, formed a sort of climax to the whole panorama, and it was more than he could endure. Sanguine by nature, Troy had a power of eluding grief by simply adjourning it. He could put off the consideration of any particular spectre till the matter had become old and softened by time. The planting of flowers on Fanny's grave had been perhaps but a species of elusion of the primary grief, and now it was as if his intention had been known and circumvented.

Almost for the first time in his life, Troy, as he stood by this dismantled grave, wished himself another man. It is seldom that a person with much animal spirit does not feel that the fact of his life being his own is the one qualification which singles it out as a more hopeful life than that of others who may actually resemble him in every particular. Troy had felt, in his transient way, hundreds of times, that he could not envy other people their condition, because the possession of that condition would have necessitated a different personality, when he desired no other than his own. He had not minded the peculiarities of his birth, the vicissitudes of his life, the meteorlike uncertainty of all that related to him, because these appertained to the hero of his story, without whom there would have been no story at all for him; and it seemed to be only in the nature of things that matters would right themselves at some proper date and wind up well. This very morning the illusion completed its disappearance, and, as it were, all of a sudden, Troy hated himself. The suddenness was probably more apparent than real. A coral reef which just comes short of the ocean surface is no more to the horizon than if it had never been begun, and the mere finishing stroke is what often appears to create an event which has long been potentially an accomplished thing.

He stood and meditated—a miserable man. Whither should he go? "He that is accursed, let him be accursed still," was the pitiless anathema written in this spoliated effort of his new-born solicitousness. A man who has spent his primal strength in journeying in one direction has not much spirit left for reversing his course. Troy had, since yesterday, faintly reversed his; but the merest opposition had disheartened him. To turn about would have been hard enough under the greatest providential encouragement; but to find that Providence, far from helping him into a new course, or showing any wish that he might adopt one, actually jeered his first trembling and critical attempt in that kind, was more than nature could bear.

He slowly withdrew from the grave. He did not attempt to fill up the hole, replace the flowers, or do anything at all. He simply threw up his cards and forswore his game for that time and always. Going out of the churchyard silently and unobserved—none of the villagers having yet risen—he passed down some fields at the back, and emerged just as secretly upon the high-road. Shortly afterwards he had gone from the village.

Meanwhile, Bathsheba remained a voluntary prisoner in the attic. The door was kept locked, except during the entries and exits of Liddy, for whom a bed had been arranged in a small adjoining room. The light of Troy's lantern in the churchyard was noticed about ten o'clock by the maid-servant, who casually glanced from the window in that direction whilst taking her supper, and she called Bathsheba's attention to it. They looked curiously at the phenomenon for a time, until Liddy was sent to bed.

Bathsheba did not sleep very heavily that night. When her attendant was unconscious and softly breathing in the next room, the mistress of the house was still looking out of the window at the faint gleam spreading from among the trees—not in a steady shine, but blinking like a revolving coast-light, though this appearance failed to suggest to her that a person was passing and repassing in front of it. Bathsheba sat here till it began to rain, and the light vanished, when she withdrew to lie restlessly in her bed and re-enact in a worn mind the lurid scene of yesternight.

Almost before the first faint sign of dawn appeared she arose again, and opened the window to obtain a full breathing of the new morning air, the panes being now wet with trembling tears left by the night rain, each one rounded with a pale lustre caught from primrose-hued slashes through a cloud low down in the awakening sky. From the trees came the sound of steady dripping upon the drifted leaves under them, and from the direction of the church she could hear another noise—peculiar, and not intermittent like the rest, the purl of water falling into a pool.

Liddy knocked at eight o'clock, and Bathsheba unlocked the door.

"What a heavy rain we've had in the night, ma'am!" said Liddy, when her enquiries about breakfast had been made.

"Yes; very heavy."

"Did you hear the strange noise from the churchyard?"

"I heard one strange noise. I've been thinking it must have been the water from the tower spouts."

"Well, that's what the shepherd was saying, ma'am. He's now gone on to see."

"Oh! Gabriel has been here this morning?"

"Only just looked in in passing—quite in his old way, which I thought he had left off lately. But the tower spouts used to spatter on the stones, and we are puzzled, for this was like the boiling of a pot."

Not being able to read, think, or work, Bathsheba asked Liddy to stay and breakfast with her. The tongue of the more childish woman still ran upon recent events. "Are you going across to the church, ma'am?" she asked.

"Not that I know of," said Bathsheba.

"I thought you might like to go and see where they have put Fanny. The trees hide the place from your window."

Bathsheba had all sorts of dreads about meeting her husband. "Has Mr. Troy been in to-night?" she said.

"No, ma'am; I think he's gone to Budmouth."

Budmouth! The sound of the word carried with it a much diminished perspective of him and his deeds; there were thirteen miles interval betwixt them now. She hated questioning Liddy about her husband's movements, and indeed had hitherto sedulously avoided doing so; but now all the house knew that there had been some dreadful disagreement between them, and it was futile to attempt disguise. Bathsheba had reached a stage at which people cease to have any appreciative regard for public opinion.

"What makes you think he has gone there?" she said.

"Laban Tall saw him on the Budmouth road this morning before breakfast."

Bathsheba was momentarily relieved of that wayward heaviness of the past twenty-four hours which had quenched the vitality of youth in her without substituting the philosophy of maturer years, and she resolved to go out and walk a little way. So when breakfast was over, she put on her bonnet, and took a direction towards the church. It was nine o'clock, and the men having returned to work again from their first meal, she was not likely to meet many of them in the road. Knowing that Fanny had been laid in the reprobates' quarter of the graveyard, called in the parish "behind church," which was invisible from the road, it was impossible to resist the impulse to enter and look upon a spot which, from nameless feelings, she at the same time dreaded to see. She had been unable to overcome an impression that some connection existed between her rival and the light through the trees.

Bathsheba skirted the buttress, and beheld the hole and the tomb, its delicately veined surface splashed and stained just as Troy had seen it and left it two hours earlier. On the other side of the scene stood Gabriel. His eyes, too, were fixed on the tomb, and her arrival having been noiseless, she had not as yet attracted his attention. Bathsheba did not at once perceive that the grand tomb and the disturbed grave were Fanny's, and she looked on both sides and around for some humbler mound, earthed up and clodded in the usual way. Then her eye followed Oak's, and she read the words with which the inscription opened:—

ERECTED BY FRANCIS TROY IN BELOVED MEMORY OF
FANNY ROBIN

Oak saw her, and his first act was to gaze enquiringly and learn how she received this knowledge of the authorship of the work, which to himself had caused considerable astonishment. But such discoveries did not much affect her now. Emotional convulsions seemed to have become the commonplaces of her history, and she bade him good-morning, and asked him to fill in the hole with the spade which was standing by. Whilst Oak was doing as she desired, Bathsheba collected the flowers, and began planting them with that sympathetic manipulation of roots and leaves which is so conspicuous in a woman's gardening, and which flowers seem to understand and thrive upon. She requested Oak to get the churchwardens to turn the leadwork at the mouth of the gurgoyle that hung gaping down upon them, that by this means the stream might be directed sideways, and a repetition of the accident prevented. Finally, with the superfluous magnanimity of a woman whose narrower instincts have brought down bitterness upon her instead of love, she wiped the mud spots from the tomb as if she rather liked its words than otherwise, and went home again.[1]

XLVII

ADVENTURES BY THE SHORE

TROY WANDERED ALONG TOWARDS THE SOUTH. A COMPOSITE FEELING, MADE UP OF disgust with the, to him, humdrum tediousness of a farmer's life, gloomy images of her who lay in the churchyard, remorse, and a general averseness to his wife's society, impelled him to seek a home in any place on earth save Weatherbury. The sad accessories of Fanny's end confronted him as vivid pictures which threatened to be indelible, and made life in Bathsheba's house intolerable. At three in the afternoon he found himself at the foot of a slope more than a mile in length, which ran to the ridge of a range of hills lying parallel with the shore, and formed a monotonous barrier between the basin of cultivated country inland and the wilder scenery of the coast. Up the hill stretched a road nearly straight and perfectly white, the two sides approaching each other in a gradual taper till they met the sky at the top about two miles off. Throughout the length of this narrow and irksome inclined plane not a sign of life was visible on this garish afternoon. Troy toiled up the road with a languor and depression greater than any he had experienced for many a day and year before. The air was warm and muggy, and the top seemed to recede as he approached.

1. The local tower and churchyard to not answer precisely to the foregoing description.

At last he reached the summit, and a wide and novel prospect burst upon him with an effect almost like that of the Pacific upon Balboa's gaze. The broad steely sea, marked only by faint lines, which had a semblance of being etched thereon to a degree not deep enough to disturb its general evenness, stretched the whole width of his front and round to the right, where, near the town and port of Budmouth, the sun bristled down upon it, and banished all colour, to substitute in its place a clear oily polish. Nothing moved in sky, land, or sea, except a frill of milkwhite foam along the nearer angles of the shore, shreds of which licked the contiguous stones like tongues.

He descended and came to a small basin of sea enclosed by the cliffs. Troy's nature freshened within him; he thought he would rest and bathe here before going farther. He undressed and plunged in. Inside the cove the water was uninteresting to a swimmer, being smooth as a pond, and to get a little of the ocean swell Troy presently swam between the two projecting spurs of rock which formed the pillars of Hercules to this miniature Mediterranean. Unfortunately for Troy a current unknown to him existed outside, which, unimportant to craft of any burden, was awkward for a swimmer who might be taken in it unawares. Troy found himself carried to the left and then round in a swoop out to sea.

He now recollected the place and its sinister character. Many bathers had there prayed for a dry death from time to time, and, like Gonzalo also, had been unanswered; and Troy began to deem it possible that he might be added to their number. Not a boat of any kind was at present within sight, but far in the distance Budmouth lay upon the sea, as it were quietly regarding his efforts, and beside the town the harbour showed its position by a dim meshwork of ropes and spars. After well-nigh exhausting himself in attempts to get back to the mouth of the cove, in his weakness swimming several inches deeper than was his wont, keeping up his breathing entirely by his nostrils, turning upon his back a dozen times over, swimming *en papillon*, and so on, Troy resolved as a last resource to tread water at a slight incline, and so endeavour to reach the shore at any point, merely giving himself a gentle impetus inwards whilst carried on in the general direction of the tide. This, necessarily a slow process, he found to be not altogether so difficult, and though there was no choice of a landing-place—the objects on shore passing by him in a sad and slow procession—he perceptibly approached the extremity of a spit of land yet further to the right, now well defined against the sunny portion of the horizon. While the swimmer's eye's were fixed upon the spit as his only means of salvation on this side of the Unknown, a moving object broke the outline of the extremity, and immediately a ship's boat appeared, manned with several sailor lads, her bows towards the sea.

All Troy's vigour spasmodically revived to prolong the struggle yet a little further. Swimming with his right arm, he held up his left to hail them, splashing upon the waves, and shouting with all his might. From the position of the setting sun his white form was distinctly visible upon the now deep-hued bosom of the sea to the east of the boat, and the men saw him at once. Backing their oars and putting the boat about, they pulled towards him with a will, and in five or six minutes from the time of his first halloo, two of the sailors hauled him in over the stern.

They formed part of a brig's crew, and had come ashore for sand. Lending him what little clothing they could spare among them as a slight protection against the rapidly cooling air, they agreed to land him in the morning; and without further delay, for it was growing late, they made again towards the roadstead where their vessel lay.

And now night drooped slowly upon the wide watery levels in front; and at no great distance from them, where the shore-line curved round, and formed a long riband of shade upon the horizon, a series of points of yellow light began to start into existence, denoting the spot to be the site of Budmouth, where the lamps were being lighted along the parade. The cluck of their oars was the only sound of any distinctness upon the sea, and as they laboured amid the thickening shades the lamp-lights grew larger, each appearing to send a flaming sword deep down into the waves before it, until there arose, among other dim shapes of the kind, the form of the vessel for which they were bound.

XLVIII

DOUBTS ARISE—DOUBTS LINGER

BATHSHEBA UNDERWENT THE ENLARGEMENT OF HER HUSBAND'S ABSENCE FROM HOURS to days with a slight feeling of surprise, and a slight feeling of relief; yet neither sensation rose at any time far above the level commonly designated as indifference. She belonged to him: the certainties of that position were so well defined, and the reasonable probabilities of its issue so bounded, that she could not speculate on contingencies. Taking no further interest in herself as a splendid woman, she acquired the indifferent feelings of an outsider in contemplating her probable fate as a singular wretch; for Bathsheba drew herself and her future in colours that no reality could exceed for darkness. Her original vigorous pride of youth had sickened, and with it had declined all her anxieties about coming years, since anxiety recognises a better and a worse alternative, and Bathsheba had made up her mind that alternatives on any noteworthy scale had ceased for her. Soon, or later—and that not very late— her husband would be home again. And then the days of their tenancy of the Upper Farm would be numbered. There had originally been shown by the agent to the estate some distrust of Bathsheba's tenure as James Everdene's successor, on the score of her sex, and her youth, and her beauty; but the peculiar nature of her uncle's will, his own frequent testimony before his death to her cleverness in such a pursuit, and her vigorous marshalling of the numerous flocks and herds which came suddenly into her hands before negotiations were concluded, had won confidence in her powers, and no further objections had been raised. She had latterly been in great doubt as to what the legal effects of her marriage would be upon her position; but no notice had been taken as yet of her change of name, and only one point was clear— that in the event of her own or her husband's inability to meet the agent at the forthcoming January rent-day, very little consideration would be shown, and, for that matter, very little would be deserved. Once out of the farm the approach of poverty would be sure.

Hence Bathsheba lived in a perception that her purposes were broken off. She was not a woman who could hope on without good materials for the process, differing thus from the less far-sighted and energetic, though more petted ones of the sex, with whom hope goes on as a sort of clockwork which the merest food and shelter are sufficient to wind up; and perceiving clearly that her mistake had been a fatal one, she accepted her position, and waited coldly for the end.

The first Saturday after Troy's departure she went to Casterbridge alone, a journey she had not before taken since her marriage. On this Saturday Bathsheba was passing slowly on foot through the crowd of rural business-men gathered as usual in front of the market-house, who were as usual gazed upon by the burghers with feelings that those healthy lives were dearly paid for by exclusion from possible aldermanship, when a man, who had apparently been following her, said some words to another on her left hand. Bathsheba's ears were keen as those of any wild animal, and she distinctly heard what the speaker said, though her back was towards him.

"I am looking for Mrs. Troy. Is that she there?"

"Yes; that's the young lady, I believe," said the person addressed.

"I have some awkward news to break to her. Her husband is drowned."

As if endowed with the spirit of prophecy, Bathsheba gasped out, "No, it is not true; it cannot be true!" Then she said and heard no more. The ice of self-command which had latterly gathered over her was broken, and the currents burst forth again, and overwhelmed her. A darkness came into her eyes, and she fell.

But not to the ground. A gloomy man, who had been observing her from under the portico of the old corn-exchange when she passed through the group without, stepped quickly to her side at the moment of her exclamation, and caught her in his arms as she sank down.

"What is it?" said Boldwood, looking up at the bringer of the big news, as he supported her.

"Her husband was drowned this week while bathing in Lulwind Cove. A coastguardsman found his clothes, and brought them into Budmouth yesterday."

Thereupon a strange fire lighted up Boldwood's eye, and his face flushed with the suppressed excitement of an unutterable thought. Everybody's glance was now centred upon him and the unconscious Bathsheba. He lifted her bodily off the ground, and smoothed down the folds of her dress as a child might have taken a storm-beaten bird and arranged its ruffled plumes, and bore her along the pavement to the King's Arms Inn. Here he passed with her under the archway into a private room; and by the time he had deposited—so loathly—the precious burden upon a sofa, Bathsheba had opened her eyes. Remembering all that had occurred, she murmured, "I want to go home!"

Boldwood left the room. He stood for a moment in the passage to recover his senses. The experience had been too much for his consciousness to keep up with, and now that he had grasped it it had gone again. For those few heavenly, golden moments she had been in his arms. What did it matter about her not knowing it? She had been close to his breast; he had been close to hers.

He started onward again, and sending a woman to her, went out to ascertain all the facts of the case. These appeared to be limited to what he had already heard. He then ordered her horse to be put into the gig, and when all was ready returned to inform her. He found that, though still pale and unwell, she had in the meantime sent for the Budmouth man who brought the tidings, and learnt from him all there was to know.

Being hardly in a condition to drive home as she had driven to town, Boldwood, with every delicacy of manner and feeling, offered to get her a driver, or to give her a seat in his phaeton, which was more comfortable than her own conveyance. These proposals Bathsheba gently declined, and the farmer at once departed.

About half an hour later she invigorated herself by an effort, and took her seat and the reins as usual—in external appearance much as if nothing had happened. She went out of the town by a tortuous back street, and drove slowly along, unconscious of the road and the scene. The first shades of evening were showing themselves when Bathsheba reached home, where, silently alighting and leaving the horse in the hands of the boy, she proceeded at once upstairs. Liddy met her on the landing. The news had preceded Bathsheba to Weatherbury by half an hour, and Liddy looked enquiringly into her mistress's face. Bathsheba had nothing to say.

She entered her bedroom and sat by the window, and thought and thought till night enveloped her, and the extreme lines only of her shape were visible. Somebody came to the door, knocked, and opened it.

"Well, what is it, Liddy?" she said.

"I was thinking there must be something got for you to wear," said Liddy, with hesitation.

"What do you mean?"

"Mourning."

"No, no, no," said Bathsheba hurriedly.

"But I suppose there must be something done for poor—"

"Not at present, I think. It is not necessary."

"Why not, ma'am?"

"Because he's still alive."

"How do you know that?" said Liddy, amazed.

"I don't know it. But wouldn't it have been different, or shouldn't I have heard more, or wouldn't they have found him, Liddy?—or—I don't know how it is, but death would have been different from how this is. I am perfectly convinced that he is still alive!"

Bathsheba remained firm in this opinion till Monday, when two circumstances conjoined to shake it. The first was a short paragraph in the local newspaper, which, beyond making by a methodising pen formidable presumptive evidence of Troy's death by drowning, contained the important testimony of a young Mr. Barker, M.D., of Budmouth, who spoke to being an eyewitness of the accident, in a letter to the editor. In this he stated that he was passing over the cliff on the remoter side of the cove just as the sun was setting. At that time he saw a bather carried along in the current outside the mouth of the cove, and guessed in an instant that there was but a poor chance for him unless he should be possessed of unusual muscular powers. He drifted behind a projection of the coast, and Mr. Barker followed along the shore in the same direction. But by the time that he could reach an elevation sufficiently great to command a view of the sea beyond, dusk had set in, and nothing further was to be seen.

The other circumstance was the arrival of his clothes, when it became necessary for her to examine and identify them—though this had virtually been done long before by those who inspected the letters in his pockets. It was so evident to her in the midst of her agitation that Troy had undressed in the full conviction of dressing again almost immediately, that the notion that anything but death could have prevented him was a perverse one to entertain.

Then Bathsheba said to herself that others were assured in their opinion; strange that she should not be. A strange reflection occurred to her, causing her face to flush. Suppose that Troy had followed Fanny into another world. Had he done this intentionally, yet contrived to make his death appear like an accident? Nevertheless, this thought of how the apparent might differ from the real—made vivid by her bygone jealousy of Fanny, and the remorse he had shown that night—did not blind her to the perception of a likelier difference, less tragic, but to herself far more disastrous.

When alone late that evening beside a small fire, and much calmed down, Bathsheba took Troy's watch into her hand, which had been restored to her with the rest of the articles belonging to him. She opened the case as he had opened it before her a week ago. There was the little coil of pale hair which had been as the fuze to this great explosion.

"He was hers and she was his; they should be gone together," she said. "I am nothing to either of them, and why should I keep her hair?" She took it in her hand, and held it over the fire. "No—I'll not burn it—I'll keep it in memory of her, poor thing!" she added, snatching back her hand.

XLIX

Oak's Advancement—A Great Hope

THE LATER AUTUMN AND THE WINTER DREW ON APACE, AND THE LEAVES LAY THICK upon the turf of the glades and the mosses of the woods. Bathsheba, having previously been living in a state of suspended feeling which was not suspense, now lived in a mood of quietude which was not precisely peacefulness. While she had known him to be alive she could have thought of his death with equanimity; but now that it might be she had lost him, she regretted that he was not hers still. She kept the farm going, raked in her profits without caring keenly about them, and expended money on ventures because she had done so in bygone days, which, though not long gone by, seemed infinitely removed from her present. She looked back upon that past over a great gulf, as if she were now a dead person, having the faculty of meditation still left in her, by means of which, like the mouldering gentlefolk of the poet's story, she could sit and ponder what a gift life used to be.

However, one excellent result of her general apathy was the long-delayed installation of Oak as bailiff; but he having virtually exercised that function for a long time already, the change, beyond the substantial increase of wages it brought, was little more than a nominal one addressed to the outside world.

Boldwood lived secluded and inactive. Much of his wheat and all his barley of that season had been spoilt by the rain. It sprouted, grew into intricate mats, and was ultimately thrown to the pigs in armfuls. The strange neglect which had produced this ruin and waste became the subject of whispered talk among all the people round; and it was elicited from one of Boldwood's men that forgetfulness had nothing to do with it, for he had been reminded of the danger to his corn as many times and as persistently as inferiors dared to do. The sight of the pigs turning in disgust from the rotten ears seemed to arouse Boldwood, and he one evening sent for Oak. Whether it was suggested by Bathsheba's recent act of promotion or not, the farmer proposed at the interview that Gabriel should undertake the superintendence of the Lower Farm as well as of Bathsheba's, because of the necessity Boldwood felt for such aid, and the impossibility of discovering a more trustworthy man. Gabriel's malignant star was assuredly setting fast.

Bathsheba, when she learnt of this proposal—for Oak was obliged to consult her—at first languidly objected. She considered that the two farms together were too extensive for the observation of one man. Boldwood, who was apparently determined by personal rather than commercial reasons, suggested that Oak should be furnished with a horse for his sole use, when the plan would present no difficulty, the two farms lying side by side. Boldwood did not directly communicate with her during these negotiations, only speaking to Oak, who was the go-between throughout. All was harmoniously arranged at last, and we now see Oak mounted on a strong cob, and daily trotting the length and breadth of about two thousand acres in a cheerful spirit of surveillance, as if the crops all belonged to him—the actual mistress of the one-half and the master of the other, sitting in their respective homes in gloomy and sad seclusion.

Out of this there arose, during the spring succeeding, a talk in the parish that Gabriel Oak was feathering his nest fast.

"Whatever d'ye think," said Susan Tall, "Gable Oak is coming it quite the dand. He now wears shining boots with hardly a hob in 'em, two or three times a-week, and a tall hat a-Sundays, and 'a hardly knows the name of smock-frock. When I see people strut enough to be cut up into bantam cocks, I stand dormant with wonder, and says no more!"

It was eventually known that Gabriel, though paid a fixed wage by Bathsheba independent of the fluctuations of agricultural profits, had made an engagement with Boldwood by which Oak was to receive a share of the receipts—a small share certainly, yet it was money of a higher quality than mere wages, and capable of expansion in a way that wages were not. Some were beginning to consider Oak a "near" man, for though his condition had thus far improved, he lived in no better style than before, occupying the same cottage, paring his own potatoes, mending his stockings, and sometimes even making his bed with his own hands. But as Oak was not only provokingly indifferent to public opinion, but a man who clung persistently to old habits and usages, simply because they were old, there was room for doubt as to his motives.

A great hope had latterly germinated in Boldwood, whose unreasoning devotion to Bathsheba could only be characterised as a fond madness which neither time nor circumstance, evil nor good report, could weaken or destroy. This fevered hope had grown up again like a grain of mustard-seed during the quiet which followed the hasty conjecture that Troy was drowned. He nourished it fearfully, and almost shunned the contemplation of it in earnest, lest facts should reveal the wildness of the dream. Bathsheba having at last been persuaded to wear mourning, her appearance as she entered the church in that guise was in itself a weekly addition to his faith that a time was coming—very far off perhaps, yet surely nearing—when his waiting on events should have its reward. How long he might have to wait he had not yet closely considered. What he would try to recognise was that the severe schooling she had been subjected to had made Bathsheba much more considerate than she had formerly been of the feelings of others, and he trusted that, should she be willing at any time in the future to marry any man at all, that man would be himself. There was a substratum of good feeling in her: her self-reproach for the injury she had thoughtlessly done him might be depended upon now to a much greater extent than before her infatuation and disappointment. It would be possible to approach her by the channel of her good nature, and to suggest a friendly businesslike compact between them for fulfilment at some future day, keeping the passionate side of his desire entirely out of her sight. Such was Boldwood's hope.

To the eyes of the middle-aged, Bathsheba was perhaps additionally charming just now. Her exuberance of spirit was pruned down; the original phantom of delight had shown herself to be not too bright for human nature's daily food, and she had been able to enter this second poetical phase without losing much of the first in the process.

Bathsheba's return from a two months' visit to her old aunt at Norcombe afforded the impassioned and yearning farmer a pretext for enquiring directly after her—now possibly in the ninth month of her widowhood—and endeavouring to get a notion of her state of mind regarding him. This occurred in the middle of the haymaking, and Boldwood contrived to be near Liddy, who was assisting in the fields.

"I am glad to see you out-of-doors, Lydia," he said pleasantly.

She simpered, and wondered in her heart why he should speak so frankly to her.

"I hope Mrs. Troy is quite well after her long absence," he continued, in a manner expressing that the coldest-hearted neighbour could scarcely say less about her.

"She is quite well, sir."

"And cheerful, I suppose."

"Yes, cheerful."

"Fearful, did you say?"

"O no. I merely said she was cheerful."

"Tells you all her affairs?"

"No, sir."

"Some of them?"

"Yes, sir."

"Mrs. Troy puts much confidence in you, Lydia; and very wisely, perhaps."

"She do, sir. I've been with her all through her troubles, and was with her at the time of Mr. Troy's going and all. And if she were to marry again I expect I should bide with her."

"She promises that you shall—quite natural," said the strategic lover, throbbing throughout him at the presumption which Liddy's words appeared to warrant—that his darling had thought of remarriage.

"No—she doesn't promise it exactly. I merely judge on my own account."

"Yes, yes, I understand. When she alludes to the possibility of marrying again, you conclude—"

"She never do allude to it, sir," said Liddy, thinking how very stupid Mr. Boldwood was getting.

"Of course not," he returned hastily, his hope falling again. "You needn't take quite such long reaches with your rake, Lydia—short and quick ones are best. Well, perhaps, as she is absolute mistress again now, it is wise of her to resolve never to give up her freedom."

"My mistress did certainly once say, though not seriously, that she supposed she might marry again at the end of seven years from last year, if she cared to risk Mr. Troy's coming back and claiming her."

"Ah, six years from the present time. Said that she might. She might marry at once in every reasonable person's opinion, whatever the lawyers may say to the contrary."

"Have you been to ask them?" said Liddy innocently.

"Not I," said Boldwood, growing red. "Liddy, you needn't stay here a minute later than you wish, so Mr. Oak says. I am now going on a little farther. Good-afternoon."

He went away vexed with himself, and ashamed of having for this one time in his life done anything which could be called underhand. Poor Boldwood had no more skill in finesse than a battering-ram, and he was uneasy with a sense of having made himself to appear stupid and, what was worse, mean. But he had, after all, lighted upon one fact by way of repayment. It was a singularly fresh and fascinating fact, and though not without its sadness it was pertinent and real. In little more than six years from this time Bathsheba might certainly marry him. There was something definite in that hope, for admitting that there might have been no deep thought in her words to Liddy about marriage, they showed at least her creed on the matter.

This pleasant notion was now continually in his mind. Six years were a long time, but how much shorter than never, the idea he had for so long been obliged to endure! Jacob had served twice seven years for Rachel: what were six for such a woman as this? He tried to like the notion of waiting for her better than that of winning her at once. Boldwood felt his love to be so deep and strong and eternal, that it was possible she had never yet known its full volume, and this patience in delay would afford him an opportunity of giving sweet proof on the point. He would annihilate the six years of his life as if they were minutes— so little did he value his time on earth beside her love. He would let her see, all those six years of intangible ethereal courtship, how little care he had for anything but as it bore upon the consummation.

Meanwhile the early and the late summer brought round the week in which Greenhill Fair was held. This fair was frequently attended by the folk of Weatherbury.

L

The Sheep Fair—Troy Touches His Wife's Hand

Greenhill was the Nijni Novgorod of South Wessex; and the busiest, merriest, noisiest day of the whole statute number was the day of the sheep fair. This yearly gathering was upon the summit of a hill which retained in good preservation the remains of an ancient earthwork, consisting of a huge rampart and entrenchment of an oval form encircling the top of the hill, though somewhat broken down here and there. To each of the two chief openings on opposite sides a winding road ascended, and the level green space of ten or fifteen acres enclosed by the bank was the site of the fair. A few permanent erections dotted the spot, but the majority of visitors patronised canvas alone for resting and feeding under during the time of their sojourn here.

Shepherds who attended with their flocks from long distances started from home two or three days, or even a week, before the fair, driving their charges a few miles each day—

not more than ten or twelve—and resting them at night in hired fields by the wayside at previously chosen points, where they fed, having fasted since morning. The shepherd of each flock marched behind, a bundle containing his kit for the week strapped upon his shoulders, and in his hand his crook, which he used as the staff of his pilgrimage. Several of the sheep would get worn and lame, and occasionally a lambing occurred on the road. To meet these contingencies, there was frequently provided, to accompany the flocks from the remoter points, a pony and waggon into which the weakly ones were taken for the remainder of the journey.

The Weatherbury Farms, however, were no such long distance from the hill, and those arrangements were not necessary in their case. But the large united flocks of Bathsheba and Farmer Boldwood formed a valuable and imposing multitude which demanded much attention, and on this account Gabriel, in addition to Boldwood's shepherd and Cain Ball, accompanied them along the way, through the decayed old town of Kingsbere, and upward to the plateau—old George the dog of course behind them.

When the autumn sun slanted over Greenhill this morning and lighted the dewy flat upon its crest, nebulous clouds of dust were to be seen floating between the pairs of hedges which streaked the wide prospect around in all directions. These gradually converged upon the base of the hill, and the flocks became individually visible, climbing the serpentine ways which led to the top. Thus, in a slow procession, they entered the opening to which the roads tended, multitude after multitude, horned and hornless—blue flocks and red flocks, buff flocks and brown flocks, even green and salmon-tinted flocks, according to the fancy of the colourist and custom of the farm. Men were shouting, dogs were barking, with greatest animation, but the thronging travellers in so long a journey had grown nearly indifferent to such terrors, though they still bleated piteously at the unwontedness of their experiences, a tall shepherd rising here and there in the midst of them, like a gigantic idol amid a crowd of prostrate devotees.

The great mass of sheep in the fair consisted of South Downs and the old Wessex horned breeds; to the latter class Bathsheba's and Farmer Boldwood's mainly belonged. These filed in about nine o'clock, their vermiculated horns lopping gracefully on each side of their cheeks in geometrically perfect spirals, a small pink and white ear nestling under each horn. Before and behind came other varieties, perfect leopards as to the full rich substance of their coats, and only lacking the spots. There were also a few of the Oxfordshire breed, whose wool was beginning to curl like a child's flaxen hair, though surpassed in this respect by the effeminate Leicesters, which were in turn less curly than the Cotswolds. But the most picturesque by far was a small flock of Exmoors, which chanced to be there this year. Their pied faces and legs, dark and heavy horns, tresses of wool hanging round their swarthy foreheads, quite relieved the monotony of the flocks in that quarter.

All these bleating, panting, and weary thousands had entered and were penned before the morning had far advanced, the dog belonging to each flock being tied to the corner of the pen containing it. Alleys for pedestrians intersected the pens, which soon became crowded with buyers and sellers from far and near.

In another part of the hill an altogether different scene began to force itself upon the eye towards mid-day. A circular tent, of exceptional newness and size, was in course of erection here. As the day drew on, the flocks began to change hands, lightening the shepherd's responsibilities; and they turned their attention to this tent and enquired of a man at work there, whose soul seemed concentrated on tying a bothering knot in no time, what was going on.

"The Royal Hippodrome Performance of Turpin's Ride to York and the Death of Black Bess," replied the man promptly, without turning his eyes or leaving off tying.

As soon as the tent was completed the band struck up highly stimulating harmonies, and the announcement was publicly made, Black Bess standing in a conspicuous position on the outside, as a living proof, if proof were wanted, of the truth of the oracular utterances from the stage over which the people were to enter. These were so convinced by such genuine appeals to heart and understanding both that they soon began to crowd in abundantly, among the foremost being visible Jan Coggan and Joseph Poorgrass, who were holiday keeping here to-day.

"That's the great ruffen pushing me!" screamed a woman in front of Jan over her shoulder at him when the rush was at its fiercest.

"How can I help pushing ye when the folk behind push me?" said Coggan, in a deprecating tone, turning his head towards the aforesaid folk as far as he could without turning his body, which was jammed as in a vice.

There was a silence; then the drums and trumpets again sent forth their echoing notes. The crowd was again ecstasied, and gave another lurch in which Coggan and Poorgrass were again thrust by those behind upon the women in front.

"O that helpless feymels should be at the mercy of such ruffens!" exclaimed one of these ladies again, as she swayed like a reed shaken by the wind.

"Now," said Coggan, appealing in an earnest voice to the public at large as it stood clustered about his shoulder-blades, "did ye ever hear such a onreasonable woman as that? Upon my carcase, neighbours, if I could only get out of this cheesewring, the damn women might eat the show for me!"

"Don't ye lose yer temper, Jan!" implored Joseph Poorgrass, in a whisper. "They might get their men to murder us, for I think by the shine of their eyes that they be a sinful form of womankind."

Jan held his tongue, as if he had no objection to be pacified to please a friend, and they gradually reached the foot of the ladder, Poorgrass being flattened like a jumping-jack, and the sixpence, for admission, which he had got ready half an hour earlier, having become so reeking hot in the tight squeeze of his excited hand that the woman in spangles, brazen rings set with glass diamonds, and with chalked face and shoulders, who took the money of him, hastily dropped it again from a fear that some trick had been played to burn her fingers. So they all entered, and the cloth of the tent, to the eyes of an observer on the outside, became bulged into innumerable pimples such as we observe on a sack of potatoes, caused by the various human heads, backs, and elbows at high pressure within.

At the rear of the large tent there were two small dressing-tents. One of these, alloted to the male performers, was partitioned into halves by a cloth; and in one of the divisions there was sitting on the grass, pulling on a pair of jack-boots, a young man whom we instantly recognise as Sergeant Troy.

Troy's appearance in this position may be briefly accounted for. The brig aboard which he was taken in Budmouth Roads was about to start on a voyage, though somewhat short of hands. Troy read the articles and joined, but before they sailed a boat was despatched across the bay to Lulwind Cove; as he had half expected, his clothes were gone.

He ultimately worked his passage to the United States, where he made a precarious living in various towns as Professor of Gymnastics, Sword Exercise, Fencing, and Pugilism. A few months were sufficient to give him a distaste for this kind of life. There was a certain animal form of refinement in his nature; and however pleasant a strange condition might be whilst privations were easily warded off, it was disadvantageously coarse when money was short. There was ever present, too, the idea that he could claim a home and its comforts did he but choose to return to England and Weatherbury Farm. Whether Bathsheba thought him dead was a frequent subject of curious conjecture. To England he did return at last; but the fact of drawing nearer to Weatherbury abstracted its fascinations, and his intention to enter his old groove at the place became modified. It was with gloom he considered on landing at Liverpool that if he were to go home his reception would be of a kind very unpleasant to contemplate; for what Troy had in the way of emotion was an occasional fitful sentiment which sometimes caused him as much inconvenience as emotion of a strong and healthy kind. Bathsheba was not a woman to be made a fool of, or a woman to suffer in silence; and how could he endure existence with a spirited wife to whom at first entering he would be beholden for food and lodging? Moreover, it was not at all unlikely that his wife would fail at her farming, if she had not already done so; and he would then become liable for her maintenance: and what a life such a future of poverty with her would be, the spectre of Fanny constantly between them, harrowing his temper and embittering her words! Thus, for reasons touching on distaste, regret, and shame commingled, he put off his return from day to day, and would have decided to put it off altogether if he could have found anywhere else the ready-made establishment which existed for him there.

At this time—the July preceding the September in which we find at Greenhill Fair— he fell in with a travelling circus which was performing in the outskirts of a northern town. Troy introduced himself to the manager by taming a restive horse of the troupe, hitting a suspended apple with a pistol-bullet fired from the animal's back when in full gallop, and other feats. For his merits in these—all more or less based upon his experiences as a dragoon-guardsman—Troy was taken into the company, and the play of Turpin was prepared with a view to his personation of the chief character. Troy was not greatly elated by the appreciative spirit in which he was undoubtedly treated, but he thought the engagement might afford him a few weeks for consideration. It was thus carelessly, and without having formed any definite plan for the future, that Troy found himself at Greenhill Fair with the rest of the company on this day.

And now the mild autumn sun got lower, and in front of the pavilion the following incident had taken place. Bathsheba—who was driven to the fair that day by her odd man Poorgrass—had, like everyone else, read or heard the announcement that Mr. Francis, the Great Cosmopolitan Equestrian and Roughrider, would enact the part of Turpin, and she was not yet too old and careworn to be without a little curiosity to see him. This particular show was by far the largest and grandest in the fair, a horde of little shows grouping themselves under its shade like chickens around a hen. The crowd had passed in, and Boldwood, who had been watching all the day for an opportunity of speaking to her, seeing her comparatively isolated, came up to her side.

"I hope the sheep have done well to-day, Mrs. Troy?" he said nervously.

"O yes, thank you," said Bathsheba, colour springing up in the centre of her cheeks. "I was fortunate enough to sell them all just as we got upon the hill, so we hadn't to pen at all."

"And now you are entirely at leisure?"

"Yes, except that I have to see one more dealer in two hours' time: otherwise I should be going home. I was looking at this large tent and the announcement. Have you ever seen the play of 'Turpin's Ride to York'? Turpin was a real man, was he not?"

"O yes, perfectly true—all of it. Indeed, I think I've heard Jan Coggan say that a relation of his knew Tom King, Turpin's friend, quite well."

"Coggan is rather given to strange stories connected with his relations, we must remember. I hope they can all be believed."

"Yes, yes; we know Coggan. But Turpin is true enough. You have never seen it played, I suppose?"

"Never. I was not allowed to go into these places when I was young. Hark! What's that prancing? How they shout!"

"Black Bess just started off, I suppose. Am I right in supposing you would like to see the performance, Mrs. Troy? Please excuse my mistake, if it is one; but if you would like to, I'll get a seat for you with pleasure." Perceiving that she hesitated, he added, "I myself shall not stay to see it: I've seen it before."

Now Bathsheba did care a little to see the show, and had only withheld her feet from the ladder because she feared to go in alone. She had been hoping that Oak might appear, whose assistance in such cases was always accepted as an inalienable right, but Oak was nowhere to be seen; and hence it was that she said, "Then if you will just look in first, to see if there's room, I think I will go in for a minute or two."

And so a short time after this Bathsheba appeared in the tent with Boldwood at her elbow, who, taking her to a "reserved" seat, again withdrew.

This feature consisted of one raised bench in a very conspicuous part of the circle, covered with red cloth, and floored with a piece of carpet, and Bathsheba immediately found, to her confusion, that she was the single reserved individual in the tent, the rest of the crowded spectators, one and all, standing on their legs on the borders of the arena, where they got twice as good a view of the performance for half the money. Hence as many eyes were turned upon her, enthroned alone in this place of honour, against a scarlet background, as upon the ponies and clown who were engaged in preliminary exploits in the centre, Turpin not having yet appeared. Once there, Bathsheba was forced to make the best of it and remain: she sat down, spreading her skirts with some dignity over the unoccupied space on each side of her, and giving a new and feminine aspect to the pavilion. In a few minutes she noticed the fat red nape of Coggan's neck among those standing just below her, and Joseph Poorgrass's saintly profile a little further on.

The interior was shadowy with a peculiar shade. The strange luminous semi-opacities of fine autumn afternoons and eves intensified into Rembrandt effects the few yellow sunbeams which came through holes and divisions in the canvas, and spirted like jets of gold-dust across the dusky blue atmosphere of haze pervading the tent, until they alighted on inner surfaces of cloth opposite, and shone like little lamps suspended there.

Troy, on peeping from his dressing-tent through a slit for a reconnoitre before entering, saw his unconscious wife on high before him as described, sitting as queen of the tournament. He started back in utter confusion, for although his disguise effectually concealed his personality, he instantly felt that she would be sure to recognise his voice. He had several times during the day thought of the possibility of some Weatherbury person or other appearing and recognising him; but he had taken the risk carelessly. If they see me, let them, he had said. But here was Bathsheba in her own person; and the reality of the scene was so much intenser than any of his prefigurings that he felt he had not half enough considered the point.

She looked so charming and fair that his cool mood about Weatherbury people was changed. He had not expected her to exercise this power over him in the twinkling of an eye. Should he go on, and care nothing? He could not bring himself to do that. Beyond a politic wish to remain unknown, there suddenly arose in him now a sense of shame at the possibility that his attractive young wife, who already despised him, should despise him more by discovering him in so mean a condition after so long a time. He actually blushed at the thought, and was vexed beyond measure that his sentiments of dislike towards Weatherbury should have led him to dally about the country in this way.

But Troy was never more clever than when absolutely at his wit's end. He hastily thrust aside the curtain dividing his own little dressing space from that of the manager and proprietor, who now appeared as the individual called Tom King as far down as his waist, and as the aforesaid respectable manager thence to his toes.

"Here's the devil to pay!" said Troy.

"How's that?"

"Why, there's a blackguard creditor in the tent I don't want to see, who'll discover me and nab me as sure as Satan if I open my mouth. What's to be done?"

"You must appear now, I think."

"I can't."

"But the play must proceed."

"Do you give out that Turpin has got a bad cold, and can't speak his part, but that he'll perform it just the same without speaking."

The proprietor shook his head.

"Anyhow, play or no play, I won't open my mouth," said Troy firmly.

"Very well, then let me see. I tell you how we'll manage," said the other, who perhaps felt it would be extremely awkward to offend his leading man just at this time. "I won't tell 'em anything about your keeping silence; go on with the piece and say nothing, doing what you can by a judicious wink now and then, and a few indomitable nods in the heroic places, you know. They'll never find out that the speeches are omitted."

This seemed feasible enough, for Turpin's speeches were not many or long, the fascination of the piece lying entirely in the action; and accordingly the play began, and at the appointed time Black Bess leapt into the grassy circle amid the plaudits of the spectators. At the turnpike scene, where Bess and Turpin are hotly pursued at midnight by the officers, and the half-awake gatekeeper in his tasselled nightcap denies that any horseman has passed, Coggan uttered a broad-chested "Well done!" which could be heard all over the fair above the bleating, and Poorgrass smiled delightedly with a nice sense of dramatic contrast between our hero, who coolly leaps the gate, and halting justice in the form of his enemies, who must needs pull up cumbersomely and wait to be let through. At the death of Tom King, he could not refrain from seizing Coggan by the hand, and whispering, with tears in his eyes, "Of course he's not really shot, Jan—only seemingly!" And when the last sad scene came on, and the body of the gallant and faithful Bess had to be carried out on a shutter by twelve volunteers from among the spectators, nothing could restrain Poorgrass from lending a hand, exclaiming, as he asked Jan to join him, " 'Twill be something to tell of at Warren's in future years, Jan, and hand down to our children." For many a year in Weatherbury, Joseph told, with the air of a man who had had experiences in his time, that he touched with his own hand the hoof of Bess as she lay upon the board upon his shoulder. If, as some thinkers hold, immortality consists in being enshrined in others' memories, then did Black Bess become immortal that day if she never had done so before.

Meanwhile Troy had added a few touches to his ordinary make-up for the character, the more effectually to disguise himself, and though he had felt faint qualms on first entering, the metamorphosis effected by judiciously "lining" his face with a wire rendered him safe from the eyes of Bathsheba and her men. Nevertheless, he was relieved when it was got through.

There was a second performance in the evening, and the tent was lighted up. Troy had taken his part very quietly this time, venturing to introduce a few speeches on occasion; and was just concluding it when, whilst standing at the edge of the circle contiguous to the first row of spectators, he observed within a yard of him the eye of a man darted keenly into his side features. Troy hastily shifted his position, after having recognised in the scrutineer the knavish bailiff Pennyways, his wife's sworn enemy, who still hung about the outskirts of Weatherbury.

At first Troy resolved to take no notice and abide by circumstances. That he had been recognised by this man was highly probable; yet there was room for a doubt. Then the great objection he had felt to allowing news of his proximity to precede him to Weatherbury in the event of his return, based on a feeling that knowledge of his present occupation would discredit him still further in his wife's eyes, returned in full force. Moreover, should he resolve not to return at all, a tale of his being alive and being in the neighbourhood would be awkward; and he was anxious to acquire a knowledge of his wife's temporal affairs before deciding which to do.

In this dilemma Troy at once went out to reconnoitre. It occurred to him that to find Pennyways, and make a friend of him if possible, would be a very wise act. He had put on a thick beard borrowed from the establishment, and in this he wandered about the fairfield. It was now almost dark, and respectable people were getting their carts and gigs ready to go home.

The largest refreshment booth in the fair was provided by an innkeeper from a neighbouring town. This was considered an unexceptionable place for obtaining the necessary food and rest: Host Trencher (as he was jauntily called by the local newspaper) being a substantial man of high repute for catering through all the country round. The tent was divided into first and second-class compartments, and at the end of the first-class division was a yet further enclosure for the most exclusive, fenced off from the body of the tent by a luncheon-bar, behind which the host himself stood bustling about in white apron and shirt-sleeves, and looking as if he had never lived anywhere but under canvas all his life. In these penetralia were chairs and a table, which, on candles being lighted, made quite a cozy and luxurious show, with an urn, plated tea and coffee pots, china tea-cups, and plum cakes.

Troy stood at the entrance to the booth, where a gipsy-woman was frying pancakes over a little fire of sticks and selling them at a penny a-piece, and looked over the heads of the people within. He could see nothing of Pennyways, but he soon discerned Bathsheba through an opening into the reserved space at the further end. Troy thereupon retreated, went round the tent into the darkness, and listened. He could hear Bathsheba's voice immediately inside the canvas; she was conversing with a man. A warmth overspread his face: surely she was not so unprincipled as to flirt in a fair! He wondered if, then, she reckoned upon his death as an absolute certainty. To get at the root of the matter, Troy took a penknife from his pocket and softly made two little cuts crosswise in the cloth, which, by folding back the corners, left a hole the size of a wafer. Close to this he placed his face, withdrawing it again in a movement of surprise; for his eye had been within twelve inches of the top of Bathsheba's head. It was too near to be convenient. He made another hole a little to one side and lower down, in a shaded place beside her chair, from which it was easy and safe to survey her by looking horizontally.

Troy took in the scene completely now. She was leaning back, sipping a cup of tea that she held in her hand, and the owner of the male voice was Boldwood, who had apparently just brought the cup to her. Bathsheba, being in a negligent mood, leant so idly against the canvas that it was pressed to the shape of her shoulder, and she was, in fact, as good as in Troy's arms; and he was obliged to keep his breast carefully backward that she might not feel its warmth through the cloth as he gazed in.

Troy found unexpected chords of feeling to be stirred again within him as they had been stirred earlier in the day. She was handsome as ever, and she was his. It was some minutes before he could counteract his sudden wish to go in, and claim her. Then he thought how the proud girl who had always looked down upon him even whilst it was to love him, would hate him on discovering him to be a strolling player. Were he to make himself known, that chapter of his life must at all risks be kept forever from her and from the Weatherbury people, or his name would be a byword throughout the parish. He would be nick-named "Turpin" as long as he lived. Assuredly before he could claim her these few past months of his existence must be entirely blotted out.

"Shall I get you another cup before you start, ma'am?" said Farmer Boldwood.

"Thank you," said Bathsheba. "But I must be going at once. It was great neglect in that man to keep me waiting here till so late. I should have gone two hours ago, if it had not been for him. I had no idea of coming in here; but there's nothing so refreshing as a cup of tea, though I should never have got one if you hadn't helped me."

Troy scrutinised her cheek as lit by the candles, and watched each varying shade thereon, and the white shell-like sinuosities of her little ear. She took out her purse and was insisting to Boldwood on paying for her tea for herself, when at this moment Pennyways entered the tent. Troy trembled: here was his scheme for respectability endangered at once. He was about to leave his hole of espial, attempt to follow Pennyways, and find out if the ex-bailiff had recognised him, when he was arrested by the conversation, and found he was too late.

"Excuse me, ma'am," said Pennyways; "I've some private information for your ear alone."

"I cannot hear it now," she said coldly. That Bathsheba could not endure this man was evident; in fact, he was continually coming to her with some tale or other, by which he might creep into favour at the expense of persons maligned.

"I'll write it down," said Pennyways confidently. He stooped over the table, pulled a leaf from a warped pocket-book, and wrote upon the paper, in a round hand—

"Your husband is here. I've seen him. Who's the fool now?"

This he folded small, and handed towards her. Bathsheba would not read it; she would not even put out her hand to take it. Pennyways, then, with a laugh of derision, tossed it into her lap, and, turning away, left her.

From the words and action of Pennyways, Troy, though he had not been able to see what the ex-bailiff wrote, had not a moment's doubt that the note referred to him. Nothing that he could think of could be done to check the exposure. "Curse my luck!" he whispered, and added imprecations which rustled in the gloom like a pestilent wind. Meanwhile Boldwood said, taking up the note from her lap—

"Don't you wish to read it, Mrs. Troy? If not, I'll destroy it."

"Oh, well," said Bathsheba carelessly, "perhaps it is unjust not to read it; but I can guess what it is about. He wants me to recommend him, or it is to tell me of some little scandal or another connected with my work-people. He's always doing that."

Bathsheba held the note in her right hand. Boldwood handed towards her a plate of cut bread-and-butter; when, in order to take a slice, she put the note into her left hand, where she was still holding the purse, and then allowed her hand to drop beside her close to the canvas. The moment had come for saving his game, and Troy impulsively felt that he would play the card. For yet another time he looked at the fair hand, and saw the pink finger-tips, and the blue veins of the wrist, encircled by a bracelet of coral chippings which she wore: how familiar it all was to him! Then, with the lightning action in which he was such an adept, he noiselessly slipped his hand under the bottom of the tent-cloth, which was far from being pinned tightly down, lifted it a little way, keeping his eye to the hole, snatched the note from her fingers, dropped the canvas, and ran away in the gloom towards the bank and ditch, smiling at the scream of astonishment which burst from her. Troy then slid down on the outside of the rampart, hastened round in the bottom of the entrenchment to a distance of a hundred yards, ascended again, and crossed boldly in a slow walk towards the front entrance of the tent. His object was now to get to Pennyways, and prevent a repetition of the announcement until such time as he should choose.

Troy reached the tent door, and standing among the groups there gathered, looked anxiously for Pennyways, evidently not wishing to make himself prominent by enquiring for him. One or two men were speaking of a daring attempt that had just been made to rob a young lady by lifting the canvas of the tent beside her. It was supposed that the rogue had imagined a slip of paper which she held in her hand to be a bank-note, for he had seized it, and made off with it, leaving her purse behind. His chagrin and disappointment at discovering its worthlessness would be a good joke, it was said. However, the occurrence seemed to have become known to few, for it had not interrupted a fiddler, who had lately begun playing by the door of the tent, nor the four bowed old men with grim countenances and walking-sticks in hand, who were dancing "Major Malley's Reel" to the tune. Behind these stood Pennyways. Troy glided up to him, beckoned, and whispered a few words; and with a mutual glance of concurrence the two men went into the night together.

LI

BATHSHEBA TALKS WITH HER OUTRIDER

THE ARRANGEMENT FOR GETTING BACK AGAIN TO WEATHERBURY HAD BEEN THAT OAK should take the place of Poorgrass in Bathsheba's conveyance and drive her home, it being discovered late in the afternoon that Joseph was suffering from his old complaint, a multiplying eye, and was, therefore, hardly trustworthy as coachman and protector to a woman. But Oak had found himself so occupied, and was full of so many cares relative to those portions of Boldwood's flocks that were not disposed of, that Bathsheba, without telling Oak or anybody, resolved to drive home herself, as she had many times done from Casterbridge Market, and trust to her good angel for performing the journey unmolested. But having fallen in with Farmer Boldwood accidentally (on her part at least) at the refreshment-tent, she found it impossible to refuse his offer to ride on horseback beside her as escort. It had grown twilight before she was aware, but Boldwood assured her that there was no cause for uneasiness, as the moon would be up in half an hour.

Immediately after the incident in the tent she had risen to go—now absolutely alarmed and really grateful for her old lover's protection—though regretting Gabriel's absence, whose company she would have much preferred, as being more proper as well as more pleasant, since he was her own managing-man and servant. This, however, could not be helped; she would not, on any consideration, treat Boldwood harshly, having once already ill-used him, and the moon having risen, and the gig being ready, she drove across the hill-top in the wending ways which led downwards—to oblivious obscurity, as it seemed, for the moon and the hill it flooded with light were in appearance on a level, the rest of the world lying as a vast shady concave between them. Boldwood mounted his horse, and followed in close attendance behind. Thus they descended into the lowlands, and the sounds of those left on the hill came like voices from the sky, and the lights were as those of a camp in heaven. They soon passed the merry stragglers in the immediate vicinity of the hill, traversed Kingsbere, and got upon the high-road.

The keen instincts of Bathsheba had perceived that the farmer's staunch devotion to herself was still undiminished, and she sympathised deeply. The sight had quite depressed her this evening; had reminded her of her folly; she wished anew, as she had wished many months ago, for some means of making reparation for her fault. Hence her pity for the man who so persistently loved on to his own injury and permanent gloom had betrayed Bathsheba into an injudicious considerateness of manner, which appeared almost like tenderness, and gave new vigour to the exquisite dream of a Jacob's seven years' service in poor Boldwood's mind.

He soon found an excuse for advancing from his position in the rear, and rode close by her side. They had gone two or three miles in the moonlight, speaking desultorily across the wheel of her gig concerning the fair, farming, Oak's usefulness to them both, and other indifferent subjects, when Boldwood said suddenly and simply—

"Mrs. Troy, you will marry again some day?"

This point-blank query unmistakably confused her, and it was not till a minute or more had elapsed that she said, "I have not seriously thought of any such subject."

"I quite understand that. Yet your late husband has been dead nearly one year, and—"

"You forget that his death was never absolutely proved, and may not have taken place; so that I may not be really a widow," she said, catching at the straw of escape that the fact afforded.

"Not absolutely proved, perhaps, but it was proved circumstantially. A man saw him drowning, too. No reasonable person has any doubt of his death; nor have you, ma'am, I should imagine."

"O yes I have, or I should have acted differently," she said, gently. "From the first I have had a strange unaccountable feeling that he could not have perished. But I have been able to explain that in several ways since. But were I half persuaded that I shall see him no more, I am far from thinking of marriage with another. I should be very contemptible to indulge in such a thought."

They were silent now a while, and having struck into an unfrequented track across a common, the creaks of Boldwood's saddle and her gig springs were all the sounds to be heard. Boldwood ended the pause.

"Do you remember when I carried you fainting in my arms into the King's Arms, in Casterbridge? Every dog has his day: that was mine."

"I know—I know it all," she said, hurriedly.

"I, for one, shall never cease regretting that events so fell out as to deny you to me."

"I, too, am very sorry," she said, and then checked herself. "I mean, you know, I am sorry you thought I—"

"I have always this dreary pleasure in thinking over those past times with you—that I was something to you before *he* was anything, and that you belonged *almost* to me. But, of course, that's nothing. You never liked me."

"I did; and respected you, too."

"Do you now?"

"Yes."

"Which?"

"How do you mean which?"

"Do you like me, or do you respect me?"

"I don't know—at least, I cannot tell you. It is difficult for a woman to define her feelings in language which is chiefly made by men to express theirs. My treatment of you was thoughtless, inexcusable, wicked! I shall eternally regret it. If there had been anything I could have done to make amends I would most gladly have done it—there was nothing on earth I so longed to do as to repair the error. But that was not possible."

"Don't blame yourself—you were not so far in the wrong as you suppose. Bathsheba, suppose you had real complete proof that you are what, in fact, you are—a widow— would you repair the old wrong to me by marrying me?"

"I cannot say. I shouldn't yet, at any rate."

"But you might at some future time of your life?"

"O yes, I might at some time."

"Well, then, do you know that without further proof of any kind you may marry again in about six years from the present—subject to nobody's objection or blame?"

"O yes," she said, quickly. "I know all that. But don't talk of it—seven or six years—where may we all be by that time?"

"They will soon glide by, and it will seem an astonishingly short time to look back upon when they are past—much less than to look forward to now."

"Yes, yes; I have found that in my own experience."

"Now listen once more," Boldwood pleaded. "If I wait that time, will you marry me? You own that you owe me amends—let that be your way of making them."

"But, Mr. Boldwood—six years—"

"Do you want to be the wife of any other man?"

"No indeed! I mean, that I don't like to talk about this matter now. Perhaps it is not proper, and I ought not to allow it. My husband may be living, as I said. Let us drop it for the present, please do!"

"Of course, I'll drop the subject if you wish. But propriety has nothing to do with reasons. I am a middle-aged man, willing to protect you for the remainder of our lives. On your side, at least, there is no passion or blamable haste—on mine, perhaps, there is. But I can't help seeing that if you choose from a feeling of pity, and, as you say, a wish to make amends, to make a bargain with me for a far-ahead time—an agreement which will set all things right and make me happy, late though it may be—there is no fault to be found with you as a woman. Hadn't I the first place beside you? Haven't you been almost mine once already? Surely you can say to me as much as this, you will have me back again should circumstances permit? Now, pray speak! O Bathsheba, promise—it is only a little promise—that if you marry again, you will marry me!"

His tone was so excited that she almost feared him at this moment, even whilst she sympathised. It was a simple physical fear—the weak of the strong; there was no emotional aversion or inner repugnance. She said, with some distress in her voice, for she remembered vividly his outburst on the Yalbury Road, and shrank from a repetition of his anger:—

"I will never marry another man whilst you wish me to be your wife, whatever comes—but to say more—you have taken me so by surprise—"

"But let it stand in these simple words—that in six years' time you will be my wife? Unexpected accidents we'll not mention, because those, of course, must be given way to. Now, this time I know you will keep your word."

"That's why I hesitate to give it."

"But do give it! Remember the past, and be kind."

She breathed; and then said mournfully: "O what shall I do? I don't love you, and I much fear that I never shall love you as much as a woman ought to love a husband. If you, sir, know that, and I can yet give you happiness by a mere promise to marry at the end of six years, if my husband should not come back, it is a great honour to me. And if you value such an act of friendship from a woman who doesn't esteem herself as she did, and has little love left, why I—I will—"

"Promise!"

"—Consider, if I cannot promise soon."

"But soon is perhaps never?"

"O no, it is not! I mean soon. Christmas, we'll say."

"Christmas!" He said nothing further till he added: "Well, I'll say no more to you about it till that time."

Bathsheba was in a very peculiar state of mind, which showed how entirely the soul is the slave of the body, the ethereal spirit dependent for its quality upon the tangible flesh and blood. It is hardly too much to say that she felt coerced by a force stronger than her own will, not only into the act of promising upon this singularly remote and vague matter, but into the emotion of fancying that she ought to promise. When the weeks intervening between the night of this conversation and Christmas day began perceptibly to diminish, her anxiety and perplexity increased.

One day she was led by an accident into an oddly confidential dialogue with Gabriel about her difficulty. It afforded her a little relief—of a dull and cheerless kind. They were auditing accounts, and something occurred in the course of their labours which led Oak to say, speaking of Boldwood, "He'll never forget you, ma'am, never."

Then out came her trouble before she was aware; and she told him how she had again got into the toils; what Boldwood had asked her, and how he was expecting her assent. "The most mournful reason of all for my agreeing to it," she said sadly, "and the true reason why I think to do so for good or for evil, is this—it is a thing I have not breathed to a living soul as yet—I believe that if I don't give my word, he'll go out of his mind."

"Really, do ye?" said Gabriel, gravely.

"I believe this," she continued, with reckless frankness; "and Heaven knows I say it in a spirit the very reverse of vain, for I am grieved and troubled to my soul about it—I believe I hold that man's future in my hand. His career depends entirely upon my treatment of him. O Gabriel, I tremble at my responsibility, for it is terrible!"

"Well, I think this much, ma'am, as I told you years ago," said Oak, "that his life is a total blank whenever he isn't hoping for 'ee; but I can't suppose—I hope that nothing so dreadful hangs on to it as you fancy. His natural manner has always been dark and strange, you know. But since the case is so sad and oddlike, why don't ye give the conditional promise? I think I would."

"But is it right? Some rash acts of my past life have taught me that a watched woman must have very much circumspection to retain only a very little credit, and I do want and long to be discreet in this! And six years—why we may all be in our graves by that time, even if Mr. Troy does not come back again, which he may not impossibly do! Such thoughts give a sort of absurdity to the scheme. Now, isn't it preposterous, Gabriel? However he came to dream of it, I cannot think. But is it wrong? You know—you are older than I."

"Eight years older, ma'am."

"Yes, eight years—and is it wrong?"

"Perhaps it would be an uncommon agreement for a man and woman to make: I don't see anything really wrong about it," said Oak slowly. "In fact the very thing that makes it doubtful if you ought to marry en under any condition, that is, your not caring about him—for I may suppose—"

"Yes, you may suppose that love is wanting," she said shortly. "Love is an utterly bygone, sorry, worn-out, miserable thing with me—for him or anyone else."

"Well, your want of love seems to me the one thing that takes away harm from such an agreement with him. If wild heat had to do wi' it, making ye long to overcome the awkwardness about your husband's vanishing, it mid be wrong; but a cold-hearted agreement to oblige a man seems different, somehow. The real sin, ma'am in my mind, lies in thinking of ever wedding wi' a man you don't love honest and true."

"That I'm willing to pay the penalty of," said Bathsheba, firmly. "You know, Gabriel, this is what I cannot get off my conscience—that I once seriously injured him in sheer idleness. If I had never played a trick upon him, he would never have wanted to marry me. O if I could only pay some heavy damages in money to him for the harm I did, and so get the sin off my soul that way! . . . Well, there's the debt, which can only be discharged in one way, and I believe I am bound to do it if it honestly lies in my power, without any consideration of my own future at all. When a rake gambles away his expectations, the fact that it is an inconvenient debt doesn't make him the less liable. I've been a rake, and the single point I ask you is, considering that my own scruples, and the fact that in the eye of the law my husband is only missing, will keep any man from marrying me until seven years have passed—am I free to entertain such an idea, even though 'tis a sort of penance—for it will be that? I *hate* the act of marriage under such circumstances, and the class of women I should seem to belong to by doing it!"

"It seems to me that all depends upon whe'r you think, as everybody else do, that your husband is dead."

"I shall get to, I suppose, because I cannot help feeling what would have brought him back long before this time if he had lived."

"Well, then, in a religious sense you will be as free to *think* o' marrying again as any real widow of one year's standing. But why don't ye ask Mr. Thirdly's advice on how to treat Mr. Boldwood?"

"No. When I want a broad-minded opinion for general enlightenment, distinct from special advice, I never go to a man who deals in the subject professionally. So I like the parson's opinion on law, the lawyer's on doctoring, the doctor's on business, and my businessman's—that is, yours—on morals."

"And on love—"

"My own."

"I'm afraid there's a hitch in that argument," said Oak, with a grave smile.

She did not reply at once, and then saying, "Good-evening, Mr. Oak," went away.

She had spoken frankly, and neither asked nor expected any reply from Gabriel more satisfactory than that she had obtained. Yet in the centremost parts of her complicated heart there existed at this minute a little pang of disappointment, for a reason she would not allow herself to recognise. Oak had not once wished her free that he might marry her himself—had not once said, "I could wait for you as well as he." That was the insect sting. Not that she would have listened to any such hypothesis. O no—for wasn't she saying all the time that such thoughts of the future were improper, and wasn't Gabriel far too poor a man to speak sentiment to her? Yet he might have just hinted about that old love of his, and asked, in a playful offhand way, if he might speak of it. It would have seemed pretty and sweet, if no more; and then she would have shown how kind and inoffensive a woman's "No" can sometimes be. But to give such cool advice—the very advice she had asked for—it ruffled our heroine all the afternoon.

LII

CONVERGING COURSES

I

CHRISTMAS-EVE CAME, AND A PARTY THAT BOLDWOOD WAS TO GIVE IN THE EVENING was the great subject of talk in Weatherbury. It was not that the rarity of Christmas parties in the parish made this one a wonder, but that Boldwood should be the giver. The announcement had had an abnormal and incongruous sound, as if one should hear of croquet-playing in a cathedral aisle, or that some much-respected judge was going upon the stage. That the party was intended to be a truly jovial one there was no room for doubt. A large bough of mistletoe had been brought from the woods that day, and suspended in the hall of the bachelor's home. Holly and ivy had followed in armfuls. From six that morning till past noon the huge wood fire in the kitchen roared and sparkled at its highest, the kettle, the sauce-pan, and the three-legged pot appearing in the midst of the flames like Shadrach, Meshach, and Abednego; moreover, roasting and basting operations were continually carried on in front of the genial blaze.

As it grew later the fire was made up in the large long hall into which the staircase descended, and all incumbrances were cleared out for dancing. The log which was to form the back-brand of the evening fire was the uncleft trunk of a tree, so unwieldy that it could be neither brought nor rolled to its place; and accordingly two men were to be observed dragging and heaving it in by chains and levers as the hour of assembly drew near.

In spite of all this, the spirit of revelry was wanting in the atmosphere of the house. Such a thing had never been attempted before by its owner, and it was now done as by a wrench. Intended gaieties would insist upon appearing like solemn grandeurs, the organization of the whole effort was carried out coldly by hirelings, and a shadow seemed to move about the rooms, saying that the proceedings were unnatural to the place and the lone man who lived therein, and hence not good.

II

BATHSHEBA WAS AT THIS TIME IN HER ROOM, DRESSING FOR THE EVENT. SHE HAD CALLED for candles, and Liddy entered and placed one on each side of her mistress's glass.

"Don't go away, Liddy," said Bathsheba, almost timidly. "I am foolishly agitated—I cannot tell why. I wish I had not been obliged to go to this dance; but there's no escaping now. I have not spoken to Mr. Boldwood since the autumn, when I promised to see him at Christmas on business, but I had no idea there was to be anything of this kind."

"But I would go now," said Liddy, who was going with her; for Boldwood had been indiscriminate in his invitations.

"Yes, I shall make my appearance, of course," said Bathsheba. "But I am *the cause* of the party, and that upsets me!—Don't tell, Liddy."

"O no, ma'am. You the cause of it, ma'am?"

"Yes. I am the reason of the party—I. If it had not been for me, there would never have been one. I can't explain any more—there's no more to be explained. I wish I had never seen Weatherbury."

"That's wicked of you—to wish to be worse off than you are."

"No, Liddy. I have never been free from trouble since I have lived here, and this party is likely to bring me more. Now, fetch my black silk dress, and see how it sits upon me."

"But you will leave off that, surely, ma'am? You have been a widow-lady fourteen months, and ought to brighten up a little on such a night as this."

"Is it necessary? No; I will appear as usual, for if I were to wear any light dress people would say things about me, and I should seem to be rejoicing when I am solemn all the time. The party doesn't suit me a bit; but never mind, stay and help to finish me off."

III

BOLDWOOD WAS DRESSING ALSO AT THIS HOUR. A TAILOR FROM CASTERBRIDGE WAS with him, assisting him in the operation of trying on a new coat that had just been brought home.

Never had Boldwood been so fastidious, unreasonable about the fit, and generally difficult to please. The tailor walked round and round him, tugged at the waist, pulled the sleeve, pressed out the collar, and for the first time in his experience Boldwood was not bored. Times had been when the farmer had exclaimed against all such niceties as childish, but now no philosophic or hasty rebuke whatever was provoked by this man for attaching as much importance to a crease in the coat as to an earthquake in South America. Boldwood at last expressed himself nearly satisfied, and paid the bill, the tailor passing out of the door just as Oak came in to report progress for the day.

"Oh, Oak," said Boldwood. "I shall of course see you here to-night. Make yourself merry. I am determined that neither expense nor trouble shall be spared."

"I'll try to be here, sir, though perhaps it may not be very early," said Gabriel, quietly. "I am glad indeed to see such a change in 'ee from what it used to be."

"Yes—I must own it—I am bright to-night: cheerful and more than cheerful—so much so that I am almost sad again with the sense that all of it is passing away. And sometimes, when I am excessively hopeful and blithe, a trouble is looming in the distance: so that I often get to look upon gloom in me with content, and to fear a happy mood. Still this may be absurd—I feel that it is absurd. Perhaps my day is dawning at last."

"I hope it 'ill be a long and a fair one."

"Thank you—thank you. Yet perhaps my cheerfulness rests on a slender hope. And yet I trust my hope. It is faith, not hope. I think this time I reckon with my host.—Oak, my hands are a little shaky, or something: I can't tie this neckerchief properly. Perhaps you will tie it for me. The fact is, I have not been well lately, you know."

"I am sorry to hear that, sir."

"Oh, it's nothing. I want it done as well as you can, please. Is there any late knot in fashion, Oak?"

"I don't know, sir," said Oak. His tone had sunk to sadness.

Boldwood approached Gabriel, and as Oak tied the neckerchief the farmer went on feverishly—

"Does a woman keep her promise, Gabriel?"

"If it is not inconvenient to her she may."

"—Or rather an implied promise."

"I won't answer for her implying," said Oak, with faint bitterness. "That's a word as full o' holes as a sieve with them."

"Oak, don't talk like that. You have got quite cynical lately—how is it? We seem to have shifted our positions: I have become the young and hopeful man, and you the old and unbelieving one. However, does a woman keep a promise, not to marry, but to enter on an engagement to marry at some time? Now you know women better than I—tell me."

"I am afeard you honour my understanding too much. However, she may keep such a promise, if it is made with an honest meaning to repair a wrong."

"It has not gone far yet, but I think it will soon—yes, I know it will," he said, in an impulsive whisper. "I have pressed her upon the subject, and she inclines to be kind to me, and to think of me as a husband at a long future time, and that's enough for me. How can I expect more? She has a notion that a woman should not marry within seven years of her husband's disappearance—that her own self shouldn't, I mean—because his body was not found. It may be merely this legal reason which influences her, or it may be a religious one, but she is reluctant to talk on the point. Yet she has promised—implied—that she will ratify an engagement to-night."

"Seven years," murmured Oak.

"No, no—it's no such thing!" he said, with impatience. "Five years, nine months, and a few days. Fifteen months nearly have passed since he vanished, and is there anything so wonderful in an engagement of little more than five years?"

"It seems long in a forward view. Don't build too much upon such promises, sir. Remember, you have once be'n deceived. Her meaning may be good; but there—she's young yet."

"Deceived? Never!" said Boldwood, vehemently. "She never promised me at that first time, and hence she did not break her promise! If she promises me, she'll marry me. Bathsheba is a woman to her word."

IV

T ROY WAS SITTING IN A CORNER OF THE WHITE HART TAVERN AT CASTERBRIDGE, SMOK- ing and drinking a steaming mixture from a glass. A knock was given at the door, and Pennyways entered.

"Well, have you seen him?" Troy enquired, pointing to a chair.

"Boldwood?"

"No—Lawyer Long."

"He wadn' at home. I went there first, too."

"That's a nuisance."

" 'Tis rather, I suppose."

"Yet I don't see that, because a man appears to be drowned and was not, he should be liable for anything. I shan't ask any lawyer—not I."

"But that's not it, exactly. If a man changes his name and so forth, and takes steps to deceive the world and his own wife, he's a cheat, and that in the eye of the law is ayless a rogue, and that is ayless a lammocken vagabond; and that's a punishable situation."

"Ha-ha! Well done, Pennyways." Troy had laughed, but it was with some anxiety that he said, "Now, what I want to know is this, do you think there's really anything going on between her and Boldwood? Upon my soul, I should never have believed it! How she must detest me! Have you found out whether she has encouraged him?"

"I haen't been able to learn. There's a deal of feeling on his side seemingly, but I don't answer for her. I didn't know a word about any such thing till yesterday, and all I heard then was that she was gwine to the party at his house to-night. This is the first time she has ever gone there, they say. And they say that she've not so much as spoke to him since they were at Greenhill Fair: but what can folk believe o't? However, she's not fond of him— quite offish and quite careless, I know."

"I'm not so sure of that. . . . She's a handsome woman, Pennyways, is she not? Own that you never saw a finer or more splendid creature in your life. Upon my honour, when I set eyes upon her that day I wondered what I could have been made of to be able to leave her by herself so long. And then I was hampered with that bothering show, which I'm free of at last, thank the stars." He smoked on a while, and then added, "How did she look when you passed by yesterday?"

"Oh, she took no great heed of me, ye may well fancy; but she looked well enough, far's I know. Just flashed her haughty eyes upon my poor scram body, and then let them go past me to what was yond, much as if I'd been no more than a leafless tree. She had just got off her mare to look at the last wring-down of cider for the year; she had been riding, and so her colours were up and her breath rather quick, so that her bosom plimmed and fell—plimmed and fell—every time plain to my eye. Ay, and there were the fellers round her wringing down the cheese and bustling about and saying, 'Ware o' the pommy, ma'am: 'twill spoil yer gown.' 'Never mind me,' says she. Then Gabe brought her some of the new cider, and she must needs go drinking it through a strawmote, and not in a nateral way at all. 'Liddy,' says she, 'bring indoors a few gallons, and I'll make some cider-wine.' Sergeant, I was no more to her than a morsel of scroff in the fuel-house!"

"I must go and find her out at once—O yes, I see that—I must go. Oak is head man still, isn't he?"

"Yes, 'a b'lieve. And at Little Weatherbury Farm too. He manages everything."

" 'Twill puzzle him to manage her, or any other man of his compass!"

"I don't know about that. She can't do without him, and knowing it well he's pretty independent. And she've a few soft corners to her mind, though I've never been able to get into one, the devil's in't!"

"Ah, baily, she's a notch above you, and you must own it: a higher class of animal— a finer tissue. However, stick to me, and neither this haughty goddess, dashing piece of womanhood, Juno-wife of mine (Juno was a goddess, you know), nor anybody else shall hurt you. But all this wants looking into, I perceive. What with one thing and another, I see that my work is well cut out for me."

V

"HOW DO I LOOK TO-NIGHT, LIDDY?" SAID BATHSHEBA, GIVING A FINAL ADJUSTMENT TO her dress before leaving the glass.

"I never saw you look so well before. Yes—I'll tell you when you looked like it—that night, a year and a half ago, when you came in so wildlike, and scolded us for making remarks about you and Mr. Troy."

"Everybody will think that I am setting myself to captivate Mr. Boldwood, I suppose," she murmured. "At least they'll say so. Can't my hair be brushed down a little flatter? I dread going—yet I dread the risk of wounding him by staying away."

"Anyhow, ma'am, you can't well be dressed plainer than you are, unless you go in sackcloth at once. 'Tis your excitement is what makes you look so noticeable to-night."

"I don't know what's the matter, I feel wretched at one time, and buoyant at another. I wish I could have continued quite alone as I have been for the last year or so, with no hopes and no fears, and no pleasure and no grief."

"Now just suppose Mr. Boldwood should ask you—only just suppose it—to run away with him, what would you do, ma'am?"

"Liddy—none of that," said Bathsheba, gravely. "Mind, I won't hear joking on any such matter. Do you hear?"

"I beg pardon, ma'am. But knowing what rum things we women be, I just said—however, I won't speak of it again."

"No marrying for me yet for many a year; if ever, 'twill be for reasons very, very different from those you think, or others will believe! Now get my cloak, for it is time to go."

VI

"OAK," SAID BOLDWOOD, "BEFORE YOU GO I WANT TO MENTION WHAT HAS BEEN PASSing in my mind lately—that little arrangement we made about your share in the farm I mean. That share is small, too small, considering how little I attend to business now, and how much time and thought you give to it. Well, since the world is brightening for me, I want to show my sense of it by increasing your proportion in the partnership. I'll make a memorandum of the arrangement which struck me as likely to be convenient, for I haven't time to talk about it now; and then we'll discuss it at our leisure. My intention is ultimately to retire from the management altogether, and until you can take all the expenditure upon your shoulders, I'll be a sleeping partner in the stock. Then, if I marry her—and I hope—I feel I shall, why—"

"Pray don't speak of it, sir," said Oak, hastily. "We don't know what may happen. So many upsets may befall 'ee. There's many a slip, as they say—and I would advise you— I know you'll pardon me this once—not to be *too sure*."

"I know, I know. But the feeling I have about increasing your share is on account of what I know of you. Oak, I have learnt a little about your secret: your interest in her is more than that of bailiff for an employer. But you have behaved like a man, and I, as a sort of successful rival—successful partly through your goodness of heart—should like definitely to show my sense of your friendship under what must have been a great pain to you."

"O that's not necessary, thank 'ee," said Oak, hurriedly. "I must get used to such as that; other men have, and so shall I."

Oak then left him. He was uneasy on Boldwood's account, for he saw anew that this constant passion of the farmer made him not the man he once had been.

As Boldwood continued a while in his room alone—ready and dressed to receive his company—the mood of anxiety about his appearance seemed to pass away, and to be succeeded by a deep solemnity. He looked out of the window, and regarded the dim outline of the trees upon the sky, and the twilight deepening to darkness.

Then he went to a locked closet, and took from a locked drawer therein a small circular case the size of a pill-box, and was about to put it into his pocket. But he lingered to open the cover and take a momentary glance inside. It contained a woman's finger-ring, set all the way round with small diamonds, and from its appearance had evidently been recently purchased. Boldwood's eyes dwelt upon its many sparkles a long time, though that its material aspect concerned him little was plain from his manner and mien, which were those of a mind following out the presumed thread of that jewel's future history.

The noise of wheels at the front of the house became audible. Boldwood closed the box, stowed it away carefully in his pocket, and went out upon the landing. The old man who was his indoor factotum came at the same moment to the foot of the stairs.

"They be coming, sir—lots of 'em—a-foot and a-driving!"

"I was coming down this moment. Those wheels I heard—is it Mrs. Troy?"

"No, sir—'tis not she yet."

A reserved and sombre expression had returned to Boldwood's face again, but it poorly cloaked his feelings when he pronounced Bathsheba's name; and his feverish anxiety continued to show its existence by a galloping motion of his fingers upon the side of his thigh as he went down the stairs.

VII

HOW DOES THIS COVER ME?" SAID TROY TO PENNYWAYS. "NOBODY WOULD RECOGNISE me now, I'm sure."

He was buttoning on a heavy grey overcoat of Noachian cut, with cape and high collar, the latter being erect and rigid, like a girdling wall, and nearly reaching to the verge of a travelling cap which was pulled down over his ears.

Pennyways snuffed the candle, and then looked up and deliberately inspected Troy.

"You've made up your mind to go then?" he said.

"Made up my mind? Yes; of course I have."

"Why not write to her? 'Tis a very queer corner that you have got into, sergeant. You see all these things will come to light if you go back, and they won't sound well at all. Faith, if I was you I'd even bide as you be—a single man of the name of Francis. A good wife is good, but the best wife is not so good as no wife at all. Now that's my outspoke mind, and I've been called a long-headed feller here and there."

"All nonsense!" said Troy, angrily. "There she is with plenty of money, and a house and farm, and horses, and comfort, and here am I living from hand to mouth—a needy adventurer. Besides, it is no use talking now; it is too late, and I am glad of it; I've been seen and recognised here this very afternoon. I should have gone back to her the day after the fair, if it hadn't been for you talking about the law, and rubbish about getting a separation; and I don't put it off any longer. What the deuce put it into my head to run away at all, I can't think! Humbugging sentiment—that's what it was. But what man on earth was to know that his wife would be in such a hurry to get rid of his name!"

"I should have known it. She's bad enough for anything."

"Pennyways, mind who you are talking to."

"Well, sergeant, all I say is this, that if I were you I'd go abroad again where I came from—'tisn't too late to do it now. I wouldn't stir up the business and get a bad name for the sake of living with her—for all that about your play-acting is sure to come out, you know, although you think otherwise. My eyes and limbs, there'll be a racket if you go back just now—in the middle of Boldwood's Christmasing!"

"H'm, yes. I expect I shall not be a very welcome guest if he has her there," said the sergeant, with a slight laugh. "A sort of Alonzo the Brave; and when I go in the guests will sit in silence and fear, and all laughter and pleasure will be hushed, and the lights in the chamber burn blue, and the worms—Ugh, horrible!—Ring for some more brandy, Pennyways, I felt an awful shudder just then! Well, what is there besides? A stick—I must have a walking-stick."

Pennyways now felt himself to be in something of a difficulty, for should Bathsheba and Troy become reconciled it would be necessary to regain her good opinion if he would secure the patronage of her husband. "I sometimes think she likes you yet, and is a good woman at bottom," he said, as a saving sentence. "But there's no telling to a certainty from a body's outside. Well, you'll do as you like about going, of course, sergeant, and as for me, I'll do as you tell me."

"Now, let me see what the time is," said Troy, after emptying his glass in one draught as he stood. "Half-past six o'clock. I shall not hurry along the road, and shall be there then before nine."

LIII

CONCURRITUR—HORÆ MOMENTO

OUTSIDE THE FRONT OF BOLDWOOD'S HOUSE A GROUP OF MEN STOOD IN THE DARK, with their faces towards the door, which occasionally opened and closed for the passage of some guest or servant, when a golden rod of light would stripe the ground for the moment and vanish again, leaving nothing outside but the glowworm shine of the pale lamp amid the evergreens over the door.

"He was seen in Casterbridge this afternoon—so the boy said," one of them remarked in a whisper. "And I for one believe it. His body was never found, you know."

" 'Tis a strange story," said the next. "You may depend upon't that she knows nothing about it."

"Not a word."

"Perhaps he don't mean that she shall," said another man.

"If he's alive and here in the neighbourhood, he means mischief," said the first. "Poor young thing: I do pity her, if 'tis true. He'll drag her to the dogs."

"O no; he'll settle down quiet enough," said one disposed to take a more hopeful view of the case.

"What a fool she must have been ever to have had anything to do with the man! She is so self-willed and independent too, that one is more minded to say it serves her right than pity her."

"No, no! I don't hold with 'ee there. She was no otherwise than a girl mind, and how could she tell what the man was made of? If 'tis really true, 'tis too hard a punishment, and more than she ought to hae.—Hullo, who's that?" This was to some footsteps that were heard approaching.

"William Smallbury," said a dim figure in the shades, coming up and joining them. "Dark as a hedge, to-night, isn't it? I all but missed the plank over the river ath'art there in the bottom—never did such a thing before in my life. Be ye any of Boldwood's workfolk?" He peered into their faces.

"Yes—all o' us. We met here a few minutes ago."

"Oh, I hear now—that's Sam Samway: thought I knowed the voice, too. Going in?"

"Presently. But I say, William," Samway whispered, "have ye heard this strange tale?"

"What—that about Sergeant Troy being seen, d'ye mean, souls?" said Smallbury, also lowering his voice.

"Ay: in Casterbridge."

"Yes, I have. Laban Tall named a hint of it to me but now—but I don't think it. Hark, here Laban comes himself, 'a b'lieve." A footstep drew near.

"Laban?"

"Yes, 'tis I," said Tall.

"Have ye heard any more about that?"

"No," said Tall, joining the group. "And I'm inclined to think we'd better keep quiet. If so be 'tis not true, 'twill flurry her, and do her much harm to repeat it; and if so be 'tis true, 'twill do no good to forestall her time o' trouble. God send that it mid be a lie, for though Henery Fray and some of 'em do speak against her, she's never been anything but fair to me. She's hot and hasty, but she's a brave girl who'll never tell a lie however much the truth may harm her, and I've no cause to wish her evil."

"She never do tell women's little lies, that's true; and 'tis a thing that can be said of very few. Ay, all the harm she thinks she says to yer face: there's nothing underhand wi' her."

They stood silent then, every man busied with his own thoughts, during which interval sounds of merriment could be heard within. Then the front door again opened, the rays streamed out, the well-known form of Boldwood was seen in the rectangular area of light, the door closed, and Boldwood walked slowly down the path.

" 'Tis master," one of the men whispered, as he neared them. "We'd better stand quiet—he'll go in again directly. He would think it unseemly o' us to be loitering here."

Boldwood came on, and passed by the men without seeing them, they being under the bushes on the grass. He paused, leant over the gate, and breathed a long breath. They heard low words come from him.

"I hope to God she'll come, or this night will be nothing but misery to me! O my darling, my darling, why do you keep me in suspense like this?"

He said this to himself, and they all distinctly heard it. Boldwood remained silent after that, and the noise from indoors was again just audible, until, a few minutes later, light wheels could be distinguished coming down the hill. They drew nearer, and ceased at the gate. Boldwood hastened back to the door, and opened it; and the light shone upon Bathsheba coming up the path.

Boldwood compressed his emotion to mere welcome: the men marked her light laugh and apology as she met him: he took her into the house; and the door closed again.

"Gracious heaven, I didn't know it was like that with him!" said one of the men. "I thought that fancy of his was over long ago."

"You don't know much of master, if you thought that," said Samway.

"I wouldn't he should know we heard what 'a said for the world," remarked a third.

"I wish we had told of the report at once," the first uneasily continued. "More harm may come of this than we know of. Poor Mr. Boldwood, it will be hard upon en. I wish Troy was in—Well, God forgive me for such a wish! A scoundrel to play a poor wife such tricks. Nothing has prospered in Weatherbury since he came here. And now I've no heart to go in. Let's look into Warren's for a few minutes first, shall us, neighbours?"

Samway, Tall, and Smallbury agreed to go to Warren's, and went out at the gate, the remaining ones entering the house. The three soon drew near the malt-house, approaching it from the adjoining orchard, and not by way of the street. The pane of glass was illuminated as usual. Smallbury was a little in advance of the rest, when, pausing, he turned suddenly to his companions and said, "Hist! See there."

The light from the pane was now perceived to be shining not upon the ivied wall as usual, but upon some object close to the glass. It was a human face.

"Let's come closer," whispered Samway; and they approached on tiptoe. There was no disbelieving the report any longer. Troy's face was almost close to the pane, and he was looking in. Not only was he looking in, but he appeared to have been arrested by a conversation which was in progress in the malt-house, the voices of the interlocutors being those of Oak and the maltster.

"The spree is all in her honour, isn't it—hey?" said the old man. "Although he made believe 'tis only keeping up o' Christmas?"

"I cannot say," replied Oak.

"O 'tis true enough, faith. I cannot understand Farmer Boldwood being such a fool at his time of life as to ho and hanker after this woman in the way 'a do, and she not care a bit about en."

The men, after recognising Troy's features, withdrew across the orchard as quietly as they had come. The air was big with Bathsheba's fortunes to-night: every word everywhere concerned her. When they were quite out of earshot all by one instinct paused.

"It gave me quite a turn—his face," said Tall, breathing.

"And so it did me," said Samway. "What's to be done?"

"I don't see that 'tis any business of ours," Smallbury murmured dubiously.

"But it is! 'Tis a thing which is everybody's business," said Samway. "We know very well that master's on a wrong tack, and that she's quite in the dark, and we should let 'em know at once. Laban, you know her best—you'd better go and ask to speak to her."

"I bain't fit for any such thing," said Laban, nervously. "I should think William ought to do it if anybody. He's oldest."

"I shall have nothing to do with it," said Smallbury. " 'Tis a ticklish business altogether. Why, he'll go on to her himself in a few minutes, ye'll see."

"We don't know that he will. Come, Laban."

"Very well, if I must I must, I suppose," Tall reluctantly answered. "What must I say?"

"Just ask to see master."

"O no; I shan't speak to Mr. Boldwood. If I tell anybody, 'twill be mistress."

"Very well," said Samway.

Laban then went to the door. When he opened it the hum of bustle rolled out as a wave upon a still strand—the assemblage being immediately inside the hall—and was deadened to a murmur as he closed it again. Each man waited intently, and looked around at the dark tree tops gently rocking against the sky and occasionally shivering in a slight wind, as if he took interest in the scene, which neither did. One of them began walking up and down, and then came to where he started from and stopped again, with a sense that walking was a thing not worth doing now.

"I should think Laban must have seen mistress by this time," said Smallbury, breaking the silence. "Perhaps she won't come and speak to him."

The door opened. Tall appeared, and joined them.

"Well?" said both.

"I didn't like to ask for her after all," Laban faltered out. "They were all in such a stir, trying to put a little spirit into the party. Somehow the fun seems to hang fire, though everything's there that a heart can desire, and I couldn't for my soul interfere and throw damp upon it—if 'twas to save my life, I couldn't!"

"I suppose we had better all go in together," said Samway, gloomily. "Perhaps I may have a chance of saying a word to master."

So the men entered the hall, which was the room selected and arranged for the gathering because of its size. The younger men and maids were at last just beginning to dance. Bathsheba had been perplexed how to act, for she was not much more than a slim young maid herself, and the weight of stateliness sat heavy upon her. Sometimes she thought she ought not to have come under any circumstances; then she considered what cold unkindness that would have been, and finally resolved upon the middle course of staying for about an hour only, and gliding off unobserved, having from the first made up her mind that she could on no account dance, sing, or take any active part in the proceedings.

Her allotted hour having been passed in chatting and looking on, Bathsheba told Liddy not to hurry herself, and went to the small parlour to prepare for departure, which, like the hall, was decorated with holly and ivy, and well lighted up.

Nobody was in the room, but she had hardly been there a moment when the master of the house entered.

"Mrs. Troy—you are not going?" he said. "We've hardly begun!"

"If you'll excuse me, I should like to go now." Her manner was restive, for she remembered her promise, and imagined what he was about to say. "But as it is not late," she added, "I can walk home, and leave my man and Liddy to come when they choose."

"I've been trying to get an opportunity of speaking to you," said Boldwood. "You know perhaps what I long to say?"

Bathsheba silently looked on the floor.

"You do give it?" he said, eagerly.

"What?" she whispered.

"Now, that's evasion! Why, the promise. I don't want to intrude upon you at all, or to let it become known to anybody. But do give your word! A mere business compact, you know, between two people who are beyond the influence of passion." Boldwood knew how false this picture was as regarded himself; but he had proved that it was the only tone in which she would allow him to approach her. "A promise to marry me at the end of five years and three-quarters. You owe it to me!"

"I feel that I do," said Bathsheba; "that is, if you demand it. But I am a changed woman—an unhappy woman—and not—not—"

"You are still a very beautiful woman," said Boldwood. Honesty and pure conviction suggested the remark, unaccompanied by any perception that it might have been adopted by blunt flattery to soothe and win her.

However, it had not much effect now, for she said, in a passionless murmur which was in itself a proof of her words: "I have no feeling in the matter at all. And I don't at all know what is right to do in my difficult position, and I have nobody to advise me. But I give my promise, if I must. I give it as the rendering of a debt, conditionally, of course, on my being a widow."

"You'll marry me between five and six years hence?"

"Don't press me too hard. I'll marry nobody else."

"But surely you will name the time, or there's nothing in the promise at all?"

"O, I don't know, pray let me go!" she said, her bosom beginning to rise. "I am afraid what to do! I want to be just to you, and to be that seems to be wronging myself, and perhaps it is breaking the commandments. There is considerable doubt of his death, and then it is dreadful; let me ask a solicitor, Mr. Boldwood, if I ought or no!"

"Say the words, dear one, and the subject shall be dismissed; a blissful loving intimacy of six years, and then marriage—O Bathsheba, say them!" he begged in a husky voice, unable to sustain the forms of mere friendship any longer. "Promise yourself to me; I deserve it, indeed I do, for I have loved you more than anybody in the world! And if I said hasty words and showed uncalled-for heat of manner towards you, believe me, dear, I did not mean to distress you; I was in agony, Bathsheba, and I did not know what I said. You wouldn't let a dog suffer what I have suffered, could you but know it! Sometimes I shrink from your knowing what I have felt for you, and sometimes I am distressed that all of it you never will know. Be gracious, and give up a little to me, when I would give up my life for you!"

The trimmings of her dress, as they quivered against the light, showed how agitated she was, and at last she burst out crying. "And you'll not—press me—about anything more—if I say in five or six years?" she sobbed, when she had power to frame the words.

"Yes, then I'll leave it to time."

"Very well. If he does not return, I'll marry you in six years from this day, if we both live," she said solemnly.

"And you'll take this as a token from me."

Boldwood had come close to her side, and now he clasped one of her hands in both his own, and lifted it to his breast.

"What is it? Oh I cannot wear a ring!" she exclaimed, on seeing what he held; "besides, I wouldn't have a soul know that it's an engagement! Perhaps it is improper? Besides, we are not engaged in the usual sense, are we? Don't insist, Mr. Boldwood—don't!" In her trouble at not being able to get her hand away from him at once, she stamped passionately on the floor with one foot, and tears crowded to her eyes again.

"It means simply a pledge—no sentiment—the seal of a practical compact," he said more quietly, but still retaining her hand in his firm grasp. "Come, now!" And Boldwood slipped the ring on her finger.

"I cannot wear it," she said, weeping as if her heart would break. "You frighten me, almost. So wild a scheme! Please let me go home!"

"Only to-night: wear it just to-night, to please me!"

Bathsheba sat down in a chair, and buried her face in her handkerchief, though Boldwood kept her hand yet. At length she said, in a sort of hopeless whisper—

"Very well, then, I will to-night, if you wish it so earnestly. Now loosen my hand; I will, indeed I will wear it to-night."

"And it shall be the beginning of a pleasant secret courtship of six years, with a wedding at the end?"

"It must be, I suppose, since you will have it so!" she said, fairly beaten into non-resistance.

Boldwood pressed her hand, and allowed it to drop in her lap. "I am happy now," he said. "God bless you!"

He left the room, and when he thought she might be sufficiently composed sent one of the maids to her. Bathsheba cloaked the effects of the late scene as she best could, followed the girl, and in a few moments came downstairs with her hat and cloak on, ready to go. To get to the door it was necessary to pass through the hall, and before doing so she paused on the bottom of the staircase which descended into one corner, to take a last look at the gathering.

There was no music or dancing in progress just now. At the lower end, which had been arranged for the work-folk specially, a group conversed in whispers, and with clouded looks. Boldwood was standing by the fireplace, and he, too, though so absorbed in visions arising from her promise that he scarcely saw anything, seemed at that moment to have observed their peculiar manner, and their looks askance.

"What is it you are in doubt about, men?" he said.

One of them turned and replied uneasily: "It was something Laban heard of, that's all, sir."

"News? Anybody married or engaged, born or dead?" enquired the farmer, gaily. "Tell it to us, Tall. One would think from your looks and mysterious ways that it was something very dreadful indeed."

"O no, sir, nobody is dead," said Tall.

"I wish somebody was," said Samway, in a whisper.

"What do you say, Samway?" asked Boldwood, somewhat sharply. "If you have anything to say, speak out; if not, get up another dance."

"Mrs. Troy has come downstairs," said Samway to Tall. "If you want to tell her, you had better do it now."

"Do you know what they mean?" the farmer asked Bathsheba, across the room.

"I don't in the least," said Bathsheba.

There was a smart rapping at the door. One of the men opened it instantly, and went outside.

"Mrs. Troy is wanted," he said, on returning.

"Quite ready," said Bathsheba. "Though I didn't tell them to send."

"It is a stranger, ma'am," said the man by the door.

"A stranger?" she said.

"Ask him to come in," said Boldwood.

The message was given, and Troy, wrapped up to his eyes as we have seen him, stood in the doorway.

There was an unearthly silence, all looking towards the new-comer. Those who had just learnt that he was in the neighbourhood recognised him instantly; those who did not were perplexed. Nobody noted Bathsheba. She was leaning on the stairs. Her brow had heavily contracted; her whole face was pallid, her lips apart, her eyes rigidly staring at their visitor.

Boldwood was among those who did not notice that he was Troy. "Come in, come in!" he repeated, cheerfully, "and drain a Christmas beaker with us, stranger!"

Troy next advanced into the middle of the room, took off his cap, turned down his coat-collar, and looked Boldwood in the face. Even then Boldwood did not recognise that the impersonator of Heaven's persistent irony towards him, who had once before broken in upon his bliss, scourged him, and snatched his delight away, had come to do these things a second time. Troy began to laugh a mechanical laugh: Boldwood recognised him now.

Troy turned to Bathsheba. The poor girl's wretchedness at this time was beyond all fancy or narration. She had sunk down on the lowest stair; and there she sat, her mouth blue and dry, and her dark eyes fixed vacantly upon him, as if she wondered whether it were not all a terrible illusion.

Then Troy spoke. "Bathsheba, I come here for you!"

She made no reply.

"Come home with me: come!"

Bathsheba moved her feet a little, but did not rise.

Troy went across to her.

"Come, madam, do you hear what I say?" he said, peremptorily.

A strange voice came from the fireplace—a voice sounding far off and confined, as if from a dungeon. Hardly a soul in the assembly recognised the thin tones to be those of Boldwood. Sudden despair had transformed him.

"Bathsheba, go with your husband!"

Nevertheless, she did not move. The truth was that Bathsheba was beyond the pale of activity—and yet not in a swoon. She was in a state of mental *gutta serena*; her mind was for the minute totally deprived of light at the same time no obscuration was apparent from without.

Troy stretched out his hand to pull her towards him, when she quickly shrank back. This visible dread of him seemed to irritate Troy, and he seized her arm and pulled it sharply. Whether his grasp pinched her, or whether his mere touch was the cause, was never known, but at the moment of his seizure she writhed, and gave a quick, low scream.

The scream had been heard but a few seconds when it was followed by a sudden deafening report that echoed through the room and stupefied them all. The oak partition shook with the concussion, and the place was filled with grey smoke.

In bewilderment they turned their eyes to Boldwood. At his back, as stood before the fireplace, was a gun-rack, as is usual in farmhouses, constructed to hold two guns. When Bathsheba had cried out in her husband's grasp, Boldwood's face of gnashing despair had changed. The veins had swollen, and a frenzied look had gleamed in his eye. He had turned quickly, taken one of the guns, cocked it, and at once discharged it at Troy.

Troy fell. The distance apart of the two men was so small that the charge of shot did not spread in the least, but passed like a bullet into his body. He uttered a long guttural sigh—there was a contraction—an extension—then his muscles relaxed, and he lay still.

Boldwood was seen through the smoke to be now again engaged with the gun. It was double-barrelled, and he had, meanwhile, in some way fastened his handkerchief to the trigger, and with his foot on the other end was in the act of turning the second barrel upon himself. Samway his man was the first to see this, and in the midst of the general horror darted up to him. Boldwood had already twitched the handkerchief, and the gun exploded a second time, sending its contents, by a timely blow from Samway, into the beam which crossed the ceiling.

"Well, it makes no difference!" Boldwood gasped. "There is another way for me to die."

Then he broke from Samway, crossed the room to Bathsheba, and kissed her hand. He put on his hat, opened the door, and went into the darkness, nobody thinking of preventing him.

LIV

AFTER THE SHOCK

B OLDWOOD PASSED INTO THE HIGH-ROAD, AND TURNED IN THE DIRECTION OF CASTER-bridge. Here he walked at an even, steady pace over Yalbury Hill, along the dead level beyond, mounted Mellstock Hill, and between eleven and twelve o'clock crossed the Moor into the town. The streets were nearly deserted now, and the waving lamp-flames only lighted up rows of grey shop-shutters, and strips of white paving upon which his step echoed as he passed along. He turned to the right, and halted before an archway of heavy stonework, which was closed by an iron-studded pair of doors. This was the entrance to the gaol, and over it a lamp was fixed, the light enabling the wretched traveller to find a bell-pull.

The small wicket at last opened, and a porter appeared. Boldwood stepped forward, and said something in a low tone, when, after a delay, another man came. Boldwood entered, and the door was closed behind him, and he walked the world no more.

Long before this time Weatherbury had been thoroughly aroused, and the wild deed which had terminated Boldwood's merrymaking became known to all. Of those out of the house Oak was one of the first to hear of the catastrophe, and when he entered the room, which was about five minutes after Boldwood's exit, the scene was terrible. All the female guests were huddled aghast against the walls like sheep in a storm, and the men were bewildered as to what to do. As for Bathsheba, she had changed. She was sitting on the floor beside the body of Troy, his head pillowed in her lap, where she had herself lifted it. With one hand she held her handkerchief to his breast and covered the wound, though scarcely a single drop of blood had flowed, and with the other she tightly clasped one of his. The household convulsion had made her herself again. The temporary coma had ceased, and activity had come with the necessity for it. Deeds of endurance, which seem ordinary in philosophy, are rare in conduct, and Bathsheba was astonishing all around her now, for her philosophy was her conduct, and she seldom thought practicable what she did not practise. She was of the stuff of which great men's mothers are made. She was indispensable to high generation, hated at tea parties, feared in shops, and loved at crises. Troy recumbent in his wife's lap formed now the sole spectacle in the middle of the spacious room.

"Gabriel," she said, automatically, when he entered, turning up a face of which only the well-known lines remained to tell him it was hers, all else in the picture having faded quite. "Ride to Casterbridge instantly for a surgeon. It is, I believe, useless, but go. Mr. Boldwood has shot my husband."

Her statement of the fact in such quiet and simple words came with more force than a tragic declamation, and had somewhat the effect of setting the distorted images in each mind present into proper focus. Oak, almost before he had comprehended anything beyond the briefest abstract of the event, hurried out of the room, saddled a horse and rode away. Not till he had ridden more than a mile did it occur to him that he would have done better by sending some other man on this errand, remaining himself in the house. What had become of Boldwood? He should have been looked after. Was he mad—had there been a quarrel? Then how had Troy got there? Where had he come from? How did this remarkable reappearance effect itself when he was supposed by many to be at the bottom of the sea? Oak had in some slight measure been prepared for the presence of Troy by hearing a rumour of his return just before entering Boldwood's house; but before he had weighed that information, this fatal event had been superimposed. However, it was too late now to think of sending another messenger, and he rode on, in the excitement of these self-enquiries not discerning, when about three miles from Casterbridge, a square-figured pedestrian passing along under the dark hedge in the same direction as his own.

The miles necessary to be traversed, and other hindrances incidental to the lateness of the hour and the darkness of the night, delayed the arrival of Mr. Aldritch, the surgeon; and more than three hours passed between the time at which the shot was fired and that of his entering the house. Oak was additionally detained in Casterbridge through having to give notice to the authorities of what had happened; and he then found that Boldwood had also entered the town, and delivered himself up.

In the meantime the surgeon, having hastened into the hall at Boldwood's, found it in darkness and quite deserted. He went on to the back of the house, where he discovered in the kitchen an old man, of whom he made enquiries.

"She's had him took away to her own house, sir," said his informant.

"Who has?" said the doctor.

"Mrs. Troy. 'A was quite dead, sir."

This was astonishing information. "She had no right to do that," said the doctor. "There will have to be an inquest, and she should have waited to know what to do."

"Yes, sir; it was hinted to her that she had better wait till the law was known. But she said law was nothing to her, and she wouldn't let her dear husband's corpse bide neglected for folks to stare at for all the crowners in England."

Mr. Aldritch drove at once back again up the hill to Bathsheba's. The first person he met was poor Liddy, who seemed literally to have dwindled smaller in these few latter hours. "What has been done?" he said.

"I don't know, sir," said Liddy, with suspended breath. "My mistress has done it all."

"Where is she?"

"Upstairs with him, sir. When he was brought home and taken upstairs, she said she wanted no further help from the men. And then she called me, and made me fill the bath, and after that told me I had better go and lie down because I looked so ill. Then she locked herself into the room alone with him, and would not let a nurse come in, or anybody at all. But I thought I'd wait in the next room in case she should want me. I heard her moving about inside for more than an hour, but she only came out once, and that was for more candles, because hers had burnt down into the socket. She said we were to let her know when you or Mr. Thirdly came, sir."

Oak entered with the parson at this moment, and they all went upstairs together, preceded by Liddy Smallbury. Everything was silent as the grave when they paused on the landing. Liddy knocked, and Bathsheba's dress was heard rustling across the room: the key turned in the lock, and she opened the door. Her looks were calm and nearly rigid, like a slightly animated bust of Melpomene.

"Oh, Mr. Aldritch, you have come at last," she murmured from her lips merely, and threw back the door. "Ah, and Mr. Thirdly. Well, all is done, and anybody in the world may see him now." She then passed by him, crossed the landing, and entered another room.

Looking into the chamber of death she had vacated they saw by the light of the candles which were on the drawers a tall straight shape lying at the further end of the bedroom, wrapped in white. Everything around was quite orderly. The doctor went in, and after a few minutes returned to the landing again, where Oak and the parson still waited.

"It is all done, indeed, as she says," remarked Mr. Aldritch, in a subdued voice. "The body has been undressed and properly laid out in grave clothes. Gracious Heaven—this mere girl! She must have the nerve of a stoic!"

"The heart of a wife merely," floated in a whisper about the ears of the three, and turning they saw Bathsheba in the midst of them. Then, as if at that instant to prove that her fortitude had been more of will than of spontaneity, she silently sank down between them and was a shapeless heap of drapery on the floor. The simple consciousness that superhuman strain was no longer required had at once put a period to her power to continue it.

They took her away into a further room, and the medical attendance which had been useless in Troy's case was invaluable in Bathsheba's, who fell into a series of fainting-fits that had a serious aspect for a time. The sufferer was got to bed, and Oak, finding from the bulletins that nothing really dreadful was to be apprehended on her score, left the house. Liddy kept watch in Bathsheba's chamber, where she heard her mistress moaning in whispers through the dull slow hours of that wretched night: "Oh it is my fault—how can I live! O Heaven, how can I live!"

LV

THE MARCH FOLLOWING—"BATHSHEBA BOLDWOOD"

WE PASS RAPIDLY ON INTO THE MONTH OF MARCH, TO A BREEZY DAY WITHOUT SUNshine, frost, or dew. On Yalbury Hill, about midway between Weatherbury and Casterbridge, where the turnpike road passes over the crest, a numerous concourse of people had gathered, the eyes of the greater number being frequently stretched afar in a northerly direction. The groups consisted of a throng of idlers, a party of javelin-men, and two trumpeters, and in the midst were carriages, one of which contained the high sheriff. With the idlers, many of whom had mounted to the top of a cutting formed for the road, were several Weatherbury men and boys—among others Poorgrass, Coggan, and Cain Ball.

At the end of half an hour a faint dust was seen in the expected quarter, and shortly after a travelling-carriage, bringing one of the two judges on the Western Circuit, came up the hill and halted on the top. The judge changed carriages whilst a flourish was blown by the big-cheeked trumpeters, and a procession being formed of the vehicles and javelin-men, they all proceeded towards the town, excepting the Weatherbury men, who as soon as they had seen the judge move off returned home again to their work.

"Joseph, I zeed you squeezing close to the carriage," said Coggan, as they walked. "Did ye notice my lord judge's face?"

"I did," said Poorgrass. "I looked hard at en, as if I would read his very soul; and there was mercy in his eyes—or to speak with the exact truth required of us at this solemn time, in the eye that was towards me."

"Well, I hope for the best," said Coggan, "though bad that must be. However, I shan't go to the trial, and I'd advise the rest of ye that bain't wanted to bide away. 'Twill disturb his mind more than anything to see us there staring at him as if he were a show."

"The very thing I said this morning," observed Joseph. " 'Justice is come to weigh him in the balances,' I said in my reflectious way, 'and if he's found wanting, so be it unto him,' and a bystander said 'Hear, hear! A man who can talk like that ought to be heard.' But I don't like dwelling upon it, for my few words are my few words, and not much; though the speech of some men is rumoured abroad as though by nature formed for such."

"So 'tis, Joseph. And now, neighbours, as I said, every man bide at home."

The resolution was adhered to; and all waited anxiously for the news next day. Their suspense was diverted, however, by a discovery which was made in the afternoon, throwing more light on Boldwood's conduct and condition than any details which had preceded it.

That he had been from the time of Greenhill Fair until the fatal Christmas Eve in excited and unusual moods was known to those who had been intimate with him; but nobody imagined that there had shown in him unequivocal symptoms of the mental derangement which Bathsheba and Oak, alone of all others and at different times, had momentarily suspected. In a locked closet was now discovered an extraordinary collection of articles. There were several sets of ladies' dresses in the piece, of sundry expensive materials; silks and satins, poplins and velvets, all of colours which from Bathsheba's style of dress might have been judged to be her favourites. There were two muffs, sable and ermine. Above all there was a case of jewellery, containing four heavy gold bracelets and several lockets and rings, all of fine quality and manufacture. These things had been bought in Bath and other towns from time to time, and brought home by stealth. They were all carefully packed in paper, and each package was labelled "Bathsheba Boldwood," a date being subjoined six years in advance in every instance.

These somewhat pathetic evidences of a mind crazed with care and love were the subject of discourse in Warren's malt-house when Oak entered from Casterbridge with tidings of sentence. He came in the afternoon, and his face, as the kiln glow shone upon it, told the tale sufficiently well. Boldwood, as everyone supposed he would do, had pleaded guilty, and had been sentenced to death.

The conviction that Boldwood had not been morally responsible for his later acts now became general. Facts elicited previous to the trial had pointed strongly in the same direction, but they had not been of sufficient weight to lead to an order for an examination into the state of Boldwood's mind. It was astonishing, now that a presumption of insanity was raised, how many collateral circumstances were remembered to which a condition of mental disease seemed to afford the only explanation—among others, the unprecedented neglect of his corn-stacks in the previous summer.

A petition was addressed to the Home Secretary, advancing the circumstances which appeared to justify a request for a reconsideration of the sentence. It was not "numerously signed" by the inhabitants of Casterbridge, as is usual in such cases, for Boldwood had never made many friends over the counter. The shops thought it very natural that a man who, by importing direct from the producer, had daringly set aside the first great principle of provincial existence, namely, that God made country villages to supply customers to county towns, should have confused ideas about the Decalogue. The prompters were a few merciful men who had perhaps too feelingly considered the facts latterly unearthed, and the result was that evidence was taken which it was hoped might remove the crime, in a moral point of view, out of the category of wilful murder, and lead it to be regarded as a sheer outcome of madness.

The upshot of the petition was waited for in Weatherbury with solicitous interest. The execution had been fixed for eight o'clock on a Saturday morning about a fortnight after the sentence was passed, and up to Friday afternoon no answer had been received. At that time Gabriel came from Casterbridge Gaol, whither he had been to wish Boldwood good-bye, and turned down a by-street to avoid the town. When past the last house he heard a hammering, and lifting his bowed head he looked back for a moment. Over the chimneys he could see the upper part of the gaol entrance, rich and glowing in the afternoon sun, and some moving figures were there. They were carpenters lifting a post into a vertical position within the parapet. He withdrew his eyes quickly, and hastened on.

It was dark when he reached home, and half the village was out to meet him.

"No tidings," Gabriel said, wearily. "And I'm afraid there's no hope. I've been with him more than two hours."

"Do ye think he *really* was out of his mind when he did it?" said Smallbury.

"I can't honestly say that I do," Oak replied. "However, that we can talk of another time. Has there been any change in mistress this afternoon?"

"None at all."

"Is she downstairs?"

"No. And getting on so nicely as she was too. She's but very little better now again than she was at Christmas. She keeps on asking if you be come, and if there's news, till one's wearied out wi' answering her. Shall I go and say you've come?"

"No," said Oak. "There's a chance yet; but I couldn't stay in town any longer—after seeing him too. So Laban—Laban is here, isn't he?"

"Yes," said Tall.

"What I've arranged is, that you shall ride to town the last thing to-night; leave here about nine, and wait a while there, getting home about twelve. If nothing has been received by eleven to-night, they say there's no chance at all."

"I do so hope his life will be spared," said Liddy. "If it is not, she'll go out of her mind too. Poor thing; her sufferings have been dreadful; she deserves anybody's pity."

"Is she altered much?" said Coggan.

"If you haven't seen poor mistress since Christmas, you wouldn't know her," said Liddy. "Her eyes are so miserable that she's not the same woman. Only two years ago she was a romping girl, and now she's this!"

Laban departed as directed, and at eleven o'clock that night several of the villagers strolled along the road to Casterbridge and awaited his arrival—among them Oak, and nearly all the rest of Bathsheba's men. Gabriel's anxiety was great that Boldwood might be saved, even though in his conscience he felt that he ought to die; for there had been qualities in the farmer which Oak loved. At last, when they all were weary the tramp of a horse was heard in the distance—

> *First dead, as if on turf it trode,*
> *Then, clattering, on the village road*
> *In other pace than forth he yode.*

"We shall soon know now, one way or other," said Coggan, and they all stepped down from the bank on which they had been standing into the road, and the rider pranced into the midst of them.

"Is that you, Laban?" said Gabriel.

"Yes—'tis come. He's not to die. 'Tis confinement during Her Majesty's pleasure."

"Hurrah!" said Coggan, with a swelling heart. "God's above the devil yet!"

LVI

BEAUTY IN LONELINESS—AFTER ALL

B ATHSHEBA REVIVED WITH THE SPRING. THE UTTER PROSTRATION THAT HAD FOLLOWED the low fever from which she had suffered diminished perceptibly when all uncertainty upon every subject had come to an end.

But she remained alone now for the greater part of her time, and stayed in the house, or at furthest went into the garden. She shunned everyone, even Liddy, and could be brought to make no confidences, and to ask for no sympathy.

As the summer drew on she passed more of her time in the open air, and began to examine into farming matters from sheer necessity, though she never rode out or personally superintended as at former times. One Friday evening in August she walked a little way along the road and entered the village for the first time since the sombre event of the preceding Christmas. None of the old colour had as yet come to her cheek, and its absolute paleness was heightened by the jet black of her gown, till it appeared preternatural. When she reached a little shop at the other end of the place, which stood nearly opposite to the churchyard, Bathsheba heard singing inside the church, and she knew that the singers were practising. She crossed the road, opened the gate, and entered the graveyard, the high sills of the church windows effectually screening her from the eyes of those gathered within. Her stealthy walk was to the nook wherein Troy had worked at planting flowers upon Fanny Robin's grave, and she came to the marble tombstone.

A motion of satisfaction enlivened her face as she read the complete inscription. First came the words of Troy himself:—

> ERECTED BY FRANCIS TROY
> IN BELOVED MEMORY OF
> FANNY ROBIN,
> WHO DIED OCTOBER 9, 18—,
> AGED 20 YEARS.

Underneath this was now inscribed in new letters:—

In the same Grave lie
The Remains of the aforesaid
Francis Troy,
Who died December 24th, 18—,
Aged 26 years.

Whilst she stood and read and meditated the tones of the organ began again in the church, and she went with the same light step round to the porch and listened. The door was closed, and the choir was learning a new hymn. Bathsheba was stirred by emotions which latterly she had assumed to be altogether dead within her. The little attenuated voices of the children brought to her ear in distinct utterance the words they sang without thought or comprehension—

Lead, kindly Light, amid the encircling gloom,
Lead Thou me on.

Bathsheba's feeling was always to some extent dependent upon her whim, as is the case with many other women. Something big came into her throat and an uprising to her eyes—and she thought that she would allow the imminent tears to flow if they wished. They did flow and plenteously, and one fell upon the stone bench beside her. Once that she had begun to cry for she hardly knew what, she could not leave off for crowding thoughts she knew too well. She would have given anything in the world to be, as those children were, unconcerned at the meaning of their words, because too innocent to feel the necessity for any such expression. All the impassioned scenes of her brief experience seemed to revive with added emotion at that moment, and those scenes which had been without emotion during enactment had emotion then. Yet grief came to her rather as a luxury than as the scourge of former times.

Owing to Bathsheba's face being buried in her hands she did not notice a form which came quietly into the porch, and on seeing her, first moved as if to retreat, then paused and regarded her. Bathsheba did not raise her head for some time, and when she looked round her face was wet, and her eyes drowned and dim. "Mr. Oak," exclaimed she, disconcerted, "how long have you been here?"

"A few minutes, ma'am," said Oak, respectfully.

"Are you going in?" said Bathsheba; and there came from within the church as from a prompter—

I loved the garish day, and, spite of fears,
Pride ruled my will: remember not past years.

"I was," said Gabriel. "I am one of the bass singers, you know. I have sung bass for several months."

"Indeed: I wasn't aware of that. I'll leave you, then."

Which I have loved long since, and lost a while,

sang the children.

"Don't let me drive you away, mistress. I think I won't go in to-night."

"O no—you don't drive me away."

Then they stood in a state of some embarrassment, Bathsheba trying to wipe her dreadfully drenched and inflamed face without his noticing her. At length Oak said, "I've not seen you—I mean spoken to you—since ever so long, have I?" But he feared to bring distressing memories back, and interrupted himself with: "Were you going into church?"

"No," she said. "I came to see the tombstone privately—to see if they had cut the inscription as I wished. Mr. Oak, you needn't mind speaking to me, if you wish to, on the matter which is in both our minds at this moment."

"And have they done it as you wished?" said Oak.

"Yes. Come and see it, if you have not already."

So together they went and read the tomb. "Eight months ago!" Gabriel murmured when he saw the date. "It seems like yesterday to me."

"And to me as if it were years ago—long years, and I had been dead between. And now I am going home, Mr. Oak."

Oak walked after her. "I wanted to name a small matter to you as soon as I could," he said with hesitation. "Merely about business, and I think I may just mention it now, if you'll allow me."

"O yes, certainly."

"It is that I may soon have to give up the management of your farm, Mrs. Troy. The fact is, I am thinking of leaving England—not yet, you know—next spring."

"Leaving England!" she said, in surprise and genuine disappointment. "Why, Gabriel, what are you going to do that for?"

"Well, I've thought it best," Oak stammered out. "California is the spot I've had in my mind to try."

"But it is understood everywhere that you are going to take poor Mr. Boldwood's farm on your own account?"

"I've had the refusal o' it 'tis true; but nothing is settled yet, and I have reasons for gieing up. I shall finish out my year there as manager for the trustees, but no more."

"And what shall I do without you? Oh, Gabriel, I don't think you ought to go away. You've been with me so long—through bright times and dark times—such old friends as we are—that it seems unkind almost. I had fancied that if you leased the other farm as master, you might still give a helping look across at mine. And now going away!"

"I would have willingly."

"Yet now that I am more helpless than ever you go away!"

"Yes, that's the ill fortune o' it," said Gabriel, in a distressed tone. "And it is because of that very helplessness that I feel bound to go. Good-afternoon, ma'am," he concluded, in evident anxiety to get away, and at once went out of the churchyard by a path she could follow on no pretence whatever.

Bathsheba went home, her mind occupied with a new trouble, which being rather harassing than deadly was calculated to do good by diverting her from the chronic gloom of her life. She was set thinking a great deal about Oak and of his wish to shun her; and there occurred to Bathsheba several incidents of her latter intercourse with him, which, trivial when singly viewed, amounted together to a perceptible disinclination for her society. It broke upon her at length as a great pain that her last old disciple was about to forsake her and flee. He who had believed in her and argued on her side when all the rest of the world was against her, had at last like the others become weary and neglectful of the old cause, and was leaving her to fight her battles alone.

Three weeks went on, and more evidence of his want of interest in her was forthcoming. She noticed that instead of entering the small parlour or office where the farm accounts were kept, and waiting, or leaving a memorandum as he had hitherto done during her seclusion, Oak never came at all when she was likely to be there, only entering at unseasonable hours when her presence in that part of the house was least to be expected. Whenever he wanted directions he sent a message, or note with neither heading nor signature, to which she was obliged to reply in the same offhand style. Poor Bathsheba began to suffer now from the most torturing sting of all—a sensation that she was despised.

The autumn wore away gloomily enough amid these melancholy conjectures, and Christmas-day came, completing a year of her legal widowhood, and two years and a quarter of her life alone. On examining her heart it appeared beyond measure strange that the subject of which the season might have been supposed suggestive—the event in the hall at Boldwood's—was not agitating her at all; but instead, an agonising conviction that everybody abjured her—for what she could not tell—and that Oak was the ringleader of the recusants. Coming out of church that day she looked round in hope that Oak, whose bass voice she had heard rolling out from the gallery overhead in a most unconcerned manner, might chance to linger in her path in the old way. There he was, as usual, coming down the path behind her. But on seeing Bathsheba turn, he looked aside, and as soon as he got beyond the gate, and there was the barest excuse for a divergence, he made one, and vanished.

The next morning brought the culminating stroke; she had been expecting it long. It was a formal notice by letter from him that he should not renew his engagement with her for the following Lady-day.

Bathsheba actually sat and cried over this letter most bitterly. She was aggrieved and wounded that the possession of hopeless love from Gabriel, which she had grown to regard as her inalienable right for life, should have been withdrawn just at his own pleasure in this way. She was bewildered too by the prospect of having to rely on her own resources again: it seemed to herself that she never could again acquire energy sufficient to go to market, barter, and sell. Since Troy's death Oak had attended all sales and fairs for her, transacting her business at the same time with his own. What should she do now? Her life was becoming a desolation.

So desolate was Bathsheba this evening, that in an absolute hunger for pity and sympathy, and miserable in that she appeared to have outlived the only true friendship she had ever owned, she put on her bonnet and cloak and went down to Oak's house just after sunset, guided on her way by the pale primrose rays of a crescent moon a few days old.

A lively firelight shone from the window, but nobody was visible in the room. She tapped nervously, and then thought it doubtful if it were right for a single woman to call upon a bachelor who lived alone, although he was her manager, and she might be supposed to call on business without any real impropriety. Gabriel opened the door, and the moon shone upon his forehead.

"Mr. Oak," said Bathsheba faintly.

"Yes; I am Mr. Oak," said Gabriel. "Who have I the honour—O how stupid of me, not to know you, mistress!"

"I shall not be your mistress much longer, shall I, Gabriel?" she said, in pathetic tones.

"Well, no. I suppose—But come in, ma'am. Oh—and I'll get a light," Oak replied, with some awkwardness.

"No; not on my account."

"It is so seldom that I get a lady visitor that I'm afraid I haven't proper accommodation. Will you sit down, please? Here's a chair, and there's one, too. I am sorry that my chairs all have wood seats, and are rather hard, but I—was thinking of getting some new ones." Oak placed two or three for her.

"They are quite easy enough for me."

So down she sat, and down sat he, the fire dancing in their faces, and upon the old furniture,

> *all a-sheenen*
> *Wi' long years o' handlen,*[1]

that formed Oak's array of household possessions, which sent back a dancing reflection in reply. It was very odd to these two persons, who knew each other passing well, that the mere circumstance of their meeting in a new place and in a new way should make them so awkward and constrained. In the fields, or at her house, there had never been any embarrassment; but now that Oak had become the entertainer their lives seemed to be moved back again to the days when they were strangers.

"You'll think it strange that I have come, but—"

"O no; not at all."

"But I thought—Gabriel, I have been uneasy in the belief that I have offended you, and that you are going away on that account. It grieved me very much, and I couldn't help coming."

"Offended me! As if you could do that, Bathsheba!"

"Haven't I?" she asked, gladly. "But, what are you going away for else?"

"I am not going to emigrate, you know; I wasn't aware that you would wish me not to when I told 'ee, or I shouldn't ha' thought of doing it," he said, simply. "I have arranged for Little Weatherbury Farm, and shall have it in my own hands at Lady-day. You know I've had a share in it for some time. Still, that wouldn't prevent my attending to your business as before, hadn't it been that things have been said about us."

"What?" said Bathsheba in surprise. "Things said about you and me! What are they?"

"I cannot tell you."

"It would be wiser if you were to, I think. You have played the part of mentor to me many times, and I don't see why you should fear to do it now."

"It is nothing that you have done, this time. The top and tail o't is this—that I am sniffing about here, and waiting for poor Boldwood's farm, with a thought of getting you some day."

1. W. Barnes.

"Getting me! What does that mean?"

"Marrying of 'ee, in plain British. You asked me to tell, so you mustn't blame me."

Bathsheba did not look quite so alarmed as if a cannon had been discharged by her ear, which was what Oak had expected. "Marrying me! I didn't know it was that you meant," she said, quietly. "Such a thing as that is too absurd—too soon—to think of, by far!"

"Yes; of course, it is too absurd. I don't desire any such thing; I should think that was plain enough by this time. Surely, surely you be the last person in the world I think of marrying. It is too absurd, as you say."

" 'Too—s-s-soon' were the words I used."

"I must beg your pardon for correcting you, but you said, 'too absurd,' and so do I."

"I beg your pardon too!" she returned, with tears in her eyes. " 'Too soon' was what I said. But it doesn't matter a bit—not at all—but I only meant, 'too soon.' Indeed, I didn't, Mr. Oak, and you must believe me!"

Gabriel looked her long in the face, but the firelight being faint there was not much to be seen. "Bathsheba," he said, tenderly and in surprise, and coming closer: "if I only knew one thing—whether you would allow me to love you and win you, and marry you after all—if I only knew that!"

"But you never will know," she murmured.

"Why?"

"Because you never ask."

"Oh—Oh!" said Gabriel, with a low laugh of joyousness. "My own dear—"

"You ought not to have sent me that harsh letter this morning," she interrupted. "It shows you didn't care a bit about me, and were ready to desert me like all the rest of them! It was very cruel of you, considering I was the first sweetheart that you ever had, and you were the first I ever had; and I shall not forget it!"

"Now, Bathsheba, was ever anybody so provoking?" he said, laughing. "You know it was purely that I, as an unmarried man, carrying on a business for you as a very taking young woman, had a proper hard part to play—more particular that people knew I had a sort of feeling for 'ee; and I fancied, from the way we were mentioned together, that it might injure your good name. Nobody knows the heat and fret I have been caused by it."

"And was that all?"

"All."

"O, how glad I am I came!" she exclaimed, thankfully, as she rose from her seat. "I have thought so much more of you since I fancied you did not want even to see me again. But I must be going now, or I shall be missed. Why Gabriel," she said, with a slight laugh, as they went to the door, "it seems exactly as if I had come courting you—how dreadful!"

"And quite right, too," said Oak. "I've danced at your skittish heels, my beautiful Bathsheba, for many a long mile, and many a long day; and it is hard to begrudge me this one visit."

He accompanied her up the hill, explaining to her the details of his forthcoming tenure of the other farm. They spoke very little of their mutual feeling; pretty phrases and warm expressions being probably unnecessary between such tried friends. Theirs was that substantial affection which arises (if any arises at all) when the two who are thrown together begin first by knowing the rougher sides of each other's character, and not the best till further on, the romance growing up in the interstices of a mass of hard prosaic reality. This good-fellowship—*camaraderie*—usually occurring through similarity of pursuits, is unfortunately seldom superadded to love between the sexes, because men and women associate, not in their labours, but in their pleasures merely. Where, however, happy circumstance permits its development, the compounded feeling proves itself to be the only love which is strong as death—that love which many waters cannot quench, nor the floods drown, beside which the passion usually called by the name is evanescent as steam.

LVII

A FOGGY NIGHT AND MORNING—CONCLUSION

T HE MOST PRIVATE, SECRET, PLAINEST WEDDING THAT IT IS POSSIBLE TO HAVE."
Those had been Bathsheba's words to Oak one evening, some time after the event of the preceding chapter, and he meditated a full hour by the clock upon how to carry out her wishes to the letter.

"A license—O yes, it must be a license," he said to himself at last. "Very well, then; first, a license."

On a dark night, a few days later, Oak came with mysterious steps from the surrogate's door in Casterbridge. On the way home he heard a heavy tread in front of him, and, overtaking the man, found him to be Coggan. They walked together into the village until they came to a little lane behind the church, leading down to the cottage of Laban Tall, who had lately been installed as clerk of the parish, and was yet in mortal terror at church on Sundays when he heard his lone voice among certain hard words of the Psalms, whither no man ventured to follow him.

"Well, good-night, Coggan," said Oak, "I'm going down this way."

"Oh!" said Coggan, surprised; "what's going on to-night then, make so bold, Mr. Oak?"

It seemed rather ungenerous not to tell Coggan, under the circumstances, for Coggan had been true as steel all through the time of Gabriel's unhappiness about Bathsheba, and Gabriel said, "You can keep a secret, Coggan?"

"You've proved me, and you know."

"Yes, I have, and I do know. Well, then, mistress and I mean to get married to-morrow morning."

"Heaven's high tower! And yet I've thought of such a thing from time to time; true, I have. But keeping it so close! Well, there, 'tis no consarn of of mine, and I wish 'ee joy o' her."

"Thank you, Coggan. But I assure 'ee that this great hush is not what I wished for at all, or what either of us would have wished if it hadn't been for certain things that would make a gay wedding seem hardly the thing. Bathsheba has a great wish that all the parish shall not be in church, looking at her—she's shylike and nervous about it, in fact—so I be doing this to humour her."

"Ay, I see: quite right, too, I suppose I must say. And you be now going down to the clerk."

"Yes; you may as well come with me."

"I am afeard your labour in keeping it close will be throwed away," said Coggan, as they walked along. "Labe Tall's old woman will horn it all over parish in half an hour."

"So she will, upon my life; I never thought of that," said Oak, pausing. "Yet I must tell him to-night, I suppose, for he's working so far off, and leaves early."

"I'll tell 'ee how we could tackle her," said Coggan. "I'll knock and ask to speak to Laban outside the door, you standing in the background. Then he'll come out, and you can tell yer tale. She'll never guess what I want en for; and I'll make up a few words about the farm-work, as a blind."

This scheme was considered feasible; and Coggan advanced boldly, and rapped at Mrs. Tall's door. Mrs. Tall herself opened it.

"I wanted to have a word with Laban."

"He's not at home, and won't be this side of eleven o'clock. He've been forced to go over to Yalbury since shutting out work. I shall do quite as well."

"I hardly think you will. Stop a moment"; and Coggan stepped round the corner of the porch to consult Oak.

"Who's t'other man, then?" said Mrs. Tall.

"Only a friend," said Coggan.

"Say he's wanted to meet mistress near church-hatch to-morrow morning at ten," said Oak, in a whisper. "That he must come without fail, and wear his best clothes."

"The clothes will floor us as safe as houses!" said Coggan.

"It can't be helped," said Oak. "Tell her."

So Coggan delivered the message. "Mind, het or wet, blow or snow, he must come," added Jan. "'Tis very particular, indeed. The fact is, 'tis to witness her sign some law-work about taking shares wi' another farmer for a long span o' years. There, that's what 'tis, and now I've told 'ee, Mother Tall, in a way I shouldn't ha' done if I hadn't loved 'ee so hopeless well."

Coggan retired before she could ask any further; and next they called at the vicar's in a manner which excited no curiosity at all. Then Gabriel went home, and prepared for the morrow.

"Liddy," said Bathsheba, on going to bed that night, "I want you to call me at seven o'clock to-morrow, in case I shouldn't wake."

"But you always do wake afore then, ma'am."

"Yes, but I have something important to do, which I'll tell you of when the time comes, and it's best to make sure."

Bathsheba, however, awoke voluntarily at four, nor could she by any contrivance get to sleep again. About six, being quite positive that her watch had stopped during the night, she could wait no longer. She went and tapped at Liddy's door, and after some labour awoke her.

"But I thought it was I who had to call you?" said the bewildered Liddy. "And it isn't six yet."

"Indeed it is; how can you tell such a story, Liddy! I know it must be ever so much past seven. Come to my room as soon as you can; I want you to give my hair a good brushing."

When Liddy came to Bathsheba's room her mistress was already waiting. Liddy could not understand this extraordinary promptness. "Whatever *is* going on, ma'am?" she said.

"Well, I'll tell you," said Bathsheba, with a mischievous smile in her bright eyes. "Farmer Oak is coming here to dine with me to-day!"

"Farmer Oak—and nobody else?—you two alone?"

"Yes."

"But is it safe, ma'am, after what's been said?" asked her companion, dubiously. "A woman's good name is such a perishable article that—"

Bathsheba laughed with a flushed cheek, and whispered in Liddy's ear, although there was nobody present. Then Liddy stared and exclaimed, "Souls alive, what news! It makes my heart go quite bumpity-bump!"

"It makes mine rather furious, too," said Bathsheba. "However, there's no getting out of it now!"

It was a damp disagreeable morning. Nevertheless, at twenty minutes to ten o'clock, Oak came out of his house, and

> *Went up the hill side*
> *With that sort of stride*
> *A man puts out when walking in search of a bride,*

and knocked at Bathsheba's door. Ten minutes later a large and a smaller umbrella might have been seen moving from the same door, and through the mist along the road to the church. The distance was not more than a quarter of a mile, and these two sensible persons deemed it unnecessary to drive. An observer must have been very close indeed to discover that the forms under the umbrellas were those of Oak and Bathsheba, arm-in-arm for the first time in their lives, Oak in a great-coat extending to his knees, and Bathsheba in a cloak that reached her clogs. Yet, though so plainly dressed, there was a certain rejuvenated appearance about her:—

> *As though a rose should shut and be a bud again.*

Repose had again incarnadined her cheeks; and having, at Gabriel's request, arranged her hair this morning as she had worn it years ago on Norcombe Hill, she seemed in his eyes remarkably like the girl of that fascinating dream, which, considering that she was now only three or four-and-twenty, was perhaps not very wonderful. In the church were Tall, Liddy, and the parson, and in a remarkably short space of time the deed was done.

The two sat down very quietly to tea in Bathsheba's parlour in the evening of the same day, for it had been arranged that Farmer Oak should go there to live, since he had as yet neither money, house, nor furniture worthy of the name, though he was on a sure way towards them, whilst Bathsheba was, comparatively, in a plethora of all three.

Just as Bathsheba was pouring out a cup of tea, their ears were greeted by the firing of a cannon, followed by what seemed like a tremendous blowing of trumpets, in the front of the house.

"There!" said Oak, laughing, "I knew those fellows were up to something, by the look on their faces."

Oak took up the light and went into the porch, followed by Bathsheba with a shawl over her head. The rays fell upon a group of male figures gathered upon the gravel in front, who, when they saw the newly-married couple in the porch, set up a loud "Hurrah!" and at the same moment bang again went the cannon in the background, followed by a hideous clang of music from a drum, tambourine, clarionet, serpent, hautboy, tenor-viol, and double-bass—the only remaining relics of the true and original Weatherbury band—venerable worm-eaten instruments, which had celebrated in their own persons the victories of Marlborough, under the fingers of the forefathers of those who played them now. The performers came forward, and marched up to the front.

"Those bright boys, Mark Clark and Jan, are at the bottom of all this," said Oak. "Come in, souls, and have something to eat and drink wi' me and my wife."

"Not to-night," said Mr. Clark, with evident self-denial. "Thank ye all the same; but we'll call at a more seemly time. However, we couldn't think of letting the day pass without a note of admiration of some sort. If ye could send a drop of som'at down to Warren's, why so it is. Here's long life and happiness to neighbour Oak and his comely bride!"

"Thank ye; thank ye all," said Gabriel. "A bit and a drop shall be sent to Warren's for ye at once. I had a thought that we might very likely get a salute of some sort from our old friends, and I was saying so to my wife but now."

"Faith," said Coggan, in a critical tone, turning to his companions, "the man hev learnt to say 'my wife' in a wonderful naterel way, considering how very youthful he is in wedlock as yet—hey, neighbours all?"

"I never heerd a skilful old married feller of twenty years' standing pipe 'my wife' in a more used note than 'a did," said Jacob Smallbury. "It might have been a little more true to nater if 't had been spoke a little chillier, but that wasn't to be expected just now."

"That improvement will come wi' time," said Jan, twirling his eye.

Then Oak laughed, and Bathsheba smiled (for she never laughed readily now), and their friends turned to go.

"Yes; I suppose that's the size o't," said Joseph Poorgrass with a cheerful sigh as they moved away; "and I wish him joy o' her; though I were once or twice upon saying to-day with holy Hosea, in my scripture manner, which is my second nature, 'Ephraim is joined to idols: let him alone.' But since 'tis as 'tis, why, it might have been worse, and I feel my thanks accordingly."

THE END

THE RETURN OF THE NATIVE

Map of the
WESSEX
of the
Novels and Poems

Scale of Miles

Emery Walker sc.

Fictions names as *Exonbury*
Real names as Portsmouth

The Channel

"To sorrow
I bade good morrow,
And thought to leave her far away behind;
But cheerly, cheerly,
She loves me dearly;
She is so constant to me, and so kind.
I would decieve her,
And so leave her,
But ah! she is so constant and so kind."

PREFACE

THE DATE AT WHICH THE FOLLOWING EVENTS ARE ASSUMED TO HAVE OC-curred may be set down as between 1840 and 1850, when the old watering-place herein called "Budmouth" still retained sufficient afterglow from its Georgian gaiety and prestige to lend it an absorbing attractiveness to the romantic and imaginative soul of a lonely dweller inland.

Under the general name of "Egdon Heath," which has been given to the sombre scene of the story, are united or typified heaths of various real names, to the number of at least a dozen; these being virtually one in character and aspect, though their original unity, or partial unity, is now somewhat disguised by intrusive strips and slices brought under the plough with varying degrees of success, or planted to woodland.

It is pleasant to dream that some spot in the extensive tract whose south-western quarter is here described, may be the heath of that traditional King of Wessex—Lear.

T. H.
July 1895

Contents

BOOK FIRST

THE THREE WOMEN

I

A Face on which Time makes but Little Impression

A SATURDAY AFTERNOON IN NOVEMBER WAS APPROACHING THE TIME OF TWILIGHT, and the vast tract of unenclosed wild known as Egdon Heath embrowned itself moment by moment. Overhead the hollow stretch of whitish cloud shutting out the sky was as a tent which had the whole heath for its floor.

The heaven being spread with this pallid screen and the earth with the darkest vegetation, their meeting-line at the horizon was clearly marked. In such contrast the heath wore the appearance of an instalment of night which had taken up its place before its astronomical hour was come: darkness had to a great extent arrived hereon, while day stood distinct in the sky. Looking upwards, a furze-cutter would have been inclined to continue work; looking down, he would have decided to finish his faggot and go home. The distant rims of the world and of the firmament seemed to be a division in time no less than a division in matter. The face of the heath by its mere complexion added half an hour to evening; it could in like manner retard the dawn, sadden noon, anticipate the frowning of storms scarcely generated, and intensify the opacity of a moonless midnight to a cause of shaking and dread.

In fact, precisely at this transitional point of its nightly roll into darkness the great and particular glory of the Egdon waste began, and nobody could be said to understand the heath who had not been there at such a time. It could best be felt when it could not clearly be seen, its complete effect and explanation lying in this and the succeeding hours before the next dawn; then, and only then, did it tell its true tale. The spot was, indeed, a near relation of night, and when night showed itself an apparent tendency to gravitate together could be perceived in its shades and the scene. The sombre stretch of rounds and hollows seemed to rise and meet the evening gloom in pure sympathy, the heath exhaling darkness as rapidly as the heavens precipitated it. And so the obscurity in the air and the obscurity in the land closed together in a black fraternisation towards which each advanced half-way.

The place became full of a watchful intentness now; for when other things sank brooding to sleep the heath appeared slowly to awake and listen. Every night its Titanic form seemed to await something; but it had waited thus, unmoved, during so many centuries, through the crises of so many things, that it could only be imagined to await one last crisis—the final overthrow.

It was a spot which returned upon the memory of those who loved it with an aspect of peculiar and kindly congruity. Smiling champaigns of flowers and fruit hardly do this, for they are permanently harmonious only with an existence of better reputation as to its issues than the present. Twilight combined with the scenery of Egdon Heath to evolve a thing majestic without severity, impressive without showiness, emphatic in its admonitions, grand in its simplicity. The qualifications which frequently invest the façade of a prison with far more dignity than is found in the façade of a palace double its size lent to this heath a sublimity in which spots renowned for beauty of the accepted kind are utterly wanting. Fair prospects wed happily with fair times; but alas, if times be not fair! Men have

oftener suffered from the mockery of a place too smiling for their reason than from the oppression of surroundings oversadly tinged. Haggard Egdon appealed to a subtler and
scarcer instinct, to a more recently learnt emotion, than that which responds to the sort of
beauty called charming and fair.

Indeed, it is a question if the exclusive reign of this orthodox beauty is not approaching its last quarter. The new Vale of Tempe may be a gaunt waste in Thule; human souls
may find themselves in closer and closer harmony with external things wearing a sombre-
ness distasteful to our race when it was young. The time seems near, if it has not actually
arrived, when the chastened sublimity of a moor, a sea, or a mountain will be all of nature
that is absolutely in keeping with the moods of the more thinking among mankind. And
ultimately, to the commonest tourist, spots like Iceland may become what the vineyards
and myrtle-gardens of South Europe are to him now; and Heidelberg and Baden be passed
unheeded as he hastens from the Alps to the sand-dunes of Scheveningen.

The most thorough-going ascetic could feel that he had a natural right to wander on
Egdon: he was keeping within the line of legitimate indulgence when he laid himself open
to influences such as these. Colours and beauties so far subdued were, at least, the
birthright of all. Only in summer days of highest feather did its mood touch the level of
gaiety. Intensity was more usually reached by way of the solemn than by way of the brilliant, and such a sort of intensity was often arrived at during winter darkness, tempests,
and mists. Then Egdon was aroused to reciprocity; for the storm was its lover, and the
wind its friend. Then it became the home of strange phantoms; and it was found to be the
hitherto unrecognised original of those wild regions of obscurity which are vaguely felt
to be compassing us about in midnight dreams of flight and disaster, and are never thought
of after the dream till revived by scenes like this.

It was at present a place perfectly accordant with man's nature—neither ghastly, hateful, nor ugly: neither commonplace, unmeaning, nor tame; but, like man, slighted and enduring; and withal singularly colossal and mysterious in its swarthy monotony. As with
some persons who have long lived apart, solitude seemed to look out of its countenance.
It had a lonely face, suggesting tragical possibilities.

This obscure, obsolete, superseded country figures in Domesday. Its condition is
recorded therein as that of heathy, furzy, briary wilderness—"Bruaria." Then follows the
length and breadth in leagues; and, though some uncertainty exists as to the exact extent of
this ancient lineal measure, it appears from the figures that the area of Egdon down to the
present day has but little diminished. "Turbaria Bruaria"—the right of cutting heath-turf—
occurs in charters relating to the district. "Overgrown with heth and mosse," says Leland
of the same dark sweep of country.

Here at least were intelligible facts regarding landscape—far-reaching proofs productive of genuine satisfaction. The untameable, Ishmaelitish thing that Egdon now was
it always had been. Civilisation was its enemy; and ever since the beginning of vegetation
its soil had worn the same antique brown dress, the natural and invariable garment of the
particular formation. In its venerable one coat lay a certain vein of satire on human vanity
in clothes. A person on a heath in raiment of modern cut and colours has more or less an
anomalous look. We seem to want the oldest and simplest human clothing where the clothing of the earth is so primitive.

To recline on a stump of thorn in the central valley of Egdon, between afternoon and night, as now, where the eye could reach nothing of the world outside the summits and shoulders of heathland which filled the whole circumference of its glance, and to know that everything around and underneath had been from prehistoric times as unaltered as the stars overhead, gave ballast to the mind adrift on change, and harassed by the irrepressible New. The great inviolate place had an ancient permanence which the sea cannot claim. Who can say of a particular sea that it is old? Distilled by the sun, kneaded by the moon, it is renewed in a year, in a day, or in an hour. The sea changed, the fields changed, the rivers, the villages, and the people changed, yet Egdon remained. Those surfaces were neither so steep as to be destructible by weather, nor so flat as to be the victims of floods and deposits. With the exception of an aged highway, and a still more aged barrow presently to be referred to—themselves almost crystallised to natural products by long-continuance—even the trifling irregularities were not caused by pickaxe, plough, or spade, but remained as the very finger-touches of the last geological change.

The above-mentioned highway traversed the lower levels of the heath, from one horizon to another. In many portions of its course it overlaid an old vicinal way, which branched from the great Western road of the Romans, the Via Iceniana, or Ikenild Street, hard by. On the evening under consideration it would have been noticed that, though the gloom had increased sufficiently to confuse the minor features of the heath, the white surface of the road remained almost as clear as ever.

II

HUMANITY APPEARS UPON THE SCENE, HAND IN HAND WITH TROUBLE

ALONG THE ROAD WALKED AN OLD MAN. HE WAS WHITE-HEADED AS A MOUNTAIN, bowed in the shoulders, and faded in general aspect. He wore a glazed hat, an ancient boat-cloak, and shoes; his brass buttons bearing an anchor upon their face. In his hand was a silver-headed walking-stick, which he used as a veritable third leg, perseveringly dotting the ground with its point at every few inches' interval. One would have said that he had been, in his day, a naval officer of some sort or other.

Before him stretched the long, laborious road, dry, empty, and white. It was quite open to the heath on each side, and bisected that vast dark surface like the parting-line on a head of black hair, diminishing and bending away on the furthest horizon.

The old man frequently stretched his eyes ahead to gaze over the tract that he had yet to traverse. At length he discerned, a long distance in front of him, a moving spot, which appeared to be a vehicle, and it proved to be going the same way as that in which he himself was journeying. It was the single atom of life that the scene contained, and it only served to render the general loneliness more evident. Its rate of advance was slow, and the old man gained upon it sensibly.

When he drew nearer he perceived it to be a spring van, ordinary in shape, but singular in colour, this being a lurid red. The driver walked beside it; and, like his van, he was completely red. One dye of that tincture covered his clothes, the cap upon his head, his boots, his face, and his hands. He was not temporarily overlaid with the colour: it permeated him.

The old man knew the meaning of this. The traveller with the cart was a reddleman—a person whose vocation it was to supply farmers with redding for their sheep. He was one of a class rapidly becoming extinct in Wessex, filling at present in the rural world the place which, during the last century, the dodo occupied in the world of animals. He is a curious, interesting, and nearly perished link between obsolete forms of life and those which generally prevail.

The decayed officer, by degrees, came up alongside his fellow-wayfarer, and wished him good evening. The reddleman turned his head, and replied in sad and occupied tones. He was young, and his face, if not exactly handsome, approached so near to handsome that nobody would have contradicted an assertion that it really was so in its natural colour. His eye, which glared so strangely through his stain, was in itself attractive—keen as that of a bird of prey, and blue as autumn mist. He had neither whisker nor moustache, which allowed the soft curves of the lower part of his face to be apparent. His lips were thin, and though, as it seemed, compressed by thought, there was a pleasant twitch at their corners now and then. He was clothed throughout in a tight-fitting suit of corduroy, excellent in quality, not much worn, and well-chosen for its purpose; but deprived of its original colour by his trade. It showed to advantage the good shape of his figure. A certain well-to-do air about the man suggested that he was not poor for his degree. The natural query of an observer would have been, Why should such a promising being as this have hidden his prepossessing exterior by adopting that singular occupation?

After replying to the old man's greeting he showed no inclination to continue in talk, although they still walked side by side, for the elder traveller seemed to desire company. There were no sounds but that of the booming wind upon the stretch of tawny herbage around them, the crackling wheels, the tread of the men, and the footsteps of the two shaggy ponies which drew the van. They were small, hardy animals, of a breed between Galloway and Exmoor, and were known as "heath-croppers" here.

Now, as they thus pursued their way, the reddleman occasionally left his companion's side, and, stepping behind the van, looked into its interior through a small window. The look was always anxious. He would then return to the old man, who made another remark about the state of the country and so on, to which the reddleman again abstractedly replied, and then again they would lapse into silence. The silence conveyed to neither any sense of awkwardness; in these lonely places wayfarers, after a first greeting, frequently plod on for miles without speech; contiguity amounts to a tacit conversation where, otherwise than in cities, such contiguity can be put an end to on the merest inclination, and where not to put an end to it is intercourse in itself.

Possibly these two might not have spoken again till their parting, had it not been for the reddleman's visits to his van. When he returned from his fifth time of looking in the old man said, "You have something inside there besides your load?"

"Yes."

"Somebody who wants looking after?"

"Yes."

Not long after this a faint cry sounded from the interior. The reddleman hastened to the back, looked in, and came away again.

"You have a child there, my man?"

"No, sir, I have a woman."

"The deuce you have! Why did she cry out?"

"Oh, she has fallen asleep, and not being used to travelling, she's uneasy, and keeps dreaming."

"A young woman?"

"Yes, a young woman."

"That would have interested me forty years ago. Perhaps she's your wife?"

"My wife!" said the other bitterly. "She's above mating with such as I. But there's no reason why I should tell you about that."

"That's true. And there's no reason why you should not. What harm can I do to you or to her?"

The reddleman looked in the old man's face. "Well, sir," he said at last, "I knew her before to-day, though perhaps it would have been better if I had not. But she's nothing to me, and I am nothing to her; and she wouldn't have been in my van if any better carriage had been there to take her."

"Where, may I ask?"

"At Anglebury."

"I know the town well. What was she doing there?"

"Oh, not much—to gossip about. However, she's tired to death now, and not at all well, and that's what makes her so restless. She dropped off into a nap about an hour ago, and 'twill do her good."

"A nice-looking girl, no doubt?"

"You would say so."

The other traveller turned his eyes with interest towards the van-window, and, without withdrawing them, said, "I presume I might look in upon her?"

"No," said the reddleman abruptly. "It is getting too dark for you to see much of her; and, more than that, I have no right to allow you. Thank God she sleeps so well: I hope she won't wake till she's home."

"Who is she? One of the neighbourhood?"

" 'Tis no matter who, excuse me."

"It is not that girl of Blooms-End, who has been talked about more or less lately? If so, I know her; and I can guess what has happened."

" 'Tis no matter. . . . Now, sir, I am sorry to say that we shall soon have to part company. My ponies are tired, and I have further to go, and I am going to rest them under this bank for an hour."

The elder traveller nodded his head indifferently, and the reddleman turned his horses and van in upon the turf, saying, "Good-night." The old man replied, and proceeded on his way as before.

The reddleman watched his form as it diminished to a speck on the road and became absorbed in the thickening films of night. He then took some hay from a truss which was slung up under the van, and, throwing a portion of it in front of the horses, made a pad of the rest, which he laid on the ground beside his vehicle. Upon this he sat down, leaning his back against the wheel. From the interior a low soft breathing came to his ear. It appeared to satisfy him, and he musingly surveyed the scene, as if considering the next step that he should take.

To do things musingly, and by small degrees, seemed, indeed, to be a duty in the Egdon valleys at this transitional hour, for there was that in the condition of the heath itself which resembled protracted and halting dubiousness. It was the quality of the repose appertaining to the scene. This was not the repose of actual stagnation, but the apparent repose of incredible slowness. A condition of healthy life so nearly resembling the torpor of death is a noticeable thing of its sort; to exhibit the inertness of the desert, and at the same time to be exercising powers akin to those of the meadow, and even of the forest, awakened in those who thought of it the attentiveness usually engendered by understatement and reserve.

The scene before the reddleman's eyes was a gradual series of ascents from the level of the road backward into the heart of the heath. It embraced hillocks, pits, ridges, acclivities, one behind the other, till all was finished by a high hill cutting against the still light sky. The traveller's eye hovered about these things for a time, and finally settled upon one noteworthy object up there. It was a barrow. This bossy projection of earth above its natural level occupied the loftiest ground of the loneliest height that the heath contained. Although from the vale it appeared but as a wart on an Atlantean brow, its actual bulk was great. It formed the pole and axis of this heathery world.

As the resting man looked at the barrow he became aware that its summit, hitherto the highest object in the whole prospect round, was surmounted by something higher. It rose from the semi-globular mound like a spike from a helmet. The first instinct of an imaginative stranger might have been to suppose it the person of one of the Celts who built the barrow, so far had all of modern date withdrawn from the scene. It seemed a sort of last man among them, musing for a moment before dropping into eternal night with the rest of his race.

There the form stood, motionless as the hill beneath. Above the plain rose the hill, above the hill rose the barrow, and above the barrow rose the figure. Above the figure was nothing that could be mapped elsewhere than on a celestial globe.

Such a perfect, delicate, and necessary finish did the figure give to the dark pile of hills that it seemed to be the only obvious justification of their outline. Without it, there was the dome without the lantern; with it the architectural demands of the mass were satisfied. The scene was strangely homogeneous. The vale, the upland, the barrow, and the figure above it amounted only to unity. Looking at this or that member of the group was not observing a complete thing, but a fraction of a thing.

The form was so much like an organic part of the entire motionless structure that to see it move would have impressed the mind as a strange phenomenon. Immobility being the chief characteristic of that whole which the person formed portion of, the discontinuance of immobility in any quarter suggested confusion.

Yet that is what happened. The figure perceptibly gave up its fixity, shifted a step or two, and turned round. As if alarmed, it descended on the right side of the barrow, with the glide of a water-drop down a bud, and then vanished. The movement had been sufficient to show more clearly the characteristics of the figure, and that it was a woman's.

The reason of her sudden displacement now appeared. With her dropping out of sight on the right side, a new-comer, bearing a burden, protruded into the sky on the left side, ascended the tumulus, and deposited the burden on the top. A second followed, then a third, a fourth, a fifth, and ultimately the whole barrow was peopled with burdened figures.

The only intelligible meaning in this sky-backed pantomime of silhouettes was that the woman had no relation to the forms who had taken her place, was sedulously avoiding these, and had come thither for another object than theirs. The imagination of the observer clung by preference to that vanished, solitary figure, as to something more interesting, more important, more likely to have a history worth knowing than these new-comers, and unconsciously regarded them as intruders. But they remained, and established themselves; and the lonely person who hitherto had been queen of the solitude did not at present seem likely to return.

III

THE CUSTOM OF THE COUNTRY

HAD A LOOKER-ON BEEN POSTED IN THE IMMEDIATE VICINITY OF THE BARROW, HE would have learned that these persons were boys and men of the neighbouring hamlets. Each, as he ascended the barrow, had been heavily laden with furze-faggots, carried upon the shoulder by means of a long stake sharpened at each end for impaling them easily—two in front and two behind. They came from a part of the heath a quarter of a mile to the rear, where furze almost exclusively prevailed as a product.

Every individual was so involved in furze by his method of carrying the faggots that he appeared like a bush on legs till he had thrown them down. The party had marched in trail, like a travelling flock of sheep; that is to say, the strongest first, the weak and young behind.

The loads were all laid together, and a pyramid of furze thirty feet in circumference now occupied the crown of the tumulus, which was known as Rainbarrow for many miles round. Some made themselves busy with matches, and in selecting the driest tufts of furze, others in loosening the bramble bonds which held the faggots together. Others, again, while this was in progress, lifted their eyes and swept the vast expanse of country commanded by their position, now lying nearly obliterated by shade. In the valleys of the heath nothing save its own wild face was visible at any time of day; but this spot commanded a horizon enclosing a tract of far extent, and in many cases lying beyond the heath country. None of its features could be seen now, but the whole made itself felt as a vague stretch of remoteness.

While the men and lads were building the pile, a change took place in the mass of shade which denoted the distant landscape. Red suns and tufts of fire one by one began to arise, flecking the whole country round. They were the bonfires of other parishes and hamlets that were engaged in the same sort of commemoration. Some were distant, and stood in a dense atmosphere, so that bundles of pale strawlike beams radiated around them in the shape of a fan. Some were large and near, glowing scarlet-red from the shade, like wounds in a black hide. Some were Mænades, with winy faces and blown hair. These tinctured the silent bosom of the clouds above them and lit up their ephemeral caves, which seemed thenceforth to become scalding caldrons. Perhaps as many as thirty bonfires could be counted within the whole bounds of the district; and as the hour may be told on a clockface when the figures themselves are invisible, so did the men recognise the locality of each fire by its angle and direction, though nothing of the scenery could be viewed.

The first tall flame from Rainbarrow sprang into the sky, attracting all eyes that had been fixed on the distant conflagrations back to their own attempt in the same kind. The cheerful blaze streaked the inner surface of the human circle—now increased by other stragglers, male and female—with its own gold livery, and even overlaid the dark turf around with a lively luminousness, which softened off into obscurity where the barrow rounded downwards out of sight. It showed the barrow to be the segment of a globe, as perfect as on the day when it was thrown up, even the little ditch remaining from which the earth was dug. Not a plough had ever disturbed a grain of that stubborn soil. In the heath's barrenness to the farmer lay its fertility to the historian. There had been no obliteration, because there had been no tending.

It was as if the bonfire-makers were standing in some radiant upper storey of the world, detached from and independent of the dark stretches below. The heath down there was now a vast abyss, and no longer a continuation of what they stood on; for their eyes, adapted to the blaze, could see nothing of the deeps beyond its influence. Occasionally, it is true, a more vigorous flare than usual from their faggots sent darting lights like aides-de-camp down the inclines to some distant bush, pool, or patch of white sand, kindling these to replies of the same colour, till all was lost in darkness again. Then the whole black phenomenon beneath represented Limbo as viewed from the brink by the sublime Florentine in his vision, and the muttered articulations of the wind in the hollows were as complaints and petitions from the "souls of mighty worth" suspended therein.

It was as if these men and boys had suddenly dived into past ages, and fetched therefrom an hour and deed which had before been familiar with this spot. The ashes of the original British pyre which blazed from that summit lay fresh and undisturbed in the barrow beneath their tread. The flames from funeral piles long ago kindled there had shone down upon the lowlands as these were shining now. Festival fires to Thor and Woden had followed on the same ground and duly had their day. Indeed, it is pretty well known that such blazes as this the heathmen were now enjoying are rather the lineal descendants from jumbled Druidical rites and Saxon ceremonies than the invention of popular feeling about Gunpowder Plot.

Moreover to light a fire is the instinctive and resistant act of man when, at the winter ingress, the curfew is sounded throughout Nature. It indicates a spontaneous, Promethean rebelliousness against that fiat that this recurrent season shall bring foul times, cold darkness, misery and death. Black chaos comes, and the fettered gods of the earth say, Let there be light.

The brilliant lights and sooty shades which struggled upon the skin and clothes of the persons standing round caused their lineaments and general contours to be drawn with Düreresque vigour and dash. Yet the permanent moral expression of each face it was impossible to discover, for as the nimble flames towered, nodded, and swooped through the surrounding air, the blots of shade and flakes of light upon the countenances of the group changed shape and position endlessly. All was unstable; quivering as leaves, evanescent as lightning. Shadowy eyesockets, deep as those of a death's head, suddenly turned into pits of lustre: a lantern-jaw was cavernous, then it was shining; wrinkles were emphasised to ravines, or obliterated entirely by a changed ray. Nostrils were dark wells; sinews in old necks were gilt mouldings; things with no particular polish on them were glazed; bright objects, such as the tip of a furze-hook one of the men carried, were as glass; eyeballs glowed like little lanterns. Those whom Nature had depicted as merely quaint became grotesque, the grotesque became preternatural; for all was in extremity.

Hence it may be that the face of an old man, who had like others been called to the heights by the rising flames, was not really the mere nose and chin that it appeared to be, but an appreciable quantity of human countenance. He stood complacently sunning himself in the heat. With a speäker, or stake, he tossed the outlying scraps of fuel into the conflagration, looking at the midst of the pile, occasionally lifting his eyes to measure the height of the flame, or to follow the great sparks which rose with it and sailed away into darkness. The beaming sight, and the penetrating warmth, seemed to breed in him a cumulative cheerfulness, which soon amounted to delight. With his stick in his hand he began to jig a private minuet, a bunch of copper seals shining and swinging like a pendulum from under his waistcoat: he also began to sing, in the voice of a bee up a flue—

> The king' call'd down' his no-bles all',
> By one', by two', by three';
> Earl Mar'-shal, I'll' go shrive' the queen',
> And thou' shalt wend' with me'.
>
> A boon', a boon', quoth Earl' Mar-shal',
> And fell' on his bend'-ded knee',
> That what'-so-e'er' the queen' shall say',
> No harm' there-of' may be'.

Want of breath prevented a continuance of the song, and the breakdown attracted the attention of a firm-standing man of middle age, who kept each corner of his crescent-shaped mouth rigorously drawn back into his cheek, as if to do away with any suspicion of mirthfulness which might erroneously have attached to him.

"A fair stave, Grandfer Cantle; but I am afeard 'tis too much for the mouldy weasand of such a old man as you," he said to the wrinkled reveller. "Dostn't wish th' wast three sixes again, Grandfer, as you was when you first learnt to sing it?"

"Hey?" said Grandfer Cantle, stopping in his dance.

"Dostn't wish was young again, I say? There's a hole in thy poor bellows now-a-days seemingly."

"But there's good art in me. If I couldn't make a little wind go a long ways I should seem no younger than the most aged man, should I, Timothy?"

"And how about the new-married folks down there at the Quiet Woman Inn?" the other enquired, pointing towards a dim light in the direction of the distant highway, but considerably apart from where the reddleman was at that moment resting. "What's the rights of the matter about 'em? You ought to know, being an understanding man."

"But a little rakish, hey? I own to it. Master Cantle is that, or he's nothing. Yet 'tis a gay fault, neighbour Fairway, that age will cure."

"I heard that they were coming home to-night. By this time they must have come. What besides?"

"The next thing is for us to go and wish 'em joy, I suppose?"

"Well, no."

"No? Now, I thought we must. *I* must, or 'twould be very unlike me—the first in every spree that's going!

> *Do thou' put on' a fri'-ar's coat',*
> *And I'll' put on' a-no'-ther,*
> *And we' will to' Queen Ele'anor go',*
> *Like Fri'ar and' his bro'-ther.*

"I met Mis'ess Yeobright, the young bride's aunt, last night, and she told me that her son Clym was coming home a' Christmas. Wonderful clever, 'a believe—ah, I should like to have all that's under that young man's hair. Well, then, I spoke to her in my well-known merry way, and she said, 'O that what's shaped so venerable should talk like a fool!'—that's what she said to me. I don't care for her, be jowned if I do, and so I told her. 'Be jowned if I care for 'ee,' I said. I had her there—hey?"

"I rather think she had you," said Fairway.

"No," said Grandfer Cantle, his countenance slightly flagging. " 'Tisn't so bad as that with me?"

"Seemingly 'tis; however, is it because of the wedding that Clym is coming home a' Christmas—to make a new arrangement because his mother is now left in the house alone?"

"Yes, yes—that's it. But, Timothy, hearken to me," said the Grandfer earnestly. "Though known as such a joker, I be an understanding man if you catch me serious, and I am serious now. I can tell 'ee lots about the married couple. Yes, this morning at six o'clock they went up the country to do the job, and neither vell nor mark have been seen of 'em since, though I reckon that this afternoon has brought 'em home again, man and woman—wife, that is. Isn't it spoke like a man, Timothy, and wasn't Mis'ess Yeobright wrong about me?"

"Yes, it will do. I didn't know the two had walked together since last fall, when her aunt forbad the banns. How long has this new set-to been in mangling then? Do you know, Humphrey?"

"Yes, how long?" said Grandfer Cantle smartly, likewise turning to Humphrey. "I ask that question."

"Ever since her aunt altered her mind, and said she might hae the man after all," replied Humphrey, without removing his eyes from the fire. He was a somewhat solemn young fellow, and carried the hook and leather gloves of a furze-cutter, his legs, by reason of that occupation, being sheathed in bulging leggings as stiff as the Philistine's greaves of brass. "That's why they went away to be married, I count. You see, after kicking up such a nunny-watch and forbidding the banns 'twould have made Mis'ess Yeobright seem foolishlike to have a banging wedding in the same parish all as if she'd never gainsaid it."

"Exactly—seem foolishlike; and that's very bad for the poor things that be so, though I only guess as much, to be sure," said Grandfer Cantle, still strenuously preserving a sensible bearing and mien.

"Ah, well, I was at church that day," said Fairway, "which was a very curious thing to happen."

"If 'twasn't my name's Simple," said the Grandfer emphatically. "I ha'n't been there to-year; and now the winter is a-coming on I won't say I shall."

"I ha'n't been these three years," said Humphrey; "for I'm so dead sleepy of a Sunday; and 'tis so terrible far to get there; and when you do get there 'tis such a mortal poor chance that you'll be chose for up above, when so many bain't, that I bide at home and don't go at all."

"I not only happened to be there," said Fairway, with a fresh collection of emphasis, "but I was sitting in the same pew as Mis'ess Yeobright. And though you may not see it as such, it fairly made my blood run cold to hear her. Yes, it is a curious thing; but it made my blood run cold, for I was close at her elbow." The speaker looked round upon the bystanders, now drawing closer to hear him, with his lips gathered tighter than ever in the rigorousness of his descriptive moderation.

" 'Tis a serious job to have things happen to 'ee there," said a woman behind.

" 'Ye are to declare it,' wez the parson's words," Fairway continued. "And then up stood a woman at my side—a-touching of me. 'Well, be damned if there isn't Mis'ess Yeobright a-standing up,' I said to myself. Yes, neighbours, though I was in the temple of prayer that's what I said. 'Tis against my conscience to curse and swear in company, and I hope any woman here will overlook it. Still what I did say I did say, and 'twould be a lie if I didn't own it."

"So 'twould, neighbour Fairway."

" 'Be damned if there isn't Mis'ess Yeobright a-standing up,' I said," the narrator repeated, giving out the bad word with the same passionless severity of face as before, which proved how entirely necessity and not gusto had to do with the iteration. "And the next thing I heard was, 'I forbid the banns,' from her. 'I'll speak to you after the service,' said the parson, in quite a homely way—yes, turning all at once into a common man no holier than you or I. Ah, her face was pale! Maybe you can call to mind that monument in church—the cross-legged soldier that have had his nose knocked away by the schoolchildren? Well, he would about have matched that woman's face, when she said, 'I forbid the banns.' "

The audience cleared their throats and tossed a few stalks into the fire, not because these deeds were urgent, but to give themselves time to weigh the moral of the story.

"I'm sure when I heard they'd been forbid I felt as glad as if anybody had gied me sixpence," said an earnest voice—that of Olly Dowden, a woman who lived by making heath brooms, or besoms. Her nature was to be civil to enemies as well as to friends, and grateful to all the world for letting her remain alive.

"And now the maid have married him just the same," said Humphrey.

"After that Mis'ess Yeobright came round and was quite agreeable," Fairway resumed, with an unheeding air, to show that his words were no appendage to Humphrey's, but the result of independent reflection.

"Supposing they were ashamed, I don't see why they shouldn't have done it here-right," said a wide-spread woman whose stays creaked like shoes whenever she stooped or turned. " 'Tis well to call the neighbours together and to hae a good racket once now and then; and it may as well be when there's a wedding as at tide-times. I don't care for close ways."

"Ah, now, you'd hardly believe it, but I don't care for gay weddings," said Timothy Fairway, his eyes again travelling round. "I hardly blame Thomasin Yeobright and neighbour Wildeve for doing it quiet, if I must own it. A wedding at home means five and six-handed reels by the hour; and they do a man's legs no good when he's over forty."

"True. Once at the woman's house you can hardly say nay to being one in a jig, knowing all the time that you be expected to make yourself worth your victuals."

"You be bound to dance at Christmas because 'tis the time o' year; you must dance at weddings because 'tis the time o' life. At christenings folk will even smuggle in a reel or two, if 'tis no further on than the first or second chiel. And this is not naming the songs you've got to sing. . . . For my part I like a good hearty funeral as well as anything. You've as splendid victuals and drink as at other parties, and even better. And it don't wear your legs to stumps in talking over a poor fellow's ways as it do to stand up in hornpipes."

"Nine folks out of ten would own 'twas going too far to dance then, I suppose?" said Grandfer Cantle enquiringly.

" 'Tis the only sort of party a staid man can feel safe at after the mug have been round a few times."

"Well, I can't understand a quiet ladylike little body like Tamsin Yeobright caring to be married in such a mean way," said Susan Nunsuch, the wide woman, who preferred the original subject. " 'Tis worse than the poorest do. And I shouldn't have cared about the man, though some may say he's good-looking."

"To give him his due he's a clever, learned fellow in his way—a'most as clever as Clym Yeobright used to be. He was brought up to better things than keeping the Quiet Woman. An engineer—that's what the man was, as we know; but he threw away his chance, and so 'a took a public-house to live. His learning was no use to him at all."

"Very often the case," said Olly, the besom-maker. "And yet how people do strive after it and get it! The class of folk that couldn't use to make a round O to save their bones from the pit can write their names now without a sputter of the pen, oftentimes without a single blot: what do I say?—why, almost without a desk to lean their stomachs and elbows upon."

"True: 'tis amazing what a polish the world have been brought to," said Humphrey.

"Why, afore I went a soldier in the Bang-up Locals (as we was called), in the year four," chimed in Grandfer Cantle brightly, "I didn't know no more what the world was like than the commonest man among ye. And now, jown it all, I won't say what I bain't fit for, hey?"

"Couldst sign the book, no doubt," said Fairway, "if wast young enough to join hands with a woman again, like Wildeve and Mis'ess Tamsin, which is more than Humph there could do, for he follows his father in learning. Ah, Humph, well I can mind when I was married how I zid thy father's mark staring me in the face as I went to put down my name. He and your mother were the couple married just afore we were, and there stood thy father's cross with arms stretched out like a great banging scarecrow. What a terrible black cross that was—thy father's very likeness in en! To save my soul I couldn't help laughing when I zid en, though all the time I was as hot as dog-days, what with the marrying, and what with the woman a-hanging to me, and what with Jack Changley and a lot more chaps grinning at me through church-window. But the next moment a strawmote would have knocked me down, for I called to mind that if thy father and mother had had high words once, they'd been at it twenty times since they'd been man and wife, and I zid myself as the next poor stunpoll to get into the same mess. . . . Ah—well, what a day 'twas!"

"Wildeve is older than Tamsin Yeobright by a good-few summers. A pretty maid too she is. A young woman with a home must be a fool to tear her smock for a man like that."

The speaker, a peat-or turf-cutter, who had newly joined the group, carried across his shoulder the singular heart-shaped spade of large dimensions used in that species of labour; and its well-whetted edge gleamed like a silver bow in the beams of the fire.

"A hundred maidens would have had him if he'd asked 'em," said the wide woman.

"Didst ever know a man, neighbour, that no woman at all would marry?" enquired Humphrey.

"I never did," said the turf-cutter.

"Nor I," said another.

"Nor I," said Grandfer Cantle.

"Well, now, I did once," said Timothy Fairway, adding more firmness to one of his legs. "I did know of such a man. But only once, mind." He gave his throat a thorough rake round, as if it were the duty of every person not to be mistaken through thickness of voice. "Yes, I knew of such a man," he said.

"And what ghastly gallicrow might the poor fellow have been like, Master Fairway?" asked the turf-cutter.

"Well, 'a was neither a deaf man, nor a dumb man, nor a blind man. What 'a was I don't say."

"Is he known in these parts?" said Olly Dowden.

"Hardly," said Timothy; "but I name no name. . . . Come, keep the fire up there, youngsters."

"Whatever is Christian Cantle's teeth a-chattering for?" said a boy from amid the smoke and shades on the other side of the blaze. "Be ye a-cold, Christian?"

A thin jibbering voice was heard to reply, "No, not at all."

"Come forward, Christian, and show yourself. I didn't know you were here," said Fairway, with a humane look across towards that quarter.

Thus requested, a faltering man, with reedy hair, no shoulders, and a great quantity of wrist and ankle beyond his clothes, advanced a step or two by his own will, and was pushed by the will of others half-a-dozen steps more. He was Grandfer Cantle's youngest son.

"What be ye quaking for, Christian?" said the turf-cutter kindly.

"I'm the man."

"What man?"

"The man no woman will marry."

"The deuce you be!" said Timothy Fairway, enlarging his gaze to cover Christian's whole surface and a great deal more; Grandfer Cantle meanwhile staring as a hen stares at the duck she has hatched.

"Yes, I be he; and it makes me afeard," said Christian. "D'ye think 'twill hurt me? I shall always say I don't care, and swear to it, though I do care all the while."

"Well, be damned if this isn't the queerest start ever I know'd," said Mr. Fairway. "I didn't mean you at all. There's another in the country, then! Why did ye reveal yer misfortune, Christian?"

" 'Twas to be if 'twas, I suppose. I can't help it, can I?" He turned upon them his painfully circular eyes, surrounded by concentric lines like targets.

"No, that's true. But 'tis a melancholy thing, and my blood ran cold when you spoke, for I felt there were two poor fellows where I had thought only one. 'Tis a sad thing for ye, Christian. How'st know the women won't hae thee?"

"I've asked 'em."

"Sure I should never have thought you had the face. Well, and what did the last one say to ye? Nothing that can't be got over, perhaps, after all?"

" 'Get out of my sight, you slack-twisted, slim-looking fool,' was the woman's words to me."

"Not encouraging, I own," said Fairway. " 'Get out of my sight, you slack-twisted, slim-looking fool,' is rather a hard way of saying No. But even that might be overcome by time and patience, so as to let a few grey hairs show themselves in the hussy's head. How old be you, Christian?"

"Thirty-one last tatie-digging, Mister Fairway."

"Not a boy—not a boy. Still there's hope yet."

"That's my age by baptism, because that's put down in the great book of the Judgment—that they keep in church vestry; but mother told me I was born some time afore I was christened."

"Ah!"

"But she couldn't tell when, to save her life, except that there was no moon."

"No moon: that's bad. Hey, neighbours, that's bad for him!"

"Yes, 'tis bad," said Grandfer Cantle, shaking his head.

"Mother know'd 'twas no moon, for she asked another woman that had an almanac, as she did whenever a boy was born to her, because of the saying, 'No moon, no man,' which made her afeard every man-child she had. Do ye really think it serious, Mister Fairway, that there was no moon?"

"Yes; 'No moon, no man.' 'Tis one of the truest sayings ever spit out. The boy never comes to anything that's born at new moon. A bad job for thee, Christian, that you should have showed your nose then of all days in the month."

"I suppose the moon was terrible full when you were born?" said Christian, with a look of hopeless admiration at Fairway.

"Well, 'a was not new," Mr. Fairway replied, with a disinterested gaze.

"I'd sooner go without drink at Lammas-tide than be a man of no moon," continued Christian, in the same shattered recitative. " 'Tis said I be only the rames of a man, and no good for my race at all; and I suppose that's the cause o't."

"Ay," said Grandfer Cantle, somewhat subdued in spirit; "and yet his mother cried for scores of hours when 'a was a boy, for fear he should outgrow hisself and go for a soldier."

"Well, there's many just as bad as he," said Fairway. "Wethers must live their time as well as other sheep, poor soul."

"So perhaps I shall rub on? Ought I to be afeared o' nights, Master Fairway?"

"You'll have to lie alone all your life; and 'tis not to married couples but to single sleepers that a ghost shows hisself when 'a do come. One has been seen lately, too. A very strange one."

"No—don't talk about it if 'tis agreeable of ye not to! 'Twill make my skin crawl when I think of it in bed alone. But you will—ah, you will, I know, Timothy; and I shall dream all night o't! A very strange one? What sort of a spirit did ye mean when ye said, a very strange one, Timothy?—no, no—don't tell me."

"I don't half believe in spirits myself. But I think it ghostly enough—what I was told. 'Twas a little boy that zid it."

"What was it like?—no, don't—"

"A red one. Yes, most ghosts be white; but this is as if it had been dipped in blood."

Christian drew a deep breath without letting it expand his body, and Humphrey said, "Where has it been seen?"

"Not exactly here; but in this same heth. But 'tisn't a thing to talk about. What do ye say," continued Fairway in brisker tones, and turning upon them as if the idea had not been Grandfer Cantle's—"what do you say to giving the new man and wife a bit of a song to-night afore we go to bed—being their wedding-day? When folks are just married 'tis as well to look glad o't, since looking sorry won't unjoin 'em. I am no drinker, as we know, but when the women-folk and youngsters have gone home we can drop down across to the Quiet Woman, and strike up a ballet in front of the married folks' door. 'Twill please the young wife, and that's what I should like to do, for many's the skinful I've had at her hands when she lived with her aunt at Blooms-End."

"Hey? And so we will!" said Grandfer Cantle, turning so briskly that his copper seals swung extravagantly. "I'm as dry as a kex with biding up here in the wind, and I haven't seen the colour of drink since nammet-time to-day. 'Tis said that the last brew at the Woman is very pretty drinking. And, neighbours, if we should be a little late in the finishing, why, to-morrow's Sunday, and we can sleep it off!"

"Grandfer Cantle! you take things very careless for an old man," said the wide woman.

"I take things careless; I do—too careless to please the women! Klk! I'll sing the 'Jovial Crew,' or any other song, when a weak old man would cry his eyes out. Jown it; I am up for anything.

> The king' look'd o'-ver his left' shoul-der',
> And a grim' look look'-ed hee',
> Earl Mar'-shal, he said', but for' my oath'
> Or hang'-ed thou' shouldst bee'.

"Well, that's what we'll do," said Fairway. "We'll give 'em a song, an' it please the Lord. What's the good of Thomasin's cousin Clym a-coming home after the deed's done? He should have come afore, if so be he wanted to stop it, and marry her himself."

"Perhaps he's coming to bide with his mother a little time, as she must feel lonely now the maid's gone."

"Now, 'tis very odd, but I never feel lonely—no, not at all," said Grandfer Cantle. "I am as brave in the night-time as a' admiral!"

The bonfire was by this time beginning to sink low, for the fuel had not been of that substantial sort which can support a blaze long. Most of the other fires within the wide horizon were also dwindling weak. Attentive observation of their brightness, colour, and length of existence would have revealed the quality of the material burnt; and through that, to some extent the natural produce of the district in which each bonfire was situate. The clear, kingly effulgence that had characterised the majority expressed a heath and furze country like their own, which in one direction extended an unlimited number of miles: the rapid flares and extinctions at other points of the compass showed the lightest of fuel—straw, beanstalks, and the usual waste from arable land. The most enduring of all— steady unaltering eyes like Planets—signified wood, such as hazel-branches, thorn-faggots, and stout billets. Fires of the last-mentioned materials were rare, and though comparatively small in magnitude beside the transient blazes, now began to get the best of them by mere long-continuance. The great ones had perished, but these remained. They occupied the remotest visible positions—sky-backed summits rising out of rich coppice and plantation districts to the north, where the soil was different, and heath foreign and strange.

Save one; and this was the nearest of any, the moon of the whole shining throng. It lay in a direction precisely opposite to that of the little window in the vale below. Its nearness was such that, notwithstanding its actual smallness, its glow infinitely transcended theirs.

This quiet eye had attracted attention from time to time; and when their own fire had become sunken and dim it attracted more; some even of the wood fires more recently lighted had reached their decline, but no change was perceptible here.

"To be sure, how near that fire is!" said Fairway. "Seemingly. I can see a fellow of some sort walking round it. Little and good must be said of that fire, surely."

"I can throw a stone there," said the boy.

"And so can I!" said Grandfer Cantle.

"No, no, you can't, my sonnies. That fire is not much less than a mile and a half off, for all that 'a seems so near."

" 'Tis in the heath, but not furze," said the turf-cutter.

" 'Tis cleft-wood, that's what 'tis," said Timothy Fairway. "Nothing would burn like that except clean timber. And 'tis on the knap afore the old captain's house at Mistover. Such a queer mortal as that man is! To have a little fire inside your own bank and ditch, that nobody else may enjoy it or come anigh it! And what a zany an old chap must be, to light a bonfire when there's no youngsters to please."

"Cap'n Vye has been for a long walk to-day, and is quite tired out," said Grandfer Cantle, "so 'tisn't likely to be he."

"And he would hardly afford good fuel like that," said the wide woman.

"Then it must be his grand-daughter," said Fairway. "Not that a body of her age can want a fire much."

"She is very strange in her ways, living up there by herself, and such things please her," said Susan.

"She's a well-favoured maid enough," said Humphrey the furze-cutter; "especially when she's got one of her dandy gowns on."

"That's true," said Fairway. "Well, let her bonfire burn an't will. Ours is well-nigh out by the look o't."

"How dark 'tis now the fire's gone down!" said Christian Cantle, looking behind him with his hare eyes. "Don't ye think we'd better get home-along, neighbours? The heth isn't haunted, I know; but we'd better get home. . . . Ah, what was that?"

"Only the wind," said the turf-cutter.

"I don't think Fifth-of-Novembers ought to be kept up by night except in towns. It should be by day in outstep, ill-accounted places like this!"

"Nonsense, Christian. Lift up your spirits like a man! Susy, dear, you and I will have a jig—hey, my honey?—before 'tis quite too dark to see how well-favoured you be still, though so many summers have passed since your husband, a son of a witch, snapped you up from me."

This was addressed to Susan Nunsuch; and the next circumstance of which the beholders were conscious was a vision of the matron's broad form whisking off towards the space whereon the fire had been kindled. She was lifted bodily by Mr. Fairway's arm, which had been flung round her waist before she had become aware of his intention. The site of the fire was now merely a circle of ashes flecked with red embers and sparks, the furze having burnt completely away. Once within the circle he whirled her round and round in a dance. She was a woman noisily constructed; in addition to her enclosing framework of whalebone and lath, she wore pattens summer and winter, in wet weather and in dry, to preserve her boots from wear; and when Fairway began to jump about with her, the clicking of the pattens, the creaking of the stays, and her screams of surprise, formed a very audible concert.

"I'll crack thy numskull for thee, you mandy chap," said Mrs. Nunsuch, as she helplessly danced round with him, her feet playing like drumsticks among the sparks. "My ankles were all in a fever afore, from walking through that prickly furze, and now you must make 'em worse with these vlankers!"

The vagary of Timothy Fairway was infectious. The turf-cutter seized old Olly Dowden, and, somewhat more gently, poussetted with her likewise. The young men were not slow to imitate the example of their elders, and seized the maids; Grandfer Cantle and his stick jigged in the form of a three-legged object among the rest; and in half a minute all that could be seen on Rainbarrow was a whirling of dark shapes amid a boiling confusion of sparks, which leapt around the dancers as high as their waists. The chief noises were women's shrill cries, men's laughter, Susan's stays and pattens, Olly Dowden's "heu-heu-heu!" and the strumming of the wind upon the furze-bushes, which formed a kind of tune to the demoniac measure they trod. Christian alone stood aloof, uneasily rocking himself as he murmured, "They ought not to do it—how the vlankers do fly! 'tis tempting the Wicked one, 'tis."

"What was that?" said one of the lads, stopping.

"Ah—where?" said Christian, hastily closing up to the rest.

The dancers all lessened their speed.

" 'Twas behind you, Christian, that I heard it—down here."

"Yes—'tis behind me!" Christian said. "Matthew, Mark, Luke, and John, bless the bed that I lie on; four angels guard—"

"Hold your tongue. What is it?" said Fairway.

"Hoi-i-i-i!" cried a voice from the darkness.

"Halloo-o-o-o!" said Fairway.

"Is there any cart-track up across here to Mis'ess Yeobright's, of Blooms-End?" came to them in the same voice, as a long, slim indistinct figure approached the barrow.

"Ought we not to run home as hard as we can, neighbours, as 'tis getting late?" said Christian. "Not run away from one another, you know; run close together, I mean."

"Scrape up a few stray locks of furze, and make a blaze, so that we can see who the man is," said Fairway.

When the flame arose it revealed a young man in tight raiment, and red from top to toe. "Is there a track across here to Mis'ess Yeobright's house?" he repeated.

"Ay—keep along the path down there."

"I mean a way two horses and a van can travel over?"

"Well, yes; you can get up the vale below here with time. The track is rough, but if you've got a light your horses may pick along wi' care. Have ye brought your cart far up, neighbour reddleman?"

"I've left it in the bottom, about half a mile back. I stepped on in front to make sure of the way, as 'tis night-time, and I han't been here for so long."

"Oh, well you can get up," said Fairway. "What a turn it did give me when I zid him!" he added to the whole group, the reddleman included. "Lord's sake, I thought, whatever fiery mommet is this come to trouble us? No slight to your looks, reddleman, for ye bain't bad-looking in the groundwork, though the finish is queer. My meaning is just to say how curious I felt. I half thought it 'twas the devil or the red ghost the boy told of."

"It gied me a turn likewise," said Susan Nunsuch, "for I had a dream last night of a death's head."

"Don't ye talk o't no more," said Christian. "If he had a handkerchief over his head he'd look for all the world like the Devil in the picture of the Temptation."

"Well, thank you for telling me," said the young reddleman, smiling faintly. "And good-night t'ye all."

He withdrew from their sight down the barrow.

"I fancy I've seen that young man's face before," said Humphrey. "But where, or how, or what his name is, I don't know."

The reddleman had not been gone more than a few minutes when another person approached the partially revived bonfire. It proved to be a well-known and respected widow of the neighbourhood, of a standing which can only be expressed by the word genteel. Her face, encompassed by the blackness of the receding heath, showed whitely, and without half-lights, like a cameo.

She was a woman of middle-age, with well-formed features of the type usually found where perspicacity is the chief quality enthroned within. At moments she seemed to be regarding issues from a Nebo denied to others around. She had something of an estranged mien: the solitude exhaled from the heath was concentrated in this face that had risen from it. The air with which she looked at the heathmen betokened a certain unconcern at their presence, or at what might be their opinions of her for walking in that lonely spot at such an hour, thus indirectly implying that in some respect or other they were not up to her level. The explanation lay in the fact that though her husband had been a small farmer she herself was a curate's daughter, who had once dreamt of doing better things.

Persons with any weight of character carry, like planets, their atmospheres along with them in their orbits; and the matron who entered now upon the scene could, and usually did, bring her own tone into a company. Her normal manner among the heath-folk had that reticence which results from the consciousness of superior communicative power. But the effect of coming into society and light after lonely wandering in darkness is a sociability in the comer above its usual pitch, expressed in the features even more than in words.

"Why, 'tis Mis'ess Yeobright," said Fairway. "Mis'ess Yeobright, not ten minutes ago a man was here asking for you—a reddleman."

"What did he want?" said she.

"He didn't tell us."

"Something to sell, I suppose; what it can be I am at a loss to understand."

"I am glad to hear that your son Mr. Clym is coming home at Christmas, ma'am," said Sam, the turf-cutter. "What a dog he used to be for bonfires!"

"Yes. I believe he is coming," she said.

"He must be a fine fellow by this time," said Fairway.

"He is a man now," she replied quietly.

" 'Tis very lonesome for 'ee in the heth to-night, mis'ess," said Christian, coming from the seclusion he had hitherto maintained. "Mind you don't get lost. Egdon Heth is a bad place to get lost in, and the winds do huffle queerer to-night than ever I heard 'em afore. Them that know Egdon best have been pixy-led here at times."

"Is that you, Christian?" said Mrs. Yeobright. "What made you hide away from me?"

" 'Twas that I didn't know you in this light, mis'ess; and being a man of the mournfullest make, I was scared a little, that's all. Oftentimes if you could see how terrible down I get in my mind, 'twould make 'ee quite nervous for fear I should die by my hand."

"You don't take after your father," said Mrs. Yeobright, looking towards the fire, where Grandfer Cantle, with some want of originality, was dancing by himself among the sparks, as the others had done before.

"Now, Grandfer," said Timothy Fairway, "we are ashamed of ye. A reverent old patriarch man as you be—seventy if a day—to go hornpiping like that by yourself!"

"A harrowing old man, Mis'ess Yeobright," said Christian despondingly. "I wouldn't live with him a week, so playward as he is, if I could get away."

" 'Twould be more seemly in ye to stand still and welcome Mis'ess Yeobright, and you the venerablest here, Grandfer Cantle," said the besom-woman.

"Faith, and so it would," said the reveller, checking himself repentantly. "I've such a bad memory, Mis'ess Yeobright, that I forget how I'm looked up to by the rest of 'em. My spirits must be wonderful good, you'll say? But not always. 'Tis a weight upon a man to be looked up to as commander, and I often feel it."

"I am sorry to stop the talk," said Mrs. Yeobright. "But I must be leaving you now. I am crossing the heath towards my niece's new home, who is returning to-night with her husband; and hearing Olly's voice I came up here to ask her if she would soon be going home; I should like her to walk with me, as her way is mine."

"Ay, sure, ma'am, I'm just thinking of moving," said Olly.

"Why, you'll be safe to meet the reddleman that I told ye of," said Fairway. "He's only gone back to get his van. We heard that your niece and her husband were coming straight home as soon as they were married, and we are going down there shortly, to give 'em a song o' welcome."

"Thank you indeed," said Mrs. Yeobright.

"But we shall take a shorter cut through the furze than you can go with long clothes; so we won't trouble you to wait."

"Very well—are you ready, Olly?"

"Yes, ma'am. And there's a light shining from your niece's window, see. It will help to keep us in the path."

She indicated the faint light at the bottom of the valley which Fairway had pointed out; and the two women descended the barrow.

IV

THE HALT ON THE TURNPIKE ROAD

DOWN, DOWNWARD THEY WENT, AND YET FURTHER DOWN—THEIR DESCENT AT EACH step seeming to outmeasure their advance. Their skirts were scratched noisily by the furze, their shoulders brushed by the ferns, which, though dead and dry, stood erect as when alive, no sufficient winter weather having as yet arrived to beat them down. Their Tartarean situation might by some have been called an imprudent one for two unattended women. But these shaggy recesses were at all seasons a familiar surrounding to Olly and Mrs. Yeobright; and the addition of darkness lends no frightfulness to the face of a friend.

"And so Tamsin has married him at last," said Olly, when the incline had become so much less steep that their footsteps no longer required undivided attention.

Mrs. Yeobright answered slowly, "Yes: at last."

"How you will miss her—living with ye as a daughter, as she always have."

"I do miss her."

Olly, though without the tact to perceive when remarks were untimely, was saved by her very simplicity from rendering them offensive. Questions that would have been resented in others she could ask with impunity. This accounted for Mrs. Yeobright's acquiescence in the revival of an evidently sore subject.

"I was quite strook to hear you'd agreed to it, ma'am, that I was," continued the besom-maker.

"You were not more struck by it than I should have been last year this time, Olly. There are a good many sides to that wedding. I could not tell you all of them, even if I tried."

"I felt myself that he was hardly solid-going enough to mate with your family. Keeping an inn—what is it? But 'a's clever, that's true, and they say he was an engineering gentleman once, but has come down by being too outwardly given."

"I saw that, upon the whole, it would be better she should marry where she wished."

"Poor little thing, her feelings got the better of her, no doubt. 'Tis nature. Well, they may call him what they will—he've several acres of heth ground broke up here, besides the public-house, and the heth-croppers, and his manners be quite like a gentleman's. And what's done cannot be undone."

"It cannot," said Mrs. Yeobright. "See, here's the waggon-track at last. Now we shall get along better."

The wedding subject was no further dwelt upon; and soon a faint diverging path was reached, where they parted company, Olly first begging her companion to remind Mr. Wildeve that he had not sent her sick husband the bottle of wine promised on the occasion of his marriage. The besom-maker turned to the left towards her own house, behind a spur of the hill, and Mrs. Yeobright followed the straight track, which further on joined the highway by the Quiet Woman Inn, whither she supposed her niece to have returned with Wildeve from their wedding at Anglebury that day.

She first reached Wildeve's Patch, as it was called, a plot of land redeemed from the heath, and after long and laborious years brought into cultivation. The man who had discovered that it could be tilled died of the labour: the man who succeeded him in possession ruined himself in fertilising it. Wildeve came like Amerigo Vespucci, and received the honours due to those who had gone before.

When Mrs. Yeobright had drawn near to the inn, and was about to enter, she saw a horse and vehicle some two hundred yards beyond it, coming towards her, a man walking alongside with a lantern in his hand. It was soon evident that this was the reddleman who had enquired for her. Instead of entering the inn at once, she walked by it and towards the van.

The conveyance came close, and the man was about to pass her with little notice, when she turned to him and said, "I think you have been enquiring for me? I am Mrs. Yeobright of Blooms-End."

The reddleman started, and held up his finger. He stopped the horses, and beckoned to her to withdraw with him a few yards aside, which she did, wondering.

"You don't know me, ma'am, I suppose?" he said.

"I do not," said she. "Why, yes, I do! You are young Venn—your father was a dairy-man somewhere here?"

"Yes; and I knew your niece, Miss Tamsin, a little. I have something bad to tell you."

"About her—no? She has just come home, I believe, with her husband. They arranged to return this afternoon—to the inn beyond here."

"She's not there."

"How do you know?"

"Because she's here. She's in my van," he added slowly.

"What new trouble has come?" murmured Mrs. Yeobright, putting her hand over her eyes.

"I can't explain much, ma'am. All I know is that, as I was going along the road this morning, about a mile out of Anglebury, I heard something trotting after me like a doe, and looking round there she was, white as death itself. 'Oh, Diggory Venn!' she said, 'I thought 'twas you: will you help me? I am in trouble.' "

"How did she know your Christian name?" said Mrs. Yeobright doubtingly.

"I had met her as a lad before I went away in this trade. She asked then if she might ride, and then down she fell in a faint. I picked her up and put her in, and there she has been ever since. She has cried a good deal, but she has hardly spoke; all she has told me being that she was to have been married this morning. I tried to get her to eat something, but she couldn't; and at last she fell asleep."

"Let me see her at once," said Mrs. Yeobright, hastening towards the van.

The reddleman followed with the lantern, and, stepping up first, assisted Mrs. Yeobright to mount beside him. On the door being opened she perceived at the end of the van an extemporised couch, around which was hung apparently all the drapery that the reddleman possessed, to keep the occupant of the little couch from contact with the red materials of his trade. A young girl lay thereon, covered with a cloak. She was asleep, and the light of the lantern fell upon her features.

A fair, sweet, and honest country face was revealed, reposing in a nest of wavy chestnut hair. It was between pretty and beautiful. Though her eyes were closed, one could easily imagine the light necessarily shining in them as the culmination of the luminous workmanship around. The groundwork of the face was hopefulness; but over it now lay like a foreign substance a film of anxiety and grief. The grief had been there so shortly as to have abstracted nothing of the bloom which had as yet but given a dignity to what it might eventually undermine. The scarlet of her lips had not had time to abate, and just now it appeared still more intense by the absence of the neighbouring and more transient colour of her cheek. The lips frequently parted, with a murmur of words. She seemed to belong rightly to a madrigal—to require viewing through rhyme and harmony.

One thing at least was obvious: she was not made to be looked at thus. The reddleman had appeared conscious of as much, and, while Mrs. Yeobright looked in upon her, he cast his eyes aside with a delicacy which well became him. The sleeper apparently thought so too, for the next moment she opened her own.

The lips then parted with something of anticipation, something more of doubt; and her several thoughts and fractions of thoughts, as signalled by the changes on her face, were exhibited by the light to the utmost nicety. An ingenuous, transparent life was disclosed; as if the flow of her existence could be seen passing within her. She understood the scene in a moment.

"O yes, it is I, aunt," she cried. "I know how frightened you are, and how you cannot believe it; but all the same, it is I who have come home like this!"

"Tamsin, Tamsin!" said Mrs. Yeobright, stooping over the young woman and kissing her. "O my dear girl!"

Thomasin was now on the verge of a sob; but by an unexpected self-command she uttered no sound. With a gentle panting breath she sat upright.

"I did not expect to see you in this state, any more than you me," she went on quickly. "Where am I, aunt?"

"Nearly home, my dear. In Egdon Bottom. What dreadful thing is it?"

"I'll tell you in a moment. So near, are we? Then I will get out and walk. I want to go home by the path."

"But this kind man who has done so much will, I am sure, take you right on to my house?" said the aunt, turning to the reddleman, who had withdrawn from the front of the van on the awakening of the girl, and stood in the road.

"Why should you think it necessary to ask me? I will, of course," said he.

"He is indeed kind," murmured Thomasin. "I was once acquainted with him, aunt, and when I saw him to-day I thought I should prefer his van to any conveyance of a stranger. But I'll walk now. Reddleman, stop the horses, please."

The man regarded her with tender reluctance, but stopped them.

Aunt and niece then descended from the van, Mrs. Yeobright saying to its owner, "I quite recognise you now. What made you change from the nice business your father left you?"

"Well, I did," he said, and looked at Thomasin, who blushed a little. "Then you'll not be wanting me any more to-night, ma'am?"

Mrs. Yeobright glanced around at the dark sky, at the hills, at the perishing bonfires, and at the lighted window of the inn they had neared. "I think not," she said, "since Thomasin wishes to walk. We can soon run up the path and reach home: we know it well."

And after a few further words they parted, the reddleman moving onwards with his van, and the two women remaining standing in the road. As soon as the vehicle and its driver had withdrawn so far as to be beyond all possible reach of her voice, Mrs. Yeobright turned to her niece.

"Now, Thomasin," she said sternly, "what's the meaning of this disgraceful performance?"

V

PERPLEXITY AMONG HONEST PEOPLE

THOMASIN LOOKED AS IF QUITE OVERCOME BY HER AUNT'S CHANGE OF MANNER. "IT means just what it seems to mean: I am—not married," she replied faintly. "Excuse me—for humiliating you, aunt, by this mishap: I am sorry for it. But I cannot help it."

"Me? Think of yourself first."

"It was nobody's fault. When we got there the parson wouldn't marry us because of some trifling irregularity in the license."

"What irregularity?"

"I don't know. Mr. Wildeve can explain. I did not think when I went away this morning that I should come back like this." It being dark, Thomasin allowed her emotion to escape her by the silent way of tears, which could roll down her cheek unseen.

"I could almost say that it serves you right—if I did not feel that you don't deserve it," continued Mrs. Yeobright, who, possessing two distinct moods in close contiguity, a gentle mood and an angry, flew from one to the other without the least warning. "Remember, Thomasin, this business was none of my seeking; from the very first, when you began to feel foolish about that man, I warned you he would not make you happy. I felt it so strongly that I did what I would never have believed myself capable of doing—stood up in the church, and made myself the public talk for weeks. But having once consented, I don't submit to these fancies without good reason. Marry him you must after this."

"Do you think I wish to do otherwise for one moment?" said Thomasin, with a heavy sigh. "I know how wrong it was of me to love him, but don't pain me by talking like that, aunt! You would not have had me stay there with him, would you?—and your house is the only home I have to return to. He says we can be married in a day or two."

"I wish he had never seen you."

"Very well; then I will be the miserablest woman in the world, and not let him see me again. No, I won't have him!"

"It is too late to speak so. Come with me. I am going to the inn to see if he has returned. Of course I shall get to the bottom of this story at once. Mr. Wildeve must not suppose he can play tricks upon me, or any belonging to me."

"It was not that. The licence was wrong, and he couldn't get another the same day. He will tell you in a moment how it was, if he comes."

"Why didn't he bring you back?"

"That was me!" again sobbed Thomasin. "When I found we could not be married I didn't like to come back with him, and I was very ill. Then I saw Diggory Venn, and was glad to get him to take me home. I cannot explain it any better, and you must be angry with me if you will."

"I shall see about that," said Mrs. Yeobright; and they turned towards the inn, known in the neighbourhood as the Quiet Woman, the sign of which represented the figure of a matron carrying her head under her arm. The front of the house was towards the heath and Rainbarrow, whose dark shape seemed to threaten it from the sky. Upon the door was a neglected brass plate, bearing the unexpected inscription, "Mr. Wildeve, Engineer"—a useless yet cherished relic from the time when he had been started in that profession in an office at Budmouth by those who had hoped much from him, and had been disappointed. The garden was at the back, and behind this ran a still deep stream, forming the margin of the heath in this direction, meadow-land appearing beyond the stream.

But the thick obscurity permitted only sky-lines to be visible of any scene at present. The water at the back of the house could be heard, idly spinning whirlpools in its creep between the rows of dry feather-headed reeds which formed a stockade along each bank. Their presence was denoted by sounds as of a congregation praying humbly, produced by their rubbing against each other in the slow wind.

The window, whence the candle-light had shone up the vale to the eyes of the bonfire group, was uncurtained, but the sill lay too high for a pedestrian on the outside to look over it into the room. A vast shadow, in which could be dimly traced portions of a masculine contour, blotted half the ceiling.

"He seems to be at home," said Mrs. Yeobright.

"Must I come in, too, aunt?" asked Thomasin faintly. "I suppose not; it would be wrong."

"You must come, certainly—to confront him, so that he may make no false representations to me. We shall not be five minutes in the house, and then we'll walk home."

Entering the open passage, she tapped at the door of the private parlour, unfastened it, and looked in.

The back and shoulders of a man came between Mrs. Yeobright's eyes and the fire. Wildeve, whose form it was, immediately turned, arose, and advanced to meet his visitors.

He was quite a young man, and of the two properties, form and motion, the latter first attracted the eye in him. The grace of his movement was singular: it was the pantomimic expression of a lady-killing career. Next came into notice the more material qualities, among which was a profuse crop of hair impending over the top of his face, lending to his forehead the high-cornered outline of an early Gothic shield; and a neck which was smooth and round as a cylinder. The lower half of his figure was of light build. Altogether he was one in whom no man would have seen anything to admire, and in whom no woman would have seen anything to dislike.

He discerned the young girl's form in the passage, and said, "Thomasin, then, has reached home. How could you leave me in that way, darling?" And turning to Mrs. Yeo-bright: "It was useless to argue with her. She would go, and go alone."

"But what's the meaning of it all?" demanded Mrs. Yeobright haughtily.

"Take a seat," said Wildeve, placing chairs for the two women. "Well, it was a very stupid mistake, but such mistakes will happen. The licence was useless at Anglebury. It was made out for Budmouth, but as I didn't read it I wasn't aware of that."

"But you had been staying at Anglebury?"

"No. I had been at Budmouth—till two days ago—and that was where I had intended to take her; but when I came to fetch her we decided upon Anglebury, forgetting that a new licence would be necessary. There was not time to get to Budmouth afterwards."

"I think you are very much to blame," said Mrs. Yeobright.

"It was quite my fault we chose Anglebury," Thomasin pleaded. "I proposed it be-cause I was not known there."

"I know so well that I am to blame that you need not remind me of it," replied Wildeve shortly.

"Such things don't happen for nothing," said the aunt. "It is a great slight to me and my family; and when it gets known there will be a very unpleasant time for us. How can she look her friends in the face to-morrow? It is a very great injury, and one I cannot eas-ily forgive. It may even reflect on her character."

"Nonsense," said Wildeve.

Thomasin's large eyes had flown from the face of one to the face of the other during this discussion, and she now said anxiously, "Will you allow me, aunt, to talk it over alone with Damon for five minutes? Will you, Damon?"

"Certainly, dear," said Wildeve, "if your aunt will excuse us." He led her into an ad-joining room, leaving Mrs. Yeobright by the fire.

As soon as they were alone, and the door closed, Thomasin said, turning up her pale, tearful face to him, "It is killing me, this, Damon! I did not mean to part from you in anger at Anglebury this morning; but I was frightened, and hardly knew what I said. I've not let aunt know how much I have suffered to-day; and it is so hard to command my face and voice, and to smile as if it were a slight thing to me; but I try to do so, that she may not be still more indignant with you. I know you could not help it, dear, what-ever aunt may think."

"She is very unpleasant."

"Yes," Thomasin murmured, "and I suppose I seem so now. . . . Damon, what do you mean to do about me?"

"Do about you?"

"Yes. Those who don't like you whisper things which at moments make me doubt you. We mean to marry, I suppose, don't we?"

"Of course we do. We have only to go to Budmouth on Monday, and we marry at once."

"Then do let us go!—O Damon, what you make me say!" She hid her face in her handkerchief. "Here am I asking you to marry me; when by rights you ought to be on your knees imploring me, your cruel mistress, not to refuse you, and saying it would break your heart if I did. I used to think it would be pretty and sweet like that; but how different!"

"Yes, real life is never at all like that."

"But I don't care personally if it never takes place," she added with a little dignity; "no, I can live without you. It is aunt I think of. She is so proud, and thinks so much of her family respectability, that she will be cut down with mortification if this story should get abroad before—it is done. My cousin Clym, too, will be much wounded."

"Then he will be very unreasonable. In fact, you are all rather unreasonable."

Thomasin coloured a little, and not with love. But whatever the momentary feeling which caused that flush in her, it went as it came, and she humbly said, "I never mean to be, if I can help it. I merely feel that you have my aunt to some extent in your power at last."

"As a matter of justice it is almost due to me," said Wildeve. "Think what I have gone through to win her consent; the insult that it is to any man to have the banns forbidden: the double insult to a man unlucky enough to be cursed with sensitiveness, and blue demons, and Heaven knows what, as I am. I can never forget those banns. A harsher man would rejoice now in the power I have of turning upon your aunt by going no further in the business."

She looked wistfully at him with her sorrowful eyes as he said those words, and her aspect showed that more than one person in the room could deplore the possession of sensitiveness. Seeing that she was really suffering he seemed disturbed and added, "This is merely a reflection, you know. I have not the least intention to refuse to complete the marriage, Tamsie mine—I could not bear it."

"You could not, I know!" said the fair girl, brightening. "You, who cannot bear the sight of pain in even an insect, or any disagreeable sound, or unpleasant smell even, will not long cause pain to me and mine."

"I will not, if I can help it."

"Your hand upon it, Damon."

He carelessly gave her his hand.

"Ah, by my crown, what's that?" he said suddenly.

There fell upon their ears the sound of numerous voices singing in front of the house. Among these two made themselves prominent by their peculiarity: one was a very strong bass, the other a wheezy thin piping. Thomasin recognised them as belonging to Timothy Fairway and Grandfer Cantle respectively.

"What does it mean—it is not skimmity-riding, I hope?" she said, with a frightened gaze at Wildeve.

"Of course not; no, it is that the heath-folk have come to sing to us a welcome. This is intolerable!" He began pacing about, the men outside singing cheerily—

> *He told' her that she' was the joy' of his life',*
> *And if' she'd con-sent' he would make her his wife';*
> *She could' not refuse' him; to church' so they went',*
> *Young Will was forgot', and young Sue' was con-tent';*
> *And then' was she kiss'd' and set down' on his knee',*
> *No man' in the world' was so lov'-ing as he'!*

Mrs. Yeobright burst in from the outer room. "Thomasin, Thomasin!" she said, looking indignantly at Wildeve; "here's a pretty exposure! Let us escape at once. Come!"

It was, however, too late to get away by the passage. A rugged knocking had begun upon the door of the front room. Wildeve, who had gone to the window, came back.

"Stop!" he said imperiously, putting his hand upon Mrs. Yeobright's arm. "We are regularly besieged. There are fifty of them out there if there's one. You stay in this room with Thomasin; I'll go out and face them. You must stay now, for my sake, till they are gone, so that it may seem as if all was right. Come, Tamsie dear, don't go making a scene—we must marry after this; that you can see as well as I. Sit still, that's all—and don't speak much. I'll manage them. Blundering fools!"

He pressed the agitated girl into a seat, returned to the outer room and opened the door. Immediately outside, in the passage, appeared Grandfer Cantle singing in concert with those still standing in front of the house. He came into the room and nodded abstractedly to Wildeve, his lips still parted, and his features excruciatingly strained in the emission of the chorus. This being ended, he said heartily, "Here's welcome to the new-made couple, and God bless 'em!"

"Thank you," said Wildeve, with dry resentment, his face as gloomy as a thunder-storm.

At the Grandfer's heels now came the rest of the group, which included Fairway, Christian, Sam the turf-cutter, Humphrey, and a dozen others. All smiled upon Wildeve, and upon his tables and chairs likewise, from a general sense of friendliness towards the articles as well as towards their owner.

"We be not here afore Mrs. Yeobright after all," said Fairway, recognising the matron's bonnet through the glass partition which divided the public apartment they had entered from the room where the women sat. "We struck down across, d'ye see, Mr. Wildeve, and she went round by the path."

"And I see the young bride's little head!" said Grandfer, peeping in the same direction, and discerning Thomasin, who was waiting beside her aunt in a miserable and awkward way. "Not quite settled yet—well, well, there's plenty of time."

Wildeve made no reply; and probably feeling that the sooner he treated them the sooner they would go, he produced a stone jar, which threw a warm halo over matters at once.

"That's a drop of the right sort, I can see," said Grandfer Cantle, with the air of a man too well-mannered to show any hurry to taste it.

"Yes," said Wildeve, " 'tis some old mead. I hope you will like it."

"Oh ay," replied the guests, in the hearty tones natural when the words demanded by politeness coincide with those of deepest feeling. "There isn't a prettier drink under the sun."

"I'll take my oath there isn't," added Grandfer Cantle. "All that can be said against mead is that 'tis rather heady, and apt to lie about a man a good while. But to-morrow's Sunday, thank God."

"I feel'd for all the world like some bold soldier after I had had some once," said Christian.

"You shall feel so again," said Wildeve, with condescension, "Cups or glasses, gentlemen?"

"Well, if you don't mind, we'll have the beaker, and pass 'en round; 'tis better than heling it out in dribbles."

"Jown the slippery glasses," said Grandfer Cantle. "What's the good of a thing that you can't put down in the ashes to warm, hey, neighbours; that's what I ask?"

"Right, Grandfer," said Sam; and the mead then circulated.

"Well," said Timothy Fairway, feeling demands upon his praise in some form or other, " 'tis a worthy thing to be married, Mr. Wildeve; and the woman you've got is a dimant, so says I. Yes," he continued, to Grandfer Cantle, raising his voice so as to be heard through the partition; "her father (inclining his head towards the inner room) was as good a feller as ever lived. He always had his great indignation ready against anything underhand."

"Is that very dangerous?" said Christian.

"And there were few in these parts that were up-sides with him," said Sam. "Whenever a club walked he'd play the clarinet in the band that marched before 'em as if he'd never touched anything but a clarinet all his life. And then, when they got to church-door he'd throw down the clarinet, mount the gallery, snatch up the bass-viol, and rozum away as if he'd never played anything but a bass-viol. Folk would say—folk that knowed what a true stave was—'Surely, surely that's never the same man that I zid handling the clarinet so masterly by now!' "

"I can mind it," said the furze-cutter. " 'Twas a wonderful thing that one body could hold it all and never mix the fingering."

"There was Kingsbere church likewise," Fairway recommenced, as one opening a new vein of the same mine of interest.

Wildeve breathed the breath of one intolerably bored, and glanced through the partition at the prisoners.

"He used to walk over there of a Sunday afternoon to visit his old acquaintance Andrew Brown, the first clarinet there; a good man enough, but rather screechy in his music, if you can mind?"

" 'A was."

"And neighbour Yeobright would take Andrey's place for some part of the service, to let Andrey have a bit of a nap, as any friend would naturally do."

"As any friend would," said Grandfer Cantle, the other listeners expressing the same accord by the shorter way of nodding their heads.

"No sooner was Andrey asleep and the first whiff of neighbour Yeobright's wind had got inside Andrey's clarinet than everyone in church felt in a moment there was a great soul among 'em. All heads would turn, and they'd say, 'Ah, I thought 'twas he!' One Sunday I can well mind—a bass-viol day that time, and Yeobright had brought his own. 'Twas the Hundred-and-thirty-third to 'Lydia'; and when they'd come to 'Ran down his beard and o'er his robes its costly moisture shed,' neighbour Yeobright, who had just warmed to his work, drove his bow into them strings that glorious grand that he e'en a'most sawed the bass-viol into two pieces. Every winder in church rattled as if 'twere a thunder-storm. Old Pa'son Williams lifted his hands in his great holy surplice as natural as if he'd been in common clothes, and seemed to say to hisself, 'Oh for such a man in our parish!' But not a soul in Kingsbere could hold a candle to Yeobright."

"Was it quite safe when the winder shook?" Christian enquired.

He received no answer; all for the moment sitting rapt in admiration of the performance described. As with Farinelli's singing before the princesses, Sheridan's renowned

Begum Speech, and other such examples, the fortunate condition of its being forever lost to the world invested the deceased Mr. Yeobright's *tour de force* on that memorable afternoon with a cumulative glory which comparative criticism, had that been possible, might considerably have shorn down.

"He was the last you'd have expected to drop off in the prime of life," said Humphrey.

"Ah, well: he was looking for the earth some months afore he went. At that time women used to run for smocks and gown-pieces at Greenhill Fair, and my wife that is now, being a long-legged slittering maid, hardly husband-high, went with the rest of the maidens, for 'a was a good runner afore she got so heavy. When she came home I said—we were then just beginning to walk together—'What have ye got, my honey?' 'I've won—well, I've won—a gown-piece,' says she, her colours coming up in a moment. 'Tis a smock for a crown, I thought; and so it turned out. Ay, when I think what she'll say to me now without a mossel of red in her face, it do seem strange that 'a wouldn't say such a little thing then. . . . However, then she went on, and that's what made me bring up the story, 'Well, whatever clothes I've won, white or figured, for eyes to see or for eyes not to see' ('a could do a pretty stroke of modesty in those days), 'I'd sooner have lost it than have seen what I have. Poor Mr. Yeobright was took bad directly he reached the fair ground, and was forced to go home again.' That was the last time he ever went out of the parish."

" 'A faltered on from one day to another, and then we heard he was gone."

"D'ye think he had great pain when 'a died?" said Christian.

"O no: quite different. Nor any pain of mind. He was lucky enough to be God A'mighty's own man."

"And other folk—d'ye think 'twill be much pain to 'em, Mister Fairway?"

"That depends on whether they be afeard."

"I bain't afeard at all, I thank God!" said Christian strenuously. "I'm glad I bain't, for then 'twon't pain me. . . . I don't think I be afeard—or if I be I can't help it, and I don't deserve to suffer. I wish I was not afeard at all!"

There was a solemn silence, and looking from the window, which was unshuttered and unblinded, Timothy said, "Well, what a fess little bonfire that one is, out by Cap'n Vye's! 'Tis burning just the same now as ever, upon my life."

All glances went through the window, and nobody noticed that Wildeve disguised a brief, tell-tale look. Far away up the sombre valley of heath, and to the right of Rainbarrow, could indeed be seen the light, small, but steady and persistent as before.

"It was lighted before ours was," Fairway continued; "and yet everyone in the country round is out afore 'n."

"Perhaps there's meaning in it!" murmured Christian.

"How meaning?" said Wildeve sharply.

Christian was too scattered to reply, and Timothy helped him.

"He means, sir, that the lonesome dark-eyed creature up there that some say is a witch—ever I should call a fine young woman such a name—is always up to some odd conceit or other; and so perhaps 'tis she."

"I'd be very glad to ask her in wedlock, if she'd hae me and take the risk of her wild dark eyes ill-wishing me," said Grandfer Cantle staunchly.

"Don't ye say it, father!" implored Christian.

"Well, be dazed if he who do marry the maid won't hae an uncommon picture for his best parlour," said Fairway in a liquid tone, placing down the cup of mead at the end of a good pull.

"And a partner as deep as the North Star," said Sam, taking up the cup and finishing the little that remained.

"Well, really, now I think we must be moving," said Humphrey, observing the emptiness of the vessel.

"But we'll gie 'em another song?" said Grandfer Cantle. "I'm as full of notes as a bird!"

"Thank you, Grandfer," said Wildeve. "But we will not trouble you now. Some other day must do for that—when I have a party."

"Be jown'd if I don't learn ten new songs for't, or I won't learn a line!" said Grandfer Cantle. "And you may be sure I won't disappoint ye by biding away, Mr. Wildeve."

"I quite believe you," said that gentleman.

All then took their leave, wishing their entertainer long life and happiness as a married man, with recapitulations which occupied some time. Wildeve attended them to the door, beyond which the deep-dyed upward stretch of heath stood awaiting them, an amplitude of darkness reigning from their feet almost to the zenith, where a definite form first became visible in the lowering forehead of Rainbarrow. Diving into the dense obscurity in a line headed by Sam the turf-cutter, they pursued their trackless way home.

When the scratching of the furze against their leggings had fainted upon the ear, Wildeve returned to the room where he had left Thomasin and her aunt. The women were gone.

They could only have left the house in one way, by the back-window; and this was open.

Wildeve laughed to himself, remained a moment thinking, and idly returned to the front-room. Here his glance fell upon a bottle of wine which stood on the mantelpiece. "Ah—old Dowden!" he murmured; and going to the kitchen door shouted, "Is anybody here who can take something to old Dowden?"

There was no reply. The room was empty, the lad who acted as his factotum having gone to bed. Wildeve came back, put on his hat, took the bottle, and left the house, turning the key in the door, for there was no guest at the inn to-night. As soon as he was on the road the little bonfire on Mistover Knap again met his eye.

"Still waiting, are you, my lady?" he murmured.

However, he did not proceed that way just then; but leaving the hill to the left of him, he stumbled over a rutted road that brought him to a cottage which, like all other habitations on the heath at this hour, was only saved from being invisible by a faint shine from its bedroom-window. This house was the home of Olly Dowden, the besom-maker, and he entered.

The lower-room was in darkness; but by feeling his way he found a table, whereon he placed the bottle, and a minute later emerged again upon the heath. He stood and looked north-east at the undying little fire—high up above him, though not so high as Rainbarrow.

We have been told what happens when a woman deliberates; and the epigram is not always terminable with woman, provided that one be in the case, and that a fair one. Wildeve stood, and stood longer, and breathed perplexedly, and then said to himself with resignation, "Yes—by Heaven, I must go to her, I suppose!"

Instead of turning in the direction of home, he pressed on rapidly by a path under Rainbarrow towards what was evidently a signal light.

VI

THE FIGURE AGAINST THE SKY

WHEN THE WHOLE EGDON CONCOURSE HAD LEFT THE SITE OF THE BONFIRE TO ITS accustomed loneliness, a closely wrapped female figure approached the barrow from that quarter of the heath in which the little fire lay. Had the reddleman been watching he might have recognised her as the woman who had first stood there so singularly, and vanished at the approach of strangers. She ascended to her old position at the top, where the red coals of the perishing fire greeted her like living eyes in the corpse of day. There she stood still, around her stretching the vast night atmosphere, whose incomplete darkness in comparison with the total darkness of the heath below it might have represented a venial beside a mortal sin.

That she was tall and straight in build, that she was ladylike in her movements, was all that could be learnt of her just now, her form being wrapped in a shawl folded in the old cornerwise fashion, and her head in a large kerchief, a protection not superfluous at this hour and place. Her back was towards the wind, which blew from the north-west; but whether she had avoided that aspect because of the chilly gusts which played about her exceptional position, or because her interest lay in the south-east, did not at first appear.

Her reason for standing so dead still as the pivot of this circle of heath-country was just as obscure. Her extraordinary fixity, her conspicuous loneliness, her heedlessness of night, betokened among other things an utter absence of fear. A tract of country unaltered from that sinister condition which made Cæsar anxious every year to get clear of its glooms before the autumnal equinox, a kind of landscape and weather which leads travellers from the South to describe our island as Homer's Cimmerian land, was not, on the face of it, friendly to women.

It might reasonably have been supposed that she was listening to the wind, which rose somewhat as the night advanced, and laid hold of the attention. The wind, indeed, seemed made for the scene, as the scene seemed made for the hour. Part of its tone was quite special; what was heard there could be heard nowhere else. Gusts in innumerable series followed each other from the north-west, and when each one of them raced past the sound of its progress resolved into three. Treble, tenor, and bass notes were to be found therein. The general ricochet of the whole over pits and prominences had the gravest pitch of the chime. Next there could be heard the baritone buzz of a holly tree. Below these in force, above them in pitch, a dwindled voice strove hard at a husky tune, which was the peculiar local sound alluded to. Thinner and less immediately traceable than the other two, it was far more impressive than either. In it lay what may be called the linguistic peculiarity of the heath; and being audible nowhere on earth off a heath, it afforded a shadow of reason for the woman's tenseness, which continued as unbroken as ever.

Throughout the blowing of these plaintive November winds that note bore a great resemblance to the ruins of human song which remain to the throat of fourscore and ten. It was a worn whisper, dry and papery, and it brushed so distinctly across the ear that, by the accustomed, the material minutiae in which it originated could be realised as by touch. It was the united products of infinitesimal vegetable causes, and these were neither stems, leaves, fruit, blades, prickles, lichen, nor moss.

They were the mummied heath-bells of the past summer, originally tender and purple, now washed colourless by Michaelmas rains, and dried to dead skins by October suns. So low was an individual sound from these that a combination of hundreds only just emerged from silence, and the myriads of the whole declivity reached the woman's ear but as a shrivelled and intermittent recitative. Yet scarcely a single accent among the many afloat to-night could have such power to impress a listener with thoughts of its origin. One inwardly saw the infinity of those combined multitudes; and perceived that each of the tiny trumpets was seized on, entered, scoured and emerged from by the wind as thoroughly as if it were as vast as a crater.

"The spirit moved them." A meaning of the phrase forced itself upon the attention; and an emotional listener's fetichistic mood might have ended in one of more advanced quality. It was not, after all, that the left-hand expanse of old blooms spoke, or the right-hand, or those of the slope in front; but it was the single person of something else speaking through each in turn.

Suddenly, on the barrow, there mingled with all this wild rhetoric of night a sound which modulated so naturally into the rest that its beginning and ending were hardly to be distinguished. The bluffs, and the bushes, and the heather-bells had broken silence; at last, so did the woman; and her articulation was but as another phrase of the same discourse as theirs. Thrown out on the winds it became twined in with them, and with them it flew away.

What she uttered was a lengthened sighing, apparently at something in her mind which had led to her presence here. There was a spasmodic abandonment about it as if, in allowing herself to utter the sound, the woman's brain had authorised what it could not regulate. One point was evident in this; that she had been existing in a suppressed state, and not in one of languor, or stagnation.

Far away down the valley the faint shine from the window of the inn still lasted on; and a few additional moments proved that the window, or what was within it, had more to do with the woman's sigh than had either her own actions or the scene immediately around. She lifted her left hand, which held a closed telescope. This she rapidly extended, as if she were well accustomed to the operation, and raising it to her eye directed it towards the light beaming from the inn.

The handkerchief which had hooded her head was now a little thrown back, her face being somewhat elevated. A profile was visible against the dull monochrome of cloud around her; and it was as though side shadows from the features of Sappho and Mrs. Siddons had converged upwards from the tomb to form an image like neither but suggesting both. This, however, was mere superficiality. In respect of character a face may make certain admissions by its outline; but it fully confesses only in its changes. So much is this the case that what is called the play of the features often helps more in understanding a man or woman than the earnest labours of all the other members together. Thus the night revealed little of her whose form it was embracing, for the mobile parts of her countenance could not be seen.

At last she gave up her spying attitude, closed the telescope, and turned to the decaying embers. From these no appreciable beams now radiated, except when a more than usually smart gust brushed over their faces and raised a fitful glow which came and went like the blush of a girl. She stooped over the silent circle, and selecting from the brands a piece of stick which bore the largest live coal at its end, brought it to where she had been standing before.

She held the brand to the ground, blowing the red coal with her mouth at the same time; till it faintly illuminated the sod, and revealed a small object, which turned out to be an hour-glass, though she wore a watch. She blew long enough to show that the sand had all slipped through.

"Ah!" she said, as if surprised.

The light raised by her breath had been very fitful, and a momentary irradiation of flesh was all that it had disclosed of her face. That consisted of two matchless lips and a cheek only, her head being still enveloped. She threw away the stick, took the glass in her hand, the telescope under her arm, and moved on.

Along the ridge ran a faint foot-track, which the lady followed. Those who knew it well called it a path; and, while a mere visitor would have passed it unnoticed even by day, the regular haunters of the heath were at no loss for it at midnight. The whole secret of following these incipient paths, when there was not light enough in the atmosphere to show a turnpike road, lay in the development of the sense of touch in the feet, which comes with years of night-rambling in little-trodden spots. To a walker practised in such places a difference between impact on maiden herbage, and on the crippled stalks of a slight footway, is perceptible through the thickest boot or shoe.

The solitary figure who walked this beat took no notice of the windy tune still played on the dead heath-bells. She did not turn her head to look at a group of dark creatures further on, who fled from her presence as she skirted a ravine where they fed. They were about a score of the small wild ponies known as heath-croppers. They roamed at large on the undulations of Egdon, but in numbers too few to detract much from the solitude.

The pedestrian noticed nothing just now, and a clue to her abstraction was afforded by a trivial incident. A bramble caught hold of her skirt, and checked her progress. Instead of putting it off and hastening along, she yielded herself up to the pull, and stood passively still. When she began to extricate herself it was by turning round and round, and so unwinding the prickly switch. She was in a desponding reverie.

Her course was in the direction of the small undying fire which had drawn the attention of the men on Rainbarrow and of Wildeve in the valley below. A faint illumination from its rays began to glow upon her face, and the fire soon revealed itself to be lit, not on the level ground, but on a salient corner or redan of earth, at the junction of two converging bank fences. Outside was a ditch, dry except immediately under the fire, where there was a large pool, bearded all round by heather and rushes. In the smooth water of the pool the fire appeared upside down.

The banks meeting behind were bare of a hedge, save such as was formed by disconnected tufts of furze, standing upon stems along the top, like impaled heads above a city wall. A white mast, fitted up with spars and other nautical tackle, could be seen rising against the dark clouds whenever the flames played brightly enough to reach it. Altogether the scene had much the appearance of a fortification upon which had been kindled a beacon fire.

Nobody was visible; but ever and anon a whitish something moved above the bank from behind, and vanished again. This was a small human hand, in the act of lifting pieces of fuel into the fire; but for all that could be seen the hand, like that which troubled Belshazzar, was there alone. Occasionally an ember rolled off the bank, and dropped with a hiss into the pool.

At one side of the pool rough steps built of clods enabled anyone who wished to do so to mount the bank; which the woman did. Within was a paddock in an uncultivated state, though bearing evidence of having once been tilled; but the heath and fern had insidiously crept in, and were reasserting their old supremacy. Further ahead were dimly visible an irregular dwelling-house, garden, and outbuildings, backed by a clump of firs.

The young lady—for youth had revealed its presence in her buoyant bound up the bank—walked along the top instead of descending inside, and came to the corner where the fire was burning. One reason for the permanence of the blaze was now manifest: the fuel consisted of hard pieces of wood, cleft and sawn—the knotty boles of old thorn trees which grew in twos and threes about the hillsides. A yet unconsumed pile of these lay in the inner angle of the bank; and from this corner the upturned face of a little boy greeted her eyes. He was dilatorily throwing up a piece of wood into the fire every now and then, a business which seemed to have engaged him a considerable part of the evening, for his face was somewhat weary.

"I am glad you have come, Miss Eustacia," he said, with a sigh of relief. "I don't like biding by myself."

"Nonsense. I have only been a little way for a walk. I have been gone only twenty minutes."

"It seemed long," murmured the sad boy. "And you have been so many times."

"Why, I thought you would be pleased to have a bonfire. Are you not much obliged to me for making you one?"

"Yes; but there's nobody here to play wi' me."

"I suppose nobody has come while I've been away?"

"Nobody except your grand-father: he looked out-of-doors once for 'ee. I told him you were walking round upon the hill to look at the other bonfires."

"A good boy."

"I think I hear him coming again, miss."

An old man came into the remoter light of the fire from the direction of the homestead. He was the same who had overtaken the reddleman on the road that afternoon. He looked wistfully to the top of the bank at the woman who stood there, and his teeth, which were quite unimpaired, showed like parian from his parted lips.

"When are you coming indoors, Eustacia?" he asked. " 'Tis almost bed-time. I've been home these two hours, and am tired out. Surely 'tis somewhat childish of you to stay out playing at bonfires so long, and wasting such fuel. My precious thorn roots, the rarest of all firing, that I laid by on purpose for Christmas—you have burnt 'em nearly all!"

"I promised Johnny a bonfire, and it pleases him not to let it go out just yet," said Eustacia, in a way which told at once that she was absolute queen here. "Grand-father, you go in to bed. I shall follow you soon. You like the fire, don't you, Johnny?"

The boy looked up doubtfully at her and murmured, "I don't think I want it any longer."

Her grand-father had turned back again, and did not hear the boy's reply. As soon as the white-haired man had vanished she said in a tone of pique to the child, "Ungrateful little boy, how can you contradict me? Never shall you have a bonfire again unless you keep it up now. Come, tell me you like to do things for me, and don't deny it."

The repressed child said, "Yes, I do, miss," and continued to stir the fire perfunctorily.

"Stay a little longer and I will give you a crooked sixpence," said Eustacia, more gently. "Put in one piece of wood every two or three minutes, but not too much at once. I am going to walk along the ridge a little longer, but I shall keep on coming to you. And if you hear a frog jump into the pond with a flounce, like a stone thrown in, be sure you run and tell me, because it is a sign of rain."

"Yes, Eustacia."

"Miss Vye, sir."

"Miss Vy—stacia."

"That will do. Now put in one stick more."

The little slave went on feeding the fire as before. He seemed a mere automaton, galvanised into moving and speaking by the wayward Eustacia's will. He might have been the brass statue which Albertus Magnus is said to have animated just so far as to make it chatter, and move, and be his servant.

Before going on her walk again the young girl stood still on the bank for a few instants and listened. It was to the full as lonely a place as Rainbarrow, though at rather a lower level; and it was more sheltered from wind and weather on account of the few firs to the north. The bank which enclosed the homestead, and protected it from the lawless state of the world without, was formed of thick square clods, dug from the ditch on the outside, and built up with a slight batter or incline, which forms no slight defense where hedges will not grow because of the wind and the wilderness, and where wall materials are unattainable. Otherwise the situation was quite open, commanding the whole length of the valley which reached to the river behind Wildeve's house. High above this to the right, and much nearer thitherward than the Quiet Woman Inn, the blurred contour of Rainbarrow obstructed the sky.

After her attentive survey of the wild slopes and hollow ravines a gesture of impatience escaped Eustacia. She vented petulant words every now and then; but there were sighs between her words, and sudden listenings between her sighs. Descending from her perch she again sauntered off towards Rainbarrow, though this time she did not go the whole way.

Twice she reappeared at intervals of a few minutes, and each time she said—

"Not any flounce into the pond yet, little man?"

"No, Miss Eustacia," the child replied.

"Well," she said at last, "I shall soon be going in; and then I will give you the crooked sixpence, and let you go home."

"Thank'ee, Miss Eustacia," said the tired stoker, breathing more easily. And Eustacia again strolled away from the fire, but this time not towards Rainbarrow. She skirted the bank and went round to the wicket before the house, where she stood motionless looking at the scene.

Fifty yards off rose the corner of the two converging banks, with the fire upon it: within the bank, lifting up to the fire one stick at a time, just as before, the figure of the little child. She idly watched him as he occasionally climbed up in the nook of the bank and stood beside the brands. The wind blew the smoke, and the child's hair, and the corner of his pinafore, all in the same direction: the breeze died, and the pinafore and hair lay still, and the smoke went up straight.

While Eustacia looked on from this distance the boy's form visibly started: he slid down the bank and ran across towards the white gate.

"Well?" said Eustacia.

"A hop-frog have jumped into the pond. Yes, I heard 'en!"

"Then it is going to rain, and you had better go home. You will not be afraid?" She spoke hurriedly, as if her heart had leapt into her throat at the boy's words.

"No, because I shall hae the crooked sixpence."

"Yes, here it is. Now run as fast as you can—not that way—through the garden here. No other boy in the heath has had such a bonfire as yours."

The boy, who clearly had had too much of a good thing, marched away into the shadows with alacrity. When he was gone Eustacia, leaving her telescope and hour-glass by the gate, brushed forward from the wicket towards the angle of the bank, under the fire.

Here, screened by the outwork, she waited. In a few moments a splash was audible from the pond outside. Had the child been there he would have said that a second frog had jumped in; but by most people the sound would have been likened to the fall of a stone into the water. Eustacia stepped upon the bank.

"Yes?" she said, and held her breath.

Thereupon the contour of a man became dimly visible against the low-reaching sky over the valley, beyond the outer margin of the pool. He came round it and leapt upon the bank beside her. A low laugh escaped her—the third utterance which the girl had indulged in to-night. The first, when she stood upon Rainbarrow, had expressed anxiety; the second, on the ridge, had expressed impatience; the present was one of triumphant pleasure. She let her joyous eyes rest upon him without speaking, as upon some wondrous thing she had created out of chaos.

"I have come," said the man, who was Wildeve. "You give me no peace. Why do you not leave me alone? I have seen your bonfire all the evening." The words were not without emotion, and retained their level tone as if by a careful equipoise between imminent extremes.

At this unexpectedly repressing manner in her lover the girl seemed to repress herself also. "Of course you have seen my fire," she answered with languid calmness, artificially maintained. "Why shouldn't I have a bonfire on the Fifth of November, like other denizens of the heath?"

"I knew it was meant for me."

"How did you know it? I have had no word with you since you—you chose her, and walked about with her, and deserted me entirely, as if I had never been yours life and soul so irretrievably!"

"Eustacia! could I forget that last autumn at this same day of the month and at this same place you lighted exactly such a fire as a signal for me to come and see you? Why should there have been a bonfire again by Captain Vye's house if not for the same purpose?"

"Yes, yes—I own it," she cried under her breath, with a drowsy fervour of manner and tone which was quite peculiar to her. "Don't begin speaking to me as you did, Damon; you will drive me to say words I would not wish to say to you. I had given you up, and re-solved not to think of you any more; and then I heard the news, and I came out and got the fire ready because I thought that you had been faithful to me."

"What have you heard to make you think that?" said Wildeve, astonished.

"That you did not marry her!" she murmured exultingly. "And I knew it was because you loved me best, and couldn't do it. . . . Damon, you have been cruel to me to go away, and I have said I would never forgive you. I do not think I can forgive you entirely, even now—it is too much for a woman of any spirit to quite overlook."

"If I had known you wished to call me up here only to reproach me, I wouldn't have come."

"But I don't mind it, and I do forgive you now that you have not married her, and have come back to me!"

"Who told you that I had not married her?"

"My grand-father. He took a long walk to-day, and as he was coming home he over-took some person who told him of a broken-off wedding: he thought it might be yours; and I knew it was."

"Does anybody else know?"

"I suppose not. Now, Damon, do you see why I lit my signal fire? You did not think I would have lit it if I had imagined you to have become the husband of this woman. It is insulting my pride to suppose that."

Wildeve was silent: it was evident that he had supposed as much.

"Did you indeed think I believed you were married?" she again demanded earnestly. "Then you wronged me; and upon my life and heart I can hardly bear to recognise that you have such ill thoughts of me! Damon, you are not worthy of me: I see it, and yet I love you. Never mind: let it go—I must bear your mean opinion as best I may. . . . It is true, is it not," she added, with ill-concealed anxiety, on his making no demonstration, "that you could not bring yourself to give me up, and are still going to love me best of all?"

"Yes; or why should I have come?" he said touchily. "Not that fidelity will be any great merit in me after your kind speech about my unworthiness, which should have been said by myself if by anybody, and comes with an ill grace from you. However, the curse of inflammability is upon me, and I must live under it, and take any snub from a woman. It has brought me down from engineering to innkeeping: what lower stage it has in store for me I have yet to learn." He continued to look upon her gloomily.

She seized the moment, and throwing back the shawl so that the firelight shone full upon her face and throat, said with a smile, "Have you seen anything better than that in your travels?"

Eustacia was not one to commit herself to such a position without good ground. He said quietly, "No."

"Not even on the shoulders of Thomasin?"

"Thomasin is a pleasing and innocent woman."

"That's nothing to do with it," she cried with quick passionateness. "We will leave her out; there are only you and me now to think of." After a long look at him she resumed with the old quiescent warmth: "Must I go on weakly confessing to you things a woman ought to conceal; and own that no words can express how gloomy I have been because of that dreadful belief I held till two hours ago——that you had quite deserted me?"

"I am sorry I caused you that pain."

"But perhaps it is not wholly because of you that I get gloomy," she archly added. "It is in my nature to feel like that. It was born in my blood, I suppose."

"Hypochondriasis."

"Or else it was coming into this wild heath. I was happy enough at Budmouth. O the times, O the days at Budmouth! But Egdon will be brighter again now."

"I hope it will," said Wildeve moodily. "Do you know the consequence of this recall to me, my old darling? I shall come to see you again as before, at Rainbarrow."

"Of course you will."

"And yet I declare that until I got here to-night I intended, after this one good-bye, never to meet you again."

"I don't thank you for that," she said, turning away, while indignation spread through her like subterranean heat. "You may come again to Rainbarrow if you like, but you won't see me; and you may call, but I shall not listen; and you may tempt me, but I won't give myself to you any more."

"You have said as much before, sweet; but such natures as yours don't so easily adhere to their words. Neither, for the matter of that, do such natures as mine."

"This is the pleasure I have won by my trouble," she whispered bitterly. "Why did I try to recall you? Damon, a strange warring takes place in my mind occasionally. I think when I become calm after your woundings, 'Do I embrace a cloud of common fog after all?' You are a chameleon, and now you are at your worst colour. Go home, or I shall hate you!"

He looked absently towards Rainbarrow while one might have counted twenty, and said, as if he did not much mind all this, "Yes, I will go home. Do you mean to see me again?"

"If you own to me that the wedding is broken off because you love me best."

"I don't think it would be good policy," said Wildeve, smiling. "You would get to know the extent of your power too clearly."

"But tell me!"

"You know."

"Where is she now?"

"I don't know. I prefer not to speak of her to you. I have not yet married her: I have come in obedience to your call. That is enough."

"I merely lit that fire because I was dull, and thought I would get a little excitement by calling you up and triumphing over you as the Witch of Endor called up Samuel. I determined you should come; and you have come! I have shown my power. A mile and half hither, and a mile and half back again to your home——three miles in the dark for me. Have I not shown my power?"

He shook his head at her. "I know you too well, my Eustacia; I know you too well.

There isn't a note in you which I don't know; and that hot little bosom couldn't play such a cold-blooded trick to save its life. I saw a woman on Rainbarrow at dusk looking down towards my house. I think I drew out you before you drew out me."

The revived embers of an old passion glowed clearly in Wildeve now; and he leant forward as if about to put his face towards her cheek.

"O no," she said, intractably moving to the other side of the decayed fire. "What did you mean by that?"

"Perhaps I may kiss your hand?"

"No, you may not."

"Then I may shake your hand?"

"No."

"Then I wish you good-night without caring for either. Good-bye, good-bye."

She returned no answer, and with the bow of a dancing-master he vanished on the other side of the pool as he had come.

Eustacia sighed: it was no fragile maiden sigh, but a sigh which shook her like a shiver. Whenever a flash of reason darted like an electric light upon her lover—as it sometimes would—and showed his imperfections, she shivered thus. But it was over in a second, and she loved on. She knew that he trifled with her; but she loved on. She scattered the half-burnt brands, went indoors immediately, and up to her bedroom without a light. Amid the rustles which denoted her to be undressing in the darkness other heavy breaths frequently came; and the same kind of shudder occasionally moved through her when, ten minutes later, she lay on her bed asleep.

VII

QUEEN OF NIGHT

EUSTACIA VYE WAS THE RAW MATERIAL OF A DIVINITY. ON OLYMPUS SHE WOULD HAVE done well with a little preparation. She had the passions and instincts which make a model goddess, that is, those which make not quite a model woman. Had it been possible for the earth and mankind to be entirely in her grasp for a while, she had handled the distaff, the spindle, and the shears at her own free will, few in the world would have noticed the change of government. There would have been the same inequality of lot, the same heaping up of favours here, of contumely there, the same generosity before justice, the same perpetual dilemmas, the same captious alteration of caresses and blows that we endure now.

She was in person full-limbed and somewhat heavy; without ruddiness, as without pallor; and soft to the touch as a cloud. To see her hair was to fancy that a whole winter did not contain darkness enough to form its shadow: it closed over her forehead like night-fall extinguishing the western glow.

Her nerves extended into those tresses, and her temper could always be softened by stroking them down. When her hair was brushed she would instantly sink into stillness and look like the Sphinx. If, in passing under one of the Egdon banks, any of its thick skeins were caught, as they sometimes were, by a prickly tuft of the large *Ulex Europœus*—which will act as a sort of hairbrush—she would go back a few steps, and pass against it a second time.

She had Pagan eyes, full of nocturnal mysteries. Their light, as it came and went, and came again, was partially hampered by their oppressive lids and lashes; and of these the under lid was much fuller than it usually is with English women. This enabled her to indulge in reverie without seeming to do so: she might have been believed capable of sleeping without closing them up. Assuming that the souls of men and women were visible essences, you could fancy the colour of Eustacia's soul to be flamelike. The sparks from it that rose into her dark pupils gave the same impression.

The mouth seemed formed less to speak than to quiver, less to quiver than to kiss. Some might have added, less to kiss than to curl. Viewed sideways, the closing-line of her lips formed, with almost geometric precision, the curve so well known in the arts of design as the cima-recta, or ogee. The sight of such a flexible bend as that on grim Egdon was quite an apparition. It was felt at once that the mouth did not come over from Sleswig with a band of Saxon pirates whose lips met like the two halves of a muffin. One had fancied that such lip-curves were mostly lurking underground in the South as fragments of forgotten marbles. So fine were the lines of her lips that, though full, each corner of her mouth was as clearly cut as the point of a spear. This keenness of corner was only blunted when she was given over to sudden fits of gloom, one of the phases of the night-side of sentiment which she knew too well for her years.

Her presence brought memories of such things as Bourbon roses, rubies, and tropical midnights; her moods recalled lotus-eaters and the march in "Athalie"; her motions, the ebb and flow of the sea; her voice, the viola. In a dim light, and with a slight rearrangement of her hair, her general figure might have stood for that of either of the higher female deities. The new moon behind her head, an old helmet upon it, a diadem of accidental dewdrops round her brow, would have been adjuncts sufficient to strike the note of Artemis, Athena, or Hera respectively, with as close an approximation to the antique as that which passes muster on many respected canvases.

But celestial imperiousness, love, wrath, and fervour had proved to be somewhat thrown away on netherward Egdon. Her power was limited, and the consciousness of this limitation had biassed her development. Egdon was her Hades, and since coming there she had imbibed much of what was dark in its tone, though inwardly and eternally unreconciled thereto. Her appearance accorded well with this smouldering rebelliousness, and the shady splendour of her beauty was the real surface of the sad and stifled warmth within her. A true Tartarean dignity sat upon her brow, and not factitiously or with marks of constraint, for it had grown in her with years.

Across the upper part of her head she wore a thin fillet of black velvet, restraining the luxuriance of her shady hair, in a way which added much to this class of majesty by irregularly clouding her forehead. "Nothing can embellish a beautiful face more than a narrow band drawn over the brow," says Richter. Some of the neighbouring girls wore coloured ribbon for the same purpose, and sported metallic ornaments elsewhere; but if anyone suggested coloured ribbon and metallic ornaments to Eustacia Vye she laughed and went on.

Why did a woman of this sort live on Egdon Heath? Budmouth was her native place, a fashionable seaside resort at that date. She was the daughter of the bandmaster of a regiment which had been quartered there—a Corfiote by birth, and a fine musician—who met his future wife during her trip thither with her father the captain, a man of good family. The marriage was scarcely in accord with the old man's wishes, for the bandmaster's pockets were as light as his occupation. But the musician did his best; adopted his wife's name, made England permanently his home, took great trouble with his child's education, the expenses of which were defrayed by the grand-father, and throve as the chief local musician till her mother's death, when he left off thriving, drank, and died also. The girl was left to the care of her grand-father, who, since three of his ribs became broken in a shipwreck, had lived in this airy perch on Egdon, a spot which had taken his fancy because the house was to be had for next to nothing, and because a remote blue tinge on the horizon between the hills, visible from the cottage door, was traditionally believed to be the English Channel. She hated the change; she felt like one banished; but here she was forced to abide.

Thus it happened that in Eustacia's brain were juxtaposed the strangest assortment of ideas, from old time and from new. There was no middle distance in her perspective: romantic recollections of sunny afternoons on an esplanade, with military bands, officers, and gallants around, stood like gilded letters upon the dark tablet of surrounding Egdon. Every bizarre effect that could result from the random intertwining of watering-place glitter with the grand solemnity of a heath, was to be found in her. Seeing nothing of human life now, she imagined all the more of what she had seen.

Where did her dignity come from? By a latent vein from Alcinous' line, her father hailing from Phæacia's isle?—or from Fitzalan and De Vere, her maternal grand-father having had a cousin in the peerage? Perhaps it was the gift of Heaven—a happy convergence of natural laws. Among other things opportunity had of late years been denied her of learning to be undignified, for she lived lonely. Isolation on a heath renders vulgarity well-nigh impossible. It would have been as easy for the heath-ponies, bats, and snakes to be vulgar as for her. A narrow life in Budmouth might have completely demeaned her.

The only way to look queenly without realms or hearts to queen it over is to look as if you had lost them; and Eustacia did that to a triumph. In the captain's cottage she could suggest mansions she had never seen. Perhaps that was because she frequented a vaster mansion than any of them, the open hills. Like the summer condition of the place around her, she was an embodiment of the phrase "a populous solitude"—apparently so listless, void, and quiet, she was really busy and full.

To be loved to madness—such was her great desire. Love was to her the one cordial which could drive away the eating loneliness of her days. And she seemed to long for the abstraction called passionate love more than for any particular lover.

She could show a most reproachful look at times, but it was directed less against human beings than against certain creatures of her mind, the chief of these being Destiny, through whose interference she dimly fancied it arose that love alighted only on gliding youth—that any love she might win would sink simultaneously with the sand in the glass. She thought of it with an ever-growing consciousness of cruelty, which tended to breed actions of reckless unconventionality, framed to snatch a year's, a week's, even an hour's passion from anywhere while it could be won. Through want of it she had sung without being merry, possessed without enjoying, outshone without triumphing. Her loneliness deepened her desire. On Egdon, coldest and meanest kisses were at famine prices; and where was a mouth matching hers to be found?

Fidelity in love for fidelity's sake had less attraction for her than for most women: fidelity because of love's grip had much. A blaze of love, and extinction, was better than a lantern glimmer of the same which should last long years. On this head she knew by prevision what most women learn only by experience: she had mentally walked round love, told the towers thereof, considered its palaces; and concluded that love was but a doleful joy. Yet she desired it, as one in a desert would be thankful for brackish water.

She often repeated her prayers; not at particular times, but, like the unaffectedly devout, when she desired to pray. Her prayer was always spontaneous, and often ran thus, "O deliver my heart from this fearful gloom and loneliness: send me great love from somewhere, else I shall die."

Her high gods were William the Conqueror, Strafford, and Napoleon Buonaparte, as they had appeared in the Lady's History used at the establishment in which she was educated. Had she been a mother she would have christened her boys such names as Saul or Sisera in preference to Jacob or David, neither of whom she admired. At school she had used to side with the Philistines in several battles, and had wondered if Pontius Pilate were as handsome as he was frank and fair.

Thus she was a girl of some forwardness of mind, indeed, weighed in relation to her situation among the very rereward of thinkers, very original. Her instincts towards social noncomformity were at the root of this. In the matter of holidays, her mood was that of horses who, when turned out to grass, enjoy looking upon their kind at work on the highway. She only valued rest to herself when it came in the midst of other people's labour. Hence she hated Sundays when all was at rest, and often said they would be the death of her. To see the heathmen in their Sunday condition, that is, with their hands in their pockets, their boots newly oiled, and not laced up (a particularly Sunday sign), walking leisurely among the turves and furze-faggots they had cut during the week, and kicking them critically as if their use were unknown, was a fearful heaviness to her. To relieve the tedium of this untimely day she would overhaul the cupboards containing her grandfather's old charts and other rubbish, humming Saturday-night ballads of the country people the while. But on Saturday nights she would frequently sing a psalm, and it was always on a week-day that she read the Bible, that she might be unoppressed with a sense of doing her duty.

Such views of life were to some extent the natural begettings of her situation upon her nature. To dwell on a heath without studying its meanings was like wedding a foreigner without learning his tongue. The subtle beauties of the heath were lost to Eustacia; she only caught its vapours. An environment which would have made a contented woman a poet, a suffering woman a devotee, a pious woman a psalmist, even a giddy woman thoughtful, made a rebellious woman saturnine.

Eustacia had got beyond the vision of some marriage of inexpressible glory; yet, though her emotions were in full vigour, she cared for no meaner union. Thus we see her in a strange state of isolation. To have lost the godlike conceit that we may do what we will, and not to have acquired a homely zest for doing what we can, shows a grandeur of temper which cannot be objected to in the abstract, for it denotes a mind that, though dis-

appointed, forswears compromise. But, if congenial to philosophy, it is apt to be dangerous to the commonwealth. In a world where doing means marrying, and the commonwealth is one of hearts and hands, the same peril attends the condition.

And so we see our Eustacia—for at times she was not altogether unlovable—arriving
at that stage of enlightenment which feels that nothing is worthwhile, and filling up the
spare hours of her existence by idealising Wildeve for want of a better object. This was
the sole reason of his ascendency: she knew it herself. At moments her pride rebelled
against her passion for him, and she even had longed to be free. But there was only one circumstance which could dislodge him, and that was the advent of a greater man.

For the rest, she suffered much from depression of spirits, and took slow walks to recover
them, in which she carried her grand-father's telescope and her grand-mother's hour-glass—
the latter because of a peculiar pleasure she derived from watching a material representation
of time's gradual glide away. She seldom schemed, but when she did scheme, her plans
showed rather the comprehensive strategy of a general than the small arts called womanish,
though she could utter oracles of Delphian ambiguity when she did not choose to be direct.
In heaven she will probably sit between the Héloïses and the Cleopatras.

VIII

THOSE WHO ARE FOUND WHERE THERE IS SAID TO BE NOBODY

AS SOON AS THE SAD LITTLE BOY HAD WITHDRAWN FROM THE FIRE HE CLASPED THE
money tight in the palm of his hand, as if thereby to fortify his courage, and began
to run. There was really little danger in allowing a child to go home alone on this part of
Egdon Heath. The distance to the boy's house was not more than three-eighths of a mile,
his father's cottage, and one other a few yards further on, forming part of the small hamlet of Mistover Knap: the third and only remaining house was that of Captain Vye and Eustacia, which stood quite away from the small cottages, and was the loneliest of lonely
houses on these thinly populated slopes.

He ran until he was out of breath, and then, becoming more courageous, walked
leisurely along, singing in an old voice a little song about a sailor-boy and a fair one, and
bright gold in store. In the middle of this the child stopped: from a pit under the hill ahead
of him shone a light, whence proceeded a cloud of floating dust and a smacking noise.

Only unusual sights and sounds frightened the boy. The shrivelled voice of the heath
did not alarm him, for that was familiar. The thorn-bushes which arose in his path from
time to time were less satisfactory, for they whistled gloomily, and had a ghastly habit after
dark of putting on the shapes of jumping madmen, sprawling giants, and hideous cripples.
Lights were not uncommon this evening, but the nature of all of them was different from
this. Discretion rather than terror prompted the boy to turn back instead of passing the
light, with a view of asking Miss Eustacia Vye to let her servant accompany him home.

When the boy had reascended to the top of the valley he found the fire to be still burning on the bank, though lower than before. Beside it, instead of Eustacia's solitary form,

he saw two persons, the second being a man. The boy crept along under the bank to ascertain from the nature of the proceedings if it would be prudent to interrupt so splendid a creature as Miss Eustacia on his poor trivial account.

After listening under the bank for some minutes to the talk he turned in a perplexed and doubting manner and began to withdraw as silently as he had come. That he did not, upon the whole, think it advisable to interrupt her conversation with Wildeve, without being prepared to bear the whole weight of her displeasure, was obvious.

Here was a Scyllæo-Charybdean position for a poor boy. Pausing when again safe from discovery he finally decided to face the pit phenomenon as the lesser evil. With a heavy sigh he retraced the slope, and followed the path he had followed before.

The light had gone, the rising dust had disappeared—he hoped forever. He marched resolutely along, and found nothing to alarm him till, coming within a few yards of the sandpit, he heard a slight noise in front, which led him to halt. The halt was but momentary, for the noise resolved itself into the steady bites of two animals grazing.

"Two he'th-croppers down here," he said aloud. "I have never known 'em come down so far afore."

The animals were in the direct line of his path, but that the child thought little of; he had played round the fetlocks of horses from his infancy. On coming nearer, however, the boy was somewhat surprised to find that the little creatures did not run off, and that each wore a clog, to prevent his going astray; this signified that they had been broken in. He could now see the interior of the pit, which, being in the side of the hill, had a level entrance. In the innermost corner the square outline of a van appeared, with its back towards him. A light came from the interior, and threw a moving shadow upon the vertical face of gravel at the further side of the pit into which the vehicle faced.

The child assumed that this was the cart of a gypsy, and his dread of those wanderers reached but to that mild pitch which titillates rather than pains. Only a few inches of mud wall kept him and his family from being gypsies themselves. He skirted the gravel-pit at a respectful distance, ascended the slope, and came forward upon the brow, in order to look into the open door of the van and see the original of the shadow.

The picture alarmed the boy. By a little stove inside the van sat a figure red from head to heels—the man who had been Thomasin's friend. He was darning a stocking, which was red like the rest of him. Moreover, as he darned he smoked a pipe, the stem and bowl of which were red also.

At this moment one of the heath-croppers feeding in the outer shadows was audibly shaking off the clog attached to its foot. Aroused by the sound, the reddleman laid down his stocking, lit a lantern which hung beside him, and came out from the van. In sticking up the candle he lifted the lantern to his face, and the light shone into the whites of his eyes and upon his ivory teeth, which, in contrast with the red surrounding, lent him a startling aspect enough to the gaze of a juvenile. The boy knew too well for his peace of mind upon whose lair he had lighted. Uglier persons than gypsies were known to cross Egdon at times, and a reddleman was one of them.

"How I wish 'twas only a gypsy!" he murmured.

The man was by this time coming back from the horses. In his fear of being seen the boy rendered detection certain by nervous motion. The heather and peat stratum overhung the brow of the pit in mats, hiding the actual verge. The boy had stepped beyond the solid ground; the heather now gave way, and down he rolled over the scarp of grey sand to the very foot of the man.

The red man opened the lantern and turned it upon the figure of the prostrate boy.

"Who be ye?" he said.

"Johnny Nunsuch, master!"

"What were you doing up there?"

"I don't know."

"Watching me, I suppose?"

"Yes, master."

"What did you watch me for?"

"Because I was coming home from Miss Vye's bonfire."

"Beest hurt?"

"No."

"Why, yes, you be: your hand is bleeding. Come under my tilt and let me tie it up."

"Please let me look for my sixpence."

"How did you come by that?"

"Miss Vye gied it to me for keeping up her bonfire."

The sixpence was found, and the man went to the van, the boy behind, almost holding his breath.

The man took a piece of rag from a satchel containing sewing materials, tore off a strip, which, like everything else, was tinged red, and proceeded to bind up the wound.

"My eyes have got foggylike—please may I sit down, master?" said the boy.

"To be sure, poor chap. 'Tis enough to make you feel fainty. Sit on that bundle."

The man finished tying up the gash, and the boy said, "I think I'll go home now, master."

"You are rather afraid of me. Do you know what I be?"

The child surveyed his vermilion figure up and down with much misgiving, and finally said, "Yes."

"Well, what?"

"The reddleman!" he faltered.

"Yes, that's what I be. Though there's more than one. You little children think there's only one cuckoo, one fox, one giant, one devil, and one reddleman, when there's lots of us all."

"Is there? You won't carry me off in your bags, will ye, master? 'Tis said that the reddleman will sometimes."

"Nonsense. All that reddlemen do is sell reddle. You see all these bags at the back of my cart? They are not full of little boys—only full of red stuff."

"Was you born a reddleman?"

"No, I took to it. I should be as white as you if I were to give up the trade—that is, I should be white in time—perhaps six months: not at first, because 'tis grow'd into my skin and won't wash out. Now, you'll never be afraid of a reddleman again, will ye?"

"No, never. Willy Orchard said he seed a red ghost here t'other day—perhaps that was you?"

"I was here t'other day."

"Were you making that dusty light I saw by now?"

"O yes: I was beating out some bags. And have you had a good bonfire up there? I saw the light. Why did Miss Vye want a bonfire so bad that she should give you sixpence to keep it up?"

"I don't know. I was tired, but she made me bide and keep up the fire just the same, while she kept going up across Rainbarrow way."

"And how long did that last?"

"Until a hopfrog jumped into the pond."

The reddleman suddenly ceased to talk idly. "A hopfrog?" he enquired. "Hopfrogs don't jump into ponds this time of year."

"They do, for I heard one."

"Certain-sure?"

"Yes. She told me afore that I should hear'n; and so I did. They say she's clever and deep, and perhaps she charmed 'en to come."

"And what then?"

"Then I came down here, and I was afeard, and I went back; but I didn't like to speak to her, because of the gentleman, and I came on here again."

"A gentleman—ah! What did she say to him, my man?"

"Told him she supposed he had not married the other woman because he liked his old sweetheart best; and things like that."

"What did the gentleman say to her, my sonny?"

"He only said he did like her best, and how he was coming to see her again under Rainbarrow o' nights."

"Ha!" cried the reddleman, slapping his hand against the side of his van so that the whole fabric shook under the blow. "That's the secret o't!"

The little boy jumped clean from the stool.

"My man, don't you be afraid," said the dealer in red, suddenly becoming gentle. "I forgot you were here. That's only a curious way reddlemen have of going mad for a moment; but they don't hurt anybody. And what did the lady say then?"

"I can't mind. Please, Master Reddleman, may I go home-along now?"

"Ay, to be sure you may. I'll go a bit of ways with you."

He conducted the boy out of the gravel-pit and into the path leading to his mother's cottage. When the little figure had vanished in the darkness the reddleman returned, resumed his seat by the fire, and proceeded to darn again.

IX

LOVE LEADS A SHREWD MAN INTO STRATEGY

REDDLEMEN OF THE OLD SCHOOL ARE NOW BUT SELDOM SEEN. SINCE THE INTRODUCtion of railways Wessex farmers have managed to do without these Mephistophelian visitants, and the bright pigment so largely used by shepherds in preparing sheep for the fair is obtained by other routes. Even those who yet survive are losing the poetry of existence which characterised them when the pursuit of the trade meant periodical journeys to the pit whence the material was dug, a regular camping out from month to month, except in the depth of winter, a peregrination among farms which could be counted by the hundred, and in spite of this Arab existence the preservation of that respectability which is ensured by the never-failing production of a well-lined purse.

Reddle spreads its lively hues over everything it lights on, and stamps unmistakably, as with the mark of Cain, any person who has handled it half an hour.

A child's first sight of a reddleman was an epoch in his life. That blood-coloured figure was a sublimation of all the horrid dreams which had afflicted the juvenile spirit since imagination began. "The reddleman is coming for you!" had been the formulated threat of Wessex mothers for many generations. He was successfully supplanted for a while, at the beginning of the present century, by Buonaparte; but as process of time rendered the latter personage stale and ineffective the older phrase resumed its early prominence. And now the reddleman has in his turn followed Buonaparte to the land of worn-out bogeys, and his place is filled by modern inventions.

The reddleman lived like a gypsy; but gypsies he scorned. He was about as thriving as travelling basket and mat makers; but he had nothing to do with them. He was more decently born and brought up than the cattle-drovers who passed and repassed him in his wanderings; but they merely nodded to him. His stock was more valuable than that of pedlars; but they did not think so, and passed his cart with eyes straight ahead. He was such an unnatural colour to look at that the men of round-abouts and wax-work shows seemed gentlemen beside him; but he considered them low company, and remained aloof. Among all these squatters and folks of the road the reddleman continually found himself; yet he was not of them. His occupation tended to isolate him, and isolated he was mostly seen to be.

It was sometimes suggested that reddlemen were criminals for whose misdeeds other men wrongfully suffered: that in escaping the law they had not escaped their own consciences, and had taken to the trade as a lifelong penance. Else why should they have chosen it? In the present case such a question would have been particularly apposite. The reddleman who had entered Egdon that afternoon was an instance of the pleasing being wasted to form the ground-work of the singular, when an ugly foundation would have done just as well for that purpose. The one point that was forbidding about this reddleman was his colour. Freed from that he would have been as agreeable a specimen of rustic manhood as one would often see. A keen observer might have been inclined to think—which was, indeed, partly the truth—that he had relinquished his proper station in life for want of interest in it. Moreover, after looking at him one would have hazarded the guess that good-nature, and an acuteness as extreme as it could be without verging on craft, formed the frame-work of his character.

While he darned the stocking his face became rigid with thought. Softer expressions followed this, and then again recurred the tender sadness which had sat upon him during his drive along the highway that afternoon. Presently his needle stopped. He laid down the stocking, arose from his seat, and took a leathern pouch from a hook in the corner of the van. This contained among other articles a brown-paper packet, which, to judge from the hingelike character of its worn folds, seemed to have been carefully opened and closed a good many times. He sat down on a three-legged milking-stool that formed the only seat in the van, and, examining his packet by the light of a candle, took thence an old letter and spread it open. The writing had originally been traced on white paper, but the letter had now assumed a pale red tinge from the accident of his situation; and the black strokes of writing thereon looked like the twigs of a winter hedge against a vermilion sunset. The letter bore a date some two years previous to that time, and was signed "Thomasin Yeobright." It ran as follows:—

DEAR DIGGORY VENN—The question you put when you overtook me coming home from Pond-close gave me such a surprise that I am afraid I did not make you exactly understand what I meant. Of course, if my aunt had not met me I could have explained all then at once, but as it was there was no chance. I have been quite uneasy since, as you know I do not wish to pain you, yet I fear I shall be doing so now in contradicting what I seemed to say then. I cannot, Diggory, marry you, or think of letting you call me your sweetheart. I could not, indeed, Diggory. I hope you will not much mind my saying this, and feel in a great pain. It makes me very sad when I think it may, for I like you very much, and I always put you next to my cousin Clym in my mind. There are so many reasons why we cannot be married that I can hardly name them all in a letter. I did not in the least expect that you were going to speak on such a thing when you followed me, because I had never thought of you in the sense of a lover at all. You must not becall me for laughing when you spoke; you mistook when you thought I laughed at you as a foolish man. I laughed because the idea was so odd, and not at you at all. The great reason with my own personal self for not letting you court me is, that I do not feel the things a woman ought to feel who consents to walk with you with the meaning of being your wife. It is not as you think, that I have another in my mind, for I do not encourage anybody, and never have in my life. Another reason is my aunt. She would not, I know, agree to it, even if I wished to have you. She likes you very well, but she will want me to look a little higher than a small dairy-farmer, and marry a professional man. I hope you will not set your heart against me for writing plainly, but I felt you might try to see me again, and it is better that we should not meet. I shall always think of you as a good man, and be anxious for your well-doing. I send this by Jane Orchard's little maid—And remain Diggory, your faithful friend,

THOMASIN YEOBRIGHT

To MR. VENN, Dairy-farmer.

Since the arrival of that letter, on a certain autumn morning long ago, the reddleman and Thomasin had not met till to-day. During the interval he had shifted his position even further from hers than it had originally been, by adopting the reddle trade; though he was really in very good circumstances still. Indeed, seeing that his expenditure was only one-fourth of his income, he might have been called a prosperous man.

Rejected suitors take to roaming as naturally as unhived bees; and the business to which he had cynically devoted himself was in many ways congenial to Venn. But his wanderings, by mere stress of old emotions, had frequently taken an Egdon direction, though he never intruded upon her who attracted him thither. To be in Thomasin's heath, and near her, yet unseen, was the one ewe-lamb of pleasure left to him.

Then came the incident of that day, and the reddleman, still loving her well, was excited by this accidental service to her at a critical juncture to vow an active devotion to her cause, instead of, as hitherto, sighing and holding aloof. After what had happened it was impossible that he should not doubt the honesty of Wildeve's intentions. But her hope was apparently centred upon him; and dismissing his regrets Venn determined to aid her to be happy in her own chosen way. That this way was, of all others, the most distressing to himself, was awkward enough; but the reddleman's love was generous.

His first active step in watching over Thomasin's interests was taken about seven o'clock the next evening, and was dictated by the news which he had learnt from the sad boy. That Eustacia was somehow the cause of Wildeve's carelessness in relation to the marriage had at once been Venn's conclusion on hearing of the secret meeting between them. It did not occur to his mind that Eustacia's love-signal to Wildeve was the tender effect upon the deserted beauty of the intelligence which her grand-father had brought home. His instinct was to regard her as a conspirator against rather than as an antecedent obstacle to Thomasin's happiness.

During the day he had been exceedingly anxious to learn the condition of Thomasin; but he did not venture to intrude upon a threshold to which he was a stranger, particularly at such an unpleasant moment as this. He had occupied his time in moving with his ponies and load to a new point in the heath, eastward to his previous station; and here he selected a nook with a careful eye to shelter from wind and rain, which seemed to mean that his stay there was to be a comparatively extended one. After this he returned on foot some part of the way that he had come; and, it being now dark, he diverged to the left till he stood behind a holly-bush on the edge of a pit not twenty yards from Rainbarrow.

He watched for a meeting there, but he watched in vain. Nobody except himself came near the spot that night.

But the loss of his labour produced little effect upon the reddleman. He had stood in the shoes of Tantalus, and seemed to look upon a certain mass of disappointment as the natural preface to all realisations, without which preface they would give cause for alarm.

The same hour the next evening found him again at the same place; but Eustacia and Wildeve, the expected trysters, did not appear.

He pursued precisely the same course yet four nights longer, and without success. But on the next, being the day-week of their previous meeting, he saw a female shape floating along the ridge and the outline of a young man ascending from the valley. They met in the little ditch encircling the barrow—the original excavation from which it had been thrown up by the ancient British people.

The reddleman, stung with suspicion of wrong to Thomasin, was aroused to strategy in a moment. He instantly left the bush and crept forward on his hands and knees. When he had got as close as he might safely venture without discovery he found that, owing to a cross-wind, the conversation of the trysting pair could not be overheard.

Near him, as in divers places about the heath, were areas strewn with large turves, which lay edgeways and upside-down awaiting removal by Timothy Fairway, previous to the winter weather. He took two of these as he lay, and dragged them over him till one covered his head and shoulders, the other his back and legs. The reddleman would now have been quite invisible, even by daylight; the turves, standing upon him with the heather upwards, looked precisely as if they were growing. He crept along again, and the turves upon his back crept with him. Had he approached without any covering the chances are that he would not have been perceived in the dusk; approaching thus, it was as though he burrowed underground. In this manner he came quite close to where the two were standing.

"Wish to consult me on the matter?" reached his ears in the rich, impetuous accents of Eustacia Vye. "Consult me? It is an indignity to me to talk so: I won't bear it any longer!" She began weeping. "I have loved you, and have shown you that I loved you, much to my regret; and yet you can come and say in that frigid way that you wish to consult with me whether it would not be better to marry Thomasin. Better—of course it would be. Marry her: she is nearer to your own position in life than I am!"

"Yes, yes; that's very well," said Wildeve peremptorily. "But we must look at things as they are. Whatever blame may attach to me for having brought it about, Thomasin's position is at present much worse than yours. I simply tell you that I am in a strait."

"But you shall not tell me! You must see that it is only harassing me. Damon, you have not acted well; you have sunk in my opinion. You have not valued my courtesy—the courtesy of a lady in loving you—who used to think of far more ambitious things. But it was Thomasin's fault. She won you away from me, and she deserves to suffer for it. Where is she staying now? Not that I care, nor where I am myself. Ah, if I were dead and gone how glad she would be! Where is she, I ask?"

"Thomasin is now staying at her aunt's shut up in a bedroom, and keeping out of everybody's sight," he said indifferently.

"I don't think you care much about her even now," said Eustacia with sudden joyousness; "for if you did you wouldn't talk so coolly about her. Do you talk so coolly to her about me? Ah, I expect you do! Why did you originally go away from me? I don't think I can ever forgive you, except on one condition, that whenever you desert me, you come back again, sorry that you served me so."

"I never wish to desert you."

"I do not thank you for that. I should hate it to be all smooth. Indeed, I think I like you to desert me a little once now and then. Love is the dismallest thing where the lover is quite honest. O, it is a shame to say so; but it is true!" She indulged in a little laugh. "My low spirits begin at the very idea. Don't you offer me tame love, or away you go!"

"I wish Tamsie were not such a confoundedly good little woman," said Wildeve, "so that I could be faithful to you without injuring a worthy person. It is I who am the sinner after all; I am not worth the little finger of either of you."

"But you must not sacrifice yourself to her from any sense of justice," replied Eustacia quickly. "If you do not love her it is the most merciful thing in the long run to leave her as she is. That's always the best way. There, now I have been unwomanly, I suppose. When you have left me, I am always angry with myself for things that I have said to you."

Wildeve walked a pace or two among the heather without replying. The pause was filled up by the intonation of a pollard thorn a little way to windward, the breezes filtering through its unyielding twigs as through a strainer. It was as if the night sang dirges with clenched teeth.

She continued, half sorrowfully, "Since meeting you last, it has occurred to me once or twice that perhaps it was not for love of me you did not marry her. Tell me, Damon: I'll try to bear it. Had I nothing whatever to do with the matter?"

"Do you press me to tell?"

"Yes, I must know. I see I have been too ready to believe in my own power."

"Well, the immediate reason was that the license would not do for the place, and before I could get another she ran away. Up to that point you had nothing to do with it. Since then her aunt has spoken to me in a tone which I don't at all like."

"Yes, yes! I am nothing in it—I am nothing in it. You only trifle with me. Heaven, what can I, Eustacia Vye, be made of to think so much of you!"

"Nonsense; do not be so passionate. . . . Eustacia, how we roved among these bushes last year, when the hot days had got cool, and the shades of the hills kept us almost invisible in the hollows!"

She remained in moody silence till she said, "Yes; and how I used to laugh at you for daring to look up to me! But you have well made me suffer for that since."

"Yes, you served me cruelly enough until I thought I had found someone fairer than you. A blessed find for me, Eustacia."

"Do you still think you found somebody fairer?"

"Sometimes I do, sometimes I don't. The scales are balanced so nicely that a feather would turn them."

"But don't you really care whether I meet you or whether I don't?" she said slowly.

"I care a little, but not enough to break my rest," replied the young man languidly. "No, all that's past. I find there are two flowers where I thought there was only one. Perhaps there are three, or four, or any number as good as the first. . . . Mine is a curious fate. Who would have thought that all this could happen to me?"

She interrupted with a suppressed fire of which either love or anger seemed an equally possible issue, "Do you love me now?"

"Who can say?"

"Tell me; I will know it!"

"I do, and I do not," said he mischievously. "That is, I have my times and my seasons. One moment you are too tall, another moment you are too do-nothing, another too melancholy, another too dark, another I don't know what, except—that you are not the whole world to me that you used to be, my dear. But you are a pleasant lady to know, and nice to meet, and I daresay as sweet as ever—almost."

Eustacia was silent, and she turned from him, till she said, in a voice of suspended mightiness, "I am for a walk, and this is my way."

"Well, I can do worse than follow you."

"You know you can't do otherwise, for all your moods and changes!" she answered defiantly. "Say what you will; try as you may; keep away from me all that you can—you will never forget me. You will love me all your life long. You would jump to marry me!"

"So I would!" said Wildeve. "Such strange thoughts as I've had from time to time, Eustacia; and they come to me this moment. You hate the heath as much as ever; that I know."

"I do," she murmured deeply. " 'Tis my cross, my misery, and will be my death!"

"I abhor it too," said he. "How mournfully the wind blows round us now!"

She did not answer. Its tone was indeed solemn and pervasive. Compound utterances addressed themselves to their senses, and it was possible to view by ear the features of the neighbourhood. Acoustic pictures were returned from the darkened scenery; they could hear where the tracts of heather began and ended; where the furze was growing stalky and tall; where it had been recently cut; in what direction the fir-clump lay, and how near was the pit in which the hollies grew; for these differing features had their voices no less than their shapes and colours.

"God, how lonely it is!" resumed Wildeve. "What are picturesque ravines and mists to us who see nothing else? Why should we stay here? Will you go with me to America? I have kindred in Wisconsin."

"That wants consideration."

"It seems impossible to do well here, unless one were a wild bird or a landscape-painter. Well?"

"Give me time," she softly said, taking his hand. "America is so far away. Are you going to walk with me a little way?"

As Eustacia uttered the latter words she retired from the base of the barrow, and Wildeve followed her, so that the reddleman could hear no more.

He lifted the turves and arose. Their black figures sank and disappeared from against the sky. They were as two horns which the sluggish heath had put forth from its crown, like a mollusc, and had now again drawn in.

The reddleman's walk across the vale, and over into the next where his cart lay, was not sprightly for a slim young fellow of twenty-four. His spirit was perturbed to aching. The breezes that blew around his mouth in that walk carried off upon them the accents of a commination.

He entered the van, where there was a fire in a stove. Without lighting his candle he sat down at once on the three-legged stool, and pondered on what he had seen and heard touching that still loved-one of his. He uttered a sound which was neither sigh nor sob, but was even more indicative than either of a troubled mind.

"My Tamsie," he whispered heavily. "What can be done? Yes, I will see that Eustacia Vye."

X

A DESPERATE ATTEMPT AT PERSUASION

THE NEXT MORNING, AT THE TIME WHEN THE HEIGHT OF THE SUN APPEARED VERY IN-significant from any part of the heath as compared with the altitude of Rainbarrow, and when all the little hills in the lower levels were like an archipelago in a fog-formed Ægean, the reddleman came from the brambled nook which he had adopted as his quarters and ascended the slopes of Mistover Knap.

Though these shaggy hills were apparently so solitary, several keen round eyes were always ready on such a wintry morning as this to converge upon a passer-by. Feathered species sojourned here in hiding which would have created wonder if found elsewhere. A bustard haunted the spot, and not many years before this five and twenty might have been seen in Egdon at one time. Marsh-harriers looked up from the valley by Wildeve's. A cream-coloured courser had used to visit this hill, a bird so rare that not more than a dozen have ever been seen in England; but a barbarian rested neither night nor day till he had shot the African truant, and after that event cream-coloured coursers thought fit to enter Egdon no more.

A traveller who should walk and observe any of these visitants as Venn observed them now could feel himself to be in direct communication with regions unknown to man. Here in front of him was a wild mallard—just arrived from the home of the north wind. The creature brought within him an amplitude of Northern knowledge. Glacial catastrophes, snow-storm episodes, glittering auroral effects, Polaris in the zenith, Franklin underfoot—the category of his commonplaces was wonderful. But the bird, like many other philosophers, seemed as he looked at the reddleman to think that a present moment of comfortable reality was worth a decade of memories.

Venn passed on through these towards the house of the isolated beauty who lived up among them and despised them. The day was Sunday; but as going to church, except to be married or buried, was exceptional at Egdon, this made little difference. He had determined upon the bold stroke of asking for an interview with Miss Vye—to attack her position as Thomasin's rival either by art or by storm, showing therein, somewhat too conspicuously, the want of gallantry characteristic of a certain astute sort of men, from clowns to kings. The great Frederick making war on the beautiful Archduchess, Napoleon refusing terms to the beautiful Queen of Prussia, were not more dead to difference of sex than the reddleman was, in his peculiar way, in planning the displacement of Eustacia.

To call at the captain's cottage was always more or less an undertaking for the inferior inhabitants. Though occasionally chatty, his moods were erratic, and nobody could be certain how he would behave at any particular moment. Eustacia was reserved, and lived very much to herself. Except the daughter of one of the cotters, who was their servant, and a lad who worked in the garden and stable, scarcely anyone but themselves ever entered the house. They were the only genteel people of the district except the Yeobrights, and though far from rich, they did not feel that necessity for preserving a friendly face towards every man, bird, and beast which influenced their poorer neighbours.

When the reddleman entered the garden the old man was looking through his glass at the stain of blue in the distant landscape, the little anchors on his buttons twinkling in the sun. He recognised Venn as his companion on the highway, but made no remark on that circumstance, merely saying, "Ah, reddleman—you here? Have a glass of grog?"

Venn declined, on the plea of it being too early, and stated that his business was with Miss Vye. The captain surveyed him from cap to waistcoat and from waistcoat to leggings for a few moments, and finally asked him to go indoors.

Miss Vye was not to be seen by anybody just then; and the reddleman waited in the window-bench of the kitchen, his hands hanging across his divergent knees, and his cap hanging from his hands.

"I suppose the young lady is not up yet?" he presently said to the servant.

"Not quite yet. Folks never call upon ladies at this time of day."

"Then I'll step outside," said Venn. "If she is willing to see me, will she please send out word, and I'll come in."

The reddleman left the house and loitered on the hill adjoining. A considerable time elapsed, and no request for his presence was brought. He was beginning to think that his scheme had failed, when he beheld the form of Eustacia herself coming leisurely towards him. A sense of novelty in giving audience to that singular figure had been sufficient to draw her forth.

She seemed to feel, after a bare look at Diggory Venn, that the man had come on a strange errand, and that he was not so mean as she had thought him; for her close approach did not cause him to writhe uneasily, or shift his feet, or show any of those little signs which escape an ingenuous rustic at the advent of the uncommon in womankind. On his enquiring if he might have a conversation with her she replied, "Yes, walk beside me"; and continued to move on.

Before they had gone far it occurred to the perspicacious reddleman that he would have acted more wisely by appearing less unimpressionable, and he resolved to correct the error as soon as he could find opportunity.

"I have made so bold, miss, as to step across and tell you some strange news which has come to my ears about that man."

"Ah! what man?"

He jerked his elbow to the south-east—the direction of the Quiet Woman.

Eustacia turned quickly to him. "Do you mean Mr. Wildeve?"

"Yes, there is trouble in a household on account of him, and I have come to let you know of it, because I believe you might have power to drive it away."

"I? What is the trouble?"

"It is quite a secret. It is that he may refuse to marry Thomasin Yeobright after all."

Eustacia, though set inwardly pulsing by his words, was equal to her part in such a drama as this. She replied coldly, "I do not wish to listen to this, and you must not expect me to interfere."

"But, miss, you will hear one word?"

"I cannot. I am not interested in the marriage, and even if I were I could not compel Mr. Wildeve to do my bidding."

"As the only lady on the heath I think you might," said Venn with subtle indirectness. "This is how the case stands. Mr. Wildeve would marry Thomasin at once, and make all matters smooth, if so be there were not another woman in the case. This other woman is some person he has picked up with, and meets on the heath occasionally, I believe. He will never marry her, and yet through her he may never marry the woman who loves him dearly. Now, if you, miss, who have so much sway over us men-folk, were to insist that he should treat your young neighbour Tamsin with honourable kindness and give up the other woman, he would perhaps do it, and save her a good deal of misery."

"Ah, my life!" said Eustacia, with a laugh which unclosed her lips so that the sun shone into her mouth as into a tulip, and lent it a similar scarlet fire. "You think too much of my influence over men-folk indeed, reddleman. If I had such a power as you imagine I would go straight and use it for the good of anybody who has been kind to me—which Thomasin Yeobright has not particularly, to my knowledge."

"Can it be that you really don't know of it—how much she had always thought of you?"

"I have never heard a word of it. Although we live only two miles apart I have never been inside her aunt's house in my life."

The superciliousness that lurked in her manner told Venn that thus far he had utterly failed. He inwardly sighed and felt it necessary to unmask his second argument.

"Well, leaving that out of the question, 'tis in your power, I assure you, Miss Vye, to do a great deal of good to another woman."

She shook her head.

"Your comeliness is law with Mr. Wildeve. It is law with all men who see ye. They say, 'This well-favoured lady coming—what's her name? How handsome!' Handsomer than Thomasin Yeobright," the reddleman persisted, saying to himself, "God forgive a rascal for lying!" And she was handsomer, but the reddleman was far from thinking so. There was a certain obscurity in Eustacia's beauty, and Venn's eye was not trained. In her winter dress, as now, she was like the tiger-beetle, which, when observed in dull situations, seems to be of the quietest neutral colour, but under a full illumination blazes with dazzling splendour.

Eustacia could not help replying, though conscious that she endangered her dignity thereby. "Many women are lovelier than Thomasin," she said; "so not much attaches to that."

The reddleman suffered the wound and went on: "He is a man who notices the looks of women, and you could twist him to your will like withywind, if you only had the mind."

"Surely what she cannot do who has been so much with him I cannot do living up here away from him."

The reddleman wheeled and looked her in the face. "Miss Vye!" he said.

"Why do you say that—as if you doubted me?" She spoke faintly, and her breathing was quick. "The idea of your speaking in that tone to me!" she added, with a forced smile of hauteur. "What could have been in your mind to lead you to speak like that?"

"Miss Vye, why should you make-believe that you don't know this man?—I know why, certainly. He is beneath you, and you are ashamed."

"You are mistaken. What do you mean?"

The reddleman had decided to play the card of truth. "I was at the meeting by Rainbarrow last night and heard every word," he said. "The woman that stands between Wildeve and Thomasin is yourself."

It was a disconcerting lift of the curtain, and the mortification of Candaules' wife glowed in her. The moment had arrived when her lip would tremble in spite of herself, and when the gasp could no longer be kept down.

"I am unwell," she said hurriedly. "No—it is not that—I am not in a humour to hear you further. Leave me, please."

"I must speak, Miss Vye, in spite of paining you. What I would put before you is this. However it may come about—whether she is to blame, or you—her case is without doubt worse than yours. Your giving up Mr. Wildeve will be a real advantage to you, for how could you marry him? Now she cannot get off so easily—everybody will blame her if she loses him. Then I ask you—not because her right is best, but because her situation is worst—to give him up to her."

"No—I won't, I won't!" she said impetuously, quite forgetful of her previous manner towards the reddleman as an underling. "Nobody has ever been served so! It was going on well—I will not be beaten down—by an inferior woman like her. It is very well for you to come and plead for her, but is she not herself the cause of all her own trouble? Am I not to show favour to any person I may choose without asking permission of a parcel of cottagers? She has come between me and my inclination, and now that she finds herself rightly punished she gets you to plead for her!"

"Indeed," said Venn earnestly, "she knows nothing whatever about it. It is only I who ask you to give him up. It will be better for her and you both. People will say bad things if they find out that a lady secretly meets a man who has ill-used another woman."

"I have *not* injured her: he was mine before he was hers! He came back—because—because he liked me best!" she said wildly. "But I lose all self-respect in talking to you. What am I giving way to!"

"I can keep secrets," said Venn gently. "You need not fear. I am the only man who knows of your meetings with him. There is but one thing more to speak of, and then I will be gone. I heard you say to him that you hated living here—that Egdon Heath was a jail to you."

"I did say so. There is a sort of beauty in the scenery, I know; but it is a jail to me. The man you mention does not save me from that feeling, though he lives here. I should have cared nothing for him had there been a better person near."

The reddleman looked hopeful: after these words from her his third attempt seemed promising. "As we have now opened our minds a bit, miss," he said, "I'll tell you what I have got to propose. Since I have taken to the reddle trade I travel a good deal, as you know."

She inclined her head, and swept round so that her eyes rested in the misty vale beneath them.

"And in my travels I go near Budmouth. Now Budmouth is a wonderful place—wonderful—a great salt sheening sea bending into the land like a bow—thousands of gentlepeople walking up and down—bands of music playing—officers by sea and officers by land walking among the rest—out of every ten folks you meet nine of 'em in love."

"I know it," she said disdainfully. "I know Budmouth better than you. I was born there. My father came to be a military musician there from abroad. Ah, my soul, Budmouth! I wish I was there now."

The reddleman was surprised to see how a slow fire could blaze on occasion. "If you were, miss," he replied, "in a week's time you would think no more of Wildeve than of one of those he'th-croppers that we see yond. Now, I could get you there."

"How?" said Eustacia, with intense curiosity in her heavy eyes.

"My uncle has been for five and twenty years the trusty man of a rich widow-lady who has a beautiful house facing the sea. This lady has become old and lame, and she wants a young company-keeper to read and sing to her, but can't get one to her mind to save her life, though she've advertised in the papers, and tried half-a-dozen. She would jump to get you, and uncle would make it all easy."

"I should have to work, perhaps?"

"No, not real work: you'd have a little to do, such as reading and that. You would not be wanted till New Year's Day."

"I knew it meant work," she said, drooping to languor again.

"I confess there would be a trifle to do in the way of amusing her; but though idle people might call it work, working people would call it play. Think of the company and the life you'd lead, miss; the gaiety you'd see, and the gentleman you'd marry. My uncle is to enquire for a trustworthy young lady from the country, as she don't like town girls."

"It is to wear myself out to please her! and I won't go. O, if I could live in a gay town as a lady should, and go my own ways, and do my own doings, I'd give the wrinkled half of my life! Yes, reddleman, that would I."

"Help me to get Thomasin happy, miss, and the chance shall be yours," urged her companion.

"Chance!—'tis no chance," she said proudly. "What can a poor man like you offer me, indeed?—I am going indoors. I have nothing more to say. Don't your horses want feeding, or your reddlebags want mending, or don't you want to find buyers for your goods, that you stay idling here like this?"

Venn spoke not another word. With his hands behind him he turned away, that she might not see the hopeless disappointment in his face. The mental clearness and power he had found in this lonely girl had indeed filled his manner with misgiving even from the first few minutes of close quarters with her. Her youth and situation had led him to expect a simplicity quite at the beck of his method. But a system of inducement which might have carried weaker country lasses along with it had merely repelled Eustacia. As a rule, the word Budmouth meant fascination on Egdon. That rising port and watering-place, if truly mirrored in the minds of the heath-folk, must have combined, in a charming and indescribable manner, a Carthaginian bustle of building with Tarentine luxuriousness and Baian health and beauty. Eustacia felt little less extravagantly about the place; but she would not sink her independence to get there.

When Diggory Venn had gone quite away, Eustacia walked to the bank and looked down the wild and picturesque vale towards the sun, which was also in the direction of Wildeve's. The mist had now so far collapsed that the tips of the trees and bushes around his house could just be discerned, as if boring upwards through a vast white cobweb which cloaked them from the day. There was no doubt that her mind was inclined thitherward; indefinitely, fancifully—twining and untwining about him as the single object within her horizon on which dreams might crystallise. The man who had begun by being merely her amusement, and would never have been more than her hobby but for his skill in deserting her at the right moments, was now again her desire. Cessation in his love-making had revivified her love. Such feeling as Eustacia had idly given to Wildeve was dammed into a flood by Thomasin. She had used to tease Wildeve, but that was before another had favoured him. Often a drop of irony into an indifferent situation renders the whole piquant.

"I will never give him up—never!" she said impetuously.

The reddleman's hint that rumour might show her to disadvantage had no permanent terror for Eustacia. She was as unconcerned at that contingency as a goddess at a lack of linen. This did not originate in inherent shamelessness, but in her living too far from the world to feel the impact of public opinion. Zenobia in the desert could hardly have cared what was said about her at Rome. As far as social ethics were concerned Eustacia approached the savage state, though in emotion she was all the while an epicure. She had advanced to the secret recesses of sensuousness, yet had hardly crossed the threshold of conventionality.

XI

THE DISHONESTY OF AN HONEST WOMAN

THE REDDLEMAN HAD LEFT EUSTACIA'S PRESENCE WITH DESPONDING VIEWS ON Thomasin's future happiness; but he was awakened to the fact that one other channel remained untried by seeing, as he followed the way to his van, the form of Mrs. Yeobright slowly walking towards the Quiet Woman. He went across to her; and could almost perceive in her anxious face that this journey of hers to Wildeve was undertaken with the same object as his own to Eustacia.

She did not conceal the fact. "Then," said the reddleman, "you may as well leave it alone, Mrs. Yeobright."

"I half think so myself," she said. "But nothing else remains to be done besides pressing the question upon him."

"I should like to say a word first," said Venn firmly. "Mr. Wildeve is not the only man who has asked Thomasin to marry him; and why should not another have a chance? Mrs. Yeobright, I should be glad to marry your niece, and would have done it any time these last two years. There, now it is out, and I have never told anybody before but herself."

Mrs. Yeobright was not demonstrative, but her eyes involuntarily glanced towards his singular though shapely figure.

"Looks are not everything," said the reddleman, noticing the glance. "There's many a calling that don't bring in so much as mine, if it comes to money; and perhaps I am not so much worse off than Wildeve. There is nobody so poor as these professional fellows who have failed; and if you shouldn't like my redness—well, I am not red by birth, you know; I only took to this business for a freak; and I might turn my hand to something else in good time."

"I am much obliged to you for your interest in my niece; but I fear there would be objections. More than that, she is devoted to this man."

"True; or I shouldn't have done what I have this morning."

"Otherwise there would be no pain in the case, and you would not see me going to his house now. What was Thomasin's answer when you told her of your feelings?"

"She wrote that you would object to me; and other things."

"She was in a measure right. You must not take this unkindly: I merely state it as a truth. You have been good to her, and we do not forget it. But as she was unwilling on her own account to be your wife, that settles the point without my wishes being concerned."

"Yes. But there is a difference between then and now, ma'am. She is distressed now, and I have thought that if you were to talk to her about me, and think favourably of me yourself, there might be a chance of winning her round, and getting her quite independent of this Wildeve's backward and forward play, and his not knowing whether he'll have her or no."

Mrs. Yeobright shook her head. "Thomasin thinks, and I think with her, that she ought to be Wildeve's wife, if she means to appear before the world without a slur upon her name. If they marry soon, everybody will believe that an accident did really prevent the wedding. If not, it may cast a shade upon her character—at any rate make her ridiculous. In short, if it is anyhow possible they must marry now."

"I thought that till half an hour ago. But, after all, why should her going off with him to Anglebury for a few hours do her any harm? Anybody who knows how pure she is will feel any such thought to be quite unjust. I have been trying this morning to help on this marriage with Wildeve—yes, I, ma'am—in the belief that I ought to do it, because she was so wrapped up in him. But I much question if I was right, after all. However, nothing came of it. And now I offer myself."

Mrs. Yeobright appeared disinclined to enter further into the question. "I fear I must go on," she said. "I do not see that anything else can be done."

And she went on. But though this conversation did not divert Thomasin's aunt from her purposed interview with Wildeve, it made a considerable difference in her mode of conducting that interview. She thanked God for the weapon which the reddleman had put into her hands.

Wildeve was at home when she reached the inn. He showed her silently into the parlour, and closed the door. Mrs. Yeobright began—

"I have thought it my duty to call to-day. A new proposal has been made to me, which has rather astonished me. It will affect Thomasin greatly; and I have decided that it should at least be mentioned to you."

"Yes? What is it?" he said civilly.

"It is, of course, in reference to her future. You may not be aware that another man has shown himself anxious to marry Thomasin. Now, though I have not encouraged him yet, I cannot conscientiously refuse him a chance any longer. I don't wish to be short with you; but I must be fair to him and to her."

"Who is the man?" said Wildeve with surprise.

"One who has been in love with her longer than she has with you. He proposed to her two years ago. At that time she refused him."

"Well?"

"He has seen her lately, and has asked me for permission to pay his addresses to her. She may not refuse him twice."

"What is his name?"

Mrs. Yeobright declined to say. "He is a man Thomasin likes," she added, "and one whose constancy she respects at least. It seems to me that what she refused then she would be glad to get now. She is much annoyed at her awkward position."

"She never once told me of this old lover."

"The gentlest women are not such fools as to show *every* card."

"Well, if she wants him I suppose she must have him."

"It is easy enough to say that; but you don't see the difficulty. He wants her much more than she wants him; and before I can encourage anything of the sort I must have a clear understanding from you that you will not interfere to injure an arrangement which I promote in the belief that it is for the best. Suppose, when they are engaged, and everything is smoothly arranged for their marriage, that you should step between them and renew your suit? You might not win her back, but you might cause much unhappiness."

"Of course I should do no such thing," said Wildeve "But they are not engaged yet. How do you know that Thomasin would accept him?"

"That's a question I have carefully put to myself; and upon the whole the probabilities are in favour of her accepting him in time. I flatter myself that I have some influence over her. She is pliable, and I can be strong in my recommendations of him."

"And in your disparagement of me at the same time."

"Well, you may depend upon my not praising you," she said drily. "And if this seems like manoeuvring, you must remember that her position is peculiar, and that she has been hardly used. I shall also be helped in making the match by her own desire to escape from the humiliation of her present state; and a woman's pride in these cases will lead her a very great way. A little managing may be required to bring her round; but I am equal to that, provided that you agree to the one thing indispensable; that is, to make a distinct declaration that she is to think no more of you as a possible husband. That will pique her into accepting him."

"I can hardly say that just now, Mrs. Yeobright. It is so sudden."

"And so my whole plan is interfered with! It is very inconvenient that you refuse to help my family even to the small extent of saying distinctly you will have nothing to do with us."

Wildeve reflected uncomfortably. "I confess I was not prepared for this," he said. "Of course I'll give her up if you wish, if it is necessary. But I thought I might be her husband."

"We have heard that before."

"Now, Mrs. Yeobright, don't let us disagree. Give me a fair time. I don't want to stand in the way of any better chance she may have; only I wish you had let me know earlier. I will write to you or call in a day or two. Will that suffice?"

"Yes," she replied, "provided you promise not to communicate with Thomasin without my knowledge."

"I promise that," he said. And the interview then terminated, Mrs. Yeobright returning homeward as she had come.

By far the greatest effect of her simple strategy on that day was, as often happens, in a quarter quite outside her view when arranging it. In the first place, her visit sent Wildeve the same evening after dark to Eustacia's house at Mistover.

At this hour the lonely dwelling was closely blinded and shuttered from the chill and darkness without. Wildeve's clandestine plan with her was to take a little gravel in his hand and hold it to the crevice at the top of the window-shutter, which was on the outside, so that it should fall with a gentle rustle, resembling that of a mouse, between shutter and glass. This precaution in attracting her attention was to avoid arousing the suspicions of her grand-father.

The soft words, "I hear; wait for me," in Eustacia's voice from within told him that she was alone.

He waited in his customary manner by walking round the enclosure and idling by the pool, for Wildeve was never asked into the house by his proud though condescending mistress. She showed no sign of coming out in a hurry. The time wore on, and he began to grow impatient. In the course of twenty minutes she appeared from round the corner, and advanced as if merely taking an airing.

"You would not have kept me so long had you known what I come about," he said with bitterness. "Still, you are worth waiting for."

"What has happened?" said Eustacia. "I did not know you were in trouble. I too am gloomy enough."

"I am not in trouble," said he. "It is merely that affairs have come to a head, and I must take a clear course."

"What course is that?" she asked with attentive interest.

"And can you forget so soon what I proposed to you the other night? Why, take you from this place, and carry you away with me abroad."

"I have not forgotten. But why have you come so unexpectedly to repeat the question, when you only promised to come next Saturday? I thought I was to have plenty of time to consider."

"Yes, but the situation is different now."

"Explain to me."

"I don't want to explain, for I may pain you."

"But I must know the reason of this hurry."

"It is simply my ardour, dear Eustacia. Everything is smooth now."

"Then why are you so ruffled?"

"I am not aware of it. All is as it should be. Mrs. Yeobright—but she is nothing to us."

"Ah, I knew she had something to do with it! Come, I don't like reserve."

"No—she has nothing. She only says she wishes me to give up Thomasin because another man is anxious to marry her. The woman, now she no longer needs me, actually shows off!" Wildeve's vexation had escaped him in spite of himself.

Eustacia was silent a long while. "You are in the awkward position of an official who is no longer wanted," she said in a changed tone.

"It seems so. But I have not yet seen Thomasin."

"And that irritates you. Don't deny it, Damon. You are actually nettled by this slight from an unexpected quarter."

"Well?"

"And you come to get me because you cannot get her. This is certainly a new position altogether. I am to be a stop-gap."

"Please remember that I proposed the same thing the other day."

Eustacia again remained in a sort of stupefied silence. What curious feeling was this coming over her? Was it really possible that her interest in Wildeve had been so entirely the result of antagonism that the glory and the dream departed from the man with the first sound that he was no longer coveted by her rival? She was, then, secure of him at last. Thomasin no longer required him. What a humiliating victory! He loved her best, she thought; and yet—dared she to murmur such treacherous criticism ever so softly?—what was the man worth whom a woman inferior to herself did not value? The sentiment which lurks more or less in all animate nature—that of not desiring the undesired of others— was lively as a passion in the supersubtle, epicurean heart of Eustacia. Her social superiority over him, which hitherto had scarcely ever impressed her, became unpleasantly insistent, and for the first time she felt that she had stooped in loving him.

"Well, darling, you agree?" said Wildeve.

"If it could be London, or even Budmouth, instead of America," she murmured languidly. "Well, I will think. It is too great a thing for me to decide offhand. I wish I hated the heath less—or loved you more."

"You can be painfully frank. You loved me a month ago warmly enough to go anywhere with me."

"And you loved Thomasin."

"Yes, perhaps that was where the reason lay," he returned, with almost a sneer. "I don't hate her now."

"Exactly. The only thing is that you can no longer get her."

"Come—no taunts, Eustacia, or we shall quarrel. If you don't agree to go with me, and agree shortly, I shall go by myself."

"Or try Thomasin again. Damon, how strange it seems that you could have married her or me indifferently, and only have come to me because I am—cheapest! Yes, yes—it is true. There was a time when I should have exclaimed against a man of that sort, and been quite wild; but it is all past now."

"Will you go, dearest? Come secretly with me to Bristol, marry me, and turn our backs upon this dog-hole of England forever? Say Yes."

"I want to get away from here at almost any cost," she said with weariness, "but I don't like to go with you. Give me more time to decide."

"I have already," said Wildeve. "Well, I give you one more week."

"A little longer, so that I may tell you decisively. I have to consider so many things. Fancy Thomasin being anxious to get rid of you! I cannot forget it."

"Never mind that. Say Monday week. I will be here precisely at this time."

"Let it be at Rainbarrow," said she. "This is too near home; my grand-father may be walking out."

"Thank you, dear. On Monday week at this time I will be at the Barrow. Till then good-bye."

"Good-bye. No, no, you must not touch me now. Shaking hands is enough till I have made up my mind."

Eustacia watched his shadowy form till it had disappeared. She placed her hand to her forehead and breathed heavily; and then her rich, romantic lips parted under that homely impulse—a yawn. She was immediately angry at having betrayed even to herself the possible evanescence of her passion for him. She could not admit at once that she might have over-estimated Wildeve, for to perceive his mediocrity now was to admit her own great folly heretofore. And the discovery that she was the owner of a disposition so purely that of the dog in the manger, had something in it which at first made her ashamed.

The fruit of Mrs. Yeobright's diplomacy was indeed remarkable, though not as yet of the kind she had anticipated. It had appreciably influenced Wildeve, but it was influencing Eustacia far more. Her lover was no longer to her an exciting man whom many women strove for, and herself could only retain by striving with them. He was a superfluity.

She went indoors in that peculiar state of misery which is not exactly grief, and which especially attends the dawnings of reason in the latter days of an ill-judged, transient love. To be conscious that the end of the dream is approaching, and yet has not absolutely come, is one of the most wearisome as well as the most curious stages along the course between the beginning of a passion and its end.

Her grand-father had returned, and was busily engaged in pouring some gallons of newly arrived rum into the square bottles of his square cellaret. Whenever these home supplies were exhausted he would go to the Quiet Woman, and, standing with his back to the fire, grog in hand, tell remarkable stories of how he had lived seven years under the water-line of his ship, and other naval wonders, to the natives, who hoped too earnestly for a treat of ale from the teller to exhibit any doubts of his truth.

He had been there this evening. "I suppose you have heard the Egdon news, Eustacia?" he said, without looking up from the bottles. "The men have been talking about it at the Woman as if it were of national importance."

"I have heard none," she said.

"Young Clym Yeobright, as they call him, is coming home next week to spend Christmas with his mother. He is a fine fellow by this time, it seems. I suppose you remember him?"

"I never saw him in my life."

"Ah, true; he left before you came here. I well remember him as a promising boy."

"Where has he been living all these years?"

"In that rookery of pomp and vanity, Paris, I believe."

Book Second

The Arrival

I

TIDINGS OF THE COMER

O N THE FINE DAYS AT THIS TIME OF THE YEAR, AND EARLIER, CERTAIN EPHEMERAL operations were apt to disturb, in their trifling way, the majestic calm of Egdon Heath. They were activities which, beside those of a town, a village, or even a farm, would have appeared as the ferment of stagnation merely, a creeping of the flesh of somnolence. But here, away from comparisons, shut in by the stable hills, among which mere walking had the novelty of pageantry, and where any man could imagine himself to be Adam without the least difficulty, they attracted the attention of every bird within eye-shot, every reptile not yet asleep, and set the surrounding rabbits curiously watching from hillocks at a safe distance.

The performance was that of bringing together and building into a stack the furze-faggots which Humphrey had been cutting for the captain's use during the foregoing fine days. The stack was at the end of the dwelling, and the men engaged in building it were Humphrey and Sam, the old man looking on.

It was a fine and quiet afternoon, about three o'clock; but the winter solstice having stealthily come on, the lowness of the sun caused the hour to seem later than it actually was, there being little here to remind an inhabitant that he must unlearn his summer experience of the sky as a dial. In the course of many days and weeks sunrise had advanced its quarters from north-east to south-east, sunset had receded from north-west to south-west; but Egdon had hardly heeded the change.

Eustacia was indoors in the dining-room, which was really more like a kitchen, having a stone floor and a gaping chimney-corner. The air was still, and while she lingered a moment here alone sounds of voices in conversation came to her ears directly down the chimney. She entered the recess, and, listening, looked up the old irregular shaft, with its cavernous hollows, where the smoke blundered about on its way to the square bit of sky at the top, from which the daylight struck down with a pallid glare upon the tatters of soot draping the flue as sea-weed drapes a rocky fissure.

She remembered: the furze-stack was not far from the chimney, and the voices were those of the workers.

Her grand-father joined in the conversation. "That lad ought never to have left home. His father's occupation would have suited him best, and the boy should have followed on. I don't believe in these new moves in families. My father was a sailor, so was I, and so should my son have been if I had had one."

"The place he's been living at is Paris," said Humphrey, "and they tell me 'tis where the king's head was cut off years ago. My poor mother used to tell me about that business. 'Hummy,' she used to say, 'I was a young maid then, and as I was at home ironing mother's caps one afternoon the parson came in and said, 'They've cut the king's head off, Jane; and what 'twill be next God knows.' "

"A good many of us knew as well as He before long," said the captain, chuckling. "I lived seven years under water on account of it in my boyhood—in that damned surgery of the *Triumph*, seeing men brought down to the cockpit with their legs and arms blown to Jericho. . . . And so the young man has settled in Paris. Manager to a diamond merchant, or some such thing, is he not?"

"Yes, sir, that's it. 'Tis a blazing great business that he belongs to, so I've heard his mother say—like a king's palace, as far as diments go."

"I can well mind when he left home," said Sam.

" 'Tis a good thing for the feller," said Humphrey. "A sight of times better to be selling diments than nobbling about here."

"It must cost a good few shillings to deal at such a place."

"A good few indeed, my man," replied the captain. "Yes, you may make away with a deal of money and be neither drunkard nor glutton."

"They say, too, that Clym Yeobright is become a real perusing man, with the strangest notions about things. There, that's because he went to school early, such as the school was."

"Strange notions, has he?" said the old man. "Ah, there's too much of that sending to school in these days! It only does harm. Every gate-post and barn's door you come to is sure to have some bad word or other chalked upon it by the young rascals: a woman can hardly pass for shame sometimes. If they'd never been taught how to write they wouldn't have been able to scribble such villainy. Their fathers couldn't do it, and the country was all the better for it."

"Now, I should think, cap'n, that Miss Eustacia had about as much in her head that comes from books as anybody about here?"

"Perhaps if Miss Eustacia, too, had less romantic nonsense in her head it would be better for her," said the captain shortly; after which he walked away.

"I say, Sam," observed Humphrey when the old man was gone, "she and Clym Yeobright would make a very pretty pigeon pair—hey? If they wouldn't I'll be dazed! Both of one mind about niceties for certain, and learned in print, and always thinking about high doctrine—there couldn't be a better couple if they were made o' purpose. Clym's family is as good as hers. His father was a farmer, that's true; but his mother was a sort of lady, as we know. Nothing would please me better than to see them two man and wife."

"They'd look very natty, arm-in-crook together, and their best clothes on, whether or no, if he's at all the well-favoured fellow he used to be."

"They would, Humphrey. Well, I should like to see the chap terrible much after so many years. If I knew for certain when he was coming I'd stroll out three or four miles to meet him and help carry anything for'n; though I suppose he's altered from the boy he was. They say he can talk French as fast as a maid can eat blackberries; and if so, depend upon it we who have stayed at home shall seem no more than scroff in his eyes."

"Coming across the water to Budmouth by steamer, isn't he?"

"Yes; but how he's coming from Budmouth I don't know."

"That's a bad trouble about his cousin Thomasin. I wonder such a nice-notioned fellow as Clym likes to come home into it. What a nunnywatch we were in, to be sure, when we heard they weren't married at all, after singing to 'em as man and wife that night! Be dazed if I should like a relation of mine to have been made such a fool of by a man. It makes the family look small."

"Yes. Poor maid, her heart has ached enough about it. Her health is suffering from it,

I hear, for she will bide entirely indoors. We never see her out now, scampering over the furze with a face as red as a rose, as she used to do."

"I've heard she wouldn't have Wildeve now if he asked her."

"You have? 'Tis news to me."

While the furze-gatherers had desultorily conversed thus Eustacia's face gradually bent to the hearth in a profound reverie, her toe unconsciously tapping the dry turf which lay burning at her feet.

The subject of their discourse had been keenly interesting to her. A young and clever man was coming into that lonely heath from, of all contrasting places in the world, Paris. It was like a man coming from heaven. More singular still, the heathmen had instinctively coupled her and this man together in their minds as a pair born for each other.

That five minutes of overhearing furnished Eustacia with visions enough to fill the whole blank afternoon. Such sudden alternations from mental vacuity do sometimes occur thus quietly. She could never have believed in the morning that her colourless inner world would before night become as animated as water under a microscope, and that without the arrival of a single visitor. The words of Sam and Humphrey on the harmony between the unknown and herself had on her mind the effect of the invading Bard's prelude in the *Castle of Indolence*, at which myriads of imprisoned shapes arose where had previously appeared the stillness of a void.

Involved in these imaginings she knew nothing of time. When she became conscious of externals it was dusk. The furze-rick was finished; the men had gone home. Eustacia went upstairs, thinking that she would take a walk at this her usual time; and she determined that her walk should be in the direction of Blooms-End, the birthplace of young Yeobright and the present home of his mother. She had no reason for walking elsewhere, and why should she not go that way? The scene of a day-dream is sufficient for a pilgrimage at nineteen. To look at the palings before the Yeobrights' house had the dignity of a necessary performance. Strange that such a piece of idling should have seemed an important errand.

She put on her bonnet, and, leaving the house, descended the hill on the side towards Blooms-End, where she walked slowly along the valley for a distance of a mile and a half. This brought her to a spot in which the green bottom of the dale began to widen, the furze-bushes to recede yet further from the path on each side, till they were diminished to an isolated one here and there by the increasing fertility of the soil. Beyond the irregular carpet of grass was a row of white palings, which marked the verge of the heath in this latitude. They showed upon the dusky scene that they bordered as distinctly as white lace on velvet. Behind the white palings was a little garden; behind the garden an old, irregular, thatched house, facing the heath, and commanding a full view of the valley. This was the obscure, removed spot to which was about to return a man whose latter life had been passed in the French capital—the centre and vortex of the fashionable world.

II

THE PEOPLE AT BLOOMS-END MAKE READY

ALL THAT AFTERNOON THE EXPECTED ARRIVAL OF THE SUBJECT OF EUSTACIA'S ruminations created a bustle of preparation at Blooms-End. Thomasin had been persuaded by her aunt, and by an instinctive impulse of loyalty towards her cousin Clym, to bestir herself on his account with an alacrity unusual in her during these most sorrowful days of her life. At the time that Eustacia was listening to the rick-makers' conversation on Clym's return, Thomasin was climbing into a loft over her aunt's fuel-house, where the store-apples were kept, to search out the best and largest of them for the coming holiday-time.

The loft was lighted by a semicircular hole, through which the pigeons crept to their lodgings in the same high quarters of the premises; and from this hole the sun shone in a bright yellow patch upon the figure of the maiden as she knelt and plunged her naked arms into the soft brown fern, which, from its abundance, was used on Egdon in packing away stores of all kinds. The pigeons were flying about her head with the greatest unconcern, and the face of her aunt was just visible above the floor of the loft, lit by a few stray motes of light, as she stood half-way up the ladder, looking at a spot into which she was not climber enough to venture.

"Now a few russets, Tamsin. He used to like them almost as well as ribstones."

Thomasin turned and rolled aside the fern from another nook, where more mellow fruit greeted her with its ripe smell. Before picking them out she stopped a moment.

"Dear Clym, I wonder how your face looks now?" she said, gazing abstractedly at the pigeon-hole, which admitted the sunlight so directly upon her brown hair and transparent tissues that it almost seemed to shine through her.

"If he could have been dear to you in another way," said Mrs. Yeobright from the ladder, "this might have been a happy meeting."

"Is there any use in saying what can do no good, aunt?"

"Yes," said her aunt, with some warmth. "To thoroughly fill the air with the past misfortune, so that other girls may take warning and keep clear of it."

Thomasin lowered her face to the apples again. "I am a warning to others, just as thieves and drunkards and gamblers are," she said in a low voice. "What a class to belong to! Do I really belong to them? 'Tis absurd! Yet why, aunt, does everybody keep on making me think that I do, by the way they behave towards me? Why don't people judge me by my acts? Now, look at me as I kneel here, picking up these apples—do I look like a lost woman? . . . I wish all good women were as good as I!" she added vehemently.

"Strangers don't see you as I do," said Mrs. Yeobright; "they judge from false report. Well, it is a silly job, and I am partly to blame."

"How quickly a rash thing can be done!" replied the girl. Her lips were quivering, and tears so crowded themselves into her eyes that she could hardly distinguish apples from fern as she continued industriously searching to hide her weakness.

"As soon as you have finished getting the apples," her aunt said, descending the ladder, "come down, and we'll go for the holly. There is nobody on the heath this afternoon, and you need not fear being stared at. We must get some berries, or Clym will never believe in our preparations."

Thomasin came down when the apples were collected, and together they went through the white palings to the heath beyond. The open hills were airy and clear, and the remote atmosphere appeared, as it often appears on a fine winter day, in distinct planes of illumination independently toned, the rays which lit the nearer tracts of landscape streaming visibly across those further off; a stratum of ensaffroned light was imposed on a stratum of deep blue, and behind these lay still remoter scenes wrapped in frigid grey.

They reached the place where the hollies grew, which was in a conical pit, so that the tops of the trees were not much above the general level of the ground. Thomasin stepped up into a fork of one of the bushes, as she had done under happier circumstances on many similar occasions, and with a small chopper that they had brought she began to lop off the heavily berried boughs.

"Don't scratch your face," said her aunt, who stood at the edge of the pit, regarding the girl as she held on amid the glistening green and scarlet masses of the tree. "Will you walk with me to meet him this evening?"

"I should like to. Else it would seem as if I had forgotten him," said Thomasin, tossing out a bough. "Not that that would matter much; I belong to one man; nothing can alter that. And that man I must marry, for my pride's sake."

"I am afraid——" began Mrs. Yeobright.

"Ah, you think, 'That weak girl—how is she going to get a man to marry her when she chooses?' But let me tell you one thing, aunt: Mr. Wildeve is not a profligate man, any more than I am an improper woman. He has an unfortunate manner, and doesn't try to make people like him if they don't wish to do it of their own accord."

"Thomasin," said Mrs. Yeobright quietly, fixing her eye upon her niece, "do you think you deceive me in your defence of Mr. Wildeve?"

"How do you mean?"

"I have long had a suspicion that your love for him has changed its colour since you have found him not to be the saint you thought him, and that you act a part to me."

"He wished to marry me, and I wish to marry him."

"Now, I put it to you: would you at this present moment agree to be his wife if that had not happened to entangle you with him?"

Thomasin looked into the tree and appeared much disturbed. "Aunt," she said presently, "I have, I think, a right to refuse to answer that question."

"Yes, you have."

"You may think what you choose. I have never implied to you by word or deed that I have grown to think otherwise of him, and I never will. And I shall marry him."

"Well, wait till he repeats his offer. I think he may do it, now that he knows— something I told him. I don't for a moment dispute that it is the most proper thing for you to marry him. Much as I have objected to him in bygone days, I agree with you now, you may be sure. It is the only way out of a false position, and a very galling one."

"What did you tell him?"

"That he was standing in the way of another lover of yours."

"Aunt," said Thomasin, with round eyes, "what *do* you mean?"

"Don't be alarmed; it was my duty. I can say no more about it now, but when it is over I will tell you exactly what I said, and why I said it."

Thomasin was perforce content.

"And you will keep the secret of my would-be marriage from Clym for the present?" she next asked.

"I have given my word to. But what is the use of it? He must soon know what has happened. A mere look at your face will show him that something is wrong."

Thomasin turned and regarded her aunt from the tree. "Now, hearken to me," she said, her delicate voice expanding into firmness by a force which was other than physical. "Tell him nothing. If he finds out that I am not worthy to be his cousin, let him. But, since he loved me once, we will not pain him by telling him my trouble too soon. The air is full of the story, I know; but gossips will not dare to speak of it to him for the first few days. His closeness to me is the very thing that will hinder the tale from reaching him early. If I am not made safe from sneers in a week or two I will tell him myself."

The earnestness with which Thomasin spoke prevented further objections. Her aunt simply said, "Very well. He should by rights have been told at the time that the wedding was going to be. He will never forgive you for your secrecy."

"Yes, he will, when he knows it was because I wished to spare him, and that I did not expect him home so soon. And you must not let me stand in the way of your Christmas party. Putting it off would only make matters worse."

"Of course I shall not. I do not wish to show myself beaten before all Egdon, and the sport of a man like Wildeve. We have enough berries now, I think, and we had better take them home. By the time we have decked the house with this and hung up the mistletoe, we must think of starting to meet him."

Thomasin came out of the tree, shook from her hair and dress the loose berries which had fallen thereon, and went down the hill with her aunt, each woman bearing half the gathered boughs. It was now nearly four o'clock, and the sunlight was leaving the vales. When the west grew red the two relatives came again from the house and plunged into the heath in a different direction from the first, towards a point in the distant highway along which the expected man was to return.

III

HOW A LITTLE SOUND PRODUCED A GREAT DREAM

EUSTACIA STOOD JUST WITHIN THE HEATH, STRAINING HER EYES IN THE DIRECTION OF Mrs. Yeobright's house and premises. No light, sound, or movement was perceptible there. The evening was chilly; the spot was dark and lonely. She inferred that the guest had not yet come; and after lingering ten or fifteen minutes she turned again towards home.

She had not far retraced her steps when sounds in front of her betokened the approach of persons in conversation along the same path. Soon their heads became visible against the sky. They were walking slowly; and though it was too dark for much discovery of character from aspect, the gait of them showed that they were not workers on the heath. Eustacia stepped a little out of the foot-track to let them pass. They were two women and a man; and the voices of the women were those of Mrs. Yeobright and Thomasin.

They went by her, and at the moment of passing appeared to discern her dusky form. There came to her ears in a masculine voice, "Good-night!"

She murmured a reply, glided by them, and turned round. She could not, for a moment, believe that chance, unrequested, had brought into her presence the soul of the house she had gone to inspect, the man without whom her inspection would not have been thought of.

She strained her eyes to see them, but was unable. Such was her intentness, however, that it seemed as if her ears were performing the functions of seeing as well as hearing. This extension of power can almost be believed in at such moments. The deaf Dr. Kitto was probably under the influence of a parallel fancy when he described his body as having become, by long endeavour, so sensitive to vibrations that he had gained the power of perceiving by it as by ears.

She could follow every word that the ramblers uttered. They were talking no secrets. They were merely indulging in the ordinary vivacious chat of relatives who have long been parted in person though not in soul. But it was not to the words that Eustacia listened; she could not even have recalled, a few minutes later, what the words were. It was to the alternating voice that gave out about one-tenth of them—the voice that had wished her good-night. Sometimes this throat uttered Yes, sometimes it uttered No; sometimes it made enquiries about a timeworn denizen of the place. Once it surprised her notions by remarking upon the friendliness and geniality written in the faces of the hills around.

The three voices passed on, and decayed and died out upon her ear. Thus much had been granted her; and all besides withheld. No event could have been more exciting. During the greater part of the afternoon she had been entrancing herself by imagining the fascination which must attend a man come direct from beautiful Paris—laden with its atmosphere, familiar with its charms. And this man had greeted her.

With the departure of the figures the profuse articulations of the women wasted away from her memory; but the accents of the other stayed on. Was there anything in the voice of Mrs. Yeobright's son—for Clym it was—startling as a sound? No: it was simply comprehensive. All emotional things were possible to the speaker of that "good-night." Eustacia's imagination supplied the rest—except the solution to one riddle. What *could* the tastes of that man be who saw friendliness and geniality in these shaggy hills?

On such occasions as this a thousand ideas pass through a highly charged woman's head; and they indicate themselves on her face; but the changes, though actual, are minute. Eustacia's features went through a rhythmical succession of them. She glowed; remembering the mendacity of the imagination, she flagged; then she freshened; then she fired; then she cooled again. It was a cycle of aspects, produced by a cycle of visions.

Eustacia entered her own house; she was excited. Her grand-father was enjoying himself over the fire, raking about the ashes and exposing the red-hot surface of the turves, so that their lurid glare irradiated the chimney-corner with the hues of a furnace.

"Why is it that we are never friendly with the Yeobrights?" she said, coming forward and stretching her soft hands over the warmth. "I wish we were. They seem to be very nice people."

"Be hanged if I know why," said the captain. "I liked the old man well enough, though he was as rough as a hedge. But you would never have cared to go there, even if you might have, I am well sure."

"Why shouldn't I?"

"Your town tastes would find them far too countrified. They sit in the kitchen, drink mead and elder-wine, and sand the floor to keep it clean. A sensible way of life; but how would you like it?"

"I thought Mrs. Yeobright was a ladylike woman? A curate's daughter, was she not?"

"Yes; but she was obliged to live as her husband did; and I suppose she has taken kindly to it by this time. Ah, I recollect that I once accidentally offended her, and I have never seen her since."

That night was an eventful one to Eustacia's brain, and one which she hardly ever forgot. She dreamt a dream; and few human beings, from Nebuchadnezzar to the Swaffham tinker, ever dreamed a more remarkable one. Such an elaborately developed, perplexing, exciting dream was certainly never dreamed by a girl in Eustacia's situation before. It had as many ramifications as the Cretan labyrinth, as many fluctuations as the Northern Lights, as much colour as a parterre in June, and was as crowded with figures as a coronation. To Queen Scheherazade the dream might have seemed not far removed from commonplace; and to a girl just returned from all the courts of Europe it might have seemed not more than interesting. But amid the circumstances of Eustacia's life it was as wonderful as a dream could be.

There was, however, gradually evolved from its transformation scenes a less extravagant episode, in which the heath dimly appeared behind the general brilliancy of the action. She was dancing to wondrous music, and her partner was the man in silver armour, who had accompanied her through the previous fantastic changes, the visor of his helmet being closed. The mazes of the dance were ecstatic. Soft whispering came into her ear from under the radiant helmet, and she felt like a woman in Paradise. Suddenly these two wheeled out from the mass of dancers, dived into one of the pools of the heath, and came out somewhere beneath into an iridescent hollow, arched with rainbows. "It must be here," said the voice by her side, and blushingly looking up she saw him removing his casque to kiss her. At that moment there was a cracking noise, and his figure fell into fragments like a pack of cards.

She cried aloud. "O that I had seen his face!"

Eustacia awoke. The cracking had been that of the window-shutter downstairs, which the maid-servant was opening to let in the day, now slowly increasing to Nature's meagre allowance at this sickly time of the year. "O that I had seen his face!" she said again. " 'Twas meant for Mr. Yeobright!"

When she became cooler she perceived that many of the phases of the dream had naturally arisen out of the images and fancies of the day before. But this detracted little from its interest, which lay in the excellent fuel it provided for newly kindled fervour. She was at the modulating point between indifference and love, at the stage called "having a fancy for." It occurs once in the history of the most gigantic passions, and it is a period when they are in the hands of the weakest will.

The perfervid woman was by this time half in love with a vision. The fantastic nature of her passion, which lowered her as an intellect, raised her as a soul. If she had had a little more self-control she would have attenuated the emotion to nothing by sheer reasoning, and so have killed it off. If she had had a little less pride she might have gone and circumambulated the Yeobrights' premises at Blooms-End at any maidenly sacrifice until she had seen him. But Eustacia did neither of these things. She acted as the most exemplary might have acted, being so influenced; she took an airing twice or thrice a day upon the Egdon hills, and kept her eyes employed.

The first occasion passed, and he did not come that way.

She promenaded a second time, and was again the sole wanderer there.

The third time there was a dense fog: she looked around, but without much hope. Even if he had been walking within twenty yards of her she could not have seen him.

At the fourth attempt to encounter him it began to rain in torrents, and she turned back.

The fifth sally was in the afternoon: it was fine, and she remained out long, walking to the very top of the valley in which Blooms-End lay. She saw the white paling about half a mile off; but he did not appear. It was almost with heart-sickness that she came home, and with a sense of shame at her weakness. She resolved to look for the man from Paris no more.

But Providence is nothing if not coquettish; and no sooner had Eustacia formed this resolve than the opportunity came which, while sought, had been entirely withholden.

IV

EUSTACIA IS LED ON TO AN ADVENTURE

IN THE EVENING OF THIS LAST DAY OF EXPECTATION, WHICH WAS THE TWENTY-THIRD OF December, Eustacia was at home alone. She had passed the recent hour in lamenting over a rumour newly come to her ears—that Yeobright's visit to his mother was to be of short duration, and would end some time the next week. "Naturally," she said to herself. A man in the full swing of his activities in a gay city could not afford to linger long on Egdon Heath. That she would behold face to face the owner of the awakening voice within the limits of such a holiday was most unlikely, unless she were to haunt the environs of his mother's house like a robin, to do which was difficult and unseemly.

The customary expedient of provincial girls and men in such circumstances is church-going. In an ordinary village or country town one can safely calculate that, either on Christmas-day or the Sunday contiguous, any native home for the holidays, who has not through age or *ennui* lost the appetite for seeing and being seen, will turn up in some pew or other, shining with hope, self-consciousness, and new clothes. Thus the congregation on Christmas morning is mostly a Tussaud collection of celebrities who have been born in the neighbourhood. Hither the mistress, left neglected at home all the year, can steal and observe the development of the returned lover who has forgotten her, and think as she watches him over her Prayer-book that he may throb with a renewed fidelity when novelties have lost their charm. And hither a comparatively recent settler like Eustacia may be-

take herself to scrutinise the person of a native son who left home before her advent upon
the scene, and consider if the friendship of his parents be worth cultivating during his next
absence in order to secure a knowledge of him on his next return.

But these tender schemes were not feasible among the scattered inhabitants of Egdon
Heath. In name they were parishioners, but virtually they belonged to no parish at all. People who came to these few isolated houses to keep Christmas with their friends remained
in their friends' chimney-corners drinking mead and other comforting liquors till they left
again for good and all. Rain, snow, ice, mud everywhere around, they did not care to
trudge two or three miles to sit wet-footed and splashed to the nape of their necks among
those who, though in some measure neighbours, lived close to the church, and entered it
clean and dry. Eustacia knew it was ten to one that Clym Yeobright would go to no church
at all during his few days of leave, and that it would be a waste of labour for her to go driving the pony and gig over a bad road in hope to see him there.

It was dusk, and she was sitting by the fire in the dining-room or hall, which they occupied at this time of the year in preference to the parlour, because of its large hearth, constructed for turf-fires, a fuel the captain was partial to in the winter season. The only
visible articles in the room were those on the window-sill, which showed their shapes
against the low sky: the middle article being the old hour-glass, and the other two a pair of
ancient British urns which had been dug from a barrow near, and were used as flower-pots
for two razor-leaved cactuses. Somebody knocked at the door. The servant was out; so was
her grand-father. The person, after waiting a minute, came in and tapped at the door of
the room.

"Who's there?" said Eustacia.

"Please, Cap'n Vye, will you let us—"

Eustacia arose and went to the door. "I cannot allow you to come in so boldly. You
should have waited."

"The cap'n said I might come in without any fuss," was answered in a lad's pleasant
voice.

"Oh, did he?" said Eustacia more gently. "What do you want, Charley?"

"Please will your grand-father lend us his fuel-house to try over our parts in, to-night
at seven o'clock?"

"What, are you one of the Egdon mummers for this year?"

"Yes, miss. The cap'n used to let the old mummers practise here."

"I know it. Yes, you may use the fuel-house if you like," said Eustacia languidly.

The choice of Captain Vye's fuel-house as the scene of rehearsal was dictated by the
fact that his dwelling was nearly in the centre of the heath. The fuel-house was as roomy
as a barn, and was a most desirable place for such a purpose. The lads who formed the
company of players lived at different scattered points around, and by meeting in this spot
the distances to be traversed by all the comers would be about equally proportioned.

Of mummers and mumming Eustacia had the greatest contempt. The mummers
themselves were not afflicted with any such feeling for their art, though at the same time
they were not enthusiastic. A traditional pastime is to be distinguished from a mere revival
in no more striking feature than in this, that while in the revival all is excitement and fervour, the survival is carried on with a stolidity and absence of stir which sets one wondering why a thing that is done so perfunctorily should be kept up at all. Like Balaam and

other unwilling prophets, the agents seem moved by an inner compulsion to say and do their allotted parts whether they will or no. This unweeting manner of performance is the true ring by which, in this refurbishing age, a fossilised survival may be known from a spurious reproduction.

The piece was the well-known play of *Saint George*, and all who were behind the scenes assisted in the preparations, including the women of each household. Without the cooperation of sisters and sweethearts the dresses were likely to be a failure; but on the other hand, this class of assistance was not without its drawbacks. The girls could never be brought to respect tradition in designing and decorating the armour; they insisted on attaching loops and bows of silk and velvet in any situation pleasing to their taste. Gorget, gusset, basinet, cuirass, gauntlet, sleeve, all alike in the view of these feminine eyes were practicable spaces whereon to sew scraps of fluttering colour.

It might be that Joe, who fought on the side of Christendom, had a sweetheart, and that Jim, who fought on the side of the Moslem, had one likewise. During the making of the costumes it would come to the knowledge of Joe's sweetheart that Jim's was putting brilliant silk scallops at the bottom of her lover's surcoat, in addition to the ribbons of the visor, the bars of which, being invariably formed of coloured strips about half an inch wide hanging before the face, were mostly of that material. Joe's sweetheart straightway placed brilliant silk on the scallops of the hem in question, and, going a little further, added ribbon tufts to the shoulder-pieces. Jim's, not to be outdone, would affix bows and rosettes everywhere.

The result was that in the end the Valiant Soldier, of the Christian army, was distinguished by no peculiarity of accoutrement from the Turkish Knight; and what was worse, on a casual view Saint George himself might be mistaken for his deadly enemy, the Saracen. The guisers themselves, though inwardly regretting this confusion of persons, could not afford to offend those by whose assistance they so largely profited, and the innovations were allowed to stand.

There was, it is true, a limit to this tendency to uniformity. The Leech or Doctor preserved his character intact: his darker habiliments, peculiar hat, and the bottle of physic slung under his arm, could never be mistaken. And the same might be said of the conventional figure of Father Christmas, with his gigantic club, an older man, who accompanied the band as general protector in long night journeys from parish to parish, and was bearer of the purse.

Seven o'clock, the hour of the rehearsal, came round, and in a short time Eustacia could hear voices in the fuel-house. To dissipate in some trifling measure her abiding sense of the murkiness of human life she went to the "linhay" or lean-to shed, which formed the root-store of their dwelling and abutted on the fuel-house. Here was a small rough hole in the mud wall, originally made for pigeons, through which the interior of the next shed could be viewed. A light came from it now; and Eustacia stepped upon a stool to look in upon the scene.

On a ledge in the fuel-house stood three tall rushlights, and by the light of them seven or eight lads were marching about, haranguing, and confusing each other, in endeavours to perfect themselves in the play. Humphrey and Sam, the furze- and turf-cutters, were there looking on, so also was Timothy Fairway, who leant against the wall and prompted the boys from memory, interspersing among the set words remarks and anecdotes of the superior days when he and others were the Egdon mummers-elect that these lads were now.

"Well, ye be as well up to it as ever ye will be," he said. "Not that such mumming would have passed in our time. Harry as the Saracen should strut a bit more, and John needn't holler his inside out. Beyond that perhaps you'll do. Have you got all your clothes ready?"

"We shall by Monday."

"Your first outing will be Monday night, I suppose?"

"Yes. At Mrs. Yeobright's."

"Oh, Mrs. Yeobright's. What makes her want to see ye? I should think a middle-aged woman was tired of mumming."

"She's got up a bit of a party, because 'tis the first Christmas that her son Clym has been home for a long time."

"To be sure, to be sure—her party! I am going myself. I almost forgot it, upon my life."

Eustacia's face flagged. There was to be a party at the Yeobrights'; she, naturally, had nothing to do with it. She was a stranger to all such local gatherings, and had always held them as scarcely appertaining to her sphere. But had she been going, what an opportunity would have been afforded her of seeing the man whose influence was penetrating her like summer sun! To increase that influence was coveted excitement; to cast it off might be to regain serenity; to leave it as it stood was tantalising.

The lads and men prepared to leave the premises, and Eustacia returned to her fire-side. She was immersed in thought, but not for long. In a few minutes the lad Charley, who had come to ask permission to use the place, returned with the key to the kitchen. Eustacia heard him, and opening the door into the passage said, "Charley, come here."

The lad was surprised. He entered the front-room not without blushing; for he, like many, had felt the power of this girl's face and form.

She pointed to a seat by the fire, and entered the other side of the chimney-corner herself. It could be seen in her face that whatever motive she might have had in asking the youth indoors would soon appear.

"Which part do you play, Charley—the Turkish Knight, do you not?" enquired the beauty, looking across the smoke of the fire to him on the other side.

"Yes, miss, the Turkish Knight," he replied diffidently.

"Is yours a long part?"

"Nine speeches, about."

"Can you repeat them to me? If so I should like to hear them."

The lad smiled into the glowing turf and began—

> *Here come I, a Turkish Knight,*
> *Who learnt in Turkish land to fight,*

continuing the discourse throughout the scenes to the concluding catastrophe of his fall by the hand of Saint George.

Eustacia had occasionally heard the part recited before. When the lad ended she began, precisely in the same words, and ranted on without hitch or divergence till she too reached the end. It was the same thing, yet how different. Like in form, it had the added softness and finish of a Raffaelle after Perugino, which, while faithfully reproducing the original subject, entirely distances the original art.

Charley's eyes rounded with surprise. "Well, you be a clever lady!" he said, in admiration. "I've been three weeks learning mine."

"I have heard it before," she quietly observed. "Now, would you do anything to please me, Charley?"

"I'd do a good deal, miss."

"Would you let me play your part for one night?"

"O, miss! But your woman's gown—you couldn't."

"I can get boy's clothes—at least all that would be wanted besides the mumming dress. What should I have to give you to lend me your things, to let me take your place for an hour or two on Monday night, and on no account to say a word about who or what I am? You would, of course, have to excuse yourself from playing that night, and to say that somebody—a cousin of Miss Vye's—would act for you. The other mummers have never spoken to me in their lives, so that it would be safe enough; and if it were not, I should not mind. Now, what must I give you to agree to this? Half-a-crown?"

The youth shook his head

"Five shillings?"

He shook his head again. "Money won't do it," he said, brushing the iron head of the fire-dog with the hollow of his hand.

"What will, then, Charley?" said Eustacia in a disappointed tone.

"You know what you forbade me at the may-poling, miss," murmured the lad, without looking at her, and still stroking the fire-dog's head.

"Yes," said Eustacia, with a little more hauteur. "You wanted to join hands with me in the ring, if I recollect?"

"Half an hour of that, and I'll agree, miss."

Eustacia regarded the youth steadfastly. He was three years younger than herself, but apparently not backward for his age. "Half an hour of what?" she said, though she guessed what.

"Holding your hand in mine."

She was silent. "Make it a quarter of an hour," she said

"Yes, Miss Eustacia—I will, if I may kiss it too. A quarter of an hour. And I'll swear to do the best I can to let you take my place without anybody knowing. Don't you think somebody might know your tongue, miss?"

"It is possible. But I will put a pebble in my mouth to make is less likely. Very well; you shall be allowed to have my hand as soon as you bring the dress and your sword and staff. I don't want you any longer now."

Charley departed, and Eustacia felt more and more interest in life. Here was something to do: here was someone to see, and a charmingly adventurous way to see him. "Ah," she said to herself, "want of an object to live for—that's all is the matter with me!"

Eustacia's manner was as a rule of a slumberous sort, her passions being of the massive rather than the vivacious kind. But when aroused she would make a dash which, just for the time, was not unlike the move of a naturally lively person.

On the question of recognition she was somewhat indifferent. By the acting lads themselves she was not likely to be known. With the guests who might be assembled she was hardly so secure. Yet detection, after all, would be no such dreadful thing. The fact only could be detected, her true motive never. It would be instantly set down as the passing freak of a girl whose ways were already considered singular. That she was doing for an earnest reason what would most naturally be done in jest was at any rate a safe secret.

The next evening Eustacia stood punctually at the fuel-house door, waiting for the dusk which was to bring Charley with the trappings. Her grand-father was at home to-night, and she would be unable to ask her confederate indoors.

He appeared on the dark ridge of heathland, like a fly on a negro, bearing the articles with him, and came up breathless with his walk.

"Here are the things," he whispered, placing them upon the threshold. "And now, Miss Eustacia——"

"The payment. It is quite ready. I am as good as my word."

She leant against the doorpost, and gave him her hand. Charley took it in both his own with a tenderness beyond description, unless it was like that of a child holding a captured sparrow.

"Why, there's a glove on it!" he said in a deprecating way.

"I have been walking," she observed.

"But, miss!"

"Well—it is hardly fair." She pulled off the glove, and gave him her bare hand.

They stood together minute after minute, without further speech, each looking at the blackening scene, and each thinking his and her own thoughts.

"I think I won't use it all up to-night," said Charley devotedly, when six or eight minutes had been passed by him caressing her hand. "May I have the other few minutes another time?"

"As you like," said she without the least emotion. "But it must be over in a week. Now, there is only one thing I want you to do: to wait while I put on the dress, and then to see if I do my part properly. But let me look first indoors."

She vanished for a minute or two, and went in. Her grand-father was safely asleep in his chair. "Now, then," she said, on returning, "walk down the garden a little way, and when I am ready I'll call you."

Charley walked and waited, and presently heard a soft whistle. He returned to the fuel-house door.

"Did you whistle, Miss Vye?"

"Yes; come in," reached him in Eustacia's voice from a back quarter. "I must not strike a light till the door is shut, or it may be seen shining. Push your hat into the hole through to the wash-house, if you can feel your way across."

Charley did as commanded, and she struck the light revealing herself to be changed in sex, brilliant in colours, and armed from top to toe. Perhaps she quailed a little under Charley's vigorous gaze, but whether any shyness at her male attire appeared upon her countenance could not be seen by reason of the strips of ribbon which used to cover the face in mumming costumes, representing the barred visor of the medieval helmet.

"It fits pretty well," she said, looking down at the white overalls, "except that the tunic, or whatever you call it, is long in the sleeve. The bottom of the overalls I can turn up inside. Now pay attention."

Eustacia then proceeded in her delivery, striking the sword against the staff or lance at the minatory phrases, in the orthodox mumming manner, and strutting up and down. Charley seasoned his admiration with criticism of the gentlest kind, for the touch of Eustacia's hand yet remained with him.

"And now for your excuse to the others," she said. "Where do you meet before you go to Mrs. Yeobright's?"

"We thought of meeting here, miss, if you have nothing to say against it. At eight o'clock, so as to get there by nine."

"Yes. Well, you of course must not appear. I will march in about five minutes late, ready-dressed, and tell them that you can't come. I have decided that the best plan will be for you to be sent somewhere by me, to make a real thing of the excuse. Our two heath-croppers are in the habit of straying into the meads, and to-morrow evening you can go and see if they are gone there. I'll manage the rest. Now you may leave me."

"Yes, miss. But I think I'll have one minute more of what I am owed, if you don't mind."

Eustacia gave him her hand as before.

"One minute," she said, and counted on till she reached seven or eight minutes. Hand and person she then withdrew to a distance of several feet, and recovered some of her old dignity. The contract completed, she raised between them a barrier impenetrable as a wall.

"There, 'tis all gone; and I didn't mean quite all," he said, with a sigh.

"You had good measure," said she, turning away.

"Yes, miss. Well, 'tis over, and now I'll get home-along."

V

THROUGH THE MOONLIGHT

THE NEXT EVENING THE MUMMERS WERE ASSEMBLED IN THE SAME SPOT, AWAITING THE entrance of the Turkish Knight.

"Twenty minutes after eight by the Quiet Woman, and Charley not come."

"Ten minutes past by Blooms-End."

"It wants ten minutes to, by Grandfer Cantle's watch."

"And 'tis five minutes past by the captain's clock."

On Egdon there was no absolute hour of the day. The time at any moment was a number of varying doctrines professed by the different hamlets, some of them having originally grown up from a common root, and then become divided by secession, some having been alien from the beginning. West Egdon believed in Blooms-End time, East Egdon in the time of the Quiet Woman Inn. Grandfer Cantle's watch had numbered many followers in years gone by, but since he had grown older faiths were shaken. Thus, the mummers having gathered hither from scattered points, each came with his own tenets on early and late; and they waited a little longer as a compromise.

Eustacia had watched the assemblage through the hole; and seeing that now was the proper moment to enter, she went from the "linhay" and boldly pulled the bobbin of the fuel-house door. Her grand-father was safe at the Quiet Woman.

"Here's Charley at last! How late you be, Charley."

" 'Tis not Charley," said the Turkish Knight from within his visor. " 'Tis a cousin of Miss Vye's, come to take Charley's place from curiosity. He was obliged to go and look for the heath-croppers that have got into the meads, and I agreed to take his place, as he knew he couldn't come back here again to-night. I know the part as well as he."

Her graceful gait, elegant figure, and dignified manner in general won the mummers to the opinion that they had gained by the exchange, if the new-comer were perfect in his part.

"It don't matter—if you be not too young," said Saint George. Eustacia's voice had sounded somewhat more juvenile and fluty than Charley's.

"I know every word of it, I tell you," said Eustacia decisively. Dash being all that was required to carry her triumphantly through, she adopted as much as was necessary. "Go ahead, lads, with the try-over. I'll challenge any of you to find a mistake in me."

The play was hastily rehearsed, whereupon the other mummers were delighted with the new knight. They extinguished the candles at half-past eight, and set out upon the heath in the direction of Mrs. Yeobright's house at Bloom's-End.

There was a slight hoar-frost that night, and the moon, though not more than half full, threw a spirited and enticing brightness upon the fantastic figures of the mumming band, whose plumes and ribbons rustled in their walk like autumn leaves. Their path was not over Rainbarrow now, but down a valley which left that ancient elevation a little to the east. The bottom of the vale was green to a width of ten yards or thereabouts, and the shining facets of frost upon the blades of grass seemed to move on with the shadows of those they surrounded. The masses of furze and heath to the right and left were dark as ever; a mere half-moon was powerless to silver such sable features as theirs.

Half an hour of walking and talking brought them to the spot in the valley where the grass riband widened and led down to the front of the house. At sight of the place Eustacia, who had felt a few passing doubts during her walk with the youths, again was glad that the adventure had been undertaken. She had come out to see a man who might possibly have the power to deliver her soul from a most deadly oppression. What was Wildeve? Interesting, but inadequate. Perhaps she would see a sufficient hero to-night.

As they drew nearer to the front of the house the mummers became aware that music and dancing were briskly flourishing within. Every now and then a long low note from the serpent, which was the chief wind instrument played at these times, advanced further into the heath than the thin treble part, and reached their ears alone; and next a more than usual loud tread from a dancer would come the same way. With nearer approach these fragmentary sounds became pieced together, and were found to be the salient points of the tune called "Nancy's Fancy."

He was there, of course. Who was she that he danced with? Perhaps some unknown woman, far beneath herself in culture, was by the most subtle of lures sealing his fate this very instant. To dance with a man is to concentrate a twelvemonth's regulation fire upon him in the fragment of an hour. To pass to courtship without acquaintance, to pass to marriage without courtship, is a skipping of terms reserved for those alone who tread this royal road. She would see how his heart lay by keen observation of them all.

The enterprising lady followed the mumming company through the gate in the white paling, and stood before the open porch. The house was encrusted with heavy thatchings, which dropped between the upper windows: the front, upon which the moonbeams directly played, had originally been white; but a huge pyracanth now darkened the greater portion.

It became at once evident that the dance was proceeding immediately within the surface of the door, no apartment intervening. The brushing of skirts and elbows, sometimes the bumping of shoulders, could be heard against the very panels. Eustacia, though living within two miles of the place, had never seen the interior of this quaint old habitation. Between Captain Vye and the Yeobrights there had never existed much acquaintance, the former having come as a stranger and purchased the long-empty house at Mistover Knap not long before the death of Mrs. Yeobright's husband; and with that event and the departure of her son such friendship as had grown up became quite broken off.

"Is there no passage inside the door, then?" asked Eustacia as they stood within the porch.

"No," said the lad who played the Saracen. "The door opens right upon the front sitting-room, where the spree's going on."

"So that we cannot open the door without stopping the dance."

"That's it. Here we must bide till they have done, for they always bolt the back door after dark."

"They won't be much longer," said Father Christmas.

This assertion, however, was hardly borne out by the event. Again the instruments ended the tune; again they recommenced with as much fire and pathos as if it were the first strain. The air was now that one without any particular beginning, middle, or end, which perhaps, among all the dances which throng an inspired fiddler's fancy, best conveys the idea of the interminable—the celebrated "Devil's Dream." The fury of personal movement that was kindled by the fury of the notes could be approximately imagined by these outsiders under the moon, from the occasional kicks of toes and heels against the door, whenever the whirl round had been of more than customary velocity.

The first five minutes of listening was interesting enough to the mummers. The five minutes extended to ten minutes, and these to a quarter of an hour; but no signs of ceasing were audible in the lively Dream. The bumping against the door, the laughter, the stamping, were all as vigorous as ever, and the pleasure in being outside lessened considerably.

"Why does Mrs. Yeobright give parties of this sort?" Eustacia asked, a little surprised to hear merriment so pronounced.

"It is not one of her bettermost parlour-parties. She's asked the plain neighbours and workpeople without drawing any lines, just to give 'em a good supper and such like. Her son and she wait upon the folks."

"I see," said Eustacia.

" 'Tis the last strain, I think," said Saint George, with his ear to the panel. "A young man and woman have just swung into this corner, and he's saying to her, 'Ah, the pity; 'tis over for us this time, my own.' "

"Thank God," said the Turkish Knight, stamping, and taking from the wall the conventional staff that each of the mummers carried. Her boots being thinner than those of the young men, the hoar had damped her feet and made them cold.

"Upon my song 'tis another ten minutes for us," said the Valiant Soldier, looking through the keyhole as the tune modulated into another without stopping. "Grandfer Cantle is standing in this corner, waiting his turn."

" 'Twon't be long; 'tis a six-handed reel," said the Doctor.

"Why not go in, dancing or no? They sent for us," said the Saracen.

"Certainly not," said Eustacia authoritatively, as she paced smartly up and down from door to gate to warm herself. "We should burst into the middle of them and stop the dance, and that would be unmannerly."

"He thinks himself somebody because he has had a bit more schooling than we," said the Doctor.

"You may go to the deuce!" said Eustacia.

There was a whispered conversation between three or four of them, and one turned to her.

"Will you tell us one thing?" he said, not without gentleness. "Be you Miss Vye? We think you must be."

"You may think what you like," said Eustacia slowly. "But honourable lads will not tell tales upon a lady."

"We'll say nothing, miss. That's upon our honour."

"Thank you," she replied.

At this moment the fiddles finished off with a screech, and the serpent emitted a last note that nearly lifted the roof. When, from the comparative quiet within, the mummers judged that the dancers had taken their seats, Father Christmas advanced, lifted the latch, and put his head inside the door.

"Ah, the mummers, the mummers!" cried several guests at once. "Clear a space for the mummers."

Hump-backed Father Christmas then made a complete entry, swinging his huge club, and in a general way clearing the stage for the actors proper, while he informed the company in smart verse that he was come, welcome or welcome not; concluding his speech with

> *Make room, make room, my gallant boys,*
> *And give us space to rhyme;*
> *We've come to show Saint George's play,*
> *Upon this Christmas time.*

The guests were now arranging themselves at one end of the room, the fiddler was mending a string, the serpent-player was emptying his mouthpiece, and the play began. First of those outside the Valiant Soldier entered, in the interest of Saint George—

> *Here come I, the Valiant Soldier;*
> *Slasher is my name;*

and so on. This speech concluded with a challenge to the infidel, at the end of which it was Eustacia's duty to enter as the Turkish Knight. She, with the rest who were not yet on, had hitherto remained in the moonlight which streamed under the porch. With no apparent effort or backwardness she came in, beginning—

> *Here come I, a Turkish Knight,*
> *Who learnt in Turkish land to fight;*
> *I'll fight this man with courage bold:*
> *If his blood's hot I'll make it cold!*

During her declamation Eustacia held her head erect, and spoke as roughly as she could, feeling pretty secure from observation. But the concentration upon her part necessary to prevent discovery, the newness of the scene, the shine of the candles, and the confusing effect upon her vision of the ribboned visor which hid her features, left her absolutely unable to perceive who were present as spectators. On the further side of a table bearing candles she could faintly discern faces, and that was all.

Meanwhile Jim Starks as the Valiant Soldier had come forward, and, with a glare upon the Turk, replied—

> *If, then, thou art that Turkish Knight,*
> *Draw out thy sword, and let us fight!*

And fight they did; the issue of the combat being that the Valiant Soldier was slain by a preternaturally inadequate thrust from Eustacia, Jim, in his ardour for genuine histrionic art, coming down like a log upon the stone floor with force enough to dislocate his shoulder. Then, after more words from the Turkish Knight, rather too faintly delivered, and statements that he'd fight Saint George and all his crew, Saint George himself magnificently entered with the well-known flourish—

> *Here come I, Saint George, the valiant man,*
> *With naked sword and spear in hand,*
> *Who fought the dragon and brought him to the slaughter,*
> *And by this won fair Sabra, the King of Egypt's daughter;*
> *What mortal man would dare to stand*
> *Before me with my sword in hand?*

This was the lad who had first recognised Eustacia; and when she now, as the Turk, replied with suitable defiance, and at once began the combat, the young fellow took especial care to use his sword as gently as possible. Being wounded, the Knight fell upon one knee, according to the direction. The Doctor now entered, restored the Knight by giving him a draught from the bottle which he carried, and the fight was again resumed, the Turk sinking by degrees until quite overcome—dying as hard in this venerable drama as he is said to do at the present day.

This gradual sinking to the earth was, in fact, one reason why Eustacia had thought that the part of the Turkish Knight, though not the shortest, would suit her best. A direct fall from upright to horizontal, which was the end of the other fighting characters, was not an elegant or decorous part for a girl. But it was easy to die like a Turk, by a dogged decline.

Eustacia was now among the number of the slain, though not on the floor, for she had managed to sink into a sitting position against the clock-case, so that her head was well elevated. The play proceeded between Saint George, the Saracen, the Doctor, and Father Christmas; and Eustacia, having no more to do, for the first time found leisure to observe the scene round, and to search for the form that had drawn her hither.

VI

THE TWO STAND FACE TO FACE

THE ROOM HAD BEEN ARRANGED WITH A VIEW TO THE DANCING, THE LARGE OAK TABLE having been moved back till it stood as a breastwork to the fireplace. At each end, behind, and in the chimney-corner were grouped the guests, many of them being warm-faced and panting, among whom Eustacia cursorily recognised some well-to-do persons from beyond the heath. Thomasin, as she had expected, was not visible, and Eustacia recollected that a light had shone from an upper window when they were outside—the window, probably, of Thomasin's room. A nose, chin, hands, knees, and toes projected from the seat within the chimney opening, which members she found to unite in the person of Grandfer Cantle, Mrs. Yeobright's occasional assistant in the garden, and therefore one of the invited. The smoke went up from an Etna of turf in front of him, played round the notches of the chimney-crook, struck against the salt-box, and got lost among the flitches.

Another part of the room soon riveted her gaze. At the other side of the chimney stood the settle, which is the necessary supplement to a fire so open that nothing less than a strong breeze will carry up the smoke. It is, to the hearths of old-fashioned cavernous fireplaces, what the east belt of trees is to the exposed country estate, or the north wall to the garden. Outside the settle candles gutter, locks of hair wave, young women shiver, and old men sneeze. Inside is Paradise. Not a symptom of a draught disturbs the air; the sitters' backs are as warm as their faces, and songs and old tales are drawn from the occupants by the comfortable heat, like fruit from melon-plants in a frame.

It was, however, not with those who sat in the settle that Eustacia was concerned. A face showed itself with marked distinctness against the dark-tanned wood of the upper part. The owner, who was leaning against the settle's outer end, was Clement Yeobright, or Clym, as he was called here; she knew it could be nobody else. The spectacle constituted an area of two feet in Rembrandt's intensest manner. A strange power in the lounger's appearance lay in the fact that, though his whole figure was visible, the observer's eye was only aware of his face.

To one of middle age the countenance was that of a young man, though a youth might hardly have seen any necessity for the term of immaturity. But it was really one of those faces which convey less the idea of so many years as its age than of so much experience as its store. The number of their years may have adequately summed up Jared, Mahalaleel, and the rest of the antediluvians, but the age of a modern man is to be measured by the intensity of his history.

The face was well shaped, even excellently. But the mind within was beginning to use it as a mere waste tablet whereon to trace its idiosyncrasies as they developed themselves. The beauty here visible would in no long time be ruthlessly overrun by its parasite, thought, which might just as well have fed upon a plainer exterior where there was nothing it could harm. Had Heaven preserved Yeobright from a wearing habit of meditation, people would have said, "A handsome man." Had his brain unfolded under sharper contours they would have said, "A thoughtful man." But an inner strenuousness was preying upon an outer symmetry, and they rated his look as singular.

Hence people who began by beholding him ended by perusing him. His countenance was overlaid with legible meanings. Without being thought-worn he yet had certain marks derived from a perception of his surroundings, such as are not unfrequently found on men at the end of the four or five years of endeavour which follow the close of placid pupilage. He already showed that thought is a disease of flesh, and indirectly bore evidence that ideal physical beauty is incompatible with emotional development and a full recognition of the coil of things. Mental luminousness must be fed with the oil of life, even though there is already a physical need for it; and the pitiful sight of two demands on one supply was just showing itself here.

When standing before certain men the philosopher regrets that thinkers are but perishable tissue, the artist that perishable tissue has to think. Thus to deplore, each from his point of view, the mutually destructive interdependence of spirit and flesh would have been instinctive with these in critically observing Yeobright.

As for his look, it was a natural cheerfulness striving against depression from without, and not quite succeeding. The look suggested isolation, but it revealed something more. As is usual with bright natures, the deity that lies ignominiously chained within an ephemeral human carcase shone out of him like a ray.

The effect upon Eustacia was palpable. The extraordinary pitch of excitement that she had reached beforehand would, indeed, have caused her to be influenced by the most commonplace man. She was troubled at Yeobright's presence.

The remainder of the play ended: the Saracen's head was cut off, and Saint George stood as victor. Nobody commented, any more than they would have commented on the fact of mushrooms coming in autumn or snowdrops in spring. They took the piece as phlegmatically as did the actors themselves. It was a phase of cheerfulness which was, as a matter of course, to be passed through every Christmas; and there was no more to be said.

They sang the plaintive chant which follows the play, during which all the dead men rise to their feet in a silent and awful manner, like the ghosts of Napoleon's soldiers in the Midnight Review. Afterwards the door opened, and Fairway appeared on the threshold, accompanied by Christian and another. They had been waiting outside for the conclusion of the play, as the players had waited for the conclusion of the dance.

"Come in, come in," said Mrs. Yeobright; and Clym went forward to welcome them. "How is it you are so late? Grandfer Cantle has been here ever so long, and we thought you'd have come with him, as you live so near one another."

"Well, I should have come earlier," Mr. Fairway said, and paused to look along the beam of the ceiling for a nail to hang his hat on; but, finding his accustomed one to be occupied by the mistletoe, and all the nails in the walls to be burdened with bunches of holly, he at last relieved himself of the hat by ticklishly balancing it between the candle-box and the head of the clock-case. "I should have come earlier, ma'am," he resumed, with a more composed air, "but I know what parties be, and how there's none too much room in folks' houses at such times, so I thought I wouldn't come till you'd got settled a bit."

"And I thought so too, Mrs. Yeobright," said Christian earnestly; "but Father there was so eager that he had no manners at all, and left home almost afore 'twas dark. I told him 'twas barely decent in a' old man to come so oversoon; but words be wind."

"Klk! I wasn't going to bide waiting about, till half the game was over! I'm as light as a kite when anything's going on!" crowed Grandfer Cantle from the chimney-seat.

Fairway had meanwhile concluded a critical gaze at Yeobright. "Now, you may not believe it," he said to the rest of the room, "but I should never have knowed this gentleman if I had met him anywhere off his own he'th: he's altered so much."

"You too have altered, and for the better, I think, Timothy," said Yeobright, surveying the firm figure of Fairway.

"Master Yeobright, look me over too. I have altered for the better, haven't I, hey?" said Grandfer Cantle, rising, and placing himself something above half a foot from Clym's eye, to induce the most searching criticism.

"To be sure we will," said Fairway, taking the candle and moving it over the surface of the Grandfer's countenance, the subject of his scrutiny irradiating himself with light and pleasant smiles, and giving himself jerks of juvenility.

"You haven't changed much," said Yeobright.

"If there's any difference, Grandfer is younger," appended Fairway decisively.

"And yet not my own doing, and I feel no pride in it," said the pleased ancient. "But I can't be cured of my vagaries; them I plead guilty to. Yes, Master Cantle always was that, as we know. But I am nothing by the side of you, Mister Clym."

"Nor any o' us," said Humphrey, in a low rich tone of admiration, not intended to reach anybody's ears.

"Really, there would have been nobody here who could have stood as decent second to him, or even third, if I hadn't been a soldier in the Bang-up Locals (as we was called for our smartness)," said Grandfer Cantle. "And even as 'tis we all look a little scammish beside him. But in the year four 'twas said there wasn't a finer figure in the whole South Wessex than I, as I looked when dashing past the shop-winders with the rest of our company on the day we ran out o' Budmouth because it was thoughted that Boney had landed round the point. There was I, straight as a young poplar, wi' my firelock, and my bagnet, and my spatterdashes, and my stock sawing my jaws off, and my accoutrements sheening like the seven stars! Yes, neighbours, I was a pretty sight in my soldiering days. You ought to have seen me in four!"

" 'Tis his mother's side where Master Clym's figure comes from, bless ye," said Timothy. "I know'd her brothers well. Longer coffins were never made in the whole country of South Wessex, and 'tis said that poor George's knees were crumpled up a little e'en as 'twas."

"Coffins, where?" enquired Christian, drawing nearer. "Have the ghost of one appeared to anybody, Master Fairway?"

"No, no. Don't let your mind so mislead your ears, Christian; and be a man," said Timothy reproachfully.

"I will." said Christian. "But now I think o't my shadder last night seemed just the shape of a coffin. What is it a sign of when your shade's like a coffin, neighbours? It can't be nothing to be afeared of, I suppose?"

"Afeared, no!" said the Grandfer. "Faith, I was never afeard of nothing except Boney, or I shouldn't ha' been the soldier I was. Yes, 'tis a thousand pities you didn't see me in four!"

By this time the mummers were preparing to leave; but Mrs. Yeobright stopped them by asking them to sit down and have a little supper. To this invitation Father Christmas, in the name of them all, readily agreed.

Eustacia was happy in the opportunity of staying a little longer. The cold and frosty night without was doubly frigid to her. But the lingering was not without its difficulties. Mrs. Yeobright, for want of room in the larger apartment, placed a bench for the mummers immediately inside the pantry-door, which opened from the sitting-room. Here they seated themselves in a row, the door being left open; thus they were still virtually in the same apartment. Mrs. Yeobright now murmured a few words to her son, who crossed the room to the pantry, striking his head against the mistletoe as he passed, and brought the mummers beef and bread, cake, pastry, mead, and elder-wine, the waiting being done by him and his mother, that the little maid-servant might sit as guest. The mummers doffed their helmets, and began to eat and drink.

"But you will surely have some?" said Clym to the Turkish Knight, as he stood before that warrior, tray in hand. She had refused, and still sat covered, only the sparkle of her eyes being visible between the ribbons which covered her face.

"None, thank you," replied Eustacia.

"He's quite a youngster," said the Saracen apologetically, "and you must excuse him. He's not one of the old set, but have jined us because t'other couldn't come."

"But he will take something?" persisted Yeobright. "Try a glass of mead or elder-wine."

"Yes, you had better try that," said the Saracen. "It will keep the cold out going home-along."

Though Eustacia could not eat without uncovering her face she could drink easily enough beneath her disguise. The elder-wine was accordingly accepted, and the glass vanished inside the ribbons.

At moments during this performance Eustacia was half in doubt about the security of her position; yet it had a fearful joy. A series of attentions paid to her, and yet not to her but to some imaginary person, by the first man she had ever been inclined to adore, complicated her emotions indescribably. She had loved him partly because he was exceptional in this scene, partly because she had determined to love him, chiefly because she was in desperate need of loving somebody after wearying of Wildeve. Believing that she must love him in spite of herself, she had been influenced after the fashion of the second Lord Lyttleton and other persons, who have dreamed that they were to die on a certain day, and by stress of a morbid imagination have actually brought about that event. Once let a maiden admit the possibility of her being stricken with love for someone at a certain hour and place, and the thing is as good as done.

Did anything at this moment suggest to Yeobright the sex of the creature whom that fantastic guise enclosed, how extended was her scope both in feeling and in making others feel, and how far her compass transcended that of her companions in the band? When the disguised Queen of Love appeared before Æneas a preternatural perfume accompanied her presence and betrayed her quality. If such a mysterious emanation ever was projected by the emotions of an earthly woman upon their object, it must have signified Eustacia's presence to Yeobright now. He looked at her wistfully, then seemed to fall into a reverie, as if he were forgetting what he observed. The momentary situation ended, he passed on, and Eustacia sipped her wine without knowing what she drank. The man for whom she had predetermined to nourish a passion went into the small room, and across it to the further extremity.

The mummers, as has been stated, were seated on a bench, one end of which extended into the small apartment, or pantry, for want of space in the outer room. Eustacia, partly from shyness, had chosen the innermost seat, which thus commanded a view of the interior of the pantry as well as the room containing the guests. When Clym passed down the pantry her eyes followed him in the gloom which prevailed there. At the remote end was a door which, just as he was about to open it for himself, was opened by somebody within; and light streamed forth.

The person was Thomasin, with a candle, looking anxious, pale, and interesting. Yeobright appeared glad to see her, and pressed her hand. "That's right, Tamsie," he said heartily, as though recalled to himself by the sight of her: "you have decided to come down. I am glad of it."

"Hush—no, no," she said quickly. "I only came to speak to you."

"But why not join us?"

"I cannot. At least I would rather not. I am not well enough, and we shall have plenty of time together now you are going to be home a good long holiday."

"It isn't nearly so pleasant without you. Are you really ill?"

"Just a little, my old cousin—here," she said, playfully sweeping her hand across her heart.

"Ah, Mother should have asked somebody else to be present to-night, perhaps?"

"O no, indeed. I merely stepped down, Clym, to ask you—" Here he followed her through the doorway into the private room beyond, and, the door closing, Eustacia and the mummer who sat next to her, the only other witness of the performance, saw and heard no more.

The heat flew to Eustacia's head and cheeks. She instantly guessed that Clym, having been home only these two or three days, had not as yet been made acquainted with Thomasin's painful situation with regard to Wildeve; and seeing her living there just as she had been living before he left home, he naturally suspected nothing. Eustacia felt a wild jealousy of Thomasin on the instant. Though Thomasin might possibly have tender sentiments towards another man as yet, how long could they be expected to last when she was shut up here with this interesting and travelled cousin of hers? There was no knowing what affection might not soon break out between the two, so constantly in each other's society, and not a distracting object near. Clym's boyish love for her might have languished, but it might easily be revived again.

Eustacia was nettled by her own contrivances. What a sheer waste of herself to be dressed thus while another was shining to advantage! Had she known the full effect of the encounter she would have moved heaven and earth to get here in a natural manner. The power of her face all lost, the charm of her emotions all disguised, the fascinations of her coquetry denied existence, nothing but a voice left to her: she had a sense of the doom of Echo. "Nobody here respects me," she said. She had overlooked the fact that, in coming as a boy among other boys, she would be treated as a boy. The slight, though of her own causing, and self-explanatory, she was unable to dismiss as unwittingly shown, so sensitive had the situation made her.

Women have done much for themselves in histrionic dress. To look far below those who, like a certain fair personator of Polly Peachum early in the last century, and another of Lydia Languish early in this, have won not only love but ducal coronets into the bargain, whole shoals of them have reached to the initial satisfaction of getting love almost whence they would. But the Turkish Knight was denied even the chance of achieving this by the fluttering ribbons which she dared not brush aside.

Yeobright returned to the room without his cousin. When within two or three feet of Eustacia he stopped, as if again arrested by a thought. He was gazing at her. She looked another way, disconcerted, and wondered how long this purgatory was to last. After lingering a few seconds he passed on again.

To court their own discomfiture by love is a common instinct with certain perfervid women. Conflicting sensations of love, fear, and shame reduced Eustacia to a state of the utmost uneasiness. To escape was her great and immediate desire. The other mummers appeared to be in no hurry to leave; and murmuring to the lad who sat next to her that she preferred waiting for them outside the house, she moved to the door as imperceptibly as possible, opened it, and slipped out.

The calm, lone scene reassured her. She went forward to the palings and leant over them, looking at the moon. She had stood thus but a little time when the door again opened. Expecting to see the remainder of the band Eustacia turned; but no—Clym Yeobright came out as softly as she had done, and closed the door behind him.

He advanced and stood beside her. "I have an odd opinion," he said, "and should like to ask you a question. Are you a woman—or am I wrong?"

"I am a woman."

His eyes lingered on her with great interest. "Do girls often play as mummers now? They never used to."

"They don't now."

"Why did you?"

"To get excitement and shake off depression," she said in low tones.

"What depressed you?"

"Life."

"That's a cause of depression a good many have to put up with."

"Yes."

A long silence. "And do you find excitement?" asked Clym at last.

"At this moment, perhaps."

"Then you are vexed at being discovered?"

"Yes; though I thought I might be."

"I would gladly have asked you to our party had I known you wished to come. Have I ever been acquainted with you in my youth?"

"Never."

"Won't you come in again, and stay as long as you like?"

"No. I wish not to be further recognised."

"Well, you are safe with me." After remaining in thought a minute he added gently, "I will not intrude upon you longer. It is a strange way of meeting, and I will not ask why I find a cultivated woman playing such a part as this."

She did not volunteer the reason which he seemed to hope for, and he wished her good-night, going thence round to the back of the house, where he walked up and down by himself for some time before re-entering.

Eustacia, warmed with an inner fire, could not wait for her companions after this. She flung back the ribbons from her face, opened the gate, and at once struck into the heath. She did not hasten along. Her grand-father was in bed at this hour, for she so frequently walked upon the hills on moonlight nights that he took no notice of her comings and goings, and, enjoying himself in his own way, left her to do likewise. A more important subject than that of getting indoors now engrossed her. Yeobright, if he had the least curiosity, would infallibly discover her name. What then? She first felt a sort of exultation at the way in which the adventure had terminated, even though at moments between her exultations she was abashed and blushful. Then this consideration recurred to chill her: What was the use of her exploit? She was at present a total stranger to the Yeobright family. The unreasonable nimbus of romance with which she had encircled that man might be her misery. How could she allow herself to become so infatuated with a stranger? And to fill the cup of her sorrow there would be Thomasin, living day after day in inflammable proximity to him; for she had just learnt that, contrary to her first belief, he was going to stay at home some considerable time.

She reached the wicket at Mistover Knap, but before opening it she turned and faced the heath once more. The form of Rainbarrow stood above the hills, and the moon stood above Rainbarrow. The air was charged with silence and frost. The scene reminded Eustacia of a circumstance which till that moment she had totally forgotten. She had promised to meet Wildeve by the Barrow this very night at eight, to give a final answer to his pleading for an elopement.

She herself had fixed the evening and the hour. He had probably come to the spot, waited there in the cold, and been greatly disappointed.

"Well, so much the better: it did not hurt him," she said serenely. Wildeve had at present the rayless outline of the sun through smoked glass, and she could say such things as that with the greatest facility.

She remained deeply pondering; and Thomasin's winning manner towards her cousin arose again upon Eustacia's mind.

"O that she had been married to Damon before this!" she said. "And she would if it hadn't been for me! If I had only known—if I had only known!"

Eustacia once more lifted her deep stormy eyes to the moonlight, and, sighing that tragic sigh of hers which was so much like a shudder, entered the shadow of the roof. She threw off her trappings in the outhouse, rolled them up, and went indoors to her chamber.

VII

A COALITION BETWEEN BEAUTY AND ODDNESS

THE OLD CAPTAIN'S PREVAILING INDIFFERENCE TO HIS GRAND-DAUGHTER'S MOVEMENTS left her free as a bird to follow her own courses; but it so happened that he did take upon himself the next morning to ask her why she had walked out so late.

"Only in search of events, grand-father," she said, looking out of the window with that drowsy latency of manner which discovered so much force behind it whenever the trigger was pressed.

"Search of events—one would think you were one of the bucks I knew at one and twenty."

"It is lonely here."

"So much the better. If I were living in a town my whole time would be taken up in looking after you. I fully expected you would have been home when I returned from the Woman."

"I won't conceal what I did. I wanted an adventure, and I went with the mummers. I played the part of the Turkish Knight."

"No, never? Ha, ha! Good gad! I didn't expect it of you, Eustacia."

"It was my first performance, and it certainly will be my last. Now I have told you— and remember it is a secret."

"Of course. But, Eustacia, you never did—ha! ha! Dammy, how 'twould have pleased me forty years ago! But remember, no more of it, my girl. You may walk on the heath night or day, as you choose, so that you don't bother me; but no figuring in breeches again."

"You need have no fear for me, grand-papa."

Here the conversation ceased, Eustacia's moral training never exceeding in severity a dialogue of this sort, which, if it ever became profitable to good works, would be a result not dear at the price. But her thoughts soon strayed far from her own personality; and, full of a passionate and indescribable solicitude for one to whom she was not even a name, she went forth into the amplitude of tanned wild around her, restless as Ahasuerus the Jew. She was about half a mile from her residence when she beheld a sinister redness arising from a ravine a little way in advance—dull and lurid like a flame in sunlight, and she guessed it to signify Diggory Venn.

When the farmers who had wished to buy in a new stock of reddle during the last month had enquired where Venn was to be found, people replied, "On Egdon Heath." Day after day the answer was the same. Now, since Egdon was populated with heath-croppers and furze-cutters rather than with sheep and shepherds, and the downs where most of the latter were to be found lay some to the north, some to the west of Egdon, his reason for camping about there like Israel in Zin was not apparent. The position was central and occasionally desirable. But the sale of reddle was not Diggory's primary object in remaining on the heath, particularly at so late a period of the year, when most travellers of his class had gone into winter quarters.

Eustacia looked at the lonely man. Wildeve had told her at their last meeting that Venn had been thrust forward by Mrs. Yeobright as one ready and anxious to take his place as Thomasin's betrothed. His figure was perfect, his face young and well outlined, his eye bright, his intelligence keen, and his position one which he could readily better if he chose. But in spite of possibilities it was not likely that Thomasin would accept this Ishmaelitish creature while she had a cousin like Yeobright at her elbow, and Wildeve at the same time not absolutely indifferent. Eustacia was not long in guessing that poor Mrs. Yeobright, in her anxiety for her niece's future, had mentioned this lover to stimulate the zeal of the other. Eustacia was on the side of the Yeobrights now, and entered into the spirit of the aunt's desire.

"Good-morning, miss," said the reddleman, taking off his cap of hareskin, and apparently bearing her no ill-will from recollection of their last meeting.

"Good-morning, reddleman," she said, hardly troubling to lift her heavily shaded eyes to his. "I did not know you were so near. Is your van here too?"

Venn moved his elbow towards a hollow in which a dense brake of purple-stemmed brambles had grown to such vast dimensions as almost to form a dell. Brambles, though churlish when handled, are kindly shelter in early winter, being the latest of the deciduous bushes to lose their leaves. The roof and chimney of Venn's caravan showed behind the tracery and tangles of the brake.

"You remain near this part?" she asked with more interest.

"Yes, I have business here."

"Not altogether the selling of reddle?"

"It has nothing to do with that."

"It has to do with Miss Yeobright?"

Her face seemed to ask for an armed peace, and he therefore said frankly, "Yes, miss; it is on account of her."

"On account of your approaching marriage with her?"

Venn flushed through his stain. "Don't make sport of me, Miss Vye," he said.

"It isn't true?"

"Certainly not."

She was thus convinced that the reddleman was a mere *pis aller* in Mrs. Yeobright's mind; one, moreover, who had not even been informed of his promotion to that lowly standing. "It was a mere notion of mine," she said quietly; and was about to pass by without further speech, when, looking round to the right, she saw a painfully well-known figure serpentining upwards by one of the little paths which led to the top where she stood. Owing to the necessary windings of his course his back was at present towards them. She glanced quickly round; to escape that man there was only one way. Turning to Venn, she said, "Would you allow me to rest a few minutes in your van? The banks are damp for sitting on."

"Certainly, miss; I'll make a place for you."

She followed him behind the dell of brambles to his wheeled dwelling, into which Venn mounted, placing the three-legged stool just within the door.

"That is the best I can do for you," he said, stepping down and retiring to the path, where he resumed the smoking of his pipe as he walked up and down.

Eustacia bounded into the vehicle and sat on the stool, ensconced from view on the side towards the trackway. Soon she heard the brushing of other feet than the reddleman's, a not very friendly "Good-day" uttered by two men in passing each other, and then the dwindling of the footfall of one of them in a direction onwards. Eustacia stretched her neck forward till she caught a glimpse of a receding back and shoulders; and she felt a wretched twinge of misery, she knew not why. It was the sickening feeling which, if the changed heart has any generosity at all in its composition, accompanies the sudden sight of a once-loved one who is beloved no more.

When Eustacia descended to proceed on her way the reddleman came near. "That was Mr. Wildeve who passed, miss," he said slowly, and expressed by his face that he expected her to feel vexed at having been sitting unseen.

"Yes, I saw him coming up the hill," replied Eustacia. "Why should you tell me that?" It was a bold question, considering the reddleman's knowledge of her past love; but her undemonstrative manner had power to repress the opinions of those she treated as remote from her.

"I am glad to hear that you can ask it," said the reddleman bluntly. "And, now I think of it, it agrees with what I saw last night."

"Ah—what was that?" Eustacia wished to leave him, but wished to know.

"Mr. Wildeve stayed at Rainbarrow a long time waiting for a lady who didn't come."

"You waited too, it seems?"

"Yes, I always do. I was glad to see him disappointed. He will be there again to-night."

"To be again disappointed. The truth is, reddleman, that that lady, so far from wishing to stand in the way of Thomasin's marriage with Mr. Wildeve, would be very glad to promote it."

Venn felt much astonishment at this avowal, though he did not show it clearly; that exhibition may greet remarks which are one remove from expectation, but it is usually withheld in complicated cases of two removes and upwards. "Indeed, miss," he replied.

"How do you know that Mr. Wildeve will come to Rainbarrow again to-night?" she asked.

"I heard him say to himself that he would. He's in a regular temper."

Eustacia looked for a moment what she felt, and she murmured, lifting her deep dark eyes anxiously to his, "I wish I knew what to do. I don't want to be uncivil to him; but I don't wish to see him again; and I have some few little things to return to him."

"If you choose to send 'em by me, miss, and a note to tell him that you wish to say no more to him, I'll take it for you quite privately. That would be the most straightforward way of letting him know your mind."

"Very well," said Eustacia. "Come towards my house, and I will bring it out to you."

She went on, and as the path was an infinitely small parting in the shaggy locks of the heath, the reddleman followed exactly in her trail. She saw from a distance that the captain was on the bank sweeping the horizon with his telescope; and bidding Venn to wait where he stood, she entered the house alone.

In ten minutes she returned with a parcel and a note, and said, in placing them in his hand, "Why are you so ready to take these for me?"

"Can you ask that?"

"I suppose you think to serve Thomasin in some way by it. Are you as anxious as ever to help on her marriage?"

Venn was a little moved. "I would sooner have married her myself," he said in a low voice. "But what I feel is that if she cannot be happy without him I will do my duty in helping her to get him, as a man ought."

Eustacia looked curiously at the singular man who spoke thus. What a strange sort of love, to be entirely free from that quality of selfishness which is frequently the chief constituent of the passion, and sometimes its only one! The reddleman's disinterestedness was so well deserving of respect that it overshot respect by being barely comprehended; and she almost thought it absurd.

"Then we are both of one mind at last," she said.

"Yes," replied Venn gloomily. "But if you would tell me, miss, why you take such an interest in her, I should be easier. It is so sudden and strange."

Eustacia appeared at a loss. "I cannot tell you that, reddleman," she said coldly.

Venn said no more. He pocketed the letter, and, bowing to Eustacia, went away.

Rainbarrow had again become blended with night when Wildeve ascended the long acclivity at its base. On his reaching the top a shape grew up from the earth immediately behind him. It was that of Eustacia's emissary. He slapped Wildeve on the shoulder. The feverish young innkeeper and ex-engineer started like Satan at the touch of Ithuriel's spear.

"The meeting is always at eight o'clock, at this place," said Venn, "and here we are—we three."

"We three?" said Wildeve, looking quickly round.

"Yes; you, and I, and she. This is she." He held up the letter and parcel.

Wildeve took them wonderingly. "I don't quite see what this means," he said. "How do you come here? There must be some mistake."

"It will be cleared from your mind when you have read the letter. Lanterns for one." The reddleman struck a light, kindled an inch of tallow-candle which he had brought, and sheltered it with his cap.

"Who are you?" said Wildeve, discerning by the candle-light an obscure rubicundity of person in his companion. "You are the reddleman I saw on the hill this morning—why, you are the man who—"

"Please read the letter."

"If you had come from the other one I shouldn't have been surprised," murmured Wildeve as he opened the letter and read. His face grew serious.

To Mr. Wildeve—After some thought I have decided once and for all that we must hold no further communication. The more I consider the matter the more I am convinced that there must be an end to our acquaintance. Had you been uniformly faithful to me throughout these two years you might now have some ground for accusing me of heartlessness; but if you calmly consider what I bore during the period of your desertion, and how I passively put up with your courtship of another without once interfering, you will, I think, own that I have a right to consult my own feelings when you come back to me again. That these are not what they were towards you may, perhaps, be a fault in me, but it is one which you can scarcely reproach me for when you remember how you left me for Thomasin.

The little articles you gave me in the early part of our friendship are returned by the bearer of this letter. They should rightly have been sent back when I first heard of your engagement to her.

                                                                    EUSTACIA

By the time that Wildeve reached her name the blankness with which he had read the first half of the letter intensified to mortification. "I am made a great fool of, one way and another," he said pettishly. "Do you know what is in this letter?"

The reddleman hummed a tune.

"Can't you answer me?" asked Wildeve warmly.

"Ru-um-tum-tum," sang the reddleman.

Wildeve stood looking on the ground beside Venn's feet, till he allowed his eyes to travel upwards over Diggory's form, as illuminated by the candle, to his head and face. "Ha-ha! Well, I suppose I deserve it, considering how I have played with them both," he said at last, as much to himself as to Venn. "But of all the odd things that ever I knew, the oddest is that you should so run counter to your own interests as to bring this to me."

"My interests?"

"Certainly. 'Twas your interest not to do anything which would send me courting Thomasin again, now she has accepted you—or something like it. Mrs. Yeobright says you are to marry her. 'Tisn't true, then?"

"Good Lord! I heard of this before, but didn't believe it. When did she say so?"

Wildeve began humming as the reddleman had done.

"I don't believe it now," cried Venn.

"Ru-um-tum-tum," sang Wildeve.

"O Lord—how we can imitate!" said Venn contemptuously. "I'll have this out. I'll go straight to her."

Diggory withdrew with an emphatic step, Wildeve's eye passing over his form in withering derision, as if he were no more than a heath-cropper. When the reddleman's figure could no longer be seen, Wildeve himself descended and plunged into the rayless hollow of the vale.

To lose the two women—he who had been the well-beloved of both—was too ironical an issue to be endured. He could only decently save himself by Thomasin; and once he became her husband, Eustacia's repentance, he thought, would set in for a long and bitter term. It was no wonder that Wildeve, ignorant of the new man at the back of the scene, should have supposed Eustacia to be playing a part. To believe that the letter was not the result of some momentary pique, to infer that she really gave him up to Thomasin, would have required previous knowledge of her transfiguration by that man's influence. Who was to know that she had grown generous in the greediness of a new passion, that in coveting one cousin she was dealing liberally with another, that in her eagerness to appropriate she gave way?

Full of this resolve to marry in haste, and wring the heart of the proud girl, Wildeve went his way.

Meanwhile Diggory Venn had returned to his van, where he stood looking thoughtfully into the stove. A new vista was opened up to him. But, however promising Mrs. Yeobright's views of him might be as a candidate for her niece's hand, one condition was indispensable to the favour of Thomasin herself, and that was a renunciation of his present wild mode of life. In this he saw little difficulty.

He could not afford to wait till the next day before seeing Thomasin and detailing his plan. He speedily plunged himself into toilet operations, pulled a suit of cloth clothes from a box, and in about twenty minutes stood before the van-lantern as a reddleman in nothing but his face, the vermilion shades of which were not to be removed in a day. Closing the door and fastening it with a padlock, Venn set off towards Blooms-End.

He had reached the white palings and laid his hand upon the gate when the door of the house opened, and quickly closed again. A female form had glided in. At the same time a man, who had seemingly been standing with the woman in the porch, came forward from the house till he was face to face with Venn. It was Wildeve again.

"Man alive, you've been quick at it," said Diggory sarcastically.

"And you slow, as you will find," said Wildeve. "And," lowering his voice, "you may as well go back again now. I've claimed her, and got her. Good-night, reddleman!" Thereupon Wildeve walked away.

Venn's heart sank within him, though it had not risen unduly high. He stood leaning over the palings in an indecisive mood for nearly a quarter of an hour. Then he went up the garden-path, knocked, and asked for Mrs. Yeobright.

Instead of requesting him to enter, she came to the porch. A discourse was carried on between them in low measured tones for the space of ten minutes or more. At the end of the time Mrs. Yeobright went in, and Venn sadly retraced his steps into the heath. When he had again regained his van he lit the lantern, and with an apathetic face at once began to pull off his best clothes, till in the course of a few minutes he reappeared as the confirmed and irretrievable reddleman that he had seemed before.

VIII

FIRMNESS IS DISCOVERED IN A GENTLE HEART

ON THAT EVENING THE INTERIOR OF BLOOMS-END, THOUGH COSY AND COMFORTABLE, had been rather silent. Clym Yeobright was not at home. Since the Christmas party he had gone on a few days' visit to a friend about ten miles off.

The shadowy form seen by Venn to part from Wildeve in the porch, and quickly withdraw into the house, was Thomasin's. On entering she threw down a cloak which had been carelessly wrapped round her, and came forward to the light, where Mrs. Yeobright sat at her work-table, drawn up within the settle, so that part of it projected into the chimney-corner.

"I don't like your going out after dark alone, Tamsin," said her aunt quietly, without looking up from her work.

"I have only been just outside the door."

"Well?" enquired Mrs. Yeobright, struck by a change in the tone of Thomasin's voice, and observing her. Thomasin's cheek was flushed to a pitch far beyond that which it had reached before her troubles, and her eyes glittered.

"It was *he* who knocked," she said.

"I thought as much."

"He wishes the marriage to be at once."

"Indeed! What—is he anxious?" Mrs. Yeobright directed a searching look upon her niece. "Why did not Mr. Wildeve come in?"

"He did not wish to. You are not friends with him, he says. He would like the wedding to be the day after to-morrow, quite privately; at the church of his parish—not at ours."

"Oh! And what did you say?"

"I agreed to it," Thomasin answered firmly. "I am a practical woman now. I don't believe in hearts at all. I would marry him under any circumstances since—since Clym's letter."

A letter was lying on Mrs. Yeobright's work-basket, and at Thomasin's words her aunt reopened it, and silently read for the tenth time that day:—

What is the meaning of this silly story that people are circulating about Thomasin and Mr. Wildeve? I should call such a scandal humiliating if there was the least chance of its being true. How could such a gross falsehood have arisen? It is said that one should go abroad to hear news of home, and I appear to have done it. Of course I contradict the tale everywhere; but it is very vexing, and I wonder how it could have originated. It is too ridiculous that such a girl as Thomasin could so mortify us as to get jilted on the wedding-day. What has she done?

"Yes," Mrs. Yeobright said sadly, putting down the letter. "If you think you can marry him, do so. And since Mr. Wildeve wishes it to be unceremonious, let it be that too. I can do nothing. It is all in your own hands now. My power over your welfare came to an end when you left this house to go with him to Anglebury." She continued, half in bitterness, "I may almost ask, why do you consult me in the matter at all? If you had gone and married him without saying a word to me, I could hardly have been angry—simply because, poor girl, you can't do a better thing."

"Don't say that and dishearten me."

"You are right: I will not."

"I do not plead for him, aunt. Human nature is weak, and I am not a blind woman to insist that he is perfect. I did think so, but I don't now. But I know my course, and you know that I know it. I hope for the best."

"And so do I, and we will both continue to," said Mrs. Yeobright, rising and kissing her. "Then the wedding, if it comes off, will be on the morning of the very day Clym comes home?"

"Yes. I decided that it ought to be over before he came. After that you can look him in the face, and so can I. Our concealments will matter nothing."

Mrs. Yeobright moved her head in thoughtful assent, and presently said, "Do you wish me to give you away? I am willing to undertake that, you know, if you wish, as I was last time. After once forbidding the banns, I think I can do no less."

"I don't think I will ask you to come," said Thomasin reluctantly, but with decision. "It would be unpleasant, I am almost sure. Better let there be only strangers present, and none of my relations at all. I would rather have it so. I do not wish to do anything which may touch your credit, and I feel that I should be uncomfortable if you were there, after what has passed. I am only your niece, and there is no necessity why you should concern yourself more about me."

"Well, he has beaten us," her aunt said. "It really seems as if he had been playing with you in this way in revenge for my humbling him as I did by standing up against him at first."

"O no, aunt," murmured Thomasin.

They said no more on the subject then. Diggory Venn's knock came soon after; and Mrs. Yeobright, on returning from her interview with him in the porch, carelessly observed, "Another lover has come to ask for you."

"No?"

"Yes; that queer young man Venn."

"Asks to pay his addresses to me?"

"Yes; and I told him he was too late."

Thomasin looked silently into the candle-flame. "Poor Diggory!" she said, and then aroused herself to other things.

The next day was passed in mere mechanical deeds of preparation, both the women being anxious to immerse themselves in these to escape the emotional aspect of the situation. Some wearing apparel and other articles were collected anew for Thomasin, and remarks on domestic details were frequently made, so as to obscure any inner misgivings about her future as Wildeve's wife.

The appointed morning came. The arrangement with Wildeve was that he should meet her at the church to guard against any unpleasant curiosity which might have affected them had they been seen walking off together in the usual country way.

Aunt and niece stood together in the bedroom where the bride was dressing. The sun, where it could catch it, made a mirror of Thomasin's hair, which she always wore braided. It was braided according to a calendric system: the more important the day the more numerous the strands in the braid. On ordinary working-days she braided it in threes; on ordinary Sundays in fours; at May-polings, gypsyings, and the like, she braided it in fives. Years ago she had said that when she married she would braid it in sevens. She had braided it in sevens to-day.

"I have been thinking that I will wear my blue silk after all," she said. "It *is* my wedding day, even though there may be something sad about the time. I mean," she added, anxious to correct any wrong impression, "not sad in itself, but in its having had great disappointment and trouble before it."

Mrs. Yeobright breathed in a way which might have been called a sigh. "I almost wish Clym had been at home," she said. "Of course you chose the time because of his absence."

"Partly. I have felt that I acted unfairly to him in not telling him all; but, as it was done not to grieve him, I thought I would carry out the plan to its end, and tell the whole story when the sky was clear."

"You are a practical little woman," said Mrs. Yeobright, smiling. "I wish you and he—no, I don't wish anything. There, it is nine o'clock," she interrupted, hearing a whizz and a dinging downstairs.

"I told Damon I would leave at nine," said Thomasin, hastening out of the room.

Her aunt followed. When Thomasin was going up the little walk from the door to the wicket gate, Mrs. Yeobright looked reluctantly at her, and said, "It is a shame to let you go alone."

"It is necessary," said Thomasin.

"At any rate," added her aunt with forced cheerfulness, "I shall call upon you this afternoon, and bring the cake with me. If Clym has returned by that time he will perhaps come too. I wish to show Mr. Wildeve that I bear him no ill-will. Let the past be forgotten.

Well, God bless you! There, I don't believe in old superstitions, but I'll do it." She threw a slipper at the retreating figure of the girl, who turned, smiled, and went on again.

A few steps further, and she looked back. "Did you call me, aunt?" she tremulously enquired. "Good-bye!"

Moved by an uncontrollable feeling as she looked upon Mrs. Yeobright's worn, wet face, she ran back, when her aunt came forward, and they met again. "O—Tamsie," said the elder, weeping, "I don't like to let you go."

"I—I am—" Thomasin began, giving way likewise. But, quelling her grief, she said "Good-bye!" again and went on.

Then Mrs. Yeobright saw a little figure wending its way between the scratching furze-bushes, and diminishing far up the valley—a pale-blue spot in a vast field of neutral brown, solitary and undefended except by the power of her own hope.

But the worst feature in the case was one which did not appear in the landscape; it was the man.

The hour chosen for the ceremony by Thomasin and Wildeve had been so timed as to enable her to escape the awkwardness of meeting her cousin Clym, who was returning the same morning. To own to the partial truth of what he had heard would be distressing as long as the humiliating position resulting from the event was unimproved. It was only after a second and successful journey to the altar that she could lift up her head and prove the failure of the first attempt a pure accident.

She had not been gone from Blooms-End more than half an hour when Yeobright came up the road from the other direction and entered the house.

"I had an early breakfast," he said to his mother after greeting her. "Now I could eat a little more."

They sat down to the repeated meal, and he went on in a low, anxious voice, apparently imagining that Thomasin had not yet come downstairs, "What's this I have heard about Thomasin and Mr. Wildeve?"

"It is true in many points," said Mrs. Yeobright quietly; "but it is all right now, I hope." She looked at the clock.

"True?"

"Thomasin is gone to him to-day."

Clym pushed away his breakfast. "Then there is a scandal of some sort, and that's what's the matter with Thomasin. Was it this that made her ill?"

"Yes. Not a scandal: a misfortune. I will tell you all about it, Clym. You must not be angry, but you must listen, and you'll find that what we have done has been done for the best."

She then told him the circumstances. All that he had known of the affair before he returned from Paris was that there had existed an attachment between Thomasin and Wildeve, which his mother had at first discountenanced, but had since, owing to the arguments of Thomasin, looked upon in a little more favourable light. When she, therefore, proceeded to explain all he was greatly surprised and troubled.

"And she determined that the wedding should be over before you came back," said Mrs. Yeobright, "that there might be no chance of her meeting you, and having a very painful time of it. That's why she has gone to him; they have arranged to be married this morning."

"But I can't understand it," said Yeobright, rising. " 'Tis so unlike her. I can see why you did not write to me after her unfortunate return home. But why didn't you let me know when the wedding was going to be—the first time?"

"Well, I felt vexed with her just then. She seemed to me to be obstinate; and when I found that you were nothing in her mind I vowed that she should be nothing in yours. I felt that she was only my niece after all; I told her she might marry, but that I should take no interest in it, and should not bother you about it either."

"It wouldn't have been bothering me. Mother, you did wrong."

"I thought it might disturb you in your business, and that you might throw up your situation, or injure your prospects in some way because of it, so I said nothing. Of course, if they had married at that time in a proper manner, I should have told you at once."

"Tamsin actually being married while we are sitting here!"

"Yes. Unless some accident happens again, as it did the first time. It may, considering he's the same man."

"Yes, and I believe it will. Was it right to let her go? Suppose Wildeve is really a bad fellow?"

"Then he won't come, and she'll come home again."

"You should have looked more into it."

"It is useless to say that," his mother answered, with an impatient look of sorrow. "You don't know how bad it has been here with us all these weeks, Clym. You don't know what a mortification anything of that sort is to a woman. You don't know the sleepless nights we've had in this house, and the almost bitter words that have passed between us since that Fifth of November. I hope never to pass seven such weeks again. Tamsin has not gone outside the door, and I have been ashamed to look anybody in the face; and now you blame me for letting her do the only thing that can be done to set that trouble straight."

"No," he said slowly. "Upon the whole I don't blame you. But just consider how sudden it seems to me. Here was I, knowing nothing; and then I am told all at once that Tamsie is gone to be married. Well, I suppose there was nothing better to do. Do you know, mother," he continued after a moment or two, looking suddenly interested in his own past history, "I once thought of Tamsin as a sweetheart? Yes, I did. How odd boys are! And when I came home and saw her this time she seemed so much more affectionate than usual, that I was quite reminded of those days, particularly on the night of the party, when she was unwell. We had the party just the same—was not that rather cruel to her?"

"It made no difference. I had arranged to give one, and it was not worthwhile to make more gloom than necessary. To begin by shutting ourselves up and telling you of Tamsin's misfortunes would have been a poor sort of welcome."

Clym remained thinking. "I almost wish you had not had that party," he said; "and for other reasons. But I will tell you in a day or two. We must think of Tamsin now."

They lapsed into silence. "I'll tell you what," said Yeobright again, in a tone which showed some slumbering feeling still. "I don't think it kind to Tamsin to let her be married like this, and neither of us there to keep up her spirits or care a bit about her. She hasn't disgraced herself, or done anything to deserve that. It is bad enough that the wedding should be so hurried and unceremonious, without our keeping away from it in addition. Upon my soul, 'tis almost a shame. I'll go."

"It is over by this time," said his mother with a sigh; "unless they were late, or he—"

"Then I shall be soon enough to see them come out. I don't quite like your keeping me in ignorance, mother, after all. Really, I half hope he has failed to meet her!"

"And ruined her character?"

"Nonsense: that wouldn't ruin Thomasin."

He took up his hat and hastily left the house. Mrs. Yeobright looked rather unhappy, and sat still, deep in thought. But she was not long left alone. A few minutes later Clym came back again, and in his company came Diggory Venn.

"I find there isn't time for me to get there," said Clym.

"Is she married?" Mrs. Yeobright enquired, turning to the reddleman a face in which a strange strife of wishes, for and against, was apparent.

Venn bowed. "She is, ma'am."

"How strange it sounds," murmured Clym.

"And he didn't disappoint her this time?" said Mrs. Yeobright.

"He did not. And there is now no slight on her name. I was hastening ath'art to tell you at once, as I saw you were not there."

"How came you to be there? How did you know it?" she asked.

"I have been in that neighbourhood for some time, and I saw them go in," said the reddleman. "Wildeve came up to the door, punctual as the clock. I didn't expect it of him." He did not add, as he might have added, that how he came to be in that neighbourhood was not by accident; that, since Wildeve's resumption of his right to Thomasin, Venn, with the thoroughness which was part of his character, had determined to see the end of the episode.

"Who was there?" said Mrs. Yeobright.

"Nobody hardly. I stood right out of the way, and she did not see me." The reddleman spoke huskily, and looked into the garden.

"Who gave her away?"

"Miss Vye."

"How very remarkable! Miss Vye! It is to be considered an honour, I suppose?"

"Who's Miss Vye?" said Clym.

"Captain Vye's grand-daughter, of Mistover Knap."

"A proud girl from Budmouth," said Mrs. Yeobright. "One not much to my liking. People say she's a witch, but of course that's absurd."

The reddleman kept to himself his acquaintance with that fair personage, and also that Eustacia was there because he went to fetch her, in accordance with a promise he had previously given as soon as he learnt that the marriage was to take place. He merely said, in continuation of the story—

"I was sitting on the churchyard-wall when they came up, one from one way, the other from the other; and Miss Vye was walking thereabouts, looking at the head-stones. As soon as they had gone in I went to the door, feeling I should like to see it, as I knew her so well. I pulled off my boots because they were so noisy, and went up into the gallery. I saw then that the parson and clerk were already there."

"How came Miss Vye to have anything to do with it, if she was only on a walk that way?"

"Because there was nobody else. She had gone into the church just before me, not into the gallery. The parson looked round before beginning, and as she was the only one near he beckoned to her, and she went up to the rails. After that, when it came to signing the book, she pushed up her veil and signed; and Tamsin seemed to thank her for her kindness." The reddleman told the tale thoughtfully, for there lingered upon his vision the changing colour of Wildeve, when Eustacia lifted the thick veil which had concealed her from recognition and looked calmly into his face. "And then," said Diggory sadly, "I came away, for her history as Tamsin Yeobright was over."

"I offered to go," said Mrs. Yeobright regretfully. "But she said it was not necessary."

"Well, it is no matter," said the reddleman. "The thing is done at last as it was meant to be at first, and God send her happiness. Now I'll wish you good-morning."

He placed his cap on his head and went out.

From that instant of leaving Mrs. Yeobright's door, the reddleman was seen no more in or about Egdon Heath for a space of many months. He vanished entirely. The nook among the brambles where his van had been standing was as vacant as ever the next morning, and scarcely a sign remained to show that he had been there, excepting a few straws, and a little redness on the turf, which was washed away by the next storm of rain.

The report that Diggory had brought of the wedding, correct as far as it went, was deficient in one significant particular, which had escaped him through his being at some distance back in the church. When Thomasin was tremblingly engaged in signing her name Wildeve had flung towards Eustacia a glance that said plainly, "I have punished you now." She had replied in a low tone—and he little thought how truly—"You mistake; it gives me sincerest pleasure to see her your wife to-day."

BOOK THIRD

THE FASCINATION

I

"My Mind to me a Kingdom is"

IN CLYM YEOBRIGHT'S FACE COULD BE DIMLY SEEN THE TYPICAL COUNTENANCE OF THE future. Should there be a classic period to art hereafter, its Pheidias may produce such faces. The view of life as a thing to be put up with, replacing that zest for existence which was so intense in early civilisations, must ultimately enter so thoroughly into the constitution of the advanced races that its facial expression will become accepted as a new artistic departure. People already feel that a man who lives without disturbing a curve of feature, or setting a mark of mental concern anywhere upon himself, is too far removed from modern perceptiveness to be a modern type. Physically beautiful men—the glory of the race when it was young—are almost an anachronism now; and we may wonder whether, at some time or other, physically beautiful women may not be an anachronism likewise.

The truth seems to be that a long line of disillusive centuries has permanently displaced the Hellenic idea of life, or whatever it may be called. What the Greeks only suspected we know well; what their Æschylus imagined our nursery children feel. That old-fashioned revelling in the general situation grows less and less possible as we uncover the defects of natural laws, and see the quandary that man is in by their operation.

The lineaments which will get embodied in ideals based upon this new recognition will probably be akin to those of Yeobright. The observer's eye was arrested, not by his face as a picture, but by his face as a page; not by what it was, but by what it recorded. His features were attractive in the light of symbols, as sounds intrinsically common become attractive in language, and as shapes intrinsically simple become interesting in writing.

He had been a lad of whom something was expected. Beyond this all had been chaos. That he would be successful in an original way, or that he would go to the dogs in an original way, seemed equally probable. The only absolute certainty about him was that he would not stand still in the circumstances amid which he was born.

Hence, when his name was casually mentioned by neighbouring yeomen, the listener said, "Ah, Clym Yeobright: what is he doing now?" When the instinctive question about a person is, What is he doing? it is felt that he will be found to be, like most of us, doing nothing in particular. There is an indefinite sense that he must be invading some region of singularity, good or bad. The devout hope is that he is doing well. The secret faith is that he is making a mess of it. Half-a-dozen comfortable market-men, who were habitual callers at the Quiet Woman as they passed by in their carts, were partial to the topic. In fact, though they were not Egdon men, they could hardly avoid it while they sucked their long clay tubes and regarded the heath through the window. Clym had been so inwoven with the heath in his boyhood that hardly anybody could look upon it without thinking of him. So the subject recurred: if he were making a fortune and a name, so much the better for him; if he were making a tragical figure in the world, so much the better for a narrative.

The fact was that Yeobright's fame had spread to an awkward extent before he left home. "It is bad when your fame outruns your means," said the Spanish Jesuit Gracian. At the age of six he had asked a Scripture riddle: "Who was the first man known to wear breeches?" and applause had resounded from the very verge of the heath. At seven he painted the Battle of Waterloo with tiger-lily pollen and black-currant juice, in the absence of water-colours. By the time he reached twelve he had in this manner been heard of as artist and scholar for at least two miles round. An individual whose fame spreads three or four thousand yards in the time taken by the fame of others similarly situated to travel six or eight hundred, must of necessity have something in him. Possibly Clym's fame, like Homer's, owed something to the accidents of his situation; nevertheless famous he was.

He grew up and was helped out in life. That waggery of fate which started Clive as a writing clerk, Gay as a linen-draper, Keats as a surgeon, and a thousand others in a thousand other odd ways, banished the wild and ascetic heath lad to a trade whose sole concern was with the especial symbols of self-indulgence and vainglory.

The details of this choice of a business for him it is not necessary to give. At the death of his father a neighbouring gentleman had kindly undertaken to give the boy a start; and this assumed the form of sending him to Budmouth. Yeobright did not wish to go there, but it was the only feasible opening. Thence he went to London; and thence, shortly after, to Paris, where he had remained till now.

Something being expected of him, he had not been at home many days before a great curiosity as to why he stayed on so long began to arise in the heath. The natural term of a holiday had passed, yet he still remained. On the Sunday morning following the week of Thomasin's marriage a discussion on this subject was in progress at a hair-cutting before Fairway's house. Here the local barbering was always done at this hour on this day; to be followed by the great Sunday wash of the inhabitants at noon, which in its turn was followed by the great Sunday dressing an hour later. On Egdon Heath Sunday proper did not begin till dinner-time, and even then it was a somewhat battered specimen of the day.

These Sunday-morning hair-cuttings were performed by Fairway; the victim sitting on a chopping-block in front of the house, without a coat, and the neighbours gossiping around, idly observing the locks of hair as they rose upon the wind after the snip, and flew away out of sight to the four quarters of the heavens. Summer and winter the scene was the same, unless the wind were more than usually blusterous, when the stool was shifted a few feet round the corner. To complain of cold in sitting out-of-doors, hatless and coatless, while Fairway told true stories between the cuts of the scissors, would have been to pronounce yourself no man at once. To flinch, exclaim, or move a muscle of the face at the small stabs under the ear received from those instruments, or at scarifications of the neck by the comb, would have been thought a gross breach of good manners, considering that Fairway did it all for nothing. A bleeding about the poll on Sunday afternoons was amply accounted for by the explanation, "I have had my hair cut, you know."

The conversation on Yeobright had been started by a distant view of the young man rambling leisurely across the heath before them.

"A man who is doing well elsewhere wouldn't bide here two or three weeks for nothing," said Fairway. "He's got some project in 's head—depend upon that."

"Well, 'a can't keep a diment shop here," said Sam.

"I don't see why he should have had them two heavy boxes home if he had not been going to bide; and what there is for him to do here the Lord in heaven knows."

Before many more surmises could be indulged in Yeobright had come near; and seeing the hair-cutting group he turned aside to join them. Marching up, and looking critically at their faces for a moment, he said, without introduction, "Now, folks, let me guess what you have been talking about."

"Ay, sure, if you will," said Sam.

"About me."

"Now, it is a thing I shouldn't have dreamed of doing, otherwise," said Fairway in a tone of integrity; "but since you have named it, Master Yeobright, I'll own that we was talking about 'ee. We were wondering what could keep you home here mollyhorning about when you have made such a world-wide name for yourself in the nick-nack trade— now, that's the truth o't."

"I'll tell you," said Yeobright, with unexpected earnestness. "I am not sorry to have the opportunity. I've come home because, all things considered, I can be a trifle less useless here than anywhere else. But I have only lately found this out. When I first got away from home I thought this place was not worth troubling about. I thought our life here was contemptible. To oil your boots instead of blacking them, to dust your coat with a switch instead of a brush: was there ever anything more ridiculous? I said."

"So 'tis; so 'tis!"

"No, no—you are wrong; it isn't."

"Beg your pardon, we thought that was your maning?"

"Well, this became very depressing as time went on. I found that I was trying to be like people who had hardly anything in common with myself. I was endeavouring to put off one sort of life for another sort of life, which was not better than the life I had known before. It was simply different."

"True; a sight different," said Fairway.

"Yes, Paris must be a taking place," said Humphrey. "Grand shop-winders, trumpets, and drums; and here be we out-of-doors in all winds and weathers—"

"But you mistake me," pleaded Clym. "All this was very depressing. But not so depressing as something I next perceived—that my business was the idlest, vainest, most effeminate business that ever a man could be put to. That decided me: I would give it up and try to follow some rational occupation among the people I knew best, and to whom I could be of most use. I have come home; and this is how I mean to carry out my plan. I shall keep a school as near to Egdon as possible, so as to be able to walk over here and have a night-school in my mother's house. But I must study a little at first, to get properly qualified. Now, neighbours, I must go."

And Clym resumed his walk across the heath.

"He'll never carry it out in the world," said Fairway. "In a few weeks he'll learn to see things otherwise."

" 'Tis good-hearted of the young man," said another. "But, for my part, I think he had better mind his business."

II

THE NEW COURSE CAUSES DISAPPOINTMENT

YEOBRIGHT LOVED HIS KIND. HE HAD A CONVICTION THAT THE WANT OF MOST MEN WAS knowledge of a sort which brings wisdom rather than affluence. He wished to raise the class at the expense of individuals rather than individuals at the expense of the class. What was more, he was ready at once to be the first unit sacrificed.

In passing from the bucolic to the intellectual life the intermediate stages are usually two at least, frequently many more; and one of those stages is almost sure to be worldly advanced. We can hardly imagine bucolic placidity quickening to intellectual aims without imagining social aims as the transitional phase. Yeobright's local peculiarity was that in striving at high thinking he still cleaved to plain living—nay, wild and meagre living in many respects, and brotherliness with clowns.

He was a John the Baptist who took ennoblement rather than repentance for his text. Mentally he was in a provincial future, that is, he was in many points abreast with the central town thinkers of his date. Much of this development he may have owed to his studious life in Paris, where he had become acquainted with ethical systems popular at the time.

In consequence of this relatively advanced position, Yeobright might have been called unfortunate. The rural world was not ripe for him. A man should be only partially before his time: to be completely to the vanward in aspirations is fatal to fame. Had Philip's warlike son been intellectually so far ahead as to have attempted civilisation without bloodshed, he would have been twice the godlike hero that he seemed, but nobody would have heard of an Alexander.

In the interests of renown the forwardness should lie chiefly in the capacity to handle things. Successful propagandists have succeeded because the doctrine they bring into form is that which their listeners have for some time felt without being able to shape. A man who advocates aesthetic effort and deprecates social effort is only likely to be understood by a class to which social effort has become a stale matter. To argue upon the possibility of culture before luxury to the bucolic world may be to argue truly, but it is an attempt to disturb a sequence to which humanity has been long accustomed. Yeobright preaching to the Egdon eremites that they might rise to a serene comprehensiveness without going through the process of enriching themselves was not unlike arguing to ancient Chaldeans that in ascending from earth to the pure empyrean it was not necessary to pass first into the intervening heaven of ether.

Was Yeobright's mind well-proportioned? No. A well-proportioned mind is one which shows no particular bias; one of which we may safely say that it will never cause its owner to be confined as a madman, tortured as a heretic, or crucified as a blasphemer. Also, on the other hand, that it will never cause him to be applauded as a prophet, revered as a priest, or exalted as a king. Its usual blessings are happiness and mediocrity. It produces the poetry of Rogers, the paintings of West, the statecraft of North, the spiritual guidance of Sumner; enabling its possessors to find their way to wealth, to wind up well, to step with dignity off the stage, to die comfortably in their beds, and to get the decent monument which, in many cases, they deserve. It never would have allowed Yeobright to do such a ridiculous thing as throw up his business to benefit his fellow-creatures.

He walked along towards home without attending to paths. If anyone knew the heath well, it was Clym. He was permeated with its scenes, with its substance, and with its odours. He might be said to be its product. His eyes had first opened thereon; with its appearance all the first images of his memory were mingled; his estimate of life had been coloured by it; his toys had been the flint knives and arrow-heads which he found there, wondering why stones should "grow" to such odd shapes; his flowers, the purple bells and yellow gorse; his animal kingdom, the snakes and croppers; his society, its human haunters. Take all the varying hates felt by Eustacia Vye towards the heath, and translate them into loves, and you have the heart of Clym. He gazed upon the wide prospect as he walked, and was glad.

To many persons this Egdon was a place which had slipped out of its century generations ago, to intrude as an uncouth object into this. It was an obsolete thing, and few cared to study it. How could this be otherwise in the days of square fields, plashed hedges, and meadows watered on a plan so rectangular that on a fine day they looked like silver gridirons? The farmer, in his ride, who could smile at artificial grasses, look with solicitude at the coming corn, and sigh with sadness at the fly-eaten turnips, bestowed upon the distant upland of heath nothing better than a frown. But as for Yeobright, when he looked from the heights on his way he could not help indulging in a barbarous satisfaction at observing that, in some of the attempts at reclamation from the waste, tillage, after holding on for a year or two, had receded again in despair, the ferns and furze-tufts stubbornly reasserting themselves.

He descended into the valley, and soon reached his home at Blooms-End. His mother was snipping dead leaves from the window-plants. She looked up at him as if she did not understand the meaning of his long stay with her; her face had worn that look for several days. He could perceive that the curiosity which had been shown by the hair-cutting group amounted in his mother to concern. But she had asked no question with her lips, even when the arrival of his trunks suggested that he was not going to leave her soon. Her silence besought an explanation of him more loudly than words.

"I am not going back to Paris again, mother," he said. "At least, in my old capacity. I have given up the business."

Mrs. Yeobright turned in pained surprise. "I thought something was amiss, because of the boxes. I wonder you did not tell me sooner."

"I ought to have done it. But I have been in doubt whether you would be pleased with my plan. I was not quite clear on a few points myself. I am going to take an entirely new course."

"I am astonished, Clym. How can you want to do better than you've been doing?"

"Very easily. But I shall not do better in the way you mean; I suppose it will be called doing worse. But I hate that business of mine, and I want to do some worthy thing before I die. As a schoolmaster I think to do it—a schoolmaster to the poor and ignorant, to teach them what nobody else will."

"After all the trouble that has been taken to give you a start, and when there is nothing to do but to keep straight on towards affluence, you say you will be a poor man's schoolmaster. Your fancies will be your ruin, Clym."

Mrs. Yeobright spoke calmly, but the force of feeling behind the words was but too apparent to one who knew her as well as her son did. He did not answer. There was in his face that hopelessness of being understood which comes when the objector is constitutionally beyond the reach of a logic that, even under favouring conditions, is almost too coarse a vehicle for the subtlety of the argument.

No more was said on the subject till the end of dinner. His mother then began, as if there had been no interval since the morning. "It disturbs me, Clym, to find that you have come home with such thoughts as those. I hadn't the least idea that you meant to go backward in the world by your own free choice. Of course, I have always supposed you were going to push straight on, as other men do—all who deserve the name—when they have been put in a good way of doing well."

"I cannot help it," said Clym, in a troubled tone. "Mother, I hate the flashy business. Talk about men who deserve the name, can any man deserving the name waste his time in that effeminate way, when he sees half the world going to ruin for want of somebody to buckle to and teach them how to breast the misery they are born to? I get up every morning and see the whole creation groaning and travailing in pain, as St. Paul says, and yet there am I, trafficking in glittering splendours with wealthy women and titled libertines, and pandering to the meanest vanities—I, who have health and strength enough for anything. I have been troubled in my mind about it all the year, and the end is that I cannot do it any more."

"Why can't you do it as well as others?"

"I don't know, except that there are many things other people care for which I don't; and that's partly why I think I ought to do this. For one thing, my body does not require much of me. I cannot enjoy delicacies; good things are wasted upon me. Well, I ought to turn that defect to advantage, and by being able to do without what other people require I can spend what such things cost upon anybody else."

Now, Yeobright, having inherited some of these very instincts from the woman before him, could not fail to awaken a reciprocity in her through her feelings, if not by arguments, disguise it as she might for his good. She spoke with less assurance. "And yet you might have been a wealthy man if you had only persevered. Manager to that large diamond establishment—what better can a man wish for? What a post of trust and respect! I suppose you will be like your father; like him, you are getting weary of doing well."

"No," said her son; "I am not weary of that, though I am weary of what you mean by it. Mother, what is doing well?"

Mrs. Yeobright was far too thoughtful a woman to be content with ready definitions, and, like the "What is wisdom?" of Plato's Socrates, and the "What is truth?" of Pontius Pilate, Yeobright's burning question received no answer.

The silence was broken by the clash of the garden gate, a tap at the door, and its opening. Christian Cantle appeared in the room in his Sunday clothes.

It was the custom on Egdon to begin the preface to a story before absolutely entering the house, so as to be well in for the body of the narrative by the time visitor and visited stood face to face. Christian had been saying to them while the door was leaving its latch, "To think that I, who go from home but once in a while, and hardly then, should have been there this morning!"

" 'Tis news you have brought us, then, Christian?" said Mrs. Yeobright.

"Ay, sure, about a witch, and ye must overlook my time o' day; for, says I, 'I must go and tell 'em, though they won't have half done dinner.' I assure ye it made me shake like a driven leaf. Do ye think any harm will come o't?"

"Well—what?"

"This morning at church we was all standing up, and the pa'son said, 'Let us pray.' 'Well,' thinks I, 'one may as well kneel as stand'; so down I went; and, more than that, all the rest were as willing to oblige the man as I. We hadn't been hard at it for more than a minute when a most terrible screech sounded through church, as if somebody had just gied up their heart's blood. All the folk jumped up, and then we found that Susan Nunsuch had pricked Miss Vye with a long stocking-needle, as she had threatened to do as soon as ever she could get the young lady to church, where she don't come very often. She've waited for this chance for weeks, so as to draw her blood and put an end to the bewitching of Susan's children that has been carried on so long. Sue followed her into church, sat next to her, and as soon as she could find a chance in went the stocking-needle into my lady's arm."

"Good heaven, how horrid!" said Mrs. Yeobright.

"Sue pricked her that deep that the maid fainted away; and as I was afeard there might be some tumult among us, I got behind the bass-viol and didn't see no more. But they carried her out into the air, 'tis said; but when they looked round for Sue she was gone. What a scream that girl gied, poor thing! There were the pa'son in his surplice holding up his hand and saying, 'Sit down, my good people, sit down!' But the deuce a bit would they sit down. O, and what d'ye think I found out, Mrs. Yeobright? The pa'son wears a suit of clothes under his surplice!—I could see his black sleeves when he held up his arm."

" 'Tis a cruel thing," said Yeobright.

"Yes," said his mother.

"The nation ought to look into it," said Christian. "Here's Humphrey coming, I think."

In came Humphrey. "Well, have ye heard the news? But I see you have. 'Tis a very strange thing that whenever one of Egdon folk goes to church some rum job or other is sure to go on. The last time one of us was there was when neighbour Fairway went in the fall; and that was the day you forbad the banns, Mrs. Yeobright."

"Has this cruelly treated girl been able to walk home?" said Clym.

"They say she got better, and went home very well. And now I've told it I must be moving homeward myself."

"And I," said Humphrey. "Truly now we shall see if there's anything in what folks say about her."

When they were gone into the heath again Yeobright said quietly to his mother, "Do you think I have turned teacher too soon?"

"It is right that there should be schoolmasters, and missionaries, and all such men," she replied. "But it is right, too, that I should try to lift you out of this life into something richer, and that you should not come back again, and be as if I had not tried at all."

Later in the day Sam, the turf-cutter, entered. "I've come a-borrowing, Mrs. Yeobright. I suppose you have heard what's been happening to the beauty on the hill?"

"Yes, Sam: half-a-dozen have been telling us."

"Beauty?" said Clym.

"Yes, tolerably well-favoured," Sam replied. "Lord! all the country owns that 'tis one of the strangest things in the world that such a woman should have come to live up there."

"Dark or fair?"

"Now, though I've seen her twenty times, that's a thing I cannot call to mind."

"Darker than Tamsin," murmured Mrs. Yeobright.

"A woman who seems to care for nothing at all, as you may say."

"She is melancholy, then?" enquired Clym.

"She mopes about by herself, and don't mix in with the people."

"Is she a young lady inclined for adventures?"

"Not to my knowledge."

"Doesn't join in with the lads in their games, to get some sort of excitement in this lonely place?"

"No."

"Mumming, for instance?"

"No. Her notions be different. I should rather say her thoughts were far away from here, with lords and ladies she'll never know, and mansions she'll never see again."

Observing that Clym appeared singularly interested Mrs. Yeobright said rather uneasily to Sam, "You see more in her than most of us do. Miss Vye is to my mind too idle to be charming. I have never heard that she is of any use to herself or to other people. Good girls don't get treated as witches even on Egdon."

"Nonsense—that proves nothing either way," said Yeobright.

"Well, of course I don't understand such niceties," said Sam, withdrawing from a possibly unpleasant argument; "and what she is we must wait for time to tell us. The business that I have really called about is this, to borrow the longest and strongest rope you have. The captain's bucket has dropped into the well, and they are in want of water; and as all the chaps are at home to-day we think we can get it out for him. We have three cart-ropes already, but they won't reach to the bottom."

Mrs. Yeobright told him that he might have whatever ropes he could find in the outhouse, and Sam went out to search. When he passed by the door Clym joined him, and accompanied him to the gate.

"Is this young witch-lady going to stay long at Mistover?" he asked.

"I should say so."

"What a cruel shame to ill-use her! She must have suffered greatly—more in mind than in body."

" 'Twas a graceless trick—such a handsome girl, too. You ought to see her, Mr. Yeobright, being a young man come from far, and with a little more to show for your years than most of us."

"Do you think she would like to teach children?" said Clym.

Sam shook his head. "Quite a different sort of body from that, I reckon."

"O, it was merely something which occurred to me. It would of course be necessary to see her and talk it over—not an easy thing, by the way, for my family and hers are not very friendly."

"I'll tell you how you mid see her, Mr. Yeobright," said Sam. "We are going to grapple for the bucket at six o'clock to-night at her house, and you could lend a hand. There's five or six coming, but the well is deep, and another might be useful, if you don't mind appearing in that shape. She's sure to be walking round."

"I'll think of it," said Yeobright; and they parted.

He thought of it a good deal; but nothing more was said about Eustacia inside the house at that time. Whether this romantic martyr to superstition and the melancholy mummer he had conversed with under the full moon were one and the same person remained as yet a problem.

III

THE FIRST ACT IN A TIMEWORN DRAMA

THE AFTERNOON WAS FINE, AND YEOBRIGHT WALKED ON THE HEATH FOR AN HOUR WITH his mother. When they reached the lofty ridge which divided the valley of Blooms-End from the adjoining valley they stood still and looked round. The Quiet Woman Inn was visible on the low margin of the heath in one direction, and afar on the other hand rose Mistover Knap.

"You mean to call on Thomasin?" he enquired.

"Yes. But you need not come this time," said his mother.

"In that case I'll branch off here, mother. I am going to Mistover."

Mrs. Yeobright turned to him enquiringly.

"I am going to help them get the bucket out of the captain's well," he continued. "As it is so very deep I may be useful. And I should like to see this Miss Vye—not so much for her good looks as for another reason."

"Must you go?" his mother asked.

"I thought to."

And they parted. "There is no help for it," murmured Clym's mother gloomily as he withdrew. "They are sure to see each other. I wish Sam would carry his news to other houses than mine."

Clym's retreating figure got smaller and smaller as it rose and fell over the hillocks on his way. "He is tender-hearted," said Mrs. Yeobright to herself while she watched him; "otherwise it would matter little. How he's going on!"

He was, indeed, walking with a will over the furze, as straight as a line, as if his life depended upon it. His mother drew a long breath, and turned to go back by the way she had come. The evening films began to make nebulous pictures of the valleys, but the high lands still were raked by the declining rays of the winter sun, which glanced on Clym as he walked forward, eyed by every rabbit and fieldfare around, a long shadow advancing in front of him.

On drawing near to the furze-covered bank and ditch which fortified the captain's dwelling he could hear voices within, signifying that operations had been already begun. At the side-entrance gate he stopped and looked over.

Half-a-dozen able-bodied men were standing in a line from the well-mouth, holding a rope which passed over the well-roller into the depths below. Fairway, with a piece of smaller rope round his body, made fast to one of the standards, to guard against accidents, was leaning over the opening, his right hand clasping the vertical rope that descended into the well.

"Now, silence, folks," said Fairway.

The talking ceased, and Fairway gave a circular motion to the rope, as if he were stirring batter. At the end of a minute a dull splashing reverberated from the bottom of the well; the helical twist he had imparted to the rope had reached the grapnel below.

"Haul!" said Fairway; and the men who held the rope began to gather it over the wheel.

"I think we've got sommat," said one of the haulers-in.

"Then pull steady," said Fairway.

They gathered up more and more, till a regular dripping into the well could be heard below. It grew smarter with the increasing height of the bucket, and presently a hundred and fifty feet of rope had been pulled in.

Fairway then lit a lantern, tied it to another cord, and began lowering it into the well beside the first. Clym came forward and looked down. Strange humid leaves, which knew nothing of the seasons of the year, and quaint-natured moss were revealed on the well-side as the lantern descended; till its rays fell upon a confused mass of rope and bucket dangling in the dank, dark air.

"We've only got en by the edge of the hoop—steady, for God's sake!" said Fairway.

They pulled with the greatest gentleness, till the wet bucket appeared about two yards below them, like a dead friend come to earth again. Three or four hands were stretched out, then jerk went the rope, whizz went the wheel, the two foremost haulers fell backward, the beating of a falling body was heard, receding down the sides of the well, and a thunderous uproar arose at the bottom. The bucket was gone again.

"Damn the bucket!" said Fairway.

"Lower again," said Sam.

"I'm as stiff as a ram's horn stooping so long," said Fairway, standing up and stretching himself till his joints creaked.

"Rest a few minutes, Timothy," said Yeobright. "I'll take your place."

The grapnel was again lowered. Its smart impact upon the distant water reached their ears like a kiss, whereupon Yeobright knelt down, and leaning over the well began dragging the grapnel round and round as Fairway had done.

"Tie a rope round him—it is dangerous!" cried a soft and anxious voice somewhere above them.

Everybody turned. The speaker was a woman, gazing down upon the group from an upper window, whose panes blazed in the ruddy glare from the west. Her lips were parted and she appeared for the moment to forget where she was.

The rope was accordingly tied round his waist, and the work proceeded. At the next haul the weight was not heavy, and it was discovered that they had only secured a coil of the rope detached from the bucket. The tangled mass was thrown into the background. Humphrey took Yeobright's place, and the grapnel was lowered again.

Yeobright retired to the heap of recovered rope in a meditative mood. Of the identity between the lady's voice and that of the melancholy mummer he had not a moment's doubt. "How thoughtful of her!" he said to himself.

Eustacia, who had reddened when she perceived the effect of her exclamation upon the group below, was no longer to be seen at the window, though Yeobright scanned it wistfully. While he stood there the men at the well succeeded in getting up the bucket without a mishap. One of them went to enquire for the captain, to learn what orders he wished to give for mending the well-tackle. The captain proved to be away from home; and Eustacia appeared at the door and came out. She had lapsed into an easy and dignified calm, far removed from the intensity of life in her words of solicitude for Clym's safety.

"Will it be possible to draw water here to-night?" she enquired.

"No, miss; the bottom of the bucket is clean knocked out. And as we can do no more now we'll leave off, and come again to-morrow morning."

"No water," she murmured, turning away.

"I can send you up some from Blooms-End," said Clym, coming forward and raising his hat as the men retired.

Yeobright and Eustacia looked at each other for one instant, as if each had in mind those few moments during which a certain moonlit scene was common to both. With the glance the calm fixity of her features sublimed itself to an expression of refinement and warmth: it was like garish noon rising to the dignity of sunset in a couple of seconds.

"Thank you; it will hardly be necessary," she replied.

"But if you have no water?"

"Well, it is what I call no water," she said, blushing, and lifting her long-lashed eyelids as if to lift them were a work requiring consideration. "But my grand-father calls it water enough. This is what I mean."

She moved away a few yards, and Clym followed. When she reached the corner of the enclosure, where the steps were formed for mounting the boundary bank, she sprang up with a lightness which seemed strange after her listless movement towards the well. It incidentally showed that her apparent languor did not arise from lack of force.

Clym ascended behind her, and noticed a circular burnt patch at the top of the bank. "Ashes?" he said.

"Yes," said Eustacia. "We had a little bonfire here last Fifth of November, and those are the marks of it."

On that spot had stood the fire she had kindled to attract Wildeve.

"That's the only kind of water we have," she continued, tossing a stone into the pool, which lay on the outside of the bank like the white of an eye without its pupil. The stone fell with a flounce, but no Wildeve appeared on the other side, as on a previous occasion there. "My grand-father says he lived for more than twenty years at sea on water twice as bad as that," she went on, "and considers it quite good enough for us here on an emergency."

"Well, as a matter of fact there are no impurities in the water of these pools at this time of the year. It has only just rained into them."

She shook her head. "I am managing to exist in a wilderness, but I cannot drink from a pond," she said.

Clym looked towards the well, which was now deserted, the men having gone home. "It is a long way to send for spring-water," he said, after a silence. "But since you don't like this in the pond, I'll try to get you some myself." He went back to the well. "Yes, I think I could do it by tying on this pail."

"But, since I would not trouble the men to get it, I cannot in conscience let you."

"I don't mind the trouble at all."

He made fast the pail to the long coil of rope, put it over the wheel, and allowed it to descend by letting the rope slip through his hands. Before it had gone far, however, he checked it.

"I must make fast the end first, or we may lose the whole," he said to Eustacia, who had drawn near. "Could you hold this a moment, while I do it—or shall I call your servant?"

"I can hold it," said Eustacia; and he placed the rope in her hands, going then to search for the end.

"I suppose I may let it slip down?" she enquired.

"I would advise you not to let it go far," said Clym. "It will get much heavier, you will find."

However, Eustacia had begun to pay out. While he was tying she cried, "I cannot stop it!"

Clym ran to her side, and found he could only check the rope by twisting the loose part round the upright post, when it stopped with a jerk. "Has it hurt you?"

"Yes," she replied.

"Very much?"

"No; I think not." She opened her hands. One of them was bleeding; the rope had dragged off the skin. Eustacia wrapped it in her handkerchief.

"You should have let go," said Yeobright. "Why didn't you?"

"You said I was to hold on. . . . This is the second time I have been wounded to-day."

"Ah, yes; I have heard of it. I blush for my native Egdon. Was it a serious injury you received in church, Miss Vye?"

There was such an abundance of sympathy in Clym's tone that Eustacia slowly drew up her sleeve and disclosed her round white arm. A bright red spot appeared on its smooth surface, like a ruby on Parian marble.

"There it is," she said, putting her finger against the spot.

"It was dastardly of the woman," said Clym. "Will not Captain Vye get her punished?"

"He is gone from home on that very business. I did not know that I had such a magic reputation."

"And you fainted?" said Clym, looking at the scarlet little puncture as if he would like to kiss it and make it well.

"Yes, it frightened me. I had not been to church for a long time. And now I shall not go again for ever so long—perhaps never. I cannot face their eyes after this. Don't you think it dreadfully humiliating? I wished I was dead for hours after, but I don't mind now."

"I have come to clean away these cobwebs," said Yeobright. "Would you like to help me—by high class teaching? We might benefit them much."

"I don't quite feel anxious to. I have not much love for my fellow-creatures. Sometimes I quite hate them."

"Still I think that if you were to hear my scheme you might take an interest in it. There is no use in hating people—if you hate anything, you should hate what produced them."

"Do you mean Nature? I hate her already. But I shall be glad to hear your scheme at any time."

The situation had now worked itself out, and the next natural thing was for them to part. Clym knew this well enough, and Eustacia made a move of conclusion; yet he looked at her as if he had one word more to say. Perhaps if he had not lived in Paris it would never have been uttered.

"We have met before," he said, regarding her with rather more interest than was necessary.

"I do not own it," said Eustacia, with a repressed, still look.

"But I may think what I like."

"Yes."

"You are lonely here."

"I cannot endure the heath, except in its purple season. The heath is a cruel taskmaster to me."

"Can you say so?" he asked. "To my mind it is most exhilarating, and strengthening, and soothing. I would rather live on these hills than anywhere else in the world."

"It is well enough for artists; but I never would learn to draw."

"And there is a very curious Druidical stone just out there." He threw a pebble in the direction signified. "Do you often go to see it?"

"I was not even aware there existed any such curious Druidical stone. I am aware that there are Boulevards in Paris."

Yeobright looked thoughtfully on the ground. "That means much," he said.

"It does indeed," said Eustacia.

"I remember when I had the same longing for town bustle. Five years of a great city would be a perfect cure for that."

"Heaven send me such a cure! Now, Mr. Yeobright, I will go indoors and plaster my wounded hand."

They separated, and Eustacia vanished in the increasing shade. She seemed full of many things. Her past was a blank, her life had begun. The effect upon Clym of this meeting he did not fully discover till some time after. During his walk home his most intelligible sensation was that his scheme had somehow become glorified. A beautiful woman had been intertwined with it.

On reaching the house he went up to the room which was to be made his study, and occupied himself during the evening in unpacking his books from the boxes and arranging them on shelves. From another box he drew a lamp and a can of oil. He trimmed the lamp, arranged his table, and said, "Now, I am ready to begin."

He rose early the next morning, read two hours before breakfast by the light of his lamp—read all the morning, all the afternoon. Just when the sun was going down his eyes felt weary, and he leant back in his chair.

His room overlooked the front of the premises and the valley of the heath beyond. The lowest beams of the winter sun threw the shadow of the house over the palings, across the grass margin of the heath, and far up the vale, where the chimney outlines and those of the surrounding tree-tops stretched forth in long dark prongs. Having been seated at work all day, he decided to take a turn upon the hills before it got dark; and, going out forthwith, he struck across the heath towards Mistover.

It was an hour and a half later when he again appeared at the garden gate. The shutters of the house were closed, and Christian Cantle, who had been wheeling manure about the garden all day, had gone home. On entering he found that his mother, after waiting a long time for him, had finished her meal.

"Where have you been, Clym?" she immediately said. "Why didn't you tell me that you were going away at this time?"

"I have been on the heath."

"You'll meet Eustacia Vye if you go up there."

Clym paused a minute. "Yes, I met her this evening," he said, as though it were spoken under the sheer necessity of preserving honesty.

"I wondered if you had."

"It was no appointment."

"No; such meetings never are."

"But you are not angry, mother?"

"I can hardly say that I am not. Angry? No. But when I consider the usual nature of the drag which causes men of promise to disappoint the world I feel uneasy."

"You deserve credit for the feeling, Mother. But I can assure you that you need not be disturbed by it on my account."

"When I think of you and your new crotchets," said Mrs. Yeobright, with some emphasis, "I naturally don't feel so comfortable as I did a twelvemonth ago. It is incredible to me that a man accustomed to the attractive women of Paris and elsewhere should be so easily worked upon by a girl in a heath. You could just as well have walked another way."

"I had been studying all day."

"Well, yes," she added more hopefully, "I have been thinking that you might get on as a schoolmaster, and rise that way, since you really are determined to hate the course you were pursuing."

Yeobright was unwilling to disturb this idea, though his scheme was far enough removed from one wherein the education of youth should be made a mere channel of social ascent. He had no desires of that sort. He had reached the stage in a young man's life when the grimness of the general human situation first becomes clear; and the realisation of this causes ambition to halt a while. In France it is not uncustomary to commit suicide at this stage; in England we do much better, or much worse, as the case may be.

The love between the young man and his mother was strangely invisible now. Of love it may be said, the less earthly the less demonstrative. In its absolutely indestructible form it reaches a profundity in which all exhibition of itself is painful. It was so with these. Had conversations between them been overheard, people would have said, "How cold they are to each other!"

His theory and his wishes about devoting his future to teaching had made an impression on Mrs. Yeobright. Indeed, how could it be otherwise when he was a part of her— when their discourses were as if carried on between the right and the left hands of the same body? He had despaired of reaching her by argument; and it was almost as a discovery to him that he could reach her by a magnetism which was as superior to words as words are to yells.

Strangely enough he began to feel now that it would not be so hard to persuade her who was his best friend that comparative poverty was essentially the higher course for him, as to reconcile to his feelings the act of persuading her. From every provident point of view his mother was so undoubtedly right, that he was not without a sickness of heart in finding he could shake her.

She had a singular insight into life, considering that she had never mixed with it. There are instances of persons who, without clear ideas of the things they criticise, have yet had clear ideas of the relations of those things. Blacklock, a poet blind from his birth, could describe visual objects with accuracy; Professor Sanderson, who was also blind, gave excellent lectures on colour, and taught others the theory of ideas which they had and he had not. In the social sphere these gifted ones are mostly women; they can watch a world which they never saw, and estimate forces of which they have only heard. We call it intuition.

What was the great world to Mrs. Yeobright? A multitude whose tendencies could be perceived, though not its essences. Communities were seen by her as from a distance; she saw them as we see the throngs which cover the canvases of Sallaert, Van Alsloot, and others of that school—vast masses of beings, jostling, zigzagging, and processioning in definite directions, but whose features are indistinguishable by the very comprehensiveness of the view.

One could see that, as far as it had gone, her life was very complete on its reflective side. The philosophy of her nature, and its limitation by circumstances, was almost written in her movements. They had a majestic foundation, though they were far from being majestic; and they had a groundwork of assurance, but they were not assured. As her once elastic walk had become deadened by time, so had her natural pride of life been hindered in its blooming by her necessities.

The next slight touch in the shaping of Clym's destiny occurred a few days after. A barrow was opened on the heath, and Yeobright attended the operation, remaining away from his study during several hours. In the afternoon Christian returned from a journey in the same direction, and Mrs. Yeobright questioned him.

"They have dug a hole, and they have found things like flower-pots upside down, Mis'ess Yeobright; and inside these be real charnel bones. They have carried 'em off to men's houses; but I shouldn't like to sleep where they will bide. Dead folks have been known to come and claim their own. Mr. Yeobright had got one pot of the bones, and was going to bring 'em home—real skellington bones—but 'twas ordered otherwise. You'll be relieved to hear that he gave away his pot and all, on second thoughts; and a blessed thing for ye, Mis'ess Yeobright, considering the wind o' nights."

"Gave it away?"

"Yes. To Miss Vye. She has a cannibal taste for such churchyard furniture seemingly."

"Miss Vye was there too?"

"Ay, 'a b'lieve she was."

When Clym came home, which was shortly after, his mother said, in a curious tone, "The urn you had meant for me you gave away."

Yeobright made no reply; the current of her feeling was too pronounced to admit it.

The early weeks of the year passed on. Yeobright certainly studied at home, but he also walked much abroad, and the direction of his walk was always towards some point of a line between Mistover and Rainbarrow.

The month of March arrived, and the heath showed its first signs of awakening from winter trance. The awakening was almost feline in its stealthiness. The pool outside the bank by Eustacia's dwelling, which seemed as dead and desolate as ever to an observer who moved and made noises in his observation, would gradually disclose a state of great animation when silently watched awhile. A timid animal world had come to life for the season. Little tadpoles and efts began to bubble up through the water, and to race along beneath it; toads made noises like very young ducks, and advanced to the margin in twos and threes; overhead, bumble-bees flew hither and thither in the thickening light, their drone coming and going like the sound of a gong.

On an evening such as this Yeobright descended into the Blooms-End valley from beside that very pool, where he had been standing with another person quite silently and quite long enough to hear all this puny stir of resurrection in nature; yet he had not heard it. His walk was rapid as he came down, and he went with a springy tread. Before entering upon his mother's premises he stopped and breathed. The light which shone forth on him from the window revealed that his face was flushed and his eye bright. What it did not show was something which lingered upon his lips like a seal set there. The abiding presence of this impress was so real that he hardly dared to enter the house, for it seemed as if his mother might say, "What red spot is that glowing upon your mouth so vividly?"

But he entered soon after. The tea was ready, and he sat down opposite his mother. She did not speak many words; and as for him, something had been just done and some words had been just said on the hill which prevented him from beginning a desultory chat. His mother's taciturnity was not without ominousness, but he appeared not to care. He knew why she said so little, but he could not remove the cause of her bearing towards him. These half-silent sittings were far from uncommon with them now. At last Yeobright made a beginning of what was intended to strike at the whole root of the matter.

"Five days have we sat like this at meals with scarcely a word. What's the use of it, mother?"

"None," said she, in a heart-swollen tone. "But there is only too good a reason."

"Not when you know all. I have been wanting to speak about this, and I am glad the subject is begun. The reason, of course, is Eustacia Vye. Well, I confess I have seen her lately, and have seen her a good many times."

"Yes, yes; and I know what that amounts to. It troubles me, Clym. You are wasting your life here; and it is solely on account of her. If it had not been for that woman you would never have entertained this teaching scheme at all."

Clym looked hard at his mother. "You know that is not it," he said.

"Well, I know you had decided to attempt it before you saw her; but that would have ended in intentions. It was very well to talk of, but ridiculous to put in practice. I fully expected that in the course of a month or two you would have seen the folly of such self-sacrifice, and would have been by this time back again to Paris in some business or other. I can understand objections to the diamond trade—I really was thinking that it might be inadequate to the life of a man like you even though it might have made you a millionaire. But now I see how mistaken you are about this girl I doubt if you could be correct about other things."

"How am I mistaken in her?"

"She is lazy and dissatisfied. But that is not all of it. Supposing her to be as good a woman as any you can find, which she certainly is not, why do you wish to connect your-self with anybody at present?"

"Well, there are practical reasons," Clym began, and then almost broke off under an overpowering sense of the weight of argument which could be brought against his state-ment. "If I take a school an educated woman would be invaluable as a help to me."

"What! you really mean to marry her?"

"It would be premature to state that plainly. But consider what obvious advantages there would be in doing it. She—"

"Don't suppose she has any money. She hasn't a farthing."

"She is excellently educated, and would make a good matron in a boarding-school. I candidly own that I have modified my views a little, in deference to you; and it should sat-isfy you. I no longer adhere to my intention of giving with my own mouth rudimentary education to the lowest class. I can do better. I can establish a good private school for farm-ers' sons, and without stopping the school I can manage to pass examinations. By this means, and by the assistance of a wife like her—"

"Oh, Clym!"

"I shall ultimately, I hope, be at the head of one of the best schools in the county."

Yeobright had enunciated the word "her" with a fervour which, in conversation with a mother, was absurdly indiscreet. Hardly a maternal heart within the four seas could in such circumstances, have helped being irritated at that ill-timed betrayal of feeling for a new woman.

"You are blinded, Clym," she said warmly. "It was a bad day for you when you first set eyes on her. And your scheme is merely a castle in the air built on purpose to justify this folly which has seized you, and to salve your conscience on the irrational situation you are in."

"Mother, that's not true," he firmly answered.

"Can you maintain that I sit and tell untruths, when all I wish to do is to save you from sorrow? For shame, Clym! But it is all through that woman—a hussy!"

Clym reddened like fire and rose. He placed his hand upon his mother's shoulder and said, in a tone which hung strangely between entreaty and command, "I won't hear it. I may be led to answer you in a way which we shall both regret."

His mother parted her lips to begin some other vehement truth, but on looking at him she saw that in his face which led her to leave the words unsaid. Yeobright walked once or twice across the room, and then suddenly went out of the house. It was eleven o'clock when he came in, though he had not been further than the precincts of the garden. His mother was gone to bed. A light was left burning on the table, and supper was spread. Without stopping for any food he secured the doors and went upstairs.

IV

AN HOUR OF BLISS AND MANY HOURS OF SADNESS

THE NEXT DAY WAS GLOOMY ENOUGH AT BLOOMS-END. YEOBRIGHT REMAINED IN HIS study, sitting over the open books; but the work of those hours was miserably scant. Determined that there should be nothing in his conduct towards his mother resembling sullenness, he had occasionally spoken to her on passing matters, and would take no notice of the brevity of her replies. With the same resolve to keep up a show of conversation he said, about seven o'clock in the evening, "There's an eclipse of the moon to-night. I am going out to see it." And, putting on his overcoat, he left her.

The low moon was not as yet visible from the front of the house, and Yeobright climbed out of the valley until he stood in the full flood of her light. But even now he walked on, and his steps were in the direction of Rainbarrow.

In half an hour he stood at the top. The sky was clear from verge to verge, and the moon flung her rays over the whole heath, but without sensibly lighting it, except where paths and water-courses had laid bare the white flints and glistening quartz sand, which made streaks upon the general shade. After standing awhile he stooped and felt the heather. It was dry, and he flung himself down upon the barrow, his face towards the moon, which depicted a small image of herself in each of his eyes.

He had often come up here without stating his purpose to his mother; but this was the first time that he had been ostensibly frank as to his purpose while really concealing it. It was a moral situation which, three months earlier, he could hardly have credited of himself. In returning to labour in this sequestered spot he had anticipated an escape from the chafing of social necessities; yet behold they were here also. More than ever he longed to be in some world where personal ambition was not the only recognised form of progress—such, perhaps, as might have been the case at some time or other in the silvery globe then shining upon him. His eye travelled over the length and breadth of that distant country—over the Bay of Rainbows, the sombre Sea of Crises, the Ocean of Storms, the Lake of Dreams, the vast Walled Plains, and the wondrous Ring Mountains—till he almost felt himself to be voyaging bodily through its wild scenes, standing on its hollow hills, traversing its deserts, descending its vales and old sea bottoms, or mounting to the edges of its craters.

While he watched the far-removed landscape a tawny stain grew into being on the lower verge: the eclipse had begun. This marked a preconcerted moment: for the remote celestial phenomenon had been pressed into sublunary service as a lover's signal. Yeobright's mind flew back to earth at the sight; he arose, shook himself and listened. Minute after minute passed by, perhaps ten minutes passed, and the shadow on the moon perceptibly widened. He heard a rustling on his left hand, a cloaked figure with an upturned face appeared at the base of the Barrow, and Clym descended. In a moment the figure was in his arms, and his lips upon hers.

"My Eustacia!"

"Clym, dearest!"

Such a situation had less than three months brought forth.

They remained long without a single utterance, for no language could reach the level of their condition: words were as the rusty implements of a bygone barbarous epoch, and only to be occasionally tolerated.

"I began to wonder why you did not come," said Yeobright, when she had withdrawn a little from his embrace.

"You said ten minutes after the first mark of shade on the edge of the moon, and that's what it is now."

"Well, let us only think that here we are."

Then, holding each other's hand, they were again silent, and the shadow on the moon's disc grew a little larger.

"Has it seemed long since you last saw me?" she asked.

"It has seemed sad."

"And not long? That's because you occupy yourself, and so blind yourself to my absence. To me, who can do nothing, it has been like living under stagnant water."

"I would rather bear tediousness, dear, than have time made short by the means that mine has been shortened."

"In what way is that? You have been thinking you wished you did not love me."

"How can a man wish that, and yet love on? No, Eustacia."

"Men can, women cannot."

"Well, whatever I may have thought, one thing is certain—I do love you—past all compass and description. I love you to oppressiveness—I, who have never before felt more than a pleasant passing fancy for any woman I have ever seen. Let me look right into your moonlit face and dwell on every line and curve in it! Only a few hair-breadths make the difference between this face and faces I have seen many times before I knew you; yet what a difference—the difference between everything and nothing at all. One touch on that mouth again! there, and there, and there. Your eyes seem heavy, Eustacia."

"No, it is my general way of looking. I think it arises from my feeling sometimes an agonising pity for myself that I ever was born."

"You don't feel it now?"

"No. Yet I know that we shall not love like this always. Nothing can ensure the continuance of love. It will evaporate like a spirit, and so I feel full of fears."

"You need not."

"Ah, you don't know. You have seen more than I, and have been into cities and among people that I have only heard of, and have lived more years than I; but yet I am older at this than you. I loved another man once, and now I love you."

"In God's mercy don't talk so, Eustacia!"

"But I do not think I shall be the one who wearies first. It will, I fear, end in this way: your mother will find out that you meet me, and she will influence you against me!"

"That can never be. She knows of these meetings already."

"And she speaks against me?"

"I will not say."

"There, go away! Obey her. I shall ruin you. It is foolish of you to meet me like this. Kiss me, and go away forever. Forever—do you hear?—forever!"

"Not I."

"It is your only chance. Many a man's love has been a curse to him."

"You are desperate, full of fancies, and wilful; and you misunderstand. I have an additional reason for seeing you to-night besides love of you. For though, unlike you, I feel our affection may be eternal, I feel with you in this, that our present mode of existence cannot last."

"O! 'tis your mother. Yes, that's it! I knew it."

"Never mind what it is. Believe this, I cannot let myself lose you. I must have you always with me. This very evening I do not like to let you go. There is only one cure for this anxiety, dearest—you must be my wife."

She started: then endeavoured to say calmly, "Cynics say that cures the anxiety by curing the love."

"But you must answer me. Shall I claim you some day—I don't mean at once?"

"I must think," Eustacia murmured. "At present speak of Paris to me. Is there any place like it on earth?"

"It is very beautiful. But will you be mine?"

"I will be nobody else's in the world—does that satisfy you?"

"Yes, for the present."

"Now tell me of the Tuilleries, and the Louvre," she continued evasively.

"I hate talking of Paris! Well, I remember one sunny room in the Louvre which would make a fitting place for you to live in—the Galerie d'Apollon. Its windows are mainly east; and in the early morning, when the sun is bright, the whole apartment is in a perfect blaze of splendour. The rays bristle and dart from the encrustations of gilding to the magnificent inlaid coffers, from the coffers to the gold and silver plate, from the plate to the jewels and precious stones, from these to the enamels, till there is a perfect network of light which quite dazzles the eye. But now, about our marriage——"

"And Versailles—the King's Gallery is some such gorgeous room, is it not?"

"Yes. But what's the use of talking of gorgeous rooms? By the way, the Little Trianon would suit us beautifully to live in, and you might walk in the gardens in the moonlight and think you were in some English shrubbery; it is laid out in English fashion."

"I should hate to think that!"

"Then you could keep to the lawn in front of the Grand Palace. All about there you would doubtless feel in a world of historical romance."

He went on, since it was all new to her, and described Fontainebleau, St. Cloud, the Bois, and many other familiar haunts of the Parisians; till she said—

"When used you to go to these places?"

"On Sundays."

"Ah, yes. I dislike English Sundays. How I should chime in with their manners over there! Dear Clym, you'll go back again?"

Clym shook his head, and looked at the eclipse.

"If you'll go back again I'll—be something," she said tenderly, putting her head near his breast. "If you'll agree I'll give my promise, without making you wait a minute longer."

"How extraordinary that you and my mother should be of one mind about this!" said Yeobright. "I have vowed not to go back, Eustacia. It is not the place I dislike; it is the occupation."

"But you can go in some other capacity."

"No. Besides, it would interfere with my scheme. Don't press that, Eustacia. Will you marry me?"

"I cannot tell."

"Now—never mind Paris; it is no better than other spots. Promise, sweet!"

"You will never adhere to your education plan, I am quite sure; and then it will be all right for me; and so I promise to be yours forever and ever."

Clym brought her face towards his by a gentle pressure of the hand, and kissed her.

"Ah! but you don't know what you have got in me," she said. "Sometimes I think there is not that in Eustacia Vye which will make a good homespun wife. Well, let it go—see how our time is slipping, slipping, slipping!" She pointed towards the half-eclipsed moon.

"You are too mournful."

"No. Only I dread to think of anything beyond the present. What is, we know. We are together now, and it is unknown how long we shall be so: the unknown always fills my mind with terrible possibilities, even when I may reasonably expect it to be cheerful. . . . Clym, the eclipsed moonlight shines upon your face with a strange foreign colour, and shows its shape as if it were cut out in gold. That means that you should be doing better things than this."

"You are ambitious, Eustacia—no, not exactly ambitious, luxurious. I ought to be of the same vein, to make you happy, I suppose. And yet, far from that, I could live and die in a hermitage here, with proper work to do."

There was that in his tone which implied distrust of his position as a solicitous lover, a doubt if he were acting fairly towards one whose tastes touched his own only at rare and infrequent points. She saw his meaning, and whispered, in a low, full accent of eager assurance, "Don't mistake me, Clym: though I should like Paris, I love you for yourself alone. To be your wife and live in Paris would be heaven to me; but I would rather live with you in a hermitage here than not be yours at all. It is gain to me either way, and very great gain. There's my too candid confession."

"Spoken like a woman. And now I must soon leave you. I'll walk with you towards your house."

"But must you go home yet?" she asked. "Yes, the sand has nearly slipped away, I see, and the eclipse is creeping on more and more. Don't go yet! Stop till the hour has run itself out; then I will not press you any more. You will go home and sleep well; I keep sighing in my sleep! Do you ever dream of me?"

"I cannot recollect a clear dream of you."

"I see your face in every scene of my dreams, and hear your voice in every sound. I wish I did not. It is too much what I feel. They say such love never lasts. But it must! And yet once, I remember, I saw an officer of the Hussars ride down the street at Budmouth, and though he was a total stranger and never spoke to me, I loved him till I thought I should really die of love—but I didn't die, and at last I left off caring for him. How terrible it would be if a time should come when I could not love you, my Clym!"

"Please don't say such reckless things. When we see such a time at hand we will say, 'I have outlived my faith and purpose,' and die. There, the hour has expired: now let us walk on."

Hand in hand they went along the path towards Mistover. When they were near the house he said, "It is too late for me to see your grand-father to-night. Do you think he will object to it?"

"I will speak to him. I am so accustomed to be my own mistress that it did not occur to me that we should have to ask him."

Then they lingeringly separated, and Clym descended towards Blooms-End.

And as he walked further and further from the charmed atmosphere of his Olympian girl his face grew sad with a new sort of sadness. A perception of the dilemma in which his love had placed him came back in full force. In spite of Eustacia's apparent willingness to wait through the period of an unpromising engagement, till he should be established in his new pursuit, he could not but perceive at moments that she loved him rather as a visitant from a gay world to which she rightly belonged than as a man with a purpose opposed to that recent past of his which so interested her. Often at their meetings a word or a sigh escaped her. It meant that, though she made no conditions as to his return to the French capital, this was what she secretly longed for in the event of marriage; and it robbed him of many an otherwise pleasant hour. Along with that came the widening breach between himself and his mother. Whenever any little occurrence had brought into more prominence than usual the disappointment that he was causing her it had sent him on lone and moody walks; or he was kept awake a great part of the night by the turmoil of spirit which such a recognition created. If Mrs. Yeobright could only have been led to see what a sound and worthy purpose this purpose of his was and how little it was being affected by his devotion to Eustacia, how differently would she regard him!

Thus as his sight grew accustomed to the first blinding halo kindled about him by love and beauty, Yeobright began to perceive what a strait he was in. Sometimes he wished that he had never known Eustacia, immediately to retract the wish as brutal. Three antagonistic growths had to be kept alive: his mother's trust in him, his plan for becoming a teacher, and Eustacia's happiness. His fervid nature could not afford to relinquish one of these, though two of the three were as many as he could hope to preserve. Though his love was as chaste as that of Petrarch for his Laura, it had made fetters of what previously was only a difficulty. A position which was not too simple when he stood whole-hearted had become indescribably complicated by the addition of Eustacia. Just when his mother was beginning to tolerate one scheme he had introduced another still bitterer than the first, and the combination was more than she could bear.

V

SHARP WORDS ARE SPOKEN, AND A CRISIS ENSUES

WHEN YEOBRIGHT WAS NOT WITH EUSTACIA HE WAS SITTING SLAVISHLY OVER HIS books; when he was not reading he was meeting her. These meetings were carried on with the greatest secrecy.

One afternoon his mother came home from a morning visit to Thomasin. He could see from a disturbance in the lines of her face that something had happened.

"I have been told an incomprehensible thing," she said mournfully. "The captain has let out at the Woman that you and Eustacia Vye are engaged to be married."

"We are," said Yeobright. "But it may not be yet for a very long time."

"I should hardly think it *would* be yet for a very long time! You will take her to Paris, I suppose?" She spoke with weary hopelessness.

"I am not going back to Paris."

"What will you do with a wife, then?"

"Keep a school in Budmouth, as I have told you."

"That's incredible! The place is overrun with schoolmasters. You have no special qualifications. What possible chance is there for such as you?"

"There is no chance of getting rich. But with my system of education, which is as new as it is true, I shall do a great deal of good to my fellow-creatures."

"Dreams, dreams! If there had been any system left to be invented they would have found it out at the universities long before this time."

"Never, mother. They cannot find it out, because their teachers don't come in contact with the class which demands such a system—that is, those who have had no preliminary training. My plan is one for instilling high knowledge into empty minds without first cramming them with what has to be uncrammed again before true study begins."

"I might have believed you if you had kept yourself free from entanglements; but this woman—if she had been a good girl it would have been bad enough; but being—"

"She is a good girl."

"So you think. A foreign bandmaster's daughter! What has her life been? Her surname even is not her true one."

"She is Captain Vye's grand-daughter, and her father merely took her mother's name. And she is a lady by instinct."

"They call him 'captain,' but anybody is captain."

"He was in the Royal Navy!"

"No doubt he has been to sea in some tub or other. Why doesn't he look after her? No lady would rove about the heath at all hours of the day and night as she does. But that's not all of it. There was something queer between her and Thomasin's husband at one time—I am as sure of it as that I stand here."

"Eustacia has told me. He did pay her a little attention a year ago; but there's no harm in that. I like her all the better."

"Clym," said his mother with firmness, "I have no proofs against her, unfortunately. But if she makes you a good wife, there has never been a bad one."

"Believe me, you are almost exasperating," said Yeobright vehemently. "And this very day I had intended to arrange a meeting between you. But you give me no peace; you try to thwart my wishes in everything."

"I hate the thought of any son of mine marrying badly! I wish I had never lived to see this; it is too much for me—it is more than I thought!" She turned to the window. Her breath was coming quickly, and her lips were pale, parted, and trembling.

"Mother," said Clym, "whatever you do, you will always be dear to me—that you know. But one thing I have a right to say, which is, that at my age I am old enough to know what is best for me."

Mrs. Yeobright remained for some time silent and shaken, as if she could say no more.

Then she replied, "Best? Is it best for you to injure your prospects for such a voluptuous, idle woman as that? Don't you see that by the very fact of your choosing her you prove that you do not know what is best for you? You give up your whole thought—you set your whole soul—to please a woman."

"I do. And that woman is you."

"How can you treat me so flippantly!" said his mother, turning again to him with a tearful look. "You are unnatural, Clym, and I did not expect it."

"Very likely," said he cheerlessly. "You did not know the measure you were going to mete me, and therefore did not know the measure that would be returned to you again."

"You answer me; you think only of her. You stick to her in all things."

"That proves her to be worthy. I have never yet supported what is bad. And I do not care only for her. I care for you and for myself, and for anything that is good. When a woman once dislikes another she is merciless!"

"O Clym! please don't go setting down as my fault what is your obstinate wrong-headedness. If you wished to connect yourself with an unworthy person why did you come home here to do it? Why didn't you do it in Paris?—it is more the fashion there. You have come only to distress me, a lonely woman, and shorten my days! I wish that you would bestow your presence where you bestow your love!"

Clym said huskily, "You are my mother. I will say no more—beyond this, that I beg your pardon for having thought this my home. I will no longer inflict myself upon you; I'll go." And he went out with tears in his eyes.

It was a sunny afternoon at the beginning of summer, and the moist hollows of the heath had passed from their brown to their green stage. Yeobright walked to the edge of the basin which extended down from Mistover and Rainbarrow. By this time he was calm, and he looked over the landscape. In the minor valleys, between the hillocks which diversified the contour of the vale, the fresh young ferns were luxuriantly growing up, ultimately to reach a height of five or six feet. He descended a little way, flung himself down in a spot where a path emerged from one of the small hollows, and waited. Hither it was that he had promised Eustacia to bring his mother this afternoon, that they might meet and be friends. His attempt had utterly failed.

He was in a nest of vivid green. The ferny vegetation round him, though so abundant, was quite uniform: it was a grove of machine-made foliage, a world of green triangles with saw-edges, and not a single flower. The air was warm with a vaporous warmth, and the stillness was unbroken. Lizards, grasshoppers, and ants were the only living things to be beheld. The scene seemed to belong to the ancient world of the carboniferous period, when the forms of plants were few, and of the fern kind; when there was neither bud nor blossom, nothing but a monotonous extent of leafage, amid which no bird sang.

When he had reclined for some considerable time, gloomily pondering, he discerned above the ferns a drawn bonnet of white silk approaching from the left, and Yeobright knew directly that it covered the head of her he loved. His heart awoke from its apathy to a warm excitement, and, jumping to his feet, he said aloud, "I knew she was sure to come."

She vanished in a hollow for a few moments, and then her whole form unfolded itself from the brake.

"Only you here?" she exclaimed, with a disappointed air, whose hollowness was proved by her rising redness and her half-guilty low laugh. "Where is Mrs. Yeobright?"

"She has not come," he replied in a subdued tone.

"I wish I had known that you would be here alone," she said seriously, "and that we were going to have such an idle, pleasant time as this. Pleasure not known beforehand is half wasted; to anticipate it is to double it. I have not thought once to-day of having you all to myself this afternoon, and the actual moment of a thing is so soon gone."

"It is indeed."

"Poor Clym!" she continued, looking tenderly into his face. "You are sad. Something has happened at your home. Never mind what is—let us only look at what seems."

"But, darling, what shall we do?" said he.

"Still go on as we do now—just live on from meeting to meeting, never minding about another day. You, I know, are always thinking of that—I can see you are. But you must not—will you, dear Clym?"

"You are just like all women. They are ever content to build their lives on any incidental position that offers itself; whilst men would fain make a globe to suit them. Listen to this, Eustacia. There is a subject I have determined to put off no longer. Your sentiment on the wisdom of *Carpe diem* does not impress me to-day. Our present mode of life must shortly be brought to an end."

"It is your mother!"

"It is. I love you none the less in telling you; it is only right you should know."

"I have feared my bliss," she said, with the merest motion of her lips. "It has been too intense and consuming."

"There is hope yet. There are forty years of work in me yet, and why should you despair? I am only at an awkward turning. I wish people wouldn't be so ready to think that there is no progress without uniformity."

"Ah—your mind runs off to the philosophical side of it. Well, these sad and hopeless obstacles are welcome in one sense, for they enable us to look with indifference upon the cruel satires that Fate loves to indulge in. I have heard of people, who, upon coming suddenly into happiness, have died from anxiety lest they should not live to enjoy it. I felt myself in that whimsical state of uneasiness lately; but I shall be spared it now. Let us walk on."

Clym took the hand which was already bared for him—it was a favourite way with them to walk bare hand in bare hand—and led her through the ferns. They formed a very comely picture of love at full flush, as they walked along the valley that late afternoon, the sun sloping down on their right, and throwing their thin spectral shadows, tall as poplar trees, far out across the furze and fern. Eustacia went with her head thrown back fancifully, a certain glad and voluptuous air of triumph pervading her eyes at having won by her own unaided self a man who was her perfect complement in attainments, appearance, and age. On the young man's part, the paleness of face which he had brought with him from Paris, and the incipient marks of time and thought, were less perceptible than when he returned, the healthful and energetic sturdiness which was his by nature having partially recovered its original proportions. They wandered onward till they reached the nether margin of the heath, where it became marshy, and merged in moorland.

"I must part from you here, Clym," said Eustacia.

They stood still and prepared to bid each other farewell. Everything before them was on a perfect level. The sun, resting on the horizon line, streamed across the ground from between copper-coloured and lilac clouds, stretched out in flats beneath a sky of pale soft green. All dark objects on the earth that lay towards the sun were overspread by a purple haze, against which groups of wailing gnats shone out, rising upwards and dancing about like sparks of fire.

"O! this leaving you is too hard to bear!" exclaimed Eustacia in a sudden whisper of anguish. "Your mother will influence you too much; I shall not be judged fairly, it will get afloat that I am not a good girl, and the witch story will be added to make me blacker!"

"They cannot. Nobody dares to speak disrespectfully of you or of me."

"Oh how I wish I was sure of never losing you—that you could not be able to desert me anyhow!"

Clym stood silent a moment. His feelings were high, the moment was passionate, and he cut the knot.

"You shall be sure of me, darling," he said, folding her in his arms. "We will be married at once."

"O Clym!"

"Do you agree to it?"

"If—If we can."

"We certainly can, both being of full age. And I have not followed my occupation all these years without having accumulated money; and if you will agree to live in a tiny cottage somewhere on the heath, until I take a house in Budmouth for the school, we can do it at a very little expense."

"How long shall we have to live in the tiny cottage, Clym?"

"About six months. At the end of that time I shall have finished my reading—yes, we will do it, and this heart-aching will be over. We shall, of course, live in absolute seclusion, and our married life will only begin to outward view when we take the house in Budmouth, where I have already addressed a letter on the matter. Would your grand-father allow you?"

"I think he would—on the understanding that it should not last longer than six months."

"I will guarantee that, if no misfortune happens."

"If no misfortune happens," she repeated slowly.

"Which is not likely. Dearest, fix the exact day."

And then they consulted on the question, and the day was chosen. It was to be a fortnight from that time.

This was the end of their talk, and Eustacia left him. Clym watched her as she retired towards the sun. The luminous rays wrapped her up with her increasing distance, and the rustle of her dress over the sprouting sedge and grass died away. As he watched, the dead flat of the scenery overpowered him, though he was fully alive to the beauty of that untarnished early summer green which was worn for the nonce by the poorest blade. There was something in its oppressive horizontality which too much reminded him of the arena of life; it gave him a sense of bare equality with, and no superiority to, a single living thing under the sun.

Eustacia was now no longer the goddess but the woman to him, a being to fight for, support, help, be maligned for. Now that he had reached a cooler moment he would have preferred a less hasty marriage; but the card was laid, and he determined to abide by the game. Whether Eustacia was to add one other to the list of those who love too hotly to love long and well, the forthcoming event was certainly a ready way of proving.

VI

YEOBRIGHT GOES, AND THE BREACH IS COMPLETE

ALL THAT EVENING SMART SOUNDS DENOTING AN ACTIVE PACKING UP CAME FROM Yeobright's room to the ears of his mother downstairs.

Next morning he departed from the house and again proceeded across the heath. A long day's march was before him, his object being to secure a dwelling to which he might take Eustacia when she became his wife. Such a house, small, secluded, and with its windows boarded up, he had casually observed a month earlier, near a village about five miles off; and thither he directed his steps to-day.

The weather was far different from that of the evening before. The yellow and vapoury sunset which had wrapped up Eustacia from his parting gaze had presaged change. It was one of those not infrequent days of an English June which are as wet and boisterous as November. The cold clouds hastened on in a body, as if painted on a moving slide. Vapours from other continents arrived upon the wind, which curled and parted round him as he walked on.

At length Clym reached the margin of a fir and beech plantation that had been enclosed from heath land in the year of his birth. Here the trees, laden heavily with their new and humid leaves, were now suffering more damage than during the highest winds of winter, when the boughs are especially disincumbered to do battle with the storm. The wet young beeches were undergoing amputations, bruises, cripplings, and harsh lacerations, from which the wasting sap would bleed for many a day to come, and which would leave scars visible till the day of their burning. Each stem was wrenched at the root, where it moved like a bone in its socket, and at every onset of the gale convulsive sounds came from the branches, as if pain were felt. In a neighbouring brake a finch was trying to sing; but the wind blew under his feathers till they stood on end, twisted round his little tail, and made him give up his song.

Yet a few yards to Yeobright's left, on the open heath, how ineffectively gnashed the storm! Those gusts which tore the trees merely waved the furze and heather in a light caress. Egdon was made for such times as these.

Yeobright reached the empty house about mid-day. It was almost as lonely as that of Eustacia's grand-father, but the fact that it stood near a heath was disguised by a belt of firs which almost enclosed the premises. He journeyed on about a mile further to the village in which the owner lived, and, returning with him to the house, arrangements were completed, and the man undertook that one room at least should be ready for occupation the next day. Clym's intention was to live there alone until Eustacia should join him on their wedding-day.

Then he turned to pursue his way homeward through the drizzle that had so greatly transformed the scene. The ferns, among which he had lain in comfort yesterday, were dripping moisture from every frond, wetting his legs through as he brushed past; and the fur of the rabbits leaping before him was clotted into dark locks by the same watery surrounding.

He reached home damp and weary enough after his ten-mile walk. It had hardly been a propitious beginning, but he had chosen his course, and would show no swerving. The evening and the following morning were spent in concluding arrangements for his departure. To stay at home a minute longer than necessary after having once come to his determination would be, he felt, only to give new pain to his mother by some word, look, or deed.

He had hired a conveyance and sent off his goods by two o'clock that day. The next step was to get some furniture, which, after serving for temporary use in the cottage, would be available for the house at Budmouth when increased by goods of a better description. A mart extensive enough for the purpose existed at Anglebury, some miles beyond the spot chosen for his residence, and there he resolved to pass the coming night.

It now only remained to wish his mother good-bye. She was sitting by the window as usual when he came downstairs.

"Mother, I am going to leave you," he said, holding out his hand.

"I thought you were, by your packing," replied Mrs. Yeobright in a voice from which every particle of emotion was painfully excluded.

"And you will part friends with me?"

"Certainly, Clym."

"I am going to be married on the twenty-fifth."

"I thought you were going to be married."

"And then—and then you must come and see us. You will understand me better after that, and our situation will not be so wretched as it is now."

"I do not think it likely I shall come to see you."

"Then it will not be my fault or Eustacia's, Mother. Good-bye!"

He kissed her cheek, and departed in great misery, which was several hours in lessening itself to a controllable level. The position had been such that nothing more could be said without, in the first place, breaking down a barrier; and that was not to be done.

No sooner had Yeobright gone from his mother's house than her face changed its rigid aspect for one of blank despair. After a while she wept, and her tears brought some relief. During the rest of the day she did nothing but walk up and down the garden path in a state bordering on stupefaction. Night came, and with it but little rest. The next day, with an instinct to do something which should reduce prostration to mournfulness, she went to her son's room, and with her own hands arranged it in order, for an imaginary time when he should return again. She gave some attention to her flowers, but it was perfunctorily bestowed, for they no longer charmed her.

It was a great relief when, early in the afternoon, Thomasin paid her an unexpected visit. This was not the first meeting between the relatives since Thomasin's marriage; and past blunders having been in a rough way rectified, they could always greet each other with pleasure and ease.

The oblique band of sunlight which followed her through the door became the young wife well. It illuminated her as her presence illuminated the heath. In her movements, in her gaze, she reminded the beholder of the feathered creatures who lived around her home. All similes and allegories concerning her began and ended with birds. There was as much variety in her motions as in their flight. When she was musing she was a kestrel, which hangs in the air by an invisible motion of its wings. When she was in a high wind her light body was blown against trees and banks like a heron's. When she was frightened she darted noiselessly like a kingfisher. When she was serene she skimmed like a swallow, and that is how she was moving now.

"You are looking very blithe, upon my word, Tamsie," said Mrs. Yeobright, with a sad smile. "How is Damon?"

"He is very well."

"Is he kind to you, Thomasin?" And Mrs. Yeobright observed her narrowly.

"Pretty fairly."

"Is that honestly said?"

"Yes, aunt. I would tell you if he were unkind." She added, blushing, and with hesitation, "He—I don't know if I ought to complain to you about this, but I am not quite sure what to do. I want some money, you know, aunt—some to buy little things for myself—and he doesn't give me any. I don't like to ask him; and yet, perhaps, he doesn't give it me because he doesn't know. Ought I to mention it to him, aunt?"

"Of course you ought. Have you never said a word on the matter?"

"You see, I had some of my own," said Thomasin evasively, "and I have not wanted any of his until lately. I did just say something about it last week; but he seems—not to remember."

"He must be made to remember. You are aware that I have a little box full of spade-guineas, which your uncle put into my hands to divide between yourself and Clym whenever I chose. Perhaps the time has come when it should be done. They can be turned into sovereigns at any moment."

"I think I should like to have my share—that is, if you don't mind."

"You shall, if necessary. But it is only proper that you should first tell your husband distinctly that you are without any, and see what he will do."

"Very well, I will . . . aunt, I have heard about Clym. I know you are in trouble about him, and that's why I have come."

Mrs. Yeobright turned away, and her features worked in her attempt to conceal her feelings. Then she ceased to make any attempt, and said, weeping, "O Thomasin, do you think he hates me? How can he bear to grieve me so, when I have lived only for him through all these years?"

"Hate you—no," said Thomasin soothingly. "It is only that he loves her too well. Look at it quietly—do. It is not so very bad of him. Do you know, I thought it not the worst match he could have made. Miss Vye's family is a good one on her mother's side; and her father was a romantic wanderer—a sort of Greek Ulysses."

"It is no use, Thomasin; it is no use. Your intention is good; but I will not trouble you to argue. I have gone through the whole that can be said on either side times, and many times. Clym and I have not parted in anger; we have parted in a worse way. It is not a passionate quarrel that would have broken my heart; it is the steady opposition and persistence in going wrong that he has shown. O Thomasin, he was so good as a little boy—so tender and kind!"

"He was, I know."

"I did not think one whom I called mine would grow up to treat me like this. He spoke to me as if I opposed him to injure him. As though I could wish him ill!"

"There are worse women in the world than Eustacia Vye."

"There are too many better; that's the agony of it. It was she, Thomasin, and she only, who led your husband to act as he did: I would swear it!"

"No," said Thomasin eagerly. "It was before he knew me that he thought of her, and it was nothing but a mere flirtation."

"Very well; we will let it be so. There is little use in unravelling that now. Sons must be blind if they will. Why is it that a woman can see from a distance what a man cannot see close? Clym must do as he will—he is nothing more to me. And this is maternity—to give one's best years and best love to ensure the fate of being despised!"

"You are too unyielding. Think how many mothers there are whose sons have brought them to public shame by real crimes before you feel so deeply a case like this."

"Thomasin, don't lecture me—I can't have it. It is the excess above what we expect that makes the force of the blow, and that may not be greater in their case than in mine: they may have foreseen the worst. . . . I am wrongly made, Thomasin," she added, with a mournful smile. "Some widows can guard against the wounds their children give them by turning their hearts to another husband and beginning life again. But I always was a poor, weak, one-idea'd creature—I had not the compass of heart nor the enterprise for that. Just as forlorn and stupefied as I was when my husband's spirit flew away I have sat ever since—never attempting to mend matters at all. I was comparatively a young woman then, and I might have had another family by this time, and have been comforted by them for the failure of this one son."

"It is more noble in you that you did not."

"The more noble, the less wise."

"Forget it, and be soothed, dear aunt. And I shall not leave you alone for long. I shall come and see you every day."

And for one week Thomasin literally fulfilled her word. She endeavoured to make light of the wedding; and brought news of the preparations, and that she was invited to be present. The next week she was rather unwell, and did not appear. Nothing had as yet been done about the guineas, for Thomasin feared to address her husband again on the subject, and Mrs. Yeobright had insisted upon this.

One day just before this time Wildeve was standing at the door of the Quiet Woman. In addition to the upward path through the heath to Rainbarrow and Mistover, there was a road which branched from the highway a short distance below the inn, and ascended to Mistover by a circuitous and easy incline. This was the only route on that side for vehicles to the captain's retreat. A light cart from the nearest town descended the road, and the lad who was driving pulled up in front of the inn for something to drink.

"You come from Mistover?" said Wildeve.

"Yes. They are taking in good things up there. Going to be a wedding." And the driver buried his face in his mug.

Wildeve had not received an inkling of the fact before, and a sudden expression of pain overspread his face. He turned for a moment into the passage to hide it. Then he came back again.

"Do you mean Miss Vye?" he said. "How is it—that she can be married so soon?"

"By the will of God and a ready young man, I suppose."

"You don't mean Mr. Yeobright?"

"Yes. He has been creeping about with her all the spring."

"I suppose—she was immensely taken with him?"

"She is crazy about him, so their general servant of all work tells me. And that lad Charley that looks after the horse is all in a daze about it. The stun-poll has got fondlike of her."

"Is she lively—is she glad? Going to be married so soon—well!"

"It isn't so very soon."

"No; not so very soon."

Wildeve went indoors to the empty room, a curious heart-ache within him. He rested his elbow upon the mantelpiece and his face upon his hand. When Thomasin entered the room he did not tell her of what he had heard. The old longing for Eustacia had reappeared in his soul: and it was mainly because he had discovered that it was another man's intention to possess her.

To be yearning for the difficult, to be weary of that offered; to care for the remote, to dislike the near; it was Wildeve's nature always. This is the true mark of the man of sentiment. Though Wildeve's fevered feeling had not been elaborated to real poetical compass, it was of the standard sort. His might have been called the Rousseau of Egdon.

VII

The Morning and the Evening of a Day

THE WEDDING MORNING CAME. NOBODY WOULD HAVE IMAGINED FROM APPEARANCES that Blooms-End had any interest in Mistover that day. A solemn stillness prevailed around the house of Clym's mother, and there was no more animation indoors. Mrs. Yeobright, who had declined to attend the ceremony, sat by the breakfast-table in the old room which communicated immediately with the porch, her eyes listlessly directed towards the open door. It was the room in which, six months earlier, the merry Christmas party had met, to which Eustacia came secretly and as a stranger. The only living thing that entered now was a sparrow; and seeing no movements to cause alarm, he hopped boldly round the room, endeavoured to go out by the window, and fluttered among the pot-flowers. This roused the lonely sitter, who got up, released the bird, and went to the door. She was expecting Thomasin, who had written the night before to state that the time had come when she would wish to have the money and that she would if possible call this day.

Yet Thomasin occupied Mrs. Yeobright's thoughts but slightly as she looked up the valley of the heath, alive with butterflies, and with grasshoppers whose husky noises on every side formed a whispered chorus. A domestic drama, for which the preparations were now being made a mile or two off, was but little less vividly present to her eyes than if enacted before her. She tried to dismiss the vision, and walked about the garden-plot; but her eyes ever and anon sought out the direction of the parish church to which Mistover belonged, and her excited fancy clove the hills which divided the building from her eyes. The morning wore away. Eleven o'clock struck: could it be that the wedding was then in progress? It must be so. She went on imagining the scene at the church to which he had by this time taken his bride. She pictured the little group of children by the gate as the pony-carriage drove up, in which, as Thomasin had learnt, they were going to perform the short journey. Then she saw them enter and proceed to the chancel and kneel; and the service seemed to go on.

She covered her face with her hands. "O, it is a mistake!" she groaned. "And he will rue it some day, and think of me!"

While she remained thus, overcome by her forebodings, the old clock indoors whizzed forth twelve strokes. Soon after, faint sounds floated to her ear from afar over the hills. The breeze came from that quarter, and it had brought with it the notes of distant bells, gaily starting off in a peal: one, two, three, four, five. The ringers at East Egdon were announcing the nuptials of Eustacia and her son.

"Then it is over," she murmured. "Well, well! and life too will be over soon. And why should I go on scalding my face like this? Cry about one thing in life, cry about all; one thread runs through the whole piece. And yet we say, 'a time to laugh!' "

Towards evening Wildeve came. Since Thomasin's marriage Mrs. Yeobright had shown him that grim friendliness which at last arises in all such cases of undesired affinity. The vision of what ought to have been is thrown aside in sheer weariness, and browbeaten human endeavour listlessly makes the best of the fact that is. Wildeve, to do him justice, had behaved very courteously to his wife's aunt; and it was with no surprise that she saw him enter now.

"Thomasin has not been able to come, as she promised to do," he replied to her enquiry, which had been anxious, for she knew that her niece was badly in want of money. "The captain came down last night and personally pressed her to join them to-day. So, not to be unpleasant, she determined to go. They fetched her in the pony-chaise, and are going to bring her back."

"Then it is done," said Mrs. Yeobright. "Have they gone to their new home?"

"I don't know. I have had no news from Mistover since Thomasin left to go."

"You did not go with her?" said she, as if there might be good reasons why.

"I could not," said Wildeve, reddening slightly. "We could not both leave the house; it was rather a busy morning, on account of Anglebury Great Market. I believe you have something to give to Thomasin? If you like, I will take it."

Mrs. Yeobright hesitated, and wondered if Wildeve knew what the something was. "Did she tell you of this?" she enquired.

"Not particularly. She casually dropped a remark about having arranged to fetch some article or other."

"It is hardly necessary to send it. She can have it whenever she chooses to come."

"That won't be yet. In the present state of her health she must not go on walking so much as she has done." He added, with a faint twang of sarcasm, "What wonderful thing is it that I cannot be trusted to take?"

"Nothing worth troubling you with."

"One would think you doubted my honesty," he said, with a laugh, though his colour rose in a quick resentfulness frequent with him.

"You need think no such thing," said she drily. "It is simply that I, in common with the rest of the world, feel that there are certain things which had better be done by certain people than by others."

"As you like, as you like," said Wildeve laconically. "It is not worth arguing about. Well, I think I must turn homeward again, as the inn must not be left long in charge of the lad and the maid only."

He went his way, his farewell being scarcely so courteous as his greeting. But Mrs. Yeobright knew him thoroughly by this time, and took little notice of his manner, good or bad.

When Wildeve was gone Mrs. Yeobright stood and considered what would be the best course to adopt with regard to the guineas, which she had not liked to entrust to Wildeve. It was hardly credible that Thomasin had told him to ask for them, when the necessity for them had arisen from the difficulty of obtaining money at his hands. At the same time Thomasin really wanted them, and might be unable to come to Blooms-End for another week at least. To take or send the money to her at the inn would be impolite, since Wildeve would pretty surely be present, or would discover the transaction; and if, as her aunt suspected, he treated her less kindly than she deserved to be treated, he might then get the whole sum out of her gentle hands. But on this particular evening Thomasin was at Mistover, and anything might be conveyed to her there without the knowledge of her husband. Upon the whole the opportunity was worth taking advantage of.

Her son, too, was there, and was now married. There could be no more proper moment to render him his share of the money than the present. And the chance that would be afforded her, by sending him this gift, of showing how far she was from bearing him ill-will, cheered the sad mother's heart.

She went upstairs and took from a locked drawer a little box, out of which she poured a hoard of broad unworn guineas that had lain there many a year. There were a hundred in all, and she divided them into two heaps, fifty in each. Tying up these in small canvas bags, she went down to the garden and called to Christian Cantle, who was loitering about in hope of a supper which was not really owed him. Mrs. Yeobright gave him the money-bags, charged him to go to Mistover, and on no account to deliver them into anyone's hands save her son's and Thomasin's. On further thought she deemed it advisable to tell Christian precisely what the two bags contained, that he might be fully impressed with their importance. Christian pocketed the money-bags, promised the greatest carefulness, and set out on his way.

"You need not hurry," said Mrs. Yeobright. "It will be better not to get there till after dusk, and then nobody will notice you. Come back here to supper, if it is not too late."

It was nearly nine o'clock when he began to ascend the vale towards Mistover; but the long days of summer being at their climax, the first obscurity of evening had only just begun to tan the landscape. At this point of his journey Christian heard voices, and found that they proceeded from a company of men and women who were traversing a hollow ahead of him, the tops only of their heads being visible.

He paused and thought of the money he carried. It was almost too early even for Christian seriously to fear robbery; nevertheless he took a precaution which ever since his boyhood he had adopted whenever he carried more than two or three shillings upon his person—a precaution somewhat like that of the owner of the Pitt Diamond when filled with similar misgivings. He took off his boots, untied the guineas, and emptied the contents of one little bag into the right boot, and of the other into the left, spreading them as flatly as possible over the bottom of each, which was really a spacious coffer by no means limited to the size of the foot. Pulling them on again and lacing them to the very top, he proceeded on his way, more easy in his head than under his soles.

His path converged towards that of the noisy company, and on coming nearer he found to his relief that they were several Egdon people whom he knew very well, while with them walked Fairway, of Blooms-End.

"What! Christian going too?" said Fairway as soon as he recognised the new-comer. "You've got no young woman nor wife to your name to gie a gown-piece to, I'm sure."

"What d'ye mean?" said Christian.

"Why, the raffle. The one we go to every year. Going to the raffle as well as ourselves?"

"Never knew a word o't. Is it like cudgel-playing or other sportful forms of bloodshed? I don't want to go, thank you, Mister Fairway, and no offence."

"Christian don't know the fun o't, and 'twould be a fine sight for him," said a buxom woman. "There's no danger at all, Christian. Every man puts in a shilling apiece, and one wins a gown-piece for his wife or sweetheart if he's got one."

"Well, as that's not my fortune there's no meaning in it to me. But I should like to see the fun, if there's nothing of the black art in it, and if a man may look on without cost or getting into any dangerous wrangle?"

"There will be no uproar at all," said Timothy. "Sure, Christian, if you'd like to come we'll see there's no harm done."

"And no ba'dy gaieties, I suppose? You see, neighbours, if so, it would be setting father a bad example, as he is so light moral'd. But a gown-piece for a shilling, and no black art—'tis worth looking in to see, and it wouldn't hinder me half an hour. Yes, I'll come, if you'll step a little way towards Mistover with me afterwards, supposing night should have closed in, and nobody else is going that way?"

One or two promised; and Christian, diverging from his direct path, turned round to the right with his companions towards the Quiet Woman.

When they entered the large common-room of the inn they found assembled there about ten men from among the neighbouring population, and the group was increased by the new contingent to double that number. Most of them were sitting round the room in seats divided by wooden elbows like those of crude cathedral stalls, which were carved with the initials of many an illustrious drunkard of former times who had passed his days and his nights between them, and now lay as an alcoholic cinder in the nearest churchyard. Among the cups on the long table before the sitters lay an open parcel of light drapery— the gown-piece, as it was called—which was to be raffled for. Wildeve was standing with his back to the fireplace, smoking a cigar; and the promoter of the raffle, a packman from a distant town, was expatiating upon the value of the fabric as material for a summer dress.

"Now, gentlemen," he continued, as the new-comers drew up to the table, "there's five have entered, and we want four more to make up the number. I think, by the faces of those gentlemen who have just come in, that they are shrewd enough to take advantage of this rare opportunity of beautifying their ladies at a very trifling expense."

Fairway, Sam, and another placed their shillings on the table, and the man turned to Christian.

"No, sir," said Christian, drawing back, with a quick gaze of misgiving. "I am only a poor chap come to look on, an it please ye, sir. I don't so much as know how you do it. If so be I was sure of getting it I would put down the shilling; but I couldn't otherwise."

"I think you might almost be sure," said the pedlar. "In fact, now I look into your face, even if I can't say you are sure to win, I can say that I never saw anything look more like winning in my life."

"You'll anyhow have the same chance as the rest of us," said Sam.

"And the extra luck of being the last comer," said another.

"And I was born wi' a caul, and perhaps can be no more ruined than drowned?" Christian added, beginning to give way.

Ultimately Christian laid down his shilling, the raffle began, and the dice went round. When it came to Christian's turn he took the box with a trembling hand, shook it fearfully, and threw a pair-royal. Three of the others had thrown common low pairs, and all the rest mere points.

"The gentleman looked like winning, as I said," observed the chapman blandly. "Take it, sir; the article is yours."

"Haw-haw-haw!" said Fairway. "I'm damned if this isn't the quarest start that ever I knowed!"

"Mine?" asked Christian, with a vacant stare from his target eyes. "I—I haven't got neither maid, wife, nor widder belonging to me at all, and I'm afeard it will make me laughed at to ha'e it, Master Traveller. What with being curious to join in I never thought of that! What shall I do wi' a woman's clothes in my bedroom, and not lose my decency!"

"Keep 'em, to be sure," said Fairway, "if it is only for luck. Perhaps 'twill tempt some woman that thy poor carcase had no power over when standing empty-handed."

"Keep it, certainly," said Wildeve, who had idly watched the scene from a distance.

The table was then cleared of the articles, and the men began to drink.

"Well, to be sure!" said Christian, half to himself. "To think I should have been born so lucky as this, and not have found it out until now! What curious creatures these dice be—powerful rulers of us all, and yet at my command! I am sure I never need be afeared of anything after this." He handled the dice fondly one by one. "Why, sir," he said in a confidential whisper to Wildeve, who was near his left hand, "if I could only use this power that's in me of multiplying money I might do some good to a near relation of yours, seeing what I've got about me of hers—eh?" He tapped one of his money-laden boots upon the floor.

"What do you mean?" said Wildeve.

"That's a secret. Well, I must be going now." He looked anxiously towards Fairway.

"Where are you going?" Wildeve asked.

"To Mistover Knap. I have to see Mrs. Thomasin there—that's all."

"I am going there, too, to fetch Mrs. Wildeve. We can walk together."

Wildeve became lost in thought, and a look of inward illumination came into his eyes. It was money for his wife that Mrs. Yeobright could not trust him with. "Yet she could trust this fellow," he said to himself. "Why doesn't that which belongs to the wife belong to the husband too?"

He called to the pot-boy to bring him his hat, and said, "Now, Christian, I am ready."

"Mr. Wildeve," said Christian timidly, as he turned to leave the room, "would you mind lending me them wonderful little things that carry my luck inside 'em, that I might practise a bit by myself, you know?" He looked wistfully at the dice and box lying on the mantelpiece.

"Certainly," said Wildeve carelessly. "They were only cut out by some lad with his knife, and are worth nothing." And Christian went back and privately pocketed them.

Wildeve opened the door and looked out. The night was warm and cloudy. "By Gad! 'tis dark," he continued. "But I suppose we shall find our way."

"If we should lose the path it might be awkward," said Christian. "A lantern is the only shield that will make it safe for us."

"Let's have a lantern by all means." The stable-lantern was fetched and lighted. Christian took up his gown-piece, and the two set out to ascend the hill.

Within the room the men fell into chat till their attention was for a moment drawn to the chimney-corner. This was large, and, in addition to its proper recess, contained within its jambs, like many on Egdon, a receding seat, so that a person might sit there absolutely unobserved, provided there was no fire to light him up, as was the case now and throughout the summer. From the niche a single object protruded into the light from the candles on the table. It was a clay pipe, and its colour was reddish. The men had been attracted to this object by a voice behind the pipe asking for a light.

"Upon my life, it fairly startled me when the man spoke!" said Fairway, handing a candle. "Oh—'tis the reddleman! You've kept a quiet tongue, young man."

"Yes, I had nothing to say," observed Venn. In a few minutes he arose and wished the company good-night.

Meanwhile Wildeve and Christian had plunged into the heath.

It was a stagnant, warm, and misty night, full of all the heavy perfumes of new vegetation not yet dried by hot sun, and among these particularly the scent of the fern. The lantern, dangling from Christian's hand, brushed the feathery fronds in passing by, disturbing moths and other winged insects, which flew out and alighted upon its horny panes.

"So you have money to carry to Mrs. Wildeve?" said Christian's companion, after a silence. "Don't you think it very odd that it shouldn't be given to me?"

"As man and wife be one flesh, 'twould have been all the same, I should think," said Christian. "But my strict documents was, to give the money into Mrs. Wildeve's hand: and 'tis well to do things right."

"No doubt," said Wildeve. Any person who had known the circumstances might have perceived that Wildeve was mortified by the discovery that the matter in transit was money, and not, as he had supposed when at Blooms-End, some fancy nick-nack which only interested the two women themselves. Mrs. Yeobright's refusal implied that his honour was not considered to be of sufficiently good quality to make him a safer bearer of his wife's property.

"How very warm it is to-night, Christian!" he said, panting, when they were nearly under Rainbarrow. "Let us sit down for a few minutes, for Heaven's sake."

Wildeve flung himself down on the soft ferns; and Christian, placing the lantern and parcel on the ground, perched himself in a cramped position hard by, his knees almost touching his chin. He presently thrust one hand into his coat-pocket and began shaking it about.

"What are you rattling in there?" said Wildeve.

"Only the dice, sir," said Christian, quickly withdrawing his hand. "What magical machines these little things be, Mr. Wildeve! 'Tis a game I should never get tired of. Would you mind my taking 'em out and looking at 'em for a minute, to see how they are made? I didn't like to look close before the other men, for fear they should think it bad manners in me." Christian took them out and examined them in the hollow of his hand by the lantern light. "That these little things should carry such luck, and such charm, and such a spell, and such power in 'em, passes all I ever heard or zeed," he went on, with a fascinated gaze at the dice, which, as is frequently the case in country places, were made of wood, the points being burnt upon each face with the end of a wire.

"They are a great deal in a small compass, you think?"

"Yes. Do ye suppose they really be the devil's playthings, Mr. Wildeve? If so, 'tis no good sign that I be such a lucky man."

"You ought to win some money, now that you've got them. Any woman would marry you then. Now is your time, Christian, and I would recommend you not to let it slip. Some men are born to luck, some are not. I belong to the latter class."

"Did you ever know anybody who was born to it besides myself?"

"O yes. I once heard of an Italian, who sat down at a gaming-table, with only a louis (that's a foreign sovereign) in his pocket. He played on for twenty-four hours, and won ten thousand pounds, stripping the bank he had played against. Then there was another man who had lost a thousand pounds, and went to the broker's next day to sell stock, that he might pay the debt. The man to whom he owed the money went with him in a hackney-coach; and to pass the time they tossed who should pay the fare. The ruined man won, and the other was tempted to continue the game, and they played all the way. When the coachman stopped he was told to drive home again: the whole thousand pounds had been won back by the man who was going to sell."

"Ha—ha—splendid!" exclaimed Christian. "Go on—go on!"

"Then there was a man of London, who was only a waiter at White's club-house. He began playing first half-crown stakes, and then higher and higher, till he became very rich, got an appointment in India, and rose to be Governor of Madras. His daughter married a member of parliament, and the Bishop of Carlisle stood godfather to one of the children."

"Wonderful! Wonderful!"

"And once there was a young man in America who gambled till he had lost his last dollar. He staked his watch and chain; and lost as before: staked his umbrella; lost again: staked his hat; lost again: staked his coat and stood in his shirt-sleeves; lost again. Began taking off his breeches, and then a looker-on gave him a trifle for his pluck. With this he won. Won back his coat, won back his hat, won back his umbrella, his watch, his money, and went out of the door a rich man."

"Oh, 'tis too good—it takes away my breath! Mr. Wildeve, I think I will try another shilling with you, as I am one of that sort; no danger can come o't, and you can afford to lose."

"Very well," said Wildeve, rising. Searching about with the lantern, he found a large flat stone, which he placed between himself and Christian, and sat down again. The lantern was opened to give more light, and its rays directed upon the stone. Christian put down a shilling, Wildeve another, and each threw. Christian won. They played for two. Christian won again.

"Let us try four," said Wildeve. They played for four. This time the stakes were won by Wildeve.

"Ah, those little accidents will, of course, sometimes happen to the luckiest man," he observed.

"And now I have no more money!" explained Christian excitedly. "And yet, if I could go on, I should get it back again, and more. I wish this was mine." He struck his boot upon the ground, so that the guineas chinked within.

"What! you have not put Mrs. Wildeve's money there?"

"Yes. 'Tis for safety. Is it any harm to raffle with a married lady's money when, if I win, I shall only keep my winnings, and give her her own all the same; and if t'other man wins, her money will go to the lawful owner?"

"None at all."

Wildeve had been brooding ever since they started on the mean estimation in which he was held by his wife's friends; and it cut his heart severely. As the minutes passed he had gradually drifted into a revengeful intention without knowing the precise moment of forming it. This was to teach Mrs. Yeobright a lesson, as he considered it to be; in other words, to show her if he could, that her niece's husband was the proper guardian of her niece's money.

"Well, here goes!" said Christian, beginning to unlace one boot. "I shall dream of it nights and nights, I suppose; but I shall always swear my flesh don't crawl when I think o't!"

He thrust his hand into the boot and withdrew one of poor Thomasin's precious guineas, piping hot. Wildeve had already placed a sovereign on the stone. The game was then resumed. Wildeve won first, and Christian ventured another, winning himself this time. The game fluctuated, but the average was in Wildeve's favour. Both men became so absorbed in the game that they took no heed of anything but the pigmy objects immediately beneath their eyes; the flat stone, the open lantern, the dice, and the few illuminated fern-leaves which lay under the light, were the whole world to them.

At length Christian lost rapidly; and presently, to his horror, the whole fifty guineas belonging to Thomasin had been handed over to his adversary.

"I don't care—I don't care!" he moaned, and desperately set about untying his left boot to get at the other fifty. "The devil will toss me into the flames on his three-pronged fork for this night's work, I know! But perhaps I shall win yet, and then I'll get a wife to sit up with me o' nights and I won't be afeard, I won't! Here's another for'ee, my man!" He slapped another guinea down upon the stone, and the dice-box was rattled again.

Time passed on. Wildeve began to be as excited as Christian himself. When commencing the game his intention had been nothing further than a bitter practical joke on Mrs. Yeobright. To win the money, fairly or otherwise, and to hand it contemptuously to Thomasin in her aunt's presence, had been the dim outline of his purpose. But men are drawn from their intentions even in the course of carrying them out, and it was extremely doubtful, by the time the twentieth guinea had been reached, whether Wildeve was conscious of any other intention than that of winning for his own personal benefit. Moreover, he was now no longer gambling for his wife's money, but for Yeobright's; though of this fact Christian, in his apprehensiveness, did not inform him till afterwards.

It was nearly eleven o'clock, when, with almost a shriek, Christian placed Yeobright's last bright guinea upon the stone. In thirty seconds it had gone the way of its companions.

Christian turned and flung himself on the ferns in a convulsion of remorse. "O, what shall I do with my wretched self?" he groaned. "What shall I do? Will any good Heaven hae mercy upon my wicked soul?"

"Do? Live on just the same."

"I won't live on just the same! I'll die! I say you are a—a—"

"A man sharper than my neighbour."

"Yes, a man sharper than my neighbour; a regular sharper!"

"Poor chips-in-porridge, you are very unmannerly."

"I don't know about that! And I say you be unmannerly! You've got money that isn't your own. Half the guineas are poor Mr. Clym's."

"How's that?"

"Because I had to gie fifty of 'em to him. Mrs. Yeobright said so."

"Oh? . . . Well, 'twould have been more graceful of her to have given them to his wife Eustacia. But they are in my hands now."

Christian pulled on his boots, and with heavy breathings, which could be heard to some distance, dragged his limbs together, arose, and tottered away out of sight. Wildeve set about shutting the lantern to return to the house, for he deemed it too late to go to Mistover to meet his wife, who was to be driven home in the captain's four-wheel. While he was closing the little horn door a figure rose from behind a neighbouring bush and came forward into the lantern light. It was the reddleman approaching.

VIII

A NEW FORCE DISTURBS THE CURRENT

WILDEVE STARED. VENN LOOKED COOLLY TOWARDS WILDEVE, AND, WITHOUT A WORD being spoken, he deliberately sat himself down where Christian had been seated, thrust his hand into his pocket, drew out a sovereign, and laid it on the stone.

"You have been watching us from behind that bush?" said Wildeve.

The reddleman nodded. "Down with your stake," he said. "Or haven't you pluck enough to go on?"

Now, gambling is a species of amusement which is much more easily begun with full pockets than left off with the same; and though Wildeve in a cooler temper might have prudently declined this invitation, the excitement of his recent success carried him completely away. He placed one of the guineas on a slab beside the reddleman's sovereign. "Mine is a guinea," he said.

"A guinea that's not your own," said Venn sarcastically.

"It is my own," answered Wildeve haughtily. "It is my wife's, and what is hers is mine."

"Very well; let's make a beginning." He shook the box, and threw eight, ten, and nine; the three casts amounted to twenty-seven.

This encouraged Wildeve. He took the box; and his three casts amounted to forty-five.

Down went another of the reddleman's sovereigns against his first one which Wildeve laid. This time Wildeve threw fifty-one points, but no pair. The reddleman looked grim, threw a raffle of aces, and pocketed the stakes.

"Here you are again," said Wildeve contemptuously. "Double the stakes." He laid two of Thomasin's guineas, and the reddleman his two pounds. Venn won again. New stakes were laid on the stone, and the gamblers proceeded as before.

Wildeve was a nervous and excitable man; and the game was beginning to tell upon his temper. He writhed, fumed, shifted his seat; and the beating of his heart was almost audible. Venn sat with lips impassively closed and eyes reduced to a pair of unimportant twinkles; he scarcely appeared to breathe. He might have been an Arab, or an automaton; he would have been like a red-sandstone statue but for the motion of his arm with the dice-box.

The game fluctuated, now in favour of one, now in favour of the other, without any great advantage on the side of either. Nearly twenty minutes were passed thus. The light of the candle had by this time attracted heath-flies, moths, and other winged creatures of night, which floated round the lantern, flew into the flame, or beat about the faces of the two players.

But neither of the men paid much attention to these things, their eyes being concentrated upon the little flat stone, which to them was an arena vast and important as a battle-field. By this time a change had come over the game; the reddleman won continually. At length sixty guineas—Thomasin's fifty, and ten of Clym's—had passed into his hands. Wildeve was reckless, frantic, exasperated.

" 'Won back his coat,' " said Venn slily.

Another throw, and the money went the same way.

" 'Won back his hat,' " continued Venn.

"Oh, oh!" said Wildeve.

" 'Won back his watch, won back his money, and went out of the door a rich man,' " added Venn sentence by sentence, as stake after stake passed over to him.

"Five more!" shouted Wildeve, dashing down the money. "And three casts be hanged—one shall decide."

The red automaton opposite lapsed into silence, nodded, and followed his example. Wildeve rattled the box, and threw a pair of sixes and five points. He clapped his hands; "I have done it this time—hurrah!"

"There are two playing, and only one has thrown," said the reddleman, quietly bringing down the box. The eyes of each were then so intently converged upon the stone that one could fancy their beams were visible, like rays in a fog.

Venn lifted the box, and behold a triplet of sixes was disclosed.

Wildeve was full of fury. While the reddleman was grasping the stakes Wildeve seized the dice and hurled them, box and all, into the darkness, uttering a fearful imprecation. Then he arose and began stamping up and down like a madman.

"It is all over, then?" said Venn.

"No, no!" cried Wildeve. "I mean to have another chance yet. I must!"

"But, my good man, what have you done with the dice?"

"I threw them away—it was a momentary irritation. What a fool I am! Here—come and help me to look for them—we must find them again."

Wildeve snatched up the lantern and began anxiously prowling among the furze and fern.

"You are not likely to find them there," said Venn, following. "What did you do such a crazy thing as that for? Here's the box. The dice can't be far off."

Wildeve turned the light eagerly upon the spot where Venn had found the box, and mauled the herbage right and left. In the course of a few minutes one of the dice was found. They searched on for some time, but no other was to be seen.

"Never mind," said Wildeve; "let's play with one."

"Agreed," said Venn.

Down they sat again, and recommenced with single guinea stakes; and the play went on smartly. But Fortune had unmistakably fallen in love with the reddleman to-night. He won steadily, till he was the owner of fourteen more of the gold pieces. Seventy-nine of the hundred guineas were his, Wildeve possessing only twenty-one. The aspect of the two opponents was now singular. Apart from motions, a complete diorama of the fluctuations of the game went on in their eyes. A diminutive candle-flame was mirrored in each pupil, and it would have been possible to distinguish therein between the moods of hope and the moods of abandonment, even as regards the reddleman, though his facial muscles betrayed nothing at all. Wildeve played on with the recklessness of despair.

"What's that?" he suddenly exclaimed, hearing a rustle; and they both looked up.

They were surrounded by dusky forms between four and five feet high, standing a few paces beyond the rays of the lantern. A moment's inspection revealed that the encircling figures were heath-croppers, their heads being all towards the players, at whom they gazed intently.

"Hoosh!" said Wildeve; and the whole forty or fifty animals at once turned and galloped away. Play was again resumed.

Ten minutes passed away. Then a large death's head moth advanced from the obscure outer air, wheeled twice round the lantern, flew straight at the candle, and extinguished it by the force of the blow. Wildeve had just thrown, but had not lifted the box to see what he had cast; and now it was impossible.

"What the infernal!" he shrieked. "Now, what shall we do? Perhaps I have thrown six—have you any matches?"

"None," said Venn.

"Christian had some—I wonder where he is. Christian!"

But there was no reply to Wildeve's shout, save a mournful whining from the herons which were nesting lower down the vale. Both men looked blankly round without rising. As their eyes grew accustomed to the darkness they perceived faint greenish points of light among the grass and fern. These lights dotted the hillside like stars of a low magnitude.

"Ah—glowworms," said Wildeve. "Wait a minute. We can continue the game."

Venn sat still, and his companion went hither and thither till he had gathered thirteen glowworms—as many as he could find in a space of four or five minutes—upon a foxglove leaf which he pulled for the purpose. The reddleman vented a low humorous laugh when he saw his adversary return with these. "Determined to go on, then?" he said drily.

"I always am!" said Wildeve angrily. And shaking the glowworms from the leaf he ranged them with a trembling hand in a circle on the stone, leaving a space in the middle for the descent of the dice-box, over which the thirteen tiny lamps threw a pale phosphoric shine. The game was again renewed. It happened to be that season of the year at which glowworms put forth their greatest brilliancy, and the light they yielded was more than ample for the purpose, since it is possible on such nights to read the handwriting of a letter by the light of two or three.

The incongruity between the men's deeds and their environment was great. Amid the soft juicy vegetation of the hollow in which they sat, the motionless and the uninhabited solitude, intruded the chink of guineas, the rattle of dice, the exclamations of the reckless players.

Wildeve had lifted the box as soon as the lights were obtained, and the solitary die proclaimed that the game was still against him.

"I won't play any more: you've been tampering with the dice," he shouted.

"How—when they were your own?" said the reddleman.

"We'll change the game: the lowest point shall win the stake—it may cut off my ill luck. Do you refuse?"

"No—go on," said Venn.

"O, there they are again—damn them!" cried Wildeve, looking up. The heath-croppers had returned noiselessly, and were looking on with erect heads just as before, their timid eyes fixed upon the scene, as if they were wondering what mankind and candle-light could have to do in these haunts at this untoward hour.

"What a plague those creatures are—staring so!" he said, and flung a stone, which scattered them; when the game was continued as before.

Wildeve had now ten guineas left; and each laid five. Wildeve threw three points; Venn two, and raked in the coins. The other seized the die, and clenched his teeth upon it in sheer rage, as if he would bite it in pieces. "Never give in—here are my last five!" he cried, throwing them down. "Hang the glowworms—they are going out. Why don't you burn, you little fools? Stir them up with a thorn."

He probed the glowworms with a bit of stick, and rolled them over, till the bright side of their tails was upwards.

"There's light enough. Throw on," said Venn.

Wildeve brought down the box within the shining circle and looked eagerly. He had thrown ace. "Well done!—I said it would turn, and it has turned." Venn said nothing; but his hand shook slightly.

He threw ace also.

"O!" said Wildeve. "Curse me!"

The die smacked the stone a second time. It was ace again. Venn looked gloomy, threw: the die was seen to be lying in two pieces, the cleft sides uppermost.

"I've thrown nothing at all," he said.

"Serves me right—I split the die with my teeth. Here—take your money. Blank is less than one."

"I don't wish it."

"Take it, I say—you've won it!" And Wildeve threw the stakes against the reddle-man's chest. Venn gathered them up, arose, and withdrew from the hollow, Wildeve sitting stupefied.

When he had come to himself he also arose, and, with the extinguished lantern in his hand, went towards the high-road. On reaching it he stood still. The silence of night pervaded the whole heath except in one direction; and that was towards Mistover. There he could hear the noise of light wheels, and presently saw two carriage-lamps descending the hill. Wildeve screened himself under a bush and waited.

The vehicle came on and passed before him. It was a hired carriage, and behind the coachman were two persons whom he knew well. There sat Eustacia and Yeobright, the arm of the latter being round her waist. They turned the sharp corner at the bottom towards the temporary home which Clym had hired and furnished, about three miles to the eastward.

Wildeve forgot the loss of the money at the sight of his lost love, whose preciousness in his eyes was increasing in geometrical progression with each new incident that reminded him of their hopeless division. Brimming with the subtilised misery that he was capable of feeling, he followed the opposite way towards the inn.

About the same moment that Wildeve stepped into the highway Venn also had reached it at a point a hundred yards further on; and he, hearing the same wheels, likewise waited till the carriage should come up. When he saw who sat therein he seemed to be disappointed. Reflecting a minute or two, during which interval the carriage rolled on, he crossed the road, and took a short cut through the furze and heath to a point where the turnpike road bent round in ascending a hill. He was now again in front of the carriage, which presently came up at a walking pace. Venn stepped forward and showed himself.

Eustacia started when the lamp shone upon him, and Clym's arm was involuntarily withdrawn from her waist. He said, "What, Diggory? You are having a lonely walk."

"Yes—I beg your pardon for stopping you," said Venn. "But I am waiting about for Mrs. Wildeve: I have something to give her from Mrs. Yeobright. Can you tell me if she's gone home from the party yet?"

"No. But she will be leaving soon. You may possibly meet her at the corner."

Venn made a farewell obeisance, and walked back to his former position, where the by-road from Mistover joined the highway. Here he remained fixed for nearly half an hour; and then another pair of lights came down the hill. It was the old-fashioned wheeled nondescript belonging to the captain, and Thomasin sat in it alone, driven by Charley.

The reddleman came up as they slowly turned the corner. "I beg pardon for stopping you, Mrs. Wildeve," he said. "But I have something to give you privately from Mrs. Yeobright." He handed a small parcel; it consisted of the hundred guineas he had just won, roughly twisted up in a piece of paper.

Thomasin recovered from her surprise, and took the packet. "That's all, ma'am—I wish you good-night," he said, and vanished from her view.

Thus Venn, in his anxiety to rectify matters, had placed in Thomasin's hands not only the fifty guineas which rightly belonged to her, but also the fifty intended for her cousin Clym. His mistake had been based upon Wildeve's words at the opening of the game, when he indignantly denied that the guinea was not his own. It had not been comprehended by the reddleman that at half-way through the performance the game was continued with the money of another person; and it was an error which afterwards helped to cause more misfortune than treble the loss in money value could have done.

The night was now somewhat advanced; and Venn plunged deeper into the heath, till he came to a ravine where his van was standing—a spot not more than two hundred yards from the site of the gambling bout. He entered this movable home of his, lit his lantern, and, before closing his door for the night, stood reflecting on the circumstances of the preceding hours. While he stood the dawn grew visible in the north-east quarter of the heavens, which, the clouds having cleared off, was bright with a soft sheen at this midsummer time, though it was only between one and two o'clock. Venn, thoroughly weary, then shut his door and flung himself down to sleep.

BOOK FOURTH

THE CLOSED DOOR

I

THE RENCOUNTER BY THE POOL

THE JULY SUN SHONE OVER EGDON AND FIRED ITS CRIMSON HEATHER TO SCARLET. It was the one season of the year, and the one weather of the season, in which the heath was gorgeous. This flowering period represented the second or noontide division in the cycle of those superficial changes which alone were possible here; it followed the green or young-fern period, representing the morn, and preceded the brown period, when the heath-bells and ferns would wear the russet tinges of evening; to be in turn displaced by the dark hue of the winter period, representing night.

Clym and Eustacia, in their little house at Alderworth, were living on with a monotony which was delightful to them. The heath and changes of weather were quite blotted out from their eyes for the present. They were enclosed in a sort of luminous mist, which hid from them surroundings of any inharmonious colour, and gave to all things the character of light. When it rained they were charmed, because they could remain indoors together all day with such a show of reason; when it was fine they were charmed, because they could sit together on the hills. They were like those double stars which revolve round and round each other, and from a distance appear to be one. The absolute solitude in which they lived intensified their reciprocal thoughts; yet some might have said that it had the disadvantage of consuming their mutual affections at a fearfully prodigal rate. Yeobright did not fear for his own part; but recollection of Eustacia's old speech about the evanescence of love, now apparently forgotten by her, sometimes caused him to ask himself a question; and he recoiled at the thought that the quality of finiteness was not foreign to Eden.

When three or four weeks had been passed thus, Yeobright resumed his reading in earnest. To make up for lost time he studied indefatigably, for he wished to enter his new profession with the least possible delay.

Now, Eustacia's dream had always been that, once married to Clym, she would have the power of inducing him to return to Paris. He had carefully withheld all promise to do so; but would he be proof against her coaxing and argument? She had calculated to such a degree on the probability of success that she had represented Paris, and not Budmouth, to her grand-father as in all likelihood their future home. Her hopes were bound up in this dream. In the quiet days since their marriage, when Yeobright had been poring over her lips, her eyes, and the lines of her face, she had mused and mused on the subject, even while in the act of returning his gaze; and now the sight of the books, indicating a future which was antagonistic to her dream, struck her with a positively painful jar. She was hoping for the time when, as the mistress of some pretty establishment, however small, near a Parisian Boulevard, she would be passing her days on the skirts at least of the gay world, and catching stray wafts from those town pleasures she was so well fitted to enjoy. Yet Yeobright was as firm in the contrary intention as if the tendency of marriage were rather to develop the fantasies of young philanthropy than to sweep them away.

Her anxiety reached a high pitch; but there was something in Clym's undeviating manner which made her hesitate before sounding him on the subject. At this point in their experience, however, an incident helped her. It occurred one evening about six weeks after their union, and arose entirely out of the unconscious misapplication of Venn of the fifty guineas intended for Yeobright.

A day or two after the receipt of the money Thomasin had sent a note to her aunt to thank her. She had been surprised at the largeness of the amount; but as no sum had ever been mentioned she set that down to her late uncle's generosity. She had been strictly charged by her aunt to say nothing to her husband of this gift; and Wildeve, as was natural enough, had not brought himself to mention to his wife a single particular of the midnight scene in the heath. Christian's terror, in like manner, had tied his tongue on the share he took in that proceeding; and hoping that by some means or other the money had gone to its proper destination, he simply asserted as much, without giving details.

Therefore, when a week or two had passed away, Mrs. Yeobright began to wonder why she never heard from her son of the receipt of the present; and to add gloom to her perplexity came the possibility that resentment might be the cause of his silence. She could hardly believe as much, but why did he not write? She questioned Christian, and the confusion in his answers would at once have led her to believe that something was wrong, had not one-half of his story been corroborated by Thomasin's note.

Mrs. Yeobright was in this state of uncertainty when she was informed one morning that her son's wife was visiting her grand-father at Mistover. She determined to walk up the hill, see Eustacia, and ascertain from her daughter-in-law's lips whether the family guineas, which were to Mrs. Yeobright what family jewels are to wealthier dowagers, had miscarried or not.

When Christian learnt where she was going his concern reached its height. At the moment of her departure he could prevaricate no longer, and, confessing to the gambling, told her the truth as far as he knew it—that the guineas had been won by Wildeve.

"What, is he going to keep them?" Mrs. Yeobright cried.

"I hope and trust not!" moaned Christian. "He's a good man, and perhaps will do right things. He said you ought to have gied Mr. Clym's share to Eustacia, and that's perhaps what he'll do himself."

To Mrs. Yeobright, as soon as she could calmly reflect, there was much likelihood in this, for she could hardly believe that Wildeve would really appropriate money belonging to her son. The intermediate course of giving it to Eustacia was the sort of thing to please Wildeve's fancy. But it filled the mother with anger none the less. That Wildeve should have got command of the guineas after all, and should rearrange the disposal of them, placing Clym's share in Clym's wife's hands, because she had been his own sweetheart, and might be so still, was as irritating a pain as any that Mrs. Yeobright had ever borne.

She instantly dismissed the wretched Christian from her employ for his conduct in the affair; but, feeling quite helpless and unable to do without him, told him afterwards that he might stay a little longer if he chose. Then she hastened off to Eustacia, moved by a much less promising emotion towards her daughter-in-law than she had felt half an hour earlier, when planning her journey. At that time it was to enquire in a friendly spirit if there had been any accidental loss; now it was to ask plainly if Wildeve had privately given her money which had been intended as a sacred gift to Clym.

She started at two o'clock, and her meeting with Eustacia was hastened by the appearance of the young lady beside the pool and bank which bordered her grand-father's premises, where she stood surveying the scene, and perhaps thinking of the romantic en-actments it had witnessed in past days. When Mrs. Yeobright approached, Eustacia sur-veyed her with the calm stare of a stranger.

The mother-in-law was the first to speak. "I was coming to see you," she said.

"Indeed!" said Eustacia with surprise, for Mrs. Yeobright, much to the girl's mortifi-cation, had refused to be present at the wedding. "I did not at all expect you."

"I was coming on business only," said the visitor, more coldly than at first. "Will you excuse my asking this—Have you received a gift from Thomasin's husband?"

"A gift?"

"I mean money!"

"What—I myself?"

"Well, I meant yourself, privately—though I was not going to put it in that way."

"Money from Mr. Wildeve? No—never! Madam, what do you mean by that?" Eusta-cia fired up all too quickly, for her own consciousness of the old attachment between her-self and Wildeve led her to jump to the conclusion that Mrs. Yeobright also knew of it, and might have come to accuse her of receiving dishonourable presents from him now.

"I simply ask the question," said Mrs. Yeobright. "I have been—"

"You ought to have better opinions of me—I feared you were against me from the first!" exclaimed Eustacia

"No. I was simply for Clym," replied Mrs. Yeobright, with too much emphasis in her earnestness. "It is the instinct of everyone to look after their own."

"How can you imply that he required guarding against me?" cried Eustacia, passion-ate tears in her eyes. "I have not injured him by marrying him! What sin have I done that you should think so ill of me? You had no right to speak against me to him when I have never wronged you."

"I only did what was fair under the circumstances," said Mrs. Yeobright more softly. "I would rather not have gone into this question at present, but you compel me. I am not ashamed to tell you the honest truth. I was firmly convinced that he ought not to marry you—therefore I tried to dissuade him by all the means in my power. But it is done now, and I have no idea of complaining any more. I am ready to welcome you."

"Ah, yes, it is very well to see things in that business point of view," murmured Eu-stacia with a smothered fire of feeling. "But why should you think there is anything be-tween me and Mr. Wildeve? I have a spirit as well as you. I am indignant; and so would any woman be. It was a condescension in me to be Clym's wife, and not a manoeuvre, let me remind you; and therefore I will not be treated as a schemer whom it becomes neces-sary to bear with because she has crept into the family."

"Oh!" said Mrs. Yeobright, vainly endeavouring to control her anger. "I have never heard anything to show that my son's lineage is not as good as the Vyes'—perhaps better. It is amusing to hear you talk of condescension."

"It was condescension, nevertheless," said Eustacia vehemently. "And if I had known then what I know now, that I should be living in this wild heath a month after my marriage, I—I should have thought twice before agreeing."

"It would be better not to say that; it might not sound truthful. I am not aware that any deception was used on his part—I know there was not—whatever might have been the case on the other side."

"This is too exasperating!" answered the younger woman huskily, her face crimsoning, and her eyes darting light. "How can you dare to speak to me like that? I insist upon repeating to you that had I known that my life would from my marriage up to this time have been as it is, I should have said *No*. I don't complain. I have never uttered a sound of such a thing to him; but it is true. I hope therefore that in the future you will be silent on my eagerness. If you injure me now you injure yourself."

"Injure you? Do you think I am an evil-disposed person?"

"You injured me before my marriage, and you have now suspected me of secretly favouring another man for money!"

"I could not help what I thought. But I have never spoken of you outside my house."

"You spoke of me within it, to Clym, and you could not do worse."

"I did my duty."

"And I'll do mine."

"A part of which will possibly be to set him against his mother. It is always so. But why should I not bear it as others have borne it before me!"

"I understand you," said Eustacia, breathless with emotion. "You think me capable of every bad thing. Who can be worse than a wife who encourages a lover, and poisons her husband's mind against his relative? Yet that is now the character given to me. Will you not come and drag him out of my hands?"

Mrs. Yeobright gave back heat for heat.

"Don't rage at me, madam! It ill becomes your beauty, and I am not worth the injury you may do it on my account, I assure you. I am only a poor old woman who has lost a son."

"If you had treated me honourably you would have had him still," Eustacia said, while scalding tears trickled from her eyes. "You have brought yourself to folly; you have caused a division which can never be healed!"

"I have done nothing. This audacity from a young woman is more than I can bear."

"It was asked for: you have suspected me, and you have made me speak of my husband in a way I would not have done. You will let him know that I have spoken thus, and it will cause misery between us. Will you go away from me? You are no friend!"

"I will go when I have spoken a word. If anyone says I have come here to question you without good grounds for it, that person speaks untruly. If anyone says that I attempted to stop your marriage by any but honest means, that person, too, does not speak the truth. I have fallen on an evil time; God has been unjust to me in letting you insult me! Probably my son's happiness does not lie on this side of the grave, for he is a foolish man who neglects the advice of his parent. You, Eustacia, stand on the edge of a precipice without knowing it. Only show my son one-half the temper you have shown me to-day—and you may before long—and you will find that though he is as gentle as a child with you now, he can be as hard as steel!"

The excited mother then withdrew, and Eustacia, panting, stood looking into the pool.

II

HE IS SET UPON BY ADVERSITIES BUT HE SINGS A SONG

THE RESULT OF THAT UNPROPITIOUS INTERVIEW WAS THAT EUSTACIA, INSTEAD OF PASSing the afternoon with her grand-father, hastily returned home to Clym, where she arrived three hours earlier than she had been expected.

She came indoors with her face flushed, and her eyes still showing traces of her recent excitement. Yeobright looked up astonished; he had never seen her in any way approaching to that state before. She passed him by, and would have gone upstairs unnoticed, but Clym was so concerned that he immediately followed her.

"What is the matter, Eustacia?" he said. She was standing on the hearthrug in the bed-room, looking upon the floor, her hands clasped in front of her, her bonnet yet unremoved. For a moment she did not answer; and then she replied in a low voice—

"I have seen your mother; and I will never see her again!"

A weight fell like a stone upon Clym. That same morning, when Eustacia had arranged to go and see her grand-father, Clym had expressed a wish that she would drive down to Blooms-End and enquire for her mother-in-law, or adopt any other means she might think fit to bring about a reconciliation. She had set out gaily; and he had hoped for much.

"Why is this?" he asked.

"I cannot tell—I cannot remember. I met your mother. And I will never meet her again."

"Why?"

"What do I know about Mr. Wildeve now? I won't have wicked opinions passed on me by anybody. Oh! it was too humiliating to be asked if I had received any money from him, or encouraged him, or something of the sort—I don't exactly know what!"

"How could she have asked you that?"

"She did."

"Then there must have been some meaning in it. What did my mother say besides?"

"I don't know what she said, except in so far as this, that we both said words which can never be forgiven!"

"O, there must be some misapprehension. Whose fault was it that her meaning was not made clear?"

"I would rather not say. It may have been the fault of the circumstances, which were awkward at the very least. O Clym—I cannot help expressing it—this is an unpleasant position that you have placed me in. But you must improve it—yes, say you will—for I hate it all now! Yes, take me to Paris, and go on with your old occupation, Clym! I don't mind how humbly we live there at first, if it can only be Paris, and not Egdon Heath."

"But I have quite given up that idea," said Yeobright, with surprise. "Surely I never led you to expect such a thing?"

"I own it. Yet there are thoughts which cannot be kept out of mind, and that one was mine. Must I not have a voice in the matter, now I am your wife and the sharer of your doom?"

"Well, there are things which are placed beyond the pale of discussion; and I thought this was specially so, and by mutual agreement."

"Clym, I am unhappy at what I hear," she said in a low voice; and her eyes drooped, and she turned away.

This indication of an unexpected mine of hope in Eustacia's bosom disconcerted her husband. It was the first time that he had confronted the fact of the indirectness of a woman's movement towards her desire. But his intention was unshaken, though he loved Eustacia well. All the effect that her remark had upon him was a resolve to chain himself more closely than ever to his books, so as to be the sooner enabled to appeal to substantial results from another course in arguing against her whim.

Next day the mystery of the guineas was explained. Thomasin paid them a hurried visit, and Clym's share was delivered up to him by her own hands. Eustacia was not present at the time.

"Then this is what my mother meant," exclaimed Clym. "Thomasin, do you know that they have had a bitter quarrel?"

There was a little more reticence now than formerly in Thomasin's manner towards her cousin. It is the effect of marriage to engender in several directions some of the reserve it annihilates in one. "Your mother told me," she said quietly. "She came back to my house after seeing Eustacia."

"The worst thing I dreaded has come to pass. Was Mother much disturbed when she came to you, Thomasin?"

"Yes."

"Very much indeed?"

"Yes."

Clym leant his elbow upon the post of the garden gate, and covered his eyes with his hand.

"Don't trouble about it, Clym. They may get to be friends."

He shook his head. "Not two people with inflammable natures like theirs. Well, what must be will be."

"One thing is cheerful in it—the guineas are not lost."

"I would rather have lost them twice over than have had this happen."

Amid these jarring events Yeobright felt one thing to be indispensable—that he should speedily make some show of progress in his scholastic plans. With this view he read far into the small hours during many nights.

One morning, after a severer strain than usual, he awoke with a strange sensation in his eyes. The sun was shining directly upon the window-blind, and at his first glance thitherward a sharp pain obliged him to close his eyelids quickly. At every new attempt to look about him the same morbid sensibility to light was manifested, and excoriating tears ran down his cheeks. He was obliged to tie a bandage over his brow while dressing; and during the day it could not be abandoned. Eustacia was thoroughly alarmed. On finding that the case was no better the next morning they decided to send to Anglebury for a surgeon.

Towards evening he arrived, and pronounced the disease to be acute inflammation induced by Clym's night studies, continued in spite of a cold previously caught, which had weakened his eyes for the time.

Fretting with impatience at this interruption to a task he was so anxious to hasten, Clym was transformed into an invalid. He was shut up in a room from which all light was excluded, and his condition would have been one of absolute misery had not Eustacia read to him by the glimmer of a shaded lamp. He hoped that the worst would soon be over; but at the surgeon's third visit he learnt to his dismay that although he might venture out-of-doors with shaded eyes in the course of a month, all thought of pursuing his work, or of reading print of any description, would have to be given up for a long time to come.

One week and another week wore on, and nothing seemed to lighten the gloom of the young couple. Dreadful imaginings occurred to Eustacia, but she carefully refrained from uttering them to her husband. Suppose he should become blind, or, at all events, never recover sufficient strength of sight to engage in an occupation which would be congenial to her feelings, and conduce to her removal from this lonely dwelling among the hills? That dream of beautiful Paris was not likely to cohere into substance in the presence of this misfortune. As day after day passed by, and he got no better, her mind ran more and more in this mournful groove, and she would go away from him into the garden and weep despairing tears.

Yeobright thought he would send for his mother; and then he thought he would not. Knowledge of his state could only make her the more unhappy; and the seclusion of their life was such that she would hardly be likely to learn the news except through a special messenger. Endeavouring to take the trouble as philosophically as possible, he waited on till the third week had arrived, when he went into the open air for the first time since the attack. The surgeon visited him again at this stage, and Clym urged him to express a distinct opinion. The young man learnt with added surprise that the date at which he might expect to resume his labours was as uncertain as ever, his eyes being in that peculiar state which, though affording him sight enough for walking about, would not admit of their being strained upon any definite object without incurring the risk of reproducing ophthalmia in its acute form.

Clym was very grave at the intelligence, but not despairing. A quiet firmness, and even cheerfulness, took possession of him. He was not to be blind; that was enough. To be doomed to behold the world through smoked glass for an indefinite period was bad enough, and fatal to any kind of advance; but Yeobright was an absolute stoic in the face of mishaps which only affected his social standing; and, apart from Eustacia, the humblest walk of life would satisfy him if it could be made to work in with some form of his culture scheme. To keep a cottage night-school was one such form; and his affliction did not master his spirit as it might otherwise have done.

He walked through the warm sun westward into those tracts of Egdon with which he was best acquainted, being those lying nearer to his old home. He saw before him in one of the valleys the gleaming of whetted iron, and advancing, dimly perceived that the shine came from the tool of a man who was cutting furze. The worker recognised Clym, and Yeobright learnt from the voice that the speaker was Humphrey.

Humphrey expressed his sorrow at Clym's condition; and added, "Now, if yours was low-class work like mine, you could go on with it just the same."

"Yes; I could," said Yeobright musingly. "How much do you get for cutting these faggots?"

"Half-a-crown a hundred, and in these long days I can live very well on the wages."

During the whole of Yeobright's walk home to Alderworth he was lost in reflections which were not of an unpleasant kind. On his coming up to the house Eustacia spoke to him from the open window, and he went across to her.

"Darling," he said, "I am much happier. And if my mother were reconciled to me and to you I should, I think, be happy quite."

"I fear that will never be," she said, looking afar with her beautiful stormy eyes. "How *can* you say 'I am happier,' and nothing changed?"

"It arises from my having at last discovered something I can do, and get a living at, in this time of misfortune."

"Yes?"

"I am going to be a furze- and turf-cutter."

"No, Clym!" she said, the slight hopefulness previously apparent in her face going off again, and leaving her worse than before.

"Surely I shall. Is it not very unwise in us to go on spending the little money we've got when I can keep down expenditures by an honest occupation? The out-door exercise will do me good, and who knows but that in a few months I shall be able to go on with my reading again?"

"But my grand-father offers to assist us, if we require assistance."

"We don't require it. If I go furze-cutting we shall be fairly well off."

"In comparison with slaves, and the Israelites in Egypt, and such people!" A bitter tear rolled down Eustacia's face, which he did not see. There had been *nonchalance* in his tone, showing her that he felt no absolute grief at a consummation which to her was a positive horror.

The very next day Yeobright went to Humphrey's cottage, and borrowed of him leggings, gloves, a whetstone, and a hook, to use till he should be able to purchase some for himself. Then he sallied forth with his new fellow-labourer and old acquaintance, and selecting a spot where the furze grew thickest he struck the first blow in his adopted calling. His sight, like the wings in *Rasselas*, though useless to him for his grand purpose, sufficed for this strait, and he found that when a little practise should have hardened his palms against blistering he would be able to work with ease.

Day after day he rose with the sun, buckled on his leggings, and went off to the rendezvous with Humphrey. His custom was to work from four o'clock in the morning till noon; then, when the heat of the day was at its highest, to go home and sleep for an hour or two; afterwards coming out again and working till dusk at nine.

This man from Paris was now so disguised by his leather accoutrements, and by the goggles he was obliged to wear over his eyes, that his closest friend might have passed by without recognising him. He was a brown spot in the midst of an expanse of olive-green gorse, and nothing more. Though frequently depressed in spirit when not actually at work, owing to thoughts of Eustacia's position and his mother's estrangement, when in the full swing of labour he was cheerfully disposed and calm.

His daily life was of a curious microscopic sort, his whole world being limited to a circuit of a few feet from his person. His familiars were creeping and winged things, and they seemed to enroll him in their band. Bees hummed around his ears with an intimate air, and tugged at the heath and furze-flowers at his side in such numbers as to weigh them down to the sod. The strange amber-coloured butterflies which Egdon produced, and which were never seen elsewhere, quivered in the breath of his lips, alighted upon his bowed back, and sported with the glittering point of his hook as he flourished it up and down. Tribes of emerald-green grasshoppers leaped over his feet, falling awkwardly on their backs, heads, or hips, like unskilful acrobats, as chance might rule; or engaged themselves in noisy flirtations under the fern-fronds with silent ones of homely hue. Huge flies, ignorant of larders and wire-netting, and quite in a savage state, buzzed about him without knowing that he was a man. In and out of the fern-dells snakes glided in their most brilliant blue and yellow guise, it being the season immediately following the shedding of their old skins, when their colours are brightest. Litters of young rabbits came out from their forms to sun themselves upon hillocks, the hot beams blazing through the delicate tissue of each thin-fleshed ear, and firing it to a blood-red transparency in which the veins could be seen.

The monotony of his occupation soothed him, and was in itself a pleasure. A forced limitation of effort offered a justification of homely courses to an unambitious man, whose conscience would hardly have allowed him to remain in such obscurity while his powers were unimpeded. Hence Yeobright sometimes sang to himself, and when obliged to accompany Humphrey in search of brambles for faggot-bonds he would amuse his companion with sketches of Parisian life and character, and so while away the time.

On one of these warm afternoons Eustacia walked out alone in the direction of Yeobright's place of work. He was busily chopping away at the furze, a long row of faggots which stretched downward from his position representing the labour of the day. He did not observe her approach, and she stood close to him, and heard his undercurrent of song. It shocked her. To see him there, a poor afflicted man, earning money by the sweat of his brow, had at first moved her to tears; but to hear him sing and not at all rebel against an occupation which, however satisfactory to himself, was degrading to her, as an educated lady-wife, wounded her through. Unconscious of her presence, he still went on singing:—

> Le point du jour
> A nos bosquets rend toute leur parure;
> Flore est plus belle à son retour;
> L'oiseau reprend doux chant d'amour;
> Tout célèbre dans la nature
> Le point du jour.

> Le point du jour
> Cause parfois, cause douleur extrême
> Que l'espace des nuits est court
> Pour le berger brûlant d'amour,
> Forcé de quitter ce qu'il aime
> Au point du jour.

It was bitterly plain to Eustacia that he did not care much about social failure; and the proud fair woman bowed her head and wept in sick despair at thought of the blasting effect upon her own life of that mood and condition in him. Then she came forward.

"I would starve rather than do it!" she exclaimed vehemently. "And you can sing! I will go and live with my grand-father again!"

"Eustacia! I did not see you, though I noticed something moving," he said gently. He came forward, pulled off his huge leather glove, and took her hand. "Why do you speak in such a strange way? It is only a little old song which struck my fancy when I was in Paris, and now just applies to my life with you. Has your love for me all died, then, because my appearance is no longer that of a fine gentleman?"

"Dearest, you must not question me unpleasantly, or it may make me not love you."

"Do you believe it possible that I would run the risk of doing that?"

"Well, you follow out your own ideas, and won't give in to mine when I wish you to leave off this shameful labour. Is there anything you dislike in me that you act so contrarily to my wishes? I am your wife, and why will you not listen? Yes, I am your wife indeed!"

"I know what that tone means."

"What tone?"

"The tone in which you said, 'Your wife indeed.' It meant, 'Your wife, worse luck.' "

"It is hard in you to probe me with that remark. A woman may have reason, though she is not without heart, and if I felt 'worse luck,' it was no ignoble feeling—it was only too natural. There, you see that at any rate I do not attempt untruths. Do you remember how, before we were married, I warned you that I had not good wifely qualities?"

"You mock me to say that now. On that point at least the only noble course would be to hold your tongue, for you are still queen of me, Eustacia, though I may no longer be king of you."

"You are my husband. Does not that content you?"

"Not unless you are my wife without regret."

"I cannot answer you. I remember saying that I should be a serious matter on your hands."

"Yes, I saw that."

"Then you were too quick to see! No true lover would have seen any such thing; you are too severe upon me, Clym—I won't like your speaking so at all."

"Well, I married you in spite of it, and don't regret doing so. How cold you seem this afternoon! and yet I used to think there never was a warmer heart than yours."

"Yes, I fear we are cooling—I see it as well as you," she sighed mournfully. "And how madly we loved two months ago! You were never tired of contemplating me, nor I of contemplating you. Who could have thought then that by this time my eyes would not seem so very bright to yours, nor your lips so very sweet to mine? Two months—is it possible? Yes, 'tis too true!"

"You sigh, dear, as if you were sorry for it; and that's a hopeful sign."

"No. I don't sigh for that. There are other things for me to sigh for, or any other woman in my place."

"That your chances in life are ruined by marrying in haste an unfortunate man?"

"Why will you force me, Clym, to say bitter things? I deserve pity as much as you. As much?—I think I deserve it more. For you can sing! It would be a strange hour which should catch me singing under such a cloud as this! Believe me, sweet, I could weep to a degree that would astonish and confound such an elastic mind as yours. Even had you felt careless about your own affliction, you might have refrained from singing out of sheer pity for mine. God! if I were a man in such a position I would curse rather than sing."

Yeobright placed his hand upon her arm. "Now, don't you suppose, my inexperienced girl, that I cannot rebel, in high Promethean fashion, against the gods and fate as well as you. I have felt more steam and smoke of that sort than you have ever heard of. But the more I see of life the more do I perceive that there is nothing particularly great in its greatest walks, and therefore nothing particularly small in mine of furze-cutting. If I feel that the greatest blessings vouchsafed to us are not very valuable, how can I feel it to be any great hardship when they are taken away? So I sing to pass the time. Have you indeed lost all tenderness for me, that you begrudge me a few cheerful moments?"

"I have still some tenderness left for you."

"Your words have no longer their old flavour. And so love dies with good fortune!"

"I cannot listen to this, Clym—it will end bitterly," she said in a broken voice. "I will go home."

III

SHE GOES OUT TO BATTLE AGAINST DEPRESSION

A FEW DAYS LATER, BEFORE THE MONTH OF AUGUST HAD EXPIRED, EUSTACIA AND YEO-bright sat together at their early dinner.

Eustacia's manner had become of late almost apathetic. There was a forlorn look about her beautiful eyes which, whether she deserved it or not, would have excited pity in the breast of anyone who had known her during the full flush of her love for Clym. The feelings of husband and wife varied, in some measure, inversely with their positions. Clym, the afflicted man, was cheerful; and he even tried to comfort her, who had never felt a moment of physical suffering in her whole life.

"Come, brighten up, dearest; we shall be all right again. Some day perhaps I shall see as well as ever. And I solemnly promise that I'll leave off cutting furze as soon as I have the power to do anything better. You cannot seriously wish me to stay idling at home all day?"

"But it is so dreadful—a furze-cutter! and you a man who have lived about the world, and speak French, and German, and who are fit for what is so much better than this."

"I suppose when you first saw me and heard about me I was wrapped in a sort of golden halo to your eyes—a man who knew glorious things, and had mixed in brilliant scenes—in short, an adorable, delightful, distracting hero?"

"Yes," she said, sobbing.

"And now I am a poor fellow in brown leather."

"Don't taunt me. But enough of this. I will not be depressed any more. I am going from home this afternoon, unless you greatly object. There is to be a village picnic—a gypsying, they call it—at East Egdon, and I shall go."

"To dance?"

"Why not? You can sing."

"Well, well, as you will. Must I come to fetch you?"

"If you return soon enough from your work. But do not inconvenience yourself about it. I know the way home, and the heath has no terror for me."

"And can you cling to gaiety so eagerly as to walk all the way to a village festival in search of it?"

"Now, you don't like my going alone! Clym, you are not jealous?"

"No. But I would come with you if it could give you any pleasure; though, as things stand, perhaps you have too much of me already. Still, I somehow wish that you did not want to go. Yes, perhaps I am jealous; and who could be jealous with more reason than I, a half-blind man, over such a woman as you?"

"Don't think like it. Let me go, and don't take all my spirits away!"

"I would rather lose all my own, my sweet wife. Go and do whatever you like. Who can forbid your indulgence in any whim? You have all my heart yet, I believe; and because you bear with me, who am in truth a drag upon you, I owe you thanks. Yes, go alone and shine. As for me, I will stick to my doom. At that kind of meeting people would shun me. My hook and gloves are like the St. Lazarus rattle of the leper, warning the world to get out of the way of a sight that would sadden them." He kissed her, put on his leggings, and went out.

When he was gone she rested her head upon her hands and said to herself, "Two wasted lives—his and mine. And I am come to this! Will it drive me out of my mind?"

She cast about for any possible course which offered the least improvement on the existing state of things, and could find none. She imagined how all those Budmouth ones who should learn what had become of her would say, "Look at the girl for whom nobody was good enough!" To Eustacia the situation seemed such a mockery of her hopes that death appeared the only door of relief if the satire of Heaven should go much further.

Suddenly she aroused herself and exclaimed, "But I'll shake it off. Yes, I *will* shake it off! No one shall know my suffering. I'll be bitterly merry, and ironically gay, and I'll laugh in derision. And I'll begin by going to this dance on the green."

She ascended to her bedroom and dressed herself with scrupulous care. To an onlooker her beauty would have made her feelings almost seem reasonable. The gloomy corner into which accident as much as indiscretion had brought this woman might have led even a moderate partisan to feel that she had cogent reasons for asking the Supreme Power by what right a being of such exquisite finish had been placed in circumstances calculated to make of her charms a curse rather than a blessing.

It was five in the afternoon when she came out from the house ready for her walk. There was material enough in the picture for twenty new conquests. The rebellious sadness that was rather too apparent when she sat indoors without a bonnet was cloaked and softened by her out-door attire, which always had a sort of nebulousness about it, devoid of harsh edges anywhere; so that her face looked from its environment as from a cloud, with no noticeable lines of demarcation between flesh and clothes. The heat of the day had scarcely declined as yet, and she went along the sunny hills at a leisurely pace, there being ample time for her idle expedition. Tall ferns buried her in their leafage whenever her path lay through them, which now formed miniature forests, though not one stem of them would remain to bud the next year.

The site chosen for the village festivity was one of the lawnlike oases which were occasionally, yet not often, met with on the plateaux of the heath district. The brakes of furze and fern terminated abruptly round the margin, and the grass was unbroken. A green cattle-track skirted the spot, without, however, emerging from the screen of fern, and this path Eustacia followed, in order to reconnoitre the group before joining it. The lusty notes of the East Egdon band had directed her unerringly, and she now beheld the musicians themselves, sitting in a blue waggon with red wheels scrubbed as bright as new, and arched with sticks, to which boughs and flowers were tied. In front of this was the grand central dance of fifteen or twenty couples, flanked by minor dances of inferior individuals whose gyrations were not always in strict keeping with the tune.

The young men wore blue and white rosettes, and with a flush on their faces footed it to the girls, who, with the excitement and the exercise, blushed deeper than the pink of their numerous ribbons. Fair ones with long curls, fair ones with short curls, fair ones with love-locks, fair ones with braids, flew round and round; and a beholder might well have wondered how such a prepossessing set of young women of like size, age, and disposition, could have been collected together where there were only one or two villages to choose from. In the background was one happy man dancing by himself, with closed eyes, totally oblivious of all the rest. A fire was burning under a pollard thorn a few paces off, over which three kettles hung in a row. Hard by was a table where elderly dames prepared tea, but Eustacia looked among them in vain for the cattle-dealer's wife who had suggested that she should come, and had promised to obtain a courteous welcome for her.

This unexpected absence of the only local resident whom Eustacia knew considerably damaged her scheme for an afternoon of reckless gaiety. Joining in became a matter of difficulty, notwithstanding that, were she to advance, cheerful dames would come forward with cups of tea and make much of her as a stranger of superior grace and knowledge to themselves. Having watched the company through the figures of two dances, she decided to walk a little further, to a cottage where she might get some refreshment, and then return homeward in the shady time of evening.

This she did; and by the time that she retraced her steps towards the scene of the gypsying, which it was necessary to repass on her way to Alderworth, the sun was going down. The air was now so still that she could hear the band afar off, and it seemed to be playing with more spirit, if that were possible, than when she had come away. On reaching the hill the sun had quite disappeared; but this made little difference either to Eustacia or to the revellers, for a round yellow moon was rising behind her, though its rays had not yet outmastered those from the west. The dance was going on just the same, but strangers had arrived and formed a ring around the figure, so that Eustacia could stand among these without a chance of being recognised.

A whole village-full of sensuous emotion, scattered abroad all the year long, surged here in a focus for an hour. The forty hearts of those waving couples were beating as they had not done since, twelve months before, they had come together in similar jollity. For the time Paganism was revived in their hearts, the pride of life was all in all, and they adored none other than themselves.

How many of those impassioned but temporary embraces were destined to become perpetual was possibly the wonder of some of those who indulged in them, as well as of Eustacia who looked on. She began to envy those pirouetters, to hunger for the hope and happiness which the fascination of the dance seemed to engender within them. Desperately fond of dancing herself, one of Eustacia's expectations of Paris had been the opportunity it might afford her of indulgence in this favourite pastime. Unhappily, that expectation was now extinct within her forever.

Whilst she abstractedly watched them spinning and fluctuating in the increasing moonlight she suddenly heard her name whispered by a voice over her shoulder. Turning in surprise, she beheld at her elbow one whose presence instantly caused her to flush to the temples.

It was Wildeve. Till this moment he had not met her eye since the morning of his marriage, when she had been loitering in the church, and had startled him by lifting her veil and coming forward to sign the register as witness. Yet why the sight of him should have instigated that sudden rush of blood she could not tell.

Before she could speak he whispered, "Do you like dancing as much as ever?"

"I think I do," she replied in a low voice.

"Will you dance with me?"

"It would be a great change for me; but will it not seem strange?"

"What strangeness can there be in relations dancing together?"

"Ah—yes, relations. Perhaps none."

"Still, if you don't like to be seen, pull down your veil; though there is not much risk of being known by this light. Lots of strangers are here."

She did as he suggested; and the act was a tacit acknowledgment that she accepted his offer.

Wildeve gave her his arm and took her down on the outside of the ring to the bottom of the dance, which they entered. In two minutes more they were involved in the figure and began working their way upwards to the top. Till they had advanced half-way thither Eustacia wished more than once that she had not yielded to his request; from the middle to the top she felt that, since she had come out to seek pleasure, she was only doing a natural thing to obtain it. Fairly launched into the ceaseless glides and whirls which their new position as top couple opened up to them, Eustacia's pulses began to move too quickly for longer rumination of any kind.

Through the length of five and twenty couples they threaded their giddy way, and a new vitality entered her form. The pale ray of evening lent a fascination to the experience. There is a certain degree and tone of light which tends to disturb the equilibrium of the senses, and to promote dangerously the tenderer moods; added to movement, it drives the emotions to rankness, the reason becoming sleepy and unperceiving in inverse proportion; and this light fell now upon these two from the disc of the moon. All the dancing girls felt the symptoms, but Eustacia most of all. The grass under their feet became trodden away, and the hard, beaten surface of the sod, when viewed aslant towards the moonlight, shone like a polished table. The air became quite still; the flag above the waggon which held the musicians clung to the pole, and the players appeared only in outline against the sky; except when the circular mouths of the trombone, ophicleide, and French horn gleamed out like huge eyes from the shade of their figures. The pretty dresses of the maids lost their subtler day colours and showed more or less of a misty white. Eustacia floated round and round on Wildeve's arm, her face rapt and statuesque; her soul had passed away from and forgotten her features, which were left empty and quiescent, as they always are when feeling goes beyond their register.

How near she was to Wildeve! it was terrible to think of. She could feel his breathing, and he, of course, could feel hers. How badly she had treated him! yet, here they were treading one measure. The enchantment of the dance surprised her. A clear line of difference divided like a tangible fence her experience within this maze of motion from her experience without it. Her beginning to dance had been like a change of atmosphere; outside, she had been steeped in arctic frigidity by comparison with the tropical sensations here. She had entered the dance from the troubled hours of her late life as one might enter a brilliant chamber after a night walk in a wood. Wildeve by himself would have been merely an agitation; Wildeve added to the dance, and the moonlight, and the secrecy, began to be a delight. Whether his personality supplied the greater part of this sweetly compounded feeling, or whether the dance and the scene weighed the more therein, was a nice point upon which Eustacia herself was entirely in a cloud.

People began to say "Who are they?" but no invidious enquiries were made. Had Eustacia mingled with the other girls in their ordinary daily walks the case would have been different: here she was not inconvenienced by excessive inspection, for all were wrought to their brightest grace by the occasion. Like the planet Mercury surrounded by the lustre of sunset, her permanent brilliancy passed without much notice in the temporary glory of the situation.

As for Wildeve, his feelings are easy to guess. Obstacles were a ripening sun to his love, and he was at this moment in a delirium of exquisite misery. To clasp as his for five minutes what was another man's through all the rest of the year was a kind of thing he of all men could appreciate. He had long since begun to sigh again for Eustacia; indeed, it may be asserted that signing the marriage register with Thomasin was the natural signal to his heart to return to its first quarters, and that the extra complication of Eustacia's marriage was the one addition required to make that return compulsory.

Thus, for different reasons, what was to the rest an exhilarating movement was to these two a riding upon the whirlwind. The dance had come like an irresistible attack upon whatever sense of social order there was in their minds, to drive them back into old paths which were now doubly irregular. Through three dances in succession they spun their way; and then, fatigued with the incessant motion, Eustacia turned to quit the circle in which she had already remained too long. Wildeve led her to a grassy mound a few yards distant, where she sat down, her partner standing beside her. From the time that he addressed her at the beginning of the dance till now they had not exchanged a word.

"The dance and the walking have tired you?" he said tenderly.

"No; not greatly."

"It is strange that we should have met here of all places, after missing each other so long."

"We have missed because we tried to miss, I suppose."

"Yes. But you began that proceeding—by breaking a promise."

"It is scarcely worthwhile to talk of that now. We have formed other ties since then—you no less than I."

"I am sorry to hear that your husband is ill."

"He is not ill—only incapacitated."

"Yes: that is what I mean. I sincerely sympathise with you in your trouble. Fate has treated you cruelly."

She was silent a while. "Have you heard that he has chosen to work as a furze-cutter?" she said in a low, mournful voice.

"It has been mentioned to me," answered Wildeve hesitatingly. "But I hardly believed it."

"It is true. What do you think of me as a furze-cutter's wife?"

"I think the same as ever of you, Eustacia. Nothing of that sort can degrade you: you ennoble the occupation of your husband."

"I wish I could feel it."

"Is there any chance of Mr. Yeobright getting better?"

"He thinks so. I doubt it."

"I was quite surprised to hear that he had taken a cottage. I thought, in common with other people, that he would have taken you off to a home in Paris immediately after you had married him. 'What a gay, bright future she has before her!' I thought. He will, I suppose, return there with you, if his sight gets strong again?"

Observing that she did not reply he regarded her more closely. She was almost weeping. Images of a future never to be enjoyed, the revived sense of her bitter disappointment, the picture of the neighbour's suspended ridicule which was raised by Wildeve's words, had been too much for proud Eustacia's equanimity.

Wildeve could hardly control his own too forward feelings when he saw her silent perturbation. But he affected not to notice this, and she soon recovered her calmness.

"You did not intend to walk home by yourself?" he asked.

"O yes," said Eustacia. "What could hurt me on this heath, who have nothing?"

"The first half of my way home is the same as yours. I shall be glad to keep you company as far as Throope Corner." Seeing that Eustacia sat on in hesitation he added, "Perhaps you think it unwise to be seen in the same road with me after the events of last summer?"

"Indeed I think no such thing," she said haughtily. "I shall accept whose company I choose, for all that may be said by the miserable inhabitants of Egdon."

"Then let us walk on—if you are ready. Our nearest way is towards that holly-bush with the dark shadow that you see down there."

Eustacia arose, and walked beside him in the direction signified, brushing her way over the damping heath and fern, and followed by the strains of the merrymakers, who still kept up the dance. The moon had now waxed bright and silvery, but the heath was proof against such illumination, and there was to be observed the striking scene of a dark, rayless tract of country, under an atmosphere charged from its zenith to its extremities with whitest light. To an eye above them their two faces would have appeared amid the expanse like two pearls on a table of ebony.

On this account the irregularities of the path were not visible, and Wildeve occasionally stumbled; whilst Eustacia found it necessary to perform some graceful feats of balancing whenever a small tuft of heather or root of furze protruded itself through the grass of the narrow track and entangled her feet. At these junctures in her progress a hand was invariably stretched forward to steady her, holding her firmly until smooth ground was again reached, when the hand was again withdrawn to a respectful distance.

They performed the journey for the most part in silence, and drew near to Throope Corner, a few hundred yards from which a short path branched away to Eustacia's house. By degrees they discerned coming towards them a pair of human figures, apparently of the male sex.

When they came a little nearer Eustacia broke the silence by saying, "One of those men is my husband. He promised to come to meet me."

"And the other is my greatest enemy," said Wildeve.

"It looks like Diggory Venn."

"That is the man."

"It is an awkward meeting," said she; "but such is my fortune. He knows too much about me, unless he could know more, and so prove to himself that what he now knows counts for nothing. Well, let it be: you must deliver me up to them."

"You will think twice before you direct me to do that. Here is a man who has not forgotten an item in our meetings at Rainbarrow: he is in company with your husband. Which of them, seeing us together here, will believe that our meeting and dancing at the gypsy party was by chance?"

"Very well," she whispered gloomily. "Leave me before they come up."

Wildeve bade her a tender farewell, and plunged across the fern and furze, Eustacia slowly walking on. In two or three minutes she met her husband and his companion.

"My journey ends here for to-night, reddleman," said Yeobright as soon as he perceived her. "I turn back with this lady. Good-night."

"Good-night, Mr. Yeobright," said Venn. "I hope to see you better soon."

The moonlight shone directly upon Venn's face as he spoke, and revealed all its lines to Eustacia. He was looking suspiciously at her. That Venn's keen eye had discerned what Yeobright's feeble vision had not—a man in the act of withdrawing from Eustacia's side—was within the limits of the probable.

If Eustacia had been able to follow the reddleman she would soon have found striking confirmation of her thought. No sooner had Clym given her his arm and led her off the scene than the reddleman turned back from the beaten track towards East Egdon, whither he had been strolling merely to accompany Clym in his walk, Diggory's van being again in the neighbourhood. Stretching out his long legs, he crossed the pathless portion of the heath somewhat in the direction which Wildeve had taken. Only a man accustomed to nocturnal rambles could at this hour have descended those shaggy slopes with Venn's velocity without falling headlong into a pit, or snapping off his leg by jamming his foot into some rabbit-burrow. But Venn went on without much inconvenience to himself, and the course of his scamper was towards the Quiet Woman Inn. This place he reached in about half an hour, and he was well aware that no person who had been near Throope Corner when he started could have got down here before him.

The lonely inn was not yet closed, though scarcely an individual was there, the business done being chiefly with travellers who passed the inn on long journeys, and these had now gone on their way. Venn went to the public-room, called for a mug of ale, and enquired of the maid in an indifferent tone if Mr. Wildeve was at home.

Thomasin sat in an inner room and heard Venn's voice. When customers were present she seldom showed herself, owing to her inherent dislike for the business; but perceiving that no one else was there to-night she came out.

"He is not at home yet, Diggory," she said pleasantly. "But I expected him sooner. He has been to East Egdon to buy a horse."

"Did he wear a light wideawake?"

"Yes."

"Then I saw him at Throope Corner, leading one home," said Venn drily. "A beauty, with a white face and a mane as black as night. He will soon be here, no doubt." Rising and looking for a moment at the pure, sweet face of Thomasin, over which a shadow of sadness had passed since the time when he had last seen her, he ventured to add, "Mr. Wildeve seems to be often away at this time."

"O yes," cried Thomasin in what was intended to be a tone of gaiety. "Husbands will play the truant, you know. I wish you could tell me of some secret plan that would help me to keep him home at my will in the evenings."

"I will consider if I know of one," replied Venn in that same light tone which meant no lightness. And then he bowed in a manner of his own invention and moved to go. Thomasin offered him her hand; and without a sigh, though with food for many, the reddleman went out.

When Wildeve returned, a quarter of an hour later, Thomasin said simply, and in the abashed manner usual with her now, "Where is the horse, Damon?"

"O, I have not bought it, after all. The man asks too much."

"But somebody saw you at Throope Corner leading it home—a beauty, with a white face and a mane as black as night."

"Ah!" said Wildeve, fixing his eyes upon her; "who told you that?"

"Venn the reddleman."

The expression of Wildeve's face became curiously condensed. "That is a mistake— it must have been someone else," he said slowly and testily, for he perceived that Venn's counter-moves had begun again.

IV

ROUGH COERCION IS EMPLOYED

THOSE WORDS OF THOMASIN, WHICH SEEMED SO LITTLE, BUT MEANT SO MUCH, RE-mained in the ears of Diggory Venn: "Help me to keep him home in the evenings."

On this occasion Venn had arrived on Egdon Heath only to cross to the other side: he had no further connection with the interests of the Yeobright family, and he had a business of his own to attend to. Yet he suddenly began to feel himself drifting into the old track of manoeuvring on Thomasin's account.

He sat in his van and considered. From Thomasin's words and manner he had plainly gathered that Wildeve neglected her. For whom could he neglect her if not for Eustacia? Yet it was scarcely credible that things had come to such a head as to indicate that Eustacia systematically encouraged him. Venn resolved to reconnoitre somewhat carefully the lonely path which led along the hills from Wildeve's dwelling to Clym's house at Alderworth.

At this time, as has been seen, Wildeve was quite innocent of any predetermined act of intrigue, and except at the dance on the green he had not once met Eustacia since her marriage. But that the spirit of intrigue was in him had been shown by a recent romantic habit of his: a habit of going out after dark and strolling towards Alderworth, there look-ing at the moon and stars, looking at Eustacia's house, and walking back at leisure.

Accordingly, when watching on the night after the festival, the reddleman saw him ascend by the little path, lean over the front gate of Clym's garden, sigh, and turn to go back again. It was plain that Wildeve's intrigue was rather ideal than real. Venn retreated before him down the hill to a place where the path was merely a deep groove between the heather; here he mysteriously bent over the ground for a few minutes, and retired. When Wildeve came on to that spot his ankle was caught by something, and he fell headlong.

As soon as he had recovered the power of respiration he sat up and listened. There was not a sound in the gloom beyond the spiritless stir of the summer wind. Feeling about for the obstacle which had flung him down, he discovered that two tufts of heath had been tied together across the path, forming a loop, which to a traveller was certain overthrow. Wildeve pulled off the string that bound them, and went on with tolerable quickness. On reaching home he found the cord to be of a reddish colour. It was just what he had expected.

Although his weaknesses were not specially those akin to physical fear, this species of *coup-de-Jarnac* from one he knew too well troubled the mind of Wildeve. But his movements were unaltered thereby. A night or two later he again went along the vale to Alderworth, taking the precaution of keeping out of any path. The sense that he was watched, that craft was employed to circumvent his errant tastes, added piquancy to a journey so entirely sentimental, so long as the danger was of no fearful sort. He imagined that Venn and Mrs. Yeobright were in league, and felt that there was a certain legitimacy in combating such a coalition.

The heath to-night appeared to be totally deserted; and Wildeve, after looking over Eustacia's garden gate for some little time, with a cigar in his mouth, was tempted by the fascination that emotional smuggling had for his nature to advance towards the window, which was not quite closed, the blind being only partly drawn down. He could see into the room, and Eustacia was sitting there alone. Wildeve contemplated her for a minute, and then retreating into the heath beat the ferns lightly, whereupon moths flew out alarmed. Securing one, he returned to the window, and holding the moth to the chink, opened his hand. The moth made towards the candle upon Eustacia's table, hovered round it two or three times, and flew into the flame.

Eustacia started up. This had been a well-known signal in old times when Wildeve had used to come secretly wooing to Mistover. She at once knew that Wildeve was outside, but before she could consider what to do her husband came in from upstairs. Eustacia's face burnt crimson at the unexpected collision of incidents, and filled it with an animation that it too frequently lacked.

"You have a very high colour, dearest," said Yeobright, when he came close enough to see it. "Your appearance would be no worse if it were always so."

"I am warm," said Eustacia. "I think I will go into the air for a few minutes."

"Shall I go with you?"

"O no. I am only going to the gate."

She arose, but before she had time to get out of the room a loud rapping began upon the front-door.

"I'll go—I'll go," said Eustacia in an unusually quick tone for her; and she glanced eagerly towards the window whence the moth had flown; but nothing appeared there.

"You had better not at this time of the evening," he said. Clym stepped before her into the passage, and Eustacia waited, her somnolent manner covering her inner heat and agitation.

She listened, and Clym opened the door. No words were uttered outside, and presently he closed it and came back, saying, "Nobody was there. I wonder what that could have meant?"

He was left to wonder during the rest of the evening, for no explanation offered itself, and Eustacia said nothing, the additional fact that she knew of only adding more mystery to the performance.

Meanwhile a little drama had been acted outside which saved Eustacia from all possibility of compromising herself that evening at least. Whilst he had been preparing his moth-signal another person had come behind him up to the gate. This man, who carried a gun in his hand, looked on for a moment at the other's operation by the window, walked up to the house, knocked at the door, and then vanished round the corner and over the hedge.

"Damn him!" said Wildeve. "He has been watching me again."

As his signal had been rendered futile by this uproarious rapping Wildeve withdrew, passed out at the gate, and walked quickly down the path without thinking of anything except getting away unnoticed. Half-way down the hill, the path ran near a knot of stunted hollies, which in the general darkness of the scene stood as the pupil in a black eye. When Wildeve reached this point a report startled his ear, and a few spent gunshots fell among the leaves around him.

There was no doubt that he himself was the cause of that gun's discharge; and he rushed into the clump of hollies, beating the bushes furiously with his stick; but nobody was there. This attack was a more serious matter than the last, and it was some time before Wildeve recovered his equanimity. A new and most unpleasant system of menace had begun, and the intent appeared to be to do him grievous bodily harm. Wildeve had looked upon Venn's first attempt as a species of horse-play, which the reddleman had indulged in for want of knowing better; but now the boundary-line was passed which divides the annoying from the perilous.

Had Wildeve known how thoroughly in earnest Venn had become he might have been still more alarmed. The reddleman had been almost exasperated by the sight of Wildeve outside Clym's house, and he was prepared to go to any lengths short of absolutely shooting him, to terrify the young innkeeper out of his recalcitrant impulses. The doubtful legitimacy of such rough coercion did not disturb the mind of Venn. It troubles few such minds in such cases, and sometimes this is not to be regretted. From the impeachment of Strafford to Farmer Lynch's short way with the scamps of Virginia there have been many triumphs of justice which are mockeries of law.

About half a mile below Clym's secluded dwelling lay a hamlet where lived one of the two constables who preserved the peace in the parish of Alderworth, and Wildeve went straight to the constable's cottage. Almost the first thing that he saw on opening the door was the constable's truncheon hanging to a nail, as if to assure him that here were the means to his purpose. On enquiry, however, of the constable's wife he learnt that the constable was not at home. Wildeve said he would wait.

The minutes ticked on, and the constable did not arrive. Wildeve cooled down from his state of high indignation to a restless dissatisfaction with himself, the scene, the constable's wife, and the whole set of circumstances. He arose and left the house. Altogether, the experience of that evening had had a cooling, not to say a chilling, effect on misdirected tenderness, and Wildeve was in no mood to ascend again to Alderworth after night-fall in hope of a stray glance from Eustacia.

Thus far the reddleman had been tolerably successful in his rude contrivances for keeping down Wildeve's inclination to rove in the evening. He had nipped in the bud the possible meeting between Eustacia and her old lover this very night. But he had not antic-ipated that the tendency of his action would be to divert Wildeve's movement rather than to stop it. The gambling with the guineas had not conduced to make him a welcome guest to Clym; but to call upon his wife's relative was natural, and he was determined to see Eu-stacia. It was necessary to choose some less untoward hour than ten o'clock at night. "Since it is unsafe to go in the evening," he said, "I'll go by day."

Meanwhile Venn had left the heath and gone to call upon Mrs. Yeobright, with whom he had been on friendly terms since she had learnt what a providential counter-move he had made towards the restitution of the family guineas. She wondered at the lateness of his call, but had no objection to see him.

He gave her a full account of Clym's affliction, and of the state in which he was living; then, referring to Thomasin, touched gently upon the apparent sadness of her days. "Now, ma'am, depend upon it," he said, "you couldn't do a better thing for either of 'em than to make yourself at home in their houses, even if there should be a little rebuff at first."

"Both she and my son disobeyed me in marrying; therefore I have no interest in their households. Their troubles are of their own making." Mrs. Yeobright tried to speak se-verely; but the account of her son's state had moved her more than she cared to show.

"Your visits would make Wildeve walk straighter than he is inclined to do, and might prevent unhappiness up the hill."

"What do you mean?"

"I saw something to-night up there which I didn't like at all. I wish your son's house and Mr. Wildeve's were a hundred miles apart instead of two or three."

"Then there *was* an understanding between him and Clym's wife when he made a fool of Thomasin!"

"We'll hope there's no understanding now."

"And our hope will probably be very vain. O Clym! O Thomasin!"

"There's no harm done yet. In fact, I've persuaded Wildeve to mind his own business."

"How?"

"O, not by talking—by a plan of mine called the silent system."

"I hope you'll succeed."

"I shall if you help me by calling and making friends with your son. You'll have a chance then of using your eyes."

"Well, since it has come to this," said Mrs. Yeobright sadly, "I will own to you, red-dleman, that I thought of going. I should be much happier if we were reconciled. The marriage is unalterable, my life may be cut short, and I should wish to die in peace. He is my only son; and since sons are made of such stuff I am not sorry I have no other. As for Thomasin, I never expected much from her; and she has not disappointed me. But I for-gave her long ago; and I forgive him now. I'll go."

At this very time of the reddleman's conversation with Mrs. Yeobright at Blooms-End another conversation on the same subject was languidly proceeding at Alderworth.

All the day Clym had borne himself as if his mind were too full of its own matter to allow him to care about outward things, and his words now showed what had occupied his thoughts. It was just after the mysterious knocking that he began the theme. "Since I have been away to-day, Eustacia, I have considered that something must be done to heal up this ghastly breach between my dear mother and myself. It troubles me."

"What do you propose to do?" said Eustacia abstractedly, for she could not clear away from her the excitement caused by Wildeve's recent manoeuvre for an interview.

"You seem to take a very mild interest in what I propose, little or much," said Clym, with tolerable warmth.

"You mistake me," she answered, reviving at his reproach. "I am only thinking."

"What of?"

"Partly of that moth whose skeleton is getting burnt up in the wick of the candle," she said slowly. "But you know I always take an interest in what you say."

"Very well, dear. Then I think I must go and call upon her. . . ." He went on with tender feeling: "It is a thing I am not at all too proud to do, and only a fear that I might irritate her has kept me away so long. But I must do something. It is wrong in me to allow this sort of thing to go on."

"What have you to blame yourself about?"

"She is getting old, and her life is lonely, and I am her only son."

"She has Thomasin."

"Thomasin is not her daughter; and if she were that would not excuse me. But this is beside the point. I have made up my mind to go to her, and all I wish to ask you is whether you will do your best to help me—that is, forget the past; and if she shows her willingness to be reconciled, meet her half-way by welcoming her to our house, or by accepting a welcome to hers?"

At first Eustacia closed her lips as if she would rather do anything on the whole globe than what he suggested. But the lines of her mouth softened with thought, though not so far as they might have softened; and she said, "I will put nothing in your way; but after what has passed it is asking too much that I go and make advances."

"You never distinctly told me what did pass between you."

"I could not do it then, nor can I now. Sometimes more bitterness is sown in five minutes than can be got rid of in a whole life; and that may be the case here." She paused a few moments, and added, "If you had never returned to your native place, Clym, what a blessing it would have been for you! . . . It has altered the destinies of—"

"Three people."

"Five," Eustacia thought; but she kept that in.

V

THE JOURNEY ACROSS THE HEATH

THURSDAY, THE THIRTY-FIRST OF AUGUST, WAS ONE OF A SERIES OF DAYS DURING WHICH snug houses were stifling, and when cool draughts were treats; when cracks appeared in clayey gardens, and were called "earthquakes" by apprehensive children; when loose spokes were discovered in the wheels of carts and carriages; and when stinging insects haunted the air, the earth, and every drop of water that was to be found.

In Mrs. Yeobright's garden large-leaved plants of a tender kind flagged by ten o'clock in the morning; rhubarb bent downward at eleven; and even stiff cabbages were limp by noon.

It was about eleven o'clock on this day that Mrs. Yeobright started across the heath towards her son's house, to do her best in getting reconciled with him and Eustacia, in conformity with her words to the reddleman. She had hoped to be well advanced in her walk before the heat of the day was at its highest, but after setting out she found that this was not to be done. The sun had branded the whole heath with his mark, even the purple heath-flowers having put on a brownness under the dry blazes of the few preceding days. Every valley was filled with air like that of a kiln, and the clean quartz sand of the winter water-courses, which formed summer paths, had undergone a species of incineration since the drought had set in.

In cool, fresh weather Mrs. Yeobright would have found no inconvenience in walking to Alderworth, but the present torrid attack made the journey a heavy undertaking for a woman past middle age; and at the end of the third mile she wished that she had hired Fair-way to drive her a portion at least of the distance. But from the point at which she had ar-rived it was as easy to reach Clym's house as to get home again. So she went on, the air around her pulsating silently, and oppressing the earth with lassitude. She looked at the sky overhead, and saw that the sapphirine hue of the zenith in spring and early summer had been replaced by a metallic violet.

Occasionally she came to a spot where independent worlds of ephemerons were pass-ing their time in mad carousal, some in the air, some on the hot ground and vegetation, some in the tepid and stringy water of a nearly dried pool. All the shallower ponds had de-creased to a vaporous mud amid which the maggoty shapes of innumerable obscure crea-tures could be indistinctly seen, heaving and wallowing with enjoyment. Being a woman not disinclined to philosophise she sometimes sat down under her umbrella to rest and to watch their happiness, for a certain hopefulness as to the result of her visit gave ease to her mind, and between important thoughts left it free to dwell on any infinitesimal matter which caught her eyes.

Mrs. Yeobright had never before been to her son's house, and its exact position was unknown to her. She tried one ascending path and another, and found that they led her astray. Retracing her steps she came again to an open level, where she perceived at a dis-tance a man at work. She went towards him and enquired the way.

The labourer pointed out the direction, and added, "Do you see that furze-cutter, ma'am, going up that footpath yond?"

Mrs. Yeobright strained her eyes, and at last said that she did perceive him.

"Well, if you follow him you can make no mistake. He's going to the same place, ma'am."

She followed the figure indicated. He appeared of a russet hue, not more distinguishable from the scene around him than the green caterpillar from the leaf it feeds on. His progress when actually walking was more rapid than Mrs. Yeobright's; but she was enabled to keep at an equable distance from him by his habit of stopping whenever he came to a brake of brambles, where he paused a while. On coming in her turn to each of these spots she found half-a-dozen long limp brambles which he had cut from the bush during his halt and laid out straight beside the path. They were evidently intended for furze-faggot bonds which he meant to collect on his return.

The silent being who thus occupied himself seemed to be of no more account in life than an insect. He appeared as a mere parasite of the heath, fretting its surface in his daily labour as a moth frets a garment, entirely engrossed with its products, having no knowledge of anything in the world but fern, furze, heath, lichens, and moss.

The furze-cutter was so absorbed in the business of his journey that he never turned his head; and his leather-legged and gauntleted form at length became to her as nothing more than a moving handpost to show her the way. Suddenly she was attracted to his individuality by observing peculiarities in his walk. It was a gait she had seen somewhere before; and the gait revealed the man to her, as the gait of Ahimaaz in the distant plain made him known to the watchman of the king. "His walk is exactly as my husband's used to be," she said; and then the thought burst upon her that the furze-cutter was her son.

She was scarcely able to familiarise herself with this strange reality. She had been told that Clym was in the habit of cutting furze, but she had supposed that he occupied himself with the labour only at odd times, by way of useful pastime; yet she now beheld him as a furze-cutter and nothing more—wearing the regulation dress of the craft, and thinking the regulation thoughts, to judge by his motions. Planning a dozen hasty schemes for at once preserving him and Eustacia from this mode of life she throbbingly followed the way, and saw him enter his own door.

At one side of Clym's house was a knoll, and on the top of the knoll a clump of fir trees so highly thrust up into the sky that their foliage from a distance appeared as a black spot in the air above the crown of the hill. On reaching this place Mrs. Yeobright felt distressingly agitated, weary, and unwell. She ascended, and sat down under their shade to recover herself, and to consider how best to break the ground with Eustacia, so as not to irritate a woman underneath whose apparent indolence lurked passions even stronger and more active than her own.

The trees beneath which she sat were singularly battered, rude, and wild, and for a few minutes Mrs. Yeobright dismissed thoughts of her own storm-broken and exhausted state to contemplate theirs. Not a bough in the nine trees which composed the group but was splintered, lopped, and distorted by the fierce weather that there held them at its mercy whenever it prevailed. Some were blasted and split as if by lightning, black stains as from fire marking their sides, while the ground at their feet was strewn with dead fir-needles and heaps of cones blown down in the gales of past years. The place was called the Devil's Bellows, and it was only necessary to come there on a March or November night to discover the forcible reasons for that name. On the present heated afternoon, when no perceptible wind was blowing, the trees kept up a perpetual moan which one could hardly believe to be caused by the air.

Here she sat for twenty minutes or more ere she could summon resolution to go down to the door, her courage being lowered to zero by her physical lassitude. To any other person than a mother it might have seemed a little humiliating that she, the elder of the two women, should be the first to make advances. But Mrs. Yeobright had well considered all that, and she only thought how best to make her visit appear to Eustacia not abject but wise.

From her elevated position the exhausted woman could perceive the roof of the house below, and the garden and the whole enclosure of the little domicile. And now, at the moment of rising, she saw a second man approaching the gate. His manner was peculiar, hesitating, and not that of a person come on business or by invitation. He surveyed the house with interest, and then walked round and scanned the outer boundary of the garden, as one might have done had it been the birthplace of Shakespeare, the prison of Mary Stuart, or the Château of Hougomont. After passing round and again reaching the gate he went in. Mrs. Yeobright was vexed at this, having reckoned on finding her son and his wife by themselves; but a moment's thought showed her that the presence of an acquaintance would take off the awkwardness of her first appearance in the house, by confining the talk to general matters until she had begun to feel comfortable with them. She came down the hill to the gate, and looked into the hot garden.

There lay the cat asleep on the bare gravel of the path, as if beds, rugs, and carpets were unendurable. The leaves of the hollyhocks hung like half-closed umbrellas, the sap almost simmered in the stems, and foliage with a smooth surface glared like metallic mirrors. A small apple tree, of the sort called Ratheripe, grew just inside the gate, the only one which thrived in the garden, by reason of the lightness of the soil; and among the fallen apples on the ground beneath were wasps rolling drunk with the juice, or creeping about the little caves in each fruit which they had eaten out before stupefied by its sweetness. By the door lay Clym's furze-hook and the last handful of faggot-bonds she had seen him gather; they had plainly been thrown down there as he entered the house.

VI

A CONJUNCTURE, AND ITS RESULT UPON THE PEDESTRIAN

WILDEVE, AS HAS BEEN STATED, WAS DETERMINED TO VISIT EUSTACIA BOLDLY, BY DAY, and on the easy terms of a relation, since the reddleman had spied out and spoilt his walks to her by night. The spell that she had thrown over him in the moonlight dance made it impossible for a man having no strong puritan force within him to keep away altogether. He merely calculated on meeting her and her husband in an ordinary manner, chatting a little while, and leaving again. Every outward sign was to be conventional; but the one great fact would be there to satisfy him: he would see her. He did not even desire Clym's absence, since it was just possible that Eustacia might resent any situation which could compromise her dignity as a wife, whatever the state of her heart towards him. Women were often so.

He went accordingly; and it happened that the time of his arrival coincided with that of Mrs. Yeobright's pause on the hill near the house. When he had looked round the premises in the manner she had noticed he went and knocked at the door. There was a few minutes' interval, and then the key turned in the lock, the door opened, and Eustacia herself confronted him.

Nobody could have imagined from her bearing now that here stood the woman who had joined with him in the impassioned dance of the week before, unless indeed he could have penetrated below the surface and gauged the real depth of that still stream.

"I hope you reached home safely?" said Wildeve.

"O yes," she carelessly returned.

"And were you not tired the next day? I feared you might be."

"I was rather. You need not speak low—nobody will overhear us. My small servant is gone on an errand to the village."

"Then Clym is not at home?"

"Yes, he is."

"O! I thought that perhaps you had locked the door because you were alone and were afraid of tramps."

"No—here is my husband."

They had been standing in the entry. Closing the front-door and turning the key, as before, she threw open the door of the adjoining room and asked him to walk in. Wildeve entered, the room appearing to be empty; but as soon as he had advanced a few steps he started. On the hearthrug lay Clym asleep. Beside him were the leggings, thick boots, leather gloves, and sleeve-waistcoat in which he worked.

"You may go in; you will not disturb him," she said, following behind. "My reason for fastening the door is that he may not be intruded upon by any chance comer while lying here, if I should be in the garden or upstairs."

"Why is he sleeping there?" said Wildeve in low tones.

"He is very weary. He went out at half-past four this morning, and has been working ever since. He cuts furze because it is the only thing he can do that does not put any strain upon his poor eyes." The contrast between the sleeper's appearance and Wildeve's at this moment was painfully apparent to Eustacia, Wildeve being elegantly dressed in a new summer suit and light hat; and she continued: "Ah! you don't know how differently he appeared when I first met him, though it is such a little while ago. His hands were as white and soft as mine; and look at them now, how rough and brown they are! His complexion is by nature fair, and that rusty look he has now, all of a colour with his leather clothes, is caused by the burning of the sun."

"Why does he go out at all?" Wildeve whispered.

"Because he hates to be idle; though what he earns doesn't add much to our exchequer. However, he says that when people are living upon their capital they must keep down current expenses by turning a penny where they can."

"The fates have not been kind to you, Eustacia Yeobright."

"I have nothing to thank them for."

"Nor has he—except for their one great gift to him."

"What's that?"

Wildeve looked her in the eyes.

Eustacia blushed for the first time that day. "Well, I am a questionable gift," she said quietly. "I thought you meant the gift of content—which he has, and I have not."

"I can understand content in such a case—though how the outward situation can attract him puzzles me."

"That's because you don't know him. He's an enthusiast about ideas, and careless about outward things. He often reminds me of the Apostle Paul."

"I am glad to hear that he's so grand in character as that."

"Yes; but the worst of it is that though Paul was excellent as a man in the Bible he would hardly have done in real life."

Their voices had instinctively dropped lower, though at first they had taken no particular care to avoid awakening Clym. "Well, if that means that your marriage is a misfortune to you, you know who is to blame," said Wildeve.

"The marriage is no misfortune in itself," she said, showing more emotion than had as yet appeared in her. "It is simply the accident which has happened since that has been the cause of my ruin. I have certainly got thistles for figs in a worldly sense, but how could I tell what time would bring forth?"

"Sometimes, Eustacia, I think it is a judgment upon you. You rightly belonged to me, you know; and I had no idea of losing you."

"No, it was not my fault! Two could not belong to you; and remember that, before I was aware, you turned aside to another woman. It was cruel levity in you to do that. I never dreamt of playing such a game on my side till you began it on yours."

"I meant nothing by it," replied Wildeve. "It was a mere interlude. Men are given to the trick of having a passing fancy for somebody else in the midst of a permanent love, which reasserts itself afterwards just as before. On account of your rebellious manner to me I was tempted to go further than I should have done; and when you still would keep playing the same tantalising part I went further still, and married her." Turning and looking again at the unconscious form of Clym, he murmured, "I am afraid that you don't value your prize, Clym. . . . He ought to be happier than I in one thing at least. He may know what it is to come down in the world, and to be afflicted with a great personal calamity; but he probably doesn't know what it is to lose the woman he loved."

"He is not ungrateful for winning her," whispered Eustacia, "and in that respect he is a good man. Many women would go far for such a husband. But do I desire unreasonably much in wanting what is called life—music, poetry, passion, war, and all the beating and pulsing that are going on in the great arteries of the world? That was the shape of my youthful dream; but I did not get it. Yet I thought I saw the way to it in my Clym."

"And you only married him on that account?"

"There you mistake me. I married him because I loved him, but I won't say that I didn't love him partly because I thought I saw a promise of that life in him."

"You have dropped into your old mournful key."

"But I am not going to be depressed," she cried excitedly. "I began a new system by going to that dance, and I mean to stick to it. Clym can sing merrily; why should not I?"

Wildeve looked thoughtfully at her. "It is easier to say you will sing than to do it; though if I could I would encourage you in your attempt. But as life means nothing to me, without one thing which is now impossible, you will forgive me for not being able to encourage you."

"Damon, what is the matter with you, that you speak like that?" she asked, raising her deep shady eyes to his.

"That's a thing I shall never tell plainly; and perhaps if I try to tell you in riddles you will not care to guess them."

Eustacia remained silent for a minute, and she said, "We are in a strange relationship to-day. You mince matters to an uncommon nicety. You mean, Damon, that you still love me. Well, that gives me sorrow, for I am not made so entirely happy by my marriage that I am willing to spurn you for the information, as I ought to do. But we have said too much about this. Do you mean to wait until my husband is awake?"

"I thought to speak to him; but it is unnecessary, Eustacia, if I offend you by not forgetting you, you are right to mention it; but do not talk of spurning."

She did not reply, and they stood looking musingly at Clym as he slept on in that profound sleep which is the result of physical labour carried on in circumstances that wake no nervous fear.

"God, how I envy him that sweet sleep!" said Wildeve. "I have not slept like that since I was a boy—years and years ago."

While they thus watched him a click at the gate was audible, and a knock came to the door. Eustacia went to a window and looked out.

Her countenance changed. First she became crimson, and then the red subsided till it even partially left her lips.

"Shall I go away?" said Wildeve, standing up.

"I hardly know."

"Who is it?"

"Mrs. Yeobright. O, what she said to me that day! I cannot understand this visit—what does she mean? And she suspects that past time of ours."

"I am in your hands. If you think she had better not see me here I'll go into the next room."

"Well, yes: go."

Wildeve at once withdrew; but before he had been half a minute in the adjoining apartment Eustacia came after him.

"No," she said, "we won't have any of this. If she comes in she must see you—I have done no wrong. But how can I open the door to her, when she dislikes me—wishes to see not me, but her son? I won't open the door!"

Mrs. Yeobright knocked again more loudly.

"Her knocking will, in all likelihood, awaken him," continued Eustacia; "and then he will let her in himself. Ah—listen."

They could hear Clym moving in the other room, as if disturbed by the knocking, and he uttered the word "Mother."

"Yes—he is awake—he will go to the door," she said, with a breath of relief. "Come this way. I have a bad name with her, and you must not be seen. Thus I am obliged to act by stealth, not because I do ill, but because others are pleased to say so."

By this time she had taken him to the back-door, which was open, disclosing a path leading down the garden. "Now, one word, Damon," she remarked as he stepped forth.

"This is your first visit here; let it be your last. We have been hot lovers in our time, but it won't do now. Good-bye."

"Good-bye," said Wildeve. "I have had all I came for, and I am satisfied."

"What was it?"

"A sight of you. Upon my eternal honour I came for no more."

Wildeve kissed his hand to the beautiful girl he addressed, and passed into the garden, where she watched him down the path, over the stile at the end, and into the ferns outside, which brushed his hips as he went along, and became lost in their thickets. When he had quite gone she slowly turned, and directed her attention to the interior of the house.

But it was possible that her presence might not be desired by Clym and his mother at this moment of their first meeting, or that it would be superfluous. At all events, she was in no hurry to meet Mrs. Yeobright. She resolved to wait till Clym came to look for her, and glided back into the garden. Here she idly occupied herself for a few minutes, till finding no notice was taken of her she retraced her steps, advancing to the front entrance, where she listened for voices in the parlour. But hearing none she opened the door and went in. To her astonishment Clym lay precisely as Wildeve and herself had left him, his sleep apparently unbroken. He had been disturbed and made to dream and murmur by the knocking, but he had not awakened. Eustacia hastened to the door, and in spite of her reluctance to open it to a woman who had spoken of her so bitterly, she unfastened it and looked out. Nobody was to be seen. There, by the scraper, lay Clym's hook and the handful of faggot-bonds he had brought home; in front of her were the empty path, the garden gate standing slightly ajar; and, beyond, the great valley of purple heath thrilling silently in the sun. Mrs. Yeobright was gone.

Clym's mother was at this time following a path which lay hidden from Eustacia by a shoulder of the hill. Her walk thither from the garden gate had been hasty and determined, as of a woman who was now no less anxious to escape from the scene than she had previously been to enter it. Her eyes were fixed on the ground; within her two sights were graven— that of Clym's hook and brambles at the door, and that of a woman's face at a window. Her lips trembled, becoming unnaturally thin as she murmured, " 'Tis too much—Clym, how can he bear to do it! He is at home; and yet he lets her shut the door against me!"

In her anxiety to get out of the direct view of the house she had diverged from the straightest path homeward, and while looking about to regain it she came upon a little boy gathering whortleberries in a hollow. The boy was Johnny Nunsuch, who had been Eustacia's stoker at the bonfire, and, with the tendency of a minute body to gravitate towards a greater, he began hovering round Mrs. Yeobright as soon as she appeared, and trotted on beside her without perceptible consciousness of his act.

Mrs. Yeobright spoke to him as one in a mesmeric sleep. " 'Tis a long way home, my child, and we shall not get there till evening."

"I shall," said her small companion. "I am going to play marnels afore supper, and we go to supper at six o'clock, because Father comes home. Does your father come home at six too?"

"No: he never comes; nor my son either, nor anybody."

"What have made you so down? Have you seen a ooser?"

"I have seen what's worse—a woman's face looking at me through a window-pane."

"Is that a bad sight?"

"Yes. It is always a bad sight to see a woman looking out at a weary wayfarer and not letting her in."

"Once when I went to Throope Great Pond to catch effets I seed myself looking up at myself, and I was frightened and jumped back like anything."

. . . "If they had only shown signs of meeting my advances half-way how well it might have been done! But there is no chance. Shut out! She must have set him against me. Can there be beautiful bodies without hearts inside? I think so. I would not have done it against a neighbour's cat on such a fiery day as this!"

"What is it you say?"

"Never again—never! Not even if they send for me!"

"You must be a very curious woman to talk like that."

"O no, not at all," she said, returning to the boy's prattle. "Most people who grow up and have children talk as I do. When you grow up your mother will talk as I do too."

"I hope she won't; because 'tis very bad to talk nonsense."

"Yes, child; it is nonsense, I suppose. Are you not nearly spent with the heat?"

"Yes. But not so much as you be."

"How do you know?"

"Your face is white and wet, and your head is hanging-downlike."

"Ah, I am exhausted from inside."

"Why do you, every time you take a step, go like this?" The child in speaking gave to his motion the jerk and limp of an invalid.

"Because I have a burden which is more than I can bear."

The little boy remained silently pondering, and they tottered on side by side until more than a quarter of an hour had elapsed, when Mrs. Yeobright, whose weakness plainly increased, said to him, "I must sit down here to rest."

When she had seated herself he looked long in her face and said, "How funny you draw your breath—like a lamb when you drive him till he's nearly done for. Do you always draw your breath like that?"

"Not always." Her voice was now so low as to be scarcely above a whisper.

"You will go to sleep there, I suppose, won't you? You have shut your eyes already."

"No. I shall not sleep much till—another day, and then I hope to have a long, long one—very long. Now can you tell me if Bottom Pond is dry this summer?"

"Bottom Pond is, but Moreford Pool isn't, because he is deep, and is never dry—'tis just over there."

"Is the water clear?"

"Yes, middling—except where the heath-croppers walk into it."

"Then, take this, and go as fast as you can, and dip me up the clearest you can find. I am very faint."

She drew from the small willow reticule that she carried in her hand an old-fashioned china tea-cup without a handle; it was one of half-a-dozen of the same sort lying in the reticule, which she had preserved ever since her childhood, and had brought with her to-day as a small present for Clym and Eustacia.

The boy started on his errand, and soon came back with the water, such as it was. Mrs. Yeobright attempted to drink, but it was so warm as to give her nausea, and she threw it away. Afterwards she still remained sitting, with her eyes closed.

The boy waited, played near her, caught several of the little brown butterflies which abounded, and then said as he waited again, "I like going on better than biding still. Will you soon start again?"

"I don't know."

"I wish I might go on by myself," he resumed, fearing, apparently, that he was to be pressed into some unpleasant service. "Do you want me any more, please?"

Mrs. Yeobright made no reply.

"What shall I tell Mother?" the boy continued.

"Tell her you have seen a broken-hearted woman cast off by her son."

Before quite leaving her he threw upon her face a wistful glance, as if he had misgivings on the generosity of forsaking her thus. He gazed into her face in a vague, wondering manner, like that of one examining some strange old manuscript the key to whose characters is undiscoverable. He was not so young as to be absolutely without a sense that sympathy was demanded, he was not old enough to be free from the terror felt in childhood at beholding misery in adult quarters hitherto deemed impregnable; and whether she were in a position to cause trouble or to suffer from it, whether she and her affliction were something to pity or something to fear, it was beyond him to decide. He lowered his eyes and went on without another word. Before he had gone half a mile he had forgotten all about her, except that she was a woman who had sat down to rest.

Mrs. Yeobright's exertions, physical and emotional, had well-nigh prostrated her; but she continued to creep along in short stages with long breaks between. The sun had now got far to the west of south and stood directly in her face, like some merciless incendiary, brand in hand, waiting to consume her. With the departure of the boy all visible animation disappeared from the landscape, though the intermittent husky notes of the male grasshoppers from every tuft of furze were enough to show that amid the prostration of the larger animal species an unseen insect world was busy in all the fulness of life.

At length she reached a slope about two-thirds of the whole distance from Alderworth to her own home, where a little patch of shepherd's-thyme intruded upon the path; and she sat down upon the perfumed mat it formed there. In front of her a colony of ants had established a thoroughfare across the way, where they toiled a never-ending and heavy-laden throng. To look down upon them was like observing a city street from the top of a tower. She remembered that this bustle of ants had been in progress for years at the same spot—doubtless those of the old times were the ancestors of these which walked there now. She leant back to obtain more thorough rest, and the soft eastern portion of the sky was as great a relief to her eyes as the thyme was to her head. While she looked a heron arose on that side of the sky and flew on with his face towards the sun. He had come dripping wet from some pool in the valleys, and as he flew the edges and lining of his wings, his thighs, and his breast were so caught by the bright sunbeams that he appeared as if formed of burnished silver. Up in the zenith where he was seemed a free and happy place, away from all contact with the earthly ball to which she was pinioned; and she wished that she could arise uncrushed from its surface and fly as he flew then.

But, being a mother, it was inevitable that she should soon cease to ruminate upon her own condition. Had the track of her next thought been marked by a streak in the air, like the path of a meteor, it would have shown a direction contrary to the heron's, and have descended to the eastward upon the roof of Clym's house.

VII

THE TRAGIC MEETING OF TWO OLD FRIENDS

HE IN THE MEANTIME HAD AROUSED HIMSELF FROM SLEEP, SAT UP, AND LOOKED AROUND. Eustacia was sitting in a chair hard by him, and though she held a book in her hand she had not looked into it for some time.

"Well, indeed!" said Clym, brushing his eyes with his hands. "How soundly I have slept! I have had such a tremendous dream, too: one I shall never forget."

"I thought you had been dreaming," said she.

"Yes. It was about my mother. I dreamt that I took you to her house to make up differences, and when we got there we couldn't get in, though she kept on crying to us for help. However, dreams are dreams. What o'clock is it, Eustacia?"

"Half-past two."

"So late, is it? I didn't mean to stay so long. By the time I have had something to eat it will be after three."

"Ann is not come back from the village, and I thought I would let you sleep on till she returned."

Clym went to the window and looked out. Presently he said, musingly, "Week after week passes, and yet mother does not come. I thought I should have heard something from her long before this."

Misgiving, regret, fear, resolution, ran their swift course of expression in Eustacia's dark eyes. She was face to face with a monstrous difficulty, and she resolved to get free of it by postponement.

"I must certainly go to Blooms-End soon," he continued, "and I think I had better go alone." He picked up his leggings and gloves, threw them down again, and added, "As dinner will be so late to-day I will not go back to the heath, but work in the garden till the evening, and then, when it will be cooler, I will walk to Blooms-End. I am quite sure that if I make a little advance mother will be willing to forget all. It will be rather late before I can get home, as I shall not be able to do the distance either way in less than an hour and a half. But you will not mind for one evening, dear? What are you thinking of to make you look so abstracted?"

"I cannot tell you," she said heavily. "I wish we didn't live here, Clym. The world seems all wrong in this place."

"Well—if we make it so. I wonder if Thomasin has been to Blooms-End lately. I hope so. But probably not, as she is, I believe, expecting to be confined in a month or so. I wish I had thought of that before. Poor Mother must indeed be very lonely."

"I don't like you going to-night."

"Why not to-night?"

"Something may be said which will terribly injure me."

"My mother is not vindictive," said Clym, his colour faintly rising.

"But I wish you would not go," Eustacia repeated in a low tone. "If you agree not to go to-night I promise to go by myself to her house to-morrow, and make it up with her, and wait till you fetch me."

"Why do you want to do that at this particular time, when at every previous time that I have proposed it you have refused?"

"I cannot explain further than that I should like to see her alone before you go," she answered, with an impatient move of her head, and looking at him with an anxiety more frequently seen upon those of a sanguine temperament than upon such as herself.

"Well, it is very odd that just when I had decided to go myself you should want to do what I proposed long ago. If I wait for you to go to-morrow another day will be lost; and I know I shall be unable to rest another night without having been. I want to get this settled, and will. You must visit her afterwards: it will be all the same."

"I could even go with you now?"

"You could scarcely walk there and back without a longer rest than I shall take. No, not to-night, Eustacia."

"Let it be as you say, then," she replied in the quiet way of one who, though willing to ward off evil consequences by a mild effort, would let events fall out as they might sooner than wrestle hard to direct them.

Clym then went into the garden; and a thoughtful languor stole over Eustacia for the remainder of the afternoon, which her husband attributed to the heat of the weather.

In the evening he set out on the journey. Although the heat of summer was yet intense the days had considerably shortened, and before he had advanced a mile on his way all the heath purples, browns, and greens had merged in a uniform dress without airiness or graduation, and broken only by touches of white where the little heaps of clean quartz sand showed the entrance to a rabbit burrow, or where the white flints of a footpath lay like a thread over the slopes. In almost every one of the isolated and stunted thorns which grew here and there a night-hawk revealed his presence by whirring like the clack of a mill as long as he could hold his breath, then stopping, flapping his wings, wheeling round the bush, alighting, and after a silent interval of listening beginning to whirr again. At each brushing of Clym's feet white miller-moths flew into the air just high enough to catch upon their dusty wings the mellowed light from the west, which now shone across the depressions and levels of the ground without falling thereon to light them up.

Yeobright walked on amid this quiet scene with a hope that all would soon be well. At length he came to a spot where a soft perfume was wafted across his path, and he stood still for a moment to inhale the familiar scent. It was the place at which, four hours earlier, his mother had sat down exhausted on the knoll covered with shepherd's-thyme. While he stood a sound between a breathing and a moan suddenly reached his ears.

He looked to where the sound came from; but nothing appeared there save the verge of the hillock stretching against the sky in an unbroken line. He moved a few steps in that direction, and now he perceived a recumbent figure almost close to his feet.

Among the different possibilities as to the person's individuality there did not for a moment occur to Yeobright that it might be one of his own family. Sometimes furze-cutters had been known to sleep out-of-doors at these times, to save a long journey homeward and back again; but Clym remembered the moan and looked closer, and saw that the form was feminine; and a distress came over him like cold air from a cave. But he was not absolutely certain that the woman was his mother till he stooped and beheld her face, pallid, and with closed eyes.

His breath went, as it were, out of his body, and the cry of anguish which would have escaped him died upon his lips. During the momentary interval that elapsed before he became conscious that something must be done all sense of time and place left him, and it seemed as if he and his mother were as when he was a child with her many years ago on this heath at hours similar to the present. Then he awoke to activity; and bending yet lower he found that she still breathed, and that her breath though feeble was regular, except when disturbed by an occasional gasp.

"O, what is it! Mother, are you very ill—you are not dying?" he cried, pressing his lips to her face. "I am your Clym. How did you come here? What does it all mean?"

At that moment the chasm in their lives which his love for Eustacia had caused was not remembered by Yeobright, and to him the present joined continuously with that friendly past that had been their experience before the division.

She moved her lips, appeared to know him, but could not speak; and then Clym strove to consider how best to move her, as it would be necessary to get her away from the spot before the dews were intense. He was able-bodied, and his mother was thin. He clasped his arms round her, lifted her a little, and said, "Does that hurt you?"

She shook her head, and he lifted her up; then, at a slow pace, went onward with his load. The air was now completely cool; but whenever he passed over a sandy patch of ground uncarpeted with vegetation there was reflected from its surface into his face the heat which it had imbibed during the day. At the beginning of his undertaking he had thought but little of the distance which yet would have to be traversed before Blooms-End could be reached; but though he had slept that afternoon he soon began to feel the weight of his burden. Thus he proceeded, like Æneas with his father; the bats circling round his head, nightjars flapping their wings within a yard of his face, and not a human being within call.

While he was yet nearly a mile from the house his mother exhibited signs of restlessness under the constraint of being borne along, as if his arms were irksome to her. He lowered her upon his knees and looked around. The point they had now reached, though far from any road, was not more than a mile from the Blooms-End cottages occupied by Fairway, Sam, Humphrey, and the Cantles. Moreover, fifty yards off stood a hut, built of clods and covered with thin turves, but now entirely disused. The simple outline of the lonely shed was visible, and thither he determined to direct his steps. As soon as he arrived he laid her down carefully by the entrance, and then ran and cut with his pocketknife an armful of the dryest fern. Spreading this within the shed, which was entirely open on one side, he placed his mother thereon: then he ran with all his might towards the dwelling of Fairway.

Nearly a quarter of an hour had passed, disturbed only by the broken breathing of the sufferer, when moving figures began to animate the line between heath and sky. In a few moments Clym arrived with Fairway, Humphrey, and Susan Nunsuch; Olly Dowden, who had chanced to be at Fairway's, Christian and Grandfer Cantle following helter-skelter behind. They had brought a lantern and matches, water, a pillow, and a few other articles which had occurred to their minds in the hurry of the moment. Sam had been despatched back again for brandy, and a boy brought Fairway's pony, upon which he rode off to the nearest medical man, with directions to call at Wildeve's on his way, and inform Thomasin that her aunt was unwell.

Sam and the brandy soon arrived, and it was administered by the light of the lantern; after which she became sufficiently conscious to signify by signs that something was wrong with her foot. Olly Dowden at length understood her meaning, and examined the foot indicated. It was swollen and red. Even as they watched the red began to assume a more livid colour, in the midst of which appeared a scarlet speck, smaller than a pea, and it was found to consist of a drop of blood, which rose above the smooth flesh of her ankle in a hemisphere.

"I know what it is," cried Sam. "She has been stung by an adder!"

"Yes," said Clym instantly. "I remember when I was a child seeing just such a bite. O, my poor mother!"

"It was my father who was bit," said Sam. "And there's only one way to cure it. You must rub the place with the fat of other adders, and the only way to get that is by frying them. That's what they did for him."

" 'Tis an old remedy," said Clym distrustfully, "and I have doubts about it. But we can do nothing else till the doctor comes."

" 'Tis a sure cure," said Olly Dowden, with emphasis. "I've used it when I used to go out nursing."

"Then we must pray for daylight, to catch them," said Clym gloomily.

"I will see what I can do," said Sam.

He took a green hazel which he had used as a walking-stick, split it at the end, inserted a small pebble, and with the lantern in his hand went out into the heath. Clym had by this time lit a small fire, and despatched Susan Nunsuch for a frying-pan. Before she had re-turned Sam came in with three adders, one briskly coiling and uncoiling in the cleft of the stick, and the other two hanging dead across it.

"I have only been able to get one alive and fresh as he ought to be," said Sam. "These limp ones are two I killed to-day at work; but as they don't die till the sun goes down they can't be very stale meat."

The live adder regarded the assembled group with a sinister look in its small black eye, and the beautiful brown and jet pattern on its back seemed to intensify with indignation. Mrs. Yeobright saw the creature, and the creature saw her: she quivered throughout, and averted her eyes.

"Look at that," murmured Christian Cantle. "Neighbours, how do we know but that something of the old serpent in God's garden, that gied the apple to the young woman with no clothes, lives on in adders and snakes still? Look at his eye—for all the world like a villainous sort of black currant. 'Tis to be hoped he can't ill-wish us! There's folks in heath who've been overlooked already. I will never kill another adder as long as I live."

"Well, 'tis right to be afeard of things, if folks can't help it," said Grandfer Cantle. " 'Twould have saved me many a brave danger in my time."

"I fancy I heard something outside the shed," said Christian. "I wish troubles would come in the daytime, for then a man could show his courage, and hardly beg for mercy of the most broomstick old woman he should see, if he was a brave man, and able to run out of her sight!"

"Even such an ignorant fellow as I should know better than do that," said Sam.

"Well, there's calamities where we least expect it, whether or no. Neighbours, if Mrs. Yeobright were to die, d'ye think we should be took up and tried for the manslaughter of a woman?"

"No, they couldn't bring it in that," said Sam, "unless they could prove we had been poachers at some time of our lives. But she'll fetch round."

"Now, if I had been stung by ten adders I should hardly have lost a day's work for't," said Grandfer Cantle. "Such is my spirit when I am on my mettle. But perhaps 'tis natural in a man trained for war. Yes, I've gone through a good deal; but nothing ever came amiss to me after I joined the Locals in four." He shook his head and smiled at a mental picture of himself in uniform. "I was always first in the most galliantest scrapes in my younger days!"

"I suppose that was because they always used to put the biggest fool afore," said Fairway from the fire, beside which he knelt, blowing it with his breath.

"D'ye think so, Timothy?" said Grandfer Cantle, coming forward to Fairway's side, with sudden depression in his face. "Then a man may feel for years that he is good solid company, and be wrong about himself after all?"

"Never mind that question, Grandfer. Stir your stumps and get some more sticks. 'Tis very nonsense of an old man to prattle so when life and death's in mangling."

"Yes, yes," said Grandfer Cantle, with melancholy conviction. "Well, this is a bad night altogether for them that have done well in their time; and if I were ever such a dab at the hautboy or tenor-viol, I shouldn't have the heart to play tunes upon 'em now."

Susan now arrived with the frying-pan, when the live adder was killed and the heads of the three taken off. The remainders, being cut into lengths and split open, were tossed into the pan, which began hissing and crackling over the fire. Soon a rill of clear oil trickled from the carcases, whereupon Clym dipped the corner of his handkerchief into the liquid and anointed the wound.

VIII

EUSTACIA HEARS OF GOOD FORTUNE AND BEHOLDS EVIL

IN THE MEANTIME EUSTACIA, LEFT ALONE IN HER COTTAGE AT ALDERWORTH, HAD BECOME considerably depressed by the posture of affairs. The consequences which might result from Clym's discovery that his mother had been turned from his door that day were likely to be disagreeable, and this was a quality in events which she hated as much as the dreadful.

To be left to pass the evening by herself was irksome to her at any time, and this evening it was more irksome than usual by reason of the excitements of the past hours. The two visits had stirred her into restlessness. She was not wrought to any great pitch of uneasiness by the probability of appearing in an ill light in the discussion between Clym and his mother, but she was wrought to vexation; and her slumbering activities were quickened to the extent of wishing that she had opened the door. She had certainly believed that Clym was awake, and the excuse would be an honest one as far as it went; but nothing could save her from censure in refusing to answer at the first knock. Yet, instead of blaming herself for the issue she laid the fault upon the shoulders of some indistinct, colossal Prince of the World, who had framed her situation and ruled her lot.

At this time of the year it was pleasanter to walk by night than by day, and when Clym had been absent about an hour she suddenly resolved to go out in the direction of Blooms-End, on the chance of meeting him on his return. When she reached the garden gate she heard wheels approaching, and looking round beheld her grand-father coming up in his car.

"I can't stay a minute, thank ye," he answered to her greeting. "I am driving to East Egdon; but I came round here just to tell you the news. Perhaps you have heard—about Mr. Wildeve's fortune?"

"No," said Eustacia blankly.

"Well, he has come into a fortune of eleven thousand pounds—uncle died in Canada, just after hearing that all his family, whom he was sending home, had gone to the bottom in the *Cassiopeia*; so Wildeve has come into everything, without in the least expecting it."

Eustacia stood motionless a while. "How long has he known of this?" she asked.

"Well, it was known to him this morning early, for I knew it at ten o'clock, when Charley came back. Now, he is what I call a lucky man. What a fool you were, Eustacia!"

"In what way?" she said, lifting her eyes in apparent calmness.

"Why, in not sticking to him when you had him."

"Had him, indeed!"

"I did not know there had ever been anything between you till lately; and, faith, I should have been hot and strong against it if I had known; but since it seems that there was some sniffing between ye, why the deuce didn't you stick to him?"

Eustacia made no reply, but she looked as if she could say as much upon that subject as he if she chose.

"And how is your poor purblind husband?" continued the old man. "Not a bad fellow either, as far as he goes."

"He is quite well."

"It is a good thing for his cousin what-d'ye-call-her? By George, you ought to have been in that galley, my girl! Now I must drive on. Do you want any assistance? What's mine is yours, you know."

"Thank you, grand-father, we are not in want at present," she said coldly. "Clym cuts furze, but he does it mostly as a useful pastime, because he can do nothing else."

"He is paid for his pastime, isn't he? Three shillings a hundred, I heard."

"Clym has money," she said, colouring; "but he likes to earn a little."

"Very well; good-night." And the captain drove on.

When her grand-father was gone Eustacia went on her way mechanically; but her thoughts were no longer concerning her mother-in-law and Clym. Wildeve, notwithstanding his complaints against his fate, had been seized upon by destiny and placed in the sunshine once more. Eleven thousand pounds! From every Egdon point of view he was a rich man. In Eustacia's eyes, too, it was an ample sum—one sufficient to supply those wants of hers which had been stigmatised by Clym in his more austere moods as vain and luxurious. Though she was no lover of money she loved what money could bring; and the new accessories she imagined around him clothed Wildeve with a great deal of interest. She recollected now how quietly well-dressed he had been that morning: he had probably put on his newest suit, regardless of damage by briars and thorns. And then she thought of his manner towards herself.

"O I see it, I see it," she said. "How much he wishes he had me now, that he might give me all I desire!"

In recalling the details of his glances and words—at the time scarcely regarded—it became plain to her how greatly they had been dictated by his knowledge of this new event. "Had he been a man to bear a jilt ill-will he would have told me of his good fortune in crowing tones; instead of doing that he mentioned not a word, in deference to my misfortunes, and merely implied that he loved me still, as one superior to him."

Wildeve's silence that day on what had happened to him was just the kind of behaviour calculated to make an impression on such a woman. Those delicate touches of good taste were, in fact, one of the strong points in his demeanour towards the other sex. The peculiarity of Wildeve was that, while at one time passionate, upbraiding, and resentful towards a woman, at another he would treat her with such unparalleled grace as to make previous neglect appear as no discourtesy, injury as no insult, interference as a delicate attention, and the ruin of her honour as excess of chivalry. This man, whose admiration to-day Eustacia had disregarded, whose good wishes she had scarcely taken the trouble to accept, whom she had shown out of the house by the back-door, was the possessor of eleven thousand pounds—a man of fair professional education, and one who had served his articles with a civil engineer.

So intent was Eustacia upon Wildeve's fortunes that she forgot how much closer to her own course were those of Clym; and instead of walking on to meet him at once she sat down upon a stone. She was disturbed in her reverie by a voice behind, and turning her head beheld the old lover and fortunate inheritor of wealth immediately beside her.

She remained sitting, though the fluctuation in her look might have told any man who knew her so well as Wildeve that she was thinking of him.

"How did you come here?" she said in her clear low tone. "I thought you were at home."

"I went on to the village after leaving your garden; and now I have come back again: that's all. Which way are you walking, may I ask?"

She waved her hand in the direction of Blooms-End. "I am going to meet my husband. I think I may possibly have got into trouble whilst you were with me to-day."

"How could that be?"

"By not letting in Mrs. Yeobright."

"I hope that visit of mine did you no harm."

"None. It was not your fault," she said quietly.

By this time she had risen; and they involuntarily sauntered on together, without speaking, for two or three minutes; when Eustacia broke silence by saying, "I assume I must congratulate you."

"On what? O yes; on my eleven thousand pounds, you mean. Well, since I didn't get something else, I must be content with getting that."

"You seem very indifferent about it. Why didn't you tell me to-day when you came?" she said in the tone of a neglected person. "I heard of it quite by accident."

"I did mean to tell you," said Wildeve. "But I—well, I will speak frankly—I did not like to mention it when I saw, Eustacia, that your star was not high. The sight of a man lying wearied out with hard work, as your husband lay, made me feel that to brag of my own fortune to you would be greatly out of place. Yet, as you stood there beside him, I could not help feeling too that in many respects he was a richer man than I."

At this Eustacia said, with slumbering mischievousness, "What, would you exchange with him—your fortune for me?"

"I certainly would," said Wildeve.

"As we are imagining what is impossible and absurd, suppose we change the subject?"

"Very well; and I will tell you of my plans for the future, if you care to hear them. I shall permanently invest nine thousand pounds, keep one thousand as ready money, and with the remaining thousand travel for a year or so."

"Travel? What a bright idea! Where will you go to?"

"From here to Paris, where I shall pass the winter and spring. Then I shall go to Italy, Greece, Egypt, and Palestine, before the hot weather comes on. In the summer I shall go to America; and then, by a plan not yet settled, I shall go to Australia and round to India. By that time I shall have begun to have had enough of it. Then I shall probably come back to Paris again, and there I shall stay as long as I can afford to."

"Back to Paris again," she murmured in a voice that was nearly a sigh. She had never once told Wildeve of the Parisian desires which Clym's description had sown in her; yet here was he involuntarily in a position to gratify them. "You think a good deal of Paris?" she added.

"Yes. In my opinion it is the central beauty-spot of the world."

"And in mine! And Thomasin will go with you?"

"Yes, if she cares to. She may prefer to stay at home."

"So you will be going about, and I shall be staying here!"

"I suppose you will. But we know whose fault that is."

"I am not blaming you," she said quickly.

"Oh, I thought you were. If ever you *should* be inclined to blame me, think of a certain evening by Rainbarrow, when you promised to meet me and did not. You sent me a letter; and my heart ached to read that as I hope yours never will. That was one point of divergence. I then did something in haste. . . . But she is a good woman, and I will say no more."

"I know that the blame was on my side that time," said Eustacia. "But it had not always been so. However, it is my misfortune to be too sudden in feeling. O, Damon, don't reproach me any more—I can't bear that."

They went on silently for a distance of a mile and more, when Eustacia said suddenly, "Haven't you come out of your way, Mr. Wildeve?"

"My way is anywhere to-night. I will go with you as far as the hill on which we can see Blooms-End, as it is getting late for you to be alone."

"Don't trouble. I am not obliged to be out at all. I think I would rather you did not accompany me further. This sort of thing would have an odd look if known."

"Very well, I will leave you." He took her hand unexpectedly, and kissed it—for the first time since her marriage. "What light is that on the hill?" he added, as it were to hide the caress.

She looked, and saw a flickering firelight proceeding from the open side of a hovel a little way before them. The hovel, which she had hitherto always found empty, seemed to be inhabited now.

"Since you have come so far," said Eustacia, "will you see me safely past that hut? I thought I should have met Clym somewhere about here, but as he doesn't appear I will hasten on and get to Blooms-End before he leaves."

They advanced to the turf-shed, and when they got near it the firelight and the lantern inside showed distinctly enough the form of a woman reclining on a bed of fern, a group of heath men and women standing around her. Eustacia did not recognise Mrs. Yeobright in the reclining figure, nor Clym as one of the standers-by till she came close. Then she quickly pressed her hand up on Wildeve's arm and signified to him to come back from the open side of the shed into the shadow.

"It is my husband and his mother," she whispered in an agitated voice. "What can it mean? Will you step forward and tell me?"

Wildeve left her side and went to the back wall of the hut. Presently Eustacia perceived that he was beckoning to her, and she advanced and joined him.

"It is a serious case," said Wildeve.

From their position they could hear what was proceeding inside.

"I cannot think where she could have been going," said Clym to someone. "She had evidently walked a long way, but even when she was able to speak just now she would not tell me where. What do you really think of her?"

"There is a great deal to fear," was gravely answered, in a voice which Eustacia recognised as that of the only surgeon in the district. "She has suffered somewhat from the bite of the adder; but it is exhaustion which has overpowered her. My impression is that her walk must have been exceptionally long."

"I used to tell her not to overwalk herself this weather," said Clym, with distress. "Do you think we did well in using the adder's fat?"

"Well, it is a very ancient remedy—the old remedy of the viper-catchers, I believe," replied the doctor. "It is mentioned as an infallible ointment by Hoffman, Mead, and I think the Abbé Fontana. Undoubtedly it was as good a thing as you could do; though I question if some other oils would not have been equally efficacious."

"Come here, come here!" was then rapidly said in anxious female tones; and Clym and the doctor could be heard rushing forward from the back part of the shed, where they had been standing.

"O, what is it?" whispered Eustacia.

" 'Twas Thomasin who spoke," said Wildeve. "Then they have fetched her. I wonder if I had better go in—yet it might do harm."

For a long time there was utter silence among the group within; and it was broken at last by Clym saying, in an agonised voice, "O doctor, what does it mean?"

The doctor did not reply at once; ultimately he said, "She is sinking fast. Her heart was previously affected, and physical exhaustion has dealt the finishing blow."

Then there was a weeping of women, then waiting, then hushed exclamations, then a strange gasping sound, then a painful stillness.

"It is all over," said the doctor.

Further back in the hut the cotters whispered, "Mrs. Yeobright is dead."

Almost at the same moment the two watchers observed the form of a small old-fashioned child entering at the open side of the shed. Susan Nunsuch, whose boy it was, went forward to the opening and silently beckoned to him to go back.

"I've got something to tell 'ee, mother," he cried in a shrill tone. "That woman asleep there walked along with me to-day; and she said I was to say that I had seed her, and she was a broken-hearted woman and cast off by her son, and then I came on home."

A confused sob as from a man was heard within, upon which Eustacia gasped faintly, "That's Clym—I must go to him—yet dare I do it? No: come away!"

When they had withdrawn from the neighbourhood of the shed she said huskily, "I am to blame for this. There is evil in store for me."

"Was she not admitted to your house after all?" Wildeve enquired.

"No; and that's where it all lies! Oh, what shall I do! I shall not intrude upon them: I shall go straight home. Damon, good-bye! I cannot speak to you any more now."

They parted company; and when Eustacia had reached the next hill she looked back. A melancholy procession was wending its way by the light of the lantern from the hut towards Blooms-End. Wildeve was nowhere to be seen.

BOOK FIFTH

THE DISCOVERY

I

"Wherefore is Light given to him that is in Misery"

ONE EVENING, ABOUT THREE WEEKS AFTER THE FUNERAL OF MRS. YEOBRIGHT, when the silver face of the moon sent a bundle of beams directly upon the floor of Clym's house at Alderworth, a woman came forth from within. She reclined over the garden gate as if to refresh herself a while. The pale lunar touches which make beauties of hags lent divinity to this face, already beautiful.

She had not long been there when a man came up the road and with some hesitation said to her, "How is he to-night, ma'am, if you please?"

"He is better, though still very unwell, Humphrey," replied Eustacia.

"Is he light-headed, ma'am?"

"No. He is quite sensible now."

"Do he rave about his mother just the same, poor fellow?" continued Humphrey.

"Just as much, though not quite so wildly," she said in a low voice.

"It was very unfortunate, ma'am, that the boy Johnny should ever ha' told him his mother's dying words, about her being broken-hearted and cast off by her son. 'Twas enough to upset any man alive."

Eustacia made no reply beyond that of a slight catch in her breath, as of one who fain would speak but could not; and Humphrey, finding that she was disinclined to say more, went home again.

Eustacia turned, entered the house, and ascended to the front bedroom, where a shaded light was burning. In the bed lay Clym, pale, haggard, wide awake, tossing to one side and to the other, his eyes lit by a hot light, as if the fire in their pupils were burning up their substance.

"Is it you, Eustacia?" he said as she sat down.

"Yes, Clym. I have been down to the gate. The moon is shining beautifully, and there is not a leaf stirring."

"Shining, is it? What's the moon to a man like me? Let it shine—let anything be, so that I never see another day! . . . Eustacia, I don't know where to look: my thoughts go through me like swords. O, if any man wants to make himself immortal by painting a picture of wretchedness, let him come here!"

"Why do you say so?"

"I cannot help feeling that I did my best to kill her."

"No, Clym."

"Yes, it was so; it is useless to excuse me! My conduct to her was too hideous—I made no advances; and she could not bring herself to forgive me. Now she is dead! If I had only shown myself willing to make it up with her sooner, and we had been friends, and then she had died, it wouldn't be so hard to bear. But I never went near her house, so she never came near mine, and didn't know how welcome she would have been—that's what troubles me. She did not know I was going to her house that very night, for she was too insensible to understand me. If she had only come to see me! I longed that she would. But it was not to be."

There escaped from Eustacia one of those shivering sighs which used to shake her like a pestilent blast. She had not yet told.

But Yeobright was too deeply absorbed in the ramblings incidental to his remorseful state to notice her. During his illness he had been continually talking thus. Despair had been added to his original grief by the unfortunate disclosure of the boy who had received the last words of Mrs. Yeobright—words too bitterly uttered in an hour of misapprehension. Then his distress had overwhelmed him, and he longed for death, as a field labourer longs for the shade. It was the pitiful sight of a man standing in the very focus of sorrow. He continually bewailed his tardy journey to his mother's house, because it was an error which could never be rectified, and insisted that he must have been horribly perverted by some fiend not to have thought before that it was his duty to go to her, since she did not come to him. He would ask Eustacia to agree with him in his self-condemnation; and when she, seared inwardly by a secret she dared not tell, declared that she could not give an opinion, he would say, "That's because you didn't know my mother's nature. She was always ready to forgive if asked to do so; but I seemed to her to be as an obstinate child, and that made her unyielding. Yet not unyielding: she was proud and reserved, no more. . . . Yes, I can understand why she held out against me so long. She was waiting for me. I daresay she said a hundred times in her sorrow, 'What a return he makes for all the sacrifices I have made for him!' I never went to her! When I set out to visit her it was too late. To think of that is nearly intolerable!"

Sometimes his condition had been one of utter remorse, unsoftened by a single tear of pure sorrow: and then he writhed as he lay, fevered far more by thought than by physical ills. "If I could only get one assurance that she did not die in a belief that I was resentful," he said one day when in this mood, "it would be better to think of than a hope of heaven. But that I cannot do."

"You give yourself up too much to this wearying despair," said Eustacia. "Other men's mothers have died."

"That doesn't make the loss of mine less. Yet it is less the loss than the circumstances of the loss. I sinned against her, and on that account there is no light for me."

"She sinned against you, I think."

"No: she did not. I committed the guilt; and may the whole burden be upon my head!"

"I think you might consider twice before you say that," Eustacia replied. "Single men have, no doubt, a right to curse themselves as much as they please; but men with wives involve two in the doom they pray down."

"I am in too sorry a state to understand what you are refining on," said the wretched man. "Day and night shout at me, 'You have helped to kill her.' But in loathing myself I may, I own, be unjust to you, my poor wife. Forgive me for it, Eustacia, for I scarcely know what I do."

Eustacia was always anxious to avoid the sight of her husband in such a state as this, which had become as dreadful to her as the trial scene was to Judas Iscariot. It brought before her eyes the spectre of a worn-out woman knocking at a door which she would not open; and she shrank from contemplating it. Yet it was better for Yeobright himself when he spoke openly of his sharp regret, for in silence he endured infinitely more, and would sometimes remain so long in a tense, brooding mood, consuming himself by the gnawing of his thought, that it was imperatively necessary to make him talk aloud, that his grief might in some degree expend itself in the effort.

Eustacia had not been long indoors after her look at the moonlight when a soft foot-step came up to the house, and Thomasin was announced by the woman downstairs.

"Ah, Thomasin! Thank you for coming to-night," said Clym when she entered the room. "Here am I, you see. Such a wretched spectacle am I, that I shrink from being seen by a single friend, and almost from you."

"You must not shrink from me, dear Clym," said Thomasin earnestly, in that sweet voice of hers which came to a sufferer like fresh air into a Black Hole. "Nothing in you can ever shock me or drive me away. I have been here before, but you don't remember it."

"Yes, I do; I am not delirious, Thomasin, nor have I been so at all. Don't you believe that if they say so. I am only in great misery at what I have done: and that, with the weak-ness, makes me seem mad. But it has not upset my reason. Do you think I should remem-ber all about my mother's death if I were out of my mind? No such good luck. Two months and a half, Thomasin, the last of her life, did my poor mother live alone, distracted and mourning because of me; yet she was unvisited by me, though I was living only five miles off. Two months and a half—seventy-five days did the sun rise and set upon her in that deserted state which a dog didn't deserve! Poor people who had nothing in common with her would have cared for her, and visited her had they known her sickness and lone-liness; but I, who should have been all to her, stayed away like a cur. If there is any justice in God let Him kill me now. He has nearly blinded me, but that is not enough. If He would only strike me with more pain I would believe in Him forever!"

"Hush, hush! O, pray, Clym, don't, don't say it!" implored Thomasin, affrighted into sobs and tears; while Eustacia, at the other side of the room, though her pale face remained calm, writhed in her chair. Clym went on without heeding his cousin.

"But I am not worth receiving further proof even of Heaven's reprobation. Do you think, Thomasin, that she knew me—that she did not die in that horrid mistaken notion about my not forgiving her, which I can't tell you how she acquired? If you could only as-sure me of that! Do you think so, Eustacia? Do speak to me."

"I think I can assure you that she knew better at last," said Thomasin. The pallid Eu-stacia said nothing.

"Why didn't she come to my house? I would have taken her in and showed her how I loved her in spite of all. But she never came; and I didn't go to her, and she died on the heath like an animal kicked out, nobody to help her till it was too late. If you could have seen her, Thomasin, as I saw her—a poor dying woman, lying in the dark upon the bare ground, moaning, nobody near, believing she was utterly deserted by all the world, it would have moved you to anguish, it would have moved a brute. And this poor woman my mother! No wonder she said to the child, 'You have seen a broken-hearted woman.' What a state she must have been brought to, to say that! and who can have done it but I? It is too dreadful to think of, and I wish I could be punished more heavily than I am. How long was I what they called out of my senses?"

"A week, I think."

"And then I became calm."

"Yes, for four days."

"And now I have left off being calm."

"But try to be quiet: please do, and you will soon be strong. If you could remove that impression from your mind—"

"Yes, yes," he said impatiently. "But I don't want to get strong. What's the use of my getting well? It would be better for me if I die, and it would certainly be better for Eustacia. Is Eustacia there?"

"Yes."

"It would be better for you, Eustacia, if I were to die?"

"Don't press such a question, dear Clym."

"Well, it really is but a shadowy supposition; for unfortunately I am going to live. I feel myself getting better. Thomasin, how long are you going to stay at the inn, now that all this money has come to your husband?"

"Another month or two, probably; until my illness is over. We cannot get off till then. I think it will be a month or more."

"Yes, yes. Of course. Ah, Cousin Tamsie, you will get over your trouble—one little month will take you through it, and bring something to console you; but I shall never get over mine, and no consolation will come!"

"Clym, you are unjust to yourself. Depend upon it, aunt thought kindly of you. I know that, if she had lived, you would have been reconciled with her."

"But she didn't come to see me, though I asked her, before I married, if she would come. Had she come, or had I gone there, she would never have died saying, 'I am a broken-hearted woman, cast off by my son.' My door has always been open to her—a welcome here has always awaited her. But that she never came to see."

"You had better not talk any more now, Clym," said Eustacia faintly, from the other part of the room, for the scene was growing intolerable to her.

"Let me talk to you instead for the little time I shall be here," Thomasin said soothingly. "Consider what a one-sided way you have of looking at the matter, Clym. When she said that to the little boy you had not found her and taken her into your arms; and it might have been uttered in a moment of bitterness. It was rather like aunt to say things in haste. She sometimes used to speak so to me. Though she did not come I am convinced that she thought of coming to see you. Do you suppose a man's mother could live two or three months without one forgiving thought? She forgave me; and why should she not have forgiven you?"

"You laboured to win her round; I did nothing. I, who was going to teach people the higher secrets of happiness, did not know how to keep out of that gross misery which the most untaught are wise enough to avoid."

"How did you get here to-night, Thomasin?" said Eustacia.

"Damon set me down at the end of the lane. He has driven into the village on business, and he will come and pick me up by and by."

Accordingly they soon after heard the noise of wheels. Wildeve had come, and was waiting outside with his horse and gig.

"Send out and tell him I will be down in two minutes," said Thomasin.

"I will run down myself," said Eustacia.

She went down. Wildeve had alighted, and was standing before the horse's head when Eustacia opened the door. He did not turn for a moment, thinking the comer Thomasin. Then he looked, startled ever so little, and said one word: "Well?"

"I have not yet told him," she replied in a whisper.

"Then don't do so till he is well—it will be fatal, you are ill yourself."

"I am wretched. . . . O Damon," she said, bursting into tears, "I—I can't tell you how unhappy I am! I can hardly bear this. I can tell nobody of my trouble—nobody knows of it but you."

"Poor girl!" said Wildeve, visibly affected at her distress, and at last led on so far as to take her hand. "It is hard, when you have done nothing to deserve it, that you should have got involved in such a web as this. You were not made for these sad scenes. I am to blame most. If I could only have saved you from it all!"

"But, Damon, please pray tell me what I must do? To sit by him hour after hour, and hear him reproach himself as being the cause of her death, and to know that I am the sinner, if any human being is at all, drives me into cold despair. I don't know what to do. Should I tell him or should I not tell him? I always am asking myself that. O, I want to tell him; and yet I am afraid. If he finds it out he must surely kill me, for nothing else will be in proportion to his feelings now. 'Beware the fury of a patient man' sounds day by day in my ears as I watch him."

"Well, wait till he is better, and trust to chance. And when you tell, you must only tell part—for his own sake."

"Which part should I keep back?"

Wildeve paused. "That I was in the house at the time," he said in a low tone.

"Yes; it must be concealed, seeing what has been whispered. How much easier are hasty actions than speeches that will excuse them!"

"If he were only to die—" Wildeve murmured.

"Do not think of it! I would not buy hope of immunity by so cowardly a desire even if I hated him. Now I am going up to him again. Thomasin bade me tell you she would be down in a few minutes. Good-bye."

She returned, and Thomasin soon appeared. When she was seated in the gig with her husband, and the horse was turning to go off, Wildeve lifted his eyes to the bedroom-windows. Looking from one of them he could discern a pale, tragic face watching him drive away. It was Eustacia's.

II

A LURID LIGHT BREAKS IN UPON A DARKENED UNDERSTANDING

CLYM'S GRIEF BECAME MITIGATED BY WEARING ITSELF OUT. HIS STRENGTH RETURNED, and a month after the visit of Thomasin he might have been seen walking about the garden. Endurance and despair, equanimity and gloom, the tints of health and the pallor of death, mingled weirdly in his face. He was now unnaturally silent upon all of the past that related to his mother; and though Eustacia knew that he was thinking of it none the less, she was only too glad to escape the topic ever to bring it up anew. When his mind had been weaker his heart had led him to speak out; but reason having now somewhat recovered itself he sank into taciturnity.

One evening when he was thus standing in the garden, abstractedly spudding up a weed with his stick, a bony figure turned the corner of the house and came up to him.

"Christian, isn't it?" said Clym. "I am glad you have found me out. I shall soon want you to go to Blooms-End and assist me in putting the house in order. I suppose it is all locked up as I left it?"

"Yes, Mister Clym."

"Have you dug up the potatoes and other roots?"

"Yes, without a drop o' rain, thank God. But I was coming to tell 'ee of something else which is quite different from what we have lately had in the family. I am sent by the rich gentleman at the Woman, that we used to call the landlord, to tell 'ee that Mrs. Wildeve is doing well of a girl, which was born punctually at one o'clock at noon, or a few minutes more or less; and 'tis said that expecting of this increase is what have kept 'em there since they came into their money."

"And she is getting on well, you say?"

"Yes, sir. Only Mr. Wildeve is twanky because 'tisn't a boy—that's what they say in the kitchen, but I was not supposed to notice that."

"Christian, now listen to me."

"Yes, sure, Mr. Yeobright."

"Did you see my mother the day before she died?"

"No, I did not."

Yeobright's face expressed disappointment.

"But I zeed her the morning of the same day she died."

Clym's look lighted up. "That's nearer still to my meaning," he said.

"Yes, I know 'twas the same day; for she said, 'I be going to see him, Christian; so I shall not want any vegetables brought in for dinner.' "

"See whom?"

"See you. She was going to your house, you understand."

Yeobright regarded Christian with intense surprise. "Why did you never mention this?" he said. "Are you sure it was my house she was coming to?"

"O yes. I didn't mention it because I've never zeed you lately. And as she didn't get there it was all nought, and nothing to tell."

"And I have been wondering why she should have walked in the heath on that hot day! Well, did she say what she was coming for? It is a thing, Christian, I am very anxious to know."

"Yes, Mister Clym. She didn't say it to me, though I think she did to one here and there."

"Do you know one person to whom she spoke of it?"

"There is one man, please, sir, but I hope you won't mention my name to him, as I have seen him in strange places, particular in dreams. One night last summer he glared at me like Famine and Sword, and it made me feel so low that I didn't comb out my few hairs for two days. He was standing, as it might be, Mister Yeobright, in the middle of the path to Mistover, and your mother came up, looking as pale—"

"Yes, when was that?"

"Last summer, in my dream."

"Pooh! Who's the man?"

"Diggory, the reddleman. He called upon her and sat with her the evening before she set out to see you. I hadn't gone home from work when he came up to the gate."

"I must see Venn—I wish I had known it before," said Clym anxiously. "I wonder why he has not come to tell me?"

"He went out of Egdon Heath the next day, so would not be likely to know you wanted him."

"Christian," said Clym, "you must go and find Venn. I am otherwise engaged, or I would go myself. Find him at once, and tell him I want to speak to him."

"I am a good hand at hunting up folk by day," said Christian, looking dubiously round at the declining light; "but as to night-time, never is such a bad hand as I, Mister Yeobright."

"Search the heath when you will, so that you bring him soon. Bring him to-morrow, if you can."

Christian then departed. The morrow came, but no Venn. In the evening Christian arrived, looking very weary. He had been searching all day, and had heard nothing of the reddleman.

"Inquire as much as you can to-morrow without neglecting your work," said Yeobright. "Don't come again till you have found him."

The next day Yeobright set out for the old house at Blooms-End, which, with the garden, was now his own. His severe illness had hindered all preparations for his removal thither; but it had become necessary that he should go and overlook its contents, as administrator to his mother's little property; for which purpose he decided to pass the next night on the premises.

He journeyed onward, not quickly or decisively, but in the slow walk of one who has been awakened from a stupefying sleep. It was early afternoon when he reached the valley. The expression of the place, the tone of the hour, were precisely those of many such occasions in days gone by; and these antecedent similarities fostered the illusion that she, who was there no longer, would come out to welcome him. The garden gate was locked and the shutters were closed, just as he himself had left them on the evening after the funeral. He unlocked the gate, and found that a spider had already constructed a large web, tying the door to the lintel, on the supposition that it was never to be opened again. When he had entered the house and flung back the shutters he set about his task of overhauling the cupboards and closets, burning papers, and considering how best to arrange the place for Eustacia's reception, until such time as he might be in a position to carry out his long-delayed scheme, should that time ever arrive.

As he surveyed the rooms he felt strongly disinclined for the alterations which would have to be made in the time-honoured furnishing of his parents and grand-parents, to suit Eustacia's modern ideas. The gaunt oak-cased clock, with the picture of the Ascension on the door-panel and the Miraculous Draught of Fishes on the base; his grand-mother's corner cupboard with the glass door, through which the spotted china was visible; the dumb-waiter; the wooden tea-trays; the hanging fountain with the brass tap—whither would these venerable articles have to be banished?

He noticed that the flowers in the window had died for want of water, and he placed them out upon the ledge, that they might be taken away. While thus engaged he heard footsteps on the gravel without, and somebody knocked at the door.

Yeobright opened it, and Venn was standing before him.

"Good-morning," said the reddleman. "Is Mrs. Yeobright at home?"

Yeobright looked upon the ground. "Then you have not seen Christian or any of the Egdon folks?" he said.

"No. I have only just returned after a long stay away. I called here the day before I left."

"And you have heard nothing?"

"Nothing."

"My mother is—dead."

"Dead!" said Venn mechanically.

"Her home now is where I shouldn't mind having mine."

Venn regarded him, and then said, "If I didn't see your face I could never believe your words. Have you been ill?"

"I had an illness."

"Well, the change! When I parted from her a month ago everything seemed to say that she was going to begin a new life."

"And what seemed came true."

"You say right, no doubt. Trouble has taught you a deeper vein of talk than mine. All I meant was regarding her life here. She has died too soon."

"Perhaps through my living too long. I have had a bitter experience on that score this last month, Diggory. But come in; I have been wanting to see you."

He conducted the reddleman into the large room where the dancing had taken place the previous Christmas; and they sat down in the settle together. "There's the cold fireplace, you see," said Clym. "When that half-burnt log and those cinders were alight she was alive! Little has been changed here yet. I can do nothing. My life creeps like a snail."

"How came she to die?" said Venn.

Yeobright gave him some particulars of her illness and death, and continued: "After this no kind of pain will ever seem more than an indisposition to me.—I began saying that I wanted to ask you something, but I stray from subjects like a drunken man. I am anxious to know what my mother said to you when she last saw you. You talked with her a long time, I think?"

"I talked with her more than half an hour."

"About me?"

"Yes. And it must have been on account of what we said that she was on the heath. Without question she was coming to see you."

"But why should she come to see me if she felt so bitterly against me? There's the mystery."

"Yet I know she quite forgave 'ee."

"But, Diggory—would a woman, who had quite forgiven her son, say, when she felt herself ill on the way to his house, that she was broken-hearted because of his ill-usage? Never!"

"What I know is, that she didn't blame you at all. She blamed herself for what had happened, and only herself. I had it from her own lips."

"You had it from her lips that I had *not* ill-treated her; and at the same time another had it from her lips that I *had* ill-treated her? My mother was no impulsive woman who changed her opinion every hour without reason. How can it be, Venn, that she should have told such different stories in close succession?"

"I cannot say. It is certainly odd, when she had forgiven you, and had forgiven your wife, and was going to see ye on purpose to make friends."

"If there was one thing wanting to bewilder me it was this incomprehensible thing! . . . Diggory, if we, who remain alive, were only allowed to hold conversation with the dead— just once, a bare minute, even through a screen of iron bars, as with persons in prison— what we might learn! How many who now ride smiling would hide their heads! And this mystery—I should then be at the bottom of it at once. But the grave has forever shut her in; and how shall it be found out now?"

No reply was returned by his companion, since none could be given; and when Venn left, a few minutes later, Clym had passed from the dulness of sorrow to the fluctuation of carking incertitude.

He continued in the same state all the afternoon. A bed was made up for him in the same house by a neighbour, that he might not have to return again the next day; and when he retired to rest in the deserted place it was only to remain awake hour after hour thinking the same thoughts. How to discover a solution to this riddle of death seemed a query of more importance than highest problems of the living. There was housed in his memory a vivid picture of the face of a little boy as he entered the hovel where Clym's mother lay. The round eyes, eager gaze, the piping voice which enunciated the words, had operated like stilettos on his brain.

A visit to the boy suggested itself as a means of gleaning new particulars; though it might be quite unproductive. To probe a child's mind after the lapse of six weeks, not for facts which the child had seen and understood, but to get at those which were in their nature beyond him, did not promise much; yet when every obvious channel is blocked we grope towards the small and obscure. There was nothing else left to do; after that he would allow the enigma to drop into the abyss of undiscoverable things.

It was about daybreak when he had reached this decision, and he at once arose. He locked up the house and went out into the green patch which merged in heather further on. In front of the white garden-palings the path branched into three like a broad-arrow. The road to the right led to the Quiet Woman and its neighbourhood; the middle track led to Mistover Knap; the left-hand track led over the hill to another part of Mistover, where the child lived. On inclining into the latter path Yeobright felt a creeping chilliness, familiar enough to most people, and probably caused by the unsunned morning air. In after days he thought of it as a thing of singular significance.

When Yeobright reached the cottage of Susan Nunsuch, the mother of the boy he sought, he found that the inmates were not yet astir. But in upland hamlets the transition from a-bed to abroad is surprisingly swift and easy. There no dense partition of yawns and toilets divides humanity by night from humanity by day. Yeobright tapped at the upper window-sill, which he could reach with his walking-stick; and in three or four minutes the woman came down.

It was not till this moment that Clym recollected her to be the person who had behaved so barbarously to Eustacia. It partly explained the insuavity with which the woman greeted him. Moreover, the boy had been ailing again; and Susan now, as ever since the night when he had been pressed into Eustacia's service at the bonfire, attributed his indispositions to Eustacia's influence as a witch. It was one of those sentiments which lurk like moles underneath the visible surface of manners, and may have been kept alive by Eustacia's entreaty to the captain, at the time that he had intended to prosecute Susan for the pricking in church, to let the matter drop; which he accordingly had done.

Yeobright overcame his repugnance, for Susan had at least borne his mother no ill-will. He asked kindly for the boy; but her manner did not improve.

"I wish to see him," continued Yeobright, with some hesitation; "to ask him if he remembers anything more of his walk with my mother than what he has previously told."

She regarded him in a peculiar and criticising manner. To anybody but a half-blind man it would have said, "You want another of the knocks which have already laid you so low."

She called the boy downstairs, asked Clym to sit down on a stool, and continued, "Now, Johnny, tell Mr. Yeobright anything you can call to mind."

"You have not forgotten how you walked with the poor lady on that hot day?" said Clym.

"No," said the boy.

"And what she said to you?"

The boy repeated the exact words he had used on entering the hut. Yeobright rested his elbow on the table and shaded his face with his hand; and the mother looked as if she wondered how a man could want more of what had stung him so deeply.

"She was going to Alderworth when you first met her?"

"No; she was coming away."

"That can't be."

"Yes; she walked along with me. I was coming away, too."

"Then where did you first see her?"

"At your house."

"Attend, and speak the truth!" said Clym sternly.

"Yes, sir; at your house was where I seed her first."

Clym started up, and Susan smiled in an expectant way which did not embellish her face; it seemed to mean, "Something sinister is coming!"

"What did she do at my house?"

"She went and sat under the trees at the Devil's Bellows."

"Good God! this is all news to me!"

"You never told me this before?" said Susan.

"No, mother; because I didn't like to tell 'ee I had been so far. I was picking black-hearts, and they don't grow nearer."

"What did she do then?" said Yeobright.

"Looked at a man who came up and went into your house."

"That was myself—a furze-cutter, with brambles in his hand."

"No; 'twas not you. 'Twas a gentleman. You had gone in afore."

"Who was he?"

"I don't know."

"Now tell me what happened next."

"The poor lady went and knocked at your door, and the lady with black hair looked out of the side-window at her."

The boy's mother turned to Clym and said, "This is something you didn't expect?"

Yeobright took no more notice of her than if he had been of stone. "Go on, go on," he said hoarsely to the boy.

"And when she saw the young lady look out of the window the old lady knocked again; and when nobody came she took up the furze-hook and looked at it, and put it down again, and then she looked at the faggot-bonds; and then she went away, and walked across to me, and blowed her breath very hard, like this. We walked on together, she and I, and I talked to her and she talked to me a bit, but not much, because she couldn't blow her breath."

"O!" murmured Clym, in a low tone, and bowed his head. "Let's have more," he said.

"She couldn't talk much, and she couldn't walk; and her face was, O so queer!"

"How was her face?"

"Like yours is now."

The woman looked at Yeobright, and beheld him colourless, in a cold sweat. "Isn't there meaning in it?" she said stealthily. "What do you think of her now?"

"Silence!" said Clym fiercely. And, turning to the boy, "And then you left her to die?"

"No," said the woman, quickly and angrily. "He did not leave her to die! She sent him away. Whoever says he forsook her says what's not true."

"Trouble no more about that," answered Clym, with a quivering mouth. "What he did is a trifle in comparison with what he saw. Door kept shut, did you say? Kept shut, she looking out of window? Good heart of God!—what does it mean?"

The child shrank away from the gaze of his questioner.

"He said so," answered the mother, "and Johnny's a God-fearing boy and tells no lies."

" 'Cast off by my son!' No, by my best life, dear mother, it is not so! But by your son's, your son's—May all murderesses get the torment they deserve!"

With these words Yeobright went forth from the little dwelling. The pupils of his eyes, fixed steadfastly on blankness, were vaguely lit with an icy shine; his mouth had passed into the phase more or less imaginatively rendered in studies of Oedipus. The strangest deeds were possible to his mood. But they were not possible to his situation. Instead of there being before him the pale face of Eustacia, and a masculine shape unknown, there was only the imperturbable countenance of the heath, which, having defied the cataclysmal onsets of centuries, reduced to insignificance by its seamed and antique features the wildest turmoil of a single man.

III

EUSTACIA DRESSES HERSELF ON A BLACK MORNING

A CONSCIOUSNESS OF A VAST IMPASSIVITY IN ALL WHICH LAY AROUND HIM TOOK POSsession even of Yeobright in his wild walk towards Alderworth. He had once before felt in his own person this overpowering of the fervid by the inanimate; but then it had tended to enervate a passion far sweeter than that which at present pervaded him. It was once when he stood parting from Eustacia in the moist still levels beyond the hills.

But dismissing all this he went onward again, and came to the front of his house. The blinds of Eustacia's bedroom were still closely drawn, for she was no early riser. All the life visible was in the shape of a solitary thrush cracking a small snail upon the door-stone for his breakfast, and his tapping seemed a loud noise in the general silence which prevailed; but on going to the door Clym found it unfastened, the young girl who attended upon Eustacia being astir in the back part of the premises. Yeobright entered and went straight to his wife's room.

The noise of his arrival must have aroused her, for when he opened the door she was standing before the looking-glass in her night-dress, the ends of her hair gathered into one hand, with which she was coiling the whole mass round her head, previous to beginning toilette operations. She was not a woman given to speaking first at a meeting, and she allowed Clym to walk across in silence, without turning her head. He came behind her, and she saw his face in the glass. It was ashy, haggard, and terrible. Instead of starting towards him in sorrowful surprise, as even Eustacia, undemonstrative wife as she was, would have done in days before she burdened herself with a secret, she remained motionless, looking at him in the glass. And while she looked the carmine flush with which warmth and sound sleep had suffused her cheeks and neck, dissolved from view, and the deathlike pallor in his face flew across into hers. He was close enough to see this, and the sight instigated his tongue.

"You know what is the matter," he said huskily. "I see it in your face."

Her hand relinquished the rope of hair and dropped to her side, and the pile of tresses, no longer supported, fell from the crown of her head about her shoulders and over the white night-gown. She made no reply.

"Speak to me," said Yeobright peremptorily.

The blanching process did not cease in her, and her lips now became as white as her face. She turned to him and said, "Yes, Clym, I'll speak to you. Why do you return so early? Can I do anything for you?"

"Yes, you can listen to me. It seems that my wife is not very well?"

"Why?"

"Your face, my dear; your face. Or perhaps it is the pale morning light which takes your colour away? Now I am going to reveal a secret to you. Ha-ha!"

"O, that is ghastly!"

"What?"

"Your laugh."

"There's reason for ghastliness. Eustacia; you have held my happiness in the hollow of your hand, and like a devil you have dashed it down!"

She started back from the dressing-table, retreated a few steps from him, and looked him in the face. "Ah! you think to frighten me," she said, with a slight laugh. "Is it worth while? I am undefended, and alone."

"How extraordinary!"

"What do you mean?"

"As there is ample time I will tell you, though you know well enough. I mean that it is extraordinary that you should be alone in my absence. Tell me, now, where is he who was with you on the afternoon of the thirty-first of August? Under the bed? Up the chimney?"

A shudder overcame her and shook the light fabric of her night-dress throughout. "I do not remember dates so exactly," she said. "I cannot recollect that anybody was with me besides yourself."

"The day I mean," said Yeobright, his voice growing louder and harsher, "was the day you shut the door against my mother and killed her. O, it is too much—too bad!" He leant over the footpiece of the bedstead for a few moments, with his back towards her; then rising again: "Tell me, tell me! tell me—do you hear?" he cried, rushing up to her and seizing her by the loose folds of her sleeve.

The superstratum of timidity which often overlies those who are daring and defiant at heart had been passed through, and the mettlesome substance of the woman was reached. The red blood inundated her face, previously so pale.

"What are you going to do?" she said in a low voice, regarding him with a proud smile. "You will not alarm me by holding on so; but it would be a pity to tear my sleeve."

Instead of letting go he drew her closer to him. "Tell me the particulars of—my mother's death," he said in a hard, panting whisper; "or—I'll—I'll—"

"Clym," she answered slowly, "do you think you dare do anything to me that I dare not bear? But before you strike me listen. You will get nothing from me by a blow, even though it should kill me, as it probably will. But perhaps you do not wish me to speak—killing may be all you mean?"

"Kill you! Do you expect it?"

"I do."

"Why?"

"No less degree of rage against me will match your previous grief for her."

"Phew—I shall not kill you," he said contemptuously, as if under a sudden change of purpose. "I did think of it; but—I shall not. That would be making a martyr of you, and sending you to where she is; and I would keep you away from her till the universe come to an end, if I could."

"I almost wish you would kill me," said she with gloomy bitterness. "It is with no strong desire, I assure you, that I play the part I have lately played on earth. You are no blessing, my husband."

"You shut the door—you looked out of the window upon her—you had a man in the house with you—you sent her away to die. The inhumanity—the treachery—I will not touch you—stand away from me—and confess every word!"

"Never! I'll hold my tongue like the very death that I don't mind meeting, even though I can clear myself of half you believe by speaking. Yes. I will! Who of any dignity would take the trouble to clear cobwebs from a wild man's mind after such language as this? No; let him go on, and think his narrow thoughts, and run his head into the mire. I have other cares."

" 'Tis too much—but I must spare you."

"Poor charity."

"By my wretched soul you sting me, Eustacia! I can keep it up, and hotly too. Now, then, madam, tell me his name!"

"Never, I am resolved."

"How often does he write to you? Where does he put his letters—when does he meet you? Ah, his letters! Do you tell me his name?"

"I do not."

"Then I'll find it myself." His eyes had fallen upon a small desk that stood near, on which she was accustomed to write her letters. He went to it. It was locked.

"Unlock this!"

"You have no right to say it. That's mine."

Without another word he seized the desk and dashed it to the floor. The hinge burst open, and a number of letters tumbled out.

"Stay!" said Eustacia, stepping before him with more excitement than she had hitherto shown.

"Come, come! stand away! I must see them."

She looked at the letters as they lay, checked her feeling, and moved indifferently aside; when he gathered them up, and examined them.

By no stretch of meaning could any but a harmless construction be placed upon a single one of the letters themselves. The solitary exception was an empty envelope directed to her, and the handwriting was Wildeve's. Yeobright held it up. Eustacia was doggedly silent.

"Can you read, madam? Look at this envelope. Doubtless we shall find more soon, and what was inside them. I shall no doubt be gratified by learning in good time what a well-finished and full-blown adept in a certain trade my lady is."

"Do you say it to me—do you?" she gasped.

He searched further, but found nothing more. "What was in this letter?" he said.

"Ask the writer. Am I your hound that you should talk to me in this way?"

"Do you brave me? do you stand me out, mistress? Answer. Don't look at me with those eyes as if you would bewitch me again! Sooner than that I die. You refuse to answer?"

"I wouldn't tell you after this, if I were as innocent as the sweetest babe in heaven!"

"Which you are not."

"Certainly I am not absolutely," she replied. "I have not done what you suppose; but if to have done no harm at all is the only innocence recognised, I am beyond forgiveness. But I require no help from your conscience."

"You can resist, and resist again! Instead of hating you I could, I think, mourn for and pity you, if you were contrite, and would confess all. Forgive you I never can. I don't speak of your lover—I will give you the benefit of the doubt in that matter, for it only affects me personally. But the other: had you half-killed *me*, had it been that you wilfully took the sight away from these feeble eyes of mine, I could have forgiven you. But *that's* too much for nature!"

"Say no more. I will do without your pity. But I would have saved you from uttering what you will regret."

"I am going away now. I shall leave you."

"You need not go, as I am going myself. You will keep just as far away from me by staying here."

"Call her to mind—think of her—what goodness there was in her: it showed in every line of her face! Most women, even when but slightly annoyed, show a flicker of evil in some curl of the mouth or some corner of the cheek; but as for her, never in her angriest moments was there anything malicious in her look. She was angered quickly, but she forgave just as readily, and underneath her pride there was the meekness of a child. What came of it?—what cared you? You hated her just as she was learning to love you. O! couldn't you see what was best for you, but must bring a curse upon me, and agony and death upon her, by doing that cruel deed! What was the devil's name who was keeping you company and causing you to add cruelty to her to your wrong to me? Was it Wildeve? Was it poor Thomasin's husband? Heaven, what wickedness! Lost your voice, have you? It is natural after detection of that most noble trick. . . . Eustacia, didn't any tender thought of your own mother lead you to think of being gentle to mine at such a time of weariness? Did not one grain of pity enter your heart as she turned away? Think what a vast opportunity was then lost of beginning a forgiving and honest course. Why did not you kick him out, and let her in, and say I'll be an honest wife and a noble woman from this hour? Had I told you to go and quench eternally our last flickering chance of happiness here you could have done no worse. Well, she's asleep now; and have you a hundred gallants, neither they nor you can insult her any more."

"You exaggerate fearfully," she said in a faint, weary voice; "but I cannot enter into my defence—it is not worth doing. You are nothing to me in future, and the past side of the story may as well remain untold. I have lost all through you, but I have not complained. Your blunders and misfortunes may have been a sorrow to you, but they have been a wrong to me. All persons of refinement have been scared away from me since I sank into the mire of marriage. Is this your cherishing—to put me into a hut like this, and keep me like the wife of a hind? You deceived me—not by words, but by appearances, which are less seen through than words. But the place will serve as well as any other—as somewhere to pass from—into my grave." Her words were smothered in her throat, and her head drooped down.

"I don't know what you mean by that. Am I the cause of your sin?" (Eustacia made a trembling motion towards him.) "What, you can begin to shed tears and offer me your hand? Good God! can you? No, not I. I'll not commit the fault of taking that." (The hand she had offered dropped nervelessly, but the tears continued flowing.) "Well, yes, I'll take it, if only for the sake of my own foolish kisses that were wasted there before I knew what I cherished. How bewitched I was! How could there be any good in a woman that everybody spoke ill of?"

"O, O, O!" she cried, breaking down at last; and, shaking with sobs which choked her, she sank upon her knees. "O, will you have done! O, you are too relentless—there's a limit to the cruelty of savages! I have held out long—but you crush me down. I beg for mercy—I cannot bear this any longer—it is inhuman to go further with this! If I had—killed your—mother with my own hand—I should not deserve such a scourging to the bone as this. O, O! God have mercy upon a miserable woman! . . . You have beaten me in this game—I beg you to stay your hand in pity! . . . I confess that I—wilfully did not undo the door the first time she knocked—but—I—should have unfastened it the second—if I had not thought you had gone to do it yourself. When I found you had not I opened it, but she was gone. That's the extent of my crime—towards *her*. Best natures commit bad faults sometimes, don't they?—I think they do. Now I will leave you—forever and ever!"

"Tell all, and I *will* pity you. Was the man in the house with you Wildeve?"

"I cannot tell," she said desperately through her sobbing. "Don't insist further—I cannot tell. I am going from this house. We cannot both stay here."

"You need not go: I will go. You can stay here."

"No, I will dress, and then I will go."

"Where?"

"Where I came from, or *else*where."

She hastily dressed herself, Yeobright moodily walking up and down the room the whole of the time. At last all her things were on. Her little hands quivered so violently as she held them to her chin to fasten her bonnet that she could not tie the strings, and after a few moments she relinquished the attempt. Seeing this he moved forward and said, "Let me tie them."

She assented in silence, and lifted her chin. For once at least in her life she was totally oblivious of the charm of her attitude. But he was not, and he turned his eyes aside, that he might not be tempted to softness.

The strings were tied; she turned from him. "Do you still prefer going away yourself to my leaving you?" he enquired again.

"I do."

"Very well—let it be. And when you will confess to the man I may pity you."

She flung her shawl about her and went downstairs, leaving him standing in the room.

Eustacia had not long been gone when there came a knock at the door of the bedroom; and Yeobright said, "Well?"

It was the servant; and she replied, "Somebody from Mrs. Wildeve's have called to tell 'ee that the mis'ess and the baby are getting on wonderful well, and the baby's name is to be Eustacia Clementine." And the girl retired.

"What a mockery!" said Clym. "This unhappy marriage of mine to be perpetuated in that child's name!"

IV

THE MINISTRATIONS OF A HALF-FORGOTTEN ONE

EUSTACIA'S JOURNEY WAS AT FIRST AS VAGUE IN DIRECTION AS THAT OF THISTLEDOWN on the wind. She did not know what to do. She wished it had been night instead of morning, that she might at least have borne her misery without the possibility of being seen. Going listlessly along between the dying ferns and the wet white spiders' webs, she at length turned her steps towards her grand-father's house. On reaching it she found the front-door closed and locked. Mechanically she went round to the end where the stable was, and on looking in at the stable-door she saw Charley standing within.

"Captain Vye is not at home?" she said.

"No, ma'am," said the lad in a flutter of feeling; "he's gone to Weatherbury, and won't be home till night. And the servant is gone home for a holiday. So the house is locked up."

Eustacia's face was not visible to Charley as she stood at the doorway, her back being to the sky, and the stable but indifferently lighted; but the wildness of her manner arrested his attention. She turned and walked away across the enclosure to the gate, and was hidden by the bank.

When she had disappeared Charley, with misgiving in his eyes, slowly came from the stable-door, and going to another point in the bank he looked over. Eustacia was leaning against it on the outside, her face covered with her hands, and her head pressing the dewy heather which bearded the bank's outer side. She appeared to be utterly indifferent to the circumstance that her bonnet, hair, and garments were becoming wet and disarranged by the moisture of her cold, harsh pillow. Clearly something was wrong.

Charley had always regarded Eustacia as Eustacia had regarded Clym when she first beheld him—as a romantic and sweet vision, scarcely incarnate. He had been so shut off from her by the dignity of her look and the pride of her speech, except at that one blissful interval when he was allowed to hold her hand, that he had hardly deemed her a woman, wingless and earthly, subject to household conditions and domestic jars. The inner details of her life he had only conjectured. She had been a lovely wonder, predestined to an orbit in which the whole of his own was but a point; and this sight of her leaning like a helpless, despairing creature against a wild wet bank, filled him with an amazed horror. He could no longer remain where he was. Leaping over, he came up, touched her with his finger, and said tenderly, "You are poorly, ma'am. What can I do?"

Eustacia started up, and said, "Ah, Charley—you have followed me. You did not think when I left home in the summer that I should come back like this!"

"I did not, dear ma'am. Can I help you now?"

"I am afraid not. I wish I could get into the house. I feel giddy—that's all."

"Lean on my arm, ma'am, till we get to the porch; and I will try to open the door."

He supported her to the porch, and there depositing her on a seat hastened to the back, climbed to a window by the help of a ladder, and descending inside opened the door. Next he assisted her into the room, where there was an old-fashioned horsehair settee as large as a donkey-waggon. She lay down here, and Charley covered her with a cloak he found in the hall.

"Shall I get you something to eat and drink?" he said.

"If you please, Charley. But I suppose there is no fire?"

"I can light it, ma'am."

He vanished, and she heard a splitting of wood and a blowing of bellows; and presently he returned, saying, "I have lighted a fire in the kitchen, and now I'll light one here."

He lit the fire, Eustacia dreamily observing him from her couch. When it was blazing up he said, "Shall I wheel you round in front of it, ma'am, as the morning is chilly?"

"Yes, if you like."

"Shall I go and bring the breakfast now?"

"Yes, do," she murmured languidly.

When he had gone, and the dull sounds occasionally reached her ears of his movements in the kitchen, she forgot where she was, and had for a moment to consider by an effort what the sounds meant. After an interval which seemed short to her whose thoughts were elsewhere, he came in with a tray on which steamed tea and toast.

"Place it on the table," she said. "I shall be ready soon."

He did so, and retired to the door: when, however, he perceived that she did not move he came back a few steps.

"Let me hold it to you, if you don't wish to get up," said Charley. He brought the tray to the front of the couch, where he knelt down, adding, "I will hold it for you."

Eustacia sat up and poured out a cup of tea. "You are very kind to me, Charley," she murmured as she sipped.

"Well, I ought to be," said he diffidently, taking great trouble not to rest his eyes upon her, though this was their only natural position, Eustacia being immediately before him. "You have been kind to me."

"How have I?" said Eustacia.

"You let me hold your hand when you were a maiden at home."

"Ah, so I did. Why did I do that? My mind is lost—it had to do with the mumming, had it not?"

"Yes, you wanted to go in my place."

"I remember. I do indeed remember—too well!"

She again became utterly downcast; and Charley, seeing that she was not going to eat or drink any more, took away the tray.

Afterwards he occasionally came in to see if the fire was burning, to ask her if she wanted anything, to tell her that the wind had shifted from south to west, to ask her if she would like him to gather her some blackberries; to all which enquiries she replied in the negative or with indifference.

She remained on the settee some time longer, when she aroused herself and went upstairs. The room in which she had formerly slept still remained much as she had left it, and the recollection that this forced upon her of her own greatly changed and infinitely worsened situation again set on her face the undetermined and formless misery which it had worn on her first arrival. She peeped into her grand-father's room, through which the fresh autumn air was blowing from the open window. Her eye was arrested by what was a familiar sight enough, though it broke upon her now with a new significance.

It was a brace of pistols, hanging near the head of her grand-father's bed, which he always kept there loaded, as a precaution against possible burglars, the house being very lonely. Eustacia regarded them long, as if they were the page of a book in which she read a new and a strange matter. Quickly, like one afraid of herself, she returned downstairs and stood in deep thought.

"If I could only do it!" she said. "It would be doing much good to myself and all connected with me, and no harm to a single one."

The idea seemed to gather force within her, and she remained in a fixed attitude nearly ten minutes, when a certain finality was expressed in her gaze, and no longer the blankness of indecision.

She turned and went up the second time—softly and stealthily now—and entered her grand-father's room, her eyes at once seeking the head of the bed. The pistols were gone.

The instant quashing of her purpose by their absence affected her brain as a sudden vacuum affects the body: she nearly fainted. Who had done this? There was only one person on the premises besides herself. Eustacia involuntarily turned to the open window which overlooked the garden as far as the bank that bounded it. On the summit of the latter stood Charley, sufficiently elevated by its height to see into the room. His gaze was directed eagerly and solicitously upon her.

She went downstairs to the door and beckoned to him.

"You have taken them away?"

"Yes, ma'am."

"Why did you do it?"

"I saw you looking at them too long."

"What has that to do with it?"

"You have been heart-broken all the morning, as if you did not want to live."

"Well?"

"And I could not bear to leave them in your way. There was meaning in your look at them."

"Where are they now?"

"Locked up."

"Where?"

"In the stable."

"Give them to me."

"No, ma'am."

"You refuse?"

"I do. I care too much for you to give 'em up."

She turned aside, her face for the first time softening from the stony immobility of the earlier day, and the corners of her mouth resuming something of that delicacy of cut which was always lost in her moments of despair. At last she confronted him again.

"Why should I not die if I wish?" she said tremulously. "I have made a bad bargain with life, and I am weary of it—weary. And now you have hindered my escape. O, why did you, Charley! What makes death painful except the thought of others' grief?—and that is absent in my case, for not a sigh would follow me!"

"Ah, it is trouble that has done this! I wish in my very soul that he who brought it about might die and rot, even if 'tis transportation to say it!"

"Charley, no more of that. What do you mean to do about this you have seen?"

"Keep it close as night, if you promise not to think of it again."

"You need not fear. The moment has passed. I promise." She then went away, entered the house, and lay down.

Later in the afternoon her grand-father returned. He was about to question her categorically; but on looking at her he withheld his words.

"Yes, it is too bad to talk of," she slowly returned in answer to his glance. "Can my old room be got ready for me to-night, grand-father? I shall want to occupy it again."

He did not ask what it all meant, or why she had left her husband, but ordered the room to be prepared.

V

AN OLD MOVE INADVERTENTLY REPEATED

CHARLEY'S ATTENTIONS TO HIS FORMER MISTRESS WERE UNBOUNDED. THE ONLY SOLACE to his own trouble lay in his attempts to relieve hers. Hour after hour he considered her wants: he thought of her presence there with a sort of gratitude, and, while uttering imprecations on the cause of her unhappiness, in some measure blessed the result. Perhaps she would always remain there, he thought, and then he would be as happy as he had been before. His dread was lest she should think fit to return to Alderworth, and in that dread his eyes, with all the enquisitiveness of affection, frequently sought her face when she was not observing him, as he would have watched the head of a stockdove to learn if it contemplated flight. Having once really succoured her, and possibly preserved her from the rashest of acts, he mentally assumed in addition a guardian's responsibility for her welfare.

For this reason he busily endeavoured to provide her with pleasant distractions, bringing home curious objects which he found in the heath, such as white trumpet-shaped mosses, red-headed lichens, stone arrow-heads used by the old tribes on Egdon, and faceted crystals from the hollows of flints. These he deposited on the premises in such positions that she should see them as if by accident.

A week passed, Eustacia never going out of the house. Then she walked into the enclosed plot and looked through her grand-father's spy-glass, as she had been in the habit of doing before her marriage. One day she saw, at a place where the high-road crossed the distant valley, a heavily laden waggon passing along. It was piled with household furniture. She looked again and again, and recognised it to be her own. In the evening her grand-father came indoors with a rumour that Yeobright had removed that day from Alderworth to the old house at Blooms-End.

On another occasion when reconnoitring thus she beheld two female figures walking in the vale. The day was fine and clear; and the persons not being more than half a mile off she could see their every detail with the telescope. The woman walking in front carried a white bundle in her arms, from one end of which hung a long appendage of drapery; and when the walkers turned, so that the sun fell more directly upon them, Eustacia could see that the object was a baby. She called Charley, and asked him if he knew who they were, though she well guessed.

"Mrs. Wildeve and the nurse-girl," said Charley.

"The nurse is carrying the baby?" said Eustacia.

"No, 'tis Mrs. Wildeve carrying that," he answered, "and the nurse walks behind carrying nothing."

The lad was in good spirits that day, for the fifth of November had again come round, and he was planning yet another scheme to divert her from her too absorbing thoughts. For two successive years his mistress had seemed to take pleasure in lighting a bonfire on the bank overlooking the valley; but this year she had apparently quite forgotten the day and the customary deed. He was careful not to remind her, and went on with his secret preparations for a cheerful surprise, the more zealously that he had been absent last time and unable to assist. At every vacant minute he hastened to gather furze-stumps, thorn-tree roots, and other solid materials from the adjacent slopes, hiding them from cursory view.

The evening came, and Eustacia was still seemingly unconscious of the anniversary. She had gone indoors after her survey through the glass, and had not been visible since. As soon as it was quite dark Charley began to build the bonfire, choosing precisely that spot on the bank which Eustacia had chosen at previous times.

When all the surrounding bonfires had burst into existence Charley kindled his, and arranged its fuel so that it should not require tending for some time. He then went back to the house, and lingered round the door and windows till she should by some means or other learn of his achievement and come out to witness it. But the shutters were closed, the door remained shut, and no heed whatever seemed to be taken of his performance. Not liking to call her he went back and replenished the fire, continuing to do this for more than half an hour. It was not till his stock of fuel had greatly diminished that he went to the back door and sent in to beg that Mrs. Yeobright would open the window-shutters and see the sight outside.

Eustacia, who had been sitting listlessly in the parlour, started up at the intelligence and flung open the shutters. Facing her on the bank blazed the fire, which at once sent a ruddy glare into the room where she was, and overpowered the candles.

"Well done, Charley!" said Captain Vye from the chimney-corner. "But I hope it is not my wood that he's burning. . . . Ah, it was this time last year that I met with that man Venn, bringing home Thomasin Yeobright—to be sure it was! Well, who would have thought that girl's troubles would have ended so well? What a snipe you were in that matter, Eustacia! Has your husband written to you yet?"

"No," said Eustacia, looking vaguely through the window at the fire, which just then so much engaged her mind that she did not resent her grand-father's blunt opinion. She could see Charley's form on the bank, shovelling and stirring the fire; and there flashed upon her imagination some other form which that fire might call up.

She left the room, put on her garden-bonnet and cloak, and went out. Reaching the bank she looked over with a wild curiosity and misgiving, when Charley said to her, with a pleased sense of himself, "I made it o' purpose for you, ma'am."

"Thank you," she said hastily. "But I wish you to put it out now."

"It will soon burn down," said Charley, rather disappointed. "Is it not a pity to knock it out?"

"I don't know," she musingly answered.

They stood in silence, broken only by the crackling of the flames, till Charley, perceiving that she did not want to talk to him, moved reluctantly away.

Eustacia remained within the bank looking at the fire, intending to go indoors, yet lingering still. Had she not by her situation been inclined to hold in indifference all things honoured of the gods and of men she would probably have come away. But her state was so hopeless that she could play with it. To have lost is less disturbing than to wonder if we may possibly have won: and Eustacia could now, like other people at such a stage, take a standing-point outside herself, observe herself as a disinterested spectator, and think what a sport for Heaven this woman Eustacia was.

While she stood she heard a sound. It was the splash of a stone in the pond.

Had Eustacia received the stone full in the bosom her heart could not have given a more decided thump. She had thought of the possibility of such a signal in answer to that which had been unwittingly given by Charley; but she had not expected it yet. How prompt Wildeve was! Yet how could he think her capable of deliberately wishing to renew their assignations now? An impulse to leave the spot, a desire to stay, struggled within her; and the desire held its own. More than that it did not do, for she refrained even from ascending the bank and looking over. She remained motionless, not disturbing a muscle of her face or raising her eyes; for were she to turn up her face the fire on the bank would shine upon it, and Wildeve might be looking down.

There was a second splash into the pond.

Why did he stay so long without advancing and looking over? Curiosity had its way: she ascended one or two of the earth-steps in the bank and glanced out.

Wildeve was before her. He had come forward after throwing the last pebble, and the fire now shone into each of their faces from the bank stretching breast-high between them.

"I did not light it!" cried Eustacia quickly. "It was lit without my knowledge. Don't, don't come over to me!"

"Why have you been living here all these days without telling me? You have left your home. I fear I am something to blame in this?"

"I did not let in his mother; that's how it is!"

"You do not deserve what you have got, Eustacia; you are in great misery; I see it in your eyes, your mouth, and all over you. My poor, poor girl!" He stepped over the bank. "You are beyond everything unhappy!"

"No, no; not exactly—"

"It has been pushed too far—it is killing you: I do think it!"

Her usually quiet breathing had grown quicker with his words. "I—I—" she began, and then burst into quivering sobs, shaken to the very heart by the unexpected voice of pity—a sentiment whose existence in relation to herself she had almost forgotten.

This outbreak of weeping took Eustacia herself so much by surprise that she could not leave off, and she turned aside from him in some shame, though turning hid nothing from him. She sobbed on desperately; then the outpour lessened, and she became quieter. Wildeve had resisted the impulse to clasp her, and stood without speaking.

"Are you not ashamed of me, who used never to be a crying animal?" she asked in a weak whisper as she wiped her eyes. "Why didn't you go away? I wish you had not seen quite all that; it reveals too much by half."

"You might have wished it, because it makes me as sad as you," he said with emotion and deference. "As for revealing—the word is impossible between us two."

"I did not send for you—don't forget it, Damon; I am in pain, but I did not send for you! As a wife, at least, I've been straight."

"Never mind—I came. O, Eustacia, forgive me for the harm I have done you in these two past years! I see more and more that I have been your ruin."

"Not you. This place I live in."

"Ah, your generosity may naturally make you say that. But I am the culprit. I should either have done more or nothing at all."

"In what way?"

"I ought never to have hunted you out; or, having done it, I ought to have persisted in retaining you. But of course I have no right to talk of that now. I will only ask this: can I do anything for you? Is there anything on the face of the earth that a man can do to make you happier than you are at present? If there is, I will do it. You may command me, Eustacia, to the limit of my influence; and don't forget that I am richer now. Surely something can be done to save you from this! Such a rare plant in such a wild place it grieves me to see. Do you want anything bought? Do you want to go anywhere? Do you want to escape the place altogether? Only say it, and I'll do anything to put an end to those tears, which but for me would never have been at all."

"We are each married to another person," she said faintly; "and assistance from you would have an evil sound—after—after—"

"Well, there's no preventing slanderers from having their fill at any time; but you need not be afraid. Whatever I may feel I promise you on my word of honour never to speak to you about—or act upon—until you say I may. I know my duty to Thomasin quite as well as I know my duty to you as a woman unfairly treated. What shall I assist you in?"

"In getting away from here."

"Where do you wish to go to?"

"I have a place in my mind. If you could help me as far as Budmouth I can do all the rest. Steamers sail from there across the Channel, and so I can get to Paris, where I want to be. Yes," she pleaded earnestly, "help me to get to Budmouth harbour without my grand-father's or my husband's knowledge, and I can do all the rest."

"Will it be safe to leave you there alone?"

"Yes, yes. I know Budmouth well."

"Shall I go with you? I am rich now."

She was silent.

"Say yes, sweet!"

She was silent still.

"Well, let me know when you wish to go. We shall be at our present house till December; after that we remove to Casterbridge. Command me in anything till that time."

"I will think of this," she said hurriedly. "Whether I can honestly make use of you as a friend, or must close with you as a lover—that is what I must ask myself. If I wish to go and decide to accept your company I will signal to you some evening at eight o'clock punctually, and this will mean that you are to be ready with a horse and trap at twelve o'clock the same night to drive me to Budmouth harbour in time for the morning boat."

"I will look out every night at eight, and no signal shall escape me."

"Now please go away. If I decide on this escape I can only meet you once more unless—I cannot go without you. Go—I cannot bear it longer. Go—go!"

Wildeve slowly went up the steps and descended into the darkness on the other side; and as he walked he glanced back, till the bank blotted out her form from his further view.

VI

THOMASIN ARGUES WITH HER COUSIN,
AND HE WRITES A LETTER

YEOBRIGHT WAS AT THIS TIME AT BLOOMS-END, HOPING THAT EUSTACIA WOULD RETURN to him. The removal of furniture had been accomplished only that day, though Clym had lived in the old house for more than a week. He had spent the time in working about the premises, sweeping leaves from the garden-paths, cutting dead stalks from the flowerbeds, and nailing up creepers which had been displaced by the autumn winds. He took no particular pleasure in these deeds, but they formed a screen between himself and despair. Moreover, it had become a religion with him to preserve in good condition all that had lapsed from his mother's hands to his own.

During these operations he was constantly on the watch for Eustacia. That there should be no mistake about her knowing where to find him he had ordered a notice-board to be affixed to the garden gate at Alderworth, signifying in white letters whither he had removed. When a leaf floated to the earth he turned his head, thinking it might be her footfall. A bird searching for worms in the mould of the flower-beds sounded like her hand on the latch of the gate; and at dusk, when soft, strange ventriloquisms came from holes in the ground, hollow stalks, curled dead leaves, and other crannies wherein breezes, worms, and insects can work their will, he fancied that they were Eustacia, standing without and breathing wishes of reconciliation.

Up to this time he had persevered in his resolve not to invite her back. At the same time the severity with which he had treated her lulled the sharpness of his regret for his mother, and awoke some of his old solicitude for his mother's supplanter. Harsh feelings produce harsh usage, and this by reaction quenches the sentiments that gave it birth. The more he reflected the more he softened. But to look upon his wife as innocence in distress was impossible, though he could ask himself whether he had given her quite time enough—if he had not come a little too suddenly upon her on that sombre morning.

Now that the first flush of his anger had paled he was disinclined to ascribe to her more than an indiscreet friendship with Wildeve; for there had not appeared in her manner the signs of dishonour. And this once admitted, an absolutely dark interpretation of her act towards his mother was no longer forced upon him.

On the evening of the fifth November his thoughts of Eustacia were intense. Echoes from those past times when they had exchanged tender words all the day long came like the diffused murmur of a seashore left miles behind. "Surely," he said, "she might have brought herself to communicate with me before now, and confess honestly what Wildeve was to her."

Instead of remaining at home that night he determined to go and see Thomasin and her husband. If he found opportunity he would allude to the cause of the separation between Eustacia and himself, keeping silence, however, on the fact that there was a third person in his house when his mother was turned away. If it proved that Wildeve was innocently there he would doubtless openly mention it. If he were there with unjust intentions Wildeve, being a man of quick feeling, might possibly say something to reveal the extent to which Eustacia was compromised.

But on reaching his cousin's house he found that only Thomasin was at home, Wildeve being at that time on his way towards the bonfire innocently lit by Charley at Mistover. Thomasin then, as always, was glad to see Clym, and took him to inspect the sleeping baby, carefully screening the candle-light from the infant's eyes with her hand.

"Tamsin, have you heard that Eustacia is not with me now?" he said when they had sat down again.

"No," said Thomasin, alarmed.

"And not that I have left Alderworth?"

"No. I never hear tidings from Alderworth unless you bring them. What is the matter?"

Clym in a disturbed voice related to her his visit to Susan Nunsuch's boy, the revelation he had made, and what had resulted from his charging Eustacia with having wilfully and heartlessly done the deed. He suppressed all mention of Wildeve's presence with her.

"All this, and I not knowing it!" murmured Thomasin in an awestruck tone. "Terrible! What could have made her—O, Eustacia! And when you found it out you went in hot haste to her? Were you too cruel?—or is she really so wicked as she seems?"

"Can a man be too cruel to his mother's enemy?"

"I can fancy so."

"Very well, then—I'll admit that he can. But now what is to be done?"

"Make it up again—if a quarrel so deadly can ever be made up. I almost wish you had not told me. But do try to be reconciled. There are ways, after all, if you both wish to."

"I don't know that we do both wish to make it up," said Clym. "If she had wished it, would she not have sent to me by this time?"

"You seem to wish to, and yet you have not sent to her."

"True; but I have been tossed to and fro in doubt if I ought, after such strong provocation. To see me now, Thomasin, gives you no idea of what I have been; of what depths I have descended to in these few last days. O, it was a bitter shame to shut out my mother like that! Can I ever forget it, or even agree to see her again?"

"She might not have known that anything serious would come of it, and perhaps she did not mean to keep aunt out altogether."

"She says herself that she did not. But the fact remains that keep her out she did."

"Believe her sorry, and send for her."

"How if she will not come?"

"It will prove her guilty, by showing that it is her habit to nourish enmity. But I do not think that for a moment."

"I will do this. I will wait for a day or two longer—not longer than two days certainly; and if she does not send to me in that time I will indeed send to her. I thought to have seen Wildeve here to-night. Is he from home?"

Thomasin blushed a little. "No," she said. "He is merely gone out for a walk."

"Why didn't he take you with him? The evening is fine. You want fresh air as well as he."

"Oh, I don't care for going anywhere; besides, there is baby."

"Yes, yes. Well, I have been thinking whether I should not consult your husband about this as well as you," said Clym steadily.

"I fancy I would not," she quickly answered. "It can do no good."

Her cousin looked her in the face. No doubt Thomasin was ignorant that her husband had any share in the events of that tragic afternoon; but her countenance seemed to signify that she concealed some suspicion or thought of the reputed tender relations between Wildeve and Eustacia in days gone by.

Clym, however, could make nothing of it, and he rose to depart, more in doubt than when he came.

"You will write to her in a day or two?" said the young woman earnestly. "I do so hope the wretched separation may come to an end."

"I will," said Clym; "I don't rejoice in my present state at all."

And he left her and climbed over the hill to Blooms-End. Before going to bed he sat down and wrote the following letter:—

MY DEAR EUSTACIA—I must obey my heart without consulting my reason too closely. Will you come back to me? Do so, and the past shall never be mentioned. I was too severe; but O, Eustacia, the provocation! You don't know, you never will know, what those words of anger cost me which you drew down upon yourself. All that an honest man can promise you I promise now, which is that from me you shall never suffer anything on this score again. After all the vows we have made, Eustacia, I think we had better pass the remainder of our lives in trying to keep them. Come to me, then, even if you reproach me. I have thought of your sufferings that morning on which I parted from you; I know they were genuine, and they are as much as you ought to bear. Our love must still continue. Such hearts as ours would never have been given us but to be concerned with each other. I could not ask you back at first, Eustacia, for I was unable to persuade myself that he who was with you was not there as a lover. But if you will come and explain distracting appearances I do not question that you can show your honesty to me. Why have you not come before? Do you think I will not listen to you? Surely not, when you remember the kisses and vows we exchanged under the summer moon. Return then, and you shall be warmly welcomed. I can no longer think of you to your prejudice—I am but too much absorbed in justifying you.—Your husband as ever,

CLYM

"There," he said, as he laid it in his desk, "that's a good thing done. If she does not come before to-morrow night I will send it to her."

Meanwhile, at the house he had just left Thomasin sat sighing uneasily. Fidelity to her husband had that evening induced her to conceal all suspicion that Wildeve's interest in Eustacia had not ended with his marriage. But she knew nothing positive; and though Clym was her well-beloved cousin there was one nearer to her still.

When, a little later, Wildeve returned from his walk to Mistover, Thomasin said, "Damon, where have you been? I was getting quite frightened, and thought you had fallen into the river. I dislike being in the house by myself."

"Frightened?" he said, touching her cheek as if she were some domestic animal. "Why, I thought nothing could frighten you. It is that you are getting proud, I am sure, and don't like living here since we have risen above our business. Well, it is a tedious matter, this getting a new house; but I couldn't have set about it sooner, unless our ten thousand pounds had been a hundred thousand, when we could have afforded to despise caution."

"No—I don't mind waiting—I would rather stay here twelve months longer than run any risk with baby. But I don't like your vanishing so in the evenings. There's something on your mind—I know there is, Damon. You go about so gloomily, and look at the heath as if it were somebody's gaol instead of a nice wild place to walk in."

He looked towards her with pitying surprise. "What, do you like Egdon Heath?" he said.

"I like what I was born near to; I admire its grim old face."

"Pooh, my dear. You don't know what you like."

"I am sure I do. There's only one thing unpleasant about Egdon."

"What's that?"

"You never take me with you when you walk there. Why do you wander so much in it yourself if you so dislike it?"

The enquiry, though a simple one, was plainly disconcerting, and he sat down before replying. "I don't think you often see me there. Give an instance."

"I will," she answered triumphantly. "When you went out this evening I thought that as baby was asleep I would see where you were going to so mysteriously without telling me. So I ran out and followed behind you. You stopped at the place where the road forks, looked round at the bonfires, and then said, 'Damn it, I'll go!' And you went quickly up the left-hand road. Then I stood and watched you."

Wildeve frowned, afterwards saying, with a forced smile, "Well, what wonderful discovery did you make?"

"There—now you are angry, and we won't talk of this any more." She went across to him, sat on a footstool, and looked up in his face.

"Nonsense!" he said; "that's how you always back out. We will go on with it now we have begun. What did you next see? I particularly want to know."

"Don't be like that, Damon!" she murmured. "I didn't see anything. You vanished out of sight, and then I looked round at the bonfires and came in."

"Perhaps this is not the only time you have dogged my steps. Are you trying to find out something bad about me?"

"Not at all! I have never done such a thing before, and I shouldn't have done it now if words had not sometimes been dropped about you."

"What *do* you mean?" he impatiently asked.

"They say—they say you used to go to Alderworth in the evenings, and it puts into my mind what I have heard about—"

Wildeve turned angrily and stood up in front of her. "Now," he said, flourishing his hand in the air, "just out with it, madam! I demand to know what remarks you have heard."

"Well, I heard that you used to be very fond of Eustacia—nothing more than that, though told more in a bit-by-bit way. You ought not to be angry!"

He observed that her eyes were brimming with tears. "Well," he said, "there is nothing new in that, and of course I don't mean to be rough towards you, so you need not cry. Now, don't let us speak of the subject any more."

And no more was said, Thomasin being glad enough of a reason for not mentioning Clym's visit to her that evening, and his story.

VII

THE NIGHT OF THE SIXTH OF NOVEMBER

HAVING RESOLVED ON FLIGHT EUSTACIA AT TIMES SEEMED ANXIOUS THAT SOMETHING should happen to thwart her own intention. The only event that could really change her position was the appearance of Clym. The glory which had encircled him as her lover was departed now; yet some good simple quality of his would occasionally return to her memory and stir a momentary throb of hope that he would again present himself before her. But calmly considered it was not likely that such a severance as now existed would ever close up: she would have to live on as a painful object, isolated, and out of place. She had used to think of the heath alone as an uncongenial spot to be in; she felt it now of the whole world.

Towards evening on the sixth her determination to go away again revived. About four o'clock she packed up anew the few small articles she had brought in her flight from Alderworth, and also some belonging to her which had been left here: the whole formed a bundle not too large to be carried in her hand for a distance of a mile or two. The scene without grew darker; mud-coloured clouds bellied downwards from the sky like vast hammocks slung across it, and with the increase of night a stormy wind arose; but as yet there was no rain.

Eustacia could not rest indoors, having nothing more to do, and she wandered to and fro on the hill, not far from the house she was soon to leave. In these desultory ramblings she passed the cottage of Susan Nunsuch, a little lower down than her grand-father's. The door was ajar, and a riband of bright firelight fell over the ground without. As Eustacia crossed the firebeams she appeared for an instant as distinct as a figure in a phantasmagoria— a creature of light surrounded by an area of darkness: the moment passed, and she was absorbed in night again.

A woman who was sitting inside the cottage had seen and recognised her in that momentary irradiation. This was Susan herself, occupied in preparing a posset for her little boy, who, often ailing, was now seriously unwell. Susan dropped the spoon, shook her fist at the vanished figure, and then proceeded with her work in a musing, absent way.

At eight o'clock, the hour at which Eustacia had promised to signal Wildeve if ever she signalled at all, she looked around the premises to learn if the coast was clear, went to the furze-rick, and pulled thence a long-stemmed bough of that fuel. This she carried to the corner of the bank, and, glancing behind to see if the shutters were all closed, she struck a light, and kindled the furze. When it was thoroughly ablaze Eustacia took it by the stem and waved it in the air above her head till it had burned itself out.

She was gratified, if gratification were possible to such a mood, by seeing a similar light in the vicinity of Wildeve's residence a minute or two later. Having agreed to keep watch at this hour every night, in case she should require assistance, this promptness proved how strictly he had held to his word. Four hours after the present time, that is, at midnight, he was to be ready to drive her to Budmouth, as prearranged.

Eustacia returned to the house. Supper having been got over she retired early, and sat in her bedroom waiting for the time to go by. The night being dark and threatening, Captain Vye had not strolled out to gossip in any cottage or to call at the inn, as was sometimes his custom on these long autumn nights; and he sat sipping grog alone downstairs. About ten o'clock there was a knock at the door. When the servant opened it the rays of the candle fell upon the form of Fairway.

"I was a-forced to go to Lower Mistover to-night," he said; "and Mr. Yeobright asked me to leave this here on my way; but, faith, I put it in the lining of my hat, and thought no more about it till I got back and was hasping my gate before going to bed. So I have run back with it at once."

He handed in a letter and went his way. The girl brought it to the captain, who found that it was directed to Eustacia. He turned it over and over, and fancied that the writing was her husband's, though he could not be sure. However, he decided to let her have it at once if possible, and took it upstairs for that purpose; but on reaching the door of her room and looking in at the keyhole he found there was no light within, the fact being that Eustacia, without undressing, had flung herself upon the bed, to rest and gather a little strength for her coming journey. Her grand-father concluded from what he saw that he ought not to disturb her; and descending again to the parlour he placed the letter on the mantelpiece to give it to her in the morning.

At eleven o'clock he went to bed himself, smoked for some time in his bedroom, put out his light at half-past eleven, and then, as was his invariable custom, pulled up the blind before getting into bed, that he might see which way the wind blew on opening his eyes in the morning, his bedroom window commanding a view of the flagstaff and vane. Just as he had lain down he was surprised to observe the white pole of the staff flash into existence like a streak of phosphorus drawn downwards across the shade of night without. Only one explanation met this—a light had been suddenly thrown upon the pole from the direction of the house. As everybody had retired to rest the old man felt it necessary to get out of bed, open the window softly, and look to the right and left. Eustacia's bedroom was lighted up, and it was the shine from her window which had lighted the pole. Wondering what had aroused her he remained undecided at the window, and was thinking of fetching the letter to slip it under her door, when he heard a slight brushing of garments on the partition dividing his room from the passage.

The captain concluded that Eustacia, feeling wakeful, had gone for a book, and would have dismissed the matter as unimportant if he had not also heard her distinctly weeping.

"She is thinking of that husband of hers," he said to himself. "Ah, the silly goose! she had no business to marry him. I wonder if that letter is really his?"

He arose, threw his boat-cloak round him, opened the door, and said, "Eustacia!" There was no answer. "Eustacia!" he repeated louder, "there is a letter on the mantelpiece for you."

But no response was made to this statement save an imaginary one from the wind, which seemed to gnaw at the corners of the house, and the stroke of a few drops of rain upon the windows.

He went on to the landing, and stood waiting nearly five minutes. Still she did not return. He went back for a light, and prepared to follow her; but first he looked into her bedroom. There, on the outside of the quilt, was the impression of her form, showing that the bed had not been opened; and, what was more significant, she had not taken her candlestick downstairs. He was now thoroughly alarmed; and hastily putting on his clothes he descended to the front-door, which he himself had bolted and locked. It was now unfastened. There was no longer any doubt that Eustacia had left the house at this midnight hour; and whither could she have gone? To follow her was almost impossible. Had the dwelling stood in an ordinary road, two persons setting out, one in each direction, might have made sure of overtaking her; but it was a hopeless task to seek for anybody on a heath in the dark, the practicable directions for flight across it from any point being as numerous as the meridians radiating from the pole. Perplexed what to do, he looked into the parlour, and was vexed to find that the letter still lay there untouched.

At half-past eleven, finding that the house was silent, Eustacia had lighted her candle, put on some warm outer wrappings, taken her bag in her hand, and, extinguishing the light again, descended the staircase. When she got into the outer air she found that it had begun to rain, and as she stood pausing at the door it increased, threatening to come on heavily. But having committed herself to this line of action there was no retreating for bad weather, since Wildeve had been communicated with, and was probably even then waiting for her. The gloom of the night was funereal; all nature seemed clothed in crape. The spiky points of the fir trees behind the house rose into the sky like the turrets and pinnacles of an abbey. Nothing below the horizon was visible save a light which was still burning in the cottage of Susan Nunsuch.

Eustacia opened her umbrella and went out from the enclosure by the steps over the bank, after which she was beyond all danger of being perceived. Skirting the pool she followed the path towards Rainbarrow, occasionally stumbling over twisted furze-roots, tufts of rushes, or oozing lumps of fleshy fungi, which at this season lay scattered about the heath like the rotten liver and lungs of some colossal animal. The moon and stars were closed up by cloud and rain to the degree of extinction. It was a night which led the traveller's thoughts instinctively to dwell on nocturnal scenes of disaster in the chronicles of the world, on all that is terrible and dark in history and legend—the last plague of Egypt, the destruction of Sennacherib's host, the agony in Gethsemane.

Eustacia at length reached Rainbarrow, and stood still there to think. Never was harmony more perfect than that between the chaos of her mind and the chaos of the world without. A sudden recollection had flashed on her this moment: she had not money enough for undertaking a long journey. Amid the fluctuating sentiments of the day her unpractical mind had not dwelt on the necessity of being well-provided, and now that she thoroughly realised the conditions she sighed bitterly and ceased to stand erect, gradually crouching down under the umbrella as if she were drawn into the Barrow by a hand from beneath. Could it be that she was to remain a captive still? Money: she had never felt its value before. Even to efface herself from the country means were required. To ask Wildeve for pecuniary aid without allowing him to accompany her was impossible to a woman with a shadow of pride left in her: to fly as his mistress—and she knew that he loved her—was of the nature of humiliation.

Anyone who had stood by now would have pitied her, not so much on account of her exposure to weather, and isolation from all of humanity except the mouldered remains inside the Barrow; but for that other form of misery which was denoted by the slightly rocking movement that her feelings imparted to her person. Extreme unhappiness weighed visibly upon her. Between the drippings of the rain from her umbrella to her mantel, from her mantel to the heather, from the heather to the earth, very similar sounds could be heard coming from her lips; and the tearfulness of the outer scene was repeated upon her face. The wings of her soul were broken by the cruel obstructiveness of all about her; and even had she seen herself in a promising way of getting to Budmouth, entering a steamer, and sailing to some opposite port, she would have been but little more buoyant, so fearfully malignant were other things. She uttered words aloud. When a woman in such a situation, neither old, deaf, crazed, nor whimsical, takes upon herself to sob and soliloquise aloud there is something grievous the matter.

"Can I go, can I go?" she moaned. "He's not *great* enough for me to give myself to— he does not suffice for my desire! . . . If he had been a Saul or a Bonaparte—ah! But to break my marriage vow for him—it is too poor a luxury! . . . And I have no money to go alone! And if I could, what comfort to me? I must drag on next year, as I have dragged on this year, and the year after that as before. How I have tried and tried to be a splendid woman, and how destiny has been against me! . . . I do not deserve my lot!" she cried in a frenzy of bitter revolt. "O, the cruelty of putting me into this ill-conceived world! I was capable of much; but I have been injured and blighted and crushed by things beyond my control! O, how hard it is of Heaven to devise such tortures for me, who have done no harm to Heaven at all!"

The distant light which Eustacia had cursorily observed in leaving the house came, as she had divined, from the cottage-window of Susan Nunsuch. What Eustacia did not divine was the occupation of the woman within at that moment. Susan's sight of her passing figure earlier in the evening, not five minutes after the sick boy's exclamation, "Mother, I do feel so bad!" persuaded the matron that an evil influence was certainly exercised by Eustacia's propinquity.

On this account Susan did not go to bed as soon as the evening's work was over, as she would have done at ordinary times. To counteract the malign spell which she imagined poor Eustacia to be working, the boy's mother busied herself with a ghastly invention of superstition, calculated to bring powerlessness, atrophy, and annihilation on any human being against whom it was directed. It was a practice well known on Egdon at that date, and one that is not quite extinct at the present day.

She passed with her candle into an inner room, where, among other utensils, were two large brown pans, containing together perhaps a hundredweight of liquid honey, the produce of the bees during the foregoing summer. On a shelf over the pans was a smooth and solid yellow mass of a hemispherical form, consisting of beeswax from the same take of honey. Susan took down the lump, and, cutting off several thin slices, heaped them in an iron ladle, with which she returned to the living-room, and placed the vessel in the hot ashes of the fireplace. As soon as the wax had softened to the plasticity of dough she kneaded the pieces together. And now her face became more intent. She began moulding the wax; and it was evident from her manner of manipulation that she was endeavouring to give it some preconceived form. The form was human.

By warming and kneading, cutting and twisting, dismembering and rejoining the incipient image she had in about a quarter of an hour produced a shape which tolerably well resembled a woman, and was about six inches high. She laid it on the table to get cold and hard. Meanwhile she took the candle and went upstairs to where the little boy was lying.

"Did you notice, my dear, what Mrs. Eustacia wore this afternoon besides the dark dress?"

"A red ribbon round her neck."

"Anything else?"

"No—except sandal-shoes."

"A red ribbon and sandal-shoes," she said to herself.

Mrs. Nunsuch went and searched till she found a fragment of the narrowest red ribbon, which she took downstairs and tied round the neck of the image. Then fetching ink and a quill from the rickety bureau by the window, she blackened the feet of the image to the extent presumably covered by shoes; and on the instep of each foot marked cross-lines in the shape taken by the sandal-strings of those days. Finally she tied a bit of black thread round the upper part of the head, in faint resemblance to a snood worn for confining the hair.

Susan held the object at arm's length and contemplated it with a satisfaction in which there was no smile. To anybody acquainted with the inhabitants of Egdon Heath the image would have suggested Eustacia Yeobright.

From her work-basket in the window-seat the woman took a paper of pins, of the old long and yellow sort, whose heads were disposed to come off at their first usage. These she began to thrust into the image in all directions, with apparently excruciating energy. Probably as many as fifty were thus inserted, some into the head of the wax model, some into the shoulders, some into the trunk, some upwards through the soles of the feet, till the figure was completely permeated with pins.

She turned to the fire. It had been of turf; and though the high heap of ashes which turf fires produce was somewhat dark and dead on the outside, upon raking it abroad with the shovel the inside of the mass showed a glow of red heat. She took a few pieces of fresh turf from the chimney-corner and built them together over the glow, upon which the fire brightened. Seizing with the tongs the image that she had made of Eustacia, she held it in the heat, and watched it as it began to waste slowly away. And while she stood thus engaged there came from between her lips a murmur of words.

It was a strange jargon—the Lord's Prayer repeated backwards—the incantation usual in proceedings for obtaining unhallowed assistance against an enemy. Susan uttered the lugubrious discourse three times slowly, and when it was completed the image had considerably diminished. As the wax dropped into the fire a long flame arose from the spot, and curling its tongue round the figure ate still further into its substance. A pin occasionally dropped with the wax, and the embers heated it red as it lay.

VIII

RAIN, DARKNESS, AND ANXIOUS WANDERERS

WHILE THE EFFIGY OF EUSTACIA WAS MELTING TO NOTHING, AND THE FAIR WOMAN herself was standing on Rainbarrow, her soul in an abyss of desolation seldom plumbed by one so young, Yeobright sat lonely at Blooms-End. He had fulfilled his word to Thomasin by sending off Fairway with the letter to his wife, and now waited with increased impatience for some sound or signal of her return. Were Eustacia still at Mistover the very least he expected was that she would send him back a reply to-night by the same hand; though, to leave all to her inclination, he had cautioned Fairway not to ask for an answer. If one were told or handed to him he was to bring it immediately; if not, he was to go straight home without troubling to come round to Blooms-End again that night.

But secretly Clym had a more pleasing hope. Eustacia might possibly decline to use her pen—it was rather her way to work silently—and surprise him by appearing at his door.

To Clym's regret it began to rain and blow hard as the evening advanced. The wind rasped and scraped at the corners of the house, and filliped the eaves-droppings like peas against the panes. He walked restlessly about the untenanted rooms, stopping strange noises in windows and doors by jamming splinters of wood into the casements and crevices, and pressing together the lead-work of the quarries where it had become loosened from the glass. It was one of those nights when cracks in the walls of old churches widen, when ancient stains on the ceilings of decayed manor-houses are renewed and enlarged from the size of a man's hand to an area of many feet. The little gate in the palings before his dwelling continually opened and clicked together again, but when he looked out eagerly nobody was there; it was as if invisible shapes of the dead were passing in on their way to visit him.

Between ten and eleven o'clock, finding that neither Fairway nor anybody else came to him, he retired to rest, and despite his anxieties soon fell asleep. His sleep, however, was not very sound, by reason of the expectancy he had given way to, and he was easily awakened by a knocking which began at the door about an hour after. Clym arose and looked out of the window. Rain was still falling heavily, the whole expanse of heath before him emitting a subdued hiss under the downpour. It was too dark to see anything at all.

"Who's there?" he cried.

Light footsteps shifted their position in the porch, and he could just distinguish in a plaintive female voice the words, "O Clym, come down and let me in!"

He flushed hot with agitation. "Surely it is Eustacia!" he murmured. If so, she had indeed come to him unawares.

He hastily got a light, dressed himself, and went down. On his flinging open the door the rays of the candle fell upon a woman closely wrapped up, who at once came forward.

"Thomasin!" he exclaimed in an indescribable tone of disappointment. "It is Thomasin, and on such a night as this! O, where is Eustacia?"

Thomasin it was, wet, frightened, and panting.

"Eustacia? I don't know, Clym; but I can think," she said with much perturbation. "Let me come in and rest—I will explain this. There is a great trouble brewing—my husband and Eustacia!"

"What, what?"

"I think my husband is going to leave me or do something dreadful—I don't know what—Clym, will you go and see? I have nobody to help me but you! Eustacia has not yet come home?"

"No."

She went on breathlessly: "Then they are going to run off together! He came indoors to-night about eight o'clock and said in an offhand way, 'Tamsie, I have just found that I must go a journey.' 'When?' I said. 'To-night,' he said. 'Where?' I asked him. 'I cannot tell you at present,' he said; 'I shall be back again to-morrow.' He then went and busied himself in looking up his things, and took no notice of me at all. I expected to see him start, but he did not, and then it came to be ten o'clock, when he said, 'You had better go to bed.' I didn't know what to do, and I went to bed. I believe he thought I fell asleep, for half an hour after that he came up and unlocked the oak chest we keep money in when we have much in the house and took out a roll of something which I believe was bank-notes, though I was not aware that he had 'em there. These he must have got from the bank when he went there the other day. What does he want bank-notes for, if he is only going off for a day? When he had gone down I thought of Eustacia, and how he had met her the night before—I know he did meet her, Clym, for I followed him part of the way; but I did not like to tell you when you called, and so make you think ill of him, as I did not think it was so serious. Then I could not stay in bed: I got up and dressed myself, and when I heard him out in the stable I thought I would come and tell you. So I came downstairs without any noise and slipped out."

"Then he was not absolutely gone when you left?"

"No. Will you, dear Cousin Clym, go and try to persuade him not to go? He takes no notice of what I say, and puts me off with the story of his going on a journey, and will be home to-morrow, and all that; but I don't believe it. I think you could influence him."

"I'll go," said Clym. "O, Eustacia!"

Thomasin carried in her arms a large bundle; and having by this time seated herself she began to unroll it, when a baby appeared as the kernel to the husks—dry, warm, and unconscious of travel or rough weather. Thomasin briefly kissed the baby, and then found time to begin crying as she said, "I brought baby, for I was afraid what might happen to her. I suppose it will be her death, but I couldn't leave her with Rachel!"

Clym hastily put together the logs on the hearth, raked abroad the embers, which were scarcely yet extinct, and blew up a flame with the bellows.

"Dry yourself," he said. "I'll go and get some more wood."

"No, no—don't stay for that. I'll make up the fire. Will you go at once—please will you?"

Yeobright ran upstairs to finish dressing himself. While he was gone another rapping came to the door. This time there was no delusion that it might be Eustacia's: the footsteps just preceding it had been heavy and slow. Yeobright, thinking it might possibly be Fairway with a note in answer, descended again and opened the door.

"Captain Vye?" he said to a dripping figure.

"Is my grand-daughter here?" said the captain.

"No."

"Then where is she?"

"I don't know."

"But you ought to know—you are her husband."

"Only in name apparently," said Clym with rising excitement. "I believe she means to elope to-night with Wildeve. I am just going to look to it."

"Well, she has left my house; she left about half an hour ago. Who's sitting there?"

"My cousin Thomasin."

The captain bowed in a preoccupied way to her. "I only hope it is no worse than an elopement," he said.

"Worse? What's worse than the worst a wife can do?"

"Well, I have been told a strange tale. Before starting in search of her I called up Charley, my stable-lad. I missed my pistols the other day."

"Pistols?"

"He said at the time that he took them down to clean. He has now owned that he took them because he saw Eustacia looking curiously at them; and she afterwards owned to him that she was thinking of taking her life, but bound him to secrecy, and promised never to think of such a thing again. I hardly suppose she will ever have bravado enough to use one of them; but it shows what has been lurking in her mind; and people who think of that sort of thing once think of it again."

"Where are the pistols?"

"Safely locked up. O no, she won't touch them again. But there are more ways of letting out life than through a bullet-hole. What did you quarrel about so bitterly with her to drive her to all this? You must have treated her badly indeed. Well, I was always against the marriage, and I was right."

"Are you going with me?" said Yeobright, paying no attention to the captain's latter remark. "If so I can tell you what we quarrelled about as we walk along."

"Where to?"

"To Wildeve's—that was her destination, depend upon it."

Thomasin here broke in, still weeping: "He said he was only going on a sudden short journey; but if so why did he want so much money? O, Clym, what do you think will happen? I am afraid that you, my poor baby, will soon have no father left to you!

"I am off now," said Yeobright, stepping into the porch.

"I would fain go with ye," said the old man doubtfully. "But I begin to be afraid that my legs will hardly carry me there such a night as this. I am not so young as I was. If they are interrupted in their flight she will be sure to come back to me, and I ought to be at the house to receive her. But be it as 'twill I can't walk to the Quiet Woman, and that's an end on't. I'll go straight home."

"It will perhaps be best," said Clym. "Thomasin, dry yourself, and be as comfortable as you can."

With this he closed the door upon her, and left the house in company with Captain Vye, who parted from him outside the gate, taking the middle path, which led to Mistover. Clym crossed by the right-hand track towards the inn.

Thomasin, being left alone, took off some of her wet garments, carried the baby upstairs to Clym's bed, and then came down to the sitting-room again, where she made a larger fire, and began drying herself. The fire soon flared up the chimney, giving the room an appearance of comfort that was doubled by contrast with the drumming of the storm without, which snapped at the window-panes and breathed into the chimney strange low utterances that seemed to be the prologue to some tragedy.

But the least part of Thomasin was in the house, for her heart being at ease about the little girl upstairs she was mentally following Clym on his journey. Having indulged in this imaginary peregrination for some considerable interval, she became impressed with a sense of the intolerable slowness of time. But she sat on. The moment then came when she could scarcely sit longer; and it was like a satire on her patience to remember that Clym could hardly have reached the inn as yet. At last she went to the baby's bedside. The child was sleeping soundly; but her imagination of possibly disastrous events at her home, the predominance within her of the unseen over the seen, agitated her beyond endurance. She could not refrain from going down and opening the door. The rain still continued, the candle-light falling upon the nearest drops and making glistening darts of them as they descended across the throng of invisible ones behind. To plunge into that medium was to plunge into water slightly diluted with air. But the difficulty of returning to her house at this moment made her all the more desirous of doing so: anything was better than suspense. "I have come here well enough," she said, "and why shouldn't I go back again? It is a mistake for me to be away."

She hastily fetched the infant, wrapped it up, cloaked herself as before, and shovelling the ashes over the fire, to prevent accidents, went into the open air. Pausing first to put the door-key in its old place behind the shutter, she resolutely turned her face to the confronting pile of firmamental darkness beyond the palings, and stepped into its midst. But Thomasin's imagination being so actively engaged elsewhere, the night and the weather had for her no terror beyond that of their actual discomfort and difficulty.

She was soon ascending Blooms-End valley and traversing the undulations on the side of the hill. The noise of the wind over the heath was shrill, and as if it whistled for joy at finding a night so congenial as this. Sometimes the path led her to hollows between thickets of tall and dripping bracken, dead, though not yet prostrate, which enclosed her like a pool. When they were more than usually tall she lifted the baby to the top of her head, that it might be out of the reach of their drenching fronds. On higher ground, where the wind was brisk and sustained, the rain flew in a level flight without sensible descent, so that it was beyond all power to imagine the remoteness of the point at which it left the bosoms of the clouds. Here self-defence was impossible, and individual drops stuck into her like the arrows into Saint Sebastian. She was enabled to avoid puddles by the nebulous paleness which signified their presence, though beside anything less dark than the heath they themselves would have appeared as blackness.

Yet in spite of all this Thomasin was not sorry that she had started. To her there were not, as to Eustacia, demons in the air, and malice in every bush and bough. The drops which lashed her face were not scorpions, but prosy rain; Egdon in the mass was no monster whatever, but impersonal open ground. Her fears of the place were rational, her dislikes of its worst moods reasonable. At this time it was in her view a windy, wet place, in which a person might experience much discomfort, lose the path without care, and possibly catch cold.

If the path is well known the difficulty at such times of keeping therein is not altogether great, from its familiar feel to the feet; but once lost it is irrecoverable. Owing to her baby, who somewhat impeded Thomasin's view forward and distracted her mind, she did at last lose the track. This mishap occurred when she was descending an open slope about two-thirds home. Instead of attempting, by wandering hither and thither, the hopeless task of finding such a mere thread, she went straight on, trusting for guidance to her general knowledge of the district, which was scarcely surpassed by Clym's or by that of the heath-croppers themselves.

At length Thomasin reached a hollow and began to discern through the rain a faint blotted radiance, which presently assumed the oblong form of an open door. She knew that no house stood hereabouts, and was soon aware of the nature of the door by its height above the ground.

"Why, it is Diggory Venn's van, surely!" she said.

A certain secluded spot near Rainbarrow was, she knew, often Venn's chosen centre when staying in this neighbourhood; and she guessed at once that she had stumbled upon this mysterious retreat. The question arose in her mind whether or not she should ask him to guide her into the path. In her anxiety to reach home she decided that she would appeal to him, notwithstanding the strangeness of appearing before his eyes at this place and season. But when, in pursuance of this resolve, Thomasin reached the van and looked in she found it to be untenanted; though there was no doubt that it was the reddleman's. The fire was burning in the stove, the lantern hung from the nail. Round the doorway the floor was merely sprinkled with rain, and not saturated, which told her that the door had not long been opened.

While she stood uncertainly looking in Thomasin heard a footstep advancing from the darkness behind her; and turning, beheld the well-known form in corduroy, lurid from head to foot, the lantern beams falling upon him through an intervening gauze of raindrops.

"I thought you went down the slope," he said, without noticing her face. "How do you come back here again?"

"Diggory?" said Thomasin faintly.

"Who are you?" said Venn, still unperceiving. "And why were you crying so just now?"

"O, Diggory! don't you know me?" said she. "But of course you don't, wrapped up like this. What do you mean? I have not been crying here, and I have not been here before."

Venn then came nearer till he could see the illuminated side of her form.

"Mrs. Wildeve!" he exclaimed, starting. "What a time for us to meet! And the baby too! What dreadful thing can have brought you out on such a night as this?"

She could not immediately answer; and without asking her permission he hopped into his van, took her by the arm, and drew her up after him.

"What is it?" he continued when they stood within.

"I have lost my way coming from Blooms-End, and I am in a great hurry to get home. Please show me as quickly as you can! It is so silly of me not to know Egdon better, and I cannot think how I came to lose the path. Show me quickly, Diggory, please."

"Yes, of course. I will go with ye. But you came to me before this, Mrs. Wildeve?"

"I only came this minute."

"That's strange. I was lying down here asleep about five minutes ago, with the door shut to keep out the weather, when the brushing of a woman's clothes over the heath-bushes just outside woke me up (for I don't sleep heavy) and at the same time I heard a sobbing or crying from the same woman. I opened my door and held out my lantern, and just as far as the light would reach I saw a woman: she turned her head when the light sheened on her, and then hurried on downhill. I hung up the lantern, and was curious enough to pull on my things and dog her a few steps, but I could see nothing of her any more. That was where I had been when you came up; and when I saw you I thought you were the same one."

"Perhaps it was one of the heath-folk going home?"

"No, it couldn't be. 'Tis too late. The noise of her gown over the he'th was of a whistling sort that nothing but silk will make."

"It wasn't I, then. My dress is not silk, you see. . . . Are we anywhere in a line between Mistover and the inn?"

"Well, yes; not far out."

"Ah, I wonder if it was she! Diggory, I must go at once!"

She jumped down from the van before he was aware, when Venn unhooked the lantern and leaped down after her. "I'll take the baby, ma'am," he said. "You must be tired out by the weight."

Thomasin hesitated a moment, and then delivered the baby into Venn's hands. "Don't squeeze her, Diggory," she said, "or hurt her little arm; and keep the cloak close over her like this, so that the rain may not drop in her face."

"I will," said Venn earnestly. "As if I could hurt anything belonging to you!"

"I only meant accidentally," said Thomasin.

"The baby is dry enough, but you are pretty wet," said the reddleman when, in closing the door of his cart to padlock it, he noticed on the floor a ring of water-drops where her cloak had hung from her.

Thomasin followed him as he wound right and left to avoid the larger bushes, stopping occasionally and covering the lantern, while he looked over his shoulder to gain some idea of the position of Rainbarrow above them, which it was necessary to keep directly behind their backs to preserve a proper course.

"You are sure the rain does not fall upon baby?"

"Quite sure. May I ask how old he is, ma'am?"

"He!" said Thomasin reproachfully. "Anybody can see better than that in a moment. She is nearly two months old. How far is it now to the inn?"

"A little over a quarter of a mile."

"Will you walk a little faster?"

"I was afraid you could not keep up."

"I am very anxious to get there. Ah, there is a light from the window!"

" 'Tis not from the window. That's a gig-lamp, to the best of my belief."

"O!" said Thomasin in despair. "I wish I had been there sooner—give me the baby, Diggory—you can go back now."

"I must go all the way," said Venn. "There is a quag between us and that light, and you will walk into it up to your neck unless I take you round."

"But the light is at the inn, and there is no quag in front of that."

"No, the light is below the inn some two or three hundred yards."

"Never mind," said Thomasin hurriedly. "Go towards the light, and not towards the inn."

"Yes," answered Venn, swerving round in obedience; and, after a pause, "I wish you would tell me what this great trouble is. I think you have proved that I can be trusted."

"There are some things that cannot be—cannot be told to—" And then her heart rose into her throat, and she could say no more.

IX

SIGHTS AND SOUNDS DRAW THE WANDERERS TOGETHER

HAVING SEEN EUSTACIA'S SIGNAL FROM THE HILL AT EIGHT O'CLOCK, WILDEVE IMMEDIately prepared to assist her in her flight, and, as he hoped, accompany her. He was somewhat perturbed, and his manner of informing Thomasin that he was going on a journey was in itself sufficient to rouse her suspicions. When she had gone to bed he collected the few articles he would require, and went upstairs to the money-chest, whence he took a tolerably bountiful sum in notes, which had been advanced to him on the property he was so soon to have in possession, to defray expenses incidental to the removal.

He then went to the stable and coach-house to assure himself that the horse, gig, and harness were in a fit condition for a long drive. Nearly half an hour was spent thus, and on returning to the house Wildeve had no thought of Thomasin being anywhere but in bed. He had told the stable-lad not to stay up, leading the boy to understand that his departure would be at three or four in the morning; for this, though an exceptional hour, was less strange than midnight, the time actually agreed on, the packet from Budmouth sailing between one and two.

At last all was quiet, and he had nothing to do but to wait. By no effort could he shake off the oppression of spirits which he had experienced ever since his last meeting with Eustacia, but he hoped there was that in his situation which money could cure. He had persuaded himself that to act not ungenerously towards his gentle wife by settling on her the half of his property, and with chivalrous devotion towards another and greater woman by sharing her fate, was possible. And though he meant to adhere to Eustacia's instructions to the letter, to deposit her where she wished and to leave her, should that be her will, the spell that she had cast over him intensified, and his heart was beating fast in the anticipated futility of such commands in the face of a mutual wish that they should depart their lot together.

He would not allow himself to dwell long upon these conjectures, maxims, and hopes, and at twenty minutes to twelve he again went softly to the stable, harnessed the horse, and lit the lamps; whence, taking the horse by the head, he led him with the covered car out of the yard to a spot by the roadside some quarter of a mile below the inn.

Here Wildeve waited, slightly sheltered from the driving rain by a high bank that had been cast up at this place. Along the surface of the road where lit by the lamps the loosened gravel and small stones scudded and clicked together before the wind, which, leaving them in heaps, plunged into the heath and boomed across the bushes into darkness. Only one sound rose above this din of weather, and that was the roaring of a ten-hatch weir a few yards further on, where the road approached the river which formed the boundary of the heath in this direction.

He lingered on in perfect stillness till he began to fancy that the midnight hour must have struck. A very strong doubt had arisen in his mind if Eustacia would venture down the hill in such weather; yet knowing her nature he felt that she might. "Poor thing! 'tis like her ill-luck," he murmured.

At length he turned to the lamp and looked at his watch. To his surprise it was nearly a quarter past midnight. He now wished that he had driven up the circuitous road to Mistover, a plan not adopted because of the enormous length of the route in proportion to that of the pedestrian's path down the open hillside, and the consequent increase of labour for the horse.

At this moment a footstep approached; but the light of the lamps being in a different direction the comer was not visible. The step paused, then came on again.

"Eustacia?" said Wildeve.

The person came forward, and the light fell upon the form of Clym, glistening with wet, whom Wildeve immediately recognised; but Wildeve, who stood behind the lamp, was not at once recognised by Yeobright.

He stopped as if in doubt whether this waiting vehicle could have anything to do with the flight of his wife or not. The sight of Yeobright at once banished Wildeve's sober feelings, who saw him again as the deadly rival from whom Eustacia was to be kept at all hazards. Hence Wildeve did not speak, in the hope that Clym would pass by without particular enquiry.

While they both hung thus in hesitation a dull sound became audible above the storm and wind. Its origin was unmistakable—it was the fall of a body into the stream adjoining, apparently at a point near the weir.

Both started. "Good God! can it be she?" said Clym.

"Why should it be she?" said Wildeve, in his alarm forgetting that he had hitherto screened himself.

"Ah!—that's you, you traitor, is it?" cried Yeobright. "Why should it be she? Because last week she would have put an end to her life if she had been able. She ought to have been watched! Take one of the lamps and come with me."

Yeobright seized the one on his side and hastened on; Wildeve did not wait to unfasten the other, but followed at once along the meadow-track to the weir, a little in the rear of Clym.

Shadwater Weir had at its foot a large circular pool, fifty feet in diameter, into which the water flowed through ten huge hatches, raised and lowered by a winch and cogs in the ordinary manner. The sides of the pool were of masonry, to prevent the water from washing away the bank; but the force of the stream in winter was sometimes such as to undermine the retaining wall and precipitate it into the hole. Clym reached the hatches, the frame-work of which was shaken to its foundations by the velocity of the current. Nothing but the froth of the waves could be discerned in the pool below. He got upon the plank bridge over the race, and holding to the rail, that the wind might not blow him off, crossed to the other side of the river. There he leant over the wall and lowered the lamp, only to behold the vortex formed at the curl of the returning current.

Wildeve meanwhile had arrived on the former side, and the light from Yeobright's lamp shed a flecked and agitated radiance across the weir-pool, revealing to the ex-engineer the tumbling courses of the currents from the hatches above. Across this gashed and puckered mirror a dark body was slowly borne by one of the backward currents.

"O, my darling!" exclaimed Wildeve in an agonised voice; and, without showing sufficient presence of mind even to throw off his great-coat, he leaped into the boiling hole.

Yeobright could now also discern the floating body, though but indistinctly; and imagining from Wildeve's plunge that there was life to be saved he was about to leap after. Bethinking himself of a wiser plan he placed the lamp against a post to make it stand upright, and running round to the lower part of the pool, where there was no wall, he sprang in and boldly waded upwards towards the deeper portion. Here he was taken off his legs, and in swimming was carried round into the centre of the basin, where he perceived Wildeve struggling.

While these hasty actions were in progress here, Venn and Thomasin had been toiling through the lower corner of the heath in the direction of the light. They had not been near enough to the river to hear the plunge, but they saw the removal of the carriage-lamp, and watched its motion into the mead. As soon as they reached the car and horse Venn guessed that something new was amiss, and hastened to follow in the course of the moving light. Venn walked faster than Thomasin, and came to the weir alone.

The lamp placed against the post by Clym still shone across the water, and the reddleman observed something floating motionless. Being incumbered with the infant he ran back to meet Thomasin.

"Take the baby, please, Mrs. Wildeve," he said hastily. "Run home with her, call the stable-lad, and make him send down to me any men who may be living near. Somebody has fallen into the weir."

Thomasin took the child and ran. When she came to the covered car the horse, though fresh from the stable, was standing perfectly still, as if conscious of misfortune. She saw for the first time whose it was. She nearly fainted, and would have been unable to proceed another step but that the necessity of preserving the little girl from harm nerved her to an amazing self-control. In this agony of suspense she entered the house, put the baby in a place of safety, woke the lad and the female domestic, and ran out to give the alarm at the nearest cottage.

Diggory, having returned to the brink of the pool, observed that the small upper hatches or floats were withdrawn. He found one of these lying upon the grass, and taking it under one arm, and with his lantern in his hand, entered at the bottom of the pool as Clym had done. As soon as he began to be in deep water he flung himself across the hatch; thus supported he was able to keep afloat as long as he chose, holding the lantern aloft with his disengaged hand. Propelled by his feet he steered round and round the pool, ascending each time by one of the back streams and descending in the middle of the current.

At first he could see nothing. Then amidst the glistening of the whirlpools and the white clots of foam he distinguished a woman's bonnet floating alone. His search was now under the left wall, when something came to the surface almost close beside him. It was not, as he had expected, a woman, but a man. The reddleman put the ring of the lantern between his teeth, seized the floating man by the collar, and, holding on to the hatch with his remaining arm, struck out into the strongest race, by which the unconscious man, the hatch, and himself were carried down the stream. As soon as Venn found his feet dragging over the pebbles of the shallower part below he secured his footing and waded towards the brink. There, where the water stood at about the height of his waist, he flung away the hatch, and attempted to drag forth the man. This was a matter of great difficulty, and he found as the reason that the legs of the unfortunate stranger were tightly embraced by the arms of another man, who had hitherto been entirely beneath the surface.

At this moment his heart bounded to hear footsteps running towards him, and two men, roused by Thomasin, appeared at the brink above. They ran to where Venn was, and helped him in lifting out the apparently drowned persons, separating them, and laying them out upon the grass. Venn turned the light upon their faces. The one who had been uppermost was Yeobright; he who had been completely submerged was Wildeve.

"Now we must search the hole again," said Venn. "A woman is in there somewhere. Get a pole."

One of the men went to the foot-bridge and tore off the handrail. The reddleman and the two others then entered the water together from below as before, and with their united force probed the pool forwards to where it sloped down to its central depth. Venn was not mistaken in supposing that any person who had sunk for the last time would be washed down to this point, for when they had examined to about half-way across something impeded their thrust.

"Pull it forward," said Venn, and they raked it in with the pole till it was close to their feet.

Venn vanished under the stream, and came up with an armful of wet drapery enclosing a woman's cold form, which was all that remained of the desperate Eustacia.

When they reached the bank there stood Thomasin, in a stress of grief, bending over the two unconscious ones who already lay there. The horse and car were brought to the nearest point in the road, and it was the work of a few minutes only to place the three in the vehicle. Venn led on the horse, supporting Thomasin upon his arm, and the two men followed, till they reached the inn.

The woman who had been shaken out of her sleep by Thomasin had hastily dressed herself and lighted a fire, the other servant being left to snore on in peace at the back of the house. The insensible forms of Eustacia, Clym, and Wildeve were then brought in and laid on the carpet, with their feet to the fire, when such restorative processes as could be thought of were adopted at once, the stableman being in the meantime sent for a doctor. But there seemed to be not a whiff of life in either of the bodies. Then Thomasin, whose stupor of grief had been thrust off a while by frantic action, applied a bottle of hartshorn to Clym's nostrils, having tried it in vain upon the other two. He sighed.

"Clym's alive!" she exclaimed.

He soon breathed distinctly, and again and again did she attempt to revive her husband by the same means; but Wildeve gave no sign. There was too much reason to think that he and Eustacia both were forever beyond the reach of stimulating perfumes. Their exertions did not relax till the doctor arrived, when one by one, the senseless three were taken upstairs and put into warm beds.

Venn soon felt himself relieved from further attendance, and went to the door, scarcely able yet to realise the strange catastrophe that had befallen the family in which he took so great an interest. Thomasin surely would be broken down by the sudden and overwhelming nature of this event. No firm and sensible Mrs. Yeobright lived now to support the gentle girl through the ordeal; and, whatever an unimpassioned spectator might think of her loss of such a husband as Wildeve, there could be no doubt that for the moment she was distracted and horrified by the blow. As for himself, not being privileged to go to her and comfort her, he saw no reason for waiting longer in a house where he remained only as a stranger.

He returned across the heath to his van. The fire was not yet out, and everything remained as he had left it. Venn now bethought himself of his clothes, which were saturated with water to the weight of lead. He changed them, spread them before the fire, and lay down to sleep. But it was more than he could do to rest here while excited by a vivid imagination of the turmoil they were in at the house he had quitted, and, blaming himself for coming away, he dressed in another suit, locked up the door, and again hastened across to the inn. Rain was still falling heavily when he entered the kitchen. A bright fire was shining from the hearth, and two women were bustling about, one of whom was Olly Dowden.

"Well, how is it going on now?" said Venn in a whisper.

"Mr. Yeobright is better; but Mrs. Yeobright and Mr. Wildeve are dead and cold. The doctor says they were quite gone before they were out of the water."

"Ah! I thought as much when I hauled 'em up. And Mrs. Wildeve?"

"She is as well as can be expected. The doctor had her put between blankets, for she was almost as wet as they that had been in the river, poor young thing. You don't seem very dry, reddleman."

"Oh, 'tis not much. I have changed my things. This is only a little dampness I've got coming through the rain again."

"Stand by the fire. Mis'ess says you be to have whatever you want, and she was sorry when she was told that you'd gone away."

Venn drew near to the fireplace, and looked into the flames in an absent mood. The steam came from his leggings and ascended the chimney with the smoke, while he thought of those who were upstairs. Two were corpses, one had barely escaped the jaws of death, another was sick and a widow. The last occasion on which he had lingered by that fireplace was when the raffle was in progress; when Wildeve was alive and well; Thomasin active and smiling in the next room; Yeobright and Eustacia just made husband and wife, and Mrs. Yeobright living at Blooms-End. It had seemed at that time that the then position of affairs was good for at least twenty years to come. Yet, of all the circle, he himself was the only one whose situation had not materially changed.

While he ruminated a footstep descended the stairs. It was the nurse, who brought in her hand a rolled mass of wet paper. The woman was so engrossed with her occupation that she hardly saw Venn. She took from a cupboard some pieces of twine, which she strained across the fireplace, tying the end of each piece to the firedog, previously pulled forward for the purpose, and, unrolling the wet papers, she began pinning them one by one to the strings in a manner of clothes on a line.

"What be they?" said Venn.

"Poor master's bank-notes," she answered. "They were found in his pocket when they undressed him."

"Then he was not coming back again for some time?" said Venn.

"That we shall never know," said she.

Venn was loth to depart, for all on earth that interested him lay under this roof. As nobody in the house had any more sleep that night, except the two who slept forever, there was no reason why he should not remain. So he retired into the niche of the fireplace where he had used to sit, and there he continued, watching the steam from the double row of bank-notes as they waved backwards and forwards in the draught of the chimney till their flaccidity was changed to dry crispness throughout. Then the woman came and unpinned them, and, folding them together, carried the handful upstairs. Presently the doctor appeared from above with the look of a man who could do no more, and, pulling on his gloves, went out of the house, the trotting of his horse soon dying away upon the road.

At four o'clock there was a gentle knock at the door. It was from Charley, who had been sent by Captain Vye to enquire if anything had been heard of Eustacia. The girl who admitted him looked in his face as if she did not know what answer to return, and showed him in to where Venn was seated, saying to the reddleman, "Will you tell him, please?"

Venn told. Charley's only utterance was a feeble, indistinct sound. He stood quite still; then he burst out spasmodically, "I shall see her once more?"

"I daresay you may see her," said Diggory gravely. "But hadn't you better run and tell Captain Vye?"

"Yes, yes. Only I do hope I shall see her just once again."

"You shall," said a low voice behind; and starting round they beheld by the dim light, a thin, pallid, almost spectral form, wrapped in a blanket, and looking like Lazarus coming from the tomb.

It was Yeobright. Neither Venn nor Charley spoke, and Clym continued: "You shall see her. There will be time enough to tell the captain when it gets daylight. You would like to see her too—would you not, Diggory? She looks very beautiful now."

Venn assented by rising to his feet, and with Charley he followed Clym to the foot of the staircase, where he took off his boots; Charley did the same. They followed Yeobright upstairs to the landing, where there was a candle burning, which Yeobright took in his hand, and with it led the way into an adjoining room. Here he went to the bedside and folded back the sheet.

They stood silently looking upon Eustacia, who, as she lay there still in death, eclipsed all her living phases. Pallor did not include all the quality of her complexion, which seemed more than whiteness; it was almost light. The expression of her finely carved mouth was pleasant, as if a sense of dignity had just compelled her to leave off speaking. Eternal rigidity had seized upon it in a momentary transition between fervour and resignation. Her black hair was looser now than either of them had ever seen it before, and surrounded her brow like a forest. The stateliness of look which had been almost too marked for a dweller in a country domicile had at last found an artistically happy background.

Nobody spoke, till at length Clym covered her and turned aside. "Now come here," he said.

They went to a recess in the same room, and there, on a smaller bed, lay another figure—Wildeve. Less repose was visible in his face than in Eustacia's, but the same luminous youthfulness overspread it, and the least sympathetic observer would have felt at sight of him now that he was born for a higher destiny than this. The only sign upon him of his recent struggle for life was in his finger-tips, which were worn and sacrificed in his dying endeavours to obtain a hold on the face of the weir-wall.

Yeobright's manner had been so quiet, he had uttered so few syllables since his reappearance, that Venn imagined him resigned. It was only when they had left the room and stood upon the landing that the true state of his mind was apparent. Here he said, with a wild smile, inclining his head towards the chamber in which Eustacia lay, "She is the second woman I have killed this year. I was a great cause of my mother's death; and I am the chief cause of hers."

"How?" said Venn.

"I spoke cruel words to her, and she left my house. I did not invite her back till it was too late. It is I who ought to have drowned myself. It would have been a charity to the living had the river overwhelmed me and borne her up. But I cannot die. Those who ought to have lived lie dead; and here am I alive!"

"But you can't charge yourself with crimes in that way," said Venn. "You may as well say that the parents be the cause of a murder by the child, for without the parents the child would never have been begot."

"Yes, Venn, that is very true; but you don't know all the circumstances. If it had pleased God to put an end to me it would have been a good thing for all. But I am getting used to the horror of my existence. They say that a time comes when men laugh at misery through long acquaintance with it. Surely that time will soon come to me!"

"Your aim has always been good," said Venn. "Why should you say such desperate things?"

"No, they are not desperate. They are only hopeless; and my great regret is that for what I have done no man or law can punish me!"

BOOK SIXTH

AFTERCOURSES

I

THE INEVITABLE MOVEMENT ONWARD

THE STORY OF THE DEATHS OF EUSTACIA AND WILDEVE WAS TOLD THROUGHOUT Egdon, and far beyond, for many weeks and months. All the known incidents of their love were enlarged, distorted, touched up, and modified, till the original reality bore but a slight resemblance to the counterfeit presentation by surrounding tongues. Yet, upon the whole, neither the man nor the woman lost dignity by sudden death. Misfortune had struck them gracefully, cutting off their erratic histories with a catastrophic dash, instead of, as with many, attenuating each life to an uninteresting meagreness, through long years of wrinkles, neglect, and decay.

On those most nearly concerned the effect was somewhat different. Strangers who had heard of many such cases now merely heard of one more; but immediately where a blow falls no previous imaginings amount to appreciable preparation for it. The very suddenness of her bereavement dulled, to some extent, Thomasin's feelings; yet, irrationally enough, a consciousness that the husband she had lost ought to have been a better man did not lessen her mourning at all. On the contrary, this fact seemed at first to set off the dead husband in his young wife's eyes, and to be the necessary cloud to the rainbow.

But the horrors of the unknown had passed. Vague misgivings about her future as a deserted wife were at an end. The worst had once been matter of trembling conjecture; it was now matter of reason only, a limited badness. Her chief interest, the little Eustacia, still remained. There was humility in her grief, no defiance in her attitude; and when this is the case a shaken spirit is apt to be stilled.

Could Thomasin's mournfulness now and Eustacia's serenity during life have been reduced to common measure, they would have touched the same mark nearly. But Thomasin's former brightness made shadow of that which in a sombre atmosphere was light itself.

The spring came and calmed her; the summer came and soothed her; the autumn arrived, and she began to be comforted, for her little girl was strong and happy, growing in size and knowledge every day. Outward events flattered Thomasin not a little. Wildeve had died intestate, and she and the child were his only relatives. When administration had been granted, all the debts paid, and the residue of her husband's uncle's property had come into her hands, it was found that the sum waiting to be invested for her own and the child's benefit was little less than ten thousand pounds.

Where should she live? The obvious place was Blooms-End. The old rooms, it is true, were not much higher than the between-decks of a frigate, necessitating a sinking in the floor under the new clock-case she brought from the inn, and the removal of the handsome brass knobs on its head, before there was height for it to stand; but, such as the rooms were, there were plenty of them, and the place was endeared to her by every early recollection. Clym very gladly admitted her as a tenant, confining his own existence to two rooms at the top of the back staircase, where he lived on quietly, shut off from Thomasin and the three servants she had thought fit to indulge in now that she was a mistress of money, going his own ways, and thinking his own thoughts.

His sorrows had made some change in his outward appearance; and yet the alteration was chiefly within. It might have been said that he had a wrinkled mind. He had no enemies, and he could get nobody to reproach him, which was why he so bitterly reproached himself.

He did sometimes think he had been ill-used by fortune, so far as to say that to be born is a palpable dilemma, and that instead of men aiming to advance in life with glory they should calculate how to retreat out of it without shame. But that he and his had been sarcastically and pitilessly handled in having such irons thrust into their souls he did not maintain long. It is usually so, except with the sternest of men. Human beings, in their generous endeavour to construct a hypothesis that shall not degrade a First Cause, have always hesitated to conceive a dominant power of lower moral quality than their own; and, even while they sit down and weep by the waters of Babylon, invent excuses for the oppression which prompts their tears.

Thus, though words of solace were vainly uttered in his presence, he found relief in a direction of his own choosing when left to himself. For a man of his habits the house and the hundred and twenty pounds a year which he had inherited from his mother were enough to supply all worldly needs. Resources do not depend upon gross amounts, but upon the proportion of givings to takings.

He frequently walked the heath alone, when the past seized upon him with its shadowy hand, and held him there to listen to its tale. His imagination would then people the spot with its ancient inhabitants: forgotten Celtic tribes trod their tracks about him, and he could almost live among them, look in their faces, and see them standing beside the barrows which swelled around, untouched and perfect as at the time of their erection. Those of the dyed barbarians who had chosen the cultivable tracts were, in comparison with those who had left their marks here, as writers on paper beside writers on parchment. Their records had perished long ago by the plough, while the works of these remained. Yet they all had lived and died unconscious of the different fates awaiting their works. It reminded him that unforeseen factors operate in the production of immortality.

Winter again came round, with its winds, frosts, tame robins, and sparkling starlight. The year previous Thomasin had hardly been conscious of the season's advance; this year she laid her heart open to external influences of every kind. The life of this sweet cousin, her baby, and her servants, came to Clym's senses only in the form of sounds through a wood partition as he sat over books of exceptionally large type; but his ear became at last so accustomed to these slight noises from the other part of the house that he almost could witness the scenes they signified. A faint beat of half-seconds conjured up Thomasin rocking the cradle, a wavering hum meant that she was singing the baby to sleep, a crunching of sand as between millstones raised the picture of Humphrey's, Fairway's, or Sam's heavy feet crossing the stone floor of the kitchen; a light boyish step, and a gay tune in a high key, betokened a visit from Grandfer Cantle; a sudden break-off in the Grandfer's utterances implied the application to his lips of a mug of small beer; a bustling and slamming of doors meant starting to go to market; for Thomasin, in spite of her added scope of gentility, led a ludicrously narrow life, to the end that she might save every possible pound for her little daughter.

One summer day Clym was in the garden, immediately outside the parlour-window, which was as usual open. He was looking at the pot-flowers on the sill; they had been revived and restored by Thomasin to the state in which his mother had left them. He heard a slight scream from Thomasin, who was sitting inside the room.

"O, how you frightened me!" she said to someone who had entered. "I thought you were the ghost of yourself."

Clym was curious enough to advance a little further and look in at the window. To his astonishment there stood within the room Diggory Venn, no longer a reddleman, but exhibiting the strangely altered hues of an ordinary Christian countenance, white shirt-front, light flowered waistcoat, blue-spotted neckerchief, and bottle-green coat. Nothing in this appearance was at all singular but the fact of its great difference from what he had formerly been. Red, and all approach to red, was carefully excluded from every article of clothes upon him; for what is there that persons just out of harness dread so much as reminders of the trade which has enriched them?

Yeobright went round to the door and entered.

"I was so alarmed!" said Thomasin, smiling from one to the other. "I couldn't believe that he had got white of his own accord! It seemed supernatural."

"I gave up dealing in reddle last Christmas," said Venn. "It was a profitable trade, and I found that by that time I had made enough to take the dairy of fifty cows that my father had in his lifetime. I always thought of getting to that place again if I changed at all; and now I am there."

"How did you manage to become white, Diggory?" Thomasin asked.

"I turned so by degrees, ma'am."

"You look much better than ever you did before."

Venn appeared confused; and Thomasin, seeing how inadvertently she had spoken to a man who might possibly have tender feelings for her still, blushed a little. Clym saw nothing of this, and added good-humouredly—

"What shall we have to frighten Thomasin's baby with, now you have become a human being again?"

"Sit down, Diggory," said Thomasin, "and stay to tea."

Venn moved as if he would retire to the kitchen, when Thomasin said with pleasant pertness as she went on with some sewing, "Of course you must sit down here. And where does your fifty-cow dairy lie, Mr. Venn?"

"At Stickleford—about two miles to the right of Alderworth, ma'am, where the meads begin. I have thought that if Mr. Yeobright would like to pay me a visit sometimes he shouldn't stay away for want of asking. I'll not bide to tea this afternoon, thank'ee, for I've got something on hand that must be settled. 'Tis Maypole-day to-morrow, and the Shadwater folk have clubbed with a few of your neighbours here to have a pole just outside your palings in the heath, as it is a nice green place." Venn waved his elbow towards the patch in front of the house. "I have been talking to Fairway about it," he continued, "and I said to him that before we put up the pole it would be as well to ask Mrs. Wildeve."

"I can say nothing against it," she answered. "Our property does not reach an inch further than the white palings."

"But you might not like to see a lot of folk going crazy round a stick, under your very nose?"

"I shall have no objection at all."

Venn soon after went away, and in the evening Yeobright strolled as far as Fairway's cottage. It was a lovely May sunset, and the birch trees which grew on this margin of the vast Egdon wilderness had put on their new leaves, delicate as butterflies' wings, and diaphanous as amber. Beside Fairway's dwelling was an open space recessed from the road, and here were now collected all the young people from within a radius of a couple of miles. The pole lay with one end supported on a trestle, and women were engaged in wreathing it from the top downwards with wild-flowers. The instincts of merry England lingered on here with exceptional vitality, and the symbolic customs which tradition has attached to each season of the year were yet a reality on Egdon. Indeed, the impulses of all such outlandish hamlets are pagan still: in these spots homage to nature, self-adoration, frantic gaieties, fragments of Teutonic rites to divinities whose names are forgotten, seem in some way or other to have survived medieval doctrine.

Yeobright did not interrupt the preparations, and went home again. The next morning, when Thomasin withdrew the curtains of her bedroom-window, there stood the Maypole in the middle of the green, its top cutting into the sky. It had sprung up in the night, or rather early morning, like Jack's bean-stalk. She opened the casement to get a better view of the garlands and posies that adorned it. The sweet perfume of the flowers had already spread into the surrounding air, which, being free from every taint, conducted to her lips a full measure of the fragrance received from the spire of blossom in its midst. At the top of the pole were crossed hoops decked with small flowers; beneath these came a milk-white zone of Maybloom; then a zone of bluebells, then of cowslips, then of lilacs, then of ragged-robins, daffodils, and so on, till the lowest stage was reached. Thomasin noticed all these, and was delighted that the May-revel was to be so near.

When afternoon came people began to gather on the green, and Yeobright was interested enough to look out upon them from the open window of his room. Soon after this Thomasin walked out from the door immediately below and turned her eyes up to her cousin's face. She was dressed more gaily than Yeobright had ever seen her dressed since the time of Wildeve's death, eighteen months before; since the day of her marriage even she had not exhibited herself to such advantage.

"How pretty you look to-day, Thomasin!" he said. "Is it because of the Maypole?"

"Not altogether." And then she blushed and dropped her eyes, which he did not specially observe, though her manner seemed to him to be rather peculiar, considering that she was only addressing himself. Could it be possible that she had put on her summer clothes to please him?

He recalled her conduct towards him throughout the last few weeks, when they had often been working together in the garden, just as they had formerly done when they were boy and girl under his mother's eye. What if her interest in him were not so entirely that of a relative as it had formerly been? To Yeobright any possibility of this sort was a serious matter; and he almost felt troubled at the thought of it. Every pulse of loverlike feeling which had not been stilled during Eustacia's lifetime had gone into the grave with her. His passion for her had occurred too far on in his manhood to leave fuel enough on hand for another fire of that sort, as may happen with more boyish loves. Even supposing him capable of loving again, that love would be a plant of slow and laboured growth, and in the end only small and sickly, like an autumn-hatched bird.

He was so distressed by this new complexity that when the enthusiastic brass band arrived and struck up, which it did about five o'clock, with apparently wind enough among its members to blow down his house, he withdrew from his rooms by the back-door, went down the garden, through the gate in the hedge, and away out of sight. He could not bear to remain in the presence of enjoyment to-day, though he had tried hard.

Nothing was seen of him for four hours. When he came back by the same path it was dusk, and the dews were coating every green thing. The boisterous music had ceased; but, entering the premises as he did from behind, he could not see if the May party had all gone till he had passed through Thomasin's division of the house to the front-door. Thomasin was standing within the porch alone.

She looked at him reproachfully. "You went away just when it began, Clym," she said.

"Yes. I felt I could not join in. You went out with them, of course?"

"No, I did not."

"You appeared to be dressed on purpose."

"Yes, but I could not go out alone; so many people were there. One is there now."

Yeobright strained his eyes across the dark-green patch beyond the paling, and near the black form of the Maypole he discerned a shadowy figure, sauntering idly up and down. "Who is it?" he said.

"Mr. Venn," said Thomasin.

"You might have asked him to come in, I think, Tamsie. He has been very kind to you first and last."

"I will now," she said; and, acting on the impulse, went through the wicket to where Venn stood under the Maypole.

"It is Mr. Venn, I think?" she enquired.

Venn started as if he had not seen her—artful man that he was—and said, "Yes."

"Will you come in?"

"I am afraid that I—"

"I have seen you dancing this evening, and you had the very best of the girls for your partners. Is it that you won't come in because you wish to stand here, and think over the past hours of enjoyment?"

"Well, that's partly it," said Mr. Venn, with ostentatious sentiment. "But the main reason why I am biding here like this is that I want to wait till the moon rises."

"To see how pretty the Maypole looks in the moonlight?"

"No. To look for a glove that was dropped by one of the maidens."

Thomasin was speechless with surprise. That a man who had to walk some four or five miles to his home should wait here for such a reason pointed to only one conclusion: the man must be amazingly interested in that glove's owner.

"Were you dancing with her, Diggory?" she asked, in a voice which revealed that he had made himself considerably more interesting to her by this disclosure.

"No," he sighed.

"And you will not come in, then?"

"Not to-night, thank you, ma'am."

"Shall I lend you a lantern to look for the young person's glove, Mr. Venn?"

"O no; it is not necessary, Mrs. Wildeve, thank you. The moon will rise in a few minutes."

Thomasin went back to the porch. "Is he coming in?" said Clym, who had been waiting where she had left him.

"He would rather not to-night," she said, and then passed by him into the house; whereupon Clym too retired to his own rooms.

When Clym was gone Thomasin crept upstairs in the dark, and, just listening by the cot, to assure herself that the child was asleep, she went to the window, gently lifted the corner of the white curtain, and looked out. Venn was still there. She watched the growth of the faint radiance appearing in the sky by the eastern hill, till presently the edge of the moon burst upwards and flooded the valley with light. Diggory's form was now distinct on the green; he was moving about in a bowed attitude, evidently scanning the grass for the precious missing article, walking in zigzags right and left till he should have passed over every foot of the ground.

"How very ridiculous!" Thomasin murmured to herself, in a tone which was intended to be satirical. "To think that a man should be so silly as to go mooning about like that for a girl's glove! A respectable dairyman, too, and a man of money as he is now. What a pity!"

At last Venn appeared to find it; whereupon he stood up and raised it to his lips. Then placing it in his breast-pocket—the nearest receptacle to a man's heart permitted by modern raiment—he ascended the valley in a mathematically direct line towards his distant home in the meadows.

II

THOMASIN WALKS IN A GREEN PLACE BY THE ROMAN ROAD

CLYM SAW LITTLE OF THOMASIN FOR SEVERAL DAYS AFTER THIS; AND WHEN THEY MET she was more silent than usual. At length he asked her what she was thinking of so intently.

"I am thoroughly perplexed," she said candidly. "I cannot for my life think who it is that Diggory Venn is so much in love with. None of the girls at the Maypole were good enough for him, and yet she must have been there."

Clym tried to imagine Venn's choice for a moment; but ceasing to be interested in the question he went on again with his gardening.

No clearing up of the mystery was granted her for some time. But one afternoon Thomasin was upstairs getting ready for a walk, when she had occasion to come to the landing and call "Rachel." Rachel was a girl about thirteen, who carried the baby out for airings; and she came upstairs at the call.

"Have you seen one of my last new gloves about the house, Rachel?" enquired Thomasin. "It is the fellow to this one."

Rachel did not reply.

"Why don't you answer?" said her mistress.

"I think it is lost, ma'am."

"Lost? Who lost it? I have never worn them but once."

Rachel appeared as one dreadfully troubled, and at last began to cry. "Please, ma'am, on the day of the Maypole I had none to wear, and I seed yours on the table, and I thought

I would borrow 'em. I did not mean to hurt 'em at all, but one of them got lost. Somebody gave me some money to buy another pair for you, but I have not been able to go anywhere to get 'em."

"Who's somebody?"

"Mr. Venn."

"Did he know it was my glove?"

"Yes. I told him."

Thomasin was so surprised by the explanation that she quite forgot to lecture the girl, who glided silently away. Thomasin did not move further than to turn her eyes upon the grass-plat where the Maypole had stood. She remained thinking, then said to herself that she would not go out that afternoon, but would work hard at the baby's unfinished lovely plaid frock, cut on the cross in the newest fashion. How she managed to work hard, and yet do no more than she had done at the end of two hours, would have been a mystery to anyone not aware that the recent incident was of a kind likely to divert her industry from a manual to a mental channel.

Next day she went her ways as usual, and continued her custom of walking in the heath with no other companion than little Eustacia, now of the age when it is a matter of doubt with such characters whether they are intended to walk through the world on their hands or on their feet; so that they get into painful complications by trying both. It was very pleasant to Thomasin, when she had carried the child to some lonely place, to give her a little private practice on the green turf and shepherd's-thyme, which formed a soft mat to fall headlong upon them when equilibrium was lost.

Once, when engaged in this system of training, and stooping to remove bits of stick, fern-stalks, and other such fragments from the child's path, that the journey might not be brought to an untimely end by some insuperable barrier a quarter of an inch high, she was alarmed by discovering that a man on horseback was almost close beside her, the soft natural carpet having muffled the horse's tread. The rider, who was Venn, waved his hat in the air and bowed gallantly.

"Diggory, give me my glove," said Thomasin, whose manner it was under any circumstances to plunge into the midst of a subject which engrossed her.

Venn immediately dismounted, put his hand in his breast-pocket, and handed the glove.

"Thank you. It was very good of you to take care of it."

"It is very good of you to say so."

"O no. I was quite glad to find you had it. Everybody gets so indifferent that I was surprised to know you thought of me."

"If you had remembered what I was once you wouldn't have been surprised."

"Ah, no," she said quickly. "But men of your character are mostly so independent."

"What is my character?" he asked.

"I don't exactly know," said Thomasin simply, "except it is to cover up your feelings under a practical manner, and only to show them when you are alone."

"Ah, how do you know that?" said Venn strategically.

"Because," said she, stopping to put the little girl, who had managed to get herself upside down, right end up again, "because I do."

"You mustn't judge by folks in general," said Venn. "Still I don't know much what feelings are now-a-days. I have got so mixed up with business of one sort and t'other that my soft sentiments are gone off in vapour like. Yes, I am given up body and soul to the making of money. Money is all my dream."

"O Diggory, how wicked!" said Thomasin reproachfully, and looking at him in exact balance between taking his words seriously and judging them as said to tease her.

"Yes, 'tis rather a rum course," said Venn, in the bland tone of one comfortably resigned to sins he could no longer overcome.

"You, who used to be so nice!"

"Well, that's an argument I rather like, because what a man has once been he may be again." Thomasin blushed. "Except that it is rather harder now," Venn continued.

"Why?" she asked.

"Because you be richer than you were at that time."

"O no—not much. I have made it nearly all over to the baby, as it was my duty to do, except just enough to live on."

"I am rather glad of that," said Venn softly, and regarding her from the corner of his eye, "for it makes it easier for us to be friendly."

Thomasin blushed again, and, when a few more words had been said of a not unpleasing kind, Venn mounted his horse and rode on.

This conversation had passed in a hollow of the heath near the old Roman road, a place much frequented by Thomasin. And it might have been observed that she did not in future walk that way less often from having met Venn there now. Whether or not Venn abstained from riding thither because he had met Thomasin in the same place might easily have been guessed from her proceedings about two months later in the same year.

III

THE SERIOUS DISCOURSE OF CLYM WITH HIS COUSIN

THROUGHOUT THIS PERIOD YEOBRIGHT HAD MORE OR LESS PONDERED ON HIS DUTY TO his cousin Thomasin. He could not help feeling that it would be a pitiful waste of sweet material if the tender-natured thing should be doomed from this early stage of her life onwards to dribble away her winsome qualities on lonely gorse and fern. But he felt this as an economist merely, and not as a lover. His passion for Eustacia had been a sort of conserve of his whole life, and he had nothing more of that supreme quality left to bestow. So far the obvious thing was not to entertain any idea of marriage with Thomasin, even to oblige her.

But this was not all. Years ago there had been in his mother's mind a great fancy about Thomasin and himself. It had not positively amounted to a desire, but it had always been a favourite dream. That they should be man and wife in good time, if the happiness of neither were endangered thereby, was the fancy in question. So that what course save one was there now left for any son who reverenced his mother's memory as Yeobright did? It is an unfortunate fact that any particular whim of parents, which might have been dispersed by half an hour's conversation during their lives, becomes sublimated by their deaths into a fiat the most absolute, with such results to conscientious children as those parents, had they lived, would have been the first to decry.

Had only Yeobright's own future been involved he would have proposed to Thomasin with a ready heart. He had nothing to lose by carrying out a dead mother's hope. But he dreaded to contemplate Thomasin wedded to the mere corpse of a lover that he now felt himself to be. He had but three activities alive in him. One was his almost daily walk to the little graveyard wherein his mother lay; another, his just as frequent visits by night to the more distant enclosure which numbered his Eustacia among its dead; the third was self-preparation for a vocation which alone seemed likely to satisfy his cravings—that of an itinerant preacher of the eleventh commandment. It was difficult to believe that Thomasin would be cheered by a husband with such tendencies as these.

Yet he resolved to ask her, and let her decide for herself. It was even with a pleasant sense of doing his duty that he went downstairs to her one evening for this purpose, when the sun was sending up on the valley the same long shadow of the housetop that he had seen lying there times out of number while his mother lived.

Thomasin was not in her room, and he found her in the front garden. "I have long been wanting, Thomasin," he began, "to say something about a matter that concerns both our futures."

"And you are going to say it now?" she remarked quickly, colouring as she met his gaze. "Do stop a minute, Clym, and let me speak first, for oddly enough, I have been wanting to say something to you."

"By all means say on, Tamsie."

"I suppose nobody can overhear us?" she went on, casting her eyes around and lowering her voice. "Well, first you will promise me this—that you won't be angry and call me anything harsh if you disagree with what I propose?"

Yeobright promised, and she continued: "What I want is your advice, for you are my relation—I mean, a sort of guardian to me—aren't you, Clym?"

"Well, yes, I suppose I am; a sort of guardian. In fact, I am, of course," he said, altogether perplexed as to her drift.

"I am thinking of marrying," she then observed blandly. "But I shall not marry unless you assure me that you approve of such a step. Why don't you speak?"

"I was taken rather by surprise. But, nevertheless, I am very glad to hear such news. I shall approve, of course, dear Tamsie. Who can it be? I am quite at a loss to guess. No I am not—'tis the old doctor!—not that I mean to call him old, for he is not very old after all. Ah—I noticed when he attended you last time!"

"No, no," she said hastily. " 'Tis Mr. Venn."

Clym's face suddenly became grave.

"There, now, you don't like him, and I wish I hadn't mentioned him!" she exclaimed almost petulantly. "And I shouldn't have done it, either, only he keeps on bothering me so till I don't know what to do!"

Clym looked at the heath. "I like Venn well enough," he answered at last. "He is a very honest and at the same time astute man. He is clever too, as is proved by his having got you to favour him. But really, Thomasin, he is not quite—"

"Gentleman enough for me? That is just what I feel. I am sorry now that I asked you, and I won't think any more of him. At the same time I must marry him if I marry anybody—that I *will* say!"

"I don't see that," said Clym, carefully concealing every clue to his own interrupted intention, which she plainly had not guessed. "You might marry a professional man, or somebody of that sort, by going into the town to live and forming acquaintances there."

"I am not fit for town life—so very rural and silly as I always have been. Do not you yourself notice my countrified ways?"

"Well, when I came home from Paris I did, a little; but I don't now."

"That's because you have got countrified too. O, I couldn't live in a street for the world! Egdon is a ridiculous old place; but I have got used to it, and I couldn't be happy anywhere else at all."

"Neither could I," said Clym.

"Then how could you say that I should marry some town man? I am sure, say what you will, that I must marry Diggory, if I marry at all. He has been kinder to me than anybody else, and has helped me in many ways that I don't know of!" Thomasin almost pouted now.

"Yes, he has," said Clym in a neutral tone. "Well, I wish with all my heart that I could say, marry him. But I cannot forget what my mother thought on that matter, and it goes rather against me not to respect her opinion. There is too much reason why we should do the little we can to respect it now."

"Very well, then," sighed Thomasin. "I will say no more."

"But you are not bound to obey my wishes. I merely say what I think."

"O no—I don't want to be rebellious in that way," she said sadly. "I had no business to think of him—I ought to have thought of my family. What dreadfully bad impulses there are in me!" Her lip trembled, and she turned away to hide a tear.

Clym, though vexed at what seemed her unaccountable taste, was in a measure relieved to find that at any rate the marriage question in relation to himself was shelved. Through several succeeding days he saw her at different times from the window of his room moping disconsolately about the garden. He was half angry with her for choosing Venn; then he was grieved at having put himself in the way of Venn's happiness, who was, after all, as honest and persevering a young fellow as any on Egdon, since he had turned over a new leaf. In short, Clym did not know what to do.

When next they met she said abruptly, "He is much more respectable now than he was then!"

"Who? O yes—Diggory Venn."

"Aunt only objected because he was a reddleman."

"Well, Thomasin, perhaps I don't know all the particulars of my mother's wish. So you had better use your own discretion."

"You will always feel that I slighted your mother's memory."

"No, I will not. I shall think you are convinced that, had she seen Diggory in his present position, she would have considered him a fitting husband for you. Now, that's my real feeling. Don't consult me any more, but do as you like, Thomasin. I shall be content."

It is to be supposed that Thomasin was convinced; for a few days after this, when Clym strayed into a part of the heath that he had not lately visited, Humphrey, who was at work there, said to him, "I am glad to see that Mrs. Wildeve and Venn have made it up again, seemingly."

"Have they?" said Clym abstractedly.

"Yes; and he do contrive to stumble upon her whenever she walks out on fine days with the chiel. But, Mr. Yeobright, I can't help feeling that your cousin ought to have married you. 'Tis a pity to make two chimley-corners where there need be only one. You could get her away from him now, 'tis my belief, if you were only to set about it."

"How can I have the conscience to marry after having driven two women to their deaths? Don't think such a thing, Humphrey. After my experience I should consider it too much of a burlesque to go to church and take a wife. In the words of Job, 'I have made a covenant with mine eyes; why then should I think upon a maid?' "

"No, Mr. Clym, don't fancy that about driving two women to their deaths. You shouldn't say it."

"Well, we'll leave that out," said Yeobright. "But anyhow the times have set a mark upon me which wouldn't look well in a love-making scene. I have two ideas in my head, and no others. I am going to keep a night-school; and I am going to turn preacher. What have you got to say to that, Humphrey?"

"I'll come and hear ye with all my heart."

"Thanks. 'Tis all I wish."

As Clym descended into the valley Thomasin came down by the other path, and met him at the gate. "What do you think I have to tell you, Clym?" she said, looking archly over her shoulder at him.

"I can guess," he replied.

She scrutinised his face. "Yes, you guess right. It is going to be after all. He thinks I may as well make up my mind, and I have got to think so too. It is to be on the twenty-fifth of next month, if you don't object."

"Do what you think right, dear. I am only too glad that you see your way clear to happiness again. My sex owes you every amends for the treatment you received in days gone by."

IV

Cheerfulness again asserts itself at Blooms-End, and Clym finds his Vocation

Anybody who had passed through Blooms-End about eleven o'clock on the morning fixed for the wedding would have found that, while Yeobright's house was comparatively quiet, sounds denoting great activity came from the dwelling of his nearest neighbour, Timothy Fairway. It was chiefly a noise of feet, briskly crunching hither and thither over the sanded floor within. One man only was visible outside, and he seemed to be later at an appointment than he had intended to be, for he hastened up to the door, lifted the latch, and walked in without ceremony.

The scene within was not quite the customary one. Standing about the room was the little knot of men who formed the chief part of the Egdon coterie, there being present Fairway himself, Grandfer Cantle, Humphrey, Christian, and one or two turf-cutters. It was a warm day, and the men were as a matter of course in their shirt-sleeves, except Christian, who had always a nervous fear of parting with a scrap of his clothing when in anybody's house but his own. Across the stout oak table in the middle of the room was thrown a mass of striped linen, which Grandfer Cantle held down on one side, and Humphrey on the other, while Fairway rubbed its surface with a yellow lump, his face being damp and creased with the effort of the labour.

"Waxing a bed-tick, souls?" said the new-comer.

"Yes, Sam," said Grandfer Cantle, as a man too busy to waste words. "Shall I stretch this corner a shade tighter, Timothy?"

Fairway replied, and the waxing went on with unabated vigour. " 'Tis going to be a good bed, by the look o't," continued Sam, after an interval of silence. "Who may it be for?"

" 'Tis a present for the new folks that's going to set up housekeeping," said Christian, who stood helpless and overcome by the majesty of the proceedings.

"Ah, to be sure; and a valuable one, 'a b'lieve."

"Beds be dear to fokes that don't keep geese, bain't they, Mister Fairway?" said Christian, as to an omniscient being.

"Yes," said the furze-dealer, standing up, giving his forehead a thorough mopping, and handing the beeswax to Humphrey, who succeeded at the rubbing forthwith. "Not that this couple be in want of one, but 'twas well to show 'em a bit of friendliness at this great racketing vagary of their lives. I set up both my own daughters in one when they was married, and there have been feathers enough for another in the house the last twelve months. Now then, neighbours, I think we have laid on enough wax. Grandfer Cantle, you turn the tick the right way outwards, and then I'll begin to shake in the feathers."

When the bed was in proper trim Fairway and Christian brought forward vast paper bags, stuffed to the full, but light as balloons, and began to turn the contents of each into the receptacle just prepared. As bag after bag was emptied, airy tufts of down and feathers floated about the room in increasing quantity till, through a mishap of Christian's, who shook the contents of one bag outside the tick, the atmosphere of the room became dense with gigantic flakes, which descended upon the workers like a windless snowstorm.

"I never saw such a clumsy chap as you, Christian," said Grandfer Cantle severely. "You might have been the son of a man that's never been outside Blooms-End in his life for all the wit you have. Really all the soldiering and smartness in the world in the father seems to count for nothing in forming the nater of the son. As far as that chiel Christian is concerned I might as well have stayed at home and seed nothing, like all the rest of ye here. Though, as far as myself is concerned, a dashing spirit has counted for sommat, to be sure!"

"Don't ye let me down so, father; I feel no bigger than a ninepin after it. I've made but a bruckle hit, I'm afeard."

"Come, come. Never pitch yerself in such a low key as that, Christian; you should try more," said Fairway.

"Yes, you should try more," echoed the Grandfer with insistence, as if he had been the first to make the suggestion. "In common conscience every man ought either to marry or go for a soldier. 'Tis a scandal to the nation to do neither one nor t'other. I did both, thank God! Neither to raise men nor to lay 'em low—that shows a poor do-nothing spirit indeed."

"I never had the nerve to stand fire," faltered Christian. "But as to marrying, I own I've asked here and there, though without much fruit from it. Yes, there's some house or other that might have had a man for a master—such as he is—that's now ruled by a woman alone. Still it might have been awkward if I had found her; for, d'ye see, neighbours, there'd have been nobody left at home to keep down father's spirits to the decent pitch that becomes a old man."

"And you've your work cut out to do that, my son," said Grandfer Cantle smartly. "I wish that the dread of infirmities was not so strong in me!—I'd start the very first thing to-morrow to see the world over again! But seventy-one, though nothing at home, is a high figure for a rover. . . . Ay, seventy-one, last Candlemas-day. Gad, I'd sooner have it in guineas than in years!" And the old man sighed.

"Don't you be mournful, Grandfer," said Fairway. "Empt some more feathers into the bed-tick, and keep up yer heart. Though rather lean in the stalks you be a green-leaved old man still. There's time enough left to ye yet to fill whole chronicles."

"Begad, I'll go to 'em, Timothy—to the married pair!" said Granfer Cantle in an encouraged voice, and starting round briskly. "I'll go to 'em to-night and sing a wedding song, hey? 'Tis like me to do so, you know; and they'd see it as such. My 'Down in Cupid's Gardens' was well liked in four; still, I've got others as good, and even better. What do you say to my

'She cal'-led to' her love'
From the lat'-tice a-bove,
"O come in' from the fog'-gy fog'-gy dew." '

'Twould please 'em well at such a time! Really, now I come to think of it, I haven't turned my tongue in my head to the shape of a real good song since Old Midsummer night, when we had the 'Barley Mow' at the Woman; and 'tis a pity to neglect your strong point where there's few that have the compass for such things!"

"So 'tis, so 'tis," said Fairway. "Now gie the bed a shake down. We've put in seventy pounds of best feathers, and I think that's as many as the tick will fairly hold. A bit and a drap wouldn't be amiss now, I reckon. Christian, maul down the victuals from corner-cupboard if canst reach, man, and I'll draw a drap o' sommat to wet it with."

They sat down to a lunch in the midst of their work, feathers around, above, and below them; the original owners of which occasionally came to the open door and cackled begrudgingly at sight of such a quantity of their old clothes.

"Upon my soul I shall be chokt," said Fairway when, having extracted a feather from his mouth, he found several others floating on the mug as it was handed round.

"I've swallered several; and one had a tolerable quill," said Sam placidly from the corner.

"Hullo—what's that—wheels I hear coming?" Grandfer Cantle exclaimed, jumping up and hastening to the door. "Why, 'tis they back again: I didn't expect 'em yet this half-hour. To be sure, how quick marrying can be done when you are in the mind for't!"

"O yes, it can soon be *done*," said Fairway, as if something should be added to make the statement complete.

He arose and followed the Grandfer, and the rest also went to the door. In a moment an open fly was driven past, in which sat Venn and Mrs. Venn, Yeobright, and a grand relative of Venn's who had come from Budmouth for the occasion. The fly had been hired at the nearest town, regardless of distance and cost, there being nothing on Egdon Heath, in Venn's opinion, dignified enough for such an event when such a woman as Thomasin was the bride; and the church was too remote for a walking bridal-party.

As the fly passed the group which had run out from the homestead they shouted "Hurrah!" and waved their hands; feathers and down floating from their hair, their sleeves, and the folds of their garments at every motion, and Grandfer Cantle's seals dancing merrily in the sunlight as he twirled himself about. The driver of the fly turned a supercilious gaze upon them; he even treated the wedded pair themselves with something of condescension; for in what other state than heathen could people, rich or poor, exist who were doomed to abide in such a world's end as Egdon? Thomasin showed no such superiority to the group at the door, fluttering her hand as quickly as a bird's wing towards them, and asking Diggory, with tears in her eyes, if they ought not to alight and speak to these kind neighbours. Venn, however, suggested that, as they were all coming to the house in the evening, this was hardly necessary.

After this excitement the saluting party returned to their occupation, and the stuffing and sewing were soon afterwards finished, when Fairway harnessed a horse, wrapped up the cumbrous present, and drove off with it in the cart to Venn's house at Stickleford.

Yeobright, having filled the office at the wedding service which naturally fell to his hands, and afterwards returned to the house with the husband and wife, was indisposed to take part in the feasting and dancing that wound up the evening. Thomasin was disappointed.

"I wish I could be there without dashing your spirits," he said. "But I might be too much like the skull at the banquet."

"No, no."

"Well, dear, apart from that, if you would excuse me, I should be glad. I know it seems unkind; but, dear Thomasin, I fear I should not be happy in the company—there, that's the truth of it. I shall always be coming to see you at your new home, you know, so that my absence now will not much matter."

"Then I give in. Do whatever will be most comfortable to yourself."

Clym retired to his lodging at the housetop much relieved, and occupied himself during the afternoon in noting down the heads of a sermon, with which he intended to initiate all that really seemed practicable of the scheme that had originally brought him hither, and that he had so long kept in view under various modifications, and through evil and good report. He had tested and weighed his convictions again and again, and saw no reason to alter them, though he had considerably lessened his plan. His eyesight, by long humouring in his native air, had grown stronger, but not sufficiently strong to warrant his attempting his extensive educational project. Yet he did not repine: there was still more than enough of an unambitious sort to tax all his energies and occupy all his hours.

Evening drew on, and sounds of life and movement in the lower part of the domicile became more pronounced, the gate in the palings clicking incessantly. The party was to be an early one, and all the guests were assembled long before it was dark. Yeobright went down the back staircase and into the heath by another path than that in front, intending to walk in the open air till the party was over, when he would return to wish Thomasin and her husband good-bye as they departed. His steps were insensibly bent towards Mistover by the path that he had followed on that terrible morning when he learnt the strange news from Susan's boy.

He did not turn aside to the cottage, but pushed on to an eminence, whence he could see over the whole quarter that had once been Eustacia's home. While he stood observing the darkening scene somebody came up. Clym, seeing him but dimly, would have let him pass by silently, had not the pedestrian, who was Charley, recognised the young man and spoken to him.

"Charley, I have not seen you for a length of time," said Yeobright. "Do you often walk this way?"

"No," the lad replied. "I don't often come outside the bank."

"You were not at the Maypole."

"No," said Charley, in the same listless tone. "I don't care for that sort of thing now."

"You rather liked Miss Eustacia, didn't you?" Yeobright gently asked. Eustacia had frequently told him of Charley's romantic attachment.

"Yes, very much. Ah, I wish——"

"Yes?"

"I wish, Mr. Yeobright, you could give me something to keep that once belonged to her—if you don't mind."

"I shall be very happy to. It will give me very great pleasure, Charley. Let me think what I have of hers that you would like. But come with me to the house, and I'll see."

They walked towards Blooms-End together. When they reached the front it was dark, and the shutters were closed, so that nothing of the interior could be seen.

"Come round this way," said Clym. "My entrance is at the back for the present."

The two went round and ascended the crooked stair in darkness till Clym's sitting-room on the upper floor was reached, where he lit a candle, Charley entering gently behind. Yeobright searched his desk, and taking out a sheet of tissue-paper unfolded from it two or three undulating locks of raven hair, which fell over the paper like black streams. From these he selected one, wrapped it up, and gave it to the lad, whose eyes had filled with tears. He kissed the packet, put it in his pocket, and said in a voice of emotion, "O, Mr. Clym, how good you are to me!"

"I will go a little way with you," said Clym. And amid the noise of merriment from below they descended. Their path to the front led them close to a little side-window, whence the rays of candles streamed across the shrubs. The window, being screened from general observation by the bushes, had been left unblinded, so that a person in this private nook could see all that was going on within the room which contained the wedding-guests, except in so far as vision was hindered by the green antiquity of the panes.

"Charley, what are they doing?" said Clym. "My sight is weaker again to-night, and the glass of this window is not good."

Charley wiped his own eyes, which were rather blurred with moisture, and stepped closer to the casement. "Mr. Venn is asking Christian Cantle to sing," he replied; "and

Christian is moving about in his chair as if he were much frightened at the question, and his father has struck up a stave instead of him."

"Yes, I can hear the old man's voice," said Clym. "So there's to be no dancing, I suppose. And is Thomasin in the room? I see something moving in front of the candles that resembles her shape, I think."

"Yes. She do seem happy. She is red in the face, and laughing at something Fairway has said to her. O my!"

"What noise was that?" said Clym.

"Mr. Venn is so tall that he knocked his head against the beam in gieing a skip as he passed under. Mrs. Venn hev run up quite frightened and now she's put her hand to his head to feel if there's a lump. And now they be all laughing again as if nothing had happened."

"Do any of them seem to care about my not being there?" Clym asked.

"No, not a bit in the world. Now they are all holding up their glasses and drinking somebody's health."

"I wonder if it is mine?"

"No, 'tis Mr. and Mrs. Venn's, because he is making a hearty sort of speech. There—now Mrs. Venn has got up, and is going away to put on her things, I think."

"Well, they haven't concerned themselves about me, and it is quite right they should not. It is all as it should be, and Thomasin at least is happy. We will not stay any longer now, as they will soon be coming out to go home."

He accompanied the lad into the heath on his way home, and, returning alone to the house a quarter of an hour later, found Venn and Thomasin ready to start, all the guests having departed in his absence. The wedded pair took their seats in the four-wheeled dog-cart which Venn's head milker and handy man had driven from Stickleford to fetch them in; little Eustacia and the nurse were packed securely upon the open flap behind; and the milker, on an ancient overstepping pony, whose shoes clashed like cymbals at every tread, rode in the rear, in the manner of a body-servant of the last century.

"Now we leave you in absolute possession of your own house again," said Thomasin as she bent down to wish her cousin good-night. "It will be rather lonely for you, Clym, after the hubbub we have been making."

"O, that's no inconvenience," said Clym, smiling rather sadly. And then the party drove off and vanished in the night-shades, and Yeobright entered the house. The ticking of the clock was the only sound that greeted him, for not a soul remained; Christian, who acted as cook, valet, and gardener to Clym, sleeping at his father's house. Yeobright sat down in one of the vacant chairs, and remained in thought a long time. His mother's old chair was opposite; it had been sat in that evening by those who had scarcely remembered that it ever was hers. But to Clym she was almost a presence there, now as always. Whatever she was in other people's memories, in his she was the sublime saint whose radiance even his tenderness for Eustacia could not obscure. But his heart was heavy; that mother had *not* crowned him in the day of his espousals and in the day of the gladness of his heart. And events had borne out the accuracy of her judgment, and proved the devotedness of her care. He should have heeded her for Eustacia's sake even more than for his own. "It was all my fault," he whispered. "O, my mother, my mother! would to God that I could live my life again, and endure for you what you endured for me!"

* * *

On the Sunday after this wedding an unusual sight was to be seen on Rainbarrow. From a distance there simply appeared to be a motionless figure standing on the top of the tumulus, just as Eustacia had stood on that lonely summit some two years and a half before. But now it was fine warm weather, with only a summer breeze blowing, and early afternoon instead of dull twilight. Those who ascended to the immediate neighbourhood of the Barrow perceived that the erect form in the centre, piercing the sky, was not really alone. Round him upon the slopes of the Barrow a number of heathmen and women were reclining or sitting at their ease. They listened to the words of the man in their midst, who was preaching, while they abstractedly pulled heather, stripped ferns, or tossed pebbles down the slope. This was the first of a series of moral lectures or Sermons on the Mount, which were to be delivered from the same place every Sunday afternoon as long as the fine weather lasted.

The commanding elevation of Rainbarrow had been chosen for two reasons: first, that it occupied a central position among the remote cottages around; secondly, that the preacher thereon could be seen from all adjacent points as soon as he arrived at his post, the view of him being thus a convenient signal to those stragglers who wished to draw near. The speaker was bareheaded, and the breeze at each waft gently lifted and lowered his hair, somewhat too thin for a man of his years, these still numbering less than thirty-three. He wore a shade over his eyes, and his face was pensive and lined; but, though these bodily features were marked with decay there was no defect in the tones of his voice, which were rich, musical, and stirring. He stated that his discourses to people were to be sometimes secular, and sometimes religious, but never dogmatic; and that his texts would be taken from all kinds of books. This afternoon the words were as follows:—

" 'And the king rose up to meet her, and bowed himself unto her, and sat down on his throne, and caused a seat to be set for the king's mother; and she sat on his right hand. Then she said, I desire one small petition of thee; I pray thee say me not nay. And the king said unto her, Ask on, my mother: for I will not say thee nay.' "

Yeobright had, in fact, found his vocation in the career of an itinerant open-air preacher and lecturer on morally unimpeachable subjects; and from this day he laboured incessantly in that office, speaking not only in simple language on Rainbarrow and in the hamlets round, but in a more cultivated strain elsewhere—from the steps and porticoes of town-halls, from market-crosses, from conduits, on esplanades and on wharves, from the parapets of bridges, in barns and outhouses, and all other such places in the neighbouring Wessex towns and villages. He left alone creeds and systems of philosophy, finding enough and more than enough to occupy his tongue in the opinions and actions common to all good men. Some believed him, and some believed not; some said that his words were commonplace, others complained of his want of theological doctrine; while others again remarked that it was well enough for a man to take to preaching who could not see to do anything else. But everywhere he was kindly received, for the story of his life had become generally known.

THE END

THE MAYOR OF CASTERBRIDGE

Map of the
WESSEX
of the
Novels and Poems

Scale of Miles

The Channel

Bristol Channel

Oriens

Septentrio

Occidens

Meridies

Emery Walker sc.

Fictitious names as
Exonbury
Real names as
Portsmouth

Isles of
Lyonesse

Land's End

PREFACE

R EADERS OF THE FOLLOWING STORY WHO HAVE NOT YET ARRIVED AT MIDDLE AGE ARE asked to bear in mind that, in the days recalled by the tale, the home Corn Trade, on which so much of the action turns, had an importance that can hardly be realised by those accustomed to the sixpenny loaf of the present date, and to the present indifference of the public to harvest weather.

The incidents narrated arise mainly out of three events, which changed to range themselves in the order and at or about the intervals of time here given, in the real history of the town called Casterbridge and the neighbouring country. They were the sale of a wife by her husband, the uncertain harvests which immediately preceded the repeal of the Corn Laws, and the visit of a Royal personage to the aforesaid part of England.

The present edition of the volume contains nearly a chapter which has never yet appeared in any English copy, though it was printed in the serial issue of the tale, and in the American edition. The restoration was made at the instance of some good judges across the Atlantic, who strongly represented that the home edition suffered from the omission. Some shorter passages and names, omitted or altered for reasons which no longer exist, in the original printing of both English and American editions, have also been replaced or inserted for the first time.

The story is more particularly a study of one man's deeds and character than, perhaps, any other of those included in my little Exhibition of Wessex life. Objections have been raised to the Scotch language of Mr. Farfrae, the second character; and one of his fellow-countrymen went so far as to declare that men beyond the Tweed did not and never could say "warrld," "cannet," "advairrtisment," and so on. As this gentleman's pronunciation in correcting me seemed to my Southron ear an exact repetition of what my spelling implied, I was not struck with the truth of his remark, and somehow we did not get any forwarder in the matter. It must be remembered that the Scotchman of the tale is represented not as he would appear to other Scotchmen, but as he would appear to people of outer regions. Moreover, no attempt is made herein to reproduce his entire pronunciation phonetically, any more than that of the Wessex speakers. I should add, however, that this new edition of the book has had the accidental advantage of a critical overlooking by a professor of the tongue in question—one of undoubted authority—in fact he is a gentleman who adopted it for urgent personal reasons in the first year of his existence.

Furthermore, a charming non-Scottish lady, of strict veracity and admitted penetration, the wife of a well-known Caledonian, came to the writer shortly after the story was first published, and enquired if Farfrae were not drawn from her husband, for he seemed to her to be the living portrait of that (doubtless) happy man. It hap-

pened that I had never thought of her husband in constructing Farfrae. I trust therefore that Farfrae may be allowed to pass, if not as a Scotchman to Scotchmen, as a
Scotchman to Southerners.

T. H.
February 1895

I

ONE EVENING OF LATE SUMMER, BEFORE THE PRESENT CENTURY HAD REACHED ITS thirtieth year, a young man and woman, the latter carrying a child, were approaching the large village of Weydon-Priors, in Upper Wessex, on foot. They were plainly but not ill clad, though the thick hoar of dust which had accumulated on their shoes and garments from an obviously long journey lent a disadvantageous shabbiness to their appearance just now.

The man was of fine figure, swarthy, and stern in aspect; and he showed in profile a facial angle so slightly inclined as to be almost perpendicular. He wore a short jacket of brown corduroy, newer than the remainder of his suit, which was a fustian waistcoat with white horn buttons, breeches of the same, tanned leggings, and a straw hat overlaid with black glazed canvas. At his back he carried by a looped strap a rush basket, from which protruded at one end the crutch of a hay-knife, a wimble for hay-bonds being also visible in the aperture. His measured, springless walk was the walk of the skilled countryman as distinct from the desultory shamble of the general labourer; while in the turn and plant of each foot there was, further, a dogged and cynical indifference, personal to himself, showing its presence even in the regularly interchanging fustian folds, now in the left leg, now in the right, as he paced along.

What was really peculiar, however, in this couple's progress, and would have attracted the attention of any casual observer otherwise disposed to overlook them, was the perfect silence they preserved. They walked side by side in such a way as to suggest afar off the low, easy, confidential chat of people full of reciprocity; but on closer view it could be discerned that the man was reading, or pretending to read, a ballad sheet which he kept before his eyes with some difficulty by the hand that was passed through the basket strap. Whether this apparent cause were the real cause, or whether it were an assumed one to escape an intercourse that would have been irksome to him, nobody but himself could have said precisely; but his taciturnity was unbroken, and the woman enjoyed no society whatever from his presence. Virtually she walked the highway alone, save for the child she bore. Sometimes the man's bent elbow almost touched her shoulder, for she kept as close to his side as was possible without actual contact; but she seemed to have no idea of taking his arm, nor he of offering it; and far from exhibiting surprise at his ignoring silence she appeared to receive it as a natural thing. If any word at all were uttered by the little group, it was an occasional whisper of the woman to the child—a tiny girl in short clothes and blue boots of knitted yarn—and the murmured babble of the child in reply.

The chief—almost the only—attraction of the young woman's face was its mobility. When she looked down sideways to the girl she became pretty, and even handsome, particularly that in the action her features caught slantwise the rays of the strongly coloured sun, which made transparencies of her eyelids and nostrils and set fire on her lips. When she plodded on in the shade of the hedge, silently thinking, she had the hard, half-apathetic expression of one who deems anything possible at the hands of Time and Chance except, perhaps, fair play. The first phase was the work of Nature, the second probably of civilization.

That the man and woman were husband and wife, and the parents of the girl in arms there could be little doubt. No other than such relationship would have accounted for the atmosphere of stale familiarity which the trio carried along with them like a nimbus as they moved down the road.

The wife mostly kept her eyes fixed ahead, though with little interest—the scene for that matter being one that might have been matched at almost any spot in any county in England at this time of the year; a road neither straight nor crooked, neither level nor hilly, bordered by hedges, trees, and other vegetation, which had entered the blackened-green stage of colour that the doomed leaves pass through on their way to dingy, and yellow, and red. The grassy margin of the bank, and the nearest hedgerow boughs, were powdered by the dust that had been stirred over them by hasty vehicles, the same dust as it lay on the road deadening their footfalls like a carpet; and this, with the aforesaid total absence of conversation, allowed every extraneous sound to be heard.

For a long time there was none, beyond the voice of a weak bird singing a trite old evening song that might doubtless have been heard on the hill at the same hour, and with the self-same trills, quavers, and breves, at any sunset of that season for centuries untold. But as they approached the village sundry distant shouts and rattles reached their ears from some elevated spot in that direction, as yet screened from view by foliage. When the out-lying houses of Weydon-Priors could just be described, the family group was met by a turnip-hoer with his hoe on his shoulder, and his dinner-bag suspended from it. The reader promptly glanced up.

"Any trade doing here?" he asked phlegmatically, designating the village in his van by a wave of the broadsheet. And thinking the labourer did not understand him, he added, "Anything in the hay-trussing line?"

The turnip-hoer had already begun shaking his head. "Why, save the man, what wisdom's in him that 'a should come to Weydon for a job of that sort this time o' year?"

"Then is there any house to let—a little small new cottage just a-builded, or such like?" asked the other.

The pessimist still maintained a negative. "Pulling down is more the nater of Weydon. There were five houses cleared away last year, and three this; and the volk nowhere to go—no, not so much as a thatched hurdle; that's the way o' Weydon-Priors."

The hay-trusser, which he obviously was, nodded with some superciliousness. Looking towards the village, he continued, "There is something going on here, however, is there not?"

"Ay. 'Tis Fair Day. Though what you hear now is little more than the clatter and scurry of getting away the money o' children and fools, for the real business is done earlier than this. I've been working within sound o't all day, but I didn't go up—not I. 'Twas no business of mine."

The trusser and his family proceeded on their way, and soon entered the Fair-field, which showed standing-places and pens where many hundreds of horses and sheep had been exhibited and sold in the forenoon, but were now in great part taken away. At present, as their informant had observed, but little real business remained on hand, the chief being the sale by auction of a few inferior animals, that could not otherwise be disposed of, and had been absolutely refused by the better class of traders, who came and went early. Yet the crowd was denser now than during the morning hours, the frivolous contingent of visitors, including journeymen out for a holiday, a stray soldier or two come on furlough, village shopkeepers, and the like, having latterly flocked in; persons whose activities found a congenial field among the peep-shows, toy-stands, waxworks, inspired monsters, disinterested medical men who travelled for the public good, thimble-riggers, nick-nack vendors, and readers of Fate.

Neither of our pedestrians had much heart for these things, and they looked around for a refreshment tent among the many which dotted the down. Two, which stood nearest to them in the ochreous haze of expiring sunlight, seemed almost equally inviting. One was formed of new, milk-hued canvas, and bore red flags on its summit; it announced "Good Home-brewed Beer, Ale, and Cyder." The other was less new; a little iron stove-pipe came out of it at the back, and in front appeared the placard, "Good Furmity Sold Hear." The man mentally weighed the two inscriptions and inclined to the former tent.

"No—no—the other one," said the woman. "I always like furmity; and so does Elizabeth-Jane; and so will you. It is nourishing after a long hard day."

"I've never tasted it," said the man. However, he gave way to her representations, and they entered the furmity booth forthwith.

A rather numerous company appeared within, seated at the long narrow tables that ran down the tent on each side. At the upper end stood a stove, containing a charcoal fire, over which hung a large three-legged crock, sufficiently polished round the rim to show that it was made of bell-metal. A haggish creature of about fifty presided, in a white apron, which as it threw an air of respectability over her as far as it extended, was made so wide as to reach nearly round her waist. She slowly stirred the contents of the pot. The dull scrape of her large spoon was audible throughout the tent as she thus kept from burning the mixture of corn in the grain, flour, milk, raisins, currants, and what not, that composed the antiquated slop in which she dealt. Vessels holding the separate ingredients stood on a white-clothed table of boards and trestles close by.

The young man and woman ordered a basin each of the mixture, steaming hot, and sat down to consume it at leisure. This was very well so far, for furmity, as the woman had said, was nourishing, and as proper a food as could be obtained within the four seas; though, to those not accustomed to it, the grains of wheat swollen as large as lemon-pips, which floated on its surface, might have a deterrent effect at first.

But there was more in that tent than met the cursory glance; and the man, with the instinct of a perverse character, scented it quickly. After a mincing attack on his bowl, he watched the hag's proceedings from the corner of his eye, and saw the game she played. He winked to her, and passed up his basin in reply to her nod; when she took a bottle from under the table, slily measured out a quantity of its contents, and tipped the same into the man's furmity. The liquor poured in was rum. The man as slily sent back money in payment.

He found the concoction, thus strongly laced, much more to his satisfaction than it had been in its natural state. His wife had observed the proceeding with much uneasiness; but he persuaded her to have hers laced also, and she agreed to a milder allowance after some misgiving.

The man finished his basin, and called for another, the rum being signalled for in yet stronger proportion. The effect of it was soon apparent in his manner, and his wife but too sadly perceived that in strenuously steering off the rocks of the licensed liquor-tent she had only got into maelstrom depths here amongst the smugglers.

The child began to prattle impatiently, and the wife more than once said to her husband, "Michael, how about our lodging? You know we may have trouble in getting it if we don't go soon."

But he turned a deaf ear to those birdlike chirpings. He talked loud to the company. The child's black eyes, after slow, round, ruminating gazes at the candles when they were lighted, fell together; then they opened, then shut again, and she slept.

At the end of the first basin the man had risen to serenity; at the second he was jovial; at the third, argumentative; at the fourth, the qualities signified by the shape of his face, the occasional clench of his mouth, and the fiery spark of his dark eye, began to tell in his conduct; he was overbearing—even brilliantly quarrelsome.

The conversation took a high turn, as it often does on such occasions. The ruin of good men by bad wives, and, more particularly, the frustration of many a promising youth's high aims and hopes and the extinction of his energies by an early imprudent marriage, was the theme.

"I did for myself that way thoroughly," said the trusser, with a contemplative bitterness that was well-nigh resentful. "I married at eighteen, like the fool that I was; and this is the consequence o't." He pointed at himself and family with a wave of the hand intended to bring out the penuriousness of the exhibition.

The young woman his wife, who seemed accustomed to such remarks, acted as if she did not hear them, and continued her intermittent private words of tender trifles to the sleeping and waking child, who was just big enough to be placed for a moment on the bench beside her when she wished to ease her arms. The man continued—

"I haven't more than fifteen shillings in the world, and yet I am a good experienced hand in my line. I'd challenge England to beat me in the fodder business; and if I were a free man again, I'd be worth a thousand pound before I'd done o't. But a fellow never knows these little things till all chance of acting upon 'em is past."

The auctioneer selling the old horses in the field outside could be heard saying, "Now this is the last lot—now who'll take the last lot for a song? Shall I say forty shillings? 'Tis a very promising broodmare, a trifle over five years old, and nothing the matter with the hoss at all, except that she's a little holler in the back and had her left eye knocked out by the kick of another, her own sister, coming along the road."

"For my part I don't see why men who have got wives and don't want 'em, shouldn't get rid of 'em as these gipsy fellows do their old horses," said the man in the tent. "Why shouldn't they put 'em up and sell 'em by auction to men who are in need of such articles? Hey? Why, begad, I'd sell mine this minute if anybody would buy her!"

"There's them that would do that," some of the guests replied, looking at the woman, who was by no means ill-favoured.

"True," said a smoking gentleman, whose coat had the fine polish about the collar, elbows, seams, and shoulder-blades that long-continued friction with grimy surfaces will produce, and which is usually more desired on furniture than on clothes. From his appearance he had possibly been in former time groom or coachman to some neighbouring county family. "I've had my breedings in as good circles, I may say, as any man," he added, "and I know true cultivation, or nobody do; and I can declare she's got it—in the bone, mind ye, I say—as much as any female in the fair—though it may want a little bringing out." Then, crossing his legs, he resumed his pipe with a nicely-adjusted gaze at a point in the air.

The fuddled young husband stared for a few seconds at this unexpected praise of his wife, half in doubt of the wisdom of his own attitude towards the possessor of such qualities. But he speedily lapsed into his former conviction, and said harshly—

"Well, then, now is your chance; I am open to an offer for this gem o' creation."

She turned to her husband and murmured, "Michael, you have talked this nonsense in public places before. A joke is a joke, but you may make it once too often, mind!"

"I know I've said it before; I meant it. All I want is a buyer."

At the moment a swallow, one among the last of the season, which had by chance found its way through an opening into the upper part of the tent, flew to and fro in quick curves above their heads, causing all eyes to follow it absently. In watching the bird till it made its escape the assembled company neglected to respond to the workman's offer, and the subject dropped.

But a quarter of an hour later the man, who had gone on lacing his furmity more and more heavily, though he was either so strong-minded or such an intrepid toper that he still appeared fairly sober, recurred to the old strain, as in a musical fantasy the instrument fetches up the original theme. "Here—I am waiting to know about this offer of mine. The woman is no good to me. Who'll have her?"

The company had by this time decidedly degenerated, and the renewed enquiry was received with a laugh of appreciation. The woman whispered; she was imploring and anxious: "Come, come, it is getting dark, and this nonsense won't do. If you don't come along, I shall go without you. Come!"

She waited and waited; yet he did not move. In ten minutes the man broke in upon the desultory conversation of the furmity drinkers with, "I asked this question, and nobody answered to 't. Will any Jack Rag or Tom Straw among ye buy my goods?"

The woman's manner changed, and her face assumed the grim shape and colour of which mention has been made.

"Mike, Mike," she said; "this is getting serious. Oh!—too serious!"

"Will anybody buy her?" said the man.

"I wish somebody would," said she firmly. "Her present owner is not at all to her liking!"

"Nor you to mine," said he. "So we are agreed about that. Gentlemen, you hear? It's an agreement to part. She shall take the girl if she wants to, and go her ways. I'll take my tools, and go my ways. 'Tis simple as Scripture history. Now then, stand up, Susan, and show yourself."

"Don't, my chiel," whispered a buxom staylace dealer in voluminous petticoats, who sat near the woman; "yer good man don't know what he's saying."

The woman, however, did stand up. "Now, who's auctioneer?" cried the hay-trusser.

"I be," promptly answered a short man, with a nose resembling a copper knob, a damp voice, and eyes like button-holes. "Who'll make an offer for this lady?"

The woman looked on the ground, as if she maintained her position by a supreme effort of will.

"Five shillings," said someone, at which there was a laugh.

"No insults," said the husband. "Who'll say a guinea?"

Nobody answered; and the female dealer in staylaces interposed.

"Behave yerself moral, good man, for Heaven's love! Ah, what a cruelty is the poor soul married to! Bed and board is dear at some figures 'pon my 'vation 'tis!"

"Set it higher, auctioneer," said the trusser.

"Two guineas!" said the auctioneer; and no one replied.

"If they don't take her for that, in ten seconds they'll have to give more," said the husband. "Very well. Now, auctioneer, add another."

"Three guineas—going for three guineas!" said the rheumy man.

"No bid?" said the husband. "Good Lord, why she's cost me fifty times the money, if a penny. Go on."

"Four guineas!" cried the auctioneer.

"I'll tell ye what—I won't sell her for less than five," said the husband, bringing down his fist so that the basins danced. "I'll sell her for five guineas to any man that will pay me the money, and treat her well; and he shall have her forever, and never hear aught o' me. But she shan't go for less. Now then—five guineas—and she's yours. Susan, you agree?"

She bowed her head with absolute indifference.

"Five guineas," said the auctioneer, "or she'll be withdrawn. Do anybody give it? The last time. Yes or no?"

"Yes," said a loud voice from the doorway.

All eyes were turned. Standing in the triangular opening which formed the door of the tent was a sailor, who, unobserved by the rest, had arrived there within the last two or three minutes. A dead silence followed his affirmation.

"You say you do?" asked the husband, staring at him.

"I say so," replied the sailor.

"Saying is one thing, and paying is another. Where's the money?"

The sailor hesitated a moment, looked anew at the woman, came in, unfolded five crisp pieces of paper, and threw them down upon the table cloth. They were Bank-of-England notes for five pounds. Upon the face of this he clinked down the shillings severally—one, two, three, four, five.

The sight of real money in full amount, in answer to a challenge for the same till then deemed slightly hypothetical, had a great effect upon the spectators. Their eyes became riveted upon the faces of the chief actors, and then upon the notes as they lay, weighted by the shillings, on the table.

Up to this moment it could not positively have been asserted that the man, in spite of his tantalizing declaration, was really in earnest. The spectators had indeed taken the proceedings throughout as a piece of mirthful irony carried to extremes; and had assumed that, being out of work, he was, as a consequence, out of temper with the world, and society, and his nearest kin. But with the demand and response of real cash the jovial frivolity of the scene departed. A lurid colour seemed to fill the tent, and change the aspect of all therein. The mirth-wrinkles left the listeners' faces, and they waited with parting lips.

"Now," said the woman, breaking the silence, so that her low dry voice sounded quite loud, "before you go further, Michael, listen to me. If you touch that money, I and this girl go with the man. Mind, it is a joke no longer."

"A joke? Of course it is not a joke!" shouted her husband, his resentment rising at her suggestion. "I take the money; the sailor takes you. That's plain enough. It has been done elsewhere—and why not here?"

" 'Tis quite on the understanding that the young woman is willing," said the sailor blandly. "I wouldn't hurt her feelings for the world."

"Faith, nor I," said her husband. "But she is willing, provided she can have the child. She said so only the other day when I talked o't!"

"That you swear?" said the sailor to her.

"I do," said she, after glancing at her husband's face and seeing no repentance there.

"Very well, she shall have the child, and the bargain's complete," said the trusser. He took the sailor's notes and deliberately folded them, and put them with the shillings in a high remote pocket, with an air of finality.

The sailor looked at the woman and smiled. "Come along!" he said kindly. "The little one too—the more the merrier!" She paused for an instant, with a close glance at him. Then dropping her eyes again, and saying nothing, she took up the child and followed him as he made towards the door. On reaching it, she turned, and pulling off her wedding-ring, flung it across the booth in the hay-trusser's face.

"Mike," she said, "I've lived with thee a couple of years, and had nothing but temper! Now I'm no more to 'ee; I'll try my luck elsewhere. 'Twill be better for me and the child, both. So good-bye!"

Seizing the sailor's arm with her right hand, and mounting the little girl on her left, she went out of the tent sobbing bitterly.

A stolid look of concern filled the husband's face, as if, after all, he had not quite anticipated this ending; and some of the guests laughed.

"Is she gone?" he said.

"Faith, ay; she's gone clane enough," said some rustics near the door.

He rose and walked to the entrance with the careful tread of one conscious of his alcoholic load. Some others followed, and they stood looking into the twilight. The difference between the peacefulness of inferior nature and the wilful hostilities of mankind was very apparent at this place. In contrast with the harshness of the act just ended within the tent was the sight of several horses crossing their necks and rubbing each other lovingly as they waited in patience to be harnessed for the homeward journey. Outside the fair, in the valleys and woods, all was quiet. The sun had recently set, and the west heaven was hung with rosy cloud, which seemed permanent, yet slowly changed. To watch it was like looking at some grand feat of stagery from a darkened auditorium. In presence of this scene, after the other, there was a natural instinct to abjure man as the blot on an otherwise kindly universe; till it was remembered that all terrestrial conditions were intermittent, and that mankind might some night be innocently sleeping when these quiet objects were raging loud.

"Where do the sailor live?" asked a spectator, when they had vainly gazed around.

"God knows that," replied the man who had seen high life. "He's without doubt a stranger here."

"He came in about five minutes ago," said the furmity woman, joining the rest with her hands on her hips. "And then 'a stepped back, and then 'a looked in again. I'm not a penny the better for him."

"Serves the husband well be-right," said the staylace vendor. "A comely respectable body like her—what can a man want more? I glory in the woman's sperrit. I'd ha' done it myself—od send if I wouldn't, if a husband had behaved so to me! I'd go, and 'a might call, and call, till his keacorn was raw; but I'd never come back—no, not till the great trumpet, would I!"

"Well, the woman will be better off," said another of a more deliberative turn. "For seafaring natures be very good shelter for shorn lambs, and the man do seem to have plenty of money, which is what she's not been used to lately, by all showings."

"Mark me—I'll not go after her!" said the trusser, returning doggedly to his seat. "Let her go! If she's up to such vagaries she must suffer for 'em. She'd no business to take the maid—'tis my maid; and if it were the doing again she shouldn't have her!"

Perhaps from some little sense of having countenanced an indefensible proceeding, perhaps because it was late, the customers thinned away from the tent shortly after this episode. The man stretched his elbows forward on the table leant his face upon his arms, and soon began to snore. The furmity seller decided to close for the night, and after seeing the rum-bottles, milk, corn, raisins, &c., that remained on hand, loaded into the cart, came to where the man reclined. She shook him, but could not wake him. As the tent was not to be struck that night, the fair continuing for two or three days, she decided to let the sleeper, who was obviously no tramp, stay where he was, and his basket with him. Extinguishing the last candle, and lowering the flap of the tent, she left it, and drove away.

II

THE MORNING SUN WAS STREAMING THROUGH THE CREVICES OF THE CANVAS WHEN THE man awoke. A warm glow pervaded the whole atmosphere of the marquee, and a single big blue fly buzzed musically round and round it. Besides the buzz of the fly there was not a sound. He looked about—at the benches—at the table supported by trestles—at his basket of tools—at the stove where the furmity had been boiled—at the empty basins—at some shed grains of wheat—at the corks which dotted the grassy floor. Among the odds and ends he discerned a little shining object, and picked it up. It was his wife's ring.

A confused picture of the events of the previous evening seemed to come back to him, and he thrust his hand into his breast-pocket. A rustling revealed the sailor's bank-notes thrust carelessly in.

This second verification of his dim memories was enough; he knew now they were not dreams. He remained seated, looking on the ground for some time. "I must get out of this as soon as I can," he said deliberately at last, with the air of one who could not catch his thoughts without pronouncing them. "She's gone—to be sure she is—gone with that sailor who bought her, and little Elizabeth-Jane. We walked here, and I had the furmity, and rum in it—and sold her. Yes, that's what's happened and here am I. Now, what am I to do—am I sober enough to walk, I wonder?" He stood up, found that he was in fairly good condition for progress, unencumbered. Next he shouldered his tool basket, and found he could carry it. Then lifting the tent-door he emerged into the open air.

Here the man looked around with gloomy curiosity. The freshness of the September morning inspired and braced him as he stood. He and his family had been weary when they arrived the night before, and they had observed but little of the place; so that he now beheld it as a new thing. It exhibited itself as the top of an open down, bounded on one extreme by a plantation, and approached by a winding road. At the bottom stood the village which lent its name to the upland and the annual fair that was held thereon. The spot stretched downward into valleys, and onward to other uplands, dotted with barrows, and trenched with the remains of prehistoric forts. The whole scene lay under the rays of a newly risen sun, which had not as yet dried a single blade of the heavily dewed grass, whereon the shadows of the yellow and red vans were projected far away, those thrown by the felloe of each wheel being elongated in shape to the orbit of a comet. All the gypsies and showmen who had remained on the ground lay snug within their carts and tents, or wrapped in horse-cloths under them, and were silent and still as death, with the exception of an occasional snore that revealed their presence. But the Seven Sleepers had a dog; and dogs of the mysterious breeds that vagrants own, that are as much like cats as dogs, and as much like foxes as cats, also lay about here. A little one started up under one of the carts, barked as a matter of principle, and quickly lay down again. He was the only positive spectator of the hay-trusser's exit from the Weydon Fair-field.

This seemed to accord with his desire. He went on in silent thought, unheeding the yellowhammers which flitted about the hedges with straws in their bills, the crowns of the mushrooms, and the tinkling of local sheep-bells, whose wearers had had the good fortune not to be included in the fair. When he reached a lane, a good mile from the scene of the previous evening, the man pitched his basket and leant upon a gate. A difficult problem or two occupied his mind.

"Did I tell my name to anybody last night, or didn't I tell my name?" he said to himself; and at last concluded that he did not. His general demeanour was enough to show how he was surprised and nettled that his wife had taken him so literally—as much could be seen in his face, and in the way he nibbled a straw which he pulled from the hedge. He knew that she must have been somewhat excited to do this; moreover, she must have believed that there was some sort of binding force in the transaction. On this latter point he felt almost certain, knowing her freedom from levity of character, and the extreme simplicity of her intellect. There may, too, have been enough recklessness and resentment beneath her ordinary placidity to make her stifle any momentary doubts. On a previous occasion when he had declared, during a fuddle, that he would dispose of her as he had done, she had replied that she would not hear him say that many times more before it happened, in the resigned tones of a fatalist. . . . "Yet she knows I am not in my senses when I do that?" he exclaimed. "Well, I must walk about till I find her. . . . Seize her, why didn't she know better than bring me into this disgrace!" he roared out. "She wasn't queer if I was. 'Tis like Susan to show such idiotic simplicity. Meek—that meekness has done me more harm than the bitterest temper!"

When he was calmer he turned to his original conviction that he must somehow find her and his little Elizabeth-Jane, and put up with the shame as best he could. It was of his own making, and he ought to bear it. But first he resolved to register an oath, a greater oath than he had ever sworn before: and to do it properly he required a fit place and imagery; for there was something fetichistic in this man's beliefs.

He shouldered his basket and moved on, casting his eyes inquisitively round upon the landscape as he walked, and at the distance of three or four miles perceived the roofs of a village and the tower of a church. He instantly made towards the latter object. The village was quite still, it being that motionless hour of rustic daily life which fills the interval between the departure of the field-labourers to their work, and the rising of their wives and daughters to prepare the breakfast for their return. Hence he reached the church without observation, and the door being only latched he entered. The hay-trusser deposited his basket by the font, went up the nave till he reached the altar-rails, and opening the gate entered the sacrarium, where he seemed to feel a sense of the strangeness for a moment; then he knelt upon the foot-pace. Dropping his head upon the clamped book which lay on the Communion-table, he said aloud—

"I, Michael Henchard, on this morning of the sixteenth of September, do take an oath before God here in this solemn place that I will avoid all strong liquors for the space of twenty years to come, being a year for every year that I have lived. And this I swear upon the book before me; and may I be strook dumb, blind, and helpless, if I break this my oath!"

When he had said it and kissed the big book, the hay-trusser arose, and seemed relieved at having made a start in a new direction. While standing in the porch a moment, he saw a thick jet of wood smoke suddenly start up from the red chimney of a cottage near, and knew that the occupant had just lit her fire. He went round to the door, and the housewife agreed to prepare him some breakfast for a trifling payment, which was done. Then he started on the search for his wife and child.

The perplexing nature of the undertaking became apparent soon enough. Though he examined and enquired, and walked hither and thither day after day, no such characters as those he described had anywhere been seen since the evening of the fair. To add to the difficulty, he could gain no sound of the sailor's name. As money was short with him, he decided, after some hesitation, to spend the sailor's money in the prosecution of this search; but it was equally in vain. The truth was, that a certain shyness of revealing his conduct prevented Michael Henchard from following up the investigation with the loud hue-and-cry such a pursuit demanded to render it effectual; and it was probably for this reason that he obtained no clue, though everything was done by him that did not involve an explanation of the circumstances under which he had lost her.

Weeks counted up to months, and still he searched on, maintaining himself by small jobs of work in the intervals. By this time he had arrived at a seaport, and there he derived intelligence that persons answering somewhat to his description had emigrated a little time before. Then he said he would search no longer, and that he would go and settle in the district which he had had for some time in his mind. Next day he started, journeying southwestward, and did not pause, except for nights' lodgings, till he reached the town of Casterbridge, in a far distant part of Wessex.

III

THE HIGHROAD INTO THE VILLAGE OF WEYDON-PRIORS WAS AGAIN CARPETED WITH dust. The trees had put on as of yore their aspect of dingy green, and where the Henchard family of three had once walked along, two persons not unconnected with the family walked now.

The scene in its broad aspect had so much of its previous character, even to the voices and rattle from the neighbouring village down, that it might for that matter have been the afternoon following the previously recorded episode. Change was only to be observed in details; but here it was obvious that a long procession of years had passed by. One of the two who walked the road was she who had figured as the young wife of Henchard on the previous occasion; now her face had lost much of its rotundity; her skin had undergone a textural change; and though her hair had not lost colour, it was considerably thinner than heretofore. She was dressed in the mourning clothes of a widow. Her companion, also in black, appeared as a well-formed young woman about eighteen, completely possessed of that ephemeral precious essence youth, which is itself beauty, irrespective of complexion or contour.

A glance was sufficient to inform the eye that this was Susan Henchard's grown-up daughter. While life's middle summer had set its hardening mark on the mother's face, her former springlike specialities were transferred so dexterously by Time to the second figure, her child, that the absence of certain facts within her mother's knowledge from the girl's mind would have seemed for the moment, to one reflecting on those facts, to be a curious imperfection in Nature's powers of continuity.

They walked with joined hands, and it could be perceived that this was the act of simple affection. The daughter carried in her outer hand a withy basket of old-fashioned make; the mother a blue bundle, which contrasted oddly with her black stuff gown.

Reaching the outskirts of the village they pursued the same track as formerly, and ascended to the fair. Here, too, it was evident that the years had told. Certain mechanical improvements might have been noticed in the roundabouts and highfliers, machines for testing rustic strength and weight, and in the erections devoted to shooting for nuts. But the real business of the fair had considerably dwindled. The new periodical great markets of neighbouring towns were beginning to interfere seriously with the trade carried on here for centuries. The pens for sheep, the tie-ropes for horses, were about half as long as they had been. The stalls of tailors, hosiers, coopers, linen-drapers, and other such trades had almost disappeared, and the vehicles were far less numerous. The mother and daughter threaded the crowd for some little distance, and then stood still.

"Why did we hinder our time by coming in here? I thought you wished to get onward?" said the maiden.

"Yes, my dear Elizabeth-Jane," explained the other. "But I had a fancy for looking up here."

"Why?"

"It was here I first met with Newson—on such a day as this."

"First met with father here? Yes, you have told me so before. And now he's drowned and gone from us!" As she spoke the girl drew a card from her pocket and looked at it with a sigh. It was edged with black, and inscribed within a design resembling a mural tablet were the words, "In affectionate memory of Richard Newson, mariner, who was unfortunately lost at sea, in the month of November 184—, aged forty-one years."

"And it was here," continued her mother, with more hesitation, "that I last saw the relation we are going to look for—Mr. Michael Henchard."

"What is his exact kin to us, mother? I have never clearly had it told me."

"He is, or was—for he may be dead—a connection by marriage," said her mother deliberately.

"That's exactly what you have said a score of times before!" replied the young woman, looking about her inattentively. "He's not a near relation, I suppose?"

"Not by any means."

"He was a hay-trusser, wasn't he, when you last heard of him?"

"He was."

"I suppose he never knew me?" the girl innocently continued.

Mrs. Henchard paused for a moment, and answered un-easily, "Of course not, Elizabeth-Jane. But come this way." She moved on to another part of the field.

"It is not much use enquiring here for anybody, I should think," the daughter observed, as she gazed roundabout. "People at fairs change like the leaves of trees; and I daresay you are the only one here to-day who was here all those years ago."

"I am not so sure of that," said Mrs. Newson, as she now called herself, keenly eyeing something under a green bank a little way off. "See there."

The daughter looked in the direction signified. The object pointed out was a tripod of sticks stuck into the earth, from which hung a three-legged crock, kept hot by a smouldering wood fire beneath. Over the pot stooped an old woman haggard, wrinkled, and almost in rags. She stirred the contents of the pot with a large spoon, and occasionally croaked in a broken voice, "Good furmity sold here!"

It was indeed the former mistress of the furmity tent—once thriving, cleanly, white-aproned, and chinking with money—now tentless, dirty, owning no tables or benches, and having scarce any customers except two small whity-brown boys, who came up and asked for "A ha'p'orth, please—good measure," which she served in a couple of chipped yellow basins of commonest clay.

"She was here at that time," resumed Mrs. Newson, making a step as if to draw nearer.

"Don't speak to her—it isn't respectable!" urged the other.

"I will just say a word—you, Elizabeth-Jane, can stay here."

The girl was not loth, and turned to some stalls of coloured prints while her mother went forward. The old woman begged for the latter's custom as soon as she saw her, and responded to Mrs. Henchard-Newson's request for a pennyworth with more alacrity than she had shown in selling sixpennyworths in her younger days. When the *soi-disant* widow had taken the basin of thin poor slop that stood for the rich concoction of the former time, the hag opened a little basket behind the fire, and looking up slily, whispered, "Just a thought o' rum in it?—smuggled, you know—say two penn'orth—'twill make it slip down like cordial!"

Her customer smiled bitterly at this survival of the old trick, and shook her head with a meaning the old woman was far from translating. She pretended to eat a little of the furmity with the leaden spoon offered, and as she did so said blandly to the hag, "You've seen better days?"

"Ah, ma'am—well ye may say it!" responded the old woman, opening the sluices of her heart forthwith. "I've stood in this fair-ground, maid, wife, and widow, these nine-and-thirty years, and in that time have known what it was to do business with the richest stomachs in the land! Ma'am, you'd hardly believe that I was once the owner of a great pavilion-tent that was the attraction of the fair. Nobody could come, nobody could go, without having a dish of Mrs. Goodenough's furmity. I knew the clergy's taste, the dandy gent's taste; I knew the town's taste, the country's taste. I even knowed the taste of the coarse shameless females. But Lord's my life—the world's no memory; straightforward dealings don't bring profit—'tis the sly and the underhand that get on in these times!"

Mrs. Newson glanced round—her daughter was still bending over the distant stalls. "Can you call to mind," she said cautiously to the old woman, "the sale of a wife by her husband in your tent eighteen years ago to-day?"

The hag reflected, and half shook her head. "If it had been a big thing I should have minded it in a moment," she said. "I can mind every serious fight o' married parties, every murder, every manslaughter, even every pocket-picking—leastwise large ones—that 't has been my lot to witness. But a selling? Was it done quietlike?"

"Well, yes. I think so."

The furmity woman half shook her head again. "And yet," she said, "I do. At any rate, I can mind a man doing something o' the sort—a man in a cord jacket, with a basket of tools; but, Lord bless ye, we don't gi'e it head-room, we don't, such as that. The only reason why I can mind the man is that he came back here to the next year's fair, and told me quite privatelike that if a woman ever asked for him I was to say he had gone to— where?—Casterbridge—yes—to Casterbridge, said he. But, Lord's my life, I shouldn't ha' thought of it again!"

Mrs. Newson would have rewarded the old woman as far as her small means afforded had she not discreetly borne in mind that it was by that unscrupulous person's liquor her husband had been degraded. She briefly thanked her informant, and rejoined Elizabeth, who greeted her with, "Mother, do let's get on—it was hardly respectable for you to buy refreshments there. I see none but the lowest do."

"I have learned what I wanted, however," said her mother quietly. "The last time our relative visited this fair he said he was living at Casterbridge. It is a long, long way from here, and it was many years ago that he said it, but there I think we'll go."

With this they descended out of the fair, and went onward to the village, where they obtained a night's lodging.

IV

Henchard's wife acted for the best, but she had involved herself in difficulties. A hundred times she had been upon the point of telling her daughter Elizabeth-Jane the true story of her life, the tragical crisis of which had been the transaction at Weydon Fair, when she was not much older than the girl now beside her. But she had refrained. An innocent maiden had thus grown up in the belief that the relations between the genial sailor and her mother were the ordinary ones that they had always appeared to be. The risk of endangering a child's strong affection by disturbing ideas which had grown with her growth was to Mrs. Henchard too fearful a thing to contemplate. It had seemed, indeed, folly to think of making Elizabeth-Jane wise.

But Susan Henchard's fear of losing her dearly loved daughter's heart by a revelation had little to do with any sense of wrong-doing on her own part. Her simplicity—the original ground of Henchard's contempt for her—had allowed her to live on in the conviction that Newson had acquired a morally real and justifiable right to her by his purchase—though the exact bearings and legal limits of that right were vague. It may seem strange to sophisticated minds that a sane young matron could believe in the seriousness of such a transfer; and were there not numerous other instances of the same belief the thing might scarcely be credited. But she was by no means the first or last peasant woman who had religiously adhered to her purchaser, as too many rural records show.

The history of Susan Henchard's adventures in the interim can be told in two or three sentences. Absolutely helpless, she had been taken off to Canada where they had lived several years without any great worldly success, though she worked as hard as any woman could to keep their cottage cheerful and well-provided. When Elizabeth-Jane was about twelve years old the three returned to England, and settled at Falmouth, where Newson made a living for a few years as boatman and general handy shoreman.

He then engaged in the Newfoundland trade, and it was during this period that Susan had an awakening. A friend to whom she confided her history ridiculed her grave acceptance of her position; and all was over with her peace of mind. When Newson came home at the end of one winter he saw that the delusion he had so carefully sustained had vanished forever.

There was then a time of sadness, in which she told him her doubts if she could live with him longer. Newson left home again on the Newfoundland trade when the season came round. The vague news of his loss at sea a little later on solved a problem which had become torture to her meek conscience. She saw him no more.

Of Henchard they heard nothing. To the liege subjects of Labour, the England of those days was a continent, and a mile a geographical degree.

Elizabeth-Jane developed early into womanliness. One day, a month or so after receiving intelligence of Newson's death off the Bank of Newfoundland, when the girl was about eighteen, she was sitting on a willow chair in the cottage they still occupied, working twine nets for the fishermen. Her mother was in a back corner of the same room, engaged in the same labour; and dropping the heavy wood needle she was filling she surveyed her daughter thoughtfully. The sun shone in at the door upon the young woman's head and hair, which was worn loose, so that the rays streamed into its depths as into a hazel copse. Her face, though somewhat wan and incomplete, possessed the raw materials of beauty in a promising degree. There was an under-handsomeness in it, struggling to reveal itself through the provisional curves of immaturity, and the casual disfigurements that resulted from the straitened circumstances of their lives. She was handsome in the bone, hardly as yet handsome in the flesh. She possibly might never be fully handsome, unless the carking accidents of her daily existence could be evaded before the mobile parts of her countenance had settled to their final mould.

The sight of the girl made her mother sad—not vaguely but by logical inference. They both were still in that strait-waistcoat of poverty from which she had tried so many times to be delivered for the girl's sake. The woman had long perceived how zealously and constantly the young mind of her companion was struggling for enlargement; and yet now, in her eighteenth year, it still remained but little unfolded. The desire—sober and repressed—of Elizabeth-Jane's heart was indeed to see, to hear, and to understand. How could she become a woman of wider knowledge, higher repute—"better," as she termed it—this was her constant enquiry of her mother. She sought further into things than other girls in her position ever did, and her mother groaned as she felt she could not aid in the search.

The sailor, was now lost to them; and Susan's staunch, religious adherence to him as her husband in principle, till her views had been disturbed by enlightenment, was demanded no more. She asked herself whether the present moment, now that she was a free woman again, were not as opportune a one as she would find in a world where everything had been so inopportune, for making a desperate effort to advance Elizabeth. To pocket her pride and search for the first husband seemed, wisely or not, the best initiatory step. He had possibly drunk himself into his tomb. But he might, on the other hand, have had too much sense to do so; for in her time with him he had been given to bouts only, and was not a habitual drunkard.

At any rate, the propriety of returning to him, if he lived, was unquestionable. The awkwardness of searching for him lay in enlightening Elizabeth, a proceeding which her mother could not endure to contemplate. She finally resolved to undertake the search without confiding to the girl her former relations with Henchard, leaving it to him if they found him to take what steps he might choose to that end. This will account for their conversation at the fair, and the half-informed state at which Elizabeth was led onward.

In this attitude they proceeded on their journey, trusting solely to the dim light afforded of Henchard's whereabouts by the furmity woman. The strictest economy was indispensable. Sometimes they might have been seen on foot, sometimes on farmers' waggons, sometimes in carriers' vans; and thus they drew near to Casterbridge. Elizabeth-Jane discovered to her alarm that her mother's health was not what it once had been, and there was ever and anon in her talk that renunciatory tone which showed that, but for the girl, she would not be very sorry to quit a life she was growing thoroughly weary of.

It was on a Friday evening, near the middle of September and just before dusk, that they reached the summit of a hill within a mile of the place they sought. There were high-banked hedges to the coach-road here, and they mounted upon the green turf within, and sat down. The spot commanded a full view of the town and its environs.

"What an old-fashioned place it seems to be!" said Elizabeth-Jane, while her silent mother mused on other things than topography. "It is huddled all together; and it is shut in by a square wall of trees, like a plot of garden ground by a box-edging."

Its squareness was, indeed, the characteristic which most struck the eye in this antiquated borough, the borough of Casterbridge—at that time, recent as it was, untouched by the faintest sprinkle of modernism. It was compact as a box of dominoes. It had no suburbs—in the ordinary sense. Country and town met at a mathematical line.

To birds of the more soaring kind Casterbridge must have appeared on this fine evening as a mosaic-work of subdued reds, browns, greys, and crystals, held together by a rectangular frame of deep green. To the level eye of humanity it stood as an indistinct mass behind a dense stockade of limes and chestnuts, set in the midst of miles of rotund down and concave field. The mass became gradually dissected by the vision into towers, gables, chimneys, and casements, the highest glazings shining bleared and bloodshot with the coppery fire they caught from the belt of sunlit cloud in the west.

From the centre of each side of this tree-bound square ran avenues east, west, and south into the wide expanse of corn-land and combe to the distance of a mile or so. It was by one of these avenues that the pedestrians were about to enter. Before they had risen to proceed, two men passed outside the hedge, engaged in argumentative conversation.

"Why, surely," said Elizabeth, as they receded, "those men mentioned the name of Henchard in their talk—the name of our relative?"

"I thought so too," said Mrs. Newson.

"That seems a hint to us that he is still here."

"Yes."

"Shall I run after them, and ask them about him—"

"No, no, no! Not for the world just yet. He may be in the workhouse, or in the stocks, for all we know."

"Dear me—why should you think that, mother?"

" 'Twas just something to say—that's all! But we must make private enquiries."

Having sufficiently rested, they proceeded on their way at evenfall. The dense trees of the avenue rendered the road dark as a tunnel, though the open land on each side was still under a faint daylight; in other words, they passed down a midnight between two gloamings. The features of the town had a keen interest for Elizabeth's mother, now that the human side came to the fore. As soon as they had wandered about they could see that the stockade of gnarled trees which framed in Casterbridge was itself an avenue, standing on a low green bank or escarpment, with a ditch yet visible without. Within the avenue and bank was a wall more or less discontinuous, and within the wall were packed the abodes of the burghers.

Though the two women did not know it, these external features were but the ancient defences of the town, planted as a promenade.

The lamplights now glimmered through the engirdling trees, conveying a sense of great snugness and comfort inside, and rendering at the same time the unlighted country without strangely solitary and vacant in aspect, considering its nearness to life. The difference between burgh and champaign was increased, too, by sounds which now reached them above others—the notes of a brass band. The travellers returned into the High Street, where there were timber houses with overhanging stories, whose small-paned lattices were screened by dimity curtains on a drawing-string, and under whose barge-boards old cobwebs waved in the breeze. There were houses of brick-nogging, which derived their chief support from those adjoining. There were slate roofs patched with tiles, and tile roofs patched with slate, with occasionally a roof of thatch.

The agricultural and pastoral character of the people upon whom the town depended for its existence was shown by the class of objects displayed in the shop-windows. Scythes, reap-hooks, sheep-shears, bill-hooks, spades, mattocks, and hoes at the iron-monger's; bee-hives, butter-firkins, churns, milking stools and pails, hay-rakes, field-flagons, and seed-lips at the cooper's; cart-ropes and plough-harness at the saddler's; carts, wheelbarrows, and mill-gear at the wheelwright's and machinist's; horse-embrocations at the chemist's; at the glover's and leather-cutter's, hedging-gloves, thatchers' knee-caps, ploughmen's leggings, villagers' pattens and clogs.

They came to a grizzled church, whose massive square tower rose unbroken into the darkening sky, the lower parts being illuminated by the nearest lamps sufficiently to show how completely the mortar from the joints of the stonework had been nibbled out by time and weather, which had planted in the crevices thus made little tufts of stone-crop and grass almost as far up as the very battlements. From this tower the clock struck eight, and thereupon a bell began to toll with a peremptory clang. The curfew was still rung in Casterbridge, and it was utilised by the inhabitants as a signal for shutting their shops. No sooner did the deep notes of the bell throb between the house-fronts than a clatter of shutters arose through the whole length of the High Street. In a few minutes business at Casterbridge was ended for the day.

Other clocks struck eight from time to time—one gloomily from the gaol, another from the gable of an almshouse, with a preparative creak of machinery, more audible than the note of the bell; a row of tall, varnished case-clocks from the interior of a clock-maker's shop joined in one after another just as the shutters were enclosing them, like a row of actors delivering their final speeches before the fall of the curtain; then chimes were heard stammering out the Sicilian Mariners' Hymn; so that chronologists of the advanced school were appreciably on their way to the next hour before the whole business of the old one was satisfactorily wound up.

In an open space before the church walked a woman with her gown-sleeves rolled up so high that the edge of her under-linen was visible, and her skirt tucked up through her pocket hole. She carried a load under her arm from which she was pulling pieces of bread, and handing them to some other women who walked with her, which pieces they nibbled critically. The sight reminded Mrs. Henchard-Newson and her daughter that they had an appetite; and they enquired of the woman for the nearest baker's.

"Ye may as well look for manna-food as good bread in Casterbridge just now," she said, after directing them. "They can blare their trumpets and thump their drums, and have their roaring dinners"—waving her hand towards a point further along the street, where the brass band could be seen standing in front of an illuminated building—"but we must needs be put-to for want of a wholesome crust. There's less good bread than good beer in Casterbridge now."

"And less good beer than swipes," said a man with his hands in his pockets.

"How does it happen there's no good bread?" asked Mrs. Henchard.

"Oh, 'tis the corn-factor—he's the man that our millers and bakers all deal wi', and he has sold 'em growed wheat, which they didn't know was growed, so they say, till the dough ran all over the ovens like quicksilver; so that the loaves be as flat as toads, and like suet pudden inside. I've been a wife, and I've been a mother, and I never see such unprincipled bread in Casterbridge as this before.—But you must be a real stranger here not to know what's made all the poor volks plim like blowed bladders this week?"

"I am," said Elizabeth's mother shyly.

Not wishing to be observed further till she knew more of her future in this place, she withdrew with her daughter from the speaker's side. Getting a couple of biscuits at the shop indicated as a temporary substitute for a meal, they next bent their steps instinctively to where the music was playing.

V

A FEW SCORE YARDS BROUGHT THEM TO THE SPOT WHERE THE TOWN BAND WAS NOW shaking the window-panes with the strains of "The Roast Beef of Old England."

The building before whose doors they had pitched their music-stands was the chief hotel in Casterbridge—namely, the King's Arms. A spacious bow-window projected into the street over the main portico, and from the open sashes came the babble of voices, the jingle of glasses, and the drawing of corks. The blinds, moreover, being left unclosed, the whole interior of this room could be surveyed from the top of some steps opposite, for which reason a knot of idlers had gathered there.

"We might, perhaps, after all, make a few enquiries about—our relation Mr. Henchard," whispered Mrs. Newson who, since her entry into Casterbridge, had seemed strangely weak and agitated, "And this, I think, would be a good place for trying it—just to ask, you know, how he stands in the town—if he is here, as I think he must be. You, Elizabeth-Jane, had better be the one to do it. I'm too worn out to do anything—pull down your fall first."

She sat down upon the lowest step, and Elizabeth-Jane obeyed her directions and stood among the idlers.

"What's going on to-night?" asked the girl, after singling out an old man, and standing by him long enough to acquire a neighbourly right of converse.

"Well, ye must be a stranger sure," said the old man, without taking his eyes from the window. "Why, 'tis a great public dinner of the gentlepeople and such like leading volk—wi' the Mayor in the chair. As we plainer fellows baint invited, they leave the winder-shutters open that we may get jist a sense o't out here. If you mount the steps you can see 'em. That's Mr. Henchard, the Mayor, at the end of the table, a facing ye; and that's the Council men right and left. . . . Ah, lots of them when they begun life were no more than I be now!"

"Henchard!" said Elizabeth-Jane, surprised, but by no means suspecting the whole force of the revelation. She ascended to the top of the door-steps.

Her mother, though her head was bowed, had already caught from the inn-window tones that strangely riveted her attention, before the old man's words, "Mr. Henchard, the Mayor," reached her ears. She arose, and stepped up to her daughter's side as soon as she could do so without showing exceptional eagerness.

The interior of the hotel dining-room was spread out before her, with its tables, and glass, and plate, and inmates. Facing the window, in the chair of dignity, sat a man about forty years of age; of heavy frame, large features, and commanding voice; his general build being rather coarse than compact. He had a rich complexion, which verged on swarthiness, a flashing black eye, and dark, bushy brows and hair. When he indulged in an occasional loud laugh at some remark among the guests, his large mouth parted so far back as to show to the rays of the chandelier a full score or more of the two-and-thirty sound white teeth that he obviously still could boast of.

That laugh was not encouraging to strangers; and hence it may have been well that it was rarely heard. Many theories might have been built upon it. It fell in well with conjectures of a temperament which would have no pity for weakness, but would be ready to yield ungrudging admiration to greatness and strength. Its producer's personal goodness, if he had any, would be of a very fitful cast—an occasional almost oppressive generosity rather than a mild and constant kindness.

Susan Henchard's husband—in law, at least—sat before them, matured in shape, stiffened in line, exaggerated in traits; disciplined, thought-marked—in a word, older. Elizabeth, encumbered with no recollections as her mother was, regarded him with nothing more than the keen curiosity and interest which the discovery of such unexpected social standing in the long-sought relative naturally begot. He was dressed in an old-fashioned evening suit, an expanse of frilled shirt showing on his broad breast; jewelled studs, and a heavy gold chain. Three glasses stood at his right hand; but, to his wife's surprise, the two for wine were empty, while the third, a tumbler, was half full of water.

When last she had seen him he was sitting in a corduroy jacket, fustian waistcoat and breeches, and tanned leather leggings, with a basin of hot furmity before him. Time, the magician, had wrought much here. Watching him, and thus thinking of past days, she became so moved that she shrank back against the jamb of the deep doorway to which the steps gave access, the shadow from it conveniently hiding her features. She forgot her daughter, till a touch from Elizabeth-Jane aroused her. "Have you seen him, mother?" whispered the girl.

"Yes, yes," answered her companion hastily. "I have seen him, and it is enough for me! Now I only want to go—pass away—die."

"Why—oh what?" She drew closer, and whispered in her mother's ear, "Does he seem to you not likely to befriend us? I thought he looked a generous man. What a gentleman he is, isn't he? and how his diamond studs shine! How strange that you should have said he might be in the stocks, or in the workhouse, or dead! Did ever anything go more by contraries! Why do you feel so afraid of him? I am not at all; I'll call upon him—he can but say he don't own such remote kin."

"I don't know at all—I can't tell what to set about. I feel so down."

"Don't be that, mother, now we have got here and all! Rest there where you be a little while—I will look on and find out more about him."

"I don't think I can ever meet Mr. Henchard. He is not how I thought he would be—he overpowers me! I don't wish to see him any more."

"But wait a little time and consider."

Elizabeth-Jane had never been so much interested in anything in her life as in their present position, partly from the natural elation she felt at discovering herself akin to a coach; and she gazed again at the scene. The younger guests were talking and eating with animation; their elders were searching for tit-bits, and sniffing and grunting over their plates like sows nuzzling for acorns. Three drinks seemed to be sacred to the company—port, sherry, and rum; outside which old-established trinity few or no palates ranged.

A row of ancient rummers with ground figures on their sides, and each primed with a spoon, was now placed down the table, and these were promptly filled with grog at such high temperatures as to raise serious considerations for the articles exposed to its vapours. But Elizabeth-Jane noticed that, though this filling went on with great promptness up and down the table, nobody filled the Mayor's glass, who still drank large quantities of water from the tumbler behind the clump of crystal vessels intended for wine and spirits.

"They don't fill Mr. Henchard's wine-glasses," she ventured to say to her elbow acquaintance, the old man.

"Ah, no; don't ye know him to be the celebrated abstaining worthy of that name? He scorns all tempting liquors; never touches nothing. O yes, he've strong qualities that way. I have heard tell that he sware a gospel oath in bygone times, and has bode by it ever since. So they don't press him, knowing it would be unbecoming in the face of that: for yer gospel oath is a serious thing."

Another elderly man, hearing this discourse, now joined in by enquiring, "How much longer have he got to suffer from it, Solomon Longways?"

"Another two year, they say. I don't know the why and the wherefore of his fixing such a time, for 'a never has told anybody. But 'tis exactly two calendar years longer, they say. A powerful mind to hold out so long!"

"True. . . . But there's great strength in hope. Knowing that in four-and-twenty months' time ye'll be out of your bondage, and able to make up for all you've suffered, by partaking without stint—why, it keeps a man up, no doubt."

"No doubt, Christopher Coney, no doubt. And 'a must need such reflections—a lonely widow man," said Longways.

"When did he lose his wife?" asked Elizabeth.

"I never knowed her. 'Twas afore he came to Casterbridge," Solomon Longways replied with terminative emphasis, as if the fact of his ignorance of Mrs. Henchard were sufficient to deprive her history of all interest. "But I know that 'a's a banded teetotaller, and that if any of his men be ever so little overtook by a drop he's down upon 'em as stern as the Lord upon the jovial Jews."

"Has he many men, then?" said Elizabeth-Jane.

"Many! Why, my good maid, he's the powerfullest member of the Town Council, and quite a principal man in the country round besides. Never a big dealing in wheat, barley, oats, hay, roots, and suchlike but Henchard's got a hand in it. Ay, and he'll go into other things too; and that's where he makes his mistake. He worked his way up from nothing when 'a came here; and now he's a pillar of the town. Not but what he's been shaken a little to-year about this bad corn he has supplied in his contracts. I've seen the sun rise over Durnover Moor these nine-and-sixty year, and though Mr. Henchard has never cussed me unfairly ever since I've worked for'n, seeing I be but a little small man, I must say that I have never before tasted such rough bread as has been made from Henchard's wheat lately. 'Tis that growed out that ye could a'most call it malt, and there's a list at bottom o' the loaf as thick as the sole of one's shoe."

The band now struck up another melody, and by the time it was ended the dinner was over, and speeches began to be made. The evening being calm, and the windows still open, these orations could be distinctly heard. Henchard's voice arose above the rest; he was telling a story of his hay-dealing experiences, in which he had outwitted a sharper who had been bent upon outwitting him.

"Ha-ha-ha!" responded his audience at the upshot of the story; and hilarity was general till a new voice arose with, "This is all very well; but how about the bad bread?"

It came from the lower end of the table, where there sat a group of minor tradesmen who, although part of the company, appeared to be a little below the social level of the others; and who seemed to nourish a certain independence of opinion, and carry on discussions not quite in harmony with those at the head; just as the west end of a church is sometimes persistently found to sing out of time and tune with the leading spirits in the chancel.

This interruption about the bad bread afforded infinite satisfaction to the loungers outside, several of whom were in the mood which finds its pleasure in others' discomfiture; and hence they echoed pretty freely, "Hey! How about the bad bread, Mr. Mayor?" Moreover, feeling none of the restraints of those who shared the feast, they could afford to add, "You rather ought to tell the story o' that, sir!"

The interruption was sufficient to compel the Mayor to notice it.

"Well, I admit that the wheat turned out badly," he said. "But I was taken in in buying it as much as the bakers who bought it o' me."

"And the poor folk who had to eat it whether or no," said the inharmonious man outside the window.

Henchard's face darkened. There was temper under the thin bland surface—the temper which, artificially intensified, had banished a wife nearly a score of years before.

"You must make allowances for the accidents of a large business," he said. "You must bear in mind that the weather just at the harvest of that corn was worse than we have known it for years. However, I have mended my arrangements on account o't. Since I have found my business too large to be well looked after by myself alone, I have advertised for a thorough good man as manager of the corn department. When I've got him you will find these mistakes will no longer occur—matters will be better looked into."

"But what are you going to do to repay us for the past?" enquired the man who had before spoken, and who seemed to be a baker or miller. "Will you replace the grown flour we've still got by sound grain?"

Henchard's face had become still more stern at these interruptions, and he drank from his tumbler of water as if to calm himself or gain time. Instead of vouchsafing a direct reply, he stiffly observed—

"If anybody will tell me how to turn grown wheat into wholesome wheat I'll take it back with pleasure. But it can't be done."

Henchard was not to be drawn again. Having said this, he sat down.

VI

NOW THE GROUP OUTSIDE THE WINDOW HAD WITHIN THE LAST FEW MINUTES BEEN REinforced by new arrivals, some of them respectable shopkeepers and their assistants, who had come out for a whiff of air after putting up the shutters for the night; some of them of a lower class. Distinct from either there appeared a stranger—a young man of remarkably pleasant aspect—who carried in his hand a carpet-bag of the smart floral pattern prevalent in such articles at that time.

He was fair and ruddy, bright-eyed, and slight in build. He might possibly have passed by without stopping at all, or at most for half a minute to glance in at the scene, had not his advent coincided with the discussion on corn and bread; in which event this history had never been enacted. But the subject seemed to arrest him, and he whispered some enquiries of the other bystanders, and remained listening.

When he heard Henchard's closing words, "It can't be done," he smiled impulsively, drew out his pocket-book, and wrote down a few words by the aid of the light in the window. He tore out the leaf, folded and directed it, and seemed about to throw it in through the open sash upon the dining-table; but, on second thoughts, edged himself through the loiterers, till he reached the door of the hotel, where one of the waiters who had been serving inside was now idly leaning against the doorpost.

"Give this to the Mayor at once," he said, handing in his hasty note.

Elizabeth-Jane had seen his movements and heard the words, which attracted her both by their subject and by their accent—a strange one for those parts. It was quaint and northerly.

The waiter took the note, while the young stranger continued—

"And can ye tell me of a respectable hotel that's a little more moderate than this?"

The waiter glanced indifferently up and down the street.

"They say the Three Mariners, just below here, is a very good place," he languidly answered; "but I have never stayed there myself."

The Scotchman, as he seemed to be, thanked him, and strolled on in the direction of the Three Mariners aforesaid, apparently more concerned about the question of an inn than about the fate of his note, now that the momentary impulse of writing it was over. While he was disappearing slowly down the street the waiter left the door, and Elizabeth-Jane saw with some interest the note brought into the dining-room and handed to the Mayor.

Henchard looked at it carelessly, unfolded it with one hand, and glanced it through. Thereupon it was curious to note an unexpected effect. The nettled, clouded aspect which had held possession of his face since the subject of his corn-dealings had been broached, changed itself into one of arrested attention. He read the note slowly, and fell into thought, not moody, but fitfully intense, as that of a man who has been captured by an idea.

By this time toasts and speeches had given place to songs, the wheat subject being quite forgotten. Men were putting their heads together in twos and threes, telling good stories, with pantomimic laughter which reached convulsive grimace. Some were beginning to look as if they did not know how they had come there, what they had come for, or how they were going to get home again; and provisionally sat on with a dazed smile. Square-built men showed a tendency to become hunchbacks; men with a dignified presence lost it in a curious obliquity of figure, in which their features grew disarranged and one-sided; whilst the heads of a few who had dined with extreme thoroughness were somehow sinking into their shoulders, the corners of their mouth and eyes being bent upwards by the subsidence. Only Henchard did not conform to these flexuous changes; he remained stately and vertical, silently thinking.

The clock struck nine. Elizabeth-Jane turned to her companion. "The evening is drawing on, mother," she said. "What do you propose to do?"

She was surprised to find how irresolute her mother had become. "We must get a place to lie down in," she murmured. "I have seen—Mr. Henchard; and that's all I wanted to do."

"That's enough for to-night, at any rate," Elizabeth-Jane replied soothingly. "We can think to-morrow what is best to do about him. The question now is—is it not?—how shall we find a lodging?"

As her mother did not reply Elizabeth-Jane's mind reverted to the words of the waiter, that the Three Mariners was an inn of moderate charges. A recommendation good for one person was probably good for another. "Let's go where the young man has gone to," she said. "He is respectable. What do you say?"

Her mother assented, and down the street they went.

In the meantime the Mayor's thoughtfulness, engendered by the note as stated, continued to hold him in abstraction; till, whispering to his neighbour to take his place, he found opportunity to leave the chair. This was just after the departure of his wife and Elizabeth.

Outside the door of the assembly-room he saw the waiter, and beckoning to him, asked who had brought the note which had been handed in a quarter of an hour before.

"A young man, sir—a sort of traveller. He was a Scotchman seemingly."

"Did he say how he had got it?"

"He wrote it himself, sir, as he stood outside the window."

"Oh—wrote it himself. . . . Is the young man in the hotel?"

"No, sir. He went to the Three Mariners, I believe."

The mayor walked up and down the vestibule of the hotel with his hands under his coat-tails, as if he were merely seeking a cooler atmosphere than that of the room he had quitted. But there could be no doubt that he was in reality still possessed to the full by the new idea, whatever that might be. At length he went back to the door of the dining-room, paused, and found that the songs, toasts, and conversation were proceeding quite satisfactorily without his presence. The Corporation, private residents, and major and minor tradesmen had, in fact, gone in for comforting beverages to such an extent that they had quite forgotten, not only the Mayor, but all those vast, political, religious, and social differences which they felt necessary to maintain in the daytime, and which separated them like iron grills. Seeing this the Mayor took his hat, and when the waiter had helped him on with a thin holland overcoat, went out and stood under the portico.

Very few persons were now in the street; and his eyes, by a sort of attraction, turned and dwelt upon a spot about a hundred yards further down. It was the house to which the writer of the note had gone—the Three Mariners—whose two prominent gables, bow-window, and passage-light could be seen from where he stood. Having kept his eyes on it for a while, he strolled in that direction.

This ancient house of accommodation for man and beast, now, unfortunately, pulled down, was built of mellow sandstone, with mullioned windows of the same material, markedly out of perpendicular from the settlement of foundations. The bay-window projecting into the street, whose interior was so popular among the frequenters of the inn, was closed with shutters, in each of which appeared a heart-shaped aperture, somewhat more attenuated in the right and left ventricles than is seen in Nature. Inside these illuminated holes, at a distance of about three inches, were ranged at this hour, as every passer knew, the ruddy polls of Billy Wills the glazier, Smart the shoemaker, Buzzford the general dealer, and others of a secondary set of worthies, of a grade somewhat below that of the diners at the King's Arms, each with his yard of clay.

A four-centred Tudor arch was over the entrance, and over the arch the signboard,

now visible in the rays of an opposite lamp. Hereon the Mariners, who had been represented by the artist as persons of two dimensions only—in other words, flat as a shadow—
were standing in a row in paralyzed attitudes. Being on the sunny side of the street the
three comrades had suffered largely from warping, splitting, fading, and shrinkage, so that
they were but a half-invisible film upon the reality of the grain, and knots, and nails, which
composed the signboard. As a matter of fact, this state of things was not so much owing
to Stannidge the landlord's neglect, as from the lack of a painter in Casterbridge who
would undertake to reproduce the features of men so traditional.

A long, narrow, dimly-lit passage gave access to the inn, within which passage the
horses going to their stalls at the back, and the coming and departing human guests,
rubbed shoulders indiscriminately, the latter running no slight risk of having their toes
trodden upon by the animals. The good stabling and the good ale of the Mariners, though
somewhat difficult to reach on account of there being but this narrow way to both, were
nevertheless perseveringly sought out by the sagacious old heads who knew what was
what in Casterbridge.

Henchard stood without the inn for a few instants; then lowering the dignity of his
presence as much as possible by buttoning the brown holland coat over his shirt-front,
and in other ways toning himself down to his ordinary everyday appearance, he entered
the inn-door.

VII

ELIZABETH-JANE AND HER MOTHER HAD ARRIVED SOME TWENTY MINUTES EARLIER.
Outside the house they had stood and considered whether even this homely place,
though recommended as moderate, might not be too serious in its prices for their light
pockets. Finally, however, they had found courage to enter, and duly met Stannidge the
landlord; a silent man, who drew and carried frothing measures to this room and to that,
shoulder to shoulder with his waiting-maids—a stately slowness, however, entering into
his ministrations by contrast with theirs, as became one whose service was somewhat optional. It would have been altogether optional but for the orders of the landlady, a person
who sat in the bar, corporeally motionless, but with a flitting eye and quick ear, with which
she observed and heard through the open door and hatchway the pressing needs of customers whom her husband overlooked though close at hand. Elizabeth and her mother
were passively accepted as sojourners, and shown to a small bedroom under one of the
gables, where they sat down.

The principle of the inn seemed to be to compensate for the antique awkwardness,
crookedness, and obscurity of the passages, floors, and windows, by quantities of clean
linen spread about everywhere, and this had a dazzling effect upon the travellers.

" 'Tis too good for us—we can't meet it!" said the elder woman, looking round the
apartment with misgiving as soon as they were left alone.

"I fear it is, too," said Elizabeth. "But we must be respectable."

"We must pay our way even before we must be respectable," replied her mother. "Mr.

Henchard is too high for us to make ourselves known to him, I much fear; so we've only our own pockets to depend on."

"I know what I'll do," said Elizabeth-Jane, after an interval of waiting, during which their needs seemed quite forgotten under the press of business below. And leaving the room, she descended the stairs and penetrated to the bar.

If there was one good thing more than another which characterised this single-hearted girl, it was a willingness to sacrifice her personal comfort and dignity to the common weal.

"As you seem busy here to-night, and mother's not well off, might I take out part of our accommodation by helping?" she asked of the landlady.

The latter, who remained as fixed in the arm-chair as if she had been melted into it when in a liquid state, and could not now be unstuck, looked the girl up and down enquiringly, with her hands on the chair-arms. Such arrangements as the one Elizabeth proposed were not uncommon in country villages; but, though Casterbridge was old-fashioned, the custom was well-nigh obsolete here. The mistress of the house, however, was an easy woman to strangers, and she made no objection. Thereupon Elizabeth, being instructed by nods and motions from the taciturn landlord as to where she could find the different things, trotted up and downstairs with materials for her own and her parent's meal.

While she was doing this, the wood partition in the centre of the house thrilled to its centre with the tugging of a bell-pull upstairs. A bell below tinkled a note that was feebler in sound than the twanging of wires and cranks that had produced it.

" 'Tis the Scotch gentleman," said the landlady omnisciently; and turning her eyes to Elizabeth, "Now then, can you go and see if his supper is on the tray? If it is you can take it up to him. The front-room over this."

Elizabeth-Jane, though hungry, willingly postponed serving herself a while, and applied to the cook in the kitchen whence she brought forth the tray of supper viands, and proceeded with it upstairs to the apartment indicated. The accommodation of the Three Mariners was far from spacious, despite the fair area of ground it covered. The room demanded by intrusive beams and rafters, partitions, passages, staircases, disused ovens, settles, and four-posters, left comparatively small quarters for human beings. Moreover, this being at a time before home-brewing was abandoned by the smaller victuallers, and a house in which the twelve-bushel strength was still religiously adhered to by the landlord in his ale, the quality of the liquor was the chief attraction of the premises, so that everything had to make way for utensils and operations in connection therewith. Thus Elizabeth found that the Scotchman was located in a room quite close to the small one that had been allotted to herself and her mother.

When she entered, nobody was present but the young man himself—the same whom she had seen lingering without the windows of the King's Arms Hotel. He was now idly reading a copy of the local paper, and was hardly conscious of her entry, so that she looked at him quite coolly, and saw how his forehead shone where the light caught it, and how nicely his hair was cut, and the sort of velvet-pile or down that was on the skin at the back of his neck, and how his cheek was so truly curved as to be part of a globe, and how clearly drawn were the lids and lashes which hid his bent eyes.

She set down the tray, spread his supper, and went away without a word. On her arrival below the landlady, who was as kind as she was fat and lazy, saw that Elizabeth-Jane was rather tired, though in her earnestness to be useful she was waiving her own needs altogether. Mrs. Stannidge thereupon said, with a considerate peremptoriness, that she and her mother had better take their own suppers if they meant to have any.

Elizabeth fetched their simple provisions, as she had fetched the Scotchman's, and went up to the little chamber where she had left her mother, noiselessly pushing open the door with the edge of the tray. To her surprise her mother, instead of being reclined on the bed where she had left her was in an erect position, with lips parted. At Elizabeth's entry she lifted her finger.

The meaning of this was soon apparent. The room allotted to the two women had at one time served as a dressing-room to the Scotchman's chamber, as was evidenced by signs of a door of communication between them—now screwed up, and pasted over with the wall paper. But, as is frequently the case with hotels of far higher pretensions than the Three Mariners, every word spoken in either of these rooms was distinctly audible in the other. Such sounds came through now.

Thus silently conjured, Elizabeth deposited the tray, and her mother whispered as she drew near, " 'Tis he."

"Who?" said the girl.

"The Mayor."

The tremors in Susan Henchard's tone might have led any person, but one so perfectly unsuspicious of the truth as the girl was, to surmise some closer connection than the admitted simple kinship as a means of accounting for them.

Two men were indeed talking in the adjoining chamber, the young Scotchman and Henchard, who, having entered the inn while Elizabeth-Jane was in the kitchen waiting for the supper, had been deferentially conducted upstairs by host Stannidge himself. The girl noiselessly laid out their little meal, and beckoned to her mother to join her, which Mrs. Henchard mechanically did, her attention being fixed on the conversation through the door.

"I merely strolled in on my way home to ask you a question about something that has excited my curiosity," said the Mayor, with careless geniality. "But I see you have not finished supper."

"Ay, but I will be done in a little! Ye needn't go, sir. Take a seat. I've almost done, and it makes no difference at all."

Henchard seemed to take the seat offered, and in a moment he resumed: "Well, first I should ask, did you write this?" A rustling of paper followed.

"Yes, I did," said the Scotchman.

"Then," said Henchard, "I am under the impression that we have met by accident while waiting for the morning to keep an appointment with each other? My name is Henchard; ha'n't you replied to an advertisement for a corn-factor's manager that I put into the paper—ha'n't you come here to see me about it?"

"No," said the Scotchman, with some surprise.

"Surely you are the man," went on Henchard insistingly, "who arranged to come and see me? Joshua, Joshua, Jipp—Jopp—what was his name?"

"You're wrong!" said the young man. "My name is Donald Farfrae. It is true I am in the corren trade—but I have replied to no advairrtisment, and arranged to see no one. I am on my way to Bristol—from there to the other side of the warrld, to try my fortune in the great wheat-growing districts of the West! I have some inventions useful to the trade, and there is no scope for developing them heere."

"To America—well, well," said Henchard, in a tone of disappointment, so strong as to make itself felt like a damp atmosphere. "And yet I could have sworn you were the man!"

The Scotchman murmured another negative, and there was a silence, till Henchard resumed: "Then I am truly and sincerely obliged to you for the few words you wrote on that paper."

"It was nothing, sir."

"Well, it has a great importance for me just now. This row about my grown wheat, which I declare to Heaven I didn't know to be bad till the people came complaining, has put me to my wits' end. I've some hundreds of quarters of it on hand; and if your renovating process will make it wholesome, why, you can see what a quag 'twould get me out of. I saw in a moment there might be truth in it. But I should like to have it proved; and of course you don't care to tell the steps of the process sufficiently for me to do that, without my paying ye well for't first."

The young man reflected a moment or two. "I don't know that I have any objection," he said. "I'm going to another country, and curing bad corn is not the line I'll take up there. Yes, I'll tell ye the whole of it—you'll make more out of it heere than I will in a foreign country. Just look heere a minute, sir. I can show ye by a sample in my carpet-bag."

The click of a lock followed, and there was a sifting and rustling; then a discussion about so many ounces to the bushel, and drying, and refrigerating, and so on.

"These few grains will be sufficient to show ye with," came in the young fellow's voice; and after a pause, during which some operation seemed to be intently watched by them both, he exclaimed, "There, now, do you taste that."

"It's complete!—quite restored, or—well—nearly."

"Quite enough restored to make good seconds out of it," said the Scotchman. "To fetch it back entirely is impossible; Nature won't stand so much as that, but heere you go a great way towards it. Well, sir, that's the process; I don't value it, for it can be but of little use in countries where the weather is more settled than in ours; and I'll be only too glad if it's of service to you."

"But hearken to me," pleaded Henchard. "My business, you know, is in corn and in hay; but I was brought up as a hay-trusser simply, and hay is what I understand best, though I now do more in corn than in the other. If you'll accept the place, you shall manage the corn branch entirely, and receive a commission in addition to salary."

"You're liberal—very liberal; but no, no—I cannet!" the young man still replied, with some distress in his accents.

"So be it!" said Henchard conclusively. "Now—to change the subject—one good turn deserves another; don't stay to finish that miserable supper. Come to my house, I can find something better for ye than cold ham and ale."

Donald Farfrae was grateful—said he feared he must decline—that he wished to leave early next day.

"Very well," said Henchard quickly, "please yourself. But I tell you, young man, if this holds good for the bulk, as it has done for the sample, you have saved my credit, stranger though you be. What shall I pay you for this knowledge?"

"Nothing at all, nothing at all. It may not prove necessary to ye to use it often, and I don't value it at all. I thought I might just as well let ye know, as you were in a difficulty, and they were harrd upon ye."

Henchard paused. "I shan't soon forget this," he said. "And from a stranger! . . . I couldn't believe you were not the man I had engaged! Says I to myself, 'He knows who I am, and recommends himself by this stroke.' And yet it turns out, after all, that you are not the man who answered my advertisement, but a stranger!"

"Ay, ay; that's so," said the young man.

Henchard again suspended his words, and then his voice came thoughtfully: "Your forehead, Farfrae, is something like my poor brother's—now dead and gone; and the nose, too, isn't unlike his. You must be, what—five foot nine, I reckon? I am six foot one and a half out of my shoes. But what of that? In my business, 'tis true that strength and bustle build up a firm. But judgment and knowledge are what keep it established. Unluckily, I am bad at science, Farfrae; bad at figures—a rule o' thumb sort of man. You are just the reverse—I can see that. I have been looking for such as you these two year, and yet you are not for me. Well, before I go, let me ask this: Though you are not the young man I thought you were, what's the difference? Can't ye stay just the same? Have you really made up your mind about this American notion? I won't mince matters. I feel you would be invaluable to me—that needn't be said—and if you will bide and be my manager, I will make it worth your while."

"My plans are fixed," said the young man, in negative tones. "I have formed a scheme, and so we need na say any more about it. But will you not drink with me, sir? I find this Casterbridge ale warreming to the stomach."

"No, no; I fain would, but I can't," said Henchard gravely, the scraping of his chair informing the listeners that he was rising to leave. "When I was a young man I went in for that sort of thing too strong—far too strong—and was well-nigh ruined by it! I did a deed on account of it which I shall be ashamed of to my dying day. It made such an impression on me that I swore, there and then, that I'd drink nothing stronger than tea for as many years as I was old that day. I have kept my oath; and though, Farfrae, I am sometimes that dry in the dog days that I could drink a quarter-barrel to the pitching, I think o' my oath, and touch no strong drink at all."

"I'll no' press ye, sir—I'll no' press ye. I respect your vow."

"Well, I shall get a manager somewhere, no doubt," said Henchard, with strong feeling in his tones. "But it will be long before I see one that would suit me so well!"

The young man appeared much moved by Henchard's warm convictions of his value. He was silent till they reached the door. "I wish I could stay—sincerely I would like to," he replied. "But no—it cannet be! it cannet! I want to see the warrld."

VIII

T HUS THEY PARTED; AND ELIZABETH-JANE AND HER MOTHER REMAINED EACH IN HER thoughts over their meal, the mother's face being strangely bright since Henchard's avowal of shame for a past action. The quivering of the partition to its core presently denoted that Donald Farfrae had again rung his bell, no doubt to have his supper removed; for humming a tune, and walking up and down, he seemed to be attracted by the lively bursts of conversation and melody from the general company below. He sauntered out upon the landing, and descended the staircase.

When Elizabeth-Jane had carried down his supper tray, and also that used by her mother and herself, she found the bustle of serving to be at its height below, as it always was at this hour. The young woman shrank from having anything to do with the ground floor serving, and crept silently about observing the scene—so new to her, fresh from the seclusion of a seaside cottage. In the general sitting-room, which was large, she remarked the two or three dozen strong-backed chairs that stood round against the wall, each fitted with its genial occupant; the sanded floor; the black settle which, projecting endwise from the wall within the door, permitted Elizabeth to be a spectator of all that went on without herself being particularly seen.

The young Scotchman had just joined the guests. These, in addition to the respectable master-tradesmen occupying the seats of privileges in the bow-window and its neighbourhood, included an inferior set at the unlighted end, whose seats were mere benches against the wall, and who drank from cups instead of from glasses. Among the latter she noticed some of those personages who had stood outside the windows of the King's Arms.

Behind their backs was a small window, with a wheel ventilator in one of the panes, which would suddenly start off spinning with a jingling sound, as suddenly stop, and as suddenly start again.

While thus furtively making her survey, the opening words of a song greeted her ears from the front of the settle, in a melody and accent of peculiar charm. There had been some singing before she came down; and now the Scotchman had made himself so soon at home that, at the request of some of the master-tradesmen, he, too, was favouring the room with a ditty.

Elizabeth-Jane was fond of music; she could not help pausing to listen; and the longer she listened the more she was enraptured. She had never heard any singing like this; and it was evident that the majority of the audience had not heard such frequently, for they were attentive to a much greater degree than usual. They neither whispered, nor drank, nor dipped their pipe-stems in their ale to moisten them, nor pushed the mug to their neighbours. The singer himself grew emotional, till she could imagine a tear in his eye as the words went on:—

> *It's hame, and it's hame, hame fain would I be,*
> *O hame, hame, hame to my ain countree!*
> *There's an eye that ever weeps, and a fair face will be fain,*
> *As I pass through Annan Water with my bonnie bands again;*
> *When the flower is in the bud, and the leaf upon the tree,*
> *The lark shall sing me hame to my ain countree!*

There was a burst of applause, and a deep silence which was even more eloquent than the applause. It was of such a kind that the snapping of a pipe-stem too long for him by old Solomon Longways, who was one of those gathered at the shady end of the room, seemed a harsh and irreverent act. Then the ventilator in the window-pane spasmodically started off for a new spin, and the pathos of Donald's song was temporarily effaced.

" 'Twas not amiss—not at all amiss!" muttered Christopher Coney, who was also present. And removing his pipe a finger's breadth from his lips, he said aloud, "Draw on with the next verse, young gentleman, please."

"Yes. Let's have it again, stranger," said the glazier, a stout, bucket-headed man, with a white apron rolled up round his waist. "Folks don't lift up their hearts like that in this part of the world." And turning aside, he said in undertones, "Who is the young man?—Scotch, d'ye say?"

"Yes, straight from the mountains of Scotland, I believe," replied Coney.

Young Farfrae repeated the last verse. It was plain that nothing so pathetic had been heard at the Three Mariners for a considerable time. The difference of accent, the excitability of the singer, the intense local feeling, and the seriousness with which he worked himself up to a climax, surprised this set of worthies, who were only too prone to shut up their emotions with caustic words.

"Danged if our country down here is worth singing about like that!" continued the glazier, as the Scotchman again melodised with a dying fall, "My ain countree!" "When you take away from among us the fools and the rogues, and the lammigers, and the wanton hussies, and the slatterns, and such like, there's cust few left to ornament a song with in Casterbridge, or the country round."

"True," said Buzzford, the dealer, looking at the grain of the table. "Casterbridge is a old, hoary place o' wickedness, by all account. 'Tis recorded in history that we rebelled against the King one or two hundred years ago, in the time of the Romans, and that lots of us was hanged on Gallows Hill, and quartered, and our different jints sent about the country like butcher's meat; and for my part I can well believe it."

"What did ye come away from yer own country for, young maister, if ye be so wownded about it?" enquired Christopher Coney, from the background, with the tone of a man who preferred the original subject. "Faith, it wasn't worth your while on our account, for as Maister Billy Wills says, we be bruckle folk here—the best o' us hardly honest sometimes, what with hard winters, and so many mouths to fill, and God-a'mighty sending his little taties so terrible small to fill 'em with. We don't think about flowers and fair faces, not we—except in the shape o' cauliflowers and pigs' chaps."

"But, no!" said Donald Farfrae, gazing round into their faces with earnest concern; "the best of ye hardly honest—not that surely? None of ye has been stealing what didn't belong to him?"

"Lord! no, no!" said Solomon Longways, smiling grimly. "That's only his random way o' speaking. 'A was always such a man of underthoughts." (And reprovingly towards Christopher): "Don't ye be so over-familiar with a gentleman that ye know nothing of—and that's travelled a'most from the North Pole."

Christopher Coney was silenced, and as he could get no public sympathy, he mumbled his feelings to himself: "Be dazed, if I loved my country half as well as the young feller do, I'd live by claning my neighbour's pigsties afore I'd go away! For my part I've no more love for my country than I have for Botany Bay!"

"Come," said Longways; "let the young man draw onward with his ballet, or we shall be here all night."

"That's all of it," said the singer apologetically.

"Soul of my body, then we'll have another!" said the general dealer.

"Can you turn a strain to the ladies, sir?" enquired a fat woman with a figured purple apron, the waist-string of which was overhung so far by her sides as to be invisible.

"Let him breathe—let him breathe, Mother Cuxsom. He hain't got his second wind yet," said the master glazier.

"Oh yes, but I have!" exclaimed the young man; and he at once rendered "O Nannie" with faultless modulations, and another or two of the like sentiment, winding up at their earnest request with "Auld Lang Syne."

By this time he had completely taken possession of the hearts of the Three Mariners' inmates, including even old Coney. Notwithstanding an occasional odd gravity which awoke their sense of the ludicrous for the moment, they began to view him through a golden haze which the tone of his mind seemed to raise around him. Casterbridge had sentiment— Casterbridge had romance; but this stranger's sentiment was of differing quality. Or rather, perhaps, the difference was mainly superficial; he was to them like the poet of a new school who takes his contemporaries by storm; who is not really new, but is the first to articulate what all his listeners have felt, though but dumbly till then.

The silent landlord came and leant over the settle while the young man sang; and even Mrs. Stannidge managed to unstick herself from the frame-work of her chair in the bar, and get as far as the doorpost, which movement she accomplished by rolling herself round, as a cask is trundled on the chine by a drayman without losing much of its perpendicular.

"And are you going to bide in Casterbridge, sir?" she asked.

"Ah—no!" said the Scotchman, with melancholy fatality in his voice, "I'm only passing thirrough! I am on my way to Bristol, and on frae there to foreign parts."

"We be truly sorry to hear it," said Solomon Longways. "We can ill afford to lose tuneful wynd-pipes like yours when they fall among us. And verily, to mak' acquaintance with a man a-come from so far, from the land o' perpetual snow, as we may say, where wolves and wild boars and other dangerous animalcules be as common as blackbirds here-about—why, 'tis a thing we can't do everyday; and there's good sound information for bide-at-homes like we when such a man opens his mouth."

"Nay, but ye mistake my country," said the young man, looking round upon them with tragic fixity, till his eye lighted up and his cheek kindled with a sudden enthusiasm to right their errors. "There are not perpetual snow and wolves at all in it!—except snow in winter, and—well—a little in summer just sometimes, and a 'gaberlunzie' or two stalking about here and there, if ye may call them dangerous. Eh, but you should take a summer jarreny to Edinboro', and Arthur's Seat, and all round there, and then go on to the lochs, and all the Highland scenery—in May and June—and you would never say 'tis the land of wolves and perpetual snow!"

"Of course not—it stands to reason," said Buzzford. " 'Tis barren ignorance that leads to such words. He's a simple home-spun man, that never was fit for good company—think nothing of him, sir."

"And do ye carry your flock bed, and your quilt, and your crock, and your bit of chiney? or do ye go in bare bones, as I may say?" enquired Christopher Coney.

"I've sent on my luggage—though it isn't much; for the voyage is long." Donald's eyes dropped into a remote gaze as he added: "But I said to myself, 'Never a one of the prizes of life will I come by unless I undertake it!' and I decided to go."

A general sense of regret, in which Elizabeth-Jane shared not least, made itself apparent in the company. As she looked at Farfrae from the back of the settle, she decided that his statements showed him to be no less thoughtful than his fascinating melodies revealed him to be cordial and impassioned. She admired the serious light in which he looked at serious things. He had seen no jest in ambiguities and roguery, as the Casterbridge toss-pots had done; and rightly not—there was none. She disliked those wretched humours of Christopher Coney and his tribe; and he did not appreciate them. He seemed to feel exactly as she felt about life and its surroundings—that they were a tragical, rather than a comical, thing; that though one could be gay on occasion, moments of gaiety were interludes, and no part of the actual drama. It was extraordinary how similar their views were.

Though it was still early, the young Scotchman expressed his wish to retire, whereupon the landlady whispered to Elizabeth to run upstairs and turn down his bed. She took a candlestick and proceeded on her mission, which was the act of a few moments only. When, candle in hand, she reached the top of the stairs on her way down again, Mr. Farfrae was at the foot coming up. She could not very well retreat; they met and passed in the turn of the staircase.

She must have appeared interesting in some way—notwithstanding her plain dress—or rather, possibly, in consequence of it, for she was a girl characterised by earnestness and soberness of mien, with which simple drapery accorded well. Her face flushed, too, at the slight awkwardness of the meeting, and she passed him with her eyes bent on the candle-flame that she carried just below her nose. Thus it happened that when confronting her he smiled; and then, with the manner of a temporarily light-hearted man, who has started himself on a flight of song whose momentum he cannot readily check, he softly tuned an old ditty that she seemed to suggest—

> As I came in by my bower door,
> As day was waxin' wearie,
> Oh wha came tripping down the stair
> But bonnie Peg my dearie.

Elizabeth-Jane, rather disconcerted, hastened on; and the Scotchman's voice died away, humming more of the same within the closed door of his room.

Here the scene and sentiment ended for the present. When, soon after, the girl rejoined her mother, the latter was still in thought—on quite another matter than a young man's song.

"We've made a mistake," she whispered (that the Scotchman might not overhear). "On no account ought ye to have helped serve here to-night. Not because of ourselves, but for the sake of *him*. If he should befriend us, and take us up, and then find out what you did when staying here, 'twould grieve and wound his natural pride as Mayor of the town."

Elizabeth, who would perhaps have been more alarmed at this than her mother had she known the real relationship, was not much disturbed about it as things stood. Her "he" was another man than her poor mother's. "For myself," she said, "I didn't at all mind waiting a little upon him. He's so respectable, and educated—far above the rest of 'em in the inn. They thought him very simple not to know their grim broad way of talking about themselves here. But of course he didn't know—he was too refined in his mind to know such things!" Thus she earnestly pleaded.

Meanwhile, the "he" of her mother was not so far away as even they thought. After leaving the Three Mariners he had sauntered up and down the empty High Street, passing and repassing the inn in his promenade. When the Scotchman sang, his voice had reached Henchard's ears through the heart-shaped holes in the window-shutters, and had led him to pause outside them a long while.

"To be sure, to be sure, how that fellow does draw me!" he had said to himself. "I suppose 'tis because I'm so lonely. I'd have given him a third share in the business to have stayed!"

IX

WHEN ELIZABETH-JANE OPENED THE HINGED CASEMENT NEXT MORNING THE MELLOW air brought in the feel of imminent autumn almost as distinctly as if she had been in the remotest hamlet. Casterbridge was the complement of the rural life around; not its urban opposite. Bees and butterflies in the corn-fields at the top of the town, who desired to get to the meads at the bottom, took no circuitous course, but flew straight down High Street without any apparent consciousness that they were traversing strange latitudes. And in autumn airy spheres of thistledown floated into the same street, lodged upon the shop fronts, blew into drains; and innumerable tawny and yellow leaves skimmed along the pavement, and stole through people's doorways into their passages with a hesitating scratch on the floor, like the skirts of timid visitors.

Hearing voices, one of which was close at hand, she withdrew her head and glanced from behind the window-curtains. Mr. Henchard—now habited no longer as a great personage, but as a thriving man of business—was pausing on his way up the middle of the street, and the Scotchman was looking from the window adjoining her own. Henchard, it appeared, had gone a little way past the inn before he had noticed his acquaintance of the previous evening. He came back a few steps, Donald Farfrae opening the window further.

"And you are off soon, I suppose?" said Henchard upwards.

"Yes—almost this moment, sir," said the other. "Maybe I'll walk on till the coach makes up on me."

"Which way?"

"The way ye are going."

"Then shall we walk together to the top o' town?"

"If ye'll wait a minute," said the Scotchman.

In a few minutes the latter emerged, bag in hand. Henchard looked at the bag as at an enemy. It showed there was no mistake about the young man's departure. "Ah, my lad," he said, "you should have been a wise man, and have stayed with me."

"Yes, yes—it might have been wiser," said Donald, looking microscopically at the houses that were furthest off. "It is only telling ye the truth when I say my plans are vague."

They had by this time passed on from the precincts of the inn, and Elizabeth-Jane heard no more. She saw that they continued in conversation, Henchard turning to the other occasionally, and emphasizing some remark with a gesture. Thus they passed the King's Arms Hotel, the Market House, St. Peter's churchyard wall, ascending to the upper end of the long street till they were small as two grains of corn; when they bent suddenly to the right into the Bristol Road, and were out of view.

"He was a good man—and he's gone," she said to herself. "I was nothing to him, and there was no reason why he should have wished me good-bye."

The simple thought, with its latent sense of slight, had moulded itself out of the following little fact: when the Scotchman came out at the door he had by accident glanced up at her; and then he had looked away again without nodding, or smiling, or saying a word.

"You are still thinking, mother," she said, when she turned inwards.

"Yes; I am thinking of Mr. Henchard's sudden liking for that young man. He was always so. Now, surely, if he takes so warmly to people who are not related to him at all, may he not take as warmly to his own kin?"

While they debated this question a procession of five large waggons went past, laden with hay up to the bedroom windows. They came in from the country, and the steaming horses had probably been travelling a great part of the night. To the shaft of each hung a little board, on which was painted in white letters, "Henchard, corn-factor and hay-merchant." The spectacle renewed his wife's conviction that, for her daughter's sake, she should strain a point to rejoin him.

The discussion was continued during breakfast, and the end of it was that Mrs. Henchard decided, for good or for ill, to send Elizabeth-Jane with a message to Henchard, to the effect that his relative Susan, a sailor's widow, was in the town; leaving it to him to say whether or not he would recognise her. What had brought her to this determination were chiefly two things. He had been described as a lonely widower; and he had expressed shame for a past transaction of his life. There was promise in both.

"If he says no," she enjoined, as Elizabeth-Jane stood, bonnet on, ready to depart; "if he thinks it does not become the good position he has reached to in the town, to own—to let us call on him as—his distant kinfolk, say, 'Then, sir, we would rather not intrude; we will leave Casterbridge as quietly as we have come, and go back to our own country.' . . . I almost feel that I would rather he did say so, as I have not seen him for so many years, and we are so—little allied to him!"

"And if he say yes?" enquired the more sanguine one.

"In that case," answered Mrs. Henchard cautiously, "ask him to write me a note, saying when and how he will see us—or *me*."

Elizabeth-Jane went a few steps towards the landing. "And tell him," continued her mother, "that I fully know I have no claim upon him—that I am glad to find he is thriving; that I hope his life may be long and happy—there, go." Thus with a half-hearted willingness, a smothered reluctance, did the poor forgiving woman start her unconscious daughter on this errand.

It was about ten o'clock, and market-day, when Elizabeth paced up the High Street, in no great hurry; for to herself her position was only that of a poor relation deputed to hunt up a rich one. The front-doors of the private houses were mostly left open at this warm autumn time, no thought of umbrella stealers disturbing the minds of the placid burgesses.

Hence, through the long, straight, entrance passages thus unclosed could be seen, as through tunnels, the mossy gardens at the back, glowing with nasturtiums, fuchsias, scarlet geraniums, "bloody warriors," snapdragons, and dahlias, this floral blaze being backed by crusted grey stone-work remaining from a yet remoter Casterbridge than the venerable one visible in the street. The old-fashioned fronts of these houses, which had older than old-fashioned backs, rose sheer from the pavement, into which the bow-windows protruded like bastions, necessitating a pleasing *chassez-déchassez* movement to the time-pressed pedestrian at every few yards. He was bound also to evolve other Terpsichorean figures in respect of door-steps, scrapers, cellar-hatches, church buttresses, and the overhanging angles of walls which, originally unobtrusive, had become bow-legged and knock-kneed.

In addition to these fixed obstacles which spoke so cheerfully of individual unrestraint as to boundaries, movables occupied the path and roadway to a perplexing extent. First the vans of the carriers in and out of Casterbridge, who hailed from Mellstock, Weatherbury, The Hintocks, Sherton-Abbas, Kingsbere, Overcombe, and many other towns and villages round. Their owners were numerous enough to be regarded as a tribe, and had almost distinctiveness enough to be regarded as a race. Their vans had just arrived, and were drawn up on each side of the street in close file, so as to form at places a wall between the pavement and the roadway. Moreover every shop pitched out half its contents upon trestles and boxes on the kerb, extending the display each week a little further and further into the roadway, despite the expostulations of the two feeble old constables, until there remained but a tortuous defile for carriages down the centre of the street, which afforded fine opportunities for skill with the reins. Over the pavement on the sunny side of the way hung shopblinds so constructed as to give the passenger's hat a smart buffet off his head, as from the unseen hands of Cranstoun's Goblin Page, celebrated in romantic lore.

Horses for sale were tied in rows, their fore-legs on the pavement, their hind-legs in the street, in which position they occasionally nipped little boys by the shoulder who were passing to school. And any inviting recess in front of a house that had been modestly kept back from the general line was utilised by pig-dealers as a pen for their stock.

The yeomen, farmers, dairymen, and townsfolk, who came to transact business in these ancient streets, spoke in other ways than by articulation. Not to hear the words of your interlocutor in metropolitan centres is to know nothing of his meaning. Here the face, the arms, the hat, the stick, the body throughout spoke equally with the tongue. To express satisfaction the Casterbridge market-man added to his utterance a broadening of the cheeks, a crevicing of the eyes, a throwing back of the shoulders, which was intelligible from the other end of the street. If he wondered, though all Henchard's carts and waggons were rattling past him, you knew it from perceiving the inside of his crimson mouth, and a targetlike circling of his eyes. Deliberation caused sundry attacks on the moss of adjoining walls with the end of his stick, a change of his hat from the horizontal to the less so; a sense of tediousness announced itself in a lowering of the person by spreading the knees to a lozenge-shaped aperture and contorting the arms. Chicanery, subterfuge, had hardly a place in the streets of this honest borough to all appearance; and it was said that the lawyers in the Court House hard by occasionally threw in strong arguments for the other side out of pure generosity (though apparently by mischance) when advancing their own.

Thus Casterbridge was in most respects but the pole, focus, or nerve-knot of the surrounding country life; differing from the many manufacturing towns which are as foreign bodies set down, like boulders on a plain, in a green world with which they have nothing in common. Casterbridge lived by agriculture at one remove further from the fountainhead than the adjoining villages—no more. The townsfolk understood every fluctuation in the rustic's condition, for it affected their receipts as much as the labourer's; they entered into the troubles and joys which moved the aristocratic families ten miles round—for the same reason. And even at the dinner-parties of the professional families the subjects of discussion were corn, cattle-disease, sowing and reaping, fencing and planting; while politics were viewed by them less from their own standpoint of burgesses with rights and privileges than from the standpoint of their country neighbours.

All the venerable contrivances and confusions which delighted the eye by their quaintness, and in a measure reasonableness, in this rare old market-town, were metropolitan novelties to the unpractised eyes of Elizabeth-Jane, fresh from netting fish-seines in a seaside cottage. Very little enquiry was necessary to guide her footsteps. Henchard's house was one of the best, faced with dull red-and-grey old brick. The front door was open, and, as in other houses, she could see through the passage to the end of the garden—nearly a quarter of a mile off.

Mr. Henchard was not in the house, but in the store-yard. She was conducted into the mossy garden, and through a door in the wall, which was studded with rusty nails speaking of generations of fruit-trees that had been trained there. The door opened upon the yard, and here she was left to find him as she could. It was a place flanked by hay-barns, into which tons of fodder, all in trusses, were being packed from the waggons she had seen pass the inn that morning. On other sides of the yard were wooden granaries on stone staddles, to which access was given by Flemish ladders, and a store-house several floors high. Wherever the doors of these places were open, a closely packed throng of bursting wheat-sacks could be seen standing inside, with the air of awaiting a famine that would not come.

She wandered about this place, uncomfortably conscious of the impending interview, till she was quite weary of searching; she ventured to enquire of a boy in what quarter Mr. Henchard could be found. He directed her to an office which she had not seen before, and knocking at the door she was answered by a cry of "Come in."

Elizabeth turned the handle; and there stood before her, bending over some sample-bags on a table, not the corn-merchant, but the young Scotchman Mr. Farfrae—in the act of pouring some grains of wheat from one hand to the other. His hat hung on a peg behind him, and the roses of his carpet-bag glowed from the corner of the room.

Having toned her feelings and arranged words on her lips for Mr. Henchard, and for him alone, she was for the moment confounded.

"Yes, what it is?" said the Scotchman, like a man who permanently ruled there.

She said she wanted to see Mr. Henchard.

"Ah, yes; will you wait a minute? He's engaged just now," said the young man, apparently not recognizing her as the girl at the inn. He handed her a chair, bade her sit down and turned to his sample-bags again. While Elizabeth-Jane sits waiting in great amaze at the young man's presence we may briefly explain how he came there.

When the two new acquaintances had passed out of sight that morning towards the

Bath and Bristol road they went on silently, except for a few commonplaces, till they had gone down an avenue on the town walls called the Chalk Walk, leading to an angle where the North and West escarpments met. From this high corner of the square earthworks a vast extent of country could be seen. A footpath ran steeply down the green slope, conducting from the shady promenade on the walls to a road at the bottom of the scarp. It was by this path the Scotchman had to descend.

"Well, here's success to ye," said Henchard, holding out his right hand and leaning with his left upon the wicket which protected the descent. In the act there was the inelegance of one whose feelings are nipped and wishes defeated. "I shall often think of this time, and of how you came at the very moment to throw a light upon my difficulty."

Still holding the young man's hand he paused, and then added deliberately: "Now I am not the man to let a cause be lost for want of a word. And before ye are gone forever I'll speak. Once more, will ye stay? There it is, flat and plain. You can see that it isn't all selfishness that makes me press 'ee; for my business is not quite so scientific as to require an intellect entirely out of the common. Others would do for the place without doubt. Some selfishness perhaps there is, but there is more; it isn't for me to repeat what. Come bide with me—and name your own terms. I'll agree to 'em willingly and 'ithout a word of gainsaying; for, hang it, Farfrae, I like thee well!"

The young man's hand remained steady in Henchard's for a moment or two. He looked over the fertile country that stretched beneath them, then backward along the shaded walk reaching to the top of the town. His face flushed.

"I never expected this—I did not!" he said. "It's Providence! Should anyone go against it? No; I'll not go to America; I'll stay and be your man!"

His hand, which had lain lifeless in Henchard's, returned the latter's grasp.

"Done," said Henchard.

"Done," said Donald Farfrae.

The face of Mr. Henchard beamed forth a satisfaction that was almost fierce in its strength. "Now you are my friend!" he exclaimed. "Come back to my house; let's clinch it at once by clear terms, so as to be comfortable in our minds." Farfrae caught up his bag and retraced the North-West Avenue in Henchard's company as he had come. Henchard was all confidence now.

"I am the most distant fellow in the world when I don't care for a man," he said. "But when a man takes my fancy he takes it strong. Now I am sure you can eat another breakfast? You couldn't have eaten much so early, even if they had anything at that place to gi'e thee, which they hadn't; so come to my house and we will have a solid, staunch tuck-in, and settle terms in black-and-white if you like; though my word's my bond. I can always make a good meal in the morning. I've got a splendid cold pigeon-pie going just now. You can have some home-brewed if you want to, you know."

"It is too airly in the morning for that," said Farfrae with a smile.

"Well, of course, I didn't know. I don't drink it because of my oath, but I am obliged to brew for my workpeople."

Thus talking they returned, and entered Henchard's premises by the back way or traffic entrance. Here the matter was settled over the breakfast, at which Henchard heaped the young Scotchman's plate to a prodigal fulness. He would not rest satisfied till Farfrae had written for his luggage from Bristol, and despatched the letter to the post-office. When it was done this man of strong impulses declared that his new friend should take up his abode in his house—at least till some suitable lodgings could be found.

He then took Farfrae round and showed him the place, and the stores of grain, and other stock; and finally entered the offices where the younger of them has already been discovered by Elizabeth.

X

WHILE SHE STILL SAT UNDER THE SCOTCHMAN'S EYES A MAN CAME UP TO THE DOOR, reaching it as Henchard opened the door of the inner office to admit Elizabeth. The new-comer stepped forward like the quicker cripple at Bethesda, and entered in her stead. She could hear his words to Henchard: "Joshua Jopp, sir—by appointment—the new manager."

"The new manager!—he's in his office," said Henchard bluntly.

"In his office!" said the man, with a stultified air.

"I mentioned Thursday," said Henchard; "and as you did not keep your appointment, I have engaged another manager. At first I thought he must be you. Do you think I can wait when business is in question?"

"You said Thursday or Saturday, sir," said the new-comer, pulling out a letter.

"Well, you are too late," said the corn-factor. "I can say no more."

"You as good as engaged me," murmured the man.

"Subject to an interview," said Henchard. "I am sorry for you—very sorry indeed. But it can't be helped."

There was no more to be said, and the man came out, encountering Elizabeth-Jane in his passage. She could see that his mouth twitched with anger, and that bitter disappointment was written in his face everywhere.

Elizabeth-Jane now entered, and stood before the master of the premises. His dark pupils—which always seemed to have a red spark of light in them, though this could hardly be a physical fact—turned indifferently round under his dark brows until they rested on her figure. "Now then, what is it, my young woman?" he said blandly.

"Can I speak to you—not on business, sir?" said she.

"Yes—I suppose." He looked at her more thoughtfully.

"I am sent to tell you, sir," she innocently went on, "that a distant relative of yours by marriage, Susan Newson, a sailor's widow, is in the town; and to ask whether you would wish to see her."

The rich *rouge-et-noir* of his countenance underwent a slight change. "Oh—Susan is—still alive?" he asked with difficulty.

"Yes, sir."

"Are you her daughter?"

"Yes, sir—her only daughter."

"What—do you call yourself—your Christian name?"

"Elizabeth-Jane, sir."

"Newson?"

"Elizabeth-Jane Newson."

This at once suggested to Henchard that the transaction of his early married life at Weydon Fair was unrecorded in the family history. It was more than he could have expected. His wife had behaved kindly to him in return for his unkindness, and had never proclaimed her wrong to her child or to the world.

"I am—a good deal interested in your news," he said. "And as this is not a matter of business, but pleasure, suppose we go indoors."

It was with a gentle delicacy of manner, surprising to Elizabeth, that he showed her out of the office and through the outer room, where Donald Farfrae was overhauling bins and samples with the enquiring inspection of a beginner in charge. Henchard preceded her through the door in the wall to the suddenly changed scene of the garden and flowers, and onward into the house. The dining-room to which he introduced her still exhibited the remnants of the lavish breakfast laid for Farfrae. It was furnished to profusion with heavy mahogany furniture of the deepest red-Spanish hues. Pembroke tables, with leaves hanging so low that they well-nigh touched the floor, stood against the walls on legs and feet shaped like those of an elephant, and on one lay three huge folio volumes—a Family Bible, a "Josephus," and a "Whole Duty of Man." In the chimney-corner was a fire-grate with a fluted semi-circular back, having urns and festoons cast in relief thereon, and the chairs were of the kind which, since that day, has cast lustre upon the names of Chippendale and Sheraton, though, in point of fact, their patterns may have been such as those illustrious carpenters never saw or heard of.

"Sit down—Elizabeth-Jane—sit down," he said, with a shake in his voice as he uttered her name, and sitting down himself he allowed his hands to hang between his knees while he looked upon the carpet. "Your mother, then, is quite well?"

"She is rather worn out, sir, with travelling."

"A sailor's widow—when did he die?"

"Father was lost last spring."

Henchard winced at the word "father," thus applied. "Do you and she come from abroad—America or Australia?" he asked.

"No. We have been in England some years. I was twelve when we came here from Canada."

"Ah; exactly." By such conversation he discovered the circumstances which had enveloped his wife and her child in such total obscurity that he had long ago believed them to be in their graves. These things being clear, he returned to the present. "And where is your mother staying?"

"At the Three Mariners."

"And you are her daughter Elizabeth-Jane?" repeated Henchard. He arose, came close to her, and glanced in her face. "I think," he said, suddenly turning away with a wet eye, "you shall take a note from me to your mother. I should like to see her. . . . She is not left very well off by her late husband?" His eye fell on Elizabeth's clothes, which, though a respectable suit of black, and her very best, were decidedly old-fashioned even to Casterbridge eyes.

"Not very well," she said, glad that he had divined this without her being obliged to express it.

He sat down at the table and wrote a few lines, next taking from his pocket-book a five-pound note, which he put in the envelope with the letter, adding to it, as by an after-thought, five shillings. Sealing the whole up carefully, he directed it to "Mrs. Newson, Three Mariners Inn," and handed the packet to Elizabeth.

"Deliver it to her personally, please," said Henchard. "Well, I am glad to see you here, Elizabeth-Jane—very glad. We must have a long talk together—but not just now."

He took her hand at parting, and held it so warmly that she, who had known so little friendship, was much affected, and tears rose to her aërial-grey eyes. The instant that she was gone Henchard's state showed itself more distinctly; having shut the door he sat in his dining-room stiffly erect, gazing at the opposite wall as if he read his history there.

"Begad!" he suddenly exclaimed, jumping up. "I didn't think of that. Perhaps these are impostors—and Susan and the child dead after all!"

However, a something in Elizabeth-Jane soon assured him that, as regarded her, at least, there could be little doubt. And a few hours would settle the question of her mother's identity; for he had arranged in his note to see her that evening.

"It never rains but it pours!" said Henchard. His keenly excited interest in his new friend the Scotchman was now eclipsed by this event; and Donald Farfrae saw so little of him during the rest of the day that he wondered at the suddenness of his employer's moods.

In the meantime Elizabeth had reached the inn. Her mother, instead of taking the note with the curiosity of a poor woman expecting assistance, was much moved at sight of it. She did not read it at once, asking Elizabeth to describe her reception, and the very words Mr. Henchard used. Elizabeth's back was turned when her mother opened the letter. It ran thus:—

Meet me at eight o'clock this evening, if you can, at the Ring on the Budmouth road. The place is easy to find. I can say no more now. The news upsets me almost. The girl seems to be in igno-rance. Keep her so till I have seen you.   *M. H.*

He said nothing about the enclosure of five guineas. The amount was significant; it may tacitly have said to her that he bought her back again. She waited restlessly for the close of the day, telling Elizabeth-Jane that she was invited to see Mr. Henchard; that she would go alone. But she said nothing to show that the place of meeting was not at his house, nor did she hand the note to Elizabeth.

XI

THE RING AT CASTERBRIDGE WAS MERELY THE LOCAL NAME OF ONE OF THE FINEST Roman Amphitheatres, if not the very finest, remaining in Britain.

Casterbridge announced old Rome in every street, alley, and precinct. It looked Roman, bespoke the art of Rome, concealed dead men of Rome. It was impossible to dig more than a foot or two deep about the town fields and gardens without coming upon some tall soldier or other of the Empire, who had lain there in his silent unobtrusive rest for a space of fifteen hundred years. He was mostly found lying on his side, in an oval scoop in the chalk, like a chicken in its shell; his knees drawn up to his chest; sometimes with the remains of his spear against his arm, a fibula or brooch of bronze on his breast or forehead, an urn at his knees, a jar at his throat, a bottle at his mouth; and mystified conjecture pouring down upon him from the eyes of Casterbridge street boys and men, who had turned a moment to gaze at the familiar spectacle as they passed by.

Imaginative inhabitants, who would have felt an unpleasantness at the discovery of a comparatively modern skeleton in their gardens, were quite unmoved by these hoary shapes. They had lived so long ago, their time was so unlike the present, their hopes and motives were so widely removed from ours, that between them and the living there seemed to stretch a gulf too wide for even a spirit to pass.

The Amphitheatre was a huge circular enclosure, with a notch at opposite extremities of its diameter north and south. From its sloping internal form it might have been called the spittoon of the Jötuns. It was to Casterbridge what the ruined Coliseum is to modern Rome, and was nearly of the same magnitude. The dusk of evening was the proper hour at which a true impression of this suggestive place could be received. Standing in the middle of the arena at that time there by degrees became apparent its real vastness, which a cursory view from the summit at noon-day was apt to obscure. Melancholy, impressive, lonely, yet accessible from every part of the town, the historic circle was the frequent spot for appointments of a furtive kind. Intrigues were arranged there; tentative meetings were there experimented after divisions and feuds. But one kind of appointment—in itself the most common of any—seldom had place in the Amphitheatre: that of happy lovers.

Why, seeing that it was pre-eminently an airy, accessible, and sequestered spot for interviews, the cheerfullest form of those occurrences never took kindly to the soil of the ruin, would be a curious enquiry. Perhaps it was because its associations had about them something sinister. Its history proved that. Apart from the sanguinary nature of the games originally played therein, such incidents attached to its past as these: that for scores of years the town-gallows had stood at one corner; that in 1705 a woman who had murdered her husband was half-strangled and then burnt there in the presence of ten thousand spectators. Tradition reports that at a certain stage of the burning her heart burst and leapt out of her body, to the terror of them all, and that not one of those ten thousand people ever cared particularly for hot roast after that. In addition to these old tragedies, pugilistic encounters almost to the death had come off down to recent dates in that secluded arena, entirely invisible to the outside world save by climbing to the top of the enclosure, which few townspeople in the daily round of their lives ever took the trouble to do. So that, though close to the turnpike road, crimes might be perpetrated there unseen at mid-day.

Some boys had latterly tried to impart gaiety to the ruin by using the central arena as a cricket-ground. But the game usually languished for the aforesaid reason—the dismal privacy which the earthen circle enforced, shutting out every appreciative passer's vision, every commendatory remark from outsiders—everything, except the sky; and to play at games in such circumstances was like acting to an empty house. Possibly, too, the boys were timid, for some old people said that at certain moments in the summer-time, in broad daylight, persons sitting with a book, or dozing in the arena had, on lifting their eyes, beheld the slopes lined with a gazing legion of Hadrian's soldiery as if watching the gladiatorial combat; and had heard the roar of their excited voices, that the scene would remain but a moment, like a lightning flash, and then disappear.

It was related that there still remained under the south entrance excavated cells for the reception of the wild animals and athletes who took part in the games. The arena was still smooth and circular, as if used for its original purpose not so very long ago. The sloping pathways by which spectators had ascended to their seats were pathways yet. But the whole was grown over with grass, which now, at the end of summer, was bearded with withered bents that formed waves under the brush of the wind, returning to the attentive ear Æolian modulations, and detaining for moments the flying globes of thistledown.

Henchard had chosen this spot as being the safest from observation which he could think of for meeting his long-lost wife, and at the same time as one easily to be found by a stranger after nightfall. As Mayor of the town, with a reputation to keep up, he could not invite her to come to his house till some definite course had been decided on.

Just before eight he approached the deserted earth-work and entered by the south path which descended over the *débris* of the former dens. In a few moments he could discern a female figure creeping in by the great north gap, or public gateway. They met in the middle of the arena. Neither spoke just at first—there was no necessity for speech—and the poor woman leant against Henchard, who supported her in his arms.

"I don't drink," he said in a low, halting, apologetic voice. "You hear, Susan?—I don't drink now—I haven't since that night." Those were his first words.

He felt her bow her head in acknowledgment that she understood. After a minute or two he again began:

"If I had known you were living, Susan! But there was every reason to suppose you and the child were dead and gone. I took every possible step to find you—travelled—advertised. My opinion at last was that you had started for some colony with that man, and had been drowned on your voyage out. Why did you keep silent like this?"

"O Michael! because of him—what other reason could there be? I thought I owed him faithfulness to the end of one of our lives—foolishly I believed there was something solemn and binding in the bargain; I thought that even in honour I dared not desert him when he had paid so much for me in good faith. I meet you now only as his widow—I consider myself that, and that I have no claim upon you. Had he not died I should never have come—never! Of that you may be sure."

"Tut-tut! How could you be so simple?"

"I don't know. Yet it would have been very wicked—if I had not thought like that!" said Susan, almost crying.

"Yes—yes—so it would. It is only that which makes me feel 'ee an innocent woman. But—to lead me into this!"

"What, Michael?" she asked, alarmed.

"Why, this difficulty about our living together again, and Elizabeth-Jane. She cannot be told all—she would so despise us both that—I could not bear it!"

"That was why she was brought up in ignorance of you. I could not bear it either."

"Well—we must talk of a plan for keeping her in her present belief, and getting matters straight in spite of it. You have heard I am in a large way of business here—that I am Mayor of the town, and churchwarden, and I don't know what all?"

"Yes," she murmured.

"These things, as well as the dread of the girl discovering our disgrace, makes it necessary to act with extreme caution. So that I don't see how you two can return openly to my house as the wife and daughter I once treated badly, and banished from me; and there's the rub o't."

"We'll go away at once. I only came to see——"

"No, no, Susan; you are not to go—you mistake me!" he said with kindly severity. "I have thought of this plan: that you and Elizabeth take a cottage in the town as the widow Mrs. Newson and her daughter; that I meet you, court you, and marry you. Elizabeth-Jane coming to my house as my step-daughter. The thing is so natural and easy that it is half done in thinking o't. This would leave my shady, head-strong, disgraceful life as a young man absolutely unopened; the secret would be yours and mine only; and I should have the pleasure of seeing my own only child under my roof, as well as my wife."

"I am quite in your hands, Michael," she said meekly. "I came here for the sake of Elizabeth; for myself, if you tell me to leave again to-morrow morning, and never come near you more, I am content to go."

"Now, now; we don't want to hear that," said Henchard gently. "Of course you won't leave again. Think over the plan I have proposed for a few hours; and if you can't hit upon a better one we'll adopt it. I have to be away for a day or two on business, unfortunately; but during that time you can get lodgings—the only ones in the town fit for you are those over the china-shop in High Street—and you can also look for a cottage."

"If the lodgings are in High Street they are dear, I suppose?"

"Never mind—you *must* start genteel if our plan is to be carried out. Look to me for money. Have you enough till I come back?"

"Quite," said she.

"And are you comfortable at the inn?"

"O yes."

"And the girl is quite safe from learning the shame of her case and ours?—that's what makes me most anxious of all."

"You would be surprised to find how unlikely she is to dream of the truth. How could she ever suppose such a thing?"

"True!"

"I like the idea of repeating our marriage," said Mrs. Henchard, after a pause. "It seems the only right course, after all this. Now I think I must go back to Elizabeth-Jane, and tell her that our kinsman, Mr. Henchard, kindly wishes us to stay in the town."

"Very well—arrange that yourself. I'll go some way with you."

"No, no. Don't run any risk!" said his wife anxiously. "I can find my way back—it is not late. Please let me go alone."

"Right," said Henchard. "But just one word. Do you forgive me, Susan?"

She murmured something; but seemed to find it difficult to frame her answer.

"Never mind—all in good time," said he. "Judge me by my future works—good-bye!"

He retreated, and stood at the upper side of the Amphitheatre while his wife passed out through the lower way, and descended under the trees to the town. Then Henchard himself went homeward, going so fast that by the time he reached his door he was almost upon the heels of the unconscious woman from whom he had just parted. He watched her up the street, and turned into his house.

XII

O<small>N ENTERING HIS OWN DOOR, AFTER WATCHING HIS WIFE OUT OF SIGHT, THE MAYOR</small> walked on through the tunnel-shaped passage into the garden, and thence by the back-door towards the stores and granaries. A light shone from the office-window, and there being no blind to screen the interior Henchard could see Donald Farfrae still seated where he had left him, initiating himself into the managerial work of the house by over-hauling the books. Henchard entered, merely observing, "Don't let me interrupt you, if ye will stay so late."

He stood behind Farfrae's chair, watching his dexterity in clearing up the numerical fogs which had been allowed to grow so thick in Henchard's books as almost to baffle even the Scotchman's perspicacity. The corn-factor's mien was half admiring, and yet it was not without a dash of pity for the tastes of anyone who could care to give his mind to such finnikin details. Henchard himself was mentally and physically unfit for grubbing sub-tleties from soiled paper; he had in a modern sense received the education of Achilles, and found penmanship a tantalizing art.

"You shall do no more to-night," he said at length, spreading his great hand over the paper. "There's time enough to-morrow. Come indoors with me and have some supper. Now you shall! I am determined on't." He shut the account-books with friendly force.

Donald had wished to get to his lodgings; but he already saw that his friend and em-ployer was a man who knew no moderation in his requests and impulses, and he yielded gracefully. He liked Henchard's warmth, even if it inconvenienced him; the great differ-ence in their characters adding to the liking.

They locked up the office, and the young man followed his companion through the private little door which, admitting directly into Henchard's garden, permitted a passage from the utilitarian to the beautiful at one step. The garden was silent, dewy, and full of perfume. It extended a long way back from the house, first as lawn and flower-beds, then as fruit-garden, where the long-tied espaliers, as old as the old house itself, had grown so stout, and cramped, and gnarled that they had pulled their stakes out of the ground and stood distorted and writhing in vegetable agony, like leafy Laocoons. The flowers which smelt so sweetly were not discernible; and they passed through them into the house.

The hospitalities of the morning were repeated, and when they were over Henchard said, "Pull your chair round to the fireplace, my dear fellow, and let's make a blaze—there's nothing I hate like a black grate, even in September." He applied a light to the laid-in fuel, and a cheerful radiance spread around.

"It is odd," said Henchard, "that two men should meet as we have done on a purely business ground, and that at the end of the first day I should wish to speak to 'ee on a fam-ily matter. But, damn it all, I am a lonely man, Farfrae: I have nobody else to speak to; and why shouldn't I tell it to 'ee?"

"I'll be glad to hear it, if I can be of any service," said Donald, allowing his eyes to travel over the intricate wood-carvings of the chimney-piece, representing garlanded lyres, shields, and quivers, on either side of a draped ox-skull, and flanked by heads of Apollo and Diana in low relief.

"I've not been always what I am now," continued Henchard, his firm deep voice being ever so little shaken. He was plainly under that strange influence which sometimes prompts men to confide to the new-found friend what they will not tell to the old. "I began life as a working hay-trusser, and when I was eighteen I married on the strength o' my calling. Would you think me a married man?"

"I heard in the town that you were a widower."

"Ah, yes—you would naturally have heard that. Well, I lost my wife eighteen years ago—by my own fault. . . . This is how it came about. One summer evening I was travelling for employment, and she was walking at my side, carying the baby, our only child. We came to a booth in a country fair. I was a drinking man at that time."

Henchard paused a moment, threw himself back so that his elbow rested on the table, his forehead being shaded by his hand, which, however, did not hide the marks of introspective inflexibility on his features as he narrated in fullest detail the incidents of the transaction with the sailor. The tinge of indifference which had at first been visible in the Scotchman now disappeared.

Henchard went on to describe his attempts to find his wife; the oath he swore; the solitary life he led during the years which followed. "I have kept my oath for eighteen years," he went on; "I have risen to what you see me now."

"Ay!"

"Well—no wife could I hear of in all that time; and being by nature something of a woman-hater, I have found it no hardship to keep mostly at a distance from the sex. No wife could I hear of, I say, till this very day. And now—she has come back."

"Come back, has she!"

"This morning—this very morning. And what's to be done?"

"Can ye no' take her and live with her, and make some amends?"

"That's what I've planned and proposed. But, Farfrae," said Henchard gloomily, "by doing right with Susan I wrong another innocent woman."

"Ye don't say that?"

"In the nature of things, Farfrae, it is almost impossible that a man of my sort should have the good fortune to tide through twenty years o' life without making more blunders than one. It has been my custom for many years to run across to Jersey in the way of business, particularly in the potato and root season. I do a large trade wi' them in that line. Well, one autumn when stopping there I fell quite ill, and in my illness I sank into one of those gloomy fits I sometimes suffer from, on account o' the loneliness of my domestic life, when the world seems to have the blackness of hell, and, like Job, I could curse the day that gave me birth."

"Ah, now, I never feel like it," said Farfrae.

"Then pray to God that you never may, young man. While in this state I was taken pity on by a woman—a young lady I should call her, for she was of good family, well bred, and well educated—the daughter of some harum-scarum military officer who had got into difficulties, and had his pay sequestrated. He was dead now, and her mother too, and she was as lonely as I. This young creature was staying at the boarding-house where I happened to have my lodging; and when I was pulled down she took upon herself to nurse me. From that she got to have a foolish liking for me. Heaven knows why, for I wasn't worth it. But being together in the same house, and her feeling warm, we got naturally intimate.

I won't go into particulars of what our relations were. It is enough to say that we honestly meant to marry. There arose a scandal, which did me no harm, but was of course ruin to her. Though, Farfrae, between you and me, as man and man, I solemnly declare that philandering with womankind has neither been my vice nor my virtue. She was terribly careless of appearances, and I was perhaps more, because o' my dreary state; and it was through this that the scandal arose. At last I was well, and came away. When I was gone she suffered much on my account, and didn't forget to tell me so in letters one after another; till, latterly, I felt I owed her something, and thought that, as I had not heard of Susan for so long, I would make this other one the only return I could make, and ask her if she would run the risk of Susan being alive (very slight as I believed) and marry me, such as I was. She jumped for joy, and we should no doubt soon have been married—but, behold, Susan appears!"

Donald showed his deep concern at a complication so far beyond the degree of his simple experiences.

"Now see what injury a man may cause around him! Even after that wrong-doing at the fair when I was young, if I had never been so selfish as to let this giddy girl devote herself to me over at Jersey, to the injury of her name, all might now be well. Yet, as it stands, I must bitterly disappoint one of these women; and it is the second. My first duty is to Susan—there's no doubt about that."

"They are both in a very melancholy position, and that's true!" murmured Donald.

"They are! For myself I don't care—'twill all end one way. But these two." Henchard paused in reverie. "I feel I should like to treat the second, no less than the first, as kindly as a man can in such a case."

"Ah, well, it cannet be helped!" said the other, with philosophic woefulness. "You mun write to the young lady, and in your letter you must put it plain and honest that it turns out she cannet be your wife, the first having come back; that ye cannet see her more; and that—ye wish her weel."

"That won't do. 'Od seize it, I must do a little more than that! I must—though she did always brag about her rich uncle or rich aunt, and her expectations from 'em—I must send a useful sum of money to her, I suppose—just as a little recompense, poor girl. . . . Now, will you help me in this, and draw up an explanation to her of all I've told ye, breaking it as gently as you can? I'm so bad at letters."

"And I will."

"Now, I haven't told you quite all yet. My wife Susan has my daughter with her— the baby that was in her arms at the fair; and this girl knows nothing of me beyond that I am some sort of relation by marriage. She has grown up in the belief that the sailor to whom I made over her mother, and who is now dead, was her father, and her mother's husband. What her mother has always felt, she and I together feel now—that we can't proclaim our disgrace to the girl by letting her know the truth. Now what would you do?—I want your advice."

"I think I'd run the risk, and tell her the truth. She'll forgive ye both."

"Never!" said Henchard. "I am not going to let her know the truth. Her mother and I be going to marry again; and it will not only help us to keep our child's respect, but it will be more proper. Susan looks upon herself as the sailor's widow, and won't think o' living with me as formerly without another religious ceremony—and she's right."

Farfrae thereupon said no more. The letter to the young Jersey woman was carefully framed by him, and the interview ended, Henchard saying, as the Scotchman left, "I feel it a great relief, Farfrae, to tell some friend o' this! You see now that the Mayor of Caster-bridge is not so thriving in his mind as it seems he might be from the state of his pocket."

"I do. And I'm sorry for ye!" said Farfrae.

When he was gone Henchard copied the letter, and, enclosing a cheque, took it to the post-office, from which he walked back thoughtfully.

"Can it be that it will go off so easily!" he said. "Poor thing—God knows! Now then, to make amends to Susan!"

XIII

THE COTTAGE WHICH MICHAEL HENCHARD HIRED FOR HIS WIFE SUSAN, UNDER HER name of Newson—in pursuance of their plan—was in the upper or western part of the town, near the wall, and the avenue which overshadowed it. The evening sun seemed to shine more yellowly there than anywhere else this autumn—stretching its rays, as the hours grew later, under the lowest sycamore boughs, and steeping the ground-floor of the dwelling, with its green shutters, in a substratum of radiance which the foliage screened from the upper parts. Beneath these sycamores on the town walls could be seen from the sitting-room the tumuli and earth forts of the distant uplands; making it altogether a pleasant spot, with the usual touch of melancholy that a past-marked prospect lends.

As soon as the mother and daughter were comfortably installed, with a white-aproned servant and all complete, Henchard paid them a visit, and remained to tea. During the entertainment Elizabeth was carefully hoodwinked by the very general tone of the conversation that prevailed—a proceeding which seemed to afford some humour to Henchard, though his wife was not particularly happy in it. The visit was repeated again and again with businesslike determination by the Mayor, who seemed to have schooled himself into a course of strict mechanical rightness towards this woman of prior claim, at any expense to the later one and to his own sentiments.

One afternoon the daughter was not indoors when Henchard came, and he said drily, "This is a very good opportunity for me to ask you to name the happy day, Susan."

The poor woman smiled faintly; she did not enjoy pleasantries on a situation into which she had entered solely for the sake of her girl's reputation. She liked them so little, indeed, that there was room for wonder why she had countenanced deception at all, and had not bravely let the girl know her history. But the flesh is weak; and the true explanation came in due course.

"O Michael!" she said, "I am afraid all this is taking up your time and giving trouble—when I did not expect any such thing!" And she looked at him and at his dress as a man of affluence, and at the furniture he had provided for the room—ornate and lavish to her eyes.

"Not at all," said Henchard, in rough benignity. "This is only a cottage—it costs me next to nothing. And as to taking up my time"—here his red and black visage kindled with satisfaction—"I've a splendid fellow to superintend my business now—a man whose like

I've never been able to lay hands on before. I shall soon be able to leave everything to him, and have more time to call my own than I've had for these last twenty years."

Henchard's visits here grew so frequent and so regular that it soon became whispered, and then openly discussed in Casterbridge that the masterful, coercive Mayor of the town was raptured and enervated by the genteel widow, Mrs. Newson. His well-known haughty indifference to the society of womankind, his silent avoidance of converse with the sex, contributed a piquancy to what would otherwise have been an unromantic matter enough. That such a poor fragile woman should be his choice was inexplicable, except on the ground that the engagement was a family affair in which sentimental passion had no place; for it was known that they were related in some way. Mrs. Henchard was so pale that the boys called her "The Ghost." Sometimes Henchard overheard this epithet when they passed together along the Walks—as the avenues on the walls were named—at which his face would darken with an expression of destructiveness towards the speakers ominous to see; but he said nothing.

He pressed on the preparations for his union, or rather reunion, with this pale creature in a dogged, unflinching spirit which did credit to his conscientiousness. Nobody would have conceived from his outward demeanour that there was no amatory fire or pulse of romance acting as stimulant to the bustle going on in his gaunt, great house; nothing but three large resolves—one, to make amends to his neglected Susan; another, to provide a comfortable home for Elizabeth-Jane under his paternal eye; and a third, to castigate himself with the thorns which these restitutory acts brought in their train; among them the lowering of his dignity in public opinion by marrying so comparatively humble a woman.

Susan Henchard entered a carriage for the first time in her life when she stepped into the plain brougham which drew up at the door on the wedding-day to take her and Elizabeth-Jane to church. It was a windless morning of warm November rain, which floated down like meal, and lay in a powdery form on the nap of hats and coats. Few people had gathered round the church door, though they were well packed within. The Scotchman, who assisted as groomsman, was of course the only one present, beyond the chief actors, who knew the true situation of the contracting parties. He, however, was too inexperienced, too thoughtful, too judicial, too strongly conscious of the serious side of the business, to enter into the scene in its dramatic aspect. That required the special genius of Christopher Coney, Solomon Longways, Buzzford, and their fellows. But they knew nothing of the secret; though, as the time for coming out of church drew on, they gathered on the pavement adjoining, and expounded the subject according to their lights.

" 'Tis five-and-forty years since I had my settlement in this here town," said Coney; "but daze me if I ever see a man wait so long before to take so little! There's a chance even for thee after this, Nance Mockridge." The remark was addressed to a woman who stood behind his shoulder—the same who had exhibited Henchard's bad bread in public when Elizabeth and her mother entered Casterbridge.

"Be cust if I'd marry any such as he, or thee either," replied that lady. "As for thee, Christopher, we know what ye be, and the less said the better. And as for he—well, there— (lowering her voice) 'tis said 'a was a poor parish 'prentice—I wouldn't say it for all the world—but 'a was a poor parish 'prentice, that began life wi' no more belonging to 'en than a carrion crow."

"And now he's worth ever so much a minute," murmured Longways. "When a man is said to be worth so much a minute, he's a man to be considered!"

Turning, he saw a circular disc reticulated with creases, and recognised the smiling countenance of the fat woman who had asked for another song at the Three Mariners. "Well, Mother Cuxsom," he said, "how's this? Here's Mrs. Newson, a mere skellinton, has got another husband to keep her, while a woman of your tonnage have not."

"I have not. Nor another to beat me. . . . Ah, yes, Cuxsom's gone, and so shall leather breeches!"

"Yes; with the blessing of God leather breeches shall go."

" 'Tisn't worth my old while to think of another husband," continued Mrs. Cuxsom. "And yet I'll lay my life I'm as respectable born as she."

"True; your mother was a very good woman—I can mind her. She were rewarded by the Agricultural Society for having begot the greatest number of healthy children without parish assistance, and other virtuous marvels."

" 'Twas that that kept us so low upon ground—that great family."

"Ay. Where the pigs be many the wash runs thin."

"And dostn't mind how mother would sing, Christopher?" continued Mrs. Cuxsom, kindling at the retrospection; "and how we went with her to the party at Mellstock, do ye mind?—at old Dame Ledlow's, farmer Shinar's sister, do ye mind?—she we used to call Toad-skin, because her face were so yaller and freckled, do ye mind?"

"I do, hee-hee, I do!" said Christopher Coney.

"And well do I—for I was getting up husband-high at that time—one-half girl, and t'other half woman, as one may say. And canst mind"—she prodded Solomon's shoulder with her finger-tip, while her eyes twinkled between the crevices of their lids—"canst mind the sherry-wine, and the zilver-snuffers, and how Joan Dummett was took bad when we were coming home, and Jack Griggs was forced to carry her through the mud; and how 'a let her fall in Dairyman Sweet-apple's cow-barton, and we had to clane her gown wi' grass—never such a mess as a' were in?"

"Ay—that I do—hee-hee, such doggery as there was in them ancient days, to be sure! Ah, the miles I used to walk then; and now I can hardly step over a furrow!"

Their reminiscences were cut short by the appearance of the reunited pair—Henchard looking round upon the idlers with that ambiguous gaze of his, which at one moment seemed to mean satisfaction, and at another fiery disdain.

"Well—there's a difference between 'em, though he do call himself a teetotaller," said Nance Mockridge. "She'll wish her cake dough afore she's done of him. There's a blue-beardy look about 'en; and 'twill out in time."

"Stuff—he's well enough! Some folk want their luck buttered. If I had a choice as wide as the ocean sea I wouldn't wish for a better man. A poor twanking woman like her—'tis a godsend for her, and hardly a pair of jumps or night-rail to her name."

The plain little brougham drove off in the mist, and the idlers dispersed. "Well, we hardly know how to look at things in these times!" said Solomon. "There was a man dropped down dead yesterday, not so very many miles from here; and what wi' that, and this moist weather, 'tis scarce worth one's while to begin any work o' consequence to-day. I'm in such a low key with drinking nothing but small table ninepenny this last week or two that I shall call and warm up at the Mar'ners as I pass along."

"I don't know but that I may as well go with 'ee, Solomon," said Christopher; "I'm as clammy as a cockle-snail."

XIV

A MARTINMAS SUMMER OF MRS. HENCHARD'S LIFE SET IN WITH HER ENTRY INTO HER HUS-band's large house and respectable social orbit; and it was as bright as such summers well can be. Lest she should pine for deeper affection than he could give he made a point of showing some semblance of it in external action. Among other things he had the iron railings, that had smiled sadly in dull rust for the last eighty years, painted a bright green, and the heavy-barred, small-paned Georgian sash windows enlivened with three coats of white. He was as kind to her as a man, mayor, and churchwarden could possibly be. The house was large, the rooms lofty, and the landings wide; and the two unassuming women scarcely made a perceptible addition to its contents.

To Elizabeth-Jane the time was a most triumphant one. The freedom she experienced, the indulgence with which she was treated, went beyond her expectations. The reposeful, easy, affluent life to which her mother's marriage had introduced her was, in truth, the beginning of a great change in Elizabeth. She found she could have nice personal possessions and ornaments for the asking, and, as the medieval saying puts it, "Take, have, and keep, are pleasant words." With peace of mind came development, and with development beauty. Knowledge—the result of great natural insight—she did not lack; learning, accomplishments—those, alas, she had not; but as the winter and spring passed by her thin face and figure filled out in rounder and softer curves; the lines and contractions upon her young brow went away; the muddiness of skin which she had looked upon as her lot by nature departed with a change to abundance of good things, and a bloom came upon her cheek. Perhaps, too, her grey, thoughtful eyes revealed an arch gaiety sometimes; but this was infrequent; the sort of wisdom which looked from their pupils did not readily keep company with these lighter moods. Like all people who have known rough times, light-heartedness seemed to her too irrational and inconsequent to be indulged in except as a reckless dram now and then; for she had been too early habituated to anxious reasoning to drop the habit suddenly. She felt none of those ups and downs of spirit which beset so many people without cause; never—to paraphrase a recent poet—never a gloom in Elizabeth-Jane's soul but she well knew how it came there; and her present cheerfulness was fairly proportionate to her solid guarantees for the same.

It might have been supposed that, given a girl rapidly becoming good-looking, comfortably circumstanced, and for the first time in her life commanding ready money, she would go and make a fool of herself by dress. But no. The reasonableness of almost everything that Elizabeth did was nowhere more conspicuous than in this question of clothes. To keep in the rear of opportunity in matters of indulgence is as valuable a habit as to keep abreast of opportunity in matters of enterprise. This unsophisticated girl did it by an innate perceptiveness that was almost genius. Thus she refrained from bursting out like a water-flower that spring, and clothing herself in puffings and knick-knacks, as most of the Casterbridge girls would have done in her circumstances. Her triumph was tempered by circumspection; she had still that field-mouse fear of the coulter of destiny despite fair promise, which is common among the thoughtful who have suffered early from poverty and oppression.

"I won't be too gay on any account," she would say to herself. "It would be tempting Providence to hurl mother and me down, and afflict us again as He used to do."

We now see her in a black silk bonnet, velvet mantle or silk spencer, dark dress, and carrying a sunshade. In this latter article she drew the line at fringe, and had it plain edged, with a little ivory ring for keeping it closed. It was odd about the necessity for that sunshade. She discovered that with the clarification of her complexion and the birth of pink cheeks her skin had grown more sensitive to the sun's rays. She protected those cheeks forthwith, deeming spotlessness part of womanliness.

Henchard had become very fond of her, and she went out with him more frequently than with her mother now. Her appearance one day was so attractive that he looked at her critically.

"I happened to have the ribbon by me, so I made it up," she faltered, thinking him perhaps dissatisfied with some rather bright trimming she had donned for the first time.

"Ay—of course—to be sure," he replied in his leonine way. "Do as you like—or rather as your mother advises ye. 'Od send—I've nothing to say to't!"

Indoors she appeared with her hair divided by a parting that arched like a white rainbow from ear to ear. All in front of this line was covered with a thick encampment of curls; all behind was dressed smoothly, and drawn to a knob.

The three members of the family were sitting at breakfast one day, and Henchard was looking silently, as he often did, at this head of hair, which in colour was brown—rather light than dark. "I thought Elizabeth-Jane's hair—didn't you tell me that Elizabeth-Jane's hair promised to be black when she was a baby?" he said to his wife.

She looked startled, jerked his foot warningly, and murmured, "Did I?"

As soon as Elizabeth was gone to her own room Henchard resumed. "Begad, I nearly forgot myself just now! What I meant was that the girl's hair certainly looked as if it would be darker, when she was a baby."

"It did; but they alter so," replied Susan.

"Their hair gets darker, I know—but I wasn't aware it lightened ever?"

"Oh yes." And the same uneasy expression came out on her face, to which the future held the key. It passed as Henchard went on:

"Well, so much the better. Now Susan, I want to have her called Miss Henchard—not Miss Newson. Lots o' people do it already in carelessness—it is her legal name—so it may as well be made her usual name—I don't like t'other name at all for my own flesh and blood. I'll advertise it in the Casterbridge paper—that's the way they do it. She won't object."

"No. Oh no. But—"

"Well, then, I shall do it," he said, peremptorily. "Surely, if she's willing, you must wish it as much as I?"

"O yes—if she agrees let us do it by all means," she replied.

Then Mrs. Henchard acted somewhat inconsistently; it might have been called falsely, but that her manner was emotional and full of the earnestness of one who wishes to do right at great hazard. She went to Elizabeth-Jane, whom she found sewing in her own sitting-room upstairs, and told her what had been proposed about her surname. "Can you agree—is it not a slight upon Newson—now he's dead and gone?"

Elizabeth reflected. "I'll think of it, mother," she answered.

When, later in the day, she saw Henchard, she adverted to the matter at once, in a way which showed that the line of feeling started by her mother had been persevered in. "Do you wish this change so very much, sir?" she asked.

"Wish it? Why, my blessed fathers, what an ado you women make about a trifle! I proposed it—that's all. Now, 'Lizabeth-Jane, just please yourself. Curse me if I care what you do. Now, you understand, don't 'ee go agreeing to it to please me."

Here the subject dropped, and nothing more was said, and nothing was done, and Elizabeth still passed as Miss Newson, and not by her legal name.

Meanwhile the great corn and hay traffic conducted by Henchard throve under the management of Donald Farfrae as it had never thriven before. It had formerly moved in jolts; now it went on oiled casters. The old crude *vivâ voce* system of Henchard, in which everything depended upon his memory, and bargains were made by the tongue alone, was swept away. Letters and ledgers took the place of "I'll do't," and "you shall hae't"; and, as in all such cases of advance, the rugged picturesqueness of the old method disappeared with its inconveniences.

The position of Elizabeth-Jane's room—rather high in the house, so that it commanded a view of the hay-stores and granaries across the garden—afforded her opportunity for accurate observation of what went on there. She saw that Donald and Mr. Henchard were inseparables. When walking together Henchard would lay his arm familiarly on his manager's shoulder, as if Farfrae were a younger brother, bearing so heavily that his slight frame bent under the weight. Occasionally she would hear a perfect cannonade of laughter from Henchard, arising from something Donald had said, the latter looking quite innocent and not laughing at all. In Henchard's somewhat lonely life he evidently found the young man as desirable for comradeship as he was useful for consultations. Donald's brightness of intellect maintained in the corn-factor the admiration it had won at the first hour of their meeting. The poor opinion, and but ill-concealed, that he entertained of the slim Farfrae's physical girth, strength, and dash was more than counterbalanced by the immense respect he had for his brains.

Her quiet eye discerned that Henchard's tigerish affection for the younger man, his constant liking to have Farfrae near him, now and then resulted in a tendency to domineer, which, however, was checked in a moment when Donald exhibited marks of real offence. One day, looking down on their figures from on high, she heard the latter remark, as they stood in the doorway between the garden and yard, that their habit of walking and driving about together rather neutralised Farfrae's value as a second pair of eyes, which should be used in places where the principal was not. " 'Od damn it," cried Henchard, "what's all the world! I like a fellow to talk to. Now come along and hae some supper, and don't take too much thought about things, or ye'll drive me crazy."

When she walked with her mother, on the other hand, she often beheld the Scotchman looking at them with a curious interest. The fact that he had met her at the Three Mariners was insufficient to account for it, since on the occasions on which she had entered his room he had never raised his eyes. Besides, it was at her mother more particularly than at herself that he looked, to Elizabeth-Jane's half-conscious, simple-minded, perhaps pardonable, disappointment. Thus she could not account for this interest by her own attractiveness, and she decided that it might be apparent only—a way of turning his eyes that Mr. Farfrae had.

She did not divine the ample explanation of his manner, without personal vanity, that was afforded by the fact of Donald being the depositary of Henchard's confidence in respect of his past treatment of the pale, chastened mother who walked by her side. Her conjectures on that past never went further than faint ones based on things casually heard and seen—mere guesses that Henchard and her mother might have been lovers in their younger days, who had quarrelled and parted.

Casterbridge, as has been hinted, was a place deposited in the block upon a corn-field. There was no suburb in the modern sense, or transitional intermixture of town and down. It stood, with regard to the wide fertile land adjoining, clean-cut and distinct, like a chess-board on a green table cloth. The farmer's boy could sit under his barley-mow and pitch a stone into the office-window of the town-clerk; reapers at work among the sheaves nodded to acquaintances standing on the pavement-corner; the red-robed judge, when he condemned a sheep-stealer, pronounced sentence to the tune of Baa, that floated in at the window from the remainder of the flock browsing hard by; and at executions the waiting crowd stood in a meadow immediately before the drop, out of which the cows had been temporarily driven to give the spectators room.

The corn grown on the upland side of the borough was garnered by farmers who lived in an eastern purlieu called Durnover. Here wheat-ricks overhung the old Roman street, and thrust their eaves against the church-tower; green-thatched barns, with door-ways as high as the gates of Solomon's temple, opened directly upon the main thoroughfare. Barns indeed were so numerous as to alternate with every half-dozen houses along the way. Here lived burgesses who daily walked the fallow; shepherds in an intra-mural squeeze. A street of farmers' homesteads—a street ruled by a mayor and corporation, yet echoing with the thump of the flail, the flutter of the winnowing-fan, and the purr of the milk into the pails—a street which had nothing urban in it whatever—this was the Durnover end of Casterbridge.

Henchard, as was natural, dealt largely with this nursery or bed of small farmers close at hand—and his waggons were often down that way. One day, when arrangements were in progress for getting home corn from one of the aforesaid farms, Elizabeth-Jane received a note by hand, asking her to oblige the writer by coming at once to a granary on Durnover Hill. As this was the granary whose contents Henchard was removing, she thought the request had something to do with his business, and proceeded thither as soon as she had put on her bonnet. The granary was just within the farm-yard, and stood on stone staddles, high enough for persons to walk under. The gates were open, but nobody was within. However, she entered and waited. Presently she saw a figure approaching the gate—that of Donald Farfrae. He looked up at the church clock, and came in. By some unaccountable shyness, some wish not to meet him there alone, she quickly ascended the step-ladder leading to the granary door, and entered it before he had seen her. Farfrae advanced, imagining himself in solitude; and a few drops of rain beginning to fall he moved and stood under the shelter where she had just been standing. Here he leant against one of the staddles, and gave himself up to patience. He, too, was plainly expecting someone; could it be herself? If so, why? In a few minutes he looked at his watch, and then pulled out a note, a duplicate of the one she had herself received.

This situation began to be very awkward, and the longer she waited the more awkward it became. To emerge from a door just above his head and descend the ladder, and show she had been in hiding there, would look so very foolish that she still waited on. A winnowing machine stood close beside her, and to relieve her suspense she gently moved the handle; whereupon a cloud of wheat husks flew out into her face, and covered her clothes and bonnet, and stuck into the fur of her victorine. He must have heard the slight movement for he looked up, and then ascended the steps.

"Ah—it's Miss Newson," he said as soon as he could see into the granary. "I didn't know you were there. I have kept the appointment, and am at your service."

"O Mr. Farfrae," she faltered; "so have I. But I didn't know it was you who wished to see me, otherwise I—"

"I wished to see you? Oh no—at least, that is, I am afraid there may be a mistake."

"Didn't you ask me to come here? Didn't you write this?" Elizabeth held out her note.

"No. Indeed, at no hand would I have thought of it! And for you—didn't you ask me? This is not your writing?" And he held up his.

"By no means."

"And is that really so! Then it's somebody wanting to see us both. Perhaps we would do well to wait a little longer."

Acting on this consideration they lingered, Elizabeth-Jane's face being arranged to an expression of preternatural composure, and the young Scot, at every footstep in the street without, looking from under the granary to see if the passer were about to enter and declare himself their summoner. They watched individual drops of rain creeping down the thatch of the opposite rick—straw after straw—till they reached the bottom; but nobody came, and the granary roof began to drip.

"The person is not likely to be coming," said Farfrae. "It's a trick perhaps, and if so, it's a great pity to waste our time like this, and so much to be done."

" 'Tis a great liberty," said Elizabeth.

"It's true, Miss Newson. We'll hear news of this some day, depend on't, and who it was that did it. I wouldn't stand for it hindering myself; but you, Miss Newson—"

"I don't mind—much,' she replied.

"Neither do I."

They lapsed again into silence. "You are anxious to get back to Scotland, I suppose, Mr. Farfrae?" she enquired.

"Oh no, Miss Newson. Why would I be?"

"I only supposed you might be from the song you sang at the Three Mariners—about Scotland and home, I mean—which you seemed to feel so deep down in your heart; so that we all felt for you."

"Ay—and I did sing there—I did—But, Miss Newson"—and Donald's voice musically undulated between two semi-tones as it always did when he became earnest—"it's well you feel a song, for a few minutes, and your eyes they get quite tearful; but you finish it, and for all you felt you don't mind it or think of it again for a long while. O no, I don't want to go back! Yet I'll sing the song to you wi' pleasure whenever you like. I could sing it now, and not mind at all!"

"Thank you, indeed. But I fear I must go—rain or no."

"Ay! Then, Miss Newson, ye had better say nothing about this hoax, and take no heed of it. And if the person should say anything to you, be civil to him or her, as if you did not mind it—so you'll take the clever person's laugh away." In speaking his eyes became fixed upon her dress, still sown with wheat husks. "There's husks and dust on you. Perhaps you don't know it?" he said, in tones of extreme delicacy. "And it's very bad to let rain come upon clothes when there's chaff on them. It washes in and spoils them. Let me help you— blowing is the best."

As Elizabeth neither assented nor dissented Donald Farfrae began blowing her back hair, and her side hair, and her neck, and the crown of her bonnet, and the fur of her victorine, Elizabeth saying, "Oh, thank you," at every puff. At last she was fairly clean, though Farfrae, having got over his first concern at the situation, seemed in no manner of hurry to be gone.

"Ah—now I'll go and get ye an umbrella," he said.

She declined the offer, stepped out and was gone. Farfrae walked slowly after, looking thoughtfully at her diminishing figure, and whistling in undertones, "As I came down through Cannobie."

XV

AT FIRST MISS NEWSON'S BUDDING BEAUTY WAS NOT REGARDED WITH MUCH INTEREST by anybody in Casterbridge. Donald Farfrae's gaze, it is true, was now attracted by the Mayor's so-called step-daughter, but he was only one. The truth is that she was but a poor illustrative instance of the prophet Baruch's sly definition: "The virgin that loveth to go gay."

When she walked abroad she seemed to be occupied with an inner chamber of ideas, and to have slight need for visible objects. She formed curious resolves on checking gay fancies in the matter of clothes, because it was inconsistent with her past life to blossom gaudily the moment she had become possessed of money. But nothing is more insidious than the evolution of wishes from mere fancies, and of wants from mere wishes. Henchard gave Elizabeth-Jane a box of delicately-tinted gloves one spring day. She wanted to wear them to show her appreciation of his kindness, but she had no bonnet that would harmonise. As an artistic indulgence she thought she would have such a bonnet. When she had a bonnet that would go with the gloves she had no dress that would go with the bonnet. It was now absolutely necessary to finish; she ordered the requisite article, and found that she had no sunshade to go with the dress. In for a penny in for a pound; she bought the sunshade, and the whole structure was at last complete.

Everybody was attracted, and some said that her bygone simplicity was the art that conceals art, the "delicate imposition" of Rochefoucauld; she had produced an effect, a contrast, and it had been done on purpose. As a matter of fact this was not true, but it had its result; for as soon as Casterbridge thought her artful it thought her worth notice. "It is the first time in my life that I have been so much admired," she said to herself; "though perhaps it is by those whose admiration is not worth having."

But Donald Farfrae admired her, too; and altogether the time was an exciting one; sex had never before asserted itself in her so strongly, for in former days she had perhaps been too impersonally human to be distinctively feminine. After an unprecedented success one day she came indoors, went upstairs, and leant upon her bed face downwards quite forgetting the possible creasing and damage. "Good Heaven," she whispered, "can it be? Here am I setting up as the town beauty!"

When she had thought it over, her usual fear of exaggerating appearances engendered a deep sadness. "There is something wrong in all this," she mused. "If they only knew what an unfinished girl I am—that I can't talk Italian, or use globes, or show any of the accomplishments they learn at boarding-schools, how they would despise me! Better sell all this finery and buy myself grammar-books and dictionaries and a history of all the philosophies!"

She looked from the window and saw Henchard and Farfrae in the hay-yard talking, with that impetuous cordiality on the Mayor's part, and genial modesty on the younger man's, that was now so generally observable in their intercourse. Friendship between man and man; what a rugged strength there was in it, as evinced by these two. And yet the seed that was to lift the foundation of this friendship was at that moment taking root in a chink of its structure.

It was about six o'clock; the men were dropping off homeward one by one. The last to leave was a round-shouldered, blinking young man of nineteen or twenty, whose mouth fell ajar on the slightest provocation, seemingly because there was no chin to support it. Henchard called aloud to him as he went out of the gate, "Here—Abel Whittle!"

Whittle turned, and ran back a few steps. "Yes, sir," he said, in breathless deprecation, as if he knew what was coming next.

"Once more—be in time to-morrow morning. You see what's to be done, and you hear what I say, and you know I'm not going to be trifled with any longer."

"Yes, sir." Then Abel Whittle left, and Henchard and Farfrae; and Elizabeth saw no more of them.

Now there was good reason for this command on Henchard's part. Poor Abel, as he was called, had an inveterate habit of over-sleeping himself and coming late to his work. His anxious will was to be among the earliest; but if his comrades omitted to pull the string that he always tied round his great toe and left hanging out the window for that purpose, his will was as wind. He did not arrive in time.

As he was often second hand at the hay-weighing, or at the crane which lifted the sacks, or was one of those who had to accompany the waggons into the country to fetch away stacks that had been purchased, this affliction of Abel's was productive of much inconvenience. For two mornings in the present week he had kept the others waiting nearly an hour; hence Henchard's threat. It now remained to be seen what would happen to-morrow.

Six o'clock struck, and there was no Whittle. At half-past six Henchard entered the yard; the waggon was horsed that Abel was to accompany; and the other man had been waiting twenty minutes. Then Henchard swore, and Whittle coming up breathless at that instant, the corn-factor turned on him, and declared with an oath that this was the last time; that if he were behind once more, by God, he would come and drag him out o' bed.

"There is sommit wrong in my make, your worshipful!" said Abel, "especially in the inside, whereas my poor dumb brain gets as dead as a clot afore I've said my few scrags of prayers. Yes—it came on as a stripling, just afore I'd got man's wages, whereas I never enjoy my bed at all, for no sooner do I lie down than I be asleep, and afore I be awake I be up. I've fretted my gizzard green about it, maister, but what can I do? Now last night, afore I went to bed, I only had a scantling o' cheese and—"

"I don't want to hear it!" roared Henchard. "To-morrow the waggons must start at four, and if you're not here, stand clear. I'll mortify thy flesh for thee!"

"But let me clear up my points, your worshipful—"

Henchard turned away.

"He asked me and he questioned me, and then 'a wouldn't hear my points!" said Abel, to the yard in general. "Now, I shall twitch like a moment-hand all night to-night for fear o' him!"

The journey to be taken by the waggons next day was a long one into Blackmoor Vale, and at four o'clock lanterns were moving about the yard. But Abel was missing. Before either of the other men could run to Abel's and warn him Henchard appeared in the garden doorway. "Where's Abel Whittle? Not come after all I've said? Now I'll carry out my word, by my blessed fathers—nothing else will do him any good! I'm going up that way."

Henchard went off, entered Abel's house, a little cottage in Back Street, the door of which was never locked because the inmates had nothing to lose. Reaching Whittle's bedside the corn-factor shouted a bass note so vigorously that Abel started up instantly, and beholding Henchard standing over him, was galvanised into spasmodic movements which had not much relation to getting on his clothes.

"Out of bed, sir, and off to the granary, or you leave my employ to-day! 'Tis to teach ye a lesson. March on; never mind your breeches!"

The unhappy Whittle threw on his sleeve waistcoat, and managed to get into his boots at the bottom of the stairs, while Henchard thrust his hat over his head. Whittle then trotted on down Back Street, Henchard walking sternly behind.

Just at this time Farfrae, who had been to Henchard's house to look for him, came out of the back gate, and saw something white fluttering in the morning gloom, which he soon perceived to be part of Abel's shirt that showed below his waistcoat.

"For maircy's sake, what object's this?" said Farfrae, following Abel into the yard, Henchard being some way in the rear by this time.

"Ye see, Mr. Farfrae," gibbered Abel with a resigned smile of terror, "he said he'd mortify my flesh if so be I didn't get up sooner, and now he's a doing on't! Ye see it can't be helped, Mr. Farfrae; things do happen queer sometimes! Yes—I'll go to Blackmoor Vale half naked as I be, since he do command; but I shall kill myself afterwards; I can't outlive the disgrace, for the women-folk will be looking out of their winders at my mortification all the way along, and laughing me to scorn as a man 'ithout breeches! You know how I feel such things, Maister Farfrae, and how forlorn thoughts get hold upon me. Yes—I shall do myself harm—I feel it coming on!"

"Get back home, and slip on your breeches, and come to wark like a man! If ye go not, you'll ha'e your death standing there!"

"I'm afeard I mustn't! Mr. Henchard said—"

"I don't care what Mr. Henchard said, nor anybody else! 'Tis simple foolishness to do this. Go and dress yourself instantly, Whittle."

"Hullo, hullo!" said Henchard, coming up behind. "Who's sending him back?"

All the men looked towards Farfrae.

"I am," said Donald. "I say this joke has been carried far enough."

"And I say it hasn't! Get up in the waggon, Whittle."

"Not if I am manager," said Farfrae. "He either goes home, or I march out of this yard for good."

Henchard looked at him with a face stern and red. But he paused for a moment, and their eyes met. Donald went up to him, for he saw in Henchard's look that he began to regret this.

"Come," said Donald quietly, "a man o' your position should ken better, sir! It is tyrannical and no worthy of you."

" 'Tis not tyrannical!" murmured Henchard, like a sullen boy. "It is to make him remember!" He presently added, in a tone of one bitterly hurt: "Why did you speak to me before them like that, Farfrae? You might have stopped till we were alone. Ah—I know why! I've told ye the secret o' my life—fool that I was to do't—and you take advantage of me!"

"I had forgot it," said Farfrae simply.

Henchard looked on the ground, said nothing more, and turned away. During the day Farfrae learnt from the men that Henchard had kept Abel's old mother in coals and snuff all the previous winter, which made him less antagonistic to the corn-factor. But Henchard continued moody and silent, and when one of the men enquired of him if some oats should be hoisted to an upper floor or not, he said shortly, "Ask Mr. Farfrae. He's master here!"

Morally he was; there could be no doubt of it. Henchard, who had hitherto been the most admired man in his circle, was the most admired no longer. One day the daughters of a deceased farmer in Durnover wanted an opinion of the value of their haystack, and sent a messenger to ask Mr. Farfrae to oblige them with one. The messenger, who was a child, met in the yard not Farfrae, but Henchard.

"Very well," he said. "I'll come."

"But please will Mr. Farfrae come?" said the child.

"I am going that way. . . . Why Mr. Farfrae?" said Henchard, with the fixed look of thought. "Why do people always want Mr. Farfrae?"

"I suppose because they like him so—that's what they say."

"Oh—I see—that's what they say—hey? They like him because he's cleverer than Mr. Henchard, and because he knows more; and, in short, Mr. Henchard can't hold a candle to him—hey?"

"Yes—that's just it, sir—some of it."

"Oh, there's more? Of course there's more! What besides? Come, here's a sixpence for a fairing."

" 'And he's better tempered, and Henchard's a fool to him,' they say. And when some of the women were a-walking home they said, 'He's a diment—he's a chap o' wax—he's the best—he's the horse for my money,' says they. And they said, 'He's the most understanding man o' them two by long chalks. I wish he was the master instead of Henchard,' they said."

"They'll talk any nonsense," Henchard replied with covered gloom. "Well, you can go now. And I am coming to value the hay, d'ye hear?—I." The boy departed, and Henchard murmured, "Wish he were master here, do they?"

He went towards Durnover. On his way he overtook Farfrae. They walked on together, Henchard looking mostly on the ground.

"You're no yoursel' the day?" Donald enquired.

"Yes, I am very well," said Henchard.

"But ye are a bit down—surely ye are down? Why, there's nothing to be angry about! 'Tis splendid stuff that we've got from Blackmoor Vale. By the by, the people in Durnover want their hay valued."

"Yes. I am going there."

"I'll go with ye."

As Henchard did not reply Donald practised a piece of music *sotto voce*, till, getting near the bereaved people's door, he stopped himself with—

"Ah, as their father is dead, I won't go on with such as that. How could I forget?"

"Do you care so very much about hurting folks' feelings?" observed Henchard with a half sneer. "You do, I know—especially mine!"

"I am sorry if I have hurt yours, sir," replied Donald, standing still, with a second expression of the same sentiment in the regretfulness of his face. "Why should you say it—think it?"

The cloud lifted from Henchard's brow, and as Donald finished the corn-merchant turned to him, regarding his breast rather than his face.

"I have been hearing things that vexed me," he said. " 'Twas that made me short in my manner—made me overlook what you really are. Now, I don't want to go in here about this hay—Farfrae, you can do it better than I. They sent for ye, too. I have to attend a meeting of the Town Council at eleven, and 'tis drawing on for't."

They parted thus in renewed friendship, Donald forbearing to ask Henchard for meanings that were not very plain to him. On Henchard's part there was now again repose; and yet, whenever he thought of Farfrae, it was with a dim dread; and he often regretted that he had told the young man his whole heart, and confided to him the secrets of his life.

XVI

O N THIS ACCOUNT HENCHARD'S MANNER TOWARDS FARFRAE INSENSIBLY BECAME MORE reserved. He was courteous—too courteous—and Farfrae was quite surprised at the good breeding which now for the first time showed itself among the qualities of a man he had hitherto thought undisciplined, if warm and sincere. The corn-factor seldom or never again put his arm upon the young man's shoulder so as to nearly weigh him down with the pressure of mechanised friendship. He left off coming to Donald's lodgings and shouting into the passage. "Hoy, Farfrae, boy, come and have some dinner with us! Don't sit here in solitary confinement!" But in the daily routine of their business there was little change.

Thus their lives rolled on till a day of public rejoicing was suggested to the country at large in celebration of a national event that had recently taken place.

For some time Casterbridge, by nature slow, made no response. Then one day Donald Farfrae broached the subject to Henchard by asking if he would have any objection to lend some rick-cloths to himself and a few others, who contemplated getting up an entertainment of some sort on the day named, and required a shelter for the same, to which they might charge admission at the rate of so much a head.

"Have as many cloths as you like," Henchard replied.

When his manager had gone about the business Henchard was fired with emulation. It certainly had been very remiss of him, as Mayor, he thought, to call no meeting ere this, to discuss what should be done on this holiday. But Farfrae had been so cursed quick in his movements as to give old-fashioned people in authority no chance of the initiative. However, it was not too late; and on second thoughts he determined to take upon his own shoulders the responsibility of organizing some amusements, if the other Councilmen would leave the matter in his hands. To this they quite readily agreed, the majority being fine old crusted characters who had a decided taste for living without worry.

So Henchard set about his preparations for a really brilliant thing—such as should be worthy of the venerable town. As for Farfrae's little affair, Henchard nearly forgot it; except once now and then when, on it coming into his mind, he said to himself, "Charge admission at so much a head—just like a Scotchman!—who is going to pay anything a head?" The diversions which the Mayor intended to provide were to be entirely free.

He had grown so dependent upon Donald that he could scarcely resist calling him in to consult. But by sheer self-coercion he refrained. No, he thought, Farfrae would be suggesting such improvements in his damned luminous way, that in spite of himself he, Henchard, would sink to the position of second fiddle, and only scrape harmonies to his manager's talents.

Everybody applauded the Mayor's proposed entertainment, especially when it became known that he meant to pay for it all himself.

Close to the town was an elevated green spot surrounded by an ancient square earthwork—earthworks square, and not square, were as common as blackberries hereabout—a spot whereon the Casterbridge people usually held any kind of merry-making, meeting, or sheep-fair that required more space than the streets would afford. On one side it sloped to the river Froom, and from any point a view was obtained of the country round for many miles. This pleasant upland was to be the scene of Henchard's exploit.

He advertised about the town, in long posters of a pink colour, that games of all sorts would take place here; and set to work a little battalion of men under his own eye. They erected greasy-poles for climbing, with smoked hams and local cheeses at the top. They placed hurdles in rows for jumping over; across the river they laid a slippery pole, with a live pig of the neighbourhood tied at the other end, to become the property of the man who could walk over and get it. There were also provided wheelbarrows for racing, donkeys for the same, a stage for boxing, wrestling, and drawing blood generally; sacks for jumping in. Moreover, not forgetting his principles, Henchard provided a mammoth tea, of which everybody who lived in the borough was invited to partake without payment. The tables were laid parallel with the inner slope of the rampart, and awnings were stretched overhead.

Passing to and fro the Mayor beheld the unattractive exterior of Farfrae's erection in the West Walk, rick-cloths of different sizes and colours being hung up to the arching trees without any regard to appearance. He was easy in his mind now, for his own preparations far transcended these.

The morning came. The sky, which had been remarkably clear down to within a day or two, was overcast, and the weather threatening, the wind having an unmistakable hint of water in it. Henchard wished he had not been quite so sure about the continuance of a fair season. But it was too late to modify or postpone, and the proceedings went on. At twelve o'clock the rain began to fall, small and steady, commencing and increasing so insensibly that it was difficult to state exactly when dry weather ended or wet established itself. In an hour the slight moisture resolved itself into a monotonous smiting of earth by heaven, in torrents to which no end could be prognosticated.

A number of people had heroically gathered in the field but by three o'clock Henchard discerned that his project was doomed to end in failure. The hams at the top of the poles dripped watered smoke in the form of a brown liquor, the pig shivered in the wind, the grain of the deal tables showed through the sticking table cloths, for the awning allowed the rain to drift under at its will, and to enclose the sides at this hour seemed a useless undertaking. The landscape over the river disappeared; the wind played on the tent-cords in Æolian improvisations, and at length rose to such a pitch that the whole erection slanted to the ground, those who had taken shelter within it having to crawl out on their hands and knees.

But towards six the storm abated, and a drier breeze shook the moisture from the grass bents. It seemed possible to carry out the programme after all. The awning was set up again; the band was called out from its shelter, and ordered to begin, and where the tables had stood a place was cleared for dancing.

"But where are the folk?" said Henchard, after the lapse of half an hour, during which time only two men and a woman had stood up to dance. "The shops are all shut. Why don't they come?"

"They are at Farfrae's affair in the West Walk," answered a councilman who stood in the field with the Mayor.

"A few, I suppose. But where are the body o 'em?"

"All out-of-doors are there."

"Then the more fools they!"

Henchard walked away moodily. One or two young fellows gallantly came to climb the poles, to save the hams from being wasted; but as there were no spectators, and the whole scene presented the most melancholy appearance, Henchard gave orders that the proceedings were to be suspended, and the entertainment closed, the food to be distributed among the poor people of the town. In a short time nothing was left in the field but a few hurdles, the tents, and the poles.

Henchard returned to his house, had tea with his wife and daughter, and then walked out. It was now dusk. He soon saw that the tendency of all promenaders was towards a particular spot in the Walks, and eventually proceeded thither himself. The notes of a stringed band came from the enclosure that Farfrae had erected—the pavilion, as he called it—and when he reached it he perceived that a gigantic tent had been ingeniously constructed without poles or ropes. The densest point of the avenue of sycamores had been selected, where the boughs made a closely interlaced vault overhead; to these boughs the canvas had been hung, and a barrel roof was the result. The end towards the wind was enclosed, the other end was open. Henchard went round and saw the interior.

In form it was like the nave of a cathedral with one gable removed, but the scene within was anything but devotional. A reel or fling of some sort was in progress; and the usually sedate Farfrae was in the midst of the other dancers in the costume of a wild Highlander, flinging himself about and spinning to the tune. For a moment Henchard could not help laughing. Then he perceived the immense admiration for the Scotchman that revealed itself in the women's faces; and when this exhibition was over, and a new dance proposed, and Donald had disappeared for a time to return in his natural garments, he had an un-limited choice of partners, every girl being in a coming-on disposition towards one who so thoroughly understood the poetry of motion as he.

All the town crowded to the Walk, such a delightful idea of a ball-room never having occurred to the inhabitants before. Among the rest of the onlookers were Elizabeth and her mother—the former thoughtful yet much interested, her eyes beaming with a longing lingering light, as if Nature had been advised by Correggio in their creation. The dancing progressed with unabated spirit, and Henchard walked and waited till his wife should be disposed to go home. He did not care to keep in the light, and when he went into the dark it was worse, for there he heard remarks of a kind which were becoming too frequent:

"Mr. Henchard's rejoicings couldn't say good-morning to this," said one. "A man must be a headstrong stunpoll to think folk would go up to that bleak place to-day."

The other answered that people said it was not only in such things as those that the Mayor was wanting. "Where would his business be if it were not for this young fellow? 'Twas verily Fortune sent him to Henchard. His accounts were like a bramblewood when Mr. Farfrae came. He used to reckon his sacks by chalk strokes all in a row like garden-palings, measure his ricks by stretching with his arms, weigh his trusses by a lift, judge his hay by a 'chaw,' and settle the price with a curse. But now this accomplished young man does it all by ciphering and mensuration. Then the wheat—that sometimes used to taste so strong o' mice when made into bread that people could fairly tell the breed—Farfrae has a plan for purifying, so that nobody would dream the smallest four-legged beast had walked over it once. Oh yes, everybody is full of him, and the care Mr. Henchard has to keep him, to be sure!" concluded this gentleman.

"But he won't do it for long, good-now," said the other.

"No!" said Henchard to himself behind the tree. "Or if he do, he'll be honeycombed clean out of all the character and standing that he's built up in these eighteen year!"

He went back to the dancing pavilion. Farfrae was footing a quaint little dance with Elizabeth-Jane—an old country thing, the only one she knew, and though he consider-ately toned down his movements to suit her demurer gait, the pattern of the shining little nails in the soles of his boots became familiar to the eyes of every bystander. The tune had enticed her into it; being a tune of a busy, vaulting, leaping sort—some low notes on the silver string of each fiddle, then a skipping on the small, like running up and down ladders—"Miss M'Leod of Ayr" was its name, so Mr. Farfrae had said, and that it was very popular in his own country.

It was soon over, and the girl looked at Henchard for approval; but he did not give it. He seemed not to see her. "Look here, Farfrae," he said, like one whose mind was else-where, "I'll go to Port-Bredy Great Market to-morrow myself. You can stay and put things right in your clothes-box, and recover strength to your knees after your vagaries." He planted on Donald an antagonistic glare that had begun as a smile.

Some other townsmen came up, and Donald drew aside. "What's this, Henchard," said Alderman Tubber, applying his thumb to the corn-factor like a cheese-taster. "An op-position randy to yours, eh? Jack's as good as his master, eh? Cut ye out quite, hasn't he?"

"You see, Mr. Henchard," said the lawyer, another good-natured friend, "where you made the mistake was in going so far afield. You should have taken a leaf out of his book, and have had your sports in a sheltered place like this. But you didn't think of it, you see; and he did, and that's where he's beat you."

"He'll be top-sawyer soon of you two, and carry all afore him," added jocular Mr. Tubber.

"No," said Henchard gloomily. "He won't be that, because he's shortly going to leave me." He looked towards Donald, who had come near. "Mr. Farfrae's time as my manager is drawing to a close—isn't it, Farfrae?"

The young man, who could now read the lines and folds of Henchard's strongly-traced face as if they were clear verbal inscriptions, quietly assented; and when people deplored the fact, and asked why it was, he simply replied that Mr. Henchard no longer required his help.

Henchard went home, apparently satisfied. But in the morning, when his jealous temper had passed away, his heart sank within him at what he had said and done. He was the more disturbed when he found that this time Farfrae was determined to take him at his word.

XVII

ELIZABETH-JANE HAD PERCEIVED FROM HENCHARD'S MANNER THAT IN ASSENTING TO dance she had made a mistake of some kind. In her simplicity she did not know what it was till a hint from a nodding acquaintance enlightened her. As the Mayor's step-daughter, she learnt, she had not been quite in her place in treading a measure amid such a mixed throng as filled the dancing pavilion.

Thereupon her ears, cheeks, and chin glowed like live coals at the dawning of the idea that her tastes were not good enough for her position, and would bring her into disgrace.

This made her very miserable, and she looked about for her mother; but Mrs. Henchard, who had less idea of conventionality than Elizabeth herself, had gone away, leaving her daughter to return at her own pleasure. The latter moved on into the dark dense old avenues, or rather vaults of living woodwork, which ran along the town boundary, and stood reflecting.

A man followed in a few minutes, and her face being towards the shine from the tent he recognised her. It was Farfrae—just come from the dialogue with Henchard which had signified his dismissal.

"And it's you, Miss Newson?—and I've been looking for ye everywhere!" he said, overcoming a sadness imparted by the estrangement with the corn-merchant. "May I walk on with you as far as your street-corner?"

She thought there might be something wrong in this, but did not utter any objection. So together they went on, first down the West Walk, and then into the Bowling Walk, till Farfrae said, "It's like that I'm going to leave you soon."

She faltered, "Why?"

"Oh—as a mere matter of business—nothing more. But we'll not concern ourselves about it—it is for the best. I hoped to have another dance with you."

She said she could not dance—in any proper way.

"Oh, but you do! It's the feeling for it rather than the learning of steps that makes pleasant dancers. . . . I fear I offended your father by getting up this! And now, perhaps, I'll have to go to another part o' the warrld altogether!"

This seemed such a melancholy prospect that Elizabeth-Jane breathed a sigh—letting it off in fragments that he might not hear her. But darkness makes people truthful, and the Scotchman went on impulsively—perhaps he had heard her after all:

"I wish I was richer, Miss Newson; and your stepfather had not been offended, I would ask you something in a short time—yes, I would ask you to-night. But that's not for me!"

What he would have asked her he did not say, and instead of encouraging him she remained incompetently silent. Thus afraid one of another they continued their promenade along the walls till they got near the bottom of the Bowling Walk; twenty steps further and the trees would end, and the street-corner and lamps appear. In consciousness of this they stopped.

"I never found out who it was that sent us to Durnover granary on a fool's errand that day," said Donald, in his undulating tones. "Did ye ever know yourself, Miss Newson?"

"Never," said she.

"I wonder why they did it!"

"For fun, perhaps."

"Perhaps it was not for fun. It might have been that they thought they would like us to stay waiting there, talking to one another? Ay, well! I hope you Casterbridge folk will not forget me if I go."

"That I'm sure we won't!" she said earnestly. "I—wish you wouldn't go at all."

They had got into the lamplight. "Now, I'll think over that," said Donald Farfrae. "And I'll not come up to your door; but part from you here; lest it make your father more angry still."

They parted, Farfrae returning into the dark Bowling Walk, and Elizabeth-Jane going up the street. Without any consciousness of what she was doing she started running with all her might till she reached her father's door. "Oh dear me—what am I at?" she thought, as she pulled up breathless.

Indoors she fell to conjecturing the meaning of Farfrae's enigmatic words about not daring to ask her what he fain would. Elizabeth, that silent observing woman, had long noted how he was rising in favour among the townspeople; and knowing Henchard's nature now she had feared that Farfrae's days as manager were numbered; so that the announcement gave her little surprise. Would Mr. Farfrae stay in Casterbridge despite his words and her father's dismissal? His occult breathings to her might be solvable by his course in that respect.

The next day was windy—so windy that walking in the garden she picked up a portion of the draft of a letter on business in Donald Farfrae's writing, which had flown over the wall from the office. The useless scrap she took indoors, and began to copy the calligraphy, which she much admired. The letter began "Dear Sir," and presently writing on a loose slip "Elizabeth-Jane," she laid the latter over "Sir," making the phrase "Dear Elizabeth-Jane." When she saw the effect a quick red ran up her face and warmed her through, though nobody was there to see what she had done. She quickly tore up the slip, and threw it away. After this she grew cool and laughed at herself, walked about the room, and laughed again; not joyfully, but distressfully rather.

It was quickly known in Casterbridge that Farfrae and Henchard had decided to dispense with each other. Elizabeth-Jane's anxiety to know if Farfrae were going away from the town reached a pitch that disturbed her, for she could no longer conceal from herself the cause. At length the news reached her that he was not going to leave the place. A man following the same trade as Henchard, but on a very small scale, had sold his business to Farfrae, who was forthwith about to start as corn and hay-merchant on his own account.

Her heart fluttered when she heard of this step of Donald's, proving that he meant to remain; and yet, would a man who cared one little bit for her have endangered his suit by setting up a business in opposition to Mr. Henchard's? Surely not; and it must have been a passing impulse only which had led him to address her so softly.

To solve the problem whether her appearance on the evening of the dance were such as to inspire a fleeting love at first sight, she dressed herself up exactly as she had dressed then—the muslin, the spencer, the sandals, the parasol—and looked in the mirror. The picture glassed back was, in her opinion, precisely of such a kind as to inspire that fleeting regard, and no more—"just enough to make him silly, and not enough to keep him so," she said luminously; and Elizabeth thought, in a much lower key, that by this time he had discovered how plain and homely was the informing spirit of that pretty outside.

Hence, when she felt her heart going out to him, she would say to herself with a mock pleasantry that carried an ache with it, "No, no, Elizabeth-Jane—such dreams are not for you!" She tried to prevent herself from seeing him, and thinking of him; succeeding fairly well in the former attempt, in the latter not so completely.

Henchard, who had been hurt at finding that Farfrae did not mean to put up with his temper any longer, was incensed beyond measure when he learnt what the young man had done as an alternative. It was in the town-hall, after a Council meeting, that he first became aware of Farfrae's *coup* for establishing himself independently in the town; and his voice might have been heard as far as the town-pump expressing his feelings to his fellow-councilmen. Those tones showed that, though under a long reign of self-control he had become Mayor and churchwarden and what not, there was still the same unruly volcanic stuff beneath the rind of Michael Henchard as when he had sold his wife at Weydon Fair.

"Well, he's a friend of mine, and I'm a friend of his—or if we are not, what are we? 'Od send, if I've not been his friend, who has, I should like to know? Didn't he come here without a sound shoe to his voot? Didn't I keep him here—help him to a living? Didn't I help him to money, or whatever he wanted? I stuck out for no terms—I said 'Name your own price.' I'd have shared my last crust with that young fellow at one time, I liked him so well. And now he's defied me! But damn him, I'll have a tussle with him now—at fair buying and selling, mind—at fair buying and selling! And if I can't overbid such a stripling as he, then I'm not wo'th a varden! We'll show that we know our business as well as one here and there!"

His friends of the Corporation did not specially respond. Henchard was less popular now than he had been when nearly two years before, they had voted him to the chief magistracy on account of his amazing energy. While they had collectively profited by this quality of the corn-factor's, they had been made to wince individually on more than one occasion. So he went out of the hall and down the street alone.

Reaching home he seemed to recollect something with a sour satisfaction. He called Elizabeth-Jane. Seeing how he looked when she entered she appeared alarmed.

"Nothing to find fault with," he said, observing her concern. "Only I want to caution you, my dear. That man, Farfrae—it is about him. I've seen him talking to you two or three times—he danced with 'ee at the rejoicings, and came home with 'ee. Now, now, no blame to you. But just harken: Have you made him any foolish promise? Gone the least bit beyond sniff and snaff at all?"

"No. I have promised him nothing."

"Good. All's well that ends well. I particularly wish you not to see him again."

"Very well, sir."

"You promise?"

She hesitated for a moment, and then said—

"Yes, if you much wish it."

"I do. He's an enemy to our house!"

When she had gone he sat down, and wrote in a heavy hand to Farfrae thus:—

SIR—I make request that henceforth you and my step-daughter be as strangers to each other. She on her part has promised to welcome no more addresses from you; and I trust, therefore, you will not attempt to force them upon her.

M. HENCHARD

One would almost have supposed Henchard to have had policy to see that no better *modus vivendi* could be arrived at with Farfrae than by encouraging him to become his son-in-law. But such a scheme for buying over a rival had nothing to recommend it to the Mayor's headstrong faculties. With all domestic *finesse* of that kind he was hopelessly at variance. Loving a man or hating him, his diplomacy was as wrongheaded as a buffalo's; and his wife had not ventured to suggest the course which she, for many reasons, would have welcomed gladly.

Meanwhile, Donald Farfrae had opened the gates of commerce on his own account at a spot on Durnover Hill—as far as possible from Henchard's stores, and with every intention of keeping clear of his former friend and employer's customers. There was, it seemed to the younger man, room for both of them and to spare. The town was small, but the corn and hay-trade was proportionately large, and with his native sagacity he saw opportunity for a share of it.

So determined was he to do nothing which should seem like trade-antagonism to the Mayor that he refused his first customer—a large farmer of good repute—because Henchard and this man had dealt together within the preceding three months.

"He was once my friend," said Farfrae, "and it's not for me to take business from him. I am sorry to disappoint you, but I cannot hurt the trade of a man who's been so kind to me."

In spite of this praiseworthy course the Scotchman's trade increased. Whether it were that his northern energy was an over-mastering force among the easy-going Wessex worthies, or whether it was sheer luck, the fact remained that whatever he touched he prospered in. Like Jacob in Padan-Aram, he would no sooner humbly limit himself to the ringstraked-and-spotted exceptions of trade than the ringstraked-and-spotted would multiply and prevail.

But most probably luck had little to do with it. Character is Fate, said Novalis, and Farfrae's character was just the reverse of Henchard's, who might not inaptly be described as Faust has been described—as a vehement gloomy being who had quitted the ways of vulgar men, without light to guide him on a better way.

Farfrae duly received the request to discontinue attentions to Elizabeth-Jane. His acts of that kind had been so slight that the request was almost superfluous. Yet he had felt a considerable interest in her, and after some cogitation he decided that it would be as well to enact no Romeo part just then—for the young girl's sake no less than his own. Thus the incipient attachment was stifled down.

A time came when, avoid collision with his former friend as he might, Farfrae was compelled, in sheer self-defence, to close with Henchard in mortal commercial combat. He could no longer parry the fierce attacks of the latter by simple avoidance. As soon as their war of prices began everybody was interested, and some few guessed the end. It was, in some degree, Northern insight matched against Southern doggedness—the dirk against the cudgel—and Henchard's weapon was one which, if it did not deal ruin at the first or second stroke, left him afterwards well-nigh at his antagonist's mercy.

Almost every Saturday they encountered each other amid the crowd of farmers which thronged about the market-place in the weekly course of their business. Donald was always ready, and even anxious, to say a few friendly words; but the Mayor invariably gazed stormfully past him, like one who had endured and lost on his account, and could in no sense forgive the wrong; nor did Farfrae's snubbed manner of perplexity at all appease him. The large farmers, corn-merchants, millers, auctioneers, and others had each an official stall in the corn-market room, with their names painted thereon; and when to the familiar series of "Henchard," "Everdene," "Shinar," "Darton," and so on, was added one inscribed "Farfrae," in staring new letters, Henchard was stung into bitterness; like Bellerophon, he wandered away from the crowd, cankered in soul.

From that day Donald Farfrae's name was seldom mentioned in Henchard's house. If at breakfast or dinner Elizabeth-Jane's mother inadvertently alluded to her favourite's movements, the girl would implore her by a look to be silent; and her husband would say, "What—are you, too, my enemy?"

XVIII

THERE CAME A SHOCK WHICH HAD BEEN FORESEEN FOR SOME TIME BY ELIZABETH, AS THE box passenger foresees the approaching jerk from some channel across the highway.

Her mother was ill—too unwell to leave her room. Henchard, who treated her kindly, except in moments of irritation, sent at once for the richest, busiest doctor, whom he supposed to be the best. Bed-time came, and they burnt a light all night. In a day or two she rallied.

Elizabeth, who had been staying up, did not appear at breakfast on the second morning, and Henchard sat down alone. He was startled to see a letter for him from Jersey in a writing he knew too well, and had expected least to behold again. He took it up in his hands and looked at it as at a picture, a vision, a vista of past enactments; and then he read it as an unimportant finale to conjecture.

The writer said that she at length perceived how impossible it would be for any further communications to proceed between them now that his remarriage had taken place. That such reunion had been the only straightforward course open to him she was bound to admit. "On calm reflection, therefore," she went on, "I quite forgive you for landing me in such a dilemma, remembering that you concealed nothing before our ill-advised acquaintance; and that you really did set before me in your grim way the fact of there being a certain risk in intimacy with you, slight as it seemed to be after fifteen or sixteen years of silence on your wife's part. I thus look upon the whole as a misfortune of mine, and not a fault of yours.

"So that, Michael, I must ask you to overlook those letters with which I pestered you day after day in the heat of my feelings. They were written whilst I thought your conduct to me cruel; but now I know more particulars of the position you were in I see how inconsiderate my reproaches were.

"Now you will, I am sure, perceive that the one condition which will make any future happiness possible for me, is that the past connection between our lives be kept secret outside this isle. Speak of it I know you will not; and I can trust you not to write of it. One safeguard more remains to be mentioned—that no writings of mine, or trifling articles belonging to me, should be left in your possession through neglect or forgetfulness. To this end may I request you to return to me any such you may have, particularly the letters written in the first abandonment of feeling.

"For the handsome sum you forwarded to me as a plaster to the wound, I heartily thank you.

"I am now on my way to Bristol, to see my only relative. She is rich, and I hope will do something for me. I shall return through Casterbridge and Budmouth, where I shall take the packet-boat. Can you meet me with the letters and other trifles? I shall be in the coach which changes horses at the Antelope Hotel at half-past five Wednesday evening; I shall be wearing a Paisley shawl with a red centre, and thus may easily be found. I should prefer this plan of receiving them to having them sent.—I remain still, yours ever,

"LUCETTA"

Henchard breathed heavily. "Poor thing—better you had not known me! Upon my heart and soul, if ever I should be left in a position to carry out that marriage with thee, I *ought* to do it—I ought to do it, indeed!"

The contingency that he had in his mind was, of course, the death of Mrs. Henchard.

As requested, he sealed up Lucetta's letters, and put the parcel aside till the day she had appointed; this plan of returning them by hand being apparently a little *ruse* of the young lady for exchanging a word or two with him on past times. He would have preferred not to see her; but deeming that there could be no great harm in acquiescing thus far, he went at dusk and stood opposite the coach-office.

The evening was chilly, and the coach was late. Henchard crossed over to it while the horses were being changed; but there was no Lucetta inside or out. Concluding that something had happened to modify her arrangements he gave the matter up and went home, not without a sense of relief.

Meanwhile Mrs. Henchard was weakening visibly. She could not go out-of-doors any more. One day, after much thinking which seemed to distress her, she said she wanted to write something. A desk was put upon her bed with pen and paper, and at her request she was left alone. She remained writing for a short time, folded her paper carefully, called Elizabeth-Jane to bring a taper and wax, and then, still refusing assistance, sealed up the sheet, directed it, and locked it in her desk. She had directed it in these words:—

"Mr. Michael Henchard. Not to be opened till Elizabeth-Jane's wedding-day."

The latter sat up with her mother to the utmost of her strength night after night. To learn to take the universe seriously there is no quicker way than to watch—to be a "waker," as the country-people call it. Between the hours at which the last toss-pot went by and the first sparrow shook himself, the silence in Casterbridge—barring the rare sound of the watchman—was broken in Elizabeth's ear only by the time-piece in the bedroom ticking frantically against the clock on the stairs; ticking harder and harder till it seemed to clang like a gong; and all this while the subtle-souled girl asking herself why she was born, why sitting in a room, and blinking at the candle; why things around her had taken the shape they wore in preference to every other possible shape. Why they stared at her so helplessly, as if waiting for the touch of some wand that should release them from terrestrial constraint; what that chaos called consciousness, which spun in her at this moment like a top, tended to, and began in. Her eyes fell together; she was awake, yet she was asleep.

A word from her mother roused her. Without preface, and as the continuation of a scene already progressing in her mind, Mrs. Henchard said: "You remember the note sent to you and Mr. Farfrae—asking you to meet someone in Durnover Barton—and that you thought it was a trick to make fools of you?"

"Yes."

"It was not to make fools of you—it was done to bring you together. 'Twas I did it."

"Why?" said Elizabeth, with a start.

"I—wanted you to marry Mr. Farfrae."

"O mother!" Elizabeth-Jane bent down her head so much that she looked quite into her own lap. But as her mother did not go on, she said, "What reason?"

"Well, I had a reason. 'Twill out one day. I wish it could have been in my time! But there—nothing is as you wish it! Henchard hates him."

"Perhaps they'll be friends again," murmured the girl.

"I don't know—I don't know." After this her mother was silent, and dozed; and she spoke on the subject no more.

Some little time later on, Farfrae was passing Henchard's house on a Sunday morning, when he observed that the blinds were all down. He rang the bell so softly that it only sounded a single full note and a small one; and then he was informed that Mrs. Henchard was dead—just dead—that very hour.

At the town-pump there were gathered when he passed a few old inhabitants, who came there for water whenever they had, as at present, spare time to fetch it, because it was purer from that original fount than from their own wells. Mrs. Cuxsom, who had been standing there for an indefinite time with her pitcher, was describing the incidents of Mrs. Henchard's death, as she had learnt them from the nurse.

"And she was white as marble-stone," said Mrs. Cuxsom. "And likewise such a thoughtful woman, too—ah, poor soul—that a' minded every little thing that wanted tending. 'Yes,' says she, 'when I'm gone, and my last breath's blowed, look in the top drawer o' the chest in the back-room by the window, and you'll find all my coffin clothes; a piece of flannel—that's to put under me, and the little piece is to put under my head; and my new stockings for my feet—they are folded alongside, and all my other things. And there's four ounce pennies, the heaviest I could find, a-tied up in bits of linen, for weights—two for my right eye and two for my left,' she said. 'And when you've used 'em, and my eyes don't open no more, bury the pennies, good souls and don't ye go spending 'em, for I shouldn't like it. And open the windows as soon as I am carried out, and make it as cheerful as you can for Elizabeth-Jane.' "

"Ah, poor heart!"

"Well, and Martha did it, and buried the ounce pennies in the garden. But if ye'll believe words, that man, Christopher Coney, went and dug 'em up, and spent 'em at the Three Mariners. 'Faith,' he said, 'why should death rob life o' fourpence? Death's not of such good report that we should respect 'en to that extent,' says he."

" 'Twas a cannibal deed!" deprecated her listeners.

"Gad, then I won't quite ha'e it," said Solomon Longways. "I say it to-day, and 'tis a Sunday morning, and I wouldn't speak wrongfully for a zilver zixpence at such a time. I don't see noo harm in it. To respect the dead is sound doxology; and I wouldn't sell skellintons—leastwise respectable skellintons—to be varnished for 'natomies, except I were out o' work. But money is scarce, and throats get dry. Why *should* death rob life o' fourpence? I say there was no treason in it."

"Well, poor soul; she's helpless to hinder that or anything now," answered Mother Cuxsom. "And all her shining keys will be took from her, and her cupboards opened; and little things a' didn't wish seen, anybody will see; and her wishes and ways will all be as nothing!"

XIX

H ENCHARD AND ELIZABETH SAT CONVERSING BY THE FIRE. IT WAS THREE WEEKS AFTER Mrs. Henchard's funeral, the candles were not lighted, and a restless, acrobatic flame, poised on a coal, called from the shady walls the smiles of all shapes that could respond—the old pier-glass, with gilt columns and huge entablature, the picture-frames, sundry knobs and handles, and the brass rosette at the bottom of each riband bell-pull on either side of the chimney-piece.

"Elizabeth, do you think much of old times?" said Henchard.

"Yes, sir; often," she said.

"Who do you put in your pictures of 'em?"

"Mother and father—nobody else hardly."

Henchard always looked like one bent on resisting pain when Elizabeth-Jane spoke of Richard Newson as "father." "Ah! I am out of all that, am I not?" he said. . . . "Was Newson a kind father?"

"Yes, sir; very."

Henchard's face settled into an expression of stolid loneliness which gradually modulated into something softer. "Suppose I had been your real father?" he said. "Would you have cared for me as much as you cared for Richard Newson?"

"I can't think it," she said quickly. "I can think of no other as my father, except my father."

Henchard's wife was dissevered from him by death; his friend and helper Farfrae by estrangement; Elizabeth-Jane by ignorance. It seemed to him that only one of them could possibly be recalled, and that was the girl. His mind began vibrating between the wish to reveal himself to her and the policy of leaving well alone, till he could no longer sit still. He walked up and down, and then he came and stood behind her chair, looking down upon the top of her head. He could no longer restrain his impulse. "What did your mother tell you about me—my history?" he asked.

"That you were related by marriage."

"She should have told more—before you knew me! Then my task would not have been such a hard one. . . . Elizabeth, it is I who am your father, and not Richard Newson. Shame alone prevented your wretched parents from owning this to you while both of 'em were alive."

The back of Elizabeth's head remained still, and her shoulders did not denote even the movements of breathing. Henchard went on: "I'd rather have your scorn, your fear, anything than your ignorance; 'tis that I hate! Your mother and I were man and wife when we were young. What you saw was our second marriage. Your mother was too honest. We had thought each other dead—and—Newson became her husband."

This was the nearest approach Henchard could make to the full truth. As far as he personally was concerned he would have screened nothing; but he showed a respect for the young girl's sex and years worthy of a better man.

When he had gone on to give details which a whole series of slight and unregarded incidents in her past life strangely corroborated; when, in short, she believed his story to be true, she became greatly agitated, and turning round to the table flung her face upon it weeping.

"Don't cry—don't cry!" said Henchard, with vehement pathos, "I can't bear it, I won't bear it. I am your father; why should you cry? Am I so dreadful, so hateful to 'ee? Don't take against me, Elizabeth-Jane!" he cried, grasping her wet hand. "Don't take against me—though I was a drinking man once, and used your mother roughly—I'll be kinder to you than *he* was! I'll do anything, if you will only look upon me as your father!"

She tried to stand up and comfort him trustfully; but she could not; she was troubled at his presence, like the brethren at the avowal of Joseph.

"I don't want you to come to me all of a sudden," said Henchard in jerks, and moving like a great tree in a wind. "No, Elizabeth, I don't. I'll go away and not see you till tomorrow, or when you like, and then I'll show 'ee papers to prove my words. There, I am gone, and won't disturb you any more. . . . 'Twas I that chose your name, my daughter; your mother wanted it Susan. There, don't forget 'twas I gave you your name!" He went out at the door and shut her softly in, and she heard him go away into the garden. But he had not done. Before she had moved, or in any way recovered from the effect of his disclosure, he reappeared.

"One word more, Elizabeth," he said. "You'll take my surname now—hey? Your mother was against it, but it will be much more pleasant to me. 'Tis legally yours, you know. But nobody need know that. You shall take it as if by choice. I'll talk to my lawyer—I don't know the law of it exactly; but will you do this—let me put a few lines into the newspaper that such is to be your name?"

"If it is my name I must have it, mustn't I?" she asked.

"Well, well; usage is everything in these matters."

"I wonder why mother didn't wish it?"

"Oh, some whim of the poor soul's. Now get a bit of paper and draw up a paragraph as I shall tell you. But let's have a light."

"I can see by the firelight," she answered. "Yes—I'd rather."

"Very well."

She got a piece of paper, and bending over the fender, wrote at his dictation words which he had evidently got by heart from some advertisement or other—words to the effect that she, the writer, hitherto known as Elizabeth-Jane Newson, was going to call herself Elizabeth-Jane Henchard forthwith. It was done, and fastened up, and directed to the office of the *Casterbridge Chronicle*.

"Now," said Henchard, with the blaze of satisfaction that he always emitted when he had carried his point—though tenderness softened it this time—"I'll go upstairs and hunt for some documents that will prove it all to you. But I won't trouble you with them till to-morrow. Good-night, my Elizabeth-Jane!"

He was gone before the bewildered girl could realise what it all meant, or adjust her filial sense to the new centre of gravity. She was thankful that he had left her to herself for the evening, and sat down over the fire. Here she remained in silence, and wept—not for her mother now,·but for the genial sailor Richard Newson, to whom she seemed doing a wrong.

Henchard, in the meantime, had gone upstairs. Papers of a domestic nature he kept in a drawer in his bedroom, and this he unlocked. Before turning them over he leant back and indulged in reposeful thought. Elizabeth was his at last, and she was a girl of such good sense and kind heart that she would be sure to like him. He was the kind of man to whom some human object for pouring out his heart upon—were it emotive or were it choleric—was almost a necessity. The craving for his heart for the re-establishment of this tenderest human tie had been great during his wife's lifetime, and now he had submitted to its mastery without reluctance and without fear. He bent over the drawer again, and proceeded in his search.

Among the other papers had been placed the contents of his wife's little desk, the keys of which had been handed to him at her request. Here was the letter addressed to him with the restriction, *"Not to be opened till Elizabeth-Jane's wedding-day."*

Mrs. Henchard, though more patient than her husband, had been no practical hand at anything. In sealing up the sheet, which was folded and tucked in without an envelope, in the old-fashioned way, she had overlaid the junction with a large mass of wax without the requisite under-touch of the same. The seal had cracked, and the letter was open. Henchard had no reason to suppose the restriction one of serious weight, and his feeling for his late wife had not been of the nature of deep respect. "Some trifling fancy or other of poor Susan's, I suppose," he said; and without curiosity he allowed his eyes to scan the letter:—

MY DEAR MICHAEL—For the good of all three of us, I have kept one thing a secret from you till now. I hope you will understand why; I think you will; though perhaps you may not forgive me. But, dear Michael, I have done it for the best. I shall be in my grave when you read this, and Elizabeth-Jane will have a home. Don't curse me, Mike—think of how I was situated. I can hardly write it, but here it is. Elizabeth-Jane is not your Elizabeth-Jane—the child who was in my arms when you sold me. No; she died three months after that, and this living one is my other husband's. I christened her by the same name we had given to the first, and she filled up the ache I felt at the other's loss. Michael, I am dying, and I might have held my tongue; but I could not. Tell her husband of this or not, as you may judge; and forgive, if you can, a woman you once deeply wronged, as she forgives you.

SUSAN HENCHARD

Her husband regarded the paper as if it were a window-pane through which he saw for miles. His lips twitched, and he seemed to compress his frame, as if to bear better. His usual habit was not to consider whether destiny were hard upon him or not—the shape of his ideals in cases of affliction being simply a moody "I am to suffer, I perceive." "So much scourging, then, is it for me?" But now through his passionate head there stormed this thought—that the blasting disclosure was what he had deserved.

His wife's extreme reluctance to have the girl's name altered from Newson to Henchard was now accounted for fully. It furnished another illustration of that honesty in dishonesty which had characterised her in other things.

He remained unnerved and purposeless for near a couple of hours; till he suddenly said, "Ah—I wonder if it is true!"

He jumped up in an impulse, kicked off his slippers, and went with a candle to the door of Elizabeth-Jane's room, where he put his ear to the keyhole and listened. She was breathing profoundly. Henchard softly turned the handle, entered, and shading the light, approached the bedside. Gradually bringing the light from behind a screening curtain he held it in such a manner that it fell slantwise on her face without shining on her eyes. He steadfastly regarded her features.

They were fair: his were dark. But this was an unimportant preliminary. In sleep there come to the surface buried genealogical facts, ancestral curves, dead men's traits, which the mobility of daytime animation screens and overwhelms. In the present statuesque repose of the young girl's countenance Richard Newson's was unmistakably reflected. He could not endure the sight of her, and hastened away.

Misery taught him nothing more than defiant endurance of it. His wife was dead, and the first impulse for revenge died with the thought that she was beyond him. He looked out at the night as at a fiend. Henchard, like all his kind, was superstitious, and he could not help thinking that the concatenation of events this evening had produced was the scheme of some sinister intelligence bent on punishing him. Yet they had developed naturally. If he had not revealed his past history to Elizabeth he would not have searched the drawer for papers, and so on. The mockery was, that he should have no sooner taught a girl to claim the shelter of his paternity than he discovered her to have no kinship with him.

This ironical sequence of things angered him like an impish trick from a fellow-creature. Like Prester John's, his table had been spread, and infernal harpies had snatched up the food. He went out of the house, and moved sullenly onward down the pavement till he came to the bridge at the bottom of the High Street. Here he turned in upon a bypath on the river bank, skirting the north-eastern limits of the town.

These precincts embodied the mournful phases of Casterbridge life, as the south avenues embodied its cheerful moods. The whole way along here was sunless, even in summer-time; in spring, white frosts lingered here when other places were steaming with warmth; while in winter it was the seed-field of all the aches, rheumatisms, and torturing cramps of the year. The Casterbridge doctors must have pined away for want of sufficient nourishment, but for the configuration of the landscape on the north-eastern side.

The river—slow, noiseless, and dark—the Schwarzwasser of Casterbridge—ran beneath a low cliff, the two together forming a defence which had rendered walls and artificial earthworks on this side unnecessary. Here were ruins of a Franciscan priory, and a mill attached to the same, the water of which roared down a back-hatch like the voice of desolation. Above the cliff, and behind the river, rose a pile of buildings, and in the front of the pile a square mass cut into the sky. It was like a pedestal lacking its statue. This missing feature, without which the design remained incomplete, was, in truth, the corpse of a man, for the square mass formed the base of the gallows, the extensive buildings at the back being the county gaol. In the meadow where Henchard now walked the mob were wont to gather whenever an execution took place, and there to the tune of the roaring weir they stood and watched the spectacle.

The exaggeration which darkness imparted to the glooms of this region impressed Henchard more than he had expected. The lugubrious harmony of the spot with his domestic situation was too perfect for him, impatient of effects, scenes, and adumbrations. It reduced his heartburning to melancholy, and he exclaimed, "Why the deuce did I come here!" He went on past the cottage in which the old local hangman had lived and died, in times before that calling was monopolised over all England by a single gentleman; and climbed up by a steep back lane into the town.

For the sufferings of that night, engendered by his bitter disappointment, he might well have been pitied. He was like one who had half fainted, and could neither recover nor complete the swoon. In words he could blame his wife, but not in his heart; and had he obeyed the wise directions outside her letter this pain would have been spared him for long—possibly forever, Elizabeth-Jane seeming to show no ambition to quit her safe and secluded maiden courses for the speculative path of matrimony.

The morning came after this night of unrest, and with it the necessity for a plan. He was far too self-willed to recede from a position, especially as it would involve humiliation. His daughter he had asserted her to be, and his daughter she should always think herself, no matter what hyprocrisy it involved.

But he was ill-prepared for the first step in this new situation. The moment he came into the breakfast-room Elizabeth advanced with open confidence to him and took him by the arm.

"I have thought and thought all night of it," she said frankly. "And I see that everything must be as you say. And I am going to look upon you as the father that you are, and not to call you Mr. Henchard any more. It is so plain to me now. Indeed, father, it is. For, of course, you would not have done half the things you have done for me, and let me have my own way so entirely, and bought me presents, if I had only been your step-daughter!

He—Mr. Newson—whom my poor mother married by such a strange mistake" (Henchard was glad that he had disguised matters here), "was very kind—oh so kind!" (she spoke with tears in her eyes); "but that is not the same thing as being one's real father after all. Now, father, breakfast is ready!" said she cheerfully.

Henchard bent and kissed her cheek. The moment and the act he had prefigured for weeks with a thrill of pleasure; yet it was no less than a miserable insipidity to him now that it had come. His reinstation of her mother had been chiefly for the girl's sake, and the fruition of the whole scheme was such dust and ashes as this.

XX

OF ALL THE ENIGMAS WHICH EVER CONFRONTED A GIRL THERE CAN HAVE BEEN SELDOM one like that which followed Henchard's announcement of himself to Elizabeth as her father. He had done it in an ardour and an agitation which had half carried the point of affection with her; yet, behold, from the next morning onwards his manner was constrained as she had never seen it before.

The coldness soon broke out into open chiding. One grievous failing of Elizabeth's was her occasional pretty and picturesque use of dialect words—those terrible marks of the beast to the truly genteel.

It was dinner-time—they never met except at meals—and she happened to say when he was rising from table, wishing to show him something, "If you'll bide where you be a minute, father, I'll get it."

" 'Bide where you be,' " he echoed sharply, "Good God, are you only fit to carry wash to a pig-trough, that ye use such words as those?"

She reddened with shame and sadness.

"I meant 'Stay where you are,' father," she said, in a low, humble voice. "I ought to have been more careful."

He made no reply, and went out of the room.

The sharp reprimand was not lost upon her, and in time it came to pass that for "fay" she said "succeed"; that she no longer spoke of "dumbledores" but of "humble bees"; no longer said of young men and women that they "walked together," but that they were "engaged"; that she grew to talk of "greggles" as "wild hyacinths"; that when she had not slept she did not quaintly tell the servants next morning that she had been "hag-rid," but that she had "suffered from indigestion."

These improvements, however, are somewhat in advance of the story. Henchard, being uncultivated himself, was the bitterest critic the fair girl could possibly have had of her own lapses—really slight now, for she read omnivorously. A gratuitous ordeal was in store for her in the matter of her handwriting. She was passing the dining-room door one evening, and had occasion to go in for something. It was not till she had opened the door that she knew the Mayor was there in the company of a man with whom he transacted business.

"Here, Elizabeth-Jane," he said, looking round at her, "just write down what I tell you—a few words of an agreement for me and this gentleman to sign. I am a poor tool with a pen."

"Be jowned, and so be I," said the gentleman.

She brought forward blotting-book, paper, and ink, and sat down.

"Now then—'An agreement entered into this sixteenth day of October'—write that first."

She started the pen in an elephantine march across the sheet. It was a splendid round, bold hand of her own conception, a style that would have stamped a woman as Minerva's own in more recent days. But other ideas reigned then: Henchard's creed was that proper young girls wrote ladies'-hand—nay, he believed that bristling characters were as innate and inseparable a part of refined womanhood as sex itself. Hence when, instead of scribbling, like the Princess Ida—

> In such a hand as when a field of corn
> Bows all its ears before the roaring East,

Elizabeth-Jane produced a line of chain-shot and sand-bags, he reddened in angry shame for her, and, peremptorily saying, "Never mind—I'll finish it," dismissed her there and then.

Her considerate disposition became a pitfall to her now. She was, it must be admitted, sometimes provokingly and unnecessarily willing to saddle herself with manual labours. She would go to the kitchen instead of ringing, "Not to make Phœbe come up twice." She went down on her knees, shovel in hand, when the cat overturned the coal-scuttle; moreover, she would persistently thank the parlour-maid for everything, till one day, as soon as the girl was gone from the room, Henchard broke out with, "Good God, why dostn't leave off thanking that girl as if she were a goddess-born! Don't I pay her a dozen pound a year to do things for 'ee?" Elizabeth shrank so visibly at the exclamation that he became sorry a few minutes after, and said that he did not mean to be rough.

These domestic exhibitions were the small protruding needle-rocks which suggested rather than revealed what was underneath. But his passion had less terror for her than his coldness. The increasing frequency of the latter mood told her the sad news that he disliked her with a growing dislike. The more interesting that her appearance and manners became under the softening influences which she could now command, and in her wisdom did command, the more she seemed to estrange him. Sometimes she caught him looking at her with a louring invidiousness that she could hardly bear. Not knowing his secret, it was cruel mockery that she should for the first time excite his animosity when she had taken his surname.

But the most terrible ordeal was to come. Elizabeth had latterly been accustomed of an afternoon to present a cup of cider or ale and bread-and-cheese to Nance Mockridge, who worked in the yard, wimbling hay-bonds. Nance accepted this offering thankfully at first; afterwards as a matter of course. On a day when Henchard was on the premises he saw his stepdaughter enter the hay-barn on this errand; and, as there was no clear spot on which to deposit the provisions, she at once set to work arranging two trusses of hay as a table, Mockridge meanwhile standing with her hands on her hips, easefully looking at the preparations on her behalf.

"Elizabeth, come here!" said Henchard; and she obeyed.

"Why do you lower yourself so confoundedly?" he said with suppressed passion. "Haven't I told you o't fifty times? Hey? Making yourself a drudge for a common work-woman of such a character as hers! Why, ye'll disgrace me to the dust!"

Now these words were uttered loud enough to reach Nance inside the barn door, who fired up immediately at the slur upon her personal character. Coming to the door she cried, regardless of consequences, "Come to that, Mr. Henchard, I can let 'ee know she've waited on worse!"

"Then she must have had more charity than sense," said Henchard.

"Oh no, she hadn't. 'Twere not for charity but for hire; and at a public-house in this town!"

"It is not true!" cried Henchard indignantly.

"Just ask her," said Nance, folding her naked arms in such a manner that she could comfortably scratch her elbows.

Henchard glanced at Elizabeth-Jane, whose complexion, now pink and white from confinement, lost nearly all of the former colour. "What does this mean?" he said to her. "Anything or nothing?"

"It is true," said Elizabeth-Jane. "But it was only—"

"Did you do it, or didn't you? Where was it?"

"At the Three Mariners; one evening for a little while, when we were staying there."

Nance glanced triumphantly at Henchard, and sailed into the barn; for, assuming that she was to be discharged on the instant, she had resolved to make the most of her victory. Henchard, however, said nothing about discharging her. Unduly sensitive on such points by reason of his own past, he had the look of one completely ground down to the last in-dignity. Elizabeth followed him to the house like a culprit; but when she got inside she could not see him. Nor did she see him again that day.

Convinced of the scathing damage to his local repute and position that must have been caused by such a fact, though it had never before reached his own ears, Henchard showed a positive distaste for the presence of this girl not his own, whenever he encountered her. He mostly dined with the farmers at the market-room of one of the two chief hotels, leav-ing her in utter solitude. Could he have seen how she made use of those silent hours he might have found reason to reserve his judgment on her quality. She read and took notes incessantly, mastering facts with painful laboriousness, but never flinching from her self-imposed task. She began the study of Latin, incited by the Roman characteristics of the town she lived in. "If I am not well-informed it shall be by no fault of my own," she would say to herself through the tears that would occasionally glide down her peachy cheeks when she was fairly baffled by the portentous obscurity of many of these educational works.

Thus she lived on, a dumb, deep-feeling, great-eyed creature, construed by not a sin-gle contiguous being; quenching with patient fortitude her incipient interest in Farfrae, be-cause it seemed to be one-sided, unmaidenly, and unwise. True, that for reasons best known to herself, she had, since Farfrae's dismissal, shifted her quarters from the back room affording a view of the yard (which she had occupied with such zest) to a front chamber overlooking the street; but as for the young man, whenever he passed the house he seldom or never turned his head.

Winter had almost come, and unsettled weather made her still more dependent upon indoor resources. But there were certain early winter days in Casterbridge—days of firmamental exhaustion which followed angry south-westerly tempests—when, if the sun shone, the air was like velvet. She seized on these days for her periodical visits to the spot where her mother lay buried—the still-used burial-ground of the old Roman-British city, whose curious feature was this, its continuity as a place of sepulture. Mrs. Henchard's dust mingled with the dust of women who lay ornamented with glass hair-pins and amber necklaces, and men who held in their mouths coins of Hadrian, Posthumus, and the Constantines.

Half-past ten in the morning was about her hour for seeking this spot—a time when the town avenues were deserted as the avenues of Karnac. Business had long since passed down them into its daily cells, and Leisure had not arrived there. So Elizabeth-Jane walked and read, or looked over the edge of the book to think, and thus reached the churchyard.

There, approaching her mother's grave, she saw a solitary dark figure in the middle of the gravel-walk. This figure, too, was reading; but not from a book: the words which engrossed it being the inscription on Mrs. Henchard's tombstone. The personage was in mourning like herself, was about her age and size, and might have been her wraith or double, but for the fact that it was a lady much more beautifully dressed than she. Indeed, comparatively indifferent as Elizabeth-Jane was to dress, unless for some temporary whim or purpose, her eyes were arrested by the artistic perfection of the lady's appearance. Her gait, too, had a flexuousness about it, which seemed to avoid angularity of movement less from choice than from predisposition. It was a revelation to Elizabeth that human beings could reach this stage of external development—she had never suspected it. She felt all the freshness and grace to be stolen from herself on the instant by the neighbourhood of such a stranger. And this was in face of the fact that Elizabeth could now have been writ handsome, while the young lady was simply pretty.

Had she been envious she might have hated the woman; but she did not do that—she allowed herself the pleasure of feeling fascinated. She wondered where the lady had come from. The stumpy and practical walk of honest homeliness which mostly prevailed there, the two styles of dress thereabout, the simple and the mistaken, equally avouched that this figure was no Casterbridge woman's, even if a book in her hand resembling a guide-book had not also suggested it.

The stranger presently moved from the tombstone of Mrs. Henchard, and vanished behind the corner of the wall. Elizabeth went to the tomb herself; beside it were two footprints distinct in the soil, signifying that the lady had stood there a long time. She returned homeward, musing on what she had seen, as she might have mused on a rainbow or the Northern Lights, a rare butterfly or a cameo.

Interesting as things had been out-of-doors, at home it turned out to be one of her bad days. Henchard, whose two years' mayoralty was ending, had been made aware that he was not to be chosen to fill a vacancy in the list of aldermen; and that Farfrae was likely to become one of the Council. This caused the unfortunate discovery that she had played the waiting-maid in the town of which he was Mayor to rankle in his mind yet more poisonously. He had learnt by personal enquiry at the time that it was to Donald Farfrae—that treacherous upstart—that she had thus humiliated herself. And though Mrs. Stannidge seemed to attach no great importance to the incident—the cheerful souls at the Three

Mariners having exhausted its aspects long ago—such was Henchard's haughty spirit that the simple thrifty deed was regarded as little less than a social catastrophe by him.

Ever since the evening of his wife's arrival with her daughter there had been something in the air which had changed his luck. That dinner at the King's Arms with his friends had been Henchard's Austerlitz: he had had his successes since, but his course had not been upward. He was not to be numbered among the aldermen—that Peerage of burghers—as he had expected to be, and the consciousness of this soured him to-day.

"Well, where have you been?" he said to her, with offhand laconism.

"I've been strolling in the Walks and churchyard, father, till I feel quite leery." She clapped her hand to her mouth, but too late.

This was just enough to incense Henchard after the other crosses of the day. "I *won't* have you talk like that!" he thundered. " 'Leery,' indeed. One would think you worked upon a farm! One day I learn that you lend a hand in public-houses. Then I hear you talk like a clodhopper. I'm burned, if it goes on, this house can't hold us two."

The only way of getting a single pleasant thought to go to sleep upon after this was by recalling the lady she had seen that day, and hoping she might see her again.

Meanwhile Henchard was sitting up, thinking over his jealous folly in forbidding Farfrae to pay his addresses to this girl who did not belong to him, when if he had allowed them to go on he might not have been encumbered with her. At last he said to himself with satisfaction as he jumped up and went to the writing-table: "Ah! he'll think it means peace, and a marriage portion—not that I don't want my house to be troubled with her, and no portion at all!" He wrote as follows:—

SIR—On consideration, I don't wish to interfere with your courtship of Elizabeth-Jane, if you care for her. I therefore withdraw my objection; excepting in this—that the business be not carried on in my house.—Yours,   M. HENCHARD.
    Mr. Farfrae.

The morrow, being fairly fine, found Elizabeth-Jane again in the churchyard; but while looking for the lady she was startled by the apparition of Farfrae, who passed outside the gate. He glanced up for a moment from a pocket-book in which he appeared to be making figures as he went; whether or not he saw her he took no notice, and disappeared.

Unduly depressed by a sense of her own superfluity she thought he probably scorned her; and quite broken in spirit sat down on a bench. She fell into painful thought on her position, which ended with her saying quite loud, "O, I wish I was dead with dear mother!"

Behind the bench was a little promenade under the wall where people sometimes walked instead of on the gravel. The bench seemed to be touched by something; she looked round, and a face was bending over her, veiled, but still distinct, the face of the young woman she had seen yesterday.

Elizabeth-Jane looked confounded for a moment, knowing she had been overheard, though there was pleasure in her confusion. "Yes, I heard you," said the lady, in a vivacious voice, answering her look. "What can have happened?"

"I don't—I can't tell you," said Elizabeth, putting her hand to her face to hide a quick flush that had come.

There was no movement or word for a few seconds; then the girl felt that the young lady was sitting down beside her.

"I guess how it is with you," said the latter. "That was your mother." She waved her hand towards the tombstone. Elizabeth looked up at her as if enquiring of herself whether there should be confidence. The lady's manner was so desirous, so anxious, that the girl decided there should be confidence. "It was my mother," she said, "my only friend."

"But your father, Mr. Henchard. He is living?"

"Yes, he is living," said Elizabeth-Jane.

"Is he not kind to you?"

"I've no wish to complain of him."

"There has been a disagreement?"

"A little."

"Perhaps you were to blame," suggested the stranger.

"I was—in many ways," sighed the meek Elizabeth. "I swept up the coals when the servants ought to have done it; and I said I was leery;—and he was angry with me."

The lady seemed to warm towards her for that reply. "Do you know the impression your words give me?" she said ingenuously. "That he is a hot-tempered man—a little proud—perhaps ambitious; but not a bad man." Her anxiety not to condemn Henchard while siding with Elizabeth, was curious.

"Oh no; certainly not *bad*," agreed the honest girl. "And he has not even been unkind to me till lately—since mother died. But it has been very much to bear while it has lasted. All is owing to my defects, I daresay; and my defects are owing to my history."

"What is your history?"

Elizabeth-Jane looked wistfully at her questioner. She found that her questioner was looking at her; turned her eyes down; and then seemed compelled to look back again. "My history is not gay or attractive," she said. "And yet I can tell it, if you really want to know."

The lady assured her that she did want to know; whereupon Elizabeth-Jane told the tale of her life as she understood it, which was in general the true one, except that the sale at the fair had no part therein.

Contrary to the girl's expectation her new friend was not shocked. This cheered her; and it was not till she thought of returning to that home in which she had been treated so roughly of late that her spirits fell.

"I don't know how to return," she murmured. "I think of going away. But what can I do? Where can I go?"

"Perhaps it will be better soon," said her friend gently. "So I would not go far. Now what do you think of this: I shall soon want somebody to live in my house, partly as housekeeper, partly as companion; would you mind coming to me? But perhaps—"

"Oh yes," cried Elizabeth, with tears in her eyes. "I would, indeed—I would do anything to be independent; for then perhaps my father might get to love me. But, ah!"

"What?"

"I am no accomplished person. And a companion to *you* must be that."

"Oh, not necessarily."

"Not? But I can't help using rural words sometimes, when I don't mean to."

"Never mind, I shall like to know them."

"And—oh, I know I shan't do!"—she cried with a distressful laugh. "I accidentally learned to write round hand instead of ladies'-hand. And, of course, you want someone who can write that?"

"Well, no."

"What, not necessary to write ladies'-hand?" cried the joyous Elizabeth.

"Not at all."

"But where do you live?"

"In Casterbridge, or rather I shall be living here after twelve o'clock to-day."

Elizabeth expressed her astonishment.

"I have been staying at Budmouth for a few days while my house was getting ready. The house I am going into is that one they call High Place Hall—the old stone one looking down the lane to the market. Two or three rooms are fit for occupation, though not all: I sleep there to-night for the first time. Now will you think over my proposal, and meet me here the first fine day next week, and say if you are still in the same mind?"

Elizabeth, her eyes shining at this prospect of a change from an unbearable position, joyfully assented; and the two parted at the gate of the churchyard.

XXI

As a maxim glibly repeated from childhood remains practically unmarked till some mature experience enforces it, so did this High Place Hall now for the first time really show itself to Elizabeth-Jane, though her ears had heard its name on a hundred occasions.

Her mind dwelt upon nothing else but the stranger, and the house, and her own chance of living there, all the rest of the day. In the afternoon she had occasion to pay a few bills in the town and do a little shopping, when she learnt that what was a new discovery to herself had become a common topic about the streets. High Place Hall was undergoing repair; a lady was coming there to live shortly; all the shop-people knew it, and had already discounted the chance of her being a customer.

Elizabeth-Jane could, however, add a capping touch to information so new to her in the bulk. The lady, she said, had arrived that day.

When the lamps were lighted, and it was yet not so dark as to render chimneys, attics, and roofs invisible, Elizabeth, almost with a lover's feeling, thought she would like to look at the outside of High Place Hall. She went up the street in that direction.

The Hall, with its grey *façade* and parapet, was the only residence of its sort so near the centre of the town. It had, in the first place, the characteristics of a country mansion—birds' nests in its chimneys, damp nooks where fungi grew and irregularities of surface direct from Nature's trowel. At night the forms of passengers were patterned by the lamps in black shadows upon the pale walls.

This evening motes of straw lay around, and other signs of the premises having been in that lawless condition which accompanies the entry of a new tenant. The house was entirely of stone, and formed an example of dignity without great size. It was not altogether aristocratic, still less consequential, yet the old-fashioned stranger instinctively said

"Blood built it, and Wealth enjoys it" however vague his opinions of those accessories might be.

Yet as regards the enjoying it, the stranger would have been wrong, for until this very evening, when the new lady had arrived, the house had been empty for a year or two while before that interval its occupancy had been irregular. The reason of its unpopularity was soon made manifest. Some of its rooms overlooked the market-place; and such a prospect from such a house was not considered desirable or seemly by its would-be occupiers.

Elizabeth's eyes sought the upper-rooms, and saw lights there. The lady had obviously arrived. The impression that this woman of comparatively practised manner had made upon the studious girl's mind was so deep that she enjoyed standing under an opposite archway merely to think that the charming lady was inside the confronting walls, and to wonder what she was doing. Her admiration for the architecture of that front was entirely on account of the inmate it screened. Though for that matter the architecture deserved admiration, or at least study, on its own account. It was Palladian, and like most architecture erected since the Gothic age, was a compilation rather than a design. But its reasonableness made it impressive. It was not rich, but rich enough. A timely consciousness of the ultimate vanity of human architecture, no less than of other human things, had prevented artistic superfluity.

Men had still quite recently been going in and out with parcels and packing-cases, rendering the door and hall within like a public thoroughfare. Elizabeth trotted through the open door in the dusk, but becoming alarmed at her own temerity she went quickly out again by another which stood open in the lofty wall of the back court. To her surprise she found herself in one of the little-used alleys of the town. Looking round at the door which had given her egress, by the light of the solitary lamp fixed in the alley, she saw that it was arched and old—older even than the house itself. The door was studded, and the keystone of the arch was a mask. Originally the mask had exhibited a comic leer, as could still be discerned; but generations of Casterbridge boys had thrown stones at the mask, aiming at its open mouth; and the blows thereof had chipped off the lips and jaws as if they had been eaten away by disease. The appearance was so ghastly by the weakly lamp glimmer that she could not bear to look at it—the first unpleasant feature of her visit.

The position of the queer old door and the odd presence of the leering mask suggested one thing above all others as appertaining to the mansion's past history—intrigue. By the alley it had been possible to come unseen from all sorts of quarters in the town— the old play-house, the old bull-stake, the old cock-pit, the pool wherein nameless infants had been used to disappear. High Place Hall could boast of its conveniences undoubtedly.

She turned to come away in the nearest direction homeward, which was down the alley, but hearing footsteps approaching in that quarter, and having no great wish to be found in such a place at such a time, she quickly retreated. There being no other way out, she stood behind a brick pier till the intruder should have gone his ways.

Had she watched she would have been surprised. She would have seen that the pedestrian on coming up made straight for the arched doorway: that as he paused with his hand upon the latch the lamplight fell upon the face of Henchard.

But Elizabeth-Jane clung so closely to her nook that she discerned nothing of this. Henchard passed in, as ignorant of her presence as she was ignorant of his identity, and disappeared in the darkness. Elizabeth came out a second time into the alley, and made the best of her way home.

Henchard's chiding, by begetting in her a nervous fear of doing anything definable as unladylike, had operated thus curiously in keeping them unknown to each other at a critical moment. Much might have resulted from recognition—at the least a query on either side in one and the self-same form: What could he or she possibly be doing there?

Henchard, whatever his business at the lady's house, reached his own home only a few minutes later than Elizabeth-Jane. Her plan was to broach the question of leaving his roof this evening; the events of the day had urged her to the course. But its execution depended upon his mood, and she anxiously awaited his manner towards her. She found that it had changed. He showed no further tendency to be angry; he showed something worse. Absolute indifference had taken the place of irritability; and his coldness was such that it encouraged her to departure, even more than hot temper could have done.

"Father, have you any objection to my going away?" she asked.

"Going away! No—none whatever. Where are you going?"

She thought it undesirable and unnecessary to say anything at present about her destination to one who took so little interest in her. He would know that soon enough. "I have heard of an opportunity of getting more cultivated and finished, and being less idle," she answered, with hesitation. "A chance of a place in a household where I can have advantages of study, and seeing refined life."

"Then make the best of it, in Heaven's name—if you can't get cultivated where you are."

"You don't object?"

"Object—I? Ho—no! Not at all." After a pause he said, "But you won't have enough money for this lively scheme without help, you know? If you like I should be willing to make you an allowance, so that you not be bound to live upon the starvation wages refined folk are likely to pay 'ee."

She thanked him for this offer.

"It had better be done properly," he added after a pause. "A small annuity is what I should like you to have—so as to be independent of me—and so that I may be independent of you. Would that please ye?"

"Certainly."

"Then I'll see about it this very day." He seemed relieved to get her off his hands by this arrangement, and as far as they were concerned the matter was settled. She now simply waited to see the lady again.

The day and the hour came; but a drizzling rain fell. Elizabeth-Jane having now changed her orbit from one of gay independence to laborious self-help, thought the weather good enough for such declined glory as hers, if her friend would only face it—a matter of doubt. She went to the boot-room where her pattens had hung ever since her apotheosis; took them down, had their mildewed leathers blacked, and put them on as she had done in old times. Thus mounted, and with cloak and umbrella, she went off to the place of appointment—intending, if the lady were not there, to call at the house.

One side of the churchyard—the side towards the weather—was sheltered by an ancient thatched mud wall whose eaves overhung as much as one or two feet. At the back of the wall was a corn-yard with its granary and barns—the place wherein she had met Farfrae many months earlier. Under the projection of the thatch she saw a figure. The young lady had come.

Her presence so exceptionally substantiated the girl's utmost hopes that she almost feared her good fortune. Fancies find rooms in the strongest minds. Here, in a churchyard old as civilization, in the worst of weathers, was a strange woman of curious fascinations never seen elsewhere: there might be some devilry about her presence. However, Elizabeth went on to the church-tower, on whose summit the rope of a flag-staff rattled in the wind; and thus she came to the wall.

The lady had such a cheerful aspect in the drizzle that Elizabeth forgot her fancy. "Well," said the lady, a little of the whiteness of her teeth appearing with the word through the black fleece that protected her face, "have you decided?"

"Yes, quite," said the other eagerly.

"Your father is willing?"

"Yes."

"Then come along."

"When?"

"Now—as soon as you like. I had a good mind to send to you to come to my house, thinking you might not venture up here in the wind. But as I like getting out-of-doors, I thought I would come and see first."

"It was my own thought."

"That shows we shall agree. Then can you come to-day? My house is so hollow and dismal that I want some living thing there."

"I think I might be able to," said the girl, reflecting.

Voices were borne over to them at that instant on the wind and raindrops from the other side of the wall. There came such words as "sacks," "quarters," "threshing," "tailing," "next Saturday's market," each sentence being disorganised by the gusts like a face in a cracked mirror. Both the women listened.

"Who are those?" said the lady.

"One is my father. He rents that yard and barn."

The lady seemed to forget the immediate business in listening to the technicalities of the corn trade. At last she said suddenly, "Did you tell him where you were going to?"

"No."

"Oh—how was that?"

"I thought it safer to get away first—as he is so uncertain in his temper."

"Perhaps you are right. . . . Besides, I have never told you my name. It is Miss Templeman. . . . Are they gone—on the other side?"

"No. They have only gone up into the granary."

"Well, it is getting damp here. I shall expect you to-day—this evening, say, at six."

"Which way shall I come, ma'am."

"The front way—through the door. There is no other."

Elizabeth-Jane had been thinking of the door in the alley.

"Perhaps, as you have not mentioned your destination, you may as well keep silent upon it till you are clear off. Who knows but that he may alter his mind?"

Elizabeth-Jane shook her head. "On consideration I don't fear it," she said sadly. "He has grown quite cold to me."

"Very well. Six o'clock then."

When they had emerged upon the open road and parted, they found enough to do in holding their bowed umbrellas to the wind. Nevertheless the lady looked in at the corn-yard gates as she passed them, and paused on one foot for a moment. But nothing was visible there save the ricks, and the humpbacked barn, cushioned with moss, and the granary rising against the church-tower behind, where the smacking of the rope against the flag-staff still went on.

Now Henchard had not the slightest suspicion that Elizabeth-Jane's movement was to be so prompt. Hence when, just before six, he reached home and saw a fly at the door from the King's Arms, and his stepdaughter, with all her little bags and boxes, getting into it, he was taken by surprise.

"But you said I might go, father?" she explained through the carriage window.

"Said!—yes. But I thought you meant next month, or next year. 'Od, seize it—you take time by the forelock! This, then, is how you be going to treat me for all my trouble about ye?"

"O father! how can you speak like that? It is unjust of you!" she said with spirit.

"Well, well, have your own way," he replied. He entered the house, and, seeing that all her things had not yet been brought down, went up to her room to look on. He had never been there since she had occupied it. Evidences of her care, of her endeavours for improvement, were visible all around, in the form of books, sketches, maps, and little arrangements for tasteful effects. Henchard had known nothing of these efforts. He gazed at them, turned suddenly about, and came down to the door.

"Look here," he said, in an altered voice—he never called her by name now—"don't 'ee go away from me. It may be I've spoke roughly to you—but I've been grieved beyond everything by you—there's something that caused it."

"By me?" she said, with deep concern. "What have I done?"

"I can't tell you now. But if you'll stop, and go on living as my daughter, I'll tell you all in time."

But the proposal had come ten minutes too late. She was in the fly—was already, in imagination, at the house of the lady whose manner had such charms for her. "Father," she said, as considerately as she could, "I think it best for us that I go on now. I need not stay long; I shall not be far away, and if you want me badly I can soon come back again."

He nodded ever so slightly, as a receipt of her decision, and no more. "You are not going far, you say. What will be your address, in case I wish to write to you? Or am I not to know?"

"Oh yes—certainly. It is only in the town—High Place Hall."

"Where?" said Henchard, his face stilling.

She repeated the words. He neither moved nor spoke, and waving her hand to him in utmost friendliness she signified to the flyman to drive up the street.

XXII

W E GO BACK FOR A MOMENT TO THE PRECEDING NIGHT, TO ACCOUNT FOR HEN-
chard's attitude.

At the hour when Elizabeth-Jane was contemplating her stealthy reconnoitring excursion to the abode of the lady of her fancy, he had been not a little amazed at receiving
a letter by hand in Lucetta's well-known characters. The self-repression, the resignation of
her previous communication had vanished from her mood; she wrote with some of the
natural lightness which had marked her in their early acquaintance.

HIGH PLACE HALL

MY DEAR MR. HENCHARD—Don't be surprised. It is for your good and mine, as I hope,
that I have come to live at Casterbridge—for how long I cannot tell. That depends upon
another; and he is a man, and a merchant, and a Mayor, and one who has the first right to
my affections.

Seriously, *mon ami*, I am not so light-hearted as I may seem to be from this. I have
come here in consequence of hearing of the death of your wife—whom you used to think
of as dead so many years before! Poor woman, she seems to have been a sufferer, though
uncomplaining, and though weak in intellect not an imbecile. I am glad you acted fairly by
her. As soon as I knew she was no more, it was brought home to me very forcibly by my
conscience that I ought to endeavour to disperse the shade which my *étourderie* flung over
my name, by asking you to carry out your promise to me. I hope you are of the same mind,
and that you will take steps to this end. As, however, I did not know how you were situated, or what had happened since our separation, I decided to come and establish myself
here before communicating with you.

You probably feel as I do about this. I shall be able to see you in a day or two. Till then,
farewell.—Yours,

LUCETTA

P.S.—I was unable to keep my appointment to meet you for a moment or two in passing through Casterbridge the other day. My plans were altered by a family event, which it
will surprise you to hear of.

Henchard had already heard that High Place Hall was being prepared for a tenant. He
said with a puzzled air to the first person he encountered, "Who is coming to live at the Hall?"

"A lady of the name of Templeman, I believe, sir," said his informant.

Henchard thought it over. "Lucetta is related to her, I suppose," he said to himself.
"Yes, I must put her in her proper position, undoubtedly."

It was by no means with the oppression that would once have accompanied the
thought that he regarded the moral necessity now; it was, indeed, with interest, if not
warmth. His bitter disappointment at finding Elizabeth-Jane to be none of his, and himself a childless man, had left an emotional void in Henchard that he unconsciously craved
to fill. In this frame of mind, though without strong feeling, he had strolled up the alley
and into High Place Hall by the postern at which Elizabeth had so nearly encountered him.

He had gone on thence into the court, and enquired of a man whom he saw unpacking china from a crate if Miss Le Sueur was living there. Miss Le Sueur had been the name under which he had known Lucetta—or "Lucette," as she had called herself at that time.

The man replied in the negative; that Miss Templeman only had come. Henchard went away, concluding that Lucetta had not as yet settled in.

He was in this interested stage of the enquiry when he witnessed Elizabeth-Jane's departure the next day. On hearing her announce the address, there suddenly took possession of him the strange thought that Lucetta and Miss Templeman were one and the same person, for he could recall that in her season of intimacy with him the name of the rich relative whom he had deemed somewhat a mythical personage had been given as Templeman. Though not a fortune-hunter, the possibility that Lucetta had been sublimed into a lady of means by some munificent testament on the part of this relative lent a charm to her image which it might not otherwise have acquired. He was getting on towards the dead level of middle age, when material things increasingly possess the mind.

But Henchard was not left long in suspense. Lucetta was rather addicted to scribbling, as had been shown by the torrent of letters after the fiasco in their marriage arrangements, and hardly had Elizabeth gone away when another note came to the Mayor's house from High Place Hall.

"I am in residence," she said, "and comfortable, though getting here has been a wearisome undertaking. You probably know what I am going to tell you, or do you not? My good Aunt Templeman, the banker's widow, whose very existence you used to doubt, much more her affluence, has lately died, and bequeathed some of her property to me. I will not enter into details except to say that I have taken her name—as a means of escape from mine, and its wrongs.

"I am now my own mistress, and have chosen to reside in Casterbridge—to be tenant of High Place Hall, that at least you may be put to no trouble if you wish to see me. My first intention was to keep you in ignorance of the changes in my life till you should meet me in the street; but I have thought better of this.

"You probably are aware of my arrangement with your daughter, and have doubtless laughed at the—what shall I call it?—practical joke (in all affection) of my getting her to live with me. But my first meeting with her was purely an accident. Do you see, Michael, partly why I have done it?—why, to give you an excuse for coming here as if to visit *her*, and thus to form my acquaintance naturally. She is a dear, good girl, and she thinks you have treated her with undue severity. You may have done so in your haste, but not deliberately, I am sure. As the result has been to bring her to me I am not disposed to upbraid you.—In haste, yours always,

"LUCETTA"

The excitement which these announcements produced in Henchard's gloomy soul was to him most pleasurable. He sat over his dining-table long and dreamily, and by an almost mechanical transfer the sentiments which had run to waste since his estrangement from Elizabeth-Jane and Donald Farfrae gathered around Lucetta before they had grown dry. She was plainly in a very coming-on disposition for marriage. But what else could a poor woman be who had given her time and her heart to him so thoughtlessly, at that former time, as to lose her credit by it? Probably conscience no less than affection had brought her here. On the whole he did not blame her.

"The artful little woman!" he said, smiling (with reference to Lucetta's adroit and pleasant manoeuvre with Elizabeth-Jane).

To feel that he would like to see Lucetta was with Henchard to start for her house. He put on his hat and went. It was between eight and nine o'clock when he reached her door. The answer brought him was that Miss Templeman was engaged for that evening; but that she would be happy to see him the next day.

"That's rather like giving herself airs!" he thought. "And considering what we——" But after all, she plainly had not expected him, and he took the refusal quietly. Nevertheless he resolved not to go next day. "These cursed women—there's not an inch of straight grain in 'em!" he said.

Let us follow the track of Mr. Henchard's thought as if it were a clue line, and view the interior of High Place Hall on this particular evening.

On Elizabeth-Jane's arrival she had been phlegmatically asked by an elderly woman to go upstairs and take off her things. She replied with great earnestness that she would not think of giving that trouble, and on the instant divested herself of her bonnet and cloak in the passage. She was then conducted to the first floor on the landing, and left to find her way further alone.

The room disclosed was prettily furnished as a boudoir or small drawing-room, and on a sofa with two cylindrical pillows reclined a dark-haired, large-eyed, pretty woman, of unmistakably French extraction on one side or the other. She was probably some years older than Elizabeth, and had a sparkling light in her eye. In front of the sofa was a small table, with a pack of cards scattered upon it faces upward.

The attitude had been so full of abandonment that she bounded up like a spring on hearing the door open.

Perceiving that it was Elizabeth she lapsed into ease, and came across to her with a reckless skip that innate grace only prevented from being boisterous.

"Why, you are late," she said, taking hold of Elizabeth-Jane's hands.

"There were so many little things to put up."

"And you seem dead-alive and tired. Let me try to enliven you by some wonderful tricks I have learnt, to kill time. Sit there and don't move." She gathered up the pack of cards, pulled the table in front of her, and began to deal them rapidly, telling Elizabeth to choose some.

"Well, have you chosen?" she asked flinging down the last card.

"No," stammered Elizabeth, arousing herself from a reverie. "I forgot, I was thinking of—you, and me—and how strange it is that I am here."

Miss Templeman looked at Elizabeth-Jane with interest, and laid down the cards. "Ah! never mind," she said. "I'll lie here while you sit by me; and we'll talk."

Elizabeth drew up silently to the head of the sofa, but with obvious pleasure. It could be seen that in years she was younger than her entertainer, while in manner and general vision she seemed more of the sage. Miss Templeman deposited herself on the sofa in her former flexuous position, and throwing her arm above her brow—somewhat in the pose of a well-known conception of Titian's—talked up at Elizabeth-Jane invertedly across her forehead and arm.

"I must tell you something," she said. "I wonder if you have suspected it. I have only been mistress of a large house and fortune a little while."

"Oh! only a little while?" murmured Elizabeth-Jane, her countenance slightly falling.

"As a girl I lived about in garrison towns and elsewhere with my father, till I was quite flighty and unsettled. He was an officer in the army. I should not have mentioned this had I not thought it best you should know the truth."

"Yes, yes." She looked thoughtfully round the room—at the little square piano with brass inlayings, at the window-curtains, at the lamp, at the fair and dark kings and queens on the card-table, and finally at the inverted face of Lucetta Templeman, whose large lustrous eyes had such an odd effect upside-down.

Elizabeth's mind ran on acquirements to an almost morbid degree. "You speak French and Italian fluently, no doubt," she said. "I have not been able to get beyond a wretched bit of Latin yet."

"Well, for that matter, in my native isle speaking French does not go for much. It is rather the other way."

"Where is your native isle?"

It was with rather more reluctance that Miss Templeman said, "Jersey. There they speak French on one side of the street and English on the other, and a mixed tongue in the middle of the road. But it is a long time since I was there. Bath is where my people really belong to, though my ancestors in Jersey were as good as anybody in England. They were the Le Sueurs, an old family who have done great things in their time. I went back and lived there after my father's death. But I don't value such past matters, and am quite an English person in my feelings and tastes."

Lucetta's tongue had for a moment outrun her discretion. She had arrived at Casterbridge as a Bath lady, and there were obvious reasons why Jersey should drop out of her life. But Elizabeth had tempted her to make free, and a deliberately formed resolve had been broken.

It could not, however, have been broken in safer company. Lucetta's words went no further, and after this day she was so much upon her guard that there appeared no chance of her identification with the young Jersey woman who had been Henchard's dear comrade at a critical time. Not the least amusing of her safeguards was her resolute avoidance of a French word, if one by accident came to her tongue more readily than its English equivalent. She shirked it with the suddenness of the weak Apostle at the accusation, "Thy speech bewrayeth thee!"

Expectancy sat visibly upon Lucetta the next morning. She dressed herself for Mr. Henchard, and restlessly awaited his call before mid-day; as he did not come she waited on through the afternoon. But she did not tell Elizabeth that the person expected was the girl's stepfather.

They sat in adjoining windows of the same room in Lucetta's great stone mansion, netting, and looking out upon the market, which formed an animated scene. Elizabeth could see the crown of her stepfather's hat among the rest beneath, and was not aware that Lucetta watched the same object with yet intenser interest. He moved about amid the throng, at this point lively as an ant-hill; elsewhere more reposeful, and broken up by stalls of fruit and vegetables. The farmers as a rule preferred the open *carrefour* for their transactions, despite its inconvenient jostlings and the danger from crossing vehicles, to the gloomy sheltered market-room provided for them. Here they surged on this one day of the week, forming a little world of leggings, switches, and sample-bags; men of extensive stomachs, sloping like mountain sides; men whose heads in walking swayed as the trees in November gales; who in conversing varied their attitudes much, lowering themselves by spreading their knees, and thrusting their hands into the pockets of remote inner jackets. Their faces radiated tropical warmth; for though when at home their countenances varied with the seasons, their market-faces all the year round were glowing little fires.

All over-clothes here were worn as if they were an inconvenience, a hampering necessity. Some men were well-dressed; but the majority were careless in that respect, appearing in suits which were historical records of their wearer's deeds, sun-scorchings, and daily struggles for many years past. Yet many carried ruffled cheque-books in their pockets which regulated at the bank hard by a balance of never less than four figures. In fact, what these gibbous human shapes specially represented was ready money—money insistently ready—not ready next year like a nobleman's—often not merely ready at the bank like a professional man's, but ready in their large plump hands.

It happened that to-day there rose in the midst of them all two or three tall apple-trees standing as if they grew on the spot; till it was perceived that they were held by men from the cider-districts who came here to sell them, bringing the clay of their county on their boots. Elizabeth-Jane, who had often observed them, said, "I wonder if the same trees come every week?"

"What trees?" said Lucetta, absorbed in watching for Henchard.

Elizabeth replied vaguely, for an incident checked her. Behind one of the trees stood Farfrae, briskly discussing a sample-bag with a farmer. Henchard had come up, accidentally encountering the young man, whose face seemed to enquire, "Do we speak to each other?"

She saw her stepfather throw a shine into his eye which answered "No!" Elizabeth-Jane sighed.

"Are you particularly interested in anybody out there?" said Lucetta.

"Oh, no," said her companion, a quick red shooting over her face.

Luckily Farfrae's figure was immediately covered by the apple-tree.

Lucetta looked hard at her. "Quite sure?" she said.

"Oh yes," said Elizabeth-Jane.

Again Lucetta looked out. "They are all farmers I suppose?" she said.

"No. There's Mr. Bulge—he's a wine merchant; there's Benjamin Brownlet—a horse dealer; and Kitson, the pig breeder; and Yopper, the auctioneer; besides maltsters, and millers—and so on." Farfrae stood out quite distinctly now; but she did not mention him.

The Saturday afternoon slipped on thus desultorily. The market changed from the sample-showing hour to the idle hour before starting homewards, when tales were told. Henchard had not called on Lucetta, though he had stood so near. He must have been too busy, she thought. He would come on Sunday or Monday.

The days came, but not the visitor, though Lucetta repeated her dressing with scrupulous care. She was disheartened. It may at once be declared that Lucetta no longer bore towards Henchard all that warm allegiance which had characterised her in their first acquaintance; the then unfortunate issue of things had chilled pure love considerably. But there remained a conscientious wish to bring about her union with him, now that there was nothing to hinder it—to right her position—which in itself was a happiness to sigh for. With strong social reasons on her side why their marriage should take place there had ceased to be any worldly reason on his why it should be postponed, since she had succeeded to fortune.

Tuesday was the great Candlemas fair. At breakfast she said to Elizabeth-Jane quite coolly: "I imagine your father may call to see you to-day. I suppose he stands close by in the market-place, with the rest of the corn-dealers?"

She shook her head. "He won't come."

"Why?"

"He has taken against me," she said in a husky voice.

"You have quarreled more deeply than I know of."

Elizabeth, wishing to shield the man she believed to be her father from any charge of unnatural dislike, said "Yes."

"Then where you are is, of all places, the one he will avoid?"

Elizabeth nodded sadly.

Lucetta looked blank, twitched up her lovely eyebrows and lip, and burst into hysterical sobs. Here was a disaster—her ingenious scheme completely stultified.

"Oh, my dear Miss Templeman—what's the matter?" cried her companion.

"I like your company much!" said Lucetta, as soon as she could speak.

"Yes, yes—and so do I yours!" Elizabeth chimed in soothingly.

"But—but—" She could not finish the sentence, which was, naturally, that if Henchard had such a rooted dislike for the girl as now seemed to be the case, Elizabeth-Jane would have to be got rid of—a disagreeable necessity.

A provisional resource suggested itself. "Miss Henchard—will you go on an errand for me as soon as breakfast is over?—Ah, that's very good of you. Will you go and order—" Here she enumerated several commissions at sundry shops, which would occupy Elizabeth's time for the next hour or two, at least.

"And have you ever seen the Museum?"

Elizabeth-Jane had not.

"Then you should do so at once. You can finish the morning by going there. It is an old house in a back street—I forget where—but you'll find out—and there are crowds of interesting things—skeletons, teeth, old pots and pans, ancient boots and shoes, birds' eggs—all charmingly instructive. You'll be sure to stay till you get quite hungry."

Elizabeth hastily put on her things and departed. "I wonder why she wants to get rid of me to-day!" she said sorrowfully as she went. That her absence, rather than her services or instruction, was in request, had been readily apparent to Elizabeth-Jane, simple as she seemed and difficult as it was to attribute a motive for the desire.

She had not been gone ten minutes when one of Lucetta's servants was sent to Henchard's with a note. The contents were briefly:—

DEAR MICHAEL—You will be standing in view of my house to-day for two or three hours in the course of your business, so do please call and see me. I am sadly disappointed that you have not come before, for can I help anxiety about my own equivocal relation to you?—especially now my aunt's fortune has brought me more prominently before society? Your daughter's presence here may be the cause of your neglect; and I have therefore sent her away for the morning. Say you come on business—I shall be quite alone.

LUCETTA

When the messenger returned her mistress gave directions that if a gentleman called he was to be admitted at once, and sat down to await results.

Sentimentally she did not much care to see him—his delays had wearied her, but it was necessary; and with a sigh she arranged herself picturesquely in the chair; first this way, then that; next so that the light fell over her head. Next she flung herself on the couch in the cyma-recta curve which so became her, and with her arm over her brow looked towards the door. This, she decided, was the best position after all; and thus she remained till a man's step was heard on the stairs. Whereupon Lucetta, forgetting her curve (for Nature was too strong for Art as yet), jumped up, and ran and hid herself behind one of the window-curtains in a freak of timidity. In spite of the waning of passion the situation was an agitating one—she had not seen Henchard since his (supposed) temporary parting from her in Jersey.

She could hear the servant showing the visitor into the room, shutting the door upon him, and leaving as if to go and look for her mistress. Lucetta flung back the curtain with a nervous greeting. The man before her was not Henchard.

XXIII

A CONJECTURE THAT HER VISITOR MIGHT BE SOME OTHER PERSON HAD, INDEED, FLASHED through Lucetta's mind when she was on the point of bursting out; but it was just too late to recede.

He was years younger than the Mayor of Casterbridge; fair, fresh, and slenderly handsome. He wore genteel cloth leggings with white buttons, polished boots with infinite lace holes, light cord breeches under a black velveteen coat and waistcoat; and he had a silver-topped switch in his hand. Lucetta blushed, and said with a curious mixture of pout and laugh on her face—"Oh, I've made a mistake!"

The visitor, on the contrary, did not laugh half a wrinkle.

"But I'm very sorry!" he said, in deprecating tones. "I came and I enquired for Miss Henchard, and they showed me up heere, and in no case would I have caught ye so unmannerly if I had known!"

"I was the unmannerly one," said she.

"But is it that I have come to the wrong house, madam?" said Mr. Farfrae, blinking a little in his bewilderment and nervously tapping his legging with his switch.

"O no, sir—sit down. You must come and sit down now you are here," replied Lucetta kindly, to relieve his embarrassment. "Miss Henchard will be here directly."

Now this was not strictly true; but that something about the young man—that hyperborean crispness, stringency, and charm, as of a well-braced musical instrument, which had awakened the interest of Henchard, and of Elizabeth-Jane, and of the Three Mariners' jovial crew, at sight, made his unexpected presence here attractive to Lucetta. He hesitated, looked at the chair, thought there was no danger in it (though there was), and sat down.

Farfrae's sudden entry was simply the result of Henchard's permission to him to see Elizabeth, if he were minded to woo her. At first he had taken no notice of Henchard's brusque letter; but an exceptionally fortunate business transaction put him on good terms with everybody, and revealed to him that he could undeniably marry if he chose. Then who so pleasing, thrifty, and satisfactory in every way as Elizabeth-Jane? Apart from her personal recommendations, a reconciliation with his former friend Henchard would, in the natural course of things, flow from such a union. He therefore forgave the Mayor his curtness; and this morning on his way to the fair he had called at her house, where he learnt that she was staying at Miss Templeman's. A little stimulated at not finding her ready and waiting—so fanciful are men!—he hastened on to High Place Hall, to encounter no Elizabeth, but its mistress herself.

"The fair to-day seems a large one," she said when, by natural deviation, their eyes sought the busy scene without. "Your numerous fairs and markets keep me interested. How many things I think of while I watch from here!"

He seemed in doubt how to answer, and the babble without reached them as they sat—voices as of wavelets on a looping sea, one ever and anon rising above the rest. "Do you look out often?" he asked.

"Yes—very often."

"Do you look for anyone you know?"

Why should she have answered as she did?

"I look as at a picture merely. But," she went on, turning pleasantly to him, "I may do so now—I may look for you. You are always there, are you not? Ah—I don't mean it seriously! But it is amusing to look for somebody one knows in a crowd, even if one does not want him. It takes off the terrible oppressiveness of being surrounded by a throng, and having no point of junction with it through a single individual."

"Ay! Maybe you'll be very lonely, ma'am?"

"Nobody knows how lonely."

"But you are rich, they say?"

"If so, I don't know how to enjoy my riches. I came to Casterbridge thinking I should like to live here. But I wonder if I shall."

"Where did ye come from, ma'am?"

"The neighbourhood of Bath."

"And I from near Edinboro'," he murmured. "It's better to stay at home, and that's true; but a man must live where his money is made. It is a great pity, but it's always so! Yet I've done very well this year. Oh yes," he went on with ingenuous enthusiasm. "You see that man with the drab kerseymere coat? I bought largely of him in the autumn when wheat was down, and then afterwards when it rose a little I sold off all I had! It brought only a small profit to me; while the farmers kept theirs, expecting higher figures—yes, though the rats were gnawing the ricks hollow. Just when I sold the markets went lower, and I bought up the corn of those who had been holding back at less price than my first purchases. And then," cried Farfrae impetuously, his face alight, "I sold it a few weeks after, when it happened to go up again! And so, by contenting mysel' with small profits frequently repeated, I soon made five hundred pounds—yes!"—(bringing down his hand upon the table, and quite forgetting where he was)—"while the others by keeping theirs in hand made nothing at all!"

Lucetta regarded him with a critical interest. He was quite a new type of person to her. At last his eye fell upon the lady's and their glances met.

"Ay, now, I'm wearying you!" he exclaimed.

She said, "No, indeed," colouring a shade.

"What then?"

"Quite otherwise. You are most interesting."

It was now Farfrae who showed the modest pink.

"I mean all you Scotchmen," she added in hasty correction. "So free from Southern extremes. We common people are all one way or the other—warm or cold, passionate or frigid. You have both temperatures going on in you at the same time."

"But how do you mean that? Ye were best to explain clearly, ma'am."

"You are animated—then you are thinking of getting on. You are sad the next moment—then you are thinking of Scotland and friends."

"Yes. I think of home sometimes!" he said simply.

"So do I—as far as I can. But it was an old house where I was born, and they pulled it down for improvements, so I seem hardly to have any home to think of now."

Lucetta did not add, as she might have done, that the house was in St. Helier, and not in Bath.

"But the mountains, and the mists and the rocks, they are there! And don't they seem like home?"

She shook her head.

"They do to me—they do to me," he murmured. And his mind could be seen flying away northwards. Whether its origin were national or personal, it was quite true what Lucetta had said, that the curious double strands in Farfrae's thread of life—the commercial and the romantic—were very distinct at times. Like the colours in a variegated cord those contrasts could be seen intertwisted, yet not mingling.

"You are wishing you were back again," she said.

"Ah, no, ma'am," said Farfrae, suddenly recalling himself.

The fair without the windows was now raging thick and loud. It was the chief hiring fair of the year, and differed quite from the market of a few days earlier. In substance it was a whitey-brown crowd flecked with white—this being the body of labourers waiting for places. The long bonnets of the women, like waggon-tilts, their cotton gowns and checked shawls, mixed with the carters' smock-frocks; for they, too, entered into the hiring. Among the rest, at the corner of the pavement, stood an old shepherd, who attracted the eyes of Lucetta and Farfrae by his stillness. He was evidently a chastened man. The battle of life had been a sharp one with him, for, to begin with, he was a man of small frame. He was now so bowed by hard work and years that, approaching from behind, a person could hardly see his head. He had planted the stem of his crook in the gutter, and was resting upon the bow, which was polished to silver brightness by the long friction of his hands. He had quite forgotten where he was, and what he had come for, his eyes being bent on the ground. A little way off negotiations were proceeding which had reference to him; but he did not hear them, and there seemed to be passing through his mind pleasant visions of the hiring successes of his prime, when his skill laid open to him any farm for the asking.

The negotiations were between a farmer from a distant county and the old man's son. In these there was a difficulty. The farmer would not take the crust without the crumb of the bargain, in other words, the old man without the younger; and the son had a sweetheart on his present farm, who stood by, waiting the issue with pale lips.

"I'm sorry to leave ye, Nelly," said the young man with emotion. "But, you see, I can't starve father, and he's out o' work at Lady-day. 'Tis only seventy mile."

The girl's lips quivered. "Seventy mile!" she murmured. "Ah! 'tis enough! I shall never see 'ee again!" It was, indeed, a hopeless length of traction for Dan Cupid's magnet; for young men were young men at Casterbridge as elsewhere.

"Oh! no, no—I never shall," she insisted, when he pressed her hand; and she turned her face to Lucetta's wall to hide her weeping. The farmer said he would give the young man half an hour for his answer, and went away, leaving the group sorrowing.

Lucetta's eyes, full of tears, met Farfrae's. His, too, to her surprise, were moist at the scene.

"It is very hard," she said with strong feelings. "Lovers ought not to be parted like that! Oh, if I had my wish, I'd let people live and love at their pleasure!"

"Maybe I can manage that they'll not be parted," said Farfrae. "I want a young carter; and perhaps I'll take the old man too—yes; he'll not be very expensive, and doubtless he will answer ma pairrpose somehow."

"Oh, you are so good!" she cried, delighted. "Go and tell them, and let me know if you have succeeded!"

Farfrae went out, and she saw him speak to the group. The eyes of all brightened; the bargain was soon struck. Farfrae returned to her immediately it was concluded.

"It is kind-hearted of you, indeed," said Lucetta. "For my part, I have resolved that all my servants shall have lovers if they want them! Do make the same resolve!"

Farfrae looked more serious, waving his head a half turn. "I must be a little stricter than that," he said.

"Why?"

"You are a—a thriving woman; and I am a struggling hay-and-corn merchant."

"I am a very ambitious woman."

"Ah, well, I cannet explain. I don't know how to talk to ladies, ambitious or no; and that's true," said Donald with grave regret. "I try to be civil to a' folk—no more!"

"I see you are as you say," replied she, sensibly getting the upper hand in these exchanges of sentiment. Under this revelation of insight Farfrae again looked out of the window into the thick of the fair.

Two farmers met and shook hands, and being quite near the window their remarks could be heard as others' had been.

"Have you seen young Mr. Farfrae this morning?" asked one. "He promised to meet me here at the stroke of twelve; but I've gone athwart and about the fair half-a-dozen times, and never a sign of him: though he's mostly a man to his word."

"I quite forgot the engagement," murmured Farfrae.

"Now you must go," said she; "must you not?"

"Yes," he replied. But he still remained.

"You had better go," she urged. "You will lose a customer."

"Now, Miss Templeman, you will make me angry," exclaimed Farfrae.

"Then suppose you don't go; but stay a little longer?"

He looked anxiously at the farmer who was seeking him and who just then ominously walked across to where Henchard was standing, and he looked into the room and at her. "I like staying; but I fear I must go!" he said. "Business ought not to be neglected, ought it?"

"Not for a single minute."

"It's true. I'll come another time—if I may, ma'am?"

"Certainly," she said. "What has happened to us to-day is very curious."

"Something to think over when we are alone, it's like to be?"

"Oh, I don't know that. It is commonplace after all."

"No, I'll not say that. Oh no!"

"Well, whatever it has been, it is now over; and the market calls you to be gone."

"Yes, yes. Market—business! I wish there were no business in the warrld."

Lucetta almost laughed—she would quite have laughed—but that there was a little emotion going in her at the time. "How you change!" she said. "You should not change like this."

"I have never wished such things before," said the Scotchman, with a simple, shamed, apologetic look for his weakness. "It is only since coming here and seeing you!"

"If that's the case, you had better not look at me any longer. Dear me, I feel I have quite demoralised you!"

"But look or look not, I will see you in my thoughts. Well, I'll go—thank you for the pleasure of this visit."

"Thank you for staying."

"Maybe I'll get into my market-mind when I've been out a few minutes," he murmured. "But I don't know—I don't know!"

As he went she said eagerly, "You may hear them speak of me in Casterbridge as time goes on. If they tell you I'm a coquette, which some may, because of the incidents of my life, don't believe it, for I am not."

"I swear I will not!" he said fervidly.

Thus the two. She had enkindled the young man's enthusiasm till he was quite brimming with sentiment; while he, from merely affording her a new form of idleness, had gone on to wake her serious solicitude. Why was this? They could not have told.

Lucetta as a young girl would hardly have looked at a tradesman. But her ups and downs, capped by her indiscretions with Henchard had made her uncritical as to station. In her poverty she had met with repulse from the society to which she had belonged, and she had no great zest for renewing an attempt upon it now. Her heart longed for some ark into which it could fly and be at rest. Rough or smooth she did not care so long as it was warm.

Farfrae was shown out, it having entirely escaped him that he had called to see Elizabeth. Lucetta at the window watched him threading the maze of farmers and farmers' men. She could see by his gait that he was conscious of her eyes, and her heart went out to him for his modesty—pleaded with her sense of his unfitness that he might be allowed to come again. He entered the market-house, and she could see him no more.

Three minutes later, when she had left the window, knocks, not of multitude but of strength, sounded through the house, and the waiting-maid tripped up.

"The Mayor," she said.

Lucetta had reclined herself, and she was looking dreamily through her fingers. She did not answer at once, and the maid repeated the information with the addition, "And he's afraid he hasn't much time to spare, he says."

"Oh! Then tell him that as I have a headache I won't detain him to-day."

The message was taken down, and she heard the door close.

Lucetta had come to Casterbridge to quicken Henchard's feelings with regard to her. She had quickened them, and now she was indifferent to the achievement.

Her morning view of Elizabeth-Jane as a disturbing element changed, and she no longer felt strongly the necessity of getting rid of the girl for her stepfather's sake. When the young woman came in, sweetly unconscious of the turn in the tide, Lucetta went up to her, and said quite sincerely—

"I'm so glad you've come. You'll live with me a long time, won't you?"

Elizabeth as a watch-dog to keep her father off—what a new idea. Yet it was not unpleasing. Henchard had neglected her all these days, after compromising her indescribably in the past. The least he could have done when he found himself free, and herself affluent, would have been to respond heartily and promptly to her invitation.

Her emotions rose, fell, undulated, filled her with wild surmise at their suddenness; and so passed Lucetta's experiences of that day.

XXIV

POOR ELIZABETH-JANE, LITTLE THINKING WHAT HER MALIGNANT STAR HAD DONE TO blast the budding attentions she had won from Donald Farfrae, was glad to hear Lucetta's words about remaining.

For in addition to Lucetta's house being a home, that raking view of the market-place which it afforded had as much attraction for her as for Lucetta. The *carrefour* was like the regulation Open Place in spectacular dramas, where the incidents that occur always happen to bear on the lives of the adjoining residents. Farmers, merchants, dairymen, quacks, hawkers, appeared there from week to week, and disappeared as the afternoon wasted away. It was the node of all orbits.

From Saturday to Saturday was as from day to day with the two young women now. In an emotional sense they did not live at all during the intervals. Wherever they might go wandering on other days, on market-day they were sure to be at home. Both stole sly glances out of the window at Farfrae's shoulders and poll. His face they seldom saw, for, either through shyness, or not to disturb his mercantile mood, he avoided looking towards their quarters.

Thus things went on, till a certain market-morning brought a new sensation. Elizabeth and Lucetta were sitting at breakfast when a parcel containing two dresses arrived for the latter from London. She called Elizabeth from her breakfast, and entering her friend's bedroom Elizabeth saw the gowns spread out on the bed, one of a deep cherry colour, the other lighter—a glove lying at the end of each sleeve, a bonnet at the top of each neck, and parasols across the gloves, Lucetta standing beside the suggested human figure in an attitude of contemplation.

"I wouldn't think so hard about it," said Elizabeth, marking the intensity with which Lucetta was alternating the question whether this or that would suit best.

"But settling upon new clothes is so trying," said Lucetta. "You are that person" (pointing to one of the arrangements), "or you are *that* totally different person" (pointing to the other), "for the whole of the coming spring: and one of the two, you don't know which, may turn out to be very objectionable."

It was finally decided by Miss Templeman that she would be the cherry-coloured person at all hazards. The dress was pronounced to be a fit, and Lucetta walked with it into the front-room, Elizabeth following her.

The morning was exceptionally bright for the time of year. The sun fell so flat on the houses and pavement opposite Lucetta's residence that they poured their brightness into her rooms. Suddenly, after a rumbling of wheels, there were added to this steady light a fantastic series of circling irradiations upon the ceiling, and the companions turned to the window. Immediately opposite a vehicle of strange description had come to a standstill, as if it had been placed there for exhibition.

It was the new-fashioned agricultural implement called a horse-drill, till then unknown, in its modern shape, in this part of the country, where the venerable seed-lip was still used for sowing as in the days of the Heptarchy. Its arrival created about as much sensation in the corn-market as a flying machine would create at Charing Cross. The farmers crowded round it, women drew near it, children crept under and into it. The machine was painted in bright hues of green, yellow, and red, and it resembled as a whole a compound of hornet, grasshopper, and shrimp, magnified enormously. Or it might have been likened to an upright musical instrument with the front gone. That was how it struck Lucetta. "Why, it is a sort of agricultural piano," she said.

"It has something to do with corn," said Elizabeth.

"I wonder who thought of introducing it here?"

Donald Farfrae was in the minds of both as the innovator, for though not a farmer he was closely leagued with farming operations. And as if in response to their thought he came up at that moment, looked at the machine, walked round it, and handled it as if he knew something about its make. The two watchers had inwardly started at his coming, and Elizabeth left the window, went to the back of the room, and stood as if absorbed in the panelling of the wall. She hardly knew that she had done this till Lucetta, animated by the conjunction of her new attire with the sight of Farfrae, spoke out: "Let us go and look at the instrument, whatever it is."

Elizabeth-Jane's bonnet and shawl were pitchforked on in a moment, and they went out. Among all the agriculturists gathered round, the only appropriate possessor of the new machine seemed to be Lucetta, because she alone rivalled it in colour.

They examined it curiously; observing the rows of trumpet-shaped tubes one within the other, the little scoops, like revolving salt-spoons, which tossed the seed into the upper ends of the tubes that conducted it to the ground; till somebody said, "Good-morning, Elizabeth-Jane." She looked up, and there was her stepfather.

His greeting had been somewhat dry and thunderous, and Elizabeth-Jane, embarrassed out of her equanimity, stammered at random, "This is the lady I live with, father—Miss Templeman."

Henchard put his hand to his hat, which he brought down with a great wave till it met his body at the knee. Miss Templeman bowed. "I am happy to become acquainted with you, Mr. Henchard," she said. "This is a curious machine."

"Yes," Henchard replied; and he proceeded to explain it, and still more forcibly to ridicule it.

"Who brought it here?" said Lucetta.

"Oh, don't ask me, ma'am!" said Henchard. "The thing—why 'tis impossible it should act. 'Twas brought here by one of our machinists on the recommendation of a jumped-up jackanapes of a fellow who thinks—" His eye caught Elizabeth-Jane's imploring face, and he stopped, probably thinking that the suit might be progressing.

He turned to go away. Then something seemed to occur which his stepdaughter fancied must really be a hallucination of hers. A murmur apparently came from Henchard's lips in which she detected the words, "You refused to see me!" reproachfully addressed to Lucetta. She could not believe that they had been uttered by her stepfather; unless, indeed, they might have been spoken to one of the yellow-gaitered farmers near them. Yet Lucetta seemed silent, and then all thought of the incident was dissipated by the humming of a song, which sounded as though from the interior of the machine. Henchard had by this time vanished into the market-house, and both the women glanced towards the corn-drill. They could see behind it the bent back of a man who was pushing his head into the internal works to master their simple secrets. The hummed song went on—

> 'Tw—s on a s—m—r aftern—n,
> A wee be—re the s—n w—nt d—n,
> When Kitty wi' a braw n—w g—wn
> C—me ow're the h—lls to Gowrie.

Elizabeth-Jane had apprehended the singer in a moment, and looked guilty of she did not know what. Lucetta next recognised him, and more mistress of herself said archly, "The 'Lass of Gowrie' from inside of a seed-drill—what a phenomenon!"

Satisfied at last with his investigation, the young man stood upright, and met their eyes across the summit.

"We are looking at the wonderful new drill," Miss Templeman said. "But practically it is a stupid thing—is it not?" she added, on the strength of Henchard's information.

"Stupid? O no!" said Farfrae gravely. "It will revolutionise sowing heerabout! No more sowers flinging their seed about broadcast, so that some falls by the wayside and some among thorns, and all that. Each grain will go straight to its intended place, and nowhere else whatever!"

"Then the romance of the sower is gone for good," observed Elizabeth-Jane, who felt herself at one with Farfrae in Bible-reading at least. " 'He that observeth the wind shall not sow,' so the Preacher said; but his words will not be to the point any more. How things change!"

"Ay; ay. . . . It must be so!" Donald admitted, his gaze fixing itself on a blank point far away. "But the machines are already very common in the East and North of England," he added apologetically.

Lucetta seemed to be outside this train of sentiment, her acquaintance with the Scriptures being somewhat limited. "Is the machine yours?" she asked of Farfrae.

"O no, madam," said he, becoming embarrassed and deferential at the sound of her voice, though with Elizabeth Jane he was quite at his ease. "No, no—I merely recommended that it should be got."

In the silence which followed Farfrae appeared only conscious of her; to have passed from perception of Elizabeth into a brighter sphere of existence than she appertained to. Lucetta, discerning that he was much mixed that day, partly in his mercantile mood and partly in his romantic one, said gaily to him—

"Well, don't forsake the machine for us," and went indoors with her companion.

The latter felt that she had been in the way, though why was unaccountable to her. Lucetta explained the matter somewhat by saying when they were again in the sitting-room—

"I had occasion to speak to Mr. Farfrae the other day, and so I knew him this morning."

Lucetta was very kind towards Elizabeth that day. Together they saw the market thicken, and in course of time thin away with the slow decline of the sun towards the upper end of the town, its rays taking the street endways and enfilading the long thoroughfare from top to bottom. The gigs and vans disappeared one by one till there was not a vehicle in the street. The time of the riding world was over; the pedestrian world held sway. Field labourers and their wives and children trooped in from the villages for their weekly shopping, and instead of a rattle of wheels and a tramp of horses ruling the sound as earlier, there was nothing but the shuffle of many feet. All the implements were gone; all the farmers; all the moneyed class. The character of the town's trading had changed from bulk to multiplicity, and pence were handled now as pounds had been handled earlier in the day.

Lucetta and Elizabeth looked out upon this, for though it was night and the street lamps were lighted, they had kept their shutters unclosed. In the faint blink of the fire they spoke more freely.

"Your father was distant with you," said Lucetta.

"Yes." And having forgotten the momentary mystery of Henchard's seeming speech to Lucetta, she continued, "It is because he does not think I am respectable. I have tried to be so more than you can imagine, but in vain! My mother's separation from my father was unfortunate for me. You don't know what it is to have shadows like that upon your life."

Lucetta seemed to wince. "I do not—of that kind precisely," she said, "but you may feel a—sense of disgrace—shame—in other ways."

"Have you ever had any such feeling?" said the younger innocently.

"O no," said Lucetta quickly. "I was thinking of—what happens sometimes when women get themselves in strange positions in the eyes of the world from no fault of their own."

"It must make them very unhappy afterwards."

"It makes them anxious; for might not other women despise them?"

"Not altogether despise them. Yet not quite like or respect them."

Lucetta winced again. Her past was by no means secure from investigation, even in Casterbridge. For one thing, Henchard had never returned to her the cloud of letters she had written and sent him in her first excitement. Possibly they were destroyed; but she could have wished that they had never been written.

The rencounter with Farfrae and his bearings towards Lucetta had made the reflective Elizabeth more observant of her brilliant and amiable companion. A few days afterwards, when her eyes met Lucetta's as the latter was going out, she somehow knew that Miss Templeman was nourishing a hope of seeing the attractive Scotchman. The fact was printed large all over Lucetta's cheeks and eyes to anyone who could read her as Elizabeth-Jane was beginning to do. Lucetta passed on and closed the street-door.

A seer's spirit took possession of Elizabeth, impelling her to sit down by the fire and divine events so surely from data already her own that they could be held as witnessed. She followed Lucetta thus mentally—saw her encounter Donald somewhere as if by chance—saw him wear his special look when meeting women, with an added intensity because this one was Lucetta. She depicted his impassioned manner; beheld the indecision of both between their lothness to separate and their desire not to be observed; depicted their shaking of hands; how they probably parted with frigidity in their general contour and movements, only in the smaller features showing the spark of passion, thus invisible to all but themselves. This discerning silent witch had not done thinking of these things when Lucetta came noiselessly behind her, and made her start.

It was all true as she had pictured—she could have sworn it. Lucetta had a heightened luminousness in her eye over and above the advanced colour of her cheeks.

"You've seen Mr. Farfrae," said Elizabeth demurely.

"Yes," said Lucetta. "How did you know?"

She knelt down on the hearth and took her friend's hands excitedly in her own. But after all she did not say when or how she had seen him or what he had said.

That night she became restless; in the morning she was feverish; and at breakfast-time she told her companion that she had something on her mind—something which concerned a person in whom she was interested much. Elizabeth was earnest to listen and sympathise.

"This person—a lady—once admired a man much—very much," she said tentatively.

"Ah," said Elizabeth-Jane.

"They were intimate—rather. He did not think so deeply of her as she did of him. But in an impulsive moment, purely out of reparation, he proposed to make her his wife. She agreed. But there was an unsuspected hitch in the proceedings; though she had been so far compromised with him that she felt she could never belong to another man, as a pure matter of conscience, even if she should wish to. After that they were much apart, heard nothing of each other for a long time, and she felt her life quite closed up for her."

"Ah—poor girl!"

"She suffered much on account of him; though I should add that he could not altogether be blamed for what had happened. At last the obstacle which separated them was providentially removed; and he came to marry her."

"How delightful!"

"But in the interval she—my poor friend—had seen a man she liked better than him. Now comes the point: Could she in honour dismiss the first?"

"A new man she liked better—that's bad!"

"Yes," said Lucetta, looking pained at a boy who was swinging the town pump-handle. "It is bad! Though you must remember that she was forced into an equivocal position with the first man by an accident—that he was not so well educated or refined as the second, and that she had discovered some qualities in the first that rendered him less desirable as a husband than she had at first thought him to be."

"I cannot answer," said Elizabeth-Jane thoughtfully. "It is so difficult. It wants a Pope to settle that!"

"You prefer not to, perhaps?" Lucetta showed in her appealing tone how much she leant on Elizabeth's judgment.

"Yes, Miss Templeman," admitted Elizabeth. "I would rather not say."

Nevertheless, Lucetta seemed relieved by the simple fact of having opened out the situation a little, and was slowly convalescent of her headache. "Bring me a looking-glass. How do I appear to people?" she said languidly.

"Well—a little worn," answered Elizabeth, eyeing her as a critic eyes a doubtful painting; fetching the glass she enabled Lucetta to survey herself in it, which Lucetta anxiously did.

"I wonder if I wear well, as times go!" she observed after a while.

"Yes—fairly."

"Where am I worst?"

"Under your eyes—I notice a little brownness there."

"Yes. That is my worst place, I know. How many years more do you think I shall last before I get hopelessly plain?"

There was something curious in the way in which Elizabeth, though the younger, had come to play the part of experienced sage in these discussions. "It may be five years," she said judicially. "Or, with a quiet life, as many as ten. With no love you might calculate on ten."

Lucetta seemed to reflect on this as on an unalterable, impartial verdict. She told Elizabeth-Jane no more of the past attachment she had roughly adumbrated as the experiences of a third person; and Elizabeth, who in spite of her philosophy was very tender-hearted, wept that night in bed at the thought that her pretty, rich Lucetta did not treat her to the full confidence of names and dates in her confessions. For by the "she" of Lucetta's story Elizabeth had not been beguiled.

XXV

THE NEXT PHASE OF THE SUPERSESSION OF HENCHARD IN LUCETTA'S HEART WAS AN EXperiment in calling on her performed by Farfrae with some apparent trepidation. Conventionally speaking, he conversed with both Miss Templeman and her companion; but in fact it was rather that Elizabeth sat invisible in the room. Donald appeared not to see her at all, and answered her wise little remarks with curtly indifferent monosyllables, his looks and faculties hanging on the woman who could boast of a more Protean variety in her phases, moods, opinions, and also principles, than could Elizabeth. Lucetta had persisted in dragging her into the circle; but she had remained like an awkward third point which that circle would not touch.

Susan Henchard's daughter bore up against the frosty ache of the treatment, as she had borne up under worse things, and contrived as soon as possible to get out of the inharmonious room without being missed. The Scotchman seemed hardly the same Farfrae who had danced with her, and walked with her, in a delicate poise between love and friendship—that period in the history of a love when alone it can be said to be unalloyed with pain.

She stoically looked from her bedroom window, and contemplated her fate as if it were written on the top of the church-tower hard by. "Yes," she said at last, bringing down her palm upon the sill with a pat: "*He* is the second man of that story she told me!"

All this time Henchard's smouldering sentiments towards Lucetta had been fanned into higher and higher inflammation by the circumstances of the case. He was discovering that the young woman, for whom he once felt a pitying warmth which had been almost chilled out of him by reflection, was, when now qualified with a slight inaccessibility and a more matured beauty, the very being to make him satisfied with life. Day after day proved to him, by her silence, that it was no use to think of bringing her round by holding aloof; so he gave in, and called upon her again, Elizabeth-Jane being absent.

He crossed the room to her with a heavy tread of some awkwardness, his strong, warm gaze upon her—like the sun beside the moon in comparison with Farfrae's modest look—and with something of a hail-fellow bearing, as, indeed, was not unnatural. But she seemed so transubstantiated by her change of position, and held out her hand to him in such cool friendship, that he became deferential, and sat down with a perceptible loss of power. He understood but little of fashion in dress, yet enough to feel himself inadequate in appearance beside her whom he had hitherto been dreaming of as almost his property. She said something very polite about his being good enough to call. This caused him to recover balance. He looked her oddly in the face, losing his awe.

"Why, of course I have called, Lucetta," he said. "What does that nonsense mean? You know I couldn't have helped myself if I had wished—that is, if I had any kindness at all. I've called to say that I am ready, as soon as custom will permit, to give you my name in return for your devotion and what you lost by it in thinking too little of yourself and too much of me; to say that you can fix the day or month, with my full consent, whenever in your opinion it would be seemly: you know more of these things than I."

"It is full early yet," she said evasively.

"Yes, yes; I suppose it is. But you know, Lucetta, I felt directly my poor ill-used Susan died, and when I could not bear the idea of marrying again, that after what had happened between us it was my duty not to let any unnecessary delay occur before putting things to rights. Still, I wouldn't call in a hurry, because—well, you can guess how this money you've come into made me feel." His voice slowly fell; he was conscious that in this room his accents and manner wore a roughness not observable in the street. He looked about the room at the novel hangings and ingenious furniture with which she had surrounded herself.

"Upon my life, I didn't know such furniture as this could be bought in Casterbridge," he said.

"Nor can it be " said she. "Nor will it till fifty years more of civilization have passed over the town. It took a waggon and four horses to get it here."

"H'm. The fact is, your setting up like this makes my beaming towards you rather awkward."

"Why?"

An answer was not really needed, and he did not furnish one. "Well," he went on, "there's nobody in the world I would have wished to see enter into this wealth before you, Lucetta, and nobody, I am sure, who will become it more." He turned to her with congratulatory admiration so fervid that she shrank somewhat, notwithstanding that she knew him so well.

"I am greatly obliged to you for all that," said she, rather with an air of speaking ritual. The stint of reciprocal feeling was perceived, and Henchard showed chagrin at once—nobody was more quick to show that than he.

"You may be obliged or not for't. Though the things I say may not have the polish of what you've lately learnt to expect for the first time in your life, they are real, my lady Lucetta."

"That's rather a rude way of speaking to me," pouted Lucetta, with stormy eyes.

"Not at all!" replied Henchard hotly. "But there, there, I don't wish to quarrel with 'ee. I come with an honest proposal for silencing your Jersey enemies, and you ought to be thankful."

"How can you speak so!" she answered, firing quickly. "Knowing that my only crime was the indulging in a foolish girl's passion for you with too little regard for correctness, and that I was what *I* call innocent all the time they called me guilty, you ought not to be so cutting! I suffered enough at that worrying time, when you wrote to tell me of your wife's return and my consequent dismissal, and if I am a little independent now, surely the privilege is due to me!"

"Yes, it is," he said. "But it is not by what is, in this life, but by what appears, that you are judged; and I therefore think you ought to accept me—for your own good name's sake. What is known in your native Jersey may get known here."

"How you keep on about Jersey! I am English!"

"Yes, yes. Well, what do you say to my proposal?"

For the first time in their acquaintance Lucetta had the move; and yet she was backward. "For the present let things be," she said with some embarrassment. "Treat me as an acquaintance; and I'll treat you as one. Time will—" she stopped; and he said nothing to fill the gap for a-while, there being no pressure of half acquaintance to drive them into speech if they were not minded for it.

"That's the way the wind blows, is it?" he said at last grimly, nodding an affirmative to his own thoughts.

A yellow flood of reflected sunlight filled the room for a few instants. It was produced by the passing of a load of newly trussed hay from the country, in a waggon marked with Farfrae's name. Beside it rode Farfrae himself on horseback. Lucetta's face became—as a woman's face becomes when the man she loves rises upon her gaze like an apparition.

A turn of the eye by Henchard, a glance from the window, and the secret of her inaccessibility would have been revealed. But Henchard in estimating her tone was looking down so plumb-straight that he did not note the warm consciousness upon Lucetta's face.

"I shouldn't have thought it—I shouldn't have thought it of women!" he said emphatically by and by, rising and shaking himself into activity; while Lucetta was so anxious to divert him from any suspicion of the truth that she asked him to be in no hurry. Bringing him some apples, she insisted upon paring one for him.

He would not take it. "No, no; such is not for me," he said drily, and moved to the door. At going out he turned his eye upon her.

"You came to live in Casterbridge entirely on my account," he said. "Yet now you are here you won't have anything to say to my offer!"

He had hardly gone down the staircase when she dropped upon the sofa, and jumped up again in a fit of desperation. "I will love him!" she cried passionately; "as for *him*—he's hot-tempered and stern, and it would be madness to bind myself to him knowing that. I won't be a slave to the past—I'll love where I choose!"

Yet having decided to break away from Henchard, one might have supposed her capable of aiming higher than Farfrae. But Lucetta reasoned nothing: she feared hard words from the people with whom she had been earlier associated; she had no relatives left; and with native lightness of heart took kindly to what fate offered.

Elizabeth-Jane, surveying the position of Lucetta between her two lovers from the crystalline sphere of a straightforward mind, did not fail to perceive that her father, as she called him, and Donald Farfrae became more desperately enamoured of her friend everyday. On Farfrae's side it was the unforced passion of youth. On Henchard's the artificially stimulated coveting of maturer age.

The pain she experienced from the almost absolute obliviousness to her existence that was shown by the pair of them became at times half dissipated by her sense of its humourousness. When Lucetta had pricked her finger they were as deeply concerned as if she were dying; when she herself had been seriously sick or in danger they uttered a conventional word of sympathy at the news, and forgot all about it immediately. But, as regarded Henchard, this perception of hers also caused her some filial grief; she could not help asking what she had done to be neglected so, after the professions of solicitude he had made. As regarded Farfrae, she thought, after honest reflection, that it was quite natural. What was she beside Lucetta?—as one of the "meaner beauties of the night," when the moon had risen in the skies.

She had learnt the lesson of renunciation, and was as familiar with the wreck of each day's wishes as with the diurnal setting of the sun. If her earthly career had taught her few book philosophies it had at least well practised her in this. Yet her experience had consisted less in a series of pure disappointments than in a series of substitutions. Continually it had happened that what she had desired had not been granted her, and that what had been granted her she had not desired. So she viewed with an approach to equanimity the new cancelled days when Donald had been her undeclared lover, and wondered what unwished-for thing Heaven might send her in place of him.

XXVI

IT CHANCED THAT ON A FINE SPRING MORNING HENCHARD AND FARFRAE MET IN THE chestnut-walk which ran along the south wall of the town. Each had just come out from his early breakfast, and there was not another soul near. Henchard was reading a letter from Lucetta, sent in answer to a note from him, in which she made some excuse for not immediately granting him a second interview that he had desired.

Donald had no wish to enter into conversation with his former friend on their present constrained terms; neither would he pass him in scowling silence. He nodded, and Henchard did the same. They receded from each other several paces when a voice cried "Far-frae!" It was Henchard's, who stood regarding him.

"Do you remember," said Henchard, as if it were the presence of the thought and not of the man which made him speak, "do you remember my story of that second woman—who suffered for her thoughtless intimacy with me?"

"I do," said Farfrae.

"Do you remember my telling 'ee how it all began, and how it ended?

"Yes."

"Well, I have offered to marry her now that I can; but she won't marry me. Now what would you think of her—I put it to you?"

"Well, ye owe her nothing more now," said Farfrae heartily.

"It is true," said Henchard, and went on.

That he had looked up from a letter to ask his questions completely shut out from Far-frae's mind all vision of Lucetta as the culprit. Indeed, her present position was so differ-ent from that of the young woman of Henchard's story as of itself to be sufficient to blind him absolutely to her identity. As for Henchard, he was reassured by Farfrae's words and manner against a suspicion which had crossed his mind. They were not those of a con-scious rival.

Yet that there was rivalry by someone he was firmly persuaded. He could feel it in the air around Lucetta, see it in the turn of her pen. There was an antagonistic force in exer-cise, so that when he had tried to hang near her he seemed standing in a refluent current. That it was not innate caprice he was more and more certain. Her windows gleamed as if they did not want him; her curtains seem to hang slily, as if they screened an ousting pres-ence. To discover whose presence that was—whether really Farfrae's after all, or another's—he exerted himself to the utmost to see her again; and at length succeeded.

At the interview, when she offered him tea, he made it a point to launch a cautious en-quiry if she knew Mr. Farfrae.

Oh yes, she knew him, she declared; she could not help knowing almost everybody in Casterbridge, living in such a gazebo over the centre and arena of the town.

"Pleasant young fellow," said Henchard.

"Yes," said Lucetta.

"We both know him," said kind Elizabeth-Jane, to relieve her companion's divined embarrassment.

There was a knock at the door; literally, three full knocks and a little one at the end.

"That kind of knock means half-and-half—somebody between gentle and simple," said the corn-merchant to himself. "I shouldn't wonder therefore if it is he." In a few sec-onds surely enough Donald walked in.

Lucetta was full of little fidgets and flutters, which increased Henchard's suspicions without affording any special proof of their correctness. He was well-nigh ferocious at the sense of the queer situation in which he stood towards this woman. One who had re-proached him for deserting her when calumniated, who had urged claims upon his consid-eration on that account, who had lived waiting for him, who at the first decent opportunity had come to ask him to rectify, by making her his, the false position into which she had placed herself for his sake; such she had been. And now he sat at her tea-table eager to gain her attention, and, in his amatory rage, feeling the other man present to be a villain, just as any young fool of a lover might feel.

They sat stiffly side by side at the darkening table, like some Tuscan painting of the two disciples supping at Emmaus. Lucetta, forming the third and chief figure, was opposite them; Elizabeth-Jane, being out of the game, and out of the group, could observe from afar all things: that there were long spaces of taciturnity, when all exterior circumstances were subdued to the touch of spoons and china, the click of a heel on the pavement under the window, the passing of a wheelbarrow or cart, the whistling of the carter, the gush of water into householders' buckets at the town-pump opposite: the exchange of greetings among their neighbours, and the rattle of the yokes by which they carried off their evening supply.

"More bread-and-butter?" said Lucetta to Henchard and Farfrae equally, holding out between them a plateful of long slices. Henchard took a slice by one end and Donald by the other; each feeling certain he was the man meant; neither let go, and the slice came in two.

"Oh—I am so sorry!" cried Lucetta, with a nervous titter. Farfrae tried to laugh; but he was too much in love to see the incident in any but a tragic light.

"How ridiculous of all three of them!" said Elizabeth to herself.

Henchard left the house with a ton of conjecture, though without a grain of proof, that the counter-attraction was Farfrae; and therefore he would not make up his mind. Yet to Elizabeth-Jane it was plain as the town-pump that Donald and Lucetta were incipient lovers. More than once, in spite of her care, Lucetta had been unable to restrain her glance from flitting across into Farfrae's eyes like a bird to its nest. But Henchard was constructed upon too large a scale to discern such minutiae as these by an evening light, which to him were as the notes of an insect that lie above the compass of the human ear.

But he was disturbed. And the sense of occult rivalry in suitorship was so much superadded to the palpable rivalry of their business lives. To the coarse materiality of that rivalry it added an inflaming soul.

The thus vitalised antagonism took the form of action by Henchard sending for Jopp, the manager originally displaced by Farfrae's arrival. Henchard had frequently met this man about the streets, observed that his clothing spoke of neediness, heard that he lived in Mixen Lane—a back slum of the town, the *pis aller* of Casterbridge domiciliation—itself almost a proof that a man had reached a stage when he would not stick at trifles.

Jopp came after dark, by the gates of the store-yard, and felt his way through the hay and straw to the office where Henchard sat in solitude awaiting him.

"I am again out of a foreman," said the corn-factor. "Are you in a place?"

"Not so much as a beggar's, sir."

"How much do you ask?"

Jopp named his price, which was very moderate.

"When can you come?"

"At this hour and moment, sir," said Jopp, who, standing hands-pocketed at the street corner till the sun had faded the shoulders of his coat to scarecrow green, had regularly watched Henchard in the market-place, measured him, and learnt him, by virtue of the power which the still man has in his stillness of knowing the busy one better than he knows himself. Jopp too, had had a convenient experience; he was the only one in Casterbridge besides Henchard and the close-lipped Elizabeth who knew that Lucetta came truly from Jersey, and but proximately from Bath. "I know Jersey too, sir," he said. "Was living there when you used to do business that way. Oh yes—have often seen ye there."

"Indeed! Very good. Then the thing is settled. The testimonials you showed me when you first tried for't are sufficient.

That characters deteriorated in time of need possibly did not occur to Henchard. Jopp said, "Thank you," and stood more firmly, in the consciousness that at last he officially belonged to that spot.

"Now," said Henchard, digging his strong eyes into Jopp's face, "one thing is necessary to me, as the biggest corn-and-hay dealer in these parts. The Scotchman, who's taking the town trade so bold into his hands, must be cut out. D'ye hear? We two can't live side by side—that's clear and certain."

"I've seen it all," said Jopp.

"By fair competition I mean, of course," Henchard continued. "But as hard, keen, and unflinching as fair—rather more so. By such a desperate bid against him for the farmers' custom as will grind him into the ground—starve him out. I've capital, mind ye, and I can do it."

"I'm all that way of thinking," said the new foreman. Jopp's dislike of Farfrae as the man who had once ursurped his place, while it made him a willing tool, made him, at the same time, commercially as unsafe a colleague as Henchard could have chosen.

"I sometimes think," he added, "that he must have some glass that he sees next year in. He has such a knack of making everything bring him fortune."

"He's deep beyond all honest men's discerning; but we must make him shallower. We'll under-sell him, and over-buy him, and so snuff him out."

They then entered into specific details of the process by which this would be accomplished, and parted at a late hour.

Elizabeth-Jane heard by accident that Jopp had been engaged by her stepfather. She was so fully convinced that he was not the right man for the place that, at the risk of making Henchard angry, she expressed her apprehension to him when they met. But it was done to no purpose. Henchard shut up her argument with a sharp rebuff.

The season's weather seemed to favour their scheme. The time was in the years immediately before foreign competition had revolutionised the trade in grain, when still, as from the earliest ages, the wheat quotations from month to month depended entirely upon the home harvest. A bad harvest, or the prospect of one, would double the price of corn in a few weeks; and the promise of a good yield would lower it as rapidly. Prices were like the roads of the period, steep in gradient, reflecting in their phases the local conditions, without engineering, levellings, or averages.

The farmer's income was ruled by the wheat-crop within his own horizon, and the wheat-crop by the weather. Thus in person, he became a sort of flesh-barometer, with feelers always directed to the sky and wind around him. The local atmosphere was everything to him; the atmospheres of other countries a matter of indifference. The people, too, who were not farmers, the rural multitude, saw in the god of the weather a more important personage than they do now. Indeed, the feeling of the peasantry in this matter was so intense as to be almost unrealizable in these equable days. Their impulse was well-nigh to prostrate themselves in lamentation before untimely rains and tempests, which came as the Alastor of those households whose crime it was to be poor.

After midsummer they watched the weather-cocks as men waiting in antechambers watch the lackey. Sun elated them; quiet rain sobered them; weeks of watery tempest stupefied them. That aspect of the sky which they now regard as disagreeable they then beheld as as furious.

It was June, and the weather was very unfavourable. Casterbridge, being, as it were, the bell-board on which all the adjacent hamlets and villages sounded their notes, was decidedly dull. Instead of new articles in the shop-windows, those that had been rejected in the foregoing summer were brought out again; superseded reap-hooks, badly-shaped rakes, shop-worn leggings, and time-stiffened water-tights reappeared, furbished up as near to new as possible.

Henchard, backed by Jopp, read a disastrous garnering, and resolved to base his strategy against Farfrae upon that reading. But before acting he wished—what so many have wished—that he could know for certain what was at present only strong probability. He was superstitious—as such headstrong natures often are—and he nourished in his mind an idea bearing on the matter; an idea he shrank from disclosing even to Jopp.

In a lonely hamlet a few miles from the town—so lonely, that what are called lonely villages were teeming by comparison—there lived a man of curious repute as a forecaster or weather-prophet. The way to his house was crooked and miry—even difficult in the present unpropitious season. One evening when it was raining so heavily that ivy and laurel resounded like distant musketry, and an out-door man could be excused for shrouding himself to his ears and eyes, such a shrouded figure on foot might have been perceived travelling in the direction of the hazel-copse which dripped over the prophet's cot. The turnpike road became a lane, the lane a cart-track, the cart-track a bridle-path, the bridle-path a foot-way, the foot-way overgrown. The solitary walker slipped here and there, and stumbled over the natural springes formed by the brambles, till at length he reached the house, which, with its garden, was surrounded with a high, dense hedge. The cottage, comparatively a large one, had been built of mud by the occupier's own hands, and thatched also by himself. Here he had always lived, and here it was assumed he would die.

He existed on unseen supplies; for it was an anomalous thing that while there was hardly a soul in the neighbourhood but affected to laugh at this man's assertions, uttering the formula, "There's nothing in 'em," with full assurance on the surface of their faces, very few of them were unbelievers in their secret hearts. Whenever they consulted him they did it "for a fancy." When they paid him they said, "Just a trifle for Christmas," or "Candlemas," as the case might be.

He would have preferred more honesty in his clients, and less sham ridicule; but fundamental belief consoled him for superficial irony. As stated, he was enabled to live; people supported him with their backs turned. He was sometimes astonished that men could profess so little and believe so much at his house, when at church they professed so much and believed so little.

Behind his back he was called "Wide-oh," on account of his reputation; to his face "Mr." Fall.

The hedge of his garden formed an arch over the entrance, and a door was inserted as in a wall. Outside the door the tall traveller stopped, bandaged his face with a handkerchief as if he were suffering from toothache, and went up the path. The window-shutters were not closed, and he could see the prophet within, preparing his supper.

In answer to the knock Fall came to the door, candle in hand. The visitor stepped back a little from the light, and said, "Can I speak to ye?" in significant tones. The other's invitation to come in was responded to by the country formula, "This will do, thank ye," after which the householder had no alternative but to come out. He placed the candle on the corner of the dresser, took his hat from a nail, and joined the stranger in the porch, shutting the door behind him.

"I've long heard that you can—do things of a sort?" began the other, repressing his individuality as much as he could.

"Maybe so, Mr. Henchard," said the weather-caster.

"Ah—why do you call me that?" asked the visitor with a start.

"Because it's your name. Feeling you'd come, I've waited for ye; and thinking you might be leery from your walk, I laid two supper plates—look ye here." He threw open the door and disclosed the supper-table, at which appeared a second chair, knife and fork, plate and mug, as he had declared.

Henchard felt like Saul at his reception by Samuel; he remained in silence for a few moments, then throwing off the disguise of frigidity which he had hitherto preserved, he said, "Then I have not come in vain. . . . Now, for instance, can ye charm away warts?"

"Without trouble."

"Cure the evil?"

"That I've done—with consideration—if they will wear the toad-bag by night as well as by day."

"Forecast the weather?"

"With labour and time."

"Then take this," said Henchard. " 'Tis a crownpiece. Now, what is the harvest fortnight to be? When can I know?'

"I've worked it out already, and you can know at once." (The fact was that five farmers had already been there on the same errand from different parts of the country.) "By the sun, moon, and stars, by the clouds, the winds, the trees, and grass, the candle-flame and swallows, the smell of the herbs; likewise by the cats' eyes, the ravens, the leeches, the spiders, and the dungmixen, the last fortnight in August will be—rain and tempest."

"You are not certain, of course?"

"As one can be in a world where all's unsure. 'Twill be more like living in Revelations this autumn than in England. Shall I sketch it out for ye in a scheme?"

"Oh no, no," said Henchard. "I don't altogether believe in forecasts, come to second thoughts on such. But I—"

"You don't—you don't—'tis quite understood," said Wide-oh, without a sound of scorn. "You have given me a crown because you've one too many. But won't you join me at supper, now 'tis waiting and all?"

Henchard would gladly have joined; for the savour of the stew had floated from the cottage into the porch with such appetizing distinctness that the meat, the onions, the pepper, and the herbs could be severally recognised by his nose. But as sitting down to hob-

and-nob there would have seemed to mark him too implicitly as the weather-caster's apostle, he declined, and went his way.

The next Saturday Henchard bought grain to such an enormous extent that there was quite a talk about his purchases among his neighbours, the lawyer, the wine merchant, and the doctor; also on the next, and on all available days. When his granaries were full to choking all the weather-cocks of Casterbridge creaked and set their faces in another direction, as if tired of the south-west. The weather changed; the sunlight, which had been like tin for weeks, assumed the hues of topaz. The temperament of the welkin passed from the phlegmatic to the sanguine; an excellent harvest was almost a certainty; and as a consequence prices rushed down.

All these transformations, lovely to the outsider, to the wrong-headed corn-dealer were terrible. He was reminded of what he had well known before, that a man might gamble upon the square green areas of fields as readily as upon those of a card-room.

Henchard had backed bad weather, and apparently lost. He had mistaken the turn of the flood for the turn of the ebb. His dealings had been so extensive that settlement could not long be postponed, and to settle, he was obliged to sell off corn that he had bought only a few weeks before at figures higher by many shillings a quarter. Much of the corn he had never seen; it had not even been moved from the ricks in which it lay stacked miles away. Thus he lost heavily.

In the blaze of an early August day he met Farfrae in the market-place. Farfrae knew of his dealings (though he did not guess their intended bearing on himself) and commiserated him; for since their exchange of words in the South Walk they had been on stiffly speaking terms. Henchard for the moment, appeared to resent the sympathy; but he suddenly took a careless turn.

"Ho, no, no!—nothing serious, man!" he cried with fierce gaiety. "These things always happen, don't they? I know it has been said that figures have touched me tight lately; but is that anything rare? The case is not so bad as folk make out perhaps. And dammy, a man must be a fool to mind the common hazards of trade!"

But he had to enter the Casterbridge Bank that day for reasons which had never before sent him there—and to sit a long time in the partners' room with a constrained bearing. It was rumoured soon after that much real property, as well as vast stores of produce, in the town and neighborhood, which had stood in Henchard's name, was actually the property of his bankers.

Coming down the steps of the bank he encountered Jopp. The gloomy transactions just completed within had added fever to the original sting of Farfrae's sympathy that morning, which Henchard fancied might be a satire disguised, so that Jopp met with anything but a bland reception. The latter was in the act of taking off his hat to wipe his forehead, and saying, "A fine hot day," to an acquaintance.

"You can wipe and wipe, and say, 'A fine hot day,' can ye!" cried Henchard in a savage undertone, imprisoning Jopp between himself and the bank wall. "If it hadn't been for your blasted advice it might have been a fine day enough! Why did ye let me go on, hey?—when a word of doubt from you or anybody would have made me think twice! For you can never be sure of weather till 'tis past."

"My advice, sir, was to do what you thought best."

"A useful fellow! And the sooner you help somebody else in that way the better!" Henchard continued his address to Jopp in similar terms till it ended in Jopp's dismissal there and then, Henchard turning upon his heel and leaving him.

"You shall be sorry for this, sir; sorry as a man can be!" said Jopp, standing pale, and looking after the corn-merchant as he disappeared in the crowd of market-men hard by.

XXVII

IT WAS THE EVE OF HARVEST. PRICES BEING LOW FARFRAE WAS BUYING. AS WAS USUAL, after reckoning too surely on famine weather the local farmers had flown to the other extreme, and (in Farfrae's opinion) were selling off too recklessly—calculating with just a trifle too much certainty upon an abundant yield. So he went on buying old corn at its comparatively ridiculous price: for the produce of the previous year, though not large, had been of excellent quality.

When Henchard had squared his affairs in a disastrous way, and got rid of his burdensome purchases at a monstrous loss, the harvest began. There were three days of excellent weather, and then—"What if that curst conjuror should be right after all!" said Henchard.

The fact was, that no sooner had the sickles begun to play than the atmosphere suddenly felt as if cress would grow in it without other nourishment. It rubbed people's cheeks like damp flannel when they walked abroad. There was a gusty, high, warm wind; isolated raindrops starred the window-panes at remote distances: the sunlight would flap out like a quickly opened fan, throw the pattern of the window upon the floor of the room in a milky, colourless shine, and withdraw as suddenly as it had appeared.

From that day and hour it was clear that there was not to be so successful an ingathering after all. If Henchard had only waited long enough he might at least have avoided loss though he had not made a profit. But the momentum of his character knew no patience. At this turn of the scales he remained silent. The movements of his mind seemed to tend to the thought that some power was working against him.

"I wonder," he asked himself with eerie misgiving; "I wonder if it can be that somebody has been roasting a waxen image of me, or stirring an unholy brew to confound me! I don't believe in such power; and yet—what if they should ha' been doing it!" Even he could not admit that the perpetrator, if any, might be Farfrae. These isolated hours of superstition came to Henchard in time of moody depression, when all his practical largeness of view had oozed out of him.

Meanwhile Donald Farfrae prospered. He had purchased in so depressed a market that the present moderate stiffness of prices was sufficient to pile for him a large heap of gold where a little one had been.

"Why, he'll soon be Mayor!" said Henchard. It was indeed hard that the speaker should, of all others, have to follow the triumphal chariot of this man to the Capitol.

The rivalry of the masters was taken up by the men.

September night-shades had fallen upon Casterbridge; the clocks had struck half-past eight, and the moon had risen. The streets of the town were curiously silent for such a comparatively early hour. A sound of jangling horse-bells and heavy wheels passed up the street. These were followed by angry voices outside Lucetta's house, which led her and Elizabeth-Jane to run to the windows, and pull up the blinds.

The opposite Market House and Town Hall abutted against its next neighbour the Church except in the lower storey, where an arched thoroughfare gave admittance to a large square called Bull Stake. A stone post rose in the midst, to which the oxen had formerly been tied for baiting with dogs to make them tender before they were killed in the adjoining shambles. In a corner stood the stocks.

The thoroughfare leading to this spot was now blocked by two four-horse waggons and horses, one laden with hay-trusses, the leaders having already passed each other, and become entangled head to tail. The passage of the vehicles might have been practicable if empty; but built up with hay to the bedroom windows as one was, it was impossible.

"You must have done it a' purpose!" said Farfrae's waggoner. "You can hear my horses' bells half a mile such a night as this!"

"If ye'd been minding your business instead of zwailing along in such a gawk-hammer way, you would have zeed me!" retorted the wroth representative of Henchard.

However, according to the strict rule of the road it appeared that Henchard's man was most in the wrong; he therefore attempted to back into the High Street. In doing this the near hind-wheel rose against the churchyard wall and the whole mountainous load went over, two of the four wheels rising in the air, and the legs of the thill horse.

Instead of considering how to gather up the load, the two men closed in a fight with their fists. Before the first round was quite over Henchard came upon the spot, somebody having run for him.

Henchard sent the two men staggering in contrary directions by collaring one with each hand, turned to the horse that was down, and extricated him after some trouble. He then enquired into the circumstances; and seeing the state of his waggon and its load, began hotly rating Farfrae's man.

Lucetta and Elizabeth-Jane had by this time run down to the door and opened it, whence they watched the bright heap of new hay lying in the moon's rays, and passed and repassed by the forms of Henchard and the waggoners. The women had witnessed what nobody else had seen—the origin of the mishap; and Lucetta spoke.

"I saw it all, Mr. Henchard," she cried; "and your man was most in the wrong!"

Henchard paused in his harangue and turned. "Oh, I didn't notice you, Miss Templeman," said he. "My man in the wrong? Ah, to be sure; to be sure! But I beg your pardon notwithstanding. The other's is the empty waggon, and he must have been most to blame for coming on."

"No; I saw it, too," said Elizabeth-Jane. "And I can assure you he couldn't help it."

"You can't trust *their* senses!" murmured Henchard's man.

"Why not?" asked Henchard sharply.

"Why, you see, sir, all the women side with Farfrae—being a damn young dand—of the sort that he is—one that creeps into a maid's heart like the giddying worm into a sheep's brain—making crooked seem straight to their eyes!"

"But do you know who that lady is you talk about in such a fashion? Do you know that I pay my attentions to her, and have for some time? Just be careful!"

"Not I. I know nothing, sir, outside eight shillings a week."

"And that Mr. Farfrae is well aware of it? He's sharp in trade, but he wouldn't do anything so underhand as what you hint at."

Whether because Lucetta heard this low dialogue, or not, her white figure disappeared from her doorway inward, and the door was shut before Henchard could reach it to converse with her further. This disappointed him, for he had been sufficiently disturbed by what the man had said to wish to speak to her more closely. While pausing the old constable came up.

"Just see that nobody drives against that hay and waggon to-night, Stubberd," said the corn-merchant. "It must bide till the morning, for all hands are in the field still. And if any coach or road-waggon wants to come along, tell 'em they must go round by the back street, and be hanged to 'em. . . . Any case to-morrow up in Hall?"

"Yes, sir. One in number, sir."

"Oh, what's that?"

"An old flagrant female, sir, swearing and committing a nuisance in a horrible profane manner against the church wall, sir, as if 'twere no more than a pot-house! That's all, sir."

"Oh. The Mayor's out o' town, isn't he?"

"He is, sir."

"Very well, then I'll be there. Don't forget to keep an eye on that hay. Good-night t'ye."

During those moments Henchard had determined to follow up Lucetta, notwithstanding her elusiveness, and he knocked for admission.

The answer he received was an expression of Miss Templeman's sorrow at being unable to see him again that evening, because she had an engagement to go out.

Henchard walked away from the door to the opposite side of the street, and stood by his hay in a lonely reverie, the constable having strolled elsewhere, and the horses being removed. Though the moon was not bright as yet there were no lamps lighted, and he entered the shadow of one of the projecting jambs which formed the thoroughfare to Bull Stake; here he watched Lucetta's door.

Candle-lights were flitting in and out of her bedroom, and it was obvious that she was dressing for the appointment, whatever the nature of that might be at such an hour. The lights disappeared, the clock struck nine, and almost at the moment Farfrae came round the opposite corner and knocked. That she had been waiting just inside for him was certain, for she instantly opened the door herself. They went together by the way of a back lane westward, avoiding the front street; guessing where they were going, he determined to follow.

The harvest had been so delayed by the capricious weather, that whenever a fine day occurred all sinews were strained to save what could be saved of the damaged crops. On account of the rapid shortening of the days the harvesters worked by moonlight. Hence to-night the wheat-fields abutting on the two sides of the square formed by Casterbridge town were animated by the gathering hands. Their shouts and laughter had reached Henchard at the Market House, while he stood there waiting, and he had little doubt from the turn which Farfrae and Lucetta had taken that they were bound for the spot.

Nearly the whole town had gone into the fields. The Casterbridge populace still retained the primitive habit of helping one another in time of need; and thus, though the corn belonged to the farming section of the little community—that inhabiting the Durnover quarter—the remainder was no less interested in the labour of getting it home.

Reaching the top of the lane Henchard crossed the shaded avenue on the walls, slid down the green rampart, and stood amongst the stubble. The "stitches" or shocks rose like tents about the yellow expanse, those in the distance becoming lost in the moonlit hazes.

He had entered at a point removed from the scene of immediate operations; but two others had entered at that place, and he could see them winding among the shocks. They were paying no regard to the direction of their walk, whose vague serpentining soon began to bear down towards Henchard. A meeting promised to be awkward, and he therefore stepped into the hollow of the nearest shock, and sat down.

"You have my leave," Lucetta was saying gaily. "Speak what you like."

"Well, then," replied Farfrae, with the unmistakable inflection of the lover pure, which Henchard had never heard in full resonance on his lips before, "you are sure to be much sought after for your position, wealth, talents, and beauty. But will ye resist the temptation to be one of those ladies with lots of admirers—ay—and be content to have only a homely one?"

"And he the speaker?" said she, laughing. "Very well, sir, what next?"

"Ah! I'm afraid that what I feel will make me forget my manners!"

"Then I hope you'll never have any, if you lack them only for that cause." After some broken words, which Henchard lost, she added, "Are you sure you won't be jealous?"

Farfrae seemed to assure her that he would not, by taking her hand.

"You are convinced, Donald, that I love nobody else," she presently said. "But I should wish to have my own way in some things."

"In everything! What special thing did you mean?"

"If I wished not to live always in Casterbridge, for instance; on finding that I should not be happy here?"

Henchard did not hear the reply; he might have done so and much more, but he did not care to play the eavesdropper. They went on towards the scene of activity, where the sheaves were being handed, a dozen a minute, upon the carts and waggons which carried them away.

Lucetta insisted on parting from Farfrae when they drew near the workpeople. He had some business with them and, though he entreated her to wait a few minutes, she was inexorable, and tripped off homeward alone.

Henchard thereupon left the field and followed her. His state of mind was such that on reaching Lucetta's door he did not knock, but opened it, and walked straight up to her sitting-room, expecting to find her there. But the room was empty, and he perceived that in his haste he had somehow passed her on the way hither. He had not to wait many minutes, however, for he soon heard her dress rustling in the hall, followed by a soft closing of the door. In a moment she appeared.

The light was so low that she did not notice Henchard at first. As soon as she saw him she uttered a little cry, almost of terror.

"How can you frighten me so?" she exclaimed, with a flushed face. "It is past ten o'clock, and you have no right to surprise me here at such a time."

"I don't know that I've not the right. At any rate I have the excuse. Is it so necessary that I should stop to think of manners and customs?"

"It is too late for propriety, and might injure me."

"I called an hour ago, and you would not see me, and I thought you were in when I called now. It is you, Lucetta, who are doing wrong. It is not proper in 'ee to throw me over like this. I have a little matter to remind you of, which you seem to forget."

She sank into a chair, and turned pale.

"I don't want to hear it—I don't want to hear it!" she said through her hands, as he, standing close to the edge of her gown, began to allude to the Jersey days.

"But you ought to hear it," said he.

"It came to nothing; and through you. Then why not leave me the freedom that I gained with such sorrow! Had I found that you proposed to marry me for pure love I might have felt bound now. But I soon learnt that you had planned it out of mere charity— almost as an unpleasant duty—because I had nursed you, and compromised myself, and you thought you must repay me. After that I did not care for you so deeply as before."

"Why did you come here to find me, then?"

"I thought I ought to marry you for conscience' sake, since you were free, even though I—did not like you so well."

"And why then don't you think so now?"

She was silent. It was only too obvious that conscience had ruled well enough till new love had intervened and usurped that rule. In feeling this she herself forgot for the moment her partially justifying argument—that having discovered Henchard's infirmities of tem- per, she had some excuse for not risking her happiness in his hands after once escaping them. The only thing she could say was, "I was a poor girl then; and now my circum- stances have altered, so I am hardly the same person."

"That's true. And it makes the case awkward for me. But I don't want to touch your money. I am quite willing that every penny of your property shall remain to your per- sonal use. Besides, that argument has nothing in it. The man you are thinking of is no bet- ter than I."

"If you were as good as he you would leave me!" she cried passionately.

This unluckily aroused Henchard. "You cannot in honour refuse me," he said. "And unless you give me your promise this very night to be my wife, before a witness, I'll reveal our intimacy—in common fairness to other men!"

A look of resignation settled upon her. Henchard saw its bitterness; and had Lucetta's heart been given to any other man in the world than Farfrae he would probably have had pity upon her at that moment. But the supplanter was the upstart (as Henchard called him) who had mounted into prominence upon his shoulders, and he could bring himself to show no mercy.

Without another word she rang the bell, and directed that Elizabeth-Jane should be fetched from her room. The latter appeared, surprised in the midst of her lucubrations. As soon as she saw Henchard she went across to him dutifully.

"Elizabeth-Jane," he said, taking her hand, "I want you to hear this." And turning to Lucetta: "Will you, or will you not, marry me?"

"If you—wish it, I must agree!"

"You say yes?"

"I do."

No sooner had she given the promise than she fell back in a fainting state.

"What dreadful thing drives her to say this, father, when it is such a pain to her?" asked Elizabeth, kneeling down by Lucetta. "Don't compel her to do anything against her will! I have lived with her, and know that she cannot bear much."

"Don't be a no'thern simpleton!" said Henchard drily. "This promise will leave him free for you, if you want him, won't it?"

At this Lucetta seemed to wake from her swoon with a start.

"Him? Who are you talking about?" she said wildly.

"Nobody, as far as I am concerned," said Elizabeth firmly.

"Oh—well. Then it is my mistake," said Henchard. "But the business is between me and Miss Templeman. She agrees to be my wife."

"But don't dwell on it just now," entreated Elizabeth, holding Lucetta's hand.

"I don't wish to, if she promises," said Henchard.

"I have, I have," groaned Lucetta, her limbs hanging like fluid, from very misery and faintness. "Michael, please don't argue it any more!"

"I will not," he said. And taking up his hat he went away.

Elizabeth-Jane continued to kneel by Lucetta. "What is this?" she said. "You called my father 'Michael' as if you knew him well? And how is it he has got this power over you, that you promise to marry him against your will? Ah—you have many many secrets from me!"

"Perhaps you have some from me," Lucetta murmured, with closed eyes, little thinking, however, so unsuspicious was she, that the secret of Elizabeth's heart concerned the young man who had caused this damage to her own.

"I would not—do anything against you at all!" stammered Elizabeth, keeping in all signs of emotion till she was ready to burst. "I cannot understand how my father can command you so; I don't sympathise with him in it at all. I'll go to him and ask him to release you."

"No, no," said Lucetta. "Let it all be."

XXVIII

THE NEXT MORNING HENCHARD WENT TO THE TOWN HALL BELOW LUCETTA'S HOUSE, to attend Petty Sessions, being still a magistrate for the year by virtue of his late position as Mayor. In passing he looked up at her windows, but nothing of her was to be seen.

Henchard, as a Justice of the Peace, may at first seem to be an even greater incongruity than Shallow and Silence themselves. But his rough and ready perceptions, his sledge-hammer directness, had often served him better than nice legal knowledge in despatching such simple business as fell to his hands in this Court. To-day, Dr. Chalkfield, the Mayor for the year, being absent, the corn-merchant took the big chair, his eyes still abstractedly stretching out of the window to the ashlar front of High Place Hall.

There was one case only, and the offender stood before him. She was an old woman of mottled countenance, attired in a shawl of that nameless tertiary hue which comes, but cannot be made—a hue neither tawny, russet, hazel, nor ash; a sticky black bonnet that seemed to have been worn in the country of the Psalmist where the clouds drop fatness; and an apron that had been white in time so comparatively recent as still to contrast visibly with the rest of her clothes. The steeped aspect of the woman as a whole showed her to be no native of the country-side or even of a country-town.

She looked cursorily at Henchard and the second magistrate, and Henchard looked at her, with a momentary pause, as if she had reminded him indistinctly of somebody or something which passed from his mind as quickly as it had come. "Well, and what has she been doing?" he said, looking down at the charge-sheet.

"She is charged, sir, with the offence of disorderly female and nuisance," whispered Stubberd.

"Where did she do that?" said the other magistrate.

"By the church, sir, of all the horrible places in the world!—I caught her in the act, your worship."

"Stand back then," said Henchard, "and let's hear what you've got to say."

Stubberd was sworn in, the magistrate's clerk dipped his pen, Henchard being no note-taker himself, and the constable began—

"Hearing a' illegal noise I went down the street at twenty-five minutes past eleven P.M. on the night of the fifth instinct, Hannah Dominy. When I had—"

"Don't go so fast, Stubberd," said the clerk.

The constable waited, with his eyes on the clerk's pen, till the latter stopped scratching, and said, "yes." Stubberd continued: "When I had proceeded to the spot I saw defendant at another spot, namely, the gutter." He paused, watching the point of the clerk's pen again.

"Gutter, yes, Stubberd."

"Spot measuring twelve feet nine inches or thereabouts from where I—" Still careful not to outrun the clerk's penmanship, Stubberd pulled up again; for having got his evidence by heart, it was immaterial to him whereabouts he broke off.

"I object to that," spoke up the old woman, " 'spot measuring twelve feet nine or thereabouts from where I,' is not good evidence!"

The magistrates consulted, and the second one said that the bench was of opinion that twelve feet nine inches from a man on his oath was admissible evidence.

Stubberd, with a suppressed gaze of victorious rectitude at the old woman, continued: "Was standing myself. She was wambling about quite dangerous to the thoroughfare and when I approached to draw near, she insulted me."

" 'Insulted me.' . . . Yes, what did she say?"

"She said, 'Put away that dee lantern,' she says."

"Yes."

"Says she, 'Dost hear, old turmit-head? Put away that dee lantern. I have floored fellows a dee sight finer-looking than a dee fool like thee, you son of a bee, dee me if I haint,' she says."

"I object to that conversation!" interposed the old woman. "I was not capable enough to hear what I said, and what is said out of my hearing is not evidence."

There was another stoppage for consultation, a book was referred to, and finally Stubberd was allowed to go on again. The truth was that the old woman had appeared in court so many more times than the magistrates themselves, that they were obliged to keep a sharp look-out upon their procedure. However, when Stubberd had rambled on a little further Henchard broke out impatiently, "Come—we don't want to hear any more of them cust D's and B's! Say the words out like a man, and don't be so modest, Stubberd; or else leave it alone!" Turning to the woman, "Now then, have you any questions to ask him, or anything to say?"

"Yes," she replied with a twinkle in her eye; and the clerk dipped his pen.

"Twenty years ago or thereabout I was selling of furmity in a tent at Weydon Fair—"

" 'Twenty years ago'—well, that's beginning at the beginning; suppose you go back to the Creation!" said the clerk, not without satire.

But Henchard stared, and quite forgot what was evidence and what was not.

"A man and a woman with a little child came into my tent," the woman continued. "They sat down and had a basin apiece. Ah, Lord's my life! I was of a more respectable station in the world then than I am now, being a land smuggler in a large way of business; and I used to season my furmity with rum for them who asked for't. I did it for the man; and then he had more and more; till at last he quarrelled with his wife, and offered to sell her to the highest bidder. A sailor came in and bid five guineas, and paid the money, and led her away. And the man who sold his wife in that fashion is the man sitting there in the great big chair." The speaker concluded by nodding her head at Henchard and folding her arms.

Everybody looked at Henchard. His face seemed strange, and in tint as if it had been powdered over with ashes. "We don't want to hear your life and adventures," said the second magistrate sharply, filling the pause which followed. "You've been asked if you've anything to say bearing on the case."

"That bears on the case. It proves that he's no better than I, and has no right to sit there in judgment upon me."

" 'Tis a concocted story," said the clerk. "So hold your tongue!"

"No—'tis true." The words came from Henchard. " 'Tis as true as the light," he said slowly. "And upon my soul it does prove that I'm no better than she! And to keep out of any temptation to treat her hard for her revenge, I'll leave her to you."

The sensation in the court was indescribably great. Henchard left the chair, and came out, passing through a group of people on the steps and outside that was much larger than usual; for it seemed that the old furmity dealer had mysteriously hinted to the denizens of the lane in which she had been lodging since her arrival, that she knew a queer thing or two about their great local man Mr. Henchard, if she chose to tell it. This had brought them hither.

"Why are there so many idlers round the Town Hall to-day?" said Lucetta to her servant when the case was over. She had risen late, and had just looked out of the window.

"Oh, please, ma'am, 'tis this larry about Mr. Henchard. A woman has proved that before he became a gentleman he sold his wife for five guineas in a booth at a fair."

In all the accounts which Henchard had given her of the separation from his wife Susan for so many years, of his belief in her death, and so on, he had never clearly explained the actual and immediate cause of that separation. The story she now heard for the first time.

A gradual misery overspread Lucetta's face as she dwelt upon the promise wrung from her the night before. At bottom, then, Henchard was this. How terrible a contingency for a woman who should commit herself to his care.

During the day she went out to the Ring and to other places, not coming in till nearly dusk. As soon as she saw Elizabeth-Jane after her return indoors she told her that she had resolved to go away from home to the seaside for a few days—to Port-Bredy; Caster-bridge was so gloomy.

Elizabeth, seeing that she looked wan and disturbed, encouraged her in the idea, thinking a change would afford her relief. She could not help suspecting that the gloom which seemed to have come over Casterbridge in Lucetta's eyes might be partially owing to the fact that Farfrae was away from home.

Elizabeth saw her friend depart for Port-Bredy, and took charge of High Place Hall till her return. After two or three days of solitude and incessant rain Henchard called at the house. He seemed disappointed to hear of Lucetta's absence and though he nodded with outward indifference he went away handling his beard with a nettled mien.

The next day he called again. "Is she come now?" he asked.

"Yes. She returned this morning," replied his stepdaughter. "But she is not indoors. She has gone for a walk along the turnpike road to Port-Bredy. She will be home by dusk."

After a few words, which only served to reveal his restless impatience, he left the house again.

XXIX

AT THIS HOUR LUCETTA WAS BOUNDING ALONG THE ROAD TO PORT-BREDY JUST AS Elizabeth had announced. That she had chosen for her afternoon walk the road along which she had returned to Casterbridge three hours earlier in a carriage was curious—if anything should be called curious in concatenations of phenomena wherein each is known to have its accounting cause. It was the day of the chief market—Saturday—and Farfrae for once had been missed from his corn-stand in the dealers' room. Nevertheless, it was known that he would be home that night—"for Sunday," as Casterbridge expressed it.

Lucetta, in continuing her walk, had at length reached the end of the ranked trees which bordered the highway in this and other directions out of the town. This end marked a mile; and here she stopped.

The spot was a vale between two gentle acclivities, and the road, still adhering to its Roman foundation, stretched onward straight as a surveyor's line till lost to sight on the most distant ridge. There was neither hedge nor tree in the prospect now, the road cling-ing to the stubby expanse of corn-land like a stripe to an undulating garment. Near her was a barn—the single building of any kind within her horizon.

She strained her eyes up the lessening road, but nothing appeared thereon—not so much as a speck. She sighed one word—"Donald!" and turned her face to the town for retreat.

Here the case was different. A single figure was approaching her—Elizabeth-Jane's. Lucetta, in spite of her loneliness, seemed a little vexed. Elizabeth's face, as soon as she recognised her friend, shaped itself into affectionate lines while yet beyond speaking distance. "I suddenly thought I would come and meet you," she said, smiling.

Lucetta's reply was taken from her lips by an unexpected diversion. A by-road on her right hand descended from the fields into the highway at the point where she stood, and down the track a bull was rambling uncertainly towards her and Elizabeth, who, facing the other way, did not observe him.

In the latter quarter of each year cattle were at once the mainstay and the terror of families about Casterbridge and its neighbourhood, where breeding was carried on with Abrahamic success. The head of stock driven into and out of the town at this season to be sold by the local auctioneer was very large; and all these horned beasts, in travelling to and fro, sent women and children to shelter as nothing else could do. In the main the animals would have walked along quietly enough; but the Casterbridge tradition was that to drive stock it was indispensable that hideous cries, coupled with Yahoo antics and gestures, should be used, large sticks flourished, stray dogs called in, and in general everything done that was likely to infuriate the viciously disposed and terrify the mild. Nothing was commoner than for a householder on going out of his parlour to find his hall or passage full of little children, nursemaids, aged women, or a ladies' school, who apologised for their presence by saying, "A bull passing down street from the sale."

Lucetta and Elizabeth regarded the animal in doubt, he meanwhile drawing vaguely towards them. It was a large specimen of the breed, in colour rich dun, though disfigured at present by splotches of mud about his seamy sides. His horns were thick and tipped with brass; his two nostrils like the Thames Tunnel as seen in the perspective toys of yore. Between them, through the gristle of his nose, was a stout copper ring, welded on, and irremovable as Gurth's collar of brass. To the ring was attached an ash staff about a yard long, which the bull with the motions of his head flung about like a flail.

It was not till they observed this dangling stick that the young women were really alarmed; for it revealed to them that the bull was an old one, too savage to be driven, which had in some way escaped, the staff being the means by which the drover controlled him and kept his horns at arms' length.

They looked round for some shelter or hiding-place, and thought of the barn hard by. As long as they had kept their eyes on the bull he had shown some deference in his manner of approach; but no sooner did they turn their backs to seek the barn than he tossed his head and decided to thoroughly terrify them. This caused the two helpless girls to run wildly, whereupon the bull advanced in a deliberate charge.

The barn stood behind a green slimy pond, and it was closed save as to one of the usual pair of doors facing them, which had been propped open by a hurdle-stick, and for this opening they made. The interior had been cleared by a recent bout of threshing except at one end, where there was a stack of dry clover. Elizabeth-Jane took in the situation. "We must climb up there," she said.

But before they had even approached it they heard the bull scampering through the pond without, and in a second he dashed into the barn, knocking down the hurdle-stake in passing; the heavy door slammed behind him; and all three were imprisoned in the barn together. The mistaken creature saw them, and stalked towards the end of the barn into which they had fled. The girls doubled so adroitly that their pursuer was against the wall when the fugitives were already half-way to the other end. By the time that his length would allow him to turn and follow them thither they had crossed over; thus the pursuit went on, the hot air from his nostrils blowing over them like a sirocco, and not a moment being attainable by Elizabeth or Lucetta in which to open the door. What might have happened had their situation continued cannot be said; but in a few moments a rattling of the door distracted their adversary's attention, and a man appeared. He ran forward towards the leading-staff, seized it, and wrenched the animal's head as if he would snap it off. The wrench was in reality so violent that the thick neck seemed to have lost its stiffness and to become half-paralyzed, whilst the nose dropped blood. The premeditated human contrivance of the nose-ring was too cunning for impulsive brute force, and the creature flinched.

The man was seen in the partial gloom to be large-framed and unhesitating. He led the bull to the door, and the light revealed Henchard. He made the bull fast without, and re-entered to the succour of Lucetta; for he had not perceived Elizabeth, who had climbed on to the clover-heap. Lucetta was hysterical, and Henchard took her in his arms and carried her to the door.

"You—have saved me!" she cried, as soon as she could speak.

"I have returned your kindness," he responded tenderly. "You once saved me."

"How—comes it to be you—you?" she asked, not heeding his reply.

"I came out here to look for you. I have been wanting to tell you something these two or three days; but you have been away, and I could not. Perhaps you cannot talk now?"

"Oh—no! Where is Elizabeth?"

"Here am I!" cried the missing one cheerfully; and without waiting for the ladder to be placed she slid down the face of the clover-stack to the floor.

Henchard supporting Lucetta on one side, and Elizabeth-Jane on the other, they went slowly along the rising road. They had reached the top and were descending again when Lucetta, now much recovered, recollected that she had dropped her muff in the barn.

"I'll run back," said Elizabeth-Jane. "I don't mind it at all, as I am not tired as you are." She thereupon hastened down again to the barn, the others pursuing their way.

Elizabeth soon found the muff, such an article being by no means small at that time. Coming out she paused to look for a moment at the bull, now rather to be pitied with his bleeding nose, having perhaps rather intended a practical joke than a murder. Henchard had secured him by jamming the staff into the hinge of the barn-door, and wedging it there with a stake. At length she turned to hasten onward after her contemplation, when she saw a green-and-black gig approaching from the contrary direction, the vehicle being driven by Farfrae.

His presence here seemed to explain Lucetta's walk that way. Donald saw her, drew up, and was hastily made acquainted with what had occurred. At Elizabeth-Jane mentioning how greatly Lucetta had been jeopardised, he exhibited an agitation different in kind no less than in intensity from any she had seen in him before. He became so absorbed in the circumstance that he scarcely had sufficient knowledge of what he was doing to think of helping her up beside him.

"She has gone on with Mr. Henchard, you say?" he enquired at last.

"Yes. He is taking her home. They are almost there by this time."

"And you are sure she can get home?"

Elizabeth-Jane was quite sure.

"Your stepfather saved her?"

"Entirely."

Farfrae checked his horse's pace; she guessed why. He was thinking that it would be best not to intrude on the other two just now. Henchard had saved Lucetta, and to provoke a possible exhibition of her deeper affection for himself was as ungenerous as it was unwise.

The immediate subject of their talk being exhausted she felt more embarrassed at sitting thus beside her past lover; but soon the two figures of the others were visible at the entrance to the town. The face of the woman was frequently turned back, but Farfrae did not whip on the horse. When these reached the town walls Henchard and his companion had disappeared down the street; Farfrae set down Elizabeth-Jane, on her expressing a particular wish to alight there, and drove round to the stables at the back of his lodgings.

On this account he entered the house through his garden, and going up to his apartments found them in a particularly disturbed state, his boxes being hauled out upon the landing, and his bookcase standing in three pieces. These phenomena, however, seemed to cause him not the least surprise. "When will everything be sent up?" he said to the mistress of the house, who was superintending.

"I am afraid not before eight, sir," said she. "You see we wasn't aware till this morning that you were going to move, or we could have been forwarder."

"A—well, never mind, never mind!" said Farfrae cheerily. "Eight o'clock will do well enough if it be not later. Now, don't ye be standing here talking, or it will be twelve, I doubt." Thus speaking he went out by the front-door and up the street.

During this interval Henchard and Lucetta had had experiences of a different kind. After Elizabeth's departure for the muff the corn-merchant opened himself frankly, holding her hand within his arm, though she would fain have withdrawn it. "Dear Lucetta, I have been very, very anxious to see you these two or three days," he said, "ever since I saw you last! I have thought over the way I got your promise that night. You said to me, 'If I were a man I should not insist.' That cut me deep. I felt that there was some truth in it. I don't want to make you wretched; and to marry me just now would do that as nothing else could—it is but too plain. Therefore I agree to an indefinite engagement—to put off all thought of marriage for a year or two."

"But—but—can I do nothing of a different kind?" said Lucetta. "I am full of gratitude to you—you have saved my life. And your care of me is like coals of fire on my head! I am a monied person now. Surely I can do something in return for your goodness—something practical?"

Henchard remained in thought. He had evidently not expected this. "There is one thing you might do, Lucetta," he said. "But not exactly of that kind."

"Then of what kind is it?" she asked with renewed misgiving.

"I must tell you a secret to ask it.—You may have heard that I have been unlucky this year? I did what I have never done before—speculated rashly; and I lost. That's just put me in a strait."

"And you would wish me to advance some money?"

"No, no!" said Henchard, almost in anger. "I'm not the man to sponge on a woman, even though she may be so nearly my own as you. No, Lucetta; what you can do is this; and it would save me. My great creditor is Grower, and it is at his hands I shall suffer if at anybody's; while a fortnight's forbearance on his part would be enough to allow me to pull through. This may be got out of him in one way—that you would let it be known to him that you are my intended—that we are to be quietly married in the next fortnight.—Now stop, you haven't heard all! Let him have this story, without, of course, any prejudice to the fact that the actual engagement between us is to be a long one. Nobody else need know: you could go with me to Mr. Grower and just let me speak to ye before him as if we were on such terms. We'll ask him to keep it secret. He will willingly wait then. At the fortnight's end I shall be able to face him; and I can coolly tell him all is postponed between us for a year or two. Not a soul in the town need know how you've helped me. Since you wish to be of use, there's your way."

It being now what the people called the "pinking in" of the day, that is, the quarter-hour just before dusk, he did not at first observe the result of his own words upon her.

"If it were anything else," she began, and the dryness of her lips was represented in her voice.

"But it is such a little thing!" he said, with a deep reproach. "Less than you have offered—just the beginning of what you have so lately promised! I could have told him as much myself, but he would not have believed me."

"It is not because I won't—it is because I absolutely can't," she said, with rising distress.

"You are provoking!" he burst out. "It is enough to make me force you to carry out at once what you have promised."

"I cannot!" she insisted desperately.

"Why? When I have only within these few minutes released you from your promise to do the thing offhand."

"Because—he was a witness!"

"Witness? Of what?"

"If I must tell you—. Don't, don't upbraid me!"

"Well! Let's hear what you mean?"

"Witness of my marriage—Mr. Grower was!"

"Marriage?"

"Yes. With Mr. Farfrae. O Michael! I am already his wife. We were married this week at Port-Bredy. There were reasons against our doing it here. Mr. Grower was a witness because he happened to be at Port-Bredy at the time."

Henchard stood as if idiotised. She was so alarmed at his silence that she murmured something about lending him sufficient money to tide over the perilous fortnight.

"Married him?" said Henchard at length. "My good—what, married him whilst—bound to marry me?"

"It was like this," she explained, with tears in her eyes and quavers in her voice; "don't—don't be cruel! I loved him so much, and I thought you might tell him of the past—and that grieved me! And then, when I had promised you, I learnt of the rumour that you had—sold your first wife at a fair like a horse or cow! How could I keep my promise after hearing that? I could not risk myself in your hands; it would have been letting myself down to take your name after such a scandal. But I knew I should lose Donald if I did not secure him at once—for you would carry out your threat of telling him of our former acquaintance, as long as there was a chance of keeping me for yourself by doing so. But you will not do so now, will you, Michael; for it is too late to separate us?"

The notes of St. Peter's bells in full peal had been wafted to them while she spoke; and now the genial thumping of the town band, renowned for its unstinted use of the drumstick, throbbed down the street.

"Then this racket they are making is on account of it, I suppose?" said he.

"Yes—I think he has told them, or else Mr. Grower has. . . . May I leave you now? My—he was detained at Port-Bredy to-day, and sent me on a few hours before him."

"Then it is *his wife's* life I have saved this afternoon."

"Yes—and he will be forever grateful to you."

"I am much obliged to him. . . . oh, you false woman!" burst from Henchard. "You promised me!"

"Yes, yes! But it was under compulsion, and I did not know all your past—"

"And now I've a mind to punish you as you deserve! One word to this bran-new husband of how you courted me, and your precious happiness is blown to atoms!"

"Michael—pity me, and be generous!"

"You don't deserve pity! You did; but you don't now."

"I'll help you to pay off your debt."

"A pensioner of Farfrae's wife—not I! Don't stay with me longer—I shall say something worse. Go home!"

She disappeared under the trees of the south walk as the band came round the corner, awaking the echoes of every stock and stone in celebration of her happiness. Lucetta took no heed, but ran up the back street and reached her own home unperceived.

XXX

FARFRAE'S WORDS TO HIS LANDLADY HAD REFERRED TO THE REMOVAL OF HIS BOXES AND other effects from his late lodgings to Lucetta's house. The work was not heavy, but it had been much hindered on account of the frequent pauses necessitated by exclamations of surprise at the event, of which the good woman had been briefly informed by letter a few hours earlier.

At the last moment of leaving Port-Bredy, Farfrae, like John Gilpin, had been detained by important customers, whom, even in the exceptional circumstances, he was not the man to neglect. Moreover, there was a convenience in Lucetta arriving first at her house. Nobody there as yet knew what had happened; and she was best in a position to break the news to the inmates, and give directions for her husband's accommodation. He had, therefore, sent on his two-days' bride in a hired brougham, whilst he went across the country to a certain group of wheat- and barley-ricks a few miles off, telling her the hour at which he might be expected the same evening. This accounted for her trotting out to meet him after their separation of four hours.

By a strenuous effort, after leaving Henchard, she calmed herself in readiness to receive Donald at High Place Hall when he came on from his lodgings. One supreme fact empowered her to this, the sense that, come what would, she had secured him. Half an hour after her arrival he walked in, and she met him with a relieved gladness, which a month's perilous absence could not have intensified.

"There is one thing I have not done; and yet it is important," she said earnestly, when she had finished talking about the adventure with the bull. "That is, broken the news of our marriage to my dear Elizabeth-Jane."

"Ah, and you have not?" he said thoughtfully. "I gave her a lift from the barn homewards; but I did not tell her either; for I thought she might have heard of it in the town, and was keeping back her congratulations from shyness, and all that."

"She can hardly have heard of it. But I'll find out; I'll go to her now. And, Donald, you don't mind her living on with me just the same as before? She is so quiet and unassuming."

"O no, indeed I don't," Farfrae answered with, perhaps, a faint awkwardness. "But I wonder if she would care to?"

"Oh yes!" said Lucetta eagerly. "I am sure she would like to. Besides, poor thing, she has no other home."

Farfrae looked at her and saw that she did not suspect the secret of her more reserved friend. He liked her all the better for the blindness. "Arrange as you like with her, by all means," he said. "It is I who have come to your house, not you to mine."

"I'll run and speak to her," said Lucetta.

When she got upstairs to Elizabeth-Jane's room the latter had taken off her out-door things, and was resting over a book. Lucetta found in a moment that she had not yet learnt the news.

"I did not come down to you, Miss Templeman," she said simply. "I was coming to ask if you had quite recovered from your fright, but I found you had a visitor. What are the bells ringing for, I wonder? And the band, too, is playing. Somebody must be married; or else they are practising for Christmas."

Lucetta uttered a vague "Yes," and seating herself by the other young woman looked musingly at her. "What a lonely creature you are," she presently said; "never knowing what's going on, or what people are talking about everywhere with keen interest. You should get out, and gossip about as other women do, and then you wouldn't be obliged to ask me a question of that kind. Well, now, I have something to tell you."

Elizabeth-Jane said she was so glad, and made herself receptive.

"I must go rather a long way back," said Lucetta, the difficulty of explaining herself satisfactorily to the pondering one beside her growing more apparent at each syllable. "You remember that trying case of conscience I told you of some time ago—about the first lover and the second lover?" She let out in jerky phrases a leading word or two of the story she had told.

"O yes—I remember; the story of *your friend*," said Elizabeth drily, regarding the irises of Lucetta's eyes as though to catch their exact shade. "The two lovers—the old one and the new: how she wanted to marry the second, but felt she ought to marry the first; so that the good she would have done she did not, and the evil that she would not, that she did—exactly like the Apostle Paul."

"Oh no; she didn't do evil exactly!" said Lucetta hastily.

"But you said that she—or as I may say *you*"—answered Elizabeth, dropping the mask, "were in honour and conscience bound to marry the first?"

Lucetta's blush at being seen through came and went again before she replied anxiously, "You will never breathe this, will you, Elizabeth-Jane?"

"Certainly not, if you say not."

"Then I will tell you that the case is more complicated—worse, in fact—than it seemed in my story. I and the first man were thrown together in a strange way, and felt that we ought to be united, as the world had talked of us. He was a widower, as he supposed. He had not heard of his first wife for many years. But the wife returned, and we parted. She is now dead; and the husband comes paying me addresses again, saying, 'Now we'll complete our purpose.' But, Elizabeth-Jane, all this amounts to a new courtship of me by him; I was absolved from all vows by the return of the other woman."

"Have you not lately renewed your promise?" said the younger with quiet surmise. She had divined Man Number One.

"That was wrung from me by a threat."

"Yes, it was. But I think when anyone gets coupled up with a man in the past so unfortunately as you have done she ought to become his wife if she can, even if she were not the sinning party."

Lucetta's countenance lost its sparkle. "He turned out to be a man I should be afraid to marry," she pleaded. "Really afraid! And it was not till after my renewed promise that I knew it."

"Then there is only one course left to honesty. You must remain a single woman."

"But think again! Do consider—"

"I am certain," interrupted her companion hardily. "I have guessed very well who the man is. My father; and I say it is him or nobody for you."

Any suspicion of impropriety was to Elizabeth-Jane like a red rag to a bull. Her craving for correctness of procedure was, indeed, almost vicious. Owing to her early troubles with regard to her mother, a semblance of irregularity had terrors for her which those whose names are safeguarded from suspicion know nothing of. "You ought to marry Mr. Henchard or nobody—certainly not another man!" she went on with a quivering lip, in whose movement two passions shared.

"I don't admit that!" said Lucetta passionately.

"Admit it or not, it is true!"

Lucetta covered her eyes with her right hand, as if she could plead no more, holding out her left to Elizabeth-Jane.

"Why, you *have* married him!" cried the latter, jumping up with pleasure after a glance at Lucetta's fingers. "When did you do it? Why did you not tell me, instead of teasing me like this? How very honourable of you! He did treat my mother badly once, it seems, in a moment of intoxication. And it is true that he is stern sometimes. But you will rule him entirely, I am sure, with your beauty and wealth and accomplishments. You are the woman he will adore, and we shall all three be happy together now!"

"Oh, my Elizabeth-Jane!" cried Lucetta distressfully. " 'Tis somebody else that I have married! I was so desperate—so afraid of being forced to anything else—so afraid of revelations that would quench his love for me, that I resolved to do it offhand, come what might, and purchase a week of happiness at any cost!"

"You—have—married Mr. Farfrae!" cried Elizabeth-Jane, in Nathan tones.

Lucetta bowed. She had recovered herself.

"The bells are ringing on that account," she said. "My husband is downstairs. He will live here till a more suitable house is ready for us; and I have told him that I want you to stay with me just as before."

"Let me think of it alone," the girl quickly replied, corking up the turmoil of her feeling with grand control.

"You shall. I am sure we shall be happy together."

Lucetta departed to join Donald below, a vague uneasiness floating over her joy at seeing him quite at home there. Not on account of her friend Elizabeth did she feel it: for of the bearings of Elizabeth-Jane's emotions she had not the least suspicion; but on Henchard's alone.

Now the instant decision of Susan Henchard's daughter was to dwell in that house no more. Apart from her estimate of the propriety of Lucetta's conduct, Farfrae had been so nearly her avowed lover that she felt she could not abide there.

It was still early in the evening when she hastily put on her things and went out. In a few minutes, knowing the ground, she had found a suitable lodging, and arranged to enter it that night. Returning and entering noiselessly she took off her pretty dress and arrayed herself in a plain one, packing up the other to keep as her best; for she would have to be very economical now. She wrote a note to leave for Lucetta, who was closely shut up in the drawing-room with Farfrae; and then Elizabeth-Jane called a man with a wheelbarrow; and seeing her boxes put into it she trotted off down the street to her rooms. They were in the street in which Henchard lived, and almost opposite his door.

Here she sat down and considered the means of subsistence. The little annual sum settled on her by her stepfather would keep body and soul together. A wonderful skill in netting of all sorts—acquired in childhood by making seines in Newson's home—might serve her in good stead; and her studies, which were pursued unremittingly, might serve her in still better.

By this time the marriage that had taken place was known throughout Casterbridge; had been discussed noisily on kerbstones, confidentially behind counters, and jovially at the Three Mariners. Whether Farfrae would sell his business and set up for a gentleman on his wife's money, or whether he would show independence enough to stick to his trade in spite of his brilliant alliance, was a great point of interest.

XXXI

THE RETORT OF THE FURMITY-WOMAN BEFORE THE MAGISTRATES HAD SPREAD; AND IN four-and-twenty hours there was not a person in Casterbridge who remained unacquainted with the story of Henchard's mad freak at Weydon Priors Fair, long years before. The amends he had made in after life were lost sight of in the dramatic glare of the original act. Had the incident been well known of old and always, it might by this time have grown to be lightly regarded as the rather tall wild oat, but well-nigh the single one, of a young man with whom the steady and mature (if somewhat headstrong) burgher of to-day had scarcely a point in common. But the act having lain as dead and buried ever since, the interspace of years was unperceived; and the black spot of his youth wore the aspect of a recent crime.

Small as the court incident had been in itself, it formed the edge or turn in the incline of Henchard's fortunes. On that day—almost at that minute—he passed the ridge of prosperity and honour, and began to descend rapidly on the other side. It was strange how soon he sank in esteem. Socially he had received a startling fillip downwards; and, having already lost commercial buoyancy from rash transactions, the velocity of his descent in both aspects became accelerated every hour.

He now gazed more at the pavements, and less at the house-fronts, when he walked about; more at the feet and leggings of men, and less into the pupils of their eyes with the blazing regard which formerly had made them blink.

New events combined to undo him. It had been a bad year for others besides himself, and the heavy failure of a debtor whom he had trusted generously completed the overthrow of his tottering credit. And now, in his desperation, he failed to preserve that strict correspondence between bulk and sample which is the soul of commerce in grain. For this, one of his men was mainly to blame; that worthy, in his great unwisdom, having picked over the sample of an enormous quantity of second-rate corn which Henchard had in hand, and removed the pinched, blasted, and smutted grains in great numbers. The produce, if honestly offered, would have created no scandal; but the blunder of misrepresentation, coming at such a moment, dragged Henchard's name into the ditch.

The details of his failure were of the ordinary kind. One day Elizabeth-Jane was passing the King's Arms, when she saw people bustling in and out more than usual when there was no market. A bystander informed her, with some surprise at her ignorance, that it was a meeting of the Commissioners under Mr. Henchard's bankruptcy. She felt quite tearful, and when she heard that he was present in the hotel she wished to go in and see him, but was advised not to intrude that day.

The room in which debtor and creditors had assembled was a front one, and Henchard, looking out of the window, had caught sight of Elizabeth-Jane through the wire blind. His examination had closed, and the creditors were leaving. The appearance of Elizabeth threw him into a reverie; till, turning his face from the window, and towering above all the rest, he called their attention for a moment more. His countenance had somewhat changed from its flush of prosperity; the black hair and whiskers were the same as ever, but a film of ash was over the rest.

"Gentlemen," he said, "over and above the assets that we've been talking about, and that appear on the balance-sheet, there be these. It all belongs to ye, as much as everything else I've got, and I don't wish to keep it from you, not I." Saying this, he took his gold watch from his pocket and laid it on the table; then his purse—the yellow canvas money-bag, such as was carried by all farmers and dealers—untying it, and shaking the money out upon the table beside the watch. The latter he drew back quickly for an instant, to remove the hair-guard made and given him by Lucetta. "There, now you have all I've got in the world," he said. "And I wish for your sakes 'twas more."

The creditors, farmers almost to a man, looked at the watch, and at the money, and into the street; when Farmer James Everdene of Weatherbury spoke.

"No, no, Henchard," he said warmly. "We don't want that. 'Tis honourable in ye; but keep it. What do you say, neighbours—do ye agree?"

"Ay, sure: we don't wish it at all," said Grower, another creditor.

"Let him keep it, of course," murmured another in the background—a silent, reserved young man named Boldwood; and the rest responded unanimously.

"Well," said the senior Commissioner, addressing Henchard, "though the case is a desperate one, I am bound to admit that I have never met a debtor who behaved more fairly. I've proved the balance-sheet to be as honestly made out as it could possibly be; we have had no trouble; there have been no evasions and no concealments. The rashness of dealing which led to this unhappy situation is obvious enough; but as far as I can see every attempt has been made to avoid wronging anybody."

Henchard was more affected by this than he cared to let them perceive, and he turned aside to the window again. A general murmur of agreement followed the Commissioner's words, and the meeting dispersed. When they were gone Henchard regarded the watch they had returned to him. " 'Tisn't mine by rights," he said to himself. "Why the devil didn't they take it?—I don't want what don't belong to me!" Moved by a recollection he took the watch to the maker's just opposite, sold it there and then for what the tradesman offered, and went with the proceeds to one among the smaller of his creditors, a cottager of Durnover, in straitened circumstances, to whom he handed the money.

When everything was ticketed that Henchard had owned, and the auctions were in progress, there was quite a sympathetic reaction in the town, which till then for some time past had done nothing but condemn him. Now that Henchard's whole career was pictured distinctly to his neighbours, and they could see how admirably he had used his one talent of energy to create a position of affluence out of absolutely nothing—which was really all he could show when he came to the town as a journeyman hay-trusser, with his wimble and knife in his basket—they wondered and regretted his fall.

Try as she might, Elizabeth could never meet with him. She believed in him still, though nobody else did; and she wanted to be allowed to forgive him for his roughness to her, and to help him in his trouble.

She wrote to him; he did not reply. She then went to his house—the great house she had lived in so happily for a time—with its front of dun brick, vitrified here and there, and its heavy sash-bars—but Henchard was to be found there no more. The ex-Mayor had left the home of his prosperity, and gone into Jopp's cottage by the Priory Mill—the sad purlieu to which he had wandered on the night of his discovery that she was not his daughter. Thither she went.

Elizabeth thought it odd that he had fixed on this spot to retire to, but assumed that necessity had no choice. Trees which seemed old enough to have been planted by the friars still stood around, and the back hatch of the original mill yet formed a cascade which had raised its terrific roar for centuries. The cottage itself was built of old stones from the long dismantled Priory, scraps of tracery, moulded window-jambs, and arch-labels, being mixed in with the rubble of the walls.

In this cottage he occupied a couple of rooms, Jopp, whom Henchard had employed, abused, cajoled, and dismissed by turns, being the householder. But even here her stepfather could not be seen.

"Not by his daughter?" pleaded Elizabeth.

"By nobody—at present: that's his order," she was informed.

Afterwards she was passing by the corn-stores and hay-barns which had been the head-quarters of his business. She knew that he ruled there no longer; but it was with amazement that she regarded the familiar gateway. A smear of decisive lead-coloured paint had been laid on to obliterate Henchard's name, though its letters dimly loomed through like ships in a fog. Over these, in fresh white, spread the name of Farfrae.

Abel Whittle was edging his skeleton in at the wicket, and she said, "Mr. Farfrae is master here?"

"Yaas, Miss Henchet," he said, "Mr. Farfrae have bought the concern and all of we work-folk with it; and 'tis better for us than 'twas—though I shouldn't say that to you as a daughter-law. We work harder, but we bain't made afeard now. It was fear made my few poor hairs so thin! No busting out, no slamming of doors, no meddling with yer eternal soul and all that; and though 'tis a shilling a week less I'm the richer man; for what's all the world if yer mind is always in a larry, Miss Henchet?"

The intelligence was in a general sense true; and Henchard's stores, which had remained in a paralyzed condition during the settlement of his bankruptcy, were stirred into activity again when the new tenant had possession. Thenceforward the full sacks, looped with the shining chain, went scurrying up and down under the cat-head, hairy arms were thrust out from the different doorways, and the grain was hauled in; trusses of hay were tossed anew in and out of the barns, and the wimbles creaked; while the scales and steel-yards began to be busy where guess-work had formerly been the rule.

XXXII

TWO BRIDGES STOOD NEAR THE LOWER PART OF CASTERBRIDGE TOWN. THE FIRST, OF weather-stained brick, was immediately at the end of High Street, where a diverging branch from that thoroughfare ran round to the low-lying Durnover lanes; so that the precincts of the bridge formed the merging point of respectability and indigence. The second bridge, of stone, was further out on the highway—in fact, fairly in the meadows, though still within the town boundary.

These bridges had speaking countenances. Every projection in each was worn down to obtuseness, partly by weather, more by friction from generations of loungers, whose toes and heels had from year to year made restless movements against these parapets, as they had stood there meditating on the aspect of affairs. In the case of the more friable bricks and stones even the flat faces were worn into hollows by the same mixed mechanism. The masonry of the top was clamped with iron at each joint; since it had been no uncommon thing for desperate men to wrench the coping off and throw it down the river, in reckless defiance of the magistrates.

For to this pair of bridges gravitated all the failures of the town; those who had failed in business, in love, in sobriety, in crime. Why the unhappy hereabout usually chose the bridges for their meditations in preference to a railing, a gate, or a stile, was not so clear.

There was a marked difference of quality between the personages who haunted the near bridge of brick and the personages who haunted the far one of stone. Those of lowest character preferred the former, adjoining the town; they did not mind the glare of the public eye. They had been of comparatively no account during their successes; and, though they might feel dispirited, they had no particular sense of shame in their ruin. Their hands were mostly kept in their pockets; they wore a leather strap round their hips or knees, and boots that required a great deal of lacing, but seemed never to get any. Instead of sighing at their adversities they spat, and instead of saying the iron had entered into their souls, they said they were down on their luck. Jopp in his time of distress had often stood here; so had Mother Cuxsom, Christopher Coney, and poor Abel Whittle.

The *misérables* who would pause on the remoter bridge were of a politer stamp. They included bankrupts, hypochondriacs, persons who were what is called "out of a situation" from fault or lucklessness, the inefficient of the professional class—shabby-genteel men, who did not know how to get rid of the weary time between breakfast and dinner, and the yet more weary time between dinner and dark. The eyes of this species were mostly directed over the parapet upon the running water below. A man seen there looking thus fixedly into the river was pretty sure to be one whom the world did not treat kindly for some reason or other. While one in straits on the townward bridge did not mind who saw him so, and kept his back to the parapet to survey the passers-by, one in straits on this never faced the road, never turned his head at coming footsteps, but, sensitive to his own condition, watched the current whenever a stranger approached, as if some strange fish interested him, though every finned thing had been poached out of the river years before.

There and thus they would muse; if their grief were the grief of oppression they would wish themselves kings; if their grief were poverty, wish themselves millionaires; if sin, they would wish they were saints or angels; if despised love, that they were some much-courted Adonis of county fame. Some had been known to stand and think so long with this fixed gaze downward that eventually they had allowed their poor carcases to follow that gaze; and they were discovered the next morning out of reach of their troubles, either here or in the deep pool called Blackwater, a little higher up the river.

To this bridge came Henchard, as other unfortunates had come before him, his way thither being by the riverside path on the chilly edge of the town. Here he was standing one windy afternoon when Durnover church clock struck five. While the gusts were bringing the notes to his ears across the damp intervening flat a man passed behind him and greeted Henchard by name. Henchard turned slightly, and saw that the corner was Jopp, his old foreman, now employed elsewhere, to whom, though he hated him, he had gone for lodgings because Jopp was the one man in Casterbridge whose observation and opinion the fallen corn-merchant despised to the point of indifference.

Henchard returned him a scarcely perceptible nod, and Jopp stopped.

"He and she are gone into their new house to-day," said Jopp.

"Oh," said Henchard absently. "Which house is that?"

"Your old one."

"Gone into my house?" And, starting up, Henchard added, " *My* house of all others in the town!"

"Well, as somebody was sure to live there, and you couldn't, it can do ye no harm that he's the man."

It was quite true: he felt that it was doing him no harm. Farfrae, who had already taken the yards and stores, had acquired possession of the house for the obvious convenience of its contiguity. And yet this act of his taking up residence within those roomy chambers while he, their former tenant, lived in a cottage, galled Henchard indescribably.

Jopp continued: "And you heard of that fellow who bought all the best furniture at your sale? He was bidding for no other than Farfrae all the while! It has never been moved out of the house, as he'd already got the lease."

"My furniture too! Surely he'll buy my body and soul likewise!"

"There's no saying he won't, if you be willing to sell." And having planted these wounds in the heart of his once imperious master Jopp went on his way; while Henchard stared and stared into the racing river till the bridge seemed moving backward with him.

The low land grew blacker, and the sky a deeper grey. When the landscape looked like a picture blotted in with ink, another traveller approached the great stone bridge. He was driving a gig, his direction being also townwards. On the round of the middle of the arch the gig stopped. "Mr. Henchard?" came from it in the voice of Farfrae. Henchard turned his face.

Finding that he had guessed rightly, Farfrae told the man who accompanied him to drive home; while he alighted and went up to his former friend.

"I have heard that you think of emigrating, Mr. Henchard?" he said. "Is it true? I have a real reason for asking."

Henchard withheld his answer for several instants, and then said, "Yes; it is true. I am going where you were going to a few years ago, when I prevented you and got you to bide here. 'Tis turn and turn about, isn't it! Do ye mind how we stood like this in the Chalk Walk when I persuaded ye to stay? You then stood without a chattel to your name, and I was the master of the house in Corn Street. But now I stand without a stick or a rag, and the master of that house is you."

"Yes, yes; that's so! It's the way o' the warrld," said Farfrae.

"Ha, ha, true!" cried Henchard, throwing himself into a mood of jocularity. "Up and down! I'm used to it. What's the odds after all!"

"Now listen to me, if it's no taking up your time," said Farfrae, "just as I listened to you. Don't go. Stay at home."

"But I can do nothing else, man!" said Henchard scornfully. "The little money I have will just keep body and soul together for a few weeks, and no more. I have not felt inclined to go back to journey-work yet; but I can't stay doing nothing, and my best chance is elsewhere."

"No; but what I propose is this—if ye will listen. Come and live in your old house. We can spare some rooms very well—I am sure my wife would not mind it at all—until there's an opening for ye."

Henchard started. Probably the picture drawn by the unsuspecting Donald of himself under the same roof with Lucetta was too striking to be received with equanimity. "No, no," he said gruffly; "we should quarrel."

"You should hae a part to yourself," said Farfrae; "and nobody to interfere wi' you. It will be a deal healthier than down there by the river where you live now."

Still Henchard refused. "You don't know what you ask," he said. "However, I can do no less than thank 'ee."

They walked into the town together side by side, as they had done when Henchard persuaded the young Scotchman to remain. "Will you come in and have some supper?"

said Farfrae when they reached the middle of the town, where their paths diverged right and left.

"No, no."

"By the by, I had nearly forgot. I bought a good deal of your furniture."

"So I have heard."

"Well, it was no that I wanted it so very much for myself; but I wish ye to pick out all that you care to have—such things as may be endeared to ye by associations, or particularly suited to your use. And take them to your own house—it will not be depriving me, we can do with less very well, and I will have plenty of opportunities of getting more."

"What—give it to me for nothing?" said Henchard. "But you paid the creditors for it!"

"Ah, yes; but maybe it's worth more to you than it is to me."

Henchard was a little moved. "I—sometimes think I've wronged ye!" he said, in tones which showed the disquietude that the night-shades hid in his face. He shook Farfrae abruptly by the hand, and hastened away as if unwilling to betray himself further. Farfrae saw him turn through the thoroughfare into Bull Stake and vanish down towards the Priory Mill.

Meanwhile Elizabeth-Jane, in an upper-room no larger than the Prophet's chamber, and with the silk attire of her palmy days packed away in a box, was netting with great industry between the hours which she devoted to studying such books as she could get hold of.

Her lodgings being nearly opposite her stepfather's former residence, now Farfrae's, she could see Donald and Lucetta speeding in and out of their door with all the bounding enthusiasm of their situation. She avoided looking that way as much as possible, but it was hardly in human nature to keep the eyes averted when the door slammed.

While living on thus quietly she heard the news that Henchard had caught cold and was confined to his room—possibly a result of standing about the meads in damp weather. She went off to his house at once. This time she was determined not to be denied admittance, and made her way upstairs. He was sitting up in the bed with a great-coat round him, and at first resented her intrusion. "Go away—go away," he said. "I don't like to see ye!"

"But, father—"

"I don't like to see ye," he repeated.

However, the ice was broken, and she remained. She made the room more comfortable, gave directions to the people below, and by the time she went away had reconciled her stepfather to her visiting him.

The effect, either of her ministrations or of her mere presence, was a rapid recovery. He soon was well enough to go out; and now things seemed to wear a new colour in his eyes. He no longer thought of emigration, and thought more of Elizabeth. The having nothing to do made him more dreary than any other circumstance; and one day, with better views of Farfrae than he had held for some time, and a sense that honest work was not a thing to be ashamed of, he stoically went down to Farfrae's yard and asked to be taken on as a journeyman hay-trusser. He was engaged at once. This hiring of Henchard was done through a foreman, Farfrae feeling that it was undesirable to come personally in contact with the ex-corn-factor more than was absolutely necessary. While anxious to help him he was well aware by this time of his uncertain temper, and thought reserved relations best. For the same reason his orders to Henchard to proceed to this and that country farm trussing in the usual way were always given through a third person.

For a time these arrangements worked well, it being the custom to truss in the respective stack-yards, before bringing it away, the hay bought at the different farms about the neighbourhood; so that Henchard was often absent at such places the whole week long. When this was all done, and Henchard had become in a measure broken in, he came to work daily on the home premises like the rest. And thus the once flourishing merchant and Mayor and what not stood as a day-labourer in the barns and granaries he formerly had owned.

"I have worked as a journeyman before now, ha'n't I?" he would say in his defiant way; "and why shouldn't I do it again?" But he looked a far different journeyman from the one he had been in his earlier days. Then he had worn clean, suitable clothes, light and cheerful in hue; leggings yellow as marigolds, corduroys immaculate as new flax, and a neckerchief like a flower-garden. Now he wore the remains of an old blue cloth suit of his gentlemanly times, a rusty silk hat, and a once black satin stock, soiled and shabby. Clad thus he went to and fro, still comparatively an active man—for he was not much over forty—and saw with the other men in the yard Donald Farfrae going in and out the green door that led to the garden, and the big house, and Lucetta.

At the beginning of the winter it was rumoured about Casterbridge that Mr. Farfrae, already in the Town Council, was to be proposed for Mayor in a year or two.

"Yes, she was wise; she was wise in her generation!" said Henchard to himself when he heard of this one day on his way to Farfrae's hay-barn. He thought it over as he wimbled his bonds, and the piece of news acted as a reviviscent breath to that old view of his— of Donald Farfrae as his triumphant rival who rode rough-shod over him.

"A fellow of his age going to be Mayor, indeed!" he murmured with a corner-drawn smile on his mouth. "But 'tis her money that floats en upward. Ha-ha—how cust odd it is! Here be I, his former master, working for him as man, and he the man standing as master, with my house and my furniture and my what-you-may-call wife all his own."

He repeated these things a hundred times a day. During the whole period of his acquaintance with Lucetta he had never wished to claim her as his own so desperately as he now regretted her loss. It was no mercenary hankering after her fortune that moved him; though that fortune had been the means of making her so much the more desired by giving her the air of independence and sauciness which attracts men of his composition. It had given her servants, house, and fine clothing—a setting that invested Lucetta with a startling novelty in the eyes of him who had known her in her narrow days.

He accordingly lapsed into moodiness, and at every allusion to the possibility of Farfrae's near election to the municipal chair his former hatred of the Scotchman returned. Concurrently with this he underwent a moral change. It resulted in his significantly saying every now and then, in tones of recklessness, "Only a fortnight more!"—"Only a dozen days!" and so forth, lessening his figures day by day.

"Why d'ye say only a dozen days?" asked Solomon Longways as he worked beside Henchard in the granary weighing oats.

"Because in twelve days I shall be released from my oath."

"What oath?"

"The oath to drink no spirituous liquid. In twelve days it will be twenty years since I swore it, and then I mean to enjoy myself, please God!"

Elizabeth-Jane sat at her window one Sunday, and while there she heard in the street below a conversation which introduced Henchard's name. She was wondering what was the matter, when a third person who was passing by asked the question in her mind.

"Michael Henchard have busted out drinking after taking nothing for twenty-one years!"

Elizabeth-Jane jumped up, put on her things, and went out.

XXXIII

A T THIS DATE THERE PREVAILED IN CASTERBRIDGE A CONVIVIAL CUSTOM—SCARCELY recognised as such, yet none the less established. On the afternoon of every Sunday a large contingent of the Casterbridge journeymen—steady church-goers and sedate characters—having attended service, filed from the church-doors across the way to the Three Mariners Inn. The rear was usually brought up by the choir, with their bass-viols, fiddles, and flutes under their arms.

The great point, the point of honour, on these sacred occasions was for each man to strictly limit himself to half-a-pint of liquor. This scrupulosity was so well understood by the landlord that the whole company was served in cups of that measure. They were all exactly alike—straight-sided, with two leafless lime-trees done in eel-brown on the sides—one towards the drinker's lips, the other confronting his comrade. To wonder how many of these cups the landlord possessed altogether was a favourite exercise of children in the marvellous. Forty at least might have been seen at these times in the large room, forming a ring round the margin of the great sixteen-legged oak table, like the monolithic circle of Stonehenge in its pristine days. Outside and above the forty cups came a circle of forty smoke-jets from forty clay pipes; outside the pipes the countenances of the forty church-goers, supported at the back by a circle of forty chairs.

The conversation was not the conversation of week-days, but a thing altogether finer in point and higher in tone. They invariably discussed the sermon, dissecting it, weighing it, as above or below the average—the general tendency being to regard it as a scientific feat or performance which had no relation to their own lives, except as between critics and the thing criticised. The bass-viol player and the clerk usually spoke with more authority than the rest on account of their official connection with the preacher.

Now the Three Mariners was the inn chosen by Henchard as the place for closing his long term of dramless years. He had so timed his entry as to be well established in the large room by the time the forty church-goers entered to their customary cups. The flush upon his face proclaimed at once that the vow of twenty-one years had lapsed, and the era of recklessness begun anew. He was seated on a small table, drawn up to the side of the massive oak board reserved for the churchmen, a few of whom nodded to him as they took their places and said, "How be ye, Mr. Henchard? Quite a stranger here."

Henchard did not take the trouble to reply for a few moments, and his eyes rested on his stretched-out legs and boots. "Yes," he said at length; "that's true. I've been down in spirit for weeks; some of ye know the cause. I am better now; but not quite serene. I want you fellows of the choir to strike up a tune; and what with that and this brew of Stannidge's, I am in hopes of getting altogether out of my minor key."

"With all my heart," said the first fiddle. "We've let back our strings, that's true, but we can soon pull 'em up again. Sound A, neighbours, and give the man a stave."

"I don't care a curse what the words be," said Henchard. "Hymns, ballets, or rantipole rubbish; the Rogue's March or the cherubim's warble—'tis all the same to me if 'tis good harmony, and well put out."

"Well—heh, heh—it may be we can do that, and not a man among us that have sat in the gallery less than twenty year," said the leader of the band. "As 'tis Sunday, neighbours, suppose we raise the Fourth Psa'am, to Samuel Wakely's tune, as improved by me?"

"Hang Samuel Wakely's tune, as improved by thee!" said Henchard. "Chuck across one of your psalters—old Wiltshire is the only tune worth singing—the psalm-tune that would make my blood ebb and flow like the sea when I was a steady chap. I'll find some words to fit en." He took one of the psalters and began turning over the leaves.

Chancing to look out of the window at that moment he saw a flock of people passing by, and perceived them to be the congregation of the upper church, now just dismissed, their sermon having been a longer one than that the lower parish was favoured with. Among the rest of the leading inhabitants walked Mr. Councillor Farfrae, with Lucetta upon his arm, the observed and imitated of all the smaller tradesmen's womankind. Henchard's mouth changed a little, and he continued to turn over the leaves.

"Now then," he said, "Psalm the Hundred-and-Ninth, to the tune of Wiltshire: verses ten to fifteen. I gi'e ye the words:

> *His seed shall orphans be, his wife*
> *A widow plunged in grief;*
> *His vagrant children beg their bread*
> *Where none can give relief.*
>
> *His ill-got riches shall be made*
> *To usurers a prey;*
> *The fruit of all his toil shall be*
> *By strangers borne away.*
>
> *None shall be found that to his wants*
> *Their mercy will extend,*
> *Or to his helpless orphan seed*
> *The least assistance lend.*
>
> *A swift destruction soon shall seize*
> *On his unhappy race;*
> *And the next age his hated name*
> *Shall utterly deface.*

"I know the Psa'am—I know the Psa'am!" said the leader hastily; "but I would as lief not sing it. 'Twasn't made for singing. We chose it once when the gypsy stole the pa'son's mare, thinking to please him, but he were quite upset. Whatever Servant David were thinking about when he made a Psalm that nobody can sing without disgracing himself, I can't fathom! Now then, the Fourth Psalm, to Samuel Wakely's tune, as improved by me."

" 'Od seize your sauce—I tell ye to sing the Hundred-and-Ninth to Wiltshire, and sing it you shall!" roared Henchard. "Not a single one of all the droning crew of ye goes out of this room till that Psalm is sung!" He slipped off the table, seized the poker, and going to the door placed his back against it. "Now then, go ahead, if you don't wish to have your cust pates broke!"

"Don't 'ee, don't 'ee take on so!—As 'tis the Sabbath-day, and 'tis Servant David's words and not ours, perhaps we don't mind for once, hey?" said one of the terrified choir, looking round upon the rest. So the instruments were tuned and the comminatory verses sung.

"Thank ye, thank ye," said Henchard in a softened voice, his eyes growing downcast, and his manner that of a man much moved by the strains. "Don't you blame David," he went on in low tones, shaking his head without raising his eyes. "He knew what he was about when he wrote that! . . . If I could afford it, be hanged if I wouldn't keep a church choir at my own expense to play and sing to me at these low, dark times of my life. But the bitter thing is, that when I was rich I didn't need what I could have, and now I be poor I can't have what I need!"

While they paused, Lucetta and Farfrae passed again, this time homeward, it being their custom to take, like others, a short walk out on the highway and back, between church and tea-time. "There's the man we've been singing about," said Henchard.

The players and singers turned their heads and saw his meaning. "Heaven forbid!" said the bass-player.

" 'Tis the man," repeated Henchard doggedly.

"Then if I'd known," said the performer on the clarionet solemnly, "that 'twas meant for a living man, nothing should have drawn out of my wynd-pipe the breath for that Psalm, so help me!"

"Nor from mine," said the first singer. "But, thought I, as it was made so long ago, and so far away, perhaps there isn't much in it, so I'll oblige a neighbour; for there's nothing to be said against the tune."

"Ah, my boys, you've sung it," said Henchard triumphantly. "As for him, it was partly by his songs that he got over me, and heaved me out. . . . I could double him up like that— and yet I don't." He laid the poker across his knee, bent it as if it were a twig, flung it down, and came away from the door.

It was at this time that Elizabeth-Jane, having heard where her stepfather was, entered the room with a pale and agonised countenance. The choir and the rest of the company moved off, in accordance with their half-pint regulation. Elizabeth-Jane went up to Henchard, and entreated him to accompany her home.

By this hour the volcanic fires of his nature had burnt down, and having drunk no great quantity as yet, he was inclined to acquiesce. She took his arm, and together they went on. Henchard walked blankly, like a blind man, repeating to himself the last words of the singers—

And the next age his hated name
Shall utterly deface!

At length he said to her, "I am a man to my word. I have kept my oath for twenty years; and now I can drink with a good conscience. . . . If I don't do for him—well, I am a fearful practical joker when I choose! He has taken away everything from me, and by heavens, if I meet him I won't answer for my deeds!"

These half-uttered words alarmed Elizabeth—all the more by reason of the still determination of Henchard's mien.

"What will you do?" she asked cautiously, while trembling with disquietude, and guessing Henchard's allusion only too well.

Henchard did not answer, and they went on till they had reached his cottage. "May I come in?" she said.

"No, no; not to-day," said Henchard; and she went away; feeling that to caution Farfrae was almost her duty, as it was certainly her strong desire.

As on the Sunday, so on the week-days, Farfrae and Lucetta might have been seen flitting about the town like two butterflies—or rather like a bee and a butterfly in league for life. She seemed to take no pleasure in going anywhere except in her husband's company; and hence when business would not permit him to waste an afternoon she remained indoors waiting for the time to pass till his return, her face being visible to Elizabeth-Jane from her window aloft. The latter, however, did not say to herself that Farfrae should be thankful for such devotion, but, full of her reading, she cited Rosalind's exclamation: "Mistress, know yourself; down on your knees and thank Heaven fasting for a good man's love."

She kept her eye upon Henchard also. One day he answered her enquiry for his health by saying that he could not endure Abel Whittle's pitying eyes upon him while they worked together in the yard. "He is such a fool," said Henchard, "that he can never get out of his mind the time when I was master there."

"I'll come and wimble for you instead of him, if you will allow me," said she. Her motive on going to the yard was to get an opportunity of observing the general position of affairs on Farfrae's premises now that her stepfather was a workman there. Henchard's threats had alarmed her so much that she wished to see his behaviour when the two were face to face.

For two or three days after her arrival Donald did not make any appearance. Then one afternoon the green door opened, and through came, first Farfrae, and at his heels Lucetta. Donald brought his wife forward without hesitation, it being obvious that he had no suspicion whatever of any antecedents in common between her and the now journeyman hay-trusser.

Henchard did not turn his eyes toward either of the pair, keeping them fixed on the bond he twisted, as if that alone absorbed him. A feeling of delicacy, which ever prompted Farfrae to avoid anything that might seem like triumphing over a fallen rival, led him to keep away from the hay-barn where Henchard and his daughter were working, and to go on to the corn department. Meanwhile Lucetta, never having been informed that Henchard had entered her husband's service, rambled straight on to the barn, where she came suddenly upon Henchard, and gave vent to a little "Oh!" which the happy and busy Donald was too far off to hear. Henchard, with withering humility of demeanour, touched the brim of his hat to her as Whittle and the rest had done, to which she breathed a dead-alive "Good-afternoon."

"I beg your pardon, ma'am?" said Henchard, as if he had not heard.

"I said good-afternoon," she faltered.

"Oh yes, good-afternoon, ma'am," he replied, touching his hat again. "I am glad to see you, ma'am." Lucetta looked embarrassed, and Henchard continued: "For we humble workmen here feel it a great honour that a lady should look in and take an interest in us."

She glanced at him entreatingly; the sarcasm was too bitter, too unendurable.

"Can you tell me the time, ma'am?" he asked.

"Yes," she said hastily; "half-past four."

"Thank 'ee. An hour and a half longer before we are released from work. Ah, ma'am, we of the lower classes know nothing of the gay leisure that such as you enjoy!"

As soon as she could do so Lucetta left him, nodded and smiled to Elizabeth-Jane, and joined her husband at the other end of the enclosure, where she could be seen leading him away by the outer gates, so as to avoid passing Henchard again. That she had been taken by surprise was obvious. The result of this casual rencounter was that the next morning a note was put into Henchard's hand by the postman.

"Will you," said Lucetta, with as much bitterness as she could put into a small communication, "will you kindly undertake not to speak to me in the biting undertones you used to-day, if I walk through the yard at any time? I bear you no ill-will, and I am only too glad that you should have employment of my dear husband; but in common fairness treat me as his wife, and do not try to make me wretched by covert sneers. I have committed no crime, and done you no injury."

"Poor fool!" said Henchard with fond savagery, holding out the note. "To know no better than commit herself in writing like this! Why, if I were to show that to her dear husband—pooh!" He threw the letter into the fire.

Lucetta took care not to come again among the hay and corn. She would rather have died than run the risk of encountering Henchard at such close quarters a second time. The gulf between them was growing wider everyday. Farfrae was always considerate to his fallen acquaintance; but it was impossible that he should not, by degrees, cease to regard the ex-corn-merchant as more than one of his other workmen. Henchard saw this, and concealed his feelings under a cover of stolidity, fortifying his heart by drinking more freely at the Three Mariners every evening.

Often did Elizabeth-Jane, in her endeavours to prevent his taking other liquor, carry tea to him in a little basket at five o'clock. Arriving one day on this errand she found her stepfather was measuring up clover-seed and rape-seed in the corn-stores on the top floor, and she ascended to him. Each floor had a door opening into the air under a cat-head, from which a chain dangled for hoisting the sacks.

When Elizabeth's head rose through the trap she perceived that the upper door was open, and that her stepfather and Farfrae stood just within it in conversation, Farfrae being nearest the dizzy edge, and Henchard a little way behind. Not to interrupt them she remained on the steps without raising her head any higher. While waiting thus she saw—or fancied she saw, for she had a terror of feeling certain—her stepfather slowly raise his hand to a level behind Farfrae's shoulders, a curious expression taking possession of his face. The young man was quite unconscious of the action, which was so indirect that, if Farfrae had observed it, he might almost have regarded it as an idle outstretching of the arm. But it would have been possible, by a comparatively light touch, to push Farfrae off his balance, and send him head over heels into the air.

Elizabeth felt quite sick at heart on thinking of what this *might* have meant. As soon as they turned she mechanically took the tea to Henchard, left it, and went away. Reflecting, she endeavoured to assure herself that the movement was an idle eccentricity, and no more. Yet, on the other hand, his subordinate position in an establishment where he once had been master might be acting on him like an irritant poison; and she finally resolved to caution Donald.

XXXIV

NEXT MORNING, ACCORDINGLY, SHE ROSE AT FIVE O'CLOCK, AND WENT INTO THE street. It was not yet light; a dense fog prevailed, and the town was as silent as it was dark, except that from the rectangular avenues which framed in the borough there came a chorus of tiny rappings, caused by the fall of water-drops condensed on the boughs; now it was wafted from the West Walk, now from the South Walk; and then from both quarters simultaneously. She moved on to the bottom of Corn Street, and, knowing his time well, waited only a few minutes before she heard the familiar bang of his door, and then his quick walk towards her. She met him at the point where the last tree of the engirding avenue flanked the last house in the street.

He could hardly discern her till, glancing enquiringly, he said, "What—Miss Henchard—and are ye up so airly?"

She asked him to pardon her for waylaying him at such an unseemly time. "But I am anxious to mention something," she said. "And I wished not to alarm Mrs. Farfrae by calling."

"Yes?" said he, with the cheeriness of a superior. "And what may it be? It's very kind of ye, I'm sure."

She now felt the difficulty of conveying to his mind the exact aspect of possibilities in her own. But she somehow began, and introduced Henchard's name. "I sometimes fear," she said with an effort, "that he may be betrayed into some attempt to—insult you, sir."

"But we are the best of friends?"

"Or to play some practical joke upon you, sir. Remember that he has been hardly used."

"But we are quite friendly?"

"Or to do something—that would injure you—hurt you—wound you." Every word cost her twice its length of pain. And she could see that Farfrae was still incredulous. Henchard, a poor man in his employ, was not to Farfrae's view the Henchard who had ruled him. Yet he was not only the same man, but that man, with his sinister qualities, formerly latent, quickened into life by his buffetings.

Farfrae, happy, and thinking no evil, persisted in making light of her fears. Thus they parted, and she went homeward, journeymen now being in the street, waggoners going to the harness-makers for articles left to be repaired, farm-horses going to the shoeing-smiths, and the sons of labour showing themselves generally on the move. Elizabeth entered her lodging unhappily, thinking she had done no good, and only made herself appear foolish by her weak note of warning.

But Donald Farfrae was one of those men upon whom an incident is never absolutely lost. He revised impressions from a subsequent point of view, and the impulsive judgment of the moment was not always his permanent one. The vision of Elizabeth's earnest face in the rimy dawn came back to him several times during the day. Knowing the solidity of her character, he did not treat her hints altogether as idle sounds.

But he did not desist from a kindly scheme on Henchard's account that engaged him just then; and when he met Lawyer Joyce, the town-clerk, later in the day, he spoke of it as if nothing had occurred to damp it.

"About that little seedsman's shop," he said; "the shop overlooking the churchyard, which is to let. It is not for myself I want it, but for our unlucky fellow-townsman Henchard. It would be a new beginning for him, if a small one; and I have told the Council that I would head a private subscription among them to set him up in it—that I would be fifty pounds, if they would make up the other fifty among them."

"Yes, yes; so I've heard; and there's nothing to say against it for that matter," the town-clerk replied, in his plain, frank way. "But, Farfrae, others see what you don't. Henchard hates ye—ay, hates ye; and 'tis right that you should know it. To my knowledge he was at the Three Mariners last night, saying in public that about you which a man ought not to say about another."

"Is that so—ah, is that so?" said Farfrae, looking down. "Why should he do it?" added the young man bitterly; "what harm have I done him that he should try to wrong me?"

"God only knows," said Joyce, lifting his eyebrows. "It shows much long-suffering in you to put up with him, and keep him in your employ."

"But I cannet discharge a man who was once a good friend to me? How can I forget that when I came here 'twas he enabled me to make a footing for mysel'? No, no. As long as I've a day's work to offer he shall do it if he chooses. 'Tis not I who will deny him such a little as that. But I'll drop the idea of establishing him in a shop till I can think more about it."

It grieved Farfrae much to give up this scheme. But a damp having been thrown over it by these and other voices in the air, he went and countermanded his orders. The then occupier of the shop was in it when Farfrae spoke to him, and feeling it necessary to give some explanation of his withdrawal from the negotiation, Donald mentioned Henchard's name, and stated that the intentions of the Council had been changed.

The occupier was much disappointed, and straight-way informed Henchard, as soon as he saw him, that a scheme of the Council for setting him up in a shop had been knocked on the head by Farfrae. And thus out of error enmity grew.

When Farfrae got indoors that evening the tea-kettle was singing on the high hob of the semi-egg-shaped grate. Lucetta, light as a sylph, ran forward and seized his hands, whereupon Farfrae duly kissed her.

"Oh!" she cried playfully, turning to the window. "See—the blinds are not drawn down, and the people can look in—what a scandal!"

When the candles were lighted, the curtains drawn, and the twain sat at tea, she noticed that he looked serious. Without directly enquiring why, she let her eyes linger solicitously on his face.

"Who has called?" he absently asked. "Any folk for me?"

"No," said Lucetta. "What's the matter, Donald?"

"Well—nothing worth talking of," he responded sadly.

"Then, never mind it. You will get through it, Scotchmen are always lucky."

"No—not always!" he said, shaking his head gloomily as he contemplated a crumb on the table. "I know many who have not been so! There was Sandy Macfarlane, who started to America to try his fortune, and he was drowned; and Archibald Leith, he was murdered! And poor Willie Dunbleeze and Maitland Macfreeze—they fell into bad courses, and went the way of all such!"

"Why—you old goosey—I was only speaking in a general sense, of course! You are always so literal. Now when we have finished tea, sing me that funny song about high-heeled shoon and siller tags, and the one-and-forty wooers."

"No, no. I couldna sing to-night! It's Henchard—he hates me; so that I may not be his friend if I would. I would understand why there should be a wee bit of envy; but I cannet see a reason for the whole intensity of what he feels. Now, can you, Lucetta? It is more like old-fashioned rivalry in love than just a bit of rivalry in trade."

Lucetta had grown somewhat wan. "No," she replied.

"I give him employment—I cannet refuse it. But neither can I blind myself to the fact that with a man of passions such as his, there is no safeguard for conduct!"

"What have you heard—O Donald, dearest?" said Lucetta in alarm. The words on her lips were "anything about me?"—but she did not utter them. She could not, however, suppress her agitation, and her eyes filled with tears.

"No, no—it is not so serious as ye fancy," declared Farfrae soothingly; though he did not know its seriousness so well as she.

"I wish you would do what we have talked of," mournfully remarked Lucetta. "Give up business, and go away from here. We have plenty of money, and why should we stay?"

Farfrae seemed seriously disposed to discuss this move, and they talked thereon till a visitor was announced. Their neighbour Alderman Vatt came in.

"You've heard, I suppose of poor Doctor Chalkfield's death? Yes—died this afternoon at five," said Mr. Vatt. Chalkfield was the Councilman who had succeeded to the Mayoralty in the preceding November.

Farfrae was sorry at the intelligence, and Mr. Vatt continued: "Well, we know he's been going some days, and as his family is well provided for we must take it all as it is. Now I have called to ask ye this—quite privately. If I should nominate ye to succeed him, and there should be no particular opposition, will ye accept the chair?"

"But there are folk whose turn is before mine; and I'm over young, and may be thought pushing!" said Farfrae after a pause.

"Not at all. I don't speak for myself only, several have named it. You won't refuse?"

"We thought of going away," interposed Lucetta, looking at Farfrae anxiously.

"It was only a fancy," Farfrae murmured. "I wouldna refuse if it is the wish of a respectable majority in the Council."

"Very well, then, look upon yourself as elected. We have had older men long enough."

When he was gone Farfrae said musingly, "See now how it's ourselves that are ruled by the powers above us! We plan this, but we do that. If they want to make me Mayor I will stay, and Henchard must rave as he will."

From this evening onward Lucetta was very uneasy. If she had not been imprudence incarnate she would not have acted as she did when she met Henchard by accident a day or two later. It was in the bustle of the market, when no one could readily notice their discourse.

"Michael," said she, "I must again ask you what I asked you months ago—to return me any letters or papers of mine that you may have—unless you have destroyed them! You must see how desirable it is that the time at Jersey should be blotted out, for the good of all parties."

"Why, bless the woman!—I packed up every scrap of your handwriting to give you in the coach—but you never appeared."

She explained how the death of her aunt had prevented her taking the journey on that day. "And what became of the parcel then?" she asked.

He could not say—he would consider. When she was gone he recollected that he had left a heap of useless papers in his former dining-room safe—built up in the wall of his old house—now occupied by Farfrae. The letters might have been amongst them.

A grotesque grin shaped itself on Henchard's face. Had that safe been opened?

On the very evening which followed this there was a great ringing of bells in Caster-bridge, and the combined brass, wood, catgut, and leather bands played round the town with more prodigality of percussion-notes than ever. Farfrae was Mayor—the two-hundredth odd of a series forming an elective dynasty dating back to the days of Charles I—and the fair Lucetta was the courted of the town. . . . But, ah! the worm i' the bud—Henchard; what he could tell!

He, in the meantime, festering with indignation at some erroneous intelligence of Farfrae's opposition to the scheme for installing him in the little seed-shop, was greeted with the news of the municipal election (which, by reason of Farfrae's comparative youth and his Scottish nativity—a thing unprecedented in the case—had an interest far beyond the ordinary). The bell-ringing and the band-playing, loud as Tamerlane's trumpet, goaded the downfallen Henchard indescribably: the ousting now seemed to him to be complete.

The next morning he went to the corn-yard as usual, and about eleven o'clock Don-ald entered through the green door, with no trace of the worshipful about him. The yet more emphatic change of places between him and Henchard which this election had es-tablished renewed a slight embarrassment in the manner of the modest young man; but Henchard showed the front of one who had overlooked all this; and Farfrae met his ameni-ties half-way at once.

"I was going to ask you," said Henchard, "about a packet that I may possibly have left in my old safe in the dining-room." He added particulars.

"If so, it is there now," said Farfrae. "I have never opened the safe at all as yet; for I keep ma papers at the bank, to sleep easy o' nights."

"It was not of much consequence—to me," said Henchard. "But I'll call for it this evening, if you don't mind?"

It was quite late when he fulfilled his promise. He had primed himself with grog, as he did very frequently now, and a curl of sardonic humour hung on his lip as he ap-proached the house, as though he were contemplating some terrible form of amusement. Whatever it was, the incident of his entry did not diminish its force, this being his first visit to the house since he had lived there as owner. The ring of the bell spoke to him like the voice of a familiar drudge who had been bribed to forsake him; the movements of the doors were revivals of dead days.

Farfrae invited him into the dining-room, where he at once unlocked the iron safe built into the wall, *his*, Henchard's safe, made by an ingenious locksmith under his direction. Farfrae drew thence the parcel, and other papers, with apologies for not having returned them.

"Never mind," said Henchard drily. "The fact is they are letters mostly. . . . Yes," he went on, sitting down and unfolding Lucetta's passionate bundle, "here they be. That ever I should see 'em again! I hope Mrs. Farfrae is well after her exertions of yesterday?"

"She has felt a bit weary; and has gone to bed early on that account."

Henchard returned to the letters, sorting them over with interest, Farfrae being seated at the other end of the dining-table. "You don't forget, of course," he resumed, "that curious chapter in the history of my past which I told you of, and that you gave me some assistance in? These letters are, in fact, related to that unhappy business. Though, thank God, it is all over now."

"What became of the poor woman?" asked Farfrae.

"Luckily she married, and married well," said Henchard. "So that these reproaches she poured out on me do not now cause me any twinges, as they might otherwise have done. . . . Just listen to what an angry woman will say!"

Farfrae, willing to humour Henchard, though quite uninterested, and bursting with yawns, gave well-mannered attention.

" 'For me,' " Henchard read, " 'there is practically no future. A creature too unconventionally devoted to you—who feels it impossible that she can be the wife of any other man; and who is yet no more to you than the first woman you meet in the street—such am I. I quite acquit you of any intention to wrong me, yet you are the door through which wrong has come to me. That in the event of your present wife's death you will place me in her position is a consolation so far as it goes—but how far does it go? Thus I sit here, forsaken by my few acquaintance, and forsaken by you!' "

"That's how she went on to me," said Henchard, "acres of words like that, when what had happened was what I could not cure."

"Yes," said Farfrae absently, "it is the way wi' women." But the fact was that he knew very little of the sex; yet detecting a sort of resemblance in style between the effusions of the woman he worshipped and those of the supposed stranger, he concluded that Aphrodite ever spoke thus, whosesoever the personality she assumed.

Henchard unfolded another letter, and read it through likewise, stopping at the subscription as before. "Her name I don't give," he said blandly. "As I didn't marry her, and another man did, I can scarcely do that in fairness to her."

"Tr-rue, tr-rue," said Farfrae. "But why didn't you marry her when your wife Susan died?" Farfrae asked this, and the other questions, in the comfortably indifferent tone of one whom the matter very remotely concerned.

"Ah—well you may ask that!" said Henchard, the new-moon-shaped grin adumbrating itself again upon his mouth. "In spite of all her protestations, when I came forward to do so, as in generosity bound, she was not the woman for me."

"She had already married another—maybe?"

Henchard seemed to think it would be sailing too near the wind to descend further into particulars, and he answered "Yes."

"The young lady must have had a heart that bore transplanting very readily!"

"She had, she had," said Henchard emphatically.

He opened a third and fourth letter, and read. This time he approached the conclusion as if the signature were indeed coming with the rest. But again he stopped short. The truth was that, as may be divined; he had quite intended to effect a grand catastrophe at the end of this drama by reading out the name; he had come to the house with no other thought. But sitting here in cold blood he could not do it. Such a wrecking of hearts appalled even him. His quality was such that he could have annihilated them both in the heat of action; but to accomplish the deed by oral poison was beyond the nerve of his enmity.

XXXV

As DONALD STATED, LUCETTA HAD RETIRED EARLY TO HER ROOM BECAUSE OF FATIGUE. She had, however, not gone to rest, but sat in the bedside chair reading and thinking over the events of the day. At the ringing of the door-bell by Henchard she wondered who it should be that would call at that comparatively late hour. The dining-room was almost under her bedroom; she could hear that somebody was admitted there, and presently the indistinct murmur of a person reading became audible.

The usual time for Donald's arrival upstairs came and passed, yet still the reading and conversation went on. This was very singular. She could think of nothing but that some extraordinary crime had been committed, and that the visitor, whoever he might be, was reading an account of it from a special edition of the *Casterbridge Chronicle*. At last she left the room, and descended the stairs. The dining-room door was ajar, and in the silence of the resting household the voice and the words were recognizable before she reached the lower flight. She stood transfixed. Her own words greeted her in Henchard's voice, like spirits from the grave.

Lucetta leant upon the banister with her cheek against the smooth hand-rail, as if she would make a friend of it in her misery. Rigid in this position, more and more words fell successively upon her ear. But what amazed her most was the tone of her husband. He spoke merely in the accents of a man who made a present of his time.

"One word," he was saying, as the crackling of paper denoted that Henchard was unfolding yet another sheet. "Is it quite fair to this young woman's memory to read at such length to a stranger what was intended for your eye alone?"

"Well, yes," said Henchard. "By not giving her name I make it an example of all womankind, and not a scandal to one."

"If I were you I would destroy them," said Farfrae, giving more thought to the letters than he had hitherto done. "As another man's wife it would injure the woman if it were known."

"No, I shall not destroy them," murmured Henchard, putting the letters away. Then he arose, and Lucetta heard no more.

She went back to her bedroom in a semi-paralyzed state. For very fear she could not undress, but sat on the edge of the bed, waiting. Would Henchard let out the secret in his parting words? Her suspense was terrible. Had she confessed all to Donald in their early acquaintance he might possibly have got over it, and married her just the same—unlikely as it had once seemed; but for her or anyone else to tell him now would be fatal.

The door slammed; she could hear her husband bolting it. After looking round in his customary way he came leisurely up the stairs. The spark in her eyes well-nigh went out when he appeared round the bedroom-door. Her gaze hung doubtful for a moment, then to her joyous amazement she saw that he looked at her with the rallying smile of one who had just been relieved of a scene that was irksome. She could hold out no longer, and sobbed hysterically.

When he had restored her Farfrae naturally enough spoke of Henchard. "Of all men he was the least desirable as a visitor," he said; "but it is my belief that he's just a bit crazed. He has been reading to me a long lot of letters relating to his past life; and I could do no less than indulge him by listening."

This was sufficient. Henchard, then, had not told. Henchard's last words to Farfrae, in short, as he stood on the door-step, had been these: "Well—I'm obliged to 'ee for listening. I may tell more about her some day."

Finding this, she was much perplexed as to Henchard's motives in opening the matter at all; for in such cases we attribute to an enemy a power of consistent action which we never find in ourselves or in our friends; and forget that abortive efforts from want of heart are as possible to revenge as to generosity.

Next morning Lucetta remained in bed, meditating how to parry this incipient attack. The bold stroke of telling Donald the truth, dimly conceived, was yet too bold; for she dreaded lest in doing so he, like the rest of the world, should believe that the episode was rather her fault than her misfortune. She decided to employ persuasion—not with Donald, but with the enemy himself. It seemed the only practicable weapon left her as a woman. Having laid her plan she rose, and wrote to him who kept her on these tenterhooks:—

"I overheard your interview with my husband last night, and saw the drift of your revenge. The very thought of it crushes me! Have pity on a distressed woman! If you could see me you would relent. You do not know how anxiety has told upon me lately. I will be at the Ring at the time you leave work—just before the sun goes down. Please come that way. I cannot rest till I have seen you face to face, and heard from your mouth that you will carry this horse-play no further."

To herself she said, on closing up her appeal: "If ever tears and pleadings have served the weak to fight the strong, let them do so now!"

With this view she made a toilette which differed from all she had ever attempted before. To heighten her natural attraction had hitherto been the unvarying endeavour of her adult life, and one in which she was no novice. But now she neglected this, and even proceeded to impair the natural presentation. She had not slept all the previous night, and this had produced upon her pretty though slightly worn features the aspect of a countenance ageing prematurely from extreme sorrow. She selected—as much from want of spirit as design—her poorest, plainest, and longest discarded attire.

To avoid the contingency of being recognised she veiled herself, and slipped out of the house quickly. The sun was resting on the hill like a drop of blood on an eyelid by the time she had got up the road opposite the amphitheatre, which she speedily entered. The interior was shadowy, and emphatic of the absence of every living thing.

She was not disappointed in the fearful hope with which she awaited him. Henchard came over the top, descended, and Lucetta waited breathlessly. But having reached the arena she saw a change in his bearing: he stood still, at a little distance from her; she could not think why.

Nor could anyone else have known. The truth was that in appointing this spot, and this hour, for the rendezvous, Lucetta had unwittingly backed up her entreaty by the strongest argument she could have used outside words, with this man of moods, glooms, and superstitions. Her figure in the midst of the huge enclosure, the unusual plainness of her dress, her attitude of hope and appeal, so strongly revived in his soul the memory of another ill-used woman who had stood there and thus in bygone days, and had now passed away into her rest, that he was unmanned, and his heart smote him for having attempted reprisals on one of a sex so weak. When he approached her, and before she had spoken a word, her point was half gained.

His manner as he had come down had been one of cynical carelessness; but he now put away his grim half-smile, and said, in a kindly subdued tone, "Good-night t'ye. Of course I'm glad to come if you want me."

"Oh, thank you," she said apprehensively.

"I am sorry to see 'ee looking so ill," he stammered, with unconcealed compunction.

She shook her head. "How can you be sorry," she asked, "when you deliberately cause it?"

"What!" said Henchard uneasily. "Is it anything I have done that has pulled you down like that?"

"It is all your doing," she said. "I have no other grief. My happiness would be secure enough but for your threats. O Michael! don't wreck me like this! You might think that you have done enough! When I came here I was a young woman; now I am rapidly becoming an old one. Neither my husband nor any other man will regard me with interest long."

Henchard was disarmed. His old feeling of supercilious pity for womankind in general was intensified by this suppliant appearing here as the double of the first. Moreover, that thoughtless want of foresight which had led to all her trouble remained with poor Lucetta still; she had come to meet him here in this compromising way without perceiving the risk. Such a woman was very small deer to hunt; he felt ashamed, lost all zest and desire to humiliate Lucetta there and then, and no longer envied Farfrae his bargain. He had married money, but nothing more. Henchard was anxious to wash his hands of the game.

"Well, what do you want me to do?" he said gently. "I am sure I shall be very willing. My reading of those letters was only a sort of practical joke, and I revealed nothing."

"To give me back the letters and any papers you may have that breathe of matrimony or worse."

"So be it. Every scrap shall be yours. . . . But, between you and me, Lucetta, he is sure to find out something of the matter, sooner or later."

"Ah!" she said with eager tremulousness; "but not till I have proved myself a faithful and deserving wife to him, and then he may forgive me everything!"

Henchard silently looked at her: he almost envied Farfrae such love as that, even now.

"H'm—I hope so," he said. "But you shall have the letters without fail. And your secret shall be kept. I swear it."

"How good you are!—how shall I get them?"

He reflected, and said he would send them the next morning. "Now don't doubt me," he added. "I can keep my word.

XXXVI

RETURNING FROM HER APPOINTMENT LUCETTA SAW A MAN WAITING BY THE LAMP NEARest to her own door. When she stopped to go in he came and spoke to her. It was Jopp.

He begged her pardon for addressing her. But he had heard that Mr. Farfrae had been applied to by a neighbouring corn-merchant to recommend a working partner; if so he wished to offer himself. He could give good security, and had stated as much to Mr. Farfrae in a letter; but he would feel much obliged if Lucetta would say a word in his favour to her husband.

"It is a thing I know nothing about," said Lucetta coldly.

"But you can testify to my trustworthiness better than anybody, ma'am," said Jopp. "I was in Jersey several years, and knew you there by sight."

"Indeed," she replied. "But I knew nothing of you."

"I think, ma'am, that a word or two from you would secure for me what I covet very much," he persisted.

She steadily refused to have anything to do with the affair, and cutting him short, because of her anxiety to get indoors before her husband should miss her, left him on the pavement.

He watched her till she had vanished, and then went home. When he got there he sat down in the fireless chimney-corner looking at the iron dogs, and the wood laid across them for heating the morning kettle. A movement upstairs disturbed him, and Henchard came down from his bedroom, where he seemed to have been rummaging boxes.

"I wish," said Henchard, "you would do me a service, Jopp, now—to-night, I mean, if you can. Leave this at Mrs. Farfrae's for her. I should take it myself, of course, but I don't wish to be seen there."

He handed a package in brown paper, sealed. Henchard had been as good as his word. Immediately on coming indoors he had searched over his few belongings; and every scrap of Lucetta's writing that he possessed was here. Jopp indifferently expressed his willingness.

"Well, how have ye got on to-day?" his lodger asked. "Any prospect of an opening?"

"I am afraid not," said Jopp, who had not told the other of his application to Farfrae.

"There never will be in Casterbridge," declared Henchard decisively. "You must roam further afield." He said good-night to Jopp, and returned to his own part of the house.

Jopp sat on till his eyes were attracted by the shadow of the candle-snuff on the wall, and looking at the original he found that it had formed itself into a head like a red-hot cauliflower. Henchard's packet next met his gaze. He knew there had been something of the nature of wooing between Henchard and the now Mrs. Farfrae; and his vague ideas on the subject narrowed themselves down to these: Henchard had a parcel belonging to Mrs. Farfrae, and he had reasons for not returning that parcel to her in person. What could be inside it? So he went on and on till, animated by resentment at Lucetta's haughtiness, as he thought it, and curiosity to learn if there were any weak sides to this transaction with Henchard, he examined the package. The pen and all its relations being awkward tools in Henchard's hands he had affixed the seals without an impression, it never occurring to him that the efficacy of such a fastening depended on this. Jopp was far less of a tyro; he lifted one of the seals with his penknife, peeped in at the end thus opened, saw that the bundle consisted of letters; and, having satisfied himself thus far, sealed up the end again by simply softening the wax with the candle, and went off with the parcel as requested.

His path was by the riverside at the foot of the town. Coming into the light at the bridge which stood at the end of High Street he beheld lounging thereon Mother Cuxsom and Nance Mockridge.

"We be just going down Mixen Lane way, to look into Peter's Finger afore creeping to bed," said Mrs. Cuxsom. "There's a fiddle and tambourine going on there. Lord, what's all the world—do ye come along too, Jopp—'twon't hinder ye five minutes."

Jopp had mostly kept himself out of this company, but present circumstances made him somewhat more reckless than usual, and without many words he decided to go to his destination that way.

Though the upper part of Durnover was mainly composed of a curious congeries of barns and farm-steads, there was a less picturesque side to the parish. This was Mixen Lane, now in great part pulled down.

Mixen Lane was the Adullam of all the surrounding villages. It was the hiding-place of those who were in distress, and in debt, and trouble of every kind. Farm-labourers and other peasants, who combined a little poaching with their farming, and a little brawling and bibbing with their poaching, found themselves sooner or later in Mixen Lane. Rural mechanics too idle to mechanise, rural servants too rebellious to serve, drifted or were forced into Mixen Lane.

The lane and its surrounding thicket of thatched cottages stretched out like a spit into the moist and misty lowland. Much that was sad, much that was low, some things that were baneful, could be seen in Mixen Lane. Vice ran freely in and out certain of the doors in the neighbourhood; recklessness dwelt under the roof with the crooked chimney; shame in some bow-windows; theft (in times of privation) in the thatched and mud-walled houses by the sallows. Even slaughter had not been altogether unknown here. In a block of cottages up an alley there might have been erected an altar to disease in years gone by. Such was Mixen Lane in the times when Henchard and Farfrae were Mayors.

Yet this mildewed leaf in the sturdy and flourishing Casterbridge plant lay close to the open country; not a hundred yards from a row of noble elms, and commanding a view across the moor of airy uplands and corn-fields, and mansions of the great. A brook divided the moor from the tenements, and to outward view there was no way across it—no way to the houses but roundabout by the road. But under every householder's stairs there was kept a mysterious plank nine inches wide; which plank was a secret bridge.

If you, as one of those refugee householders, came in from business after dark—and this was the business time here—you stealthily crossed the moor, approached the border of the aforesaid brook, and whistled opposite the house to which you belonged. A shape thereupon made its appearance on the other side bearing the bridge on end against the sky; it was lowered; you crossed, and a hand helped you to land yourself, together with the pheasants and hares gathered from neighbouring manors. You sold them slily the next morning, and the day after you stood before the magistrates with the eyes of all your sympathizing neighbours concentrated on your back. You disappeared for a time; then you were again found quietly living in Mixen Lane.

Walking along the lane at dusk the stranger was struck by two or three peculiar features therein. One was an intermittent rumbling from the back premises of the inn half-way up; this meant a skittle alley. Another was the extensive prevalence of whistling in the various domiciles—a piped note of some kind coming from nearly every open door. Another was the frequency of white aprons over dingy gowns among the women around the doorways. A white apron is a suspicious vesture in situations where spotlessness is difficult; moreover, the industry and cleanliness which the white apron expressed were belied by the postures and gaits of the women who wore it—their knuckles being mostly on their hips (an attitude which lent them the aspect of two-handled mugs), and their shoulders against doorposts; while there was a curious alacrity in the turn of each honest woman's head upon her neck, and in the twirl of her honest eyes, at any noise resembling a masculine footfall along the lane.

Yet amid so much that was bad needy respectability also found a home. Under some of the roofs abode pure and virtuous souls whose presence there was due to the iron hand of necessity, and to that alone. Families from decayed villages—families of that once bulky, but now nearly extinct, section of village society called "liviers," or lifeholders—copy-holders and others, whose roof-trees had fallen for some reason or other, compelling them to quit the rural spot that had been their home for generations—came here, unless they chose to lie under a hedge by the wayside.

The inn called Peter's Finger was the church of Mixen Lane.

It was centrally situate, as such places should be, and bore about the same social relation to the Three Mariners as the latter bore to the King's Arms. At first sight the inn was so respectable as to be puzzling. The front door was kept shut, and the step was so clean that evidently but few persons entered over its sanded surface. But at the corner of the public-house was an alley, a mere slit, dividing it from the next building. Half-way up the alley was a narrow door, shiny and paintless from the rub of infinite hands and shoulders. This was the actual entrance to the inn.

A pedestrian would be seen abstractedly passing along Mixen Lane; and then, in a moment, he would vanish, causing the gazer to blink like Ashton at the disappearance of Ravenswood. That abstracted pedestrian had edged into the slit by the adroit fillip of his person sideways; from the slit he edged into the tavern by a similar exercise of skill.

The company at the Three Mariners were persons of quality in comparison with the company which gathered here; though it must be admitted that the lowest fringe of the Mariner's party touched the crest of Peter's at points. Waifs and strays of all sorts loitered about here. The landlady was a virtuous woman who, years ago had been unjustly sent to gaol as an accessory to something or other after the fact. She underwent her year, and had worn a martyr's countenance ever since, except at times of meeting the constable who apprehended her, when she winked her eye.

To this house Jopp and his acquaintances had arrived. The settles on which they sat down were thin and tall, their tops being guyed by pieces of twine to hooks in the ceiling; for when the guests grew boisterous the settles would rock and overturn without some such security. The thunder of bowls echoed from the backyard; swingels hung behind the blower of the chimney; and ex-poachers and ex-gamekeepers, whom squires had persecuted without a cause, sat elbowing each other—men who in past times had met in fights under the moon, till lapse of sentences on the one part, and loss of favour and expulsion from service on the other, brought them here together to a common level, where they sat calmly discussing old times.

"Dost mind how you could jerk a trout ashore with a bramble, and not ruffle the stream, Charl?" a deposed keeper was saying. " 'Twas at that I caught 'ee once, if you can mind?"

"That can I. But the worst larry for me was that pheasant business at Yalbury Wood. Your wife swore false that time, Joe—oh, by Gad, she did—there's no denying it."

"How was that?" asked Jopp.

"Why—Joe closed wi' me, and we rolled down together, close to his garden hedge. Hearing the noise, out ran his wife with the oven pyle, and it being dark under the trees she couldn't see which was uppermost. 'Where beest thee, Joe, under or top?' she screeched. 'Oh—under, by Gad!' says he. She then began to rap down upon my skull, back, and ribs with the pyle till we'd roll over again. 'Where beest now, dear Joe, under or top?' she'd scream again. By George, 'twas through her I was took! And then when we got up in hall she sware that the cock pheasant was one of her rearing, when 'twas not your bird at all, Joe; 'twas Squire Brown's bird—that's whose 'twas—one that we'd picked off as we passed his wood, an hour afore. It did hurt my feelings to be so wronged! . . . Ah well—'tis over now."

"I might have had ye days afore that," said the keeper. "I was within a few yards of ye dozens of times, with a sight more of birds than that poor one."

"Yes—'tis not our greatest doings that the world gets wind of," said the furmity-woman, who, lately settled in this purlieu, sat among the rest. Having travelled a great deal in her time, she spoke with cosmopolitan largeness of idea. It was she who presently asked Jopp what was the parcel he kept so snugly under his arm.

"Ah, therein lies a grand secret," said Jopp. "It is the passion of love. To think that a woman should love one man so well, and hate another so unmercifully."

"Who's the object of your meditation, sir?"

"One that stands high in this town. I'd like to shame her! Upon my life, 'twould be as good as a play to read her love-letters, the proud piece of silk and wax-work! For 'tis her love-letters that I've got here."

"Love-letters? then let's hear 'em, good soul," said Mother Cuxsom. "Lord, do ye mind, Richard, what fools we used to be when we were younger? Getting a schoolboy to write ours for us; and giving him a penny, do ye mind, not to tell other folks what he'd put inside, do ye mind?"

By this time Jopp had pushed his finger under the seals, and unfastened the letters, tumbling them over and picking up one here and there at random, which he read aloud. These passages soon began to uncover the secret which Lucetta had so earnestly hoped to keep buried, though the epistles, being allusive only, did not make it altogether plain.

"Mrs. Farfrae wrote that!" said Nance Mockridge. " 'Tis a humbling thing for us, as respectable women, that one of the same sex could do it. And now she's vowed herself to another man!"

"So much the better for her," said the aged furmity-woman. "Ah, I saved her from a real bad marriage, and she's never been the one to thank me."

"I say, what a good foundation for a skimmity-ride," said Nance.

"True," said Mrs. Cuxsom, reflecting. " 'Tis as good a ground for a skimmity-ride as ever I knowed; and it ought not to be wasted. The last one seen in Casterbridge must have been ten years ago, if a day."

At this moment there was a shrill whistle, and the landlady said to the man who had been called Charl, " 'Tis Jim coming in. Would ye go and let down the bridge for me?"

Without replying Charl and his comrade Joe rose, and receiving a lantern from her went out at the back-door and down the garden-path, which ended abruptly at the edge of the stream already mentioned. Beyond the stream was the open moor, from which a clammy breeze smote upon their faces as they advanced. Taking up the board that had lain in readiness, one of them lowered it across the water, and the instant its further end touched the ground footsteps entered upon it, and there appeared from the shade a stalwart man with straps round his knees, a double-barrelled gun under his arm and some birds slung up behind him. They asked him if he had had much luck.

"Not much," he said indifferently. "All safe inside?"

Receiving a reply in the affirmative he went on inwards, the others withdrawing the bridge and beginning to retreat in his rear. Before, however, they had entered the house a cry of "Ahoy" from the moor led them to pause.

The cry was repeated. They pushed the lantern into an outhouse, and went back to the brink of the stream.

"Ahoy—is this the way to Casterbridge?" said someone from the other side.

"Not in particular," said Charl. "There's a river afore ye."

"I don't care—here's for through it!" said the man in the moor. "I've had travelling enough for to-day."

"Stop a minute, then," said Charl, finding that the man was no enemy. "Joe, bring the plank and lantern; here's somebody that's lost his way. You should have kept along the turnpike road, friend, and not have strook across here."

"I should—as I see now. But I saw a light here, and says I to myself, that's a short cut, depend on't."

The plank was now lowered; and the stranger's form shaped itself from the darkness. He was a middle-aged man, with hair and whiskers prematurely grey, and a broad and genial face. He had crossed on the plank without hesitation, and seemed to see nothing odd in the transit. He thanked them, and walked between them up the garden. "What place is this?" he asked, when they reached the door.

"A public-house."

"Ah. Perhaps it will suit me to put up at. Now then, come in and wet your whistle at my expense for the lift over you have given me."

They followed him into the inn, where the increased light exhibited him as one who would stand higher in an estimate by the eye than in one by the ear. He was dressed with a certain clumsy richness—his coat being furred, and his head covered by a cap of sealskin, which, though the nights were chilly, must have been warm for the day-time, spring being somewhat advanced. In his hand he carried a small mahogany case, strapped, and clamped with brass.

Apparently surprised at the kind of company which confronted him through the kitchen-door, he at once abandoned his idea of putting up at the house; but taking the situation lightly, he called for glasses of the best, paid for them as he stood in the passage, and turned to proceed on his way by the front-door. This was barred, and while the landlady was unfastening it the conversation about the skimmington was continued in the sitting-room, and reached his ears.

"What do they mean by a 'skimmity-ride'?" he asked.

"Oh, sir!" said the landlady, swinging her long ear-rings with deprecating modesty; " 'tis a' old foolish thing they do in these parts when a man's wife is—well, not too particularly his own. But as a respectable householder I don't encourage it."

"Still, are they going to do it shortly? It is a good sight to see, I suppose?"

"Well, sir!" she simpered. And then, bursting into naturalness, and glancing from the corner of her eye, " 'Tis the funniest thing under the sun! And it costs money."

"Ah! I remember hearing of some such thing. Now I shall be in Casterbridge for two or three weeks to come, and should not mind seeing the performance. Wait a moment." He turned back, entered the sitting-room, and said, "Here, good folks; I should like to see the old custom you are talking of, and I don't mind being something towards it—take that." He threw a sovereign on the table and returned to the landlady at the door, of whom, having enquired the way into the town, he took his leave.

"There were more where that one came from," said Charl when the sovereign had been taken up and handed to the landlady for safe keeping. "By George! we ought to have got a few more while we had him here."

"No, no," answered the landlady. "This is a respectable house, thank God! And I'll have nothing done but what's honourable."

"Well," said Jopp; "now we'll consider the business begun, and will soon get it in train."

"We will!" said Nance. "A good laugh warms my heart more than a cordial, and that's the truth on't."

Jopp gathered up the letters, and it being now somewhat late, he did not attempt to call at Farfrae's with them that night. He reached home, sealed them up as before, and delivered the parcel at its address next morning. Within an hour its contents were reduced to ashes by Lucetta, who, poor soul! was inclined to fall down on her knees in thankfulness that at last no evidence remained of the unlucky episode with Henchard in her past. For though hers had been rather the laxity of inadvertence than of intention, that episode, if known, was not the less likely to operate fatally between herself and her husband.

XXXVII

S UCH WAS THE STATE OF THINGS WHEN THE CURRENT AFFAIRS OF CASTERBRIDGE WERE interrupted by an event of such magnitude that its influence reached to the lowest social stratum there, stirring the depths of its society simultaneously with the preparations for the skimmington. It was one of those excitements which, when they move a country town, leave permanent mark upon its chronicles, as a warm summer permanently marks the ring in the tree-trunk corresponding to its date.

A Royal Personage was about to pass through the borough on his course further west, to inaugurate an immense engineering work out that way. He had consented to halt half an hour or so in the town, and to receive an address from the corporation of Casterbridge, which, as a representative centre of husbandry, wished thus to express its sense of the great services he had rendered to agricultural science and economics, by his zealous promotion of designs for placing the art of farming on a more scientific footing.

Royalty had not been seen in Casterbridge since the days of the third King George, and then only by candle-light for a few minutes, when that monarch, on a night-journey, had stopped to change horses at the King's Arms. The inhabitants therefore decided to make a thorough *fête carillonée* of the unwonted occasion. Half an hour's pause was not long, it is true; but much might be done in it by a judicious grouping of incidents, above all, if the weather were fine.

The address was prepared on parchment, by an artist who was handy at ornamental lettering, and was laid on with the best gold-leaf and colours that the sign-painter had in his shop. The Council had met on the Tuesday before the appointed day, to arrange the details of the procedure. While they were sitting, the door of the Council Chamber standing open, they heard a heavy footstep coming up the stairs. It advanced along the passage, and Henchard entered the room, in clothes of frayed and threadbare shabbiness, the very clothes which he had used to wear in the primal days when he had sat among them.

"I have a feeling," he said, advancing to the table and laying his hand upon the green cloth, "that I should like to join ye in this reception of our illustrious visitor. I suppose I could walk with the rest?"

Embarrassed glances were exchanged by the Council, and Grower nearly ate the end of his quill-pen, so gnawed he it during the silence. Farfrae, the young Mayor, who by virtue of his office sat in the large chair, intuitively caught the sense of the meeting, and as spokesman was obliged to utter it, glad as he would have been that the duty should have fallen to another tongue.

"I hardly see that it would be proper, Mr. Henchard," said he. "The Council are the Council, and as ye are no longer one of the body, there would be an irregularity in the proceeding. If ye were included, why not others?"

"I have a particular reason for wishing to assist at the ceremony."

Farfrae looked round. "I think I have expressed the feeling of the Council," he said.

"Yes, yes," from Dr. Bath, Lawyer Long, Alderman Tubber, and several more.

"Then I am not to be allowed to have anything to do with it officially?"

"I am afraid so; it is out of the question, indeed. But of course you can see the doings full well, such as they are to be, like the rest of the spectators."

Henchard did not reply to that very obvious suggestion, and, turning on his heel, went away.

It had been only a passing fancy of his, but opposition crystallised it into a determination. "I'll welcome his Royal Highness, or nobody shall!" he went about saying. "I am not going to be sat upon by Farfrae, or any of the rest of the paltry crew! You shall see."

The eventful morning was bright, a full-faced sun confronting early window-gazers eastward, and all perceived (for they were practised in weather-lore) that there was permanence in the glow. Visitors soon began to flock in from county houses, villages, remote copses, and lonely uplands, the latter in oiled boots and tilt bonnets, to see the reception, or if not to see it, at any rate to be near it. There was hardly a workman in the town who did not put a clean shirt on. Solomon Longways, Christopher Coney, Buzzford, and the rest of that fraternity, showed their sense of the occasion by advancing their customary eleven o'clock pint to half-past ten; from which they found a difficulty in getting back to the proper hour for several days.

Henchard had determined to do no work that day. He primed himself in the morning with a glass of rum, and walking down the street met Elizabeth-Jane, whom he had not seen for a week. "It was lucky," he said to her, "my twenty years had expired before this came on, or I should never have had the nerve to carry it out."

"Carry out what?" said she, alarmed.

"This welcome I am going to give our Royal visitor."

She was perplexed. "Shall we go and see it together?" she said.

"See it! I have other fish to fry. You see it. It will be worth seeing!"

She could do nothing to elucidate this, and decked herself out with a heavy heart. As the appointed time drew near she got sight again of her stepfather. She thought he was going to the Three Mariners; but no, he elbowed his way through the gay throng to the shop of Woolfrey, the draper. She waited in the crowd without.

In a few minutes he emerged, wearing, to her surprise, a brilliant rosette, while more surprising still, in his hand he carried a flag, of somewhat homely construction, formed by tacking one of the small Union Jacks, which abounded in the town to-day, to the end of a deal wand—probably the roller from a piece of calico. Henchard rolled up his flag on the door-step, put it under his arm, and went down the street.

Suddenly the taller members of the crowd turned their heads, and the shorter stood on tiptoe. It was said that the Royal *cortège* approached. The railway had stretched out an arm towards Casterbridge at this time, but had not reached it by several miles as yet; so that the intervening distance, as well as the remainder of the journey, was to be traversed by road in the old fashion. People thus waited—the county families in their carriages, the masses on foot—and watched the far-stretching London highway to the ringing of bells and chatter of tongues.

From the background Elizabeth-Jane watched the scene. Some seats had been arranged from which ladies could witness the spectacle, and the front seat was occupied by Lucetta, the Mayor's wife, just at present. In the road under her eyes stood Henchard. She appeared so bright and pretty that, as it seemed, he was experiencing the momentary weakness of wishing for her notice. But he was far from attractive to a woman's eye, ruled as that is so largely by the superficies of things. He was not only a journeyman, unable to appear as he formerly had appeared, but he disdained to appear as well as he might. Everybody else, from the Mayor to the washerwoman, shone in new vesture according to means; but Henchard had doggedly retained the fretted and weather-beaten garments of bygone years.

Hence, alas, this occurred: Lucetta's eyes slid over him to this side and to that without anchoring on a feature—as gaily dressed women's eyes will too often do on such occasions. Her manner signified quite plainly that she meant to know him in public no more.

But she was never tired of watching Donald, as he stood in animated converse with his friends a few yards off, wearing round his young neck the official gold chain with great square links, like that round the Royal unicorn. Every trifling emotion that her husband showed as he talked had its reflex on her face and lips, which moved in little duplicates to his. She was living his part rather than her own, and cared for no one's situation but Farfrae's that day.

At length a man stationed at the furthest turn of the high-road, namely, on the second bridge of which mention has been made, gave a signal, and the Corporation in their robes proceeded from the front of the Town Hall to the archway erected at the entrance to the town. The carriages containing the Royal visitor and his suite arrived at the spot in a cloud of dust, a procession was formed, and the whole came on to the Town Hall at a walking pace.

This spot was the centre of interest. There were a few clear yards in front of the Royal carriage; and into this space a man stepped before anyone could prevent him. It was Henchard. He had unrolled his private flag, and removing his hat he staggered to the side of the slowing vehicle, waving the Union Jack to and fro with his left hand while he blandly held out his right to the illustrious Personage.

All the ladies said with bated breath, "Oh, look there!" and Lucetta was ready to faint. Elizabeth-Jane peeped through the shoulders of those in front, saw what it was, and was terrified; and then her interest in the spectacle as a strange phenomenon got the better of her fear.

Farfrae, with Mayoral authority, immediately rose to the occasion. He seized Henchard by the shoulder, dragged him back, and told him roughly to be off. Henchard's eyes met his, and Farfrae observed the fierce light in them despite his excitement and irritation. For a moment Henchard stood his ground rigidly; then by an unaccountable impulse gave way and retired. Farfrae glanced to the ladies' gallery, and saw that his Calphurnia's cheek was pale.

"Why—it is your husband's old patron!" said Mrs. Blowbody, a lady of the neighbourhood who sat beside Lucetta.

"Patron!" said Donald's wife with quick indignation.

"Do you say the man is an acquaintance of Mr. Farfrae's?" observed Mrs. Bath, the physician's wife, a new-comer to the town through her recent marriage with the doctor.

"He works for my husband," said Lucetta.

"Oh—is that all? They have been saying to me that it was through him your husband first got a footing in Casterbridge. What stories people will tell!"

"They will indeed. It was not so at all. Donald's genius would have enabled him to get a footing anywhere, without anybody's help! He would have been just the same if there had been no Henchard in the world!"

It was partly Lucetta's ignorance of the circumstances of Donald's arrival which led her to speak thus, partly the sensation that everybody seemed bent on snubbing her at this triumphant time. The incident had occupied but a few moments, but it was necessarily witnessed by the Royal personage, who, however, with practised tact affected not to have noticed anything unusual. He alighted, the Mayor advanced, the address was read; the visitor replied, then said a few words to Farfrae, and shook hands with Lucetta as the Mayor's wife. The ceremony occupied but a few minutes, and the carriages rattled heavily as Pharaoh's chariots down Corn Street and out upon the Budmouth Road, in continuation of the journey coastward.

In the crowd stood Coney, Buzzford, and Longways. "Some difference between him now and when he zung at the Dree Mariners," said the first. " 'Tis wonderful how he could get a lady of her quality to go snacks wi' en in such quick time."

"True. Yet how folk do worship fine clothes! Now there's a better-looking woman than she that nobody notices at all, because she's akin to that hontish fellow Henchard."

"I could worship ye, Buzz, for saying that," remarked Nance Mockridge. "I do like to see the trimming pulled off such Christmas candles. I am quite unequal to the part of villain myself, or I'd gi'e all my small silver to see that lady toppered. . . . And perhaps I shall soon," she added significantly.

"That's not a noble passiont for a 'oman to keep up," said Longways.

Nance did not reply, but everyone knew what she meant. The ideas diffused by the reading of Lucetta's letters at Peter's Finger had condensed into a scandal, which was spreading like a miasmatic fog through Mixen Lane, and thence up the back streets of Casterbridge.

The mixed assemblage of idlers known to each other presently fell apart into two bands by a process of natural selection, the frequenters of Peter's Finger going off Mixen Lane–wards, where most of them lived, while Coney, Buzzford, Longways, and that connection remained in the street.

"You know what's brewing down there, I suppose?" said Buzzford mysteriously to the others.

Coney looked at him. "Not the skimmity-ride?"

Buzzford nodded.

"I have my doubts if it will be carried out," said Longways. "If they are getting it up they are keeping it mighty close.

"I heard they were thinking of it a fortnight ago, at all events."

"If I were sure o't I'd lay information," said Longways emphatically. " 'Tis too rough a joke, and apt to wake riots in towns. We know that the Scotchman is a right enough man, and that his lady has been a right enough 'oman since she came here, and if there was anything wrong about her afore, that's their business, not ours."

Coney reflected. Farfrae was still liked in the community; but it must be owned that, as the Mayor and man of money, engrossed with affairs and ambitions, he had lost in the eyes of the poorer inhabitants something of that wondrous charm which he had had for them as a light-hearted penniless young man, who sang ditties as readily as the birds in the trees. Hence the anxiety to keep him from annoyance showed not quite the ardour that would have animated it in former days.

"Suppose we make enquiration into it, Christopher," continued Longways; "and if we find there's really anything in it, drop a letter to them most concerned, and advise 'em to keep out of the way?"

This course was decided on, and the group separated, Buzzford saying to Coney, "Come, my ancient friend; let's move on. There's nothing more to see here."

These well-intentioned ones would have been surprised had they known how ripe the great jocular plot really was. "Yes, to-night," Jopp had said to the Peter's party at the corner of Mixen Lane. "As a wind-up to the Royal visit the hit will be all the more pat by reason of their great elevation to-day."

To him, at least, it was not a joke, but a retaliation.

XXXVIII

THE PROCEEDINGS HAD BEEN BRIEF—TOO BRIEF—TO LUCETTA WHOM AN INTOXICATing *Weltlust* had fairly mastered; but they had brought her a great triumph nevertheless. The shake of the Royal hand still lingered in her fingers; and the chit-chat she had overheard, that her husband might possibly receive the honour of knighthood, though idle to a degree, seemed not the wildest vision; stranger things had occurred to men so good and captivating as her Scotchman was.

After the collision with the Mayor, Henchard had withdrawn behind the ladies' stand; and there he stood, regarding with a stare of abstraction the spot on the lapel of his coat where Farfrae's hand had seized it. He put his own hand there, as if he could hardly realise such an outrage from one whom it had once been his wont to treat with ardent generosity. While pausing in this half-stupefied state the conversation of Lucetta with the other ladies reached his ears; and he distinctly heard her deny him—deny that he had assisted Donald, that he was anything more than a common journeyman.

He moved on homeward, and met Jopp in the archway to the Bull Stake. "So you've had a snub," said Jopp.

"And what if I have?" answered Henchard sternly.

"Why, I've had one too, so we are both under the same cold shade." He briefly related his attempt to win Lucetta's intercession.

Henchard merely heard his story, without taking it deeply in. His own relation to Farfrae and Lucetta overshadowed all kindred ones. He went on saying brokenly to himself, "She has supplicated to me in her time; and now her tongue won't own me nor her eyes see me! . . . And he—how angry he looked. He drove me back as if I were a bull breaking fence. . . . I took it like a lamb, for I saw it could not be settled there. He can rub brine on a green wound! . . . But he shall pay for it, and she shall be sorry. It must come to a tussle—face to face; and then we'll see how a coxcomb can front a man!"

Without further reflection the fallen merchant, bent on some wild purpose, ate a hasty dinner and went forth to find Farfrae. After being injured by him as a rival, and snubbed by him as a journeyman, the crowning degradation had been reserved for this day—that he should be shaken at the collar by him as a vagabond in the face of the whole town.

The crowds had dispersed. But for the green arches which still stood as they were erected Casterbridge life had resumed its ordinary shape. Henchard went down Corn Street till he came to Farfrae's house, where he knocked, and left a message that he would be glad to see his employer at the granaries as soon as he conveniently could come there. Having done this he proceeded round to the back and entered the yard.

Nobody was present, for, as he had been aware, the labourers and carters were enjoying a half-holiday on account of the events of the morning—though the carters would have to return for a short time later on, to feed and litter down the horses. He had reached the granary steps and was about to ascend, when he said to himself aloud, "I'm stronger than he."

Henchard returned to a shed, where he selected a short piece of rope from several pieces that were lying about; hitching one end of this to a nail, he took the other in his right hand and turned himself bodily round, while keeping his arm against his side; by this contrivance he pinioned the arm effectively. He now went up the ladders to the top floor of the corn-stores.

It was empty, except of a few sacks, and at the further end was the door often mentioned, opening under the cat-head and chain that hoisted the sacks. He fixed the door open and looked over the sill. There was a depth of thirty or forty feet to the ground; here was the spot on which he had been standing with Farfrae when Elizabeth-Jane had seen him lift his arm, with many misgivings as to what the movement portended.

He retired a few steps into the loft and waited. From this elevated perch his eyes could sweep the roofs roundabout, the upper parts of the luxurious chestnut trees, now delicate in leaves of a week's age, and the drooping boughs of the lines; Farfrae's garden and the green door leading therefrom. In course of time—he could not say how long—that green door opened and Farfrae came through. He was dressed as if for a journey. The low light of the nearing evening caught his head and face when he emerged from the shadow of the wall, warming them to a complexion of flame-colour. Henchard watched him with his mouth firmly set, the squareness of his jaw and the verticality of his profile being unduly marked.

Farfrae came on with one hand in his pocket, and humming a tune in a way which told that the words were most in his mind. They were those of the song he had sung when he arrived years before at the Three Mariners, a poor young man, adventuring for life and fortune, and scarcely knowing witherward:—

> *And here's a hand, my trusty fiere,*
> *And gie's a hand o' thine.*

Nothing moved Henchard like an old melody. He sank back. "No; I can't do it!" he gasped. "Why does the infernal fool begin that now!"

At length Farfrae was silent, and Henchard looked out of the loft door. "Will ye come up here?" he said.

"Ay, man," said Farfrae. "I couldn't see ye. What's wrang?"

A minute later Henchard heard his feet on the lowest ladder. He heard him land on the first floor, ascend and land on the second, begin the ascent to the third. And then his head rose through the trap behind.

"What are you doing up here at this time?" he asked, coming forward. "Why didn't ye take your holiday like the rest of the men?" He spoke in a tone which had just severity enough in it to show that he remembered the untoward event of the forenoon.

Henchard said nothing; but going back he closed the stair hatchway, and stamped upon it so that it went tight into its frame; he next turned to the wondering young man, who by this time observed that one of Henchard's arms was bound to his side.

"Now," said Henchard quietly, "we stand face to face—man and man. Your money and your fine wife no longer lift 'ee above me as they did but now, and my poverty does not press me down."

"What does it all mean?" asked Farfrae simply.

"Wait a bit, my lad. You should ha' thought twice before you affronted to extremes a man who had nothing to lose. I've stood your rivalry, which ruined me, and your snubbing, which humbled me; but your hustling, that disgraced me, I won't stand!"

Farfrae warmed a little at this. "Ye'd no business there," he said.

"As much as anyone among ye! What, you forward stripling, tell a man of my age he'd no business there!" The anger-vein swelled in his forehead as he spoke.

"You insulted Royalty, Henchard; and 'twas my duty, as the chief magistrate, to stop you."

"Royalty be damned," said Henchard. "I am as loyal as you, come to that!"

"I am not here to argue. Wait till you cool doon, wait till you cool; and you will see things the same way as I do."

"You may be the one to cool first," said Henchard grimly. "Now this is the case. Here be we, in this four-square loft, to finish out that little wrestle you began this morning. There's the door, forty foot above ground. One of us two puts the other out by that door—the master stays inside. If he likes he may go down afterwards and give the alarm that the other has fallen out by accident—or he may tell the truth—that's his business. As the strongest man I've tied one arm to take no advantage of 'ee. D'ye understand? Then here's at 'ee!"

There was no time for Farfrae to do aught but one thing, to close with Henchard, for the latter had come on at once. It was a wrestling match, the object of each being to give his antagonist a back fall; and on Henchard's part, unquestionably, that it should be through the door.

At the outset Henchard's hold by his only free hand, the right, was on the left side of Farfrae's collar, which he firmly grappled, the latter holding Henchard by his collar with the contrary hand. With his right he endeavoured to get hold of his antagonist's left arm, which, however, he could not do, so adroitly did Henchard keep it in the rear as he gazed upon the lowered eyes of his fair and slim antagonist.

Henchard planted the first toe forward, Farfrae crossing him with his; and thus far the struggle had very much the appearance of the ordinary wrestling of those parts. Several minutes were passed by them in this attitude, the pair rocking and writhing like trees in a gale, both preserving an absolute silence. By this time their breathing could be heard. Then Farfrae tried to get hold of the other side of Henchard's collar, which was resisted by the larger man exerting all his force in a wrenching movement, and this part of the struggle ended by his forcing Farfrae down on his knees by sheer pressure of one of his muscular arms. Hampered as he was, however, he could not keep him there, and Farfrae finding his feet again the struggle proceeded as before.

By a whirl Henchard brought Donald dangerously near the precipice; seeing his position the Scotchman for the first time locked himself to his adversary, and all the efforts of that infuriated Prince of Darkness—as he might have been called from his appearance just now—were inadequate to lift or loosen Farfrae for a time. By an extraordinary effort he succeeded at last, though not until they had got far back again from the fatal door. In doing so Henchard contrived to turn Farfrae a complete somersault. Had Henchard's other arm been free it would have been all over with Farfrae then. But again he regained his feet, wrenching Henchard's arm considerably, and causing him sharp pain, as could be seen from the twitching of his face. He instantly delivered the younger man an annihilating turn by the left fore-hip, as it used to be expressed, and following up his advantage thrust him towards the door, never loosening his hold till Farfrae's fair head was hanging over the window-sill, and his arm dangling down outside the wall.

"Now," said Henchard between his gasps, "this is the end of what you began this morning. Your life is in my hands."

"Then take it, take it!" said Farfrae. "Ye've wished to long enough!"

Henchard looked down upon him in silence, and their eyes met. "O Farfrae!—that's not true!" he said bitterly. "God is my witness that no man ever loved another as I did thee at one time. . . . And now—though I came here to kill 'ee, I cannot hurt thee! Go and give me in charge—do what you will—I care nothing for what comes of me!"

He withdrew to the back part of the loft, and flung himself into a corner upon some sacks, in the abandonment of remorse. Farfrae regarded him in silence; then went to the hatch and descended through it. Henchard would fain have recalled him, but his tongue failed in its task, and the young man's steps died on his ear.

Henchard took his full measure of shame and self-reproach. The scenes of his first acquaintance with Farfrae rushed back upon him—that time when the curious mixture of romance and thrift in the young man's composition so commanded his heart that Farfrae could play upon him as on an instrument. So thoroughly subdued was he that he remained on the sacks in a crouching attitude, unusual for a man, and for such a man. Its womanliness sat tragically on the figure of so stern a piece of virility. He heard a conversation below, the opening of the coach-house door, and the putting in of a horse, but took no notice.

Here he stayed till the thin shades thickened to opaque obscurity, and the loft-door became an oblong of grey light—the only visible shape around. At length he arose, shook the dust from his clothes wearily, felt his way to the hatch, and gropingly descended the steps till he stood in the yard.

"He thought highly of me once," he murmured. "Now he'll hate me and despise me forever!"

He became possessed by an overpowering wish to see Farfrae again that night, and by some desperate pleading to attempt the well-nigh impossible task of winning pardon for his late mad attack. But as he walked towards Farfrae's door he recalled the unheeded doings in the yard while he had lain above in a sort of stupor. Farfrae he remembered had gone to the stable and put the horse into the gig; while doing so Whittle had brought him a letter; Farfrae had then said that he would not go towards Budmouth as he had intended—that he was unexpectedly summoned to Weatherbury, and meant to call at Mellstock on his way thither, that place lying but one or two miles out of his course.

He must have come prepared for a journey when he first arrived in the yard, unsuspecting enmity; and he must have driven off (though in a changed direction) without saying a word to anyone on what had occurred between themselves.

It would therefore be useless to call at Farfrae's house till very late.

There was no help for it but to wait till his return, though waiting was almost torture to his restless and self-accusing soul. He walked about the streets and outskirts of the town, lingering here and there till he reached the stone bridge of which mention has been made, an accustomed halting-place with him now. Here he spent a long time, the purl of waters through the weirs meeting his ear, and the Casterbridge lights glimmering at no great distance off.

While leaning thus upon the parapet, his listless attention was awakened by sounds of an unaccustomed kind from the town quarter. They were a confusion of rhythmical noises, to which the streets added yet more confusion by encumbering them with echoes. His first incurious thought that the clangour arose from the town band, engaged in an attempt to round off a memorable day in a burst of evening harmony, was contradicted by certain peculiarities of reverberation. But inexplicability did not rouse him to more than a cursory heed; his sense of degradation was too strong for the admission of foreign ideas; and he leant against the parapet as before.

XXXIX

WHEN FARFRAE DESCENDED OUT OF THE LOFT BREATHLESS FROM HIS ENCOUNTER with Henchard, he paused at the bottom to recover himself. He arrived at the yard with the intention of putting the horse into the gig himself (all the men having a holiday), and driving to a village on the Budmouth Road. Despite the fearful struggle he decided still to persevere in his journey, so as to recover himself before going indoors and meeting the eyes of Lucetta. He wished to consider his course in a case so serious.

When he was just on the point of driving off Whittle arrived with a note badly addressed, and bearing the word "immediate" upon the outside. On opening it he was surprised to see that it was unsigned. It contained a brief request that he would go to Weatherbury that evening about some business which he was conducting there. Farfrae knew nothing that could make it pressing; but as he was bent upon going out he yielded to the anonymous request, particularly as he had a call to make at Mellstock which could be included in the same tour. Thereupon he told Whittle of his change of direction, in words which Henchard had overheard; and set out on his way. Farfrae had not directed his man to take the message indoors, and Whittle had not been supposed to do so on his own responsibility.

Now the anonymous letter was a well-intentioned but clumsy contrivance of Longways and other of Farfrae's men, to get him out of the way for the evening, in order that the satirical mummery should fall flat, if it were attempted. By giving open information they would have brought down upon their heads the vengeance of those among their comrades who enjoyed these boisterous old games; and therefore the plan of sending a letter recommended itself by its indirectness.

For poor Lucetta they took no protective measure, believing with the majority there was some truth in the scandal, which she would have to bear as she best might.

It was about eight o'clock, and Lucetta was sitting in the drawing-room alone. Night had set in for more than half an hour, but she had not had the candles lighted, for when Farfrae was away she preferred waiting for him by the firelight, and, if it were not too cold, keeping one of the window-sashes a little way open that the sound of his wheels might reach her ears early. She was leaning back in the chair, in a more hopeful mood than she had enjoyed since her marriage. The day had been such a success; and the temporary uneasiness which Henchard's show of effrontery had wrought in her disappeared with the quiet disappearance of Henchard himself under her husband's reproof. The floating evidences of her absurd passion for him, and its consequences, had been destroyed, and she really seemed to have no cause for fear.

The reverie in which these and other subjects mingled was disturbed by a hubbub in the distance, that increased moment by moment. It did not greatly surprise her, the afternoon having been given up to recreation by a majority of the populace since the passage of the Royal equipages. But her attention was at once riveted to the matter by the voice of a maid-servant next door, who spoke from an upper-window across the street to some other maid even more elevated than she.

"Which way be they going now?" enquired the first with interest.

"I can't be sure for a moment," said the second, "because of the malter's chimbley. Oh yes—I can see 'em. Well, I declare, I declare!"

"What, what?" from the first, more enthusiastically.

"They are coming up Corn Street after all! They sit back to back!"

"What—two of 'em—are there two figures?"

"Yes. Two images on a donkey, back to back, their elbows tied to one another's! She's facing the head, and he's facing the tail."

"Is it meant for anybody in particular?"

"Well—it mid be. The man has got on a blue coat and kerseymere leggings; he has black whiskers, and a reddish face. 'Tis a stuffed figure, with a mask."

The din was increasing now—then it lessened a little.

"There—I shan't see, after all!" cried the disappointed first maid.

"They have gone into a back street—that's all," said the one who occupied the enviable position in the attic. "There—now I have got 'em all endways nicely!"

"What's the woman like? Just say, and I can tell in a moment if 'tis meant for one I've in mind."

"My—why—'tis dressed just as *she* dressed when she sat in the front seat at the time the play-actors came to the Town Hall!"

Lucetta started to her feet, and almost at the instant the door of the room was quickly and softly opened. Elizabeth-Jane advanced into the firelight.

"I have come to see you," she said breathlessly. "I did not stop to knock—forgive me! I see you have not shut your shutters, and the window is open."

Without waiting for Lucetta's reply she crossed quickly to the window and pulled out one of the shutters. Lucetta glided to her side. "Let it be—hush!" she said peremptorily, in a dry voice, while she seized Elizabeth-Jane by the hand, and held up her finger. Their intercourse had been so low and hurried that not a word had been lost of the conversation without, which had thus proceeded:—

"Her neck is uncovered, and her hair in bands, and her back-comb in place; she's got on a puce silk, and white stockings, and coloured shoes."

Again Elizabeth-Jane attempted to close the window, but Lucetta held her by main force.

" 'Tis me!" she said, with a face pale as death. "A procession—a scandal—an effigy of me, and him!"

The look of Elizabeth betrayed that the latter knew it already.

"Let us shut it out," coaxed Elizabeth-Jane, noting that the rigid wildness of Lucetta's features was growing yet more rigid and wild with the meaning of the noise and laughter. "Let us shut it out!"

"It is of no use!" she shrieked. "He will see it, won't he? Donald will see it! He is just coming home—and it will break his heart—he will never love me any more—and oh, it will kill me—kill me!"

Elizabeth-Jane was frantic now. "Oh, can't something be done to stop it?" she cried. "Is there nobody to do it—not one?"

She relinquished Lucetta's hands, and ran to the door. Lucetta herself, saying recklessly "I will see it!" turned to the window, threw up the sash, and went out upon the balcony. Elizabeth immediately followed, and put her arm round her to pull her in. Lucetta's eyes were straight upon the spectacle of the uncanny revel, now dancing rapidly. The numerous lights round the two effigies threw them up into lurid distinctness; it was impossible to mistake the pair for other than the intended victims.

"Come in, come in," implored Elizabeth; "and let me shut the window!"

"She's me—she's me—even to the parasol—my green parasol!" cried Lucetta with a wild laugh as she stepped in. She stood motionless for one second—then fell heavily to the floor.

Almost at the instant of her fall the rude music of the skimmington ceased. The roars of sarcastic laughter went off in ripples, and the trampling died out like the rustle of a spent wind. Elizabeth was only indirectly conscious of this; she had rung the bell, and was bending over Lucetta, who remained convulsed on the carpet in the paroxysms of an epileptic seizure. She rang again and again, in vain; the probability being that the servants had all run out of the house to see more of the Daemonic Sabbath than they could see within.

At last Farfrae's man, who had been agape on the door-step, came up; then the cook. The shutters, hastily pushed to by Elizabeth, were quite closed, a light was obtained, Lucetta carried to her room, and the man sent off for a doctor. While Elizabeth was undressing her she recovered consciousness; but as soon as she remembered what had passed the fit returned.

The doctor arrived with unhoped-for promptitude; he had been standing at his door, like others, wondering what the uproar meant. As soon as he saw the unhappy sufferer he said, in answer to Elizabeth's mute appeal, "This is serious."

"It is a fit," Elizabeth said.

"Yes. But a fit in the present state of her health means mischief. You must send at once for Mr. Farfrae. Where is he?"

"He has driven into the country, sir," said the parlour-maid; "to some place on the Budmouth Road. He's likely to be back soon."

"Never mind; he must be sent for, in case he should not hurry." The doctor returned to the bedside again. The man was despatched, and they soon heard him clattering out of the yard at the back.

Meanwhile Mr. Benjamin Grower, that prominent burgess of whom mention has been already made, hearing the din of cleavers, tongs, tambourines, kits, crouds, humstrums, serpents, rams'-horns, and other historical kinds of music as he sat indoors in the High Street, had put on his hat and gone out to learn the cause. He came to the corner above Farfrae's, and soon guessed the nature of the proceedings; for being a native of the town he had witnessed such rough jests before. His first move was to search hither and thither for the constables, there were two in the town, shrivelled men whom he ultimately found in hiding up an alley, yet more shrivelled than usual, having some not ungrounded fears that they might be roughly handled if seen.

"What can we two poor lammigers do against such a multitude!" expostulated Stubberd, in answer to Mr. Grower's chiding. " 'Tis tempting 'em to commit *felo de se* upon us, and that would be the death of the perpetrator; and we wouldn't be the cause of a fellow-creature's death on no account, not we!"

"Get some help, then! Here, I'll come with you. We'll see what a few words of authority can do. Quick now; have you got your staves?"

"We didn't want the folk to notice us as law officers, being so short-handed, sir; so we pushed our Gover'ment staves up this water-pipe."

"Out with 'em, and come along, for Heaven's sake! Ah, here's Mr. Blowbody; that's lucky." (Blowbody was the third of the three borough magistrates.)

"Well, what's the row?" said Blowbody. "Got their names—hey?"

"No. Now," said Grower to one of the constables, "you go with Mr. Blowbody round by the Old Walk and come up the street; and I'll go with Stubberd straight forward. By this plan we shall have 'em between us. Get their names only: no attack or interruption."

Thus they started. But as Stubberd with Mr. Grower advanced into Corn Street, whence the sounds had proceeded, they were surprised that no procession could be seen. They passed Farfrae's, and looked to the end of the street. The lamp flames waved, the Walk trees soughed, a few loungers stood about with their hands in their pockets. Everything was as usual.

"Have you seen a motley crowd making a disturbance?" Grower said magisterially to one of these in a fustian jacket, who smoked a short pipe and wore straps round his knees.

"Beg yer pardon, sir?" blandly said the person addressed, who was no other than Charl, of Peter's Finger. Mr. Grower repeated the words.

Charl shook his head to the zero of childlike ignorance. "No; we haven't seen anything; have we, Joe? And you was here afore I."

Joseph was quite as blank as the other in his reply.

"H'm—that's odd," said Mr. Grower. "Ah—here's a respectable man coming that I know by sight. Have you," he enquired, addressing the nearing shape of Jopp, "have you seen any gang of fellows making a devil of a noise—skimmington-riding, or something of the sort?"

"Oh no—nothing, sir," Jopp replied, as if receiving the most singular news. "But I've not been far to-night, so perhaps—"

"Oh, 'twas here—just here," said the magistrate.

"Now I've noticed, come to think o't, that the wind in the Walk trees makes a peculiar poetical-like murmur to-night, sir; more than common; so perhaps 'twas that?" Jopp suggested, as he rearranged his hand in his great-coat pocket (where it ingeniously supported a pair of kitchen tongs and a cow's horn, thrust up under his waistcoat).

"No, no, no—d'ye think I'm a fool? Constable, come this way. They must have gone into the back street."

Neither in back street nor in front street, however, could the disturbers be perceived, and Blowbody and the second constable, who came up at this time, brought similar intelligence. Effigies, donkey, lanterns, band, all had disappeared like the crew of *Comus*.

"Now," said Mr. Grower, "there's only one thing more we can do. Get ye half-a-dozen helpers, and go in a body to Mixen Lane, and into Peter's Finger. I'm much mistaken if you don't find a clue to the perpetrators there."

The rusty-jointed executors of the law mustered assistance as soon as they could, and the whole party marched off to the lane of notoriety. It was no rapid matter to get there at night, not a lamp or glimmer of any sort offering itself to light the way, except an occasional pale radiance through some window-curtain, or through the chink of some door which could not be closed because of the smoky chimney within. At last they entered the inn boldly, by the till then bolted front-door, after a prolonged knocking of loudness commensurate with the importance of their standing.

In the settles of the large room, guyed to the ceiling by cords as usual for stability, an ordinary group sat drinking and smoking with statuesque quiet of demeanour. The landlady looked mildly at the invaders, saying in honest accents, "Good-evening, gentlemen; there's plenty of room. I hope there's nothing amiss?"

They looked round the room. "Surely," said Stubberd to one of the men, "I saw you by now in Corn Street—Mr. Grower spoke to 'ee?"

The man, who was Charl, shook his head absently. "I've been here this last hour, hain't I, Nance?" he said to the woman who meditatively sipped her ale near him.

"Faith, that you have. I came in for my quiet supper-time half-pint, and you were here then, as well as all the rest."

The other constable was facing the clock-case, where he saw reflected in the glass a quick motion by the landlady. Turning sharply, he caught her closing the oven-door.

"Something curious about that oven, ma'am!" he observed advancing, opening it, and drawing out a tambourine.

"Ah," she said apologetically, "that's what we keep here to use when there's a little quiet dancing. You see damp weather spoils it, so I put it there to keep it dry."

The constable nodded knowingly; but what he knew was nothing. Nohow could anything be elicited from this mute and inoffensive assembly. In a few minutes the investigators went out, and joining those of their auxiliaries who had been left at the door they pursued their way elsewhither.

XL

LONG BEFORE THIS TIME HENCHARD, WEARY OF HIS RUMINATIONS ON THE BRIDGE, HAD repaired towards the town. When he stood at the bottom of the street a procession burst upon his view, in the act of turning out of an alley just above him. The lanterns, horns, and multitude startled him; he saw the mounted images, and knew what it all meant.

They crossed the way, entered another street, and disappeared. He turned back a few steps and was lost in grave reflection, finally wending his way homeward by the obscure riverside path. Unable to rest there, he went to his stepdaughter's lodging, and was told that Elizabeth-Jane had gone to Mr. Farfrae's. Like one acting in obedience to a charm, and with a nameless apprehension, he followed in the same direction in the hope of meeting her, the roysterers having vanished. Disappointed in this he gave the gentlest of pulls to the door-bell, and then learnt particulars of what had occurred, together with the doctor's imperative orders that Farfrae should be brought home, and how they had set out to meet him on the Budmouth Road.

"But he has gone to Mellstock and Weatherbury!" exclaimed Henchard, now unspeakably grieved. "Not Budmouth way at all."

But, alas! for Henchard; he had lost his good name. They would not believe him, taking his words but as the frothy utterances of recklessness. Though Lucetta's life seemed at that moment to depend upon her husband's return (she being in great mental agony lest he should never know the unexaggerated truth of her past relations with Henchard), no messenger was despatched towards Weatherbury. Henchard, in a state of bitter anxiety and contrition, determined to seek Farfrae himself.

To this end he hastened down the town, ran along the eastern road over Durnover Moor, up the hill beyond, and thus onward in the moderate darkness of this spring night till he had reached a second and almost a third hill about three miles distant. In Yalbury Bottom, the plain at the foot of the hill, he listened. At first nothing, beyond his own heart-throbs, was to be heard but the slow wind making its moan among the masses of spruce and larch of Yalbury Wood which clothed the heights on either hand; but presently there came the sound of light wheels whetting their felloes against the newly stoned patches of road, accompanied by the distant glimmer of lights.

He knew it was Farfrae's gig descending the hill from an indescribable personality in its noise, the vehicle having been his own till bought by the Scotchman at the sale of his effects. Henchard thereupon retraced his steps along Yalbury Plain, the gig coming up with him as its driver slackened speed between two plantations.

It was a point in the highway near which the road to Mellstock branched off from the homeward direction. By diverging to that village, as he had intended to do, Farfrae might probably delay his return by a couple of hours. It soon appeared that his intention was to do so still, the light swerving towards Cuckoo Lane, the by-road aforesaid. Farfrae's off gig-lamp flashed in Henchard's face. At the same time, Farfrae discerned his late antagonist.

"Farfrae—Mr. Farfrae!" cried the breathless Henchard, holding up his hand.

Farfrae allowed the horse to turn several steps into the branch lane before he pulled up. He then drew rein, and said "Yes?" over his shoulder, as one would towards a pronounced enemy.

"Come back to Casterbridge at once!" Henchard said. "There's something wrong at your house—requiring your return. I've run all the way here on purpose to tell ye."

Farfrae was silent, and at his silence Henchard's soul sank within him. Why had he not, before this, thought of what was only too obvious? He who, four hours earlier, had enticed Farfrae into a deadly wrestle stood now in the darkness of late night-time on a lonely road, inviting him to come a particular way, where an assailant might have confederates, instead of his purposed way, where there might be a better opportunity of guarding himself from attack. Henchard could almost feel this view of things in course of passage through Farfrae's mind.

"I have to go to Mellstock," said Farfrae coldly, as he loosened his reins to move on.

"But," implored Henchard, "the matter is more serious than your business at Mellstock. It is—your wife! She is ill. I can tell you particulars as we go along."

The very agitation and abruptness of Henchard increased Farfrae's suspicion that this was a ruse to decoy him on to the next wood, where might be effectually compassed what, from policy or want of nerve, Henchard had failed to do earlier in the day. He started the horse.

"I know what you think," deprecated Henchard, running after, almost bowed down with despair as he perceived the image of unscrupulous villainy that he assumed in his former friend's eyes. "But I am not what you think!" he cried hoarsely. "Believe me, Farfrae; I have come entirely on your own and your wife's account. She is in danger. I know no more; and they want you to come. Your man has gone the other way in a mistake. O Farfrae! don't mistrust me—I am a wretched man; but my heart is true to you still!"

Farfrae, however, did distrust him utterly. He knew his wife was with child, but he had left her not long ago in perfect health; and Henchard's treachery was more credible than his story. He had in his time heard bitter ironies from Henchard's lips, and there might be ironies now. He quickened the horse's pace, and had soon risen into the high country lying between there and Mellstock, Henchard's spasmodic run after him lending yet more substance to his thought of evil purposes.

The gig and its driver lessened against the sky in Henchard's eyes; his exertions for Farfrae's good had been in vain. Over this repentant sinner, at least, there was to be no joy in heaven. He cursed himself like a less scrupulous Job, as a vehement man will do when he loses self-respect, the last mental prop under poverty. To this he had come after a time of emotional darkness of which the adjoining woodland shade afforded inadequate illustration. Presently he began to walk back again along the way by which he had arrived. Farfrae should at all events have no reason for delay upon the road by seeing him there when he took his journey homeward later on.

Arriving at Casterbridge, Henchard went again to Farfrae's house to make enquiries. As soon as the door opened anxious faces confronted his from the staircase, hall, and landing; and they all said in grievous disappointment, "Oh—it is not he!" The man, finding his mistake, had long since returned, and all hopes had centred upon Henchard.

"But haven't you found him?" said the doctor.

"Yes. . . . I cannot tell ye!" Henchard replied as he sank down on a chair within the entrance. "He can't be home for two hours."

"H'm," said the surgeon, returning upstairs.

"How is she?" asked Henchard of Elizabeth, who formed one of the group.

"In great danger, father. Her anxiety to see her husband makes her fearfully restless. Poor woman—I fear they have killed her!"

Henchard regarded the sympathetic speaker for a few instants as if she struck him in a new light; then, without further remark, went out of the door and onward to his lonely cottage. So much for man's rivalry, he thought. Death was to have the oyster, and Farfrae and himself the shells. But about Elizabeth-Jane; in the midst of his gloom she seemed to him as a pin-point of light. He had liked the look of her face as she answered him from the stairs. There had been affection in it, and above all things what he desired now was affection from anything that was good and pure. She was not his own; yet, for the first time, he had a faint dream that he might get to like her as his own—if she would only continue to love him.

Jopp was just going to bed when Henchard got home. As the latter entered the door Jopp said, "This is rather bad about Mrs. Farfrae's illness."

"Yes," said Henchard shortly, though little dreaming of Jopp's complicity in the night's harlequinade, and raising his eyes just sufficiently to observe that Jopp's face was lined with anxiety.

"Somebody has called for you," continued Jopp, when Henchard was shutting himself into his own apartment. "A kind of traveller, or sea-captain of some sort."

"Oh?—who could he be?"

"He seemed a well-be-doing man—had grey hair and a broadish face; but he gave no name, and no message."

"Nor do I gi'e him any attention." And, saying this, Henchard closed his door.

The divergence to Mellstock delayed Farfrae's return very nearly the two hours of Henchard's estimate. Among the other urgent reasons for his presence had been the need of his authority to send to Budmouth for a second physician; and when at length Farfrae did come back he was in a state bordering on distraction at his misconception of Henchard's motives.

A messenger was despatched to Budmouth, late as it had grown; the night wore on, and the other doctor came in the small hours. Lucetta had been much soothed by Donald's arrival; he seldom or never left her side; and when, immediately after his entry, she had tried to lisp out to him the secret which so oppressed her, he checked her feeble words, lest talking should be dangerous, assuring her there was plenty of time to tell him everything.

Up to this time he knew nothing of the skimmington-ride. The dangerous illness and miscarriage of Mrs. Farfrae was soon rumoured through the town, and an apprehensive guess having been given as to its cause by the leaders in the exploit, compunction and fear threw a dead silence over all particulars of their orgie; while those immediately around Lucetta would not venture to add to her husband's distress by alluding to the subject.

What, and how much, Farfrae's wife ultimately explained to him of her past entanglement with Henchard, when they were alone in the solitude of that sad night, cannot be told. That she informed him of the bare facts of her peculiar intimacy with the corn-merchant became plain from Farfrae's own statements. But in respect of her subsequent conduct—her motive in coming to Casterbridge to unite herself with Henchard—her assumed justification in abandoning him when she discovered reasons for fearing him (though in truth her inconsequent passion for another man at first sight had most to do with that abandonment)—her method of reconciling to her conscience a marriage with the second when she was in a measure committed to the first: to what extent she spoke of these things remained Farfrae's secret alone.

Besides the watchman who called the hours and weather in Casterbridge that night there walked a figure up and down Corn Street hardly less frequently. It was Henchard's, whose retiring to rest had proved itself a futility as soon as attempted; and he gave it up to go hither and thither, and make enquiries about the patient every now and then. He called as much on Farfrae's account as on Lucetta's, and on Elizabeth-Jane's even more than on either's. Shorn one by one of all other interests, his life seemed centring on the personality of the stepdaughter whose presence but recently he could not endure. To see her on each occasion of his enquiry at Lucetta's was a comfort to him.

The last of his calls was made about four o'clock in the morning, in the steely light of dawn. Lucifer was fading into day across Durnover Moor, the sparrows were just alighting into the street, and the hens had begun to cackle from the outhouses. When within a few yards of Farfrae's he saw the door gently opened, and a servant raise her hand to the knocker, to untie the piece of cloth which had muffled it. He went across, the sparrows in his way scarcely flying up from the road-litter, so little did they believe in human aggression at so early a time.

"Why do you take off that?" said Henchard.

She turned in some surprise at his presence, and did not answer for an instant or two. Recognizing him, she said, "Because they may knock as loud as they will; she will never hear it any more."

XLI

HENCHARD WENT HOME. THE MORNING HAVING NOW FULLY BROKE HE LIT HIS FIRE, AND sat abstractedly beside it. He had not sat there long when a gentle footstep approached the house and entered the passage, a finger tapping lightly at the door. Henchard's face brightened, for he knew the motions to be Elizabeth's. She came into his room, looking wan and sad.

"Have you heard?" she asked. "Mrs. Farfrae! She is—dead! Yes, indeed—about an hour ago!"

"I know it," said Henchard. "I have but lately come in from there. It is so very good of 'ee, Elizabeth, to come and tell me. You must be so tired out, too, with sitting up. Now do you bide here with me this morning. You can go and rest in the other room; and I will call 'ee when breakfast is ready."

To please him, and herself—for his recent kindliness was winning a surprised gratitude from the lonely girl—she did as he bade her, and lay down on a sort of couch which Henchard had rigged up out of a settle in the adjoining room. She could hear him moving about in his preparations; but her mind ran most strongly on Lucetta, whose death in such fulness of life and amid such cheerful hopes of maternity, was appallingly unexpected. Presently she fell asleep.

Meanwhile her stepfather in the outer room had set the breakfast in readiness; but finding that she dozed he would not call her; he waited on, looking into the fire and keeping the kettle boiling with housewifely care, as if it were an honour to have her in his house. In truth, a great change had come over him with regard to her, and he was developing the dream of a future lit by her filial presence, as though that way alone could happiness lie.

He was disturbed by another knock at the door, and rose to open it, rather deprecating a call from anybody just then. A stoutly built man stood on the door-step, with an alien, unfamiliar air about his figure and bearing—an air which might have been called colonial by people of cosmopolitan experience. It was the man who had asked the way at Peter's Finger. Henchard nodded, and looked enquiry.

"Good-morning, good-morning," said the stranger with profuse heartiness. "Is it Mr. Henchard I am talking to?"

"My name is Henchard."

"Then I've caught 'ee at home—that's right. Morning's the time for business, says I. Can I have a few words with you?"

"By all means," Henchard answered, showing the way in.

"You may remember me?" said his visitor, seating himself.

Henchard observed him indifferently, and shook his head.

"Well—perhaps you may not. My name is Newson."

Henchard's face and eyes seemed to die. The other did not notice it. "I know the name well," Henchard said at last, looking on the floor.

"I make no doubt of that. Well, the fact is, I've been looking for 'ee this fortnight past. I landed at Havenpool and went through Casterbridge on my way to Falmouth, and when I got there, they told me you had some years before been living at Casterbridge. Back came I again, and by long and by late I got here by coach, ten minutes ago. 'He lives down by the mill,' says they. So here I am. Now—that transaction between us some twenty years agone—'tis that I've called about. 'Twas a curious business. I was younger then than I am now, and perhaps the less said about it, in one sense, the better."

"Curious business! 'Twas worse than curious. I cannot even allow that I'm the man you met then. I was not in my senses, and a man's senses are himself."

"We were young and thoughtless," said Newson. "However, I've come to mend matters rather than open arguments. Poor Susan—hers was a strange experience."

"It was."

"She was a warm-hearted, home-spun woman. She was not what they call shrewd or sharp at all—better she had been."

"She was not."

"As you in all likelihood know, she was simple-minded enough to think that the sale was in a way binding. She was as guiltless o' wrong-doing in that particular as a saint in the clouds."

"I know it, I know it. I found it out directly," said Henchard, still with averted eyes. "There lay the sting o't to me. If she had seen it as what it was she would never have left me. Never! But how should she be expected to know? What advantages had she? None. She could write her own name, and no more."

"Well, it was not in my heart to undeceive her when the deed was done," said the sailor of former days. "I thought, and there was not much vanity in thinking it, that she would be happier with me. She was fairly happy, and I never would have undeceived her till the day of her death. Your child died; she had another, and all went well. But a time came—mind me, a time always does come. A time came—it was some while after she and I and the child returned from America—when somebody she had confided her history to, told her my claim to her was a mockery, and made a jest of her belief in my right. After that she was never happy with me. She pined and pined, and socked and sighed. She said she must leave me, and then came the question of our child. Then a man advised me how to act, and I did it, for I thought it was best. I left her at Falmouth, and went off to sea. When I got to the other side of the Atlantic there was a storm, and it was supposed that a lot of us, including myself, had been washed overboard. I got ashore at Newfoundland, and then I asked myself what I should do. 'Since I'm here, here I'll bide,' I thought to myself; ' 'twill be most kindness to her, now she's taken against me, to let her believe me lost, for,' I thought, 'while she supposes us both alive she'll be miserable; but if she thinks me dead she'll go back to him, and the child will have a home.' I've never returned to this country till a month ago, and I found that, as I supposed, she went to you, and my daughter with her. They told me in Falmouth that Susan was dead. But my Elizabeth-Jane— where is she?"

"Dead likewise," said Henchard doggedly. "Surely you learnt that too?"

The sailor started up, and took an enervated pace or two down the room. "Dead!" he said, in a low voice. "Then what's the use of my money to me?"

Henchard, without answering, shook his head as if that were rather a question for Newson himself than for him.

"Where is she buried?" the traveller enquired.

"Beside her mother," said Henchard, in the same stolid tones.

"When did she die?"

"A year ago and more," replied the other without hesitation.

The sailor continued standing. Henchard never looked up from the floor. At last Newson said: "My journey hither has been for nothing! I may as well go as I came! It has served me right. I'll trouble you no longer."

Henchard heard the retreating footsteps of Newson upon the sanded floor, the mechanical lifting of the latch, the slow opening and closing of the door that was natural to a baulked or dejected man; but he did not turn his head. Newson's shadow passed the window. He was gone.

Then Henchard, scarcely believing the evidence of his senses, rose from his seat amazed at what he had done. It had been the impulse of a moment. The regard he had lately acquired for Elizabeth, the new-sprung hope of his loneliness that she would be to him a daughter of whom he could feel as proud as of the actual daughter she still believed herself to be, had been stimulated by the unexpected coming of Newson to a greedy exclusiveness in relation to her; so that the sudden prospect of her loss had caused him to speak mad lies like a child, in pure mockery of consequences. He had expected questions to close in round him, and unmask his fabrication in five minutes; yet such questioning had not come. But surely they would come; Newson's departure could be but momentary; he would learn all by enquiries in the town; and return to curse him, and carry his last treasure away!

He hastily put on his hat, and went out in the direction that Newson had taken. Newson's back was soon visible up the road. Henchard followed; and saw his visitor stop at the King's Arms, where the morning coach which had brought him waited half an hour for another coach which crossed there. The coach Newson had come by was now about to move again. Newson mounted; his luggage was put in, and in a few minutes the vehicle disappeared with him.

He had not so much as turned his head. It was an act of simple faith in Henchard's words—faith so simple as to be almost sublime. The young sailor who had taken Susan Henchard on the spur of the moment and on the faith of a glance at her face, more than twenty years before, was still living and acting under the form of the grizzled traveller who had taken Henchard's words on trust so absolute as to shame him as he stood.

Was Elizabeth-Jane to remain his by virtue of this hardy invention of a moment? "Perhaps not for long," said he. Newson might converse with his fellow-travellers, some of whom might be Casterbridge people; and the trick would be discovered.

This probability threw Henchard into a defensive attitude, and instead of considering how best to right the wrong, and acquaint Elizabeth's father with the truth at once, he bethought himself of ways to keep the position he had accidentally won. Towards the young woman herself his affection grew more jealously strong with each new hazard to which his claim to her was exposed.

He watched the distant highway expecting to see Newson return on foot, enlightened and indignant, to claim his child. But no figure appeared. Possibly he had spoken to nobody on the coach, but buried his grief in his own heart.

His grief!—what was it, after all, to that which he, Henchard, would feel at the loss of her? Newson's affection, cooled by years, could not equal his who had been constantly in her presence. And thus his jealous soul speciously argued to excuse the separation of father and child.

He returned to the house half expecting that she would have vanished. No; there she was—just coming out from the inner-room, the marks of sleep upon her eyelids, and exhibiting a generally refreshed air.

"O father!" she said smiling. "I had no sooner lain down than I napped, though I did not mean to? I wonder I did not dream about poor Mrs. Farfrae, after thinking of her so; but I did not. How strange it is that we do not often dream of latest events, absorbing as they may be."

"I am glad you have been able to sleep," he said, taking her hand with anxious proprietorship—an act which gave her a pleasant surprise.

They sat down to breakfast, and Elizabeth-Jane's thoughts reverted to Lucetta. Their sadness added charm to a countenance whose beauty had ever lain in its meditative soberness.

"Father," she said, as soon as she recalled herself to the outspread meal, "it is so kind of you to get this nice breakfast with your own hands, and I idly asleep the while."

"I do it everyday," he replied. "You have left me; everybody has left me; how should I live but by my own hands."

"You are very lonely, are you not?"

"Ay, child—to a degree that you know nothing of! It is my own fault. You are the only one who has been near me for weeks. And you will come no more."

"Why do you say that? Indeed I will, if you would like to see me."

Henchard signified dubiousness. Though he had so lately hoped that Elizabeth-Jane might again live in his house as daughter, he would not ask her to do so now. Newson might return at any moment, and what Elizabeth would think of him for his deception it were best to bear apart from her.

When they had breakfasted his stepdaughter still lingered, till the moment arrived at which Henchard was accustomed to go to his daily work. Then she arose, and with assurance of coming again soon went up the hill in the morning sunlight.

"At this moment her heart is as warm towards me as mine is towards her; she would live with me here in this humble cottage for the asking! Yet before the evening probably he will have come; and then she will scorn me!"

This reflection, constantly repeated by Henchard to himself, accompanied him everywhere through the day. His mood was no longer that of the rebellious, ironical, reckless misadventurer; but the leaden gloom of one who has lost all that can make life interesting, or even tolerable. There would remain nobody for him to be proud of, nobody to fortify him; for Elizabeth-Jane would soon be but as a stranger, and worse. Susan, Farfrae, Lucetta, Elizabeth—all had gone from him, one after one, either by his fault or by his misfortune.

In place of them he had no interest, hobby, or desire. If he could have summoned music to his aid his existence might even now have been borne; for with Henchard music was of regal power. The merest trumpet or organ tone was enough to move him, and high harmonies transubstantiated him. But hard fate had ordained that he should be unable to call up this Divine spirit in his need.

The whole land ahead of him was as darkness itself; there was nothing to come, nothing to wait for. Yet in the natural course of life he might possibly have to linger on earth another thirty or forty years—scoffed at; at best pitied.

The thought of it was unendurable.

To the east of Casterbridge lay moors and meadows through which much water flowed. The wanderer in this direction who should stand still for a few moments on a quiet night, might hear singular symphonies from these waters, as from a lampless orchestra, all playing in their sundry tones from near and far parts of the moor. At a hole in a rotten weir they executed a recitative; where a tributary brook fell over a stone breastwork they trilled cheerily; under an arch they performed a metallic cymballing; and at Durnover Hole they hissed. The spot at which their instrumentation rose loudest was a place called Ten Hatches, whence during high springs there proceeded a very fugue of sounds.

The river here was deep and strong at all times, and the hatches on this account were raised and lowered by cogs and a winch. A path led from the second bridge over the highway (so often mentioned) to these Hatches, crossing the stream at their head by a narrow plank-bridge. But after night-fall human beings were seldom found going that way, the path leading only to no place in particular, and the passage being dangerous.

Henchard, however, leaving the town by the east road, proceeded to the second, or stone bridge, and thence struck into this path of solitude, following its course beside the stream till the dark shapes of the Ten Hatches cut the sheen thrown upon the river by the weak lustre that still lingered in the west. In a second or two he stood beside the weir-hole where the water was at its deepest. He looked backwards and forwards, and no creature appeared in view. He then took off his coat and hat, and stood on the brink of the stream with his hands clasped in front of him.

While his eyes were bent on the water beneath there slowly became visible a something floating in the circular pool formed by the wash of centuries; the pool he was intending to make his death-bed. At first it was indistinct, by reason of the shadow from the bank; but it emerged thence and took shape, which was that of a human body, lying stiff and stark upon the surface of the stream.

In the circular current imparted by the central flow the form was brought forward, till it passed under his eyes; and then he perceived with a sense of horror that it was *himself*. Not a man somewhat resembling him, but one in all respects his counterpart, his actual double, was floating as if dead in Ten Hatches Hole.

The sense of the supernatural was strong in this unhappy man, and he turned away as one might have done in the actual presence of an appalling miracle. He covered his eyes and bowed his head. Without looking again into the stream he took his coat and hat, and went slowly away.

Presently he found himself by the door of his own dwelling. To his surprise Elizabeth-Jane was standing there. She came forward, spoke, called him "father" just as before. Newson, then, had not even yet returned.

"I thought you seemed very sad this morning," she said, "so I have come again to see you. Not that I am anything but sad myself. But everybody and everything seem against you so, and I know you must be suffering."

How this woman divined things! Yet she had not divined their whole extremity.

He said to her, "Are miracles still worked, do ye think, Elizabeth? I am not a read man. I don't know so much as I could wish. I have tried to peruse and learn all my life; but the more I try to know the more ignorant I seem."

"I don't quite think there are any miracles now-a-days," she said.

"No interference in the case of desperate intentions, for instance? Well, perhaps not, in a direct way. Perhaps not. But will you come and walk with me, and I will show 'ee what I mean."

She agreed willingly, and he took her over the highway, and by the lonely path to Ten Hatches. He walked restlessly, as if some haunting shade, unseen of her, hovered round him and troubled his glance. She would gladly have talked of Lucetta, but feared to disturb him. When they got near the weir he stood still, and asked her to go forward and look into the pool, and tell him what she saw.

She went, and soon returned to him. "Nothing," she said.

"Go again," said Henchard, "and look narrowly."

She proceeded to the river brink a second time. On her return, after some delay, she told him that she saw something floating round and round there; but what it was she could not discern. It seemed to be a bundle of old clothes.

"Are they like mine?" asked Henchard.

"Well—they are. Dear me—I wonder if—Father, let us go away!"

"Go and look once more; and then we will get home."

She went back, and he could see her stoop till her head was close to the margin of the pool. She started up, and hastened back to his side.

"Well," said Henchard; "what do you say now?"

"Let us go home."

"But tell me—do—what is it floating there?"

"The effigy," she answered hastily. "They must have thrown it into the river higher up amongst the willows, to get rid of it in their alarm at discovery; and it must have floated down here."

"Ah—to be sure—the image o' me! But where is the other? Why that one only? . . . That performance of theirs killed her, but kept me alive!"

Elizabeth-Jane thought and thought of these words "kept me alive," as they slowly retraced their way to the town, and at length guessed their meaning. "Father!—I will not leave you alone like this!" she cried. "May I live with you, and tend upon you as I used to do? I do not mind your being poor. I would have agreed to come this morning, but you did not ask me."

"May you come to me?" he cried bitterly. "Elizabeth, don't mock me! If you only would come!"

"I will," said she.

"How will you forgive all my roughness in former days? You cannot!"

"I have forgotten it. Talk of that no more."

Thus she assured him, and arranged their plans for reunion; and at length each went home. Then Henchard shaved for the first time during many days, and put on clean linen, and combed his hair; and was as a man resuscitated thenceforward.

The next morning the fact turned out to be as Elizabeth-Jane had stated; the effigy was discovered by a cowherd, and that of Lucetta a little higher up in the same stream. But as little as possible was said of the matter, and the figures were privately destroyed.

Despite this natural solution of the mystery Henchard no less regarded it as an intervention that the figure should have been floating there. Elizabeth-Jane heard him say, "Who is such a reprobate as I! And yet it seems that even I be in Somebody's hand!"

XLII

BUT THE EMOTIONAL CONVICTION THAT HE WAS IN SOMEBODY'S HAND BEGAN TO DIE OUT of Henchard's breast as time slowly removed into distance the event which had given that feeling birth. The apparition of Newson haunted him. He would surely return.

Yet Newson did not arrive. Lucetta had been borne along the churchyard path; Casterbridge had for the last time turned its regard upon her, before proceeding to its work as if she had never lived. But Elizabeth remained undisturbed in the belief of her relationship to Henchard, and now shared his home. Perhaps, after all, Newson was gone forever.

In due time the bereaved Farfrae had learnt the, at least, proximate cause of Lucetta's illness and death; and his first impulse was naturally enough to wreak vengeance in the name of the law upon the perpetrators of the mischief. He resolved to wait till the funeral was over ere he moved in the matter. The time having come he reflected. Disastrous as the result had been, it was obviously in no way foreseen or intended by the thoughtless crew who arranged the motley procession. The tempting prospect of putting to the blush people who stand at the head of affairs—that supreme and piquant enjoyment of those who writhe under the heel of the same—had alone animated them, so far as he could see; for he knew nothing of Jopp's incitements. Other considerations were also involved. Lucetta had confessed everything to him before her death, and it was not altogether desirable to make much ado about her history, alike for her sake, for Henchard's, and for his own. To regard the event as an untoward accident seemed, to Farfrae, truest consideration for the dead one's memory, as well as best philosophy.

Henchard and himself mutually forbore to meet. For Elizabeth's sake the former had fettered his pride sufficiently to accept the small seed and root business which some of the Town Council, headed by Farfrae, had purchased to afford him a new opening. Had he been only personally concerned, Henchard, without doubt, would have declined assistance even remotely brought about by the man whom he had so fiercely assailed. But the sympathy of the girl seemed necessary to his very existence; and on her account pride itself wore the garments of humility.

Here they settled themselves; and on each day of their lives Henchard anticipated her every wish with a watchfulness in which paternal regard was heightened by a burning jealous dread of rivalry. Yet that Newson would ever now return to Casterbridge to claim her as a daughter there was little reason to suppose. He was a wanderer and a stranger, almost an alien; he had not seen his daughter for several years; his affection for her could not in the nature of things be keen; other interests would probably soon obscure his recollections of her, and prevent any such renewal of enquiry into the past as would lead to a discovery that she was still a creature of the present. To satisfy his conscience somewhat Henchard repeated to himself that the lie which had retained for him the coveted treasure had not been deliberately told to that end, but had come from him as the last defiant word of a despair which took no thought of consequences. Furthermore he pleaded within himself that no Newson could love her as he loved her, or would tend her to his life's extremity as he was prepared to do cheerfully.

Thus they lived on in the shop overlooking the churchyard, and nothing occurred to mark their days during the remainder of the year. Going out but seldom, and never on a market-day, they saw Donald Farfrae only at rarest intervals, and then mostly as a transitory object in the distance of the street. Yet he was pursuing his ordinary avocations, smiling mechanically to fellow-tradesmen, and arguing with bargainers—as bereaved men do after a while.

Time, "in his own grey style," taught Farfrae how to estimate his experience of Lucetta—all that it was, and all that it was not. There are men whose hearts insist upon a dogged fidelity to some image or cause thrown by chance into their keeping, long after their judgment has pronounced it no rarity—even the reverse, indeed; and without them the band of the worthy is incomplete. But Farfrae was not of those. It was inevitable that the insight, briskness, and rapidity of his nature should take him out of the dead blank which his loss threw about him. He could not but perceive that by the death of Lucetta he had exchanged a looming misery for a simple sorrow. After that revelation of her history, which must have come sooner or later in any circumstances, it was hard to believe that life with her would have been productive of further happiness.

But as a memory, notwithstanding such conditions, Lucetta's image still lived on with him, her weaknesses provoking only the gentlest criticism, and her sufferings attenuating wrath at her concealments to a momentary spark now and then.

By the end of a year Henchard's little retail seed and grain shop, not much larger than a cupboard, had developed its trade considerably, and the stepfather and daughter enjoyed much serenity in the pleasant, sunny corner in which it stood. The quiet bearing of one who brimmed with an inner activity characterised Elizabeth-Jane at this period. She took long walks into the country two or three times a week, mostly in the direction of Bud-mouth. Sometimes it occurred to him that when she sat with him in the evening after those invigorating walks she was civil rather than affectionate; and he was troubled; one more bitter regret being added to those he had already experienced at having, by his severe censorship, frozen up her precious affection when originally offered.

She had her own way in everything now. In going and coming, in buying and selling, her word was law.

"You have got a new muff, Elizabeth," he said to her one day quite humbly.

"Yes; I bought it," she said.

He looked at it again as it lay on an adjoining table. The fur was of a glossy brown, and, though he was no judge of such articles, he thought it seemed an unusually good one for her to possess.

"Rather costly, I suppose, my dear, was it not?" he hazarded.

"It was rather above my figure," she said quietly. "But it is not showy."

"Oh no," said the netted lion, anxious not to pique her in the least.

Some little time after, when the year had advanced into another spring, he paused opposite her empty bedroom in passing it. He thought of the time when she had cleared out of his then large and handsome house in Corn Street, in consequence of his dislike and harshness, and he had looked into her chamber in just the same way. The present room was much humbler, but what struck him about it was the abundance of books lying everywhere. Their number and quality made the meagre furniture that supported them seem absurdly disproportionate. Some, indeed many, must have been recently purchased; and though he encouraged her to buy in reason, he had no notion that she indulged her innate passion so extensively in proportion to the narrowness of their income. For the first time he felt a little hurt by what he thought her extravagance, and resolved to say a word to her about it. But, before he had found the courage to speak, an event happened which set his thoughts flying in quite another direction.

The busy time of the seed trade was over; and the quiet weeks that preceded the hay-season had come—setting their special stamp upon Casterbridge by thronging the market with wood rakes, new waggons in yellow, green, and red, formidable scythes, and pitch-forks of prong sufficient to skewer up a small family. Henchard, contrary to his wont, went out one Saturday afternoon towards the market-place, from a curious feeling that he would like to pass a few minutes on the spot of his former triumphs. Farfrae, to whom he was still a comparative stranger, stood a few steps below the Corn Exchange door—a usual position with him at this hour—and he appeared lost in thought about something he was looking at a little way off.

Henchard's eyes followed Farfrae's, and he saw that the object of his gaze was no sample-showing farmer, but his own stepdaughter, who had just come out of a shop over the way. She, on her part, was quite unconscious of his attention, and in this was less fortunate than those young women whose very plumes, like those of Juno's bird, are set with Argus eyes whenever possible admirers are within ken.

Henchard went away, thinking that perhaps there was nothing significant after all in Farfrae's look at Elizabeth-Jane at that juncture. Yet he could not forget that the Scotch-man had once shown a tender interest in her, of a fleeting kind. Thereupon promptly came to the surface that idiosyncrasy of Henchard's which had ruled his courses from the beginning, and had mainly made him what he was. Instead of thinking that a union between his cherished stepdaughter and the energetic thriving Donald was a thing to be desired for her good and his own, he hated the very possibility.

Time had been when such instinctive opposition would have taken shape in action. But he was not now the Henchard of former days. He schooled himself to accept her will, in this as in other matters, as absolute and unquestionable. He dreaded lest an antagonistic word should lose for him such regard as he had regained from her by his devotion, feeling that to retain this under separation was better than to incur her dislike by keeping her near.

But the mere thought of such separation fevered his spirit much, and in the evening he said, with the stillness of suspense: "Have you seen Mr. Farfrae to-day, Elizabeth?"

Elizabeth-Jane started at the question; and it was with some confusion that she replied "No."

"Oh—that's right—that's right. . . . It was only that I saw him in the street when we both were there." He was wondering if her embarrassment justified him in a new suspicion—that the long walks which she had latterly been taking, that the new books which had so surprised him, had anything to do with the young man. She did not enlighten him, and lest silence should allow her to shape thoughts unfavourable to their present friendly relations, he diverted the discourse into another channel.

Henchard was, by original make, the last man to act stealthily, for good or for evil. But the *solicitus timor* of his love—the dependence upon Elizabeth's regard into which he had declined (or, in another sense, to which he had advanced)—denaturalised him. He would often weigh and consider for hours together the meaning of such and such a deed or phrase of hers, when a blunt settling question would formerly have been his first instinct. And now, uneasy at the thought of a passion for Farfrae which should entirely displace her mild filial sympathy with himself, he observed her going and coming more narrowly.

There was nothing secret in Elizabeth-Jane's movements beyond what habitual reserve induced; and it may at once be owned on her account that she was guilty of occasional conversations with Donald when they chanced to meet. Whatever the origin of her walks on the Budmouth Road, her return from those walks was often coincident with Farfrae's emergence from Corn Street for a twenty minutes' blow on that rather windy highway—just to winnow the seeds and chaff out of him before sitting down to tea, as he said. Henchard became aware of this by going to the Ring, and, screened by its enclosure, keeping his eye upon the road till he saw them meet. His face assumed an expression of extreme anguish.

"Of her, too, he means to rob me!" he whispered. "But he has the right. I do not wish to interfere."

The meeting, in truth, was of a very innocent kind, and matters were by no means so far advanced between the young people as Henchard's jealous grief inferred. Could he have heard such conversation as passed he would have been enlightened thus much:—

He.—"You like walking this way, Miss Henchard—and is it not so?" (uttered in his undulatory accents, and with an appraising, pondering gaze at her).

She.—"Oh yes. I have chosen this road latterly. I have no great reason for it."

He.—"But that may make a reason for others."

She (reddening).—"I don't know that. My reason, however, such as it is, is that I wish to get a glimpse of the sea everyday."

He.—"Is it a secret why?"

She (reluctantly).—"Yes."

He (with the pathos of one of his native ballads).—"Ah, I doubt there will be any good in secrets! A secret cast a deep shadow over my life. And well you know what it was."

Elizabeth admitted that she did, but she refrained from confessing why the sea attracted her. She could not herself account for it fully, not knowing the secret possibly to be that, in addition to early marine associations, her blood was a sailor's.

"Thank you for those new books, Mr. Farfrae," she added shyly. "I wonder if I ought to accept so many!"

"Ay! why not? It gives me more pleasure to get them for you, than you to have them!"

"It cannot."

They proceeded along the road together till they reached the town, and their paths diverged.

Henchard vowed that he would leave them to their own devices, put nothing in the way of their courses, whatever they might mean. If he were doomed to be bereft of her, so it must be. In the situation which their marriage would create he could see no *locus standi* for himself at all. Farfrae would never recognise him more than superciliously; his poverty ensured that, no less than his past conduct. And so Elizabeth would grow to be a stranger to him, and the end of his life would be friendless solitude.

With such a possibility impending he could not help watchfulness. Indeed, within certain lines, he had the right to keep an eye upon her as his charge. The meetings seemed to become matters of course with them on special days of the week.

At last full proof was given him. He was standing behind a wall close to the place at which Farfrae encountered her. He heard the young man address her as "Dearest Elizabeth-Jane," and then kiss her, the girl looking quickly round to assure herself that nobody was near.

When they were gone their way Henchard came out from the wall, and mournfully followed them to Casterbridge. The chief looming trouble in this engagement had not decreased. Both Farfrae and Elizabeth-Jane, unlike the rest of the people, must suppose Elizabeth to be his actual daughter, from his own assertion while he himself had the same belief; and though Farfrae must have so far forgiven him as to have no objection to own him as a father-in-law, intimate they could never be. Thus would the girl, who was his only friend, be withdrawn from him by degrees through her husband's influence, and learn to despise him.

Had she lost her heart to any other man in the world than the one he had rivalled, cursed, wrestled with for life in days before his spirit was broken, Henchard would have said, "I am content." But content with the prospect as now depicted was hard to acquire.

There is an outer chamber of the brain in which thoughts unowned, unsolicited, and of noxious kind, are sometimes allowed to wander for a moment prior to being sent off whence they came. One of these thoughts sailed into Henchard's ken now.

Suppose he were to communicate to Farfrae the fact that his betrothed was not the child of Michael Henchard at all—legally, nobody's child; how would that correct and leading townsman receive the information? He might possibly forsake Elizabeth-Jane, and then she would be her stepsire's own again.

Henchard shuddered, and exclaimed, "God forbid such a thing! Why should I still be subject to these visitations of the devil, when I try so hard to keep him away?"

XLIII

W HAT HENCHARD SAW THUS EARLY WAS, NATURALLY ENOUGH, SEEN AT A LITTLE LATER
date by other people. That Mr. Farfrae "walked with that bankrupt Henchard's
stepdaughter, of all women," became a common topic in the town, the simple perambu-
lating term being used hereabout to signify a wooing; and the nineteen superior young
ladies of Casterbridge, who had each looked upon herself as the only woman capable of
making the merchant Councilman happy, indignantly left off going to the church Farfrae
attended, left off conscious mannerisms, left off putting him in their prayers at night
amongst their blood relations; in short, reverted to their normal courses.

Perhaps the only inhabitants of the town to whom this looming choice of the Scotchman's gave unmixed satisfaction were the members of the philosophic party, which included Longways, Christopher Coney, Billy Wills, Mr. Buzzford, and the like. The Three
Mariners having been, years before, the house in which they had witnessed the young man
and woman's first and humble appearance on the Casterbridge stage, they took a kindly
interest in their career, not unconnected, perhaps, with visions of festive treatment at their
hands hereafter. Mrs. Stannidge, having rolled into the large parlour one evening and said
that it was a wonder such a man as Mr. Farfrae, "a pillow of the town," who might have
chosen one of the daughters of the professional men or private residents, should stoop so
low, Coney ventured to disagree with her.

"No, ma'am, no wonder at all. 'Tis she that's a-stooping to he—that's my opinion. A
widow man—whose first wife was no credit to him—what is it for a young perusing
woman that's her own mistress and well-liked? But as a neat patching up of things I see
much good in it. When a man have put up a tomb of best marble-stone to the other one,
as he've done, and weeped his fill, and thought it all over, and said to hisself, 'T'other
took me in; I knowed this one first; she's a sensible piece for a partner, and there's no
faithful woman in high life now';—well, he may do worse than not to take her, if she's
tender-inclined."

Thus they talked at the Mariners. But we must guard against a too liberal use of the
conventional declaration that a great sensation was caused by the prospective event, that
all the gossips' tongues were set wagging thereby, and so on, even though such a declaration might lend some eclat to the career of our poor only heroine. When all has been said
about busy rumourers, a superficial and temporary thing is the interest of anybody in affairs which do not directly touch them. It would be a truer representation to say that Casterbridge (ever excepting the nineteen young ladies) looked up for a moment at the news,
and withdrawing its attention, went on labouring and victualling, bringing up its children,
and burying its dead, without caring a tittle for Farfrae's domestic plans.

Not a hint of the matter was thrown out to her stepfather by Elizabeth herself or by
Farfrae either. Reasoning on the cause of their reticence he concluded that, estimating him
by his past, the throbbing pair were afraid to broach the subject, and looked upon him as
an irksome obstacle whom they would be heartily glad to get out of the way. Embittered
as he was against society, this moody view of himself took deeper and deeper hold of
Henchard, till the daily necessity of facing mankind, and of them particularly Elizabeth-

Jane, became well-nigh more than he could endure. His health declined; he became morbidly sensitive. He wished he could escape those who did not want him, and hide his head forever.

But what if he were mistaken in his views, and there were no necessity that his own absolute separation from her should be involved in the incident of her marriage?

He proceeded to draw a picture of the alternative—himself living like a fangless lion about the back-rooms of a house in which his stepdaughter was mistress; an inoffensive old man, tenderly smiled on by Elizabeth, and good-naturedly tolerated by her husband. It was terrible to his pride to think of descending so low; and yet, for the girl's sake he might put up with anything; even from Farfrae; even snubbings and masterful tongue scourgings. The privilege of being in the house she occupied would almost outweigh the personal humiliation.

Whether this were a dim possibility or the reverse, the courtship—which it evidently now was—had an absorbing interest for him.

Elizabeth, as has been said, often took her walks on the Budmouth Road, and Farfrae as often made it convenient to create an accidental meeting with her there. A quarter of a mile from the highway, was the pre-historic fort called Mai Dun, of huge dimensions and many ramparts, within or upon whose enclosures a human being as seen from the road, was but an insignificant speck. Hitherward Henchard often resorted, glass in hand, and scanned the hedgeless *Via*—for it was the original track laid out by the legions of the Empire—to a distance of two or three miles, his object being to read the progress of affairs between Farfrae and his charmer.

One day Henchard was at this spot when a masculine figure came along the road from Budmouth, and lingered. Applying his telescope to his eye Henchard expected that Farfrae's features would be disclosed as usual. But the lenses revealed that to-day the man was not Elizabeth-Jane's lover.

It was one clothed as a merchant captain; and as he turned in the scrutiny of the road he revealed his face. Henchard lived a lifetime the moment he saw it. The face was Newson's.

Henchard dropped the glass, and for some seconds made no other movement. Newson waited, and Henchard waited—if that could be called a waiting which was a transfixture. But Elizabeth-Jane did not come. Something or other had caused her to neglect her customary walk that day. Perhaps Farfrae and she had chosen another road for variety's sake. But what did that amount to? She might be here to-morrow, and in any case Newson, if bent on a private meeting and a revelation of the truth to her, would soon make his opportunity.

Then he would tell her not only of his paternity, but of the ruse by which he had been once sent away. Elizabeth's strict nature would cause her for the first time to despise her stepfather, would root out his image as that of an arch-deceiver, and Newson would reign in her heart in his stead.

But Newson did not see anything of her that morning. Having stood still a while he at last retraced his steps, and Henchard felt like a condemned man who has a few hours' respite. When he reached his own house he found her there.

"O father!" she said innocently. "I have had a letter—a strange one—not signed. Somebody has asked me to meet him, either on the Budmouth Road at noon to-day, or in the evening at Mr. Farfrae's. He says he came to see me some time ago, but a trick was played him, so that he did not see me. I don't understand it; but between you and me I think Donald is at the bottom of the mystery, and that it is a relation of his who wants to pass an opinion on his choice. But I did not like to go till I had seen you. Shall I go?"

Henchard replied heavily, "Yes; go."

The question of his remaining in Casterbridge was forever disposed of by this closing in of Newson on the scene. Henchard was not the man to stand the certainty of condemnation on a matter so near his heart. And being an old hand at bearing anguish in silence, and haughty withal, he resolved to make as light as he could of his intentions, while immediately taking his measures.

He surprised the young woman, whom he had looked upon as his all in this world, by saying to her, as if he did not care about her more: "I am going to leave Casterbridge, Elizabeth-Jane."

"Leave Casterbridge!" she cried, "and leave—me?"

"Yes, this little shop can be managed by you alone as well as by us both; I don't care about shops and streets and folk—I would rather get into the country by myself, out of sight, and follow my own ways, and leave you to yours."

She looked down, and her tears fell silently. It seemed to her that this resolve of his had come on account of her attachment and its probable result. She showed her devotion to Farfrae, however, by mastering her emotion and speaking out.

"I am sorry you have decided on this," she said with difficult firmness. "For I thought it probable—possible—that I might marry Mr. Farfrae some little time hence, and I did not know that you disapproved of the step!"

"I approve of anything you desire to do, Izzy," said Henchard huskily. "If I did not approve, it would be no matter! I wish to go away. My presence might make things awkward in the future; and, in short, it is best that I go."

Nothing that her affection could urge would induce him to reconsider his determination; for she could not urge what she did not know—that when she should learn he was not related to her other than as a step-parent she would refrain from despising him, and that when she knew what he had done to keep her in ignorance she would refrain from hating him. It was his conviction that she would not so refrain; and there existed as yet neither word nor event which could argue it away.

"Then," she said at last, "you will not be able to come to my wedding; and that is not as it ought to be."

"I don't want to see it—I don't want to see it!" he exclaimed; adding more softly, "but think of me sometimes in your future life—you'll do that, Izzy?—think of me when you are living as the wife of the richest, the foremost man in the town, and don't let my sins, *when you know them all,* cause 'ee to quite forget that though I loved 'ee late I loved 'ee well."

"It is because of Donald!" she sobbed.

"I don't forbid you to marry him," said Henchard. "Promise not to quite forget me when—" He meant when Newson should come.

She promised mechanically, in her agitation; and the same evening at dusk Henchard left the town, to whose development he had been one of the chief stimulants for many years. During the day he had bought a new tool-basket, cleaned up his old hay-knife and wimble, set himself up in fresh leggings, knee-naps and corduroys, and in other ways gone back to the working clothes of his young manhood, discarding forever the shabby-genteel suit of cloth and rusty silk hat that since his decline had characterised him in the Caster-bridge street as a man who had seen better days.

He went secretly and alone, not a soul of the many who had known him being aware of his departure. Elizabeth-Jane accompanied him as far as the second bridge on the highway—for the hour of her appointment with the unguessed visitor at Farfrae's had not yet arrived—and parted from him with unfeigned wonder and sorrow—keeping him back a minute or two before finally letting him go. She watched his form diminish across the moor, the yellow straw basket at his back moving up and down with each tread, and the creases behind his knees coming and going alternately till she could no longer see them. Though she did not know it, Henchard formed at this moment much the same picture as he had presented when entering Casterbridge for the first time nearly a quarter of a cen-tury before; except, to be sure, that the serious addition to his years had considerably less-ened the spring to his stride, that his state of hopelessness had weakened him, and imparted to his shoulders, as weighted by the basket, a perceptible bend.

He went on till he came to the first milestone, which stood in the bank, half-way up a steep hill. He rested his basket on the top of the stone, placed his elbows on it, and gave way to a convulsive twitch, which was worse than a sob, because it was so hard and so dry.

"If I had only got her with me—if I only had!" he said. "Hard work would be noth-ing to me then! But that was not to be. I—Cain—go alone as I deserve—an outcast and a vagabond. But my punishment is *not* greater than I can bear!"

He sternly subdued his anguish, shouldered his basket, and went on.

Elizabeth, in the meantime, had breathed him a sigh, recovered her equanimity, and turned her face to Casterbridge. Before she had reached the first house she was met in her walk by Donald Farfrae. This was evidently not their first meeting that day; they joined hands without ceremony, and Farfrae anxiously asked, "And is he gone—and did you tell him?—I mean of the other matter—not of ours."

"He is gone; and I told him all I knew of your friend. Donald, who is he?"

"Well, well, dearie; you will know soon about that. And Mr. Henchard will hear of it if he does not go far."

"He will go far—he's bent upon getting out of sight and sound!"

She walked beside her lover, and when they reached the Town Pump, turned with him into Corn Street, instead of going straight on to her own door. At Farfrae's house they stopped and went in.

Farfrae flung open the door of the ground floor sitting-room, saying, "There he is waiting for you," and Elizabeth entered. In the arm-chair sat the broad-faced genial man who had called on Henchard on a memorable morning between one and two years before this time, and whom the latter had seen mount the coach and depart within half an hour of his arrival. It was Richard Newson. The meeting with the light-hearted father from whom she had been separated half-a-dozen years, as if by death, need hardly be detailed. It was an affecting one, apart from the question of paternity. Henchard's departure was in a mo-ment explained. When the true facts came to be handled the difficulty of restoring her to her old belief in Newson was not so great as might have seemed likely, for Henchard's conduct itself was a proof that those facts were true. Moreover, she had grown up under

Newson's paternal care; and even had Henchard been her father in nature, this father in early domiciliation might almost have carried the point against him, when the incidents of her parting with Henchard had a little worn off.

Newson's pride in what she had grown up to be was more than he could express. He kissed her again and again.

"I've saved you the trouble to come and meet me—ha-ha!" said Newson. "The fact is that Mr. Farfrae here, he said, 'Come up and stop with me for a day or two, Captain Newson, and I'll bring her round.' 'Faith,' says I, 'so I will'; and here I am."

"Well, Henchard is gone," said Farfrae, shutting the door. "He has done it all voluntarily, and, as I gather from Elizabeth, he has been very nice with her. I was got rather uneasy; but all is as it should be, and we will have no more deefficulties at all."

"Now, that's very much as I thought," said Newson, looking into the face of each by turns. "I said to myself, ay, a hundred times, when I tried to get a peep at her unknown to herself—'Depend upon it, 'tis best that I should live on quiet for a few days like this till something turns up for the better.' I now know you are all right, and what can I wish for more?"

"Well, Captain Newson, I will be glad to see ye here everyday now, since it can do no harm," said Farfrae. "And what I've been thinking is, that the wedding may as well be kept under my own roof, the house being large, and you being in lodgings by yourself—so that a great deal of trouble and expense would be saved ye?—and 'tis a convenience when a couple's married not to hae far to go to get home!"

"With all my heart," said Captain Newson; "since, as ye say, it can do no harm, now poor Henchard's gone; though I wouldn't have done it otherwise, or put myself in his way at all; for I've already in my lifetime been an intruder into his family quite as far as politeness can be expected to put up with. But what do the young woman say herself about it? Elizabeth, my child, come and hearken to what we be talking about, and not bide staring out o' the window as if ye didn't hear."

"Donald and you must settle it," murmured Elizabeth, still keeping up a scrutinizing gaze at some small object in the street.

"Well, then," continued Newson, turning anew to Farfrae with a face expressing thorough entry into the subject, "that's how we'll have it. And, Mr. Farfrae, as you provide so much, and houseroom, and all that, I'll do my part in the drinkables, and see to the rum and schiedam—maybe a dozen jars will be sufficient?—as many of the folk will be ladies, and perhaps they won't drink hard enough to make a high average in the reckoning? But you know best. I've provided for men and shipmates times enough, but I'm as ignorant as a child how many glasses of grog a woman, that's not a drinking woman, is expected to consume at these ceremonies?"

"Oh, none—we'll no want much of that—oh no!" said Farfrae, shaking his head with appalled gravity. "Do you leave all to me."

When they had gone a little further in these particulars Newson, leaning back in his chair and smiling reflectively at the ceiling, said, "I've never told ye, or have I, Mr. Farfrae, how Henchard put me off the scent that time?"

He expressed ignorance of what the Captain alluded to.

"Ah, I thought I hadn't. I resolved that I would not, I remember, not to hurt the man's name. But now he's gone I can tell ye. Why, I came to Casterbridge nine or ten months before that day last week that I found ye out. I had been here twice before then. The first time I passed through the town on my way westward, not knowing Elizabeth lived here. Then hearing at some place—I forget where—that a man of the name of Henchard had been mayor here, I came back, and called at his house one morning. The old rascal!—he said Elizabeth-Jane had died years ago."

Elizabeth now gave earnest heed to his story.

"Now, it never crossed my mind that the man was selling me a packet," contiued Newson. "And, if you'll believe me, I was that upset, that I went back to the coach that had brought me, and took passage onward without lying in the town half an hour. Ha-ha!— 'twas a good joke, and well carried out, and I give the man credit for't!"

Elizabeth-Jane was amazed at the intelligence. "A joke?—oh no!" she cried. "Then he kept you from me, father, all those months, when you might have been here?"

The father admitted that such was the case.

"He ought not to have done it!" said Farfrae.

Elizabeth sighed. "I said I would never forget him. But oh! I think I ought to forget him now!"

Newson, like a good many rovers and sojourners among strange men and strange moralities, failed to perceive the enormity of Henchard's crime, notwithstanding that he himself had been the chief sufferer therefrom. Indeed, the attack upon the absent culprit waxing serious, he began to take Henchard's part.

"Well, 'twas not ten words that he said, after all," Newson pleaded. "And how could he know that I should be such a simpleton as to believe him? 'Twas as much my fault as his, poor fellow!"

"No," said Elizabeth-Jane firmly, in her revulsion of feeling. "He knew your disposition—you always were so trusting, father; I've heard my mother say so hundreds of times—and he did it to wrong you. After weaning me from you these five years by saying he was my father, he should not have done this."

Thus they conversed; and there was nobody to set before Elizabeth any extenuation of the absent one's deceit. Even had he been present Henchard might scarce have pleaded it, so little did he value himself or his good name.

"Well, well—never mind—it is all over and past," said Newson good-naturedly. "Now, about this wedding again."

XLIV

MEANWHILE, THE MAN OF THEIR TALK HAD PURSUED HIS SOLITARY WAY EASTWARD TILL weariness overtook him, and he looked about for a place of rest. His heart was so exacerbated at parting from the girl that he could not face an inn, or even a household of the most humble kind; and entering a field he lay down under a wheat-rick, feeling no want of food. The very heaviness of his soul caused him to sleep profoundly.

The bright autumn sun shining into his eyes across the stubble awoke him the next morning early. He opened his basket and ate for his breakfast what he had packed for his supper; and in doing so overhauled the remainder of his kit. Although everything he brought necessitated carriage at his own back, he had secreted among his tools a few of Elizabeth-Jane's cast-off belongings, in the shape of gloves, shoes, a scrap of her hand-writing, and the like, and in his pocket he carried a curl of her hair. Having looked at these things he closed them up again, and went onward.

During five consecutive days Henchard's rush basket rode along upon his shoulder between the highway hedges, the new yellow of the rushes catching the eye of an occa-sional field-labourer as he glanced through the quickset, together with the wayfarer's hat and head, and down-turned face, over which the twig shadows moved in endless proces-sion. It now became apparent that the direction of his journey was Weydon Priors, which he reached on the afternoon of the sixth day.

The renowned hill, whereon the annual fair had been held for so many generations, was now bare of human beings, and almost of aught besides. A few sheep grazed thereabout, but these ran off when Henchard halted upon the summit. He deposited his basket upon the turf, and looked about with sad curiosity; till he discovered the road by which his wife and him-self had entered on the upland so memorable to both, five-and-twenty years before.

"Yes, we came up that way," he said, after ascertaining his bearings. "She was carry-ing the baby, and I was reading a ballet-sheet. Then we crossed about here—she so sad and weary, and I speaking to her hardly at all, because of my cursed pride and mortification at being poor. Then we saw the tent—that must have stood more this way." He walked to an-other spot, it was not really where the tent had stood but it seemed so to him. "Here we went in, and here we sat down. I faced this way. Then I drank, and committed my crime. It must have been just on that very pixy-ring that she was standing when she said her last words to me before going off with him; I can hear their sound now, and the sound of her sobs: 'O Mike! I've lived with thee all this while, and had nothing but temper. Now I'm no more to 'ee—I'll try my luck elsewhere.' "

He experienced not only the bitterness of a man who finds, in looking back upon an ambitious course, that what he has sacrificed in sentiment was worth as much as what he has gained in substance; but the superadded bitterness of seeing his very recantation nul-lified. He had been sorry for all this long ago; but his attempts to replace ambition by love had been as fully foiled as his ambition itself. His wronged wife had foiled them by a fraud so grandly simple as to be almost a virtue. It was an odd sequence that out of all this tam-pering with social law came that flower of Nature, Elizabeth. Part of his wish to wash his hands of life arose from his perception of its contrarious inconsistencies—of Nature's jaunty readiness to support unorthodox social principles.

He intended to go on from this place—visited as an act of penance—into another part of the country altogether. But he could not help thinking of Elizabeth, and the quarter of the horizon in which she lived. Out of this it happened that the centrifugal tendency im-parted by weariness of the world was counteracted by the centripetal influence of his love for his stepdaughter. As a consequence, instead of following a straight course yet further away from Casterbridge, Henchard gradually, almost unconsciously, deflected from that right line of his first intention; till, by degrees, his wandering, like that of the Canadian woodsman, became part of a circle, of which Casterbridge formed the centre. In ascend-ing any particular hill he ascertained the bearings as nearly as he could by means of the sun, moon, or stars, and settled in his mind the exact direction in which Casterbridge and

Elizabeth-Jane lay. Sneering at himself for his weakness, he yet every hour—nay, every few minutes—conjectured her actions for the time being—her sitting down and rising up, her goings and comings, till thought of Newson's and Farfrae's counter-influence would pass like a cold blast over a pool, and efface her image. And then he would say to himself, "O you fool! All this about a daughter who is no daughter of thine!"

At length he obtained employment at his own occupation of hay-trusser, work of that sort being in demand at this autumn time. The scene of his hiring was a pastoral farm near the old western highway, whose course was the channel of all such communications as passed between the busy centres of novelty and the remote Wessex boroughs. He had chosen the neighbourhood of this artery from a sense that, situated here, though at a distance of fifty miles, he was virtually nearer to her whose welfare was so dear than he would be at a roadless spot only half as remote.

And thus Henchard found himself again on the precise standing which he had occupied five-and-twenty years before. Externally there was nothing to hinder his making another start on the upward slope, and by his new lights achieving higher things than his soul in its half-formed state had been able to accomplish. But the ingenious machinery contrived by the Gods for reducing human possibilities of amelioration to a minimum—which arranges that wisdom to do shall come *pari passu* with the departure of zest for doing—stood in the way of all that. He had no wish to make an arena a second time of a world that had become a mere painted scene to him.

Very often, as his hay-knife crunched down among the sweet-smelling grassy stems, he would survey mankind and say to himself: "Here and everywhere be folk dying before their time like frosted leaves, though wanted by their families, the country, and the world; while I, an outcast, an encumberer of the ground, wanted by nobody, and despised by all, live on against my will!"

He often kept an eager ear upon the conversation of those who passed along the road—not from a general curiosity by any means—but in the hope that among these travellers between Casterbridge and London some would, sooner or later, speak of that place. The distance, however, was too great to lend much probability to his desire; and the highest result of his attention to wayside words was that he did indeed hear the name "Casterbridge" uttered one day by the driver of a road-waggon. Henchard ran to the gate of the field he worked in, and hailed the speaker, who was a stranger.

"Yes—I've come from there, maister," he said, in answer to Henchard's enquiry. "I trade up and down, ye know; though, what with this travelling without horses that's getting so common, my work will soon be done."

"Anything moving in the old place, mid I ask?"

"All the same as usual."

"I've heard that Mr. Farfrae, the late Mayor, is thinking of getting married. Now is that true or not?"

"I couldn't say for the life o' me. Oh no, I should think not."

"But yes, John—you forget," said a woman inside the waggon-tilt. "What were them packages we carr'd there at the beginning o' the week? Surely they said a wedding was coming off soon—on Martin's Day?"

The man declared he remembered nothing about it; and the waggon went on jangling over the hill.

Henchard was convinced that the woman's memory served her well. The date was an extremely probable one, there being no reason for delay on either side. He might, for that matter, write and enquire of Elizabeth; but his instinct for sequestration had made the course difficult. Yet before he left her, she had said that for him to be absent from her wedding was not as she wished it to be.

The remembrance would continually revive in him now that it was not Elizabeth and Farfrae who had driven him away from them, but his own haughty sense that his presence was no longer desired. He had assumed the return of Newson, without absolute proof that the Captain meant to return; still less that Elizabeth-Jane would welcome him; and with no proof whatever that if he did return he would stay. What if he had been mistaken in his views; if there had been no necessity that his own absolute separation from her he loved should be involved in these untoward incidents? To make one more attempt to be near her: to go back, to see her, to plead his cause before her, to ask forgiveness for his fraud, to endeavour strenuously to hold his own in her love; it was worth the risk of repulse, ay, of life itself.

But how to initiate this reversal of all his former resolves, without causing husband and wife to despise him for his inconsistency was a question which made him tremble and brood.

He cut and cut his trusses two days more, and then he concluded his hesitancies by a sudden reckless determination to go to the wedding festivity. Neither writing nor message would be expected of him. She had regretted his decision to be absent—his unanticipated presence would fill the little unsatisfied corner that would probably have place in her just heart without him.

To intrude as little of his personality as possible upon a gay event with which that personality could show nothing in keeping, he decided not to make his appearance till evening—when stiffness would have worn off, and a gentle wish to let bygones be bygones would exercise its sway in all hearts.

He started on foot, two mornings before St. Martin's-tide, allowing himself about sixteen miles to perform for each of the three days' journey, reckoning the wedding-day as one. There were only one town, Shottsford, of any importance along his course, and at the latter he stopped on the second night, not only to rest, but to prepare himself for the next evening.

Possessing no clothes but the working suit he stood in—now stained and distorted by their two months of hard usage, he entered a shop to make some purchases which should put him, externally at any rate, a little in harmony with the prevailing tone of the morrow. A rough yet respectable coat and hat, a new shirt and neck-cloth, were the chief of these; and having satisfied himself that in appearance at least he would not now offend her, he proceeded to the more interesting particular of buying her some present.

What should that present be? He walked up and down the street, regarding dubiously the display in the shop-windows, from a gloomy sense that what he might most like to give her would be beyond his miserable pocket. At length a caged goldfinch met his eye. The cage was a plain and small one, the shop humble, and on enquiry he concluded he could afford the modest sum asked. A sheet of newspaper was tied round the little creature's wire prison, and with the wrapped up cage in his hand Henchard sought a lodging for the night.

Next day he set out upon the last stage, and was soon within the district which had been his dealing ground in bygone years. Part of the distance he travelled by carrier, seating himself in the darkest corner at the back of that trader's van; and as the other passengers, mainly women going short journeys, mounted and alighted in front of Henchard, they talked over much local news, not the least portion of this being the wedding then in course of celebration at the town they were nearing. It appeared from their accounts that the town band had been hired for the evening party, and, lest the convivial instincts of that body should get the better of their skill, the further step had been taken of engaging the string band from Budmouth, so that there would be a reserve of harmony to fall back upon in case of need.

He heard, however, but few particulars beyond those known to him already, the incident of the deepest interest on the journey being the soft pealing of the Casterbridge bells, which reached the travellers' ears while the van paused on the top of Yalbury Hill to have the drag lowered. The time was just after twelve o'clock.

Those notes were a signal that all had gone well; that there had been no slip 'twixt cup and lip in this case; that Elizabeth-Jane and Donald Farfrae were man and wife.

Henchard did not care to ride any further with his chattering companions after hearing this sound. Indeed, it quite unmanned him; and in pursuance of his plan of not showing himself in Casterbridge street till evening, lest he should mortify Farfrae and his bride, he alighted here, with his bundle and bird-cage, and was soon left as a lonely figure on the broad white highway.

It was the hill near which he had waited to meet Farfrae, almost two years earlier, to tell him of the serious illness of his wife Lucetta. The place was unchanged; the same larches sighed the same notes; but Farfrae had another wife—and, as Henchard knew, a better one. He only hoped that Elizabeth-Jane had obtained a better home than had been hers at the former time.

He passed the remainder of the afternoon in a curious high-strung condition, unable to do much but think of the approaching meeting with her, and sadly satirise himself for his emotions thereon, as a Samson shorn. Such an innovation on Casterbridge customs as a flitting of bridegroom and bride from the town immediately after the ceremony, was not likely, but if it should have taken place he would wait till their return. To assure himself on this point he asked a market-man when near the borough if the newly-married couple had gone away, and was promptly informed that they had not; they were at that hour, according to all accounts, entertaining a houseful of guests at their home in Corn Street.

Henchard dusted his boots, washed his hands at the riverside, and proceeded up the town under the feeble lamps. He need have made no enquiries beforehand, for on drawing near Farfrae's residence it was plain to the least observant that festivity prevailed within, and that Donald himself shared it, his voice being distinctly audible in the street, giving strong expression to a song of his dear native country, that he loved so well as never to have revisited it. Idlers were standing on the pavement in front; and wishing to escape the notice of these Henchard passed quickly on to the door.

It was wide open; the hall was lighted extravagantly, and people were going up and down the stairs. His courage failed him; to enter footsore, laden, and poorly dressed into the midst of such resplendency was to bring needless humiliation upon her he loved, if not to court repulse from her husband. Accordingly he went round into the street at the back that he knew so well, entered the garden, and came quietly into the house through the kitchen, temporarily depositing the bird and cage under a bush outside, to lessen the awkwardness of his arrival.

Solitude and sadness had so emolliated Henchard that he now feared circumstances he would formerly have scorned, and he began to wish that he had not taken upon himself to arrive at such a juncture. However, his progress was made unexpectedly easy by his discovering alone in the kitchen an elderly woman who seemed to be acting as provisional housekeeper during the convulsions from which Farfrae's establishment was just then suffering. She was one of those people whom nothing surprises, and though to her, a total stranger, his request must have seemed odd, she willingly volunteered to go up and inform the master and mistress of the house that "a humble old friend" had come.

On second thought she said that he had better not wait in the kitchen, but come up into the little back-parlour, which was empty. He thereupon followed her thither, and she left him. Just as she got across the landing to the door of the best parlour a dance was struck up, and she returned to say that she would wait till that was over before announcing him— Mr. and Mrs. Farfrae having both joined in the figure.

The door of the front-room had been taken off its hinges to give more space, and that of the room Henchard sat in being ajar, he could see fractional parts of the dancers whenever their gyrations brought them near the doorway, chiefly in the shape of the skirts of dresses and streaming curls of hair; together with about three-fifths of the band in profile, including the restless shadow of a fiddler's elbow, and the tip of the bass-viol bow.

The gaiety jarred upon Henchard's spirits; and he could not quite understand why Farfrae, a much-sobered man, and a widower, who had had his trials, should have cared for it all, notwithstanding the fact that he was quite a young man still, and quickly kindled to enthusiasm by dance and song. That the quiet Elizabeth, who had long ago appraised life at a moderate value, and who knew in spite of her maidenhood that marriage was as a rule no dancing matter, should have had zest for this revelry surprised him still more. However, young people could not be quite old people, he concluded, and custom was omnipotent.

With the progress of the dance the performers spread out somewhat, and then for the first time he caught a glimpse of the once despised daughter who had mastered him, and made his heart ache. She was in a dress of white silk or satin, he was not near enough to say which—snowy white, without a tinge of milk or cream; and the expression of her face was one of nervous pleasure rather than of gaiety. Presently Farfrae came round, his exuberant Scotch movement making him conspicuous in a moment. The pair were not dancing together, but Henchard could discern that whenever the chances of the figure made them the partners of a moment their emotions breathed a much subtler essence than at other times.

By degrees Henchard became aware that the measure was trod by someone who outFarfraed Farfrae in saltatory intenseness. This was strange, and it was stranger to find that the eclipsing personage was Elizabeth-Jane's partner. The first time that Henchard saw him he was sweeping grandly round, his head quivering and low down, his legs in the form of an X and his back towards the door. The next time he came round in the other direction, his white waistcoat preceding his face, and his toes preceding his white waistcoat. That happy face—Henchard's complete discomfiture lay in it. It was Newson's, who had indeed come and supplanted him.

Henchard pushed to the door, and for some seconds made no other movement. He rose to his feet, and stood like a dark ruin, obscured by "the shade from his own soul upthrown."

But he was no longer the man to stand these reverses unmoved. His agitation was great, and he would fain have been gone, but before he could leave the dance had ended, the housekeeper had informed Elizabeth-Jane of the stranger who awaited her, and she entered the room immediately.

"Oh—it is—Mr. Henchard!" she said, starting back.

"What; Elizabeth?" he cried, as she seized her hand. "What do you say?—*Mr.* Henchard? Don't, don't scourge me like that! Call me worthless old Henchard—anything—but don't 'ee be so cold as this! Oh, my maid—I see you have another—a real father in my place. Then you know all; but don't give all your thought to him! Do ye save a little room for me!"

She flushed up, and gently drew her hand away. "I could have loved you always—I would have, gladly," she said. "But how can I when I know you have deceived me so—so bitterly deceived me! You persuaded me that my father was not my father—allowed me to live on in ignorance of the truth for years; and then when he, my warm-hearted real father, came to find me, cruelly sent him away with a wicked invention of my death, which nearly broke his heart. Oh how can I love, or do anything more for, a man who has served us like this!"

Henchard's lips half parted to begin an explanation. But he shut them up like a vice, and uttered not a sound. How should he, there and then, set before her with any effect the palliatives of his great faults—that he had himself been deceived in her identity at first, till informed by her mother's letter that his own child had died; that, in the second accusation, his lie had been the last desperate throw of a gamester who loved her affection better than his own honour? Among the many hindrances to such a pleading not the least was this, that he did not sufficiently value himself to lessen his sufferings by strenuous appeal or elaborate argument.

Waiving, therefore, his privilege of self-defence, he regarded only his discomposure. "Don't ye distress yourself on my account," he said, with proud superiority. "I would not wish it—at such a time, too, as this. I have done wrong in coming to 'ee—I see my error. But it is only for once, so forgive it. I'll never trouble 'ee again, Elizabeth-Jane—no, not to my dying day! Good-night. Good-bye!"

Then, before she could collect her thoughts, Henchard went out from her rooms, and departed from the house by the back way as he had come; and she saw him no more.

XLV

IT WAS ABOUT A MONTH AFTER THE DAY WHICH CLOSED AS IN THE LAST CHAPTER. Elizabeth-Jane had grown accustomed to the novelty of her situation, and the only difference between Donald's movements now and formerly was, that he hastened indoors rather more quickly after business hours than he had been in the habit of doing for some time.

Newson had stayed in Casterbridge three days after the wedding party (whose gaiety, as might have been surmised, was of his making rather than of the married couple's), and was stared at and honoured as became the returned Crusoe of the hour. But whether or not because Casterbridge was difficult to excite by dramatic returns and disappearances through having been for centuries an assize town, in which sensational exits from the world, antipodean absences, and such like, were half-yearly occurrences, the inhabitants did not altogether lose their equanimity on his account. On the fourth morning he was discovered disconsolately climbing a hill, in his craving to get a glimpse of the sea from somewhere or other. The contiguity of salt water proved to be such a necessity of his existence that he preferred Budmouth as a place of residence, notwithstanding the society of his daughter in the other town. Thither he went, and settled in lodgings in a green-shuttered cottage which had a bow-window, jutting out sufficiently to afford glimpses of a vertical strip of blue sea to anyone opening the sash, and leaning forward far enough to look through a narrow lane of tall intervening houses.

Elizabeth-Jane was standing in the middle of her upstairs parlour, critically surveying some rearrangement of articles with her head to one side, when the housemaid came in with the announcement, "Oh, please ma'am, we know now how that bird-cage came there."

In exploring her new domain during the first week of residence, gazing with critical satisfaction on this cheerful room and that, penetrating cautiously into dark cellars, sallying forth with gingerly tread to the garden, now leaf-strewn by autumn winds, and thus, like a wise field-marshal, estimating the capabilities of the site whereon she was about to open her housekeeping campaign—Mrs. Donald Farfrae had discovered in a screened corner a new bird-cage, shrouded in newspaper, and at the bottom of the cage a little ball of feathers—the dead body of a goldfinch. Nobody could tell her how the bird and cage had come there; though that the poor little songster had been starved to death was evident. The sadness of the incident had made an impression on her. She had not been able to forget it for days, despite Farfrae's tender banter; and now when the matter had been nearly forgotten it was again revived.

"Oh, please ma'am, we know how the bird-cage came there. That farmer's man who called on the evening of the wedding—he was seen wi' it in his hand as he came up the street; and 'tis thoughted that he put it down while he came in with his message, and then went away forgetting where he had left it."

This was enough to set Elizabeth thinking, and in thinking she seized hold of the idea, at one feminine bound, that the caged bird had been brought by Henchard for her as a wedding gift and token of repentance. He had not expressed to her any regrets or excuses for what he had done in the past; but it was a part of his nature to extenuate nothing, and live on as one of his own worst accusers. She went out, looked at the cage, buried the starved little singer, and from that hour her heart softened towards the self-alienated man.

When her husband came in she told him her solution of the bird-cage mystery; and begged Donald to help her in finding out, as soon as possible, whither Henchard had banished himself, that she might make her peace with him; try to do something to render his life less that of an outcast, and more tolerable to him. Although Farfrae had never so passionately liked Henchard as Henchard had liked him, he had, on the other hand, never so passionately hated in the same direction as his former friend had done; and he was therefore not the least indisposed to assist Elizabeth-Jane in her laudable plan.

But it was by no means easy to set about discovering Henchard. He had apparently sunk into the earth on leaving Mr. and Mrs. Farfrae's door. Elizabeth-Jane remembered what he had once attempted; and trembled.

But though she did not know it Henchard had become a changed man since then—as far, that is, as change of emotional basis can justify such a radical phrase; and she needed not to fear. In a few days Farfrae's enquiries elicited that Henchard had been seen by one who knew him walking steadily along the Melchester highway eastward, at twelve o'clock at night—in other words, retracing his steps on the road by which he had come.

This was enough; and the next morning Farfrae might have been discovered driving his gig out of Casterbridge in that direction, Elizabeth-Jane sitting beside him, wrapped in a thick flat fur—the victorine of the period—her complexion somewhat richer than formerly, and an incipient matronly dignity, which the serene Minerva-eyes of one "whose gestures beamed with mind" made becoming, settling on her face. Having herself arrived at a promising haven from at least the grosser troubles of her life, her object was to place Henchard in some similar quietude before he should sink into that lower stage of existence which was only too possible to him now.

After driving along the highway for a few miles they made further enquiries, and learnt of a road-mender, who had been working thereabouts for weeks, that he had observed such a man at the time mentioned; he had left the Melchester coachroad at Weatherbury by a forking highway which skirted the north of Egdon Heath. Into this road they directed the horse's head, and soon were bowling across that ancient country whose surface never had been stirred to a finger's depth, save by the scratchings of rabbits, since brushed by the feet of the earliest tribes. The tumuli these had left behind, dun and shagged with heather, jutted roundly into the sky from the uplands, as though they were the full breasts of Diana Multimammia supinely extended there.

They searched Egdon, but found no Henchard. Farfrae drove onward, and by the afternoon reached the neighbourhood of some extension of the heath to the north of Anglebury, a prominent feature of which, in the form of a blasted clump of firs on a summit of a hill, they soon passed under. That the road they were following had, up to this point, been Henchard's track on foot they were pretty certain; but the ramifications which now began to reveal themselves in the route made further progress in the right direction a matter of pure guess-work, and Donald strongly advised his wife to give up the search in person, and trust to other means for obtaining news of her stepfather. They were now a score of miles at least from home, but, by resting the horse for a couple of hours at a village they had just traversed, it would be possible to get back to Casterbridge that same day, while to go much further afield would reduce them to the necessity of camping out for the night, "and that will make a hole in a sovereign," said Farfrae. She pondered the position, and agreed with him.

He accordingly drew rein, but before reversing their direction paused a moment and looked vaguely round upon the wide country which the elevated position disclosed. While they looked, a solitary human form came from under the clump of trees, and crossed ahead of them. The person was some labourer; his gait was shambling, his regard fixed in front of him as absolutely as if he wore blinkers; and in his hand he carried a few sticks. Having crossed the road he descended into a ravine, where a cottage revealed itself, which he entered.

"If it were not so far away from Casterbridge I should say that must be poor Whittle. 'Tis just like him," observed Elizabeth-Jane.

"And it may be Whittle, for he's never been to the yard these three weeks, going away without saying any word at all; and I owing him for two days' work, without knowing who to pay it to."

The possibility led them to alight, and at least make an enquiry at the cottage. Farfrae hitched the reins to the gatepost, and they approached what was of humble dwellings surely the humblest. The walls, built of kneaded clay originally faced with a trowel, had been worn by years of rain-washings to a lumpy crumbling surface, channelled and sunken from its plane, its grey rents held together here and there by a leafy strap of ivy which could scarcely find substance enough for the purpose. Leaves from the fence had been blown into the corners of the doorway, and lay there undisturbed. The door was ajar; Farfrae knocked; and he who stood before them was Whittle, as they had conjectured.

His face showed marks of deep sadness, his eyes lighting on them with an unfocused gaze; and he still held in his hand the few sticks he had been out to gather. As soon as he recognised them he started.

"What, Abel Whittle; is it that ye are here?" said Farfrae.

"Ay, yes sir! You see he was kindlike to mother when she wer here below, though 'a was rough to me."

"Who are you talking of?"

"O sir—Mr. Henchet! Didn't ye know it? He's just gone—about half an hour ago, by the sun; for I've got no watch to my name."

"Not—dead?" faltered Elizabeth-Jane.

"Yes, ma'am, he's gone! He was kindlike to mother when she wer here below, sending her the best ship-coal, and hardly any ashes from it at all; and taties, and suchlike that were very needful to her. I seed en go down street on the night of your worshipful's wedding to the lady at yer side, and I thought he looked low and faltering. And I followed en over the road, and he turned and zeed me, and said 'You go back!' But I followed, and he turned again, and said, 'Do you hear, sir? Go back!' But I zeed that he was low, and I followed on still. Then 'a said, 'Whittle, what do ye follow me for when I've told ye to go back all these times?' And I said, 'Because, sir, I see things be bad with 'ee, and ye wer kindlike to mother if ye wer rough to me, and I would fain be kindlike to you.' Then he walked on, and I followed; and he never complained at me no more. We walked on like that all night; and in the blue o' the morning, when 'twas hardly day, I looked ahead o' me, and I zeed that he wambled, and could hardly drag along. By the time we had got past here, but I had seen that this house was empty as I went by, and I got him to come back; and I took down the boards from the windows, and helped him inside. 'What, Whittle,' he said, 'and can ye really be such a poor fond fool as to care for such a wretch as I!' Then I went on further, and some neighbourly woodmen lent me a bed, and a chair, and a few other traps, and we brought 'em here, and made him as comfortable as we could. But he didn't gain strength, for you see, ma'am, he couldn't eat—no, no appetite at all—and he got weaker; and to-day he died. One of the neighbours have gone to get a man to measure him."

"Dear me—is that so!" said Farfrae.

As for Elizabeth, she said nothing.

"Upon the head of his bed he pinned a piece of paper, with some writing upon it," continued Abel Whittle. "But not being a man o' letters, I can't read writing; so I don't know what it is. I can get it and show ye."

They stood in silence while he ran into the cottage; returning in a moment with a crumpled scrap of paper. On it there was penciled as follows:—

MICHAEL HENCHARD'S WILL.

That Elizabeth-Jane Farfrae be not told of my death, or made to grieve on account of me.

   & that I be not bury'd in consecrated ground.

   & that no sexton be asked to toll the bell.

   & that nobody is wished to see my dead body.

   & that no murners walk behind me at my funeral.

   & that no flours be planted on my grave,

   & that no man remember me.

   To this I put my name.

MICHAEL HENCHARD

"What are we to do?" said Donald, when he had handed the paper to her.

She could not answer distinctly. "O Donald!" she cried at last through her tears, "what bitterness lies there! Oh I would not have minded so much if it had not been for that last parting! . . . But there's no altering—so it must be."

What Henchard had written in the anguish of his dying was respected as far as practicable by Elizabeth-Jane, though less from a sense of the sacredness of last words, as such, than from her independent knowledge that the man who wrote them meant what he said. She knew the directions to be a piece of the same stuff that his whole life was made of, and hence were not to be tampered with to give herself a mournful pleasure, or her husband credit for large-heartedness.

All was over at last, even her regrets for having misunderstood him on his last visit, for not having searched him out sooner, though these were deep and sharp for a good while. From this time forward Elizabeth-Jane found herself in a latitude of calm weather, kindly and grateful in itself, and doubly so after the Capharnaum in which some of her preceding years had been spent. As the lively and sparkling emotions of her early married life cohered into an equable serenity, the finer movements of her nature found scope in discovering to the narrow-lived ones around her the secret (as she had once learnt it) of making limited opportunities endurable; which she deemed to consist in the cunning enlargement, by a species of microscopic treatment, of those minute forms of satisfaction that offer themselves to everybody not in positive pain; which, thus handled, have much of the same inspiring effect upon life as wider interests cursorily embraced.

Her teaching had a reflex action upon herself, insomuch that she thought she could perceive no great personal difference between being respected in the nether parts of Casterbridge and glorified at the uppermost end of the social world. Her position was, indeed, to a marked degree one that, in the common phrase, afforded much to be thankful for. That she was not demonstratively thankful was no fault of hers. Her experience had been of a kind to teach her, rightly or wrongly, that the doubtful honour of a brief transit through a sorry world hardly called for effusiveness, even when the path was suddenly irradiated at some half-way point by daybeams rich as hers. But her strong sense that neither she nor any human being deserved less than was given, did not blind her to the fact that there were others receiving less who had deserved much more. And in being forced to class herself among the fortunate she did not cease to wonder at the persistence of the unforeseen, when the one to whom such unbroken tranquility had been accorded in the adult stage was she whose youth had seemed to teach that happiness was but the occasional episode in a general drama of pain.

THE END

TESS OF THE D'URBERVILLES
A PURE WOMAN

" . . . Poor wounded name! My bosom as a bed
Shall lodge thee."—W. SHAKESPEARE.

General Preface to the Novels and Poems

IN ACCEPTING A PROPOSAL FOR A DEFINITIVE EDITION OF THESE PRODUCTIONS IN PROSE and verse I have found an opportunity of classifying the novels under heads that show approximately the author's aim, if not his achievement, in each book of the series at the date of its composition. Sometimes the aim was lower than at other times; sometimes, where the intention was primarily high, force of circumstances (among which the chief were the necessities of magazine publication) compelled a modification, great or slight, of the original plan. Of a few, however, of the longer novels, and of many of the shorter tales, it may be assumed that they stand to-day much as they would have stood if no accidents had obstructed the channel between the writer and the public. That many of them, if any, stand as they would stand if written *now* is not to be supposed.

In the classification of these fictitious chronicles—for which the name of "The Wessex Novels" was adopted, and is still retained—the first group is called "Novels of Character and Environment," and contains those which approach most nearly to uninfluenced works; also one or two which, whatever their quality in some few of their episodes, may claim a verisimilitude in general treatment and detail.

The second group is distinguished as "Romances and Fantasies," a sufficiently descriptive definition. The third class—"Novels of Ingenuity"—show a not infrequent disregard of the probable in the chain of events, and depend for their interest mainly on the incidents themselves. They might also be characterised as "Experiments," and were written for the nonce simply; though despite the artificiality of their fable some of their scenes are not without fidelity to life.

It will not be supposed that these differences are distinctly perceptible in every page of every volume. It was inevitable that blendings and alternations should occur in all. Moreover, as it was not thought desirable in every instance to change the arrangement of the shorter stories to which readers have grown accustomed, certain of these may be found under headings to which the acute judgment might deny appropriateness.

It has sometimes been conceived of novels that evolve their action on a circumscribed scene—as do many (though not all) of these—that they cannot be so inclusive in their exhibition of human nature as novels wherein the scenes cover large extents of country, in which events figure amid towns and cities, even wander over the four quarters of the globe. I am not concerned to argue this point further than to suggest that the conception is an untrue one in respect of the elementary passions. But I would state that the geographical limits of the stage here trodden were not absolutely forced upon the writer by circumstances; he forced them upon himself from judgment. I considered that our magnificent heritage from the Greeks in dramatic literature found sufficient room for a large proportion of its action in an extent of their country not much larger than the half-dozen counties here reunited under the old name of Wessex, that the domestic emotions have throbbed in Wessex nooks with as much intensity as in the palaces of Europe, and that, anyhow, there was quite enough human nature in Wessex for one man's literary purpose. So far was I possessed by this idea that I kept within the frontiers when it would have been easier to overleap them and give more cosmopolitan features to the narrative.

Thus, though the people in most of the novels (and in much of the shorter verse) are dwellers in a province bounded on the north by the Thames, on the south by the English Channel, on the east by a line running from Hayling Island to Windsor Forest, and on the west by the Cornish coast, they were meant to be typically and essentially those of any and every place where

Thought's the slave of life, and life time's fool,

—beings in whose hearts and minds that which is apparently local should be really universal.

But whatever the success of this intention, and the value of these novels as delineations of humanity, they have at least a humble supplementary quality of which I may be justified in reminding the reader, though it is one that was quite unintentional and unforeseen. At the dates represented in the various narrations things were like that in Wessex: the inhabitants lived in certain ways, engaged in certain occupations, kept alive certain customs, just as they are shown doing in these pages. And in particularising such I have often been reminded of Boswell's remarks on the trouble to which he was put and the pilgrimages he was obliged to make to authenticate some detail, though the labour was one which would bring him no praise. Unlike his achievement, however, on which an error would as he says have brought discredit, if these country customs and vocations, obsolete and obsolescent, had been detailed wrongly, nobody would have discovered such errors to the end of Time. Yet I have instituted enquiries to correct tricks of memory, and striven against temptations to exaggerate, in order to preserve for my own satisfaction a fairly true record of a vanishing life.

It is advisable also to state here, in response to enquiries from readers interested in landscape, prehistoric antiquities, and especially old English architecture, that the description of these backgrounds has been done from the real—that is to say, has something real from its basis, however illusively treated. Many features of the first two kinds have been given under their existing names; for instance, the Vale of Blackmoor or Blakemore, Hambledon Hill, Bulbarrow, Nettlecombe Tout, Dogbury Hill, High-Stoy, Bubb-Down Hill, The Devil's Kitchen, Cross-in-Hand, Long-Ash Lane, Benvill Lane, Giant's Hill, Crimmercrock Lane, and Stonehenge. The rivers Froom, or Frome, and Stour, are, of course, well known as such. And the further idea was that large towns and points tending to mark the outline of Wessex—such as Bath, Plymouth, The Start, Portland Bill, Southampton, etc.,—should be named clearly. The scheme was not greatly elaborated, but, whatever its value, the names remain still.

In respect of places described under fictitious or ancient names in the novels—for reasons that seemed good at the time of writing them—and kept up in the poems—discerning people have affirmed in print that they clearly recognise the originals: such as Shaftesbury in "Shaston," Sturminster Newton in "Stourcastle," Dorchester in "Casterbridge," Salisbury Plain in "The Great Plain," Cranborne Chase in "The Chase,"

Beaminster in "Emminster," Bere Regis in "Kingsbere," Woodbury Hill in "Greenhill," Wool Bridge in "Wellbridge," Hartfoot or Harput Lane in "Stagfoot Lane," Hazlebury in "Nuttlebury," Bridport in "Port Bredy," Maiden Newton in " Chalk Newton," a farm near Nettlecombe Tout in "Flintcomb Ash," Sherborne in "Sherton Abbas," Milton Abbey in "Middleton Abbey," Cerne Abbas in "Abbot's Cernel," Evershot in "Evershed," Taunton in "Toneborough," Bournemouth in "Sandbourne," Winchester in "Wintonchester," Oxford in "Christminster," Reading in "Aldbrickham," Newbury in "Kennetbridge," Wantage in "Alfredston," Basingstoke in "Stoke Barehills," and so on. Subject to the qualifications above given, that no detail is guaranteed—that the portraiture of ficti- tiously named towns and villages was only suggested by certain real places, and wantonly wanders from inventorial descriptions of them—I do not contradict these keen hunters for the real; I am satisfied with their statements as at least an indication of their interest in the scenes.

Thus much for the novels. Turning now to the verse—to myself the more individual part of my literary fruitage—I would say that, unlike some of the fiction, nothing interfered with the writer's freedom in respect of its form or content. Several of the poems—indeed many—were produced before novel-writing had been thought of as a pursuit; but few saw the light till all the novels had been published. The limited stage to which the majority of the latter confine their exhibitions has not been adhered to here in the same proportion, the dramatic part especially having a very broad theatre of action. It may thus relieve the cir- cumscribed areas treated in the prose, if such relief be needed. To be sure, one might argue that by surveying Europe from a celestial point of vision—as in *The Dynasts*—that conti- nent becomes virtually a province—a Wessex, an Attica, even a mere garden—and hence is made conform to the principle of the novels, however far it outmeasures their region. But that may be as it will.

The few volumes filled by the verse cover a producing period of some eighteen years first and last, while the seventeen or more volumes of novels represent correspondingly about four-and-twenty years. One is reminded by this disproportion in time and result how much more concise and quintessential expression becomes when given in rhythmic form than when shaped in the language of prose.

One word on what has been called the present writer's philosophy of life, as exhibited more particularly in this metrical section of his compositions. Positive views on the Whence and the Wherefore of things have never been advanced by this pen as a consis- tent philosophy. Nor is it likely, indeed, that imaginative writings extending over more than forty years would exhibit a coherent scientific theory of the universe even if it had been attempted—of that universe concerning which Spencer owns to the "paralysing thought" that possibly there exists no comprehension of it anywhere. But such objectless consistency never has been attempted, and the sentiments in the following pages have been stated truly to be mere impressions of the moment, and not convictions or arguments.

That these impressions have been condemned as "pessimistic"—as if that were a very wicked adjective—shows a curious muddle-mindedness. It must be obvious that there is a higher characteristic of philosophy than pessimism, or than meliorism, or even than the optimism of these critics—which is truth. Existence is either ordered in a certain way, or it is not so ordered, and conjectures which harmonise best with experience are removed above all comparison with other conjectures which do not so harmonise. So that to say one view is worse than other views without proving it erroneous implies the possibility of a false view being better or more expedient than a true view; and no pragmatic proppings can make that *idolum specus* stand on its feet, for it postulates a prescience denied to humanity.

And there is another consideration. Differing natures find their tongue in the presence of differing spectacles. Some natures become vocal at tragedy, some are made vocal by comedy, and it seems to me that to whichever of these aspects of life a writer's instinct for expression the more readily responds, to that he should allow it to respond. That before a contrasting side of things he remains undemonstrative need not be assumed to mean that he remains unperceiving.

It was my hope to add to these volumes of verse as many more as would make a fairly comprehensive cycle of the whole. I had wished that those in dramatic, ballad, and narrative form should include most of the cardinal situations which occur in social and public life, and those in lyric form a round of emotional experiences of some completeness. But

The little done, the undone vast!

The more written the more seems to remain to be written; and the night cometh. I realise that these hopes and plans, except possibly to the extent of a volume or two, must remain unfulfilled.

T. H.
October 1911

EXPLANATORY NOTE TO THE FIRST EDITION

THE MAIN PORTION OF THE FOLLOWING STORY APPEARED—WITH SLIGHT MODIFICA-tions—in the *Graphic* newspaper; other chapters, more especially addressed to adult readers, in the *Fortnightly Review* and the *National Observer*, as episodic sketches. My thanks are tendered to the editors and proprietors of those periodicals for enabling me now to piece the trunk and limbs of the novel together, and print it complete, as originally written two years ago.

I will just add that the story is sent out in all sincerity of purpose, as an attempt to give artistic form to a true sequence of things; and in respect of the book's opinions and senti-ments, I would ask any too genteel reader, who cannot endure to have said what everybody nowadays thinks and feels, to remember a well-worn sentence of St. Jerome's: If an offence come out of the truth, better is it that the offence come than that the truth be concealed.

T. H.
November 1891

Preface to the Fifth and Later Editions

THIS NOVEL BEING ONE WHEREIN THE GREAT CAMPAIGN OF THE HEROINE BEGINS AFTER an event in her experience which has usually been treated as fatal to her part of protagonist, or at least as the virtual ending of her enterprises and hopes, it was quite contrary to avowed conventions that the public should welcome the book, and agree with me in holding that there was something more to be said in fiction than had been said about the shaded side of a well-known catastrophe. But the responsive spirit in which *Tess of the d'Urbervilles* has been received by the readers of England and America, would seem to prove that the plan of laying down a story on the lines of tacit opinion, instead of making it to square with the merely vocal formulae of society, is not altogether a wrong one, even when exemplified in so unequal and partial an achievement as the present. For this responsiveness I cannot refrain from expressing my thanks; and my regret is that, in a world where one so often hungers in vain for friendship, where even not to be wilfully misunderstood is felt as a kindness, I shall never meet in person these appreciative readers, male and female, and shake them by the hand.

I include amongst them the reviewers—by far the majority—who have so generously welcomed the tale. Their words show that they, like the others, have only too largely repaired my defects of narration by their own imaginative intuition.

Nevertheless, though the novel was intended to be neither didactic nor aggressive, but in the scenic parts to be representative simply, and in the contemplative to be oftener charged with impressions than with convictions, there have been objectors both to the matter and to the rendering.

The more austere of these maintain a conscientious difference of opinion concerning, among other things, subjects fit for art, and reveal an inability to associate the idea of the sub-title adjective with any but the artificial and derivative meaning which has resulted to it from the ordinances of civilisation. They ignore the meaning of the word in Nature, together with all aesthetic claims upon it, not to mention the spiritual interpretation afforded by the finest side of their Christianity. Others dissent on grounds which are intrinsically no more than an assertion that the novel embodies the views of life prevalent at the end of the nineteenth century, and not those of an earlier and simpler generation—an assertion which I can only hope may be well founded. Let me repeat that a novel is an impression, not an argument; and there the matter must rest; as one is reminded by a passage which occurs in the letters of Schiller to Goethe on judges of this class: "They are those who seek only their own ideas in a representation, and prize that which should be as higher than what is. The cause of the dispute, therefore, lies in the very first principles, and it would be utterly impossible to come to an understanding with them." And again: "As soon as I observe that anyone, when judging of poetical representations, considers anything more important than the inner Necessity and Truth, I have done with him."

In the introductory words to the first edition I suggested the possible advent of the genteel person who would not be able to endure something or other in these pages. That person duly appeared among the aforesaid objectors. In one case he felt upset that it was not possible for him to read the book through three times, owing to my not having made that critical effort which "alone can prove the salvation of such an one." In another, he objected to such vulgar articles as the Devil's pitchfork, a lodging-house carving-knife, and a shame-bought parasol, appearing in a respectable story. In another place he was a gentleman who turned Christian for half an hour the better to express his grief that a disrespectful phrase about the Immortals should have been used; though the same innate gentility compelled him to excuse the author in words of pity that one cannot be too thankful for: "He does but give us of his best." I can assure this great critic that to exclaim illogically against the gods, singular or plural, is not such an original sin of mine as he seems to imagine. True, it may have some local originality; though if Shakespeare were an authority on history, which per-haps he is not, I could show that the sin was introduced into Wessex as early as the Hep-tarchy itself. Says Glo'ster in *Lear*, otherwise Ina, king of that country:

> *As flies to wanton boys are we to the gods;*
> *They kill us for their sport.*

The remaining two or three manipulators of *Tess* were of the predetermined sort whom most writers and readers would gladly forget; professed literary boxers, who put on their convictions for the occasion; modern "Hammers of Heretics"; sworn Discouragers, ever on the watch to prevent the tentative half-success from becoming the whole success later on; who pervert plain meanings, and grow personal under the name of practising the great historical method. However, they may have causes to advance, privileges to guard, traditions to keep going; some of which a mere tale-teller, who writes down how the things of the world strike him, without any ulterior intentions whatever, has overlooked, and may by pure inadvertence have run foul of when in the least aggressive mood. Perhaps some passing perception, the outcome of a dream hour, would, if generally acted on, cause such an assailant considerable inconvenience with respect to position, interests, family, servant, ox, ass, neighbour, or neighbour's wife. He therefore valiantly hides his personality behind a publisher's shutters, and cries "Shame!" So densely is the world thronged that any shift-ing of positions, even the best warranted advance, galls somebody's kibe. Such shiftings often begin in sentiment, and such sentiment sometimes begins in a novel.

July 1892

The foregoing remarks were written during the early career of this story, when a spir-ited public and private criticism of its points was still fresh to the feelings. The pages are allowed to stand for what they are worth, as something once said; but probably they would not have been written down. Even in the short time which has elapsed since the book was first published, some of the critics who provoked the reply have "gone down into silence," as if to remind one of the infinite unimportance of both their say and mine.

January 1895

The present edition of this novel contains a few pages that have never appeared in any previous edition. When the detached episodes were collected as stated in the preface of 1891, these pages were overlooked, though they were in the original manuscript. They occur in Chapter X.

Respecting the sub-title, to which allusion was made above, I may add that it was appended at the last moment, after reading the final proofs, as being the estimate left in a candid mind of the heroine's character—an estimate that nobody would be likely to dispute. It was disputed more than anything else in the book. *Melius fuerat non scribere*. But there it stands.

The novel was first published complete, in three volumes, in November 1891.

T. H.
March 1912

CONTENTS

PHASE THE FIRST

THE MAIDEN

I

ON AN EVENING IN THE LATTER PART OF MAY A MIDDLE-AGED MAN WAS WALKING homeward from Shaston to the village of Marlott, in the adjoining Vale of Blakemore or Blackmoor. The pair of legs that carried him were rickety, and there was a bias in his gait which inclined him somewhat to the left of a straight line. He occasionally gave a smart nod, as if in confirmation of some opinion, though he was not thinking of anything in particular. An empty egg-basket was slung upon his arm, the nap of his hat was ruffled, a patch being quite worn away at its brim where his thumb came in taking it off. Presently he was met by an elderly parson astride on a grey mare, who, as he rode, hummed a wandering tune.

"Good-night t'ee," said the man with the basket.

"Good-night, Sir John," said the parson.

The pedestrian, after another pace or two, halted, and turned round.

"Now, sir, begging your pardon; we met last market-day on this road about this time, and I said "Good-night," and you made reply *'Good-night, Sir John,'* as now."

"I did," said the parson.

"And once before that—near a month ago."

"I may have."

"Then what might your meaning be in calling me 'Sir John' these different times, when I be plain Jack Durbeyfield, the haggler?"

The parson rode a step or two nearer.

"It was only my whim," he said; and, after a moment's hesitation: "It was on account of a discovery I made some little time ago, whilst I was hunting up pedigrees for the new county history. I am Parson Tringham, the antiquary, of Stagfoot Lane. Don't you really know, Durbeyfield, that you are the lineal representative of the ancient and knightly family of the d'Urbervilles, who derive their descent from Sir Pagan d'Urberville, that renowned knight who came from Normandy with William the Conqueror, as appears by Battle Abbey Roll?"

"Never heard it before, sir!"

"Well it's true. Throw up your chin a moment, so that I may catch the profile of your face better. Yes, that's the d'Urberville nose and chin—a little debased. Your ancestor was one of the twelve knights who assisted the Lord of Estremavilla in Normandy in his conquest of Glamorganshire. Branches of your family held manors over all this part of England; their names appear in the Pipe Rolls in the time of King Stephen. In the reign of King John one of them was rich enough to give a manor to the Knights Hospitallers; and in Edward the Second's time your forefather Brian was summoned to Westminster to attend the great Council there. You declined a little in Oliver Cromwell's time, but to no serious extent, and in Charles the Second's reign you were made Knights of the Royal Oak for your loyalty. Ay, there have been generations of Sir Johns among you, and if knighthood were hereditary, like a baronetcy, as it practically was in old times, when men were knighted from father to son, you would be Sir John now."

"Ye don't say so!"

"In short," concluded the parson, decisively smacking his leg with his switch, "there's hardly such another family in England."

"Daze my eyes, and isn't there?" said Durbeyfield. "And here have I been knocking about, year after year, from pillar to post, as if I was no more than the commonest feller in the parish. . . . And how long hev this news about me been knowed, Pa'son Tringham?"

The clergyman explained that, as far as he was aware, it had quite died out of knowledge, and could hardly be said to be known at all. His own investigations had begun on a day in the preceding spring when, having been engaged in tracing the vicissitudes of the d'Urberville family, he had observed Durbeyfield's name on his waggon, and had thereupon been led to make enquiries about his father and grand-father till he had no doubt on the subject.

"At first I resolved not to disturb you with such a useless piece of information," said he. "However, our impulses are too strong for our judgment sometimes. I thought you might perhaps know something of it all the while."

"Well, I have heard once or twice, 'tis true, that my family had seen better days afore they came to Blackmoor. But I took no notice o't, thinking it to mean that we had once kept two horses where we now keep only one. I've got a wold silver spoon, and a wold graven seal at home, too; but, Lord, what's a spoon and seal? . . . And to think that I and these noble d'Urbervilles were one flesh all the time. 'Twas said that my gr't-grandfer had secrets, and didn't care to talk of where he came from. . . . And where do we raise our smoke, now, parson, if I may make so bold; I mean, where do we d'Urbervilles live?"

"You don't live anywhere. You are extinct—as a county family."

"That's bad."

"Yes—what the mendacious family chronicles call extinct in the male line—that is, gone down—gone under."

"Then where do we lie?"

"At Kingsbere-sub-Greenhill: rows and rows of you in your vaults, with your effigies under Purbeck-marble canopies."

"And where be our family mansions and estates?"

"You haven't any."

"Oh? No lands neither?"

"None; though you once had 'em in abundance, as I said, for your family consisted of numerous branches. In this county there was a seat of yours at Kingsbere, and another at Sherton, and another in Millpond, and another at Lullstead, and another at Wellbridge."

"And shall we ever come into our own again?"

"Ah—that I can't tell!"

"And what had I better do about it, sir?" asked Durbeyfield, after a pause.

"Oh—nothing, nothing; except chasten yourself with the thought of 'how are the mighty fallen.' It is a fact of some interest to the local historian and genealogist, nothing more. There are several families among the cottagers of this county of almost equal lustre. Good-night."

"But you'll turn back and have a quart of beer wi' me on the strength o't, Pa'son Tringham? There's a very pretty brew in tap at The Pure Drop—though, to be sure, not so good as at Rolliver's."

"No, thank you—not this evening, Durbeyfield. You've had enough already." Concluding thus the parson rode on his way, with doubts as to his discretion in retailing this curious bit of lore.

When he was gone Durbeyfield walked a few steps in a profound reverie, and then sat down upon the grassy bank by the roadside, depositing his basket before him. In a few minutes a youth appeared in the distance, walking in the same direction as that which had been pursued by Durbeyfield. The latter, on seeing him, held up his hand, and the lad quickened his pace and came near.

"Boy, take up that basket! I want 'ee to go on an errand for me."

The lathlike stripling frowned. "Who be you, then, John Durbeyfield, to order me about and call me 'boy?' You know my name as well as I know yours!"

"Do you, do you? That's the secret—that's the secret! Now obey my orders, and take the message I'm going to charge 'ee wi'. . . . Well, Fred, I don't mind telling you that the secret is that I'm one of a noble race—it has been just found out by me this present afternoon, P.M." And as he made the announcement, Durbeyfield, declining from his sitting position, luxuriously stretched himself out upon the bank among the daisies.

The lad stood before Durbeyfield, and contemplated his length from crown to toe.

"Sir John d'Urberville—that's who I am," continued the prostrate man. "That is if knights were baronets—which they be. 'Tis recorded in history all about me. Dost know of such a place, lad, as Kingsbere-sub-Greenhill?"

"Ees. I've been there to Greenhill Fair."

"Well, under the church of that city there lie—"

" 'Tisn't a city, the place I mean; leastwise 'twaddn' when I was there—'twas a little one-eyed, blinking sort o'place."

"Never you mind the place, boy, that's not the question before us. Under the church of that there parish lie my ancestors—hundreds of 'em—in coats of mail and jewels, in gr't lead coffins weighing tons and tons. There's not a man in the county o' South-Wessex that's got grander and nobler skillentons in his family than I."

"Oh?"

"Now take up that basket, and goo on to Marlott, and when you've come to The Pure Drop Inn, tell 'em to send a horse and carriage to me immed'ately, to carry me hwome. And in the bottom o' the carriage they be to put a noggin o' rum in a small bottle, and chalk it up to my account. And when you've done that goo on to my house with the basket, and tell my wife to put away that washing, because she needn't finish it, and wait till I come hwome, as I've news to tell her."

As the lad stood in a dubious attitude, Durbeyfield put his hand in his pocket, and produced a shilling, one of the chronically few that he possessed.

"Here's for your labour, lad."

This made a difference in the young man's estimate of the position.

"Yes, Sir John. Thank 'ee. Anything else I can do for 'ee, Sir John?"

"Tell 'em at hwome that I should like for supper—well, lamb's fry if they can get it; and if they can't, black-pot; and if they can't get that, well, chitterlings will do."

"Yes, Sir John."

The boy took up the basket, and as he set out the notes of a brass band were heard from the direction of the village.

"What's that?" said Durbeyfield. "Not on account o' I?"

" 'Tis the women's club-walking, Sir John. Why, your da'ter is one o' the members."

"To be sure—I'd quite forgot it in my thoughts of greater things! Well, vamp on to Marlott, will ye, and order that carriage, and maybe I'll drive round and inspect the club."

The lad departed, and Durbeyfield lay waiting on the grass and daisies in the evening sun. Not a soul passed that way for a long while, and the faint notes of the band were the only human sounds audible within the rim of blue hills.

II

THE VILLAGE OF MARLOTT LAY AMID THE NORTH-EASTERN UNDULATIONS OF THE BEAU-tiful Vale of Blakemore or Blackmoor aforesaid, an engirdled and secluded region, for the most part untrodden as yet by tourist or landscape-painter, though within a four hours' journey from London.

It is a vale whose acquaintance is best made by viewing it from the summits of the hills that surround it—except perhaps during the droughts of summer. An unguided ramble into its recesses in bad weather is apt to engender dissatisfaction with its narrow, tortuous, and miry ways.

This fertile and sheltered tract of country, in which the fields are never brown and the springs never dry, is bounded on the south by the bold chalk ridge that embraces the prominences of Hambledon Hill, Bulbarrow, Nettlecombe-Tout, Dogbury, High Stoy, and Bubb Down. The traveller from the coast, who, after plodding northward for a score of miles over calcareous downs and corn-lands, suddenly reaches the verge of one of these escarpments, is surprised and delighted to behold, extended like a map beneath him, a country differing absolutely from that which he has passed through. Behind him the hills are open, the sun blazes down upon fields so large as to give an unenclosed character to the landscape, the lanes are white, the hedges low and plashed, the atmosphere colourless. Here, in the valley, the world seems to be constructed upon a smaller and more delicate scale; the fields are mere paddocks, so reduced that from this height their hedgerows ap-pear a network of dark green threads overspreading the paler green of the grass. The at-mosphere beneath is languorous, and is so tinged with azure that what artists call the middle distance partakes also of that hue, while the horizon beyond is of the deepest ul-tramarine. Arable lands are few and limited; with but slight exceptions the prospect is a broad rich mass of grass and trees, mantling minor hills and dales within the major. Such is the Vale of Blackmoor.

The district is of historic, no less than of topographical interest. The Vale was known in former times as the Forest of White Hart, from a curious legend of King Henry III's reign, in which the killing by a certain Thomas de la Lynd of a beautiful white hart which the king had run down and spared, was made the occasion of a heavy fine. In those days, and till comparatively recent times, the country was densely wooded. Even now, traces of its earlier condition are to be found in the old oak copses and irreg-ular belts of timber that yet survive upon its slopes, and the hollow-trunked trees that shade so many of its pastures.

The forests have departed, but some old customs of their shades remain. Many, however, linger only in a metamorphosed or disguised form. The May-Day dance, for instance, was to be discerned on the afternoon under notice, in the guise of the club revel, or "club-walking," as it was there called.

It was an interesting event to the younger inhabitants of Marlott, though its real interest was not observed by the participators in the ceremony. Its singularity lay less in the retention of a custom of walking in procession and dancing on each anniversary than in the members being solely women. In men's clubs such celebrations were, though expiring, less uncommon; but either the natural shyness of the softer sex, or a sarcastic attitude on the part of male relatives, had denuded such women's clubs as remained (if any other did) of this their glory and consummation. The club of Marlott alone lived to uphold the local Cerealia. It had walked for hundreds of years, if not as benefit-club, as votive sisterhood of some sort; and it walked still.

The banded ones were all dressed in white gowns—a gay survival from Old Style days, when cheerfulness and May-time were synonyms—days before the habit of taking long views had reduced emotions to a monotonous average. Their first exhibition of themselves was in a processional march of two and two round the parish. Ideal and real clashed slightly as the sun lit up their figures against the green hedges and creeper-laced house-fronts; for, though the whole troop wore white garments, no two whites were alike among them. Some approached pure blanching; some had a bluish pallor; some worn by the older characters (which had possibly lain by folded for many a year) inclined to a cadaverous tint, and to a Georgian style.

In addition to the distinction of a white frock, every woman and girl carried in her right hand a peeled willow wand, and in her left a bunch of white flowers. The peeling of the former, and the selection of the latter, had been an operation of personal care.

There were a few middle-aged and even elderly women in the train, their silver-wiry hair and wrinkled faces, scourged by time and trouble, having almost a grotesque, certainly a pathetic, appearance in such a jaunty situation. In a true view, perhaps, there was more to be gathered and told of each anxious and experienced one, to whom the years were drawing nigh when she should say, "I have no pleasure in them," than of her juvenile comrades. But let the elder be passed over here for those under whose bodices the life throbbed quick and warm.

The young girls formed, indeed, the majority of the band, and their heads of luxuriant hair reflected in the sunshine every tone of gold, and black, and brown. Some had beautiful eyes, others a beautiful nose, others a beautiful mouth and figure: few, if any, had all. A difficulty of arranging their lips in this crude exposure to public scrutiny, an inability to balance their heads, and to dissociate self-consciousness from their features, was apparent in them, and showed that they were genuine country girls, unaccustomed to many eyes.

And as each and all of them were warmed without by the sun, so each had a private little sun for her soul to bask in; some dream, some affection, some hobby, at least some remote and distant hope which, though perhaps starving to nothing, still lived on, as hopes will. They were all cheerful, and many of them merry.

They came round by The Pure Drop Inn, and were turning out of the high-road to pass through a wicket gate into the meadows, when one of the women said—

"The Lord-a-Lord! Why, Tess Durbeyfield, if there isn't thy father riding hwome in a carriage!"

A young member of the band turned her head at the exclamation. She was a fine and handsome girl—not handsomer than some others, possibly—but her mobile peony mouth and large innocent eyes added eloquence to colour and shape. She wore a red ribbon in her hair, and was the only one of the white company who could boast of such a pronounced adornment. As she looked round Durbeyfield was seen moving along the road in a chaise belonging to The Pure Drop, driven by a frizzle-headed brawny damsel with her gown-sleeves rolled above her elbows. This was the cheerful servant of that establishment, who, in her part of factotum, turned groom and ostler at times. Durbeyfield, leaning back, and with his eyes closed luxuriously, was waving his hand above his head, and singing in a slow recitative—

"I've-got-a-gr't-family-vault-at-Kingsbere—and knighted-forefathers-in-lead-coffins-there!"

The clubbists tittered, except the girl called Tess—in whom a slow heat seemed to rise at the sense that her father was making himself foolish in their eyes.

"He's tired, that's all," she said hastily, "and he has got a lift home, because our own horse has to rest to-day."

"Bless thy simplicity, Tess," said her companions. "He's got his market-nitch. Haw-haw!"

"Look here; I won't walk another inch with you, if you say any jokes about him!" Tess cried, and the colour upon her cheeks spread over her face and neck. In a moment her eyes grew moist, and her glance drooped to the ground. Perceiving that they had really pained her they said no more, and order again prevailed. Tess's pride would not allow her to turn her head again, to learn what her father's meaning was, if he had any; and thus she moved on with the whole body to the enclosure where there was to be dancing on the green. By the time the spot was reached she had recovered her equanimity, and tapped her neighbour with her wand and talked as usual.

Tess Durbeyfield at this time of her life was a mere vessel of emotion untinctured by experience. The dialect was on her tongue to some extent, despite the village school: the characteristic intonation of that dialect for this district being the voicing approximately rendered by the syllable UR, probably as rich an utterance as any to be found in human speech. The pouted-up deep red mouth to which this syllable was native had hardly as yet settled into its definite shape, and her lower lip had a way of thrusting the middle of her top one upward, when they closed together after a word.

Phases of her childhood lurked in her aspect still. As she walked along to-day, for all her bouncing handsome womanliness, you could sometimes see her twelfth year in her cheeks, or her ninth sparkling from her eyes; and even her fifth would flit over the curves of her mouth now and then.

Yet few knew, and still fewer considered this. A small minority, mainly strangers, would look long at her in casually passing by, and grow momentarily fascinated by her freshness, and wonder if they would ever see her again: but to almost everybody she was a fine and picturesque country girl, and no more.

Nothing was seen or heard further of Durbeyfield in his triumphal chariot under the conduct of the ostleress, and the club having entered the allotted space, dancing began. As there were no men in the company the girls danced at first with each other, but when the hour for the close of labour drew on, the masculine inhabitants of the village, together with other idlers and pedestrians, gathered round the spot, and appeared inclined to negotiate for a partner.

Among these on-lookers were three young men of a superior class, carrying small knapsacks strapped to their shoulders, and stout sticks in their hands. Their general likeness to each other, and their consecutive ages, would almost have suggested that they might be, what in fact they were, brothers. The eldest wore the white tie, high waistcoat, and thin-brimmed hat of the regulation curate; the second was the normal undergraduate; the appearance of the third and youngest would hardly have been sufficient to characterise him; there was an uncribbed, uncabined aspect in his eyes and attire, implying that he had hardly as yet found the entrance to his professional groove. That he was a desultory tentative student of something and everything might only have been predicted of him.

These three brethren told casual acquaintance that they were spending their Whitsun holidays in a walking tour through the Vale of Blackmoor, their course being southwesterly from the town of Shaston on the north-east.

They leant over the gate by the highway, and enquired as to the meaning of the dance and the white-frocked maids. The two elder of the brothers were plainly not intending to linger more than a moment, but the spectacle of a bevy of girls dancing without male partners seemed to amuse the third, and make him in no hurry to move on. He unstrapped his knapsack, put it, with his stick, on the hedge-bank, and opened the gate.

"What are you going to do, Angel?" asked the eldest.

"I am inclined to go and have a fling with them. Why not all of us—just for a minute or two—it will not detain us long?"

"No—no; nonsense!" said the first. "Dancing in public with a troop of country hoydens—suppose we should be seen! Come along, or it will be dark before we get to Stourcastle, and there's no place we can sleep at nearer than that; besides, we must get through another chapter of *A Counterblast to Agnosticism* before we turn in, now I have taken the trouble to bring the book."

"All right—I'll overtake you and Cuthbert in five minutes; don't stop; I give my word that I will, Felix."

The two elder reluctantly left him and walked on, taking their brother's knapsack to relieve him in following, and the youngest entered the field.

"This is a thousand pities," he said gallantly, to two or three of the girls nearest him, as soon as there was a pause in the dance. "Where are your partners, my dears?"

"They've not left off work yet," answered one of the boldest. "They'll be here by and by. Till then, will you be one, sir?"

"Certainly. But what's one among so many!"

"Better than none. 'Tis melancholy work facing and footing it to one of your own sort, and no clipsing and colling at all. Now, pick and choose."

" 'Ssh—don't be so for'ard!" said a shyer girl.

The young man, thus invited, glanced them over, and attempted some discrimination; but, as the group were all so new to him, he could not very well exercise it. He took almost the first that came to hand, which was not the speaker, as she had expected; nor did it happen to be Tess Durbeyfield. Pedigree, ancestral skeletons, monumental record, the d'Urberville lineaments, did not help Tess in her life's battle as yet, even to the extent of attracting to her a dancing-partner over the heads of the commonest peasantry. So much for Norman blood unaided by Victorian lucre.

The name of the eclipsing girl, whatever it was, has not been handed down; but she was envied by all as the first who enjoyed the luxury of a masculine partner that evening. Yet such was the force of example that the village young men, who had not hastened to enter the gate while no intruder was in the way, now dropped in quickly, and soon the couples became leavened with rustic youth to a marked extent, till at length the plainest woman in the club was no longer compelled to foot it on the masculine side of the figure.

The church-clock struck, when suddenly the student said that he must leave—he had been forgetting himself—he had to join his companions. As he fell out of the dance his eyes lighted on Tess Durbeyfield, whose own large orbs wore, to tell the truth, the faintest aspect of reproach that he had not chosen her. He, too, was sorry then that, owing to her backwardness, he had not observed her; and with that in his mind he left the pasture.

On account of his long delay he started in a flying-run down the lane westward, and had soon passed the hollow and mounted the next rise. He had not yet overtaken his brothers, but he paused to get breath, and looked back. He could see the white figures of the girls in the green enclosure whirling about as they had whirled when he was among them. They seemed to have quite forgotten him already.

All of them, except, perhaps, one. This white shape stood apart by the hedge alone. From her position he knew it to be the pretty maiden with whom he had not danced. Trifling as the matter was, he yet instinctively felt that she was hurt by his oversight. He wished that he had asked her; he wished that he had enquired her name. She was so modest, so expressive, she had looked so soft in her thin white gown that he felt he had acted stupidly.

However, it could not be helped, and turning, and bending himself to a rapid walk, he dismissed the subject from his mind.

III

AS FOR TESS DURBEYFIELD, SHE DID NOT SO EASILY DISLODGE THE INCIDENT FROM HER consideration. She had no spirit to dance again for a long time, though she might have had plenty of partners; but, ah! they did not speak so nicely as the strange young man had done. It was not till the rays of the sun had absorbed the young stranger's retreating figure on the hill that she shook off her temporary sadness and answered her would-be partner in the affirmative.

She remained with her comrades till dusk, and participated with a certain zest in the dancing; though, being heart-whole as yet, she enjoyed treading a measure purely for its own sake; little divining when she saw "the soft torments, the bitter sweets, the pleasing pains, and the agreeable distresses" of those girls who had been wooed and won, what she herself was capable of in that kind. The struggles and wrangles of the lads for her hand in a jig were an amusement to her—no more; and when they became fierce she rebuked them.

She might have stayed even later, but the incident of her father's odd appearance and manner returned upon the girl's mind to make her anxious, and wondering what had become of him she dropped away from the dancers and bent her steps towards the end of the village at which the parental cottage lay.

While yet many score yards off, other rhythmic sounds than those she had quitted became audible to her; sounds that she knew well—so well. They were a regular series of thumpings from the interior of the house, occasioned by the violent rocking of a cradle upon a stone floor, to which movement a feminine voice kept time by singing, in a vigorous gallopade, the favourite ditty of "The Spotted Cow"—

> *I saw her lie do'—own in yon'—der green gro'—ove;*
> *Come, love!' and I'll tell' you where!'*

The cradle-rocking and the song would cease simultaneously for a moment, and an explanation at highest vocal pitch would take the place of the melody.

"God bless thy diment eyes! And thy waxen cheeks! And thy cherry mouth! And thy Cubit's thighs! And every bit o' thy blessed body!"

After this invocation the rocking and the singing would recommence, and the "Spotted Cow" proceed as before. So matters stood when Tess opened the door, and paused upon the mat within it surveying the scene.

The interior, in spite of the melody, struck upon the girl's senses with an unspeakable dreariness. From the holiday gaieties of the field—the white gowns, the nosegays, the willow-wands, the whirling movements on the green, the flash of gentle sentiment towards the stranger—to the yellow melancholy of this one-candled spectacle, what a step! Besides the jar of contrast there came to her a chill self-reproach that she had not returned sooner, to help her mother in these domesticities, instead of indulging herself out-of-doors.

There stood her mother amid the group of children, as Tess had left her, hanging over the Monday washing-tub, which had now, as always, lingered on to the end of the week. Out of that tub had come the day before—Tess felt it with a dreadful sting of remorse—the very white frock upon her back which she had so carelessly greened about the skirt on the damping grass—which had been wrung up and ironed by her mother's own hands.

As usual, Mrs. Durbeyfield was balanced on one foot beside the tub, the other being engaged in the aforesaid business of rocking her youngest child. The cradle-rockers had done hard duty for so many years, under the weight of so many children, on that flagstone floor, that they were worn nearly flat, in consequence of which a huge jerk accompanied each swing of the cot, flinging the baby from side to side like a weaver's shuttle, as Mrs. Durbeyfield, excited by her song, trod the rocker with all the spring that was left in her after a long day's seething in the suds.

Nick-knock, nick-knock, went the cradle; the candle-flame stretched itself tall, and began jigging up and down; the water dribbled from the matron's elbows, and the song galloped on to the end of the verse, Mrs. Durbeyfield regarding her daughter the while. Even now, when burdened with a young family, Joan Durbeyfield was a passionate lover of tune. No ditty floated into Blackmoor Vale from the outer world but Tess's mother caught up its notation in a week.

There still faintly beamed from the woman's features something of the freshness, and even the prettiness, of her youth; rendering it probable that the personal charms which Tess could boast of were in main part her mother's gift, and therefore unknightly, unhistorical.

"I'll rock the cradle for 'ee, mother," said the daughter gently. "Or I'll take off my best frock and help you wring up? I thought you had finished long ago."

Her mother bore Tess no ill-will for leaving the house-work to her single-handed efforts for so long; indeed, Joan seldom upbraided her thereon at any time, feeling but slightly the lack of Tess's assistance whilst her instinctive plan for relieving herself of her labours lay in postponing them. To-night, however, she was even in a blither mood than usual. There was a dreaminess, a preoccupation, an exaltation, in the maternal look which the girl could not understand.

"Well, I'm glad you've come," her mother said, as soon as the last note had passed out of her. "I want to go and fetch your father; but what's more 'n that, I want to tell 'ee what have happened. Y'll be fess enough, my poppet, when th'st know!" (Mrs. Durbeyfield habitually spoke the dialect; her daughter, who had passed the Sixth Standard in the National School under a London-trained mistress, spoke two languages: the dialect at home, more or less; ordinary English abroad and to persons of quality.)

"Since I've been away?" Tess asked.

"Ay!"

"Had it anything to do with father's making such a mommet of himself in thik carriage this afternoon? Why did 'er? I felt inclined to sink into the ground with shame!"

"That wer all a part of the larry! We've been found to be the greatest gentlefolk in the whole county—reaching all back long before Oliver Grumble's time—to the days of the Pagan Turks—with monuments, and vaults, and crests, and 'scutcheons, and the Lord knows what all. In Saint Charles's days we was made Knights o' the Royal Oak, our real name being d'Urberville! . . . Don't that make your bosom plim? 'Twas on this account that your father rode home in the vlee; not because he'd been drinking, as people supposed."

"I'm glad of that. Will it do us any good, mother?"

"O yes! 'Tis thoughted that great things may come o't. No doubt a mampus of volk of our own rank will be down here in their carriages as soon as 'tis known. Your father learnt it on his way hwome from Shaston, and he has been telling me the whole pedigree of the matter."

"Where is father now?" asked Tess suddenly.

Her mother gave irrelevant information by way of answer: "He called to see the doctor to-day in Shaston. It is not consumption at all, it seems. It is fat round his heart, 'a says. There, it is like this." Joan Durbeyfield, as she spoke, curved a sodden thumb and forefinger to the shape of the letter C, and used the other forefinger as a pointer. " 'At the present moment,' he says to your father, 'your heart is enclosed all round there, and all round there; this space is still open,' 'a says. 'As soon as it do meet, so,' "—Mrs. Durbeyfield closed her fingers into a circle complete—"off you will go like a shadder, Mr. Durbeyfield,' 'a says. 'You mid last ten years; you mid go off in ten months, or ten days.' "

Tess looked alarmed. Her father possibly to go behind the eternal cloud so soon, notwithstanding this sudden greatness!

"But where *is* father?" she asked again.

Her mother put on a deprecating look. "Now don't you be bursting out angry! The poor man—he felt so rafted after his uplifting by the pa'son's news—that he went up to Rolliver's half an hour ago. He do want to get up his strength for his journey to-morrow with that load of beehives, which must be delivered, family or no. He'll have to start shortly after twelve to-night, as the distance is so long."

"Get up his strength!" said Tess impetuously, the tears welling to her eyes. "O my God! Go to a public-house to get up his strength! And you as well agreed as he, mother!"

Her rebuke and her mood seemed to fill the whole room, and to impart a cowed look to the furniture, and candle, and children playing about, and to her mother's face.

"No," said the latter touchily, "I be not agreed. I have been waiting for 'ee to bide and keep house while I go fetch him."

"I'll go."

"O no, Tess. You see, it would be no use."

Tess did not expostulate. She knew what her mother's objection meant. Mrs. Durbeyfield's jacket and bonnet were already hanging slily upon a chair by her side, in readiness for this contemplated jaunt, the reason for which the matron deplored more than its necessity.

"And take the *Compleat Fortune-Teller* to the outhouse," Joan continued, rapidly wiping her hands, and donning the garments.

The *Compleat Fortune-Teller* was an old thick volume, which lay on a table at her elbow, so worn by pocketing that the margins had reached the edge of the type. Tess took it up, and her mother started.

This going to hunt up her shiftless husband at the inn was one of Mrs. Durbeyfield's still extant enjoyments in the muck and muddle of rearing children. To discover him at Rolliver's, to sit there for an hour or two by his side and dismiss all thought and care of the children during the interval, made her happy. A sort of halo, an occidental glow, came over life then. Troubles and other realities took on themselves a metaphysical impalpability, sinking to mere mental phenomena for serene contemplation, and no longer stood as pressing concretions which chafed body and soul. The youngsters, not immediately within sight, seemed rather bright and desirable appurtenances than otherwise; the incidents of daily life were not without humorousness and jollity in their aspect there. She felt a little as she had used to feel when she sat by her now wedded husband in the same spot during his wooing, shutting her eyes to his defects of character, and regarding him only in his ideal presentation as lover.

Tess, being left alone with the younger children, went first to the outhouse with the fortune-telling book, and stuffed it into the thatch. A curious fetichistic fear of this grimy volume on the part of her mother prevented her ever allowing it to stay in the house all night, and hither it was brought back whenever it had been consulted. Between the mother, with her fast-perishing lumber of superstitions, folk-lore, dialect, and orally transmitted ballads, and the daughter, with her trained National teachings and Standard knowledge under an infinitely Revised Code, there was a gap of two hundred years as ordinarily understood. When they were together the Jacobean and the Victorian ages were juxtaposed.

Returning along the garden path Tess mused on what the mother could have wished to ascertain from the book on this particular day. She guessed the recent ancestral discovery to bear upon it, but did not divine that it solely concerned herself. Dismissing this, however, she busied herself with sprinkling the linen dried during the daytime, in company with her nine-year-old brother Abraham, and her sister Eliza-Louisa of twelve and a half, called " 'Liza-Lu," the youngest ones being put to bed. There was an interval of four years and more between Tess and the next of the family, the two who had filled the gap having died in their infancy, and this lent her a deputy-maternal attitude when she was alone with her juniors. Next in juvenility to Abraham came two more girls, Hope and Modesty; then a boy of three, and then the baby, who had just completed his first year.

All these young souls were passengers in the Durbeyfield ship—entirely dependent on the judgment of the two Durbeyfield adults for their pleasures, their necessities, their health, even their existence. If the heads of the Durbeyfield household chose to sail into difficulty, disaster, starvation, disease, degradation, death, thither were these half-dozen little captives under hatches compelled to sail with them—six helpless creatures, who had never been asked if they wished for life on any terms, much less if they wished for it on such hard conditions as were involved in being of the shiftless house of Durbeyfield. Some people would like to know whence the poet whose philosophy is in these days deemed as profound and trustworthy as his song is breezy and pure, gets his authority for speaking of "Nature's holy plan."

It grew later, and neither father nor mother reappeared. Tess looked out of the door, and took a mental journey through Marlott. The village was shutting its eyes. Candles and lamps were being put out everywhere: she could inwardly behold the extinguisher and the extended hand.

Her mother's fetching simply meant one more to fetch. Tess began to perceive that a man in indifferent health, who proposed to start on a journey before one in the morning, ought not to be at an inn at this late hour celebrating his ancient blood.

"Abraham," she said to her little brother, "do you put on your hat—you bain't afraid?—and go up to Rolliver's, and see what has gone wi' father and mother."

The boy jumped promptly from his seat, and opened the door, and the night swallowed him up. Half an hour passed yet again; neither man, woman, nor child returned. Abraham, like his parents, seemed to have been limed and caught by the ensnaring inn.

"I must go myself," she said.

'Liza-Lu then went to bed, and Tess, locking them all in, started on her way up the dark and crooked lane or street not made for hasty progress; a street laid out before inches of land had value, and when one-handed clocks sufficiently subdivided the day.

IV

ROLLIVER'S INN, THE SINGLE ALE-HOUSE AT THIS END OF THE LONG AND BROKEN VILlage, could only boast of an off-licence; hence, as nobody could legally drink on the premises, the amount of overt accommodation for consumers was strictly limited to a little board about six inches wide and two yards long, fixed to the garden palings by pieces of wire, so as to form a ledge. On this board thirsty strangers deposited their cups as they stood in the road and drank, and threw the dregs on the dusty ground to the pattern of Polynesia, and wished they could have a restful seat inside.

Thus the strangers. But there were also local customers who felt the same wish; and where there's a will there's a way.

In a large bedroom upstairs, the window of which was thickly curtained with a great woollen shawl lately discarded by the landlady Mrs. Rolliver, were gathered on this evening nearly a dozen persons, all seeking beatitude; all old inhabitants of the nearer end of Marlott, and frequenters of this retreat. Not only did the distance to the The Pure Drop, the fully-licensed tavern at the further part of the dispersed village, render its accommodation practically unavailable for dwellers at this end; but the far more serious question, the quality of the liquor, confirmed the prevalent opinion that it was better to drink with Rolliver in a corner of the housetop than with the other landlord in a wide house.

A gaunt four-post bedstead which stood in the room afforded sitting-space for several persons gathered round three of its sides; a couple more men had elevated themselves on a chest of drawers; another rested on the oak-carved "cwoffer"; two on the wash-stand; another on the stool; and thus all were, somehow, seated at their ease. The stage of mental comfort to which they had arrived at this hour was one wherein their souls expanded beyond their skins, and spread their personalities warmly through the room. In this process the chamber and its furniture grew more and more dignified and luxurious; the shawl hanging at the window took upon itself the richness of tapestry; the brass handles of the chest of drawers were as golden knockers; and the carved bed-posts seemed to have some kinship with the magnificent pillars of Solomon's temple.

Mrs. Durbeyfield, having quickly walked hitherward after parting from Tess, opened the front door, crossed the downstairs room, which was in deep gloom, and then unfastened the stair-door like one whose fingers knew the tricks of the latches well. Her ascent of the crooked staircase was a slower process, and her face, as it rose into the light above the last stair, encountered the gaze of all the party assembled in the bedroom.

"—Being a few private friends I've asked in to keep up club-walking at my own expense," the landlady exclaimed at the sound of footsteps, as glibly as a child repeating the Catechism, while she peered over the stairs. "Oh, 'tis you, Mrs. Durbeyfield—Lard—how you frightened me!—I thought it might be some gaffer sent by Gover'ment."

Mrs. Durbeyfield was welcomed with glances and nods by the remainder of the conclave, and turned to where her husband sat. He was humming absently to himself, in a low tone: "I be as good as some folks here and there! I've got a great family vault at Kingsbere-sub-Greenhill, and finer skillentons than any man in Wessex!"

"I've something to tell 'ee that's come into my head about that—a grand projick!" whispered his cheerful wife. "Here, John, don't 'ee see me?" She nudged him, while he, looking through her as through a window-pane, went on with his recitative.

"Hush! Don't 'ee sing so loud, my good man," said the landlady; "in case any member of the Gover'ment should be passing, and take away my licends."

"He's told 'ee what's happened to us, I suppose?" asked Mrs. Durbeyfield.

"Yes—in a way. D'ye think there's any money hanging by it?"

"Ah, that's the secret," said Joan Durbeyfield sagely. "However, 'tis well to be kin to a coach, even if you don't ride in 'en." She dropped her public voice, and continued in a low tone to her husband: "I've been thinking since you brought the news that there's a great rich lady out by Trantridge, on the edge o' The Chase, of the name of d'Urberville."

"Hey—what's that?" said Sir John.

She repeated the information. "That lady must be our relation," she said. "And my projick is to send Tess to claim kin."

"There *is* a lady of the name, now you mention it," said Durbeyfield. "Pa'son Tringham didn't think of that. But she's nothing beside we—a junior branch of us, no doubt, hailing long since King Norman's day."

While this question was being discussed neither of the pair noticed, in their preoccupation, that little Abraham had crept into the room, and was awaiting an opportunity of asking them to return.

"She is rich, and she'd be sure to take notice o' the maid," continued Mrs. Durbeyfield; "and 'twill be a very good thing. I don't see why two branches o' one family should not be on visiting terms."

"Yes; and we'll all claim kin!" said Abraham brightly from under the bedstead. "And we'll all go and see her when Tess has gone to live with her; and we'll ride in her coach and wear black clothes!"

"How do you come here, child? What nonsense be ye talking! Go away, and play on the stairs till father and mother be ready! . . . Well, Tess ought to go to this other member of our family. She'd be sure to win the lady—Tess would; and likely enough 'twould lead to some noble gentleman marrying her. In short, I know it."

"How?"

"I tried her fate in the *Fortune-Teller,* and it brought out that very thing! . . . You should ha' seen how pretty she looked to-day; her skin is as sumple as a duchess's."

"What says the maid herself to going?"

"I've not asked her. She don't know there is any such lady-relation yet. But it would certainly put her in the way of a grand marriage, and she won't say nay to going."

"Tess is queer."

"But she's tractable at bottom. Leave her to me."

Though this conversation had been private, sufficient of its import reached the understandings of those around to suggest to them that the Durbeyfields had weightier concerns to talk of now than common folks had, and that Tess, their pretty eldest daughter, had fine prospects in store.

"Tess is a fine figure o' fun, as I said to myself to-day when I zeed her vamping round parish with the rest," observed one of the elderly boozers in an undertone. "But Joan Durbeyfield must mind that she don't get green malt in floor." It was a local phrase which had a peculiar meaning, and there was no reply.

The conversation became inclusive, and presently other footsteps were heard crossing the room below.

"—Being a few private friends asked in to-night to keep up club-walking at my own expense." The landlady had rapidly reused the formula she kept on hand for intruders before she recognised that the new-comer was Tess.

Even to her mother's gaze the girl's young features looked sadly out of place amid the alcoholic vapours which floated here as no unsuitable medium for wrinkled middle-age; and hardly was a reproachful flash from Tess's dark eyes needed to make her father and mother rise from their seats, hastily finish their ale, and descend the stairs behind her, Mrs. Rolliver's caution following their footsteps.

"No noise, please, if ye'll be so good, my dears; or I mid lose my licends, and be summons'd, and I don't know what all! 'Night t'ye!"

They went home together, Tess holding one arm of her father, and Mrs. Durbeyfield the other. He had, in truth, drunk very little—not a fourth of the quantity which a systematic tippler could carry to church on a Sunday afternoon without a hitch in his eastings or genuflections; but the weakness of Sir John's constitution made mountains of his petty sins in this kind. On reaching the fresh air he was sufficiently unsteady to incline the row of three at one moment as if they were marching to London, and at another as if they were marching to Bath—which produced a comical effect, frequent enough in families on nocturnal homegoings; and, like most comical effects, not quite so comic after all. The two women valiantly disguised these forced excursions and countermarches as well as they could from Durbeyfield their cause, and from Abraham, and from themselves; and so they approached by degrees their own door, the head of the family bursting suddenly into his former refrain as he drew near, as if to fortify his soul at sight of the smallness of his present residence—

"I've got a fam—ily vault at Kingsbere!"

"Hush—don't be so silly, Jacky," said his wife. "Yours is not the only family that was of 'count in wold days. Look at the Anktells, and Horseys, and the Tringhams themselves—gone to seed a'most as much as you—though you was bigger folks than they, that's true. Thank God, I was never of no family, and have nothing to be ashamed of in that way!"

"Don't you be so sure o' that. From you nater 'tis my belief you've disgraced yourselves more than any o' us, and was kings and queens outright at one time."

Tess turned the subject by saying what was far more prominent in her own mind at the moment than thoughts of her ancestry—

"I am afraid father won't be able to take the journey with the beehives to-morrow so early."

"I? I shall be all right in an hour or two," said Durbeyfield.

It was eleven o'clock before the family were all in bed, and two o'clock next morning was the latest hour for starting with the beehives if they were to be delivered to the retailers in Casterbridge before the Saturday market began, the way thither lying by bad roads over a distance of between twenty and thirty miles, and the horse and waggon being of the slowest. At half-past one Mrs. Durbeyfield came into the large bedroom where Tess and all her little brothers and sisters slept.

"The poor man can't go," she said to her eldest daughter, whose great eyes had opened the moment her mother's hand touched the door.

Tess sat up in bed, lost in a vague interspace between a dream and this information.

"But somebody must go," she replied. "It is late for the hives already. Swarming will soon be over for the year; and if we put off taking 'em till next week's market the call for 'em will be past, and they'll be thrown on our hands."

Mrs. Durbeyfield looked unequal to the emergency. "Some young feller, perhaps, would go? One of them who were so much after dancing with 'ee yesterday," she presently suggested.

"O no—I wouldn't have it for the world!" declared Tess proudly. "And letting everybody know the reason—such a thing to be ashamed of! I think *I* could go if Abraham could go with me to kip me company."

Her mother at length agreed to this arrangement. Little Abraham was aroused from his deep sleep in a corner of the same apartment, and made to put on his clothes while still mentally in the other world. Meanwhile Tess had hastily dressed herself; and the twain, lighting a lantern, went out to the stable. The rickety little waggon was already laden, and the girl led out the horse Prince, only a degree less rickety than the vehicle.

The poor creature looked wonderingly round at the night, at the lantern, at their two figures, as if he could not believe that at that hour, when every living thing was intended to be in shelter and at rest, he was called upon to go out and labour. They put a stock of candle-ends into the lantern, hung the latter to the off-side of the load, and directed the horse onward, walking at his shoulder at first during the up-hill parts of the way, in order not to overload an animal of so little vigour. To cheer themselves as well as they could, they made an artificial morning with the lantern, some bread and butter, and their own conversation, the real morning being far from come. Abraham, as he more fully awoke (for he had moved in a sort of trance so far), began to talk of the strange shapes assumed by the various dark objects against the sky; of this tree that looked like a raging tiger springing from a lair; of that which resembled a giant's head.

When they had passed the little town of Stourcastle, dumbly somnolent under its thick brown thatch, they reached higher ground. Still higher, on their left, the elevation called Bulbarrow or Bealbarrow, well-nigh the highest in South Wessex, swelled into the sky, engirdled by its earthen trenches. From hereabout the long road was fairly level for some distance onward. They mounted in front of the waggon, and Abraham grew reflective.

"Tess!" he said in a preparatory tone, after a silence.

"Yes, Abraham."

"Bain't you glad that we've become gentlefolk?"

"Not particular glad."

"But you be glad that you 'm going to marry a gentleman?"

"What?" said Tess, lifting her face.

"That our great relation will help 'ee to marry a gentleman."

"I? Our great relation? We have no such relation. What has put that into your head?"

"I heard 'em talking about it up at Rolliver's when I went to find father. There's a rich lady of our family out at Trantridge, and mother said that if you claimed kin with the lady, she'd put 'ee in the way of marrying a gentleman."

His sister became abruptly still, and lapsed into a pondering silence. Abraham talked on, rather for the pleasure of utterance than for audition, so that his sister's abstraction was of no account. He leant back against the hives, and with upturned face made observations on the stars, whose cold pulses were beating amid the black hollows above, in serene dissociation from these two wisps of human life. He asked how far away those twinklers were, and whether God was on the other side of them. But ever and anon his childish prattle recurred to what impressed his imagination even more deeply than the wonders of creation. If Tess were made rich by marrying a gentleman, would she have money enough to buy a spy-glass so large that it would draw the stars as near to her as Nettlecombe-Tout?

The renewed subject, which seemed to have impregnated the whole family, filled Tess with impatience.

"Never mind that now!" she exclaimed.

"Did you say the stars were worlds, Tess?"

"Yes."

"All like ours?"

"I don't know; but I think so. They sometimes seem to be like the apples on our stubbard-tree. Most of them splendid and sound—a few blighted."

"Which do we live on—a splendid one or a blighted one?"

"A blighted one."

" 'Tis very unlucky that we didn't pitch on a sound one, when there were so many more of 'em!"

"Yes."

"Is it like that *really*, Tess?" said Abraham, turning to her much impressed, on reconsideration of this rare information. "How would it have been if we had pitched on a sound one?"

"Well, father wouldn't have coughed and creeped about as he does, and wouldn't have got too tipsy to go on this journey; and mother wouldn't have been always washing, and never getting finished."

"And you would have been a rich lady ready-made, and not have had to be made rich by marrying a gentleman?"

"O Aby, don't—don't talk of that any more!"

Left to his reflections Abraham soon grew drowsy. Tess was not skilful in the management of a horse, but she thought that she could take upon herself the entire conduct of the load for the present, and allow Abraham to go to sleep if he wished to do so. She made him a sort of nest in front of the hives, in such a manner that he could not fall, and, taking the reins into her own hands, jogged on as before.

Prince required but slight attention, lacking energy for superfluous movements of any sort. With no longer a companion to distract her, Tess fell more deeply into reverie than ever, her back leaning against the hives. The mute procession past her shoulders of trees and hedges became attached to fantastic scenes outside reality, and the occasional heave of the wind became the sigh of some immense sad soul, conterminous with the universe in space, and with history in time.

Then, examining the mesh of events in her own life, she seemed to see the vanity of her father's pride; the gentlemanly suitor awaiting herself in her mother's fancy; to see him as a grimacing personage, laughing at her poverty, and her shrouded knightly ancestry. Everything grew more and more extravagant, and she no longer knew how time passed. A sudden jerk shook her in her seat, and Tess awoke from the sleep into which she, too, had fallen.

They were a long way further on than when she had lost consciousness, and the waggon had stopped. A hollow groan, unlike anything she had ever heard in her life, came from the front, followed by a shout of "Hoi there!"

The lantern hanging at her waggon had gone out, but another was shining in her face—much brighter than her own had been. Something terrible had happened. The harness was entangled with an object which blocked the way.

In consternation Tess jumped down, and discovered the dreadful truth. The groan had proceeded from her father's poor horse Prince. The morning mail-cart, with its two noiseless wheels, speeding along these lanes like an arrow, as it always did, had driven into her slow and unlighted equipage. The pointed shaft of the cart had entered the breast of the unhappy Prince like a sword, and from the wound his life's blood was spouting in a stream, and falling with a hiss into the road.

In her despair Tess sprang forward and put her hand upon the hole, with the only result that she became splashed from face to skirt with the crimson drops. Then she stood helplessly looking on. Prince also stood firm and motionless as long as he could; till he suddenly sank down in a heap.

By this time the mail-cart man had joined her, and began dragging and unharnessing the hot form of Prince. But he was already dead, and, seeing that nothing more could be done immediately, the mail-cart man returned to his own animal, which was uninjured.

"You was on the wrong side," he said. "I am bound to go on with the mail-bags, so that the best thing for you to do is bide here with your load. I'll send somebody to help you as soon as I can. It is getting daylight, and you have nothing to fear."

He mounted and sped on his way; while Tess stood and waited. The atmosphere turned pale, the birds shook themselves in the hedges, arose, and twittered; the lane showed all its white features, and Tess showed hers, still whiter. The huge pool of blood in front of her was already assuming the iridescence of coagulation; and when the sun rose a hundred prismatic hues were reflected from it. Prince lay alongside still and stark; his eyes half open, the hole in his chest looking scarcely large enough to have let out all that had animated him.

" 'Tis all my doing—all mine!" the girl cried, gazing at the spectacle. "No excuse for me—none. What will mother and father live on now? Aby, Aby!" She shook the child, who had slept soundly through the whole disaster. "We can't go on with our load—Prince is killed!"

When Abraham realised all, the furrows of fifty years were extemporised on his young face.

"Why, I danced and laughed only yesterday!" she went on to herself. "To think that I was such a fool!"

" 'Tis because we be on a blighted star, and not a sound one, isn't it, Tess?" murmured Abraham through his tears.

In silence they waited through an interval which seemed endless. At length a sound, and an approaching object, proved to them that the driver of the mail-cart had been as good as his word. A farmer's man from near Stourcastle came up, leading a strong cob. He was harnessed to the waggon of beehives in the place of Prince, and the load taken on towards Casterbridge.

The evening of the same day saw the empty waggon reach again the spot of the accident. Prince had lain there in the ditch since the morning; but the place of the blood-pool was still visible in the middle of the road, though scratched and scraped over by passing vehicles. All that was left of Prince was now hoisted into the waggon he had formerly hauled, and with his hoofs in the air, and his shoes shining in the setting sunlight, he retracted the eight or nine miles to Marlott.

Tess had gone back earlier. How to break the news was more than she could think. It was a relief to her tongue to find from the faces of her parents that they already knew of their loss, though this did not lessen the self-reproach which she continued to heap upon herself for her negligence.

But the very shiftlessness of the household rendered the misfortune a less terrifying one to them than it would have been to a striving family, though in the present case it meant ruin, and in the other it would only have meant inconvenience. In the Durbeyfield countenances there was nothing of the red wrath that would have burnt upon the girl from parents more ambitious for her welfare. Nobody blamed Tess as she blamed herself.

When it was discovered that the knacker and tanner would give only a very few shillings for Prince's carcase because of his decrepitude, Durbeyfield rose to the occasion.

"No," said he stoically, "I won't sell his old body. When we d'Urbervilles was knights in the land, we didn't sell our chargers for cat's meat. Let 'em keep their shillings! He 've served me well in his lifetime, and I won't part from him now."

He worked harder the next day in digging a grave for Prince in the garden than he had worked for months to grow a crop for his family. When the hole was ready, Durbeyfield and his wife tied a rope round the horse and dragged him up the path towards it, the children following in funeral-train. Abraham and 'Liza-Lu sobbed, Hope and Modest discharged their griefs in loud blares which echoed from the walls; and when Prince was tumbled in they gathered round the grave. The bread-winner had been taken away from them; what would they do?

"Is he gone to heaven?" asked Abraham, between the sobs.

Then Durbeyfield began to shovel in the earth, and the children cried anew. All except Tess. Her face was dry and pale, as though she regarded herself in the light of a murderess.

V

THE HAGGLING BUSINESS, WHICH HAD MAINLY DEPENDED ON THE HORSE, BECAME DISorganised forthwith. Distress, if not penury, loomed in the distance. Durbeyfield was what was locally called a slack-twisted fellow; he had good strength to work at times; but the times could not be relied on to coincide with the hours of requirement; and, having been unaccustomed to the regular toil of the day-labourer, he was not particularly persistent when they did so coincide.

Tess, meanwhile, as the one who had dragged her parents into this quagmire, was silently wondering what she could do to help them out of it; and then her mother broached her scheme.

"We must take the ups wi' the downs, Tess," said she; "and never could your high blood have been found out at a more called-for moment. You must try your friends. Do ye know that there is a very rich Mrs. d'Urberville living on the outskirts o' The Chase, who must be our relation? You must go to her and claim kin, and ask for some help in our trouble."

"I shouldn't care to do that," says Tess. "If there is such a lady, 'twould be enough for us if she were friendly—not to expect her to give us help."

"You could win her round to do anything, my dear. Besides, perhaps there's more in it than you know of. I've heard what I've heard, good-now."

The oppressive sense of the harm she had done led Tess to be more deferential than she might otherwise have been to the maternal wish; but she could not understand why her mother should find such satisfaction in contemplating an enterprise of, to her, such doubtful profit. Her mother might have made enquiries, and have discovered that this Mrs. d'Urberville was a lady of unequalled virtues and charity. But Tess's pride made the part of poor relation one of particular distaste to her.

"I'd rather try to get work," she murmured.

"Durbeyfield, you can settle it," said his wife, turning to where he sat in the background. "If you say she ought to go, she will go."

"I don't like my children going and making themselves beholden to strange kin," murmured he. "I'm the head of the noblest branch o' the family, and I ought to live up to it."

His reasons for staying away were worse to Tess than her own objections to going. "Well, as I killed the horse, mother," she said mournfully, "I suppose I ought to do something. I don't mind going and seeing her, but you must leave it to me about asking for help. And don't go thinking about her making a match for me—it is silly."

"Very well said, Tess!" observed her father sententiously.

"Who said I had such a thought?" asked Joan.

"I fancy it is in your mind, mother. But I'll go."

Rising early next day she walked to the hill-town called Shaston, and there took advantage of a van which twice in the week ran from Shaston eastward to Chaseborough, passing near Trantridge, the parish in which the vague and mysterious Mrs. d'Urberville had her residence.

Tess Durbeyfield's route on this memorable morning lay amid the north-eastern undulations of the Vale in which she had been born, and in which her life had unfolded. The Vale of Blackmoor was to her the world, and its inhabitants the races thereof. From the gates and stiles of Marlott she had looked down its length in the wondering days of infancy, and what had been mystery to her then was not much less than mystery to her now. She had seen daily from her chamber-window towers, villages, faint white mansions; above all the town of Shaston standing majestically on its height; its windows shining like lamps in the evening sun. She had hardly ever visited the place, only a small tract even of the Vale and its environs being known to her by close inspection. Much less had she been far outside the valley. Every contour of the surrounding hills was as personal to her as that of her relatives' faces; but for what lay beyond her judgment was dependent on the teaching of the village school, where she had held a leading place at the time of her leaving, a year or two before this date.

In those early days she had been much loved by others of her own sex and age, and had used to be seen about the village as one of three—all nearly of the same year—walking home from school side by side; Tess the middle one—in a pink print pinafore, of a finely reticulated pattern, worn over a stuff frock that had lost its original colour for a nondescript tertiary—marching on upon long stalky legs, in tight stockings which had little ladderlike holes at the knees, torn by kneeling in the roads and banks in search of vegetable and mineral treasures; her then earth-coloured hair hanging like pot-hooks; the arms of the two outside girls resting round the waist of Tess; her arms on the shoulders of the two supporters.

As Tess grew older, and began to see how matters stood, she felt quite a Malthusian towards her mother for thoughtlessly giving her so many little sisters and brothers, when it was such a trouble to nurse and provide for them. Her mother's intelligence was that of a happy child: Joan Durbeyfield was simply an additional one, and that not the eldest, to her own long family of waiters on Providence.

However, Tess became humanely beneficent towards the small ones, and to help them as much as possible she used, as soon as she left school, to lend a hand at haymaking or harvesting on neighbouring farms; or, by preference, at milking or butter-making processes, which she had learnt when her father had owned cows; and being deft-fingered it was a kind of work in which she excelled.

Every day seemed to throw upon her young shoulders more of the family burdens, and that Tess should be the representative of the Durbeyfields at the d'Urberville mansion came as a thing of course. In this instance it must be admitted that the Durbeyfields were putting their fairest side outward.

She alighted from the van at Trantridge Cross, and ascended on foot a hill in the direction of the district known as The Chase, on the borders of which, as she had been informed, Mrs. d'Urberville's seat, The Slopes, would be found. It was not a manorial home in the ordinary sense, with fields, and pastures, and a grumbling farmer, out of whom the owner had to squeeze an income for himself and his family by hook or by crook. It was more, far more; a country-house built for enjoyment pure and simple, with not an acre of troublesome land attached to it beyond what was required for residential purposes, and for a little fancy farm kept in hand by the owner, and tended by a bailiff.

The crimson brick lodge came first in sight, up to its eaves in dense evergreens. Tess thought this was the mansion itself till, passing through the side wicket with some trepidation, and onward to a point at which the drive took a turn, the house proper stood in full view. It was of recent erection—indeed almost new—and of the same rich red colour that formed such a contrast with the evergreens of the lodge. Far behind the corner of the house—which rose like a geranium bloom against the subdued colours around—stretched the soft azure landscape of The Chase—a truly venerable tract of forest land, one of the few remaining woodlands in England of undoubted primaeval date, wherein Druidical mistletoe was still found on aged oaks, and where enormous yew-trees, not planted by the hand of man, grew as they had grown when they were pollarded for bows. All this sylvan antiquity, however, though visible from The Slopes, was outside the immediate boundaries of the estate.

Everything on this snug property was bright, thriving, and well kept; acres of glass-houses stretched down the inclines to the copses at their feet. Everything looked like money—like the last coin issued from the Mint. The stables, partly screened by Austrian pines and evergreen oaks, and fitted with every late appliance, were as dignified as Chapels-of-Ease. On the extensive lawn stood an ornamental tent, its door being towards her.

Simple Tess Durbeyfield stood at gaze, in a half-alarmed attitude, on the edge of the gravel sweep. Her feet had brought her onward to this point before she had quite realised where she was; and now all was contrary to her expectation.

"I thought we were an old family; but this is all new!" she said, in her artlessness. She wished that she had not fallen in so readily with her mother's plans for "claiming kin," and had endeavoured to gain assistance nearer home.

* * *

The d'Urbervilles—or Stoke-d'Urbervilles, as they at first called themselves—who owned all this, were a somewhat unusual family to find in such an old-fashioned part of the country. Parson Tringham had spoken truly when he said that our shambling John Durbeyfield was the only really lineal representative of the old d'Urberville family existing in the county, or near it; he might have added, what he knew very well, that the Stoke-d'Urbervilles were no more d'Urbervilles of the true tree than he was himself. Yet it must be admitted that this family formed a very good stock whereon to regraft a name which sadly wanted such renovation.

When old Mr. Simon Stoke, latterly deceased, had made his fortune as an honest merchant (some said money-lender) in the North, he decided to settle as a county man in the South of England, out of hail of his business district; and in doing this he felt the necessity of recommencing with a name that would not too readily identify him with the smart tradesman of the past, and that would be less commonplace than the original bald stark words. Conning for an hour in the British Museum the pages of works devoted to extinct, half-extinct, obscured, and ruined families appertaining to the quarter of England in which he proposed to settle, he considered that *d'Urberville* looked and sounded as well as any of them: and d'Urberville accordingly was annexed to his own name for himself and his heirs eternally. Yet he was not an extravagant-minded man in this, and in constructing his family tree on the new basis was duly reasonable in framing his intermarriages and aristocratic links, never inserting a single title above a rank of strict moderation.

Of this work of imagination poor Tess and her parents were naturally in ignorance—much to their discomfiture; indeed, the very possibility of such annexations was unknown to them; who supposed that, though to be well-favoured might be the gift of fortune, a family name came by nature.

Tess still stood hesitating like a bather about to make his plunge, hardly knowing whether to retreat or to persevere, when a figure came forth from the dark triangular door of the tent. It was that of a tall young man, smoking.

He had an almost swarthy complexion, with full lips, badly moulded, though red and smooth, above which was a well-groomed black moustache with curled points, though his age could not be more than three- or four-and-twenty. Despite the touches of barbarism in his contours, there was a singular force in the gentleman's face, and in his bold rolling eye.

"Well, my Beauty, what can I do for you?" said he, coming forward. And perceiving that she stood quite confounded: "Never mind me. I am Mr. d'Urberville. Have you come to see me or my mother?"

This embodiment of a d'Urberville and a namesake differed even more from what Tess had expected than the house and grounds had differed. She had dreamed of an aged and dignified face, the sublimation of all the d'Urberville lineaments, furrowed with incarnate memories representing in hieroglyphic the centuries of her family's and England's history. But she screwed herself up to the work in hand, since she could not get out of it, and answered—

"I came to see your mother, sir."

"I am afraid you cannot see her—she is an invalid," replied the present representative of the spurious house; for this was Mr. Alec, the only son of the lately deceased gentleman. "Cannot I answer your purpose? What is the business you wish to see her about?"

"It isn't business—it is—I can hardly say what!"

"Pleasure?"

"Oh no. Why, sir, if I tell you, it will seem—"

Tess's sense of a certain ludicrousness in her errand was now so strong that, notwithstanding her awe of him, and her general discomfort at being here, her rosy lips curved towards a smile, much to the attraction of the swarthy Alexander.

"It is so very foolish," she stammered; "I fear I can't tell you!"

"Never mind; I like foolish things. Try again, my dear," said he kindly.

"Mother asked me to come," Tess continued; "and, indeed, I was in the mind to do so myself likewise. But I did not think it would be like this. I came, sir, to tell you that we are of the same family as you."

"Ho! Poor relations?"

"Yes."

"Stokes?"

"No; d'Urbervilles."

"Ay, ay; I mean d'Urbervilles."

"Our names are worn away to Durbeyfield; but we have several proofs that we are d'Urbervilles. Antiquarians hold we are—and—and we have an old seal, marked with a ramping lion on a shield, and a castle over him. And we have a very old silver spoon, round in the bowl like a little ladle, and marked with the same castle. But it is so worn that mother uses it to stir the pea-soup."

"A castle argent is certainly my crest," said he blandly. "And my arms a lion rampant."

"And so mother said we ought to make ourselves beknown to you—as we've lost our horse by a bad accident, and are the oldest branch o' the family."

"Very kind of your mother, I'm sure. And I, for one, don't regret her step." Alec looked at Tess as he spoke, in a way that made her blush a little. "And so, my pretty girl, you've come on a friendly visit to us, as relations?"

"I suppose I have," faltered Tess, looking uncomfortable again.

"Well—there's no harm in it. Where do you live? What are you?"

She gave him brief particulars; and responding to further enquiries told him that she was intending to go back by the same carrier who had brought her.

"It is a long while before he returns past Trantridge Cross. Supposing we walk round the grounds to pass the time, my pretty Coz?"

Tess wished to abridge her visit as much as possible; but the young man was pressing, and she consented to accompany him. He conducted her about the lawns, and flower-beds, and conservatories; and thence to the fruit-garden and green-houses, where he asked her if she liked strawberries.

"Yes," said Tess, "when they come."

"They are already here." D'Urberville began gathering specimens of the fruit for her, handing them back to her as he stooped; and, presently, selecting a specially fine product of the "British Queen" variety, he stood up and held it by the stem to her mouth.

"No—no!" she said quickly, putting her fingers between his hand and her lips. "I would rather take it in my own hand."

"Nonsense!" he insisted; and in a slight distress she parted her lips and took it in.

They had spent some time wandering desultorily thus, Tess eating in a half-pleased, half-reluctant state whatever d'Urberville offered her. When she could consume no more of the strawberries he filled her little basket with them; and then the two passed round to the rose trees, whence he gathered blossoms and gave her to put in her bosom. She obeyed like one in a dream, and when she could affix no more he himself tucked a bud or two into her hat, and heaped her basket with others in the prodigality of his bounty. At last, looking at his watch, he said, "Now, by the time you have had something to eat, it will be time for you to leave, if you want to catch the carrier to Shaston. Come here, and I'll see what grub I can find."

Stoke-d'Urberville took her back to the lawn and into the tent, where he left her, soon reappearing with a basket of light luncheon, which he put before her himself. It was evidently the gentleman's wish not to be disturbed in this pleasant *tête-à-tête* by the servantry.

"Do you mind my smoking?" he asked.

"Oh, not at all, sir."

He watched her pretty and unconscious munching through the skeins of smoke that pervaded the tent, and Tess Durbeyfield did not divine, as she innocently looked down at the roses in her bosom, that there behind the blue narcotic haze was potentially the "tragic mischief" of her drama—one who stood fair to be the blood-red ray in the spectrum of her young life. She had an attribute which amounted to a disadvantage just now; and it was this that caused Alec d'Urberville's eyes to rivet themselves upon her. It was a luxuriance of aspect, a fulness of growth, which made her appear more of a woman than she really was. She had inherited the feature from her mother without the quality it denoted. It had troubled her mind occasionally, till her companions had said that it was a fault which time would cure.

She soon had finished her lunch. "Now I am going home, sir," she said, rising.

"And what do they call you?" he asked, as he accompanied her along the drive till they were out of sight of the house.

"Tess Durbeyfield, down at Marlott."

"And you say your people have lost their horse?"

"I—killed him!" she answered, her eyes filling with tears as she gave particulars of Prince's death. "And I don't know what to do for father on account of it!"

"I must think if I cannot do something. My mother must find a berth for you. But, Tess, no nonsense about 'd'Urberville';—'Durbeyfield' only, you know—quite another name."

"I wish for no better, sir," said she with something of dignity.

For a moment—only for a moment—when they were in the turning of the drive, between the tall rhododendrons and conifers, before the lodge became visible, he inclined his face towards her as if—but, no: he thought better of it, and let her go.

Thus the thing began. Had she perceived this meeting's import she might have asked why she was doomed to be seen and coveted that day by the wrong man, and not by some other man, the right and desired one in all respects—as nearly as humanity can supply the right and desired; yet to him who amongst her acquaintance might have approximated to this kind, she was but a transient impression, half forgotten.

In the ill-judged execution of the well-judged plan of things the call seldom produces the comer, the man to love rarely coincides with the hour for loving. Nature does not often say "See!" to her poor creature at a time when seeing can lead to happy doing; or reply

"Here!" to a body's cry of "Where?" till the hide-and-seek has become an irksome, outworn game. We may wonder whether at the acme and summit of the human progress these anachronisms will be corrected by a finer intuition, a close interaction of the social machinery than that which now jolts us round and along; but such completeness is not to be prophesied, or even conceived as possible. Enough that in the present case, as in millions, it was not the two halves of a perfect whole that confronted each other at the perfect moment; a missing counterpart wandered independently about the earth waiting in crass obtuseness till the late time came. Out of which maladroit delay sprang anxieties, disappointments, shocks, catastrophes, and passing-strange destinies.

When d'Urberville got back to the tent he sat down astride on a chair reflecting, with a pleased gleam in his face. Then he broke into a loud laugh.

"Well, I'm damned! What a funny thing! Ha-ha-ha! And what a crumby girl!"

VI

Tess went down the hill to Trantridge Cross, and inattentively waited to take her seat in the van returning from Chaseborough to Shaston. She did not know what the other occupants said to her as she entered, though she answered them; and when they had started anew she rode along with an inward and not an outward eye.

One among her fellow-travellers addressed her more pointedly than any had spoken before: "Why, you be quite a posy! And such roses in early June!"

Then she became aware of the spectacle she presented to their surprised vision: roses at her breasts; roses in her hat; roses and strawberries in her basket to the brim. She blushed, and said confusedly that the flowers had been given to her. When the passengers were not looking she stealthily removed the more prominent blooms from her hat and placed them in the basket, where she covered them with her handkerchief. Then she fell to reflecting again, and in looking downwards a thorn of the rose remaining in her breast accidentally pricked her chin. Like all the cottagers in Blackmoor Vale, Tess was steeped in fancies and prefigurative superstitions; she thought this an ill omen—the first she had noticed that day.

The van travelled only so far as Shaston, and there were several miles of pedestrian descent from that mountain-town into the vale of Marlott. Her mother had advised her to stay here for the night, at the house of a cottage-woman they knew, if she should feel too tired to come on; and this Tess did, not descending to her home till the following afternoon.

When she entered the house she perceived in a moment from her mother's triumphant manner that something had occurred in the interim.

"Oh yes; I know all about it! I told 'ee it would be all right, and now 'tis proved!"

"Since I've been away? What has?" said Tess rather wearily.

Her mother surveyed the girl up and down with arch approval, and went on banteringly: "So you've brought 'em round!"

"How do you know, mother?"

"I've had a letter."

Tess then remembered that there would have been time for this.

"They say—Mrs. d'Urberville says—that she wants you to look after a little fowl-farm which is her hobby. But this is only her artful way of getting 'ee there without raising your hopes. She's going to own 'ee as kin—that's the meaning o't."

"But I didn't see her."

"You zid somebody, I suppose?"

"I saw her son."

"And did he own 'ee?"

"Well—he called me Coz."

"An' I knew it! Jacky—he called her Coz!" cried Joan to her husband. "Well, he spoke to his mother, of course, and she do want 'ee there."

"But I don't know that I am apt at tending fowls," said the dubious Tess.

"Then I don't know who is apt. You've be'n born in the business, and brought up in it. They that be born in a business always know more about it than any 'prentice. Besides, that's only just a show of something for you to do, that you midn't feel beholden."

"I don't altogether think I ought to go," said Tess thoughtfully. "Who wrote the letter? Will you let me look at it?"

"Mrs. d'Urberville wrote it. Here it is."

The letter was in the third person, and briefly informed Mrs. Durbeyfield that her daughter's services would be useful to that lady in the management of her poultry-farm, that a comfortable room would be provided for her if she could come, and that the wages would be on a liberal scale if they liked her.

"Oh—that's all!" said Tess.

"You couldn't expect her to throw her arms round 'ee, an' to kiss and to coll 'ee all at once."

Tess looked out of the window.

"I would rather stay here with father and you," she said.

"But why?"

"I'd rather not tell you why, mother; indeed, I don't quite know why."

A week afterwards she came in one evening from an unavailing search for some light occupation in the immediate neighbourhood. Her idea had been to get together sufficient money during the summer to purchase another horse. Hardly had she crossed the threshold before one of the children danced across the room, saying, "The gentleman's been here!"

Her mother hastened to explain, smiles breaking from every inch of her person. Mrs. d'Urberville's son had called on horseback, having been riding by chance in the direction of Marlott. He had wished to know, finally, in the name of his mother, if Tess could really come to manage the old lady's fowl-farm or not; the lad who had hitherto superintended the birds having proved untrustworthy. "Mr. d'Urberville says you must be a good girl if you are at all as you appear; he knows you must be worth your weight in gold. He is very much interested in 'ee—truth to tell."

Tess seemed for the moment really pleased to hear that she had won such high opinion from a stranger when, in her own esteem, she had sunk so low.

"It is very good of him to think that," she murmured; "and if I was quite sure how it would be living there, I would go any-when."

"He is a mighty handsome man!"

"I don't think so," said Tess coldly.

"Well, there's your chance, whether or no; and I'm sure he wears a beautiful diamond ring!"

"Yes," said little Abraham, brightly, from the window-bench; "and I seed it! and it did twinkle when he put his hand up to his mistarshers. Mother, why did our grand relation keep on putting his hand up to his mistarshers?"

"Hark at that child!" cried Mrs. Durbeyfield, with parenthetic admiration.

"Perhaps to show his diamond ring," murmured Sir John, dreamily, from his chair.

"I'll think it over," said Tess, leaving the room.

"Well, she's made a conquest o' the younger branch of us, straight off," continued the matron to her husband, "and she's a fool if she don't follow it up."

"I don't quite like my children going away from home," said the haggler. "As the head of the family, the rest ought to come to me."

"But do let her go, Jacky," coaxed his poor witless wife. "He's struck wi' her—you can see that. He called her Coz! He'll marry her, most likely, and make a lady of her; and then she'll be what her forefathers was."

John Durbeyfield had more conceit than energy or health, and this supposition was pleasant to him.

"Well, perhaps, that's what young Mr. d'Urberville means," he admitted; "and sure enough he mid have serious thoughts about improving his blood by linking on to the old line. Tess, the little rogue! And have she really paid 'em a visit to such an end as this?"

Meanwhile Tess was walking thoughtfully among the gooseberry-bushes in the garden, and over Prince's grave. When she came in her mother pursued her advantage.

"Well, what be you going to do?" she asked.

"I wish I had seen Mrs. d'Urberville," said Tess.

"I think you mid as well settle it. Then you'll see her soon enough."

Her father coughed in his chair.

"I don't know what to say!" answered the girl restlessly. "It is for you to decide. I killed the old horse, and I suppose I ought to do something to get ye a new one. But—but—I don't quite like Mr. d'Urberville being there!"

The children, who had made use of this idea of Tess being taken up by their wealthy kinsfolk (which they imagined the other family to be) as a species of dolorifuge after the death of the horse, began to cry at Tess's reluctance, and teased and reproached her for hesitating.

"Tess won't go—o—o and be made a la—a—dy of!—no, she says she wo—o—on't!" they wailed, with square mouths. "And we shan't have a nice new horse, and lots o' golden money to buy fairlings! And Tess won't look pretty in her best cloze no mo—o—ore!"

Her mother chimed in to the same tune: a certain way she had of making her labours in the house seem heavier than they were by prolonging them indefinitely, also weighed in the argument. Her father alone preserved an attitude of neutrality.

"I will go," said Tess at last.

Her mother could not repress her consciousness of the nuptial Vision conjured up by the girl's consent.

"That's right! For such a pretty maid as 'tis, this is a fine chance!"

Tess smiled crossly.

"I hope it is a chance for earning money. It is no other kind of chance. You had better say nothing of that silly sort about parish."

Mrs. Durbeyfield did not promise. She was not quite sure that she did not feel proud enough, after the visitor's remarks, to say a good deal.

Thus it was arranged; and the young girl wrote, agreeing to be ready to set out on any day on which she might be required. She was duly informed that Mrs. d'Urberville was glad of her decision, and that a spring-cart should be sent to meet her and her luggage at the top of the Vale on the day after the morrow, when she must hold herself prepared to start. Mrs. d'Urberville's handwriting seemed rather masculine.

"A cart?" murmured Joan Durbeyfield doubtingly. "It might have been a carriage for her own kin!"

Having at last taken her course Tess was less restless and abstracted, going about her business with some self-assurance in the thought of acquiring another horse for her father by an occupation which would not be onerous. She had hoped to be a teacher at the school, but the fates seemed to decide otherwise. Being mentally older than her mother she did not regard Mrs. Durbeyfield's matrimonial hopes for her in a serious aspect for a moment. The light-minded woman had been discovering good matches for her daughter almost from the year of her birth.

VII

O N THE MORNING APPOINTED FOR HER DEPARTURE TESS WAS AWAKE BEFORE DAWN— at the marginal minute of the dark when the grove is still mute, save for one prophetic bird who sings with a clear-voiced conviction that he at least knows the correct time of day, the rest preserving silence as if equally convinced that he is mistaken. She remained upstairs packing till breakfast-time, and then came down in her ordinary week-day clothes, her Sunday apparel being carefully folded in her box.

Her mother expostulated. "You will never set out to see your folks without dressing up more the dand than that?"

"But I am going to work!" said Tess.

"Well, yes," said Mrs. Durbeyfield; and in a private tone, "at first there mid be a little pretence o't.... But I think it will be wiser of 'ee to put your best side outward," she added.

"Very well; I suppose you know best," replied Tess with calm abandonment.

And to please her parent the girl put herself quite in Joan's hands, saying serenely— "Do what you like with me, mother."

Mrs. Durbeyfield was only too delighted at this tractability. First she fetched a great basin, and washed Tess's hair with such thoroughness that when dried and brushed it looked twice as much as at other times. She tied it with a broader pink ribbon than usual. Then she put upon her the white frock that Tess had worn at the club-walking, the airy fulness of which, supplementing her enlarged *coiffure*, imparted to her developing figure an amplitude which belied her age, and might cause her to be estimated as a woman when she was not much more than a child.

"I declare there's a hole in my stocking-heel!" said Tess.

"Never mind holes in your stockings—they don't speak! When I was a maid, so long as I had a pretty bonnet the devil might ha' found me in heels."

Her mother's pride in the girl's appearance led her to step back, like a painter from his easel, and survey her work as a whole.

"You must zee yourself!" she cried. "It is much better than you was t'other day."

As the looking-glass was only large enough to reflect a very small portion of Tess's person at one time, Mrs. Durbeyfield hung a black cloak outside the casement, and so made a large reflector of the panes, as it is the wont of bedecking cottagers to do. After this she went downstairs to her husband, who was sitting in the lower-room.

"I'll tell 'ee what 'tis, Durbeyfield," said she exultingly; "he'll never have the heart not to love her. But whatever you do, don't zay too much to Tess of his fancy for her, and this chance she has got. She is such an odd maid that it mid zet her against him, or against going there, even now. If all goes well, I shall certainly be for making some return to pa'son at Stagfoot Lane for telling us—dear, good man!"

However, as the moment for the girl's setting out drew nigh, when the first excitement of the dressing had passed off, a slight misgiving found place in Joan Durbeyfield's mind. It prompted the matron to say that she would walk a little way—as far as to the point where the acclivity from the valley began its first steep ascent to the outer world. At the top Tess was going to be met with the spring-cart sent by the Stoke-d'Urbervilles, and her box had already been wheeled ahead towards this summit by a lad with trucks, to be in readiness.

Seeing their mother put on her bonnet the younger children clamoured to go with her.

"I do want to walk a little-ways wi' Sissy, now she's going to marry our gentleman-cousin, and wear fine cloze!"

"Now," said Tess, flushing and turning quickly, "I'll hear no more o' that! Mother, how could you ever put such stuff into their heads?"

"Going to work, my dears, for our rich relation, and help get enough money for a new horse," said Mrs. Durbeyfield pacifically.

"Good-bye, father," said Tess, with a lumpy throat.

"Good-bye, my maid," said Sir John, raising his head from his breast as he suspended his nap, induced by a slight excess this morning in honour of the occasion. "Well, I hope my young friend will like such a comely sample of his own blood. And tell'n, Tess, that being sunk, quite, from our former grandeur, I'll sell him the title—yes, sell it—and at no onreasonable figure."

"Not for less than a thousand pound!" cried Lady Durbeyfield.

"Tell'n—I'll take a thousand pound. Well, I'll take less, when I come to think o't. He'll adorn it better than a poor lammicken feller like myself can. Tell'n he shall hae it for a hundred. But I won't stand upon trifles—tell'n he shall hae it for fifty—for twenty pound! Yes, twenty pound—that's the lowest. Dammy, family honour is family honour, and I won't take a penny less!"

Tess's eyes were too full and her voice too choked to utter the sentiments that were in her. She turned quickly, and went out.

So the girls and their mother all walked together, a child on each side of Tess, holding her hand, and looking at her meditatively from time to time, as at one who was about to do great things; her mother just behind with the smallest; the group forming a picture of honest beauty flanked by innocence, and backed by simple-souled vanity. They followed the way till they reached the beginning of the ascent, on the crest of which the vehicle from Trantridge was to receive her, this limit having been fixed to save the horse the labour of the last slope. Far away behind the first hills the clifflike dwellings of Shaston broke the line of the ridge. Nobody was visible in the elevated road which skirted the ascent save the lad whom they had sent on before them, sitting on the handle of the barrow that contained all Tess's worldly possessions.

"Bide here a bit, and the cart will soon come, no doubt," said Mrs. Durbeyfield. "Yes, I see it yonder!"

It had come—appearing suddenly from behind the forehead of the nearest upland, and stopping beside the boy with the barrow. Her mother and the children thereupon decided to go no farther, and bidding them a hasty good-bye Tess bent her steps up the hill.

They saw her white shape draw near to the spring-cart, on which her box was already placed. But before she had quite reached it another vehicle shot out from a clump of trees on the summit, came round the bend of the road there, passed the luggage-cart, and halted beside Tess, who looked up as if in great surprise.

Her mother perceived, for the first time, that the second vehicle was not a humble conveyance like the first, but a spick-and-span gig or dog-cart, highly varnished and equipped. The driver was a young man of three- or four-and-twenty, with a cigar between his teeth; wearing a dandy cap, drab jacket, breeches of the same hue, white neckcloth, stick-up collar, and brown driving-gloves—in short, he was the handsome, horsey young buck who had visited Joan a week or two before to get her answer about Tess.

Mrs. Durbeyfield clapped her hands like a child. Then she looked down, then stared again. Could she be deceived as to the meaning of this?

"Is dat the gentleman-kinsman who'll make Sissy a lady?" asked the youngest child.

Meanwhile the muslined form of Tess could be seen standing still, undecided, beside this turn-out, whose owner was talking to her. Her seeming indecision was, in fact, more than indecision: it was misgiving. She would have preferred the humble cart. The young man dismounted, and appeared to urge her to ascend. She turned her face down the hill to her relatives, and regarded the little group. Something seemed to quicken her to a determination; possibly the thought that she had killed Prince. She suddenly stepped up; he mounted beside her, and immediately whipped on the horse. In a moment they had passed the slow cart with the box, and disappeared behind the shoulder of the hill.

Directly Tess was out of sight, and the interest of the matter as a drama was at an end, the little ones' eyes filled with tears. The youngest child said, "I wish poor, poor Tess wasn't gone away to be a lady!" and, lowering the corners of his lips, burst out crying. The new point of view was infectious, and the next child did likewise, and then the next, till the whole three of them wailed loud.

There were tears also in Joan Durbeyfield's eyes as she turned to go home. But by the time she had got back to the village she was passively trusting to the favour of accident. However, in bed that night she sighed, and her husband asked her what was the matter.

"Oh, I don't know exactly," she said. "I was thinking that perhaps it would ha' been better if Tess had not gone."

"Oughtn't ye to have thought of that before?"

"Well, 'tis a chance for the maid—Still, if 'twere the doing again, I wouldn't let her go till I had found out whether the gentleman is really a good-hearted young man and choice over her as his kinswoman."

"Yes, you ought, perhaps, to ha' done that," snored Sir John.

Joan Durbeyfield always managed to find consolation somewhere: "Well, as one of the genuine stock, she ought to make her way with 'en, if she plays her trump card aright. And if he don't marry her afore he will after. For that he's all afire wi' love for her any eye can see."

"What's her trump card? Her d'Urberville blood, you mean?"

"No, stupid; her face—as 'twas mine."

VIII

H AVING MOUNTED BESIDE HER, ALEC D'URBERVILLE DROVE RAPIDLY ALONG THE CREST of the first hill, chatting compliments to Tess as they went, the cart with her box being left far behind. Rising still, an immense landscape stretched around them on every side; behind, the green valley of her birth, before, a grey country of which she knew nothing except from her first brief visit to Trantridge. Thus they reached the verge of an incline down which the road stretched in a long straight descent of nearly a mile.

Ever since the accident with her father's horse Tess Durbeyfield, courageous as she naturally was, had been exceedingly timid on wheels; the least irregularity of motion startled her. She began to get uneasy at a certain recklessness in her conductor's driving.

"You will go down slow, sir, I suppose?" she said with attempted unconcern.

D'Urberville looked round upon her, nipped his cigar with the tips of his large white centre-teeth, and allowed his lips to smile slowly of themselves.

"Why, Tess," he answered, after another whiff or two, "it isn't a brave bouncing girl like you who asks that? Why, I always go down at full gallop. There's nothing like it for raising your spirits."

"But perhaps you need not now?"

"Ah," he said, shaking his head, "there are two to be reckoned with. It is not me alone. Tib had to be considered, and she has a very queer temper."

"Who?"

"Why, this mare. I fancy she looked round at me in a very grim way just then. Didn't you notice it?"

"Don't try to frighten me, sir," said Tess stiffly.

"Well, I don't. If any living man can manage this horse I can:—I won't say any living man can do it—but if such has the power, I am he."

"Why do you have such a horse?"

"Ah, well may you ask it! It was my fate, I suppose. Tib has killed one chap; and just after I bought her she nearly killed me. And then, take my word for it, I nearly killed her. But she's touchy still, very touchy; and one's life is hardly safe behind her sometimes."

They were just beginning to descend; and it was evident that the horse, whether of her own will or of his (the latter being the more likely), knew so well the reckless performance expected of her that she hardly required a hint from behind.

Down, down, they sped, the wheels humming like a top, the dog-cart rocking right and left, its axis acquiring a slightly oblique set in relation to the line of progress; the figure of the horse rising and falling in undulations before them. Sometimes a wheel was off the ground, it seemed, for many yards; sometimes a stone was sent spinning over the hedge, and flinty sparks from the horse's hoofs outshone the daylight. The aspect of the straight road enlarged with their advance, the two banks dividing like a splitting stick; one rushing past at each shoulder.

The wind blew through Tess's white muslin to her very skin, and her washed hair flew out behind. She was determined to show no open fear, but she clutched d'Urberville's rein-arm.

"Don't touch my arm! We shall be thrown out if you do! Hold on round my waist!"

She grasped his waist, and so they reached the bottom.

"Safe, thank God, in spite of your fooling!" said she, her face on fire.

"Tess—fie! that's temper!" said d'Urberville.

" 'Tis truth."

"Well, you need not let go your hold of me so thanklessly the moment you feel yourself out of danger."

She had not considered what she had been doing; whether he were man or woman, stick or stone, in her involuntary hold on him. Recovering her reserve she sat without replying, and thus they reached the summit of another declivity.

"Now then, again!" said d'Urberville.

"No, no!" said Tess. "Show more sense, do, please."

"But when people find themselves on one of the highest points in the county, they must get down again," he retorted.

He loosened rein, and away they went a second time. D'Urberville turned his face to her as they rocked, and said, in playful raillery: "Now then, put your arms round my waist again, as you did before, my Beauty."

"Never!" said Tess independently, holding on as well as she could without touching him.

"Let me put one little kiss on those holmberry lips, Tess, or even on that warmed cheek, and I'll stop—on my honour, I will!"

Tess, surprised beyond measure, slid farther back still on her seat, at which he urged the horse anew, and rocked her the more.

"Will nothing else do?" she cried at length, in desperation, her large eyes staring at him like those of a wild animal. This dressing her up so prettily by her mother had apparently been to lamentable purpose.

"Nothing, dear Tess," he replied.

"Oh, I don't know—very well; I don't mind!" she panted miserably.

He drew rein, and as they slowed he was on the point of imprinting the desired salute, when, as if hardly yet aware of her own modesty, she dodged aside. His arms being occupied with the reins there was left him no power to prevent her manoeuvre.

"Now, damn it—I'll break both our necks!" swore her capriciously passionate companion. "So you can go from your word like that, you young witch, can you?"

"Very well," said Tess, "I'll not move since you be so determined! But I—thought you would be kind to me, and protect me, as my kinsman!"

"Kinsman be hanged! Now!"

"But I don't want anybody to kiss me, sir!" she implored, a big tear beginning to roll down her face, and the corners of her mouth trembling in her attempts not to cry. "And I wouldn't ha' come if I had known!"

He was inexorable, and she sat still, and d'Urberville gave her the kiss of mastery. No sooner had he done so than she flushed with shame, took out her handkerchief, and wiped the spot on her cheek that had been touched by his lips. His ardour was nettled at the sight, for the act on her part had been unconsciously done.

"You are mighty sensitive for a cottage girl!" said the young man.

Tess made no reply to this remark, of which, indeed, she did not quite comprehend the drift, unheeding the snub she had administered by her instinctive rub upon her cheek. She had, in fact, undone the kiss, as far as such a thing was physically possible. With a dim sense that he was vexed she looked steadily ahead as they trotted on near Melbury Down and Wingreen, till she saw, to her consternation, that there was yet another descent to be undergone.

"You shall be made sorry for that!" he resumed, his injured tone still remaining, as he flourished the whip anew. "Unless, that is, you agree willingly to let me do it again, and no handkerchief."

She sighed. "Very well, sir!" she said. "Oh—let me get my hat!"

At the moment of speaking her hat had blown off into the road, their present speed on the upland being by no means slow. D'Urberville pulled up, and said he would get it for her, but Tess was down on the other side.

She turned back and picked up the article.

"You look prettier with it off, upon my soul, if that's possible," he said, contemplating her over the back of the vehicle. "Now then, up again! What's the matter?"

The hat was in place and tied, but Tess had not stepped forward.

"No, sir," she said, revealing the red and ivory of her mouth as her eye lit in defiant triumph; "not again, if I know it!"

"What—you won't get up beside me?"

"No; I shall walk."

" 'Tis five or six miles yet to Trantridge."

"I don't care if 'tis dozens. Besides, the cart is behind."

"You artful hussy! Now, tell me—didn't you make that hat blow off on purpose? I'll swear you did!"

Her strategic silence confirmed his suspicion.

Then d'Urberville cursed and swore at her, and called her everything he could think of for the trick. Turning the horse suddenly he tried to drive back upon her, and so hem her in between the gig and the hedge. But he could not do this short of injuring her.

"You ought to be ashamed of yourself for using such wicked words!" cried Tess with spirit, from the top of the hedge into which she had scrambled. "I don't like 'ee at all! I hate and detest you! I'll go back to mother, I will!"

D'Urberville's bad temper cleared up at sight of hers; and he laughed heartily.

"Well, I like you all the better," he said. "Come, let there be peace. I'll never do it any more against your will. My life upon it now!"

Still Tess could not be induced to remount. She did not, however, object to his keeping his gig alongside her; and in this manner, at a slow pace, they advanced towards the village of Trantridge. From time to time d'Urberville exhibited a sort of fierce distress at the sight of the tramping he had driven her to undertake by his misdemeanour. She might in truth have safely trusted him now; but he had forfeited her confidence for the time, and she kept on the ground progressing thoughtfully, as if wondering whether it would be wiser to return home. Her resolve, however, had been taken, and it seemed vacillating even to childishness to abandon it now, unless for graver reasons. How could she face her parents, get back her box, and disconcert the whole scheme for the rehabilitation of her family on such sentimental grounds?

A few minutes later the chimneys of The Slopes appeared in view, and in a snug nook to the right the poultry-farm and cottage of Tess's destination.

IX

THE COMMUNITY OF FOWLS TO WHICH TESS HAD BEEN APPOINTED AS SUPERVISOR, PURveyor, nurse, surgeon, and friend, made its head-quarters in an old thatched cottage standing in an enclosure that had once been a garden, but was now a trampled and sanded square. The house was overrun with ivy, its chimney being enlarged by the boughs of the parasite to the aspect of a ruined tower. The lower-rooms were entirely given over to the birds, who walked about them with a proprietary air, as though the place had been built by themselves, and not by certain dusty copyholders who now lay east and west in the churchyard. The descendants of these bygone owners felt it almost as a slight to their family when the house which had so much of their affection, had cost so much of their forefathers' money, and had been in their possession for several generations before the d'Urbervilles came and built here, was indifferently turned into a fowl-house by Mrs. Stoke-d'Urberville as soon as the property fell into hand according to law. " 'Twas good enough for Christians in grand-father's time," they said.

The rooms wherein dozens of infants had wailed at their nursing now resounded with the tapping of nascent chicks. Distracted hens in coops occupied spots where formerly stood chairs supporting sedate agriculturists. The chimney-corner and once blazing hearth was now filled with inverted beehives, in which the hens laid their eggs; while out-of-doors the plots that each succeeding householder had carefully shaped with his spade were torn by the cocks in wildest fashion.

The garden in which the cottage stood was surrounded by a wall, and could only be entered through a door.

When Tess had occupied herself about an hour the next morning in altering and improving the arrangements, according to her skilled ideas as the daughter of a professed poulterer, the door in the wall opened and a servant in white cap and apron entered. She had come from the manor-house.

"Mrs. d'Urberville wants the fowls as usual," she said; but perceiving that Tess did not quite understand, she explained, "Mis'ess is a old lady, and blind."

"Blind!" said Tess.

Almost before her misgiving at the news could find time to shape itself she took, under her companion's direction, two of the most beautiful of the Hamburghs in her arms, and followed the maid-servant, who had likewise taken two, to the adjacent mansion, which, though ornate and imposing, showed traces everywhere on this side that some occupant of its chambers could bend to the love of dumb creatures—feathers floating within view of the front, and hen-coops standing on the grass.

In a sitting-room on the ground floor, ensconced in an arm-chair with her back to the light, was the owner and mistress of the estate, a white-haired woman of not more than sixty, or even less, wearing a large cap. She had the mobile face frequent in those whose sight has decayed by stages, has been laboriously striven after, and reluctantly let go, rather than the stagnant mien apparent in persons long sightless or born blind. Tess walked up to this lady with her feathered charges—one sitting on each arm.

"Ah, you are the young woman come to look after my birds?" said Mrs. d'Urberville, recognising a new footstep. "I hope you will be kind to them. My bailiff tells me you are quite the proper person. Well, where are they? Ah, this is Strut! But he is hardly so lively to-day, is he? He is alarmed at being handled by a stranger, I suppose. And Phena too—yes, they are a little frightened—aren't you, dears? But they will soon get used to you."

While the old lady had been speaking Tess and the other maid, in obedience to her gestures, had placed the fowls severally in her lap, and she had felt them over from head to tail, examining their beaks, their combs, the manes of the cocks, their winds, and their claws. Her touch enabled her to recognise them in a moment, and to discover if a single feather were crippled or draggled. She handled their crops, and knew what they had eaten, and if too little or too much; her face enacting a vivid pantomime of the criticisms passing in her mind.

The birds that the two girls had brought in were duly returned to the yard, and the process was repeated till all the pet cocks and hens had been submitted to the old woman—Hamburghs, Bantams, Cochins, Brahmas, Dorkings, and such other sorts as were in fashion just then—her perception of each visitor being seldom at fault as she received the bird upon her knees.

It reminded Tess of a Confirmation, in which Mrs. d'Urberville was the bishop, the fowls the young people presented, and herself and the maid-servant the parson and curate of the parish bringing them up. At the end of the ceremony Mrs. d'Urberville abruptly asked Tess, wrinkling and twitching her face into undulations, "Can you whistle?"

"Whistle, ma'am?"

"Yes, whistle tunes."

Tess could whistle like most other country girls, though the accomplishment was one which she did not care to profess in genteel company. However, she blandly admitted that such was the fact.

"Then you will have to practise it everyday. I had a lad who did it very well, but he has left. I want you to whistle to my bullfinches; as I cannot see them I like to hear them, and we teach 'em airs that way. Tell her where the cages are, Elizabeth. You must begin to-morrow, or they will go back in their piping. They have been neglected these several days."

"Mr. d'Urberville whistled to 'em this morning, ma'am," said Elizabeth.

"He! Pooh!"

The old lady's face creased into furrows of repugnance, and she made no further reply.

Thus the reception of Tess by her fancied kinswoman terminated, and the birds were taken back to their quarters. The girl's surprise at Mrs. d'Urberville's manner was not great; for since seeing the size of the house she had expected no more. But she was far from being aware that the old lady had never heard a word of the so-called kinship. She gathered that no great affection flowed between the blind woman and her son. But in that, too, she was mistaken. Mrs. d'Urberville was not the first mother compelled to love her offspring resentfully, and to be bitterly fond.

In spite of the unpleasant initiation of the day before, Tess inclined to the freedom and novelty of her new position in the morning when the sun shone, now that she was once installed there; and she was curious to test her powers in the unexpected direction asked of her, so as to ascertain her chance of retaining her post. As soon as she was alone within the walled garden she sat herself down on a coop, and seriously screwed up her mouth for the long-neglected practice. She found her former ability to have degenerated to the production of a hollow rush of wind through the lips, and no clear note at all.

She remained fruitlessly blowing and blowing, wondering how she could have so grown out of the art which had come by nature, till she became aware of a movement among the ivy-boughs which cloaked the garden-wall no less then the cottage. Looking that way she beheld a form springing from the coping to the plot. It was Alec d'Urberville, whom she had not set eyes on since he had conducted her the day before to the door of the gardener's cottage where she had lodgings.

"Upon my honour!" cried he, "there was never before such a beautiful thing in Nature or Art as you look, 'Cousin' Tess ['Cousin' had a faint ring of mockery]. I have been watching you from over the wall—sitting like *Im*-patience on a monument, and pouting up that pretty red mouth to whistling shape, and whooing and whooing, and privately swearing, and never being able to produce a note. Why, you are quite cross because you can't do it."

"I may be cross, but I didn't swear."

"Ah! I understand why you are trying—those bullies! My mother wants you to carry on their musical education. How selfish of her! As if attending to these curst cocks and hens here were not enough work for any girl. I would flatly refuse, if I were you."

"But she wants me particularly to do it, and to be ready by to-morrow morning."

"Does she? Well then—I'll give you a lesson or two."

"Oh no, you won't!" said Tess, withdrawing towards the door.

"Nonsense; I don't want to touch you. See—I'll stand on this side of the wire-netting, and you can keep on the other; so you may feel quite safe. Now, look here; you screw up your lips too harshly. There 'tis—so."

He suited the action to the word, and whistled a line of "Take, O take those lips away." But the allusion was lost upon Tess.

"Now try," said d'Urberville.

She attempted to look reserved; her face put on a sculptural severity. But he persisted in his demand, and at last, to get rid of him, she did put up her lips as directed for producing a clear note; laughing distressfully, however, and then blushing with vexation that she had laughed.

He encouraged her with "Try again!"

Tess was quite serious, painfully serious by this time; and she tried—ultimately and unexpectedly emitting a real round sound. The momentary pleasure of success got the better of her; her eyes enlarged, and she involuntarily smiled in his face.

"That's it! Now I have started you—you'll go on beautifully. There—I said I would not come near you; and, in spite of such temptation as never before fell to mortal man, I'll keep my word. . . . Tess, do you think my mother a queer old soul?"

"I don't know much of her yet, sir."

"You'll find her so; she must be, to make you learn to whistle to her bullfinches. I am rather out of her books just now, but you will be quite in favour if you treat her live-stock well. Good-morning. If you meet with any difficulties and want help here, don't go to the bailiff, come to me."

It was in the economy of this *régime* that Tess Durbeyfield had undertaken to fill a place. Her first day's experiences were fairly typical of those which followed through many succeeding days. A familiarity with Alec d'Urberville's presence—which that young man carefully cultivated in her by playful dialogue, and by jestingly calling her his cousin when they were alone—removed much of her original shyness of him, without, however, implanting any feeling which could engender shyness of a new and tenderer kind. But she was more pliable under his hands than a mere companionship would have made her, owing to her unavoidable dependence upon his mother, and, through that lady's comparative helplessness, upon him.

She soon found that whistling to the bullfinches in Mrs. d'Urberville's room was no such onerous business when she had regained the art, for she had caught from her musical mother numerous airs that suited those songsters admirably. A far more satisfactory time than when she practised in the garden was this whistling by the cages each morning. Unrestrained by the young man's presence she threw up her mouth, put her lips near the bars, and piped away in easeful grace to the attentive listeners.

Mrs. d'Urberville slept in a large four-post bedstead hung with heavy damask curtains, and the bullfinches occupied the same apartment, where they flitted about freely at certain hours, and made little white spots on the furniture and upholstery. Once while Tess was at the window where the cages were ranged, giving her lesson as usual, she thought she heard a rustling behind the bed. The old lady was not present, and turning round the girl had an impression that the toes of a pair of boots were visible below the fringe of the curtains. Thereupon her whistling became so disjointed that the listener, if such there were, must have discovered her suspicion of his presence. She searched the curtains every morning after that, but never found anybody within them. Alec d'Urberville had evidently thought better of his freak to terrify her by an ambush of that kind.

X

EVERY VILLAGE HAS ITS IDIOSYNCRASY, ITS CONSTITUTION, OFTEN ITS OWN CODE OF morality. The levity of some of the younger women in and about Trantridge was marked, and was perhaps symptomatic of the choice spirit who ruled The Slopes in that vicinity. The place had also a more abiding defect; it drank hard. The staple conversation on the farms around was on the uselessness of saving money; and smock-frocked arithmeticians, leaning on their ploughs or hoes, would enter into calculations of great nicety to prove that parish relief was a fuller provision for a man in his old age than any which could result from savings out of their wages during a whole lifetime.

The chief pleasure of these philosophers lay in going every Saturday night, when work was done, to Chaseborough, a decayed market-town two or three miles distant; and, returning in the small hours of the next morning, to spend Sunday in sleeping off the dyspeptic effects of the curious compounds sold to them as beer by the monopolisers of the once independent inns.

For a long time Tess did not join in the weekly pilgrimages. But under pressure from matrons not much older than herself—for a field-man's wages being as high at twenty-one as at forty, marriage was early here—Tess at length consented to go. Her first experience of the journey afforded her more enjoyment than she had expected, the hilariousness of the others being quite contagious after her monotonous attention to the poultry-farm all the week. She went again and again. Being graceful and interesting, standing moreover on the momentary threshold of womanhood, her appearance drew down upon her some sly regards from loungers in the streets of Chaseborough; hence, though sometimes her journey to the town was made independently, she always searched for her fellows at night-fall, to have the protection of their companionship homeward.

This had gone on for a month or two when there came a Saturday in September, on which a fair and a market coincided; and the pilgrims from Trantridge sought double delights at the inns on that account. Tess's occupations made her late in setting out, so that her comrades reached the town long before her. It was a fine September evening, just before sunset, when yellow lights struggle with blue shades in hairlike lines, and the atmosphere itself forms a prospect without aid from more solid objects, except the innumerable winged insects that dance in it. Through this low-lit mistiness Tess walked leisurely along.

She did not discover the coincidence of the market with the fair till she had reached the place, by which time it was close upon dusk. Her limited marketing was soon completed; and then as usual she began to look about for some of the Trantridge cottagers.

At first she could not find them, and she was informed that most of them had gone to what they called a private little jig at the house of a hay-trusser and peat-dealer who had transactions with their farm. He lived in an out-of-the-way nook of the townlet, and in trying to find her course thither her eyes fell upon Mr. d'Urberville standing at a street corner.

"What—my Beauty? You here so late?" he said.

She told him that she was simply waiting for company homeward.

"I'll see you again," said he over her shoulder as she went on down the back lane.

Approaching the hay-trusser's she could hear the fiddled notes of a reel proceeding from some building in the rear; but no sound of dancing was audible—an exceptional state of things for these parts, where as a rule the stamping drowned the music. The front-door being open she could see straight through the house into the garden at the back as far as the shades of night would allow; and nobody appearing to her knock she traversed the dwelling and went up the path to the outhouse whence the sound had attracted her.

It was a windowless erection used for storage, and from the open door there floated into the obscurity a mist of yellow radiance, which at first Tess thought to be illuminated smoke. But on drawing nearer she perceived that it was a cloud of dust, lit by candles within the outhouse, whose beams upon the haze carried forward the outline of the door-way into the wide night of the garden.

When she came close and looked in she beheld indistinct forms racing up and down to the figure of the dance, the silence of their footfalls arising from their being overshoe in "scroff"—that is to say, the powdery residuum from the storage of peat and other products, the stirring of which by their turbulent feet created the nebulosity that involved the scene. Through this floating, fusty *débris* of peat and hay, mixed with the perspirations and warmth of the dancers, and forming together a sort of vegeto-human pollen, the muted fiddles feebly pushed their notes, in marked contrast to the spirit with which the measure was trodden out. They coughed as they danced, and laughed as they coughed. Of the rushing couples there could barely be discerned more than the high lights—the indistinct-ness shaping them to satyrs clasping nymphs—a multiplicity of Pans whirling a multi-plicity of Syrinxes; Lotis attempting to elude Priapus, and always failing.

At intervals a couple would approach the doorway for air, and the haze no longer veil-ing their features, the demi-gods resolved themselves into the homely personalities of her own next-door neighbours. Could Trantridge in two or three short hours have metamor-phosed itself thus madly!

Some Sileni of the throng sat on benches and hay-trusses by the wall; and one of them recognised her.

"The maids don't think it respectable to dance at 'The Flower-de-Luce,'" he ex-plained. "They don't like to let everybody see which be their fancy-men. Besides, the house sometimes shuts up just when their jints begin to get greased. So we come here and send out for liquor."

"But when be any of you going home?" asked Tess with some anxiety.

"Now—a'most directly. This is all but the last jig."

She waited. The reel drew to a close, and some of the party were in the mind of start-ing. But others would not, and another dance was formed. This surely would end it, thought Tess. But it merged in yet another. She became restless and uneasy; yet, having waited so long, it was necessary to wait longer; on account of the fair the roads were dot-ted with roving characters of possibly ill intent; and, though not fearful of measurable dan-gers, she feared the unknown. Had she been near Marlott she would have had less dread.

"Don't ye be nervous, my dear good soul," expostulated, between his coughs, a young man with a wet face, and his straw hat so far back upon his head that the brim encircled it like the nimbus of a saint. "What's yer hurry? To-morrow is Sunday, thank God, and we can sleep it off in church-time. Now, have a turn with me?"

She did not abhor dancing, but she was not going to dance here. The movement grew more passionate: the fiddlers behind the luminous pillar of cloud now and then varied the air by playing on the wrong side of the bridge or with the back of the bow. But it did not matter; the panting shapes spun onwards.

They did not vary their partners if their inclination were to stick to previous ones. Changing partners simply meant that a satisfactory choice had not as yet been arrived at by one or other of the pair, and by this time every couple had been suitably matched. It was then that the ecstasy and the dream began, in which emotion was the matter of the universe, and matter but an adventitious intrusion likely to hinder you from spinning where you wanted to spin.

Suddenly there was a dull thump on the ground: a couple had fallen, and lay in a mixed heap. The next couple, unable to check its progress, came toppling over the obstacle. An inner cloud of dust rose around the prostrate figures amid the general one of the room, in which a twitching entanglement of arms and legs was discernible.

"You shall catch it for this, my gentleman, when you get home!" burst in female accents from the human heap—those of the unhappy partner of the man whose clumsiness had caused the mishap; she happened also to be his recently married wife, in which assortment there was nothing unusual at Trantridge as long as any affection remained between wedded couples; and, indeed, it was not uncustomary in their later lives, to avoid making odd lots of the single people between whom there might be a warm understanding.

A loud laugh from behind Tess's back, in the shade of the garden, united with the titter within the room. She looked round, and saw the red coal of a cigar: Alec d'Urberville was standing there alone. He beckoned to her, and she reluctantly retreated towards him.

"Well, my Beauty, what are you doing here?"

She was so tired after her long day and her walk that she confided her trouble to him—that she had been waiting ever since he saw her to have their company home, because the road at night was strange to her. "But it seems they will never leave off, and I really think I will wait no longer."

"Certainly do not. I have only a saddle-horse here to-day; but come to 'The Flower-de-Luce,' and I'll hire a trap, and drive you home with me."

Tess, though flattered, had never quite got over her original mistrust of him, and, despite their tardiness, she preferred to walk home with the work-folk. So she answered that she was much obliged to him, but would not trouble him. "I have said that I will wait for 'em, and they will expect me to now."

"Very well, Miss Independence. Please yourself. . . . Then I shall not hurry. . . . My good Lord, what a kick-up they are having there!"

He had not put himself forward into the light, but some of them had perceived him, and his presence led to a slight pause and a consideration of how the time was flying. As soon as he had relit a cigar and walked away the Trantridge people began to collect themselves from amid those who had come in from other farms, and prepared to leave in a body. Their bundles and baskets were gathered up, and half an hour later, when the clock-chime sounded a quarter past eleven, they were straggling along the lane which led up the hill towards their homes.

It was a three-mile walk, along a dry white road, made whiter to-night by the light of the moon.

Tess soon perceived as she walked in the flock, sometimes with this one, sometimes with that, that the fresh night air was producing staggerings and serpentine courses among then men who had partaken too freely; some of the more careless women also were wandering in their gait—to wit, a dark virago, Car Darch, dubbed Queen of Spades, till lately a favourite of d'Urberville's; Nancy, her sister, nick-named the Queen of Diamonds; and the young married woman who had already tumbled down. Yet however terrestrial and lumpy their appearance just now to the mean unglamoured eye, to themselves the case was different. They followed the road with a sensation that they were soaring along in a supporting medium, possessed of original and profound thoughts, themselves and surrounding nature forming an organism of which all the parts harmoniously and joyously interpenetrated each other. They were as sublime as the moon and stars above them, and the moon and stars were as ardent as they.

Tess, however, had undergone such painful experiences of this kind in her father's house, that the discovery of their condition spoilt the pleasure she was beginning to feel in the moonlight journey. Yet she stuck to the party, for reasons above given.

In the open highway they had progressed in scattered order; but now their route was through a field gate, and the foremost finding a difficulty in opening it they closed up together.

This leading pedestrian was Car the Queen of Spades, who carried a wicker-basket containing her mother's groceries, her own draperies, and other purchases for the week. The basket being large and heavy, Car had placed it for convenience of porterage on the top of her head, where it rode on in jeopardised balance as she walked with arms akimbo.

"Well—whatever is that a-creeping down thy back, Car Darch?" said one of the group suddenly.

All looked at Car. Her gown was a light cotton print, and from the back of her head a kind of rope could be seen descending to some distance below her waist, like a Chinaman's queue.

" 'Tis her hair falling down," said another.

No; it was not her hair: it was a black stream of something oozing from her basket, and it glistened like a slimy snake in the cold still rays of the moon.

" 'Tis treacle," said an observant matron.

Treacle it was. Car's poor old grand-mother had a weakness for the sweet stuff. Honey she had in plenty out of her own hives, but treacle was what her soul desired, and Car had been about to give her a treat of surprise. Hastily lowering the basket the dark girl found that the vessel containing the syrup had been smashed within.

By this time there had arisen a shout of laughter at the extraordinary appearance of Car's back, which irritated the dark queen into getting rid of the disfigurement by the first sudden means available, and independently of the help of the scoffers. She rushed excitedly into the field they were about to cross, and flinging herself flat on her back upon the grass, began to wipe her gown as well as she could by spinning horizontally on the herbage and dragging herself over it upon her elbows.

The laughter rang louder; they clung to the gate, to the posts, rested on their staves, in the weakness engendered by their convulsions at the spectacle of Car. Our heroine, who had hitherto held her peace, at this wild moment could not help joining in with the rest.

It was a misfortune—in more ways than one. No sooner did the dark queen hear the soberer richer note of Tess among those of the other workpeople than a long smouldering sense of rivalry inflamed her to madness. She sprang to her feet and closely faced the object of her dislike.

"How darest th' laugh at me, hussy!" she cried.

"I couldn't really help it when t'others did," apologised Tess, still tittering.

"Ah, th'st think th' beest everybody, dostn't, because th' beest first favourite with He just now! But stop a bit, my lady, stop a bit! I'm as good as two of such! Look here—here's at 'ee!"

To Tess's horror the dark queen began stripping off the bodice of her gown—which for the added reason of its ridiculed condition she was only too glad to be free of—till she had bared her plump neck, shoulders, and arms to the moonshine, under which they looked as luminous and beautiful as some Praxitelean creation, in their possession of the faultless rotundities of a lusty country girl. She closed her fists and squared up at Tess.

"Indeed, then, I shall not fight!" said the latter majestically; "and if I had known you was of that sort, I wouldn't have so let myself down as to come with such a whorage as this is!"

The rather too inclusive speech brought down a torrent of vituperation from other quarters upon fair Tess's unlucky head, particularly from the Queen of Diamonds, who having stood in the relations to d'Urberville that Car had also been suspected of, united with the latter against the common enemy. Several other women also chimed in, with an animus which none of them would have been so fatuous as to show but for the rollicking evening they had passed. Thereupon, finding Tess unfairly browbeaten, the husbands and lovers tried to make peace by defending her; but the result of that attempt was directly to increase the war.

Tess was indignant and ashamed. She no longer minded the loneliness of the way and the lateness of the hour; her one object was to get away from the whole crew as soon as possible. She knew well enough that the better among them would repent of their passion next day. They were all now inside the field, and she was edging back to rush off alone when a horseman emerged almost silently from the corner of the hedge that screened the road, and Alec d'Urberville looked round upon them.

"What the devil is all this row about, work-folk?" he asked.

The explanation was not readily forthcoming; and, in truth, he did not require any. Having heard their voices while yet some way off he had ridden creepingly forward, and learnt enough to satisfy himself.

Tess was standing apart from the rest, near the gate. He bent over towards her. "Jump up behind me," he whispered, "and we'll get shot of the screaming cats in a jiffy!"

She felt almost ready to faint, so vivid was her sense of the crisis. At almost any other moment of her life she would have refused such proffered aid and company, as she had refused them several times before; and now the loneliness would not of itself have forced her to do otherwise. But coming as the invitation did at the particular juncture when fear and indignation at these adversaries could be transformed by a spring of the foot into a triumph over them, she abandoned herself to her impulse, climbed the gate, put her toe upon his instep, and scrambled into the saddle behind him. The pair were speeding away into the distant grey by the time that the contentious revellers became aware of what had happened.

The Queen of Spades forgot the stain on her bodice, and stood beside the Queen of Diamonds and the new-married, staggering young woman—all with a gaze of fixity in the direction in which the horse's tramp was diminishing into silence on the road.

"What be ye looking at?" asked a man who had not observed the incident.

"Ho-ho-ho!" laughed dark Car.

"Hee-hee-hee!" laughed the tippling bride, as she steadied herself on the arm of her fond husband.

"Heu-heu-heu!" laughed dark Car's mother, stroking her moustache as she explained laconically: "Out of the frying-pan into the fire!"

Then these children of the open air, whom even excess of alcohol could scarce injure permanently, betook themselves to the field-path; and as they went there moved onward with them, around the shadow of each one's head, a circle of opalised light, formed by the moon's rays upon the glistening sheet of dew. Each pedestrian could see no halo but his or her own, which never deserted the head-shadow, whatever its vulgar unsteadiness might be; but adhered to it, and persistently beautified it; till the erratic motions seemed an inherent part of the irradiation, and the fumes of their breathing a component of the night's mist; and the spirit of the scene, and of the moonlight, and of Nature, seemed harmoniously to mingle with the spirit of wine.

XI

THE TWAIN CANTERED ALONG FOR SOME TIME WITHOUT SPEECH, TESS AS SHE CLUNG TO him still panting in her triumph, yet in other respects dubious. She had perceived that the horse was not the spirited one he sometimes rose, and felt no alarm on that score, though her seat was precarious enough despite her tight hold of him. She begged him to slow the animal to a walk which Alec accordingly did.

"Neatly done, was it not, dear Tess?" he said by and by.

"Yes!" said she. "I am sure I ought to be much obliged to you."

"And are you?"

She did not reply.

"Tess, why do you always dislike my kissing you?"

"I suppose—because I don't love you."

"You are quite sure?"

"I am angry with you sometimes!"

"Ah, I half feared as much." Nevertheless, Alec did not object to that confession. He knew that anything was better then frigidity. "Why haven't you told me when I have made you angry?"

"You know very well why. Because I cannot help myself here."

"I haven't offended you often by love-making?"

"You have sometimes."

"How many times?"

"You know as well as I—too many times."

"Every time I have tried?"

She was silent, and the horse ambled along for a considerable distance, till a faint luminous fog, which had hung in the hollows all the evening, became general and enveloped them. It seemed to hold the moonlight in suspension, rendering it more pervasive than in clear air. Whether on this account, or from absent-mindedness, or from sleepiness, she did not perceive that they had long ago passed the point at which the lane to Trantridge branched from the highway, and that her conductor had not taken the Trantridge track.

She was inexpressibly weary. She had risen at five o'clock every morning of that week, had been on foot the whole of each day, and on this evening had in addition walked the three miles to Chaseborough, waited three hours for her neighbours without eating or drinking, her impatience to start them preventing either; she had then walked a mile of the way home, and had undergone the excitement of the quarrel, till, with the slow progress of their steed, it was now nearly one o'clock. Only once, however, was she overcome by actual drowsiness. In that moment of oblivion her head sank gently against him.

D'Urberville stopped the horse, withdrew his feet from the stirrups, turned sideways on the saddle, and enclosed her waist with his arm to support her.

This immediately put her on the defensive, and with one of those sudden impulses of reprisal to which she was liable she gave him a little push from her. In his ticklish position he nearly lost his balance and only just avoided rolling over into the road, the horse, though a powerful one, being fortunately the quietest he rode.

"That is devilish unkind!" he said. "I mean no harm—only to keep you from falling."

She pondered suspiciously; till, thinking that this might after all be true, she relented, and said quite humbly, "I beg your pardon, sir."

"I won't pardon you unless you show some confidence in me. Good God!" he burst out, "what am I, to be repulsed so by a mere chit like you? For near three mortal months have you trifled with my feelings, eluded me, and snubbed me; and I won't stand it!"

"I'll leave you to-morrow, sir."

"No, you will not leave me to-morrow! Will you, I ask once more, show your belief in me by letting me clasp you with my arm? Come, between us two and nobody else, now. We know each other well; and you know that I love you, and think you the prettiest girl in the world, which you are. Mayn't I treat you as a lover?"

She drew a quick pettish breath of objection, writhing uneasily on her seat, looked far ahead, and murmured, "I don't know—I wish—how can I say yes or no when—"

He settled the matter by clasping his arm round her as he desired, and Tess expressed no further negative. Thus they sidled slowly onward till it struck her they had been advancing for an unconscionable time—far longer than was usually occupied by the short journey from Chaseborough, even at this walking pace, and that they were no longer on hard road, but in a mere trackway.

"Why, where be we?" she exclaimed.

"Passing by a wood."

"A wood—what wood? Surely we are quite out of the road?"

"A bit of The Chase—the oldest wood in England. It is a lovely night, and why should we not prolong our ride a little?"

"How could you be so treacherous!" said Tess, between archness and real dismay, and getting rid of his arm by pulling open his fingers one by one, though at the risk of slipping off herself. "Just when I've been putting such trust in you, and obliging you to please you, because I thought I had wronged you by that push! Please set me down, and let me walk home."

"You cannot walk home, darling, even if the air were clear. We are miles away from Trantridge, if I must tell you, and in this growing fog you might wander for hours among these trees."

"Never mind that," she coaxed. "Put me down, I beg you. I don't mind where it is; only let me get down, sir, please!"

"Very well, then, I will—on one condition. Having brought you here to this out-of-the-way place, I feel myself responsible for your safe-conduct home, whatever you may yourself feel about it. As to your getting to Trantridge without assistance, it is quite impossible; for, to tell the truth, dear, owing to this fog, which so disguises everything, I don't quite know where we are myself. Now, if you will promise to wait beside the horse while I walk through the bushes till I come to some road or house, and ascertain exactly our whereabouts, I'll deposit you here willingly. When I come back I'll give you full directions, and if you insist upon walking you may; or you may ride—at your pleasure."

She accepted these terms, and slid off on the near side, though not till he had stolen a cursory kiss. He sprang down on the other side.

"I suppose I must hold the horse?" said she.

"Oh no; it's not necessary," replied Alec, patting the panting creature. "He's had enough of it for to-night."

He turned the horse's head into the bushes, hitched him on to a bough, and made a sort of couch or nest for her in the deep mass of dead leaves.

"Now, you sit there," he said. "The leaves have not got damp as yet. Just give an eye to the horse—it will be quite sufficient."

He took a few steps away from her, but, returning, said, "By the by, Tess, your father has a new cob to-day. Somebody gave it to him."

"Somebody? You!"

D'Urberville nodded.

"O how very good of you that is!" she exclaimed, with a painful sense of the awkwardness of having to thank him just then.

"And the children have some toys."

"I didn't know—you ever sent them anything!" she murmured, much moved. "I almost wish you had not—yes, I almost wish it!"

"Why, dear?"

"It—hampers me so."

"Tessy—don't you love me ever so little now?"

"I'm grateful," she reluctantly admitted. "But I fear I do not—" The sudden vision of his passion for herself as a factor in this result so distressed her that, beginning with one slow tear, and then following with another, she wept outright.

"Don't cry, dear, dear one! Now sit down here, and wait till I come." She passively sat down amid the leaves he had heaped, and shivered slightly. "Are you cold?" he asked.

"Not very—a little."

He touched her with his fingers, which sank into her as into down. "You have only that puffy muslin dress on—how's that?"

"It's my best summer one. 'Twas very warm when I started, and I didn't know I was going to ride, and that it would be night."

"Nights grow chilly in September. Let me see." He pulled off a light overcoat that he had worn, and put it round her tenderly. "That's it—now you'll feel warmer," he continued. "Now, my pretty, rest there; I shall soon be back again."

Having buttoned the overcoat round her shoulders he plunged into the webs of vapour which by this time formed veils between the trees. She could hear the rustling of the branches as he ascended the adjoining slope, till his movements were no louder than the hopping of a bird, and finally died away. With the setting of the moon the pale light lessened, and Tess became invisible as she fell into reverie upon the leaves where he had left her.

In the meantime Alec d'Urberville had pushed on up the slope to clear his genuine doubt as to the quarter of The Chase they were in. He had, in fact, ridden quite at random for over an hour, taking any turning that came to hand in order to prolong companionship with her, and giving far more attention to Tess's moonlit person than to any wayside object. A little rest for the jaded animal being desirable, he did not hasten his search for landmarks. A clamber over the hill into the adjoining vale brought him to the fence of a highway whose contours he recognised, which settled the question of their whereabouts. D'Urberville thereupon turned back; but by this time the moon had quite gone down, and partly on account of the fog The Chase was wrapped in thick darkness, although morning was not far off. He was obliged to advance with outstretched hands to avoid contact with the boughs, and discovered that to hit the exact spot from which he had started was at first entirely beyond him. Roaming up and down, round and round, he at length heard a slight movement of the horse close at hand; and the sleeve of his overcoat unexpectedly caught his foot.

"Tess!" said d'Urberville.

There was no answer. The obscurity was now so great that he could see absolutely nothing but a pale nebulousness at his feet, which represented the white muslin figure he had left upon the dead leaves. Everything else was blackness alike. D'Urberville stooped; and heard a gentle regular breathing. He knelt and bent lower, till her breath warmed his face, and in a moment his cheek was in contact with hers. She was sleeping soundly, and upon her eyelashes there lingered tears.

Darkness and silence ruled everywhere around. Above them rose the primaeval yews and oaks of The Chase, in which there poised gentle roosting birds in their last nap; and about them stole the hopping rabbits and hares. But, might some say, where was Tess's guardian-angel? where was the providence of her simple faith? Perhaps, like that other god of whom the ironical Tishbite spoke, he was talking, or he was pursuing, or he was in a journey, or he was sleeping and not to be awaked.

Why it was that upon this beautiful feminine tissue, sensitive as gossamer, and practically blank as snow as yet, there should have been traced such a coarse pattern as it was doomed to receive; why so often the coarse appropriates the finer thus, the wrong man the woman, the wrong woman the man, many thousand years of analytical philosophy have failed to explain to our sense of order. One may, indeed, admit the possibility of a retribution lurking in the present catastrophe. Doubtless some of Tess d'Urberville's mailed ancestors rollicking home from a fray had dealt the same measure even more ruthlessly towards peasant girls of their time. But though to visit the sins of the fathers upon the children may be a morality good enough for divinities, it is scorned by average human nature; and it therefore does not mend the matter.

As Tess's own people down in those retreats are never tired of saying among each other in their fatalistic way: "It was to be." There lay the pity of it. An immeasurable social chasm was to divide our heroine's personality thereafter from that previous self of hers who stepped from her mother's door to try her fortune at Trantridge poultry-farm.

END OF PHASE THE FIRST

Phase the Second

Maiden No More

XII

THE BASKET WAS HEAVY AND THE BUNDLE WAS LARGE, BUT SHE LUGGED THEM along like a person who did not find her especial burden in material things. Occasionally she stopped to rest in a mechanical way by some gate or post; and then, giving the baggage another hitch upon her full round arm, went steadily on again.

It was a Sunday morning in late October, about four months after Tess Durbeyfield's arrival at Trantridge, and some few weeks subsequent to the night ride in The Chase. The time was not long past daybreak, and the yellow luminosity upon the horizon behind her back lighted the ridge towards which her face was set—the barrier of the vale wherein she had of late been a stranger—which she would have to climb over to reach her birthplace. The ascent was gradual on this side, and the soil and scenery differed much from those within Blackmore Vale. Even the character and accent of the two peoples had shades of difference, despite the amalgamating effects of a roundabout railway; so that, though less than twenty miles from the place of her sojourn at Trantridge, her native village had seemed a far-away spot. The field-folk shut in there traded northward and westward, travelled, courted, and married northward and westward, thought northward and westward; those on this side mainly directed their energies and attention to the east and south.

The incline was the same down which d'Urberville had driven her so wildly on that day in June. Tess went up the remainder of its length without stopping, and on reaching the edge of the escarpment gazed over the familiar green world beyond, now half-veiled in mist. It was always beautiful from here; it was terribly beautiful to Tess to-day, for since her eyes last fell upon it she had learnt that the serpent hisses where the sweet birds sing, and her views of life had been totally changed for her by the lesson. Verily another girl than the simple one she had been at home was she who, bowed by thought, stood still here, and turned to look behind her. She could not bear to look forward into the Vale.

Ascending by the long white road that Tess herself had just laboured up, she saw a two-wheeled vehicle, beside which walked a man, who held up his hand to attract her attention.

She obeyed the signal to wait for him with unspeculative repose, and in a few minutes man and horse stopped beside her.

"Why did you slip away by stealth like this?" said d'Urberville, with upbraiding breathlessness; "on a Sunday morning, too, when people were all in bed! I only discovered it by accident, and I have been driving like the deuce to overtake you. Just look at the mare. Why go off like this? You know that nobody wished to hinder your going. And how unnecessary it has been for you to toil along on foot, and incumber yourself with this heavy load! I have followed like a madman, simply to drive you the rest of the distance, if you won't come back."

"I shan't come back," said she.

"I thought you wouldn't—I said so! Well, then, put up your basket, and let me help you on."

She listlessly placed her basket and bundle within the dog-cart, and stepped up, and they sat side by side. She had no fear of him now, and in the cause of her confidence her sorrow lay.

D'Urberville mechanically lit a cigar, and the journey was continued with broken unemotional conversation on the commonplace objects by the wayside. He had quite forgotten his struggle to kiss her when, in the early summer, they had driven in the opposite direction along the same road. But she had not, and she sat now, like a puppet, replying to his remarks in monosyllables. After some miles they came in view of the clump of trees beyond which the village of Marlott stood. It was only then that her still face showed the least emotion, a tear or two beginning to trickle down.

"What are you crying for?" he coldly asked.

"I was only thinking that I was born over there," murmured Tess.

"Well—we must all be born somewhere."

"I wish I had never been born—there or anywhere else!"

"Pooh! Well, if you didn't wish to come to Trantridge why did you come?"

She did not reply.

"You didn't come for love of me, that I'll swear."

" 'Tis quite true. If I had gone for love o' you, if I had ever sincerely loved you, if I loved you still, I should not so loath and hate myself for my weakness as I do now! . . . My eyes were dazed by you for a little, and that was all."

He shrugged his shoulders. She resumed—

"I didn't understand your meaning till it was too late."

"That's what every woman says."

"How can you dare to use such words!" she cried, turning impetuously upon him, her eyes flashing as the latent spirit (of which he was to see more some day) awoke in her. "My God! I could knock you out of the gig! Did it never strike your mind that what every woman says some women may feel?"

"Very well," he said, laughing; "I am sorry to wound you. I did wrong—I admit it." He dropped into some little bitterness as he continued: "Only you needn't be so everlastingly flinging it in my face. I am ready to pay to the uttermost farthing. You know you need not work in the fields or the dairies again. You know you may clothe yourself with the best, instead of in the bald plain way you have lately affected, as if you couldn't get a ribbon more than you earn."

Her lip lifted slightly, though there was little scorn, as a rule, in her large and impulsive nature.

"I have said I will not take anything more from you, and I will not—I cannot! I *should* be your creature to go on doing that, and I won't!"

"One would think you were a princess from your manner, in addition to a true and original d'Urberville—ha! ha! Well, Tess, dear, I can say no more. I suppose I am a bad fellow—a damn bad fellow. I was born bad, and I have lived bad, and I shall die bad in all probability. But, upon my lost soul, I won't be bad towards you again, Tess. And if certain circumstances should arise—you understand—in which you are in the least need, the least difficulty, send me one line, and you shall have by return whatever you require. I may not be at Trantridge—I am going to London for a time—I can't stand the old woman. But all letters will be forwarded."

She said that she did not wish him to drive her further, and they stopped just under the clump of trees. D'Urberville alighted, and lifted her down bodily in his arms, afterwards placing her articles on the ground beside her. She bowed to him slightly, her eye just lingering in his; and then she turned to take the parcels for departure.

Alec d'Urberville removed his cigar, bent towards her, and said—

"You are not going to turn away like that, dear? Come!"

"If you wish," she answered indifferently. "See how you've mastered me!"

She thereupon turned round and lifted her face to his, and remained like a marble term while he imprinted a kiss upon her cheek—half perfunctorily, half as if zest had not yet quite died out. Her eyes vaguely rested upon the remotest trees in the lane while the kiss was given, as though she were nearly unconscious of what he did.

"Now the other side, for old acquaintance' sake."

She turned her head in the same passive way, as one might turn at the request of a sketcher or hairdresser, and he kissed the other side, his lips touching cheeks that were damp and smoothly chill as the skin of the mushrooms in the fields around.

"You don't give me your mouth and kiss me back. You never willingly do that—you'll never love me, I fear."

"I have said so, often. It is true. I have never really and truly loved you, and I think I never can." She added mournfully, "Perhaps, of all things, a lie on this thing would do the most good to me now; but I have honour enough left, little as 'tis, not to tell that lie. If I did love you I may have the best o' causes for letting you know it. But I don't."

He emitted a laboured breath, as if the scene were getting rather oppressive to his heart, or to his conscience, or to his gentility.

"Well, you are absurdly melancholy, Tess. I have no reason for flattering you now, and I can say plainly that you need not be so sad. You can hold your own for beauty against any woman of these parts, gentle or simple; I say it to you as a practical man and well-wisher. If you are wise you will show it to the world more than you do before it fades. . . . And yet, Tess, will you come back to me? Upon my soul I don't like to let you go like this!"

"Never, never! I made up my mind as soon as I saw—what I ought to have seen sooner; and I won't come."

"Then good-morning, my four months' cousin—good-bye!"

He leapt up lightly, arranged the reins, and was gone between the tall red-berried hedges.

Tess did not look after him, but slowly wound along the crooked lane. It was still early, and though the sun's lower limb was just free of the hill, his rays, ungenial and peering, addressed the eye rather than the touch as yet. There was not a human soul near. Sad October and her sadder self seemed the only two existences haunting that lane.

As she walked, however, some footsteps approached behind her, the footsteps of a man; and owing to the briskness of his advance he was close at her heels and had said "Good-morning" before she had been long aware of his propinquity. He appeared to be an artisan of some sort, and carried a tin pot of red paint in his hand. He asked in a businesslike manner if he should take her basket, which she permitted him to do, walking beside him.

"It is early to be astir this Sabbath morn!" he said cheerfully.

"Yes," said Tess.

"When most people are at rest from their week's work."

She also assented to this.

"Though I do more real work to-day than all the week besides."

"Do you?"

"All the week I work for the glory of man, and on Sunday for the glory of God. That's more real than the other—hey? I have a little to do here at this stile." The man turned as he spoke to an opening at the roadside leading into a pasture. "If you'll wait a moment," he added, "I shall not be long."

As he had her basket she could not well do otherwise; and she waited, observing him. He set down her basket and the tin pot, and stirring the paint with the brush that was in it began painting large square letters on the middle board of the three composing the stile, placing a comma after each word, as if to give pause while that word was driven well home to the reader's heart—

THY, DAMNATION, SLUMBERETH, NOT.
2 PET. II. 3.

Against the peaceful landscape, the pale, decaying tints of the copses, the blue air of the horizon and the lichened stile-boards, these staring vermilion words shone forth. They seemed to shout themselves out and make the atmosphere ring. Some people might have cried "Alas, poor Theology!" at the hideous defacement—the last grotesque phase of a creed which had served mankind well in its time. But the words entered Tess with accusatory horror. It was as if this man had known her recent history; yet he was a total stranger.

Having finished his text he picked up her basket, and she mechanically resumed her walk beside him.

"Do you believe what you paint?" she asked in low tones.

"Believe that tex? Do I believe in my own existence!"

"But," said she tremulously, "suppose your sin was not of your own seeking?"

He shook his head.

"I cannot split hairs on that burning query," he said. "I have walked hundreds of miles this past summer, painting these texes on every wall, gate, and stile the length and breadth of this district. I leave their application to the hearts of the people who read 'em."

"I think they are horrible," said Tess. "Crushing! killing!"

"That's what they are meant to be!" he replied in a trade voice. "But you should read my hottest ones—them I kips for slums and seaports. They'd make ye wriggle! Not but what this is a very good tex for rural districts. . . . Ah—there's a nice bit of blank wall up by that barn standing to waste. I must put one there—one that it will be good for dangerous young females like yerself to heed. Will ye wait, missy?"

"No," said she; and taking her basket Tess trudged on. A little way forward she turned her head. The old grey wall began to advertise a similar fiery lettering to the first, with a strange and unwonted mien, as if distressed at duties it had never before been called upon to perform. It was with a sudden flush that she read and realised what was to be the inscription he was now half-way through—

THOU, SHALT, NOT, COMMIT—

Her cheerful friend saw her looking, stopped his brush, and shouted—

"If you want to ask for edification on these things of moment, there's a very earnest good man going to preach a charity-sermon to-day in the parish you are going to—Mr. Clare of Emminster. I'm not of his persuasion now, but he's a good man, and he'll expound as well as any parson I know. 'Twas he began the work in me."

But Tess did not answer; she throbbingly resumed her walk, her eyes fixed on the ground. "Pooh—I don't believe God said such things!" she murmured contemptuously when her flush had died away.

A plume of smoke soared up suddenly from her father's chimney, the sight of which made her heart ache. The aspect of the interior, when she reached it, made her heart ache more. Her mother, who had just come downstairs, turned to greet her from the fireplace, where she was kindling barked-oak twigs under the breakfast kettle. The young children were still above, as was also her father, it being Sunday morning, when he felt justified in lying an additional half-hour.

"Well!—my dear Tess!" exclaimed her surprised mother, jumping up and kissing the girl. "How be ye? I didn't see you till you was in upon me! Have you come home to be married?"

"No, I have not come for that, mother."

"Then for a holiday?"

"Yes—for a holiday; for a long holiday," said Tess.

"What, isn't your cousin going to do the handsome thing?"

"He's not my cousin, and he's not going to marry me."

Her mother eyed her narrowly.

"Come, you have not told me all," she said.

Then Tess went up to her mother, put her face upon Joan's neck, and told.

"And yet th'st not got him to marry 'ee!" reiterated her mother. "Any woman would have done it but you, after that!"

"Perhaps any woman would except me."

"It would have been something like a story to come back with, if you had!" continued Mrs. Durbeyfield, ready to burst into tears of vexation. "After all the talk about you and him which has reached us here, who would have expected it to end like this! Why didn't ye think of doing some good for your family instead o' thinking only of yourself? See how I've got to teave and slave, and your poor weak father with his heart clogged like a dripping-pan. I did hope for something to come out o' this! To see what a pretty pair you and he made that day when you drove away together four months ago! See what he has given us—all, as we thought, because we were his kin. But if he's not, it must have been done because of his love for 'ee. And yet you've not got him to marry!"

Get Alec d'Urberville in the mind to marry her! He marry *her*! On matrimony he had never once said a word. And what if he had? How a convulsive snatching at social salvation might have impelled her to answer him she could not say. But her poor foolish mother little knew her present feeling towards this man. Perhaps it was unusual in the circumstances, unlucky, unaccountable; but there it was; and this, as she had said, was what made her detest herself. She had never wholly cared for him, she did not at all care for him now. She had dreaded him, winced before him, succumbed to adroit advantages he took of her helplessness; then, temporarily blinded by his ardent manners, had been stirred to confused surrender a while: had suddenly despised and disliked him, and had run away. That was all. Hate him she did not quite; but he was dust and ashes to her, and even for her name's sake she scarcely wished to marry him.

"You ought to have been more careful if you didn't mean to get him to make you his wife!"

"O mother, my mother!" cried the agonised girl, turning passionately upon her parent as if her poor heart would break. "How could I be expected to know? I was a child when I left this house four months ago. Why didn't you tell me there was danger in menfolk? Why didn't you warn me? Ladies know what to fend hands against, because they read novels that tell them of these tricks; but I never had the chance o' learning in that way, and you did not help me!"

Her mother was subdued.

"I thought if I spoke of his fond feelings and what they might lead to, you would be hontish wi' him and lose your chance," she murmured, wiping her eyes with her apron. "Well, we must make the best of it, I suppose. 'Tis nater, after all, and what do please God!"

XIII

THE EVENT OF TESS DURBEYFIELD'S RETURN FROM THE MANOR OF HER BOGUS KINSFOLK was rumoured abroad, if rumour be not too large a word for a space of a square mile. In the afternoon several young girls of Marlott, former schoolfellows and acquaintances of Tess, called to see her, arriving dressed in their best starched and ironed, as became visitors to a person who had made a transcendent conquest (as they supposed), and sat round the room looking at her with great curiosity. For the fact that it was this said thirty-first cousin, Mr. d'Urberville, who had fallen in love with her, a gentleman not altogether local, whose reputation as a reckless gallant and heart-breaker was beginning to spread beyond the immediate boundaries of Trantridge, lent Tess's supposed position, by its fearsomeness, a far higher fascination that it would have exercised if unhazardous.

Their interest was so deep that the younger ones whispered when her back was turned—

"How pretty she is; and how that best frock do set her off! I believe it cost an immense deal, and that it was a gift from him."

Tess, who was reaching up to get the tea-things from the corner-cupboard, did not hear these commentaries. If she had heard them, she might soon have set her friends right on the matter. But her mother heard, and Joan's simple vanity, having been denied the hope of a dashing marriage, fed itself as well as it could upon the sensation of a dashing flirtation. Upon the whole she felt gratified, even though such a limited and evanescent triumph should involve her daughter's reputation; it might end in marriage yet, and in the warmth of her responsiveness to their admiration she invited her visitors to stay to tea.

Their chatter, their laughter, their good-humoured innuendoes, above all, their flashes and flickerings of envy, revived Tess's spirits also; and, as the evening wore on, she caught the infection of their excitement, and grew almost gay. The marble hardness left her face, she moved with something of her old bounding step, and flushed in all her young beauty.

At moments, in spite of thought, she would reply to their enquiries with a manner of superiority, as if recognising that her experiences in the field of courtship had, indeed, been slightly enviable. But so far was she from being, in the words of Robert South, "in love with her own ruin," that the illusion was transient as lightning; cold reason came back to mock her spasmodic weakness; the ghastliness of her momentary pride would convict her, and recall her to reserved listlessness again.

And the despondency of the next morning's dawn, when it was no longer Sunday, but Monday; and no best clothes; and the laughing visitors were gone, and she awoke alone in her old bed, the innocent younger children breathing softly around her. In place of the excitement of her return, and the interest it had inspired, she saw before her a long and stony highway which she had to tread, without aid, and with little sympathy. Her depression was then terrible, and she could have hidden herself in a tomb.

In the course of a few weeks Tess revived sufficiently to show herself so far as was necessary to get to church one Sunday morning. She liked to hear the chanting—such as it was—and the old Psalms, and to join in the Morning Hymn. That innate love of melody, which she had inherited from her ballad-singing mother, gave the simplest music a power over her which could well-nigh drag her heart out of her bosom at times.

To be as much out of observation as possible for reasons of her own, and to escape the gallantries of the young men, she set out before the chiming began, and took a back seat under the gallery, close to the lumber, where only old men and women came, and where the bier stood on end among the churchyard tools.

Parishioners dropped in by twos and threes, deposited themselves in rows before her, rested three-quarters of a minute on their foreheads as if they were praying, though they were not; then sat up, and looked around. When the chants came on one of her favourites happened to be chosen among the rest—the old double chant "Langdon"— but she did not know what it was called, though she would much have liked to know. She thought, without exactly wording the thought, how strange and godlike was a composer's power, who from the grave could lead through sequences of emotion, which he alone had felt at first, a girl like her who had never heard of his name, and never would have a clue to his personality.

The people who had turned their heads turned them again as the service proceeded; and at last observing her they whispered to each other. She knew what their whispers were about, grew sick at heart, and felt that she could come to church no more.

The bedroom which she shared with some of the children formed her retreat more continually than ever. Here, under her few square yards of thatch, she watched winds, and snows, and rains, gorgeous sunsets, and successive moons at their full. So close kept she that at length almost everybody thought she had gone away.

The only exercise that Tess took at this time was after dark; and it was then, when out in the woods, that she seemed least solitary. She knew how to hit to a hair's-breadth that moment of evening when the light and the darkness are so evenly balanced that the constraint of day and the suspense of night neutralise each other, leaving absolute mental liberty. It is then that the plight of being alive becomes attenuated to its least possible dimensions. She had no fear of the shadows; her sole idea seemed to be to shun mankind—

or rather that cold accretion called the world, which, so terrible in the mass, is so unformidable, even pitiable, in its units.

On these lonely hills and dales her quiescent glide was of a piece with the element she moved in. Her flexuous and stealthy figure became an integral part of the scene. At times her whimsical fancy would intensify natural processes around her till they seemed a part of her own story. Rather they became a part of it; for the world is only a psychological phenomenon, and what they seemed they were. The midnight airs and gusts, moaning amongst the tightly-wrapped buds and bark of the winter twigs, were formulae of bitter reproach. A wet day was the expression of irremediable grief at her weakness in the mind of some vague ethical being whom she could not class definitely as the God of her childhood, and could not comprehend as any other.

But this encompassment of her own characterisation, based on shreds of convention, peopled by phantoms and voices antipathetic to her, was a sorry and mistaken creation of Tess's fancy—a cloud of moral hobgoblins by which she was terrified without reason. It was they that were out of harmony with the actual world, not she. Walking among the sleeping birds in the hedges, watching the skipping rabbits on a moonlit warren, or standing under a pheasant-laden bough, she looked upon herself as a figure of Guilt intruding into the haunts of Innocence. But all the while she was making a distinction where there was no difference. Feeling herself in antagonism she was quite in accord. She had been made to break an accepted social law, but no law known to the environment in which she fancied herself such an anomaly.

XIV

IT WAS A HAZY SUNRISE IN AUGUST. THE DENSER NOCTURNAL VAPOURS, ATTACKED BY THE warm beams, were dividing and shrinking into isolated fleeces within hollows and coverts, where they waited till they should be dried away to nothing.

The sun, on account of the mist, had a curious sentient, personal look, demanding the masculine pronoun for its adequate expression. His present aspect, coupled with the lack of all human forms in the scene, explained the old-time heliolatries in a moment. One could feel that a saner religion had never prevailed under the sky. The luminary was a golden-haired, beaming, mild-eyed, Godlike creature, gazing down in the vigour and intentness of youth upon an earth that was brimming with interest for him.

His light, a little later, broke though chinks of cottage shutters, throwing stripes like red-hot pokers upon cupboards, chests of drawers, and other furniture within; and awakening harvesters who were not already astir.

But of all ruddy things that morning the brightest were two broad arms of painted wood, which rose from the margin of yellow corn-field hard by Marlott village. They, with two others below, formed the revolving Maltese cross of the reaping-machine, which had been brought to the field on the previous evening to be ready for operations this day. The paint with which they were smeared, intensified in hue by the sunlight, imparted to them a look of having been dipped in liquid fire.

The field had already been "opened"; that is to say, a lane a few feet wide had been hand-cut through the wheat along the whole circumference of the field, for the first passage of the horses and machine.

Two groups, one of men and lads, the other of women, had come down the lane just at the hour when the shadows of the eastern hedge-top struck the west hedge midway, so that the heads of the groups were enjoying sunrise while their feet were still in the dawn. They disappeared from the lane between the two stone posts which flanked the nearest field gate.

Presently there arose from within a ticking like the love-making of the grasshopper. The machine had begun, and a moving concatenation of three horses and the aforesaid long rickety machine was visible over the gate, a driver sitting upon one of the hauling horses, and an attendant on the seat of the implement. Along one side of the field the whole wain went, the arms of the mechanical reaper revolving slowly, till it passed down the hill quite out of sight. In a minute it came up on the other side of the field at the same equable pace; the glistening brass star in the forehead of the fore horse first catching the eye as it rose into view over the stubble, then the bright arms, and then the whole machine.

The narrow lane of stubble encompassing the field grew wider with each circuit, and the standing corn was reduced to smaller area as the morning wore on. Rabbits, hares, snakes, rats, mice, retreated inwards as into a fastness, unaware of the ephemeral nature of their refuge, and of the doom that awaited them later in the day when, their covert shrinking to a more and more horrible narrowness, they were huddled together, friends and foes, till the last few yards of upright wheat fell also under the teeth of the unerring reaper, and they were everyone put to death by the sticks and stones of the harvesters.

The reaping-machine left the fallen corn behind it in little heaps, each heap being of the quantity for a sheaf; and upon these the active binders in the rear laid their hands— mainly women, but some of them men in print shirts, and trousers supported round their waists by leather straps, rendering useless the two buttons behind, which twinkled and bristled with sunbeams at every movement of each wearer, as if they were a pair of eyes in the small of his back.

But those of the other sex were the most interesting of this company of binders, by reason of the charm which is acquired by woman when she becomes part and parcel of out-door nature, and is not merely an object set down therein as at ordinary times. A field-man is a personality afield; a field-woman is a portion of the field; she has somehow lost her own margin, imbibed the essence of her surrounding, and assimilated herself with it.

The women—or rather girls, for they were mostly young—wore drawn cotton bonnets with great flapping curtains to keep off the sun, and gloves to prevent their hands being wounded by the stubble. There was one wearing a pale pink jacket, another in a cream-coloured tight-sleeved gown, another in a petticoat as red as the arms of the reaping-machine; and others, older, in the brown-rough "wropper" or over-all—the old-established and most appropriate dress of the field-woman, which the young ones were abandoning. This morning the eye returns involuntarily to the girl in the pink cotton jacket, she being the most flexuous and finely-drawn figure of them all. But her bonnet is pulled so far over her brow that none of her face is disclosed while she binds, though her complexion may be guessed from a stray twine or two of dark brown hair which extends below the curtain of her bonnet. Perhaps one reason why she seduces casual attention is that she never courts it, though the other women often gaze around them.

Her binding proceeds with clocklike monotony. From the sheaf last finished she draws a handful of ears, patting their tips with her left palm to bring them even. Then stooping low she moves forward, gathering the corn with both hands against her knees, and pushing her left gloved hand under the bundle to meet the right on the other side, holding the corn in an embrace like that of a lover. She brings the ends of the bond together, and kneels on the sheaf while she ties it, beating back her skirts now and then when lifted by the breeze. A bit of her naked arm is visible between the buff leather of the gauntlet and the sleeve of her gown; and as the day wears on its feminine smoothness becomes scarified by the stubble, and bleeds.

At intervals she stands up to rest, and to retie her disarranged apron, or to pull her bonnet straight. Then one can see the oval face of a handsome young woman with deep dark eyes and long heavy clinging tresses, which seem to clasp in a beseeching way anything they fall against. The cheeks are paler, the teeth more regular, the red lips thinner than is usual in a country-bred girl.

It is Tess Durbeyfield, otherwise d'Urberville, somewhat changed—the same, but not the same; at the present stage of her existence living as a stranger and an alien here, though it was no strange land that she was in. After a long seclusion she had come to a resolve to undertake out-door work in her native village, the busiest season of the year in the agricultural world having arrived, and nothing that she could do within the house being so remunerative for the time as harvesting in the fields.

The movements of the other women were more or less similar to Tess's, the whole bevy of them drawing together like dancers in a quadrille at the completion of a sheaf by each, everyone placing her sheaf on end against those of the rest, till a shock, or "stitch" as it was here called, of ten or a dozen was formed.

They went to breakfast, and came again, and the work proceeded as before. As the hour of eleven drew near a person watching her might have noticed that every now and then Tess's glance flitted wistfully to the brow of the hill, though she did not pause in her sheafing. On the verge of the hour the heads of a group of children, of ages ranging from six to fourteen, rose over the stubbly convexity of the hill.

The face of Tess flushed slightly, but still she did not pause.

The eldest of the comers, a girl who wore a triangular shawl, its corner draggling on the stubble, carried in her arms what at first sight seemed to be a doll, but proved to be an infant in long clothes. Another brought some lunch. The harvesters ceased working, took their provisions, and sat down against one of the shocks. Here they fell to, the men plying a stone jar freely, and passing round a cup.

Tess Durbeyfield had been one of the last to suspend her labours. She sat down at the end of the shock, her face turned somewhat away from her companions. When she had deposited herself a man in a rabbit-skin cap and with a red handkerchief tucked into his belt, held the cup of ale over the top of the shock for her to drink. But she did not accept his offer. As soon as her lunch was spread she called up the big girl her sister, and took the baby of her, who, glad to be relieved of the burden, went away to the next shock and joined the other children playing there. Tess, with a curiously stealthy yet courageous movement, and with a still rising colour, unfastened her frock and began suckling the child.

The men who sat nearest considerately turned their faces towards the other end of the field, some of them beginning to smoke; one, with absent-minded fondness, regretfully stroking the jar that would no longer yield a stream. All the women but Tess fell into animated talk, and adjusted the disarranged knots of their hair.

When the infant had taken its fill the young mother sat it upright in her lap, and looking into the far distance dandled it with a gloomy indifference that was almost dislike; then all of a sudden she fell to violently kissing it some dozens of times, as if she could never leave off, the child crying at the vehemence of an onset which strangely combined passionateness with contempt.

"She's fond of that there child, though she mid pretend to hate en, and say she wishes the baby and her too were in the churchyard," observed the woman in the red petticoat.

"She'll soon leave off saying that," replied the one in buff. "Lord, 'tis wonderful what a body can get used to o' that sort in time!"

"A little more than persuading had to do wi' the coming o't, I reckon. There were they that heard a sobbing one night last year in The Chase; and it mid ha' gone hard wi' a certain party if folks had come along."

"Well, a little more, or a little less, 'twas a thousand pities that it should have happened to she, of all others. But 'tis always the comeliest! The plain ones be as safe as churches—hey, Jenny?" The speaker turned to one of the group who certainly was not ill-defined as plain.

It was a thousand pities, indeed; it was impossible for even an enemy to feel otherwise on looking at Tess as she sat there, with her flowerlike mouth and large tender eyes, neither black nor blue nor grey nor violet; rather all those shades together, and a hundred others, which could be seen if one looked into their irises—shade behind shade—tint beyond tint—around pupils that had no bottom; an almost standard woman, but for the slight incautiousness of character inherited from her race.

A resolution which had surprised herself had brought her into the fields this week for the first time during many months. After wearing and wasting her palpitating heart with every engine of regret that lonely inexperience could devise, common sense had illumined her. She felt that she would do well to be useful again—to taste anew sweet independence at any price. The past was past; whatever it had been it was no more at hand. Whatever its consequences, time would close over them; they would all in a few years be as if they had never been, and she herself grassed down and forgotten. Meanwhile the trees were just as green as before; the birds sang and the sun shone as clearly now as ever. The familiar surroundings had not darkened because of her grief, nor sickened because of her pain.

She might have seen that what had bowed her head so profoundly—the thought of the world's concern at her situation—was founded on an illusion. She was not an existence, an experience, a passion, a structure of sensations, to anybody but herself. To all humankind besides Tess was only a passing thought. Even to friends she was no more than a frequently passing thought. If she made herself miserable the livelong night and day it was only this much to them—"Ah, she makes herself unhappy." If she tried to be cheerful, to dismiss all care, to take pleasure in the daylight, the flowers, the baby, she could only be this idea to them—"Ah, she bears it very well." Moreover, alone in a desert island would she have been wretched at what had happened to her? Not greatly. If she could have been but just created, to discover herself as a spouseless mother, with no experience of life except as the parent of a nameless child, would the position have caused her to despair? No, she would have taken it calmly, and found pleasures therein. Most of the misery had been generated by her conventional aspect, and not by her innate sensations.

Whatever Tess's reasoning, some spirit had induced her to dress herself up neatly as she had formerly done, and come out into the fields, harvest-hands being greatly in demand just then. This was why she had borne herself with dignity, and had looked people calmly in the face at times, even when holding the baby in her arms.

The harvest-men rose from the shock of corn, and stretched their limbs, and extinguished their pipes. The horses, which had been unharnessed and fed, were again attached to the scarlet machine. Tess, having quickly eaten her own meal, beckoned to her eldest sister to come and take away the baby, fastened her dress, put on the buff gloves again, and stooped anew to draw a bond from the last completed sheaf for the tying of the next.

In the afternoon and evening the proceedings of the morning were continued, Tess staying on till dusk with the body of harvesters. Then they all rode home in one of the largest waggons, in the company of a broad tarnished moon that had risen from the ground to the eastwards, its face resembling the outworn gold-leaf halo of some worm-eaten Tuscan saint. Tess's female companions sang songs, and showed themselves very sympathetic and glad at her reappearance out-of-doors, though they could not refrain from mischievously throwing in a few verses of the ballad about the maid who went to the merry green wood and came back a changed state. There are counterpoises and compensations in life; and the event which had made of her a social warning had also for the moment made her the most interesting personage in the village to many. Their friendliness won her still farther away from herself, their lively spirits were contagious, and she became almost gay.

But now that her moral sorrows were passing away a fresh one arose on the natural side of her which knew no social law. When she reached home it was to learn to her grief that the baby had been suddenly taken ill since the afternoon. Some such collapse had been probable, so tender and puny was its frame; but the event came as a shock nevertheless.

The baby's offence against society in coming into the world was forgotten by the girl-mother; her soul's desire was to continue that offence by preserving the life of the child. However, it soon grew clear that the hour of emancipation for that little prisoner of the flesh was to arrive earlier than her worst misgiving had conjectured. And when she had discovered this she was plunged into a misery which transcended that of the child's simple loss. Her baby had not been baptised.

Tess had drifted into a frame of mind which accepted passively the consideration that if she should have to burn for what she had done, burn she must, and there was an end of it. Like all village girls she was well grounded in the Holy Scriptures, and had dutifully studied the histories of Aholah and Aholibah, and knew the inferences to be drawn therefrom. But when the same question arose with regard to the baby, it had a very different colour. Her darling was about to die, and no salvation.

It was nearly bed-time, but she rushed downstairs and asked if she might send for the parson. The moment happened to be one at which her father's sense of the antique nobility of his family was highest, and his sensitiveness to the smudge which Tess had set upon that nobility most pronounced, for he had just returned from his weekly booze at Rolliver's Inn. No parson should come inside his door, he declared, prying into his affairs, just then, when, by her shame, it had become more necessary than ever to hide them. He locked the door and put the key in his pocket.

The household went to bed, and, distressed beyond measure, Tess retired also. She was continually waking as she lay, and in the middle of the night found that the baby was still worse. It was obviously dying—quietly and painlessly, but none the less surely.

In her misery she rocked herself upon the bed. The clock struck the solemn hour of one, that hour when fancy stalks outside reason, and malignant possibilities stand rock-firm as facts. She thought of the child consigned to the nethermost corner of hell, as its double doom for lack of baptism and lack of legitimacy; saw the arch-fiend tossing it with his three-pronged fork, like the one they used for heating the oven on baking days; to which picture she added many other quaint and curious details of torment sometimes taught the young in this Christian country. The lurid presentment so powerfully affected her imagination in the silence of the sleeping house that her night-gown became damp with perspiration, and the bedstead shook with each throb of her heart.

The infant's breathing grew more difficult, and the mother's mental tension increased. It was useless to devour the little thing with kisses; she could stay in bed no longer, and walked feverishly about the room.

"O merciful God, have pity; have pity upon my poor baby!" she cried. "Heap as much anger as you want to upon me, and welcome; but pity the child!"

She leant against the chest of drawers, and murmured incoherent supplications for a long while, till she suddenly started up.

"Ah! perhaps baby can be saved! Perhaps it will be just the same!"

She spoke so brightly that it seemed as though her face might have shone in the gloom surrounding her.

She lit a candle, and went to a second and a third bed under the wall, where she awoke her young sisters and brothers, all of whom occupied the same room. Pulling out the washing-stand so that she could get behind it, she poured some water from a jug, and made them kneel around, putting their hands together with fingers exactly vertical. While the children, scarcely awake, awe-stricken at her manner, their eyes growing larger and larger, remained in this position, she took the baby from her bed—a child's child—so immature as scarce to seem a sufficient personality to endow its producer with the maternal title. Tess then stood erect with the infant on her arm beside the basin, the next sister held the Prayer-book open before her, as the clerk at church held it before the parson; and thus the girl set about baptising her child.

Her figure looked singularly tall and imposing as she stood in her long white night-gown, a thick cable of twisted dark hair hanging straight down her back to her waist. The kindly dimness of the weak candle abstracted from her form and features the little blemishes which sunlight might have revealed—the stubble scratches upon her wrists, and the weariness of her eyes—her high enthusiasm having a transfiguring effect upon the face which had been her undoing, showing it as a thing of immaculate beauty, with a touch of dignity which was almost regal. The little ones kneeling round, their sleepy eyes blinking and red, awaited her preparations full of a suspended wonder which their physical heaviness at that hour would not allow to become active.

The most impressed of them said:

"Be you really going to christen him, Tess?"

The girl-mother replied in a grave affirmative.

"What's his name going to be?"

She had not thought of that, but a name suggested by a phrase in the book of Genesis came into her head as she proceeded with the baptismal service, and now she pronounced it:

"SORROW, I baptise thee in the name of the Father, and the Son, and the Holy Ghost."

She sprinkled the water, and there was silence.

"Say 'Amen,' children."

The tiny voices piped in obedient response "Amen!"

Tess went on:

"We receive this child"—and so forth—"and do sign him with the sign of the Cross."

Here she dipped her hand into the basin, and fervently drew an immense cross upon the baby with her forefinger, continuing with the customary sentences as to his manfully fighting against sin, the world, and the devil, and being a faithful soldier and servant unto his life's end. She duly went on with the Lord's Prayer, the children lisping it after her in a thin gnatlike wail, till, at the conclusion, raising their voices to clerk's pitch, they again piped into silence, "Amen!"

Then their sister, with much augmented confidence in the efficacy of the sacrament, poured forth from the bottom of her heart the thanksgiving that follows, uttering it boldly and triumphantly in the stopt-diapason note which her voice acquired when her heart was in her speech, and which will never be forgotten by those who knew her. The ecstasy of faith almost apotheosised her; it set upon her face a glowing irradiation, and brought a red spot into the middle of each cheek; while the miniature candle-flame inverted in her eye-pupils shone like a diamond. The children gazed up at her with more and more reverence, and no longer had a will for questioning. She did not look like Sissy to them now, but as a being large, towering, and awful—a divine personage with whom they had nothing in common.

Poor Sorrow's campaign against sin, the world, and the devil was doomed to be of limited brilliancy—luckily perhaps for himself, considering his beginnings. In the blue of the morning that fragile soldier and servant breathed his last, and when the other children awoke they cried bitterly, and begged Sissy to have another pretty baby.

The calmness which had possessed Tess since the christening remained with her in the infant's loss. In the daylight, indeed, she felt her terrors about his soul to have been somewhat exaggerated; whether well founded or not she had no uneasiness now, reasoning that if Providence would not ratify such an act of approximation she, for one, did not value the kind of heaven lost by the irregularity—either for herself or for her child.

So passed away Sorrow the Undesired—that intrusive creature, that bastard gift of shameless Nature who respects not the social law; a waif to whom eternal Time had been a matter of days merely, who knew not that such things as years and centuries ever were; to whom the cottage interior was the universe, the week's weather climate, new-born babyhood human existence, and the instinct to suck human knowledge.

Tess, who mused on the christening a good deal, wondered if it were doctrinally sufficient to secure a Christian burial for the child. Nobody could tell this but the parson of the parish, and he was a new-comer, and did not know her. She went to his house after dusk, and stood by the gate, but could not summon courage to go in. The enterprise would have been abandoned if she had not by accident met him coming homeward as she turned away. In the gloom she did not mind speaking freely.

"I should like to ask you something, sir."

He expressed his willingness to listen, and she told the story of the baby's illness and the extemporised ordinance.

"And now, sir," she added earnestly, "can you tell me this—will it be just the same for him as if you had baptised him?"

Having the natural feelings of a tradesman at finding that a job he should have been called in for had been unskilfully botched by his customers among themselves, he was disposed to say no. Yet the dignity of the girl, the strange tenderness in her voice, combined to affect his nobler impulses—or rather those that he had left in him after ten years of endeavour to graft technical belief on actual scepticism. The man and the ecclesiastic fought within him, and the victory fell to the man.

"My dear girl," he said, "it will be just the same."

"Then will you give him a Christian burial?" she asked quickly.

The vicar felt himself cornered. Hearing of the baby's illness, he had conscientiously gone to the house after night-fall to perform the rite, and, unaware that the refusal to admit him had come from Tess's father and not from Tess, he could not allow the plea of necessity for its irregular administration.

"Ah—that's another matter," he said.

"Another matter—why?" asked Tess, rather warmly.

"Well—I would willingly do so if only we two were concerned. But I must not—for certain reasons."

"Just for once, sir!"

"Really I must not."

"O sir!" She seized his hand as she spoke.

He withdrew it, shaking his head.

"Then I don't like you!" she burst out, "and I'll never come to your church no more!"

"Don't talk so rashly."

"Perhaps it will be just the same to him if you don't? . . . Will it be just the same? Don't for God's sake speak as saint to sinner, but as you yourself to me myself—poor me!"

How the vicar reconciled his answer with the strict notions he supposed himself to hold on these subjects it is beyond a layman's power to tell, though not to excuse. Somewhat moved, he said in this case also—

"It will be just the same."

So the baby was carried in a small deal box, under an ancient woman's shawl, to the churchyard that night, and buried by lantern-light, at the cost of a shilling and a pint of beer to the sexton, in that shabby corner of God's allotment where He lets the nettles grow, and where all unbaptised infants, notorious drunkards, suicides, and others of the conjecturally damned are laid. In spite of the untoward surroundings, however, Tess bravely made a little cross of two laths and a piece of string, and having bound it with flowers, she stuck it up at the head of the grave one evening when she could enter the churchyard without being seen, putting at the foot also a bunch of the same flowers in a little jar of water to keep them alive. What matter was it that on the outside of the jar the eye of mere observation noted the words "Keelwell's Marmalade"? The eye of maternal affection did not see them in its vision of higher things.

XV

"BY EXPERIENCE," SAYS ROGER ASCHAM, "WE FIND OUT A SHORT WAY BY A LONG WAN-dering." Not seldom that long wandering unfits us for further travel, and of what use is our experience to us then? Tess Durbeyfield's experience was of this incapacitating kind. At last she had learned what to do; but who would now accept her doing?

If before going to the d'Urbervilles' she had vigorously moved under the guidance of sundry gnomic texts and phrases known to her and to the world in general, no doubt she would never have been imposed on. But it had not been in Tess's power—nor is it in any-body's power—to feel the whole truth of golden opinions while it is possible to profit by them. She—and how many more—might have ironically said to God with Saint Augus-tine: "Thou hast counselled a better course than Thou hast permitted."

She remained in her father's house during the winter months, plucking fowls, or cram-ming turkeys and geese, or making clothes for her sisters and brothers out of some finery which d'Urberville had given her, and she had put by with contempt. Apply to him she would not. But she would often clasp her hands behind her head and muse when she was supposed to be working hard.

She philosophically noted dates as they came past in the revolution of the year; the disastrous night of her undoing at Trantridge with its dark background of The Chase; also the dates of the baby's birth and death; also her own birthday; and every other day individualised by incidents in which she had taken some share. She suddenly thought one afternoon, when looking in the glass at her fairness, that there was yet another date, of greater importance to her than those; that of her own death, when all these charms would have disappeared; a day which lay sly and unseen among all the other days of the year, giving no sign or sound when she annually passed over it; but not the less surely there. When was it? Why did she not feel the chill of each yearly encounter with such a cold relation? She had Jeremy Taylor's thought that some time in the future those who had known her would say: "It is the ——th, the day that poor Tess Durbeyfield died"; and there would be nothing singular to their minds in the statement. Of that day, doomed to be her terminus in time through all the ages, she did not know the place in month, week, season, or year.

Almost at a leap Tess thus changed from simple girl to complex woman. Symbols of reflectiveness passed into her face, and a note of tragedy at times into her voice. Her eyes grew larger and more eloquent. She became what would have been called a fine creature; her aspect was fair and arresting; her soul that of a woman whom the turbulent experiences of the last year or two had quite failed to demoralise. But for the world's opinion those ex-periences would have been simply a liberal education.

She had held so aloof of late that her trouble, never generally known, was nearly for-gotten in Marlott. But it became evident to her that she could never be really comfortable again in a place which had seen the collapse of her family's attempt to "claim kin"—and, through her, even closer union—with the rich d'Urbervilles. At least she could not be comfortable there till long years should have obliterated her keen consciousness of it. Yet even now Tess felt the pulse of hopeful life still warm within her; she might be happy in some nook which had no memories. To escape the past and all that appertained thereto was to annihilate it, and to do that she would have to get away.

Was once lost always lost really true of chastity? she would ask herself. She might prove it false if she could veil bygones. The recuperative power which pervaded organic nature was surely not denied to maidenhood alone.

She waited a long time without finding opportunity for a new departure. A particularly fine spring came round, and the stir of germination was almost audible in the buds; it moved her, as it moved the wild animals, and made her passionate to go. At last, one day in early May, a letter reached her from a former friend of her mother's, to whom she had addressed enquiries long before—a person whom she had never seen—that a skilful milkmaid was required at a dairy-house many miles to the southward, and that the dairyman would be glad to have her for the summer months.

It was not quite so far off as could have been wished; but it was probably far enough, her radius of movement and repute having been so small. To persons of limited spheres, miles are as geographical degrees, parishes as counties, counties as provinces and kingdoms.

On one point she was resolved: there should be no more d'Urberville air-castles in the dreams and deeds of her new life. She would be the dairymaid Tess, and nothing more. Her mother knew Tess's feeling on this point so well, though no words had passed between them on the subject, that she never alluded to the knightly ancestry now.

Yet such is human inconsistency that one of the interests of the new place to her was the accidental virtues of its lying near her forefathers' country (for they were not Blakemore men, though her mother was Blakemore to the bone). The dairy called Talbothays, for which she was bound, stood not remotely from some of the former estates of the d'Urbervilles, near the great family vaults of her granddames and their powerful husbands. She would be able to look at them, and think not only that d'Urberville, like Babylon, had fallen, but that the individual innocence of a humble descendant could lapse as silently. All the while she wondered if any strange good thing might come of her being in her ancestral land; and some spirit within her rose automatically as the sap in the twigs. It was unexpected youth, surging up anew after its temporary check, and bringing with it hope, and the invincible instinct towards self-delight.

END OF PHASE THE SECOND

PHASE THE THIRD

THE RALLY

XVI

O
N A THYME-SCENTED, BIRD-HATCHING MORNING IN MAY, BETWEEN TWO AND three years after the return from Trantridge—silent reconstructive years for Tess Durbeyfield—she left her home for the second time.

Having packed up her luggage so that it could be sent to her later, she started in a hired trap for the little town of Stourcastle, through which it was necessary to pass on her journey, now in a direction almost opposite to that of her first adventuring. On the curve of the nearest hill she looked back regretfully at Marlott and her father's house, although she had been so anxious to get away.

Her kindred dwelling there would probably continue their daily lives as heretofore, with no great diminution of pleasure in their consciousness, although she would be far off, and they deprived of her smile. In a few days the children would engage in their games as merrily as ever, without the sense of any gap left by her departure. This leaving of the younger children she had decided to be for the best; were she to remain they would probably gain less good by her precepts than harm by her example.

She went through Stourcastle without pausing, and onward to a junction of highways, where she could await a carrier's van that ran to the south-west; for the railways which engirdled this interior tract of country had never yet struck across it. While waiting, however, there came along a farmer in his spring-cart, driving approximately in the direction that she wished to pursue. Though he was a stranger to her she accepted his offer of a seat beside him, ignoring that its motive was a mere tribute to her countenance. He was going to Weatherbury, and by accompanying him thither she could walk the remainder of the distance instead of travelling in the van by way of Casterbridge.

Tess did not stop at Weatherbury, after this long drive, further than to make a slight nondescript meal at noon at a cottage to which the farmer recommended her. Thence she started on foot, basket in hand, to reach the wide upland of heath dividing this district from the low-lying meads of a further valley in which the dairy stood that was the aim and end of her day's pilgrimage.

Tess had never before visited this part of the country, and yet she felt akin to the landscape. Not so very far to the left of her she could discern a dark patch in the scenery, which enquiry confirmed her in supposing to be trees marking the environs of Kingsbere—in the church of which parish the bones of her ancestors—her useless ancestors—lay entombed.

She had no admiration for them now; she almost hated them for the dance they had led her; not a thing of all that had been theirs did she retain but the old seal and spoon. "Pooh—I have as much of mother as father in me!" she said. "All my prettiness comes from her, and she was only a dairymaid."

The journey over the intervening uplands and lowlands of Egdon, when she reached them, was a more troublesome walk than she had anticipated, the distance being actually but a few miles. It was two hours, owing to sundry wrong turnings, ere she found herself on a summit commanding the long-sought-for vale, the Valley of the Great Dairies, the valley in which milk and butter grew to rankness, and were produced more profusely, if less delicately, than at her home—the verdant plain so well watered by the river Var or Froom.

It was intrinsically different from the Vale of Little Dairies, Blackmoor Vale, which, save during her disastrous sojourn at Trantridge, she had exclusively known till now. The world was drawn to a larger pattern here. The enclosures numbered fifty acres instead of ten, the farmsteads were more extended, the groups of cattle formed tribes hereabout; there only families. These myriads of cows stretching under her eyes from the far east to the far west outnumbered any she had ever seen at one glance before. The green lea was speckled as thickly with them as a canvas by Van Alsloot or Sallaert with burghers. The ripe hue of the red and dun kine absorbed the evening sunlight, which the white-coated animals returned to the eye in rays almost dazzling, even at the distant elevation on which she stood.

The bird's-eye perspective before her was not so luxuriantly beautiful, perhaps, as that other one which she knew so well; yet it was more cheering. It lacked the intensely blue atmosphere of the rival vale, and its heavy soils and scents; the new air was clear, bracing, ethereal. The river itself, which nourished the grass and cows of these renowned dairies, flowed not like the streams in Blackmoor. Those were slow, silent, often turbid; flowing over beds of mud into which the incautious wader might sink and vanish unawares. The Froom waters were clear as the pure River of Life shown to the Evangelist, rapid as the shadow of a cloud, with pebbly shallows that prattled to the sky all day long. There the water-flower was the lily; the crow-foot here.

Either the change in the quality of the air from heavy to light, or the sense of being amid new scenes where there were no invidious eyes upon her, sent up her spirits wonderfully. Her hopes mingled with the sunshine in an ideal photosphere which surrounded her as she bounded along against the soft south wind. She heard a pleasant voice in every breeze, and in every bird's note seemed to lurk a joy.

Her face had latterly changed with changing states of mind, continually fluctuating between beauty and ordinariness, according as the thoughts were gay or grave. One day she was pink and flawless; another pale and tragical. When she was pink she was feeling less then when pale; her more perfect beauty accorded with her less elevated mood; her more intense mood with her less perfect beauty. It was her best face physically that was now set against the south wind.

The irresistible, universal, automatic tendency to find sweet pleasure somewhere, which pervades all life, from the meanest to the highest, had at length mastered Tess. Being even now only a young woman of twenty, one who mentally and sentimentally had not finished growing, it was impossible that any event should have left upon her an impression that was not in time capable of transmutation.

And thus her spirits, and her thankfulness, and her hopes, rose higher and higher. She tried several ballads, but found them inadequate; till, recollecting the psalter that her eyes had so often wandered over of a Sunday morning before she had eaten of the tree of knowledge, she chanted: "O ye Sun and Moon . . . O ye Stars . . . ye Green Things upon the Earth . . . ye Fowls of the Air . . . Beasts and Cattle . . . Children of Men . . . bless ye the Lord, praise Him and magnify Him forever!"

She suddenly stopped and murmured: "But perhaps I don't quite know the Lord as yet."

And probably the half-unconscious rhapsody was a Fetichistic utterance in a Mono-theistic setting; women whose chief companions are the forms and forces of out-door Nature retain in their souls far more of the Pagan fantasy of their remote forefathers than of the systematised religion taught their race at later date. However, Tess found at least approximate expression for her feelings in the old *Benedicite* that she had lisped from in-fancy; and it was enough. Such high contentment with such a slight initial performance as that of having started towards a means of independent living was a part of the Durbey-field temperament. Tess really wished to walk uprightly, while her father did nothing of the kind; but she resembled him in being content with immediate and small achievements, and in having no mind for laborious effort towards such petty social advancement as could alone be effected by a family so heavily handicapped as the once powerful d'Urbervilles were now.

There was, it might be said, the energy of her mother's unexpected family, as well as the natural energy of Tess's years, rekindled after the experience which had so over-whelmed her for the time. Let the truth be told—women do as a rule live through such hu-miliations, and regain their spirits, and again look about them with an interested eye. While there's life there's hope is a conviction not so entirely unknown to the "betrayed" as some amiable theorists would have us believe.

Tess Durbeyfield, then, in good heart, and full of zest for life, descended the Egdon slopes lower and lower towards the dairy of her pilgrimage.

The marked difference, in the final particular, between the rival vales now showed it-self. The secret of Blackmoor was best discovered from the heights around; to read aright the valley before her it was necessary to descend into its midst. When Tess had accom-plished this feat she found herself to be standing on a carpeted level, which stretched to the east and west as far as the eye could reach.

The river had stolen from the higher tracts and brought in particles to the vale all this horizontal land; and now, exhausted, aged, and attenuated, lay serpentining along through the midst of its former spoils.

Not quite sure of her direction Tess stood still upon the hemmed expanse of verdant flatness, like a fly on a billiard-table of indefinite length, and of no more consequence to the surroundings than that fly. The sole effect of her presence upon the placid valley so far had been to excite the mind of a solitary heron, which, after descending to the ground not far from her path, stood with neck erect, looking at her.

Suddenly there arose from all parts of the lowland a prolonged and repeated call— "Waow! waow! waow!"

From the furthest east to the furthest west the cries spread as if by contagion, accom-panied in some cases by the barking of a dog. It was not the expression of the valley's con-sciousness that beautiful Tess had arrived, but the ordinary announcement of milking-time—half-past four o'clock, when the dairymen set about getting in the cows.

The red and white herd nearest at hand, which had been phlegmatically waiting for the call, now trooped towards the steading in the background, their great bags of milk swinging under them as they walked. Tess followed slowly in their rear, and entered the barton by the open gate through which they had entered before her. Long thatched sheds stretched round the enclosure, their slopes encrusted with vivid green moss, and their eaves supported by wooden posts rubbed to a glossy smoothness by the flanks of infinite cows and calves of bygone years, now passed to an oblivion almost inconceivable in its profundity. Between the post were ranged the milchers, each exhibiting herself at the present moment to a whimsical eye in the rear as a circle on two stalks, down the centre of which a switch moved pendulum-wise; while the sun, lowering itself behind this patient row, threw their shadows accurately inwards upon the wall. Thus it threw shadows of these obscure and homely figures every evening with as much care over each contour as if it had been the profile of a Court beauty on a palace wall; copied them as diligently as it had copied Olympian shapes on marble *façades* long ago, or the outline of Alexander, Cæsar, and the Pharaohs.

They were the less restful cows that were stalled. Those that would stand still of their own will were milked in the middle of the yard, where many of such better behaved ones stood waiting now—all prime milchers, such as were seldom seen out of this valley, and not always within it; nourished by the succulent feed which the water-meads supplied at this prime season of the year. Those of them that were spotted with white reflected the sunshine in dazzling brilliancy, and the polished brass knobs of their horns glittered with something of military display. Their large-veined udders hung ponderous as sandbags, the teats sticking out like the legs of a gypsy's crock; and as each animal lingered for her turn to arrive the milk oozed forth and fell in drops to the ground.

XVII

THE DAIRYMAIDS AND MEN HAD FLOCKED DOWN FROM THEIR COTTAGES AND OUT OF the dairy-house with the arrival of the cows from the meads; the maids walking in patterns, not on account of the weather, but to keep their shoes above the mulch of the barton. Each girl sat down on her three-legged stool, her face sideways, her right cheek resting against the cow; and looked musingly along the animal's flank at Tess as she approached. The male milkers, with hat-brims turned down, resting flat on their foreheads and gazing on the ground, did not observe her.

One of these was a sturdy middle-aged man—whose long white "pinner" was somewhat finer and cleaner than the wraps of the others, and whose jacket underneath had a presentable marketing aspect—the master-dairyman, of whom she was in quest, his double character as a working milker and butter-maker here during six days, and on the seventh as a man in shining broad-cloth in his family pew at church, being so marked as to have inspired a rhyme—

> *Dairyman Dick*
> *All the week:—*
> *On Sundays Mister Richard Crick.*

Seeing Tess standing at gaze he went across to her.

The majority of dairymen have a cross manner at milking time, but it happened that Mr. Crick was glad to get a new hand—for the days were busy ones now—and he received her warmly; enquiring for her mother and the rest of the family—(though this as a matter of form merely, for in reality he had not been aware of Mrs. Durbeyfield's existence till apprised of the fact by a brief business-letter about Tess).

"Oh—ay, as a lad I knowed your part o' the country very well," he said terminatively. "Though I've never been there since. And a aged woman of ninety that use to live nigh here, but is dead and gone long ago, told me that a family of some such name as yours in Blackmoor Vale came originally from these parts, and that 'twere a old ancient race that had all but perished off the earth—though the new generations didn't know it. But, Lord, I took no notice of the old woman's ramblings, not I."

"Oh no—it is nothing," said Tess.

Then the talk was of business only.

"You can milk 'em clean, my maidy? I don't want my cow going azew at this time o' year."

She reassured him on that point, and he surveyed her up and down. She had been staying indoors a good deal, and her complexion had grown delicate.

"Quite sure you can stand it? 'Tis comfortable enough here for rough folk; but we don't live in a cowcumber frame."

She declared that she could stand it, and her zest and willingness seemed to win him over.

"Well, I suppose you'll want a dish o' tay, or victuals of some sort, hey? Not yet? Well, do as ye like about it. But faith, if 'twas I, I should be as dry as a kex wi' travelling so far."

"I'll begin milking now, to get my hand in," said Tess.

She drank a little milk as temporary refreshment—to the surprise—indeed, slight contempt—of Dairyman Crick, to whose mind it had apparently never occurred that milk was good as a beverage.

"Oh, if ye can swaller that, be it so," he said indifferently, while one held up the pail that she sipped from. " 'Tis what I hain't touched for years—not I. Rot the stuff; it would lie in my innerds like lead. You can try your hand upon she," he pursued, nodding to the nearest cow. "Not but what she do milk rather hard. We've hard ones and we've easy ones, like other folks. However, you'll find out that soon enough."

When Tess had changed her bonnet for a hood, and was really on her stool under the cow, and the milk was squirting from her fists into the pail, she appeared to feel that she really had laid a new foundation for her future. The conviction bred serenity, her pulse slowed, and she was able to look about her.

The milkers formed quite a little battalion of men and maids, the men operating on the hard-teated animals, the maids on the kindlier natures. It was a large dairy. There were nearly a hundred milchers under Crick's management, all told; and of the herd the master-dairyman milked six or eight with his own hands, unless away from home. These were the cows that milked hardest of all; for his journey-milkmen being more or less casually hired, he would not entrust this half-dozen to their treatment, lest, from indifference, they should not milk them fully; nor to the maids, lest they should fail in the same way for lack of finger-grip; with the result that in course of time the cows would "go azew"—that is, dry up. It was not the loss for the moment that made slack milking so serious, but that with the decline of demand there came decline, and ultimately cessation, of supply.

After Tess had settled down to her cow there was for a time no talk in the barton, and not a sound interfered with the purr of the milk-jets into the numerous pails, except a momentary exclamation to one or other of the beasts requesting her to turn round or stand still. The only movements were those of the milkers' hands up and down, and the swing of the cows' tails. Thus they all worked on, encompassed by the vast flat mead which extended to either slope of the valley—a level landscape compounded of old landscapes long forgotten, and, no doubt, differing in character very greatly from the landscape they composed now.

"To my thinking," said the dairyman, rising suddenly from a cow he had just finished off, snatching up his three-legged stool in one hand and the pail in the other, and moving on to the next hard-yielder in his vicinity; "to my thinking, the cows don't gie down their milk to-day as usual. Upon my life, if Winker do begin keeping back like this, she'll not be worth going under by midsummer."

" 'Tis because there's a new hand come among us,' said Jonathan Kail. "I've noticed such things afore."

"To be sure. It may be so. I didn't think o't."

"I've been told that it goes up into their horns at such times," said a dairymaid.

"Well, as to going up into their horns," replied Dairyman Crick dubiously, as though even witchcraft might be limited by anatomical possibilities, "I couldn't say; I certainly could not. But as nott cows will keep it back as well as the horned ones, I don't quite agree to it. Do ye know that riddle about the nott cows, Jonathan? Why do nott cows give less milk in a year than horned?"

"I don't!" interposed the milkmaid, "Why do they?"

"Because there bain't so many of 'em," said the dairyman. "Howsomever, these gam'sters do certainly keep back their milk to-day. Folks, we must lift up a stave or two— that's the only cure for't."

Songs were often resorted to in dairies hereabout as an enticement to the cows when they showed signs of withholding their usual yield; and the band of milkers at this request burst into melody—in purely businesslike tones, it is true, and with no great spontaneity; the result, according to their own belief, being a decided improvement during the song's continuance. When they had gone through fourteen or fifteen verses of a cheerful ballad about a murderer who was afraid to go to bed in the dark because he saw certain brimstone flames around him, one of the male milkers said—

"I wish singing on the stoop didn't use up so much of a man's wind! You should get your harp, sir; not but what a fiddle is best."

Tess, who had given ear to this, thought the words were addressed to the dairyman, but she was wrong. A reply, in the shape of "Why?" came as it were out of the belly of a dun cow in the stalls; it had been spoken by a milker behind the animal, whom she had not hitherto perceived.

"Oh yes; there's nothing like a fiddle," said the dairyman. "Though I do think that bulls are more moved by a tune than cows—at least that's my experience. Once there was an old aged man over at Mellstock—William Dewy by name—one of the family that used to do a good deal of business as tranters over there, Jonathan, do ye mind?—I knowed the man by sight as well as I know my own brother, in a manner of speaking. Well, this man was a coming home-along from a wedding where he had been playing his fiddle, one fine moonlight night, and for shortness' sake he took a cut across Forty-acres, a field lying that way, where a bull was out to grass. The bull seed William, and took after him, horns aground, begad; and though William runned his best, and hadn't *much* drink in him (considering 'twas a wedding, and the folks well off), he found he'd never reach the fence and get over in time to save himself. Well, as a last thought, he pulled out his fiddle as he runned, and struck up a jig, turning to the bull, and backing towards the corner. The bull softened down, and stood still, looking hard at William Dewy, who fiddled on and on; till a sort of a smile stole over the bull's face. But no sooner did William stop his playing and turn to get over hedge than the bull would stop his smiling and lower his horns towards the seat of William's breeches. Well, William had to turn about and play on, willy-nilly; and 'twas only three o'clock in the world, and 'a knowed that nobody would come that way for hours, and he so leery and tired that 'a didn't know what to do. When he had scraped till about four o'clock he felt that he verily would have to give over soon, and he said to himself, 'There's only this last tune between me and eternal welfare! Heaven save me, or I'm a done man.' Well, then he called to mind how he'd seen the cattle kneel o' Christmas Eves in the dead o' night. It was not Christmas Eve then, but it came into his head to play a trick upon the bull. So he broke into the 'Tivity Hymn, just as at Christmas carol-singing; when, lo and behold, down went the bull on his bended knees, in his ignorance, just as if 'twere the true 'Tivity night and hour. As soon as his horned friend were down, William turned, clinked off like a long-dog, and jumped safe over hedge, before the praying bull had got on his feet again to take after him. William used to say that he'd seen a man look a fool a good many times, but never such a fool as that bull looked when he found his pious feelings had been played upon, and 'twas not Christmas Eve. . . . Yes, William Dewy, that was the man's name; and I can tell you to a foot where's he a-lying in Mellstock Churchyard at this very moment—just between the second yew-tree and the north aisle."

"It's a curious story; it carries us back to medieval times, when faith was a living thing!"

The remark, singular for a dairy-yard, was murmured by the voice behind the dun cow; but as nobody understood the reference no notice was taken, except that the narrator seemed to think it might imply scepticism as to his tale.

"Well, 'tis quite true, sir, whether or no. I knowed the man well."

"Oh yes; I have no doubt of it," said the person behind the dun cow.

Tess's attention was thus attracted to the dairyman's interlocutor, of whom she could see but the merest patch, owing to his burying his head so persistently in the flank of the milcher. She could not understand why he should be addressed as "sir" even by the dairyman himself. But no explanation was discernible; he remained under the cow long enough to have milked three, uttering a private ejaculation now and then, as if he could not get on.

"Take it gentle, sir; take it gentle," said the dairyman. " 'Tis knack, not strength that does it."

"So I find," said the other, standing up at last and stretching his arms. "I think I have finished her, however, though she made my fingers ache."

Tess could then see him at full length. He wore the ordinary white pinner and leather leggings of a dairy-farmer when milking, and his boots were clogged with the mulch of the yard; but this was all his local livery. Beneath it was something educated, reserved, subtle, sad, differing.

But the details of his aspect were temporarily thrust aside by the discovery that he was one whom she had seen before. Such vicissitudes had Tess passed through since that time that for a moment she could not remember where she had met him; and then it flashed upon her that he was the pedestrian who had joined in the club-dance at Marlott—the passing stranger who had come she knew not whence, had danced with others but not with her, and slightingly left her, and gone on his way with his friends.

The flood of memories brought back by this revival of an incident anterior to her troubles produced a momentary dismay lest, recognising her also, he should by some means discover her story. But it passed away when she found no sign of remembrance in him. She saw by degrees that since their first and only encounter his mobile face had grown more thoughtful, and had acquired a young man's shapely moustache and beard—the latter of the palest straw colour where it began upon his cheeks, and deepening to a warm brown farther from its root. Under his linen milking-pinner he wore a dark velveteen jacket, cord breeches and gaiters, and a starched white shirt. Without the milking-gear nobody could have guessed what he was. He might with equal probability have been an eccentric landowner or a gentlemanly ploughman. That he was but a novice at dairy-work she had realised in a moment, from the time he had spent upon the milking of one cow.

Meanwhile many of the milkmaids had said to one another of the new-comer, "How pretty she is!" with something of real generosity and admiration, though with a half hope that the auditors would qualify the assertion—which, strictly speaking, they might have done, prettiness being an inexact definition of what struck the eye in Tess. When the milking was finished for the evening they straggled indoors, where Mrs. Crick, the dairyman's wife—who was too respectable to go out milking herself, and wore a hot stuff gown in warm weather because the dairymaids wore prints—was giving an eye to the leads and things.

Only two or three of the maids, Tess learnt, slept in the dairy-house besides herself; most of the helpers going to their homes. She saw nothing at supper-time of the superior milker who had commented on the story, and asked no questions about him, the remainder of the evening being occupied in arranging her place in the bed-chamber. It was a large room over the milk-house, some thirty feet long; the sleeping-cots of the other three indoor milkmaids being in the same apartment. They were blooming young women, and, except one, rather older than herself. By bed-time Tess was thoroughly tired, and fell asleep immediately.

But one of the girls who occupied an adjoining bed was more wakeful than Tess, and would insist upon relating to the latter various particulars of the homestead into which she had just entered. The girl's whispered words mingled with the shades, and, to Tess's drowsy mind, they seemed to be generated by the darkness in which they floated.

"Mr. Angel Clare—he that is learning milking, and that plays the harp—never says much to us. He is a pa'son's son, and is too much taken up wi' his own thoughts to notice girls. He is the dairyman's pupil—learning farming in all its branches. He has learnt sheep-farming at another place, and he's now mastering dairy-work. . . . Yes, he is quite the gentleman-born. His father is the Reverent Mr. Clare at Emminster—a good many miles from here."

"Oh—I have heard of him," said her companion, now awake. "A very earnest clergyman, is he not?"

"Yes—that he is—the earnestest man in all Wessex, they say—the last of the old Low Church sort, they tell me—for all about here be what they call High. All his sons, except our Mr. Clare, be made pa'sons too."

Tess had not at this hour the curiosity to ask why the present Mr. Clare was not made a parson like his brethren, and gradually fell asleep again, the words of her informant coming to her along with the smell of the cheeses in the adjoining cheese-loft, and the measured dripping of the whey from the wrings downstairs.

XVIII

ANGEL CLARE RISES OUT OF THE PAST NOT ALTOGETHER AS A DISTINCT FIGURE, BUT AS an appreciative voice, a long regard of fixed, abstracted eyes, and a mobility of mouth somewhat too small and delicately lined for a man's, though with an unexpectedly firm close of the lower lip now and then; enough to do away with any inference of indecision. Nevertheless, something nebulous, preoccupied, vague, in his bearing and regard, marked him as one who probably had no very definite aim or concern about his material future. Yet as a lad people had said of him that he was one who might do anything if he tried.

He was the youngest son of his father, a poor parson at the other end of the county, and had arrived at Talbothays Dairy as a six months' pupil, after going the round of some other farms, his object being to acquire a practical skill in the various processes of farming, with a view either to the Colonies, or the tenure of a home-farm, as circumstances might decide.

His entry into the ranks of the agriculturists and breeders was a step in the young man's career which had been anticipated neither by himself nor by others.

Mr. Clare the elder, whose first wife had died and left him a daughter, married a second late in life. This lady had somewhat unexpectedly brought him three sons, so that between Angel, the youngest, and his father the vicar there seemed to be almost a missing generation. Of these boys the aforesaid Angel, the child of his old age, was the only son who had not taken a University degree, though he was the single one of them whose early promise might have done full justice to an academical training.

Some two or three years before Angel's appearance at the Marlott dance, on a day when he had left school and was pursuing his studies at home, a parcel came to the vicarage from the local bookseller's, directed to the Reverend James Clare. The vicar having opened it and found it to contain a book, read a few pages; whereupon he jumped up from his seat and went straight to the shop with the book under his arm.

"Why has this been sent to my house?" he asked peremptorily, holding up the volume.

"It was ordered, sir."

"Not by me, or anyone belonging to me, I am happy to say."

The shopkeeper looked into his order-book.

"Oh, it has been misdirected, sir," he said. "It was ordered by Mr. Angel Clare, and should have been sent to him."

Mr. Clare winced as if he had been struck. He went home pale and dejected, and called Angel into his study.

"Look into this book, my boy," he said. "What do you know about it?"

"I ordered it," said Angel simply.

"What for?"

"To read."

"How can you think of reading it?"

"How can I? Why—it is a system of philosophy. There is no more moral, or even religious, work published."

"Yes—moral enough; I don't deny that. But religious!—and for *you*, who intend to be a minister of the Gospel!"

"Since you have alluded to the matter, father," said the son, with anxious thought upon his face, "I should like to say, once for all, that I should prefer not to take Orders. I fear I could not conscientiously do so. I love the Church as one loves a parent. I shall always have the warmest affection for her. There is no institution for whose history I have a deeper admiration; but I cannot honestly be ordained her minister, as my brothers are, while she refuses to liberate her mind from an untenable redemptive theolatry."

It had never occurred to the straightforward and simple-minded vicar that one of his own flesh and blood could come to this! He was stultified, shocked, paralysed. And if Angel were not going to enter the Church, what was the use of sending him to Cambridge? The University as a step to anything but ordination seemed, to this man of fixed ideas, a preface without a volume. He was a man not merely religious, but devout; a firm believer—not as the phrase is now elusively construed by theological thimble-riggers in the Church and out of it, but in the old and ardent sense of the Evangelical school: one who could

> *Indeed opine*
> *That the Eternal and Divine*
> *Did, eighteen centuries ago*
> *In very truth . . .*

Angel's father tried argument, persuasion, entreaty.

"No, father; I cannot underwrite Article Four (leave alone the rest), taking it 'in the literal and grammatical sense' as required by the Declaration; and, therefore, I can't be a parson in the present state of affairs," said Angel. "My whole instinct in matters of religion is towards reconstruction; to quote your favorite Epistle to the Hebrews, '*the removing of those things that are shaken, as of things that are made, that those things which cannot be shaken may remain.*'"

His father grieved so deeply that it made Angel quite ill to see him.

"What is the good of your mother and me economising and stinting ourselves to give you a University education, if it is not to be used for the honour and glory of God?" his father repeated.

"Why, that it may be used for the honour and glory of man, father."

Perhaps if Angel had persevered he might have gone to Cambridge like his brothers. But the vicar's view of that seat of learning as a stepping-stone to Orders alone was quite a family tradition; and so rooted was the idea in his mind that perseverance began to appear to the sensitive son akin to an intent to misappropriate a trust, and wrong the pious heads of the household, who had been and were, as his father had hinted, compelled to exercise much thrift to carry out this uniform plan of education for the three young men.

"I will do without Cambridge," said Angel at last. "I feel that I have no right to go there in the circumstances."

The effects of this decisive debate were not long in showing themselves. He spent years and years in desultory studies, undertakings, and meditations; he began to evince considerable indifference to social forms and observances. The material distinctions of rank and wealth he increasingly despised. Even the "good old family" (to use a favourite phrase of a late local worthy) had no aroma for him unless there were good new resolutions in its representatives. As a balance to these austerities, when he went to live in London to see what the world was like, and with a view to practising a profession or business there, he was carried off his head, and nearly entrapped by a woman much older than himself, though luckily he escaped not greatly the worse for the experience.

Early association with country solitudes had bred in him an unconquerable, and almost unreasonable, aversion to modern town life, and shut him out from such success as he might have aspired to by following a mundane calling in the impracticability of the spiritual one. But something had to be done; he had wasted many valuable years; and having an acquaintance who was starting on a thriving life as a Colonial farmer, it occurred to Angel that this might be a lead in the right direction. Farming, either in the Colonies, America, or at home—farming, at any rate, after becoming well qualified for the business by a careful apprenticeship—that was a vocation which would probably afford an independence without the sacrifice of what he valued even more than a competency—intellectual liberty.

So we find Angel Clare at six-and-twenty here at Talbothays as a student of kine, and, as there were no houses near at hand in which he could get a comfortable lodging, a boarder at the dairyman's.

His room was an immense attic which ran the whole length of the dairy-house. It could only be reached by a ladder from the cheese-loft, and had been closed up for a long time till he arrived and selected it as his retreat. Here Clare had plenty of space, and could often be heard by the dairy-folk pacing up and down when the household had gone to rest. A portion was divided off at one end by a curtain, behind which was his bed, the outer part being furnished as a homely sitting-room.

At first he lived up above entirely, reading a good deal, and strumming upon an old harp which he had bought at a sale, saying when in a bitter humour that he might have to get his living by it in the streets some day. But he soon preferred to read human nature by taking his meals downstairs in the general dining-kitchen, with the dairyman and his wife, and the maids and men, who all together formed a lively assembly; for though but few milking hands slept in the house, several joined the family at meals. The longer Clare resided here the less objection had he to his company, and the more did he like to share quarters with them in common.

Much to his surprise he took, indeed, a real delight in their companionship. The conventional farm-folk of his imagination—personified by the pitiable dummy known as Hodge—were obliterated after a few days' residence. At close quarters no Hodge was to be seen. At first, it is true, when Clare's intelligence was fresh from a contrasting society, these friends with whom he now hobnobbed seemed a little strange. Sitting down as a level member of the dairyman's household seemed at the outset an undignified proceeding. The ideas, the modes, the surroundings, appeared retrogressive and unmeaning. But with living on there, day after day, the acute sojourner became conscious of a new aspect in the spectacle. Without any objective change whatever, variety had taken the place of monotonousness. His host and his host's household, his men and his maids, as they became intimately known to Clare, began to differentiate themselves as in a chemical process. The thought of Pascal's was brought home to him: "A mesure qu'on a plus d'esprit, on trouve qu'il y a plus d'hommes originaux. Les gens du commun ne trouvent pas de différence entre les hommes." The typical and unvarying Hodge ceased to exist. He had been disintegrated into a number of varied fellow-creatures—beings of many minds, beings infinite in difference; some happy, many serene, a few depressed, one here and there bright even to genius, some stupid, others wanton, others austere; some mutely Miltonic, some potentially Cromwellian; into men who had private views of each other, as he had of his friends; who could applaud or condemn each other, amuse or sadden themselves by the contemplation of each other's foibles or vices; men every one of whom walked in his own individual way the road to dusty death.

Unexpectedly he began to like the out-door life for its own sake, and for what it brought, apart from its bearing on his own proposed career. Considering his position he became wonderfully free from the chronic melancholy which is taking hold of the civilised races with the decline of belief in a beneficent Power. For the first time of late years he could read as his musings inclined him, without any eye to cramming for a profession, since the few farming handbooks which he deemed it desirable to master occupied him but little time.

He grew away from old associations, and saw something new in life and humanity. Secondarily, he made close acquaintance with phenomena which he had before known but darkly—the seasons in their moods, morning and evening, night and noon, winds in their different tempers, trees, waters and mists, shades and silences, and the voices of inanimate things.

The early mornings were still sufficiently cool to render a fire acceptable in the large room wherein they breakfasted; and, by Mrs. Crick's orders, who held that he was too genteel to mess at their table, it was Angel Clare's custom to sit in the yawning chimney-corner during the meal, his cup-and-saucer and plate being placed on a hinged flap at his elbow. The light from the long, wide, mullioned window opposite shone in upon his nook, and, assisted by a secondary light of cold blue quality which shone down the chimney, enabled him to read there easily whenever disposed to do so. Between Clare and the window was the table at which his companions sat, their munching profiles rising sharp against the panes; while to the side was the milk-house door, through which were visible the rectangular leads in rows, full to the brim with the morning's milk. At the further end the great churn could be seen revolving, and its slip-slopping heard—the moving power being discernible through the window in the form of a spiritless horse walking in a circle and driven by a boy.

For several days after Tess's arrival Clare, sitting abstractedly reading from some book, periodical, or piece of music just come by post, hardly noticed that she was present at table. She talked so little, and the other maids talked so much, that the babble did not strike him as possessing a new note, and he was ever in the habit of neglecting the particulars of an outward scene for the general impression. One day, however, when he had been conning one of his music-scores, and by force of imagination was hearing the tune in his head, he lapsed into listlessness, and the music-sheet rolled to the hearth. He looked at the fire of logs, with its one flame pirouetting on the top in a dying dance after the breakfast-cooking and boiling, and it seemed to jig to his inward tune; also at the two chimney crooks dangling down from the cotterel or cross-bar, plumed with soot which quivered to the same melody; also at the half-empty kettle whining an accompaniment. The conversation at the table mixed in with his phantasmal orchestra till he thought: "What a fluty voice one of those milkmaids has! I suppose it is the new one."

Clare looked round upon her, seated with the others.

She was not looking towards him. Indeed, owing to his long silence, his presence in the room was almost forgotten.

"I don't know about ghosts," she was saying; "but I do know that our souls can be made to go outside our bodies when we are alive."

The dairyman turned to her with his mouth full, his eyes charged with serious enquiry, and his great knife and fork (breakfasts were breakfasts here) planted erect on the table, like the beginning of a gallows.

"What—really now? And is it so, maidy?" he said.

"A very easy way to feel 'em go," continued Tess, "is to lie on the grass at night and look straight up at some big bright star; and, by fixing your mind upon it, you will soon find that you are hundreds and hundreds o' miles away from your body, which you don't seem to want at all."

The dairyman removed his hard gaze from Tess, and fixed it on his wife.

"Now that's a rum thing, Christianner—hey? To think o' the miles I've vamped o' starlight nights these last thirty year, courting, or trading, or for doctor, or for nurse, and yet never had the least notion o' that till now, or felt my soul rise so much as an inch above my shirt-collar."

The general attention being drawn to her, including that of the dairyman's pupil, Tess flushed, and remarking evasively that it was only a fancy, resumed her breakfast.

Clare continued to observe her. She soon finished her eating, and having a consciousness that Clare was regarding her, began to trace imaginary patterns on the table cloth with her forefinger with the constraint of a domestic animal that perceives itself to be watched.

"What a fresh and virginal daughter of Nature that milkmaid is!" he said to himself.

And then he seemed to discern in her something that was familiar, something which carried him back into a joyous and unforeseeing past, before the necessity of taking thought had made the heavens grey. He concluded that he had beheld her before; where he could not tell. A casual encounter during some country ramble it certainly had been, and he was not greatly curious about it. But the circumstance was sufficient to lead him to select Tess in preference to the other pretty milkmaids when he wished to contemplate contiguous womankind.

XIX

IN GENERAL THE COWS WERE MILKED AS THEY PRESENTED THEMSELVES, WITHOUT FANCY or choice. But certain cows will show a fondness for a particular pair of hands, sometimes carrying this predilection so far as to refuse to stand at all except to their favourite, the pail of a stranger being unceremoniously kicked over.

It was Dairyman Crick's rule to insist on breaking down these partialities and aversions by constant interchange, since otherwise, in the event of a milkman or maid going away from the dairy, he was placed in a difficulty. The maids' private aims, however, were the reverse of the dairyman's rule, the daily selection by each damsel of the eight or ten cows to which she had grown accustomed rendering the operation on their willing udders surprising easy and effortless.

Tess, like her compeers, soon discovered which of the cows had a preference for her style of manipulation, and her fingers having become delicate from the long domiciliary imprisonments to which she had subjected herself at intervals during the last two or three years, she would have been glad to meet the milchers' views in this respect. Out of the whole ninety-five there were eight in particular—Dumpling, Fancy, Lofty, Mist, Old Pretty, Young Pretty, Tidy, and Loud—who, though the teats of one or two were as hard as carrots, gave down to her with a readiness that made her work on them a mere touch of the fingers. Knowing, however, the dairyman's wish, she endeavoured conscientiously to take the animals just as they came, expecting the very hard yielders which she could not yet manage.

But she soon found a curious correspondence between the ostensibly chance position of the cows and her wishes in this matter, till she felt that their order could not be the result of accident. The dairyman's pupil had lent a hand in getting the cows together of late, and at the fifth or sixth time she turned her eyes, as she rested against the cow, full of sly enquiry upon him.

"Mr. Clare, you have ranged the cows!" she said, blushing; and in making the accusation symptoms of a smile gently lifted her upper lip in spite of her, so as to show the tips of her teeth, the lower lip remaining severely still.

"Well, it makes no difference," said he. "You will always be here to milk them."

"Do you think so? I *hope* I shall! But I don't *know*."

She was angry with herself afterwards, thinking that he, unaware of her grave reasons for liking this seclusion, might have mistaken her meaning. She had spoken so earnestly to him, as if his presence were somehow a factor in her wish. Her misgiving was such that at dusk, when the milking was over, she walked in the garden alone, to continue her regrets that she had disclosed to him her discovery of his considerateness.

It was a typical summer evening in June, the atmosphere being in such delicate equilibrium and so transmissive that inanimate objects seemed endowed with two or three senses, if not five. There was no distinction between the near and the far, and an auditor felt close to everything within the horizon. The soundlessness impressed her as a positive entity rather than as the mere negation of noise. It was broken by the strumming of strings.

Tess had heard those notes in the attic above her head. Dim, flattened, constrained by their confinement, they had never appealed to her as now, when they wandered in the still air with a stark quality like that of nudity. To speak absolutely, both instrument and execution were poor; but the relative is all, and as she listened Tess, like a fascinated bird, could not leave the spot. Far from leaving she drew up towards the performer, keeping behind the hedge that he might not guess her presence.

The outskirt of the garden in which Tess found herself had been left uncultivated for some years, and was now damp and rank with juicy grass which sent up mists of pollen at a touch; and with tall blooming weeds emitting offensive smells—weeds whose red and yellow and purple hues formed a polychrome as dazzling as that of cultivated flowers. She went stealthily as a cat through this profusion of growth, gathering cuckoo-spittle on her skirts, cracking snails that were underfoot, staining her hands with thistle-milk and slug-slime, and rubbing off upon her naked arms sticky blights which, though snow-white on the apple-tree trunks, made madder stains on her skin; thus she drew quite near to Clare, still unobserved of him.

Tess was conscious of neither time nor space. The exaltation which she had described as being producible at will by gazing at a star, came now without any determination of hers; she undulated upon the thin notes of the second-hand harp, and their harmonies passed like breezes through her, bringing tears into her eyes. The floating pollen seemed to be his notes made visible, and the dampness of the garden the weeping of the garden's sensibility. Though near night-fall, the rank-smelling weed-flowers glowed as if they would not close for intentness, and the waves of colour mixed with the waves of sound.

The light which still shone was derived mainly from a large hole in the western bank of cloud; it was like a piece of day left behind by accident, dusk having closed in elsewhere. He concluded his plaintive melody, a very simple performance, demanding no great skill; and she waited, thinking another might be begun. But, tired of playing, he had desultorily come round the fence, and was rambling up behind her. Tess, her cheeks on fire, moved away furtively, as if hardly moving at all.

Angel, however, saw her light summer gown, and he spoke; his low tones reaching her, though he was some distance off.

"What makes you draw off in that way, Tess?" said he. "Are you afraid?"

"Oh no, sir . . . not of out-door things; especially just now when the apple-blooth is falling, and everything so green."

"But you have your indoor fears—eh?"

"Well—yes, sir."

"What of?"

"I couldn't quite say."

"The milk turning sour?"

"No."

"Life in general?"

"Yes, sir."

"Ah—so have I, very often. This hobble of being alive is rather serious, don't you think so?"

"It is—now you put it that way."

"All the same, I shouldn't have expected a young girl like you to see it so just yet. How is it you do?"

She maintained a hesitating silence.

"Come, Tess, tell me in confidence."

She thought that he meant what were the aspects of things to her, and replied shyly—

"The trees have enquisitive eyes, haven't they?—that is, seem as if they had. And the river says,—'Why do ye trouble me with your looks?' And you seem to see numbers of to-morrows just all in a line, the first of them the biggest and clearest, the others getting smaller and smaller as they stand farther away; but they all seem very fierce and cruel and as if they said, 'I'm coming! Beware of me! Beware of me!' . . . But *you,* sir, can raise up dreams with your music, and drive all such horrid fancies away!"

He was surprised to find this young woman—who though but a milkmaid had just that touch of rarity about her which might make her the envied of her housemates—shaping such sad imaginings. She was expressing in her own native phrases—assisted a little by her Sixth Standard training—feelings which might almost have been called those of the age—the ache of modernism. The perception arrested him less when he reflected that what are called advanced ideas are really in great part but the latest fashion in definition— a more accurate expression, by words in *logy* and *ism,* of sensations which men and women have vaguely grasped for centuries.

Still, it was strange that they should have come to her while yet so young; more than strange; it was impressive, interesting, pathetic. Not guessing the cause, there was nothing to remind him that experience is as to intensity, and not as to duration. Tess's passing corporeal blight had been her mental harvest.

Tess, on her part, could not understand why a man of clerical family and good education, and above physical want, should look upon it as a mishap to be alive. For the unhappy pilgrim herself there was very good reason. But how could this admirable and poetic man ever have descended into the Valley of Humiliation, have felt with the man of Uz—as she herself had felt two or three years ago—"My soul chooseth strangling and death rather than my life. I loath it; I would not live alway."

It was true that he was at present out of his class. But she knew that was only because, like Peter the Great in a shipwright's yard, he was studying what he wanted to know. He did not milk cows because he was obliged to milk cows, but because he was learning to be a rich and prosperous dairyman, landowner, agriculturist, and breeder of cattle. He would become an American or Australian Abraham, commanding like a monarch his flocks and his herds, his spotted and his ring-straked, his men-servants and his maids. At times, nevertheless, it did seem unaccountable to her that a decidedly bookish, musical, thinking young man should have chosen deliberately to be a farmer, and not a clergyman, like his father and brothers.

Thus, neither having the clue to the other's secret, they were respectively puzzled at what each revealed, and awaited new knowledge of each other's character and moods without attempting to pry into each other's history.

Every day, every hour, brought to him one more little stroke of her nature, and to her one more of his. Tess was trying to lead a repressed life, but she little divined the strength of her own vitality.

At first Tess seemed to regard Angel Clare as an intelligence rather than as a man. As such she compared him with herself; and at every discovery of the abundance of his illuminations, of the distance between her own modest mental standpoint and the unmeasurable, Andean altitude of his, she became quite dejected, disheartened from all further effort on her own part whatever.

He observed her dejection one day, when he had casually mentioned something to her about pastoral life in ancient Greece. She was gathering the buds called "lords and ladies" from the bank while he spoke.

"Why do you look so woebegone all of a sudden?" he asked.

"Oh, 'tis only—about my own self," she said, with a frail laugh of sadness, fitfully beginning to peel "a lady" meanwhile. "Just a sense of what might have been with me! My life looks as if it had been wasted for want of chances! When I see what you know, what you have read, and seen, and thought, I feel what a nothing I am! I'm like the poor Queen of Sheba who lived in the Bible. There is no more spirit in me."

"Bless my soul, don't go troubling about that! Why," he said with some enthusiasm, "I should be only too glad, my dear Tess, to help you to anything in the way of history, or any line of reading you would like to take up—"

"It is a lady again," interrupted she, holding out the bud she had peeled.

"What?"

"I meant that there are always more ladies than lords when you come to peel them."

"Never mind about the lords and ladies. Would you like to take up any course of study—history, for example?"

"Sometimes I feel I don't want to know anything more about it than I know already."

"Why not?"

"Because what's the use of learning that I am one of a long row only—finding out that there is set down in some old book somebody just like me, and to know that I shall only act her part; making me sad, that's all. The best is not to remember that your nature and your past doings have been just like thousands' and thousands', and that your coming life and doings 'll be like thousands' and thousands'."

"What, really, then, you don't want to learn anything?"

"I shouldn't mind learning why—why the sun do shine on the just and the unjust alike," she answered, with a slight quaver in her voice. "But that's what books will not tell me."

"Tess, fie for such bitterness!" Of course he spoke with a conventional sense of duty only, for that sort of wondering had not been unknown to himself in bygone days. And as he looked at the unpractised mouth and lips, he thought that such a daughter of the soil could only have caught up the sentiment by rote. She went on peeling the lords and ladies till Clare, regarding for a moment the wavelike curl of her lashes as they dropped with her bent gaze on her soft cheek, lingeringly went away. When he was gone she stood a while, thoughtfully peeling the last bud; and then, awakening from her reverie, flung it and all the crowd of floral nobility impatiently on the ground, in an ebullition of displeasure with herself for her *niaiseries*, and with a quickening warmth in her heart of hearts.

How stupid he must think her! In an access of hunger for his good opinion she bethought herself of what she had latterly endeavoured to forget, so unpleasant had been its issues—the identity of her family with that of the knightly d'Urbervilles. Barren attribute as it was, disastrous as its discovery had been in many ways to her, perhaps Mr. Clare, as a gentleman and a student of history, would respect her sufficiently to forget her

childish conduct with the lords and ladies if he knew that those Purbeck-marble and alabaster people in Kingsbere Church really represented her own lineal forefathers; that she
was no spurious d'Urberville, compounded of money and ambition like those at
Trantridge, but true d'Urberville to the bone.

But, before venturing to make the revelation, dubious Tess indirectly sounded the
dairyman as to its possible effect upon Mr. Clare, by asking the former if Mr. Clare had
any great respect for old county families when they had lost all their money and land.

"Mr. Clare," said the dairyman emphatically, "is one of the most rebellest rozums you
ever knowed—not a bit like the rest of his family; and if there's one thing that he do hate
more than another 'tis the notion of what's called a' old family. He says that it stands to
reason that old families have done their spurt of work in past days, and can't have anything
left in 'em now. There's the Billets and the Drenkhards and the Greys and the St. Quintins
and the Hardys and the Goulds, who used to own the lands for miles down this valley; you
could buy 'em all up now for an old song a'most. Why, our little Retty Priddle here, you
know, is one of the Paridelles—the old family that used to own lots o' the lands out by
King's-Hintock now owned by the Earl o' Wessex, afore even he or his was heard of. Well,
Mr. Clare found this out, and spoke quite scornful to the poor girl for days. 'Ah!' he says
to her, 'you'll never make a good dairymaid! All your skill was used up ages ago in Palestine, and you must lie fallow for a thousand years to git strength for more deeds!' A boy
came here t'other day asking for a job, and said his name was Matt, and when we asked him
his surname he said he'd never heard that 'a had any surname, and when we asked why, he
said he supposed his folks hadn't been 'stablished long enough. 'Ah! you're the very boy I
want!' says Mr. Clare, jumping up and shaking hands wi'en; 'I've great hopes of you'; and
gave him half-a-crown. O no! he can't stomach old families!"

After hearing this caricature of Clare's opinion poor Tess was glad that she had not
said a word in a weak moment about her family—even though it was so unusually old almost to have gone round the circle and become a new one. Besides, another diarygirl was
as good as she, it seemed, in that respect. She held her tongue about the d'Urberville vault,
and the Knight of the Conqueror whose name she bore. The insight afforded into Clare's
character suggested to her that it was largely owing to her supposed untraditional newness
that she had won interest in his eyes.

XX

T HE SEASON DEVELOPED AND MATURED. ANOTHER YEAR'S INSTALMENT OF FLOWERS,
   leaves, nightingales, thrushes, finches, and such ephemeral creatures, took up their
positions where only a year ago others had stood in their place when these were nothing
more than germs and inorganic particles. Rays from the sunrise drew forth the buds and
stretched them into long stalks, lifted up sap in noiseless streams, opened petals, and sucked
out scents in invisible jets and breathings.

Dairyman Crick's household of maids and men lived on comfortably, placidly, even
merrily. Their position was perhaps the happiest of all positions in the social scale, being

above the line at which neediness ends, and below the line at which the *convenances* begin to cramp natural feeling, and the stress of threadbare modishness makes too little of enough.

Thus passed the leafy time when arborescence seems to be the one thing aimed at out-of-doors. Tess and Clare unconsciously studied each other, ever balanced on the edge of a passion, yet apparently keeping out of it. All the while they were converging, under an irresistible law, as surely as two streams in one vale.

Tess had never in her recent life been so happy as she was now, possibly never would be so happy again. She was, for one thing, physically and mentally suited among these new surroundings. The sapling which had rooted down to a poisonous stratum on the spot of its sowing had been transplanted to a deeper soil. Moreover she, and Clare also, stood as yet on the debatable land between predilection and love; where no profundities have been reached; no reflections have set in, awkwardly enquiring, "Whither does this new current tend to carry me? What does it mean to my future? How does it stand towards my past?"

Tess was the merest stray phenomenon to Angel Clare as yet—a rosy warming apparition which had only just acquired the attribute of persistence in his consciousness. So he allowed his mind to be occupied with her, deeming his preoccupation to be no more than a philosopher's regard of an exceedingly novel, fresh, and interesting specimen of womankind.

They met continually; they could not help it. They met daily in that strange and solemn interval, the twilight of the morning, in the violet or pink dawn; for it was necessary to rise early, so very early, here. Milking was done betimes; and before the milking came the skimming, which began at a little past three. It usually fell to the lot of some one or other of them to wake the rest, the first being aroused by an alarm-clock; and, as Tess was the latest arrival, and they soon discovered that she could be depended upon not to sleep through the alarm as others did, this task was thrust most frequently upon her. No sooner had the hour of three struck and whizzed, than she left her room and ran to the dairyman's door; then up the ladder to Angel's, calling him in a loud whisper; then woke her fellow-milkmaids. By the time that Tess was dressed Clare was downstairs and out in the humid air. The remaining maids and the dairyman usually gave themselves another turn on the pillow, and did not appear till a quarter of an hour later.

The grey half-tones of daybreak are not the grey half-tones of the day's close, though the degree of their shade may be the same. In the twilight of the morning light seems active, darkness passive; in the twilight of evening it is the darkness which is active and crescent, and the light which is the drowsy reverse.

Being so often—possibly not always by chance—the first two persons to get up at the dairy-house, they seemed to themselves the first persons up of all the world. In these early days of her residence here Tess did not skim, but went out-of-doors at once after rising, where he was generally awaiting her. The spectral, half-compounded, aqueous light which pervaded the open mead, impressed them with a feeling of isolation, as if they were Adam and Eve. At this dim inceptive stage of the day Tess seemed to Clare to exhibit a dignified largeness both of disposition and physique, an almost regnant power, possibly because he knew that at that preternatural time hardly any woman so well endowed in person as she was likely to be walking in the open air within the boundaries of his horizon; very few in all England. Fair women are usually asleep at midsummer dawns. She was close at hand, and the rest were nowhere.

The mixed, singular, luminous gloom in which they walked along together to the spot where the cows lay, often made him think of the Resurrection hour. He little thought that the Magdalen might be at his side. Whilst all the landscape was in neutral shade his companion's face, which was the focus of his eyes, rising above the mist stratum, seemed to have a sort of phosphorescence upon it. She looked ghostly, as if she were merely a soul at large. In reality her face, without appearing to do so, had caught the cold gleam of day from the north-east; his own face, though he did not think of it, wore the same aspect to her.

It was then, as has been said, that she impressed him most deeply. She was no longer the milkmaid, but a visionary essence of woman—a whole sex condensed into one typical form. He called her Artemis, Demeter, and other fanciful names half teasingly, which she did not like because she did not understand them.

"Call me Tess," she would say askance; and he did.

Then it would grow lighter, and her features would become simply feminine; they had changed from those of a divinity who could confer bliss to those of a being who craved it.

At these non-human hours they could get quite close to the waterfowl. Herons came, with a great bold noise as of opening doors and shutters, out of the boughs of a plantation which they frequented at the side of the mead; or, if already on the spot, hardily maintained their standing in the water as the pair walked by, watching them by moving their heads round in a slow, horizontal, passionless wheel, like the turn of puppets by clockwork.

They could then see the faint summer fogs in layers, woolly, level, and apparently no thicker than counterpanes, spread about the meadows in detached remnants of small extent. On the grey moisture of the grass were marks where the cows had lain through the night—dark-green islands of dry herbage the size of their carcases, in the general sea of dew. From each island proceeded a serpentine trail, by which the cow had rambled away to feed after getting up, at the end of which trail they found her; the snoring puff from her nostrils, when she recognised them, making an intenser little fog of her own amid the prevailing one. Then they drove the animals back to the barton, or sat down to milk them on the spot, as the case might require.

Or perhaps the summer fog was more general, and the meadows lay like a white sea, out of which the scattered trees rose like dangerous rocks. Birds would soar through it into the upper radiance, and hang on the wing sunning themselves, or alight on the wet rails subdividing the mead, which now shone like glass rods. Minute diamonds of moisture from the mist hung, too, upon Tess's eyelashes, and drops upon her hair, like seed pearls. When the day grew quite strong and commonplace these dried off her; moreover, Tess then lost her strange and ethereal beauty; her teeth, lips, and eyes scintillated in the sunbeams, and she was again the dazzlingly fair dairymaid only, who had to hold her own against the other women of the world.

About this time they would hear Dairyman Crick's voice, lecturing the non-resident milkers for arriving late, and speaking sharply to old Deborah Fyander for not washing her hands.

"For Heaven's sake, pop thy hands under the pump, Deb! Upon my soul, if the London folk only knowed of thee and thy slovenly ways, they'd swaller their milk and butter more mincing than they do a'ready; and that's saying a good deal."

The milking progressed, till towards the end Tess and Clare, in common with the rest, could hear the heavy breakfast-table dragged out from the wall in the kitchen by Mrs. Crick, this being the invariable preliminary to each meal; the same horrible scrape accompanying its return journey when the table had been cleared.

XXI

THERE WAS A GREAT STIR IN THE MILK-HOUSE JUST AFTER BREAKFAST. THE CHURN RE-volved as usual, but the butter would not come. Whenever this happened the dairy was paralysed. Squish, squash, echoed the milk in the great cylinder, but never arose the sound they waited for.

Dairyman Crick and his wife, the milkmaids Tess, Marian, Retty Priddle, Izz Huett, and the married ones from the cottages; also Mr. Clare, Jonathan Kail, old Deborah, and the rest, stood gazing hopelessly at the churn; and the boy who kept the horse going outside put on moonlike eyes to show his sense of the situation. Even the melancholy horse himself seemed to look in at the window in enquiring despair at each walk round.

" 'Tis years since I went to Conjuror Trendle's son in Egdon—years!" said the dairy-man bitterly. "And he was nothing to what his father had been. I have said fifty times, if I have said once, that I don't believe in en. And I *don't* believe in en. But I shall have to go to 'n if he's alive. O yes, I shall have to go to 'n, if this sort of thing continnys!"

Even Mr. Clare began to feel tragical at the dairyman's desperation.

"Conjuror Fall, t'other side of Casterbridge, that they used to call 'Wide-O', was a very good man when I was a boy," said Jonathan Kail. "But he's rotten as touchwood by now."

"My grand-father used to go to Conjuror Mynterne, out at Owlscombe, and a clever man a' were, so I've heard grandf'er say," continued Mr. Crick. "But there's no such gen-uine folk about now-a-days!"

Mrs. Crick's mind kept nearer to the matter in hand.

"Perhaps somebody in the house is in love," she said tentatively. "I've heard tell in my younger days that that will cause it. Why, Crick—that maid we had years ago, do ye mind, and how the butter didn't come then—"

"Ah yes, yes!—but that isn't the rights o't. It had nothing to do with the love-making. I can mind all about it—'twas the damage to the churn."

He turned to Clare.

"Jack Dollop, a 'hore's-bird of a fellow we had here as milker at one time, sir, courted a young woman over at Mellstock, and deceived her as he had deceived many afore. But he had another sort o' woman to reckon wi' this time, and it was not the girl herself. One Holy Thursday, of all days in the almanack, we was here as we mid be now, only there was no churning in hand, when we zid the girl's mother coming up to the door, wi' a great brass-mounted umbrella in her hand that would ha' felled an ox, and saying 'Do Jack Dol-lop work here?—because I want him! I have a big bone to pick with he, I can assure 'n!' And some way behind her mother walked Jack's young woman, crying bitterly into her handkercher. 'O Lard, here's a time!' said Jack, looking out o' winder at 'em. 'She'll murder me! Where shall I get—where shall I—? Don't tell her where I be!' And with that he scrambled into the churn through the trap-door, and shut himself inside, just as the young woman's mother busted into the milk-house. 'The villain—where is he?' says she, 'I'll claw his face for'n, let me only catch him!' Well, she hunted about everywhere, ballyragging Jack by side and by seam, Jack lying a'most stifled inside the churn, and the poor maid—or young woman rather—standing at the door crying her eyes out. I shall never forget it, never! 'Twould have melted a marble stone! But she couldn't find him nowhere at all."

The dairyman paused, and one or two words of comment came from the listeners.

Dairyman Crick's stories often seemed to be ended when they were not really so, and strangers were betrayed into premature interjections of finality; though old friends knew better. The narrator went on—

"Well, how the old woman should have had the wit to guess it I could never tell, but she found out that he was inside that there churn. Without saying a word she took hold of the winch (it was turned by handpower then), and round she swung him, and Jack began to flop about inside. 'O Lard! stop the churn! let me out!' says he, popping out his head, 'I shall be churned into a pummy!' (he was a cowardly chap in his heart, as such men mostly be). 'Not till ye make amends for ravaging her virgin innocence!' says the old woman. 'Stop the churn, you old witch!' screams he. 'You call me old witch, do ye, you deceiver!' says she, 'when ye ought to ha' been calling me mother-law these last five months!' And on went the churn, and Jack's bones rattled round again. Well, none of us ventured to interfere; and at last 'a promised to make it right wi' her. 'Yes—I'll be as good as my word!' he said. And so it ended that day."

While the listeners were smiling their comments there was a quick movement behind their backs, and they looked round. Tess, pale-faced, had gone to the door.

"How warm 'tis to-day!" she said, almost inaudibly.

It was warm, and none of them connected her withdrawal with the reminiscences of the dairyman. He went forward and opened the door for her, saying with tender raillery—

"Why, maidy" (he frequently, with unconscious irony, gave her this pet name), "the prettiest milker I've got in my dairy; you mustn't get so fagged as this at the first breath of summer weather, or we shall be finely put to for want of 'ee by dog-days, shan't we, Mr. Clare?"

"I was faint—and—I think I am better out o' doors," she said mechanically; and disappeared outside.

Fortunately for her the milk in the revolving churn at that moment changed its squashing for a decided flick-flack.

" 'Tis coming!" cried Mrs. Crick, and the attention of all was called off from Tess.

That fair sufferer soon recovered herself externally; but she remained much depressed all the afternoon. When the evening milking was done she did not care to be with the rest of them, and went out-of-doors wandering along she knew not whither. She was wretched—O so wretched—at the perception that to her companions the dairyman's story had been rather a humorous narration than otherwise; none of them but herself seemed to see the sorrow of it; to a certainty, not one knew how cruelly it touched the tender place in her experience. The evening sun was now ugly to her, like a great inflamed wound in the sky. Only a solitary cracked-voice reed-sparrow greeted her from the bushes by the river, in a sad, machine-made tone, resembling that of a past friend whose friendship she had outworn.

In these long June days the milkmaids, and, indeed, most of the household, went to bed at sunset or sooner, the morning work before milking being so early and heavy at a time of full pails. Tess usually accompanied her fellows upstairs. To-night, however, she was the first to go to their common chamber; and she had dozed when the other girls came in. She saw them undressing in the orange light of the vanished sun, which flushed their forms with its colour; she dozed again, but she was reawakened by their voices, and quietly turned her eyes towards them.

Neither of her three chamber-companions had got into bed. They were standing in a group, in their night-gowns, barefooted, at the window, the last red rays of the west still warming their faces and necks, and the walls around them. All were watching somebody in the garden with deep interest, their three faces close together: a jovial and round one, a pale one with dark hair, and a fair one whose tresses were auburn.

"Don't push! You can see as well as I," said Retty, the auburn-haired and youngest girl, without removing her eyes from the window.

" 'Tis no use for you to be in love with him any more than me, Retty Priddle," said jolly-faced Marian, the eldest, slily. "His thoughts be of other cheeks than thine!"

Retty Priddle still looked, and the other looked again.

"There he is again!" cried Izz Huett, the pale girl with dark damp hair and keenly cut lips.

"You needn't say anything, Izz," answered Retty. "For I zid you kissing his shade."

"*What* did you see her doing?" asked Marian.

"Why—he was standing over the whey-tub to let off the whey, and the shade of his face came upon the wall behind, close to Izz, who was standing there filling a vat. She put her mouth against the wall and kissed the shade of his mouth; I zid her, though he didn't."

"O Izz Huett!" said Marian.

A rosy spot came into the middle of Izz Huett's cheek.

"Well, there was no harm in it," she declared, with attempted coolness. "And if I be in love wi' en, so is Retty, too; and so be you, Marian, come to that."

Marian's full face could not blush past its chronic pinkness.

"I!" she said. "What a tale! Ah, there he is again! Dear eyes—dear face—dear Mr. Clare!"

"There—you've owned it!"

"So have you—so have we all," said Marian, with the dry frankness of complete indifference to opinion. "It is silly to pretend otherwise amongst ourselves, though we need not own it to other folks. I would just marry 'n to-morrow!"

"So would I—and more," murmured Izz Huett.

"And I too," whispered the more timid Retty.

The listener grew warm.

"We can't all marry him," said Izz.

"We shan't, either of us; which is worse still," said the eldest. "There he is again!"

They all three blew him a silent kiss.

"Why?" asked Retty quickly.

"Because he likes Tess Durbeyfield best," said Marian, lowering her voice. "I have watched him everyday, and have found it out."

There was a reflective silence.

"But she don't care anything for 'n?" at length breathed Retty.

"Well—I sometimes think that too."

"But how silly all this is!" said Izz Huett impatiently. "Of course he won't marry any one of us, or Tess either—a gentleman's son, who's going to be a great landowner and farmer abroad! More likely to ask us to come wi'en as farm-hands at so much a year!"

One sighed, and another sighed, and Marian's plump figure sighed biggest of all. Somebody in bed hard by sighed too. Tears came into the eyes of Retty Priddle, the pretty red-haired youngest—the last bud of the Paridelles, so important in the county annals. They watched silently a little longer, their three faces still close together as before, and the triple hues of their hair mingling. But the unconscious Mr. Clare had gone indoors, and they saw him no more; and, the shades beginning to deepen, they crept into their beds. In a few minutes they heard him ascend the ladder to his own room. Marian was soon snoring, but Izz did not drop into forgetfulness for a long time. Retty Priddle cried herself to sleep.

The deeper-passioned Tess was very far from sleeping even then. This conversation was another of the bitter pills she had been obliged to swallow that day. Scarce the least feeling of jealousy arose in her breast. For that matter she knew herself to have the preference. Being more finely formed, better educated, and, though the youngest except Retty, more woman than either, she perceived that only the slightest ordinary care was necessary for holding her own in Angel Clare's heart against these her candid friends. But the grave question was, ought she to do this? There was, to be sure, hardly a ghost of a chance for either of them, in a serious sense; but there was, or had been, a chance of one or the other inspiring him with a passing fancy for her, and enjoying the pleasure of his attentions while he stayed here. Such unequal attachments had led to marriage; and she had heard from Mrs. Crick that Mr. Clare had one day asked, in a laughing way, what would be the use of his marrying a fine lady, and all the while ten thousand acres of Colonial pasture to feed, and cattle to rear, and corn to reap. A farm-woman would be the only sensible kind of wife for him. But whether Mr. Clare had spoken seriously or not, why should she, who could never conscientiously allow any man to marry her now, and who had religiously determined that she never would be tempted to do so, draw off Mr. Clare's attention from other women, for the brief happiness of sunning herself in his eyes while he remained at Talbothays?

XXII

THEY CAME DOWNSTAIRS YAWNING NEXT MORNING; BUT SKIMMING AND MILKING WERE proceeded with as usual, and they went indoors to breakfast. Dairyman Crick was discovered stamping about the house. He had received a letter, in which a customer had complained that the butter had a twang.

"And begad, so 't have!" said the dairyman, who held in his left hand a wooden slice on which a lump of butter was stuck. "Yes—taste for yourself!"

Several of them gathered round him; and Mr. Clare tasted, Tess tasted, also the other indoor milkmaids, one or two of the milking-men, and last of all Mrs. Crick, who came out from the waiting breakfast-table. There certainly was a twang.

The dairyman, who had thrown himself into abstraction to better realise the taste, and so divine the particular species of noxious weed to which it appertained, suddenly exclaimed—

" 'Tis garlic! and I thought there wasn't a blade left in that mead!"

Then all the old hands remembered that a certain dry mead, into which a few of the cows had been admitted of late, had, in years gone by, spoilt the butter in the same way. The dairyman had not recognised the taste at that time, and thought the butter bewitched.

"We must overhaul that mead," he resumed; "this mustn't continny!"

All having armed themselves with old pointed knives they went out together. As the inimical plant could only be present in very microscopic dimensions to have escaped ordinary observation, to find it seemed rather a hopeless attempt in the stretch of rich grass before them. However, they formed themselves into line, all assisting, owing to the importance of the search; the dairyman at the upper end with Mr. Clare, who had volunteered to help; then Tess, Marian, Izz Huett, and Retty; then Bill Lewell, Jonathan, and the married dairywomen—Beck Knibbs, with her woolly black hair and rolling eyes; and flaxen Frances, consumptive from the winter damps of the water-meads—who lived in their respective cottages.

With eyes fixed upon the ground they crept slowly across a strip of the field, returning a little further down in such a manner that, when they should have finished, not a single inch of the pasture but would have fallen under the eye of some one of them. It was a most tedious business, not more than half-a-dozen shoots of garlic being discoverable in the whole field; yet such was the herb's pungency that probably one bite of it by one cow had been sufficient to season the whole dairy's produce for the day.

Differing one from another in natures and moods so greatly as they did, they yet formed, bending, a curiously uniform row—automatic, noiseless; and an alien observer passing down the neighbouring lane might well have been excused for massing them as "Hodge." As they crept along, stooping low to discern the plant, a soft yellow gleam was reflected from the buttercups into their shaded faces, giving them an elfish, moonlit aspect, though the sun was pouring upon their backs in all the strength of noon.

Angel Clare, who communistically stuck to his rule of taking part with the rest in everything, glanced up now and then. It was not, of course, by accident that he walked next to Tess.

"Well, how are you?" he murmured.

"Very well, thank you, sir," she replied demurely.

As they had been discussing a score of personal matters only half an hour before, the introductory style seemed a little superfluous. But they got no further in speech just then. They crept and crept, the hem of her petticoat just touching his gaiter, and his elbow sometimes brushing hers. At last the dairyman, who came next, could stand it no longer.

"Upon my soul and body, this here stooping do fairly make my back open and shut!" he exclaimed, straightening himself slowly with an excruciated look till quite upright. "And you, maidy Tess, you wasn't well a day or two ago—this will make your head ache finely! Don't do any more, if you feel fainty; leave the rest to finish it."

Dairyman Crick withdrew, and Tess dropped behind. Mr. Clare also stepped out of line, and began privateering about for the weed. When she found him near her, her very tension at what she had heard the night before made her the first to speak.

"Don't they look pretty?" she said.

"Who?"

"Izzy Huett and Retty."

Tess had moodily decided that either of these maidens would make a good farmer's wife, and that she ought to recommend them, and obscure her own wretched charms.

"Pretty? Well, yes—they are pretty girls—fresh looking. I have often thought so."

"Though, poor dears, prettiness won't last long!"

"O no, unfortunately."

"They are excellent dairywomen."

"Yes: though not better than you."

"They skim better than I."

"Do they?"

Clare remained observing them—not without their observing him.

"She is colouring up," continued Tess heroically.

"Who?"

"Retty Priddle."

"Oh! Why is that?"

"Because you are looking at her."

Self-sacrificing as her mood might be Tess could not well go further and cry, "Marry one of them, if you really do want a dairywoman and not a lady; and don't think of marrying me!" She followed Dairyman Crick, and had the mournful satisfaction of seeing that Clare remained behind.

From this day she forced herself to take pains to avoid him—never allowing herself, as formerly, to remain long in his company, even if their juxtaposition were purely accidental. She gave the other three every chance.

Tess was woman enough to realise from their avowals to herself that Angel Clare had the honour of all the dairymaids in his keeping, and her perception of his care to avoid compromising the happiness of either in the least degree bred a tender respect in Tess for what she deemed, rightly or wrongly, the self-controlling sense of duty shown by him, a quality which she had never expected to find in one of the opposite sex, and in the absence of which more than one of the simple hearts who were his housemates might have gone weeping on her pilgrimage.

XXIII

THE HOT WEATHER OF JULY HAD CREPT UPON THEM UNAWARES, AND THE ATMOSPHERE of the flat vale hung heavy as an opiate over the dairy-folk, the cows, and the trees. Hot steaming rains fell frequently, making the grass where the cows fed yet more rank, and hindering the late haymaking in the other meads.

It was Sunday morning; the milking was done; the out-door milkers had gone home.

Tess and the other three were dressing themselves rapidly, the whole bevy having agreed to go together to Mellstock Church, which lay some three or four miles distant from the dairy-house. She had now been two months at Talbothays, and this was her first excursion.

All the preceding afternoon and night heavy thunder-storms had hissed down upon the meads, and washed some of the hay into the river; but this morning the sun shone out all the more brilliantly for the deluge, and the air was balmy and clear.

The crooked lane leading from their own parrish to Mellstock ran along the lowest levels in a portion of its length, and when the girls reached the most depressed spot they found that the result of the rain had been to flood the lane over-shoe to a distance of some fifty yards. This would have been no serious hindrance on a week-day; they would have clicked through it in their high pattens and boots quite unconcerned; but on this day of vanity, this Sun's-day, when flesh went forth to coquet with flesh while hypocritically affecting business with spiritual things; on this occasion for wearing their white stockings and thin shoes, and their pink, white, and lilac gowns, on which every mud spot would be visible, the pool was an awkward impediment. They could hear the church-bell calling— as yet nearly a mile off.

"Who would have expected such a rise in the river in summer-time!" said Marian, from the top of the roadside-bank on which they had climbed, and were maintaining a precarious footing in the hope of creeping along its slope till they were past the pool.

"We can't get there anyhow, without walking right through it, or else going round the Turnpike way; and that would make us so very late!" said Retty, pausing hopelessly.

"And I do colour up so hot, walking into church late, and all the people staring round," said Marian, "that I hardly cool down again till we get into the That-it-may-please-Thees."

While they stood clinging to the bank they heard a splashing round the bend of the road, and presently appeared Angel Clare, advancing along the lane towards them through the water.

Four hearts gave a big throb simultaneously.

His aspect was probably as un-Sabbatarian a one as a dogmatic parson's son often presented; his attire being his dairy clothes, long wading boots, a cabbage-leaf inside his hat to keep his head cool, with a thistle-spud to finish him off.

"He's not going to church," said Marian.

"No—I wish he was!" murmured Tess.

Angel, in fact, rightly or wrongly (to adopt the safe phrase of evasive controversialists), preferred sermons in stones to sermons in churches and chapels on fine summer days. This morning, moreover, he had gone out to see if the damage to the hay by the flood was considerable or not. On his walk he observed the girls from a long distance, though they had been so occupied with their difficulties of passage as not to notice him. He knew that the water had risen at that spot, and that it would quite check their progress. So he had hastened on, with a dim idea of how he could help them—one of them in particular.

The rosy-cheeked, bright-eyed quartet looked so charming in their light summer attire, clinging to the roadside-bank like pigeons on a roof-slope, that he stopped a moment to regard them before coming close. Their gauzy skirts had brushed up from the grass innumerable flies and butterflies which, unable to escape, remained caged in the transparent tissue as in an aviary. Angel's eye at last fell upon Tess, the hindmost of the four; she, being full of suppressed laughter at their dilemma, could not help meeting his glance radiantly.

He came beneath them in the water, which did not rise over his long boots; and stood looking at the entrapped flies and butterflies.

"Are you trying to get to church?" he said to Marian, who was in front, including the next two in his remark, but avoiding Tess.

"Yes, sir; and 'tis getting late; and my colour do come up so—"

"I'll carry you through the pool—every Jill of you."

The whole four flushed as if one heart beat through them.

"I think you can't, sir," said Marian.

"It is the only way for you to get past. Stand still. Nonsense—you are not too heavy! I'd carry you all four together. Now, Marian, attend," he continued, "and put your arms round my shoulders, so. Now! Hold on. That's well done."

Marian had lowered herself upon his arm and shoulder as directed, and Angel strode off with her, his slim figure, as viewed from behind, looking like the mere stem to the great nosegay suggested by hers. They disappeared round the curve of the road, and only his sousing footsteps and the top ribbon of Marian's bonnet told where they were. In a few minutes he reappeared. Izz Huett was the next in order upon the bank.

"Here he comes," she murmured, and they could hear that her lips were dry with emotion. "And I have to put my arms round his neck and look into his face as Marian did."

"There's nothing in that," said Tess quickly.

"There's a time for everything," continued Izz, unheeding. "A time to embrace, and a time to refrain from embracing; the first is now going to be mine."

"Fie—it is Scripture, Izz!"

"Yes," said Izz, "I've always a' ear at church for pretty verses."

Angel Clare, to whom three-quarters of this performance was a commonplace act of kindness, now approached Izz. She quietly and dreamily lowered herself into his arms, and Angel methodically marched off with her. When he was heard returning for the third time Retty's throbbing heart could be almost seen to shake her. He went up to the red-haired girl, and while he was seizing her he glanced at Tess. His lips could not have pronounced more plainly, "It will soon be you and I." Her comprehension appeared in her face; she could not help it. There was an understanding between them.

Poor little Retty, though by far the lightest weight, was the most troublesome of Clare's burdens. Marian had been like a sack of meal, a dead weight of plumpness under which he has literally staggered. Izz had ridden sensibly and calmly. Retty was a bunch of hysterics.

However, he got through with the disquieted creature, deposited her, and returned. Tess could see over the hedge the distant three in a group, standing as he had placed them on the next rising ground. It was now her turn. She was embarrassed to discover that excitement at the proximity of Mr. Clare's breath and eyes, which she had contemned in her companions, was intensified in herself; and as if fearful of betraying her secret she paltered with him at the last moment.

"I may be able to clim' along the bank perhaps—I can clim' better than they. You must be so tired, Mr. Clare!"

"No, no, Tess," said he quickly. And almost before she was aware she was seated in his arms and resting against his shoulder.

"Three Leahs to get one Rachel," he whispered.

"They are better women than I," she replied, magnanimously sticking to her resolve.

"Not to me," said Angel.

He saw her grow warm at this; and they went some steps in silence.

"I hope I am not too heavy?" she said timidly.

"O no. You should lift Marian! Such a lump. You are like an undulating billow warmed by the sun. And all this fluff of muslin about you is the froth."

"It is very pretty—if I seem like that to you."

"Do you know that I have undergone three-quarters of this labour entirely for the sake of the fourth quarter?"

"No."

"I did not expect such an event to-day."

"Nor I. . . . The water came up so sudden."

That the rise in the water was what she understood him to refer to, the state of her breathing belied. Clare stood still and inclinced his face towards hers.

"O Tessy!" he exclaimed.

The girl's cheeks burned to the breeze, and she could not look into his eyes for her emotion. It reminded Angel that he was somewhat unfairly taking advantage of an accidental position; and he went no further with it. No definite words of love had crossed their lips as yet, and suspension at this point was desirable now. However, he walked slowly, to make the remainder of the distance as long as possible; but at last they came to the bend, and the rest of their progress was in full view of the other three. The dry land was reached, and he set her down.

Her friends were looking with round thoughtful eyes at her and him, and she could see that they had been talking of her. He hastily bade them farewell, and splashed back along the stretch of submerged road.

The four moved on together as before, till Marian broke the silence by saying—

"No—in all truth; we have no chance against her!" She looked joylessly at Tess.

"What do you mean?" asked the latter.

"He likes 'ee best—the very best! We could see it as he brought 'ee. He would have kissed 'ee, if you had encouraged him to do it, ever so little."

"No, no," said she.

The gaiety with which they had set out had somehow vanished; and yet there was no enmity or malice between them. They were generous young souls; they had been reared in the lonely country nooks where fatalism is a strong sentiment, and they did not blame her. Such supplanting was to be.

Tess's heart ached. There was no concealing from herself the fact that she loved Angel Clare, perhaps all the more passionately from knowing that the others had also lost their hearts to him. There is contagion in this sentiment, especially among women. And yet that same hungry heart of hers compassionated her friends. Tess's honest nature had fought against this, but too feebly, and the natural result had followed.

"I will never stand in your way, nor in the way of either of you!" she declared to Retty that night in the bedroom (her tears running down). "I can't help this, my dear! I don't think marrying is in his mind at all; but if he were ever to ask me I should refuse him, as I should refuse any man."

"Oh! would you? Why?" said wondering Retty.

"It cannot be! But I will be plain. Putting myself quite on one side. I don't think he will choose either of you."

"I have never expected it—thought of it!" moaned Retty. "But O! I wish I was dead!"

The poor child, torn by a feeling which she hardly understood, turned to the other two girls who came upstairs just then.

"We be friends with her again," she said to them. "She thinks no more of his choosing her than we do."

So the reserve went off, and they were confiding and warm.

"I don't seem to care what I do now," said Marian, whose mood was turned to its lowest bass. "I was going to marry a dairyman at Stickleford, who's asked me twice; but—my soul—I would put an end to myself rather'n be his wife now! Why don't ye speak, Izz?"

"To confess, then," murmured Izz, "I made sure to-day that he was going to kiss me as he held me; and I lay still against his breast, hoping and hoping, and never moved at all. But he did not. I don't like biding here at Talbothays any longer! I shall go hwome."

The air of the sleeping-chamber seemed to palpitate with the hopeless passion of the girls. They writhed feverishly under the oppressiveness of an emotion thrust on them by cruel Nature's law—an emotion which they had neither expected nor desired. The incident of the day had fanned the flame that was burning the inside of their hearts out, and the torture was almost more than they could endure. The differences which distinguished them as individuals were abstracted by this passion, and each was but portion of one organism called sex. There was so much frankness and so little jealousy because there was no hope. Each one was a girl of fair common sense, and she did not delude herself with any vain conceits, or deny her love, or give herself airs, in the idea of outshining the others. The full recognition of the futility of their infatuation, from a social point of view; its purposeless beginning; its self-bounded outlook; its lack of everything to justify its existence in the eye of civilisation (while lacking nothing in the eye of Nature); the one fact that it did exist, ecstasising them to a killing joy; all this imparted to them a resignation, a dignity, which a practical and sordid expectation of winning him as a husband would have destroyed.

They tossed and turned on their little beds, and the cheese-wring dripped monotonously downstairs.

"B' you awake, Tess?" whispered one, half an hour later.

It was Izz Huett's voice.

Tess replied in the affirmative, whereupon also Retty and Marian suddenly flung the bedclothes off them, and sighed—

"So be we!"

"I wonder what she is like—the lady they say his family have looked out for him!"

"I wonder," said Izz.

"Some lady looked out for him?" gasped Tess, starting. "I have never heard o' that!"

"O yes—'tis whispered; a young lady of his own rank, chosen by his family; a Doctor of Divinity's daughter near his father's parish of Emminster; he don't much care for her, they say. But he is sure to marry her."

They had heard so very little of this; yet it was enough to build up wretched dolorous dreams upon, there in the shade of the night. They pictured all the details of his being won round to consent, of the wedding preparations, of the bride's happiness, of her dress and veil, of her blissful home with him, when oblivion would have fallen upon themselves as far as he and their love were concerned. Thus they talked, and ached, and wept till sleep charmed their sorrow away.

After this disclosure Tess nourished no further foolish thought that there lurked any grave and deliberate import in Clare's attentions to her. It was a passing summer love of her face, for love's own temporary sake—nothing more. And thorny crown of this sad conception was that she whom he really did prefer in a cursory way to the rest, she who knew herself to be more impassioned in nature, cleverer, more beautiful than they, was in the eyes of propriety far less worthy of him than the homelier ones whom he ignored.

XXIV

AMID THE OOZING FATNESS AND WARM FERMENTS OF THE VAR VALE, AT A SEASON WHEN the rush of juices could almost be heard below the hiss of fertilisation, it was impossible that the most fanciful love should not grow passionate. The ready bosoms existing there were impregnated by their surroundings.

July passed over their heads, and the Thermidorean weather which came in its wake seemed an effort on the part of Nature to match the state of hearts at Talbothays Dairy. The air of the place, so fresh in the spring and early summer, was stagnant and enervating now. Its heavy scents weighed upon them, and at mid-day the landscape seemed lying in a swoon. Ethiopic scorchings browned the upper slopes of the pastures, but there was still bright green herbage here where the watercourses purled. And as Clare was oppressed by the outward heats, so was he burdened inwardly by waxing fervour of passion for the soft and silent Tess.

The rains having passed the uplands were dry. The wheels of the dairyman's spring-cart, as he sped home from market, licked up the pulverised surface of the highway, and were followed by white ribands of dust, as if they had set a thin powder-train on fire. The cows jumped wildly over the five-barred barton gate, maddened by the gad-fly; Dairyman Crick kept his shirt-sleeves permanently rolled up from Monday to Saturday: open windows had no effect in ventilation without open doors, and in the dairy-garden the blackbirds and thrushes crept about under the currant-bushes, rather in the manner of quadrupeds than of winged creatures. The flies in the kitchen were lazy, teasing, and familiar, crawling about in the unwonted places, on the floors, into drawers, and over the backs of the milkmaids' hands. Conversations were concerning sunstroke; while butter-making, and still more butter-keeping, was a despair.

They milked entirely in the meads for coolness and convenience, without driving in the cows. During the day the animals obsequiously followed the shadow of the smallest tree as it moved round the stem with the diurnal roll; and when the milkers came they could hardly stand still for the flies.

On one of these afternoons four or five unmilked cows chanced to stand apart from the general herd, behind the corner of a hedge, among them being Dumpling and Old

Pretty, who loved Tess's hands above those of any other maid. When she rose from her stool under a finished cow Angel Clare, who had been observing her for some time, asked her if she would take the aforesaid creatures next. She silently assented, and with her stool at arm's length, and the pail against her knee, went round to where they stood. Soon the sound of Old Pretty's milk fizzing into the pail came through the hedge, and then Angel felt inclined to go round the corner also, to finish off a hard-yielding milcher who had strayed there, he being now as capable of this as the dairyman himself.

All the men, and some of the women, when milking, dug their foreheads into the cows and gazed into the pail. But a few—mainly the younger ones—rested their heads side-ways. This was Tess Durbeyfield's habit, her temple pressing the milcher's flank, her eyes fixed on the far end of the meadow with the quiet of one lost in meditation. She was milk-ing Old Pretty thus, and the sun chancing to be on the milking-side it shone flat upon her pink-gowned form and her white curtain-bonnet, and upon her profile, rendering it keen as a cameo cut from the dun background of the cow.

She did not know that Clare had followed her round, and that he sat under his cow watching her. The stillness of her head and features was remarkable: she might have been in a trance, her eyes open, yet unseeing. Nothing in the picture moved but Old Pretty's tail and Tess's pink hands, the latter so gently as to be a rhythmic pulsation only, as if they were obeying a reflex stimulus, like a beating heart.

How very lovable her face was to him. Yet there was nothing ethereal about it; all was real vitality, real warmth, real incarnation. And it was in her mouth that this culminated. Eyes almost as deep and speaking he had seen before, and cheeks perhaps as fair; brows as arched, a chin and throat almost as shapely; her mouth he had seen nothing to equal on the face of the earth. To a young man with the least fire in him that little upward lift in the middle of her red top lip was distracting, infatuating, maddening. He had never be-fore seen a woman's lips and teeth which forced upon his mind with such persistent iter-ation the old Elizabethan simile of roses filled with snow. Perfect, he, as a lover, might have called them offhand. But no—they were not perfect. And it was the touch of the im-perfect upon the would-be perfect that gave the sweetness, because it was that which gave the humanity.

Clare had studied the curves of those lips so many times that he could reproduce them mentally with ease: and now, as they again confronted him, clothed with colour and life, they sent an *aura* over his flesh, a breeze through his nerves, which well-nigh produced a qualm; and actually produced, by some mysterious physiological process, a prosaic sneeze.

She then became conscious that he was observing her; but she would not show it by any change of position, though the curious dreamlike fixity disappeared, and a close eye might easily have discerned that the rosiness of her face deepened, and then faded till only a tinge of it was left.

The influence that had passed into Clare like an excitation from the sky did not die down. Resolutions, reticences, prudences, fears, fell back like a defeated battalion. He jumped up from his seat, and, leaving his pail to be kicked over if the milcher had such a mind, went quickly towards the desire of his eyes, and, kneeling down beside her, clasped her in his arms.

Tess was taken completely by surprise, and she yielded to his embrace with unreflect-ing inevitableness. Having seen that it was really her lover who had advanced, and no one else, her lips parted, and she sank upon him in her momentary joy, with something very like an ecstatic cry.

He had been on the point of kissing that too tempting mouth, but he checked himself, for tender conscience' sake.

"Forgive me, Tess dear!" he whispered. "I ought to have asked. I—did not know what I was doing. I do not mean it as a liberty. I am devoted to you, Tessy, dearest, in all sincerity!"

Old Pretty by this time had looked round, puzzled; and seeing two people crouching under her where, by immemorial custom, there should have been only one, lifted her hind-leg crossly.

"She is angry—she doesn't know what we mean—she'll kick over the milk!" exclaimed Tess, gently striving to free herself, her eyes concerned with the quadruped's actions, her heart more deeply concerned with herself and Clare.

She slipped up from her seat, and they stood together, his arm still encircling her. Tess's eyes, fixed on distance, began to fill.

"Why do you cry, my darling?" he said.

"O—I don't know!" she murmured.

As she saw and felt more clearly the position she was in she became agitated and tried to withdraw.

"Well, I have betrayed my feeling, Tess, at last," said he, with a curious sigh of desperation, signifying unconsciously that his heart had outrun his judgment. "That I—love you dearly and truly I need not say. But I—it shall go no further now—it distresses you— I am as surprised as you are. You will not think I have presumed upon your defencelessness—been too quick and unreflecting, will you?"

"N'—I can't tell."

He had allowed her to free herself; and in a minute or two the milking of each was resumed. Nobody had beheld the gravitation of the two into one; and when the dairyman came round by that screened nook a few minutes later there was not a sign to reveal that the markedly sundered pair were more to each other than mere acquaintance. Yet in the interval since Crick's last view of them something had occurred which changed the pivot of the universe for their two natures; something which, had he known its quality, the dairyman would have despised, as a practical man; yet which was based upon a more stubborn and resistless tendency than a whole heap of so-called practicalities. A veil had been whisked aside; the tract of each one's outlook was to have a new horizon thenceforward— for a short time or for a long.

END OF PHASE THE THIRD

Phase the Fourth

The Consequence

XXV

CLARE, RESTLESS, WENT OUT INTO THE DUSK WHEN EVENING DREW ON, SHE WHO had won him having retired to her chamber.

The night was as sultry as the day. There was no coolness after dark unless on the grass. Roads, garden-paths, the house-fronts, the barton-walls were warm as hearths, and reflected the noontime temperature into the noctambulist's face.

He sat on the east gate of the dairy-yard, and knew not what to think of himself. Feeling had indeed smothered judgment that day.

Since the sudden embrace, three hours before, the twain had kept apart. She seemed stilled, almost alarmed, at what had occurred, while the novelty, unpremeditation, mastery of circumstance disquieted him—palpitating, contemplative being that he was. He could hardly realise their true relations to each other as yet, and what their mutual bearing should be before third parties thenceforward.

Angel had come as pupil to this dairy in the idea that his temporary existence here was to be the merest episode in his life, soon passed through and early forgotten; he had come as to a place from which as from a screened alcove he could calmly view the absorbing world without, and, apostrophising it with Walt Whitman—

> Crowds of men and women attired in the usual costumes,
> How curious you are to me!—

resolve upon a plan for plunging into that world anew. But, behold, the absorbing scene had been imported hither. What had been the engrossing world had dissolved into an uninteresting outer dumb-show; while here, in this apparently dim and unimpassioned place, novelty had volcanically started up, as it had never, for him, started up elsewhere.

Every window of the house being open Clare could hear across the yard each trivial sound of the retiring household. The dairy-house, so humble, so insignificant, so purely to him a place of constrained sojourn that he had never hitherto deemed it of sufficient importance to be reconnoitred as an object of any quality whatever in the landscape; what was it now? The aged and lichened brick gables breathed forth "Stay!" The windows smiled, the door coaxed and beckoned, the creeper blushed confederacy. A personality within it was so far-reaching in her influence as to spread into and make the bricks, mortar, and whole overhanging sky throb with a burning sensibility. Whose was this mighty personality? A milkmaid's.

It was amazing, indeed, to find how great a matter the life of the obscure dairy had become to him. And though new love was to be held partly responsible for this it was not solely so. Many besides Angel have learnt that the magnitude of lives is not as to their external displacements, but as to their subjective experiences. The impressionable peasant leads a larger, fuller, more dramatic life than the pachydermatous king. Looking at it thus he found that life was to be seen of the same magnitude here as elsewhere.

Despite his heterodoxy, faults, and weaknesses, Clare was a man with a conscience. Tess was no insignificant creature to toy with and dismiss; but a woman living her precious life—a life which, to herself who endured or enjoyed it, possessed as great a dimension as the life of the mightiest to himself. Upon her sensations the whole world depended to Tess; through her existence all her fellow-creatures existed, to her. The universe itself only came into being for Tess on the particular day in the particular year in which she was born.

This consciousness upon which he had intruded was the single opportunity of existence ever vouchsafed to Tess by an unsympathetic First Cause—her all; her every and only chance. How then should he look upon her as of less consequence than himself; as a pretty trifle to caress and grow weary of; and not deal in the greatest seriousness with the affection which he knew that he had awakened in her—so fervid and so impressionable as she was under her reserve; in order that it might not agonise and wreck her?

To encounter her daily in the accustomed manner would be to develop what had begun. Living in such close relations, to meet meant to fall into endearment; flesh and blood could not resist it; and, having arrived at no conclusion as to the issue of such a tendency, he decided to hold aloof for the present from occupations in which they would be mutually engaged. As yet the harm done was small.

But it was not easy to carry out the resolution never to approach her. He was driven towards her by every heave of his pulse.

He thought he would go and see his friends. It might be possible to sound them upon this. In less than five months his term here would have ended, and after a few additional months spent upon other farms he would be fully equipped in agricultural knowledge, and in a position to start on his own account. Would not a farmer want a wife, and should a farmer's wife be a drawing-room wax-figure, or a woman who understood farming? Notwithstanding the pleasing answer returned to him by the silence he resolved to go his journey.

One morning when they sat down to breakfast at Talbothays Dairy some maid observed that she had not seen anything of Mr. Clare that day.

"O no," said Dairyman Crick. "Mr. Clare has gone hwome to Emminster to spend a few days wi' his kinsfolk."

For four impassioned ones around that table the sunshine of the morning went out at a stroke, and the birds muffled their song. But neither girl by word or gesture revealed her blankness.

"He's getting on towards the end of his time wi' me," added the dairyman, with a phlegm which unconsciously was brutal; "and so I suppose he is beginning to see about his plans elsewhere."

"How much longer is he to bide here?" asked Izz Huett, the only one of the gloom-stricken bevy who could trust her voice with the question.

The others waited for the dairyman's answer as if their lives hung upon it; Retty, with parted lips, gazing on the table cloth, Marian with heat added to her redness, Tess throbbing and looking out at the meads.

"Well, I can't mind the exact day without looking at my memorandum-book," replied Crick, with the same intolerable unconcern. "And even that may be altered a bit. He'll bide to get a little practise in the calving out at the straw-yard, for certain. He'll hang on till the end of the year I should say."

Four months or so of torturing ecstasy in his society—of "pleasure girdled about with pain." After that the blackness of unutterable night.

*   *   *

At this moment of the morning Angel Clare was riding along a narrow lane ten miles distant from the breakfasters, in the direction of his father's vicarage at Emminster, carrying, as well as he could, a little basket which contained some black-puddings and a bottle of mead, sent by Mrs. Crick, with her kind respects, to his parents. The white lane stretched before him, and his eyes were upon it; but they were staring into next year, and not at the lane. He loved her; ought he to marry her? Dared he to marry her? What would his mother and his brothers say? What would he himself say a couple of years after the event? That would depend upon whether the germs of staunch comradeship underlay the temporary emotion, or whether it were a sensuous joy in her form only, with no substratum of everlastingness.

His father's hill-surrounded little town, the Tudor church-tower of red stone, the clump of trees near the vicarage, came at last into view beneath him, and he rode down towards the well-known gate. Casting a glance in the direction of the church before entering his home, he beheld standing by the vestry-door a group of girls, of ages between twelve and sixteen, apparently awaiting the arrival of some other one, who in a moment became visible; a figure somewhat older than the schoolgirls, wearing a broad-brimmed hat and highly-starched cambric morning-gown, with a couple of books in her hand.

Clare knew her well. He could not be sure that she observed him; he hoped she did not, so as to render it unnecessary that he should go and speak to her, blameless creature that she was. An overpowering reluctance to greet her made him decide that she had not seen him. The young lady was Miss Mercy Chant, the only daughter of his father's neighbour and friend, whom it was his parents' quiet hope that he might wed some day. She was great at Antinomianism and Bible-classes, and was plainly going to hold a class now. Clare's mind flew to the impassioned, summer-steeped heathens in the Var Vale, their rosy faces court-patched with cow-droppings; and to one the most impassioned of them all.

It was on the impulse of the moment that he had resolved to trot over to Emminster, and hence had not written to apprise his mother and father, aiming, however, to arrive about the breakfast hour, before they should have gone out to their parish duties. He was a little late, and they had already sat down to the morning meal. The group at the table jumped up to welcome him as soon as he entered. They were his father and mother, his brother the Reverend Felix—curate at a town in the adjoining county, home for the inside of a fortnight—and his other brother, the Reverend Cuthbert, the classical scholar, and Fellow and Dean of his College, down from Cambridge for the long vacation. His mother appeared in a cap and silver spectacles, and his father looked what in fact he was—an earnest, God-fearing man, somewhat gaunt, in years about sixty-five, his pale face lined with thought and purpose. Over their heads hung the picture of Angel's sister, the eldest of the family, sixteen years his senior, who had married a missionary and gone out to Africa.

Old Mr. Clare was a clergyman of a type which, within the last twenty years, has well-nigh dropped out of contemporary life. A spiritual descendant in the direct line from Wycliff, Huss, Luther, Calvin; an Evangelical of the Evangelicals, a Conversionist, a man of Apostolic simplicity in life and thought, he had in his raw youth made up his mind once for all in the deeper questions of existence, and admitted no further reasoning on them thenceforward. He was regarded even by those of his own date and school of thinking as extreme; while, on the other hand, those totally opposed to him were unwillingly won to admiration for his thoroughness, and for the remarkable power he showed in dismissing all question as to principles in his energy for applying them. He loved Paul of Tarsus, liked St. John, hated St. James as much as he dared, and regarded with mixed feelings Timothy, Titus, and Philemon. The New Testament was less a Christiad then a Pauliad to his intelligence—less an argument than an intoxication. His creed of determinism was such that it almost amounted to a vice, and quite amounted, on its negative side, to a renunciative philosophy which had cousinship with that of Schopenhauer and Leopardi. He despised the Canons and Rubric, swore by the Articles, and deemed himself consistent through the whole category—which in a way he might have been. One thing he certainly was—sincere.

To the aesthetic, sensuous, pagan pleasure in natural life and lush womanhood which his son Angel had lately been experiencing in Var Vale, his temper would have been antipathetic in a high degree, had he either by enquiry or imagination been able to apprehend it. Once upon a time Angel had been so unlucky as to say to his father, in a moment of irritation, that it might have resulted far better for mankind if Greece had been the source of the religion of modern civilisation, and not Palestine; and his father's grief was of that blank description which could not realise that there might lurk a thousandth part of a truth, much less a half truth or a whole truth, in such a proposition. He had simply preached austerely at Angel for some time after. But the kindness of his heart was such that he never resented anything for long, and welcomed his son to-day with a smile which was as candidly sweet as a child's.

Angel sat down, and the place felt like home; yet he did not so much as formerly feel himself one of the family gathered there. Every time that he returned hither he was conscious of this divergence, and since he had last shared in the vicarage life it had grown even more distinctly foreign to his own than usual. Its transcendental aspirations—still unconsciously based on the geocentric view of things, a zenithal paradise, a nadiral hell—were as foreign to his own as if they had been the dreams of people on another planet. Latterly he had seen only Life, felt only the great passionate pulse of existence, unwarped, uncontorted, untrammelled by those creeds which futilely attempt to check what wisdom would be content to regulate.

On their part they saw a great difference in him, a growing divergence from the Angel Clare of former times. It was chiefly a difference in his manner that they noticed just now, particularly his brothers. He was getting to behave like a farmer; he flung his legs about; the muscles of his face had grown more expressive; his eyes looked as much information as his tongue spoke, and more. The manner of the scholar had nearly disappeared; still more the manner of the drawing-room young man. A prig would have said that he had lost culture, and a prude that he had become coarse. Such was the contagion of domiciliary fellowship with the Talbothays nymphs and swains.

After breakfast he walked with his two brothers, non-evangelical, well-educated, hall-marked young men, correct to their remotest fibre, such unimpeachable models as are turned out yearly by the lathe of a systematic tuition. They were both somewhat short-sighted, and when it was the custom to wear a single eyeglass and string they wore a single eyeglass and string; when it was the custom to wear a double glass they wore a double glass; when it was the custom to wear spectacles they wore spectacles straightway, all without reference to the particular variety of defect in their own vision. When Wordsworth was enthroned they carried pocket copies; and when Shelley was belittled they allowed him to grow dusty on their shelves. When Correggio's Holy Families were admired, they admired Correggio's Holy Families; when he was decried in favour of Velasquez, they sedulously followed suit without any personal objection.

If these two noticed Angel's growing social ineptness, he noticed their growing mental limitations. Felix seemed to him all Church; Cuthbert all College. His Diocesan Synod and Visitations were the mainsprings of the world to the one; Cambridge to the other. Each brother candidly recognised that there were a few unimportant score of millions of outsiders in civilised society, persons who were neither University men nor churchmen; but they were to be tolerated rather than reckoned with and respected.

They were both dutiful and attentive sons, and were regular in their visits to their parents. Felix, though an offshoot from a far more recent point in the devolution of theology than his father, was less self-sacrificing and disinterested. More tolerant than his father of a contradictory opinion, in its aspect as a danger to its holder, he was less ready than his father to pardon it as a slight to his own teaching. Cuthbert was, upon the whole, the more liberal-minded, though, with greater subtlety, he had not so much heart.

As they walked along the hillside Angel's former feeling revived in him—that whatever their advantages by comparison with himself, neither saw or set forth life as it really was lived. Perhaps, as with many men, their opportunities of observation were not so good as their opportunities of expression. Neither had an adequate conception of the complicated forces at work outside the smooth and gentle current in which they and their associates floated. Neither saw the difference between local truth and universal truth; that what the inner world said in their clerical and academic hearing was quite a different thing from what the outer world was thinking.

"I suppose it is farming or nothing for you now, my dear fellow," Felix was saying, among other things, to his youngest brother, as he looked through his spectacles at the distant fields with sad austerity. "And, therefore, we must make the best of it. But I do entreat you to endeavour to keep as much as possible in touch with moral ideals. Farming, of course, means roughing it externally; but high thinking may go with plain living, nevertheless."

"Of course it may," said Angel. "Was it not proved nineteen hundred years ago—if I may trespass upon your domain a little? Why should you think, Felix, that I am likely to drop my high thinking and my moral ideals?"

"Well, I fancied, from the tone of your letters and our conversation—it may be fancy only—that you were somehow losing intellectual grasp. Hasn't it struck you, Cuthbert?"

"Now, Felix," said Angel drily, "we are very good friends, you know; each of us treading our allotted circles; but if it comes to intellectual grasp, I think you, as a contented dogmatist, had better leave mine alone, and enquire what has become of yours."

They returned down the hill to dinner, which was fixed at any time at which their father's and mother's morning work in the parish usually concluded. Convenience as regarded afternoon callers was the last thing to enter into the consideration of unselfish Mr. and Mrs. Clare; though the three sons were sufficiently in unison on this matter to wish that their parents would conform a little to modern notions.

The walk had made them hungry, Angel in particular, who was now an out-door man, accustomed to the profuse *dapes inemptæ* of the dairyman's somewhat coarsely-laden table. But neither of the old people had arrived, and it was not till the sons were almost tired of waiting that their parents entered. The self-denying pair had been occupied in coaxing the appetites of some of their sick parishioners, whom they, somewhat inconsistently, tried to keep imprisoned in the flesh, their own appetites being quite forgotten.

The family sat down to table, and a frugal meal of cold viands was deposited before them. Angel looked round for Mrs. Crick's black-puddings, which he had directed to be nicely grilled as they did them at the dairy, and of which he wished his father and mother to appreciate the marvellous herbal savours as highly as he did himself.

"Ah! you are looking for the black-puddings, my dear boy," observed Clare's mother. "But I am sure you will not mind doing without them as I am sure your father and I shall not, when you know the reason. I suggested to him that we should take Mrs. Crick's kind present to the children of the man who can earn nothing just now because of his attacks of delirium tremens; and he agreed that it would be a great pleasure to them; so we did."

"Of course," said Angel cheerfully, looking round for the mead.

"I found the mead so extremely alcoholic," continued his mother, "that it was quite unfit for use as a beverage, but as valuable as rum or brandy in an emergency; so I have put it in my medicine-closet."

"We never drink spirits at this table, on principle," added his father.

"But what shall I tell the dairyman's wife?" said Angel.

"The truth, of course," said his father.

"I rather wanted to say we enjoyed the mead and the black-puddings very much. She is a kind, jolly sort of body, and is sure to ask me directly I return."

"You cannot, if we did not," Mr. Clare answered lucidly.

"Ah—no; though that mead was a drop of pretty tipple."

"A what?" said Cuthbert and Felix both.

"Oh—'tis an expression they use down at Talbothays," replied Angel, blushing. He felt that his parents were right in their practise if wrong in their want of sentiment, and said no more.

XXVI

IT WAS NOT TILL THE EVENING, AFTER FAMILY PRAYERS, THAT ANGEL FOUND OPPORTUnity of broaching to his father one or two subjects near his heart. He had strung himself up to the purpose while kneeling behind his brothers on the carpet, studying the little nails in the heels of their walking boots. When the service was over they went out of the room with their mother, and Mr. Clare and himself were left alone.

The young man first discussed with the elder his plans for the attainment of his position as a farmer on an extensive scale—either in England or in the Colonies. His father then told him that, as he had not been put to the expense of sending Angel up to Cambridge, he had felt it his duty to set by a sum of money every year towards the purchase or lease of land for him some day, that he might not feel himself unduly slighted.

"As far as worldly wealth goes," continued his father, "you will no doubt stand far superior to your brothers in a few years."

This considerateness on old Mr. Clare's part led Angel onward to the other and dearer subject. He observed to his father that he was then six-and-twenty, and that when he should start in the farming business he would require eyes in the back of his head to see to all matters—someone would be necessary to superintend the domestic labours of his establishment whilst he was a-field. Would it not be well, therefore, for him to marry?

His father seemed to think this idea not unreasonable; and then Angel put the question—

"What kind of wife do you think would be best for me as a thrifty hard-working farmer?"

"A truly Christian woman, who will be a help and a comfort to you in your goings-out and your comings-in. Beyond that, it really matters little. Such an one can be found; indeed, my earnest-minded friend and neighbour, Dr Chant—"

"But ought she not primarily to be able to milk cows, churn good butter, make immense cheeses; know how to sit hens and turkeys and rear chickens, to direct a field of labourers in an emergency, and estimate the value of sheep and calves?"

"Yes; a farmer's wife; yes, certainly. It would be desirable." Mr. Clare, the elder, had plainly never thought of these points before. "I was going to add," he said, "that for a pure and saintly woman you will not find one more to your true advantage, and certainly not more to your mother's mind and my own, than your friend Mercy, whom you used to show a certain interest in. It is true that my neighbour Chant's daughter had lately caught up the fashion of the younger clergy round about us for decorating the Communion-table—altar, as I was shocked to hear her call it one day—with flowers and other stuff on festival occasions. But her father, who is quite as opposed to such flummery as I, says that can be cured. It is a mere girlish outbreak which, I am sure, will not be permanent."

"Yes, yes; Mercy is good and devout, I know. But, father, don't you think that a young woman equally pure and virtuous as Miss Chant, but one who, in place of that lady's ecclesiastical accomplishments, understands the duties of farm life as well as a farmer himself, would suit me infinitely better?"

His father persisted in his conviction that a knowledge of a farmer's wife's duties came second to a Pauline view of humanity; and the impulsive Angel, wishing to honour his father's feelings and to advance the cause of his heart at the same time, grew specious. He said that fate or Providence had thrown in his way a woman who possessed every qualification to be the helpmate of an agriculturist, and was decidedly of a serious turn of mind. He would not say whether or not she had attached herself to the sound Low Church School of his father; but she would probably be open to conviction on that point; she was a regular church-goer of simple faith; honest-hearted, receptive, intelligent, graceful to a degree, chaste as a vestal, and, in personal appearance, exceptionally beautiful.

"Is she of a family such as you would care to marry into—a lady, in short?" asked his startled mother, who had come softly into the study during the conversation.

"She is not what in common parlance is called a lady," said Angel, unflinchingly, "for she is a cottager's daughter, as I am proud to say. But she *is* a lady, nevertheless—in feeling and nature."

"Mercy Chant is of a very good family."

"Pooh!—what's the advantage of that, mother?" said Angel quickly. "How is family to avail the wife of a man who has to rough it as I have, and shall have to do?"

"Mercy is accomplished. And accomplishments have their charm," returned his mother, looking at him through her silver spectacles.

"As to external accomplishments, what will be the use of them in the life I am going to lead?—while as to her reading, I can take that in hand. She'll be apt pupil enough, as you would say if you knew her. She's brim full of poetry—actualised poetry, if I may use the expression. She *lives* what paper-poets only write. . . . And she is an unimpeachable Christian, I am sure; perhaps of the very tribe, genus, and species you desire to propagate."

"O Angel, you are mocking!"

"Mother, I beg pardon. But as she really does attend Church almost every Sunday morning, and is a good Christian girl, I am sure you will tolerate any social shortcomings for the sake of that quality, and feel that I may do worse than choose her." Angel waxed quite earnest on that rather automatic orthodoxy in his beloved Tess which (never dreaming that it might stand him in such good stead) he had been prone to slight when observing it practised by her and the other milkmaids, because of its obvious unreality amid beliefs essentially naturalistic.

In their sad doubts as to whether their son had himself any right whatever to the title he claimed for the unknown young woman, Mr. and Mrs. Clare began to feel it as an advantage not to be overlooked that she at least was sound in her views; especially as the conjunction of the pair must have arisen by an act of Providence; for Angel never would have made orthodoxy a condition of his choice. They said finally that it was better not to act in a hurry, but that they would not object to see her.

Angel therefore refrained from declaring more particulars now. He felt that, single-minded and self-sacrificing as his parents were, there yet existed certain latent prejudices of theirs, as middle-class people, which it would require some tact to overcome. For though legally at liberty to do as he chose, and though their daughter-in-law's qualifications could make no practical difference to their lives, in the probability of her living far away from them, he wished for affection's sake not to wound their sentiment in the most important decision of his life.

He observed his own inconsistencies in dwelling upon accidents in Tess's life as if they were vital features. It was for herself that he loved Tess; her soul, her heart, her substance—not for her skill in the dairy, her aptness as his scholar, and certainly not for her simple formal faith-professions. Her unsophisticated open-air existence required no varnish of conventionality to make it palatable to him. He held that education had as yet but little affected the beats of emotion and impulse on which domestic happiness depends. It was probable that, in the lapse of ages, improved systems of moral and intellectual training would appreciably, perhaps considerably, elevate the involuntary and even the unconscious instincts of human nature; but up to the present day culture, as far as he could see, might be said to have affected only the mental epiderm of those lives which had been brought under its influence. This belief was confirmed by his experience of women, which, having latterly been extended from the cultivated middle-class into the rural community, had taught him how much less was the intrinsic difference between the good and wise woman of one social stratum and the good and wise woman of another social stratum, than between the good and bad, the wise and the foolish, of the same stratum or class.

It was the morning of his departure. His brothers had already left the vicarage to proceed on a walking tour in the north, whence one was to return to his college, and the other to his curacy. Angel might have accompanied them, but preferred to rejoin his sweetheart at Talbothays. He would have been an awkward member of the party; for, though the most appreciative humanist, the most ideal religionist, even the best-versed Christologist of the three, there was alienation in the standing consciousness that his squareness would not fit the round hole that had been prepared for him. To neither Felix nor Cuthbert had he ventured to mention Tess.

His mother made him sandwiches, and his father accompanied him, on his own mare, a little way along the road. Having fairly well advanced his own affairs Angel listened in a willing silence, as they jogged on together through the shady lanes, to his father's account of his parish difficulties, and the coldness of brother clergymen whom he loved, because of his strict interpretations of the New Testament by the light of what they deemed a pernicious Calvinistic doctrine.

"Pernicious!" said Mr. Clare, with genial scorn; and he proceeded to recount experiences which would show the absurdity of that idea. He told of wondrous conversions of evil livers of which he had been the instrument, not only amongst the poor, but amongst the rich and well-to-do; and he also candidly admitted many failures.

As an instance of the latter, he mentioned the case of a young upstart squire named d'Urberville, living some forty miles off, in the neighbourhood of Trantridge.

"Not one of the ancient d'Urbervilles of Kingsbere and other places?" asked his son. "That curiously historic worn-out family with its ghostly legend of the coach-and-four?"

"O no. The original d'Urbervilles decayed and disappeared sixty or eighty years ago––at least, I believe so. This seems to be a new family which has taken the name; for the credit of the former knightly line I hope they are spurious, I'm sure. But it is odd to hear you express interest in old families. I thought you set less store by them even than I."

"You misapprehend me, father; you often do," said Angel with a little impatience. "Politically I am sceptical as to the virtue of their being old. Some of the wise even among themselves 'exclaim against their own succession,' as Hamlet puts it; but lyrically, dramatically, and even historically, I am tenderly attached to them."

This distinction, though by no means a subtle one, was yet too subtle for Mr. Clare the elder, and he went on with the story he had been about to relate; which was that after the death of the senior so-called d'Urberville the young man developed the most culpable passions, though he had a blind mother, whose condition should have made him know better. A knowledge of his career having come to the ears of Mr. Clare, when he was in that part of the country preaching missionary sermons, he boldly took occasion to speak to the delinquent on his spiritual state. Though he was a stranger, occupying another's pulpit, he had felt this to be his duty, and took for his text the words from St. Luke: "Thou fool, this night thy soul shall be required of thee!" The young man much resented this directness of attack, and in the war of words which followed when they met he did not scruple publicly to insult Mr. Clare, without respect for his grey hairs.

Angel flushed with distress.

"Dear father," he said sadly, "I wish you would not expose yourself to such gratuitous pain from scoundrels!"

"Pain?" said his father, his rugged face shining in the ardour of self-abnegation. "The only pain to me was pain on his account, poor, foolish young man. Do you suppose his incensed words could give me any pain, or even his blows? 'Being reviled we bless; being persecuted we suffer it; being defamed we entreat; we are made as the filth of the world, and as the offscouring of all things unto this day.' Those ancient and noble words to the Corinthians are strictly true at this present hour."

"Not blows, father? He did not proceed to blows?"

"No, he did not. Though I have borne blows from men in a mad state of intoxication."

"No!"

"A dozen times, my boy. What then? I have saved them from the guilt of murdering their own flesh and blood thereby; and they have lived to thank me, and praise God."

"May this young man do the same!" said Angel fervently. "But I fear otherwise, from what you say."

"We'll hope, nevertheless," said Mr. Clare. "And I continue to pray for him, though on this side of the grave we shall probably never meet again. But, after all, one of those poor words of mine may spring up in his heart as a good seed some day."

Now, as always, Clare's father was sanguine as a child; and though the younger could not accept his parent's narrow dogma he revered his practice, and recognised the hero under the pietist. Perhaps he revered his father's practice even more now than ever, seeing that, in the question of making Tessy his wife, his father had not once thought of enquiring whether she were well provided or penniless. The same unworldliness was what had necessitated Angel's getting a living as a farmer, and would probably keep his brothers in the position of poor parsons for the term of their activities; yet Angel admired it none the less. Indeed, despite his own heterodoxy, Angel often felt that he was nearer to his father on the human side than was either of his brethren.

XXVII

AN UP-HILL AND DOWN-HILL RIDE OF TWENTY-ODD MILES THROUGH A GARISH MID-DAY atmosphere brought him in the afternoon to a detached knoll a mile or two west of Talbothays, whence he again looked into that green trough of sappiness and humidity, the valley of the Var or Froom. Immediately he began to descend from the upland to the fat alluvial soil below, the atmosphere grew heavier; the languid perfume of the summer fruits, the mists, the hay, the flowers, formed therein a vast pool of odour which at this hour seemed to make the animals, the very bees and butterflies, drowsy. Clare was now so familiar with the spot that he knew the individual cows by their names when, a long distance off, he saw them dotted about the meads. It was with a sense of luxury that he recognised his power of viewing life here from its inner side, in a way that had been quite foreign to him in his student-days; and, much as he loved his parents, he could not help being aware that to come here, as now, after an experience of home-life, affected him like throwing off splints and bandages; even the one customary curb on the humours of English rural societies being absent in this place, Talbothays having no resident landlord.

Not a human being was out-of-doors at the dairy. The denizens were all enjoying the usual afternoon nap of an hour or so which the exceedingly early hours kept in summertime rendered a necessity. At the door the wood-hooped pails, sodden and bleached by infinite scrubbings, hung like hats on a stand upon the forked and peeled limb of an oak fixed there for that purpose; all of them ready and dry for the evening milking. Angel entered, and went through the silent passages of the house to the back quarters, where he listened for a moment. Sustained snores came from the cart-house, where some of the men were lying down; the grunt and squeal of sweltering pigs arose from the still further distance. The large-leaved rhubarb and cabbage plants slept too, their broad limp surfaces hanging in the sun like half-closed umbrellas.

He unbridled and fed his horse, and as he re-entered the house the clock struck three. Three was the afternoon skimming-hour; and, with the stroke, Clare heard the creaking of the floor-boards above, and then the touch of a descending foot on the stairs. It was Tess's, who in another moment came down before his eyes.

She had not heard him enter, and hardly realised his presence there. She was yawning, and he saw the red interior of her mouth as if it had been a snake's. She had stretched one arm so high above her coiled-up cable of hair that he could see its satin delicacy above the sunburn; her face was flushed with sleep, and her eyelids hung heavy over their pupils. The brim-fulness of her nature breathed from her. It was a moment when a woman's soul is more incarnate than at any other time; when the most spiritual beauty bespeaks itself flesh; and sex takes the outside place in the presentation.

Then those eyes flashed brightly through their filmy heaviness, before the remainder of her face was well awake. With an oddly compounded look of gladness, shyness, and surprise, she exclaimed—

"O Mr. Clare! How you frightened me—I—"

There had not at first been time for her to think of the changed relations which his declaration had introduced; but the full sense of the matter rose up in her face when she encountered Clare's tender look as he stepped forward to the bottom stair.

"Dear, darling Tessy!" he whispered, putting his arm round her, and his face to her flushed cheek. "Don't, for Heaven's sake, Mister me any more. I have hastened back so soon because of you!"

Tess's excitable heart beat against his by way of reply; and there they stood upon the red-brick floor of the entry, the sun slanting in by the window upon his back, as he held her tightly to his breast; upon her inclining face, upon the blue veins of her temple, upon her naked arm, and her neck, and into the depths of her hair. Having been lying down in her clothes she was warm as a sunned cat. At first she would not look straight up at him, but her eyes soon lifted, and his plumbed the deepness of the ever-varying pupils, with their radiating fibrils of blue, and black, and grey, and violet, while she regarded him as Eve at her second waking might have regarded Adam.

"I've got to go a-skimming," she pleaded, "and I have on'y old Deb to help me to-day. Mrs. Crick is gone to market with Mr. Crick, and Retty is not well, and the others are gone out somewhere, and won't be home till milking."

As they retreated to the milk-house Deborah Fyander appeared on the stairs.

"I have come back, Deborah," said Mr. Clare, upwards. "So I can help Tess with the skimming; and, as you are very tired, I am sure, you needn't come down till milking-time."

Possibly the Talbothays milk was not very thoroughly skimmed that afternoon. Tess was in a dream wherein familiar objects appeared as having light and shade and position, but no particular outline. Every time she held the skimmer under the pump to cool it for the work her hand trembled, the ardour of his affection being so palpable that she seemed to flinch under it like a plant in too burning a sun.

Then he pressed her again to his side, and when she had done running her forefinger round the leads to cut off the cream-edge, he cleaned it in nature's way; for the unconstrained manners of Talbothays dairy came convenient now.

"I may as well say it now as later, dearest," he resumed gently. "I wish to ask you something of a very practical nature, which I have been thinking of ever since that day last week in the meads. I shall soon want to marry, and, being a farmer, you see I shall require for my wife a woman who knows all about the management of farms. Will you be that woman, Tessy?"

He put it that way that she might not think he had yielded to an impulse of which his head would disapprove.

She turned quite careworn. She had bowed to the inevitable result of proximity, the necessity of loving him; but she had not calculated upon this sudden corollary, which, indeed, Clare had put before her without quite meaning himself to do it so soon. With pain that was like the bitterness of dissolution she murmured the words of her indispensable and sworn answer as an honourable woman.

"O Mr. Clare—I cannot be your wife—I cannot be!"

The sound of her own decision seemed to break Tess's very heart, and she bowed her face in her grief.

"But, Tess!" he said, amazed at her reply, and holding her still more greedily close. "Do you say no? Surely you love me?"

"O yes, yes! And I would rather by yours than anybody's in the world," returned the sweet and honest voice of the distressed girl. "But I *cannot* marry you!"

"Tess," he said, holding her at arm's length, "you are engaged to marry someone else!"

"No, no!"

"Then why do you refuse me?"

"I don't want to marry! I have not thought o' doing it. I cannot! I only want to love you."

"But why?"

Driven to subterfuge, she stammered—

"Your father is a parson, and your mother wouldn' like you to marry such as me. She will want you to marry a lady."

"Nonsense—I have spoken to them both. That was partly why I went home."

"I feel I cannot—never, never!" she echoed.

"Is it too sudden to be asked thus, my Pretty?"

"Yes—I did not expect it."

"If you will let it pass, please, Tessy, I will give you time," he said. "It was very abrupt to come home and speak to you all at once. I'll not allude to it again for a while."

She again took up the shining skimmer, held it beneath the pump, and began anew. But she could not, as at other times, hit the exact under-surface of the cream with the delicate dexterity required, try as she might: sometimes she was cutting down into the milk, sometimes in the air. She could hardly see, her eyes having filled with two blurring tears drawn forth by a grief which, to this her best friend and dear advocate, she could never explain.

"I can't skim—I can't!" she said, turning away from him.

Not to agitate and hinder her longer the considerate Clare began talking in a more general way:

"You quite misapprehend my parents. They are the most simple-mannered people alive, and quite unambitious. They are two of the few remaining Evangelical school. Tessy, are you an Evangelical?"

"I don't know."

"You go to church very regularly, and our parson here is not very High, they tell me."

Tess's ideas on the views of the parish clergyman, whom she heard every week, seemed to be rather more vague than Clare's, who had never heard him at all.

"I wish I could fix my mind on what I hear there more firmly than I do," she remarked as a safe generality. "It is often a great sorrow to me."

She spoke so unaffectedly that Angel was sure in his heart that his father could not object to her on religious grounds, even though she did not know whether her principles were High, Low, or Broad. He himself knew that, in reality, the confused beliefs which she held, apparently imbibed in childhood, were, if anything, Tractarian as to phraseology, and Pantheistic as to essence. Confused or otherwise, to disturb them was his last desire:

> Leave thou thy sister, when she prays,
>   Her early Heaven, her happy views;
>   Nor thou with shadow'd hint confuse
> A life that leads melodious days.

He had occasionally thought the counsel less honest than musical; but he gladly conformed to it now.

He spoke further of the incidents of his visit, of his father's mode of life, of his zeal for his principles; she grew serener, and the undulations disappeared from her skimming; as she finished one lead after another he followed her, and drew the plugs for letting down the milk.

"I fancied you looked a little downcast when you came in," she ventured to observe, anxious to keep away from the subject of herself.

"Yes—well, my father had been talking a good deal to me of his troubles and difficulties, and the subject always tends to depress me. He is so zealous that he gets many snubs and buffetings from people of a different way of thinking from himself, and I don't like to hear of such humiliations to a man of his age, the more particularly as I don't think earnestness does any good when carried so far. He has been telling me of a very unpleasant scene in which he took part quite recently. He went as the deputy of some missionary society to preach in the neighbourhood of Trantridge, a place forty miles from here, and made it his business to expostulate with a lax young cynic he met with somewhere about there—son of some landowner up that way—and who has a mother afflicted with blindness. My father addressed himself to the gentleman point-blank, and there was quite a disturbance. It was very foolish of my father, I must say, to intrude his conversation upon a stranger when the probabilities were so obvious that it would be useless. But whatever he thinks to be his duty, that he'll do, in season or out of season; and, of course, he makes many enemies, not only among the absolutely vicious, but among the easy-going, who hate being bothered. He says he glories in what happened, and that good may be done in-directly; but I wish he would not wear himself out now he is getting old, and would leave such pigs to their wallowing."

Tess's look had grown hard and worn, and her ripe mouth tragical; but she no longer showed any tremulousness. Clare's revived thoughts of his father prevented his noticing her particularly; and so they went on down the white row of liquid rectangles till they had finished and drained them off, when the other maids returned, and took their pails, and Deb came to scald out the leads for the new milk. As Tess withdrew to go a-field to the cows he said to her softly—

"And my question, Tessy?"

"O no—no!" replied she with grave hopelessness, as one who had heard anew the tur-moil of her own past in the allusion to Alec d'Urberville. "It *can't* be!"

She went out towards the mead, joining the other milkmaids with a bound, as if try-ing to make the open air drive away her sad constraint. All the girls drew onward to the spot where the cows were grazing in the farther mead, the bevy advancing with the bold grace of wild animals—the reckless unchastened motion of women accustomed to unlim-ited space—in which they abandoned themselves to the air as a swimmer to the wave. It seemed natural enough to him now that Tess was again in sight to choose a mate from un-constrained Nature, and not from the abodes of Art.

XXVIII

HER REFUSAL, THOUGH UNEXPECTED, DID NOT PERMANENTLY DAUNT CLARE. HIS EX-perience of women was great enough for him to be aware that the negative often meant nothing more than the preface to the affirmative; and it was little enough for him not to know that in the manner of the present negative there lay a great exception to the dallyings of coyness. That she had already permitted him to make love to her he read as an additional assurance, not fully trowing that in the fields and pastures to "sigh gratis" is by no means deemed waste; love-making being here more often accepted inconsider-ately and for its own sweet sake than in the carking anxious homes of the ambitious, where a girl's craving for an establishment paralyses her healthy thought of a passion as an end.

"Tess, why did you say 'no' in such a positive way?" he asked her in the course of a few days.

She started.

"Don't ask me. I told you why—partly. I am not good enough—not worthy enough."

"How? Not fine lady enough?"

"Yes—something like that," murmured she. "Your friends would scorn me."

"Indeed, you mistake them—my father and mother. As for my brothers, I don't care—" He clasped his fingers behind her back to keep her from slipping away. "Now—you did not mean it, sweet?—I am sure you did not! You have made me so restless that I cannot read, or play, or do anything. I am in no hurry, Tess, but I want to know—to hear from your own warm lips—that you will some day be mine—any time you may choose; but some day?"

She could only shake her head and look away from him.

Clare regarded her attentively, conned the characters of her face as if they had been hieroglyphics. The denial seemed real.

"Then I ought not to hold you in this way—ought I? I have no right to you—no right to seek out where you are, or walk with you! Honestly, Tess, do you love any other man?"

"How can you ask?" she said, with continued self-suppression.

"I almost know that you do not. But then, why do you repulse me?"

"I don't repulse you. I like you to—tell me you love me; and you may always tell me so as you go about with me—and never offend me."

"But you will not accept me as a husband?"

"Ah—that's different—it is for your good, indeed my dearest! O, believe me, it is only for your sake! I don't like to give myself the great happiness o' promising to be yours in that way—because—because I am *sure* I ought not to do it."

"But you will make me happy!"

"Ah—you think so, but you don't know!"

At such times as this, apprehending the grounds of her refusal to be her modest sense of incompetence in matters social and polite, he would say that she was wonderfully well-informed and versatile—which was certainly true, her natural quickness, and her admiration for him, having led her to pick up his vocabulary, his accent, and fragments of his knowledge, to a surprising extent. After these tender contests and her victory she would go away by herself under the remotest cow, if at milking-time, or into the sedge, or into her room, if at a leisure interval, and mourn silently, not a minute after an apparently phlegmatic negative.

The struggle was so fearful; her own heart was so strongly on the side of his—two ardent hearts against one poor little conscience—that she tried to fortify her resolution by every means in her power. She had come to Talbothays with a made-up mind. On no account could she agree to a step which might afterwards cause bitter rueing to her husband for his blindness in wedding her. And she held that what her conscience had decided for her when her mind was unbiassed ought not to be overruled now.

"Why don't somebody tell him all about me?" she said. "It was only forty miles off—why hasn't it reached here? Somebody must know!"

Yet nobody seemed to know; nobody told him.

For two or three days no more was said. She guessed from the sad countenances of her chamber companions that they regarded her not only as the favourite, but as the chosen; but they could see for themselves that she did not put herself in his way.

Tess had never before known a time in which the thread of her life was so distinctly twisted of two strands, positive pleasure and positive pain. At the next cheese-making the pair were again left alone together. The dairyman himself had been lending a hand; but Mr. Crick, as well as his wife, seemed latterly to have acquired a suspicion of mutual interest between these two; though they walked so circumspectly that suspicion was but of the faintest. Anyhow, the dairyman left them to themselves.

They were breaking up the masses of curd before putting them into the vats. The operation resembled the act of crumbling bread on a large scale; and amid the immaculate whiteness of the curds Tess Durbeyfield's hands showed themselves of the pinkness of the rose. Angel, who was filling the vats with his handful, suddenly ceased, and laid his hands flat upon hers. Her sleeves were rolled far above the elbow, and bending lower he kissed the inside vein of her soft arm.

Although the early September weather was sultry, her arm, from her dabbling in the curds, was as cold and damp to his mouth as a new-gathered mushroom, and tasted of the whey. But she was such a sheaf of susceptibilities that her pulse was accelerated by the touch, her blood driven to her finger-ends, and the cool arms flushed hot. Then, as though her heart had said, "Is coyness longer necessary? Truth is truth between man and woman, as between man and man," she lifted her eyes and they beamed devotedly into his, as her lip rose in a tender half-smile.

"Do you know why I did that, Tess?" he said.

"Because you love me very much!"

"Yes, and as a preliminary to a new entreaty."

"Not *again!*"

She looked a sudden fear that her resistance might break down under her own desire.

"O, Tessy!" he went on, "I *cannot* think why you are so tantalising. Why do you disappoint me so? You seem almost like a coquette, upon my life you do—a coquette of the first urban water! They blow hot and blow cold, just as you do; and it is the very last sort of thing to expect to find in a retreat like Talbothays. . . . And yet, dearest," he quickly added, observing how the remark had cut her, "I know you to be the most honest, spotless creature that ever lived. So how can I suppose you a flirt? Tess, why don't you like the idea of being my wife, if you love me as you seem to do?"

"I have never said I don't like the idea, and I never could say it; because—it isn't true!"

The stress now getting beyond endurance her lip quivered, and she was obliged to go away. Clare was so pained and perplexed that he ran after and caught her in the passage.

"Tell me, tell me!" he said, passionately clasping her, in forgetfulness of his curdy hands: "do tell me that you won't belong to anybody but me!"

"I will, I will tell you!" she exclaimed. "And I will give you a complete answer, if you will let me go now. I will tell you my experiences—all about myself—all!"

"Your experiences, dear; yes, certainly; any number." He expressed assent in loving satire, looking into her face. "My Tess has, no doubt, almost as many experiences as that wild convolvulus out there on the garden hedge, that opened itself this morning for the first time. Tell me anything, but don't use that wretched expression any more about not being worthy of me."

"I will try—not! And I'll give you my reasons to-morrow—next week."

"Say on Sunday?"

"Yes, on Sunday."

At last she got away, and did not stop in her retreat till she was in the thicket of pollard willows at the lower side of the barton, where she could be quite unseen. Here Tess flung herself down upon the rustling undergrowth of spear-grass, as upon a bed, and remained crouching in palpitating misery broken by momentary shoots of joy, which her fears about the ending could not altogether suppress.

In reality, she was drifting into acquiescence. Every see-saw of her breath, every wave of her blood, every pulse singing in her ears, was a voice that joined with nature in revolt against her scrupulousness. Reckless, inconsiderate acceptance of him; to close with him at the altar, revealing nothing, and chancing discovery; to snatch ripe pleasure before the iron teeth of pain could have time to shut upon her: that was what love counselled; and in almost a terror of ecstasy Tess divined that, despite her many months of lonely self-chastisement, wrestlings, communings, schemes to lead a future of austere isolation, love's counsel would prevail.

The afternoon advanced, and still she remained among the willows. She heard the rattle of taking down the pails from the forked stands; the "waow-waow!" which accompanied the getting together of the cows. But she did not go to the milking. They would see her agitation; and the dairyman, thinking the cause to be love alone, would good-naturedly tease her; and that harassment could not be borne.

Her lover must have guessed her overwrought state, and invented some excuse for her non-appearance, for no enquiries were made or calls given. At half-past six the sun settled down upon the levels, with the aspect of a great forge in the heavens, and presently a monstrous pumpkinlike moon arose on the other hand. The pollard willows, tortured out of their natural shape by incessant choppings, became spiny-haired monsters as they stood up against it. She went in, and upstairs without a light.

It was now Wednesday. Thursday came, and Angel looked thoughtfully at her from a distance, but intruded in no way upon her. The indoor milkmaids, Marian and the rest, seemed to guess that something definite was afoot, for they did not force any remarks upon her in the bedchamber. Friday passed; Saturday. To-morrow was the day.

"I shall give way—I shall say yes—I shall let myself marry him—I cannot help it!" she jealously panted, with her hot face to the pillow that night, on hearing one of the other girls sigh his name in her sleep. "I can't bear to let anybody have him but me! Yet it is a wrong to him, and may kill him when he knows! O my heart—O—O—O!"

XXIX

N OW, WHO MID YE THINK I'VE HEARD NEWS O' THIS MORNING?" SAID DAIRYMAN CRICK, as he sat down to breakfast next day, with a riddling gaze round upon the munching men and maids. "Now, just who mid ye think?"

One guessed, and another guessed. Mrs. Crick did not guess, because she knew already.

"Well," said the dairyman, " 'tis that slack-twisted 'hore's-bird of a feller, Jack Dollop. He's lately got married to a widow-woman."

"Not Jack Dollop? A villain—to think o' that!" said a milker.

The name entered quickly into Tess Durbeyfield's consciousness, for it was the name of the lover who had wronged his sweetheart, and had afterwards been so roughly used by the young woman's mother in the butter-churn.

"And had he married the valiant matron's daughter, as he promised?" asked Angel Clare absently, as he turned over the newspaper he was reading at the little table to which he was always banished by Mrs. Crick, in her sense of his gentility.

"Not he, sir. Never meant to," replied the dairyman. "As I say, 'tis a widow-woman, and she had money, it seems—fifty poun' a year or so; and that was all he was after. They were married in a great hurry; and then she told him that by marrying she had lost her fifty poun' a year. Just fancy the state o' my gentleman's mind at that news! Never such a cat-and-dog life as they've been leading ever since! Serve him will beright. But onluckily the poor woman gets the worst o't."

"Well, the silly body should have told en sooner that the ghost of her first man would trouble him," said Mrs. Crick.

"Ay; ay," responded the dairyman indecisively. "Still, you can see exactly how 'twas. She wanted a home, and didn't like to run the risk of losing him. Don't ye think that was something like it, maidens?"

He glanced towards the row of girls.

"She ought to ha' told him just before they went to church, when he could hardly have backed out," exclaimed Marian.

"Yes, she ought," agreed Izz.

"She must have seen what he was after, and should ha' refused him," cried Retty spasmodically.

"And what do you say, my dear?" asked the dairyman of Tess.

"I think she ought—to have told him the true state of things—or else refused him— I don't know," replied Tess, the bread-and-butter choking her.

"Be cust if I'd have done either o't," said Beck Knibbs, a married helper from one of the cottages. "All's fair in love and war. I'd ha' married en just as she did, and if he'd said two words to me about not telling him beforehand anything whatsomdever about my first chap that I hadn't chose to tell, I'd ha' knocked him down wi' the rolling-pin—a scram lit-tle feller like he! Any woman could do it."

The laughter which followed this sally was supplemented only by a sorry smile, for form's sake, from Tess. What was comedy to them was tragedy to her; and she could hardly bear their mirth. She soon rose from table, and, with an impression that Clare would soon follow her, went along a little wriggling path, now stepping to one side of the irrigating channels, and now to the other, till she stood by the main stream of the Var. Men had been cutting the water-weeds higher up the river, and masses of them were floating past her— moving islands of green crow-foot, whereon she might almost have ridden; long locks of which weed had lodged against the piles driven to keep the cows from crossing.

Yes, there was the pain of it. This question of a woman telling her story—the heavi-est of crosses to herself—seemed but amusement to others. It was as if people should laugh at martyrdom.

"Tessy!" came from behind her, and Clare sprang across the gully, alighting beside her feet. "My wife—soon!"

"No, no; I cannot. For your sake, O Mr. Clare; for your sake, I say no!"

"Tess!"

"Still I say no!" she repeated.

Not expecting this he had put his arm lightly round her waist the moment after speak-ing, beneath her hanging tail of hair. (The younger dairymaids, including Tess, break-fasted with their hair loose on Sunday mornings before building it up extra high for attending church, a style they could not adopt when milking with their heads against the cows.) If she had said "Yes" instead of "No" he would have kissed her; it had evidently been his intention; but her determined negative deterred his scrupulous heart. Their condition of domiciliary comradeship put her, as the woman, to such disadvantage by its enforced intercourse, that he felt it unfair to her to exercise any pressure of blandishment which he might have honestly employed had she been better able to avoid him. He released her momentarily-imprisoned waist, and withheld the kiss.

It all turned on that release. What had given her strength to refuse him this time was solely the tale of the widow told by the dairyman; and that would have been overcome in another moment. But Angel said no more; his face was perplexed; he went away.

Day after day they met—somewhat less constantly than before; and thus two or three weeks went by. The end of September drew near, and she could see in his eye that he might ask her again.

His plan of procedure was different now—as though he had made up his mind that her negatives were, after all, only coyness and youth startled by the novelty of the proposal. The fitful evasiveness of her manner when the subject was under discussion countenanced the idea. So he played a more coaxing game; and while never going beyond words, or attempting the renewal of caresses, he did his utmost orally.

In this way Clare persistently wooed her in undertones like that of the purling milk—at the cow's side, at skimmings, at butter-makings, at cheese-makings, among broody poultry, and among farrowing pigs—as no milkmaid was ever wooed before by such a man.

Tess knew that she must break down. Neither a religious sense of a certain moral validity in the previous union nor a conscientious wish for candour could hold out against it much longer. She loved him so passionately, and he was so godlike in her eyes; and being, though untrained, instinctively refined, her nature cried for his tutelary guidance. And thus, though Tess kept repeating to herself, "I can never be his wife," the words were vain. A proof of her weakness lay in the very utterance of what calm strength would not have taken the trouble to formulate. Every sound of his voice beginning on the old subject stirred her with a terrifying bliss, and she coveted the recantation she feared.

His manner was—what man's is not?—so much that of one who would love and cherish and defend her under any conditions, changes, charges, or revelations, that her gloom lessened as she basked in it. The season meanwhile was drawing onward to the equinox, and though it was still fine, the days were much shorter. The dairy had again worked by morning candle-light for a long time; and a fresh renewal of Clare's pleading occurred one morning between three and four.

She had run up in her bed-gown to his door to call him as usual; then had gone back to dress and call the others; and in ten minutes was walking to the head of the stairs with the candle in her hand. At the same moment he came down his steps from above in his shirt-sleeves and put his arm across the stairway.

"Now, Miss Flirt, before you go down," he said peremptorily. "It is a fortnight since I spoke, and this won't do any longer. You *must* tell me what you mean, or I shall have to leave this house. My door was ajar just now, and I saw you. For your own safety I must go. You don't know. Well? Is it to be yes at last?"

"I am only just up, Mr. Clare, and it is too early to take me to task!" she pouted. "You need not call me Flirt. 'Tis cruel and untrue. Wait till by and by. Please wait till by and by! I will really think seriously about it between now and then. Let me go downstairs!"

She looked a little like what he said she was as, holding the candle sideways, she tried to smile away the seriousness of her words.

"Call me Angel, then, and not Mr. Clare."

"Angel."

"Angel dearest—why not?"

" 'Twould mean that I agree, wouldn't it?"

"It would only mean that you love me, even if you cannot marry me; and you were so good as to own that long ago."

"Very well, then, 'Angel dearest,' if I *must*," she murmured, looking at her candle, a roguish curl coming upon her mouth, notwithstanding her suspense.

Clare had resolved never to kiss her until he had obtained her promise; but somehow, as Tess stood there in her prettily tucked-up milking gown, her hair carelessly heaped upon her head till there should be leisure to arrange it when skimming and milking were done, he broke his resolve, and brought his lips to her cheek for one moment. She passed downstairs very quickly, never looking back at him or saying another word. The other maids were already down, and the subject was not pursued. Except Marian, they all looked wistfully and suspiciously at the pair, in the sad yellow rays which the morning candles emitted in contrast with the first cold signals of the dawn without.

When skimming was done—which, as the milk diminished with the approach of autumn, was a lessening process day by day—Retty and the rest went out. The lovers followed them.

"Our tremulous lives are so different from theirs, are they not?" he musingly observed to her, as he regarded the three figures tripping before him through the frigid pallor of opening day.

"Not so very different, I think," she said.

"Why do you think that?"

"There are very few women's lives that are not—tremulous," Tess replied, pausing over the new word as if it impressed her. "There's more in those three than you think."

"What is in them?"

"Almost either of 'em," she began, "would make—perhaps would make—a properer wife than I. And perhaps they love you as well as I—almost."

"O, Tessy!"

There were signs that it was an exquisite relief to her to hear the impatient exclamation, though she had resolved so intrepidly to let generosity make one bid against herself. That was now done, and she had not the power to attempt self-immolation a second time then. They were joined by a milker from one of the cottages, and no more was said on that which concerned them so deeply. But Tess knew that this day would decide it.

In the afternoon several of the dairyman's household and assistants went down to the meads as usual, a long way from the dairy, where many of the cows were milked without being driven home. The supply was getting less as the animals advanced in calf, and the supernumerary milkers of the lush green season had been dismissed.

The work progressed leisurely. Each pailful was poured into tall cans that stood in a large spring-waggon which had been brought upon the scene; and when they were milked the cows trailed away.

Dairyman Crick, who was there with the rest, his wrapper gleaming miraculously white against a leaden evening sky, suddenly looked at his heavy watch.

"Why, 'tis later than I thought," he said. "Begad! We shan't be soon enough with this milk at the station, if we don't mind. There's no time to-day to take it home and mix it with the bulk afore sending off. It must go to station straight from here. Who'll drive it across?"

Mr. Clare volunteered to do so, though it was none of his business, asking Tess to accompany him. The evening, though sunless, had been warm and muggy for the season, and Tess had come out with her milking-hood only, naked-armed and jacketless; certainly not dressed for a drive. She therefore replied by glancing over her scant habiliments; but Clare gently urged her. She assented by relinquishing her pail and stool to the dairyman to take home; and mounted the spring-waggon beside Clare.

XXX

IN THE DIMINISHING DAYLIGHT THEY WENT ALONG THE LEVEL ROADWAY THROUGH THE meads, which stretched away into grey miles, and were backed in the extreme edge of distance by the swarthy and abrupt slopes of Egdon Heath. On its summit stood clumps and stretches of fir-trees, whose notched tips appeared like battlemented towers crowning black-fronted castles of enchantment.

They were so absorbed in the sense of being close to each other that they did not begin talking for a long while, the silence being broken only by the clucking of the milk in the tall cans behind them. The lane they followed was so solitary that the hazel nuts had remained on the boughs till they slipped from their shells, and the blackberries hung in heavy clusters. Every now and then Angel would fling the lash of his whip round one of these, pluck it off, and give it to his companion.

The dull sky soon began to tell its meaning by sending down herald-drops of rain, and the stagnant air of the day changed into a fitful breeze which played about their faces. The quicksilvery glaze on the rivers and pools vanished; from broad mirrors of light they changed to lustreless sheets of lead, with a surface like a rasp. But that spectacle did not affect her preoccupation. Her countenance, a natural carnation slightly embrowned by the season, had deepened its tinge with the beating of the raindrops; and her hair, which the pressure of the cows' flanks had, as usual, caused to tumble down from its fastenings and stray beyond the curtain of her calico bonnet, was made clammy by the moisture, till it hardly was better than sea-weed.

"I ought not to have come, I suppose," she murmured, looking at the sky.

"I am sorry for the rain," said he. "But how glad I am to have you here!"

Remote Egdon disappeared by degree behind the liquid gauze. The evening grew darker, and the roads being crossed by gates it was not safe to drive faster than at a walking pace. The air was rather chill.

"I am so afraid you will get cold, with nothing upon your arms and shoulders," he said. "Creep close to me, and perhaps the drizzle won't hurt you much. I should be sorrier still if I did not think that the rain might be helping me."

She imperceptibly crept closer, and he wrapped round them both a large piece of sail-cloth, which was sometimes used to keep the sun off the milk-cans. Tess held it from slipping off him as well as herself, Clare's hands being occupied.

"Now we are all right again. Ah—no we are not! It runs down into my neck a little, and it must still more into yours. That's better. Your arms are like wet marble, Tess. Wipe them in the cloth. Now, if you stay quiet, you will not get another drop. Well, dear—about that question of mine—that long-standing question?"

The only reply that he could hear for a little while was the smack of the horse's hoofs on the moistening road, and the cluck of the milk in the cans behind them.

"Do you remember what you said?"

"I do," she replied.

"Before we get home, mind."

"I'll try."

He said no more then. As they drove on the fragment of an old manor-house of Caroline date rose against the sky, and was in due course passed and left behind.

"That," he observed, to entertain her, "is an interesting old place—one of the several seats which belonged to an ancient Norman family formerly of great influence in this county, the d'Urbervilles. I never pass one of their residences without thinking of them. There is something very sad in the extinction of a family of renown, even if it was fierce, domineering, feudal renown."

"Yes," said Tess.

They crept along towards a point in the expanse of shade just at hand at which a feeble light was beginning to assert its presence, a spot where, by day, a fitful white streak of steam at intervals upon the dark green background denoted intermittent moments of contact between their secluded world and modern life. Modern life stretched out its steam feeler to this point three or four times a day, touched the native existences, and quickly withdrew its feeler again, as if what it touched had been uncongenial.

They reached the feeble light, which came from the smoky lamp of a little railway-station; a poor enough terrestrial star, yet in one sense of more importance to Talbothays Dairy and mankind than the celestial ones to which it stood in such humiliating contrast. The cans of new milk were unladen in the rain, Tess getting a little shelter from a neighbouring holly-tree.

Then there was the hissing of a train, which drew up almost silently upon the wet rails, and the milk was rapidly swung can by can into the truck. The light of the engine flashed for a second upon Tess Durbeyfield's figure, motionless under the great holly tree. No object could have looked more foreign to the gleaming cranks and wheels than this unsophisticated girl, with the round bare arms, the rainy face and hair, the suspended attitude of a friendly leopard at pause, the print gown of no date or fashion, and the cotton bonnet drooping on her brow.

She mounted again beside her lover, with a mute obedience characteristic of impassioned natures at times, and when they had wrapped themselves up over head and ears in the sail-cloth again, they plunged back into the now thick night. Tess was so receptive that the few minutes of contact with the whirl of material progress lingered in her thought.

"Londoners will drink it at their breakfasts to-morrow, won't they?" she asked. "Strange people that we have never seen."

"Yes—I suppose they will. Though not as we send it. When its strength has been lowered, so that it may not get up into their heads."

"Noble men and noble women, ambassadors and centurions, ladies and tradeswomen, and babies who have never seen a cow."

"Well, yes; perhaps; particularly centurions."

"Who don't know anything of us, and where it comes from; or think how we two drove miles across the moor to-night in the rain that it might reach 'em in time?"

"We did not drive entirely on account of these precious Londoners; we drove a little on our own—on account of that anxious matter which you will, I am sure, set at rest, dear Tess. Now, permit me to put it in this way. You belong to me already, you know; your heart, I mean. Does it not?"

"You know as well as I. O yes—yes!"

"Then, if your heart does, why not your hand?"

"My only reason was on account of you—on account of a question. I have something to tell you—"

"But suppose it to be entirely for my happiness, and my worldly convenience also?"

"O yes; if it is for your happiness and worldly convenience. But my life before I came here—I want—"

"Well, it is for my convenience as well as my happiness. If I have a very large farm, either English or colonial, you will be invaluable as a wife to me; better than a woman out of the largest mansion in the country. So please—please, dear Tessy, disabuse your mind of the feeling that you will stand in my way."

"But my history. I want you to know it—you must let me tell you—you will not like me so well!"

"Tell it if you wish to, dearest. This precious history then. Yes, I was born at so and so, Anno Domini—"

"I was born at Marlott," she said, catching at his words as a help, lightly as they were spoken. "And I grew up there. And I was in the Sixth Standard when I left school, and they said I had great aptness, and should make a good teacher, so it was settled that I should be one. But there was trouble in my family; father was not very industrious, and he drank a little."

"Yes, yes. Poor child! Nothing new." He pressed her more closely to his side.

"And then—there is something very unusual about it—about me. I—I was—"
Tess's breath quickened.

"Yes, dearest. Never mind."

"I—I—am not a Durbeyfield, but a d'Urberville—a descendant of the same family as those that owned the old house we passed. And—we are all gone to nothing!"

"A d'Urberville!—Indeed! And is that all the trouble, dear Tess?"

"Yes," she answered faintly.

"Well—why should I love you less after knowing this?"

"I was told by the dairyman that you hated old families."

He laughed.

"Well, it is true, in one sense. I do hate the aristocratic principle of blood before everything, and do think that as reasoners the only pedigrees we ought to respect are those spiritual ones of the wise and virtuous, without regard to corporeal paternity. But I am extremely interested in this news—you can have no idea how interested I am! Are you not interested yourself in being one of that well-known line?"

"No. I have thought it sad—especially since coming here, and knowing that many of the hills and fields I see once belonged to my father's people. But other hills and fields belonged to Retty's people, and perhaps others to Marian's, so that I don't value it particularly."

"Yes—it is surprising how many of the present tillers of the soil were once owners of it, and I sometimes wonder that a certain school of politicians don't make capital of the circumstance; but they don't seem to know it. . . . I wonder that I did not see the resemblance of your name of d'Urberville, and trace the manifest corruption. And this was the carking secret!"

She had not told. At the last moment her courage had failed her, she feared his blame for not telling him sooner; and her instinct of self-preservation was stronger than her candour.

"Of course," continued the unwitting Clare, "I should have been glad to know you to be descended exclusively from the long-suffering, dumb, unrecorded rank and file of the English nation, and not from the self-seeking few who made themselves powerful at the expense of the rest. But I am corrupted away from that by my affection for you, Tess [he laughed as he spoke], and made selfish likewise. For your own sake I rejoice in your descent. Society is hopelessly snobbish, and this fact of your extraction may make an appreciable difference to its acceptance of you as my wife, after I have made you the well-read woman that I mean to make you. My mother too, poor soul, will think so much better of you on account of it. Tess, you must spell your name correctly—d'Urberville—from this very day."

"I like the other way rather best."

"But you *must*, dearest! Good heavens, why dozens of mushroom millionaires would jump at such a possession! By the by, there's one of that kidney who has taken the name—where have I heard of him?—Up in the neighbourhood of The Chase, I think. Why, he is the very man who had that rumpus with my father I told you of. What an odd coincidence!"

"Angel, I think I would rather not take the name! It is unlucky, perhaps!"

She was agitated.

"Now then, Mistress Teresa d'Urberville, I have you. Take my name, and so you will escape yours! The secret is out, so why should you any longer refuse me?"

"If it is *sure* to make you happy to have me as your wife, and you feel that you do wish to marry me, *very, very* much—"

"I do, dearest, of course!"

"I mean, that it is only your wanting me very much, and being hardly able to keep alive without me, whatever my offences, that would make me feel I ought to say I will."

"You will—you do say it, I know! You will be mine forever and ever."

He clasped her close and kissed her.

"Yes!"

She had no sooner said it than she burst into a dry hard sobbing, so violent that it seemed to rend her. Tess was not a hysterical girl by any means, and he was surprised.

"Why do you cry, dearest?"

"I can't tell—quite!—I am so glad to think—of being yours, and making you happy!"

"But this does not seem very much like gladness, my Tessy!"

"I mean—I cry because I have broken down in my vow! I said I would die unmarried!"

"But, if you love me you would like me to be your husband?"

"Yes, yes, yes! But O, I sometimes wish I had never been born!"

"Now, my dear Tess, if I did not know that you are very much excited, and very inexperienced, I should say that remark was not very complimentary. How came you to wish that if you care for me? Do you care for me? I wish you would prove it in some way."

"How can I prove it more than I have done?" she cried, in a distraction of tenderness. "Will this prove it more?"

She clasped his neck, and for the first time Clare learnt what an impassioned woman's kisses were like upon the lips of one whom he loved with all her heart and soul, as Tess loved him.

"There—now do you believe?" she asked, flushed, and wiping her eyes.

"Yes. I never really doubted—never, never!"

So they drove on through the gloom, forming one bundle inside the sail-cloth, the horse going as he would, and the rain driving against them. She had consented. She might as well have agreed at first. The "appetite for joy" which pervades all creation, that tremendous force which sways humanity to its purpose, as the tide sways the helpless weed, was not to be controlled by vague lucubrations over the social rubric.

"I must write to my mother," she said. "You don't mind my doing that?"

"Of course not, dear child. You are a child to me, Tess, not to know how very proper it is to write to your mother at such a time, and how wrong it would be in me to object. Where does she live?"

"At the same place—Marlott. On the further side of Blackmoor Vale."

"Ah, then I *have* seen you before this summer—"

"Yes; at that dance on the green; but you would not dance with me. O, I hope that is of no ill-omen for us now!"

XXXI

TESS WROTE A MOST TOUCHING AND URGENT LETTER TO HER MOTHER THE VERY NEXT day, and by the end of the week a response to her communication arrived in Joan Durbeyfield's wandering last-century hand.

DEAR TESS—J write these few lines Hoping they will find you well, as they leave me at Present, thank God for it. Dear Tess, we are all glad to Hear that you are going really to be married soon. But with respect to your question, Tess, J say between ourselves, quite private but very strong, that on no account do you say a word of your Bygone Trouble to him. J did not tell everything to your Father, he being so Proud on account of his Respectability, which, perhaps, your Intended is the same. Many a woman—some of the Highest in the Land—have had a Trouble in their time; and why should you Trumpet yours when others don't Trumpet theirs? No girl would be such a Fool, specially as it is so long ago, and not your Fault at all. J shall answer the same if you ask me fifty times. Besides, you must bear in mind that, knowing it to be your Childish Nature to tell all that's in your heart—so simple!—J made you promise me never to let it out by Word or Deed, having your Welfare in my Mind; and you most solemnly did promise it going from this Door. J have not named either that Question or your coming marriage to your Father, as he would blab it everywhere, poor Simple Man.

Dear Tess, keep up your Spirits, and we mean to send you a Hogshead of Cyder for your Wedding, knowing there is not much in your parts, and thin Sour Stuff what there is. So no more at present, and with kind love to your Young Man.—From your affectte. Mother,

J. DURBEYFIELD

"O mother, mother!" murmured Tess.

She was recognising how light was the touch of events the most oppressive upon Mrs. Durbeyfield's elastic spirit. Her mother did not see life as Tess saw it. That haunting episode of bygone days was to her mother but a passing accident. But perhaps her mother was right as to the course to be followed, whatever she might be in her reasons. Silence seemed, on the face of it, best for her adored one's happiness: silence it should be.

Thus steadied by a command from the only person in the world who had any shadow of right to control her action, Tess grew calmer. The responsibility was shifted, and her heart was lighter than it had been for weeks. The days of declining autumn which followed her assent, beginning with the month of October, formed a season through which she lived in spiritual altitudes more nearly approaching ecstasy than any other period of her life.

There was hardly a touch of earth in her love for Clare. To her sublime trustfulness he was all that goodness could be—knew all that a guide, philosopher, and friend should know. She thought every line in the contour of his person the perfection of masculine beauty, his soul the soul of a saint, his intellect that of a seer. The wisdom of her love for him, as love, sustained her dignity; she seemed to be wearing a crown. The compassion of his love for her, as she saw it, made her lift up her heart to him in devotion. He would sometimes catch her large, worshipful eyes, that had no bottom to them, looking at him from their depths, as if she saw something immortal before her.

She dismissed the past—trod upon it and put it out, as one treads on a coal that is smouldering and dangerous.

She had not known that men could be so disinterested, chivalrous, protective, in their love for women as he. Angel Clare was far from all that she thought him in this respect; absurdly far, indeed; but he was, in truth, more spiritual than animal; he had himself well in hand, and was singularly free from grossness. Though not cold-natured, he was rather bright than hot—less Byronic than Shelleyan; could love desperately, but with a love more especially inclined to the imaginative and ethereal; it was a fastidious emotion which could jealously guard the loved-one against his very self. This amazed and enraptured Tess, whose slight experiences had been so infelicitous till now; and in her reaction from indignation against the male sex she swerved to excess of honour for Clare.

They unaffectedly sought each other's company; in her honest faith she did not disguise her desire to be with him. The sum of her instincts on this matter, if clearly stated, would have been that the elusive quality in her sex which attracts men in general might be distasteful to so perfect a man after an avowal of love, since it must in its very nature carry with it a suspicion of art.

The country custom of unreserved comradeship out-of-doors during betrothal was the only custom she knew, and to her it had no strangeness; though it seemed oddly anticipative to Clare till he saw how normal a thing she, in common with all the other dairy-folk, regarded it. Thus, during this October month of wonderful afternoons they roved along the meads by creeping paths which followed the brinks of trickling tributary brooks, hopping across by little wooden bridges to the other side, and back again. They were never out of the sound of some purling weir, whose buzz accompanied their own murmuring, while the beams of the sun, almost as horizontal as the mead itself, formed a pollen of radiance over the landscape. They saw tiny blue fogs in the shadows of trees and hedges, all the time that there was bright sunshine elsewhere. The sun was so near the ground, and the sward so flat, that the shadows of Clare and Tess would stretch a quarter of a mile ahead of them, like two long fingers pointing afar to where the green alluvial reaches abutted against the sloping sides of the vale.

Men were at work here and there—for it was the season for "taking up" the meadows, or digging the little waterways clear for the winter irrigation, and mending their banks where trodden down by the cows. The shovelfuls of loam, black as jet, brought there by the river when it was as wide as the whole valley, were an essence of soils, pounded champaigns of the past, steeped, refined, and subtilised to extraordinary richness, out of which came all the fertility of the mead, and of the cattle grazing there.

Clare hardily kept his arm round her waist in sight of these watermen, with the air of a man who was accustomed to public dalliance, though actually as shy as she who, with lips parted and eyes askance on the labourers, wore the look of a wary animal the while.

"You are not ashamed of owning me as yours before them!" she said gladly.

"O no!"

"But if it should reach the ears of your friends at Emminster that you are walking about like this with me, a milkmaid—"

"The most bewitching milkmaid ever seen."

"They might feel it a hurt to their dignity."

"My dear girl—a d'Urberville hurt the dignity of a Clare! It is a grand card to play—that of your belonging to such a family, and I am reserving it for a grand effect when we are married, and have the proofs of your descent from Parson Tringham. Apart from that, my future is to be totally foreign to my family—it will not affect even the surface of their lives. We shall leave this part of England—perhaps England itself—and what does it matter how people regard us here? You will like going, will you not?"

She could answer no more than a bare affirmative, so great was the emotion aroused in her at the thought of going through the world with him as his own familiar friend. Her feelings almost filled her ears like a babble of waves, and surged up to her eyes. She put her hand in his, and thus they went on, to a place where the reflected sun glared up from the river, under a bridge, with a molten-metallic glow that dazzled their eyes, though the sun itself was hidden by the bridge. They stood still, whereupon little furred and feathered heads popped up from the smooth surface of the water; but, finding that the disturbing presences had paused, and not passed by, they disappeared again. Upon this river-brink they lingered till the fog began to close round them—which was very early in the evening at this time of the year—settling on the lashes of her eyes, where it rested like crystals, and on his brows and hair.

They walked later on Sundays, when it was quite dark. Some of the dairy-people, who were also out-of-doors on the first Sunday evening after their engagement, heard her impulsive speeches, ecstasised to fragments, though they were too far off to hear the words discoursed; noted the spasmodic catch in her remarks, broken into syllables by the leapings of her heart, as she walked leaning on his arm; her contented pauses, the occasional little laugh upon which her soul seemed to ride—the laugh of a woman in company with the man she loves and has won from all other women—unlike anything else in nature. They marked the buoyancy of her tread, like the skim of a bird which had not quite alighted.

Her affection for him was now the breath and life of Tess's being; it enveloped her as a photosphere, irradiated her into forgetfulness of her past sorrows, keeping back the gloomy spectres that would persist in their attempts to touch her—doubt, fear, moodiness, care, shame. She knew that they were waiting like wolves just outside the circumscribing light, but she had long spells of power to keep them in hungry subjection there.

A spiritual forgetfulness co-existed with an intellectual remembrance. She walked in brightness, but she knew that in the background those shapes of darkness were always spread. They might be receding, or they might be approaching, one or the other, a little everyday.

One evening Tess and Clare were obliged to sit indoors keeping house, all the other occupants of the domicile being away. As they talked she looked thoughtfully up at him, and met his two appreciative eyes.

"I am not worthy of you—no, I am not!" she burst out, jumping up from her low stool as though appalled at his homage, and the fulness of her own joy thereat.

Clare, deeming the whole basis of her excitement to be that which was only the smaller part of it, said—

"I won't have you speak like it, dear Tess! Distinction does not consist in the facile use of a contemptible set of conventions, but in being numbered among those who are true, and honest, and just, and pure, and lovely, and of good report—as you are, my Tess."

She struggled with the sob in her throat. How often had that string of excellences made her young heart ache in church of late years, and how strange that he should have cited them now.

"Why didn't you stay and love me when I—was sixteen; living with my little sisters and brothers, and you danced on the green? O, why didn't you, why didn't you!" she said, impetuously clasping her hands.

Angel began to comfort and reassure her, thinking to himself, truly enough, what a creature of moods she was, and how careful he would have to be of her when she depended for her happiness entirely on him.

"Ah—why didn't I stay!" he said. "That is just what I feel. If I had only known! But you must not be so bitter in your regret—why should you be?"

With the woman's instinct to hide she diverged hastily—

"I should have had four years more of your heart than I can ever have now. Then I should not have wasted my time as I have done—I should have had so much longer happiness!"

It was no mature woman with a long dark vista of intrigue behind her who was tormented thus; but a girl of simple life, not yet one-and-twenty, who had been caught during her days of immaturity like a bird in a springe. To calm herself the more completely she rose from her little stool and left the room, overturning the stool with her skirts as she went.

He sat on by the cheerful firelight thrown from a bundle of green ash-sticks laid across the dogs; the sticks snapped pleasantly, and hissed out bubbles of sap from their ends. When she came back she was herself again.

"Do you not think you are just a wee bit capricious, fitful, Tess?" he said, good-humouredly, as he spread a cushion for her on the stool, and seated himself in the settle beside her. "I wanted to ask you something, and just then you ran away."

"Yes, perhaps I am capricious," she murmured. She suddenly approached him, and put a hand upon each of his arms. "No, Angel, I am not really so—by Nature, I mean!" The more particularly to assure him that she was not, she placed herself close to him in the settle, and allowed her head to find a resting-place against Clare's shoulder. "What did you want to ask me—I am sure I will answer it," she continued humbly.

"Well, you love me, and have agreed to marry me, and hence there follows a thirdly, 'When shall the day be?' "

"I like living like this."

"But I must think of starting in business on my own hook with the new year, or a little later. And before I get involved in the multifarious details of my new position, I should like to have secured my partner."

"But," she timidly answered, "to talk quite practically, wouldn't it be best not to marry till after all that?—Though I can't bear the thought o' your going away and leaving me here!"

"Of course you cannot—and it is not best in this case. I want you to help me in many ways in making my start. When shall it be? Why not a fortnight from now?"

"No," she said, becoming grave: "I have so many things to think of first."

"But—"

He drew her gently nearer to him.

The reality of marriage was startling when it loomed so near. Before discussion of the question had proceeded further there walked round the corner of the settle into the full firelight of the apartment Mr. Dairyman Crick, Mrs. Crick, and two of the milkmaids.

Tess sprang like an elastic ball from his side to her feet while her face flushed and her eyes shone in the firelight.

"I knew how it would be if I sat so close to him!" she cried, with vexation. "I said to myself, they are sure to come and catch us! But I wasn't really sitting on his knee, though it might ha' seemed as if I was almost!"

"Well—if so be you hadn't told us, I am sure we shouldn't ha' noticed that ye had been sitting anywhere at all in this light," replied the dairyman. He continued to his wife, with the stolid mien of a man who understood nothing of the emotions relating to matrimony—"Now, Christianer, that shows that folks should never fancy other folks be supposing things when they bain't. O no, I should never ha' thought a word of where she was a-sitting to, if she hadn't told me—not I."

"We are going to be married soon," said Clare, with improvised phlegm.

"Ah—and be ye! Well, I am truly glad to hear it, sir. I've thought you mid do such a thing for some time. She's too good for a dairymaid—I said so the very first day I zid her—and a prize for any man; and what's more, a wonderful woman for a gentleman-farmer's wife; he won't be at the mercy of his baily wi' her at his side."

Somehow Tess disappeared. She had been even more struck with the look of the girls who followed Crick than abashed by Crick's blunt praise.

After supper, when she reached her bedroom, they were all present. A light was burning, and each damsel was sitting up whitely in her bed, awaiting Tess, the whole like a row of avenging ghosts.

But she saw in a few moments that there was no malice in their mood. They could scarcely feel as a loss what they had never expected to have. Their condition was objective, contemplative.

"He's going to marry her!" murmured Retty, never taking eyes off Tess. "How her face do show it!"

"You *be* going to marry him?" asked Marian.

"Yes," said Tess.

"When?"

"Some day."

They thought that this was evasiveness only.

"*Yes*—going to *marry* him—a gentleman!" repeated Izz Huett.

And by a sort of fascination the three girls, one after another, crept out of their beds, and came and stood barefooted round Tess. Retty put her hands upon Tess's shoulders, as if to realise her friend's corporeality after such a miracle, and the other two laid their arms round her waist, all looking into her face.

"How it do seem! Almost more than I can think of!" said Izz Huett.

Marian kissed Tess. "Yes," she murmured as she withdrew her lips.

"Was that because of love for her, or because other lips have touched there by now?" continued Izz drily to Marian.

"I wasn't thinking o' that," said Marian simply. "I was on'y feeling all the strangeness o't—that she is to be his wife, and nobody else. I don't say nay to it, nor either of us, because we did not think of it—only loved him. Still, nobody else is to marry'n in the world—no fine lady, nobody in silks and satins; but she who do live like we."

"Are you sure you don't dislike me for it?" said Tess in a low voice.

They hung about her in their white night-gowns before replying, as if they considered their answer might lie in her look.

"I don't know—I don't know," murmured Retty Priddle. "I want to hate 'ee; but I cannot!"

"That's how I feel," echoed Izz and Marian. "I can't hate her. Somehow she hinders me!"

"He ought to marry one of you," murmured Tess.

"Why?"

"You are all better than I."

"We better than you?" said the girls in a low, slow whisper. "No, no, dear Tess!"

"You are!" she contradicted impetuously. And suddenly tearing away from their clinging arms she burst into a hysterical fit of tears, bowing herself on the chest of drawers and repeating incessantly, "O yes, yes, yes!"

Having once given way she could not stop her weeping.

"He ought to have had one of you!" she cried. "I think I ought to make him even now! You would be better for him than—I don't know what I'm saying! O! O!"

They went up to her and clasped her round, but still her sobs tore her.

"Get some water," said Marian, "She's upset by us, poor thing, poor thing!"

They gently led her back to the side of her bed, where they kissed her warmly.

"You are best for'n," said Marian. "More ladylike, and a better scholar than we, especially since he had taught 'ee so much. But even you ought to be proud. You *be* proud, I'm sure!"

"Yes, I am," she said; "and I am ashamed at so breaking down!"

When they were all in bed, and the light was out, Marian whispered across to her—

"You will think of us when you be his wife, Tess, and of how we told 'ee that we loved him, and how we tried not to hate you, and did not hate you, and could not hate you, because you were his choice, and we never hoped to be chose by him."

They were not aware that, at these words, salt, stinging tears trickled down upon Tess's pillow anew, and how she resolved, with a bursting heart, to tell all her history to Angel Clare, despite her mother's command—to let him for whom she lived and breathed despise her if he would, and her mother regard her as a fool, rather then preserve a silence which might be deemed a treachery to him, and which somehow seemed a wrong to these.

XXXII

THIS PENITENTIAL MOOD KEPT HER FROM NAMING THE WEDDING-DAY. THE BEGINNING of November found its date still in abeyance, though he asked her at the most tempting times. But Tess's desire seemed to be for a perpetual betrothal in which everything should remain as it was then.

The meads were changing now; but it was still warm enough in early afternoons before milking to idle there a-while, and the state of dairy-work at this time of year allowed a spare hour for idling. Looking over the damp sod in the direction of the sun, a glistening ripple of gossamer webs was visible to their eyes under the luminary, like the track of moonlight on the sea. Gnats, knowing nothing of their brief glorification, wandered across the shimmer of this pathway, irradiated as if they bore fire within them, then passed out of its line, and were quite extinct. In the presence of these things he would remind her that the date was still the question.

Or he would ask her at night, when he accompanied her on some mission invented by Mrs. Crick to give him the opportunity. This was mostly a journey to the farmhouse on the slopes above the vale, to enquire how the advanced cows were getting on in the straw-barton to which they were relegated. For it was a time of the year that brought great changes to the world of kine. Batches of the animals were sent away daily to this lying-in hospital, where they lived on straw till their calves were born, after which event, and as soon as the calf could walk, mother and offspring were driven back to the dairy. In the interval which elapsed before the calves were sold there was, of course, little milking to be done, but as soon as the calf had been taken away the milkmaids would have to set to work as usual.

Returning from one of these dark walks they reached a great gravel-cliff immediately over the levels, where they stood still and listened. The water was now high in the streams, squirting through the weirs, and tinkling under culverts; the smallest gullies were all full; there was no taking short cuts anywhere, and foot-passengers were compelled to follow the permanent ways. From the whole extent of the invisible vale came a multitudinous intonation; it forced upon their fancy that a great city lay below them, and that the murmur was the vociferation of its populace.

"It seems like tens of thousands of them," said Tess; "holding public-meetings in their market-places, arguing, preaching, quarrelling, sobbing, groaning, praying, and cursing."

Clare was not particularly heeding.

"Did Crick speak to you to-day, dear, about his not wanting much assistance during the winter months?"

"No."

"The cows are going dry rapidly."

"Yes. Six of seven went to the straw-barton yesterday, and three the day before, making nearly twenty in the straw already. Ah—is it that the farmer don't want my help for the calving? O, I am not wanted here any more! And I have tried so hard to—"

"Crick didn't exactly say that he would no longer require you. But, knowing what our relations were, he said in the most good-natured and respectful manner possible that he supposed on my leaving at Christmas I should take you with me, and on my asking what he would do without you he merely observed that, as a matter of fact, it was a time of year when he could do with a very little female help. I am afraid I was sinner enough to feel rather glad that he was in this way forcing your hand."

"I don't think you ought to have felt glad, Angel. Because 'tis always mournful not to be wanted, even if at the same time 'tis convenient."

"Well, it is convenient—you have admitted that." He put his finger upon her cheek. "Ah!" he said.

"What?"

"I feel the red rising up at her having been caught! But why should I trifle so! We will not trifle—life is too serious."

"It is. Perhaps I saw that before you did."

She was seeing it then. To decline to marry him after all—in obedience to her emotion of last night—and leave the dairy, meant to go to some strange place, not a dairy; for milkmaids were not in request now calving-time was coming on; to go to some arable farm where no divine being like Angel Clare was. She hated the thought, and she hated more the thought of going home.

"So that, seriously, dearest Tess," he continued, "since you will probably have to leave at Christmas, it is in every way desirable and convenient that I should carry you off then as my property. Besides, if you were not the most uncalculating girl in the world you would know that we could not go on like this forever."

"I wish we could. That it would always be summer and autumn, and you always courting me, and always thinking as much of me as you have done through the past summer-time!"

"I always shall."

"O, I know you will!" she cried, with a sudden fervour of faith in him. "Angel, I will fix the day when I will become yours for always!"

Thus at last it was arranged between them, during that dark walk home, amid the myriads of liquid voices on the right and left.

When they reached the dairy Mr. and Mrs. Crick were promptly told—with injunctions to secrecy; for each of the lovers was desirous that the marriage should be kept as private as possible. The dairyman, though he had thought of dismissing her soon, now made a great concern about losing her. What should he do about his skimming? Who would make the ornamental butter-pats for the Anglebury and Sandbourne ladies? Mrs. Crick congratulated Tess on the shilly-shallying having at last come to an end, and said that directly she set eyes on Tess she divined that she was to be the chosen one of somebody who was no common out-door man; Tess had looked so superior as she walked across the barton on that afternoon of her arrival; that she was of a good family she could have sworn. In point of fact Mrs. Crick did remember thinking that Tess was graceful and good-looking as she approached; but the superiority might have been a growth of the imagination aided by subsequent knowledge.

Tess was now carried along upon the wings of the hours, without the sense of a will. The word had been given; the number of the day written down. Her naturally bright intelligence had begun to admit the fatalistic convictions common to field-folk and those who associate more extensively with natural phenomena than with their fellow-creatures; and she accordingly drifted into that passive responsiveness to all things her lover suggested, characteristic of the frame of mind.

But she wrote anew to her mother, ostensibly to notify the wedding-day; really to again implore her advice. It was a gentleman who had chosen her, which perhaps her mother had not sufficiently considered. A post-nuptial explanation, which might be accepted with a light heart by a rougher man, might not be received with the same feeling by him. But this communication brought no reply from Mrs. Durbeyfield.

Despite Angel Clare's plausible representations to himself and to Tess of the practical need for their immediate marriage, there was in truth an element of precipitancy in the step, as became apparent at a later date. He loved her dearly, though perhaps rather ideally and fancifully than with the impassioned thoroughness of her feeling for him. He had entertained no notion, when doomed as he had thought to an unintellectual bucolic life, that such charms as he beheld in this idyllic creature would be found behind the scenes. Unsophistication was a thing to talk of; but he had not known how it really struck one until he came here. Yet he was very far from seeing his future track clearly, and it might be a year or two before he would be able to consider himself fairly started in life. The secret lay in the tinge of recklessness imparted to his career and character by the sense that he had been made to miss his true destiny through the prejudices of his family.

"Don't you think 'twould have been better for us to wait till you were quite settled in your midland farm?" she once asked timidly. (A midland farm was the idea just then.)

"To tell the truth, my Tess, I don't like you to be left anywhere away from my protection and sympathy."

The reason was a good one, so far as it went. His influence over her had been so marked that she had caught his manner and habits, his speech and phrases, his likings and his aversions. And to leave her in farmland would be to let her slip back again out of accord with him. He wished to have her under his charge for another reason. His parents had naturally desired to see her once at least before he carried her off to a distant settlement, English or colonial; and as no opinion of theirs was to be allowed to change his intention, he judged that a couple of months' life with him in lodgings whilst seeking for an advantageous opening would be of some social assistance to her at what she might feel to be a trying ordeal—her presentation to his mother at the vicarage.

Next, he wished to see a little of the working of a flour-mill, having an idea that he might combine the use of one with corn-growing. The proprietor of a large old water-mill at Wellbridge—once the mill of an Abbey—had offered him the inspection of his time-honoured mode of procedure, and a hand in the operations for a few days, whenever he should choose to come. Clare paid a visit to the place, some few miles distant, one day at this time, to enquire particulars, and returned to Talbothays in the evening. She found him determined to spend a short time at the Wellbridge flour-mills. And what had determined him? Less the opportunity of an insight into grinding and bolting than the casual fact that lodgings were to be obtained in that very farmhouse which, before its mutilation, had been the mansion of a branch of the d'Urberville family. This was always how Clare settled practical questions; by a sentiment which had nothing to do with them. They decided to go immediately after the wedding, and remain for a fortnight, instead of journeying to towns and inns.

"Then we will start off to examine some farms on the other side of London that I have heard of," he said, "and by March or April we will pay a visit to my father and mother."

Questions of procedure such as these arose and passed, and the day, the incredible day, on which she was to become his, loomed large in the near future. The thirty-first of December, New Year's Eve, was the date. His wife, she said to herself. Could it ever be? Their two selves together, nothing to divide them, every incident shared by them; why not? And yet why?

One Sunday morning Izz Huett returned from church, and spoke privately to Tess.

"You was not called home[1] this morning."

"What?"

"It should ha' been the first time of asking to-day," she answered, looking quietly at Tess. "You meant to be married New Year's Eve, deary?"

The other returned a quick affirmative.

"And there must be three times of asking. And now there be only two Sundays left between."

Tess felt her cheek paling; Izz was right; of course there must be three. Perhaps he had forgotten! If so, there must be a week's postponement, and that was unlucky. How could she remind her lover? She who had been so backward was suddenly fired with impatience and alarm lest she should lose her dear prize.

A natural incident relieved her anxiety. Izz mentioned the omission of the banns to Mrs. Crick, and Mrs. Crick assumed a matron's privilege of speaking to Angel on the point.

---

1. "Called home"—local phrase for publication of banns.

"Have ye forgot 'em, Mr. Clare? The banns, I mean."

"No, I have not forgot 'em," says Clare.

As soon as he caught Tess alone he assured her:

"Don't let them tease you about the banns. A licence will be quieter for us, and I have decided on a licence without consulting you. So if you go to church on Sunday morning you will not hear your own name, if you wished to."

"I didn't wish to hear it, dearest," she said proudly.

But to know that things were in train was an immense relief to Tess notwithstanding, who had well-nigh feared that somebody would stand up and forbid the banns on the ground of her history. How events were favouring her!

"I don't quite feel easy," she said to herself. "All this good fortune may be scourged out of me afterwards by a lot of ill. That's how Heaven mostly does. I wish I could have had common banns!"

But everything went smoothly. She wondered whether he would like her to be married in her present best white frock, or if she ought to buy a new one. The question was set at rest by his forethought, disclosed by the arrival of some large packages addressed to her. Inside them she found a whole stock of clothing, from bonnet to shoes, including a perfect morning costume, such as would well suit the simple wedding they planned. He entered the house shortly after the arrival of the packages, and heard her upstairs undoing them.

A minute later she came down with a flush on her face and tears in her eyes.

"How thoughtful you've been!" she murmured, her cheek upon his shoulder. "Even to the gloves and handkerchief! My own love—how good, how kind!"

"No, no, Tess; just an order to a tradeswoman in London—nothing more."

And to divert her from thinking too highly of him he told her to go upstairs, and take her time, and see if it all fitted; and, if not, to get the village sempstress to make a few alterations.

She did return upstairs, and put on the gown. Alone, she stood for a moment before the glass looking at the effect of her silk attire; and then there came into her head her mother's ballad of the mystic robe—

> *That never would become that wife*
> *That had once done amiss,*

which Mrs. Durbeyfield had used to sing to her as a child, so blithely and so archly, her foot on the cradle, which she rocked to the tune. Suppose this robe should betray her by changing colour, as her robe had betrayed Queen Guénever. Since she had been at the dairy she had not once thought of the lines till now.

XXXIII

ANGEL FELT THAT HE WOULD LIKE TO SPEND A DAY WITH HER BEFORE THE WEDDING, somewhere away from the dairy, as a last jaunt in her company while they were yet mere lover and mistress; a romantic day, in circumstances that would never be repeated; with that other and greater day beaming close ahead of them. During the preceding week, therefore, he suggested making a few purchases in the nearest town, and they started together.

Clare's life at the dairy had been that of a recluse in respect to the world of his own class. For months he had never gone near a town, and, requiring no vehicle, had never kept one, hiring the dairyman's cob or gig if he rode or drove. They went in the gig that day.

And then for the first time in their lives they shopped as partners in one concern. It was Christmas Eve, with its loads a holly and mistletoe, and the town was very full of strangers who had come in from all parts of the country on account of the day. Tess paid the penalty of walking about with happiness superadded to beauty on her countenance by being much stared at as she moved amid them on his arm.

In the evening they returned to the inn at which they had put up, and Tess waited in the entry while Angel went to see the horse and gig brought to the door. The general sitting-room was full of guests, who were continually going in and out. As the door opened and shut each time for the passage of these, the light within the parlour fell full upon Tess's face. Two men came out and passed by her among the rest. One of them had stared her up and down in surprise, and she fancied he was a Trantridge man, though that village lay so many miles off that Trantridge folk were rarities here.

"A comely maid that," said the other.

"True, comely enough. But unless I make a great mistake—" And he negatived the remainder of the definition forthwith.

Clare had just returned from the stable-yard, and, confronting the man on the threshold, heard the words, and saw the shrinking of Tess. The insult to her stung him to the quick, and before he had considered anything at all he struck the man on the chin with the full force of his fist, sending him staggering backwards into the passage.

The man recovered himself, and seemed inclined to come on, and Clare, stepping outside the door, put himself in a posture of defence. But his opponent began to think better of the matter. He looked anew at Tess as he passed her, and said to Clare—

"I beg pardon, sir; 'twas a complete mistake. I thought she was another woman, forty miles from here."

Clare, feeling then that he had been too hasty, and that he was, moreover, to blame for leaving her standing in an inn-passage, did what he usually did in such cases, gave the man five shillings to plaster the blow; and thus they parted, bidding each other a pacific good-night. As soon as Clare had taken the reins from the ostler, and the young couple had driven off, the two men went in the other direction.

"And was it a mistake?" said the second one.

"Not a bit of it. But I didn't want to hurt the gentleman's feelings—not I."

In the meantime the lovers were driving onward.

"Could we put off our wedding till a little later?" Tess asked in a dry dull voice. "I mean if we wished?"

"No, my love. Calm yourself. Do you mean that the fellow may have time to summon me for assault?" he asked good-humouredly.

"No—I only meant—if it should have to be put off."

What she meant was not very clear, and he directed her to dismiss such fancies from her mind, which she obediently did as well as she could. But she was grave, very grave, all the way home; till she thought, "We shall go away, a very long distance, hundreds of miles from these parts, and such as this can never happen again, and no ghost of the past reach there."

They parted tenderly that night on the landing, and Clare ascended to his attic. Tess sat up getting on with some little requisites, lest the few remaining days should not afford sufficient time. While she sat she heard a noise in Angel's room overhead, a sound of thumping and struggling. Everybody else in the house was asleep, and in her anxiety lest Clare should be ill she ran up and knocked at his door, and asked him what was the matter.

"Oh, nothing, dear," he said from within. "I am so sorry I disturbed you! But the reason is rather an amusing one: I fell asleep and dreamt that I was fighting that fellow again who insulted you and the noise you heard was my pummelling away with my fists at my portmanteau, which I pulled out to-day for packing. I am occasionally liable to these freaks in my sleep. Go to bed and think of it no more."

This was the last drachm required to turn the scale of her indecision. Declare the past to him by word of mouth she could not; but there was another way. She sat down and wrote on the four pages of a note-sheet a succinct narrative of those events of three or four years ago, put it into an envelope, and directed it to Clare. Then, lest the flesh should again be weak, she crept upstairs without any shoes and slipped the note under his door.

Her night was a broken one, as it well might be, and she listened for the first faint noise overhead. It came, as usual; he descended, as usual. She descended. He met her at the bottom of the stairs and kissed her. Surely it was as warmly as ever!

He looked a little disturbed and worn, she thought. But he said not a word to her about her revelation, even when they were alone. Could he have had it? Unless he began the subject she felt that she could say nothing. So the day passed, and it was evident that whatever he thought he meant to keep to himself. Yet he was frank and affectionate as before. Could it be that her doubts were childish? that he forgave her; that he loved her for what she was, just as she was, and smiled at her disquiet as at a foolish nightmare? Had he really received her note? She glanced into his room, and could see nothing of it. It might be that he forgave her. But even if he had not received it she had a sudden enthusiastic trust that he surely would forgive her.

Every morning and night he was the same, and thus New Year's Eve broke—the wedding-day.

The lovers did not rise at milking-time, having through the whole of this last week of their sojourn at the dairy been accorded something of the position of guests, Tess being honoured with a room of her own. When they arrived downstairs at breakfast-time they were surprised to see what effects had been produced in the large kitchen for their glory since they had last beheld it. At some unnatural hour of the morning the dairyman had caused the yawning chimney-corner to be whitened, and the brick hearth reddened, and a blazing yellow damask blower to be hung across the arch in place of the old grimy blue cotton one with a black sprig pattern which had formerly done duty here. This renovated aspect of what was the focus indeed of the room on a dull winter morning, threw a smiling demeanour over the whole apartment.

"I was determined to do summat in honour o't," said the dairyman. "And as you wouldn't hear of my gieing a rattling good randy wi' fiddles and bass-viols complete, as we should ha' done in old times, this was all I could think o' as a noiseless thing."

Tess's friends lived so far off that none could conveniently have been present at the ceremony, even had any been asked; but as a fact nobody was invited from Marlott. As for Angel's family, he had written and duly informed them of the time, and assured them that he would be glad to see one at least of them there for the day if he would like to come. His brothers had not replied at all, seeming to be indignant with him; while his father and mother had written a rather sad letter, deploring his precipitancy in rushing into marriage, but making the best of the matter by saying that, though a dairywoman was the last daughter-in-law they could have expected, their son had arrived at an age which he might be supposed to be the best judge.

This coolness in his relations distressed Clare less than it would have done had he been without the grand card with which he meant to surprise them ere long. To produce Tess, fresh from the dairy, as a d'Urberville and a lady, he had felt to be temerarious and risky; hence he had concealed her lineage till such time as, familiarised with worldly ways by a few months' travel and reading with him, he could take her on a visit to his parents, and impart the knowledge while triumphantly producing her as worthy of such an ancient line. It was a pretty lover's dream, if no more. Perhaps Tess's lineage had more value for himself than for anybody in the world beside.

Her perception that Angel's bearing towards her still remained in no whit altered by her own communication rendered Tess guiltily doubtful if he could have received it. She rose from breakfast before he had finished, and hastened upstairs. It had occurred to her to look once more into the queer gaunt room which had been Clare's den, or rather eyrie, for so long, and climbing the ladder she stood at the open door of the apartment, regarding and pondering. She stooped to the threshold of the doorway, where she had pushed in the note two or three days earlier in such excitement. The carpet reached close to the sill, and under the edge of the carpet she discerned the faint white margin of the envelope containing her letter to him, which he obviously had never seen, owing to her having in her haste thrust it beneath the carpet as well as beneath the door.

With a feeling of faintness she withdrew the letter. There it was—sealed up, just as it had left her hands. The mountain had not yet been removed. She could not let him read it now, the house being in full bustle of preparation; and descending to her own room she destroyed the letter there.

She was so pale when he saw her again that he felt quite anxious. The incident of the misplaced letter she had jumped at as if it prevented a confession; but she knew in her conscience that it need not; there was still time. Yet everything was in a stir; there was coming and going; all had to dress, the dairyman and Mrs. Crick having been asked to accompany them as witnesses; and reflection or deliberate talk was well-nigh impossible. The only minute Tess could get to be alone with Clare was when they met upon the landing.

"I am so anxious to talk to you—I want to confess all my faults and blunders!" she said with attempted lightness.

"No, no—we can't have faults talked of—you must be deemed perfect to-day at least, my Sweet!" he cried. "We shall have plenty of time, hereafter, I hope, to talk over our failings. I will confess mine at the same time."

"But it would be better for me to do it now, I think, so that you could not say—"

"Well, my quixotic one, you shall tell me anything—say, as soon as we are settled in our lodging; not now. I, too, will tell you my faults then. But do not let us spoil the day with them; they will be excellent matter for a dull time."

"Then you don't wish me to, dearest?"

"I do not, Tessy, really."

The hurry of dressing and starting left no time for more than this. Those words of his seemed to reassure her on further reflection. She was whirled onward through the next couple of critical hours by the mastering tide of her devotion to him, which closed up further meditation. Her one desire, so long resisted, to make herself his, to call him her lord, her own—then, if necessary, to die—had at last lifted her up from her plodding reflective pathway. In dressing, she moved about in a mental cloud of many-coloured idealities, which eclipsed all sinister contingencies by its brightness.

The church was a long way off, and they were obliged to drive, particularly as it was winter. A close carriage was ordered from a roadside inn, a vehicle which had been kept there ever since the old days of post-chaise travelling. It had stout wheel-spokes, and heavy felloes, a great curved bed, immense straps and springs, and a pole like a battering-ram. The postilion was a venerable "boy" of sixty—a martyr to rheumatic gout, the result of excessive exposure in youth, counteracted by strong liquors—who had stood at inn-doors doing nothing for the whole five-and-twenty years that had elapsed since he had no longer been required to ride professionally, as if expecting the old times to come back again. He had a permanent running wound on the outside of his right leg, originated by the constant bruisings of aristocratic carriage-poles during the many years that he had been in regular employ at the King's Arms, Casterbridge.

Inside this cumbrous and creaking structure, and behind this decayed conductor, the *partie carrée* took their seats—the bride and bridegroom and Mr. and Mrs. Crick. Angel would have liked one at least of his brothers to be present as groomsman, but their silence after his gentle hint to that affect by letter had signified that they did not care to come. They disapproved of the marriage, and could not be expected to countenance it. Perhaps it was as well that they could not be present. They were not worldly young fellows, but fraternising with dairy-folk would have struck unpleasantly upon their biassed niceness, apart from their views of the match.

Upheld by the momentum of the time Tess knew nothing of this; did not see anything; did not know the road they were taking to the church. She knew that Angel was close to her; all the rest was a luminous mist. She was a sort of celestial person, who owed her being to poetry—one of those classical divinities Clare was accustomed to talk to her about when they took their walks together.

The marriage being by licence there were only a dozen or so of people in the church; had there been a thousand they would have produced no more effect upon her. They were at stellar distances from her present world. In the ecstatic solemnity with which she swore her faith to him the ordinary sensibilities of sex seemed a flippancy. At a pause in the service, while they were kneeling together, she unconsciously inclined herself towards him, so that her shoulder touched his arm; she had been frightened by a passing thought, and the movement had been automatic, to assure herself that he was really there, and to fortify her belief that his fidelity would be proof against all things.

Clare knew that she loved him—every curve of her form showed that—but he did not know at that time the full depth of her devotion, its single-mindedness, its meekness; what long-suffering it guaranteed, what honesty, what endurance, what good faith.

As they came out of church the ringers swung the bells off their rests, and a modest peal of three notes broke forth—that limited amount of expression having been deemed sufficient by the church-builders for the joys of such a small parish. Passing by the tower with her husband on the path to the gate she could feel the vibrant air humming round them from the louvred belfry in a circle of sound, and it matched the highly-charged mental atmosphere in which she was living.

This condition of mind, wherein she felt glorified by an irradiation not her own, like the angel whom St. John saw in the sun, lasted till the sound of the church-bells had died away, and the emotions of the wedding service had calmed down. Her eyes could dwell upon details more clearly now, and Mr. and Mrs. Crick having directed their own gig to be sent for them, to leave the carriage to the young couple, she observed the build and character of that conveyance for the first time. Sitting in silence she regarded it long.

"I fancy you seem oppressed, Tessy," said Clare.

"Yes," she answered, putting her hand to her brow. "I tremble at many things. It is all so serious, Angel. Among other things I seem to have seen this carriage before, to be very well acquainted with it. It is very odd—I must have seen it in a dream."

"Oh—you have heard the legend of the d'Urberville Coach—that well-known superstition of this county about your family when they were very popular here; and this lumbering old thing reminds you of it."

"I have never heard of it to my knowledge," said she. "What is the legend—may I know it?"

"Well—I would rather not tell it in detail just now. A certain d'Urberville of the sixteenth or seventeenth century committed a dreadful crime in his family coach; and since that time members of the family see or hear the old coach whenever—But I'll tell you another day—it is rather gloomy. Evidently some dim knowledge of it has been brought back to your mind by the sight of this venerable caravan."

"I don't remember hearing it before," she murmured. "Is it when we are going to die, Angel, that members of my family see it, or is it when we have committed a crime?"

"Now, Tess!"

He silenced her by a kiss.

By the time they reached home she was contrite and spiritless. She was Mrs. Angel Clare, indeed, but had she any moral right to the name? Was she not more truly Mrs. Alexander d'Urberville? Could intensity of love justify what might be considered in upright souls as culpable reticence? She knew not what was expected of women in such cases; and she had no counsellor.

However, when she found herself alone in her room for a few minutes—the last day this on which she was ever to enter it—she knelt down and prayed. She tried to pray to

God, but it was her husband who really had her supplication. Her idolatry of this man was such that she herself almost feared it to be ill-omened. She was conscious of the notion expressed by Friar Laurence: "These violent delights have violent ends." It might be too desperate for human conditions—too rank, to wild, too deadly.

"O my love, my love, why do I love you so!" she whispered there alone; "for she you love is not my real self, but one in my image; the one I might have been!"

Afternoon came, and with it the hour for departure. They had decided to fulfil the plan of going for a few days to the lodgings in the old farmhouse near Wellbridge Mill, at which he meant to reside during his investigation of flour processes. At two o'clock there was nothing left to do but to start. All the servantry of the dairy were standing in the red-brick entry to see them go out, the dairyman and his wife following to the door. Tess saw her three chamber-mates in a row against the wall, pensively inclining their heads. She had much questioned if they would appear at the parting moment; but there they were, stoical and staunch to the last. She knew why the delicate Retty looked so fragile, and Izz so tragically sorrowful, and Marian so blank; and she forgot her own dogging shadow for a moment in contemplating theirs.

She impulsively whispered to him—

"Will you kiss 'em all, once, poor things, for the first and last time?"

Clare had not the least objection to such a farewell formality—which was all that it was to him—and as he passed them he kissed them in succession where they stood, saying "Good-bye" to each as he did so. When they reached the door Tess femininely glanced back to discern the effect of that kiss of charity; there was no triumph in her glance, as there might have been. If there had it would have disappeared when she saw how moved the girls all were. The kiss had obviously done harm by awakening feelings they were trying to subdue.

Of all this Clare was unconscious. Passing on to the wicket gate he shook hands with the dairyman and his wife, and expressed his last thanks to them for their attentions; after which there was a moment of silence before they had moved off. It was interrupted by the crowing of a cock. The white one with the rose comb had come and settled on the palings in front of the house, within a few yards of them, and his notes thrilled their ears through, dwindling away like echoes down a valley of rocks.

"Oh?" said Mrs. Crick. "An afternoon crow!"

Two men were standing by the yard gate, holding it open.

"That's bad," one murmured to the other, not thinking that the words could be heard by the group at the door-wicket.

The cock crew again—straight towards Clare.

"Well!" said the dairyman.

"I don't like to hear him!" said Tess to her husband. "Tell the man to drive on. Good-bye, good-bye!"

The cock crew again.

"Hoosh! Just you be off, sir, or I'll twist your neck!" said the dairyman with some irritation, turning to the bird and driving him away. And to his wife as they went indoors: "Now, to think o' that just to-day! I've not heard his crow of an afternoon all the year afore."

"It only means a change in the weather," said she; "not what you think: 'tis impossible!"

XXXIV

THEY DROVE BY THE LEVEL ROAD ALONG THE VALLEY TO A DISTANCE OF A FEW MILES, and, reaching Wellbridge, turned away from the village to the left, and over the great Elizabethan bridge which gives the place half its name. Immediately behind it stood the house wherein they had engaged lodgings, whose exterior features are so well known to all travellers through the Froom Valley; once portion of a fine manorial residence, and the property and seat of a d'Urberville, but since its partial demolition a farmhouse.

"Welcome to one of your ancestral mansions!" said Clare as he handed her down. But he regretted the pleasantry; it was too near a satire.

On entering they found that, though they had only engaged a couple of rooms, the farmer had taken advantage of their proposed presence during the coming days to pay a New Year's visit to some friends, leaving a woman from a neighbouring cottage to minister to their few wants. The absoluteness of possession pleased them, and they realised it as the first moment of their experience under their own exclusive roof-tree.

But he found that the mouldy old habitation somewhat depressed his bride. When the carriage was gone they ascended the stairs to wash their hands, the charwoman showing the way. On the landing Tess stopped and started.

"What's the matter?" said he.

"Those horrid women!" she answered with a smile. "How they frightened me."

He looked up, and perceived two life-size portraits on panels built into the masonry. As all visitors to the mansion are aware, these paintings represent women of middle age, of a date some two hundred years ago, whose lineaments once seen can never be forgotten. The long pointed features, narrow eye, and smirk of the one, so suggestive of merciless treachery; the bill-hook nose, large teeth, and bold eye of the other, suggesting arrogance to the point of ferocity, haunt the beholder afterwards in his dreams.

"Whose portraits are those?" asked Clare of the charwoman.

"I have been told by old folk that they were ladies of the d'Urberville family, the ancient lords of this manor," she said. "Owing to their being builded into the wall they can't be moved away."

The unpleasantness of the matter was that, in addition to their effect upon Tess, her fine features were unquestionably traceable in these exaggerated forms. He said nothing of this, however, and, regretting that he had gone out of his way to choose the house for their bridal time, went on into the adjoining room. The place having been rather hastily prepared for them they washed their hands in one basin. Clare touched hers under the water.

"Which are my fingers and which are yours?" he said, looking up. "They are very much mixed."

"They are all yours," said she, very prettily, and endeavoured to be gayer than she was. He had not been displeased with her thoughtfulness on such an occasion; it was what every sensible woman would show: but Tess knew that she had been thoughtful to excess, and struggled against it.

The sun was so low on that short last afternoon of the year that it shone in through a small opening and formed a golden staff which stretched across to her skirt, where it made a spot like a paint-mark set upon her. They went into the ancient parlour to tea, and here they shared their first common meal alone. Such was their childishness, or rather his, that he found it interesting to use the same bread-and-butter plate as herself, and to brush crumbs from her lips with his own. He wondered a little that she did not enter into these frivolities with his own zest.

Looking at her silently for a long time; "She is a dear dear Tess," he thought to himself, as one deciding on the true construction of a difficult passage. "Do I realise solemnly enough how utterly and irretrievably this little womanly thing is the creature of my good or bad faith and fortune? I think not. I think I could not, unless I were a woman myself. What I am in worldly estate, she is. What I become, she must become. What I cannot be, she cannot be. And shall I ever neglect her, or hurt her, or even forget to consider her? God forbid such a crime!"

They sat on over the tea-table waiting for their luggage, which the dairyman had promised to send before it grew dark. But evening began to close in, and the luggage did not arrive, and they had brought nothing more than they stood in. With the departure of the sun the calm mood of the winter day changed. Out-of-doors there began noises as of silk smartly rubbed; the restful dead leaves of the preceding autumn were stirred to irritated resurrection, and whirled about unwillingly, and tapped against the shutters. It soon began to rain.

"That cock knew the weather was going to change," said Clare.

The woman who had attended upon them had gone home for the night, but she had placed candles upon the table, and now they lit them. Each candle-flame drew towards the fireplace.

"These old houses are so draughty," continued Angel, looking at the flames, and at the grease guttering down the sides. "I wonder where that luggage is. We haven't even a brush and comb."

"I don't know," she answered, absent-minded.

"Tess, you are not a bit cheerful this evening—not at all as you used to be. Those harridans on the panels upstairs have unsettled you. I am sorry I brought you here. I wonder if you really love me, after all?"

He knew that she did, and the words had no serious intent; but she was surcharged with emotion, and winced like a wounded animal. Though she tried not to shed tears she could not help showing one or two.

"I did not mean it!" said he, sorry. "You are worried at not having your things, I know. I cannot think why old Jonathan has not come with them. Why, it is seven o'clock? Ah, there he is!"

A knock had come to the door, and, there being nobody else to answer it Clare went out. He returned to the room with a small package in his hand.

"It is not Jonathan, after all," he said.

"How vexing!" said Tess.

The packet had been brought by a special messenger, who had arrived at Talbothays from Emminster vicarage immediately after the departure of the married couple, and had followed them hither, being under injunction to deliver it into nobody's hands but theirs. Clare brought it to the light. It was less than a foot long, sewed up in canvas, sealed in red wax with his father's seal, and directed in his father's hand to "Mrs. Angel Clare."

"It is a little wedding-present for you, Tess," said he, handing it to her. "How thoughtful they are!"

Tess looked a little flustered as she took it.

"I think I would rather have you open it, dearest," said she, turning over the parcel. "I don't like to break those great seals; they look so serious. Please open it for me!"

He undid the parcel. Inside was a case of morocco leather, on the top of which lay a note and a key.

The note was for Clare, in the following words:

MY DEAR SON—Possibly you have forgotten that on the death of your godmother, Mrs. Pitney, when you were a lad, she—vain kind woman that she was—left to me a portion of the contents of her jewel-case in trust for your wife, if you should ever have one, as a mark of her affection for you and whomsoever you should choose. This trust I have fulfilled, and the diamonds have been locked up at my banker's ever since. Though I feel it to be a somewhat incongruous act in the circumstances, I am, as you will see, bound to hand over the articles to the woman to whom the use of them for her lifetime will now rightly belong, and they are therefore promptly sent. They become, I believe, heirlooms, strictly speaking, according to the terms of your godmother's will. The precise words of the clause that refers to this matter are enclosed.

"I do remember," said Clare; "but I had quite forgotten."

Unlocking the case, they found it to contain a necklace, with pendant, bracelets, and ear-rings; and also some other small ornaments.

Tess seemed afraid to touch them at first, but her eyes sparkled for a moment as much as the stones when Clare spread out the set.

"Are they mine?" she asked incredulously.

"They are, certainly," said he.

He looked into the fire. He remembered how, when he was a lad of fifteen, his godmother, the Squire's wife—the only rich person with whom he had ever come in contact—had pinned her faith to his success; had prophesied a wondrous career for him. There had seemed nothing at all out of keeping with such a conjectured career in the storing up of these showy ornaments for his wife and the wives of her descendants. They gleamed somewhat ironically now. "Yet why?" he asked himself. It was but a question of vanity throughout; and if that were admitted into one side of the equation it should be admitted into the other. His wife was a d'Urberville: whom could they become better than her?

Suddenly he said with enthusiasm—

"Tess, put them on—put them on!" And he turned from the fire to help her.

But as if by magic she had already donned them—necklace, ear-rings, bracelets, and all.

"But the gown isn't right, Tess," said Clare. "It ought to be a low one for a set of brilliants like that."

"Ought it?" said Tess.

"Yes," said he.

He suggested to her how to tuck in the upper edge of her bodice, so as to make it roughly approximate to the cut for evening wear; and when she had done this, and the pendant to the necklace hung isolated amid the whiteness of her throat, as it was designed to do, he stepped back to survey her.

"My heavens," said Clare, "how beautiful you are!"

As everybody knows, fine feathers make fine birds; a peasant girl but very moderately prepossessing to the casual observer in her simple condition and attire, will bloom as an amazing beauty if clothed as a woman of fashion with the aids that Art can render; while the beauty of the midnight crush would often cut but a sorry figure if placed inside the field-woman's wrapper upon a monotonous acreage of turnips on a dull day. He had never till now estimated the artistic excellence of Tess's limbs and features.

"If you were only to appear in a ball-room!" he said. "But no—no, dearest; I think I love you best in the wing-bonnet and cotton-frock—yes, better than in this, well as you support these dignities."

Tess's sense of her striking appearance had given her a flush of excitement, which was yet not happiness.

"I'll take them off," she said, "in case Jonathan should see me. They are not fit for me, are they? They must be sold, I suppose?"

"Let them stay a few minutes longer. Sell them? Never. It would be a breach of faith."

Influenced by a second thought she readily obeyed. She had something to tell, and there might be help in these. She sat down with the jewels upon her; and they again indulged in conjectures as to where Jonathan could possibly be with their baggage. The ale they had poured out for his consumption when he came had gone flat with long standing.

Shortly after this they began supper, which was already laid on a side-table. Ere they had finished there was a jerk in the fire-smoke, the rising skein of which bulged out into the room, as if some giant had laid his hand on the chimney-top for a moment. It had been caused by the opening of the outer door. A heavy step was now heard in the passage, and Angel went out.

"I couldn' make nobody hear at all by knocking," apologised Jonathan Kail, for it was he at last; "and as 't was raining out I opened the door. I've brought the things, sir."

"I am very glad to see them. But you are very late."

"Well, yes, sir."

There was something subdued in Jonathan Kail's tone which had not been there in the day, and lines of concern were ploughed upon his forehead in addition to the lines of years. He continued—

"We've all been gallied at the dairy at what might ha' been a most terrible affliction since you and your Mis'ess—so to name her now—left us this a'ternoon. Perhaps you ha'nt forgot the cock's afternoon crow?"

"Dear me;—what—"

"Well, some says it do mane one thing, and some another; but what's happened is that poor little Retty Priddle hev tried to drown herself."

"No! Really! Why, she bade us good-bye with the rest—"

"Yes. Well, sir, when you and your Mis'ess—so to name what she lawful is—when you two drove away, as I say, Retty and Marian put on their bonnets and went out; and as there is not much doing now, being New Year's Eve, and folks mops and brooms from what's inside 'em, nobody took much notice. They went on to Lew-Everard, where they had summut to drink, and then on they vamped to Dree-armed Cross, and there they seemed to have parted, Retty striking across the water-meads as if for home, and Marian going on to the next village, where there's another public-house. Nothing more was zeed or heard o' Retty till the waterman, on his way home, noticed something by the Great Pool; 'twas her bonnet and shawl packed up. In the water he found her. He and another man brought her home, thinking 'a was dead; but she fetched round by degrees."

Angel, suddenly recollecting that Tess was overhearing this gloomy tale, went to shut the door between the passage and the ante-room to the inner parlour where she was; but his wife, flinging a shawl round her, had come to the outer-room and was listening to the man's narrative, her eyes resting absently on the luggage and the drops of rain glistening upon it.

"And, more than this, there's Marian; she's been found dead drunk by the withy-bed—a girl who hev never been known to touch anything before except shilling ale; though, to be sure, 'a was always a good trencher-woman, as her face showed. It seems as if the maids had all gone out o' their minds!"

"And Izz?" asked Tess.

"Izz is about house as usual; but 'a do say 'a can guess how it happened; and she seems to be very low in mind about it, poor maid, as well she mid be. And so you see, sir, as all this happened just when we was packing your few traps and your Mis'ess's night-rail and dressing things into the cart, why, it belated me."

"Yes. Well, Jonathan, will you get the trunks upstairs, and drink a cup of ale, and hasten back as soon as you can, in case you should be wanted?"

Tess had gone back to the inner parlour, and sat down by the fire, looking wistfully into it. She heard Jonathan Kail's heavy footsteps up and down the stairs till he had done placing the luggage, and heard him express his thanks for the ale her husband took out to him, and for the gratuity he received. Jonathan's footsteps then died from the door, and his cart creaked away.

Angel slid forward the massive oak bar which secured the door, and coming in to where she sat over the hearth, pressed her cheeks between his hands from behind. He expected her to jump up gaily and unpack the toilet-gear that she had been so anxious about, but as she did not rise he sat down with her in the firelight, the candles on the supper-table being too thin and glimmering to interfere with its glow.

"I am so sorry you should have heard this sad story about the girls," he said. "Still, don't let it depress you. Retty was naturally morbid, you know."

"Without the least cause," said Tess. "While they who have cause to be, hide it, and pretend they are not."

This incident had turned the scale for her. They were simple and innocent girls on whom the unhappiness of unrequited love had fallen; they had deserved better at the hands of Fate. She had deserved worse—yet she was the chosen one. It was wicked of her to take all without paying. She would pay to the uttermost farthing; she would tell, there and then. This final determination she came to when she looked into the fire, he holding her hand.

A steady glare from the now flameless embers painted the sides and back of the fire-place with its colour, and the well-polished andirons, and the old brass tongs that would not meet. The underside of the mantel-shelf was flushed with the high-coloured light, and the legs of the table nearest the fire. Tess's face and neck reflected the same warmth, which each gem turned into an Aldebaran or a Sirius—a constellation of white, red, and green flashes, that interchanged their hues with her every pulsation.

"Do you remember what we said to each other this morning about telling our faults?" he asked abruptly, finding that she still remained immovable. "We spoke lightly perhaps, and you may well have done so. But for me it was no light promise. I want to make a confession to you, Love."

This, from him, so unexpectedly apposite, had the effect upon her of a Providential interposition.

"You have to confess something?" she said quickly, and even with gladness and relief.

"You did not expect it? Ah—you thought too highly of me. Now listen. Put your head there, because I want you to forgive me, and not to be indignant with me for not telling you before, as perhaps I ought to have done."

How strange it was! He seemed to be her double. She did not speak, and Clare went on—

"I did not mention it because I was afraid of endangering my chance of you, darling, the great prize of my life—my Fellowship I call you. My brother's Fellowship was won at his college, mine at Talbothays Dairy. Well, I would not risk it. I was going to tell you a month ago—at the time you agreed to be mine, but I could not; I thought it might frighten you away from me. I put it off; then I thought I would tell you yesterday, to give you a chance at least of escaping me. But I did not. And I did not this morning, when you proposed our confessing our faults on the landing—the sinner that I was! But I must, now I see you sitting there so solemnly. I wonder if you will forgive me?"

"O yes! I am sure that—"

"Well, I hope so. But wait a minute. You don't know. To begin at the beginning. Though I imagine my poor father fears that I am one of the eternally lost for my doctrines, I am of course, a believer in good morals, Tess, as much as you. I used to wish to be a teacher of men, and it was a great disappointment to me when I found I could not enter the Church. I admired spotlessness, even though I could lay no claim to it, and hated impurity, as I hope I do now. Whatever one may think of plenary inspiration, one must heartily subscribe to these words of Paul: 'Be thou an example—in word, in conversation, in charity, in spirit, in faith, in purity.' It is the only safeguard for us poor human beings. 'Integer vitae,' says a Roman poet, who is strange company for St. Paul—

> The man of upright life, from frailties free,
> Stands not in need of Moorish spear or bow.

"Well, a certain place is paved with good intentions, and having felt all that so strongly, you will see what a terrible remorse it bred in me when, in the midst of my fine aims for other people, I myself fell."

He then told her of that time of his life to which allusion has been made when, tossed about by doubts and difficulties in London, like a cork on the waves, he plunged into eight-and-forty hours' dissipation with a stranger.

"Happily I awoke almost immediately to a sense of my folly," he continued. "I would have no more to say to her, and I came home. I have never repeated the offence. But I felt I should like to treat you with perfect frankness and honour, and I could not do so without telling this. Do you forgive me?"

She pressed his hand tightly for an answer.

"Then we will dismiss it at once and forever!—too painful as it is for the occasion—and talk of something lighter."

"O, Angel—I am almost glad—because now *you* can forgive *me!* I have not made my confession. I have a confession, too—remember, I said so."

"Ah, to be sure! Now then for it, wicked little one."

"Perhaps, although you smile, it is as serious as yours, or more so."

"It can hardly be more serious, dearest."

"It cannot—O no, it cannot!" She jumped up joyfully at the hope. "No, it cannot be more serious, certainly," she cried, "because 'tis just the same! I will tell you now."

She sat down again.

Their hands were still joined. The ashes under the grate were lit by the fire vertically, like a torrid waste. Imagination might have beheld a Last Day luridness in this red-coaled glow, which fell on his face and hand, and on hers, peering into the loose hair about her brow, and firing the delicate skin underneath. A large shadow of her shape rose upon the wall and ceiling. She bent forward, at which each diamond on her neck gave a sinister wink like a toad's; and pressing her forehead against his temple she entered on her story of her acquaintance with Alec d'Urberville and its results, murmuring the words without flinching, and with her eyelids drooping down.

END OF PHASE THE FOURTH

Phase the Fifth

The Woman Pays

XXXV

HER NARRATIVE ENDED; EVEN ITS REASSERTIONS AND SECONDARY EXPLANATIONS were done. Tess's voice throughout had hardly risen higher than its opening tone; there had been no exculpatory phrase of any kind, and she had not wept.

But the complexion even of external things seemed to suffer transmutation as her announcement progressed. The fire in the grate looked impish—demoniacally funny, as if it did not care in the least about her strait. The fender grinned idly, as if it too did not care. The light from the water-bottle was merely engaged in a chromatic problem. All material objects around announced their irresponsibility with terrible iteration. And yet nothing had changed since the moments when he had been kissing her; or rather, nothing in the substance of things. But the essence of things had changed.

When she ceased the auricular impressions from their previous endearments seemed to hustle away into the corner of their brains, repeating themselves as echoes from a time of supremely purblind foolishness.

Clare performed the irrelevant act of stirring the fire; the intelligence had not even yet got to the bottom of him. After stirring the embers he rose to his feet; all the force of her disclosure had imparted itself now. His face had withered. In the strenuousness of his concentration he treadled fitfully on the floor. He could not, by any contrivance, think closely enough; that was the meaning of his vague movement. When he spoke it was in the most inadequate, commonplace voice of the many varied tones she had heard from him.

"Tess!"

"Yes, dearest."

"Am I to believe this? From your manner I am to take it as true. O you cannot be out of your mind! You ought to be! Yet you are not. . . . My wife, my Tess—nothing in you warrants such a supposition as that?"

"I am not out of my mind," she said.

"And yet—" He looked vacantly at her, to resume with dazed senses: "Why didn't you tell me before? Ah, yes, you would have told me, in a way—but I hindered you, I remember!"

These and other of his words were nothing but the perfunctory babble of the surface while the depths remained paralysed. He turned away, and bent over a chair. Tess followed him to the middle of the room where he was, and stood there staring at him with eyes that did not weep. Presently she slid down upon her knees beside his foot, and from this position she crouched in a heap.

"In the name of our love, forgive me!" she whispered with a dry mouth. "I have forgiven you for the same!"

And, as he did not answer, she said again—

"Forgive me as you are forgiven! *I* forgive *you*, Angel."

"You—yes, you do."

"But you do not forgive me?"

"O Tess, forgiveness does not apply to the case! You were one person; now you are another. My God—how can forgiveness meet such a grotesque—prestidigitation as that!"

He paused, contemplating this definition; then suddenly broke into horrible laughter—as unnatural and ghastly as a laugh in hell.

"Don't—don't! It kills me quite, that!" she shrieked. "O have mercy upon me—have mercy!"

He did not answer; and, sickly white, she jumped up.

"Angel, Angel! what do you mean by that laugh?" she cried out. "Do you know what this is to me?"

He shook his head.

"I have been hoping, longing, praying, to make you happy! I have thought what joy it will be to do it, what an unworthy wife I shall be if I do not! That's what I have felt, Angel!"

"I know that."

"I thought, Angel, that you loved me—me, my very self! If it is I you do love, O how can it be that you look and speak so? It frightens me! Having begun to love you, I love you forever—in all changes, in all disgraces, because you are yourself. I ask no more. Then how can you, O my own husband, stop loving me?"

"I repeat, the woman I have been loving is not you."

"But who?"

"Another woman in your shape."

She perceived in his words the realisation of her own apprehensive foreboding in former times. He looked upon her as a species of imposter; a guilty woman in the guise of an innocent one. Terror was upon her white face as she saw it; her cheek was flaccid, and her mouth had almost the aspect of a round little hole. The horrible sense of his view of her so deadened her that she staggered; and he stepped forward, thinking she was going to fall.

"Sit down, sit down," he said gently. "You are ill; and it is natural that you should be."

She did sit down, without knowing where she was, that strained look still upon her face, and her eyes such as to make his flesh creep.

"I don't belong to you any more, then; do I, Angel?" she asked helplessly. "It is not me, but another woman like me that he loved, he says."

The image raised caused her to take pity upon herself as one who was ill-used. Her eyes filled as she regarded her position further; she turned round and burst into a flood of self-sympathetic tears.

Clare was relieved at this change, for the effect on her of what had happened was beginning to be a trouble to him only less than the woe of the disclosure itself. He waited patiently, apathetically, till the violence of her grief had worn itself out, and her rush of weeping had lessened to a catching gasp at intervals.

"Angel," she said suddenly, in her natural tones, the insane, dry voice of terror having left her now. "Angel, am I too wicked for you and me to live together?"

"I have not been able to think what we can do."

"I shan't ask you to let me live with you, Angel, because I have no right to! I shall not write to mother and sisters to say we be married, as I said I would do; and I shan't finish the good-hussif' I cut out and meant to make while we were in lodgings."

"Shan't you?"

"No, I shan't do anything, unless you order me to; and if you go away from me I shall not follow 'ee; and if you never speak to me any more I shall not ask why, unless you tell me I may."

"And if I order you to do anything?"

"I will obey you like your wretched slave, even if it is to lie down and die."

"You are very good. But it strikes me that there is a want of harmony between your present mood of self-sacrifice and your past mood of self-preservation."

These were the first words of antagonism. To fling elaborate sarcasms at Tess, however, was much like flinging them at a dog or cat. The charms of their subtlety passed by her unappreciated, and she only received them as inimical sounds which meant that anger ruled. She remained mute, not knowing that he was smothering his affection for her. She hardly observed that a tear descended slowly upon his cheek, a tear so large that it magnified the pores of the skin over which it rolled, like the object lens of a microscope. Meanwhile reillumination as to the terrible and total change that her confession had wrought in his life, in his universe, returned to him, and he tried desperately to advance among the new conditions in which he stood. Some consequent action was necessary; yet what?

"Tess," he said, as gently as he could speak, "I cannot stay—in this room—just now. I will walk out a little way."

He quietly left the room, and the two glasses of wine that he had poured out for their supper—one for her, one for him—remained on the table untasted. This was what their *Agape* had come to. At tea, two or three hours earlier, they had, in the freakishness of affection, drunk from one cup.

The closing of the door behind him, gently as it had been pulled to, roused Tess from her stupor. He was gone; she could not stay. Hastily flinging her cloak around her she opened the door and followed, putting out the candles as if she were never coming back. The rain was over and the night was now clear.

She was soon close at his heels, for Clare walked slowly and without purpose. His form beside her light grey figure looked black, sinister, and forbidding, and she felt as sarcasm the touch of the jewels of which she had been momentarily so proud. Clare turned at hearing her footsteps, but his recognition of her presence seemed to make no difference to him, and he went on over the five yawning arches of the great bridge in front of the house.

The cow and horse tracks in the road were full of water, and rain having been enough to charge them, but not enough to wash them away. Across these minute pools the reflected stars flitted in a quick transit as she passed; she would not have known they were shining overhead if she had not seen them there—the vastest things of the universe imaged in objects so mean.

The place to which they had travelled to-day was in the same valley as Talbothays, but some miles lower down the river; and the surroundings being open she kept easily in sight of him. Away from the house the road wound through the meads, and along these she followed Clare without any attempt to come up with him or to attract him, but with dumb and vacant fidelity.

At last, however, her listless walk brought her up alongside him, and still he said nothing. The cruelty of fooled honesty is often great after enlightenment, and it was mighty in Clare now. The out-door air had apparently taken away from him all tendency to act on impulse; she knew that he saw her without irradiation—in all her bareness; that Time was chanting his satiric psalm at her then—

Behold, when thy face is made bare, he that loved thee shall hate;
Thy face shall be no more fair at the fall of thy fate.
For thy life shall fall as a leaf and be shed as the rain;
And the veil of thine head shall be grief, and the crown shall be pain.

He was still intently thinking, and her companionship had now insufficient power to break or divert the strain of thought. What a weak thing her presence must have become to him! She could not help addressing Clare.

"What have I done—what *have* I done! I have not told of anything that interferes with or belies my love for you. You don't think I planned it, do you? It is in your own mind what you are angry at, Angel; it is not in me. O, it is not in me, and I am not that deceitful woman you think me!"

"H'm—well. Not deceitful, my wife; but not the same. No, not the same. But do not make me reproach you. I have sworn that I will not; and I will do everything to avoid it."

But she went on pleading in her distraction; and perhaps said things that would have been better left to silence.

"Angel!—Angel! I was a child—a child when it happened! I knew nothing of men."

"You were more sinned against than sinning, that I admit."

"Then will you not forgive me?"

"I do forgive you, but forgiveness is not all."

"And love me?"

To this question he did not answer.

"O Angel—my mother says that it sometimes happens so!—she knows several cases where they were worse than I, and the husband has not minded it much—has got over it at least. And yet the woman had not loved him as I do you!"

"Don't, Tess; don't argue. Different societies, different manners. You almost make me say you are an unapprehending peasant woman, who have never been initiated into the proportions of social things. You don't know what you say."

"I am only a peasant by position, not by nature!"

She spoke with an impulse to anger, but it went as it came.

"So much the worse for you. I think that parson who unearthed your pedigree would have done better if he had held his tongue. I cannot help associating your decline as a family with this other fact—of your want of firmness. Decrepit families imply decrepit wills, decrepit conduct. Heaven, why did you give me a handle for despising you more by informing me of your descent! Here was I thinking you a new-sprung child of nature; there were you, the belated seedling of an effete aristocracy!"

"Lots of families are as bad as mine in that! Retty's family were once large landowners, and so were Dairyman Billett's. And the Debbyhouses, who now are carters, were once the De Bayeux family. You find such as I everywhere; 'tis a feature of our county, and I can't help it."

"So much the worse for the county."

She took these reproaches in their bulk simply, not in their particulars; he did not love her as he had loved her hitherto, and to all else she was indifferent.

They wandered on again in silence. It was said afterwards that a cottager of Wellbridge, who went out late that night for a doctor, met two lovers in the pastures, walking very slowly, without converse, one behind the other, as in a funeral procession, and the glimpse that he obtained of their faces seemed to denote that they were anxious and sad. Returning later, he passed them again in the same field, progressing just as slowly, and as regardless of the hour and of the cheerless night as before. It was only on account of his preoccupation with his own affairs, and the illness in his house, that he did not bear in mind the curious incident, which, however, he recalled a long while after.

During the interval of the cottager's going and coming, she had said to her husband—

"I don't see how I can help being the cause of much misery to you all your life. The river is down there. I can put an end to myself in it. I am not afraid."

"I don't wish to add murder to my other follies," he said.

"I will leave something to show that I did it myself—on account of my shame. They will not blame you then."

"Don't speak so absurdly—I wish not to hear it. It is nonsense to have such thoughts in this kind of case, which is rather one for satirical laughter than for tragedy. You don't in the least understand the quality of the mishap. It would be viewed in the light of a joke by nine-tenths of the world if it were known. Please oblige me by returning to the house, and going to bed."

"I will," said she dutifully.

They had rambled round by a road which led to the well-known ruins of the Cistercian abbey behind the mill, the latter having, in centuries past, been attached to the monastic establishment. The mill still worked on, food being a perennial necessity; the abbey had perished, creeds being transient. One continually sees the ministration of the temporary outlasting the ministration of the eternal. Their walk having been circuitous they were still not far from the house, and in obeying his direction she only had to reach the large stone bridge across the main river, and follow the road for a few yards. When she got back everything remained as she had left it, the fire being still burning. She did not stay downstairs for more than a minute, but proceeded to her chamber, whither the luggage had been taken. Here she sat down on the edge of the bed, looking blankly around, and presently began to undress. In removing the light towards the bedstead its rays fell upon the tester of white dimity; something was hanging beneath it, and she lifted the candle to see what it was. A bough of mistletoe. Angel had put it there; she knew that in an instant. This was the explanation of that mysterious parcel which it had been so difficult to pack and bring; whose contents he would not explain to her, saying that time would soon show her the purpose thereof. In his zest and his gaiety he had hung it there. How foolish and inopportune that mistletoe looked now.

Having nothing more to fear, having scarce anything to hope, for that he would relent there seemed no promise whatever, she lay down dully. When sorrow ceases to be speculative sleep sees her opportunity. Among so many happier moods which forbid repose this was a mood which welcomed it, and in a few minutes the lonely Tess forgot existence, surrounded by the aromatic stillness of the chamber that had once, possibly, been the bridechamber of her own ancestry.

Later on that night Clare also retraced his steps to the house. Entering softly to the sitting-room he obtained a light, and with the manner of one who had considered his course he spread his rugs upon the old horse-hair sofa which stood there, and roughly shaped it to a sleeping-couch. Before lying down he crept shoeless upstairs, and listened at the door of her apartment. Her measured breathing told that she was sleeping profoundly.

"Thank God!" murmured Clare; and yet he was conscious of a pang of bitterness at the thought—approximately true, though not wholly so—that having shifted the burden of her life to his shoulders she was now reposing without care.

He turned away to descend; then, irresolute, faced round to her door again. In the act he caught sight of one of the d'Urberville dames, whose portrait was immediately over the entrance to Tess's bedchamber. In the candle-light the painting was more than unpleasant. Sinister design lurked in the woman's features, a concentrated purpose of revenge on the other sex—so it seemed to him then. The Caroline bodice of the portrait was low—precisely as Tess's had been when he tucked it in to show the necklace; and again he experienced the distressing sensation of a resemblance between them.

The check was sufficient. He resumed his retreat and descended.

His air remained calm and cold, his small compressed mouth indexing his powers of self-control; his face wearing still that terrible sterile expression which had spread thereon since her disclosure. It was the face of a man who was no longer passion's slave, yet who found no advantage in his enfranchisement. He was simply regarding the harrowing contingencies of human experience, the unexpectedness of things. Nothing so pure, so sweet, so virginal as Tess had seemed possible all the long while that he had adored her, up to an hour ago; but

The little less, and what worlds away!

He argued erroneously when he said to himself that her heart was not indexed in the honest freshness of her face; but Tess had no advocate to set him right. Could it be possible, he continued, that eyes which as they gazed never expressed any divergence from what the tongue was telling, were yet ever seeing another world behind her ostensible one, discordant and contrasting.

He reclined on his couch in the sitting-room, and extinguished the light. The night came in, and took up its place there, unconcerned and indifferent; the night which had already swallowed up his happiness, and was now digesting it listlessly; and was ready to swallow up the happiness of a thousand other people with as little disturbance or change of mien.

XXXVI

CLARE AROSE IN THE LIGHT OF A DAWN THAT WAS ASHY AND FURTIVE, AS THOUGH ASsociated with crime. The fireplace confronted him with its extinct embers; the spread supper-table, whereon stood the two full glasses of untasted wine, now flat and filmy; her vacated seat and his own; the other articles of furniture, with their eternal look of not being able to help it, their intolerable enquiry what was to be done? From above there was no sound; but in a few minutes there came a knock at the door. He remembered that it would be the neighbouring cottager's wife, who was to minister to their wants while they remained here.

The presence of a third person in the house would be extremely awkward just now, and, being already dressed, he opened the window and informed her that they could manage to shift for themselves that morning. She had a milk-can in her hand, which he told her to leave at the door. When the dame had gone away he searched in the back quarters of the house for fuel, and speedily lit a fire. There was plenty of eggs, butter, bread, and so on in the larder, and Clare soon had breakfast laid, his experiences at the dairy having rendered him facile in domestic preparations. The smoke of the kindled wood rose from the chimney without like a lotus-headed column; local people who were passing by saw it, and thought of the newly-married couple, and envied their happiness.

Angel cast a final glance round, and then going to the foot of the stairs, called in a conventional voice—

"Breakfast is ready!"

He opened the front-door, and took a few steps in the morning air. When, after a short space, he came back she was already in the sitting-room mechanically readjusting the breakfast things. As she was fully attired, and the interval since his calling her had been but two or three minutes, she must have been dressed or nearly so before he went to summon her. Her hair was twisted up in a large round mass at the back of her head, and she had put on one of the new frocks—a pale blue woollen garment with neck-frillings of white. Her hands and face appeared to be cold, and she had possibly been sitting dressed in the bedroom a long time without any fire. The marked civility of Clare's tone in calling her seemed to have inspired her, for the moment, with a new glimmer of hope. But it soon died when she looked at him.

The pair were, in truth, but the ashes of their former fires. To the hot sorrow of the previous night had succeeded heaviness; it seemed as if nothing could kindle either of them to fervour of sensation any more.

He spoke gently to her, and she replied with a like undemonstrativeness. At last she came up to him, looking in his sharply-defined face as one who had no consciousness that her own formed a visible object also.

"Angel!" she said, and paused, touching him with her fingers lightly as a breeze, as though she could hardly believe to be there in the flesh the man who was once her lover. Her eyes were bright, her pale cheek still showed its wonted roundness, though half-dried tears had left glistening traces thereon; and the usually ripe red mouth was almost as pale as her cheek. Throbbingly alive as she was still, under the stress of her mental grief the life beat so brokenly, that a little further pull upon it would cause real illness, dull her characteristic eyes, and make her mouth thin.

She looked absolutely pure. Nature, in her fantastic trickery, had set such a seal of maidenhood upon Tess's countenance that he gazed at her with a stupefied air.

"Tess! Say it is not true! No, it is not true!"

"It is true."

"Every word?"

"Every word."

He looked at her imploringly, as if he would willingly have taken a lie from her lips, knowing it to be one, and have made of it, by some sort of sophistry, a valid denial. However, she only repeated—

"It is true."

"Is he living?" Angel then asked.

"The baby died."

"But the man?"

"He is alive."

A last despair passed over Clare's face.

"Is he in England?"

"Yes."

He took a few vague steps.

"My position—is this," he said abruptly. "I thought—any man would have thought—that by giving up all ambition to win a wife with social standing, with fortune, with knowledge of the world, I should secure rustic innocence as surely as I should secure pink cheeks; but—However, I am no man to reproach you, and I will not."

Tess felt his position so entirely that the remainder had not been needed. Therein lay just the distress of it; she saw that he had lost all round.

"Angel—I should not have let it go on to marriage with you if I had not known that, after all, there was a last way out of it for you; though I hoped you would never—"

Her voice grew husky.

"A last way?"

"I mean, to get rid of me. You *can* get rid of me."

"How?"

"By divorcing me."

"Good heavens—how can you be so simple! How can I divorce you?"

"Can't you—now I have told you? I thought my confession would give you grounds for that."

"O Tess—you are too, too—childish—unformed—crude, I suppose! I don't know what you are. You don't understand the law—you don't understand!"

"What—you cannot?"

"Indeed I cannot."

A quick shame mixed with the misery upon his listener's face.

"I thought—I thought," she whispered. "O, now I see how wicked I seem to you! Believe me—believe me, on my soul, I never thought but that you could! I hoped you would not; yet I believed, without a doubt, that you could cast me off if you were determined, and didn't love me at—at—all!"

"You were mistaken," he said.

"O, then I ought to have done it, to have done it last night! But I hadn't the courage. That's just like me!"

"The courage to do what?"

As she did not answer he took her by the hand.

"What were you thinking of doing?" he enquired.

"Of putting an end to myself."

"When?"

She writhed under this enquisitorial manner of his. "Last night," she answered.

"Where?"

"Under your mistletoe."

"My good——! How?" he asked sternly.

"I'll tell you, if you won't be angry with me!" she said, shrinking. "It was with the cord of my box. But I could not—do the last thing! I was afraid that it might cause a scandal to your name."

The unexpected quality of this confession, wrung from her, and not volunteered, shook him perceptibly. But he still held her, and, letting his glance fall from her face downwards, he said:

"Now, listen to this. You must not dare to think of such a horrible thing! How could you! You will promise me as your husband to attempt that no more."

"I am ready to promise. I saw how wicked it was."

"Wicked! The idea was unworthy of you beyond description."

"But, Angel," she pleaded, enlarging her eyes in calm unconcern upon him, "it was thought of entirely on your account—to set you free without the scandal of the divorce that I thought you would have to get. I should never have dreamt of doing it on mine. However, to do it with my own hand is too good for me, after all. It is you, my ruined husband, who ought to strike the blow. I think I should love you more, if that were possible, if you could bring yourself to do it, since there's no other way of escape for 'ee. I feel I am so utterly worthless! So very greatly in the way!"

"Ssh!"

"Well, since you say no, I won't. I have no wish opposed to yours."

He knew this to be true enough. Since the desperation of the night her activities had dropped to zero, and there was no further rashness to be feared.

Tess tried to busy herself again over the breakfast-table with more or less success, and they sat down both on the same side, so that their glances did not meet. There was at first something awkward in hearing each other eat and drink, but this could not be escaped; moreover, the amount of eating done was small on both sides. Breakfast over he rose, and telling her the hour at which he might be expected to dinner, went off to the miller's in a mechanical pursuance of the plan of studying that business, which had been his only practical reason for coming here.

When he was gone Tess stood at the window, and presently saw his form crossing the great stone bridge which conducted to the mill premises. He sank behind it, crossed the railway beyond, and disappeared. Then, without a sigh, she turned her attention to the room, and began clearing the table and setting it in order.

The charwoman soon came. Her presence was at first a strain upon Tess, but afterwards an alleviation. At half-past twelve she left her assistant alone in the kitchen, and, returning to the sitting-room, waited for the reappearance of Angel's form behind the bridge.

About one he showed himself. Her face flushed, although he was a quarter of a mile off. She ran to the kitchen to get the dinner served by the time he should enter. He went first to the room where they had washed their hands together the day before, and as he entered the sitting-room the dish-covers rose from the dishes as if by his own motion.

"How punctual!" he said.

"Yes. I saw you coming over the bridge," said she.

The meal was passed in commonplace talk of what he had been doing during the morning at the Abbey Mill, of the methods of bolting and the old-fashioned machinery, which he feared would not enlighten him greatly on modern improved methods, some of it seeming to have been in use ever since the days it ground for the monks in the adjoining conventual buildings—now a heap of ruins. He left the house again in the course of an hour, coming home at dusk, and occupying himself through the evening with his papers. She feared she was in the way, and, when the old woman was gone, retired to the kitchen, where she made herself busy as well as she could for more than an hour.

Clare's shape appeared at the door.

"You must not work like this," he said. "You are not my servant; you are my wife."

She raised her eyes, and brightened somewhat. "I may think myself that—indeed?" she murmured, in piteous raillery. "You mean in name! Well, I don't want to be anything more."

"You *may* think so, Tess! You are. What do you mean?"

"I don't know," she said hastily, with tears in her accents. "I thought I—because I am not respectable, I mean. I told you I thought I was not respectable enough long ago—and on that account I didn't want to marry you, only—only you urged me!"

She broke into sobs, and turned her back to him. It would almost have won round any man but Angel Clare. Within the remote depths of his constitution, so gentle and affectionate as he was in general, there lay hidden a hard logical deposit, like a vein of metal in a soft loam, which turned the edge of everything that attempted to traverse it. It had blocked his acceptance of the Church; it blocked his acceptance of Tess. Moreover, his affection itself was less fire than radiance, and, with regard to the other sex, when he ceased to believe he ceased to follow: contrasting in this with many impressionable natures, who remain sensuously infatuated with what they intellectually despise. He waited till her sobbing ceased.

"I wish half the women in England were as respectable as you," he said, in an ebullition of bitterness against womankind in general. "It isn't a question of respectability, but one of principle!"

He spoke such things as these and more of a kindred sort to her, being still swayed by the antipathetic wave which warps direct souls with such persistence when once their vision finds itself mocked by appearances. There was, it is true, underneath, a back current of sympathy through which a woman of the world might have conquered him. But Tess did not think of this; she took everything as her deserts, and hardly opened her mouth. The firmness of her devotion to him was indeed almost pitiful; quick-tempered as she naturally was, nothing that he could say made her unseemly; she sought not her own; was not provoked; thought no evil of his treatment of her. She might just now have been Apostolic Charity herself returned to a self-seeking modern world.

This evening, night, and morning were passed precisely as the preceding ones had been passed. On one, and only one, occasion did she—the formerly free and independent Tess—venture to make any advances. It was on the third occasion of his starting after a meal to go out to the flour-mill. As he was leaving the table he said "Good-bye," and she replied in the same words, at the same time inclining her mouth in the way of his. He did not avail himself of the invitation, saying, as he turned hastily aside—

"I shall be home punctually."

Tess shrank into herself as if she had been struck. Often enough had he tried to reach those lips against her consent—often had he said gaily that her mouth and breath tasted of the butter and eggs and milk and honey on which she mainly lived, that he drew sustenance from them, and other follies of that sort. But he did not care for them now. He observed her sudden shrinking, and said gently—

"You know, I have to think of a course. It was imperative that we should stay together a little while, to avoid the scandal to you that would have resulted from our immediate parting. But you must see it is only for form's sake."

"Yes," said Tess absently.

He went out, and on his way to the mill stood still, and wished for a moment that he had responded yet more kindly, and kissed her once at least.

Thus they lived through this despairing day or two; in the same house, truly; but more widely apart than before they were lovers. It was evident to her that he was, as he had said, living with paralysed activities, in his endeavour to think of a plan of procedure. She was awe-stricken to discover such determination under such apparent flexibility. His consistency was, indeed, too cruel. She no longer expected forgiveness now. More than once she thought of going away from him during his absence at the mill; but she feared that this, instead of benefiting him, might be the means of hampering and humiliating him yet more if it should become known.

Meanwhile Clare was meditating, verily. His thought had been unsuspended; he was becoming ill with thinking; eaten out with thinking, withered by thinking; scourged out of all his former pulsating flexuous domesticity. He walked about saying to himself, "What's to be done—what's to be done?" and by chance she overheard him. It caused her to break the reserve about their future which had hitherto prevailed.

"I suppose—you are not going to live with me—long, are you, Angel?" she asked, the sunk corners of her mouth betraying how purely mechanical were the means by which she retained that expression of chastened calm upon her face.

"I cannot" he said, "without despising myself, and what is worse, perhaps, despising you. I mean, of course, cannot live with you in the ordinary sense. At present, whatever I feel, I do not despise you. And, let me speak plainly, or you may not see all my difficulties. How can we live together while that man lives?—he being your husband in nature, and not I. If he were dead it might be different. . . . Besides, that's not all the difficulty; it lies in another consideration—one bearing upon the future of other people than ourselves. Think of years to come, and children being born to us, and this past matter getting known—for it must get known. There is not an uttermost part of the earth but somebody comes from it or goes to it from elsewhere. Well, think of wretches of our flesh and blood growing up under a taunt which they will gradually get to feel the full force of with their expanding years. What an awakening for them! What a prospect! Can you honestly say Remain, after contemplating this contingency? Don't you think we had better endure the ills we have than fly to others?"

Her eyelids, weighted with trouble, continued drooping as before.

"I cannot say Remain," she answered, "I cannot; I had not thought so far."

Tess's feminine hope—shall we confess it—had been so obstinately recuperative as to revive in her surreptitious visions of a domiciliary intimacy continued long enough to break down his coldness even against his judgment. Though unsophisticated in the usual sense, she was not incomplete; and it would have denoted deficiency of womanhood if she had not instinctively known what an argument lies in propinquity. Nothing else would serve her, she knew, if this failed. It was wrong to hope in what was of the nature of strategy, she said to herself: yet that sort of hope she could not extinguish. His last representation had now been made, and it was, as she said, a new view. She had truly never thought so far as that, and his lucid picture of possible offspring who would scorn her was one that brought deadly conviction to an honest heart which was humanitarian to its centre. Sheer experience had already taught her that, in some circumstances, there was one thing better than to lead a good life, and that was to be saved from leading any life whatever. Like all who have been previsioned by suffering, she could, in the words of M. Sully-Prudhomme, hear a penal sentence in the fiat, "You shall be born," particularly if addressed to potential issue of hers.

Yet such is the vulpine slyness of Dame Nature, that, till now, Tess had been hoodwinked by her love for Clare into forgetting it might result in vitalisations that would inflict upon others what she had bewailed as misfortune to herself.

She therefore could not withstand his argument. But with the self-combating proclivity of the supersensitive, an answer thereto arose in Clare's own mind, and he almost feared it. It was based on her exceptional physical nature; and she might have used it promisingly. She might have added besides: "On an Australian upland or Texan plain, who is to know or care about my misfortunes, or to reproach me or you?" Yet, like the majority of women, she accepted the momentary presentment as if it were the inevitable. And she may have been right. The intuitive heart of woman knoweth not only its own bitterness, but its husband's, and even if these assumed reproaches were not likely to be addressed to him or to his by strangers, they might have reached his ears from his own fastidious brain.

It was the third day of the estrangement. Some might risk the odd paradox that with more animalism he would have been the nobler man. We do not say it. Yet Clare's love was doubtless ethereal to a fault, imaginative to impracticability. With these natures, corporeal presence is something less appealing than corporeal absence; the latter creating an ideal presence that conveniently drops the defects of the real. She found that her personality did not plead her cause so forcibly as she had anticipated. The figurative phrase was true: she was another woman than the one who had excited his desire.

"I have thought over what you say," she remarked to him, moving her forefinger over the table cloth, her other hand, which bore the ring that mocked them both, supporting her forehead. "It is quite true all of it; it must be. You must go away from me."

"But what can you do?"

"I can go home."

Clare had not thought of that.

"Are you sure?" he enquired.

"Quite sure. We ought to part, and we may as well get it past and done. You once said that I was apt to win men against their better judgment; and if I am constantly before your eyes I may cause you to change your plans in opposition to your reason and wish; and afterwards your repentance and my sorrow will be terrible."

"And you would like to go home?" he asked.

"I want to leave you, and go home."

"Then it shall be so."

Though she did not look up at him, she started. There was a difference between the proposition and the covenant which she had felt only too quickly.

"I feared it would come to this," she murmured, her countenance meekly fixed. "I don't complain, Angel. I—I think it best. What you said has quite convinced me. Yes, though nobody else should reproach me if we should stay together, yet somewhen, years hence, you might get angry with me for any ordinary matter, and knowing what you do of my bygones you yourself might be tempted to say words, and they might be overheard, perhaps by my own children. O, what only hurts me now would torture and kill me then! I will go—to-morrow."

"And I shall not stay here. Though I didn't like to initiate it, I have seen that it was advisable we should part—at least for a while, till I can better see the shape that things have taken, and can write to you."

Tess stole a glance at her husband. He was pale, even tremulous; but, as before, she was appalled by the determination revealed in the depths of this gentle being she had married—the will to subdue the grosser to the subtler emotion, the substance to the conception, the flesh to the spirit. Propensities, tendencies, habits, were as dead leaves upon the tyrannous wind of his imaginative ascendency.

He may have observed her look, for he explained—

"I think of people more kindly when I am away from them"; adding cynically, "God knows; perhaps we will shake down together some day, for weariness; thousands have done it!"

That day he began to pack up, and she went upstairs and began to pack also. Both knew that it was in their two minds that they might part the next morning forever, despite the gloss of assuaging conjectures thrown over their processing because they were of the sort to whom any parting which has an air of finality is a torture. He knew, and she knew, that, though the fascination which each had exercised over the other—on her part independently of accomplishments—would probably in the first days of their separation be even more potent than ever, time must attenuate that effect; the practical arguments against accepting her as a housemate might pronounce themselves more strongly in the boreal light of a remoter view. Moreover, when two people are once parted—have abandoned a common domicile and a common environment—new growths insensibly bud upward to fill each vacated place; unforeseen accidents hinder intentions, and old plans are forgotten.

XXXVII

MIDNIGHT CAME AND PASSED SILENTLY, FOR THERE WAS NOTHING TO ANNOUNCE IT IN the Valley of the Froom.

Not long after one o'clock there was a slight creak in the darkened farmhouse once the mansion of the d'Urbervilles. Tess, who used the upper chamber, heard it and awoke. It had come from the corner step of the staircase, which, as usual, was loosely nailed. She saw the door of her bedroom open, and the figure of her husband crossed the stream of moonlight with a curiously careful tread. He was in his shirt and trousers only, and her first flush of joy died when she perceived that his eyes were fixed in an unnatural stare on vacancy. When he reached the middle of the room he stood still and murmured in tones of indescribable sadness—

"Dead! dead! dead!"

Under the influence of any strongly-disturbing force Clare would occasionally walk in his sleep, and even perform strange feats, such as he had done on the night of their return from market just before their marriage, when he re-enacted in his bedroom his combat with the man who had insulted her. Tess saw that continued mental distress had wrought him into that somnambulistic state now.

Her loyal confidence in him lay so deep down in her heart that, awake or asleep, he inspired her with no sort of personal fear. If he had entered with a pistol in his hand he would scarcely have disturbed her trust in his protectiveness.

Clare came close, and bent over her. "Dead, dead, dead!" he murmured.

After fixedly regarding her for some moments with the same gaze of unmeasurable woe he bent lower, enclosed her in his arms, and rolled her in the sheet as in a shroud. Then lifting her from the bed with as much respect as one would show to a dead body, he carried her across the room, murmuring—

"My poor, poor Tess—my dearest, darling Tess! So sweet, so good, so true!"

The words of endearment, withheld so severely in his waking hours, were inexpressibly sweet to her forlorn and hungry heart. If it had been to save her weary life she would not, by moving or struggling, have put an end to the position she found herself in. Thus she lay in absolute stillness, scarcely venturing to breathe, and, wondering what he was going to do with her, suffered herself to be borne out upon the landing.

"My wife—dead, dead!" he said.

He paused in his labours for a moment to lean with her against the banister. Was he going to throw her down? Self-solicitude was near extinction in her, and in the knowledge that he had planned to depart on the morrow, possibly for always, she lay in his arms in this precarious position with a sense rather of luxury than of terror. If they could only fall together, and both be dashed to pieces, how fit, how desirable.

However, he did not let her fall, but took advantage of the support of the handrail to imprint a kiss upon her lips—lips in the daytime scorned. Then he clasped her with a renewed firmness of hold, and descended the staircase. The creak of the loose stair did not awaken him, and they reached the ground floor safely. Freeing one of his hands from his grasp of her for a moment, he slid back the door-bar and passed out, slightly striking his stockinged toe against the edge of the door. But this he seemed not to mind, and, having room for extension in the open air, he lifted her against his shoulder, so that he could carry her with ease, the absence of clothes taking much from his burden. Thus he bore her off the premises in the direction of the river a few yards distant.

His ultimate intention, if he had any, she had not yet divined; and she found herself conjecturing on the matter as a third person might have done. So easefully had she delivered her whole being up to him that it pleased her to think he was regarding her as his absolute possession, to dispose of as he should choose. It was consoling, under the hovering terror of to-morrow's separation, to feel that he really recognised her now as his wife Tess, and did not cast her off, even if in that recognition he went so far as to arrogate to himself the right of harming her.

Ah! now she knew what he was dreaming of—that Sunday morning when he had borne her along through the water with the other dairymaids, who had loved him nearly as much as she, if that were possible, which Tess could hardly admit. Clare did not cross the bridge with her, but proceeding several paces on the same side towards the adjoining mill, at length stood still on the brink of the river.

Its waters, in creeping down these miles of meadowland, frequently divided, serpentining in purposeless curves, looping themselves around little islands that had no name, returning and re-embodying themselves as a broad main stream further on. Opposite the spot to which he had brought her was such a general confluence, and the river was proportionately voluminous and deep. Across it was a narrow foot-bridge; but now the autumn flood had washed the handrail away, leaving the bare plank only, which, lying a few inches above the speeding current, formed a giddy pathway for even steady heads; and Tess had noticed from the window of the house in the daytime young men walking across upon it as a feat in balancing. Her husband had possibly observed the same performance; anyhow, he now mounted the plank, and, sliding one foot forward, advanced along it.

Was he going to drown her? Probably he was. The spot was lonely, the river deep and wide enough to make such a purpose easy of accomplishment. He might drown her if he would; it would be better than parting to-morrow to lead severed lives.

The swift stream raced and gyrated under them, tossing, distorting, and splitting the moon's reflected face. Spots of froth travelled past, and intercepted weeds waved behind the piles. If they could both fall together into the current now, their arms would be so tightly clasped together that they could not be saved; they would go out of the world almost painlessly, and there would be no more reproach to her, or to him for marrying her. His last half-hour with her would have been a loving one, while if they lived till he awoke his daytime aversion would return, and this hour would remain to be contemplated only as a transient dream.

The impulse stirred in her, yet she dared not indulge it, to make a movement that would have precipitated them both into the gulf. How she valued her own life had been proved; but his—she had no right to tamper with it. He reached the other side with her in safety.

Here they were within a plantation which formed the Abbey grounds, and taking a new hold of her he went onward a few steps till they reached the ruined choir of the Abbey-church. Against the north wall was the empty stone coffin of an abbot, in which every tourist with a turn for grim humour was accustomed to stretch himself. In this Clare carefully laid Tess. Having kissed her lips a second time he breathed deeply, as if a greatly desired end were attained. Clare then lay down on the ground alongside, when he immediately fell into the deep dead slumber of exhaustion, and remained motionless as a log. The spurt of mental excitement which had produced the effort was now over.

Tess sat up in the coffin. The night, though dry and mild for the season, was more than sufficiently cold to make it dangerous for him to remain here long, in his half-clothed state. If he were left to himself he would in all probability stay there till the morning, and be chilled to certain death. She had heard of such deaths after sleep-walking. But how could she dare to awaken him, and let him know what he had been doing, when it would mortify him to discover his folly in respect of her? Tess, however, stepping out of her stone confine, shook him slightly, but was unable to arouse him without being violent. It was indispensable to do something, for she was beginning to shiver, the sheet being but a poor protection. Her excitement had in a measure kept her warm during the few minutes' adventure; but that beatific interval was over.

It suddenly occurred to her to try persuasion; and accordingly she whispered in his ear, with as much firmness and decision as she could summon—

"Let us walk on, darling," at the same time taking him suggestively by the arm. To her relief, he unresistingly acquiesced; her words had apparently thrown him back into his dream, which thenceforward seemed to enter on a new phase, wherein he fancied she had risen as a spirit, and was leading him to Heaven. Thus she conducted him by the arm to the stone bridge in front of their residence, crossing which they stood at the manor-house door. Tess's feet were quite bare, and the stones hurt her, and chilled her to the bone; but Clare was in his woollen stockings, and appeared to feel no discomfort.

There was no further difficulty. She induced him to lie down on his own sofa bed, and covered him up warmly, lighting a temporary fire of wood, to dry any dampness out of him. The noise of these attentions she thought might awaken him, and secretly wished that they might. But the exhaustion of his mind and body was such that he remained undisturbed.

As soon as they met the next morning Tess divined that Angel knew little or nothing of how far she had been concerned in the night's excursion, though, as regarded himself, he may have been aware that he had not lain still. In truth, he had awakened that morning from a sleep deep as annihilation; and during those first few moments in which the brain, like a Samson shaking himself, is trying its strength, he had some dim notion of an unusual nocturnal proceeding. But the realities of his situation soon displaced conjecture on the other subject.

He waited in expectancy to discern some mental pointing; he knew that if any intention of his, concluded over-night, did not vanish in the light of morning, it stood on a basis approximating to one of pure reason, even if initiated by impulse of feeling; that it was so far, therefore, to be trusted. He thus beheld in the pale morning light the resolve to separate from her; not as a hot and indignant instinct, but denuded of the passionateness which had made it scorch and burn; standing in its bones; nothing but a skeleton, but none the less there. Clare no longer hesitated.

At breakfast, and while they were packing the few remaining articles, he showed his weariness from the night's effort so unmistakeably that Tess was on the point of revealing all that had happened; but the reflection that it would anger him, grieve him, stultify him, to know that he had instinctively manifested a fondness for her of which his common sense did not approve; that his inclination had compromised his dignity when reason slept, again deterred her. It was too much like laughing at a man when sober for his erratic deeds during intoxication.

It just crossed her mind, too, that he might have a faint recollection of his tender vagary, and was disinclined to allude to it from a conviction that she would take amatory advantage of the opportunity it gave her of appealing to him anew not to go.

He had ordered by letter a vehicle from the nearest town, and soon after breakfast it arrived. She saw in it the beginning of the end—the temporary end, at least, for the revelation of his tenderness by the incident of the night raised dreams of a possible future with him. The luggage was put on the top, and the man drove them off, the miller and the old waiting-woman expressing some surprise at their precipitate departure, which Clare attributed to his discovery that the mill-work was not of the modern kind which he wished to investigate, a statement that was true so far as it went. Beyond this there was nothing in the manner of their leaving to suggest a *fiasco*, or that they were not going together to visit friends.

Their route lay near the dairy from which they had started with such solemn joy in each other a few days back, and, as Clare wished to wind up his business with Mr. Crick, Tess could hardly avoid paying Mrs. Crick a call at the same time, unless she would excite suspicion of their unhappy state.

To make the call as unobtrusive as possible they left the carriage by the wicket leading down from the high-road to the dairy-house, and descended the track on foot, side by side. The withy-bed had been cut, and they could see over the stumps the spot to which Clare had followed her when he pressed her to be his wife; to the left the enclosure in which she had been fascinated by his harp; and far away behind the cowstalls the mead which had been the scene of their first embrace. The gold of the summer picture was now grey, the colours mean, the rich soil mud, and the river cold.

Over the barton gate the dairyman saw them, and came forward, throwing into his face the kind of jocularity deemed appropriate in Talbothays and its vicinity on the reappearance of the newly-married. Then Mrs. Crick emerged from the house, and several others of their old acquaintance, though Marian and Retty did not seem to be there.

Tess valiantly bore their sly attacks and friendly humours, which affected her far otherwise than they supposed. In the tacit agreement of husband and wife to keep their estrangement a secret they behaved as would have been ordinary. And then, although she would rather there had been no word spoken on the subject, Tess had to hear in detail the story of Marian and Retty. The latter had gone home to her father's and Marian had left to look for employment elsewhere. They feared she would come to no good.

To dissipate the sadness of this recital Tess went and bade all her favourite cows goodbye, touching each of them with her hand, and as she and Clare stood side by side at leaving, as if united body and soul, there would have been something peculiarly sorry in their aspect to one who should have seen it truly; two limbs of one life, as they outwardly were, his arm touching hers, her skirts touching him, facing one way, as against all the dairy facing the other, speaking in their adieux as "we," and yet sundered like the poles. Perhaps something unusually stiff and embarrassed in their attitude, some awkwardness in acting up to their profession of unity, different from the natural shyness of young couples, may have been apparent, for when they were gone Mrs. Crick said to her husband—

"How onnatural the brightness of her eyes did seem, and how they stood like waxen images and talked as if they were in a dream! Didn't it strike 'ee that 'twas so? Tess had always sommat strange in her, and she's not now quite like the proud young bride of a well-be-doing man."

They re-entered the vehicle, and were driven along the roads towards Weatherbury and Stagfoot Lane, till they reached the Lane inn, where Clare dismissed the fly and man. They rested here a while, and entering the Vale were next driven onward towards her home by a stranger who did not know their relations. At a midway point, when Nuttlebury had been passed, and where there were cross-roads, Clare stopped the conveyance and said to Tess that if she meant to return to her mother's house it was here that he would leave her. As they could not talk with freedom in the driver's presence he asked her to accompany him for a few steps on foot along one of the branch roads; she assented, and directing the man to wait a few minutes they strolled away.

"Now, let us understand each other," he said gently. "There is no anger between us, though there is that which I cannot endure at present. I will try to bring myself to endure it. I will let you know where I go to as soon as I know myself. And if I can bring myself to bear it—if it is desirable, possible—I will come to you. But until I come to you it will be better that you should not try to come to me."

The severity of the decree seemed deadly to Tess; she saw his view of her clearly enough; he could regard her in no other light than that of one who had practised gross deceit upon him. Yet could a woman who had done even what she had done deserve all this? But she could contest the point with him no further. She simply repeated after him his own words.

"Until you come to me I must not try to come to you?"

"Just so."

"May I write to you?"

"O yes—if you are ill, or want anything at all. I hope that will not be the case; so that it may happen that I write first to you."

"I agree to the conditions, Angel; because you know best what my punishment ought to be; only—only—don't make it more than I can bear!"

That was all she said on the matter. If Tess had been artful, had she made a scene, fainted, wept hysterically, in that lonely lane, notwithstanding the fury of fastidiousness with which he was possessed, he would probably not have withstood her. But her mood of long-suffering made his way easy for him, and she herself was his best advocate. Pride, too, entered into her submission—which perhaps was a symptom of that reckless acquiescence in chance too apparent in the whole d'Urberville family—and the many effective chords which she could have stirred by an appeal were left untouched.

The remainder of their discourse was on practical matters only. He now handed her a packet containing a fairly good sum of money, which he had obtained from his bankers for the purpose. The brilliants, the interest in which seemed to be Tess's for her life only (if he understood the wording of the will), he advised her to let him send to a bank for safety; and to this she readily agreed.

These things arranged he walked with Tess back to the carriage, and handed her in. The coachman was paid and told where to drive her. Taking next his own bag and umbrella—the sole articles he had brought with him hitherwards—he bade her good-bye; and they parted there and then.

The fly moved creepingly up a hill, and Clare watched it go with an unpremeditated hope that Tess would look out of the window for one moment. But that she never thought of doing, would not have ventured to do, lying in a half-dead faint inside. Thus he beheld her recede, and in the anguish of his heart quoted a line from a poet, with peculiar emendations of his own—

God's not *in his heaven: all's* wrong *with the world!*

When Tess had passed over the crest of the hill he turned to go his own way, and hardly knew that he loved her still.

XXXVIII

As she drove on through Blackmoor Vale, and the landscape of her youth began to open around her, Tess aroused herself from her stupor. Her first thought was how would she be able to face her parents?

She reached a turnpike gate which stood upon the highway to the village. It was thrown open by a stranger, not by the old man who had kept it for many years, and to whom she had been known; he had probably left on New Year's Day, the date when such changes were made. Having received no intelligence lately from her home, she asked the turnpike-keeper for news.

"Oh—nothing, miss," he answered. "Marlott is Marlott still. Folks have died and that. John Durbeyfield, too, hev had a daughter married this week to a gentleman-farmer; not from John's own house, you know; they was married elsewhere; the gentleman being of that high standing that John's own folk was not considered well-be-doing enough to have any part in it, the bridegroom seeming not to know how't have been discovered that John is a old and ancient nobleman himself by blood, with family skillentons in their own vaults to this day, but done out of his property in the time o' the Romans. However, Sir John, as we call 'n now, kept up the wedding-day as well as he could, and stood treat to everybody in the parish; and John's wife sung songs at The Pure Drop till past eleven o'clock."

Hearing this, Tess felt so sick at heart that she could not decide to go home publicly in the fly with her luggage and belongings. She asked the turnpike-keeper if she might deposit her things at his house for a while, and, on his offering no objection, she dismissed her carriage, and went on to the village alone by a back lane.

At sight of her father's chimney she asked herself how she could possibly enter the house? Inside that cottage her relations were calmly supposing her far away on a wedding-tour with a comparatively rich man, who was to conduct her to bouncing prosperity; while here she was, friendless, creeping up to the old door quite by herself, with no better place to go to in the world.

She did not reach the house unobserved. Just by the garden-hedge she was met by a girl who knew her—one of the two or three with whom she had been intimate at school. After making a few enquiries as to how Tess came there, her friend, unheeding her tragic look, interrupted with—

"But where's thy gentleman, Tess?"

Tess hastily explained that he had been called away on business, and, leaving her interlocutor, clambered over the garden-hedge, and thus made her way to the house.

As she went up the garden-path she heard her mother singing by the back-door, coming in sight of which she perceived Mrs. Durbeyfield on the door-step in the act of wringing a sheet. Having performed this without observing Tess, she went indoors, and her daughter followed her.

The washing-tub stood in the same old place on the same old quarter-hogshead, and her mother, having thrown the sheet aside, was about to plunge her arms in anew.

"Why—Tess!—my chil'—I thought you was married!—married really and truly this time—we sent the cider—"

"Yes, mother; so I am."

"Going to be?"

"No—I am married."

"Married! Then where's thy husband?"

"Oh, he's gone away for a time."

"Gone away! When was you married, then? The day you said?"

"Yes, Tuesday, mother."

"And now 'tis on'y Saturday, and he gone away?"

"Yes; he's gone."

"What's the meaning o' that? 'Nation seize such husbands as you seem to get, say I!"

"Mother!" Tess went across to Joan Durbeyfield, laid her face upon the matron's bosom, and burst into sobs. "I don't know how to tell 'ee, mother! You said to me, and wrote to me, that I was not to tell him. But I did tell him—I couldn't help it—and he went away!"

"O you little fool—you little fool!" burst out Mrs. Durbeyfield, splashing Tess and herself in her agitation. "My good God! that ever I should ha' lived to say it, but I say it again, you little fool!"

Tess was convulsed with weeping, the tension of so many days having relaxed at last.

"I know it—I know—I know!" she gasped through her sobs. "But, O my mother, I could not help it! He was so good—and I felt the wickedness of trying to blind him as to what had happened! If—if—it were to be done again—I should do the same. I could not—I dared not—so sin—against him!"

"But you sinned enough to marry him first!"

"Yes, yes; that's where my misery do lie! But I thought he could get rid o' me by law if he were determined not to overlook it. And O, if you knew—if you could only half know how I loved him—how anxious I was to have him—and how wrung I was between caring so much for him and my wish to be fair to him!"

Tess was so shaken that she could get no further, and sank a helpless thing into a chair.

"Well, well; what's done can't be undone! I'm sure I don't know why children o' my bringing forth should all be bigger simpletons than other people's—not to know better than to blab such a thing as that, when he couldn't ha' found it out till too late!" Here Mrs. Durbeyfield began shedding tears on her own account as a mother to be pitied. "What your father will say I don't know," she continued; "for he's been talking about the wedding up at Rolliver's and The Pure Drop every day since, and about his family getting back to their rightful position through you—poor silly man!—and now you've made this mess of it! The Lord-a-Lord!"

As if to bring matters to a focus, Tess's father was heard approaching at that moment. He did not, however, enter immediately, and Mrs. Durbeyfield said that she would break the bad news to him herself, Tess keeping out of sight for the present. After her first burst of disappointment Joan began to take the mishap as she had taken Tess's original trouble, as she would have taken a wet holiday or failure in the potato-crop; as a thing which had come upon them irrespective of desert or folly; a chance external impingement to be borne with; not a lesson.

Tess retreated upstairs, and beheld casually that the beds had been shifted, and new arrangements made. Her old bed had been adapted for two younger children. There was no place here for her now.

The room below being unceiled she could hear most of what went on there. Presently her father entered, apparently carrying in a live hen. He was a foot-haggler now, having been obliged to sell his second horse, and he travelled with his basket on his arm. The hen had been carried about this morning as it was often carried, to show people that he was in his work, though it had lain, with its legs tied, under the table at Rolliver's for more than an hour.

"We've just had up a story about—" Durbeyfield began, and thereupon related in detail to his wife a discussion which had arisen at the inn about the clergy, originated by the fact of his daughter having married into a clerical family. "They was formerly styled 'sir,' like my own ancestry," he said, "though now-a-days their true style, strictly speaking, is 'clerk' only." As Tess had wished that no great publicity should be given to the event, he had mentioned no particulars. He hoped she would remove that prohibition soon. He proposed that the couple should take Tess's own name, d'Urberville, as uncorrupted. It was better than her husbands's. He asked if any letter had come from her that day.

Then Mrs. Durbeyfield informed him that no letter had come, but Tess unfortunately had come herself.

When at length the collapse was explained to him a sullen mortification, not usual with Durbeyfield, overpowered the influence of the cheering glass. Yet the intrinsic quality of the event moved his touchy sensitiveness less than its conjectured effect upon the minds of others.

"To think, now, that this was to be the end o't!" said Sir John. "And I with a family vault under that there church of Kingsbere as big as Squire Jollard's ale-cellar, and my folk lying there in sixes and sevens, as genuine county bones and marrow as any recorded in history. And now to be sure what they fellers at Rolliver's and The Pure Drop will say to me! How they'll squint and glane, and say, 'This is yer mighty match is it; this is yer getting back to the true level of yer forefathers in King Norman's time!' I feel this is too much, Joan; I shall put an end to myself, title and all—I can bear it no longer! . . . But she can make him keep her if he's married her?"

"Why, yes. But she won't think o' doing that."

"D'ye think he really have married her?—or is it like the first—"

Poor Tess, who had heard as far as this, could not bear to hear more. The perception that her word could be doubted even here, in her own parental house, set her mind against the spot as nothing else could have done. How unexpected were the attacks of destiny! And if her father doubted her a little, would not neighbours and acquaintance doubt her much? O, she could not live long at home!

A few days, accordingly, were all that she allowed herself here, at the end of which time she received a short note from Clare, informing her that he had gone to the North of England to look at a farm. In her craving for the lustre of her true position as his wife, and to hide from her parents the vast extent of the division between them, she made use of this letter as her reason for again departing, leaving them under the impression that she was setting out to join him. Still further to screen her husband from any imputation of unkindness to her, she took twenty-five of the fifty pounds Clare had given her, and handed the sum over to her mother, as if the wife of a man like Angel Clare could well afford it, saying that it was a slight return for the trouble and humiliation she had brought upon them in years past. With this assertion of her dignity she bade them farewell; and after that there were lively doing in the Durbeyfield household for some time on the strength of Tess's bounty, her mother saying, and, indeed, believing, that the rupture which had arisen between the young husband and wife had adjusted itself under their strong feeling that they could not live apart from each other.

XXXIX

I T WAS THREE WEEKS AFTER THE MARRIAGE THAT CLARE FOUND HIMSELF DESCENDING THE hill which led to the well-known parsonage of his father. With his downward course the tower of the church rose into the evening sky in a manner of enquiry as to why he had come; and no living person in the twilighted town seemed to notice him, still less to expect him. He was arriving like a ghost, and the sound of his own footsteps was almost an incumbrance to be got rid of.

The picture of life had changed for him. Before this time he had known it but speculatively; now he thought he knew it as a practical man; though perhaps he did not, even yet. Nevertheless humanity stood before him no longer in the pensive sweetness of Italian art, but in the staring and ghastly attitudes of a Wiertz Museum, and with the leer of a study by Van Beers.

His conduct during these first weeks had been desultory beyond description. After mechanically attempting to pursue his agricultural plans as though nothing unusual had happened, in the manner recommended by the great and wise men of all ages, he concluded that very few of those great and wise men had ever gone so far outside themselves as to test the feasibility of their counsel. "This is the chief thing: be not perturbed," said the Pagan moralist. That was just Clare's own opinion. But he was perturbed. "Let not your heart be troubled, neither let it be afraid," said the Nazarene. Clare chimed in cordially; but his heart was troubled all the same. How he would have liked to confront those two great thinkers, and earnestly appeal to them as fellow-man to fellow-men, and ask them to tell him their method!

His mood transmuted itself into a dogged indifference till at length he fancied he was looking on his own existence with the passive interest of an outsider.

He was embittered by the conviction that all this desolation had been brought about by the accident of her being a d'Urberville. When he found that Tess came of that exhausted ancient line, and was not of the new tribes from below, as he had fondly dreamed, why had he not stoically abandoned her, in fidelity to his principles? This was what he had got by apostasy, and his punishment was deserved.

Then he became weary and anxious, and his anxiety increased. He wondered if he had treated her unfairly. He ate without knowing that he ate, and drank without tasting. As the hours dropped past, as the motive of each act in the long series of bygone days presented itself to his view, he perceived how intimately the notion of having Tess as a dear possession was mixed up with all his schemes and words and ways.

In going hither and thither he observed in the outskirts of a small town a red-and-blue placard setting forth the great advantages of the Empire of Brazil as a field for the emigrating agriculturist. Land was offered there on exceptionally advantageous terms. Brazil somewhat attracted him as a new idea. Tess could eventually join him there, and perhaps in that country of contrasting scenes and notions and habits the conventions would not be so operative which made life with her seem impracticable to him here. In brief he was strongly inclined to try Brazil, especially as the season for going thither was just at hand.

With this view he was returning to Emminster to disclose his plan to his parents, and to make the best explanation he could make of arriving without Tess, short of revealing what had actually separated them. As he reached the door the new moon shone upon his face, just as the old one had done in the small hours of that morning when he had carried his wife in his arms across the river to the graveyard of the monks; but his face was thinner now.

Clare had given his parents no warning of his visit, and his arrival stirred the atmosphere of the vicarage as the dive of the kingfisher stirs a quiet pool. His father and mother were both in the drawing-room, but neither of his brothers was now at home. Angel entered, and closed the door quietly behind him.

"But—where's your wife, dear Angel?" cried his mother. "How you surprise us!"

"She is at her mother's—temporarily. I have come home rather in a hurry because I've decided to go to Brazil."

"Brazil! Why they are all Roman Catholics there surely!"

"Are they? I hadn't thought of that."

But even the novelty and painfulness of his going to a Papistical land could no displace for long Mr. and Mrs. Clare's natural interest in their son's marriage.

"We had your brief note three weeks ago announcing that it had taken place," said Mrs. Clare, "and your father sent your godmother's gift to her, as you know. Of course it was best that none of us should be present, especially as you preferred to marry her from the dairy, and not at her home, wherever that may be. It would have embarrassed you, and given us no pleasure. Your bothers felt that very strongly. Now it is done we do not complain, particularly if she suits you for the business you have chosen to follow instead of the ministry of the Gospel. . . . Yet I wish I could have seen her first, Angel, or have known a little more about her. We sent her no present of our own, not knowing what would best give her pleasure, but you must suppose it only delayed. Angel, there is no irritation in my mind or your father's against you for this marriage; but we have thought it much better to reserve our liking for your wife till we could see her. And now you have not brought her. It seems strange. What has happened?"

He replied that it had been thought best by them that she should to go her parents' home for the present, whilst he came there.

"I don't mind telling you, dear mother," he said, "that I always meant to keep her away from this house till I should feel she could come with credit to you. But this idea of Brazil is quite a recent one. If I do go it will be unadvisable for me to take her on this my first journey. She will remain at her mother's till I come back."

"And I shall not see her before you start?"

He was afraid they would not. His original plan had been, as he had said, to refrain from bringing her there for some little while—not to wound their prejudices—feelings— in any way; and for other reasons he had adhered to it. He would have to visit home in the course of a year, if he went out at once; and it would be possible for them to see her before he started a second time—with her.

A hastily prepared supper was brought in, and Clare made further exposition of his plans. His mother's disappointment at not seeing the bride still remained with her. Clare's late enthusiasm for Tess had infected her through her maternal sympathies, till she had almost fancied that a good thing could come out of Nazareth—a charming woman out of Talbothays Dairy. She watched her son as he ate.

"Cannot you describe her? I am sure she is very pretty, Angel."

"Of that there can be no question!" he said, with a zest which covered its bitterness.

"And that she is pure and virtuous goes without question?"

"Pure and virtuous, of course, she is."

"I can see her quite distinctly. You said the other day that she was fine in figure; roundly built; had deep red lips like Cupid's bow; dark eyelashes and brows, an immense rope of hair like a ship's cable; and large eyes violety-bluey-blackish."

"I did, mother."

"I quite see her. And living in such seclusion she naturally had scarce ever seen any young man from the world without till she saw you."

"Scarcely."

"You were her first love?"

"Of course."

"There are worse wives than these simple, rosy-mouthed, robust girls of the farm. Certainly I could have wished—well, since my son is to be an agriculturist, it is perhaps but proper that his wife should have been accustomed to an out-door life."

His father was less enquisitive; but when the time came for the chapter from the Bible which was always read before evening prayers, the vicar observed to Mrs. Clare—

"I think, since Angel has come, that it will be more appropriate to read the thirty-first of Proverbs than the chapter which we should have had in the usual course of our reading?"

"Yes, certainly," said Mrs. Clare. "The words of King Lemuel" (she could cite chapter and verse as well as her husband). "My dear son, your father has decided to read us the chapter in Proverbs in praise of a virtuous wife. We shall not need to be reminded to apply the words to the absent one. May Heaven shield her in all her ways!"

A lump rose in Clare's throat. The portable lectern was taken out from the corner and set in the middle of the fireplace, the two old servants came in, and Angel's father began to read at the tenth verse of the aforesaid chapter—

" 'Who can find a virtuous woman? for her price is far above rubies. She riseth while it is yet night, and giveth meat to her household. She girdeth her loins with strength and strengtheneth her arms. She perceiveth that her merchandise is good; her candle goeth not out by night. She looketh well to the ways of her household, and eateth not the bread of idleness. Her children arise up and call her blessed; her husband also, and he praiseth her. Many daughters have done virtuously, but thou excellest them all.' "

When prayers were over, his mother said—

"I could not help thinking how very aptly that chapter your dear father read applied, in some of its particulars, to the woman you have chosen. The perfect woman, you see, was a working woman; not an idler; not a fine lady; but one who used her hands and her head and her heart for the good of others. 'Her children arise up and call her blessed; her husband also, and he praiseth her. Many daughters have done virtuously, but she excelleth them all.' Well, I wish I could have seen her, Angel. Since she is pure and chaste she would have been refined enough for me."

Clare could bear this no longer. His eyes were full of tears, which seemed like drops of molten lead. He bade a quick good-night to these sincere and simple souls whom he loved so well; who knew neither the world, the flesh, nor the devil in their own hearts; only as something vague and external to themselves. He went to his own chamber.

His mother followed him, and tapped at his door. Clare opened it to discover her standing without, with anxious eyes.

"Angel," she asked, "is there something wrong that you go away so soon? I am quite sure you are not yourself."

"I am not, quite, mother," said he.

"About her? Now, my son, I know it is that—I know it is about her! Have you quarrelled in these three weeks?"

"We have not exactly quarrelled," he said. "But we have had a difference—"

"Angel—is she a young woman whose history will bear investigation?"

With a mother's instinct Mrs. Clare had put her finger on the kind of trouble that would cause such a disquiet as seemed to agitate her son.

"She is spotless!" he replied; and felt that if it had sent him to eternal hell there and then he would have told that lie.

"Then never mind the rest. After all, there are few purer things in nature then an unsullied country maid. Any crudeness of manner which may offend your more educated sense at first, will, I am sure, disappear under the influence or your companionship and tuition."

Such terrible sarcasm of blind magnanimity brought home to Clare the secondary perception that he had utterly wrecked his career by this marriage, which had not been among his early thoughts after the disclosure. True, on his own account he cared very little about his career; but he had wished to make it at least a respectable one on account of his parents and brothers. And now as he looked into the candle its flame dumbly expressed to him that it was made to shine on sensible people, and that it abhorred lighting the face of a dupe and a failure.

When his agitation had cooled he would be at moments incensed with his poor wife for causing a situation in which he was obliged to practise deception on his parents. He almost talked to her in his anger, as if she had been in the room. And then her cooing voice, plaintive in expostulation, disturbed the darkness, the velvet touch of her lips passed over his brow, and he could distinguish in the air the warmth of her breath.

This night the woman of his belittling deprecations was thinking how great and good her husband was. But over them both there hung a deeper shade than the shade which Angel Clare perceived, namely, the shade of his own limitations. With all his attempted independence of judgment this advanced and well-meaning young man, a sample product of the last five-and-twenty years, was yet the slave to custom and conventionality when surprised back into his early teachings. No prophet had told him, and he was not prophet enough to tell himself, that essentially this young wife of his was as deserving of the praise of King Lemuel as any other woman endowed with the same dislike of evil, her moral value having to be reckoned not by achievement but by tendency. Moreover, the figure near at hand suffers on such occasions, because it shows up its sorriness without shade; while vague figures afar off are honoured, in that their distance makes artistic virtues of their stains. In considering what Tess was not, he overlooked what she was, and forgot that the defective can be more than the entire.

XL

AT BREAKFAST BRAZIL WAS THE TOPIC, AND ALL ENDEAVOURED TO TAKE A HOPEFUL view of Clare's proposed experiment with that country's soil, notwithstanding the discouraging reports of some farm-labourers who had emigrated thither and returned home within the twelve months. After breakfast Clare went into the little town to wind up such trifling matters as he was concerned with there, and to get from the local bank all the money he possessed. On his way back he encountered Miss Mercy Chant by the church, from whose walls she seemed to be a sort of emanation. She was carrying an armful of Bibles for her class, and such was her view of life that events which produced heart-ache in others wrought beatific smiles upon her—an enviable result, although, in the opinion of Angel, it was obtained by a curiously unnatural sacrifice of humanity to mysticism.

She had learnt that he was about to leave England, and observed what an excellent and promising scheme it seemed to be.

"Yes; it is a likely scheme enough in a commercial sense, no doubt," he replied. "But, my dear Mercy, it snaps the continuity of existence. Perhaps a cloister would be preferable."

"A cloister! O, Angel Clare!"

"Well?"

"Why, you wicked man, a cloister implies a monk, and a monk Roman Catholicism."

"And Roman Catholicism sin, and sin damnation. Thou art in a parlous state, Angel Clare."

"*I* glory in my Protestantism!" she said severely.

Then Clare, thrown by sheer misery into one of the demoniacal moods in which a man does despite to his true principles, called her close to him, and fiendishly whispered in her ear the most heterodox ideas he could think of. His momentary laughter at the horror which appeared on her fair face ceased when it merged in pain and anxiety for his welfare.

"Dear Mercy," he said, "you must forgive me. I think I am going crazy!"

She thought that he was; and thus the interview ended, and Clare re-entered the vicarage. With the local banker he deposited the jewels till happier days should arise. He also paid into the bank thirty pounds—to be sent to Tess in a few months, as she might require; and wrote to her at her parents' home in Blackmoor Vale to inform her of what he had done. This amount, with the sum he had already placed in her hands—about fifty pounds—he hoped would be amply sufficient for her wants just at present, particularly as in an emergency she had been directed to apply to his father.

He deemed it best not to put his parents into communication with her by informing them of her address; and, being unaware of what had really happened to estrange the two, neither his father nor his mother suggested that he should do so. During the day he left the parsonage, for what he had to complete he wished to get done quickly.

As the last duty before leaving this part of England it was necessary for him to call at the Wellbridge farmhouse, in which he had spent with Tess the first three days of their marriage, the trifle of rent having to be paid, the key given up of the rooms they had occupied, and two or three small articles fetched away that they had left behind. It was under this roof that the deepest shadow ever thrown upon his life had stretched its gloom over him. Yet when he had unlocked the door of the sitting-room and looked into it, the memory which returned first upon him was that of their happy arrival on a similar afternoon, the first fresh sense of sharing a habitation conjointly, the first meal together, the chatting by the fire with joined hands.

The farmer and his wife were in the fields at the moment of his visit, and Clare was in the rooms alone for some time. Inwardly swollen with a renewal of sentiment that he had not quite reckoned with, he went upstairs to her chamber, which had never been his. The bed was smooth as she had made it with her own hands on the morning of leaving. The mistletoe hung under the tester just as he had placed it. Having been there three or four weeks it was turning colour, and the leaves and berries were wrinkled. Angel took it down and crushed it into the grate. Standing there he for the first time doubted whether his course in this conjecture had been a wise, much less a generous, one. But had he not been cruelly blinded? In the incoherent multitude of his emotions he knelt down at the bedside wet-eyed. "O Tess! If you had only told me sooner, I would have forgiven you!" he mourned.

Hearing a footstep below he rose and went to the top of the stairs. At the bottom of the flight he saw a woman standing, and on her turning up her face recognised the pale, dark-eyed Izz Huett.

"Mr. Clare," she said, "I've called to see you and Mrs. Clare, and to enquire if ye be well. I thought you might be back here again."

This was a girl whose secret he had guessed, but who had not yet guessed his; an honest girl who loved him—one who would have made as good, or nearly as good, a practical farmer's wife as Tess.

"I am here alone," he said; "we are not living here now." Explaining why he had come, he asked, "Which way are you going home, Izz?"

"I have no home at Talbothays Dairy now, sir," she said.

"Why is that?"

Izz looked down.

"It was so dismal there that I left! I am staying out this way." She pointed in a contrary direction, the direction in which he was journeying.

"Well—are you going there now? I can take you if you wish for a lift."

Her olive complexion grew richer in hue.

"Thank 'ee, Mr. Clare," she said.

He soon found the farmer, and settled the account for his rent and the few other items which had to be considered by reason of the sudden abandonment of the lodgings. On Clare's return to his horse and gig Izz jumped up beside him.

"I am going to leave England, Izz," he said, as they drove on. "Going to Brazil."

"And do Mrs. Clare like the notion of such a journey?" she asked.

"She is not going at present—say for a year or so. I am going out to reconnoitre—to see what life there is like."

They sped along eastward for some considerable distance, Izz making no observation.

"How are the others?" he enquired. "How is Retty?"

"She was in a sort of nervous state when I zid her last; and so thin and hollow-cheeked that 'a do seem in a decline. Nobody will ever fall in love wi' her any more," said Izz absently.

"And Marian?"

Izz lowered her voice.

"Marian drinks."

"Indeed!"

"Yes. The dairyman has got rid of her."

"And you!"

"I don't drink, and I bain't in a decline. But—I am no great things at singing afore breakfast now!"

"How is that? Do you remember how neatly you used to turn ' 'Twas down in Cupid's Gardens' and 'The Tailor's Breeches' at morning milking?"

"Ah, yes! When you first came, sir, that was. Not when you had been there a bit."

"Why was that falling-off?"

Her black eyes flashed up to his face for one moment by way of answer.

"Izz!—how weak of you—for such as I!" he said, and fell into reverie. "Then—suppose I had asked *you* to marry me?"

"If you had I should have said 'Yes,' and you would have married a woman who loved 'ee!"

"Really!"

"Down to the ground!" she whispered vehemently. "O my God! did you never guess it till now!"

By and by they reached a branch road to a village.

"I must get down. I live out there," said Izz abruptly, never having spoken since her avowal.

Clare slowed the horse. He was incensed against his fate, bitterly disposed towards social ordinances; for they had cooped him up in a corner, out of which there was no legitimate pathway. Why not be revenged on society by shaping his future domesticities loosely, instead of kissing the pedagogic rod of convention in this ensnaring manner?

"I am going to Brazil alone, Izz," said he. "I have separated from my wife for personal, not voyaging, reason. I may never live with her again. I may not be able to love you; but—will you go with me instead of her?"

"You truly wish me to go?"

"I do. I have been badly used enough to wish for relief. And you at least love me disinterestedly."

"Yes—I will go," said Izz, after a pause.

"You will? You know what it means, Izz?"

"It means that I shall live with you for the time you are over there—that's good enough for me."

"Remember, you are not to trust me in morals now. But I ought to remind you that it will be wrong-doing in the eyes of civilization—Western civilization, that is to say."

"I don't mind that; no woman do when it comes to agony-point, and there's no other way!"

"Then don't get down, but sit where you are."

He drove past the cross-roads, one mile, two miles, without showing any signs of affection.

"You love me very, very much, Izz?" he suddenly asked.

"I do—I have said I do! I loved you all the time we was at the dairy together!"

"More than Tess?"

She shook her head.

"No," she murmured, "not more than she."

"How's that?"

"Because nobody could love 'ee more than Tess did! . . . She would have laid down her life for 'ee. I could do no more."

Like the prophet on the top of Peor Izz Huett would fain have spoken perversely at such a moment, but the fascination exercised over her rougher nature by Tess's character compelled her to grace.

Clare was silent; his heart had risen at these straightforward words from such an un-expected unimpeachable quarter. In his throat was something as if a sob had solidified there. His ear repeated, *"She would have laid down her life for 'ee. I could do no more!"*

"Forget our idle talk, Izz," he said, turning the horse's head suddenly. "I don't know what I've been saying! I will now drive you back to where your lane branches off."

"So much for honesty towards 'ee! O—how can I bear it—how can I—how can I!"

Izz Huett burst into wild tears, and beat her forehead as she saw what she had done.

"Do you regret that poor little act of justice to an absent one? O, Izz, don't spoil it by regret!"

She stilled herself by degrees.

"Very well, sir. Perhaps I didn't know what I was saying, either, wh—when I agreed to go! I wish—what cannot be!"

"Because I have a loving wife already."

"Yes, yes! You have!"

They reached the corner of the lane which they had passed half an hour earlier, and she hopped down.

"Izz—please, please forget my momentary levity!" he cried. "It was so ill-considered, so ill-advised!"

"Forget it? Never, never! O, it was no levity to me!"

He felt how richly he deserved the reproach that the wounded cry conveyed, and, in a sorrow that was inexpressible, leapt down and took her hand.

"Well, but, Izz, we'll part friends, anyhow? You don't know what I've had to bear!"

She was a really generous girl, and allowed no further bitterness to mar their adieux.

"I forgive 'ee, sir!" she said.

"Now, Izz," he said, while she stood beside him there, forcing himself to the mentor's part he was far from feeling; "I want you to tell Marian when you see her that she is to be a good woman, and not to give way to folly. Promise that, and tell Retty that there are more worthy men than I in the world, that for my sake she is to act wisely and well—remember the words—wisely and well—for my sake. I send this message to them as a dying man to the dying; for I shall never see them again. And you, Izzy, you have saved me by your honest words about my wife from an incredible impulse towards folly and treachery. Women may be bad, but they are not so bad as men in these things! On that one account I can never forget you. Be always the good and sincere girl you have hitherto been; and think of me as a worthless lover, but a faithful friend. Promise."

She gave the promise.

"Heaven bless and keep you, sir. Good-bye!"

He drove on; but no sooner had Izz turned into the lane, and Clare was out of sight, than she flung herself down on the bank in a fit of racking anguish; and it was with a strained unnatural face that she entered her mother's cottage late that night. Nobody ever was told how Izz spent the dark hours that intervened between Angel Clare's parting from her and her arrival home.

Clare, too, after bidding the girl farewell, was wrought to aching thoughts and quivering lips. But his sorrow was not for Izz. That evening he was within a feather-weight's turn of abandoning his road to the nearest station, and driving across that elevated dorsal line of South Wessex which divided him from his Tess's home. It was neither a contempt for her nature, nor the probable state of her heart, which deterred him.

No; it was a sense that, despite her love, as corroborated by Izz's admission, the facts had not changed. If he was right at first, he was right now. And the momentum of the course on which he had embarked tended to keep him going in it, unless diverted by a stronger, more sustained force than had played upon him this afternoon. He could soon come back to her. He took the train that night for London, and five days after shook hands in farewell of his brothers at the port of embarkation.

XLI

FROM THE FOREGOING EVENTS OF THE WINTER-TIME LET US PRESS ON TO AN OCTOBER day, more than eight months subsequent to the parting of Clare and Tess. We discover the latter in changed conditions; instead of a bride with boxes and trunks which others bore, we see her a lonely woman with a basket and a bundle in her own porterage, as at an earlier time when she was no bride; instead of the ample means that were projected by her husband for her comfort through this probationary period, she can produce only a flattened purse.

After again leaving Marlott, her home, she had got through the spring and summer without any great stress upon her physical powers, the time being mainly spent in rendering light irregular service at dairy-work near Port-Bredy to the west of the Blackmoor Valley, equally remote from native place and from Talbothays. She preferred this to living on his allowance. Mentally she remained in utter stagnation, a condition which the mechanical occupation rather fostered than checked. Her consciousness was at that other dairy, at that other season, in the presence of the tender lover who had confronted her there—he who, the moment she had grasped him to keep for her own, had disappeared like a shape in a vision.

The dairy-work lasted only till the milk began to lessen, for she had not met with a second regular engagement as at Talbothays, but had done duty as a supernumerary only. However, as harvest was now beginning, she had simply to remove from the pasture to the stubble to find plenty of further occupation, and this continued till harvest was done.

Of the five-and-twenty pounds which had remained to her of Clare's allowance, after deducting the other half of the fifty as a contribution to her parents for the trouble and expense to which she had put them, she had as yet spent but little. But there now followed an unfortunate interval of wet weather, during which she was obliged to fall back upon her sovereigns.

She could not bear to let them go. Angel had put them into her hand, had obtained them bright and new from his bank for her; his touch had consecrated them to souvenirs of himself—they appeared to have had as yet no other history than such as was created by his and her own experiences—and to disperse them was like giving away relics. But she had to do it, and one by one they left her hands.

She had been compelled to send her mother her address from time to time, but she concealed her circumstances. When her money had almost gone a letter from her mother reached her. Joan stated that they were in dreadful difficulty; the autumn rains had gone through the thatch of the house, which required entire renewal; but this could not be done because the previous thatching had never been paid for. New rafters and a new ceiling upstairs also were required, which, with the previous bill, would amount to a sum of twenty pounds. As her husband was a man of means, and had doubtless returned by this time, could she not send them the money?

Tess had thirty pounds coming to her almost immediately from Angel's bankers, and, the case being so deplorable, as soon as the sum was received she sent the twenty as requested. Part of the remainder she was obliged to expend in winter clothing, leaving only a nominal sum for the whole inclement season at hand. When the last pound had gone, a remark of Angel's that whenever she required further resources she was to apply to his father, remained to be considered.

But the more Tess thought of the step the more reluctant was she to take it. The same delicacy, pride, false shame, whatever it may be called, on Clare's account, which had led her to hide from her own parents the prolongation of the estrangement, hindered her owning to his that she was in want after the fair allowance he had left her. They probably despised her already; how much more they would despise her in the character of a mendicant! The consequence was that by no effort could the parson's daughter-in-law bring herself to let him know her state.

Her reluctance to communicate with her husband's parents might, she thought, lessen with the lapse of time; but with her own the reverse obtained. On her leaving their house after the short visit subsequent to her marriage they were under the impression that she was ultimately going to join her husband; and from that time to the present she had done nothing to disturb their belief that she was awaiting his return in comfort, hoping against hope that his journey to Brazil would result in a short stay only, after which he would come to fetch her, or that he would write for her to join him; in any case that they would soon present a united front to their families and the world. This hope she still fostered. To let her parents know that she was a deserted wife, dependent, now that she had relieved their necessities, on her own hands for a living, after the *éclat* of a marriage which was to nullify the collapse of the first attempt, would be too much indeed.

The set of brilliants returned to her mind. Where Clare had deposited them she did not know, and it mattered little, if it were true that she could only use and not sell them. Even were they absolutely hers it would be passing mean to enrich herself by a legal title to them which was not essentially hers at all.

Meanwhile her husband's days had been by no means free from trial. At this moment he was lying ill of fever in the clay lands near Curitiba in Brazil, having been drenched with thunder-storms and persecuted by other hardships, in common with all the English farmers and farm-labourers who, just at this time, were deluded into going thither by the promises of the Brazilian Government, and by the baseless assumption that those frames which, ploughing and sowing on English uplands, had resisted all the weathers to whose moods they had been born, could resist equally well all the weathers by which they were surprised on Brazilian plains.

To return. Thus it happened that when the last of Tess's sovereigns had been spent she was unprovided with others to take their place, while on account of the season she found it increasingly difficult to get employment. Not being aware of the rarity of intelligence, energy, health, and willingness in any sphere of life, she refrained from seeking an indoor occupation; fearing towns, large houses, people of means and social sophistication, and of manners other than rural. From that direction of gentility Black Care had come. Society might be better than she supposed from her slight experience of it. But she had no proof of this, and her instinct in the circumstances was to avoid its purlieus.

The small dairies to the west, beyond Port-Bredy, in which she had served as supernumerary milkmaid during the spring and summer required no further aid. Room would probably have been made for her at Talbothays, if only out of sheer compassion; but comfortable as her life had been there she could not go back. The anti-climax would be too intolerable; and her return might bring reproach upon her idolised husband. She could not have borne their pity, and their whispered remarks to one another upon her strange situation; though she would almost have faced a knowledge of her circumstances by every individual there, so long as her story had remained isolated in the mind of each. It was the interchange of ideas about her that made her sensitiveness wince. Tess could not account for this distinction; she simply knew that she felt it.

She was now on her way to an upland farm in the centre of the county, to which she had been recommended by a wandering letter which had reached her from Marian. Marian had somehow heard that Tess was separated from her husband—probably through Izz Huett—and the good-natured and now tippling girl, deeming Tess in trouble, had hastened to notify to her former friend that she herself had gone to this upland spot after leaving the dairy, and would like to see her there, where there was room for other hands, if it was really true that she worked again as of old.

With the shortening of the days all hope of obtaining her husband's forgiveness began to leave her; and there was something of the habitude of the wild animal in the unreflecting instinct with which she rambled on—disconnecting herself by littles from her eventful past at every step, obliterating her identity, giving no thought to accidents or contingencies which might make a quick discovery of her whereabouts by others of importance to her own happiness, if not to theirs.

Among the difficulties of her lonely position not the least was the attention she excited by her appearance, a certain bearing of distinction, which she had caught from Clare, being superadded to her natural attractiveness. Whilst the clothes lasted which had been prepared for her marriage, these casual glances of interest caused her no inconvenience, but as soon as she was compelled to don the wrapper of a fieldwoman, rude words were addressed to her more than once; but nothing occurred to cause her bodily fear till a particular November afternoon.

She had preferred the country west of the River Brit to the upland farm for which she was now bound, because, for one thing, it was nearer to the home of her husband's father; and to hover about that region unrecognised, with the notion that she might decide to call at the vicarage some day, gave her pleasure. But having once decided to try the higher and drier levels, she pressed back eastward, marching afoot towards the village of Chalk-Newton, where she meant to pass the night.

The lane was long and unvaried, and, owing to the rapid shortening of the days, dusk came upon her before she was aware. She had reached the top of a hill down which the lane stretched its serpentine length in glimpses, when she heard footsteps behind her back, and in a few moments she was overtaken by a man. He stepped up alongside Tess and said—

"Good-night, my pretty maid:" to which she civilly replied.

The light still remaining in the sky lit up her face, though the landscape was nearly dark. The man turned and stared hard at her.

"Why, surely, it is the young wench who was at Trantridge a while—young Squire d'Urberville's friend? I was there at that time, though I don't live there now."

She recognised in him the well-to-do boor whom Angel had knocked down at the inn for addressing her coarsely. A spasm of anguish shot through her, and she returned him no answer.

"Be honest enough to own it, and that what I said in the town was true, though your fancy-man was so up about it—hey, my sly one? You ought to beg my pardon for that blow of his, considering."

Still no answer came from Tess. There seemed only one escape for her hunted soul. She suddenly took to her heels with the speed of the wind, and, without looking behind her, ran along the road till she came to a gate which opened directly into a plantation. Into this she plunged, and did not pause till she was deep enough in its shade to be safe against any possibility of discovery.

Under foot the leaves were dry, and the foliage of some holly-bushes which grew among the deciduous trees was dense enough to keep off draughts. She scraped together the dead leaves till she had formed them into a large heap, making a sort of nest in the middle. Into this Tess crept.

Such sleep as she got was naturally fitful; she fancied she heard strange noises, but persuaded herself that they were caused by the breeze. She thought of her husband in some vague warm clime on the other side of the globe, while she was here in the cold. Was there another such a wretched being as she in the world? Tess asked herself; and, thinking of her wasted life, said, "All is vanity." She repeated the words mechanically, till she reflected that this was a most inadequate thought for modern days. Solomon had thought as far as that more than two thousand years ago; she herself, though not in the van of thinkers, had got much further. If all were only vanity, who would mind it? All was, alas, worse than vanity—injustice, punishment, exaction, death. The wife of Angel Clare put her hand to her brow, and felt its curve, and the edges of her eye-sockets perceptible under the soft skin, and thought as she did so that a time would come when that bone would be bare. "I wish it were now," she said.

In the midst of these whimsical fancies she heard a new strange sound among the leaves. It might be the wind; yet there was scarcely any wind. Sometimes it was a palpitation, sometimes a flutter; sometimes it was a sort of gasp or gurgle. Soon she was certain that the noises came from wild creatures of some kind, the more so when, originating in the boughs overhead, they were followed by the fall of a heavy body upon the ground. Had she been ensconced here under other and more pleasant conditions she would have become alarmed; but, outside humanity, she had at present no fear.

Day at length broke in the sky. When it had been day aloft for some little while it became day in the wood.

Directly the assuring and prosaic light of the world's active hours had grown strong she crept from under her hillock of leaves, and looked around boldly. Then she perceived what had been going on to disturb her. The plantation wherein she had taken shelter ran down at this spot into a peak, which ended it hitherward, outside the hedge being arable ground. Under the trees several pheasants lay about, their rich plumage dabbled with blood; some were dead, some feebly twitching a wing, some staring up at the sky, some pulsating quickly, some contorted, some stretched out—all of them writhing in agony, except the fortunate ones whose tortures had ended during the night by the inability of nature to bear more.

Tess guessed at once the meaning of this. The birds had been driven down into this corner the day before by some shooting-party; and while those that had dropped dead under the shot, or had died before night-fall, had been searched for and carried off, many badly wounded birds had escaped and hidden themselves away, or risen among the thick boughs, where they had maintained their position till they grew weaker with loss of blood in the night-time, when they had fallen one by one as she had heard them.

She had occasionally caught glimpses of these men in girlhood, looking over hedges, or peeping through bushes, and pointing their guns, strangely accoutred, a bloodthirsty light in their eyes. She had been told that, rough and brutal as they seemed just then, they were not like this all the year round, but were, in fact, quite civil persons save during certain weeks of autumn and winter, when, like the inhabitants of the Malay Peninsula, they ran amuck, and made it their purpose to destroy life—in this case harmless feathered creatures, brought into being by artificial means solely to gratify these propensities—at once so unmannerly and so unchivalrous towards their weaker fellows in Nature's teeming family.

With the impulse of a soul who could feel for kindred sufferers as much as for herself, Tess's first thought was to put the still living birds out of their torture, and to this end with her own hands she broke the necks of as many as she could find, leaving them to lie where she had found them till the gamekeepers should come—as they probably would come—to look for them a second time.

"Poor darlings—to suppose myself the most miserable being on earth in the sight o' such misery as yours!" she exclaimed, her tears running down as she killed the birds tenderly. "And not a twinge of bodily pain about me! I be not mangled, and I be not bleeding, and I have two hands to feed and clothe me." She was ashamed of herself for her gloom of the night, based on nothing more tangible than a sense of condemnation under an arbitrary law of society which had no foundation in Nature.

XLII

IT WAS NOW BROAD DAY, AND SHE STARTED AGAIN, EMERGING CAUTIOUSLY UPON THE highway. But there was no need for caution; not a soul was at hand, and Tess went onward with fortitude, her recollection of the birds' silent endurance of their night of agony impressing upon her the relativity of sorrows and the tolerable nature of her own, if she could once rise high enough to despise opinion. But that she could not do so long as it was held by Clare.

She reached Chalk-Newton, and breakfasted at an inn, where several young men were troublesomely complimentary to her good looks. Somehow she felt hopeful, for was it not possible that her husband also might say these same things to her even yet? She was bound to take care of herself on the chance of it, and keep off these casual lovers. To this end Tess resolved to run no further risks from her appearance. As soon as she got out of the village she entered a thicket and took from her basket one of the oldest field-gowns, which she had never put on even at the dairy—never since she had worked among the stubble at Marlott. She also, by a felicitous thought, took a handkerchief from her bundle and tied it round her face under her bonnet, covering her chin and half her cheeks and temples, as if she were suffering from toothache. Then with her little scissors, by the aid of a pocket looking-glass, she mercilessly nipped her eyebrows off, and thus ensured against aggressive admiration she went on her uneven way.

"What a mommet of a maid!" said the next man who met her to a companion.

Tears came into her eyes for very pity of herself as she heard him.

"But I don't care!" she said. "O no—I don't care! I'll always be ugly now, because Angel is not here, and I have nobody to take care of me. My husband that was is gone away, and never will love me any more; but I love him just the same, and hate all other men, and like to make 'em think scornfully of me!"

Thus Tess walks on; a figure which is part of the landscape; a fieldwoman pure and simple, in winter guise; a grey serge cape, a red woollen cravat, a stuff skirt covered by a whitey-brown rough wrapper, and buff-leather gloves. Every thread of that old attire has become faded and thin under the stroke of raindrops, the burn of sunbeams, and the stress of winds. There is no sign of young passion in her now—

> *The maiden's mouth is cold*
> *. . . . .*
> *Fold over simple fold*
> *Binding her head.*

Inside this exterior, over which the eye might have roved as over a thing scarcely percipient, almost inorganic, there was the record of a pulsing life which had learnt too well, for its years, of the dust and ashes of things, of the cruelty of lust and the fragility of love.

Next day the weather was bad, but she trudged on, the honesty, directness, and impartiality of elemental enmity disconcerting her but little. Her object being a winter's occupation and a winter's home, there was no time to lose. Her experience of short hirings had been such that she was determined to accept no more.

Thus she went forward from farm to farm in the direction of the place whence Marian had written to her, which she determined to make use of as a last shift only, its rumoured stringencies being the reverse of tempting. First she enquired for the lighter kinds of employment, and, as acceptance in any variety of these grew hopeless, applied next for the less light, till, beginning with the dairy and poultry tendance that she liked best, she ended with the heavy and course pursuits which she liked least—work on arable land: work of such roughness, indeed, as she would never have deliberately volunteered for.

Towards the second evening she reached the irregular chalk table-land or plateau, bosomed with semi-globular tumuli—as if Cybele the Many-breasted were supinely extended there—which stretched between the valley of her birth and the valley of her love.

Here the air was dry and cold, and the long cart-roads were blown white and dusty within a few hours after rain. There were few trees, or none, those that would have grown in the hedges being mercilessly plashed down with the quickset by the tenant-farmers, the natural enemies of tree, bush, and brake. In the middle distance ahead of her she could see the summits of Bulbarrow and of Nettlecombe Tout, and they seemed friendly. They had a low and unassuming aspect from this upland, though as approached on the other side from Blackmoor in her childhood they were as lofty bastions against the sky. Southerly, at many miles' distance, and over the hills and ridges coastward, she could discern a surface like polished steel: it was the English Channel at a point far out towards France.

Before her, in a slight depression, were the remains of a village. She had, in fact, reached Flintcomb-Ash, the place of Marian's sojourn. There seemed to be no help for it; hither she was doomed to come. The stubborn soil around her showed plainly enough that the kind of labour in demand here was of the roughest kind; but it was time to rest from searching, and she resolved to stay, particularly as it began to rain. At the entrance to the village was a cottage whose gable jutted into the road, and before applying for a lodging she stood under its shelter, and watched the evening close in.

"Who would think I was Mrs. Angel Clare!" she said.

The wall felt warm to her back and shoulders, and she found that immediately within the gable was the cottage fireplace, the heat of which came through the bricks. She warmed her hands upon them, and also put her cheek—red and moist with the drizzle—against their comforting surface. The wall seemed to be the only friend she had. She had so little wish to leave it that she could have stayed there all night.

Tess could hear the occupants of the cottage—gathered together after their day's labour—talking to each other within, and the rattle of their supper-plates was also audible. But in the village-street she had seen no soul as yet. The solitude was at last broken by the approach of one feminine figure, who, though the evening was cold, wore the print gown and the tilt-bonnet of summer-time. Tess instinctively thought it might be Marian, and when she came near enough to be distinguishable in the gloom surely enough it was she. Marian was even stouter and redder in the face than formerly, and decidedly shabbier in attire. At any previous period of her existence Tess would hardly have cared to renew the acquaintance in such conditions; but her loneliness was excessive, and she responded readily to Marian's greeting.

Marian was quite respectful in her enquiries, but seemed much moved by the fact that Tess should still continue in no better condition than at first; though she had dimly heard of the separation.

"Tess—Mrs. Clare—the dear wife of dear he! And is it really so bad as this, my child? Why is your cwomely face tied up in such a way? Anybody been beating 'ee? Not *he?*"

"No, no, no! I merely did it not to be clipsed or colled, Marian."

She pulled off in disgust a bandage which could suggest such wild thoughts.

"And you've got no collar on" (Tess had been accustomed to wear a little white collar at the dairy).

"I know it, Marian."

"You've lost it travelling."

"I've not lost it. The truth is, I don't care anything about my looks; and so I didn't put it on."

"And you don't wear your wedding-ring?"

"Yes, I do; but not in public. I wear it round my neck on a ribbon. I don't wish people to think who I am by marriage, or that I am married at all; it would be so awkward while I lead my present life."

Marian paused.

"But you *be* a gentleman's wife; and it seems hardly fair that you should live like this!"

"O yes it is, quite fair; though I am very unhappy."

"Well, well. *He* married you—and you can be unhappy!"

"Wives are unhappy sometimes; from no fault of their husbands—from their own."

"You've no faults, deary; that I'm sure of. And he's none. So it must be something outside ye both."

"Marian, dear Marian, will you do me a good turn without asking questions? My husband has gone abroad, and somehow I have overrun my allowance, so that I have to fall back upon my old work for a time. Do not call me Mrs. Clare, but Tess, as before. Do they want a hand here?"

"O yes; they'll take one always, because few care to come. 'Tis a starve-acre place. Corn and swedes are all they grow. Though I be here myself, I feel 'tis a pity for such as you to come."

"But you used to be as good a dairywoman as I."

"Yes; but I've got out o' that since I took to drink. Lord, that's the only comfort I've got now! If you engage, you'll be set swede-hacking. That's what I be doing; but you won't like it."

"O—anything! Will you speak for me?"

"You will do better by speaking for yourself."

"Very well. Now, Marian, remember—nothing about *him*, if I get the place. I don't wish to bring his name down to the dirt."

Marian, who was really a trustworthy girl though of coarser grain than Tess, promised anything she asked.

"This is pay-night," she said, "and if you were to come with me you would know at once. I be real sorry that you are not happy; but 'tis because he's away, I know. You couldn't be unhappy if he were here, even if he gie'd ye no money—even if used you like a drudge."

"That's true; I could not!"

They walked on together, and soon reached the farmhouse, which was almost sublime in its dreariness. There was not a tree within sight; there was not, at this season, a green pasture—nothing but fallow and turnips everywhere; in large fields divided by hedges plashed to unrelieved levels.

Tess waited outside the door of the farmhouse till the group of work-folk had received their wages, and then Marian introduced her. The farmer himself, it appeared, was not at home, but his wife, who represented him this evening, made no objection to hiring Tess, on her agreeing to remain till Old Lady-Day. Female field-labour was seldom offered now, and its cheapness made it profitable for tasks which women could perform as readily as men.

Having signed the agreement, there was nothing more for Tess to do at present than to get a lodging, and she found one in the house at whose gable-wall she had warmed herself. It was a poor subsistence that she had ensured, but it would afford a shelter for the winter at any rate.

That night she wrote to inform her parents of her new address, in case a letter should arrive at Marlott from her husband. But she did not tell them of the sorriness of her situation: it might have brought reproach upon him.

XLIII

THERE WAS NO EXAGGERATION IN MARIAN'S DEFINITION OF FLINTCOMB-ASH FARM AS A starve-acre place. The single fat thing on the soil was Marian herself; and she was an importation. Of the three classes of village, the village cared for by its lord, the village cared for by itself, and the village uncared for either by itself or by its lord (in other words, the village of a resident squires's tenantry, the village of free or copy-holders, and the absentee-owner's village, farmed with the land) this place, Flintcomb-Ash, was the third.

But Tess set to work. Patience, that blending of moral courage with physical timidity, was now no longer a minor feature in Mrs. Angel Clare; and it sustained her.

The swede-field in which she and her companion were set hacking was a stretch of a hundred odd acres, in one patch, on the highest ground of the farm, rising above stony lanchets or lynchets—the outcrop of siliceous veins in the chalk formation, composed of myriads of loose white flints in bulbous, cusped, and phallic shapes. The upper half of each turnip had been eaten off by the live-stock, and it was the business of the two women to grub up the lower or earthy half of the root with a hooked fork called a hacker, that it might be eaten also. Every leaf of the vegetable having already been consumed, the whole field was in colour a desolate drab; it was a complexion without features, as if a face, from chin to brow, should be only an expanse of skin. The sky wore, in another colour, the same likeness; a white vacuity of countenance with the lineaments gone. So these two upper and nether visages confronted each other all day long, the white face looking down on the brown face, and the brown face looking up at the white face, without anything standing between them but the two girls crawling over the surface of the former like flies.

Nobody came near them, and their movements showed a mechanical regularity; their forms standing enshrouded in Hessian "wroppers"—sleeved brown pinafores, tied behind to the bottom, to keep their gowns from blowing about—scant skirts revealing boots that reached high up the ankles, and yellow sheepskin gloves with gauntlets. The pensive character which the curtained hood lent to their bent heads would have reminded the observer of some early Italian conception of the two Marys.

They worked on hour after hour, unconscious of the forlorn aspect they bore in the landscape, not thinking of the justice or injustice of their lot. Even in such a position as theirs it was possible to exist in a dream. In the afternoon the rain came on again, and Marian said that they need not work any more. But if they did not work they would not be paid; so they worked on. It was so high a situation, this field, that the rain had no occasion to fall, but raced along horizontally upon the yelling wind, sticking into them like glass splinters till they were wet through. Tess had not known till now what was really meant by that. There are degrees of dampness, and a very little is called being wet through in common talk. But to stand working slowly in a field, and feel the creep of rain-water, first in legs and shoulders, then on hips and head, then at back, front, and sides, and yet to work on till the leaden light diminishes and marks that the sun is down, demands a distinct modicum of stoicism, even of valour.

Yet they did not feel the wetness so much as might be supposed. They were both young, and they were talking of the time when they lived and loved together at Talbothays Dairy, that happy green tract of land where summer had been liberal in her gifts; in substance to all, emotionally to these. Tess would fain not have conversed with Marian of the man who was legally, if not actually, her husband; but the irresistible fascination of the subject betrayed her into reciprocating Marian's remarks. And thus, as has been said, though the damp curtains of their bonnets flapped smartly into their faces, and their wrappers clung about them to wearisomeness, they lived all this afternoon in memories of green, sunny, romantic Talbothays.

"You can see a gleam of a hill within a few miles o' Froom Valley from here when 'tis fine," said Marian.

"Ah! Can you?" said Tess, awake to the new value of this locality.

So the two forces were at work here as everywhere, the inherent will to enjoy, and the circumstantial will against enjoyment. Marian's will had a method of assisting itself by taking from her pocket as the afternoon wore on a pint bottle corked with white rag, from which she invited Tess to drink. Tess's unassisted power of dreaming, however, being enough for her sublimation at present, she declined except the merest sip, and then Marian took a pull from the spirits.

"I've got used to it," she said, "and can't leave it off now. 'Tis my only comfort—You see I lost him: you didn't; and you can do without it perhaps."

Tess thought her loss as great as Marian's, but upheld by the dignity of being Angel's wife, in the letter at least, she accepted Marian's differentiation.

Amid this scene Tess slaved in the morning frosts and in the afternoon rains. When it was not swede-grubbing it was swede-trimming, in which process they sliced off the earth and the fibres with a bill-hook before storing the roots for future use. At this occupation they could shelter themselves by a thatched hurdle if it rained; but if it was frosty even their thick leather gloves could not prevent the frozen masses they handled from biting their fingers. Still Tess hoped. She had a conviction that sooner or later the magnanimity which she persisted in reckoning as a chief ingredient of Clare's character would lead him to rejoin her.

Marian, primed to a humorous mood, would discover the queer-shaped flints afore-said, and shriek with laughter, Tess remaining severely obtuse. They often looked across the country to where the Var or Froom was know to stretch, even though they might not be able to see it; and, fixing their eyes on the cloaking grey mist, imagined the old times they had spent out there.

"Ah," said Marian, "how I should like another or two of our old set to come here! Then we could bring up Talbothays everyday here a-field, and talk of he, and of what nice times we had there, and o' the old things we used to know, and make it all come back a'most, in seeming!" Marian's eyes softened, and her voice grew vague as the visions returned. "I'll write to Izz Huett," she said. "She's biding at home doing nothing now, I know, and I'll tell her we be here, and ask her to come; and perhaps Retty is well enough now."

Tess had nothing to say against the proposal, and the next she heard of this plan for importing old Talbothays' joys was two or three days later, when Marian informed her that Izz had replied to her enquiry, and had promised to come if she could.

There had not been such a winter for years. It came on in stealthy and measured glides, like the moves of a chess-player. One morning the few lonely trees and the thorns of the hedgerows appeared as if they had put off a vegetable for an animal integument. Every twig was covered with a white nap as of fur grown from the rind during the night, giving it four times its usual stoutness; the whole bush or tree forming a staring sketch in white lines on the mournful grey of the sky and horizon. Cobwebs revealed their presence on sheds and walls where none had ever been observed till brought out into visibility by the crystallising atmosphere, hanging like loops of white worsted from salient points of the outhouses, posts, and gates.

After this season of congealed dampness came a spell of dry frost, when strange birds from behind the North Pole began to arrive silently on the upland of Flintcomb-Ash; gaunt spectral creatures with tragical eyes—eyes which had witnessed scenes of cata-clysmal horror in inaccessible polar regions of a magnitude such as no human being had ever conceived, in curdling temperatures that no man could endure; which had beheld the crash of icebergs and the slide of snow-hills by the shooting light of the Aurora; been half blinded by the whirl of colossal storms and terraqueous distortions; and retained the ex-pression of feature that such scenes had engendered. These nameless birds came quite near to Tess and Marian, but of all they had seen which humanity would never see, they brought no account. The traveller's ambition to tell was not theirs, and, with dumb im-passivity, they dismissed experiences which they did not value for the immediate incidents of this homely upland—the trivial movements of the two girls in disturbing the clods with their hackers so as to uncover something or other that these visitants relished as food.

Then one day a peculiar quality invaded the air of this open country. There came a moisture which was not of rain, and a cold which was not of frost. It chilled the eyeballs of the twain, made their brows ache, penetrated to their skeletons, affecting the surface of the body less than its core. They knew that it meant snow, and in the night the snow came. Tess, who continued to live at the cottage with the warm gable that cheered any lonely pedestrian who paused beside it, awoke in the night, and heard above the thatch noises which seemed to signify that the roof had turned itself into a gymnasium of all the winds. When she lit her lamp to get up in the morning she found that the snow had blown through a chink in the casement, forming a white cone of the finest powder against the inside, and had also come down the chimney, so that it lay sole-deep upon the floor, on which her shoes left tracks when she moved about. Without, the storm drove so fast as to create a snow-mist in the kitchen; but as yet it was too dark out-of-doors to see anything.

Tess knew that it was impossible to go on with the swedes; and by the time she had finished breakfast beside the solitary little lamp, Marian arrived to tell her that they were to join the rest of the women at reed-drawing in the barn till the weather changed. As soon, therefore, as the uniform cloak of darkness without began to turn to a disordered medley of greys, they blew out the lamp, wrapped themselves up in their thickest pinners, tied their woollen cravats round their necks and across their chests, and started for the barn. The snow had followed the birds from the polar basin as a white pillar of a cloud, and individual flakes could not be seen. The blast smelt of icebergs, arctic seas, whales, and white bears, carrying the snow so that it licked the land but did not deepen on it. They trudged onwards with slanted bodies through the flossy fields, keeping as well as they could in the shelter of hedges, which, however, acted as strainers rather than screens. The air, afflicted to pallor with the hoary multitudes that infested it, twisted and spun them eccentrically, suggesting an achromatic chaos of things. But both the young women were fairly cheerful; such weather on a dry upland is not in itself dispiriting.

"Ha-ha! the cunning northern birds knew this was coming," said Marian. "Depend upon't, they keep just in front o't all the way from the North Star. Your husband, my dear, is, I make no doubt, having scorching weather all this time. Lord, if he could only see his pretty wife now! Not that this weather hurts your beauty at all—in fact, it rather does it good."

"You mustn't talk about him to me, Marian," said Tess severely.

"Well, but—surely you care for 'n! Do you?"

Instead of answering, Tess, with tears in her eyes, impulsively faced in the direction in which she imagined South America to lie, and, putting up her lips, blew out a passionate kiss upon the snowy wind.

"Well, well, I know you do. But 'pon my body, it is a rum life for a married couple! There—I won't say another word! Well, as for the weather, it won't hurt us in the wheat-barn; but reed-drawing is fearful hard work—worse than swede-hacking. I can stand it because I'm stout; but you be slimmer than I. I can't think why maister should have set 'ee at it."

They reached the wheat-barn and entered it. One end of the long structure was full of corn; the middle was where the reed-drawing was carried on, and there had already been placed in the reed-press the evening before as many sheaves of wheat as would be sufficient for the women to draw from during the day.

"Why, here's Izz!" said Marian.

Izz it was, and she came forward. She had walked all the way from her mother's home on the previous afternoon, and, not deeming the distance so great, had been belated, arriving, however, just before the snow began, and sleeping at the ale-house. The farmer had agreed with her mother at market to take her on if she came to-day, and she had been afraid to disappoint him by delay.

In addition to Tess, Marian, and Izz, there were two women from a neighbouring village; two Amazonian sisters, whom Tess with a start remembered as Dark Car the Queen of Spades and her junior the Queen of Diamonds—those who had tried to fight with her in the midnight quarrel at Trantridge. They showed no recognition of her, and possibly had none, for they had been under the influence of liquor on that occasion, and were only temporary sojourners there as here. They did all kinds of men's work of preference, including well-sinking, hedging, ditching, and excavating, without any sense of fatigue. Noted reed-drawers were they too, and looked round upon the other three with some superciliousness.

Putting on their gloves all set to work in a row in front of the press, an erection formed of two posts connected by a cross-beam, under which the sheaves to be drawn from were laid ears outward, the beam being pegged down by pins in the uprights, and lowered as the sheaves diminished.

The day hardened in colour, the light coming in at the barn-doors upwards from the snow instead of downwards from the sky. The girls pulled handful after handful from the press; but by reason of the presence of the strange women, who were recounting scandals, Marian and Izz could not at first talk of old times as they wished to do. Presently they heard the muffled tread of a horse, and the farmer rode up to the barn-door. When he had dismounted he came close to Tess, and remained looking musingly at the side of her face. She had not turned at first, but his fixed attitude led her to look round, when she perceived that her employer was the native of Trantridge from whom she had taken flight on the high-road because of his allusion to her history.

He waited till she had carried the drawn bundles to the pile outside, when he said, "So you be the young woman who took my civility in such ill part? Be drowned if I didn't think you might be as soon as I heard of your being hired! Well, you thought you had got the better of me the first time at the inn with your fancy-man, and the second time on the road, when you bolted; but now I think I've got the better of you." He concluded with a hard laugh.

Tess, between the Amazons and the farmer like a bird caught in a clap-net, returned no answer, continuing to pull the straw. She could read character sufficiently well to know by this time that she had nothing to fear from her employer's gallantry; it was rather the tyranny induced by his mortification at Clare's treatment of him. Upon the whole she preferred that sentiment in man and felt brave enough to endure it.

"You thought I was in love with 'ee I suppose? Some women are such fools, to take every look as serious earnest. But there's nothing like a winter a-field for taking that nonsense out o' young wenches' heads; and you've signed and agreed till Lady-Day. Now, are you going to beg my pardon?"

"I think you ought to beg mine."

"Very well—as you like. But we'll see which is master here. Be they all the sheaves you've done to-day?"

"Yes, sir."

" 'Tis a very poor show. Just see what they've done over there" (pointing to the two stalwart women). "The rest, too, have done better than you."

"They've all practised it before, and I have not. And I thought it made no difference to you as it is task work, and we are only paid for what we do."

"Oh, but it does. I want the barn cleared."

"I am going to work all the afternoon instead of leaving at two as the others will do."

He looked sullenly at her and went away. Tess felt that she could not have come to a much worse place; but anything was better than gallantry. When two o'clock arrived the professional reed-drawers tossed off the last half-pint in their flagon, put down their hooks, tied their last sheaves, and went away. Marian and Izz would have done likewise, but on hearing that Tess meant to stay, to make up by longer hours for her lack of skill, they would not leave her. Looking out at the snow, which still fell, Marian exclaimed, "Now, we've got it all to ourselves." And so at last the conversation turned to their old experiences at the dairy; and, of course, the incidents of their affection for Angel Clare.

"Izz and Marian," said Mrs. Angel Clare, with a dignity which was extremely touching, seeing how very little of a wife she was: "I can't join in talk with you now, as I used to do, about Mr. Clare; you will see that I cannot; because, although he is gone away from me for the present, he is my husband."

Izz was by nature the sauciest and most caustic of all the four girls who had loved Clare. "He was a very splendid lover, no doubt," she said; "but I don't think he is a too fond husband to go away from you so soon."

"He had to go—he was obliged to go, to see about the land over there!" pleaded Tess.

"He might have tided 'ee over the winter."

"Ah—that's owing to an accident—a misunderstanding; and we won't argue it," Tess answered, with tearfulness in her words. "Perhaps there's a good deal to be said for him! He did not go away, like some husbands, without telling me; and I can always find out where he is."

After this they continued for some long time in a reverie, as they went on seizing the ears of corn, drawing out the straw, gathering it under their arms, and cutting off the ears with their bill-hooks, nothing sounding in the barn but the swish of the straw and the crunch of the hook. Then Tess suddenly flagged, and sank down upon the heap of wheat-ears at her feet.

"I knew you wouldn't be able to stand it!" cried Marian. "It wants harder flesh than yours for this work."

Just then the farmer entered. "Oh, that's how you get on when I am away," he said to her.

"But it is my own loss," she pleaded. "Not yours."

"I want it finished," he said doggedly, as he crossed the barn and went out at the other door.

"Don't 'ee mind him, there's a dear," said Marian. "I've worked here before. Now you go and lie down there, and Izz and I will make up your number."

"I don't like to let you do that. I'm taller than you, too."

However, she was so overcome that she consented to lie down a-while, and reclined on a heap of pull-tails—the refuse after the straight straw had been drawn—thrown up at the further side of the barn. Her succumbing had been as largely owning to agitation at the reopening the subject of her separation from her husband as to the hard work. She lay in a state of percipience without volition, and the rustle of the straw and the cutting of the ears by the others had the weight of bodily touches.

She could hear from her corner, in addition to these noises, the murmur of their voices. She felt certain that they were continuing the subject already broached, but their voices were so low that she could not catch the words. At last Tess grew more and more anxious to know what they were saying, and, persuading herself that she felt better, she got up and resumed work.

Then Izz Huett broke down. She had walked more than a dozen miles the previous evening, had gone to bed at midnight, and had risen again at five o'clock. Marian alone, thanks to her bottle of liquor and her stoutness of build, stood the strain upon back and arms without suffering. Tess urged Izz to leave off, agreeing, as she felt better, to finish the day without her, and make equal division of the number of sheaves.

Izz accepted the offer gratefully, and disappeared through the great door into the snowy track to her lodging. Marian, as was the case every afternoon at this time on account of the bottle, began to feel in a romantic vein.

"I should not have thought it of him—never!" she said in a dreamy tone. "And I loved him so! I didn't mind his having *you*. But this about Izz is too bad!"

Tess, in her start at the words, narrowly missed cutting off a finger with the bill-hook. "Is it about my husband?" she stammered.

"Well, yes. Izz said, 'Don't 'ee tell her'; but I am sure I can't help it! It was what he wanted Izz to do. He wanted her to go off to Brazil with him."

Tess's face faded as white as the scene without, and its curves straightened. "And did Izz refuse to go?" she asked.

"I don't know. Anyhow he changed his mind."

"Pooh—then he didn't mean it! 'Twas just a man's jest!"

"Yes he did; for he drove her a good-ways towards the station."

"He didn't take her!"

They pulled on in silence till Tess, without any premonitory symptoms, burst out crying.

"There!" said Marian. "Now I wish I hadn't told 'ee!"

"No. It is a very good thing that you have done! I have been living on in a thirtover, lackaday way, and have not seen what it may lead to! I ought to have sent him a letter oftener. He said I could not go to him, but he didn't say I was not to write as often as I liked. I won't dally like this any longer! I have been very wrong and neglectful in leaving everything to be done by him!"

The dim light in the barn grew dimmer, and they could see to work no longer. When Tess had reached home that evening, and had entered into the privacy of her little whitewashed chamber, she began impetuously writing a letter to Clare. But falling into doubt she could not finish it. Afterwards she took the ring from the ribbon on which she wore it next her heart, and retained it on her finger all night, as if to fortify herself in the sensation that she was really the wife of this elusive lover of hers, who could propose that Izz should go with him abroad, so shortly after he had left her. Knowing that, how could she write entreaties to him, or show that she cared for him any more?

XLIV

B Y THE DISCLOSURE IN THE BARN HER THOUGHTS WERE LED ANEW IN THE DIRECTION which they had taken more than once of late—to the distant Emminster vicarage. It was through her husband's parents that she had been charged to send a letter to Clare if she desired; and to write to them direct if in difficulty. But that sense of her having morally no claim upon him had always led Tess to suspend her impulse to send these notes; and to the family at the vicarage, therefore, as to her own parents since her marriage, she was virtually non-existent. This self-effacement in both directions had been quite in consonance with her independent character of desiring nothing by way of favour or pity to which she was not entitled on a fair consideration of her deserts. She had set herself to stand or fall by her qualities, and to waive such merely technical claims upon a strange family as had been established for her by the flimsy fact of a member of that family, in a season of impulse, writing his name in a church-book beside hers.

But now that she was stung to a fever by Izz's tale there was a limit to her powers of renunciation. Why had her husband not written to her? He had distinctly implied that he would at least let her know of the locality to which he had journeyed; but he had not sent a line to notify his address. Was he really indifferent? But was he ill? Was it for her to make some advance? Surely she might summon the courage of solicitude, call at the vicarage for intelligence, and express her grief at his silence. If Angel's father were the good man she had heard him represented to be, he would be able to enter into her heart-starved situation. Her social hardships she could conceal.

To leave the farm on a week-day was not in her power; Sunday was the only possible opportunity. Flintcomb-Ash being in the middle of the cretaceous table-land over which no railway had climbed as yet, it would be necessary to walk. And the distance being fifteen miles each way she would have to allow herself a long day for the undertaking by rising early.

A fortnight later, when the snow had gone, and had been followed by a hard black frost, she took advantage of the state of the roads to try the experiment. At four o'clock that Sunday morning she came downstairs and stepped out into the starlight. The weather was still favourable, the ground ringing under her feet like an anvil.

Marian and Izz were much interested in her excursion, knowing that the journey concerned her husband. Their lodgings were in a cottage a little further along the lane, but they came and assisted Tess in her departure, and argued that she should dress up in her very prettiest guise to captivate the hearts of her parents-in-law; though she, knowing of the austere and Calvinistic tenets of old Mr. Clare, was indifferent, and even doubtful. A year had now elapsed since her sad marriage, but she had preserved sufficient draperies from the wreck of her then full wardrobe to clothe her very charmingly as a simple country girl with no pretensions to recent fashion; a soft grey woollen gown, with white crape quilling against the pink skin of her face and neck, and a black velvet jacket and hat.

" 'Tis a thousand pities your husband can't see 'ee now—you do look a real beauty!" said Izz Huett, regarding Tess as she stood on the threshold between the steely starlight without and the yellow candle-light within. Izz spoke with a magnanimous abandonment of herself to the situation; she could not be—no woman with a heart bigger than a hazel-nut could be—antagonistic to Tess in her presence, the influence which she exercised over those of her own sex being of a warmth and strength quite unusual, curiously overpowering the less worthy feminine feelings of spite and rivalry.

With a final tug and touch here, and a slight brush there, they let her go; and she was absorbed into the pearly air of the fore-dawn. They heard her footsteps tap along the hard road as she stepped out to her full pace. Even Izz hoped she would win, and, though without any particular respect for her own virtue, felt glad that she had been prevented wronging her friend when momentarily tempted by Clare.

It was a year ago, all but a day, that Clare had married Tess, and only a few days less than a year that he had been absent from her. Still, to start on a brisk walk, and on such an errand as hers, on a dry clear wintry morning, through the rarefied air of these chalky hogs'-backs, was not depressing; and there is no doubt that her dream at starting was to win the heart of her mother-in-law, tell her whole history to that lady, enlist her on her side, and so gain back the truant.

In time she reached the edge of the vast escarpment below which stretched the loamy Vale of Blackmoor, now lying misty and still in the dawn. Instead of the colourless air of the uplands the atmosphere down there was a deep blue. Instead of the great enclosures of a hundred acres in which she was now accustomed to toil there were little fields below her of less than half-a-dozen acres, so numerous that they looked from this height like the meshes of a net. Here the landscape was whitey-brown; down there, as in Froom Valley, it was always green. Yet is was in that vale that her sorrow had taken shape, and she did not love it as formerly. Beauty to her, as to all who have felt, lay not in the thing, but in what the thing symbolised.

Keeping the Vale on her right she steered steadily westward; passing above the Hintocks, crossing at right-angles the high-road from Sherton-Abbas to Casterbridge, and skirting Dogbury Hill and High-Stoy, with the dell between them called "The Devil's Kitchen." Still following the elevated way she reached Cross-in-Hand, where the stone pillar stands desolate and silent, to mark the site of a miracle, or murder, or both. Three miles further she cut across the straight and deserted Roman road called Long-Ash Lane; leaving which as soon as she reached it she dipped down a hill by a transverse lane into the small town or village of Evershead, being now about half-way over the distance. She made a halt here, and breakfasted a second time, heartily enough—not at the Sow-and-Acorn, for she avoided inns, but at a cottage by the church.

The second half of her journey was through a more gentle country, by way of Benvill Lane. But as the mileage lessened between her and the spot of her pilgrimage, so did Tess's confidence decrease, and her enterprise loom out more formidably. She saw her purpose in such staring lines, and the landscape so faintly, that she was sometimes in danger of losing her way. However, about noon she paused by a gate on the edge of the basin in which Emminster and its vicarage lay.

The square tower, beneath which she knew that at that moment the vicar and his congregation were gathered, had a severe look in her eyes. She wished that she had somehow contrived to come on a week-day. Such a good man might be prejudiced against a woman who had chosen Sunday, never realising the necessities of her case. But it was incumbent upon her to go on now. She took off the thick boots in which she had walked thus far, put on her pretty thin ones of patent leather, and, stuffing the former into the hedge by the gate-post where she might readily find them again, descended the hill; the freshness of colour she had derived from the keen air thinning away in spite of her as she drew near the parsonage.

Tess hoped for some accident that might favour her, but nothing favoured her. The shrubs on the vicarage lawn rustled uncomfortably in the frosty breeze; she could not feel by any stretch of imagination, dressed to her highest as she was, that the house was the residence of near relations; and yet nothing essential, in nature or emotion, divided her from them: in pains, pleasures, thoughts, birth, death, and after-death, they were the same.

She nerved herself by an effort, entered the swing gate, and rang the door-bell. The thing was done; there could be no retreat. No; the thing was not done. Nobody answered to her ringing. The effort had to be risen to and made again. She rang a second time, and the agitation of the act, coupled with her weariness after the fifteen miles' walk, led her to support herself while she waited by resting her hand on her hip, and her elbow against the wall of the porch. The wind was so nipping that the ivy-leaves had become wizened and grey, each tapping incessantly upon its neighbour with a disquieting stir of her nerves. A piece of blood-stained paper, caught up from some meat-buyer's dust-heap, beat up and down the road without the gate; too flimsy to rest, too heavy to fly away; and a few straws kept it company.

The second peal had been louder, and still nobody came. Then she walked out of the porch, opened the gate, and passed through. And though she looked dubiously at the house-front as if inclined to return, it was with a breath of relief that she closed the gate. A feeling haunted her that she might have been recognised (though how she could not tell), and orders been given not to admit her.

Tess went as far as the corner. She had done all she could do; but determined not to escape present trepidation at the expense of future distress, she walked back again quite past the house, looking up at all the windows.

Ah—the explanation was that they were all at church, everyone. She remembered her husband saying that his father always insisted upon the household, servants included, going to morning-service, and, as a consequence, eating cold food when they came home. It was, therefore, only necessary to wait till the service was over. She would not make herself conspicuous by waiting on the spot, and she started to get past the church into the lane. But as she reached the churchyard gate the people began pouring out, and Tess found herself in the midst of them.

The Emminster congregation looked at her as only a congregation of small country-townsfolk walking home at its leisure can look at a woman out of the common whom it perceives to be a stranger. She quickened her pace, and ascended the road by which she had come, to find a retreat between its hedges till the vicar's family should have lunched, and it might be convenient for them to receive her. She soon distanced the churchgoers, except two youngish men, who, linked arm-in-arm, were beating up behind her at a quick step.

As they drew nearer she could hear their voices engaged in earnest discourse, and, with the natural quickness of a woman in her situation, did not fail to recognise in those noises the quality of her husband's tones. The pedestrians were his two brothers. Forgetting all her plans, Tess's one dread was lest they should overtake her now, in her disorganised condition, before she was prepared to confront them; for though she felt that they could not identify her she instinctively dreaded their scrutiny. The more briskly they walked the more briskly walked she. They were plainly bent upon taking a short quick stroll before going indoors to lunch or dinner, to restore warmth to limbs chilled with sitting through a long service.

Only one person had preceded Tess up the hill—a ladylike young woman, somewhat interesting, though, perhaps, a trifle *guindée* and prudish. Tess had nearly overtaken her when the speed of her brothers-in-law brought them so nearly behind her back that she could hear every word of their conversation. They said nothing, however, which particularly interested her till, observing the young lady still further in front, one of them remarked, "There is Mercy Chant. Let us overtake her."

Tess knew the name. It was the woman who had been destined for Angel's life-companion by his and her parents, and whom he probably would have married but for her intrusive self. She would have known as much without previous information if she had waited a moment, for one of the brothers proceeded to say: "Ah! poor Angel, poor Angel! I never see that nice girl without more and more regretting his precipitancy in throwing himself away upon a dairymaid, or whatever she may be. It is a queer business, apparently. Whether she has joined him yet or not I don't know; but she had not done so some months ago when I heard from him."

"I can't say. He never tells me anything now-a-days. His ill-considered marriage seems to have completed that estrangement from me which was begun by his extraordinary opinions."

Tess beat up the long hill still faster; but she could not outwalk them without exciting notice. At last they outsped her altogether, and passed her by. The young lady still further ahead heard their footsteps and turned. Then there was a greeting and a shaking of hands, and the three went on together.

They soon reached the summit of the hill, and, evidently intending this point to be the limit of their promenade, slackened pace and turned all three aside to the gate whereat Tess had paused an hour before that time to reconnoitre the town before descending into it. During their discourse one of the clerical brothers probed the hedge carefully with his umbrella, and dragged something to light.

"Here's a pair of old boots," he said. "Thrown away, I suppose, by some tramp or other."

"Some imposter who wished to come into the town barefoot, perhaps, and so excite our sympathies," said Miss Chant. "Yes, it must have been, for they are excellent walking-boots—by no means worn-out. What a wicked thing to do! I'll carry them home for some poor person."

Cuthbert Clare, who had been the one to find them, picked them up for her with the crook of his stick; and Tess's boots were appropriated.

She, who had heard this, walked past under the screen of her woollen veil, till, presently looking back, she perceived that the church party had left the gate with her boots and retreated down the hill.

Thereupon our heroine resumed her walk. Tears, blinding tears, were running down her face. She knew that it was all sentiment, all baseless impressibility, which had caused her to read the scene as her own condemnation; nevertheless she could not get over it; she could not contravene in her own defenceless person all these untoward omens. It was impossible to think of returning to the vicarage. Angel's wife felt almost as if she had been hounded up that hill like a scorned thing by those—to her—superfine clerics. Innocently as the slight had been inflicted, it was somewhat unfortunate that she had encountered the sons and not the father, who, despite his narrowness, was far less starched and ironed than they, and had to the full the gift of charity. As she again thought of her dusty boots she almost pitied those habiliments for the quizzing to which they had been subjected, and felt how hopeless life was for their owner.

"Ah!" she said, still sighing in pity of herself, "*they* didn't know that I wore those over the roughest part of the road to save these pretty ones *he* bought for me—no—they did not know it! And they didn't think that *he* chose the colour o' my pretty frock—no—how could they? If they had known perhaps they would not have cared, for they don't care much for him, poor thing!"

Then she grieved for the beloved man whose conventional standard of judgment had caused her all these latter sorrows; and she went her way without knowing that the greatest misfortune of her life was this feminine loss of courage at the last and critical moment through her estimating her father-in-law by his sons. Her present condition was precisely one which would have enlisted the sympathies of old Mr. and Mrs. Clare. Their hearts went out of them at a bound towards extreme cases, when the subtle mental troubles of the less desperate among mankind failed to win their interest or regard. In jumping at Publicans and Sinners they would forget that a word might be said for the worries of Scribes and Pharisees; and this defect or limitation might have recommended their own daughter-in-law to them at this moment as a fairly choice sort of lost person for their love.

Thereupon she began to plod back along the road by which she had come not altogether full of hope, but full of a conviction that a crisis in her life was approaching. No crisis, apparently, had supervened; and there was nothing left for her to do but to continue upon that starve-acre farm till she could again summon courage to face the vicarage. She did, indeed, take sufficient interest in herself to throw up her veil on this return journey, as if to let the world see that she could at least exhibit a face such as Mercy Chant could not show. But it was done with a sorry shake of the head. "It is nothing—it is nothing!" she said. "Nobody loves it; nobody sees it. Who cares about the looks of a castaway like me!"

Her journey back was rather a meander than a march. It had no sprightliness, no purpose; only a tendency. Along the tedious length of Benvill Lane she began to grow tired, and she leant upon gates and paused by milestones.

She did not enter any house till, at the seventh or eighth mile, she descended the steep long hill below which lay the village or townlet of Evershead, where in the morning she had breakfasted with such contrasting expectations. The cottage by the church, in which she again sat down, was almost the first at that end of the village, and while the woman fetched her some milk from the pantry, Tess, looking down the street, perceived that the place seemed quite deserted.

"The people are gone to afternoon service, I suppose?" she said.

"No, my dear," said the old woman. " 'Tis too soon for that; the bells hain't strook out yet. They be all gone to hear the preaching in yonder barn. A ranter preaches there between the services—an excellent, fiery, Christian man, they say. But, Lord, I don't go to hear'n! What comes in the regular way over the pulpit is hot enough for I."

Tess soon went onward into the village, her footsteps echoing against the houses as though it were a place of the dead. Nearing the central part her echoes were intruded on by other sounds; and seeing the barn not far off the road, she guessed these to be the utterances of the preacher.

His voice became so distinct in the still clear air that she could soon catch his sentences, though she was on the closed side of the barn. The sermon, as might be expected, was of the extremest antinomian type; on justification by faith, as expounded in the theology of St. Paul. This fixed idea of the rhapsodist was delivered with animated enthusiasm, in a manner entirely declamatory, for he had plainly no skill as a dialectician. Although Tess had not heard the beginning of the address, she learnt what the text had been from its constant iteration—

"*O foolish Galatians, who hath bewitched you, that ye should not obey the truth, before whose eyes Jesus Christ hath been evidently set forth, crucified among you?*"

Tess was all the more interested, as she stood listening behind, in finding that the preacher's doctrine was a vehement form of the views of Angel's father, and her interest intensified when the speaker began to detail his own spiritual experiences of how he had come by those views. He had, he said, been the greatest of sinners. He had scoffed; he had wantonly associated with the reckless and the lewd. But a day of awakening had come, and, in a human sense, it had been brought about mainly by the influence of a certain clergyman, whom he had at first grossly insulted; but whose parting words had sunk into his heart, and had remained there, till by the grace of Heaven they had worked this change in him, and made him what they saw him.

But more startling to Tess than the doctrine had been the voice, which, impossible as it seemed, was precisely that of Alec d'Urberville. Her face fixed in painful suspense she came round to the front of the barn, and passed before it. The low winter sun beamed directly upon the great double-doored entrance on this side; one of the doors being open, so that the rays stretched far in over the threshing-floor to the preacher and his audience, all snugly sheltered from the northern breeze. The listeners were entirely villagers, among them being the man whom she had seen carrying the red paint-pot on a former memorable occasion. But her attention was given to the central figure, who stood upon some sacks of corn, facing the people and the door. The three o'clock sun shone full upon him, and the strange enervating conviction that her seducer confronted her, which had been gaining ground in Tess ever since she had heard his words distinctly, was at last established as a fact indeed.

END OF PHASE THE FIFTH

PHASE THE SIXTH

THE CONVERT

XLV

TILL THIS MOMENT SHE HAD NEVER SEEN OR HEARD FROM D'URBERVILLE SINCE HER departure from Trantridge.

The rencounter came at a heavy moment, one of all moments calculated to permit its impact with the least emotional shock. But such was unreasoning memory that, though he stood there openly and palpably a converted man, who was sorrowing for his past irregularities, a fear overcame her, paralysing her movement so that she neither retreated nor advanced.

To think of what emanated from that countenance when she saw it last, and to behold it now! . . . There was the same handsome unpleasantness of mien, but now he wore neatly trimmed, old-fashioned whiskers, the sable moustache having disappeared; and his dress was half-clerical, a modification which had changed his expression sufficiently to abstract the dandyism from his features, and to hinder for a second her belief in his identity.

To Tess's sense there was, just at first, a ghastly *bizarrerie*, a grim incongruity, in the march of these solemn words of Scripture out of such a mouth. This too familiar intonation, less than four years earlier, had brought to her ears expressions of such divergent purpose that her heart became quite sick at the irony of the contrast.

It was less a reform than a transfiguration. The former curves of sensuousness were now modulated to lines of devotional passion. The lip-shapes that had meant seductiveness were now made to express supplication; the glow on the cheek that yesterday could be translated as riotousness was evangelised to-day into the splendour of pious rhetoric; animalism had become fanaticism; Paganism Paulinism; the bold rolling eye that had flashed upon her form in the old time with such mastery now beamed with the rude energy of a theolatry that was almost ferocious. Those black angularities which his face had used to put on when his wishes were thwarted now did duty in picturing the incorrigible backslider who would insist upon turning again to his wallowing in the mire.

The lineaments, as such, seemed to complain. They had been diverted from their hereditary connotation to signify impressions for which Nature did not intend them. Strange that their very elevation was a misapplication, that to raise seemed to falsify.

Yet could it be so? She would admit the ungenerous sentiment no longer. D'Urberville was not the first wicked man who had turned away from his wickedness to save his soul alive, and why should she deem it unnatural in him? It was but the usage of thought which had been jarred in her at hearing good new words in bad old notes. The greater the sinner the greater the saint; it was not necessary to dive far into Christian history to discover that.

Such impressions as these moved her vaguely, and without strict definiteness. As soon as the nerveless pause of her surprise would allow her to stir, her impulse was to pass on out of his sight. He had obviously not discerned her yet in her position against the sun.

But the moment that she moved again he recognised her. The effect upon her old lover was electric, far stronger than the effect of his presence upon her. His fire, the tumultuous ring of his eloquence, seemed to go out of him. His lip struggled and trembled under the words that lay upon it; but deliver them it could not as long as she faced him. His eyes, after their first glance upon her face, hung confusedly in every other direction but hers, but came back in a desperate leap every few seconds. This paralysis lasted, however, but a short time; for Tess's energies returned with the atrophy of his, and she walked as fast as she was able past the barn and onward.

As soon as she could reflect it appalled her, this change in their relative platforms. He who had wrought her undoing was now on the side of the Spirit, while she remained unregenerate. And, as in the legend, it had resulted that her Cyprian image had suddenly appeared upon his altar, whereby the fire of the priest had been well-nigh extinguished.

She went on without turning her head. Her back seemed to be endowed with a sensitiveness to ocular beams—even her clothing—so alive was she to a fancied gaze which might be resting upon her from the outside of that barn. All the way along to this point her heart had been heavy with an inactive sorrow; now there was a change in the quality of its trouble. That hunger for affection too long withheld was for the time displaced by an almost physical sense of an implacable past which still engirdled her. It intensified her consciousness of error to a practical despair; the break of continuity between her earlier and present existence, which she had hoped for, had not, after all, taken place. Bygones would never be complete bygones till she was a bygone herself.

Thus absorbed she recrossed the northern part of Long-Ash Lane at right angles, and presently saw before her the road ascending whitely to the upland along whose margin the remainder of her journey lay. Its dry pale surface stretched severely onward, unbroken by a single figure, vehicle, or mark, save some occasional brown horse-droppings which dotted its cold aridity here and there. While slowly breasting this ascent Tess became conscious of footsteps behind her, and turning she saw approaching that well-known form—so strangely accoutred as the Methodist—the one personage in all the world she wished not to encounter alone on this side of the grave.

There was not much time, however, for thought or elusion, and she yielded as calmly as she could to the necessity of letting him overtake her. She saw that he was excited, less by the speed of his walk than by the feelings within him.

"Tess!" he said.

She slackened speed without looking round.

"Tess!" he repeated. "It is I—Alec d'Urberville."

She then looked back at him, and he came up.

"I see it is," she answered coldly.

"Well—is that all? Yet I deserve no more! Of course," he added, with a slight laugh, "there is something of the ridiculous to your eyes in seeing me like this. But—I must put up with that. . . . I heard you had gone away, nobody knew where. Tess, you wonder why I have followed you?"

"I do, rather; and I would that you had not, with all my heart!"

"Yes—you may well say it," he returned grimly, as they moved onward together, she with unwilling tread. "But don't mistake me; I beg this because you may have been led to do so in noticing—if you did notice it—how your sudden appearance unnerved me down there. It was but a momentary faltering; and considering what you had been to me, it was natural enough. But will helped me through it—though perhaps you think me a humbug for saying it—and immediately afterwards I felt that, of all persons in the world whom it was my duty and desire to save from the wrath to come—sneer if you like—the woman whom I had so grievously wronged was that person. I have come with that sole purpose in view—nothing more."

There was the smallest vein of scorn in her words of rejoinder: "Have you saved yourself? Charity begins at home, they say."

"*I* have done nothing!" said he indifferently. "Heaven, as I have been telling my hearers, has done all. No amount of contempt that you can pour upon me, Tess, will equal what I have poured upon myself—the old Adam of my former years! Well, it is a strange story; believe it or not; but I can tell you the means by which my conversion was brought about, and I hope you will be interested enough at least to listen. Have you ever heard the name of the parson of Emminster—you must have done so?—old Mr. Clare; one of the most earnest of his school; one of the few intense men left in the Church; not so intense as the extreme wind of Christian believers with which I have thrown in my lot, but quite an exception among the Established clergy, the younger of whom are gradually attenuating the true doctrines by their sophistries, till they are but the shadow of what they were. I only differ from him on the question of Church and State—the interpretation of the text, 'Come out from among them and be ye separate, saith the Lord'—that's all. He is one who, I firmly believe, has been the humble means of saving more souls in this country than any other man you can name. You have heard of him?"

"I have," she said.

"He came to Trantridge two or three years ago to preach on behalf of some missionary society; and I, wretched fellow that I was, insulted him when, in his disinterestedness, he tried to reason with me and show me the way. He did not resent my conduct, he simply said that some day I should receive the first-fruits of the Spirit—that those who came to scoff sometimes remained to pray. There was a strange magic in his words. They sank into my mind. But the loss of my mother hit me most; and by degrees I was brought to see daylight. Since then my one desire has been to hand on the true view to others, and that is what I was trying to do to-day; though it is only lately that I have preached hereabout. The first months of my ministry have been spent in the North of England among strangers, where I preferred to make my earliest clumsy attempts, so as to acquire courage before undergoing that severest of all tests of one's sincerity, addressing those who have known one, and have been one's companions in the days of darkness. If you could only know, Tess, the pleasure of having a good slap at yourself, I am sure—"

"Don't go on with it!" she cried passionately, as she turned away from him to a stile by the wayside, on which she bent herself. "I can't believe in such sudden things! I feel indignant with you for talking to me like this, when you know—when you know what harm you've done me! You, and those like you, take your fill of pleasure on earth by making the life of such as me bitter and black with sorrow; and then it is a fine thing, when you have had enough of that, to think of securing your pleasure in heaven by becoming converted! Out upon such—I don't believe in you—I hate it!"

"Tess," he insisted; "don't speak so! It came to me like a jolly new idea! And you don't believe me? What don't you believe?"

"Your conversion. Your scheme of religion."

"Why?"

She dropped her voice. "Because a better man than you does not believe in such."

"What a woman's reason! Who is this better man?"

"I cannot tell you."

"Well," he declared, a resentment beneath his words seeming ready to spring out at a moment's notice, "God forbid that I should say I am a good man—and you know I don't say any such thing. I am new to goodness, truly; but new-comers see furthest sometimes."

"Yes," she replied sadly. "But I cannot believe in your conversion to a new spirit. Such flashes as you feel, Alec, I fear don't last!"

Thus speaking she turned from the stile over which she had been leaning, and faced him; whereupon his eyes, falling casually upon the familiar countenance and form, remained contemplating her. The inferior man was quiet in him now; but it was surely not extracted, nor even entirely subdued.

"Don't look at me like that!" he said abruptly.

Tess, who had been quite unconscious of her action and mien, instantly withdrew the large dark gaze of her eyes, stammering with a flush, "I beg your pardon!" And there was revived in her the wretched sentiment which had often come to her before, that in inhabiting the fleshly tabernacle with which nature had endowed her she was somehow doing wrong.

"No, no! Don't beg my pardon. But since you wear a veil to hide your good looks, why don't you keep it down?"

She pulled down the veil, saying hastily, "It was mostly to keep off the wind."

"It may seem harsh of me to dictate like this," he went on; "but it is better that I should not look too often on you. It might be dangerous."

"Ssh!" said Tess.

"Well, women's faces have had too much power over me already for me not to fear them! An evangelist has nothing to do with such as they; and it reminds me of the old times that I would forget!"

After this their conversation dwindled to a casual remark now and then as they rambled onward, Tess inwardly wondering how far he was going with her, and not liking to send him back by positive mandate. Frequently when they came to a gate or stile they found painted thereon in red or blue letters some text of Scripture, and she asked him if he knew who had been at the pains to blazon these announcements. He told her that the man was employed by himself and others who were working with him in that district, to paint these reminders that no means might be left untried which might move the hearts of a wicked generation.

At length the road touched the spot called "Cross-in-Hand." Of all spots on the bleached and desolate upland this was the most forlorn. It was so far removed from the charm which is sought in landscape by artists and view-lovers as to reach a new kind of beauty, a negative beauty of tragic tone. The place took its name from a stone pillar which stood there, a strange rude monolith, from a stratum unknown in any local quarry, on which was roughly carved a human hand. Differing accounts were given of its history and purport. Some authorities stated that a devotional cross had once formed the complete erection thereon, of which the present relic was but the stump; others that the stone as it stood was entire, and that it had been fixed there to mark a boundary or place of meeting. Anyhow, whatever the origin of the relic, there was and is something sinister, or solemn, according to mood, in the scene amid which it stands; something tending to impress the most phlegmatic passer-by.

"I think I must leave you now," he remarked, as they drew near to this spot. "I have to preach at Abbot's-Cernel at six this evening, and my way lies across to the right from here. And you upset me somewhat too, Tessy—I cannot, will not, say why. I must go away and get strength. . . . How is it that you speak so fluently now? Who has taught you such good English?"

"I have learnt things in my troubles," she said evasively.

"What troubles have you had?"

She told him of the first one—the only one that related to him.

D'Urberville was struck mute. "I knew nothing of this till now!" he next murmured. "Why didn't you write to me when you felt your trouble coming on?"

She did not reply; and he broke the silence by adding: "Well—you will see me again."

"No," she answered. "Do not again come near me!"

"I will think. But before we part come here." He stepped up to the pillar. "This was once a Holy Cross. Relics are not in my creed; but I fear you at moments—far more than you need fear me at present; and to lessen my fear, put your hand upon that stone hand, and swear that you will never tempt me—by your charms or ways."

"Good God—how can you ask what is so unnecessary! All that is furthest from my thought!"

"Yes—but swear it."

Tess, half frightened, gave way to his importunity; placed her hand upon the stone and swore.

"I am sorry you are not a believer," he continued; "that some unbeliever should have got hold of you and unsettled your mind. But no more now. At home at least I can pray for you; and I will; and who knows what may not happen? I'm off. Good-bye!"

He turned to a hunting gate in the hedge, and without letting his eyes again rest upon her leapt over, and struck out across the down in the direction of Abbot's-Cernel. As he walked his pace showed perturbation, and by and by, as if instigated by a former thought, he drew from his pocket a small book, between the leaves of which was folded a letter, worn and soiled, as from much rereading. D'Urberville opened the letter. It was dated several months before this time, and was signed by Parson Clare.

The letter began by expressing the writer's unfeigned joy at d'Urberville's conversion, and thanked him for his kindness in communicating with the parson on the subject. It expressed Mr. Clare's warm assurance of forgiveness for d'Urberville's former conduct, and his interest in the young man's plans for the future. He, Mr. Clare, would much have liked to see d'Urberville in the Church to whose ministry he had devoted so many years of his own life, and would have helped him to enter a theological college to that end; but since his correspondent had possibly not cared to do this on account of the delay it would have entailed, he was not the man to insist upon its paramount importance. Every man must work as he could best work, and in the method towards which he felt impelled by the Spirit.

D'Urberville read and reread this letter, and seemed to quiz himself cynically. He also read some passages from memoranda as he walked till his face assumed a calm, and apparently the image of Tess no longer troubled his mind.

She meanwhile had kept along the edge of the hill by which lay her nearest way home. Within the distance of a mile she met a solitary shepherd.

"What is the meaning of that old stone I have passed?" she asked of him. "Was it ever a Holy Cross?"

"Cross—no; 'twer not a cross! 'Tis a thing of ill-omen, Miss. It was put up in wuld times by the relations of a malefactor who was tortured there by nailing his hand to a post and afterwards hung. The bones lie underneath. They say he sold his soul to the devil, and that he walks at times."

She felt the *petite mort* at this unexpectedly gruesome information, and left the solitary man behind her. It was dusk when she drew near to Flintcomb-Ash, and in the lane at the entrance to the hamlet she approached a girl and her lover without their observing her. They were talking no secrets, and the clear unconcerned voice of the young woman, in response to the warmer accents of the man, spread into the chilly air as the one soothing thing within the dusky horizon, full of a stagnant obscurity upon which nothing else intruded. For a moment the voices cheered the heart of Tess, till she reasoned that this interview had its origin, on one side or the other, in the same attraction which had been the prelude to her own tribulation. When she came close the girl turned serenely and recognised her, the young man walking off in embarrassment. The woman was Izz Huett, whose interest in Tess's excursion immediately superseded her own proceedings. Tess did not explain very clearly its results, and Izz, who was a girl of tact, began to speak of her own little affair, a phase of which Tess had just witnessed.

"He is Amby Seedling, the chap who used to sometimes come and help at Talbothays," she explained indifferently. "He actually enquired and found out that I had come here, and has followed me. He says he's been in love wi' me these two years. But I've hardly answered him."

XLVI

Several days had passed since her futile journey, and Tess was a-field. The dry winter wind still blew, but a screen of thatched hurdles erected in the eye of the blast kept its force away from her. On the sheltered side was a turnip-slicing machine, whose bright blue hue of new paint seemed almost vocal in the otherwise subdued scene. Opposite its front was a long mound or "grave," in which the roots had been preserved since early winter. Tess was standing at the uncovered end, chopping off with a bill-hook the fibres and earth from each root, and throwing it after the operation into the slicer. A man was turning the handle of the machine, and from its trough came the newly-cut swedes, the fresh smell of whose yellow chips was accompanied by the sounds of the snuffling wind, the smart swish of the slicing-blades, and the choppings of the hook in Tess's leather-gloved hand.

The wide acreage of blank agricultural brownness, apparent where the swedes had been pulled, was beginning to be striped in wales of darker brown, gradually broadening to ribands. Along the edge of each of these something crept upon ten legs, moving without haste and without rest up and down the whole length of the field; it was two horses and a man, the plough going between them, turning up the cleared ground for a spring sowing.

For hours nothing relieved the joyless monotony of things. Then, far beyond the ploughing-teams, a black speck was seen. It had come from the corner of a fence, where there was a gap, and its tendency was up the incline, towards the swede-cutters. From the proportions of a mere point it advanced to the shape of a ninepin, and was soon perceived to be a man in black, arriving from the direction of Flintcomb-Ash. The man at the slicer, having nothing else to do with his eyes, continually observed the comer, but Tess, who was occupied, did not perceive him till her companion directed her attention to his approach.

It was not her hard taskmaster, Farmer Groby; it was one in a semi-clerical costume, who now represented what had once been the free-and-easy Alec d'Urberville. Not being hot at his preaching there was less enthusiasm about him now, and the presence of the grinder seemed to embarrass him. A pale distress was already on Tess's face, and she pulled her curtained hood further over it.

D'Urberville came up and said quietly—

"I want to speak to you, Tess."

"You have refused my last request, not to come near me!" said she.

"Yes, but I have a good reason."

"Well, tell it."

"It is more serious than you may think."

He glanced round to see if he were overheard. They were at some distance from the man who turned the slicer, and the movement of the machine, too, sufficiently prevented Alec's words reaching other ears. D'Urberville placed himself so as to screen Tess from the labourer, turning his back to the latter.

"It is this," he continued, with capricious compunction. "In thinking of your soul and mine when we last met, I neglected to enquire as to your worldly condition. You were well dressed, and I did not think of it. But I see now that it is hard—harder than it used to be when I—knew you—harder than you deserve. Perhaps a good deal of it is owning to me!"

She did not answer, and he watched her enquiringly, as, with bent head, her face completely screened by the hood, she resumed her trimming of the swedes. By going on with her work she felt better able to keep him outside her emotions.

"Tess," he added, with a sigh of discontent—"yours was the very worst case I ever was concerned in! I had no idea of what had resulted till you told me. Scamp that I was to foul that innocent life! The whole blame was mine—the whole unconventional business of our time at Trantridge. You, too, the real blood of which I am but the base imitation, what a blind young thing you were as to possibilities! I say in all earnestness that it is a shame for parents to bring up their girls in such dangerous ignorance of the gins and nets that the wicked may set for them, whether their motive be a good one or the result of simple indifference."

Tess still did no more than listen, throwing down one globular root and taking up another with automatic regularity, the pensive contour of the mere fieldwoman alone marking her.

"But it is not that I came to say," d'Urberville went on. "My circumstances are these. I have lost my mother since you were at Trantridge, and the place is my own. But I intend to sell it, and devote myself to missionary work in Africa. A devil of a poor hand I shall make at the trade, no doubt. However, what I want to ask you is, will you put it in my power to do my duty—to make the only reparation I can make for the trick played you:

that is, will you be my wife, and go with me? . . . I have already obtained this precious document. It was my old mother's dying wish."

He drew a piece of parchment from his pocket, with a slight fumbling of embarrassment.

"What is it?" said she.

"A marriage licence."

"O no, sir—no!" she said quickly, starting back.

"You will not? Why is that?"

And as he asked the question a disappointment which was not entirely the disappointment of thwarted duty crossed d'Urberville's face. It was unmistakably a symptom that something of his old passion for her had been revived; duty and desire ran hand-in-hand.

"Surely," he began again, in more impetuous tones, and then looked round at the labourer who turned the slicer.

Tess, too, felt that the argument could not be ended there. Informing the man that a gentleman had come to see her, with whom she wished to walk a little way, she moved off with d'Urberville across the zebra-striped field. When they reached the first newly-ploughed section he held out his hand to help her over it; but she stepped forward on the summits of the earth-rolls as if she did not see him.

"You will not marry me, Tess, and make me a self-respecting man?" he repeated, as soon as they were over the furrows.

"I cannot."

"But why?"

"You know I have no affection for you."

"But you would get to feel that in time, perhaps—as soon as you really could forgive me?"

"Never!"

"Why so positive?"

"I love somebody else."

The words seemed to astonish him.

"You do?" he cried. "Somebody else? But has not a sense of what is morally right and proper any weight with you?"

"No, no, no—don't say that!"

"Anyhow, then, your love for this other man may be only a passing feeling which you will overcome—"

"No—no."

"Yes, yes! Why not?"

"I cannot tell you."

"You must in honour!"

"Well then . . . I have married him."

"Ah!" he exclaimed; and he stopped dead and gazed at her.

"I did not wish to tell—I did not mean to!" she pleaded. "It is a secret here, or at any rate but dimly known. So will you, *please* will you, keep from questioning me? You must remember that we are now strangers."

"Strangers—are we? Strangers!"

For a moment a flash of his old irony marked his face; but he determinedly chastened it down.

"Is that man your husband?" he asked mechanically, denoting by a sign the labourer who turned the machine.

"That man!" she said proudly. "I should think not!"

"Who, then?"

"Do not ask what I do not wish to tell!" she begged, and flashed her appeal to him from her upturned face and lash-shadowed eyes.

D'Urberville was disturbed.

"But I only asked for your sake!" he retorted hotly. "Angels of heaven!—God forgive me for such an expression—I came here, I swear, as I thought for your good. Tess—don't look at me so—I cannot stand your looks! There never were such eyes, surely, before Christianity or since! There—I won't lose my head; I dare not. I own that the sight of you has waked up my love for you, which, I believed, was extinguished with all such feelings. But I thought that our marriage might be a sanctification for us both. 'The unbelieving husband is sanctified by the wife, and the unbelieving wife is sanctified by the husband,' I said to myself. But my plan is dashed from me; and I must bear the disappointment!"

He moodily reflected with his eyes on the ground.

"Married. Married! . . . Well, that being so," he added, quite calmly, tearing the licence slowly into halves and putting them in his pocket; "that being prevented, I should like to do some good to you and your husband, whoever he may be. There are many questions that I am tempted to ask, but I will not do so, of course, in opposition to your wishes. Though, if I could know your husband, I might more easily benefit him and you. Is he on this farm?"

"No," she murmured. "He is far away."

"Far away? From *you?* What sort of husband can he be?"

"O, do not speak against him! It was through you! He found out—"

"Ah, is it so! . . . That's sad, Tess!"

"Yes."

"But to stay away from you—to leave you to work like this!"

"He does not leave me to work!" she cried, springing to the defence of the absent one with all her fervour. "He don't know it! It is by my own arrangement."

"Then, does he write?"

"I—I cannot tell you. There are things which are private to ourselves."

"Of course that means that he does not. You are a deserted wife, my fair Tess!"

In an impulse he turned suddenly to take her hand; the buff-glove was on it, and he seized only the rough leather fingers which did not express the life or shape of those within.

"You must not—you must not!" she cried fearfully, slipping her hand from the glove as from a pocket, and leaving it in his grasp. "O, will you go away—for the sake of me and my husband—go, in the name of your own Christianity!"

"Yes, yes; I will," he said abruptly, and thrusting the glove back to her turned to leave. Facing round, however, he said, "Tess, as God is my judge, I meant no humbug in taking your hand!"

A pattering of hoofs on the soil of the field, which they had not noticed in their preoccupation, ceased close behind them; and a voice reached her ear:

"What the devil are you doing away from your work at this time o' day?"

Farmer Groby had espied the two figures from the distance, and had enquisitively ridden across, to learn what was their business in his field.

"Don't speak like that to her!" said d'Urberville, his face blackening with something that was not Christianity.

"Indeed, Mister! And what mid Methodist pa'sons have to do with she?"

"Who is the fellow?" asked d'Urberville, turning to Tess.

She went close up to him.

"Go—I do beg you!" she said.

"What! And leave you to that tyrant? I can see in his face what a churl he is."

"He won't hurt me. *He's* not in love with me. I can leave at Lady-Day."

"Well, I have no right but to obey, I suppose. But—well, good-bye!"

Her defender, whom she dreaded more than her assailant, having reluctantly disappeared, the farmer continued his reprimand, which Tess took with the greatest coolness, that sort of attack being independent of sex. To have as a master this man of stone, who would have cuffed her if he had dared, was almost a relief after her former experiences. She silently walked back towards the summit of the field that was the scene of her labour, so absorbed in the interview which had just taken place that she was hardly aware that the nose of Groby's horse almost touched her shoulders.

"If so be you make an agreement to work for me till Lady-Day, I'll see that you carry it out," he growled. " 'Od rot the women—now 'tis one thing, and then 'tis another. But I'll put up with it no longer!"

Knowing very well that he did not harass the other women of the farm as he harassed her out of spite for the flooring he had once received, she did for one moment picture what might have been the result if she had been free to accept the offer just made her of being the monied Alec's wife. It would have lifted her completely out of subjection, not only to her present oppressive employer, but to a whole world who seemed to despise her. "But no, no!" she said breathlessly; "I could not have married him now! He is so unpleasant to me."

That very night she began an appealing letter to Clare, concealing from him her hardships, and assuring him of her undying affection. Anyone who had been in a position to read between the lines would have seen that at the back of her great love was some monstrous fear—almost a desperation—as to some secret contingencies which were not disclosed. But again she did not finish her effusion; he had asked Izz to go with him, and perhaps he did not care for her at all. She put the letter in her box, and wondered if it would ever reach Angel's hands.

After this her daily tasks were gone through heavily enough, and brought on the day which was of great import to agriculturists—the day of the Candlemas Fair. It was at this fair that new engagements were entered into for the twelve months following the ensuing Lady-Day, and those of the farming population who thought of changing their places duly attended at the county-town where the fair was held. Nearly all the labourers on Flintcomb-Ash Farm intended flight, and early in the morning there was a general exodus in the direction of the town, which lay at a distance of from ten to a dozen miles over hilly country. Though Tess also meant to leave at the quarter-day she was one of the few who did not go to the fair, having a vaguely-shaped hope that something would happen to render another out-door engagement unnecessary.

It was a peaceful February day, of wonderful softness for the time, and one would almost have thought that winter was over. She had hardly finished her dinner when d'Urberville's figure darkened the window of the cottage wherein she was a lodger, which she had all to herself to-day.

Tess jumped up, but her visitor had knocked at the door, and she could hardly in reason run away. D'Urberville's knock, his walk up to the door, had some indescribable quality of difference from his air when she last saw him. They seemed to be acts of which the doer was ashamed. She thought that she would not open the door; but, as there was no sense in that either, she arose, and having lifted the latch stepped back quickly. He came in, saw her, and flung himself down into a chair before speaking.

"Tess—I couldn't help it!" he began desperately, as he wiped his heated face, which had also a superimposed flush of excitement. "I felt that I must call at least to ask how you are. I assure you I had not been thinking of you at all till I saw you that Sunday; now I cannot get rid of your image, try how I may! It is hard that a good woman should do harm to a bad man; yet so it is. If you would only pray for me, Tess!"

The suppressed discontent of his manner was almost pitiable, and yet Tess did not pity him.

"How can I pray for you," she said, "when I am forbidden to believe that the great Power who moves the world would alter His plans on my account?"

"You really think that?"

"Yes. I have been cured of the presumption of thinking otherwise."

"Cured? By whom?"

"By my husband, if I must tell."

"Ah—your husband—your husband! How strange it seems! I remember you hinted something of the sort the other day. What do you really believe in these matters, Tess?" he asked. "You seem to have no religion—perhaps owing to me."

"But I have. Though I don't believe in anything supernatural."

D'Urberville looked at her with misgiving.

"Then do you think that the line I take is all wrong?"

"A good deal of it."

"H'm—and yet I've felt so sure about it," he said uneasily.

"I believe in the *spirit* of the Sermon on the Mount, and so did my dear husband. . . . But I don't believe—"

Here she gave her negations.

"The fact is," said d'Urberville drily, "whatever your dear husband believed you accept, and whatever he rejected you reject, without the least enquiry or reasoning on your own part. That's just like you women. Your mind is enslaved to his."

"Ah, because he knew everything!" said she, with a triumphant simplicity of faith in Angel Clare that the most perfect man could hardly have deserved, much less her husband.

"Yes, but you should not take negative opinions wholesale from another person like that. A pretty fellow he must be to teach you such scepticism!"

"He never forced my judgment! He would never argue on the subject with me! But I looked at it in this way; what he believed, after enquiring deep into doctrines, was much more likely to be right than what I might believe, who hadn't looked into doctrines at all."

"What used he to say? He must have said something?"

She reflected; and with her acute memory for the letter of Angel Clare's remarks, even when she did not comprehend their spirit, she recalled a merciless polemical syllogism that she had heard him use when, as it occasionally happened, he indulged in a species of thinking aloud with her at his side. In delivering it she gave also Clare's accent and manner with reverential faithfulness.

"Say that again," asked d'Urberville, who had listened with the greatest attention.

She repeated the argument, and d'Urberville thoughtfully murmured the words after her.

"Anything else?" he presently asked.

"He said at another time something like this"; and she gave another, which might possibly have been parallelled in many a work of the pedigree ranging from the *Dictionnaire Philosophique* to Huxley's *Essays*.

"Ah—ha! How do you remember them?"

"I wanted to believe what he believed, though he didn't wish me to; and I managed to coax him to tell me a few of his thoughts. I can't say I quite understand that one; but I know it is right."

"H'm. Fancy your being able to teach me what you don't know yourself!"

He fell into thought.

"And so I threw in my spiritual lot with his," she resumed. "I didn't wish it to be different. What's good enough for him is good enough for me."

"Does he know that you are as big an infidel as he?"

"No—I never told him—if I am an infidel."

"Well—you are better off to-day that I am, Tess, after all! You don't believe that you ought to preach my doctrine, and, therefore, do no despite to your conscience in abstaining. I do believe I ought to preach it, but like the devils I believe and tremble, for I suddenly leave off preaching it, and give way to my passion for you."

"How?"

"Why," he said aridly; "I have come all the way here to see you to-day! But I started from home to go to Casterbridge Fair, where I have undertaken to preach the Word from a waggon at half-past two this afternoon, and where all the brethren are expecting me this minute. Here's the announcement."

He drew from his breast-pocket a poster whereon was printed the day, hour, and place of meeting, at which he, d'Urberville, would preach the Gospel as aforesaid.

"But how can you get there?" said Tess, looking at the clock.

"I cannot get there! I have come here."

"What, you have really arranged to preach, and—"

"I have arranged to preach, and I shall not be there—by reason of my burning desire to see a woman whom I once despised!—No, by my word and truth, I never despised you; if I had I should not love you now! Why I did not despise you was on account of your being unsmirched in spite of all; you withdrew yourself from me so quickly and resolutely when you saw the situation; you did not remain at my pleasure; so there was one petticoat in the world for whom I had no contempt, and you are she. But you may well despise me now! I thought I worshipped on the mountains, but I find I still serve in the groves! Ha! ha!"

"O Alec d'Urberville! what does this mean? What have I done!"

"Done?" he said, with a soulless sneer in the word. "Nothing intentionally. But you have been the means—the innocent means—of my backsliding, as they call it. I ask myself, am I, indeed, one of those 'servants of corruption' who, 'after they have escaped the pollutions of the world, are again entangled therein and overcome'—whose latter end is worse than their beginning?" He laid his hand on her shoulder. "Tess, my girl, I was on the way to, at least, social salvation till I saw you again!" he said freakishly shaking her, as if she were a child. "And why then have you tempted me? I was firm as a man could be till I saw those eyes and that mouth again—surely there never was such a maddening mouth since Eve's!" His voice sank, and a hot archness shot from his own black eyes. "You temptress, Tess; you dear damned witch of Babylon—I could not resist you as soon as I met you again!"

"I couldn't help your seeing me again!" said Tess, recoiling.

"I know it—I repeat that I do not blame you. But the fact remains. When I saw you ill-used on the farm that day I was nearly mad to think that I had no legal right to protect you—that I could not have it; whilst he who has it seems to neglect you utterly!"

"Don't speak against him—he is absent!" she cried in much excitement. "Treat him honourably—he has never wronged you! O leave his wife before any scandal spreads that may do harm to his honest name!"

"I will—I will," he said, like a man awakening from a luring dream. "I have broken my engagement to preach to those poor drunken boobies at the fair—it is the first time I have played such a practical joke. A month ago I should have been horrified at such a possibility. I'll go away—to swear—and—ah, can I! to keep away." Then, suddenly: "One clasp, Tessy—one! Only for old friendship—"

"I am without defence, Alec! A good man's honour is in my keeping—think—be ashamed!"

"Pooh! Well, yes—yes!"

He clenched his lips, mortified with himself for his weakness. His eyes were equally barren of worldly and religious faith. The corpses of those old fitful passions which had lain inanimate amid the lines of his face ever since his reformation seemed to wake and come together as in a resurrection. He went out indeterminately.

Though d'Urberville had declared that this breach of his engagement to-day was the simple backsliding of a believer, Tess's words, as echoed from Angel Clare, had made a deep impression upon him, and continued to do so after he had left her. He moved on in silence, as if his energies were benumbed by the hitherto undreamt-of possibility that his position was untenable. Reason had had nothing to do with his whimsical conversion, which was perhaps the mere freak of a careless man in search of a new sensation, and temporarily impressed by his mother's death.

The drops of logic Tess had let fall into the sea of his enthusiasm served to chill its effervescence to stagnation. He said to himself, as he pondered again and again over the crystallised phrases that she had handed on to him, "That clever fellow little thought that, by telling her those things, he might be paving my way back to her!"

XLVII

IT IS THE THRESHING OF THE LAST WHEAT-RICK AT FLINTCOMB-ASH FARM. THE DAWN OF the March morning is singularly inexpressive, and there is nothing to show where the eastern horizon lies. Against the twilight rises the trapezoidal top of the stack, which has stood forlornly here through the washing and bleaching of the wintry weather.

When Izz Huett and Tess arrived at the scene of operations only a rustling denoted that others had preceded them; to which, as the light increased, there were presently added the silhouettes of two men on the summit. They were busily "unhaling" the rick, that is, stripping off the thatch before beginning to throw down the sheaves; and while this was in progress Izz and Tess, with the other women-workers, in their whitey-brown pinners, stood waiting and shivering, Farmer Groby having insisted upon their being on the spot thus early to get the job over if possible by the end of the day. Close under the eaves of the stack, and as yet barely visible, was the red tyrant that the women had come to serve— a timber-framed construction, with straps and wheels appertaining—the threshing-machine which, whilst it was going, kept up a despotic demand upon the endurance of their muscles and nerves.

A little way off there was another indistinct figure; this one black, with a sustained hiss that spoke of strength very much in reserve. The long chimney running up beside an ash-tree, and the warmth which radiated from the spot, explained without the necessity of much daylight that here was the engine which was to act as the *primum mobile* of this little world. By the engine stood a dark motionless being, a sooty and grimy embodiment of tallness, in a sort of trance, with a heap of coals by his side: it was the engineman. The isolation of his manner and colour lent him the appearance of a creature from Tophet, who had strayed into the pellucid smokelessness of this region of yellow grain and pale soil, with which he had nothing in common, to amaze and to discompose its aborigines.

What he looked he felt. He was in the agricultural world, but not of it. He served fire and smoke; these denizens of the fields served vegetation, weather, frost, and sun. He travelled with his engine from farm to farm, from county to county, for as yet the steam threshing-machine was itinerant in this part of Wessex. He spoke in a strange northern accent; his thoughts being turned inwards upon himself, his eye on his iron charge, hardly perceiving the scenes around him, and caring for them not at all: holding only strictly necessary intercourse with the natives, as if some ancient doom compelled him to wander here against his will in the service of his Plutonic master. The long strap which ran from the driving-wheel of his engine to the red thresher under the rick was the sole tie-line between agriculture and him.

While they uncovered the sheaves he stood apathetic beside his portable repository of force, round whose hot blackness the morning air quivered. He had nothing to do with preparatory labour. His fire was waiting incandescent, his steam was at high pressure, in a few seconds he could make the long strap move at an invisible velocity. Beyond its extent the environment might be corn, straw, or chaos; it was all the same to him. If any of the autochthonous idlers asked him what he called himself, he replied shortly, "an engineer."

The rick was unhaled by full daylight; the men then took their places, the women mounted, and the work began. Farmer Groby—or, as they called him, "he"—had arrived ere this, and by his orders Tess was placed on the platform of the machine, close to the man who fed it, her business being to untie every sheaf of corn handed on to her by Izz Huett, who stood next, but on the rick; so that the feeder could seize it and spread it over the revolving drum, which whisked out every grain in one moment.

They were soon in full progress, after a preparatory hitch or two, which rejoiced the hearts of those who hated machinery. The work sped on till breakfast-time, when the thresher was stopped for half an hour; and on starting again after the meal the whole supplementary strength of the farm was thrown into the labour of constructing the straw-rick, which began to grow beside the stack of corn. A hasty lunch was eaten as they stood, without leaving their positions, and then another couple of hours brought them near to dinner-time; the inexorable wheel continuing to spin, and the penetrating hum of the thresher to thrill to the very marrow all who were near the revolving wire-cage.

The old men on the rising straw-rick talked of the past days when they had been accustomed to thresh with flails on the oaken barn-floor; when everything, even to winnowing, was effected by hand-labour, which, to their thinking, though slow, produced better results. Those, too, on the corn-rick talked a little; but the perspiring ones at the machine, including Tess, could not lighten their duties by the exchange of many words. It was the ceaselessness of the work which tried her so severely, and began to make her wish that she had never come to Flintcomb-Ash. The women on the corn-rick—Marian, who was one of them, in particular—could stop to drink ale or cold tea from the flagon now and then, or to exchange a few gossiping remarks while they wiped their faces or cleared the fragments of straw and husk from their clothing; but for Tess there was no respite; for, as the drum never stopped, the man who fed it could not stop, and she, who had to supply the man with untied sheaves, could not stop either, unless Marian changed places with her, which she sometimes did for half an hour in spite of Groby's objection that she was too slow-handed for a feeder.

For some probably economical reason it was usually a woman who was chosen for this particular duty, and Groby gave as his motive in selecting Tess that she was one of those who best combined strength with quickness in untying, and both with staying power, and this may have been true. The hum of the thresher, which prevented speech, increased to a raving whenever the supply of corn fell short of the regular quantity. As Tess and the man who fed could never turn their heads she did not know that just before the dinner-hour a person had come silently into the field by the gate, and had been standing under a second rick watching the scene, and Tess in particular. He was dressed in a tweed suit of fashionable pattern, and he twirled a gay walking-cane.

"Who is that?" said Izz Huett to Marian. She had at first addressed the enquiry to Tess, but the latter could not hear it.

"Somebody's fancy-man, I s'pose," said Marian laconically.

"I'll lay a guinea he's after Tess."

"O no. 'Tis a ranter pa'son who's been sniffing after her lately; not a dandy like this."

"Well—this is the same man."

"The same man as the preacher? But he's quite different!"

"He hev left off his black coat and white neckercher, and hev cut off his whiskers; but he's the same man for all that."

"D'ye really think so? Then I'll tell her," said Marian.

"Don't. She'll see him soon enough, good-now."

"Well. I don't think it at all right for him to join his preaching to courting a married woman, even though her husband mid be abroad, and she, in a sense, a widow."

"Oh—he can do her no harm," said Izz drily. "Her mind can no more be heaved from that one place where it do bide than a stooded waggon from the hole he's in. Lord love 'ee, neither court-paying, nor preaching, nor the seven thunders themselves, can wean a woman when 'twould be better for her that she should be weaned."

Dinner-time came, and the whirling ceased; whereupon Tess left her post, her knees trembling so wretchedly with the shaking of the machine that she could scarcely walk.

"You ought to het a quart o' drink into 'ee, as I've done," said Marian. "You wouldn't look so white then. Why, souls above us, your face is as if you'd been hagrode!"

It occurred to the good-natured Marian that, as Tess was so tired, her discovery of her visitor's presence might have the bad effect of taking away her appetite; and Marian was thinking of inducing Tess to descend by a ladder on the further side of the stack when the gentleman came forward and looked up.

Tess uttered a short little "Oh!" And a moment after she said, quickly, "I shall eat my dinner here—right on the rick."

Sometimes, when they were so far from their cottages, they all did this; but as there was rather a keen wind going to-day, Marian and the rest descended, and sat under the straw-stack.

The new-comer was, indeed, Alec d'Urberville, the late Evangelist, despite his changed attire and aspect. It was obvious at a glance that the original *Weltlust* had come back; that he had restored himself, as nearly as a man could do who had grown three or four years older, to the old jaunty, slap-dash guise under which Tess had first known her admirer, and cousin so-called. Having decided to remain where she was, Tess sat down among the bundles, out of sight of the ground, and began her meal; till, by and by, she heard footsteps on the ladder, and immediately after Alec appeared upon the stack—now an oblong and level platform of sheaves. He strode across them, and sat down opposite to her without a word.

Tess continued to eat her modest dinner, a slice of thick pancake which she had brought with her. The other work-folk were by this time all gathered under the rick, where the loose straw formed a comfortable retreat.

"I am here again, as you see," said d'Urberville.

"Why do you trouble me so!" she cried, reproach flashing from her very finger-ends.

"*I* trouble *you?* I think I may ask, why do you trouble me?"

"Sure, I don't trouble you any-when!"

"You say you don't? But you do! You haunt me. Those very eyes that you turned upon me with such a bitter flash a moment ago, they come to me just as you showed them then, in the night and in the day! Tess, ever since you told me of that child of ours, it is just as if my feelings, which have been flowing in a strong puritanical stream, had suddenly found a way open in the direction of you, and had all at once gushed through. The religious channel is left dry forthwith; and it is you who have done it!"

She gazed in silence.

"What—you have given up your preaching entirely?" she asked.

She had gathered from Angel sufficient of the incredulity of modern thought to despise flash enthusiasm; but, as a woman, she was somewhat appalled.

In affected severity d'Urberville continued—

"Entirely. I have broken every engagement since that afternoon I was to address the drunkards at Casterbridge Fair. The deuce only knows what I am thought of by the brethren. Ah-ha! The brethren! No doubt they pray for me—weep for me; for they are kind people in their way. But what do I care? How could I go on with the thing when I had lost my faith in it?—it would have been hypocrisy of the basest kind! Among them I should have stood like Hymenæus and Alexander, who were delivered over to Satan that they might learn not to blaspheme. What a grand revenge you have taken! I saw you innocent, and I deceived you. Four years after, you find me a Christian enthusiast; you then work upon me, perhaps to my complete perdition! But Tess, my coz, as I used to call you, this is only my way of talking, and you must not look so horribly concerned. Of course you have done nothing except retain your pretty face and shapely figure. I saw it on the rick before you saw me—that tight pinafore-thing sets it off, and that wing-bonnet—you field-girls should never wear those bonnets if you wish to keep out of danger." He regarded her silently for a few moments, and with a short cynical laugh resumed: "I believe that if the bachelor-apostle, whose deputy I thought I was, had been tempted by such a pretty face, he would have let go the plough for her sake as I do!"

Tess attempted to expostulate, but at this juncture all her fluency failed her, and without heeding he added:

"Well, this paradise that you supply is perhaps as good as any other, after all. But to speak seriously. Tess." D'Urberville rose and came nearer, reclining sideways amid the sheaves, and resting upon his elbow. "Since I last saw you, I have been thinking of what you said that *he* said. I have come to the conclusion that there does seem rather a want of common sense in these threadbare old propositions; how I could have been so fired by poor Parson Clare's enthusiasm, and have gone so madly to work, transcending even him, I cannot make out! As for what you said last time, on the strength of your wonderful husband's intelligence—whose name you have never told me—about having what they call an ethical system without any dogma, I don't see my way to that at all."

"Why, you can have the religion of loving-kindness and purity at least, if you can't have—what do you call it—dogma."

"O no! I'm a different sort of fellow from that! If there's nobody to say, 'Do this, and it will be a good thing for you after you are dead; do that, and if will be a bad thing for you,' I can't warm up. Hang it, I am not going to feel responsible for my deeds and passions if there's nobody to be responsible to; and if I were you, my dear, I wouldn't either!"

She tried to argue, and tell him that he had mixed in his dull brain two matters, theology and morals, which in the primitive days of mankind had been quite distinct. But owing to Angel Clare's reticence, to her absolute want of training, and to her being a vessel of emotions rather than reasons, she could not get on.

"Well, never mind," he resumed. "Here I am, my love, as in the old times!"

"Not as then—never as then—'tis different!" she entreated. "And there was never warmth with me! O why didn't you keep your faith, if the loss of it has brought you to speak to me like this!"

"Because you've knocked it out of me; so the evil be upon your sweet head! Your husband little thought how his teaching would recoil upon him! Ha-ha—I'm awfully glad you have made an apostate of me all the same! Tess, I am more taken with you than ever, and I pity you too. For all your closeness, I see you are in a bad way—neglected by one who ought to cherish you."

She could not get her morsels of food down her throat; her lips were dry, and she was ready to choke. The voices and laughs of the work-folk eating and drinking under the rick came to her as if they were a quarter of a mile off.

"It is cruelty to me!" she said. "How—how can you treat me to this talk, if you care ever so little for me?"

"True, true," he said, wincing a little. "I did not come to reproach you for my deeds. I came, Tess, to say that I don't like you to be working like this, and I have come on purpose for you. You say you have a husband who is not I. Well, perhaps you have; but I've never seen him, and you've not told me his name; and altogether he seems rather a mythological personage. However, even if you have one, I think I am nearer to you than he is. I, at any rate, try to help you out of trouble, but he does not, bless his invisible face! The words of the stern prophet Hosea that I used to read come back to me. Don't you know them, Tess?—'And she shall follow after her lover, but she shall not overtake him; and she shall seek him, but shall not find him; then shall she say, I will go and return to my first husband; for then was it better with me than now!' . . . Tess, my trap is waiting just under the hill, and—darling mine, not his!—you know the rest."

Her face had been rising to a dull crimson fire while he spoke; but she did not answer.

"You have been the cause of my backsliding," he continued, stretching his arm towards her waist; "you should be willing to share it, and leave that mule you call husband forever."

One of her leather gloves, which she had taken off to eat her skimmer-cake, lay in her lap, and without the slightest warning she passionately swung the glove by the gauntlet directly in his face. It was heavy and thick as a warrior's, and it struck him flat on the mouth. Fancy might have regarded the act as the recrudescence of a trick in which her armed progenitors were not unpractised. Alec fiercely started up from his reclining position. A scarlet oozing appeared where her blow had alighted, and in a moment the blood began dropping from his mouth upon the straw. But he soon controlled himself, calmly drew his handkerchief from his pocket, and mopped his bleeding lips.

She too had sprung up, but she sank down again.

"Now, punish me!" she said, turning up her eyes to him with the hopeless defiance of the sparrow's gaze before its captor twists its neck. "Whip me, crush me; you need not mind those people under the rick! I shall not cry out. Once victim, always victim—that's the law!"

"O no, no, Tess," he said blandly. "I can make full allowance for this. Yet you most unjustly forget one thing, that I would have married you if you had not put it out of my power to do so. Did I not ask you flatly to be my wife—hey? Answer me."

"You did."

"And you cannot be. But remember one thing!" His voice hardened as his temper got the better of him with the recollection of his sincerity in asking her and her present ingratitude, and he stepped across to her side and held her by the shoulders, so that she shook under his grasp. "Remember, my lady, I was your master once! I will be your master again. If you are any man's wife you are mine!"

The threshers now began to stir below.

"So much for our quarrel," he said, letting her go. "Now I shall leave you, and shall come again for your answer during the afternoon. You don't know me yet! But I know you."

She had not spoken again, remaining as if stunned. D'Urberville retreated over the sheaves, and descended the ladder, while the workers below rose and stretched their arms, and shook down the beer they had drunk. Then the threshing-machine started afresh; and amid the renewed rustle of the straw Tess resumed her position by the buzzing drum as one in a dream, untying sheaf after sheaf in endless succession.

XLVIII

IN THE AFTERNOON THE FARMER MADE IT KNOWN THAT THE RICK WAS TO BE FINISHED that night, since there was a moon by which they could see to work, and the man with the engine was engaged for another farm on the morrow. Hence the twanging and humming and rustling proceeded with even less intermission than usual.

It was not till "nammet"-time, about three o-clock, that Tess raised her eyes and gave a momentary glance round. She felt but little surprise at seeing that Alec d'Urberville had come back, and was standing under the hedge by the gate. He had seen her lift her eyes, and waved his hand urbanely to her, while he blew her a kiss. It meant that their quarrel was over. Tess looked down again, and carefully abstained from gazing in that direction.

Thus the afternoon dragged on. The wheat-rick shrank lower, and the straw-rick grew higher, and the corn-sacks were carted away. At six o'clock the wheat-rick was about shoulder-high from the ground. But the unthreshed sheaves remaining untouched seemed countless still, notwithstanding the enormous numbers that had been gulped down by the insatiable swallower, fed by the man and Tess, through whose two young hands the greater part of them had passed. And the immense stack of straw where in the morning there had been nothing, appeared as the *faeces* of the same buzzing red glutton. From the west sky a wrathful shine—all that wild March could afford in the way of sunset—had burst forth after the cloudy day, flooding the tired and sticky faces of the threshers, and dyeing them with a coppery light, as also the flapping garments of the women, which clung to them like dull flames.

A panting ache ran through the rick. The man who fed was weary, and Tess could see that the red nape of his neck was encrusted with dirt and husks. She still stood at her post, her flushed and perspiring face coated with the corn-dust, and her white bonnet embrowned by it. She was the only woman whose place was upon the machine so as to be shaken bodily by its spinning, and the decrease of the stack now separated her from Marian and Izz, and prevented their changing duties with her as they had done. The incessant quivering, in which every fibre of her frame participated, had thrown her into a stupefied reverie in which her arms worked on independently of her consciousness. She hardly knew where she was, and did not hear Izz Huett tell her from below that her hair was tumbling down.

By degrees the freshest among them began to grow cadaverous and saucer-eyed.

Whenever Tess lifted her head she beheld always the great upgrown straw-stack, with the men in shirt-sleeves upon it, against the grey north sky; in front of it the long red elevator like a Jacob's ladder, on which a perpetual stream of threshed straw ascended, a yellow river running up-hill, and spouting out on the top of the rick.

She knew that Alec d'Urberville was still on the scene, observing her from some point or other, though she could not say where. There was an excuse for his remaining, for when the threshed rick drew near its final sheaves a little ratting was always done, and men unconnected with the threshing sometimes dropped in for that performance—sporting characters of all descriptions, gents with terriers and facetious pipes, roughs with sticks and stones.

But there was another hour's work before the layer of live rats at the base of the stack would be reached; and as the evening light in the direction of the Giant's Hill by Abbot's-Cernel dissolved away, the white-faced moon of the season arose from the horizon that lay towards Middleton Abbey and Shottsford on the other side. For the last hour or two Marian had felt uneasy about Tess, whom she could not get near enough to speak to, the other women having kept up their strength by drinking ale, and Tess having done without it through traditionary dread, owing to its results at her home in childhood. But Tess still kept going: if she could not fill her part she would have to leave; and this contingency, which she would have regarded with equanimity and even with relief a month or two earlier, had become a terror since d'Urberville had begun to hover round her.

The sheaf-pitchers and feeders had now worked the rick so low that people on the ground could talk to them. To Tess's surprise Farmer Groby came up on the machine to her, and said that if she desired to join her friend he did not wish her to keep on any longer, and would send somebody else to take her place. The "friend" was d'Urberville, she knew, and also that this concession had been granted in obedience to the request of that friend, or enemy. She shook her head and toiled on.

The time for the rat-catching arrived at last, and the hunt began. The creatures had crept downwards with the subsidence of the rick till they were all together at the bottom, and being now uncovered from their last refuge they ran across the open ground in all directions, a loud shriek from the by this time half-tipsy Marian informing her companions that one of the rats had invaded her person—a terror which the rest of the women had guarded against by various schemes of skirt-tucking and self-elevation. The rat was at last dislodged, and, amid the barking of dogs, masculine shouts, feminine screams, oaths, stampings, and confusion as of Pandemonium, Tess untied her last sheaf; the drum slowed, the whizzing ceased, and she stepped from the machine to the ground.

Her lover, who had only looked on at the rat-catching, was promptly at her side.

"What—after all—my insulting slap, too!" said she in an underbreath. She was so utterly exhausted that she had not strength to speak louder.

"I should indeed be foolish to feel offended at anything you say or do," he answered, in the seductive voice of the Trantridge time. "How the little limbs tremble! You are as weak as a bled calf, you know you are; and yet you need have done nothing since I arrived. How could you be so obstinate? However, I have told the farmer that he has no right to employ women at steam-threshing. It is not proper work for them; and on all the better class of farms it has been given up, as he knows very well. I will walk with you as far as your home."

"O yes," she answered with a jaded gait. "Walk wi' me if you will! I do bear in mind that you came to marry me before you knew o' my state. Perhaps—perhaps you are a little better and kinder than I have been thinking you were. Whatever is meant by kindness I am grateful for; whatever is meant in any other way I am angered at. I cannot sense your meaning sometimes."

"If I cannot legitimise our former relations at least I can assist you. And I will do it with much more regard for your feelings than I formerly showed. My religious mania, or whatever it was, is over. But I retain a little good nature; I hope I do. Now Tess, by all that's tender and strong between man and woman, trust me! I have enough and more than enough to put you out of anxiety, both for yourself and your parents and sisters. I can make them all comfortable if you will only show confidence in me."

"Have you seen 'em lately?" she quickly enquired.

"Yes. They didn't know where you were. It was only by chance that I found you here."

The cold moon looked aslant upon Tess's fagged face between the twigs of the garden-hedge as she paused outside the cottage which was her temporary home, d'Urberville pausing beside her.

"Don't mention my little brothers and sisters—don't make me break down quite!" she said. "If you want to help them—God knows they need it—do it without telling me. But no, no!" she cried. "I will take nothing from you, either for them or for me!"

He did not accompany her further, since, as she lived with the household, all was public indoors. No sooner had she herself entered, laved herself in a washing-tub, and shared supper with the family than she fell into thought, and withdrawing to the table under the wall, by the light of her own little lamp wrote in a passionate mood—

MY OWN HUSBAND—Let me call you so—I must—even if it makes you angry to think of such an unworthy wife as I. I must cry to you in my trouble—I have no one else! I am so exposed to temptation, Angel. I fear to say who it is, and I do not like to write about it at all. But I cling to you in a way you cannot think! Can you not come to me now, at once, before anything terrible happens? O, I know you cannot, because you are so far away! I think I must die if you do not come soon, or tell me to come to you. The punishment you have measured out to me is deserved—I do know that—well deserved—and you are right and just to be angry with me. But, Angel, please, please, not to be just—only a little kind to me, even if I do not deserve it, and come to me! If you would come, I could die in your arms! I would be well content to do that if so be you had forgiven me!

Angel, I live entirely for you. I love you too much to blame you for going away, and I know it was necessary you should find a farm. Do not think I shall say a word of sting or bitterness. Only come back to me. I am desolate without you, my darling, O, so desolate! I do not mind having to work: but if you will send me one little line, and say, *"I am coming soon,"* I will bide on, Angel—O, so cheerfully!

It has been so much my religion ever since we were married to be faithful to you in every thought and look, that even when a man speaks a compliment to me before I am aware, it seems wronging you. Have you never felt one little bit of what you used to feel when we were at the dairy? If you have, how can you keep away from me? I am the same woman, Angel, as you fell in love with; yes, the very same!—not the one you disliked but never saw. What was the past to me as soon as I met you? It was a dead thing altogether. I

became another woman, filled full of new life from you. How could I be the early one?
Why do you not see this? Dear, if you would only be a little more conceited, and believe
in yourself so far as to see that you were strong enough to work this change in me, you
would perhaps be in a mind to come to me, your poor wife.

How silly I was in my happiness when I thought I could trust you always to love me!
I ought to have known that such as that was not for poor me. But I am sick at heart, not
only for old times, but for the present. Think—think how it do hurt my heart not to see
you ever—ever! Ah, if I could only make your dear heart ache one little minute of each
day as mine does everyday and all day long, it might lead you to show pity to your poor
lonely one.

People still say that I am rather pretty, Angel (handsome is the word they use, since I
wish to be truthful). Perhaps I am what they say. But I do not value my good looks; I only
like to have them because they belong to you, my dear, and that there may be at least one
thing about me worth your having. So much have I felt this, that when I met with annoyance on account of the same I tied up my face in a bandage as long as people would believe in it. O Angel, I tell you all this not from vanity—you will certainly know I do
not—but only that you may come to me!

If you really cannot come to me will you let me come to you? I am, as I say, worried,
pressed to do what I will not do. It cannot be that I shall yield one inch, yet I am in terror
as to what an accident might lead to, and I so defenceless on account of my first error. I
cannot say more about this—it makes me too miserable. But if I break down by falling into
some fearful snare, my last state will be worse than my first. O God, I cannot think of it!
Let me come at once, or at once come to me!

I would be content, ay, glad, to live with you as your servant, if I may not as your wife;
so that I could only be near you, and get glimpses of you, and think of you as mine.

The daylight has nothing to show me, since you are not here, and I don't like to see
the rooks and starlings in the field, because I grieve and grieve to miss you who used to see
them with me. I long for only one thing in heaven or earth or under the earth, to meet you,
my own dear! Come to me—come to me, and save me from what threatens me!—Your
faithful heart-broken   TESS

XLIX

THE APPEAL DULY FOUND ITS WAY TO THE BREAKFAST-TABLE OF THE QUIET VICARAGE
to the westward, in that valley where the air is so soft and the soil so rich that the effort of growth requires but superficial aid by comparison with the tillage at Flintcomb-
Ash, and where to Tess the human world seemed so different (though it was much the
same). It was purely for security that she had been requested by Angel to send her communications through his father, whom he kept pretty well informed of his changing addresses in the country he had gone to exploit for himself with a heavy heart.

"Now," said old Mr. Clare to his wife, when he had read the envelope, "if Angel pro-
poses leaving Rio for a visit home at the end of next month, as he told us that he hoped to

do, I think this may hasten his plans; for I believe it to be from his wife." He breathed deeply at the thought of her; and the letter was redirected to be promptly sent on to Angel.

"Dear fellow, I hope he will get home safely," murmured Mrs. Clare. "To my dying day I shall feel that he had been ill-used. You should have sent him to Cambridge in spite of his want of faith, and given him the same chance as the other boys had. He would have grown out of it under proper influence, and perhaps would have taken Orders after all. Church or no Church, it would have been fairer to him."

This was the only wail with which Mrs. Clare ever disturbed her husband's peace in respect of their sons. And she did not vent this often; for she was as considerate as she was devout, and knew that his mind too was troubled by doubts as to his justice in this matter. Only too often had she heard him lying awake at night, stifling sighs for Angel with prayers. But the uncompromising Evangelical did not even now hold that he would have been justified in giving his son, an unbeliever, the same academic advantages that he had given to the two others, when it was possible, if not probable, that those very advantages might have been used to decry the doctrines which he had made it his life's mission and desire to propagate, and the mission of his ordained sons likewise. To put with one hand a pedestal under the feet of the two faithful ones, and with the other to exalt the unfaithful by the same artificial means, he deemed to be alike inconsistent with his convictions, his position, and his hopes. Nevertheless, he loved his misnamed Angel, and in secret mourned over this treatment of him as Abraham might have mourned over the doomed Isaac while they went up the hill together. His silent self-generated regrets were far bitterer than the reproaches which his wife rendered audible.

They blamed themselves for this unlucky marriage. If Angel had never been destined for a farmer he would never have been thrown with agricultural girls. They did not distinctly know what had separated him and his wife, nor the date on which the separation had taken place. At first they had supposed it must be something of the nature of a serious aversion. But in his later letters he occasionally alluded to the intention of coming home to fetch her; from which expressions they hoped the division might not owe its origin to anything so hopelessly permanent as that. He had told them that she was with her relatives, and in their doubts they had decided not to intrude into a situation which they knew no way of bettering.

The eyes for which Tess's letter was intended were gazing at this time on a limitless expanse of country from the back of a mule which was bearing him from the interior of the South-American Continent towards the coast. His experiences of this strange land had been sad. The severe illness from which he had suffered shortly after his arrival had never wholly left him, and he had by degrees almost decided to relinquish his hope of farming here, though, as long as the bare possibility existed of his remaining, he kept this change of view a secret from his parents.

The crowds of agricultural labourers who had come out to the country in his wake, dazzled by representations of easy independence, had suffered, died, and wasted away. He would see mothers from English farms trudging along with their infants in their arms, when the child would be stricken with fever and would die; the mother would pause to dig a hole in the loose earth with her bare hands, would bury the babe therein with the same natural grave-tools, shed one tear, and again trudge on.

Angel's original intention had not been emigration to Brazil but a northern or eastern farm in his own country. He had come to this place in a fit of desperation, the Brazil movement among the English agriculturists having by chance coincided with his desire to escape from his past existence.

During this time of absence he had mentally aged a dozen years. What arrested him now as of value in life was less its beauty than its pathos. Having long discredited the old systems of mysticism, he now began to discredit the old appraisements of morality. He thought they wanted readjusting. Who was the moral man? Still more pertinently, who was the moral woman? The beauty or ugliness of a character lay not only in its achievements, but in its aims and impulses; its true history lay, not among things done, but among things willed.

How, then, about Tess?

Viewing her in these lights, a regret for his hasty judgment began to oppress him. Did he reject her eternally, or did he not? He could no longer say that he would always reject her, and not to say that was in spirit to accept her now.

This growing fondness for her memory coincided in point of time with her residence at Flintcomb-Ash, but it was before she had felt herself at liberty to trouble him with a word about her circumstances or her feelings. He was greatly perplexed; and in his perplexity as to her motives in withholding intelligence he did not enquire. Thus her silence of docility was misinterpreted. How much it really said if he had understood!—that she adhered with literal exactness to orders which he had given and forgotten; that despite her natural fearlessness she asserted no rights, admitted his judgment to be in every respect the true one, and bent her head dumbly thereto.

In the before-mentioned journey by mules through the interior of the country, another man rode beside him. Angel's companion was also an Englishman, bent on the same errand, though he came from another part of the island. They were both in a state of mental depression, and they spoke of home affairs. Confidence begat confidence. With that curious tendency evinced by men, more especially when in distant lands, to entrust to strangers details of their lives which they would on no account mention to friends, Angel admitted to this man as they rode along the sorrowful facts of his marriage.

The stranger had sojourned in many more lands and among many more peoples than Angel; to his cosmopolitan mind such deviations from the social norm, so immense to domesticity, were no more than are the irregularities of vale and mountain-chain to the whole terrestrial curve. He viewed the matter in quite a different light from Angel; thought that what Tess had been was of no importance beside what she would be, and plainly told Clare that he was wrong in coming away from her.

The next day they were drenched in a thunder-storm. Angel's companion was struck down with fever, and died by the week's end. Clare waited a few hours to bury him, and then went on his way.

The cursory remarks of the large-minded stranger, of whom he knew absolutely nothing beyond a commonplace name, were sublimed by his death, and influenced Clare more than all the reasoned ethics of the philosophers. His own parochialism made him ashamed by its contrast. His inconsistencies rushed upon him in a flood. He had persistently elevated Hellenic Paganism at the expense of Christianity; yet in that civilization an illegal surrender was not certain disesteem. Surely then he might have regarded that abhorrence of the un-intact state, which he had inherited with the creed of mysticism, as at least open to correction when the result was due to treachery. A remorse struck into him. The words of Izz Huett, never quite stilled in his memory, came back to him. He had asked Izz if she loved him, and she had replied in the affirmative. Did she love him more than Tess did? No, she had replied; Tess would lay down her life for him, and she herself could do no more.

He thought of Tess as she had appeared on the day of the wedding. How her eyes had lingered upon him; how she had hung upon his words as if they were a god's! And during the terrible evening over the hearth, when her simple soul uncovered itself to his, how pitiful her face had looked by the rays of the fire, in her inability to realise that his love and protection could possibly be withdrawn.

Thus from being her critic he grew to be her advocate. Cynical things he had uttered to himself about her; but no man can be always a cynic and live; and he withdrew them. The mistake of expressing them had arisen from his allowing himself to be influenced by general principles to the disregard of the particular instance.

But the reasoning is somewhat musty; lovers and husbands have gone over the ground before to-day. Clare had been harsh towards her; there is no doubt of it. Men are too often harsh with women they love or have loved; women with men. And yet these harshnesses are tenderness itself when compared with the universal harshness out of which they grow; the harshness of the position towards the temperament, of the means towards the aims, of to-day towards yesterday, of hereafter towards to-day.

The historic interest of her family—that masterful line of d'Urbervilles—whom he had despised as a spent force, touched his sentiments now. Why had he not known the difference between the political value and the imaginative value of these things? In the latter aspect her d'Urberville descent was a fact of great dimensions; worthless to economics, it was a most useful ingredient to the dreamer, to the moraliser on declines and falls. It was a fact that would soon be forgotten—that bit of distinction in poor Tess's blood and name, and oblivion would fall upon her hereditary link with the marble monuments and leaded skeletons at Kingsbere. So does Time ruthlessly destroy his own romances. In recalling her face again and again, he thought now that he could see therein a flash of the dignity which must have graced her granddames; and the vision sent that *aura* through his veins which he had formerly felt, and which left behind it a sense of sickness.

Despite her not inviolate past, what still abode in such a woman as Tess outvalued the freshness of her fellows. Was not the gleaning of the grapes of Ephraim better than the vintage of Abi-ezer?

So spoke love renascent, preparing the way for Tess's devoted outpouring, which was then just being forwarded to him by his father; though owing to his distance inland it was to be a long time in reaching him.

Meanwhile the writer's expectation that Angel would come in response to the entreaty was alternately great and small. What lessened it was that the facts of her life which had led to the parting had not changed—could never change; and that, if her presence had not attenuated them, her absence could not. Nevertheless she addressed her mind to the tender question of what she could do to please him best if he should arrive. Sighs were expended on the wish that she had taken more notice of the tunes he played on his harp, that she had enquired more curiously of him which were his favourite ballads among those the country-girls sang. She indirectly enquired of Amby Seedling, who had followed Izz from

Talbothays, and by chance Amby remembered that, amongst the snatches of melody in which they had indulged at the dairyman's, to induce the cows to let down their milk, Clare had seemed to like "Cupid's Gardens," "I have parks, I have hounds," and "The break o' the day"; and had seemed not to care for "The Tailor's Breeches" and "Such a beauty I did grow," excellent ditties as they were.

To perfect the ballads was now her whimsical desire. She practised them privately at odd moments, especially "The break o' the day":

> *Arise, arise, arise!*
> *And pick your love a posy,*
> *All o' the sweetest flowers*
> *That in the garden grow.*
> *The turtle doves and sma' birds*
> *In every bough a-building,*
> *So early in the May-time*
> *At the break o' the day!*

It would have melted the heart of a stone to hear her singing these ditties, whenever she worked apart from the rest of the girls in this cold dry time; the tears running down her cheeks all the while at the thought that perhaps he would not, after all, come to hear her, and the simple silly words of the songs resounding in painful mockery of the aching heart of the singer.

Tess was so wrapt up in this fanciful dream that she seemed not to know how the season was advancing; that the days had lengthened, that Lady-Day was at hand, and would soon be followed by Old Lady-Day, the end of her term here.

But before the quarter-day had quite come something happened which made Tess think of far different matters. She was at her lodging as usual one evening, sitting in the downstairs room with the rest of the family, when somebody knocked at the door and enquired for Tess. Through the doorway she saw against the declining light a figure with the height of a woman and the breadth of a child, a tall, thin, girlish creature whom she did not recognise in the twilight till the girl said "Tess!"

"What—is it 'Liza-Lu?" asked Tess, in startled accents. Her sister, whom a little over a year ago she had left at home as a child, had sprung up by a sudden shoot to a form of this presentation, of which as yet Lu seemed herself scarce able to understand the meaning. Her thin legs, visible below her once long frock now short by her growing, and her uncomfortable hands and arms, revealed her youth and inexperience.

"Yes, I have been traipsing about all day, Tess," said Lu, with unemotional gravity, "a-trying to find 'ee; and I'm very tired."

"What is the matter at home?"

"Mother is took very bad, and the doctor says she's dying, and as father is not very well neither, and says 'tis wrong for a man of such a high family as his to slave and drave at common labouring work, we don't know what to do."

Tess stood in reverie a long time before she thought of asking 'Liza-Lu to come in and sit down. When she had done so, and 'Liza-Lu was having some tea, she came to a decision. It was imperative that she should go home. Her agreement did not end till Old Lady-

Day, the sixth of April, but as the interval thereto was not a long one she resolved to run the risk of starting at once.

To go that night would be a gain of twelve hours; but her sister was too tired to undertake such a distance till the morrow. Tess ran down to where Marian and Izz lived, informed them of what had happened, and begged them to make the best of her case to the farmer. Returning, she got Lu a supper, and after that, having tucked the younger into her own bed, packed up as many of her belongings as would go into a withy basket, and started, directing Lu to follow her next morning.

L

SHE PLUNGED INTO THE CHILLY EQUINOCTIAL DARKNESS AS THE CLOCK STRUCK TEN, FOR her fifteen miles' walk under the steely stars. In lone districts night is a protection rather than a danger to a noiseless pedestrian, and knowing this Tess pursued the nearest course along by-lanes that she would almost have feared in the daytime; but marauders were wanting now, and spectral fears were driven out of her mind by thoughts of her mother. Thus she proceeded mile after mile, ascending and descending till she came to Bulbarrow, and about midnight looked from that height into the abyss of chaotic shade which was all that revealed itself of the vale on whose further side she was born. Having already traversed about five miles on the upland she had now some ten or eleven in the lowland before her journey would be finished. The winding road downwards became just visible to her under the wan starlight as she followed it, and soon she paced a soil so contrasting with that above it that the difference was perceptible to the tread and to the smell. It was the heavy clay land of Blackmoor Vale, and a part of the Vale to which turnpike roads had never penetrated. Superstitions linger longest on these heavy soils. Having once been forest, at this shadowy time it seemed to assert something of its old character, the far and the near being blended, and every tree and tall hedge making the most of its presence. The harts that had been hunted here, the witches that had been pricked and ducked, the green-spangled fairies that "whickered" at you as you passed;—the place teemed with beliefs in them still, and they formed an impish multitude now.

At Nuttlebury she passed the village inn, whose sign creaked in response to the greeting of her footsteps, which not a human soul heard but herself. Under the thatched roofs her mind's eye beheld relaxed tendons and flaccid muscles, spread out in the darkness beneath coverlets made of little purple patchwork squares, and undergoing a bracing process at the hands of sleep for renewed labour on the morrow, as soon as a hint of pink nebulosity appeared on Hambledon Hill.

At three she turned the last corner of the maze of lanes she had threaded, and entered Marlott, passing the field in which as a club-girl, she had first seen Angel Clare, when he had not danced with her; the sense of disappointment remained with her yet. In the direction of her mother's house she saw a light. It came from the bedroom window, and a branch waved in front of it and made it wink at her. As soon as she could discern the outline of the house—newly thatched with her money—it had all its old effect upon Tess's imagination. Part of her body and life it ever seemed to be; the slope of its dormers, the finish of its gables, the broken courses of brick which topped the chimney, all had something in common with her personal character. A stupefaction had come into these features, to her regard; it meant the illness of her mother.

She opened the door so softly as to disturb nobody; the lower room was vacant, but the neighbour who was sitting up with her mother came to the top of the stairs, and whispered that Mrs. Durbeyfield was no better, though she was sleeping just then. Tess prepared herself a breakfast, and then took her place as nurse in her mother's chamber.

In the morning, when she contemplated the children, they had all a curiously elongated look; although she had been away little more than a year their growth was astounding; and the necessity of applying herself heart and soul to their needs took her out of her own cares.

Her father's ill-health was the same indefinite kind, and he sat in his chair as usual. But the day after her arrival he was unusually bright. He had a rational scheme for living, and Tess asked him what it was.

"I'm thinking of sending round to all the old antiqueerians in this part of England," he said, "asking them to subscribe to a fund to maintain me. I'm sure they'd see it as a romantical, artistical, and proper thing to do. They spend lots o' money in keeping up old ruins, and finding the bones o' things, and such like; and living remains must be more interesting to 'em still, if they only knowed of me. Would that somebody would go round and tell 'em what there is living among 'em, and they thinking nothing of him! If Pa'son Tringham, who discovered me, had lived, he'd ha' done it, I'm sure."

Tess postponed her arguments on this high project till she had grappled with pressing matters in hand, which seemed little improved by her remittances. When indoor necessities had been eased she turned her attention to external things. It was now the season for planting and sowing; many gardens and allotments of the villagers had already received their spring tillage; but the garden and the allotment of the Durbeyfields were behindhand. She found, to her dismay, that this was owing to their having eaten all the seed potatoes—that last lapse of the improvident. At the earliest moment she obtained what others she could procure, and in a few days her father was well enough to see to the garden, under Tess's persuasive efforts: while she herself undertook the allotment-plot which they rented in a field a couple of hundred yards out of the village.

She liked doing it after the confinement of the sick chamber, where she was not now required by reason of her mother's improvement. Violent motion relieved thought. The plot of ground was in a high, dry, open enclosure, where there were forty or fifty such pieces, and where labour was at its briskest when the hired labour of the day had ended. Digging began usually at six o'clock, and extended indefinitely into the dusk or moonlight. Just now heaps of dead weeds and refuse were burning on many of the plots, the dry weather favouring their combustion.

One fine day Tess and 'Liza-Lu worked on here with their neighbours till the last rays of the sun smote flat upon the white pegs that divided the plots. As soon as twilight succeeded to sunset the flare of the couch-grass and cabbage-stalk fires began to light up the allotments fitfully, their outlines appearing and disappearing under the dense smoke as wafted by the wind. When a fire glowed, banks of smoke, blown level along the ground, would themselves become illuminated to an opaque lustre, screening the workpeople from one another; and meaning of the "pillar of a cloud," which was a wall by day and a light by night, could be understood.

As evening thickened some of the gardening men and women gave over for the night, but the greater number remained to get their planting done, Tess being among them, though she sent her sister home. It was on one of the couch-burning plots that she laboured with her fork, its four shining prongs resounding against the stones and dry clods in little clicks. Sometimes she was completely involved in the smoke of her fire; then it would leave her figure free, irradiated by the brassy glare from the heap. She was oddly dressed to-night, and presented a somewhat staring aspect, her attire being a gown bleached by many washings, with a short black jacket over it, the effect of the whole being that of a wedding and funeral guest in one. The women further back wore white aprons, which, with their pale faces, were all that could be seen of them in the gloom, except when at moments they caught a flash from the flames.

Westward, the wiry boughs of the bare thorn hedge which formed the boundary of the field rose against the pale opalescence of the lower sky. Above, Jupiter hung like a full-blown jonquil, so bright as almost to throw a shade. A few small nondescript stars were appearing elsewhere. In the distance a dog barked, and wheels occasionally rattled along the dry road.

Still the prongs continued to click assiduously, for it was not late; and though the air was fresh and keen there was a whisper of spring in it that cheered the workers on. Something in the place, the hour, the crackling fires, the fantastic mysteries of light and shade, made others as well as Tess enjoy being there. Night-fall, which in the frost of winter comes as a fiend and in the warmth of summer as a lover, came as a tranquilliser on this March day.

Nobody looked at his or her companions. The eyes of all were on the soil as its turned surface was revealed by the fires. Hence as Tess stirred the clods and sang her foolish little songs with scarce now a hope that Clare would ever hear them, she did not for a long time notice the person who worked nearest to her—a man in a long smock-frock who, she found, was forking the same plot as herself, and whom she supposed her father had sent there to advance the work. She became more conscious of him when the direction of his digging brought him closer. Sometimes the smoke divided them; then it swerved, and the two were visible to each other but divided from all the rest.

Tess did not speak to her fellow-worker, nor did he speak to her. Nor did she think of him further than to recollect that he had not been there when it was broad daylight, and that she did not know him as any one of the Marlott labourers, which was no wonder, her absences having been so long and frequent of late years. By and by he dug so close to her that the fire-beams were reflected as distinctly from the steel prongs of his fork as from her own. On going up to the fire to throw a pitch of dead weeds upon it, she found that he did the same on the other side. The fire flared up, and she beheld the face of d'Urberville.

The unexpectedness of his presence, the grotesqueness of his appearance in a gathered smock-frock, such as was now worn only by the most old-fashioned of the labourers, had a ghastly comicality that chilled her as to its bearing. D'Urberville emitted a low long laugh.

"If I were inclined to joke I should say, How much this seems like Paradise!" he remarked whimsically, looking at her with an inclined head.

"What do you say?" she weakly asked.

"A jester might say this is just like Paradise. You are Eve, and I am the old Other One come to tempt you in the disguise of an inferior animal. I used to be quite up in that scene of Milton's when I was theological. Some of it goes—

> *"Empress, the way is ready, and not long,*
> *Beyond a row of myrtles. . . .*
> *. . . . If thou accept*
> *My conduct, I can bring thee thither soon."*
> *"Lead then," said Eve.*

And so on. My dear Tess, I am only putting this to you as a thing that you might have supposed or said quite untruly, because you think so badly of me."

"I never said you were Satan, or thought it. I don't think of you in that way at all. My thoughts of you are quite cold, except when you affront me. What, did you come digging here entirely because of me?"

"Entirely. To see you; nothing more. The smock-frock, which I saw hanging for sale as I came along, was an after-thought, that I mightn't be noticed. I come to protest against your working like this."

"But I like doing it—it is for my father."

"Your engagement at the other place is ended?"

"Yes."

"Where are you going to next? To join your dear husband?"

She could not bear the humiliating reminder.

"O—I don't know!" she said bitterly. "I have no husband!"

"It is quite true—in the sense you mean. But you have a friend, and I have determined that you shall be comfortable in spite of yourself. When you get down to your house you will see what I have sent there for you."

"O, Alec, I wish you wouldn't give me anything at all! I cannot take it from you! I don't like—it is not right!"

"It *is* right!" he cried lightly. "I am not going to see a woman whom I feel so tenderly for as I do for you, in trouble without trying to help her."

"But I am very well off! I am only in trouble about—about—not about living at all!"

She turned, and desperately resumed her digging, tears dripping upon the fork-handle and upon the clods.

"About the children—your brothers and sisters," he resumed. "I've been thinking of them."

Tess's heart quivered—he was touching her in a weak place. He had divined her chief anxiety. Since returning home her soul had gone out to those children with an affection that was passionate.

"If your mother does not recover, somebody ought to do something for them; since your father will not be able to do much, I suppose?"

"He can with my assistance. He must!"

"And with mine."

"No, sir!"

"How damned foolish this is!" burst out d'Urberville. "Why, he thinks we are the same family; and will be quite satisfied!"

"He don't. I've undeceived him."

"The more fool you!"

D'Urberville in anger retreated from her to the hedge, where he pulled off the long smock-frock which had disguised him; and rolling it up and pushing it into the couch-fire, went away.

Tess could not get on with her digging after this; she felt restless; she wondered if he had gone back to her father's house; and taking the fork in her hand proceeded homewards.

Some twenty yards from the house she was met by one of her sisters.

"O, Tessy—what do you think! 'Liza-Lu is a-crying, and there's a lot of folk in the house, and mother is a good deal better, but they think father is dead!"

The child realised the grandeur of the news; but not as yet its sadness; and stood looking at Tess with round-eyed importance, till, beholding the effect produced upon her, she said—

"What, Tess, shan't we talk to father never no more?"

"But father was only a little bit ill!" exclaimed Tess distractedly.

'Liza-Lu came up.

"He dropped down just now, and the doctor who was there for mother said there was no chance for him, because his heart was growed in."

Yes; the Durbeyfield couple had changed places; the dying one was out of danger, and the indisposed one was dead. The news meant even more than it sounded. Her father's life had a value apart from his personal achievements, or perhaps it would not have had much. It was the last of the three lives for whose duration the house and premises were held under a lease; and it had long been coveted by the tenant-farmer for his regular labourers, who were stinted in cottage accommodation. Moreover, "liviers" were disapproved of in villages almost as much as little freeholders, because of their independence of manner, and when a lease determined it was never renewed.

Thus the Durbeyfields, once d'Urbervilles, saw descending upon them the destiny which, no doubt, when they were among the Olympians of the county, they had caused to descend many a time, and severely enough, upon the heads of such landless ones as they themselves were not. So do flux and reflux—the rhythm of change—alternate and persist in everything under the sky.

LI

AT LENGTH IT WAS THE EVE OF OLD LADY-DAY, AND THE AGRICULTURAL WORLD WAS IN a fever of mobility such as only occurs at that particular date of the year. It is a day of fulfilment; agreements for out-door service during the ensuing year, entered into at Candlemas, are to be now carried out. The labourers—or "work-folk," as they used to call themselves immemorially till the other word was introduced from without—who wish to remain no longer in old places are removing to the new farms.

These annual migrations from farm to farm were on the increase here. When Tess's mother was a child the majority of the field-folk about Marlott had remained all their lives on one farm, which had been the home also of their fathers and grand-fathers; but latterly the desire for yearly removal had risen to a high pitch. With the younger families it was a pleasant excitement which might possibly be an advantage. The Egypt of one family was the Land of Promise to the family who saw it from a distance, till by residence there it became it turn their Egypt also; and so they changed and changed.

However, all the mutations so increasingly discernible in village life did not originate entirely in the agricultural unrest. A depopulation was also going on. The village had formerly contained, side by side with the argicultural labourers, an interesting and better-informed class, ranking distinctly above the former—the class to which Tess's father and mother had belonged—and including the carpenter, the smith, the shoemaker, the huckster, together with nondescript workers other than farm-labourers; a set of people who owed a certain stability of aim and conduct to the fact of their being life-holders like Tess's father, or copyholders, or, occasionally, small freeholders. But as the long holdings fell in they were seldom again let to similar tenants, and were mostly pulled down, if not absolutely required by the farmer for his hands. Cottagers who were not directly employed on the land were looked upon with disfavour, and the banishment of some starved the trade of others, who were thus obliged to follow. These families, who had formed the backbone of the village life in the past, who were the depositaries of the village traditions, had to seek refuge in the large centres; the process, humorously designated by statisticians as "the tendency of the rural population towards the large towns," being really the tendency of water to flow up-hill when forced by machinery.

The cottage accommodation at Marlott having been in this manner considerably curtailed by demolitions, every house which remained standing was required by the agriculturist for his workpeople. Ever since the occurrence of the event which had cast such a shadow over Tess's life, the Durbeyfield family (whose descent was not credited) had been tacitly looked on as one which would have to go when their lease ended, if only in the interests of morality. It was, indeed, quite true that the household had not been shining examples either of temperance, soberness, or chastity. The father, and even the mother, had got drunk at times, the younger children seldom had gone to church, and the eldest daughter had made queer unions. By some means the village had to be kept pure. So on this, the first Lady-Day on which the Durbeyfields were expellable, the house, being roomy, was required for a carter with a large family; and Widow Joan, her daughters Tess and 'Liza-Lu, the boy Abraham and the younger children, had to go elsewhere.

On the evening preceding their removal it was getting dark betimes by reason of a drizzling rain which blurred the sky. As it was the last night they would spend in the village which had been their home and birthplace, Mrs. Durbeyfield, 'Liza-Lu, and Abraham had gone out to bid some friends good-bye, and Tess was keeping house till they should return.

She was kneeling in the window-bench, her face close to the casement, where an outer pane of rain-water was sliding down the inner pane of glass. Her eyes rested on the web of a spider, probably starved long ago, which had been mistakenly placed in a corner where no flies ever came, and shivered in the slight draught through the casement. Tess was reflecting on the position of the household, in which she perceived her own evil influence.

Had she not come home her mother and the children might probably have been allowed to stay on as weekly tenants. But she had been observed almost immediately on her return by some people of scrupulous character and great influence: they had seen her idling in the churchyard, restoring as well as she could with a little trowel a baby's obliterated grave. By this means they had found that she was living here again; her mother was scolded for "harbouring" her; sharp retorts had ensued from Joan, who had independently offered to leave at once; she had been taken at her word; and here was the result.

"I ought never to have come home," said Tess to herself, bitterly.

She was so intent upon these thoughts that she hardly at first took note of a man in a white mackintosh whom she saw riding down the street. Possibly it was owing to her face being near to the pane that he saw her so quickly, and directed his horse so close to the cottage-front that his hoofs were almost upon the narrow border for plants growing under the wall. It was not till he touched the window with his riding-crop that she observed him. The rain had nearly ceased, and she opened the casement in obedience to his gesture.

"Didn't you see me?" asked d'Urberville.

"I was not attending," she said. "I heard you, I believe, though I fancied it was a carriage and horses. I was in a sort of dream."

"Ah! you heard the d'Urberville Coach, perhaps. You know the legend, I suppose?"

"No. My—somebody was going to tell it me once, but didn't."

"If you are a genuine d'Urberville I ought not to tell you either, I suppose. As for me, I'm a sham one, so it doesn't matter. It is rather dismal. It is that this sound of a non-existent coach can only be heard by one of d'Urberville blood, and it is held to be of ill-omen to the one who hears it. It has to do with a murder, committed by one of the family, centuries ago."

"Now you have begun it, finish it."

"Very well. One of the family is said to have abducted some beautiful woman, who tried to escape from the coach in which he was carrying her off, and in the struggle he killed her—or she killed him—I forget which. Such is one version of the tale. . . . I see that your tubs and buckets are packed. Going away, aren't you?"

"Yes, to-morrow—Old Lady-Day."

"I heard you were, but could hardly believe it; it seems so sudden. Why is it?"

"Father's was the last life on the property, and when that dropped we had no further right to stay. Though we might, perhaps, have stayed as weekly tenants—if it had not been for me."

"What about you?"

"I am not a—proper woman."

D'Urberville's face flushed.

"What a blasted shame! Miserable snobs! May their dirty souls be burnt to cinders!" he exclaimed in tones of ironic resentment. "That's why you are going, is it? Turned out?"

"We are not turned out exactly; but as they said we should have to go soon, it was best to go now everybody was moving because there are better chances."

"Where are you going to?"

"Kingsbere. We have taken rooms there. Mother is so foolish about father's people that she will go there."

"But your mother's family are not fit for lodgings, and in a little hole of a town like that. Now why not come to my garden-house at Trantridge? There are hardly any poultry now, since my mother's death; but there's the house, as you know it, and the garden. It can be whitewashed in a day, and your mother can live there quite comfortably; and I will put the children to a good school. Really I ought to do something for you!"

"But we have already taken the rooms at Kingsbere!" she declared. "And we can wait there—"

"Wait—what for? For that nice husband, no doubt. Now look here, Tess, I know what men are, and, bearing in mind the *grounds* of your separation, I am quite positive he will never make it up with you. Now, though I have been your enemy, I am your friend, even if you won't believe it. Come to this cottage of mine. We'll get up a regular colony of fowls, and your mother can attend to them excellently; and the children can go to school."

Tess breathed more and more quickly, and at length she said—

"How do I know that you would do all this? Your views may change—and then—we should be—my mother would be—homeless again."

"O no—no. I would guarantee you against such as that in writing, if necessary. Think it over."

Tess shook her head. But d'Urberville persisted; she had seldom seen him so determined; he would not take a negative.

"Please just tell your mother," he said, in emphatic tones. "It is her business to judge—not yours. I shall get the house swept out and whitened to-morrow morning, and fires lit; and it will be dry by the evening, so that you can come straight there. Now mind, I shall expect you."

Tess again shook her head; her throat swelling with complicated emotion. She could not look up at d'Urberville.

"I owe you something for the past, you know," he resumed. "And you cured me, too, of that craze; so I am glad—"

"I would rather you had kept the craze, so that you had kept the practice which went with it!"

"I am glad of this opportunity of repaying you a little. To-morrow I shall expect to hear your mother's goods unloading. . . . Give me your hand on it now—dear, beautiful Tess!"

With the last sentence he had dropped his voice to a murmur, and put his hand in at the half-open casement. With stormy eyes she pulled the stay-bar quickly, and, in doing so, caught his arm between the casement and the stone mullion.

"Damnation—you are very cruel!" he said, snatching out his arm. "No, no!—I know you didn't do it on purpose. Well, I shall expect you, or your mother and children at least."

"I shall not come—I have plenty of money!" she cried.

"Where?"

"At my father-in-law's, if I ask for it."

"*If* you ask for it. But you won't, Tess; I know you; you'll never ask for it—you'll starve first!"

With these words he rode off. Just at the corner of the street he met the man with the paint-pot, who asked him if he had deserted the brethren.

"You go to the devil!" said d'Urberville.

Tess remained where she was a long while, till a sudden rebellious sense of injustice caused the region of her eyes to swell with the rush of hot tears thither. Her husband, Angel Clare himself, had, like others, dealt out hard measure to her, surely he had! She had never before admitted such a thought; but he had surely! Never in her life—she could swear it from the bottom of her soul—had she ever intended to do wrong; yet these hard judgments had come. Whatever her sins, they were not sins of intention, but of inadvertence, and why should she have been punished so persistently?

She passionately seized the first piece of paper that came to hand, and scribbled the following lines:

O why have you treated me so monstrously, Angel! I do not deserve it. I have thought it all over carefully, and I can never, never forgive you! You know that I did not intend to wrong you— why have you so wronged me? You are cruel, cruel indeed! I will try to forget you. It is all injustice I have received at your hands!   *T.*

She watched till the postman passed by, ran out to him with her epistle, and then again took her listless place inside the window-panes.

It was just as well to write like that as to write tenderly. How could he give way to entreaty? The facts had not changed: there was no new event to alter his opinion.

It grew darker, the fire-light shining over the room. The two biggest of the younger children had gone out with their mother; the four smallest, their ages ranging from three-and-a-half years to eleven, all in black frocks, were gathered round the hearth babbling their own little subjects. Tess at length joined them, without lighting a candle.

"This is the last night that we shall sleep here, dears, in the house where we were born," she said quickly. "We ought to think of it, oughtn't we?"

They all became silent; with the impressibility of their age they were ready to burst into tears at the picture of finality she had conjured up, though all the day hitherto they had been rejoicing in the idea of a new place. Tess changed the subject.

"Sing to me, dears," she said.

"What shall we sing?"

"Anything you know; I don't mind."

There was a momentary pause; it was broken, first, in one little tentative note; then a second voice strengthened it, and a third and a fourth chimed in unison, with words they had learnt at the Sunday-school—

> *Here we suffer grief and pain,*
> *Here we meet to part again;*
> *In Heaven we part no more.*

The four sang on with the phlegmatic passivity of persons who had long ago settled the question, and there being no mistake about it, felt that further thought was not required. With features strained hard to enunciate the syllables they continued to regard the centre of the flickering fire, the notes of the youngest straying over into the pauses of the rest.

Tess turned from them, and went to the window again. Darkness had now fallen without, but she put her face to the pane as though to peer into the gloom. It was really to hide her tears. If she could only believe what the children were singing; if she were only sure, how different all would now be; how confidently she would leave them to Providence and their future kingdom! But, in default of that, it behoved her to do something; to be their Providence; for to Tess, as to not a few millions of others, there was ghastly satire in the poet's lines—

Not in utter nakedness
But trailing clouds of glory do we come.

To her and her like, birth itself was an ordeal of degrading personal compulsion, whose gratuitousness nothing in the result seemed to justify, and at best could only palliate.

In the shades of the wet road she soon discerned her mother with tall 'Liza-Lu and Abraham. Mrs. Durbeyfield's pattens clicked up to the door, and Tess opened it.

"I see the tracks of a horse outside the window," said Joan. "Hev somebody called?"

"No," said Tess.

The children by the fire looked gravely at her, and one murmured—

"Why, Tess, the gentleman a-horseback!"

"He didn't call," said Tess. "He spoke to me in passing."

"Who was the gentleman?" asked the mother. "Your husband?"

"No. He'll never, never come," answered Tess in stony hopelessness.

"Then who was it?"

"Oh, you needn't ask. You've seen him before, and so have I."

"Ah! What did he say?" said Joan curiously.

"I will tell you when we are settled in our lodging at Kingsbere to-morrow—every word."

It was not her husband, she had said. Yet a consciousness that in a physical sense this man alone was her husband seemed to weigh on her more and more.

LII

DURING THE SMALL HOURS OF THE NEXT MORNING, WHILE IT WAS STILL DARK, DWELLERS near the highways were conscious of a disturbance of their night's rest by rumbling noises, intermittently continuing till daylight—noises as certain to recur in this particular first week of the month as the voice of the cuckoo in the third week of the same. They were the preliminaries of the general removal, the passing of the empty waggons and teams to fetch the goods of the migrating families; for it was always by the vehicle of the farmer who required his services that the hired man was conveyed to his destination. That this might be accomplished within the day was the explanation of the reverberation occurring so soon after midnight, the aim of the carters being to reach the door of the outgoing households by six o'clock, when the loading of their movables at once began.

But to Tess and her mother's household no such anxious farmer sent his team. They were only women; they were not regular labourers; they were not particularly required anywhere; hence they had to hire a waggon at their own expense, and got nothing sent gratuitously.

It was a relief to Tess, when she looked out of the window that morning, to find that though the weather was windy and louring, it did not rain, and that the waggon had come. A wet Lady-Day was a spectre which removing families never forgot; damp furniture, damp bedding, damp clothing accompanied it, and left a train of ills.

Her mother, 'Liza-Lu, and Abraham were also awake, but the younger children were let sleep on. The four breakfasted by the thin light, and the "house-ridding" was taken in hand.

It proceeded with some cheerfulness, a friendly neighbour or two assisting. When the large articles of furniture had been packed in position a circular nest was made of the beds and bedding, in which Joan Durbeyfield and the young children were to sit through the journey. After loading there was a long delay before the horses were brought, these having been unharnessed during the ridding; but at length, about two o'clock, the whole was under way, the cooking-pot swinging from the axle of the waggon, Mrs. Durbeyfield and family at the top, the matron having in her lap, to prevent injury to its works, the head of the clock, which, at any exceptional lurch of the waggon, struck one, or one-and-a-half, in hurt tones. Tess and the next eldest girl walked alongside till they were out of the village.

They had called on a few neighbours that morning and the previous evening, and some came to see them off, all wishing them well, though, in their secret hearts, hardly expecting welfare possible to such a family, harmless as the Durbeyfields were to all except themselves. Soon the equipage began to ascend to higher ground, and the wind grew keener with the change of level and soil.

The day being the sixth of April, the Durbeyfield waggon met many other waggons with families on the summit of the load, which was built on a well-nigh unvarying principle, as peculiar, probably, to the rural labourer as the hexagon to the bee. The groundwork of the arrangement was the family dresser, which, with its shining handles, and finger-marks, and domestic evidences thick upon it, stood importantly in front, over the tails of the shaft-horses, in its erect and natural position, like some Ark of the Covenant that they were bound to carry reverently.

Some of the households were lively, some mournful; some were stopping at the doors of wayside inns; where, in due time, the Durbeyfield menagerie also drew up to bait horses and refresh the travellers.

During the halt Tess's eyes fell upon a three-pint blue mug, which was ascending and descending through the air to and from the feminine section of a household, sitting on the summit of a load that had also drawn up at a little distance from the same inn. She followed one of the mug's journeys upward, and perceived it to be clasped by hands whose owner she well knew. Tess went towards the waggon.

"Marian and Izz!" she cried to the girls, for it was they, sitting with the moving family at whose house they had lodged. "Are you house-ridding to-day, like everybody else?"

They were, they said. It had been too rough a life for them at Flintcomb-Ash, and they had come away, almost without notice, leaving Groby to prosecute them if he chose. They told Tess their destination, and Tess told them hers.

Marian leant over the load, and lowered her voice. "Do you know that the gentleman who follows 'ee—you'll guess who I mean—came to ask for 'ee at Flintcomb after you had gone? We didn't tell'n where you was, knowing you wouldn't wish to see him."

"Ah—but I did see him!" Tess murmured. "He found me."

"And do he know where you be going?"

"I think so."

"Husband come back?"

"No."

She bade her acquaintance good-bye—for the respective carters had now come out from the inn—and the two waggons resumed their journey in opposite directions; the vehicle whereon sat Marian, Izz, and the ploughman's family with whom they had thrown in their lot, being brightly painted, and drawn by three powerful horses with shining brass ornaments on their harness; while the waggon on which Mrs. Durbeyfield and her family rode was a creaking erection that would scarcely bear the weight of the superincumbent load; one which had known no paint since it was made, and drawn by two horses only. The contrast well marked the difference between being fetched by a thriving farmer and conveying oneself whither no hirer waited one's coming.

The distance was great—too great for a day's journey—and it was with the utmost difficulty that the horses performed it. Though they had started so early it was quite late in the afternoon when they turned the flank of an eminence which formed part of the upland called Greenhill. While the horses stood to stale and breathe themselves Tess looked around. Under the hill, and just ahead of them, was the half-dead townlet of their pilgrimage, Kingsbere, where lay those ancestors of whom her father had spoken and sung to painfulness: Kingsbere, the spot of all spots in the world which could be considered the d'Urbervilles' home, since they had resided there for full five hundred years.

A man could be seen advancing from the outskirts towards them, and when he beheld the nature of their waggon-load he quickened his steps.

"You be the woman they call Mrs. Durbeyfield, I reckon?" he said to Tess's mother, who had descended to walk the remainder of the way.

She nodded. "Though widow of the late Sir John d'Urberville, poor nobleman, if I cared for my rights; and returning to the domain of his forefathers."

"Oh? Well, I know nothing about that; but if you be Mrs. Durbeyfield, I am sent to tell 'ee that the rooms you wanted be let. We didn't know that you was coming till we got your letter this morning—when 'twas too late. But no doubt you can get other lodgings somewhere."

The man had noticed the face of Tess, which had become ash-pale at his intelligence. Her mother looked hopelessly at fault. "What shall we do now, Tess?" she said bitterly. "Here's a welcome to your ancestors' lands! However, let's try further."

They moved on into the town, and tried with all their might, Tess remaining with the waggon to take care of the children whilst her mother and 'Liza-Lu made enquiries. At the last return of Joan to the vehicle, an hour later, when her search for accommodation had still been fruitless, the driver of the waggon said the goods must be unloaded, as the horses were half-dead, and he was bound to return part of the way at least that night.

"Very well—unload it here," said Joan recklessly. "I'll get shelter somewhere."

The waggon had drawn up under the churchyard wall, in a spot screened from view, and the driver, nothing loath, soon hauled down the poor heap of household goods. This done she paid him, reducing herself to almost her last shilling thereby, and he moved off and left them, only too glad to get out of further dealings with such a family. It was a dry night, and he guessed that they would come to no harm.

Tess gazed desperately at the pile of furniture. The cold sunlight of this spring evening peered invidiously upon the crocks and kettles, upon the bunches of dried herbs shivering in the breeze, upon the brass handles of the dresser, upon the wicker-cradle they had all been rocked in, and upon the well-rubbed clock-case, all of which gave out the reproachful gleam of indoor articles abandoned to the vicissitudes of a roofless exposure for which they were never made. Round about were deparked hills and slopes—now cut up into little paddocks—and the green foundations that showed where the d'Urberville mansion once had stood; also an outlying stretch of Egdon Heath that had always belonged to the estate. Hard by, the aisle of the church called the d'Urberville Aisle looked on imperturbably.

"Isn't your family vault your own freehold?" said Tess's mother, as she returned from a reconnoitre of the church and graveyard. "Why, of course 'tis, and that's where we will camp, girls, till the place of your ancestors finds us a roof! Now Tess and 'Liza and Abraham, you help me. We'll make a nest for these children, and then we'll have another look round."

Tess listlessly lent a hand, and in a quarter of an hour the old four-post bedstead was dissociated from the heap of goods, and erected under the south wall of the church, the part of the building known as the d'Urberville Aisle, beneath which the huge vaults lay. Over the tester of the bedstead was a beautiful traceried window, of many lights, its date being the fifteenth century. It was called the d'Urberville Window, and in the upper part could be discerned heraldic emblems like those on Durbeyfield's old seal and spoon.

Joan drew the curtains round the bed so as to make an excellent tent of it, and put the smaller children inside. "If it comes to the worst we can sleep there too, for one night," she said. "But let us try further on, and get something for the dears to eat! O, Tess, what's the use of your playing at marrying gentlemen, if it leaves us like this!"

Accompanied by 'Liza-Lu and the boy she again ascended the little lane which secluded the church from the townlet. As soon as they got into the street they beheld a man on horseback gazing up and down. "Ah—I'm looking for you!" he said, riding up to them. "This is indeed a family gathering on the historic spot!"

It was Alec d'Urberville. "Where is Tess?" he asked.

Personally Joan had no liking for Alec. She cursorily signified the direction of the church, and went on, d'Urberville saying that he would see them again, in case they should be still unsuccessful in their search for shelter, of which he had just heard. When they had gone d'Urberville rode to the inn, and shortly after came out on foot.

In the interim Tess, left with the children inside the bedstead, remained talking with them a while, till, seeing that no more could be done to make them comfortable just then, she walked about the churchyard, now beginning to be embrowned by the shades of nightfall. The door of the church was unfastened, and she entered it for the first time in her life.

Within the window under which the bedstead stood were the tombs of the family, covering in their dates several centuries. They were canopied, altar-shaped, and plain; their carvings being defaced and broken; their brasses torn from the matrices, the rivet-holes remaining like marten-holes in a sand-cliff. Of all the reminders that she had ever received that her people were socially extinct there was none so forcible as this spoliation.

She drew near to a dark stone on which was inscribed:

Ostium sepulchri antiquae familiae d'Urberville.

Tess did not read Church-Latin like a Cardinal, but she knew that this was the door of her ancestral sepulchre, and that the tall knights of whom her father had chanted in his cups lay inside.

She musingly turned to withdraw, passing near an altar-tomb, the oldest of them all, on which was a recumbent figure. In the dusk she had not noticed it before, and would hardly have noticed it now but for an odd fancy that the effigy moved. As soon as she drew close to it she discovered all in a moment that the figure was a living person; and the shock to her sense of not having been alone was so violent that she was quite overcome, and sank down nigh to fainting, not, however, till she had recognised Alec d'Urberville in the form.

He leapt off the slab and supported her.

"I saw you come in," he said smiling, "and got up there not to interrupt your meditations. A family gathering, is it not, with these old fellows under us here? Listen."

He stamped with his heel heavily on the floor; whereupon there arose a hollow echo from below.

"That shook them a bit, I'll warrant!" he continued. "And you thought I was the mere stone reproduction of one of them. But no. The old order changeth. The little finger of the sham d'Urberville can do more for you than the whole dynasty of the real underneath. . . . Now command me. What shall I do?"

"Go away!" she murmured.

"I will—I'll look for your mother," said he blandly. But in passing her he whispered: "Mind this; you'll be civil yet!"

When he was gone she bent down upon the entrance to the vaults, and said—

"Why am I on the wrong side of this door!"

In the meantime Marian and Izz Huett had journeyed onward with the chattels of the ploughman in the direction of their land of Canaan—the Egypt of some other family who had left it only that morning. But the girls did not for a long time think of where they were going. Their talk was of Angel Clare and Tess, and Tess's persistent lover, whose connection with her previous history they had partly heard and partly guessed ere this.

" 'Tisn't as though she had never known him afore," said Marian. "His having won her once makes all the difference in the world. 'Twould be a thousand pities if he were to tole her away again. Mr. Clare can never be anything to us, Izz; and why should we grudge him to her, and not try to mend this quarrel? If he could on'y know what straits she's put to, and what's hovering round, he might come to take care of his own."

"Could we let him know?"

They thought of this all the way to their destination; but the bustle of reestablishment in their new place took up all their attention then. But when they were settled, a month later, they heard of Clare's approaching return, though they had learnt nothing more of Tess. Upon that, agitated anew by their attachment to him, yet honourably disposed to her, Marian uncorked the penny ink-bottle they shared, and a few lines were concocted between the two girls.

HONOUR'D SIR—Look to your Wife if you do love her as much as she do love you. For she is sore put to by an Enemy in the shape of a Friend. Sir, there is one near her who ought to be Away. A woman should not be try'd beyond her Strength, and continual dropping will wear away a Stone—ay, more—a Diamond.

FROM TWO WELL-WISHERS

This they addressed to Angel Clare at the only place they had ever heard him to be connected with, Emminster vicarage; after which they continued in a mood of emotional exaltation at their own generosity, which made them sing in hysterical snatches and weep at the same time.

END OF PHASE THE SIXTH

PHASE THE SEVENTH

FULFILMENT

LIII

IT WAS EVENING AT EMMINSTER VICARAGE. THE TWO CUSTOMARY CANDLES WERE BURN-ing under their green shades in the vicar's study, but he had not been sitting there. Occasionally he came in, stirred the small fire which sufficed for the increasing mildness of the spring, and went out again; sometimes pausing at the front-door, going on to the drawing-room, then returning again to the front-door.

It faced westward, and though gloom prevailed inside, there was still light enough without to see with distinctness. Mrs. Clare, who had been sitting in the drawing-room, followed him hither.

"Plenty of time yet," said the vicar. "He doesn't reach Chalk-Newton till six, even if the train should be punctual, and ten miles of country-road, five of them in Crimmercrock Lane, are not jogged over in a hurry by our old horse."

"But he has done it in an hour with us, my dear."

"Years ago."

Thus they passed the minutes, each well knowing that this was only waste of breath, the one essential being simply to wait.

At length there was a slight noise in the lane, and the old pony-chaise appeared indeed outside the railings. They saw alight therefrom a form which they affected to recognise, but would actually have passed by in the street without identifying had he not got out of their carriage at the particular moment when a particular person was due.

Mrs. Clare rushed through the dark passage to the door, and her husband came more slowly after her.

The new arrival, who was just about to enter, saw their anxious faces in the doorway and the gleam of the west in their spectacles because they confronted the last rays of day; but they could only see his shape against the light.

"O, my boy, my boy—home again at last!" cried Mrs. Clare, who cared no more at that moment for the stains of heterodoxy which has caused all this separation than for the dust upon his clothes. What woman, indeed, among the most faithful adherents of the truth, believes the promises and threats of the Word in the sense in which she believes in her own children, or would not throw her theology to the wind if weighed against their happiness? As soon as they reached the room where the candles were lighted she looked at his face.

"O, it is not Angel—not my son—the Angel who went away!" she cried in all the irony of sorrow, as she turned herself aside.

His father, too, was shocked to see him, so reduced was that figure from its former contours by worry and the bad season that Clare had experienced, in the climate to which he had so rashly hurried in his first aversion to the mockery of events at home. You could see the skeleton behind the man, and almost the ghost behind the skeleton. He matched Crivelli's dead *Christus.* His sunken eye-pits were of morbid hue, and the light in his eyes had waned. The angular hollows and lines of his aged ancestors had succeeded to their reign in his face twenty years before their time.

"I was ill over there, you know," he said. "I am all right now."

As if, however, to falsify this assertion, his legs seemed to give way, and he suddenly sat down to save himself from falling. It was only a slight attack of faintness, resulting from the tedious day's journey, and the excitement of arrival.

"Has any letter come for me lately?" he asked. "I received the last you sent on by the merest chance, and after considerable delay through being inland; or I might have come sooner."

"It was from your wife, we supposed?"

"It was."

Only one other had recently come. They had not sent it on to him, knowing he would start for home so soon.

He hastily opened the letter produced, and was much disturbed to read in Tess's handwriting the sentiments expressed in her last hurried scrawl to him.

O why have you treated me so monstrously, Angel! I do not deserve it. I have thought it all over carefully, and I can never, never forgive you! You know that I did not intend to wrong you— why have you so wronged me? You are cruel, cruel indeed! I will try to forget you. It is all injustice I have received at your hands.   *T.*

"It is quite true!" said Angel, throwing down the letter. "Perhaps she will never be reconciled to me!"

"Don't, Angel, be so anxious about a mere child of the soil!" said his mother.

"Child of the soil! Well, we all are children of the soil. I wish she were so in the sense you mean; but let me now explain to you what I have never explained before, that her father is a descendant in the male line of one of the oldest Norman houses, like a good many others who lead obscure agricultural lives in our villages, and are dubbed 'sons of the soil.' "

He soon retired to bed; and the next morning, feeling exceedingly unwell, he remained in his room pondering. The circumstances amid which he had left Tess were such that though, while on the south of the Equator and just in receipt of her loving epistle, it had seemed the easiest thing in the world to rush back into her arms the moment he chose to forgive her, now that he had arrived it was not so easy as it had seemed. She was passionate, and her present letter, showing that her estimate of him had changed under his delay—too justly changed, he sadly owned,—made him ask himself if it would be wise to confront her unannounced in the presence of her parents. Supposing that her love had indeed turned to dislike during the last weeks of separation, a sudden meeting might lead to bitter words.

Clare therefore thought it would be best to prepare Tess and her family by sending a line to Marlott announcing his return, and his hope that she was still living with them there, as he had arranged for her to do when he left England. He despatched the enquiry that very day, and before the week was out there came a short reply from Mrs. Durbeyfield which did not remove his embarrassment, for it bore no address, though to his surprise it was not written from Marlott.

SIR—J write these few lines to say that my Daughter is away from me at present, and J am not sure when she will return, but J will let you know as Soon as she do. J do not feel at liberty to tell you Where she is temperly biding. J should say that me and my Family have left Marlott for some Time.—Yours,

J. DURBEYFIELD

It was such a relief to Clare to learn that Tess was at least apparently well that her mother's stiff reticence as to her whereabouts did not long distress him. They were all angry with him, evidently. He would wait till Mrs. Durbeyfield could inform him of Tess's return, which her letter implied to be soon. He deserved no more. His had been a love "which alters when it alteration finds". He had undergone some strange experiences in his absence; he had seen the virtual Faustina in the literal Cornelia, a spiritual Lucretia in a corporeal Phryne; he had thought of the woman taken and set in the midst as one deserving to be stoned, and of the wife of Uriah being made a queen; and he had asked himself why he had not judged Tess constructively rather than biographically, by the will rather than by the deed?

A day or two passed while he waited at his father's house for the promised second note from Joan Durbeyfield, and indirectly to recover a little more strength. The strength showed signs of coming back, but there was no sign of Joan's letter. Then he hunted up the old letter sent on to him in Brazil, which Tess had written from Flintcomb-Ash, and reread it. The sentences touched him now as much as when he had first perused them.

I must cry to you in my trouble—I have no one else. . . . I think I must die if you do not come soon, or tell me to come to you. . . . Please, please, not to be just; only a little kind to me! . . . If you would come, I could die in your arms! I would be well content to do that if so be you had forgiven me! . . . If you will send me one little line and say, I am coming soon, *I will bide on, Angel, O so cheerfully! . . . Think how it do hurt my heart not to see you ever, ever! Ah, if I could only make your dear heart ache one little minute of each day as mine does everyday and all day long, it might lead you to show pity to your poor lonely one. . . . I would be content, ay, glad, to live with you as your servant, if I may not as your wife; so that I could only be near you, and get glimpses of you, and think of you as mine. . . . I long for only one thing in heaven or earth or under the earth, to meet you, my own dear! Come to me—come to me, and save me from what threatens me.*

Clare determined that he would no longer believe in her more recent and severer regard of him; but would go and find her immediately. He asked his father if she had applied for any money during his absence. His father returned a negative, and then for the first time it occurred to Angel that her pride had stood in her way, and that she had suffered privation. From his remarks his parents now gathered the real reason of the separation; and their Christianity was such that, reprobates being their especial care, the tenderness towards Tess which her blood, her simplicity, even her poverty, had not engendered, was instantly excited by her sin.

Whilst he was hastily packing together a few articles for his journey he glanced over a poor plain missive also lately come to hand—the one from Marian and Izz Huett, beginning—

"HONOUR'D SIR—Look to your wife if you do love her as much as she do love you," and signed, "FROM TWO WELL-WISHERS."

LIV

I N A QUARTER OF AN HOUR CLARE WAS LEAVING THE HOUSE, WHENCE HIS MOTHER watched his thin figure as it disappeared into the street. He had declined to borrow his father's old mare, well knowing of its necessity to the household. He went to the inn, where he hired a trap, and could hardly wait during the harnessing. In a very few minutes after he was driving up the hill out of the town which, three or four months earlier in the year, Tess had descended with such hopes and ascended with such shattered purposes.

Benvill Lane soon stretched before him, its hedges and trees purple with buds; but he was looking at other things, and only recalled himself to the scene sufficiently to enable him to keep the way. In something less than an hour-and-a-half he had skirted the south of the King's Hintock estates and ascended to the untoward solitude of Cross-in-Hand, the unholy stone whereon Tess had been compelled by Alec d'Urberville, in his whim of reformation, to swear the strange oath that she would never wilfully tempt him again. The pale and blasted nettle-stems of the preceding year even now lingered nakedly in the banks, young green nettles of the present spring growing from their roots.

Thence he went along the verge of the upland overhanging the other Hintocks, and, turning to the right, plunged into the bracing calcareous region of Flintcomb-Ash, the address from which she had written to him in one of the letters, and which he supposed to be the place of sojourn referred to by her mother. Here, of course, he did not find her; and what added to his depression was the discovery that no "Mrs. Clare" had ever been heard of by the cottagers or by the farmer himself, though Tess was remembered well enough by her Christian name. His name she had obviously never used during their separation, and her dignified sense of their total severance was shown not much less by this abstention than by the hardships she had chosen to undergo (of which he now learnt for the first time) rather than apply to his father for more funds.

From this place they told him Tess Durbeyfield had gone, without due notice, to the home of her parents on the other side of Blackmoor, and it therefore became necessary to find Mrs. Durbeyfield. She had told him she was not now at Marlott, but had been curiously reticent as to her actual address, and the only course was to go to Marlott and enquire for it. The farmer who had been so churlish with Tess was quite smooth-tongued to Clare, and lent him a horse and man to drive him towards Marlott, the gig he had arrived in being sent back to Emminster; for the limit of a day's journey with that horse was reached.

Clare would not accept the loan of the farmer's vehicle for a further distance than to the outskirts of the Vale, and, sending it back with the man who had driven him, he put up at an inn, and next day entered on foot the region wherein was the spot of his dear Tess's birth. It was as yet too early in the year for much colour to appear in the gardens and foliage; the so-called spring was but winter overlaid with a thin coat of greenness, and it was of a parcel with his expectations.

The house in which Tess had passed the years of her childhood was now inhabited by another family who had never known her. The new residents were in the garden, taking as much interest in their own doings as if the homestead had never passed its primal time in conjunction with the histories of others, beside which the histories of these were but as a tale told by an idiot. They walked about the garden paths with thoughts of their own concerns entirely uppermost, bringing their actions at every moment in jarring collision with the dim ghosts behind them, talking as though the time when Tess lived there were not one whit intenser in story than now. Even the spring birds sang over their heads as if they thought there was nobody missing in particular.

On enquiry of these precious innocents, to whom even the name of their predecessors was a failing memory, Clare learned that John Durbeyfield was dead; that his widow and children had left Marlott, declaring that they were going to live at Kingsbere, but instead of doing so had gone on to another place they mentioned. By this time Clare abhorred the house for ceasing to contain Tess, and hastened away from its hated presence without once looking back.

His way was by the field in which he had first beheld her at the dance. It was as bad as the house—even worse. He passed on through the churchyard, where, amongst the new head-stones, he saw one of a somewhat superior design to the rest. The inscription ran thus:

IN MEMORY OF JOHN DURBEYFIELD, RIGHTLY D'URBERVILLE, OF THE ONCE POW-
ERFUL FAMILY OF THAT NAME, AND DIRECT DESCENDANT THROUGH AN ILLUS-
TRIOUS LINE FROM SIR PAGAN D'URBERVILLE, ONE OF THE KNIGHTS OF THE
CONQUEROR. DIED MARCH 10TH, 18—

HOW ARE THE MIGHTY FALLEN.

Some man, apparently the sexton, had observed Clare standing there, and drew nigh. "Ah, sir, now that's a man who didn't want to lie here, but wished to be carried to Kingsbere, where his ancestors be."

"And why didn't they respect his wish?"

"Oh—no money. Bless your soul, sir, why—there, I wouldn't wish to say it everywhere, but—even this head-stone, for all the flourish wrote upon en, is not paid for."

"Ah, who put it up?"

The man told the name of a mason in the village, and, on leaving the churchyard, Clare called at the mason's house. He found that the statement was true, and paid the bill. This done he turned in the direction of the migrants.

The distance was too long for a walk, but Clare felt such a strong desire for isolation that at first he would neither hire a conveyance nor go to a circuitous line of railway by which he might eventually reach the place. At Shaston, however, he found he must hire; but the way was such that he did not enter Joan's place till about seven o'clock in the evening, having traversed a distance of over twenty miles since leaving Marlott.

The village being small he had little difficulty in finding Mrs. Durbeyfield's tenement, which was a house in a walled garden, remote from the main road, where she had stowed away her clumsy old furniture as best she could. It was plain that for some reason or other she had not wished him to visit her, and he felt his call to be somewhat of an intrusion. She came to the door herself, and the light from the evening sky fell upon her face.

This was the first time that Clare had ever met her, but he was too preoccupied to observe more than that she was still a handsome woman, in the garb of a respectable widow. He was obliged to explain that he was Tess's husband, and his object in coming there, and he did it awkwardly enough. "I want to see her at once," he added. "You said you would write to me again, but you have not done so."

"Because she've not come home," said Joan.

"Do you know if she is well?"

"I don't. But you ought to, sir," said she.

"I admit it. Where is she staying?"

From the beginning of the interview Joan had disclosed her embarrassment by keeping her hand to the side of her cheek.

"I—don't know exactly where she is staying," she answered. "She was—but—"

"Where was she?"

"Well, she is not there now."

In her evasiveness she paused again, and the younger children had by this time crept to the door, where, pulling at his mother's skirts, the youngest murmured—

"Is this the gentleman who is going to marry Tess?"

"He has married her," Joan whispered. "Go inside."

Clare saw her efforts for reticence, and asked—

"Do you think Tess would wish me to try and find her? If not, of course—"

"I don't think she would."

"Are you sure?"

"I am sure she wouldn't."

He was turning away; and then he thought of Tess's tender letter.

"I am sure she would!" he retorted passionately. "I know her better than you do."

"That's very likely, sir; for I have never really known her."

"Please tell me her address, Mrs. Durbeyfield, in kindness to a lonely wretched man!"

Tess's mother again restlessly swept her cheek with her vertical hand, and seeing that he suffered, she at last said, in a low voice—

"She is at Sandbourne."

"Ah—where there? Sandbourne has become a large place, they say."

"I don't know more particularly than I have said—Sandbourne. For myself, I was never there."

It was apparent that Joan spoke the truth in this, and he pressed her no further.

"Are you in want of anything?" he said gently.

"No, sir," she replied. "We are fairly well provided for."

Without entering the house Clare turned away. There was a station three miles ahead, and paying off his coachman, he walked thither. The last train to Sandbourne left shortly after, and it bore Clare on its wheels.

LV

AT ELEVEN O'CLOCK THAT NIGHT, HAVING SECURED A BED AT ONE OF THE HOTELS AND telegraphed his address to his father immediately on his arrival, he walked out into the streets of Sandbourne. It was too late to call on or enquire for anyone, and he reluctantly postponed his purpose till the morning. But he could not retire to rest just yet.

This fashionable watering-place, with its eastern and its western stations, its piers, its groves of pines, its promenades, and its covered gardens, was, to Angel Clare, like a fairy place suddenly created by the stroke of a wand, and allowed to get a little dusty. An outlying eastern tract of the enormous Egdon Waste was close at hand, yet on the very verge of that tawny piece of antiquity such a glittering novelty as this pleasure city had chosen to spring up. Within the space of a mile from its outskirts every irregularity of the soil was prehistoric, every channel an undisturbed British trackway; not a sod having been turned there since the days of the Cæsars. Yet the exotic had grown here, suddenly as the prophet's gourd; and had drawn hither Tess.

By the midnight lamps he went up and down the winding way of this new world in an old one, and could discern between the trees and against the stars the lofty roofs, chimneys, gazebos, and towers of the numerous fanciful residences of which the place was composed. It was a city of detached mansions; a Mediterranean lounging-place on the English Channel; and as seen now by night it seemed even more imposing than it was.

The sea was near at hand, but not intrusive; it murmured, and he thought it was the pines; the pines murmured in precisely the same tones, and he thought they were the sea.

Where could Tess possibly be, a cottage-girl, his young wife, amidst all this wealth and fashion? The more he pondered the more was he puzzled. Were there any cows to milk here? There certainly were no fields to till. She was most probably engaged to do something in one of these large houses; and he sauntered along, looking at the chamber-windows and their lights going out one by one; and wondered which of them might be hers.

Conjecture was useless, and just after twelve o'clock he entered and went to bed. Before putting out his light he reread Tess's impassioned letter. Sleep, however, he could not—so near her, yet so far from her—and he continually lifted the window-blind and regarded the backs of the opposite houses, and wondered behind which of the sashes she reposed at that moment.

He might almost as well have sat up all night. In the morning he arose at seven, and shortly after went out, taking the direction of the chief post-office. At the door he met an intelligent postman coming out with letters for the morning delivery.

"Do you know the address of a Mrs. Clare?" asked Angel.

The postman shook his head.

Then, remembering that she would have been likely to continue the use of her maiden name, Clare said—

"Or a Miss Durbeyfield?"

"Durbeyfield?"

This also was strange to the postman addressed.

"There's visitors coming and going every day, as you know, sir," he said; "and without the name of the house 'tis impossible to find 'em."

One of his comrades hastening out at that moment, the name was repeated to him.

"I know no name of Durbeyfield; but there is the name of d'Urberville at The Herons," said the second.

"That's it!" cried Clare, pleased to think that she had reverted to the real pronunciation. "What place is The Herons?"

"A stylish lodging-house. 'Tis all lodging-houses here, bless 'ee."

Clare received directions how to find the house, and hastened thither, arriving with the milkman. The Herons, though an ordinary villa, stood in its own grounds, and was certainly the last place in which one would have expected to find lodgings, so private was its appearance. If poor Tess was a servant here, as he feared, she would go to the back-door to that milkman, and he was inclined to go thither also. However, in his doubts he turned to the front, and rang.

The hour being early the landlady herself opened the door. Clare enquired for Teresa d'Urberville or Durbeyfield.

"Mrs. d'Urberville?"

"Yes."

Tess, then, passed as a married woman, and he felt glad, even though she had not adopted his name.

"Will you kindly tell her that a relative is anxious to see her?"

"It is rather early. What name shall I give, sir?"

"Angel."

"Mr. Angel?"

"No; Angel. It is my Christian name. She'll understand."

"I'll see if she is awake."

He was shown into the front-room—the dining-room—and looked out through the spring curtains at the little lawn, and the rhododendrons and other shrubs upon it. Obviously her position was by no means so bad as he had feared, and it crossed his mind that she must somehow have claimed and sold the jewels to attain it. He did not blame her for one moment. Soon his sharpened ear detected footsteps upon the stairs, at which his heart thumped so painfully that he could hardly stand firm. "Dear me! what will she think of me, so altered as I am!" he said to himself; and the door opened.

Tess appeared on the threshold—not at all as he had expected to see her—bewilderingly otherwise, indeed. Her great natural beauty was, if not heightened, rendered more obvious by her attire. She was loosely wrapped in a cashmere dressing-gown of grey-white, embroidered in half-mourning tints, and she wore slippers of the same hue. Her neck rose out of a frill of down, and her well-remembered cable of dark-brown hair was partially coiled up in a mass at the back of her head and partly hanging on her shoulder—the evident result of haste.

He had held out his arms, but they had fallen again to his side; for she had not come forward, remaining still in the opening of the doorway. Mere yellow skeleton that he was now he felt the contrast between them, and thought his appearance distasteful to her.

"Tess!" he said huskily, "can you forgive me for going away? Can't you—come to me? How do you get to be—like this?"

"It is too late," said she, her voice sounding hard through the room, her eyes shining unnaturally.

"I did not think rightly of you—I did not see you as you were!" he continued to plead. "I have learnt to since, dearest Tessy mine!"

"Too late, too late!" she said, waving her hand in the impatience of a person whose tortures cause every instant to seem an hour. "Don't come close to me, Angel! No—you must not. Keep away."

"But don't you love me, my dear wife, because I have been so pulled down by illness? You are not so fickle—I am come on purpose for you—my mother and father will welcome you now!"

"Yes—O, yes, yes! But I say, I say it is too late."

She seemed to feel like a fugitive in a dream, who tries to move away, but cannot. "Don't you know all—don't you know it? Yet how do you come here if you do not know?"

"I enquired here and there, and I found the way."

"I waited and waited for you," she went on, her tones suddenly resuming their old fluty pathos. "But you did not come! And I wrote to you, and you did not come! He kept on saying you would never come any more, and that I was a foolish woman. He was very kind to me, and to mother, and to all of us after father's death. He—"

"I don't understand."

"He has won me back to him."

Clare looked at her keenly, then, gathering her meaning, flagged like one plague-stricken, and his glance sank; it fell on her hands, which, once rosy, were now white and more delicate.

She continued—

"He is upstairs. I hate him now, because he told me a lie—that you would not come again; and you *have* come! These clothes are what he's put upon me: I didn't care what he did wi' me! But—will you go away, Angel, please, and never come any more?"

They stood fixed, their baffled hearts looking out of their eyes with a joylessness pitiful to see. Both seemed to implore something to shelter them from reality.

"Ah—it is my fault!" said Clare.

But he could not get on. Speech was as inexpressive as silence. But he had a vague consciousness of one thing, though it was not clear to him till later; that his original Tess had spiritually ceased to recognise the body before him as hers—allowing it to drift, like a corpse upon the current, in a direction dissociated from its living will.

A few instants passed, and he found that Tess was gone. His face grew colder and more shrunken as he stood concentrated on the moment, and a minute or two after he found himself in the street, walking along he did not know whither.

LVI

M RS. BROOKS, THE LADY WHO WAS THE HOUSEHOLDER AT THE HERONS, AND OWNER OF all the handsome furniture, was not a person of an unusually curious turn of mind. She was too deeply materialised, poor woman, by her long and enforced bondage to that arithmetical demon Profit-and-Loss, to retain much curiosity for its own sake, and apart from possible lodgers' pockets. Nevertheless, the visit of Angel Clare to her well-paying tenants, Mr. and Mrs. d'Urberville, as she deemed them, was sufficiently exceptional in point of time and manner to reinvigorate the feminine proclivity which had been stifled down as useless save in its bearings on the letting trade.

Tess had spoken to her husband from the doorway, without entering the dining-room, and Mrs. Brooks, who stood within the partly-closed door of her own sitting-room at the back of the passage, could hear fragments of the conversation—if conversation it could be called—between those two wretched souls. She heard Tess reascend the stairs to the first floor, and the departure of Clare, and the closing of the front-door behind him. Then the door of the room above was shut, and Mrs. Brooks knew that Tess had re-entered her apartment. As the young lady was not fully dressed, Mrs. Brooks knew that she would not emerge again for some time.

She accordingly ascended the stairs softly, and stood at the door of the front-room— a drawing-room, connected with the room immediately behind it (which was a bedroom) by folding-doors in the common manner. This first floor, containing Mrs. Brooks's best apartments, had been taken by the week by the d'Urbervilles. The back-room was now in silence; but from the drawing-room there came sounds.

All that she could at first distinguish of them was one syllable, continually repeated in a low note of moaning, as if it came from a soul bound to some Ixionian wheel—

"O—O—O!"

Then a silence, then a heavy sigh, and again—

"O—O—O!"

The landlady looked through the keyhole. Only a small space of the room inside was visible, but within that space came a corner of the breakfast-table, which was already spread for the meal, and also a chair beside. Over the seat of the chair Tess's face was bowed, her posture being a kneeling one in front of it; her hands were clasped over her head, the skirts of her dressing-gown and the embroidery of her night-gown flowed upon the floor behind her, and her stockingless feet, from which the slippers had fallen, pro-truded upon the carpet. It was from her lips that came the murmur of unspeakable despair.

Then a man's voice from the adjoining bedroom—

"What's the matter?"

She did not answer, but went on, in a tone which was a soliloquy rather than an ex-clamation, and a dirge rather than a soliloquy. Mrs. Brooks could only catch a portion:

"And then my dear, dear husband came home to me . . . and I did not know it! . . . And you had used your cruel persuasion upon me . . . you did not stop using it—no—you did not stop! My little sisters and brothers and my mother's needs—they were the things you moved me by . . . and you said my husband would never come back—never; and you taunted me, and said what a simpleton I was to expect him! . . . And at last I believed you and gave way! . . . And then he came back! Now he is gone. Gone a second time, and I have lost him now forever . . . and he will not love me the littlest bit ever any more—only hate me! . . . O yes, I have lost him now—again because of—you!" In writhing, with her head on the chair, she turned her face towards the door, and Mrs. Brooks could see the pain upon it; and that her lips were bleeding from the clench of her teeth upon them, and that the long lashes of her closed eyes stuck in wet tags to her cheeks. She continued: "And he is dying—he looks as if he is dying! . . . And my sin will kill him and not kill me! . . . O, you have torn my life all to pieces . . . made me be what I prayed you in pity not to make me be again! . . . My own true husband will never, never—O God—I can't bear this!—I cannot!"

There were more and sharper words from the man; then a sudden rustle; she had sprung to her feet. Mrs. Brooks, thinking that the speaker was coming to rush out of the door, hastily retreated down the stairs.

She need not have done so, however, for the door of the sitting-room was not opened. But Mrs. Brooks felt it unsafe to watch on the landing again, and entered her own parlour below.

She could hear nothing through the floor, although she listened intently, and thereupon went to the kitchen to finish her interrupted breakfast. Coming up presently to the front-room on the ground floor she took up some sewing, waiting for her lodgers to ring that she might take away the breakfast, which she meant to do herself, to discover what was the matter if possible. Overhead, as she sat, she could now hear the floorboards slightly creak, as if someone were walking about, and presently the movement was explained by the rustle of garments against the banisters, the opening and the closing of the front-door, and the form of Tess passing to the gate on her way into the street. She was fully dressed now in the walking costume of a well-to-do young lady in which she had arrived, with the sole addition that over her hat and black feathers a veil was drawn.

Mrs. Brooks had not been able to catch any word of farewell, temporary or otherwise, between her tenants at the door above. They might have quarrelled, or Mr. d'Urberville might still be asleep, for he was not an early riser.

She went into the back-room which was more especially her own apartment, and continued her sewing there. The lady lodger did not return, nor did the gentleman ring his bell. Mrs. Brooks pondered on the delay, and on what probable relation the visitor who had called so early bore to the couple upstairs. In reflecting she leant back in her chair.

As she did so her eyes glanced casually over the ceiling till they were arrested by a spot in the middle of its white surface which she had never noticed there before. It was about the size of a wafer when she first observed it, but it speedily grew as large as the palm of her hand, and then she could perceive that it was red. The oblong white ceiling, with this scarlet blot in the midst, had the appearance of a gigantic ace of hearts.

Mrs. Brooks had strange qualms of misgiving. She got upon the table, and touched the spot in the ceiling with her fingers. It was damp, and she fancied that it was a blood stain.

Descending from the table, she left the parlour, and went upstairs, intending to enter the room overhead, which was the bed-chamber at the back of the drawing-room. But, nerveless woman as she had now become, she could not bring herself to attempt the handle. She listened. The dead silence within was broken only by a regular beat.

Drip, drip, drip.

Mrs. Brooks hastened downstairs, opened the front-door, and ran into the street. A man she knew, one of the workmen employed at an adjoining villa, was passing by, and she begged him to come in and go upstairs with her; she feared something had happened to one of her lodgers. The workman assented, and followed her to the landing.

She opened the door of the drawing-room, and stood back for him to pass in, entering herself behind him. The room was empty; the breakfast—a substantial repast of coffee, eggs, and a cold ham—lay spread upon the table untouched, as when she had taken it up, excepting that the carving-knife was missing. She asked the man to go through the folding-doors into the adjoining room.

He opened the doors, entered a step or two, and came back almost instantly with a rigid face. "My good God, the gentleman in bed is dead! I think he has been hurt with a knife—a lot of blood had run down upon the floor!"

The alarm was soon given, and the house which had lately been so quiet resounded with the tramp of many footsteps, a surgeon among the rest. The wound was small, but the point of the blade had touched the heart of the victim, who lay on his back, pale, fixed, dead, as if he had scarcely moved after the infliction of the blow. In a quarter of an hour the news that a gentleman who was a temporary visitor to the town had been stabbed in his bed, spread through every street and villa of the popular watering-place.

LVII

MEANWHILE ANGEL CLARE HAD WALKED AUTOMATICALLY ALONG THE WAY BY WHICH he had come, and, entering his hotel, sat down over the breakfast, staring at nothingness. He went on eating and drinking unconsciously till on a sudden he demanded his bill; having paid which he took his dressing-bag in his hand, the only luggage he had brought with him, and went out.

At the moment of his departure a telegram was handed to him—a few words from his mother, stating that they were glad to know his address, and informing him that his brother Cuthbert had proposed to and been accepted by Mercy Chant.

Clare crumpled up the paper, and followed the route to the station; reaching it, he found that there would be no train leaving for an hour and more. He sat down to wait, and having waited a quarter of an hour felt that he could wait there no longer. Broken in heart and numbed, he had nothing to hurry for; but he wished to get out of a town which had been the scene of such an experience, and turned to walk to the first station onward, and let the train pick him up there.

The highway that he followed was open, and at a little distance dipped into a valley, across which it could be seen running from edge to edge. He had traversed the greater part of this depression, and was climbing the western acclivity, when, pausing for breath, he unconsciously looked back. Why he did so he could not say, but something seemed to impel him to the act. The tapelike surface of the road diminished in his rear as far as he could see, and as he gazed a moving spot intruded on the white vacuity of its perspective.

It was a human figure running. Clare waited, with a dim sense that somebody was trying to overtake him.

The form descending the incline was a woman's, yet so entirely was his mind blinded to the idea of his wife's following him that even when she came nearer he did not recognise her under the totally changed attire in which he now beheld her. It was not till she was quite close that he could believe her to be Tess.

"I saw you—turn away from the station—just before I got there—and I have been following you all this way!"

She was so pale, so breathless, so quivering in every muscle, that he did not ask her a single question, but seizing her hand, and pulling it within his arm, he led her along. To avoid meeting any possible wayfarers he left the high-road, and took a footpath under some fir-trees. When they were deep among the moaning boughs he stopped and looked at her enquiringly.

"Angel," she said, as if waiting for this, "do you know what I have been running after you for? To tell you that I have killed him!" A pitiful white smile lit her face as she spoke.

"What!" said he, thinking from the strangeness of her manner that she was in some delirium.

"I have done it—I don't know how," she continued. "Still, I owed it to you, and to myself, Angel. I feared long ago, when I struck him on the mouth with my glove, that I might do it some day for the trap he set for me in my simple youth, and his wrong to you through me. He has come between us and ruined us, and now he can never do it any more. I never loved him at all, Angel, as I loved you. You know it, don't you? You believe it? You didn't come back to me, and I was obliged to go back to him. Why did you go away—why did you—when I loved you so? I can't think why you did it. But I don't blame you; only, Angel, will you forgive me my sin against you, now I have killed him? I thought as I ran along that you would be sure to forgive me now I have done that. It came to me as a shining light that I should get you back that way. I could not bear the loss of you any longer—you don't know how entirely I was unable to bear your not loving me! Say you do now, dear, dear husband; say you do, now I have killed him!"

"I do love you, Tess—O, I do—it is all come back!" he said, tightening his arms round her with fervid pressure. "But how do you mean—you have killed him?"

"I mean that I have," she murmured in a reverie.

"What, bodily? Is he dead?"

"Yes. He heard me crying about you, and he bitterly taunted me; and called you by a foul name; and then I did it. My heart could not bear it. He had nagged me about you before. And then I dressed myself and came away to find you."

By degrees he was inclined to believe that she had faintly attempted, at least, what she said she had done; and his horror at her impulse was mixed with amazement at the strength of her affection for himself, and at the strangeness of its quality, which had apparently extinguished her moral sense altogether. Unable to realise the gravity of her conduct she seemed at last content; and he looked at her as she lay upon his shoulder, weeping with happiness, and wondered what obscure strain in the d'Urberville blood had led to this aberration—if it were an aberration. There momentarily flashed through his mind that the family tradition of the coach and murder might have arisen because the d'Urbervilles had been known to do these things. As well as his confused and excited ideas could reason, he supposed that in the moment of mad grief of which she spoke her mind had lost its balance, and plunged her into this abyss.

It was very terrible if true; if a temporary hallucination, sad. But, anyhow, here was this deserted wife of his, this passionately-fond woman, clinging to him without a suspicion that he would be anything to her but a protector. He saw that for him to be otherwise was not, in her mind, within the region of the possible. Tenderness was absolutely dominant in Clare at last. He kissed her endlessly with his white lips, and held her hand, and said—

"I will not desert you! I will protect you by every means in my power, dearest love, whatever you may have done or not have done!"

They then walked on under the trees, Tess turning her head every now and then to look at him. Worn and unhandsome as he had become, it was plain that she did not discern the least fault in his appearance. To her he was, as of old, all that was perfection, personally and mentally. He was still her Antinous, her Apollo even; his sickly face was beautiful as the morning to her affectionate regard on this day no less than when she first beheld him; for was it not the face of the one man on earth who had loved her purely, and who had believed in her as pure!

With an instinct as to possibilities he did not now, as he had intended, make for the first station beyond the town, but plunged still farther under the firs, which here abounded for miles. Each clasping the other round the waist they promenaded over the dry bed of fir-needles, thrown into a vague intoxicating atmosphere at the consciousness of being together at last, with no living soul between them; ignoring that there was a corpse. Thus they proceeded for several miles till Tess, arousing herself, looked about her, and said, timidly—

"Are we going anywhere in particular?"

"I don't know, dearest. Why?"

"I don't know."

"Well, we might walk a few miles further, and when it is evening find lodgings somewhere or other—in a lonely cottage, perhaps. Can you walk well, Tessy?"

"O yes! I could walk forever and ever with your arm round me!"

Upon the whole it seemed a good thing to do. Thereupon they quickened their pace, avoiding high-roads, and following obscure paths tending more or less northward. But there was an unpractical vagueness in their movements throughout the day; neither one of them seemed to consider any question of effectual escape, disguise, or long concealment. Their every idea was temporary and unforefending, like the plans of two children.

At mid-day they drew near to a roadside inn, and Tess would have entered it with him to get something to eat, but he persuaded her to remain among the trees and bushes of this half-woodland, half-moorland part of the country, till he should come back. Her clothes were of recent fashion; even the ivory-handled parasol that she carried was of a shape unknown in the retired spot to which they had now wandered; and the cut of such articles would have attracted attention in the settle of a tavern. He soon returned, with food enough for half-a-dozen people and two bottles of wine—enough to last them for a day or more, should any emergency arise.

They sat down upon some dead boughs and shared their meal. Between one and two o'clock they packed up the remainder and went on again.

"I feel strong enough to walk any distance," said she.

"I think we may as well steer in a general way towards the interior of the country, where we can hide for a time, and are less likely to be looked for than anywhere near the coast," Clare remarked. "Later on, when they have forgotten us, we can make for some port."

She made no reply to this beyond that of grasping him more tightly, and straight inland they went. Though the season was an English May the weather was serenely bright, and during the afternoon it was quite warm. Through the latter miles of their walk their footpath had taken them into the depths of the New Forest, and towards evening, turning the corner of a lane, they perceived behind a brook and bridge a large board on which was painted in white letters, "This desirable Mansion to be Let Furnished"; particulars following, with directions to apply to some London agents. Passing through the gate they could see the house, an old brick building of regular design and large accommodation.

"I know it," said Clare. "It is Bramshurst Court. You can see that it is shut up, and grass is growing on the drive."

"Some of the windows are open," said Tess.

"Just to air the rooms, I suppose."

"All these rooms empty, and we without a roof to our heads!"

"You are getting tired, my Tess!" he said. "We'll stop soon." And kissing her sad mouth he again led her onwards.

He was growing weary likewise, for they had wandered a dozen or fifteen miles, and it became necessary to consider what they should do for rest. They looked from afar at isolated cottages and little inns, and were inclined to approach one of the latter, when their hearts failed them, and they sheered off. At length their gait dragged, and they stood still.

"Could we sleep under the trees?" she asked.

He thought the season insufficiently advanced.

"I have been thinking of that empty mansion we passed," he said. "Let us go back towards it again."

They retraced their steps, but it was half an hour before they stood without the entrance gate as earlier. He then requested her to stay where she was, whilst he went to see who was within.

She sat down among the bushes within the gate, and Clare crept towards the house. His absence lasted some considerable time, and when he returned Tess was wildly anxious, not for herself, but for him. He had found out from a boy that there was only an old woman in charge as caretaker, and she only came there on fine days, from the hamlet near, to open and shut the windows. She would come to shut them at sunset. "Now, we can get in through one of the lower windows, and rest there," said he.

Under his escort she went tardily forward to the main front, whose shuttered windows, like sightless eyeballs, excluded the possibility of watchers. The door was reached a few steps further, and one of the windows beside it was open. Clare clambered in, and pulled Tess in after him.

Except the hall the rooms were all in darkness, and they ascended the staircase. Up here also the shutters were tightly closed, the ventilation being perfunctorily done, for this day at least, by opening the hall-window in front and an upper-window behind. Clare unlatched the door of a large chamber, felt his way across it, and parted the shutters to the width of two or three inches. A shaft of dazzling sunlight glanced into the room, reveal-ing heavy, old-fashioned furniture, crimson damask hangings, and an enormous four-post bedstead, along the head of which were carved running figures, apparently Atalanta's race.

"Rest at last!" said he, setting down his bag and the parcel of viands.

They remained in great quietness till the caretaker should have come to shut the win-dows: as a precaution, putting themselves in total darkness by barring the shutters as be-fore, lest the woman should open the door of their chamber for any casual reason. Between six and seven o'clock she came, but did not approach the wing they were in. They heard her close the windows, fasten them, lock the door, and go away. Then Clare again stole a chink of light from the window, and they shared another meal, till by and by they were en-veloped in the shades of night which they had no candle to disperse.

LVIII

THE NIGHT WAS STRANGELY SOLEMN AND STILL. IN THE SMALL HOURS SHE WHISPERED to him the whole story of how he had walked in his sleep with her in his arms across the Froom stream, at the imminent risk of both their lives, and laid her down in the stone coffin at the ruined abbey. He had never known of that till now.

"Why didn't you tell me next day?" he said. "It might have prevented much misun-derstanding and woe."

"Don't think of what's past!" said she. "I am not going to think outside of now. Why should we! Who knows what to-morrow has in store?"

But it apparently had no sorrow. The morning was wet and foggy, and Clare, rightly informed that the caretaker only opened the windows on fine days, ventured to creep out of their chamber, and explore the house, leaving Tess asleep. There was no food on the premises, but there was water, and he took advantage of the fog to emerge from the man-sion, and fetch tea, bread, and butter from a shop in a little place two miles beyond, as also a small tin kettle and spirit-lamp, that they might get fire without smoke. His re-entry awoke her; and they breakfasted on what he had brought.

They were indisposed to stir abroad, and the day passed, and the night following, and the next, and next; till, almost without their being aware, five days had slipped by in ab-solute seclusion, not a sight or sound of a human being disturbing their peacefulness, such as it was. The changes of the weather were their only events, the birds of the New Forest their only company. By tacit consent they hardly once spoke of any incident of the past subsequent to their wedding-day. The gloomy intervening time seemed to sink into chaos, over which the present and prior times closed as if it never had been. Whenever he sug-gested that they should leave their shelter, and go forwards towards Southampton or Lon-don, she showed a strange unwillingness to move.

"Why should we put an end to all that's sweet and lovely!" she deprecated. "What must come will come." And, looking through the shutter-chink: "All is trouble outside there; inside here content."

He peeped out also. It was quite true; within was affection, union, error forgiven: outside was the inexorable.

"And—and," she said, pressing her cheek against his, "I fear that what you think of me now may not last. I do not wish to outlive your present feeling for me. I would rather not. I would rather be dead and buried when the time comes for you to despise me, so that it may never be known to me that you despised me."

"I cannot ever despise you."

"I also hope that. But considering what my life has been I cannot see why any man should, sooner or later, be able to help despising me. . . . How wickedly mad I was! Yet formerly I never could bear to hurt a fly or a worm, and the sight of a bird in a cage used often to make me cry."

They remained yet another day. In the night the dull sky cleared, and the result was that the old caretaker at the cottage awoke early. The brilliant sunrise made her unusually brisk; she decided to open the contiguous mansion immediately, and to air it thoroughly on such a day. Thus it occurred that, having arrived and opened the lower-rooms before six o'clock, she ascended to the bedchambers, and was about to turn the handle of the one wherein they lay. At that moment she fancied she could hear the breathing of persons within. Her slippers and her antiquity had rendered her progress a noiseless one so far, and she made for instant retreat; then, deeming that her hearing might have deceived her, she turned anew to the door and softly tried the handle. The lock was out of order, but a piece of furniture had been moved forward on the inside, which prevented her opening the door more than an inch or two. A stream of morning light through the shutter-chink fell upon the faces of the pair, wrapped in profound slumber, Tess's lips being parted like a half-opened flower near his cheek. The caretaker was so struck with their innocent appearance, and with the elegance of Tess's gown hanging across a chair, her silk stockings beside it, the pretty parasol, and the other habits in which she had arrived because she had none else, that her first indignation at the effrontery of tramps and vagabonds gave way to a momentary sentimentality over this genteel elopement, as it seemed. She closed the door, and withdrew as softly as she had come, to go and consult with her neighbours on the odd discovery.

Not more than a minute had elapsed after her withdrawal when Tess woke, and then Clare. Both had a sense that something had disturbed them, though they could not say what; and the uneasy feeling which it engendered grew stronger. As soon as he was dressed he narrowly scanned the lawn through the two or three inches of shutter-chink.

"I think we will leave at once," said he. "It is a fine day. And I cannot help fancying somebody is about the house. At any rate, the woman will be sure to come to-day."

She passively assented, and putting the room in order they took up the few articles that belonged to them, and departed noiselessly. When they had got into the Forest she turned to take a last look at the house.

"Ah, happy house—good-bye!" she said. "My life can only be a question of a few weeks. Why should we not have stayed there?"

"Don't say it, Tess! We shall soon get out of this district altogether. We'll continue our course as we've begun it, and keep straight north. Nobody will think of looking for us there. We shall be looked for at the Wessex ports if we are sought at all. When we are in the north we will get to a port and away."

Having thus persuaded her the plan was pursued, and they kept a bee line northward. Their long repose at the manor-house lent them walking power now; and towards mid-day they found that they were approaching the steepled city of Melchester, which lay directly in their way. He decided to rest her in a clump of trees during the afternoon, and push onward under cover of darkness. At dusk Clare purchased food as usual, and their night march began, the boundary between Upper and Mid-Wessex being crossed about eight o'clock.

To walk across country without much regard to roads was not new to Tess, and she showed her old agility in the performance. The intercepting city, ancient Melchester, they were obliged to pass through in order to take advantage of the town bridge for crossing a large river that obstructed them. It was about midnight when they went along the deserted streets, lighted fitfully by the few lamps, keeping off the pavement that it might not echo their footsteps. The graceful pile of cathedral architecture rose dimly on their left hand, but it was lost upon them now. Once out of the town they followed the turnpike road, which after a few miles plunged across an open plain.

Though the sky was dense with cloud a diffused light from some fragment of a moon had hitherto helped them a little. But the moon had now sunk, the clouds seemed to settle almost on their heads, and the night grew as dark as a cave. However, they found their way along, keeping as much on the turf as possible that their tread might not resound, which it was easy to do, there being no hedge or fence of any kind. All around was open loneliness and black solitude, over which a stiff breeze blew.

They had proceeded thus gropingly two or three miles further when on a sudden Clare became conscious of some vast erection close in his front, rising sheer from the grass. They had almost struck themselves against it.

"What monstrous place is this?" said Angel.

"It hums," said she. "Hearken!"

He listened. The wind, playing upon the edifice, produced a booming tune, like the note of some gigantic one-stringed harp. No other sound came from it, and lifting his hand and advancing a step or two, Clare felt the vertical surface of the structure. It seemed to be of solid stone, without joint or moulding. Carrying his fingers onward he found that what he had come in contact with was a colossal rectangular pillar; by stretching out his left hand he could feel a similar one adjoining. At an indefinite height overhead something made the black sky blacker, which had the semblance of a vast architrave uniting the pillars horizontally. They carefully entered beneath and between; the surfaces echoed their soft rustle; but they seemed to be still out-of-doors. The place was roofless. Tess drew her breath fearfully, and Angel, perplexed, said—

"What can it be?"

Feeling sideways they encountered another towerlike pillar, square and uncompromising as the first; beyond it another and another. The place was all doors and pillars, some connected above by continuous architraves.

"A very Temple of the Winds," he said.

The next pillar was isolated; others composed a trilithon; others were prostrate, their flanks forming a causeway wide enough for a carriage and it was soon obvious that they made up a forest of monoliths grouped upon the grassy expanse of the plain. The couple advanced further into this pavilion of the night till they stood in its midst.

"It is Stonehenge!" said Clare.

"The heathen temple, you mean?"

"Yes. Older than the centuries; older than the d'Urbervilles! Well, what shall we do, darling? We may find shelter further on."

But Tess, really tired by this time, flung herself upon an oblong slab that lay close at hand, and was sheltered from the wind by a pillar. Owing to the action of the sun during the preceding day the stone was warm and dry, in comforting contrast to the rough and chill grass around, which had damped her skirts and shoes.

"I don't want to go any further, Angel," she said stretching out her hand for his. "Can't we bide here?"

"I fear not. This spot is visible for miles by day, although it does not seem so now."

"One of my mother's people was a shepherd hereabouts, now I think of it. And you used to say at Talbothays that I was a heathen. So now I am at home."

He knelt down beside her outstretched form, and put his lips upon hers.

"Sleepy are you, dear? I think you are lying on an altar."

"I like very much to be here," she murmured. "It is so solemn and lonely—after my great happiness—with nothing but the sky above my face. It seems as if there were no folk in the world but we two; and I wish there were not—except 'Liza-Lu."

Clare though she might as well rest here till it should get a little lighter, and he flung his overcoat upon her, and sat down by her side.

"Angel, if anything happens to me, will you watch over 'Liza-Lu for my sake?" she asked, when they had listened a long time to the wind among the pillars.

"I will."

"She is so good and simple and pure. O, Angel—I wish you would marry her if you lose me, as you will do shortly. O, if you would!"

"If I lose you I lose all! And she is my sister-in-law."

"That's nothing, dearest. People marry sister-laws continually about Marlott; and 'Liza-Lu is so gentle and sweet, and she is growing so beautiful. O, I could share you with her willingly when we are spirits! If you would train her and teach her, Angel, and bring her up for your own self! . . . She had all the best of me without the bad of me; and if she were to become yours it would almost seem as if death had not divided us. . . . Well, I have said it. I won't mention it again."

She ceased, and he fell into thought. In the far north-east sky he could see between the pillars a level streak of light. The uniform concavity of black cloud was lifting bodily like the lid of a pot, letting in at the earth's edge the coming day, against which the towering monoliths and trilithons began to be blackly defined.

"Did they sacrifice to God here?" asked she.

"No," said he.

"Who to?"

"I believe to the sun. That lofty stone set away by itself is in the direction of the sun, which will presently rise behind it."

"This reminds me, dear," she said. "You remember you never would interfere with any belief of mine before we were married? But I knew your mind all the same, and I thought as you thought—not from any reasons of my own, but because you thought so. Tell me now, Angel, do you think we shall meet again after we are dead? I want to know."

He kissed her to avoid a reply at such a time.

"O, Angel—I fear that means no!" said she, with a suppressed sob. "And I wanted so to see you again—so much, so much! What—not even you and I, Angel, who love each other so well?"

Like a greater than himself, to the critical question at the critical time he did not answer; and they were again silent. In a minute or two her breathing became more regular, her clasp of his hand relaxed, and she fell asleep. The band of silver paleness along the east horizon made even the distant parts of the Great Plain appear dark and near; and the whole enormous landscape bore that impress of reserve, taciturnity, and hesitation which is usual just before day. The eastward pillars and their architraves stood up blackly against the light, and the great flame-shaped Sun-stone beyond them; and the Stone of Sacrifice midway. Presently the night wind died out, and the quivering little pools in the cuplike hollows of the stones lay still. At the same time something seemed to move on the verge of the dip eastward—a mere dot. It was the head of a man approaching them from the hollow beyond the Sun-stone. Clare wished they had gone onward, but in the circumstances decided to remain quiet. The figure came straight towards the circle of pillars in which they were.

He heard something behind him, the brush of feet. Turning, he saw over the prostrate columns another figure; then before he was aware, another was at hand on the right, under a trilithon, and another on the left. The dawn shone full on the front of the man westward, and Clare could discern from this that he was tall, and walked as if trained. They all closed in with evident purpose. Her story then was true! Springing to his feet, he looked around for a weapon, loose stone, means of escape, anything. By this time the nearest man was upon him.

"It is no use, sir," he said. "There are sixteen of us on the Plain, and the whole country is reared."

"Let her finish her sleep!" he implored in a whisper of the men as they gathered round.

When they saw where she lay, which they had not done till then, they showed no objection, and stood watching her, as still as the pillars around. He went to the stone and bent over her, holding one poor little hand; her breathing now was quick and small, like that of a lesser creature than a woman. All waited in the growing light, their faces and hands as if they were silvered, the remainder of their figures dark, the stones glistening green-grey, the Plain still a mass of shade. Soon the light was strong, and a ray shone upon her unconscious form, peering under her eyelids and waking her.

"What is it, Angel?" she said, starting up. "Have they come for me?"

"Yes, dearest," he said. "They have come."

"It is as it should be," she murmured. "Angel, I am almost glad—yes, glad! This happiness could not have lasted. It was too much. I have had enough; and now I shall not live for you to despise me!"

She stood up, shook herself, and went forward, neither of the men having moved.

"I am ready," she said quietly.

LIX

THE CITY OF WINTONCESTER, THAT FINE OLD CITY, AFORETIME CAPITAL OF WESSEX, lay amidst its convex and concave downlands in all the brightness and warmth of a July morning. The gabled brick, tile, and freestone houses had almost dried off for the season their integument of lichen, the streams in the meadows were low, and in the sloping High Street, from the West Gateway to the medieval cross, and from the medieval cross to the bridge, that leisurely dusting and sweeping was in progress which usually ushers in an old-fashioned market-day.

From the western gate aforesaid the highway, as every Wintoncestrian knows, ascends a long and regular incline of the exact length of a measured mile, leaving the houses gradually behind. Up this road from the precincts of the city two persons were walking rapidly, as if unconscious of the trying ascent—unconscious through preoccupation and not through buoyancy. They had emerged upon this road through a narrow barred wicket in a high wall a little lower down. They seemed anxious to get out of the sight of the houses and of their kind, and this road appeared to offer the quickest means of doing so. Though they were young they walked with bowed heads, which gait of grief the sun's rays smiled on pitilessly.

One of the pair was Angel Clare, the other a tall budding creature—half girl, half woman—a spiritualised image of Tess, slighter than she, but with the same beautiful eyes—Clare's sister-in-law, 'Liza-Lu. Their pale faces seemed to have shrunk to half their natural size. They moved on hand in hand, and never spoke a word, the drooping of their heads being that of Giotto's "Two Apostles."

When they had nearly reached the top of the great West Hill the clocks in the town struck eight. Each gave a start at the notes, and, walking onward yet a few steps, they reached the first milestone, standing whitely on the green margin of the grass, and backed by the down, which here was open to the road. They entered upon the turf, and, impelled by a force that seemed to overrule their will, suddenly stood still, turned, and waited in paralysed suspense beside the stone.

The prospect from this summit was almost unlimited. In the valley beneath lay the city they had just left, its more prominent buildings showing as in an isometric drawing—among them the broad cathedral tower, with its Norman windows and immense length of aisle and nave, the spires of St. Thomas's, the pinnacled tower of the College, and, more to the right, the tower and gables of the ancient hospice, where to this day the pilgrim may receive his dole of bread and ale. Behind the city swept the rotund upland of St. Catherine's Hill; further off, landscape beyond landscape, till the horizon was lost in the radiance of the sun hanging above it.

Against these far stretches of country rose, in front of the other city edifices, a large red-brick building, with level grey roofs, and rows of short barred windows bespeaking captivity, the whole contrasting greatly by its formalism with the quaint irregularities of the Gothic erections. It was somewhat disguised from the road in passing it by yews and evergreen oaks, but it was visible enough up here. The wicket from which the pair had lately emerged was in the wall of this structure. From the middle of the building an ugly flat-topped octagonal tower ascended against the east horizon, and viewed from this spot, on its shady side and against the light, it seemed the one blot on the city's beauty. Yet it was with this blot, and not with the beauty, that the two gazers were concerned.

Upon the cornice of the tower a tall staff was fixed. Their eyes were riveted on it. A few minutes after the hour had struck something moved slowly up the staff, and extended itself upon the breeze. It was a black flag.

"Justice" was done, and the President of the Immortals, in Æschylean phrase, had ended his sport with Tess. And the d'Urberville knights and dames slept on in their tombs unknowing. The two speechless gazers bent themselves down to the earth, as if in prayer, and remained thus a long time, absolutely motionless: the flag continued to wave silently. As soon as they had strength they arose, joined hands again, and went on.

THE END

JUDE THE OBSCURE

"The letter killeth"

PREFACE

THE HISTORY OF THIS NOVEL (WHOSE BIRTH IN ITS PRESENT SHAPE HAS BEEN MUCH RE-tarded by the necessities of periodical publication) is briefly as it follows. The scheme was jotted down in 1890, from notes made in 1887 and onwards, some of the circumstances being suggested by the death of a woman in the former year. The scenes were revisited in October 1892; the narrative was written in outline in 1892 and the spring of 1893, and at full length, as it now appears, from August 1893 onwards into the next year; the whole, with the exception of a few chapters, being in the hands of the publisher by the end of 1894. It was begun as a serial story in Harper's Magazine at the end of November 1894, and was continued in monthly parts.

But, as in the case of *Tess of the d'Urbervilles*, the magazine version was for various reasons abridged and modified in some degree, the present edition being the first in which the whole appears as originally written. And in the difficulty of coming to an early decision in the matter of a title, the tale was issued under a provisional name—two such titles having, in fact, been successively adopted. The present and final title, deemed on the whole the best, was one of the earliest thought of.

For a novel addressed by a man to men and women of full age; which attempts to deal unaffectedly with the fret and fever, derision and disaster, that may press in the wake of the strongest passion known to humanity; to tell, without a mincing of words, of a deadly war waged with old Apostolic desperation between flesh and spirit; and to point the tragedy of unfulfilled aims, I am not aware that there is anything in the handling to which exception can be taken.

Like former productions of this pen, *Jude the Obscure* is simply an endeavour to give shape and coherence to a series of seemings, or personal impressions, the question of their consistency or their discordance, of their permanence or their transitoriness, being regarded as not of the first moment.

T. H.
1895–1902

CONTENTS

PART FIRST

AT MARYGREEN

"Yea, many there be that have run out of their wits for women, and become servants for their sakes. Many also have perished, have erred, and sinned, for women. . . . O ye men, how can it be but women should be strong, seeing they do thus?"

—ESDRAS

I

THE SCHOOLMASTER WAS LEAVING THE VILLAGE, AND EVERYBODY SEEMED SORRY. The miller at Cresscombe lent him the small white tilted cart and horse to carry his goods to the city of his destination, about twenty miles off, such a vehicle proving of quite sufficient size for the departing teacher's effects. For the school-house had been partly furnished by the managers, and the only cumbersome article possessed by the master, in addition to the packing-case of books, was a cottage piano that he had bought at an auction during the year in which he thought of learning instrumental music. But the enthusiasm having waned he had never acquired any skill in playing, and the purchased article had been a perpetual trouble to him ever since in moving house.

The rector had gone away for the day, being a man who disliked the sight of changes. He did not mean to return till the evening, when the new school-teacher would have arrived and settled in, and everything would be smooth again.

The blacksmith, the farm bailiff, and the schoolmaster himself were standing in perplexed attitudes in the parlour before the instrument. The master had remarked that even if he got it into the cart he should not know what to do with it on his arrival at Christminster, the city he was bound for, since he was only going into temporary lodgings just at first.

A little boy of eleven, who had been thoughtfully assisting in the packing, joined the group of men, and as they rubbed their chins he spoke up, blushing at the sound of his own voice: "Aunt have got a great fuel-house, and it could be put there, perhaps, till you've found a place to settle in, sir."

"A proper good notion," said the blacksmith.

It was decided that a deputation should wait on the boy's aunt—an old maiden resident—and ask her if she would house the piano till Mr. Phillotson should send for it. The smith and the bailiff started to see about the practicability of the suggested shelter, and the boy and the schoolmaster were left standing alone.

"Sorry I am going, Jude?" asked the latter kindly.

Tears rose into the boy's eyes, for he was not among the regular day scholars, who came unromantically close to the schoolmaster's life, but one who had attended the night school only during the present teacher's term of office. The regular scholars, if the truth must be told, stood at the present moment afar off, like certain historic disciples, indisposed to any enthusiastic volunteering of aid.

The boy awkwardly opened the book he held in his hand, which Mr. Phillotson had bestowed on him as a parting gift, and admitted that he was sorry.

"So am I," said Mr. Phillotson.

"Why do you go, sir?" asked the boy.

"Ah—that would be a long story. You wouldn't understand my reasons, Jude. You will, perhaps, when you are older."

"I think I should now, sir."

"Well—don't speak of this everywhere. You know what a university is, and a university degree? It is the necessary hall-mark of a man who wants to do anything in teaching. My scheme, or dream, is to be a university graduate, and then to be ordained. By going to live at Christminster, or near it, I shall be at head-quarters, so to speak, and if my scheme is practicable at all, I consider that being on the spot will afford me a better chance of carrying it out than I should have elsewhere."

The smith and his companion returned. Old Miss Fawley's fuel-house was dry, and eminently practicable; and she seemed willing to give the instrument standing-room there. It was accordingly left in the school till the evening, when more hands would be available for removing it; and the schoolmaster gave a final glance round.

The boy Jude assisted in loading some small articles, and at nine o'clock Mr. Phillotson mounted beside his box of books and other *impedimenta*, and bade his friends good-bye.

"I sha'n't forget you, Jude," he said, smiling, as the cart moved off. "Be a good boy, remember; and be kind to animals and birds, and read all you can. And if ever you come to Christminster remember you hunt me out for old acquaintance' sake."

The cart creaked across the green, and disappeared round the corner by the rectory-house. The boy returned to the draw-well at the edge of the greensward, where he had left his buckets when he went to help his patron and teacher in the loading. There was a quiver in his lip now and after opening the well-cover to begin lowering the bucket he paused and leant with his forehead and arms against the frame-work, his face wearing the fixity of a thoughtful child's who has felt the pricks of life somewhat before his time. The well into which he was looking was as ancient as the village itself, and from his present position appeared as a long circular perspective ending in a shining disk of quivering water at a distance of a hundred feet. There was a lining of green moss near the top, and nearer still the hart's-tongue fern.

He said to himself, in the melodramatic tones of a whimsical boy, that the schoolmaster had drawn at that well scores of times on a morning like this, and would never draw there any more. "I've seen him look down into it, when he was tired with his drawing, just as I do now, and when he rested a bit before carrying the buckets home! But he was too clever to bide here any longer—a small sleepy place like this!"

A tear rolled from his eye into the depths of the well. The morning was a little foggy, and the boy's breathing unfurled itself as a thicker fog upon the still and heavy air. His thoughts were interrupted by a sudden outcry:

"Bring on that water, will ye, you idle young harlican!"

It came from an old woman who had emerged from her door towards the garden gate of a green-thatched cottage not far off. The boy quickly waved a signal of assent, drew the water with what was a great effort for one of his stature, landed and emptied the big bucket into his own pair of smaller ones, and pausing a moment for breath, started with them across the patch of clammy greensward whereon the well stood—nearly in the centre of the little village, or rather hamlet.

It was as old-fashioned as it was small, and it rested in the lap of an undulating upland adjoining the North Wessex downs. Old as it was, however, the well-shaft was probably the only relic of the local history that remained absolutely unchanged. Many of the thatched and dormered dwelling-houses had been pulled down of late years, and many trees felled on the green. Above all, the original church, hump-backed, wood-turreted, and quaintly hipped, had been taken down, and either cracked up into heaps of road-metal in the lane, or utilised as pig-sty walls, garden seats, guard-stones to fences, and rockeries in the flower-beds of the neighbourhood. In place of it a tall new building of German-Gothic design, unfamiliar to English eyes, had been erected on a new piece of ground by a certain obliterator of historic records who had run down from London and back in a day. The site whereon so long had stood the ancient temple to the Christian divinities was not even recorded on the green and level grass-plot that had immemorially been the church-yard, the obliterated graves being commemorated by ninepenny cast-iron crosses war-ranted to last five years.

II

SLENDER AS WAS JUDE FAWLEY'S FRAME HE BORE THE TWO BRIMMING HOUSE-BUCKETS OF water to the cottage without resting. Over the door was a little rectangular piece of blue board, on which was painted in yellow letters, "Drusilla Fawley, Baker." Within the little lead panes of the window—this being one of the few old houses left—were five bottles of sweets, and three buns on a plate of the willow pattern.

While emptying the buckets at the back of the house he could hear an animated conversation in progress within-doors between his great-aunt, the Drusilla of the signboard, and some other villagers. Having seen the schoolmaster depart, they were summing up particulars of the event, and indulging in predictions of his future.

"And who's he?" asked one, comparatively a stranger, when the boy entered.

"Well ye med ask it, Mrs. Williams. He's my great-nephew—come since you was last this way." The old inhabitant who answered was a tall, gaunt woman, who spoke tragically on the most trivial subject, and gave a phrase of her conversation to each auditor in turn. "He come from Mellstock, down in South Wessex, about a year ago—worse luck for 'n, Belinda" (turning to the right) "where his father was living, and was took wi' the shakings for death, and died in two days, as you know, Caroline" (turning to the left). "It would ha' been a blessing if Goddy-mighty had took thee too, wi' thy mother and father, poor use-less boy! But I've got him here to stay with me till I can see what's to be done with un, though I be obliged to let him earn any penny he can. Just now he's a-scaring of birds for Farmer Troutham. It keeps un out of mischty. Why do ye turn away, Jude?" she continued, as the boy, feeling the impact of their glances like slaps upon his face, moved aside.

The local washerwoman replied that it was perhaps a very good plan of Miss or Mrs. Fawley's (as they called her indifferently) to have him with her—"to kip 'ee company in your loneliness, fetch water, shet the winder-shetters o' nights, and help in the bit o' baking."

Miss Fawley doubted it. . . . "Why didn't ye get the schoolmaster to take 'ee to Christ-minster wi' un, and make a scholar of 'ee," she continued, in frowning pleasantry. "I'm sure he couldn't ha' took a better one. The boy is crazy for books, that he is. It runs in our family rather. His cousin Sue is just the same—so I've heard; but I have not seen the chile for years, though she was born in this place, within these four walls, as it happened. My niece and her husband, after they were married, didn' get a house of their own for some year or more; and then they only had one till—Well, I won't go into that. Jude, my chile, don't *you* ever marry. 'Tisn't for the Fawleys to take that step anymore. She, their only one, was like a chile o' my own, Belinda, till the split come! Ah, that a little maid should know such changes!"

Jude, finding the general attention again centering on himself, went out to the bake-house, where he ate the cake provided for his breakfast. The end of his spare time had now arrived, and emerging from the garden by getting over the hedge at the back he pursued a path northward, till he came to a wide and lonely depression in the general level of the up-land, which was sown as a corn-field. This vast concave was the scene of his labours for Mr. Troutham the farmer, and he descended into the midst of it.

The brown surface of the field went right up towards the sky all round, where it was lost by degrees in the mist that shut out the actual verge and accentuated the solitude. The only marks on the uniformity of the scene were a rick of last year's produce standing in the midst of the arable, the rooks that rose at his approach, and the path athwart the fal-low by which he had come, trodden now by he hardly knew whom, though once by many of his own dead family.

"How ugly it is here!" he murmured.

The fresh harrow-lines seemed to stretch like the channellings in a piece of new cor-duroy, lending a meanly utilitarian air to the expanse, taking away its gradations, and de-priving it of all history beyond that of the few recent months, though in every clod and stone there really lingered associations enough and to spare—echoes of songs from ancient harvest-days, of spoken words, and of sturdy deeds. Every inch of ground had been the site, first or last, of energy, gaiety, horse-play, bickerings, weariness. Groups of gleaners had squatted in the sun on every square yard. Love-matches that had populated the adjoin-ing hamlet had been made up there between reaping and carrying. Under the hedge which divided the field from a distant plantation girls had given themselves to lovers who would not turn their heads to look at them by the next harvest; and in that ancient corn-field many a man had made love-promises to a woman at whose voice he had trembled by the next seed-time after fulfilling them in the church adjoining. But this neither Jude nor the rooks around him considered. For them it was a lonely place, possessing, in the one view, only the quality of a work-ground, and in the other that of a granary good to feed in.

The boy stood under the rick before mentioned, and every few seconds used his clacker or rattle briskly. At each clack the rooks left off pecking, and rose and went away on their leisurely wings, burnished like tassets of mail, afterwards wheeling back and re-garding him warily, and descending to feed at a more respectful distance.

He sounded the clacker till his arm ached, and at length his heart grew sympathetic with the birds' thwarted desires. They seemed, like himself, to be living in a world which did not want them. Why should he frighten them away? They took upon them more and more the aspect of gentle friends and pensioners—the only friends he could claim as being in the least degree interested in him, for his aunt had often told him that she was not. He ceased his rattling, and they alighted anew.

"Poor little dears!" said Jude, aloud. "You *shall* have some dinner—you shall. There is enough for us all. Farmer Troutham can afford to let you have some. Eat, then, my dear little birdies, and make a good meal!"

They stayed and ate, inky spots on the nut-brown soil and Jude enjoyed their appetite.

A magic thread of fellow-feeling united his own life with theirs. Puny and sorry as those lives were, they much resembled his own.

His clacker he had by this time thrown away from him, as being a mean and sordid instrument, offensive both to the birds and to himself as their friend. All at once he became conscious of a smart blow upon his buttocks, followed by a loud clack, which announced to his surprised senses that the clacker had been the instrument of offence used. The birds and Jude started up simultaneously, and the dazed eyes of the latter beheld the farmer in person, the great Troutham himself, his red face glaring down upon Jude's cowering frame, the clacker swinging in his hand.

"So it's 'Eat, my dear birdies,' is it, young man? 'Eat, dear birdies,' indeed! I'll tickle your breeches, and see if you say, 'Eat, dear birdies,' again in a hurry! And you've been idling at the schoolmaster's too, instead of coming here, ha'n't ye, hey? That's how you earn your sixpence a day for keeping the rooks off my corn!"

Whilst saluting Jude's ears with this impassioned rhetoric, Troutham had seized his left hand with his own left, and swinging his slim frame round him at arm's-length, again struck Jude on the hind parts with the flat side of Jude's own rattle, till the field echoed with the blows, which were delivered once or twice at each revolution.

"Don't 'ee, sir—please don't 'ee!" cried the whirling child, as helpless under the centrifugal tendency of his person as a hooked fish swinging to land, and beholding the hill, the rick, the plantation, the path, and the rooks going round and round him in an amazing circular race. "I—I sir—only meant that—there was a good crop in the ground—I saw 'em sow it—and the rooks could have a little bit for dinner—and you wouldn't miss it, sir—and Mr. Phillotson said I was to be kind to 'em—O, O, O!"

This truthful explanation seemed to exasperate the farmer even more than if Jude had stoutly denied saying anything at all; and he still smacked the whirling urchin, the clacks of the instrument continuing to resound all across the field and as far as the ears of distant workers—who gathered thereupon that Jude was pursuing his business of clacking with great assiduity—and echoing from the brand-new church-tower just behind the mist, towards the building of which structure the farmer had largely subscribed, to testify his love for God and man.

Presently Troutham grew tired of his punitive task, and depositing the quivering boy on his legs, took a sixpence from his pocket and gave it him in payment for his day's work, telling him to go home and never let him see him in one of those fields again.

Jude leaped out of arm's reach, and walked along the trackway weeping—not from the pain, though that was keen enough; not from the perception of the flaw in the terrestrial scheme, by which what was good for God's birds was bad for God's gardener; but with the awful sense that he had wholly disgraced himself before he had been a year in the parish, and hence might be a burden to his great-aunt for life.

With this shadow on his mind he did not care to show himself in the village, and went homeward by a roundabout track behind a high hedge and across a pasture. Here he beheld scores of coupled earthworms lying half their length on the surface of the damp ground, as they always did in such weather at that time of the year. It was impossible to advance in regular steps without crushing some of them at each tread.

Though Farmer Troutham had just hurt him, he was a boy who could not himself bear to hurt anything. He had never brought home a nest of young birds without lying awake in misery half the night after, and often reinstating them and the nest in their original place the next morning. He could scarcely bear to see trees cut down or lopped, from a fancy that it hurt them; and late pruning, when the sap was up and the tree bled profusely, had been a positive grief to him in his infancy. This weakness of character, as it may be called, suggested that he was the sort of man who was born to ache a good deal before the fall of the curtain upon his unnecessary life should signify that all was well with him again. He carefully picked his way on tiptoe among the earthworms, without killing a single one.

On entering the cottage he found his aunt selling a penny loaf to a little girl, and when the customer was gone she said, "Well, how do you come to be back here in the middle of the morning like this?"

"I'm turned away."

"What?"

"Mr. Troutham have turned me away because I let the rooks have a few peckings of corn. And there's my wages—the last I shall ever hae!"

He threw the sixpence tragically on the table.

"Ah!" said his aunt, suspending her breath. And she opened upon him a lecture on how she would now have him all the spring upon her hands doing nothing. "If you can't skeer birds, what can ye do? There! don't ye look so deedy! Farmer Troutham is not so much better than myself, come to that. But 'tis as Job said, 'Now they that are younger than I have me in derision, whose fathers I would have disdained to have set with the dogs of my flock.' His father was my father's journeyman, anyhow, and I must have been a fool to let 'ee go to work for 'n, which I shouldn't ha' done but to keep 'ee out of mischty."

More angry with Jude for demeaning her by coming there than for dereliction of duty, she rated him primarily from that point of view, and only secondarily from a moral one.

"Not that you should have let the birds eat what Farmer Troutham planted. Of course you was wrong in that. Jude, Jude, why didstn't go off with that schoolmaster of thine to Christminster or somewhere? But, O no—poor or'nary child—there never was any sprawl on thy side of the family, and never will be!"

"Where is this beautiful city, aunt—this place where Mr. Phillotson is gone to?" asked the boy, after meditating in silence.

"Lord! you ought to know where the city of Christminster is. Near a score of miles from here. It is a place much too good for you ever to have much to do with, poor boy, I'm a-thinking."

"And will Mr. Phillotson always be there?"

"How can I tell?"

"Couldn't I go to see him?"

"Lord, no! You didn't grow up hereabout, or you wouldn't ask such as that. We've never had anything to do with folk in Christminster, nor folk in Christminster with we."

Jude went out, and, feeling more than ever his existence to be an undemanded one, he lay down upon his back on a heap of litter near the pig-sty. The fog had by this time become more translucent, and the position of the sun could be seen through it. He pulled his straw hat over his face, and peered through the interstices of the plaiting at the white brightness, vaguely reflecting. Growing up brought responsibilities, he found. Events did not rhyme quite as he had thought. Nature's logic was too horrid for him to care for. That mercy towards one set of creatures was cruelty towards another sickened his sense of harmony. As you got older, and felt yourself to be at the centre of your time, and not at a point in its circumference, as you had felt when you were little, you were seized with a sort of shuddering, he perceived. All around you there seemed to be something glaring, garish, rattling, and the noises and glares hit upon the little cell called your life, and shook it, and scorched it.

If he could only prevent himself growing up! He did not want to be a man.

Then, like the natural boy, he forgot his despondency, and sprang up. During the remainder of the morning he helped his aunt, and in the afternoon, when there was nothing more to be done, he went into the village. Here he asked a man whereabouts Christminster lay.

"Christminster? O, well, out by there yonder; though I've never bin there—not I. I've never had any business at such a place."

The man pointed north-eastward, in the very direction where lay that field in which Jude had so disgraced himself. There was something unpleasant about the coincidence for the moment, but the fearsomeness of this fact rather increased his curiosity about the city. The farmer had said he was never to be seen in that field again; yet Christminster lay across it, and the path was a public one. So, stealing out of the hamlet he descended into the same hollow which had witnessed his punishment in the morning, never swerving an inch from the path, and climbing up the long and tedious ascent on the other side till the track joined the highway by a little clump of trees. Here the ploughed land ended, and all before him was bleak open down.

III

NOT A SOUL WAS VISIBLE ON THE HEDGELESS HIGHWAY, OR ON EITHER SIDE OF IT, AND the white road seemed to ascend and diminish till it joined the sky. At the very top it was crossed at right angles by a green "ridgeway"—the Icknield Street and original Roman road through the district. This ancient track ran east and west for many miles, and down almost to within living memory had been used for driving flocks and herds to fairs and markets. But it was now neglected and overgrown.

The boy had never before strayed so far north as this from the nestling hamlet in which he had been deposited by the carrier from a railway-station southward, one dark evening some few months earlier, and till now he had had no suspicion that such a wide, flat, low-lying country lay so near at hand, under the very verge of his upland world. The whole northern semi-circle between east and west, to a distance of forty or fifty miles, spread itself before him; a bluer, moister atmosphere, evidently, than that he breathed up here.

Not far from the road stood a weather-beaten old barn of reddish-grey brick and tile. It was known as the Brown House by the people of the locality. He was about to pass it when he perceived a ladder against the eaves; and the reflection that the higher he got, the further he could see, led Jude to stand and regard it. On the slope of the roof two men were repairing the tiling. He turned into the ridgeway and drew towards the barn.

When he had wistfully watched the workmen for some time he took courage, and ascended the ladder till he stood beside them.

"Well, my lad, and what may you want up here?"

"I wanted to know where the city of Christminster is, if you please."

"Christminster is out across there, by that clump. You can see it—at least you can on a clear day. Ah, no, you can't now."

The other tiler, glad of any kind of diversion from the monotony of his labour, had also turned to look towards the quarter designated. "You can't often see it in weather like this," he said. "The time I've noticed it is when the sun is going down in a blaze of flame, and it looks like—I don't know what."

"The heavenly Jerusalem," suggested the serious urchin.

"Ay—though I should never ha' thought of it myself. . . . But I can't see no Christminster to-day."

The boy strained his eyes also; yet neither could he see the far-off city. He descended from the barn, and abandoning Christminster with the versatility of his age he walked along the ridge-track, looking for any natural objects of interest that might lie in the banks thereabout. When he repassed the barn to go back to Marygreen he observed that the ladder was still in its place, but that the men had finished their day's work and gone away.

It was waning towards evening; there was still a faint mist, but it had cleared a little except in the damper tracts of subjacent country and along the river-courses. He thought again of Christminster, and wished, since he had come two or three miles from his aunt's house on purpose, that he could have seen for once this attractive city of which he had been told. But even if he waited here it was hardly likely that the air would clear before night. Yet he was loath to leave the spot, for the northern expanse became lost to view on retreating towards the village only a few hundred yards.

He ascended the ladder to have one more look at the point the men had designated, and perched himself on the highest rung, overlying the tiles. He might not be able to come so far as this for many days. Perhaps if he prayed, the wish to see Christminster might be forwarded. People said that, if you prayed, things sometimes came to you, even though they sometimes did not. He had read in a tract that a man who had begun to build a church, and had no money to finish it, knelt down and prayed, and the money came in by the next post. Another man tried the same experiment, and the money did not come; but he found afterwards that the breeches he knelt in were made by a wicked Jew. This was not discouraging, and turning on the ladder Jude knelt on the third rung, where, resting against those above it, he prayed that the mist might rise.

He then seated himself again, and waited. In the course of ten or fifteen minutes the thinning mist dissolved altogether from the northern horizon, as it had already done elsewhere, and about a quarter of an hour before the time of sunset the westward clouds parted, the sun's position being partially uncovered, and the beams streaming out in visible lines between two bars of slaty cloud. The boy immediately looked back in the old direction.

Some way within the limits of the stretch of landscape, points of light like the topaz gleamed. The air increased in transparency with the lapse of minutes, till the topaz points showed themselves to be the vanes, windows, wet roof slates, and other shining spots upon the spires, domes, freestone-work, and varied outlines that were faintly revealed. It was Christminster, unquestionably; either directly seen, or miraged in the peculiar atmosphere.

The spectator gazed on and on till the windows and vanes lost their shine, going out almost suddenly like extinguished candles. The vague city became veiled in mist. Turning to the west, he saw that the sun had disappeared. The foreground of the scene had grown funereally dark, and near objects put on the hues and shapes of chimaeras.

He anxiously descended the ladder, and started homewards at a run, trying not to think of giants, Herne the Hunter, Apollyon lying in wait for Christian, or of the captain with the bleeding hole in his forehead and the corpses round him that remutinied every night on board the bewitched ship. He knew that he had grown out of belief in these horrors, yet he was glad when he saw the church-tower and the lights in the cottage-windows, even though this was not the home of his birth, and his great-aunt did not care much about him.

Inside and roundabout that old woman's "shop" window, with its twenty-four little panes set in lead-work, the glass of some of them oxidised with age, so that you could hardly see the poor penny articles exhibited within, and forming part of a stock which a strong man could have carried, Jude had his outer being for some long tideless time. But his dreams were as gigantic as his surroundings were small.

Through the solid barrier of cold cretaceous upland to the northward he was always beholding a gorgeous city—the fancied place he had likened to the new Jerusalem, though there was perhaps more of the painter's imagination and less of the diamond merchant's in his dreams thereof than in those of the Apocalyptic writer. And the city acquired a tangibility, a permanence, a hold on his life, mainly from the one nucleus of fact that the man for whose knowledge and purposes he had so much reverence was actually living there; not only so, but living among the more thoughtful and mentally shining ones therein.

In sad wet seasons, though he knew it must rain at Christminster too, he could hardly believe that it rained so drearily there. Whenever he could get away from the confines of the hamlet for an hour or two, which was not often, he would steal off to the Brown House on the hill and strain his eyes persistently; sometimes to be rewarded by the sight of a dome or spire, at other times by a little smoke, which in his estimate had some of the mysticism of incense.

Then the day came when it suddenly occurred to him that if he ascended to the point of view after dark, or possibly went a mile or two further, he would see the night lights of the city. It would be necessary to come back alone, but even that consideration did not deter him, for he could throw a little manliness into his mood, no doubt.

The project was duly executed. It was not late when he arrived at the place of outlook, only just after dusk; but a black north-east sky, accompanied by a wind from the same quarter, made the occasion dark enough. He was rewarded; but what he saw was not the lamps in rows, as he had half expected. No individual light was visible, only a halo or glow-fog over-arching the place against the black heavens behind it, making the light and the city seem distant but a mile or so.

He set himself to wonder on the exact point in the glow where the schoolmaster might be—he who never communicated with anybody at Marygreen now; who was as if dead to them here. In the glow he seemed to see Phillotson promenading at ease, like one of the forms in Nebuchadnezzar's furnace.

He had heard that breezes travelled at the rate of ten miles an hour, and the fact now came into his mind. He parted his lips as he faced the north-east, and drew in the wind as if it were a sweet liquor.

"You," he said, addressing the breeze caressingly, "were in Christminster city between one and two hours ago, floating along the streets, pulling round the weather-cocks, touching Mr. Phillotson's face, being breathed by him; and now you be here, breathed by me—you, the very same."

Suddenly there came along this wind something towards him—a message from the place—from some soul residing there, it seemed. Surely it was the sound of bells, the voice of the city, faint and musical, calling to him, "We are happy here!"

He had become entirely lost to his bodily situation during this mental leap, and only got back to it by a rough recalling. A few yards below the brow of the hill on which he paused a team of horses made its appearance, having reached the place by dint of half an hour's serpentine progress from the bottom of the immense declivity. They had a load of coals behind them—a fuel that could only be got into the upland by this particular route. They were accompanied by a carter, a second man, and a boy, who now kicked a large stone behind one of the wheels, and allowed the panting animals to have a long rest, while those in charge took a flagon off the load and indulged in a drink round.

They were elderly men, and had genial voices. Jude addressed them, inquiring if they had come from Christminster.

"Heaven forbid, with this load!" said they.

"The place I mean is that one yonder." He was getting so romantically attached to Christminster that, like a young lover alluding to his mistress, he felt bashful at mentioning its name again. He pointed to the light in the sky—hardly perceptible to their older eyes.

"Yes. There do seem a spot a bit brighter in the nor'-east than elsewhere, though I shouldn't ha' noticed it myself, and no doubt it med be Christminster."

Here a little book of tales which Jude had tucked up under his arm, having brought them to read on his way hither before it grew dark, slipped and fell into the road. The carter eyed him while he picked it up and straightened the leaves.

"Ah, young man," he observed, "you'd have to get your head screwed on t'other way before you could read what they read there."

"Why?" asked the boy.

"Oh, they never look at anything that folks like we can understand," the carter continued, by way of passing the time. "On'y foreign tongues used before the Flood, when no two families spoke alike. They read that sort of thing as fast as a night-hawk will whir. 'Tis all learning there—nothing but learning, except religion. And that's learning too, for I never could understand it. Yes, 'tis a serious-minded place. Not but there's wenches in the streets o' nights. . . . You know, I suppose, that they raise pa'sons there like radishes in a bed? And though it do take—how many years, Bob?—five years to turn a lirruping hobble-de-hoy chap into a solemn preaching man with no corrupt passions, they'll do it, if it can be done, and polish un off like the workmen they be, and turn un out wi' a long face, and a long black coat and waistcoat, and a religious collar and hat, same as they used to wear in the Scriptures, so that his own mother wouldn't know un sometimes. . . . There, 'tis their business, like anybody else's."

"But how should you know—"

"Now don't you interrupt, my boy. Never interrupt your senyers. Move the fore hoss aside, Bobby; here's som'at coming. . . . You must mind that I be a-talking of the college life. 'Em lives on a lofty level; there's no gainsaying it, though I myself med not think much of 'em. As we be here in our bodies on this high ground, so be they in their minds— noble-minded men enough, no doubt—some on 'em—able to earn hundreds by thinking out loud. And some on 'em be strong young fellows that can earn a'most as much in silver cups. As for music, there's beautiful music everywhere in Christminster. You med be religious, or you med not, but you can't help striking in your homely note with the rest. And there's a street in the place—the main street—that ha'n't another like it in the world. I should think I did know a little about Christminster!"

By this time the horses had recovered breath and bent to their collars again. Jude, throwing a last adoring look at the distant halo, turned and walked beside his remarkably well-informed friend, who had no objection to telling him as they moved on more yet of the city—its towers and halls and churches. The waggon turned into a cross-road, whereupon Jude thanked the carter warmly for his information, and said he only wished he could talk half as well about Christminster as he.

"Well, 'tis oonly what has come in my way," said the carter unboastfully. "I've never been there, no more than you; but I've picked up the knowledge here and there, and you be welcome to it. A-getting about the world as I do, and mixing with all classes of society, one can't help hearing of things. A friend o' mine, that used to clane the boots at the Crozier Hotel in Christminster when he was in his prime, why, I knowed un as well as my own brother in his later years."

Jude continued his walk homeward alone, pondering so deeply that he forgot to feel timid. He suddenly grew older. It had been the yearning of his heart to find something to anchor on, to cling to—for some place which he could call admirable. Should he find that place in this city if he could get there? Would it be a spot in which, without fear of farmers, or hindrance, or ridicule, he could watch and wait, and set himself to some mighty undertaking like the men of old of whom he had heard? As the halo had been to his eyes when gazing at it a quarter of an hour earlier, so was the spot mentally to him as he pursued his dark way.

"It is a city of light," he said to himself.

"The tree of knowledge grows there," he added a few steps further on.

"It is a place that teachers of men spring from and go to."

"It is what you may call a castle, manned by scholarship and religion."

After this figure he was silent a long while, till he added:

"It would just suit me."

IV

WALKING SOMEWHAT SLOWLY, BY REASON OF HIS CONCENTRATION, THE BOY—AN ANcient man in some phases of thought, much younger than his years in others—was overtaken by a light-footed pedestrian, whom, notwithstanding the gloom, he could perceive to be wearing an extraordinarily tall hat, a swallow-tailed coat, and a watch-chain that danced madly and threw around scintillations of sky-light as its owner swung along upon a pair of thin legs and noiseless boots. Jude, beginning to feel lonely, endeavoured to keep up with him.

"Well, my man! I'm in a hurry, so you'll have to walk pretty fast if you keep along-side of me. Do you know who I am?"

"Yes, I think. Physician Vilbert?"

"Ah—I'm known everywhere, I see! That comes of being a public benefactor."

Vilbert was an itinerant quack-doctor, well known to the rustic population, and absolutely unknown to anybody else, as he, indeed, took care to be, to avoid inconvenient investigations. Cottagers formed his only patients, and his Wessex-wide repute was among them alone. His position was humbler and his field more obscure than those of the quacks with capital and an organised system of advertising. He was, in fact, a survival. The distances he traversed on foot were enormous, and extended nearly the whole length and breadth of Wessex. Jude had one day seen him selling a pot of coloured lard to an old woman as a certain cure for a bad leg, the woman arranging to pay a guinea, in instalments of a shilling a fortnight, for the precious salve, which, according to the physician, could only be obtained from a particular animal which grazed on Mount Sinai, and was to be captured only at great risk to life and limb. Jude, though he already had his doubts about this gentleman's medicines, felt him to be unquestionably a travelled personage, and one who might be a trustworthy source of information on matters not strictly professional.

"I s'pose you've been to Christminster, Physician?"

"I have—many times," replied the long thin man. "That's one of my centres."

"It's a wonderful city for scholarship and religion?"

"You'd say so, my boy, if you'd seen it. Why, the very sons of the old women who do the washing of the college can talk in Latin—not good Latin, that I admit, as a critic: dog-Latin—cat-Latin, as we used to call it in my undergraduate days."

"And Greek?"

"Well—that's more for the men who are in training for bishops, that they may be able to read the New Testament in the original."

"I want to learn Latin and Greek myself."

"A lofty desire. You must get a grammar of each tongue."

"I mean to go to Christminster some day."

"Whenever you do, you say that Physician Vilbert is the only proprietor of those celebrated pills that infallibly cure all disorders of the alimentary system, as well as asthma and shortness of breath. Two and threepence a box—specially licensed by the government stamp."

"Can you get me the grammars if I promise to say it hereabout?"

"I'll sell you mine with pleasure—those I used as a student."

"O, thank you, sir!" said Jude gratefully, but in gasps, for the amazing speed of the physician's walk kept him in a dog-trot which was giving him a stitch in the side.

"I think you'd better drop behind, my young man. Now I'll tell you what I'll do. I'll get you the grammars, and give you a first lesson, if you'll remember, at every house in the village, to recommend Physician Vilbert's golden ointment, life-drops, and female pills."

"Where will you be with the grammars?"

"I shall be passing here this day fortnight at precisely this hour of five-and-twenty minutes past seven. My movements are as truly timed as those of the planets in their courses."

"Here I'll be to meet you," said Jude.

"With orders for my medicines?"

"Yes, Physician."

Jude then dropped behind, waited a few minutes to recover breath, and went home with a consciousness of having struck a blow for Christminster.

Through the intervening fortnight he ran about and smiled outwardly at his inward thoughts, as if they were people meeting and nodding to him—smiled with that singularly beautiful irradiation which is seen to spread on young faces at the inception of some glorious idea, as if a supernatural lamp were held inside their transparent natures, giving rise to the flattering fancy that heaven lies about them then.

He honestly performed his promise to the man of many cures, in whom he now sincerely believed, walking miles hither and thither among the surrounding hamlets as the physician's agent in advance. On the evening appointed he stood motionless on the plateau, at the place where he had parted from Vilbert, and there awaited his approach. The road physician was fairly up to time; but, to the surprise of Jude on striking into his pace, which the pedestrian did not diminish by a single unit of force, the latter seemed hardly to recognise his young companion, though with the lapse of the fortnight the evenings had grown light. Jude thought it might perhaps be owing to his wearing another hat, and he saluted the physician with dignity.

"Well, my boy?" said the latter abstractedly.

"I've come," said Jude.

"You? who are you? Oh yes—to be sure! Got any orders, lad?"

"Yes." And Jude told him the names and addresses of the cottagers who were willing to test the virtues of the world-renowned pills and salve. The quack mentally registered these with great care.

"And the Latin and Greek grammars?" Jude's voice trembled with anxiety.

"What about them?"

"You were to bring me yours, that you used before you took your degree."

"Ah, yes, yes! Forgot all about it—all! So many lives depending on my attention, you see, my man, that I can't give so much thought as I would like to other things."

Jude controlled himself sufficiently long to make sure of the truth; and he repeated, in a voice of dry misery, "You haven't brought 'em!"

"No. But you must get me some more orders from sick people, and I'll bring the grammars next time."

Jude dropped behind. He was an unsophisticated boy, but the gift of sudden insight which is sometimes vouchsafed to children showed him all at once what shoddy humanity the quack was made of. There was to be no intellectual light from this source. The leaves dropped from his imaginary crown of laurel; he turned to a gate, leant against it, and cried bitterly.

The disappointment was followed by an interval of blankness. He might, perhaps, have obtained grammars from Alfredston, but to do that required money, and a knowledge of what books to order; and though physically comfortable, he was in such absolute dependence as to be without a farthing of his own.

At this date Mr. Phillotson sent for his pianoforte, and it gave Jude a lead. Why should he not write to the schoolmaster, and ask him to be so kind as to get him the grammars in Christminster? He might slip a letter inside the case of the instrument, and it would be sure to reach the desired eyes. Why not ask him to send any old second-hand copies, which would have the charm of being mellowed by the university atmosphere?

To tell his aunt of his intention would be to defeat it. It was necessary to act alone.

After a further consideration of a few days he did act, and on the day of the piano's departure, which happened to be his next birthday, clandestinely placed the letter inside the packing-case, directed to his much-admired friend; being afraid to reveal the operation to his aunt Drusilla, lest she should discover his motive, and compel him to abandon his scheme.

The piano was despatched, and Jude waited days and weeks, calling every morning at the cottage post-office before his great-aunt was stirring. At last a packet did indeed arrive at the village, and he saw from the ends of it that it contained two thin books. He took it away into a lonely place, and sat down on a felled elm to open it.

Ever since his first ecstasy or vision of Christminster and its possibilities, Jude had meditated much and curiously on the probable sort of process that was involved in turning the expressions of one language into those of another. He concluded that a grammar of the required tongue would contain, primarily, a rule, prescription, or clue of the nature of a secret cipher, which, once known, would enable him, by merely applying it, to change at will all words of his own speech into those of the foreign one. His childish idea was, in fact, a pushing to the extremity of mathematical precision what is everywhere known as Grimm's Law—an aggrandisement of rough rules to ideal completeness. Thus he assumed that the words of the required language were always to be found somewhere latent in the words of the given language by those who had the art to uncover them, such art being furnished by the books aforesaid.

When, therefore, having noted that the packet bore the postmark of Christminster, he cut the string, opened the volumes, and turned to the Latin grammar, which chanced to come uppermost, he could scarcely believe his eyes.

The book was an old one—thirty years old, soiled, scribbled wantonly over with a strange name in every variety of enmity to the letterpress, and marked at random with dates twenty years earlier than his own day. But this was not the cause of Jude's amazement. He learnt for the first time that there was no law of transmutation, as in his innocence he had supposed (there was, in some degree, but the grammarian did not recognise it), but that every word in both Latin and Greek was to be individually committed to memory at the cost of years of plodding.

Jude flung down the books, lay backward along the broad trunk of the elm, and was an utterly miserable boy for the space of a quarter of an hour. As he had often done before, he pulled his hat over his face and watched the sun peering insidiously at him through the interstices of the straw. This was Latin and Greek, then, was it, this grand delusion! The charm he had supposed in store for him was really a labour like that of Israel in Egypt.

What brains they must have in Christminster and the great schools, he presently thought, to learn words one by one up to tens of thousands! There were no brains in his head equal to this business; and as the little sun-rays continued to stream in through his hat at him, he wished he had never seen a book, that he might never see another, that he had never been born.

Somebody might have come along that way who would have asked him his trouble, and might have cheered him by saying that his notions were further advanced than those of his grammarian. But nobody did come, because nobody does; and under the crushing recognition of his gigantic error Jude continued to wish himself out of the world.

V

DURING THE THREE OR FOUR SUCCEEDING YEARS A QUAINT AND SINGULAR VEHICLE might have been discerned moving along the lanes and by-roads near Marygreen, driven in a quaint and singular way.

In the course of a month or two after the receipt of the books Jude had grown callous to the shabby trick played him by the dead languages. In fact, his disappointment at the nature of those tongues had, after a while, been the means of still further glorifying the erudition of Christminster. To acquire languages, departed or living, in spite of such obstinacies as he now knew them inherently to possess, was a herculean performance which gradually led him on to a greater interest in it than in the presupposed patent process. The mountain-weight of material under which the ideas lay in those dusty volumes called the classics piqued him into a dogged, mouselike subtlety of attempt to move it piecemeal.

He had endeavoured to make his presence tolerable to his crusty maiden aunt by assisting her to the best of his ability, and the business of the little cottage bakery had grown in consequence. An aged horse with a hanging head had been purchased for eight pounds at a sale, a creaking cart with a whity-brown tilt obtained for a few pounds more, and in this turnout it became Jude's business thrice a week to carry loaves of bread to the villagers and solitary cotters immediately around Marygreen.

The singularity aforesaid lay, after all, less in the conveyance itself than in Jude's manner of conducting it along its route. Its interior was the scene of most of Jude's education by "private study." As soon as the horse had learnt the road and the houses at which he was to pause a while, the boy, seated in front, would slip the reins over his arm, ingeniously fix open, by means of a strap attached to the tilt, the volume he was reading, spread the dictionary on his knees, and plunge into the simpler passages from Cæsar, Virgil, or Horace, as the case might be, in his purblind stumbling way, and with an expenditure of labour that would have made a tender-hearted pedagogue shed tears; yet somehow getting at the meaning of what he read, and divining rather than beholding the spirit of the original, which often to his mind was something else than that which he was taught to look for.

The only copies he had been able to lay hands on were old Delphin editions, because they were superseded, and therefore cheap. But, bad for idle schoolboys, it did so happen that they were passably good for him. The hampered and lonely itinerant conscientiously covered up the marginal readings, and used them merely on points of construction, as he would have used a comrade or tutor who should have happened to be passing by. And though Jude may have had little chance of becoming a scholar by these rough and ready means, he was in the way of getting into the groove he wished to follow.

While he was busied with these ancient pages, which had already been thumbed by hands possibly in the grave, digging out the thoughts of these minds so remote, yet so near, the bony old horse pursued his rounds, and Jude would be aroused from the woes of Dido by the stoppage of his cart and the voice of some old woman crying, "Two to-day, baker, and I return this stale one."

He was frequently met in the lanes by pedestrians and others without his seeing them, and by degrees the people of the neighbourhood began to talk about his method of combining work and play (such they considered his reading to be), which, though probably convenient enough to himself, was not altogether a safe proceeding for other travellers along the same roads. There were murmurs. Then a private resident of an adjoining place informed the local policeman that the baker's boy should not be allowed to read while driving, and insisted that it was the constable's duty to catch him in the act, and take him to the police court at Alfredston, and get him fined for dangerous practices on the highway. The policeman thereupon lay in wait for Jude, and one day accosted him and cautioned him.

As Jude had to get up at three o'clock in the morning to heat the oven, and mix and set in the bread that he distributed later in the day, he was obliged to go to bed at night immediately after laying the sponge; so that if he could not read his classics on the highways, he could hardly study at all. The only thing to be done was, therefore, to keep a sharp eye ahead and around him as well as he could in the circumstances, and slip away his books as soon as anybody loomed in the distance, the policeman in particular. To do that official justice, he did not put himself much in the way of Jude's bread-cart, considering that in such a lonely district the chief danger was to Jude himself, and often on seeing the white tilt over the hedges he would move in another direction.

On a day when Fawley was getting quite advanced, being now about sixteen, and had been stumbling through the "Carmen Sæculare," on his way home, he found himself to be passing over the high edge of the plateau by the Brown House. The light had changed, and it was the sense of this which had caused him to look up. The sun was going down, and the full moon was rising simultaneously behind the woods in the opposite quarter. His mind had become so impregnated with the poem that, in a moment of the same impulsive emotion which years before had caused him to kneel on the ladder, he stopped the horse, alighted, and glancing round to see that nobody was in sight, knelt down on the roadside bank with open book. He turned first to the shiny goddess, who seemed to look so softly and critically at his doings, then to the disappearing luminary on the other hand, as he began:

Phœbe silvarumque potens Diana!

The horse stood still till he had finished the hymn, which Jude repeated under the sway of a polytheistic fancy that he would never have thought of humouring in broad daylight.

Reaching home, he mused over his curious superstition, innate or acquired, in doing this, and the strange forgetfulness which had led to such a lapse from common sense and custom in one who wished, next to being a scholar, to be a Christian divine. It had all come of reading heathen works exclusively. The more he thought of it, the more convinced he was of his inconsistency. He began to wonder whether he could be reading quite the right books for his object in life. Certainly there seemed little harmony between this pagan literature and the medieval colleges at Christminster, that ecclesiastical romance in stone.

Ultimately he decided that in his sheer love of reading he had taken up a wrong emotion for a Christian young man. He had dabbled in Clarke's Homer, but had never yet worked much at the New Testament in the Greek, though he possessed a copy, obtained by post from a second-hand bookseller. He abandoned the now familiar Ionic for a new dialect, and for a long time onward limited his reading almost entirely to the Gospels and Epistles in Griesbach's text. Moreover, on going into Alfredston one day, he was introduced to patristic literature by finding at the bookseller's some volumes of the Fathers which had been left behind by an insolvent clergyman of the neighbourhood.

As another outcome of this change of groove, he visited on Sundays all the churches within a walk, and deciphered the Latin inscriptions on fifteenth-century brasses and tombs. On one of these pilgrimages he met with a hunchbacked old woman of great intelligence, who read everything she could lay her hands on, and she told him more yet of the romantic charms of the city of light and lore. Thither he resolved as firmly as ever to go.

But how live in that city? At present he had no income at all. He had no trade or calling of any dignity or stability whatever on which he could subsist while carrying out an intellectual labour which might spread over many years.

What was most required by citizens? Food, clothing, and shelter. An income from any work in preparing the first would be too meagre; for making the second he felt a distaste; the preparation of the third requisite he inclined to. They built in a city; therefore he would learn to build. He thought of his unknown uncle, his cousin Susanna's father, an ecclesiastical worker in metal, and somehow medieval art in any material was a trade for which he had rather a fancy. He could not go far wrong in following his uncle's footsteps, and engaging himself a while with the carcases that contained the scholar souls.

As a preliminary he obtained some small blocks of freestone, metal not being available, and suspending his studies a while, occupied his spare half-hours in copying the heads and capitals in his parish church.

There was a stone-cutter of a humble kind in Alfredston, and as soon as he had found a substitute for himself in his aunt's little business, he offered his services to this man for a trifling wage. Here Jude had the opportunity of learning at least the rudiments of freestone-working. Some time later he went to a church-builder in the same place, and under the architect's direction became handy at restoring the dilapidated masonries of several village churches roundabout.

Not forgetting that he was only following up this handicraft as a prop to lean on while he prepared those greater engines which he flattered himself would be better fitted for him, he yet was interested in his pursuit on its own account. He now had lodgings during the week in the little town, whence he returned to Marygreen village every Saturday evening. And thus he reached and passed his nineteenth year.

VI

At this memorable date of his life he was, one Saturday, returning from Alfredston to Marygreen about three o'clock in the afternoon. It was fine, warm, and soft summer weather, and he walked with his tools at his back, his little chisels clinking faintly against the larger ones in his basket. It being the end of the week he had left work early, and had come out of the town by a roundabout route which he did not usually frequent, having promised to call at a flour-mill in that direction to execute a commission for his aunt.

He was in an enthusiastic mood. He seemed to see his way to living comfortably in Christminster in the course of a year or two, and knocking at the doors of one of those strongholds of learning of which he had dreamed so much. He might, of course, have gone there now, in some capacity or other, but he preferred to enter the city with a little more assurance as to means than he could be said to feel at present. A warm self-content suffused him when he considered what he had already done. Now and then as he went along he turned to face the peeps of country on either side of him. But he hardly saw them; the act was an automatic repetition of what he had been accustomed to do when less occupied; and the one matter which really engaged him was the mental estimate of his progress thus far.

"I have acquired quite an average student's power to read the common ancient classics, Latin in particular." This was true, Jude possessing a facility in that language which enabled him with great ease to himself to beguile his lonely walks by imaginary conversations therein.

"I have read two books of Homer, besides being pretty familiar with passages such as the speech of Phœnix in the ninth book, the fight of Hector and Ajax in the fourteenth, the appearance of Achilles unarmed and his heavenly armour in the eighteenth, and the funeral games in the twenty-third. I have also done some Hesiod, a little scrap of Thucydides, and a lot of the Greek Testament. . . . I wish there was only one dialect, all the same.

"I have done some mathematics, including the first six and the eleventh and twelfth books of Euclid; and algebra as far as simple equations.

"I know something of the Fathers, and something of Roman and English history.

"These things are only a beginning. But I shall not make much farther advance here, from the difficulty of getting books. Hence I must next concentrate all my energies on settling in Christminster. Once there I shall so advance, with the assistance I shall there get, that my present knowledge will appear to me but as childish ignorance. I must save money, and I will; and one of those colleges shall open its doors to me—shall welcome whom now it would spurn, if I wait twenty years for the welcome.

"I'll be D.D. before I have done!"

And then he continued to dream, and thought he might become even a bishop by leading a pure, energetic, wise, Christian life. And what an example he would set! If his income were £5000 a year, he would give away £4500 in one form and another, and live sumptuously (for him) on the remainder. Well, on second thoughts, a bishop was absurd. He would draw the line at an archdeacon. Perhaps a man could be as good and as learned and as useful in the capacity of archdeacon as in that of bishop. Yet he thought of the bishop again.

"Meanwhile I will read, as soon as I am settled in Christminster, the books I have not been able to get hold of here: Livy, Tacitus, Herodotus, Æschylus, Sophocles, Aristophanes——"

"Ha, ha, ha! Hoity-toity!" The sounds were expressed in light voices on the other side of the hedge, but he did not notice them. His thoughts went on:

"——Euripides, Plato, Aristotle, Lucretius, Epictetus, Seneca, Antoninus. Then I must master other things: the Fathers thoroughly; Bede and ecclesiastical history generally; a smattering of Hebrew——I only know the letters as yet——"

"Hoity-toity!"

"——but I can work hard. I have staying power in abundance, thank God! and it is that which tells. . . . Yes, Christminster shall be my Alma Mater; and I'll be her beloved son, in whom she shall be well pleased."

In his deep concentration on these transactions of the future Jude's walk had slackened, and he was now standing quite still, looking at the ground as though the future were thrown thereon by a magic lantern. On a sudden something smacked him sharply in the ear, and he became aware that a soft cold substance had been flung at him, and had fallen at his feet.

A glance told him what it was—a piece of flesh, the characteristic part of a barrow-pig, which the countrymen used for greasing their boots, as it was useless for any other purpose. Pigs were rather plentiful hereabout, being bred and fattened in large numbers in certain parts of North Wessex.

On the other side of the hedge was a stream, whence, as he now for the first time realised, had come the slight sounds of voices and laughter that had mingled with his dreams. He mounted the bank and looked over the fence. On the further side of the stream stood a small homestead, having a garden and pigsties attached; in front of it, beside the brook, three young women were kneeling, with buckets and platters beside them containing heaps of pigs' chitterlings, which they were washing in the running water. One or two pairs of eyes slily glanced up, and perceiving that his attention had at last been attracted, and that he was watching them, they braced themselves for inspection by putting their mouths demurely into shape and recommencing their rinsing operations with assiduity.

"Thank you!" said Jude severely.

"I *didn't* throw it, I tell you!" asserted one girl to her neighbour, as if unconscious of the young man's presence.

"Nor I," the second answered.

"O, Anny, how can you!" said the third.

"If I had thrown anything at all, it shouldn't have been that!"

"Pooh! I don't care for him!" And they laughed and continued their work, without looking up, still ostentatiously accusing each other.

Jude grew sarcastic as he wiped his face, and caught their remarks.

"*You* didn't do it—O no!" he said to the up-stream one of the three.

She whom he addressed was a fine dark-eyed girl, not exactly handsome, but capable of passing as such at a little distance, despite some coarseness of skin and fibre. She had a round and prominent bosom, full lips, perfect teeth, and the rich complexion of a Cochin hen's egg. She was a complete and substantial female animal—no more, no less; and Jude was almost certain that to her was attributable the enterprize of attracting his attention from dreams of the humaner letters to what was simmering in the minds around him.

"That you'll never be told," said she deedily.

"Whoever did it was wasteful of other people's property."

"O, that's nothing."

"But you want to speak to me, I suppose?"

"O yes; if you like to."

"Shall I clamber across, or will you come to the plank above here?"

Perhaps she foresaw an opportunity; for somehow or other the eyes of the brown girl rested in his own when he had said the words, and there was a momentary flash of intelligence, a dumb announcement of affinity *in posse* between herself and him, which, so far as Jude Fawley was concerned, had no sort of premeditation in it. She saw that he had singled her out from the three, as a woman is singled out in such cases, for no reasoned purpose of further acquaintance, but in commonplace obedience to conjunctive orders from head-quarters, unconsciously received by unfortunate men when the last intention of their lives is to be occupied with the feminine.

Springing to her feet, she said: "Bring back what is lying there."

Jude was now aware that no message on any matter connected with her father's business had prompted her signal to him. He set down his basket of tools, beat a pathway for himself with his stick, and got over the hedge. They walked in parallel lines, one on each bank of the stream, towards the small plank bridge. As the girl drew nearer to it, she gave, without Jude perceiving it, an adroit little suck to the interior of each of her cheeks in succession, by which curious and original manoeuvre she brought as by magic upon its smooth and rotund surface a perfect dimple, which she was able to retain there as long as she continued to smile. This production of dimples at will was a not unknown operation, which many attempted, but only a few succeeded in accomplishing.

They met in the middle of the plank, and Jude, tossing back her missile, seemed to expect her to explain why she had audaciously stopped him by this novel artillery instead of by hailing him.

But she, slily looking in another direction, swayed herself backwards and forwards on her hand as it clutched the rail of the bridge; till, moved by amatory curiosity, she turned her eyes critically upon him.

"You don't think I would shy things at you?"

"O no."

"We are doing this for my father, who doesn't want anything thrown away."

"What made either of the others throw it, I wonder?" Jude asked, politely accepting her assertion, though he had very large doubts as to its truth.

"Impudence. Don't tell folk it was I, mind!"

"How can I? I don't know your name."

"Ah, no. Shall I tell it to you?"

"Do!"

"Arabella Donn. I'm living here."

"I must have known it if I had often come this way. But I mostly go straight along the high-road."

"My father is a pig-breeder, and these girls are helping me wash the innerds for black-puddings and such like."

They talked a little more and a little more, as they stood regarding each other and leaning against the hand-rail of the bridge. The unvoiced call of woman to man, which was uttered very distinctly by Arabella's personality, held Jude to the spot against his intention—almost against his will, and in a way new to his experience. It is scarcely an exaggeration to say that till this moment Jude had never looked at a woman to consider her as such, but had vaguely regarded the sex as beings outside his life and purposes. He gazed from her eyes to her mouth, thence to her bosom, and to her full round naked arms, wet, mottled with the chill of the water, and firm as marble.

"What a nice-looking girl you are!" he murmured, though the words had not been necessary to express his sense of her magnetism.

"Ah, you should see me Sundays!" she said piquantly.

"I don't suppose I could?" he answered

"That's for you to think on. There's nobody after me just now, though there med be in a week or two." She had spoken this without a smile, and the dimples disappeared.

Jude felt himself drifting strangely, but could not help it. "Will you let me?"

"I don't mind."

By this time she had managed to get back one dimple by turning her face aside for a moment and repeating the odd little sucking operation before mentioned, Jude being still unconscious of more than a general impression of her appearance. "Next Sunday?" he hazarded. "To-morrow, that is?"

"Yes."

"Shall I call?"

"Yes."

She brightened with a little glow of triumph, swept him almost tenderly with her eyes in turning, and retracing her steps down the brookside grass, rejoined her companions.

Jude Fawley shouldered his tool-basket and resumed his lonely way, filled with an ardour at which he mentally stood at gaze. He had just inhaled a single breath from a new atmosphere, which had evidently been hanging round him everywhere he went, for he knew not how long, but had somehow been divided from his actual breathing as by a sheet of glass. The intentions as to reading, working, and learning, which he had so precisely formulated only a few minutes earlier, were suffering a curious collapse into a corner, he knew not how.

"Well, it's only a bit of fun," he said to himself, faintly conscious that to common sense there was something lacking, and still more obviously something redundant, in the nature of this girl who had drawn him to her, which made it necessary that he should assert mere sportiveness on his part as his reason in seeking her—something in her quite antipathetic to that side of him which had been occupied with literary study and the magnificent Christminster dream. It had been no vestal who chose *that* missile for opening her attack on him. He saw this with his intellectual eye, just for a short fleeting while, as by the light of a falling lamp one might momentarily see an inscription on a wall before being enshrouded in darkness. And then this passing discriminative power was withdrawn, and Jude was lost to all conditions of things in the advent of a fresh and wild pleasure, that of having found a new channel for emotional interest hitherto unsuspected, though it had lain close beside him. He was to meet this enkindling one of the other sex on the following Sunday.

Meanwhile the girl had joined her companions, and she silently resumed her flicking and sousing of the chitterlings in the pellucid stream.

"Catched un, my dear?" laconically asked the girl called Anny.

"I don't know. I wish I had thrown something else than that!" regretfully murmured Arabella.

"Lord! he's nobody, though you med think so. He used to drive old Drusilla Fawley's bread-cart out at Marygreen, till he 'prenticed himself at Alfredston. Since then he's been very stuck up, and always reading. He wants to be a scholar, they say."

"O, I don't care what he is, or anything about 'n. Don't you think it, my child!"

"O, don't 'ee! You needn't try to deceive us! What did you stay talking to him for, if you didn't want un? Whether you do or whether you don't, he's as simple as a child. I could see it as you courted on the bridge, when he looked at 'ee as if he had never seen a woman before in his born days. Well, he's to be had by any woman who can get him to care for her a bit, if she likes to set herself to catch him the right way."

VII

THE NEXT DAY JUDE FAWLEY WAS PAUSING IN HIS BEDROOM WITH THE SLOPING CEILING, looking at the books on the table, and then at the black mark on the plaster above them, made by the smoke of his lamp in past months.

It was Sunday afternoon, four-and-twenty hours after his meeting with Arabella Donn. During the whole bygone week he had been resolving to set this afternoon apart for a special purpose—the rereading of his Greek Testament—his new one, with better type than his old copy, following Griesbach's text as amended by numerous correctors, and with variorum readings in the margin. He was proud of the book, having obtained it by boldly writing to its London publisher, a thing he had never done before.

He had anticipated much pleasure in this afternoon's reading, under the quiet roof of his great-aunt's house as formerly, where he now slept only two nights a week. But a new thing, a great hitch, had happened yesterday in the gliding and noiseless current of his life, and he felt as a snake must feel who has sloughed off its winter skin, and cannot understand the brightness and sensitiveness of its new one.

He would not go out to meet her, after all. He sat down, opened the book, and with his elbows firmly planted on the table, and his hands to his temples began at the beginning:

Η ΚΑΙΝΗ ΔΙΑΘΗΚΗ.

.   .   .   .   .

Had he promised to call for her? Surely he had! She would wait indoors, poor girl, and waste all her afternoon on account of him. There was a something in her, too, which was very winning, apart from promises. He ought not to break faith with her. Even though he had only Sundays and week-day evenings for reading he could afford one afternoon, seeing that other young men afforded so many. After to-day he would never probably see her again. Indeed, it would be impossible, considering what his plans were.

In short, as if materially, a compelling arm of extraordinary muscular power seized hold of him—something which had nothing in common with the spirits and influences that had moved him hitherto. This seemed to care little for his reason and his will, nothing for his so-called elevated intentions, and moved him along, as a violent schoolmaster a schoolboy he has seized by the collar, in a direction which tended towards the embrace of a woman for whom he had no respect, and whose life had nothing in common with his own except locality.

Η ΚΑΙΝΗ ΔΙΑΘΗΚΗ was no more heeded, and the predestinate Jude sprang up and across the room. Foreseeing such an event he had already arrayed himself in his best clothes. In three minutes he was out of the house and descending by the path across the wide vacant hollow of corn-ground which lay between the village and the isolated house of Arabella in the dip beyond the upland.

As he walked he looked at his watch. He could be back in two hours, easily, and a good long time would still remain to him for reading after tea.

Passing the few unhealthy fir-trees and cottage where the path joined the highway he hastened along, and struck away to the left, descending the steep side of the country to the west of the Brown House. Here at the base of the chalk formation he neared the brook that oozed from it, and followed the stream till he reached her dwelling. A smell of piggeries came from the back, and the grunting of the originators of that smell. He entered the garden, and knocked at the door with the knob of his stick.

Somebody had seen him through the window, for a male voice on the inside said:

"Arabella! Here's your young man come coorting! Mizzel, my girl!"

Jude winced at the words. Courting in such a businesslike aspect as it evidently wore to the speaker was the last thing he was thinking of. He was going to walk with her, perhaps kiss her; but "courting" was too coolly purposeful to be anything but repugnant to his ideas. The door was opened and he entered, just as Arabella came downstairs in full walking attire.

"Take a chair, Mr. What's-your-name?" said her father, an energetic, black-whiskered man, in the same businesslike tones Jude had heard from outside.

"I'd rather go out at once, wouldn't you?" she whispered to Jude.

"Yes," said he. "We'll walk up to the Brown House and back, we can do it in half an hour."

Arabella looked so handsome amid her untidy surroundings that he felt glad he had come, and all the misgivings vanished that had hitherto haunted him.

First they clambered to the top of the great down, during which ascent he had occasionally to take her hand to assist her. Then they bore off to the left along the crest into the ridgeway, which they followed till it intersected the high-road at the Brown House aforesaid, the spot of his former fervid desires to behold Christminster. But he forgot them now. He talked the commonest local twaddle to Arabella with greater zest than he would have felt in discussing all the philosophies with all the Dons in the recently adored University, and passed the spot where he had knelt to Diana and Phœbus without remembering that there were any such people in the mythology, or that the Sun was anything else than a useful lamp for illuminating Arabella's face. An indescribable lightness of heel served to lift him along; and Jude, the incipient scholar, prospective D.D., Professor, Bishop, or what not, felt himself honoured and glorified by the condescension of this handsome country wench in agreeing to take a walk with him in her Sunday frock and ribbons.

They reached the Brown House barn—the point at which he had planned to turn back. While looking over the vast northern landscape from this spot, they were struck by the rising of a dense volume of smoke from the neighbourhood of the little town which lay beneath them at a distance of a couple of miles.

"It is a fire," said Arabella. "Let's run and see it—do! It is not far!"

The tenderness which had grown up in Jude's bosom left him no will to thwart her inclination now—which pleased him in affording him excuse for a longer time with her. They started off down the hill almost at a trot; but on gaining level ground at the bottom, and walking a mile, they found that the spot of the fire was much further off than it had seemed.

Having begun their journey, however, they pushed on; but it was not till five o'clock that they found themselves on the scene—the distance being altogether about half-a-dozen miles from Marygreen, and three from Arabella's. The conflagration had been got under by the time they reached it, and after a short inspection of the melancholy ruins they retraced their steps—their course lying through the town of Alfredston.

Arabella said she would like some tea, and they entered an inn of an inferior class, and gave their order. As it was not for beer they had a long time to wait. The maid-servant recognised Jude, and whispered her surprise to her mistress in the background, that he, the student "who kept hisself up so particular," should have suddenly descended so low as to keep company with Arabella. The latter guessed what was being said, and laughed as she met the serious and tender gaze of her lover—the low and triumphant laugh of a careless woman who sees she is winning her game.

They sat and looked round the room, and at the picture of Samson and Delilah which hung on the wall, and at the circular beer-stains on the table, and at the spittoons underfoot filled with sawdust. The whole aspect of the scene had that depressing effect on Jude which few places can produce like a tap-room on a Sunday evening when the setting sun is slanting in, and no liquor is going, and the unfortunate wayfarer finds himself with no other haven of rest.

It began to grow dusk. They could not wait longer, really, they said. "Yet what else can we do?" asked Jude. "It is a three-mile walk for you."

"I suppose we can have some beer," said Arabella.

"Beer, O yes. I had forgotten that. Somehow it seems odd to come to a public-house for beer on a Sunday evening."

"But we didn't."

"No, we didn't." Jude by this time wished he was out of such an uncongenial atmosphere; but he ordered the beer, which was promptly brought.

Arabella tasted it. "Ugh!" she said.

Jude tasted. "What's the matter with it?" he asked. "I don't understand beer very much now, it is true. I like it well enough, but it is bad to read on, and I find coffee better. But this seems all right."

"Adulterated—I can't touch it!" She mentioned three or four ingredients that she detected in the liquor beyond malt and hops, much to Jude's surprise.

"How much you know!" he said good-humouredly.

Nevertheless she returned to the beer and drank her share, and they went on their way. It was now nearly dark, and as soon as they had withdrawn from the lights of the town they walked closer together, till they touched each other. She wondered why he did not put his arm round her waist, but he did not; he merely said what to himself seemed a quite bold enough thing: "Take my arm."

She took it, thoroughly, up to the shoulder. He felt the warmth of her body against his, and putting his stick under his other arm held with his right hand her right as it rested in its place.

"Now we are well together, dear, aren't we?" he observed.

"Yes," said she; adding to herself: "Rather mild!"

"How fast I have become!" he was thinking.

Thus they walked till they reached the foot of the upland, where they could see the white highway ascending before them in the gloom. From this point the only way of getting to Arabella's was by going up the incline, and dipping again into her valley on the right. Before they had climbed far they were nearly run into by two men who had been walking on the grass unseen.

"These lovers—you find 'em out o' doors in all seasons and weathers—lovers and homeless dogs only," said one of the men as they vanished down the hill.

Arabella tittered lightly.

"Are we lovers?" asked Jude.

"You know best."

"But you can tell me?"

For answer she inclined her head upon his shoulder. Jude took the hint, and encircling her waist with his arm, pulled her to him and kissed her.

They walked now no longer arm in arm but, as she had desired, clasped together. After all, what did it matter since it was dark, said Jude to himself. When they were half-way up the long hill they paused as by arrangement, and he kissed her again. They reached the top, and he kissed her once more.

"You can keep your arm there, if you would like to," she said gently.

He did so, thinking how trusting she was.

Thus they slowly went towards her home. He had left his cottage at half-past three, intending to be sitting down again to the New Testament by half-past five. It was nine o'clock when, with another embrace, he stood to deliver her up at her father's door.

She asked him to come in, if only for a minute, as it would seem so odd otherwise, and as if she had been out alone in the dark. He gave way, and followed her in. Immediately that the door was opened he found, in addition to her parents, several neighbours sitting round. They all spoke in a congratulatory manner, and took him seriously as Arabella's intended partner.

They did not belong to his set or circle, and he felt out of place and embarrassed. He had not meant this: a mere afternoon of pleasant walking with Arabella, that was all he had meant. He did not stay longer than to speak to her stepmother, a simple, quiet woman without features or character; and bidding them all good-night plunged with a sense of relief into the track over the down.

But that sense was only temporary: Arabella soon reasserted her sway in his soul. He walked as if he felt himself to be another man from the Jude of yesterday. What were his books to him? what were his intentions, hitherto adhered to so strictly, as to not wasting a single minute of time day by day? "Wasting!" It depended on your point of view to define that: he was just living for the first time: not wasting life. It was better to love a woman than to be a graduate, or a parson; ay, or a pope!

When he got back to the house, his aunt had gone to bed, and a general consciousness of his neglect seemed written on the face of all things confronting him. He went upstairs without a light, and the dim interior of his room accosted him with sad inquiry. There lay his book open, just as he had left it, and the capital letters on the title-page regarded him with fixed reproach in the grey starlight, like the unclosed eyes of a dead man:

Η ΚΑΙΝΗ ΔΙΑΘΗΚΗ

.   .   .   .   .   .

Jude had to leave early next morning for his usual week of absence at lodgings; and it was with a sense of futility that he threw into his basket upon his tools and other necessaries the unread book he had brought with him.

He kept his impassioned doings a secret almost from himself. Arabella, on the contrary, made them public among all her friends and acquaintance.

Retracing by the light of dawn the road he had followed a few hours earlier, under cover of darkness, with his sweetheart by his side, he reached the bottom of the hill, where he walked slowly, and stood still. He was on the spot where he had given her the first kiss. As the sun had only just risen it was possible that nobody had passed there since. Jude looked on the ground and sighed. He looked closely, and could just discern in the damp dust the imprints of their feet as they had stood locked in each other's arms. She was not there now, and "the embroidery of imagination upon the stuff of nature" so depicted her past presence that a void was in his heart which nothing could fill. A pollard willow stood close to the place, and that willow was different from all other willows in the world. Utter annihilation of the six days which must elapse before he could see her again as he had promised would have been his intensest wish if he had had only the week to live.

An hour and a half later Arabella came along the same way with her two companions of the Saturday. She passed unheedingly the scene of the kiss, and the willow that marked it, though chattering freely on the subject to the other two.

"And what did he tell 'ee next?"

"Then he said—" And she related almost word for word some of his tenderest speeches. If Jude had been behind the fence he would have felt not a little surprised at learning how very few of his sayings and doings on the previous evening were private.

"You've got him to care for 'ee a bit, 'nation if you ha'n't!" murmured Anny judicially. "It's well to be you!"

In a few moments Arabella replied in a curiously low, fierce tone of latent sensuousness: "I've got him to care for me: yes! But I want him to more than care for me; I want him to have me—to marry me! I must have him. I can't do without him. He's the sort of man I long for. I shall go mad if I can't give myself to him altogether! I felt I should when I first saw him!"

"As he is a romancing, straightfor'ard, honest chap, he's to be had, and as a husband, if you set about catching him in the right way."

Arabella remained thinking a while. "What med be the right way?" she asked.

"O you don't know—you don't!" said Sarah, the third girl.

"On my word I don't!—No further, that is, than by plain courting, and taking care he don't go too far!"

The third girl looked at the second. "She *don't* know!"

" 'Tis clear she don't!" said Anny.

"And having lived in a town, too, as one may say! Well, we can teach 'ee som'at then, as well as you us."

"Yes. And how do you mean—a sure way to gain a man? Take me for an innocent, and have done wi' it!"

"As a husband."

"As a husband."

"A countryman that's honourable and serious-minded such as he; God forbid that I should say a sojer, or sailor, or commercial gent from the towns, or any of them that be slippery with poor women! I'd do no friend that harm!"

"Well, such as he, of course!"

Arabella's companions looked at each other, and turning up their eyes in drollery began smirking. Then one went up close to Arabella, and, although nobody was near, imparted some information in a low tone, the other observing curiously the effect upon Arabella.

"Ah!" said the last-named slowly. "I own I didn't think of that way! . . . But suppose he *isn't* honourable? A woman had better not have tried it!"

"Nothing venture nothing have! Besides, you make sure that he's honourable before you begin. You'd be safe enough with yours. I wish I had the chance! Lots of girls do it; or do you think they'd get married at all?"

Arabella pursued her way in silent thought. "I'll try it!" she whispered; but not to them.

VIII

ONE WEEK'S END JUDE WAS AS USUAL WALKING OUT TO HIS AUNT'S AT MARYGREEN from his lodging in Alfredston, a walk which now had large attractions for him quite other than his desire to see his aged and morose relative. He diverged to the right before ascending the hill with the single purpose of gaining, on his way, a glimpse of Arabella that should not come into the reckoning of regular appointments. Before quite reaching the homestead his alert eye perceived the top of her head moving quickly hither and thither over the garden hedge. Entering the gate he found that three young unfattened pigs had escaped from their sty by leaping clean over the top, and that she was endeavouring unassisted to drive them in through the door which she had set open. The lines of her countenance changed from the rigidity of business to the softness of love when she saw Jude, and she bent her eyes languishingly upon him. The animals took advantage of the pause by doubling and bolting out of the way.

"They were only put in this morning!" she cried, stimulated to pursue in spite of her lover's presence. "They were drove from Spaddleholt Farm only yesterday, where father bought 'em at a stiff price enough. They are wanting to get home again, the stupid toads! Will you shut the garden gate, dear, and help me to get 'em in? There are no men-folk at home, only mother, and they'll be lost if we don't mind."

He set himself to assist, and dodged this way and that over the potato rows and the cabbages. Every now and then they ran together, when he caught her for a moment an kissed her. The first pig was got back promptly; the second with some difficulty; the third, a long-legged creature, was more obstinate and agile. He plunged through a hole in the garden hedge, and into the lane.

"He'll be lost if I don't follow 'n!" said she. "Come along with me!"

She rushed in full pursuit out of the garden, Jude alongside her, barely contriving to keep the fugitive in sight. Occasionally they would shout to some boy to stop the animal, but he always wriggled past and ran on as before.

"Let me take your hand, darling," said Jude. "You are getting out of breath." She gave him her now hot hand with apparent willingness, and they trotted along together.

"This comes of driving 'em home," she remarked. "They always know the way back if you do that. They ought to have been carted over."

By this time the pig had reached an unfastened gate admitting to the open down, across which he sped with all the agility his little legs afforded. As soon as the pursuers had entered and ascended to the top of the high ground it became apparent that they would have to run all the way to the farmer's if they wished to get at him. From this summit he could be seen as a minute speck, following an unerring line towards the farm.

"It is no good!" cried Arabella. "He'll be there long before we get there. It don't matter now we know he's not lost or stolen on the way. They'll see it is ours, and send un back. O dear, how hot I be!"

Without relinquishing her hold of Jude's hand she swerved aside and flung herself down on the sod under a stunted thorn, precipitately pulling Jude on to his knees at the same time.

"O, I ask pardon—I nearly threw you down, didn't I! But I am so tired!"

She lay supine, and straight as an arrow, on the sloping sod of this hill-top, gazing up into the blue miles of sky, and still retaining her warm hold of Jude's hand. He reclined on his elbow near her.

"We've run all this way for nothing," she went on, her form heaving and falling in quick pants, her face flushed, her full red lips parted, and a fine dew of perspiration on her skin. "Well—why don't you speak, deary?"

"I'm blown too. It was all up-hill."

They were in absolute solitude—the most apparent of all solitudes, that of empty surrounding space. Nobody could be nearer than a mile to them without their seeing him. They were, in fact, on one of the summits of the county, and the distant landscape around Christminster could be discerned from where they lay. But Jude did not think of that then.

"O, I can see such a pretty thing up this tree," said Arabella. "A sort of a—caterpillar, of the most loveliest green and yellow you ever came across!"

"Where?" said Jude, sitting up.

"You can't see him there—you must come here," said she.

He bent nearer and put his head in front of hers. "No—I can't see it," he said.

"Why, on the limb there where it branches off—close to the moving leaf—there!" She gently pulled him down beside her.

"I don't see it," he repeated, the back of his head against her cheek. "But I can, perhaps, standing up." He stood accordingly, placing himself in the direct line of her gaze.

"How stupid you are!" she said crossly, turning away her face.

"I don't care to see it, dear: why should I?" he replied, looking down upon her. "Get up, Abby."

"Why?"

"I want you to let me kiss you. I've been waiting to ever so long!"

She rolled round her face, remained a moment looking deedily aslant at him; then with a slight curl of the lip sprang to her feet, and exclaiming abruptly "I must mizzle!" walked off quickly homeward. Jude followed and rejoined her.

"Just one!" he coaxed

"Shan't!" she said

He, surprised: "What's the matter?"

She kept her two lips resentfully together, and Jude followed her like a pet lamb till she slackened her pace and walked beside him, talking calmly on indifferent subjects, and always checking him if he tried to take her hand or clasp her waist. Thus they descended to the precincts of her father's homestead, and Arabella went in, nodding good-bye to him with a supercilious, affronted air.

"I expect I took too much liberty with her, somehow," Jude said to himself, as he withdrew with a sigh and went on to Marygreen.

On Sunday morning the interior of Arabella's home was, as usual, the scene of a grand weekly cooking, the preparation of the special Sunday dinner. Her father was shaving before a little glass hung on the mullion of the window, and her mother and Arabella herself were shelling beans hard by. A neighbour passed on her way home from morning service at the nearest church, and seeing Donn engaged at the window with the razor, nodded and came in.

She at once spoke playfully to Arabella: "I zeed 'ee running with 'un—hee-hee! I hope 'tis coming to something?"

Arabella merely threw a look of consciousness into her face without raising her eyes.

"He's for Christminster, I hear, as soon as he can get there."

"Have you heard that lately—quite lately?" asked Arabella with a jealous, tigerish indrawing of breath.

"Oh no! But it has been known a long time that it is his plan. He's on'y waiting here for an opening. Ah well: he must walk about with somebody I s'pose. Young men don't mean much now-a-days. 'Tis a sip here and a sip there with 'em. 'Twas different in my time."

When the gossip had departed Arabella said suddenly to her mother: "I want you and Father to go and enquire how the Edlins be, this evening after tea. Or no—there's evening service at Fensworth—you can walk to that."

"Oh? What's up to-night, then?"

"Nothing. Only I want the house to myself. He's shy; and I can't get un to come in when you are here. I shall let him slip through my fingers if I don't mind, much as I care for 'n!"

"If it is fine we med as well go, since you wish."

In the afternoon Arabella met and walked with Jude, who had now for weeks ceased to look into a book of Greek, Latin, or any other tongue. They wandered up the slopes till they reached the green track along the ridge, which they followed to the circular British earth-bank adjoining, Jude thinking of the great age of the trackway, and of the drovers who had frequented it, probably before the Romans knew the country. Up from the level lands below them floated the chime of church-bells. Presently they were reduced to one note, which quickened, and stopped.

"Now we'll go back," said Arabella, who had attended to the sounds.

Jude assented. So long as he was near her he minded little where he was. When they arrived at her house he said lingeringly: "I won't come in. Why are you in such a hurry to go in to-night? It is not near dark."

"Wait a moment," said she. She tried the handle of the door and found it locked.

"Ah—they are gone to church," she added. And searching behind the scraper she found the key and unlocked the door. "Now, you'll come in a moment?" she asked lightly. "We shall be all alone."

"Certainly," said Jude with alacrity, the case being unexpectedly altered.

Indoors they went. Did he want any tea? No, it was too late: he would rather sit and talk to her. She took off her jacket and hat, and they sat down—naturally enough close together.

"Don't touch me, please," she said softly. "I am part egg-shell. Or perhaps I had better put it in a safe place." She began unfastening the collar of her gown.

"What is it?" said her lover.

"An egg—a bantam's egg. I am hatching a very rare sort. I carry it about everywhere with me, and it will get hatched in less than three weeks."

"Where do you carry it?"

"Just here." She put her hand into her bosom and drew out the egg, which was wrapped in wool, outside it being a piece of pig's bladder, in case of accidents. Having exhibited it to him she put it back, "Now mind you don't come near me. I don't want to get it broke, and have to begin another."

"Why do you do such a strange thing?"

"It's an old custom. I suppose it is natural for a woman to want to bring live things into the world."

"It is very awkward for me just now," he said, laughing.

"It serves you right. There—that's all you can have of me"

She had turned round her chair, and, reaching over the back of it, presented her cheek to him gingerly.

"That's very shabby of you!"

"You should have catched me a minute ago when I had put the egg down! There!" she said defiantly, "I am without it now!" She had quickly withdrawn the egg a second time; but before he could quite reach her she had put it back as quickly, laughing with the excitement of her strategy. Then there was a little struggle, Jude making a plunge for it and capturing it triumphantly. Her face flushed; and becoming suddenly conscious he flushed also.

They looked at each other, panting; till he rose and said: "One kiss, now I can do it without damage to property; and I'll go!"

But she had jumped up too. "You must find me first!" she cried.

Her lover followed her as she withdrew. It was now dark inside the room, and the window being small he could not discover for a long time what had become of her, till a laugh revealed her to have rushed up the stairs, whither Jude rushed at her heels.

IX

IT WAS SOME TWO MONTHS LATER IN THE YEAR, AND THE PAIR HAD MET CONSTANTLY during the interval. Arabella seemed dissatisfied; she was always imagining, and waiting, and wondering.

One day she met the itinerant Vilbert. She, like all the cottagers thereabout, knew the quack well, and they began talking about her experiences. Arabella had been gloomy, but before he left her she had grown brighter. That evening she kept an appointment with Jude, who seemed sad.

"I am going away," he said to her. "I think I ought to go. I think it will be better both for you and for me. I wish some things had never begun! I was much to blame, I know. But it is never too late to mend."

Arabella began to cry. "How do you know it is not too late?" she said. "That's all very well to say! I haven't told you yet!" and she looked into his face with streaming eyes.

"What?" he asked, turning pale. "Not . . . ?"

"Yes! And what shall I do if you desert me?"

"Oh, Arabella—how can you say that, my dear! You *know* I wouldn't desert you!"

"Well then—"

"I have next to no wages as yet, you know; or perhaps I should have thought of this before. . . . But, of course, if that's the case, we must marry! What other thing do you think I could dream of doing?"

"I thought—I thought, deary, perhaps you would go away all the more for that, and leave me to face it alone!"

"You knew better! Of course I never dreamt six months ago, or even three, of marrying. It is a complete smashing up of my plans—I mean my plans before I knew you, my dear. But what are they, after all! Dreams about books, and degrees, and impossible scholarships, and all that. Certainly we'll marry: we must!"

That night he went out alone, and walked in the dark, self-communing. He knew well, too well, in the secret centre of his brain, that Arabella was not worth a great deal as a specimen of womankind. Yet, such being the custom of the rural districts among honourable young men who had drifted so far into intimacy with a woman as he unfortunately had done, he was ready to abide by what he had said, and take the consequences. For his own

soothing he kept up a factitious belief in her. His idea of her was the thing of most consequence, not Arabella herself, he sometimes said laconically.

The banns were put in and published the very next Sunday. The people of the parish
all said what a simple fool young Fawley was. All his reading had only come to this, that
he would have to sell his books to buy sauce-pans. Those who guessed the probable state
of affairs, Arabella's parents being among them, declared that it was the sort of conduct
they would have expected of such an honest young man as Jude in reparation of the wrong
he had done his innocent sweetheart. The parson who married them seemed to think it satisfactory too.

And so, standing before the aforesaid officiator, the two swore that at every other time
of their lives they would assuredly believe, feel, and desire precisely as they had believed,
felt, and desired during the few preceding weeks. What was as remarkable as the undertaking itself was the fact that nobody seemed at all surprised at what they swore.

Fawley's aunt being a baker she made him a bride-cake, saying bitterly that it was the
last thing she could do for him, poor silly fellow; and that it would have been far better if,
instead of his living to trouble her, he had gone underground years before with his father
and mother. Of this cake Arabella took some slices, wrapped them up in white note-paper,
and sent them to her companions in the pork-dressing business, Anny and Sarah, labelling
each packet *"In remembrance of good advice."*

The prospects of the newly married couple were certainly not very brilliant even to
the most sanguine mind. He, a stone-mason's apprentice, nineteen years of age, was working for half wages till he should be out of his time. His wife was absolutely useless in a
town-lodging, where he at first had considered it would be necessary for them to live. But
the urgent need of adding to income in ever so little a degree caused him to take a lonely
roadside cottage between the Brown House and Marygreen, that he might have the profits of a vegetable garden, and utilise her past experiences by letting her keep a pig. But it
was not the sort of life he had bargained for, and it was a long way to walk to and from
Alfredston everyday. Arabella, however, felt that all these makeshifts were temporary; she
had gained a husband; that was the thing—a husband with a lot of earning power in him
for buying her frocks and hats when he should begin to get frightened a bit, and stick to
his trade, and throw aside those stupid books for practical undertakings.

So to the cottage he took her on the evening of the marriage, giving up his old room
at his aunt's—where so much of the hard labour at Greek and Latin had been carried on.

A little chill overspread him at her first unrobing. A long tail of hair, which Arabella
wore twisted up in an enormous knob at the back of her head, was deliberately unfastened,
stroked out, and hung upon the looking-glass which he had bought her.

"What—it wasn't your own?" he said, with a sudden distaste for her.

"Oh no—it never is now-a-days with the better class."

"Nonsense! Perhaps not in towns. But in the country it is supposed to be different. Besides, you've enough of your own, surely?"

"Yes, enough as country notions go. But in towns the men expect more, and when I
was barmaid at Aldbrickham—"

"Barmaid at Aldbrickham?"

"Well, not exactly barmaid—I used to draw the drink at a public-house there—just
for a little time; that was all. Some people put me up to getting this, and I bought it just for

a fancy. The more you have the better in Aldbrickham, which is a finer town than all your Christminsters. Every lady of position wears false hair—the barber's assistant told me so."

Jude thought with a feeling of sickness that though this might be true to some extent, for all that he knew, many unsophisticated girls would and did go to towns and remain there for years without losing their simplicity of life and embellishments. Others, alas, had an instinct towards artificiality in their very blood, and became adepts in counterfeiting at the first glimpse of it. However, perhaps there was no great sin in a woman adding to her hair, and he resolved to think no more of it.

A new-made wife can usually manage to look interesting for a few weeks, even though the prospects of the household ways and means are cloudy. There is a certain piquancy about her situation, and her manner to her acquaintance at the sense of it, which carries off the gloom of facts, and renders even the humblest bride independent a while of the real. Mrs. Jude Fawley was walking in the streets of Alfredston one market-day with this quality in her carriage when she met Anny her former friend, whom she had not seen since the wedding.

As usual they laughed before talking; the world seemed funny to them without saying it.

"So it turned out a good plan you see!" remarked the girl to the wife. "I knew it would with such as him. He's a dear good fellow, and you ought to be proud of un."

"I am," said Mrs. Fawley quietly.

"And when do you expect—?"

"Ssh! Not at all."

"What!"

"I was mistaken."

"O, Arabella, Arabella; you be a deep one! Mistaken! well, that's clever—it's a rale stroke of genius! It is a thing I never thought o', wi' all my experience! I never thought beyond the rale thing—not that one could sham it!"

"Don't you be too quick to cry sham! 'Twasn't sham. I didn't know."

"My word—won't he be in a taking! He'll give it to 'ee o' Saturday nights! Whatever it was, he'll say it was a trick—a double one, by the Lord!"

"I'll own to the first, but not to the second. . . . Pooh—he won't care! He'll be glad I was wrong in what I said. He'll shake down, bless 'ee—men always do. What can 'em do otherwise? Married is married."

Nevertheless it was with a little uneasiness that Arabella approached the time when in the natural course of things she would have to reveal that the alarm she had raised had been without foundation. The occasion was one evening at bed-time, and they were in their chamber in the lonely cottage by the wayside, to which Jude walked home from his work everyday. He had worked hard the whole twelve hours, and had retired to rest before his wife. When she came into the room he was between sleeping and waking, and was barely conscious of her undressing before the little looking-glass as he lay.

One action of hers, however, brought him to full cognition. Her face being reflected towards him as she sat, he could perceive that she was amusing herself by artificially producing in each cheek the dimple before alluded to, a curious accomplishment of which she was mistress, effecting it by a momentary suction. It seemed to him for the first time that the dimples were far oftener absent from her face during his intercourse with her now-a-days than they had been in the earlier weeks of their acquaintance.

"Don't do that, Arabella!" he said suddenly. "There is no harm in it, but—I don't like to see you."

She turned and laughed. "Lord, I didn't know you was awake!" she said. "How countrified you are! That's nothing."

"Where did you learn it?"

"Nowhere that I know of. They used to stay without any trouble when I was at the public-house; but now they won't. My face was fatter then."

"I don't care about dimples. I don't think they improve a woman—particularly a married woman, and of full-sized figure like you."

"Most men think otherwise."

"I don't care what most men think, if they do. How do you know?"

"I used to be told so when I was serving in the tap-room."

"Ah—that public-house experience accounts for your knowing about the adulteration of the ale when we went and had some that Sunday evening. I thought when I married you that you had always lived in your father's house."

"You ought to have known better than that, and seen I was a little more finished than I could have been by staying where I was born. There was not much to do at home, and I was eating my head off, so I went away for three months."

"You'll soon have plenty to do now, dear, won't you?"

"How do you mean?"

"Why, of course—little things to make."

"Oh."

"When will it be? Can't you tell me exactly, instead of in such general terms as you have used?"

"Tell you?"

"Yes—the date."

"There's nothing to tell. I made a mistake."

"What?"

"It was a mistake."

He sat bolt upright in bed and looked at her. "How can that be?"

"People fancy wrong things sometimes."

"But—! Why, of course, so unprepared as I was, without a stick of furniture, and hardly a shilling, I shouldn't have hurried on our affair, and brought you to a half-furnished hut before I was ready, if it had not been for the news you gave me, which made it necessary to save you, ready or no. . . . Good God!"

"Don't take on, dear. What's done can't be undone."

"I have no more to say!"

He gave the answer simply, and lay down; and there was silence between them.

When Jude awoke the next morning he seemed to see the world with a different eye. As to the point in question he was compelled to accept her word; in the circumstances he could not have acted otherwise while ordinary notions prevailed. But how came they to prevail?

There seemed to him, vaguely and dimly, something wrong in a social ritual which made necessary a cancelling of well-formed schemes involving years of thought and labour, of foregoing a man's one opportunity of showing himself superior to the lower animals, and of contributing his units of work to the general progress of his generation, because of a momentary surprise by a new and transitory instinct which had nothing in it of the nature of vice, and could be only at the most called weakness. He was inclined to enquire what he had done, or she lost, for that matter, that he deserved to be caught in a gin which would cripple him, if not her also, for the rest of a lifetime? There was perhaps something fortunate in the fact that the immediate reason of his marriage had proved to be non-existent. But the marriage remained.

X

THE TIME ARRIVED FOR KILLING THE PIG WHICH JUDE AND HIS WIFE HAD FATTENED IN their sty during the autumn months, and the butchering was timed to take place as soon as it was light in the morning, so that Jude might get to Alfredston without losing more than a quarter of a day.

The night had seemed strangely silent. Jude looked out of the window long before dawn, and perceived that the ground was covered with snow—snow rather deep for the season, it seemed, a few flakes still falling.

"I'm afraid the pig-killer won't be able to come," he said to Arabella.

"O, he'll come. You must get up and make the water hot, if you want Challow to scald him. Though I like singeing best."

"I'll get up," said Jude. "I like the way of my own county."

He went downstairs, lit the fire under the copper, and began feeding it with bean-stalks, all the time without a candle, the blaze flinging a cheerful shine into the room; though for him the sense of cheerfulness was lessened by thoughts on the reason of that blaze—to heat water to scald an animal that as yet lived, and whose voice could be continually heard from a corner of the garden. At half-past six, the time of appointment with the butcher, the water boiled, and Jude's wife came downstairs.

"Is Challow come?" she asked.

"No."

They waited, and it grew lighter, with the dreary light of a snowy dawn. She went out, gazed along the road, and returning said, "He's not coming. Drunk last night, I expect. The snow is not enough to hinder him, surely!"

"Then we must put it off. It is only the water boiled for nothing. The snow may be deep in the valley."

"Can't be put off. There's no more victuals for the pig. He ate the last mixing o' barleymeal yesterday morning."

"Yesterday morning? What has he lived on since?"

"Nothing."

"What—he has been starving?"

"Yes. We always do it the last day or two, to save bother with the innerds. What ignorance, not to know that!"

"That accounts for his crying so. Poor creature!"

"Well—you must do the sticking—there's no help for it. I'll show you how. Or I'll do it myself—I think I could. Though as it is such a big pig I had rather Challow had done it. However, his basket o' knives and things have been already sent on here, and we can use 'em."

"Of course you shan't do it," said Jude. "I'll do it, since it must be done."

He went out to the sty, shovelled away the snow for the space of a couple of yards or more, and placed the stool in front, with the knives and ropes at hand. A robin peered down at the preparations from the nearest tree, and, not liking the sinister look of the scene, flew away, though hungry. By this time Arabella had joined her husband, and Jude, rope in hand, got into the sty, and noosed the affrighted animal, who, beginning with a squeak of surprise, rose to repeated cries of rage. Arabella opened the sty-door, and together they hoisted the victim on to the stool, legs upward, and while Jude held him Arabella bound him down, looping the cord over his legs to keep him from struggling.

The animal's note changed its quality. It was not now rage, but the cry of despair; long-drawn, slow and hopeless.

"Upon my soul I would sooner have gone without the pig than have had this to do!" said Jude. "A creature I have fed with my own hands."

"Don't be such a tender-hearted fool! There's the sticking-knife—the one with the point. Now whatever you do, don't stick un too deep."

"I'll stick him effectually, so as to make short work of it. That's the chief thing."

"You must not!" she cried. "The meat must be well bled, and to do that he must die slow. We shall lose a shilling a score if the meat is red and bloody! Just touch the vein, that's all. I was brought up to it, and I know. Every good butcher keeps un bleeding long. He ought to be eight or ten minutes dying, at least."

"He shall not be half a minute if I can help it, however the meat may look," said Jude determinedly. Scraping the bristles from the pig's upturned throat, as he had seen the butchers do, he slit the fat; then plunged in the knife with all his might.

" 'Od damn it all!" she cried, "that ever I should say it! You've over-stuck un! And I telling you all the time—"

"Do be quiet, Arabella, and have a little pity on the creature!"

However unworkmanlike the deed, it had been mercifully done. The blood flowed out in a torrent instead of in the trickling stream she had desired. The dying animal's cry assumed its third and final tone, the shriek of agony; his glazing eyes rivetting themselves on Arabella with the eloquently keen reproach of a creature recognizing at last the treachery of those who had seemed his only friends.

"Make un stop that!" said Arabella. "Such a noise will bring somebody or other up here, and I don't want people to know we are doing it ourselves." Picking up the knife from the ground whereon Jude had flung it, she slipped it into the gash, and slit the windpipe. The pig was instantly silent, his dying breath coming through the hole.

"That's better," she said.

"It is a hateful business!" said he.

"Pigs must be killed."

The animal heaved in a final convulsion, and, despite the rope, kicked out with all his last strength. A tablespoonful of black clot came forth, the trickling of red blood having ceased for some seconds.

"That's it; now he'll go," said she. "Artful creatures—they always keep back a drop like that as long as they can!"

The last plunge had come so unexpectedly as to make Jude stagger, and in recovering himself he kicked over the vessel in which the blood had been caught.

"There!" she cried, thoroughly in a passion. "Now I can't make any blackpot. There's a waste, all through you!"

Jude put the pan upright, but only about a third of the whole steaming liquid was left in it, the main part being splashed over the snow, and forming a dismal, sordid, ugly spectacle—to those who saw it as other than an ordinary obtaining of meat. The lips and nostrils of the animal turned livid, then white, and the muscles of his limbs relaxed.

"Thank God!" Jude said. "He's dead."

"What's God got to do with such a messy job as a pig-killing, I should like to know!" she said scornfully. "Poor folks must live."

"I know, I know," said he. "I don't scold you."

Suddenly they became aware of a voice at hand.

"Well done, young married volk! I couldn't have carried it out much better myself, cuss me if I could!" The voice, which was husky, came from the garden gate, and looking up from the scene of slaughter they saw the burly form of Mr. Challow leaning over the gate, critically surveying their performance.

" 'Tis well for 'ee to stand there and glane!" said Arabella. "Owing to your being late the meat is blooded and half spoiled! 'Twon't fetch so much by a shilling a score!"

Challow expressed his contrition. "You should have waited a bit," he said, shaking his head, "and not have done this—in the delicate state, too, that you be in at present, ma'am. 'Tis risking yourself too much."

"You needn't be concerned about that," said Arabella, laughing. Jude too laughed, but there was a strong flavour of bitterness in his amusement.

Challow made up for his neglect of the killing by zeal in the scalding and scraping. Jude felt dissatisfied with himself as a man at what he had done, though aware of his lack of common sense, and that the deed would have amounted to the same thing if carried out by deputy. The white snow, stained with the blood of his fellow-mortal, wore an illogical look to him as a lover of justice, not to say a Christian; but he could not see how the matter was to be mended. No doubt he was, as his wife had called him, a tender-hearted fool.

He did not like the road to Alfredston now. It stared him cynically in the face. The wayside objects reminded him so much of his courtship of his wife that, to keep them out of his eyes, he read whenever he could as he walked to and from his work. Yet he sometimes felt that by caring for books he was not escaping commonplace nor gaining rare ideas, every working-man being of that taste now. When passing near the spot by the stream on which he had first made her acquaintance he one day heard voices just as he had done at that earlier time. One of the girls who had been Arabella's companions was talking to a friend in a shed, himself being the subject of discourse, possibly because they had seen him in the distance. They were quite unaware that the shed-walls were so thin that he could hear their words as he passed.

"Howsomever, 'twas I put her up to it! 'Nothing venture nothing have,' I said. If I hadn't she'd no more have been his mis'ess than I."

" 'Tis my belief she knew before . . ."

What had Arabella been put up to by this woman, so that he should make her his "mis-'ess," otherwise wife? The suggestion was horridly unpleasant, and it rankled in his mind so much that instead of entering his own cottage when he reached it he flung his basket inside the garden gate and passed on, determined to go and see his old aunt and get some supper there.

This made his arrival home rather late. Arabella, however, was busy melting down lard from fat of the deceased pig, for she had been out on a jaunt all day, and so delayed her work. Dreading lest what he had heard should lead him to say something regrettable to her he spoke little. But Arabella was very talkative, and said among other things that she wanted some money. Seeing the book sticking out of his pocket she added that he ought to earn more.

"An apprentice's wages are not meant to be enough to keep a wife on, as a rule, my dear."

"Then you shouldn't have had one."

"Come, Arabella! That's too bad, when you know how it came about."

"I'll declare afore Heaven that I thought what I told you was true. Doctor Vilbert thought so. It was a good job for you that it wasn't so!"

"I don't mean that," he said hastily. "I mean before that time. I know it was not your fault; but those women friends of yours gave you bad advice. If they hadn't, or you hadn't taken it, we should at this moment have been free from a bond which, not to mince matters, galls both of us devilishly. It may be very sad, but it is true."

"Who's been telling you about my friends? What advice? I insist upon your telling me."

"Pooh—I d rather not."

"But you shall—you ought to. It is mean of 'ee not to!"

"Very well." And he hinted gently what had been revealed to him. "But I don't wish to dwell upon it. Let us say no more about it."

Her defensive manner collapsed. "That was nothing," she said, laughing coldly. "Every woman has a right to do such as that. The risk is hers."

"I quite deny it, Bella. She might if no life-long penalty attached to it for the man, or, in his default, for herself; if the weakness of the moment could end with the moment, or even with the year. But when effects stretch so far she should not go and do that which entraps a man if he is honest, or herself if he is otherwise."

"What ought I to have done?"

"Given me time. . . . Why do you fuss yourself about melting down that pig's fat tonight? Please put it away!"

"Then I must do it to-morrow morning. It won't keep."

"Very well—do."

XI

N EXT MORNING, WHICH WAS SUNDAY, SHE RESUMED OPERATIONS ABOUT TEN O'CLOCK; and the renewed work recalled the conversation which had accompanied it the night before, and put her back into the same intractable temper.

"That's the story about me in Marygreen, is it—that I entrapped 'ee? Much of a catch you were, Lord send!" As she warmed she saw some of Jude's dear ancient classics on a table where they ought not to have been laid. "I won't have them books here in the way!" she cried petulantly; and seizing them one by one she began throwing them upon the floor.

"Leave my books alone!" he said. "You might have thrown them aside if you had liked, but as to soiling them like that, it is disgusting!" In the operation of making lard Arabella's hands had become smeared with the hot grease, and her fingers consequently left very perceptible imprints on the book-covers. She continued deliberately to toss the books severally upon the floor, till Jude, incensed beyond bearing, caught her by the arms to make her leave off. Somehow, in going so, he loosened the fastening of her hair, and it rolled about her ears.

"Let me go!" she said.

"Promise to leave the books alone."

She hesitated. "Let me go!" she repeated.

"Promise!"

After a pause: "I do."

Jude relinquished his hold, and she crossed the room to the door, out of which she went with a set face, and into the highway. Here she began to saunter up and down, perversely pulling her hair into a worse disorder than he had caused, and unfastening several buttons of her gown. It was a fine Sunday morning, dry, clear and frosty, and the bells of Alfredston Church could be heard on the breeze from the north. People were going along the road, dressed in their holiday clothes; they were mainly lovers—such pairs as Jude and Arabella had been when they sported along the same track some months earlier. These pedestrians turned to stare at the extraordinary spectacle she now presented, bonnetless, her dishevelled hair blowing in the wind, her bodice apart, her sleeves rolled above her elbows for her work, and her hands reeking with melted fat. One of the passers said in mock terror: "Good Lord deliver us!"

"See how he's served me!" she cried. "Making me work Sunday mornings when I ought to be going to my church, and tearing my hair off my head, and my gown off my back!"

Jude was exasperated, and went out to drag her in by main force. Then he suddenly lost his heat. Illuminated with the sense that all was over between them, and that it mattered not what she did, or he, her husband stood still, regarding her. Their lives were ruined, he thought; ruined by the fundamental error of their matrimonial union: that of having based a permanent contract on a temporary feeling which had no necessary connection with affinities that alone render a life-long comradeship tolerable.

"Going to ill-use me on principle, as your father ill-used your mother, and your father's sister ill-used her husband?" she asked. "All you be a queer lot as husbands and wives!"

Jude fixed an arrested, surprised look on her. But she said no more, and continued her saunter till she was tired. He left the spot, and, after wandering vaguely a little while, walked in the direction of Marygreen. Here he called upon his great-aunt, whose infirmities daily increased.

"Aunt—did my father ill-use my mother, and my aunt her husband?" said Jude abruptly, sitting down by the fire.

She raised her ancient eyes under the rim of the bygone bonnet that she always wore. "Who's been telling you that?" she said.

"I have heard it spoken of, and want to know all."

"You med so well, I s'pose; though your wife—I reckon 'twas she—must have been a fool to open up that! There isn't much to know after all. Your father and mother couldn't get on together, and they parted. It was coming home from Alfredston market, when you were a baby—on the hill by the Brown House barn—that they had their last difference, and took leave of one another for the last time. Your mother soon afterwards died—she drowned herself, in short, and your father went away with you to South Wessex, and never came here any more."

Jude recalled his father's silence about North Wessex and Jude's mother, never speaking of either till his dying day.

"It was the same with your father's sister. Her husband offended her, and she so disliked living with him afterwards that she went away to London with her little maid. The Fawleys were not made for wedlock: it never seemed to sit well upon us. There's sommat in our blood that won't take kindly to the notion of being bound to do what we do readily enough if not bound. That's why you ought to have hearkened to me, and not ha' married."

"Where did Father and Mother part—by the Brown House, did you say?"

"A little further on—where the road to Fenworth branches off, and the handpost stands. A gibbet once stood there."

In the dusk of that evening Jude walked away from his old aunt's as if to go home. But as soon as he reached the open down he struck out upon it till he came to a large round pond. The frost continued, though it was not particularly sharp, and the larger stars overhead came out slow and flickering. Jude put one foot on the edge of the ice, and then the other: it cracked under his weight; but this did not deter him. He ploughed his way inward to the centre, the ice making sharp noises as he went. When just about the middle he looked around him and gave a jump. The cracking repeated itself; but he did not go down. He jumped again, but the cracking had ceased. Jude went back to the edge, and stepped upon the ground.

It was curious, he thought. What was he reserved for? He supposed he was not a sufficiently dignified person for suicide. Peaceful death abhorred him as a subject, and would not take him.

What could he do of a lower kind than self-extermination; what was there less noble, more in keeping with his present degraded position? He could get drunk. Of course that was it; he had forgotten. Drinking was the regular, stereotyped resource of the despairing worthless. He began to see now why some men boozed at inns. He struck down the hill northwards and came to an obscure public-house. On entering and sitting down the sight of the picture of Samson and Delilah on the wall caused him to recognise the place as that he had visited with Arabella on that first Sunday evening of their courtship. He called for liquor and drank briskly for an hour or more.

Staggering homeward late that night, with all his sense of depression gone, and his head fairly clear still, he began to laugh boisterously, and to wonder how Arabella would receive him in his new aspect. The house was in darkness when he entered, and in his stumbling state it was some time before he could get a light. Then he found that, though the marks of pig-dressing, of fats and scallops, were visible, the materials themselves had been taken away. A line written by his wife on the inside of an old envelope was pinned to the cotton blower of the fireplace:

"Have gone to my friends. Shall not return."

All the next day he remained at home, and sent off the carcase of the pig to Alfredston. He then cleaned up the premises, locked the door, put the key in a place she would know if she came back, and returned to his masonry at Alfredston.

At night when he again plodded home he found she had not visited the house. The next day went in the same way, and the next. Then there came a letter from her.

That she had gone tired of him she frankly admitted. He was such a slow old coach, and she did not care for the sort of life he led. There was no prospect of his ever bettering himself or her. She further went on to say that her parents had, as he knew, for some time considered the question of emigrating to Australia, the pig-jobbing business being a poor one now-a-days. They had at last decided to go, and she proposed to go with them, if he had no objection. A woman of her sort would have more chance over there than in this stupid country.

Jude replied that he had not the least objection to her going. He thought it a wise course, since she wished to go, and one that might be to the advantage of both. He enclosed in the packet containing the letter the money that had been realised by the sale of the pig, with all he had besides, which was not much.

From that day he heard no more of her except indirectly, though her father and his household did not immediately leave, but waited till his goods and other effects had been sold off. When Jude learnt that there was to be an auction at the house of the Donns he packed his own household goods into a waggon, and sent them to her at the aforesaid homestead, that she might sell them with the rest, or as many of them as she should choose.

He then went into lodgings at Alfredston, and saw in a shop-window the little handbill announcing the sale of his father-in-law's furniture. He noted its date, which came and passed without Jude's going near the place, or perceiving that the traffic out of Alfredston by the southern road was materially increased by the auction. A few days later he entered a little broker's shop in the main street of the town, and amid a heterogeneous collection of sauce-pans, a clothes-horse, rollingpin, brass candlestick, swing looking-glass, and other things at the back of the shop, evidently just brought in from a sale, he perceived a little framed photograph, which turned out to be his own portrait.

It was one which he had had specially taken and framed by a local man in bird's-eye maple, as a present for Arabella, and had duly given her on their wedding-day. On the back was still to be read, *"Jude to Arabella,"* with the date. She must have thrown it in with the rest of her property at the auction.

"Oh," said the broker, seeing him look at this and the other articles in the heap, and not perceiving that the portrait was of himself: "It is a small lot of stuff that was knocked down to me at a cottage sale out on the road to Marygreen. The frame is a very useful one, if you take out the likeness. You shall have it for a shilling."

The utter death of every tender sentiment in his wife, as brought home to him by this mute and undesigned evidence of her sale of his portrait and gift, was the conclusive little stroke required to demolish all sentiment in him. He paid the shilling, took the photograph away with him, and burnt it, frame and all, when he reached his lodging.

Two or three days later he heard that Arabella and her parents had departed. He had sent a message offering to see her for a formal leave-taking, but she had said that it would be better otherwise, since she was bent on going, which perhaps was true. On the evening following their emigration, when his day's work was done, he came out-of-doors after supper, and strolled in the starlight along the too familiar road towards the upland whereon had been experienced the chief emotions of his life. It seemed to be his own again.

He could not realise himself. On the old track he seemed to be a boy still, hardly a day older than when he had stood dreaming at the top of that hill, inwardly fired for the first time with ardours for Christminster and scholarship. "Yet I am a man," he said. "I have a wife. More, I have arrived at the still riper stage of having disagreed with her, disliked her, had a scuffle with her, and parted from her."

He remembered then that he was standing not far from the spot at which the parting between his father and his mother was said to have occurred.

A little further on was the summit, whence Christminster, or what he had taken for that city, had seemed to be visible. A milestone, now as always, stood at the roadside hard by. Jude drew near it, and felt rather than read the mileage to the city. He remembered that once on his way home he had proudly cut with his keen new chisel an inscription on the back of that milestone, embodying his aspirations. It had been done in the first week of his apprenticeship, before he had been diverted from his purposes by an unsuitable woman. He wondered if the inscription were legible still, and going to the back of the milestone brushed away the nettles. By the light of a match he could still discern what he had cut so enthusiastically so long ago:

THITHER

J. F.   ☞

The sight of it, unimpaired, within its screen of grass and nettles, lit in his soul a spark of the old fire. Surely his plan should be to move onward through good and ill—to avoid morbid sorrow even though he did see uglinesses in the world? *Bene agere et lœtari*—to do good cheerfully—which he had heard to be the philosophy of one Spinoza, might be his own even now.

He might battle with his evil star, and follow out his original intention.

By moving to a spot a little way off he uncovered the horizon in a north-easterly direction. There actually rose the faint halo, a small dim nebulousness, hardly recognizable save by the eye of faith. It was enough for him. He would go to Christminster as soon as the term of his apprenticeship expired.

He returned to his lodgings in a better mood, and said his prayers.

Part Second

At Christminster

"Save his own soul he hath no star."

—SWINBURNE

"Notitiam primosque gradus vicinia fecit;
Tempore crevit amor."

—OVID

I

T HE NEXT NOTEWORTHY MOVE IN JUDE'S LIFE WAS THAT IN WHICH HE APPEARED
gliding steadily onward through a dusky landscape of some three years' later
leafage than had graced his courtship of Arabella, and the disruption of his
coarse conjugal life with her. He was walking towards Christminster City, at a point a mile
or two to the south-west.

He had at last found himself clear of Marygreen and Alfredston: he was out of his apprenticeship, and with his tools at his back seemed to be in the way of making a new
start—the start to which, barring the interruption involved in his intimacy and married experience with Arabella, he had been looking forward for about ten years.

Jude would now have been described as a young man with a forcible, meditative, and
earnest rather than handsome cast of countenance. He was of dark complexion, with dark
harmonizing eyes, and he wore a closely trimmed black beard of more advanced growth
than is usual at his age; this, with his great mass of black curly hair, was some trouble to
him in combing and washing out the stone-dust that settled on it in the pursuit of his
trade. His capabilities in the latter, having been acquired in the country, were of an all-
round sort, including monumental stone-cutting, gothic freestone work for the restoration of churches, and carving of a general kind. In London he would probably have
become specialised and have made himself a moulding mason, a "foliage sculptor"— perhaps a "statuary."

He had that afternoon driven in a cart from Alfredston to the village nearest the city
in this direction, and was now walking the remaining four miles rather from choice than
from necessity, having always fancied himself arriving thus.

The ultimate impulse to come had had a curious origin—one more nearly related to
the emotional side of him than to the intellectual, as is often the case with young men. One
day while in lodgings at Alfredston he had gone to Marygreen to see his old aunt, and had
observed between the brass candlesticks on her mantelpiece the photograph of a pretty
girlish face, in a broad hat with radiating folds under the brim like the rays of a halo. He
had asked who she was. His grand-aunt had gruffly replied that she was his cousin Sue
Bridehead, of the inimical branch of the family; and on further questioning the old woman
had replied that the girl lived in Christminster, though she did not know where, or what
she was doing.

His aunt would not give him the photograph. But it haunted him; and ultimately
formed a quickening ingredient in his latent intent of following his friend the schoolmaster thither.

He now paused at the top of a crooked and gentle declivity, and obtained his first near
view of the city. Grey stoned and dun-roofed, it stood within hail of the Wessex border,
and almost with the tip of one small toe within it, at the northernmost point of the crinkled line along which the leisurely Thames strokes the fields of that ancient kingdom. The
buildings now lay quiet in the sunset, a vane here and there on their many spires and domes
giving sparkle to a picture of sober secondary and tertiary hues.

Reaching the bottom he moved along the level way between pollard willows growing indistinct in the twilight, and soon confronted the outmost lamps of the town—some of those lamps which had sent into the sky the gleam and glory that caught his strained gaze in his days of dreaming, so many years ago. They winked their yellow eyes at him dubiously, and as if, though they had been awaiting him all these years in disappointment at his tarrying, they did not much want him now.

He was a species of Dick Whittington whose spirit was touched to finer issues than a mere material gain. He went along the outlying streets with the cautious tread of an explorer. He saw nothing of the real city in the suburbs on this side. His first want being a lodging he scrutinised carefully such localities as seemed to offer on inexpensive terms the modest type of accommodation he demanded; and after inquiry took a room in a suburb nick-named "Beersheba," though he did not know this at the time. Here he installed himself, and having had some tea sallied forth.

It was a windy, whispering, moonless night. To guide himself he opened under a lamp a map he had brought. The breeze ruffled and fluttered it, but he could see enough to decide on the direction he should take to reach the heart of the place.

After many turnings he came up to the first ancient medieval pile that he had encountered. It was a college, as he could see by the gateway. He entered it, walked round, and penetrated to dark corners which no lamplight reached. Close to this college was another; and a little further on another; and then he began to be encircled as it were with the breath and sentiment of the venerable city. When he passed objects out of harmony with its general expression he allowed his eyes to slip over them as if he did not see them.

A bell began clanging, and he listened till a hundred and one strokes had sounded. He must have made a mistake, he thought: it was meant for a hundred.

When the gates were shut, and he could no longer get into the quadrangles, he rambled under the walls and doorways, feeling with his fingers the contours of their mouldings and carving. The minutes passed, fewer and fewer people were visible, and still he serpentined among the shadows, for had he not imagined these scenes through ten bygone years, and what mattered a night's rest for once? High against the black sky the flash of a lamp would show crocketed pinnacles and indented battlements. Down obscure alleys, apparently never trodden now by the foot of man, and whose very existence seemed to be forgotten, there would jut into the path porticoes, oriels, doorways of enriched and florid middle-age design, their extinct air being accentuated by the rottenness of the stones. It seemed impossible that modern thought could house itself in such decrepit and superseded chambers.

Knowing not a human being here, Jude began to be impressed with the isolation of his own personality, as with a self-spectre, the sensation being that of one who walked, but could not make himself seen or heard. He drew his breath pensively, and, seeming thus almost his own ghost, gave his thoughts to the other ghostly presences with which the nooks were haunted.

During the interval of preparation for this venture, since his wife and furniture's uncompromising disappearance into space, he had read and learnt almost all that could be read and learnt by one in his position, of the worthies who had spent their youth within these reverend walls, and whose souls had haunted them in their maturer age. Some of them, by the accidents of his reading, loomed out in his fancy disproportionately large by comparison with the rest. The brushing of the wind against the angles, buttresses, and door-jambs were as the passing of these only other inhabitants, the tappings of each ivy leaf on its neighbour were as the mutterings of their mournful souls, the shadows as their thin shapes in nervous movement, making him comrades in his solitude. In the gloom it was as if he ran against them without feeling their bodily frames.

The streets were now deserted, but on account of these things he could not go in. There were poets abroad, of early date and of late, from the friend and eulogist of Shakespeare down to him who has recently passed into silence, and that musical one of the tribe who is still among us. Speculative philosophers passed along, not always with wrinkled foreheads and hoary hair as in framed portraits, but pink-faced, slim, and active as in youth; modern divines sheeted in their surplices, among whom the most real to Jude Fawley were the founders of the religious school called Tractarian; the well-known three, the enthusiast, the poet, and the formularist, the echoes of whose teachings had influenced him even in his obscure home. A start of aversion appeared in his fancy to move them at sight of those other sons of the place, the form in the full-bottomed wig, statesman, rake, reasoner, and sceptic; the smoothly shaven historian so ironically civil to Christianity; with others of the same incredulous temper, who knew each quad as well as the faithful, and took equal freedom in haunting its cloisters.

He regarded the statesmen in their various types, men of firmer movement and less dreamy air; the scholar, the speaker, the plodder; the man whose mind grew with his growth in years, and the man whose mind contracted with the same.

The scientists and philologists followed on in his mind-sight in an odd impossible combination, men of meditative faces, lined foreheads, and weak-eyed as bats with constant research; then official characters—such men as Governor-Generals and Lord-Lieutenants, in whom he took little interest; Chief-Justices and Lord Chancellors, silent thin-lipped figures of whom he knew barely the names. A keener regard attached to the prelates, by reason of his own former hopes. Of them he had an ample band—some men of heart, others rather men of head; he who apologised for the Church in Latin; the saintly author of the Evening Hymn; and near them the great itinerant preacher, hymn-writer, and zealot, shadowed like Jude by his matrimonial difficulties.

Jude found himself speaking out loud, holding conversations with them, as it were, like an actor in a melodrama who apostrophises the audience on the other side of the footlights; till he suddenly ceased with a start at his absurdity. Perhaps those incoherent words of the wanderer were heard within the walls by some student or thinker over his lamp; and he may have raised his head, and wondered what voice it was, and what it betokened. Jude now perceived that, so far as solid flesh went, he had the whole aged city to himself with the exception of a belated townsman here and there, and that he seemed to be catching a cold.

A voice reached him out of the shade; a real and local voice:

"You've been a-settin' a long time on that plinth-stone, young man. What med you be up to?"

It came from a policeman who had been observing Jude without the latter observing him.

Jude went home and to bed, after reading up a little about these men and their several messages to the world from a book or two that he had brought with him concerning the sons of the University. As he drew towards sleep various memorable words of theirs that he had just been conning seemed spoken by them in muttering utterances; some audible, some unintelligible to him. One of the spectres (who afterwards mourned Christminster as "the home of lost causes," though Jude did not remember this) was now apostrophizing her thus:

"Beautiful city! so venerable, so lovely, so unravaged by the fierce intellectual life of our century, so serene! . . . Her ineffable charm keeps ever calling us to the true goal of all of us, to the ideal, to perfection."

Another voice was that of the Corn Law convert, whose phantom he had just seen in the quadrangle with the great bell. Jude thought his soul might have been shaping the historic words of his master-speech:

"Sir, I may be wrong, but my impression is that my duty towards a country threatened with famine requires that that which has been the ordinary remedy under all similar circumstances should be resorted to now, namely, that there should be free access to the food of man from whatever quarter it may come. . . . Deprive me of office to-morrow, you can never deprive me of the consciousness that I have exercised the powers committed to me from no corrupt or interested motives, from no desire to gratify ambition, for no personal gain."

Then the sly author of the immortal Chapter on Christianity: "How shall we excuse the supine inattention of the Pagan and philosophic world, to those evidences [miracles] which were presented by Omnipotence? . . . The sages of Greece and Rome turned aside from the awful spectacle, and appeared unconscious of any alterations in the moral or physical government of the world."

Then the shade of the poet, the last of the optimists:

> *How the world is made for each of us!*
>
> .   .   .   .
>
> *And each of the Many helps to recruit*
> *The life of the race by a general plan.*

Then one of the three enthusiasts he had seen just now, the author of the *Apologia*:

"My argument was . . . that absolute certitude as to the truths of natural theology was the result of an assemblage of concurring and converging probabilities . . . that probabilities which did not reach to logical certainty might create a mental certitude."

The second of them, no polemic, murmured quieter things:

> *Why should we faint, and fear to live alone,*
> *Since all alone, so Heaven has will'd, we die?*

He likewise heard some phrases spoken by the phantom with the short face, the genial Spectator:

"When I look upon the tombs of the great, every motion of envy dies in me; when I read the epitaphs of the beautiful, every inordinate desire goes out; when I meet with the grief of parents upon a tombstone, my heart melts with compassion; when I see the tombs of the parents themselves, I consider the vanity of grieving for those whom we must quickly follow."

And lastly a gentle-voiced prelate spoke, during whose meek, familiar rhyme, endeared to him from earliest childhood, Jude fell asleep:

> *Teach me to live, that I may dread*
> *The grave as little as my bed.*
> *Teach me to die . . .*

He did not wake till morning. The ghostly past seemed to have gone, and everything spoke of to-day. He started up in bed, thinking he had overslept himself, and then said:

"By Jove—I had quite forgotten my sweet-faced cousin, and that she's here all the time! . . . and my old schoolmaster, too." His words about his schoolmaster had, perhaps, less zest in them than his words concerning his cousin.

II

NECESSARY MEDITATIONS ON THE ACTUAL, INCLUDING THE MEAN BREAD-AND-CHEESE question, dissipated the phantasmal for a while, and compelled Jude to smother high thinkings under immediate needs. He had to get up, and seek for work, manual work; the only kind deemed by many of its professors to be work at all.

Passing out into the streets on this errand he found that the colleges had treacherously changed their sympathetic countenances: some were stern; some had put on the look of family vaults above ground; something barbaric loomed in the masonries of all. The spirits of the great men had disappeared.

The numberless architectural pages around him he read, naturally, less as an artist-critic of their forms than as an artizan and comrade of the dead handicraftsmen whose muscles had actually executed those forms. He examined the mouldings, stroked them as one who knew their beginning, said they were difficult or easy in the working, had taken little or much time, were trying to the arm, or convenient to the tool.

What at night had been perfect and ideal was by day the more or less defective real. Cruelties, insults, had, he perceived, been inflicted on the aged erections. The condition of several moved him as he would have been moved by maimed sentient beings. They were wounded, broken, sloughing off their outer shape in the deadly struggle against years, weather, and man.

The rottenness of these historical documents reminded him that he was not, after all, hastening on to begin the morning practically as he had intended. He had come to work, and to live by work, and the morning had nearly gone. It was, in one sense, encouraging to think that in a place of crumbling stones there must be plenty for one of his trade to do in the business of renovation. He asked his way to the workyard of the stone-cutter whose name had been given him at Alfredston; and soon heard the familiar sound of the rubbers and chisels.

The yard was a little centre of regeneration. Here, with keen edges and smooth curves, were forms in the exact likeness of those he had seen abraded and time-eaten on the walls. These were the ideas in modern prose which the lichened colleges presented in old poetry. Even some of those antiques might have been called prose when they were new. They had done nothing but wait, and had become poetical. How easy to the smallest building; how impossible to most men.

He asked for the foreman, and looked round among the new traceries, mullions, transoms, shafts, pinnacles, and battlements standing on the bankers half worked, or waiting to be removed. They were marked by precision, mathematical straightness, smoothness, exactitude: there in the old walls were the broken lines of the original idea; jagged curves, disdain of precision, irregularity, disarray.

For a moment there fell on Jude a true illumination; that here in the stone-yard was a centre of effort as worthy as that dignified by the name of scholarly study within the noblest of the colleges. But he lost it under stress of his old idea. He would accept any employment which might be offered him on the strength of his late employer's recommendation; but he would accept it as a provisional thing only. This was his form of the modern vice of unrest.

Moreover he perceived that at best only copying, patching and imitating went on here; which he fancied to be owing to some temporary and local cause. He did not at that time see that medievalism was as dead as a fern-leaf in a lump of coal; that other developments were shaping in the world around him, in which Gothic architecture and its associations had no place. The deadly animosity of contemporary logic and vision towards so much of what he held in reverence was not yet revealed.

Having failed to obtain work here as yet he went away, and thought again of his cousin, whose presence somewhere at hand he seemed to feel in wavelets of interest, if not of emotion. How he wished he had that pretty portrait of her! At last he wrote to his aunt to send it. She did so, with a request, however, that he was not to bring disturbance into the family by going to see the girl or her relations. Jude, a ridiculously affectionate fellow, promised nothing, put the photograph on the mantelpiece, kissed it—he did not know why—and felt more at home. She seemed to look down and preside over his tea. It was cheering—the one thing uniting him to the emotions of the living city.

There remained the schoolmaster—probably now a reverend parson. But he could not possibly hunt up such a respectable man just yet; so raw and unpolished was his condition, so precarious were his fortunes. Thus he still remained in loneliness. Although people moved round him he virtually saw none. Not as yet having mingled with the active life of the place it was largely non-existent to him. But the saints and prophets in the window-tracery, the paintings in the galleries, the statues, the busts, the gurgoyles, the corbel-heads—these seemed to breathe his atmosphere. Like all new-comers to a spot on which the past is deeply graven he heard that past announcing itself with an emphasis altogether unsuspected by, and even incredible to, the habitual residents.

For many days he haunted the cloisters and quadrangles of the colleges at odd minutes in passing them, surprised by impish echoes of his own footsteps, smart as the blows of a mallet. The Christminster "sentiment," as it had been called, ate further and further into him; till he probably knew more about those buildings materially, artistically, and historically, than any one of their inmates.

It was not till now, when he found himself actually on the spot of his enthusiasm, that Jude perceived how far away from the object of that enthusiasm he really was. Only a wall divided him from those happy young contemporaries of his with whom he shared a common mental life; men who had nothing to do from morning till night but to read, mark, learn, and inwardly digest. Only a wall—but what a wall!

Everyday, every hour, as he went in search of labour, he saw them going and coming also, rubbed shoulders with them, heard their voices, marked their movements. The conversation of some of the more thoughtful among them seemed oftentimes, owing to his long and persistent preparation for this place, to be peculiarly akin to his own thoughts. Yet he was as far from them as if he had been at the antipodes. Of course he was. He was a young workman in a white blouse, and with stone-dust in the creases of his clothes; and in passing him they did not even see him, or hear him, rather saw through him as through a pane of glass at their familiars beyond. Whatever they were to him, he to them was not on the spot at all; and yet he had fancied he would be close to their lives by coming there.

But the future lay ahead after all; and if he could only be so fortunate as to get into good employment he would put up with the inevitable. So he thanked God for his health and strength, and took courage. For the present he was outside the gates of everything, colleges included: perhaps some day he would be inside. Those palaces of light and leading; he might some day look down on the world through their panes.

At length he did receive a message from the stone-mason's yard—that a job was waiting for him. It was his first encouragement, and he closed with the offer promptly.

He was young and strong, or he never could have executed with such zest the undertakings to which he now applied himself, since they involved reading most of the night after working all the day. First he bought a shaded lamp for four and sixpence, and obtained a good light. Then he got pens, paper, and such other necessary books as he had been unable to obtain elsewhere. Then, to the consternation of his landlady, he shifted all the furniture of his room—a single one for living and sleeping—rigged up a curtain on a rope across the middle, to make a double chamber out of one, hung up a thick blind that nobody should know how he was curtailing the hours of sleep, laid out his books, and sat down.

Having been deeply encumbered by marrying, getting a cottage, and buying the furniture which had disappeared in the wake of his wife, he had never been able to save any money since the time of those disastrous ventures, and till his wages began to come in he was obliged to live in the narrowest way. After buying a book or two he could not even afford himself a fire; and when the nights reeked with the raw and cold air from the Meadows he sat over his lamp in a great-coat, hat, and woollen gloves.

From his window he could perceive the spire of the Cathedral, and the ogee dome under which resounded the great bell of the city. The tall tower, tall belfry-windows, and tall pinnacles of the college by the bridge he could also get a glimpse of by going to the staircase. These objects he used as stimulants when his faith in the future was dim.

Like enthusiasts in general he made no inquiries into details of procedure. Picking up general notions from casual acquaintance, he never dwelt upon them. For the present, he said to himself, the one thing necessary was to get ready by accumulating money and knowledge, and await whatever chances were afforded to such an one of becoming a son of the University. "For wisdom is a defence, and money is a defence; but the excellency of knowledge is, that wisdom giveth life to them that have it." His desire absorbed him, and left no part of him to weigh its practicability.

At this time he received a nervously anxious letter from his poor old aunt, on the subject which had previously distressed her—a fear that Jude would not be strong-minded enough to keep away from his cousin Sue Bridehead and her relations. Sue's parents, his aunt believed, had gone to London, but the girl remained at Christminster. To make her still more objectionable she was an artist or designer of some sort in what was called an ecclesiastical warehouse, which was a perfect seed-bed of idolatry, and she was no doubt abandoned to mummeries on that account—if not quite a Papist. (Miss Drusilla Fawley was of her date, Evangelical.)

As Jude was rather on an intellectual track than a theological, this news of Sue's probable opinions did not much influence him one way or the other, but the clue to her whereabouts was decidedly interesting. With an altogether singular pleasure he walked at his earliest spare minutes past the shops answering to his great-aunt's description; and beheld in one of them a young girl sitting behind a desk, who was suspiciously like the original of the portrait. He ventured to enter on a trivial errand, and having made his purchase lingered on the scene. The shop seemed to be kept entirely by women. It contained Anglican books, stationery, texts, and fancy goods: little plaster angels on brackets, Gothic-framed pictures of saints, ebony crosses that were almost crucifixes, Prayer-books that were almost missals. He felt very shy of looking at the girl in the desk; she was so pretty that he could not believe it possible that she should belong to him. Then she spoke to one of the two older women behind the counter; and he recognised in the accents certain qualities of his own voice; softened and sweetened, but his own. What was she doing? He stole a glance round. Before her lay a piece of zinc, cut to the shape of a scroll three or four feet long, and coated with a dead-surface paint on one side. Hereon she was designing or illuminating, in characters of Church text, the single word

ALLELUJA

"A sweet, saintly, Christian business, hers!" thought he.

Her presence here was now fairly enough explained, her skill in work of this sort having no doubt been acquired from her father's occupation as an ecclesiastical worker in metal. The lettering on which she was engaged was clearly intended to be fixed up in some chancel to assist devotion.

He came out. It would have been easy to speak to her there and then, but it seemed scarcely honourable towards his aunt to disregard her request so incontinently. She had used him roughly, but she had brought him up: and the fact of her being powerless to control him lent a pathetic force to a wish that would have been inoperative as an argument.

So Jude gave no sign. He would not call upon Sue just yet. He had other reasons against doing so when he had walked away. She seemed so dainty beside himself in his rough working-jacket and dusty trousers that he felt he was as yet unready to encounter her, as he had felt about Mr. Phillotson. And how possible it was that she had inherited the antipathies of her family, and would scorn him, as far as a Christian could, particularly when he had told her that unpleasant part of his history which had resulted in his becoming enchained to one of her own sex whom she would certainly not admire.

Thus he kept watch over her, and liked to feel she was there. The consciousness of her living presence stimulated him. But she remained more or less an ideal character, about whose form he began to weave curious and fantastic day-dreams.

Between two and three weeks afterwards Jude was engaged with some more men, outside Crozier College in Old-time Street, in getting a block of worked freestone from a waggon across the pavement, before hoisting it to the parapet which they were repairing. Standing in position the head man said, "Spaik when ye heave! He-ho!" And they heaved.

All of a sudden, as he lifted, his cousin stood close to his elbow, pausing a moment on the bend of her foot till the obstructing object should have been removed. She looked right into his face with liquid, untranslatable eyes, that combined, or seemed to him to combine, keenness with tenderness, and mystery with both, their expression, as well as that of her lips, taking its life from some words just spoken to a companion, and being carried on into his face quite unconsciously. She no more observed his presence than that of the dust-motes which his manipulations raised into the sunbeams.

His closeness to her was so suggestive that he trembled, and turned his face away with a shy instinct to prevent her recognizing him, though as she had never once seen him she could not possibly do so; and might very well never have heard even his name. He could perceive that though she was a country-girl at bottom, a latter girlhood of some years in London, and a womanhood here, had taken all rawness out of her.

When she was gone he continued his work, reflecting on her. He had been so caught by her influence that he had taken no count of her general mould and build. He remembered now that she was not a large figure, that she was light and slight, of the type dubbed elegant. That was about all he had seen. There was nothing statuesque in her; all was nervous motion. She was mobile, living, yet a painter might not have called her handsome or beautiful. But the much that she was surprised him. She was quite a long way removed from the rusticity that was his. How could one of his cross-grained, unfortunate, almost accursed stock, have contrived to reach this pitch of niceness? London had done it, he supposed.

From this moment the emotion which had been accumulating in his breast as the bottled-up effect of solitude and the poetised locality he dwelt in, insensibly began to precipitate itself on this half-visionary form; and he perceived that, whatever his obedient wish in a contrary direction, he would soon be unable to resist the desire to make himself known to her.

He affected to think of her quite in a family way, since there were crushing reasons why he should not and could not think of her in any other.

The first reason was that he was married, and it would be wrong. The second was that they were cousins. It was not well for cousins to fall in love even when circumstances seemed to favour the passion. The third: even were he free, in a family like his own where marriage usually meant a tragic sadness, marriage with a blood-relation would duplicate the adverse conditions, and a tragic sadness might be intensified to a tragic horror.

Therefore, again, he would have to think of Sue with only a relation's mutual interest in one belonging to him; regard her in a practical way as someone to be proud of; to talk and nod to; later on, to be invited to tea by, the emotion spent on her being rigorously that of a kinsman and well-wisher. So would she be to him a kindly star, an elevating power, a companion in Anglican worship, a tender friend.

III

B UT UNDER THE VARIOUS DETERRENT INFLUENCES JUDE'S INSTINCT WAS TO APPROACH her timidly, and the next Sunday he went to the morning service in the Cathedral-church of Cardinal College to gain a further view of her, for he had found that she frequently attended there.

She did not come, and he awaited her in the afternoon, which was finer. He knew that if she came at all she would approach the building along the eastern side of the great green quadrangle from which it was accessible, and he stood in a corner while the bell was going. A few minutes before the hour for service she appeared as one of the figures walking along under the College walls, and at sight of her he advanced up the side opposite, and followed her into the building, more than ever glad that he had not as yet revealed himself. To see her, and to be himself unseen and unknown, was enough for him at present.

He lingered a while in the vestibule, and the service was some way advanced when he was put into a seat. It was a louring, mournful, still afternoon, when a religion of some sort seems a necessity to ordinary practical men, and not only a luxury of the emotional and leisured classes. In the dim light and the baffling glare of the clerestory-windows, he could discern the opposite worshippers indistinctly only, but he saw that Sue was among them. He had not long discovered the exact seat that she occupied when the chanting of the 119th Psalm in which the choir was engaged reached its second part, *In quo corriget*, the organ changing to a pathetic Gregorian tune as the singers gave forth:

Wherewithal shall a young man cleanse his way?

It was the very question that was engaging Jude's attention at this moment. What a wicked worthless fellow he had been to give vent as he had done to an animal passion for a woman, and allow it to lead to such disastrous consequences; then to think of putting an end to himself; then to go recklessly and get drunk. The great waves of pedal music tumbled round the choir, and, nursed on the supernatural as he had been, it is not wonderful that he could hardly believe that the psalm was not specially set by some regardful Providence for this moment of his first entry into the solemn building. And yet it was the ordinary psalm for the twenty-fourth evening of the month.

The girl for whom he was beginning to nourish an extraordinary tenderness was at this time ensphered by the same harmonies as those which floated into his ears; and the thought was a delight to him. She was probably a frequenter of this place, and, steeped body and soul in church sentiment as she must be by occupation and habit, had, no doubt, much in common with him. To an impressionable and lonely young man the consciousness of having at last found anchorage for his thoughts, which promised to supply both social and spiritual possibilities, was like the dew of Hermon, and he remained throughout the service in a sustaining atmosphere of ecstasy.

Though he was loath to suspect it, some people might have said to him that the atmosphere blew as distinctly from Cyprus as from Galilee.

Jude waited till she had left her seat and passed under the screen before he himself moved. She did not look towards him, and by the time he reached the door she was half-way down the broad path. Being dressed up in his Sunday suit he was inclined to follow her and reveal himself. But he was not quite ready; and, alas, ought he to do so with the kind of feeling that was awakening in him?

For though it had seemed to have an ecclesiastical basis during the service, and he had persuaded himself that such was the case, he could not altogether be blind to the real nature of the magnetism. She was such a stranger that the kinship was affectation, and he said, "It can't be! I, a man with a wife, must not know her!" Still Sue *was* his own kin, and the fact of his having a wife, even though she was not in evidence in this hemisphere, might be a help in one sense. It would put all thought of a tender wish on his part out of Sue's mind, and make her intercourse with him free and fearless. It was with some heart-ache that he saw how little he cared for the freedom and fearlessness that would result in her from such knowledge.

Some little time before the date of this service in the cathedral the pretty, liquid-eyed, light-footed young woman Sue Bridehead had an afternoon's holiday, and leaving the ecclesiastical establishment in which she not only assisted but lodged, took a walk into the country with a book in her hand. It was one of those cloudless days which sometimes occur in Wessex and elsewhere between days of cold and wet, as if intercalated by caprice of the weather-god. She went along for a mile or two until she came to much higher ground than that of the city she had left behind her. The road passed between green fields, and coming to a stile Sue paused there, to finish the page she was reading, and then looked back at the towers and domes and pinnacles new and old.

On the other side of the stile, in the footpath, she beheld a foreigner with black hair and a sallow face, sitting on the grass beside a large square board whereon were fixed, as closely as they could stand, a number of plaster statuettes, some of them bronzed, which he was rearranging before proceeding with them on his way. They were in the main reduced copies of ancient marbles, and comprised divinities of a very different character from those the girl was accustomed to see portrayed, among them being a Venus of standard pattern, a Diana, and, of the other sex, Apollo, Bacchus, and Mars. Though the figures were many yards away from her the south-west sun brought them out so brilliantly against the green herbage that she could discern their contours with luminous distinctness; and being almost in a line between herself and the church towers of the city they awoke in her an oddly foreign and contrasting set of ideas by comparison. The man rose, and, seeing her, politely took off his cap, and cried "I-i-i-mages!" in an accent that agreed with his appearance. In a moment he dexterously lifted upon his knee the great board with its assembled notabilities divine and human, and raised it to the top of his head, bringing them on to her and resting the board on the stile. First he offered her his smaller wares—the busts of kings and queens, then a minstrel, then a winged Cupid. She shook her head.

"How much are these two?" she said, touching with her finger the Venus and the Apollo—the largest figures on the tray.

He said she should have them for ten shillings.

"I cannot afford that," said Sue. She offered considerably less, and to her surprise the image-man drew them from their wire stay and handed them over the stile. She clasped them as treasures.

When they were paid for, and the man had gone, she began to be concerned as to what she should do with them. They seemed so very large now that they were in her possession, and so very naked. Being of a nervous temperament she trembled at her enterprize. When she handled them the white pipeclay came off on her gloves and jacket. After carrying them along a little way openly an idea came to her, and, pulling some huge burdock leaves, parsley, and other rank growths from the hedge, she wrapped up her burden as well as she could in these, so that what she carried appeared to be an enormous armful of green stuff, gathered by a zealous lover of nature.

"Well, anything is better than those everlasting church fal-lals!" she said. But she was still in a trembling state, and seemed almost to wish she had not bought the figures.

Occasionally peeping inside the leaves to see that Venus's arm was not broken, she entered with her heathen load into the most Christian city in the country by an obscure street running parallel to the main one, and round a corner to the side-door of the establishment to which she was attached. Her purchases were taken straight up to her own chamber, and she at once attempted to lock them in a box that was her very own property; but finding them too cumbersome she wrapped them in large sheets of brown paper, and stood them on the floor in a corner.

The mistress of the house, Miss Fontover, was an elderly lady in spectacles, dressed almost like an abbess; a dab at Ritual, as became one of her business, and a worshipper at the ceremonial church of St. Silas, in the suburb of Beersheba before-mentioned, which Jude also had begun to attend. She was the daughter of a clergyman in reduced circumstances, and at his death, which had occurred several years before this date, she boldly avoided penury by taking over a little shop of church requisites and developing it to its present creditable proportions. She wore a cross and beads round her neck as her only ornament, and knew the Christian Year by heart.

She now came to call Sue to tea, and, finding that the girl did not respond for a moment, entered the room just as the other was hastily putting a string round each parcel.

"Something you have been buying, Miss Bridehead?" she asked, regarding the enwrapped objects.

"Yes—just something to ornament my room," said Sue.

"Well, I should have thought I had put enough here already," said Miss Fontover, looking round at the Gothic-framed prints of saints, the Church-text scrolls, and other articles which, having become too stale to sell, had been used to furnish this obscure chamber. "What is it? How bulky!" She tore a little hole, about as big as a wafer, in the brown paper, and tried to peep in. "Why, statuary? Two figures? Where did you get them?"

"O—I bought them of a travelling man who sells casts—"

"Two saints?"

"Yes."

"What ones?"

"St. Peter and St.—St. Mary Magdalen."

"Well—now come down to tea, and go and finish that organ-text, if there's light enough afterwards."

These little obstacles to the indulgence of what had been the merest passing fancy created in Sue a great zest for unpacking her objects and looking at them; and at bed-time, when she was sure of being undisturbed, she unrobed the divinities in comfort. Placing the pair of figures on the chest of drawers, a candle on each side of them, she withdrew to the bed, flung herself down thereon, and began reading a book she had taken from her box, which Miss Fontover knew nothing of. It was a volume of Gibbon, and she read the chapter dealing with the reign of Julian the Apostate. Occasionally she looked up at the statuettes, which appeared strange and out of place amid the other objects and pictures in the room, and, as if the scene suggested the action, she at length jumped up and withdrew another book from her box—a volume of verse—and turned to the familiar poem—

> *Thou hast conquered, O pale Galilean:*
> *The world has grown grey from thy breath!*

which she read to the end. Presently she put out the candles, undressed, and finally extinguished her own light.

She was of an age which usually sleeps soundly, yet to-night she kept waking up, and every time she opened her eyes there was enough diffused light from the window to show her the white plaster figures, standing on the chest of drawers in odd contrast to their environment of text and martyr, and the Gothic-framed Crucifix-picture that was only discernible now as a Latin cross, the figure thereon being obscured by the shades.

On one of these occasions the church clocks struck some small hour. It fell upon the ears of another person who sat bending over his books at a not very distant spot in the same city. Being Saturday night the morrow was one on which Jude had not set his alarm-clock to call him at his usually early time, and hence he had stayed up, as was his custom, two or three hours later than he could afford to do on any other day of the week. Just then he was earnestly reading from his Griesbach's text. At the very time that Sue was tossing, the policeman and belated citizens passing along under his window might have heard, if they had stood still, strange syllables mumbled with fervour within—words that had for Jude an indescribable enchantment: inexplicable sounds something like these:—

"All hemin heis Theos ho Pater, ex hou ta panta, kai hemeis eis auton:"

Till the sounds rolled with reverent loudness, as a book was heard to close:—

"Kai heis Kurios Iesous Christos, di hou ta panta kai hemeis di autou!"

IV

HE WAS A HANDY MAN AT HIS TRADE, AN ALL-ROUND MAN, AS ARTIZANS IN COUNTRY-towns are apt to be. In London the man who carves the boss or knob of leafage declines to cut the fragment of moulding which merges in that leafage, as if it were a degradation to do the second half of one whole. When there was not much Gothic moulding for Jude to run, or much window-tracery on the bankers, he would go out lettering monuments or tombstones, and take a pleasure in the change of handiwork.

The next time that he saw her was when he was on a ladder executing a job of this sort inside one of the churches. There was a short morning service, and when the parson entered Jude came down from his ladder, and sat with the half-dozen people forming the congregation, till the prayers should be ended, and he could resume his tapping. He did not observe till the service was half over that one of the women was Sue, who had accompanied the elderly Miss Fontover thither.

Jude sat watching her pretty shoulders, her easy, curiously nonchalant risings and sittings, and her perfunctory genuflexions, and thought what a help such an Anglican would have been to him in happier circumstances. It was not so much his anxiety to get on with his work that made him go up to it immediately the worshippers began to take their leave: it was that he dared not, in this holy spot, confront the woman who was beginning to influence him in such an indescribable manner. Those three enormous reasons why he must not attempt intimate acquaintance with Sue Bridehead now that his interest in her had shown itself to be unmistakably of a sexual kind, loomed as stubbornly as ever. But it was also obvious that man could not live by work alone; that the particular man Jude, at any rate, wanted something to love. Some men would have rushed incontinently to her, snatched the pleasure of easy friendship which she could hardly refuse, and have left the rest to chance. Not so Jude—at first.

But as the days, and still more particularly the lonely evenings, dragged along, he found himself, to his moral consternation, to be thinking more of her instead of thinking less of her, and experiencing a fearful bliss in doing what was erratic, informal, and unexpected. Surrounded by her influence all day, walking past the spots she frequented, he was always thinking of her, and was obliged to own to himself that his conscience was likely to be the loser in this battle.

To be sure she was almost an ideality to him still. Perhaps to know her would be to cure himself of this unexpected and unauthorised passion. A voice whispered that, though he desired to know her, he did not desire to be cured.

There was not the least doubt that from his own orthodox point of view the situation was growing immoral. For Sue to be the loved-one of a man who was licensed by the laws of his country to love Arabella and none other unto his life's end, was a pretty bad second beginning, when the man was bent on such a course as Jude purposed. This conviction was so real with him that one day when, as was frequent, he was at work in a neighbouring village church alone, he felt it to be his duty to pray against his weakness. But much as he wished to be an exemplar in these things he could not get on. It was quite impossible, he found, to ask to be delivered from temptation when your heart's desire was to be tempted unto seventy times seven. So he excused himself. "After all," he said, "it is not altogether an *erotolepsy* that is the matter with me, as at that first time. I can see that she is exceptionally bright; and it is partly a wish for intellectual sympathy, and a craving for loving-kindness in my solitude." Thus he went on adoring her, fearing to realise that it was human perversity. For whatever Sue's virtues, talents, or ecclesiastical saturation, it was certain that those items were not at all the cause of his affection for her.

On an afternoon at this time a young girl entered the stone-mason's yard with some hesitation, and, lifting her skirts to avoid draggling them in the white dust, crossed towards the office.

"That's a nice girl," said one of the men known as Uncle Joe.

"Who is she?" asked another.

"I don't know—I've seen her about here and there. Why, yes, she's the daughter of that clever chap Bridehead who did all the wrought ironwork at St. Luke's ten years ago, and went away to London afterwards. I don't know what he's doing now—not much I fancy—as she's come back here."

Meanwhile the young woman had knocked at the office door and asked if Mr. Jude Fawley was at work in the yard. It so happened that Jude had gone out somewhere or other that afternoon, which information she received with a look of disappointment, and went away immediately. When Jude returned they told him, and described her, whereupon he exclaimed, "Why—that's my cousin Sue!"

He looked along the street after her, but she was out of sight. He had no longer any thought of a conscientious avoidance of her, and resolved to call upon her that very evening. And when he reached his lodging he found a note from her—a first note—one of those documents which, simple and commonplace in themselves, are seen retrospectively to have been pregnant with impassioned consequences. The very unconsciousness of a looming drama which is shown in such innocent first epistles from women to men, or *vice versâ*, makes them, when such a drama follows, and they are read over by the purple or lurid light of it, all the more impressive, solemn, and in cases, terrible.

Sue's was of the most artless and natural kind. She addressed him as her dear cousin Jude; said she had only just learnt by the merest accident that he was living in Christminster, and reproached him with not letting her know. They might have had such nice times together, she said, for she was thrown much upon herself, and had hardly any congenial friend. But now there was every probability of her soon going away, so that the chance of companionship would be lost perhaps forever.

A cold sweat overspread Jude at the news that she was going away. That was a contingency he had never thought of, and it spurred him to write all the more quickly to her. He would meet her that very evening, he said, one hour from the time of writing, at the cross in the pavement which marked the spot of the martyrdoms.

When he had despatched the note by a boy he regretted that in his hurry he should have suggested to her to meet him out-of-doors, when he might have said he would call upon her. It was, in fact, the country custom to meet thus, and nothing else had occurred to him. Arabella had been met in the same way, unfortunately, and it might not seem respectable to a dear girl like Sue. However, it could not be helped now, and he moved towards the point a few minutes before the hour, under the glimmer of the newly lighted lamps.

The broad street was silent, and almost deserted, although it was not late. He saw a figure on the other side, which turned out to be hers, and they both converged towards the cross-mark at the same moment. Before either had reached it she called out to him:

"I am not going to meet you just there, for the first time in my life! Come further on."

The voice, though positive and silvery, had been tremulous. They walked on in parallel lines, and, waiting her pleasure, Jude watched till she showed signs of closing in, when he did likewise, the place being where the carriers' carts stood in the daytime, though there was none on the spot then.

"I am sorry that I asked you to meet me, and didn't call," began Jude with the bashfulness of a lover. "But I thought it would save time if we were going to walk."

"O—I don't mind that," she said with the freedom of a friend. "I have really no place to ask anybody in to. What I meant was that the place you chose was so horrid—I suppose I ought not to say horrid—I mean gloomy and inauspicious. . . . But isn't it funny to begin like this, when I don't know you yet?" She looked him up and down curiously, though Jude did not look much at her.

"You seem to know me more than I know you," she added.

"Yes—I have seen you now and then."

"And you knew who I was, and didn't speak? And now I am going away!"

"Yes. That's unfortunate. I have hardly any other friend. I have, indeed, one very old friend here somewhere, but I don't quite like to call on him just yet. I wonder if you know anything of him—Mr. Phillotson? A parson somewhere about the county I think he is."

"No—I only know of one Mr. Phillotson. He lives a little way out in the country, at Lumsdon. He's a village schoolmaster."

"Ah! I wonder if he's the same. Surely it is impossible! Only a schoolmaster still! Do you know his Christian name—is it Richard?"

"Yes—it is; I've directed books to him, though I've never seen him."

"Then he couldn't do it!"

Jude's countenance fell, for how could he succeed in an enterprize wherein the great Phillotson had failed? He would have had a day of despair if the news had not arrived during his sweet Sue's presence, but even at this moment he had visions of how Phillotson's failure in the grand University scheme would depress him when she had gone.

"As we are going to take a walk, suppose we go and call upon him?" said Jude suddenly. "It is not late."

She agreed, and they went along up a hill, and through some prettily wooded country. Presently the embattled tower and square turret of the church rose into the sky, and then the school-house. They enquired of a person in the street if Mr. Phillotson was likely to be at home, and were informed that he was always at home. A knock brought him to the school-house door, with a candle in his hand, and a look of inquiry on his face, which had grown thin and careworn since Jude last set eyes on him.

That after all these years the meeting with Mr. Phillotson should be of this homely complexion destroyed at one stroke the halo which had surrounded the schoolmaster's figure in Jude's imagination ever since their parting. It created in him at the same time a sympathy with Phillotson as an obviously much chastened and disappointed man. Jude told him his name, and said he had come to see him as an old friend who had been kind to him in his youthful days.

"I don't remember you in the least," said the schoolmaster thoughtfully. "You were one of my pupils you say? Yes, no doubt; but they number so many thousands at this time of my life, and have naturally changed so much, that I remember very few except the quite recent ones."

"It was out at Marygreen," said Jude, wishing he had not come.

"Yes. I was there a short time. And is this an old pupil, too?"

"No—that's my cousin. . . . I wrote to you for some grammars, if you recollect, and you sent them?"

"Ah—yes!—I do dimly recall that incident."

"It was very kind of you to do it. And it was you who first started me on that course. On the morning you left Marygreen, when your goods were on the waggon, you wished me good-bye, and said your scheme was to be a University man and enter the church—that a degree was the necessary hall-mark of one who wanted to do anything as a theologian or teacher."

"I remember I thought all that privately; but I wonder I did not keep my own counsel. The idea was given up years ago."

"I have never forgotten it. It was that which brought me to this part of the country, and out here to see you to-night."

"Come in," said Phillotson. "And your cousin, too."

They entered the parlour of the school-house, where there was a lamp with a paper shade, which threw the light down on three or four books. Phillotson took it off, so that they could see each other better, and the rays fell on the nervous little face and vivacious dark eyes and hair of Sue, on the earnest features of her cousin, and on the schoolmaster's own maturer face and figure, showing him to be a spare and thoughtful personage of five-and-forty, with a thin-lipped, somewhat refined mouth, a slightly stooping habit, and a black frock coat, which from continued frictions shone a little at the shoulder-blades, the middle of the back, and the elbows.

The old friendship was imperceptibly renewed, the schoolmaster speaking of his experiences, and the cousins of theirs. He told them that he still thought of the church sometimes, and that though he could not enter it as he had intended to do in former years he might enter it as a licentiate. Meanwhile, he said, he was comfortable in his present position, though he was in want of a pupil-teacher.

They did not stay to supper, Sue having to be indoors before it grew late, and the road was retraced to Christminster. Though they had talked of nothing more than general subjects Jude was surprised to find what a revelation of woman his cousin was to him. She was so vibrant that everything she did seemed to have its source in feeling. An exciting thought would make her walk ahead so fast that he could hardly keep up with her; and her sensitiveness on some points was such that it might have been misread as vanity. It was with heart-sickness he perceived that, while her sentiments towards him were those of the frankest friendliness only, he loved her more than before becoming acquainted with her; and the gloom of the walk home lay not in the night overhead, but in the thought of her departure.

"Why must you leave Christminster?" he said regretfully. "How can you do otherwise than cling to a city in whose history such men as Newman, Pusey, Ward, Keble, loom so large!"

"Yes—they do. Though how large do they loom in the history of the world? . . . What a funny reason for caring to stay! I should never have thought of it!" She laughed.

"Well—I must go," she continued. "Miss Fontover, one of the partners whom I serve, is offended with me, and I with her; and it is best to go."

"How did that happen?"

"She broke some statuary of mine."

"Oh? Wilfully?"

"Yes. She found it in my room, and though it was my property she threw it on the floor and stamped on it, because it was not according to her taste, and ground the arms and the head of one of the figures all to bits with her heel—a horrid thing!"

"Too Catholic-Apostolic for her, I suppose? No doubt she called them popish images and talked of the invocation of saints."

"No. . . . No, she didn't do that. She saw the matter quite differently."

"Ah! Then I am surprised!"

"Yes. It was for quite some other reason that she didn't like my patron-saints. So I was led to retort upon her; and the end of it was that I resolved not to stay, but to get into an occupation in which I shall be more independent."

"Why don't you try teaching again? You once did, I heard."

"I never thought of resuming it; for I was getting on as an art-designer."

"*Do* let me ask Mr. Phillotson to let you try your hand in his school? If you like it, and go to a Training College, and become a first-class certificated mistress, you get twice as large an income as any designer or church artist, and twice as much freedom."

"Well—ask him. Now I must go in. Good-bye, dear Jude! I am so glad we have met at last. We needn't quarrel because our parents did, need we?"

Jude did not like to let her quite see how much he agreed with her, and went his way to the remote street in which he had his lodging.

To keep Sue Bridehead near him was now a desire which operated without regard of consequences, and the next evening he again set out for Lumsdon, fearing to trust to the persuasive effects of a note only. The schoolmaster was unprepared for such a proposal.

"What I rather wanted was a second year's transfer, as it is called," he said. "Of course your cousin would do, personally; but she has had no experience. O—she has, has she? Does she really think of adopting teaching as a profession?"

Jude said she was disposed to do so, he thought, and his ingenious arguments on her natural fitness for assisting Mr. Phillotson, of which Jude knew nothing whatever, so influenced the schoolmaster that he said he would engage her, assuring Jude as a friend that unless his cousin really meant to follow on in the same course, and regarded this step as the first stage of an apprenticeship, of which her training in a normal school would be the second stage, her time would be wasted quite, the salary being merely nominal.

The day after this visit Phillotson received a letter from Jude, containing the information that he had again consulted his cousin, who took more and more warmly to the idea of tuition; and that she had agreed to come. It did not occur for a moment to the schoolmaster and recluse that Jude's ardour in promoting the arrangement arose from any other feelings towards Sue than the instinct of co-operation common among members of the same family.

V

THE SCHOOLMASTER SAT IN HIS HOMELY DWELLING ATTACHED TO THE SCHOOL, BOTH being modern erections; and he looked across the way at the old house in which his teacher Sue had a lodging. The arrangement had been concluded very quickly. A pupil-teacher who was to have been transferred to Mr. Phillotson's school had failed him, and Sue had been taken as stop-gap. All such provisional arrangements as these could only last till the next annual visit of H.M. Inspector, whose approval was necessary to make them permanent. Having taught for some two years in London, though she had abandoned that vocation of late, Miss Bridehead was not exactly an outsider, and Phillotson thought there would be no difficulty in retaining her services, which he already wished to do, though she had only been with him three or four weeks. He had found her quite as bright as Jude had described her; and what master-tradesman does not wish to keep an apprentice who saves him half his labour?

It was a little over half-past eight o'clock in the morning and he was waiting to see her cross the road to the school, when he would follow. At twenty minutes to nine she did cross, a light hat tossed on her head; and he watched her as a curiosity. A new emanation, which had nothing to do with her skill as a teacher, seemed to surround her this morning. He went to the school also, and Sue remained governing her class at the other end of the room, all day under his eye. She certainly was an excellent teacher.

It was part of his duty to give her private lessons in the evening, and some article in the Code made it necessary that a respectable, elderly woman should be present at these lessons when the teacher and the taught were of different sexes. Richard Phillotson thought of the absurdity of the regulation in this case, when he was old enough to be the girl's father; but he faithfully acted up to it; and sat down with her in a room where Mrs. Hawes, the widow at whose house Sue lodged, occupied herself with sewing. The regulation was, indeed, not easy to evade, for there was no other sitting-room in the dwelling.

Sometimes as she figured—it was arithmetic that they were working at—she would involuntarily glance up with a little inquiring smile at him, as if she assumed that, being the master, he must perceive all that was passing in her brain, as right or wrong. Phillotson was not really thinking of the arithmetic at all, but of her, in a novel way which somehow seemed strange to him as preceptor. Perhaps she knew that he was thinking of her thus.

For a few weeks their work had gone on with a monotony which in itself was a delight to him. Then it happened that the children were to be taken to Christminster to see an itinerant exhibition, in the shape of a model of Jerusalem, to which schools were admitted at a penny a head in the interests of education. They marched along the road two and two, she beside her class with her simple cotton sunshade, her little thumb cocked up against its stem; and Phillotson behind in his long dangling coat, handling his walking-stick genteelly, in the musing mood which had come over him since her arrival. The afternoon was one of sun and dust, and when they entered the exhibition room few people were present but themselves.

The model of the ancient city stood in the middle of the apartment, and the proprietor, with a fine religious philanthropy written on his features, walked round it with a pointer in his hand, showing the young people the various quarters and places known to them by name from reading their Bibles; Mount Moriah, the Valley of Jehoshaphat, the City of Zion, the walls and the gates, outside one of which there was a large mound like a tumulus, and on the mound a little white cross. The spot, he said, was Calvary.

"I think," said Sue to the schoolmaster, as she stood with him a little in the background, "that this model, elaborate as it is, is a very imaginary production. How does anybody know that Jerusalem was like this in the time of Christ? I am sure this man doesn't."

"It is made after the best conjectural maps, based on actual visits to the city as it now exists."

"I fancy we have had enough of Jerusalem," she said, "considering we are not descended from the Jews. There was nothing first-rate about the place, or people, after all—as there was about Athens, Rome, Alexandria, and other old cities."

"But my dear girl, consider what it is to us!"

She was silent, for she was easily repressed; and then perceived behind the group of children clustered round the model a young man in a white flannel jacket, his form being bent so low in his intent inspection of the Valley of Jehoshaphat that he was almost hidden from view by the Mount of Olives. "Look at your cousin Jude," continued the schoolmaster. "He doesn't think we have had enough of Jerusalem!"

"Ah—I didn't see him!" she cried in her quick light voice. "Jude—how seriously you are going into it!"

Jude started up from his reverie, and saw her. "O—Sue!" he said, with a glad flush of embarrassment. "These are your schoolchildren, of course! I saw that schools were admitted in the afternoons, and thought you might come; but I got so deeply interested that I didn't remember where I was. How it carries one back, doesn't it! I could examine it for hours, but I have only a few minutes, unfortunately; for I am in the middle of a job out here."

"Your cousin is so terribly clever that she criticises it unmercifully," said Phillotson, with good-humoured satire. "She is quite sceptical as to its correctness."

"No, Mr. Phillotson, I am not—altogether! I hate to be what is called a clever girl—there are too many of that sort now!" answered Sue sensitively. "I only meant—I don't know what I meant—except that it was what you don't understand!"

"*I* know your meaning," said Jude ardently (although he did not). "And I think you are quite right."

"That's a good Jude—I know *you* believe in me!" She impulsively seized his hand, and leaving a reproachful look on the schoolmaster turned away to Jude, her voice revealing a tremor which she herself felt to be absurdly uncalled for by sarcasm so gentle. She had not the least conception how the hearts of the twain went out to her at this momentary revelation of feeling, and what a complication she was building up thereby in the futures of both.

The model wore too much of an educational aspect for the children not to tire of it soon, and a little later in the afternoon they were all marched back to Lumsdon, Jude returning to his work. He watched the juvenile flock in their clean frocks and pinafores, filing down the street towards the country beside Phillotson and Sue, and a sad, dissatisfied sense of being out of the scheme of the latters' lives had possession of him. Phillotson had invited him to walk out and see them on Friday evening, when there would be no lessons to give to Sue, and Jude had eagerly promised to avail himself of the opportunity.

Meanwhile the scholars and teachers moved homewards, and the next day, on looking on the black-board in Sue's class, Phillotson was surprised to find upon it, skilfully drawn in chalk, a perspective view of Jerusalem, with every building shown in its place.

"I thought you took no interest in the model, and hardly looked at it?" he said.

"I hardly did," said she, "but I remembered that much of it."

"It is more than I had remembered myself."

Her Majesty's school-inspector was at that time paying "surprise-visits" in this neighbourhood to test the teaching unawares; and two days later, in the middle of the morning lessons, the latch of the door was softly lifted, and in walked my gentleman, the king of terrors—to pupil-teachers.

To Mr. Phillotson the surprise was not great; like the lady in the story, he had been played that trick too many times to be unprepared. But Sue's class was at the further end of the room, and her back was towards the entrance; the inspector therefore came and stood behind her and watched her teaching some half-minute before she became aware of his presence. She turned, and realised that an oft-dreaded moment had come. The effect upon her timidity was such that she uttered a cry of fright. Phillotson, with a strange instinct of solicitude quite beyond his control, was at her side just in time to prevent her falling from faintness. She soon recovered herself, and laughed; but when the inspector had gone there was a reaction, and she was so white that Phillotson took her into his room, and gave her some brandy to bring her round. She found him holding her hand.

"You ought to have told me," she gasped petulantly, "that one of the Inspector's surprise-visits was imminent! O, what shall I do! Now he'll write and tell the managers that I am no good, and I shall be disgraced forever!"

"He won't do that, my dear little girl. You are the best teacher ever I had!"

He looked so gently at her that she was moved, and regretted that she had upbraided him. When she was better she went home.

Jude in the meantime had been waiting impatiently for Friday. On both Wednesday and Thursday he had been so much under the influence of his desire to see her that he walked after dark some distance along the road in the direction of the village, and, on returning to his room to read, found himself quite unable to concentrate his mind on the page. On Friday, as soon as he had got himself up as he thought Sue would like to see him, and made a hasty tea, he set out, notwithstanding that the evening was wet. The trees overhead deepened the gloom of the hour, and they dripped sadly upon him, impressing him with forebodings—illogical forebodings; for though he knew that he loved her he also knew that he could not be more to her than he was.

On turning the corner and entering the village the first sight that greeted his eyes was that of two figures under one umbrella coming out of the vicarage gate. He was too far back for them to notice him, but he knew in a moment that they were Sue and Phillotson. The latter was holding the umbrella over her head, and they had evidently been paying a visit to the vicar—probably on some business connected with the school work. And as they walked along the wet and deserted lane Jude saw Phillotson place his arm round the girl's waist; whereupon she gently removed it; but he replaced it; and she let it remain, looking quickly round her with an air of misgiving. She did not look absolutely behind her, and therefore did not see Jude, who sank into the hedge like one struck with a blight. There he remained hidden till they had reached Sue's cottage and she had passed in, Phillotson going on to the school hard by.

"O, he's too old for her—too old!" cried Jude in all the terrible sickness of hopeless, handicapped love.

He could not interfere. Was he not Arabella's? He was unable to go on further, and retraced his steps towards Christminster. Every tread of his feet seemed to say to him that he must on no account stand in the schoolmaster's way with Sue. Phillotson was perhaps twenty years her senior, but many a happy marriage had been made in such conditions of age. The ironical clinch to his sorrow was given by the thought that the intimacy between his cousin and the schoolmaster had been brought about entirely by himself.

VI

J UDE'S OLD AND EMBITTERED AUNT LAY UNWELL AT MARYGREEN, AND ON THE FOLLOW-
ing Sunday he went to see her—a visit which was the result of a victorious struggle
against his inclination to turn aside to the village of Lumsdon and obtain a miserable interview with his cousin, in which the word nearest his heart could not be spoken, and the
sight which had tortured him could not be revealed.

His aunt was now unable to leave her bed, and a great part of Jude's short day was occupied in making arrangements for her comfort. The little bakery business had been sold
to a neighbour, and with the proceeds of this and her savings she was comfortably supplied
with necessaries, and more, a widow of the same village living with her and ministering to
her wants. It was not till the time had nearly come for him to leave that he obtained a quiet
talk with her, and his words tended insensibly towards his cousin.

"Was Sue born here?"

"She was—in this room. They were living here at that time. What made 'ee ask that?"

"O—I wanted to know."

"Now you've been seeing her!" said the harsh old woman. "And what did I tell 'ee?"

"Well—that I was not to see her."

"Have you gossiped with her?"

"Yes."

"Then don't keep it up. She was brought up by her father to hate her mother's family;
and she'll look with no favour upon a working chap like you—a townish girl as she's become by now. I never cared much about her. A pert little thing, that's what she was too
often, with her tight-strained nerves. Many's the time I've smacked her for her impertinence. Why, one day when she was walking into the pond with her shoes and stockings off,
and her petticoats pulled above her knees, afore I could cry out for shame, she said: 'Move
on, aunty! This is no sight for modest eyes!' "

"She was a little child then."

"She was twelve if a day."

"Well—of course. But now she's older she's of a thoughtful, quivering, tender nature, and as sensitive as—"

"Jude!" cried his aunt, springing up in bed. "Don't you be a fool about her!"

"No, no, of course not."

"Your marrying that woman Arabella was about as bad a thing as a man could possibly do for himself by trying hard. But she's gone to the other side of the world, and med
never trouble you again. And there'll be a worse thing if you, tied and bound as you be,
should have a fancy for Sue. If your cousin is civil to you, take her civility for what it is
worth. But anything more than a relation's good wishes it is stark madness for ye to give
her. If she's townish and wanton it med bring 'ee to ruin."

"Don't say anything against her, aunt! Don't, please!"

A relief was afforded to him by the entry of the companion and nurse of his aunt, who
must have been listening to the conversation, for she began a commentary on past years,
introducing Sue Bridehead as a character in her recollections. She described what an odd

little maid Sue had been when a pupil at the village school across the green opposite, before her father went to London—how, when the vicar arranged readings and recitations, she appeared on the platform, the smallest of them all, "in her little white frock, and shoes, and pink sash"; how she recited "Excelsior," "There was a sound of revelry by night," and "The Raven"; how during the delivery she would knit her little brows and glare round tragically, and say to the empty air, as if some real creature stood there—

> Ghastly, grim, and ancient Raven,
> Tell me what thy lordly name is,
> On the night's Plutonian shore!

"She'd bring up the nasty carrion bird that clear," corroborated the sick woman reluctantly, "as she stood there in her little sash and things, that you could see un a'most before your very eyes. You too, Jude, had the same trick as a child of seeming to see things in the air."

The neighbour told also of Sue's accomplishments in other kinds:

"She was not exactly a tomboy, you know; but she could do things that only boys do, as a rule. I've seen her hit in and steer down the long slide on yonder pond, with her little curls blowing, one of a file of twenty moving along against the sky like shapes painted on glass, and up the back slide without stopping. All boys except herself; and then they'd cheer her, and then she'd say, 'Don't be saucy, boys,' and suddenly run indoors. They'd try to coax her out again. But 'a wouldn't come."

These retrospective visions of Sue only made Jude the more miserable that he was unable to woo her, and he left the cottage of his aunt that day with a heavy heart. He would fain have glanced into the school to see the room in which Sue's little figure had so glorified itself; but he checked his desire and went on.

It being Sunday evening, some villagers who had known him during his residence here were standing in a group in their best clothes. Jude was startled by a salute from one of them:

"Ye've got there right enough, then!"

Jude showed that he did not understand.

"Why, to the seat of l'arning—the 'City of Light' you used to talk to us about as a little boy! Is it all you expected of it?"

"Yes; more!" cried Jude.

"When I was there once for an hour I didn't see much in it for my part; auld crumbling buildings, half church, half almshouse, and not much going on at that."

"You are wrong, John; there is more going on than meets the eye of a man walking through the streets. It is a unique centre of thought and religion—the intellectual and spiritual granary of this country. All that silence and absence of goings-on is the stillness of infinite motion—the sleep of the spinning-top, to borrow the simile of a writer."

"O, well, it med be all that, or it med not. As I say, I didn't see nothing of it the hour or two I was there; so I went in and had a pot o' beer, and a penny loaf, and a ha'porth o' cheese, and waited till it was time to come along home. You've j'ined a College by this time, I suppose?"

"Ah, no!" said Jude. "I am almost as far off that as ever."

"How so?"

Jude slapped his pocket.

"Just what we thought! Such places be not for such as you—only for them with plenty o' money."

"There you are wrong," said Jude, with some bitterness. "They are for such ones!"

Still, the remark was sufficient to withdraw Jude's attention from the imaginative world he had lately inhabited, in which an abstract figure, more or less himself, was steeping his mind in a sublimation of the arts and sciences, and making his calling and election sure to a seat in the paradise of the learned. He was set regarding his prospects in a cold northern light. He had lately felt that he could not quite satisfy himself in his Greek—in the Greek of the dramatists particularly. So fatigued was he sometimes after his day's work that he could not maintain the critical attention necessary for thorough application. He felt that he wanted a coach—a friend at his elbow to tell him in a moment what sometimes would occupy him a weary month in extracting from unanticipative, clumsy books.

It was decidedly necessary to consider facts a little more closely than he had done of late. What was the good, after all, of using up his spare hours in a vague labour called "private study" without giving an outlook on practicabilities?

"I ought to have thought of this before," he said, as he journeyed back. "It would have been better never to have embarked in the scheme at all than to do it without seeing clearly where I am going, or what I am aiming at. . . . This hovering outside the walls of the colleges, as if expecting some arm to be stretched out from them to lift me inside, won't do! I must get special information."

The next week accordingly he sought it. What at first seemed an opportunity occurred one afternoon when he saw an elderly gentleman, who had been pointed out as the Head of a particular College, walking in the public path of a parklike enclosure near the spot at which Jude chanced to be sitting. The gentleman came nearer, and Jude looked anxiously at his face. It seemed benign, considerate, yet rather reserved. On second thoughts Jude felt that he could not go up and address him; but he was sufficiently influenced by the incident to think what a wise thing it would be for him to state his difficulties by letter to some of the best and most judicious of these old masters, and obtain their advice.

During the next week or two he accordingly placed himself in such positions about the city as would afford him glimpses of several of the most distinguished among the Provosts, Wardens, and other Heads of Houses; and from those he saw he ultimately selected five whose physiognomies seemed to say to him that they were appreciative and farseeing men. To these five he addressed letters, briefly stating his difficulties, and asking their opinion on his stranded situation.

When the letters were posted Jude mentally began to criticise them; he wished they had not been sent. "It is just one of those intrusive, vulgar, pushing applications which are so common in these days," he thought. "Why couldn't I know better than address utter strangers in such a way? I may be an impostor, and idle scamp, a man with a bad character, for all that they know to the contrary. . . . Perhaps that's what I am!"

Nevertheless, he found himself clinging to the hope of some reply as to his one last chance of redemption. He waited day after day, saying that it was perfectly absurd to expect, yet expecting. While he waited he was suddenly stirred by news about Phillotson. Phillotson was giving up the school near Christminster, for a larger one further south, in

Mid-Wessex. What this meant; how it would affect his cousin; whether, as seemed possible, it was a practical move of the schoolmaster's towards a larger income, in view of a provision for two instead of one, he would not allow himself to say. And the tender relations between Phillotson and the young girl of whom Jude was passionately enamoured effectually made it repugnant to Jude's tastes to apply to Phillotson for advice on his own scheme.

Meanwhile the academic dignitaries to whom Jude had written vouchsafed no answer, and the young man was thus thrown back entirely on himself, as formerly, with the added gloom of a weakened hope. By indirect inquiries he soon perceived clearly, what he had long uneasily suspected, that to qualify himself for certain open scholarships and exhibitions was the only brilliant course. But to do this a good deal of coaching would be necessary, and much natural ability. It was next to impossible that a man reading on his own system, however widely and thoroughly, even over the prolonged period of ten years, should be able to compete with those who had passed their lives under trained teachers and had worked to ordained lines.

The other course, that of buying himself in, so to speak, seemed the only one really open to men like him, the difficulty being simply of a material kind. With the help of his information he began to reckon the extent of this material obstacle, and ascertained, to his dismay, that, at the rate at which, with the best of fortune, he would be able to save money, fifteen years must elapse before he could be in a position to forward testimonials to the Head of a College and advance to a matriculation examination. The undertaking was hopeless.

He saw what a curious and cunning glamour the neighbourhood of the place had exercised over him. To get there and live there, to move among the churches and halls and become imbued with the *genius loci,* had seemed to his dreaming youth, as the spot shaped its charms to him from its halo on the horizon, the obvious and ideal thing to do. "Let me only get there," he had said with the fatuousness of Crusoe over his big boat, "and the rest is but a matter of time and energy." It would have been far better for him in every way if he had never come within sight and sound of the delusive precincts, had gone to some busy commercial town with the sole object of making money by his wits, and thence surveyed his plan in true perspective. Well, all that was clear to him amounted to this, that the whole scheme had burst up, like an iridescent soap-bubble, under the touch of a reasoned inquiry. He looked back at himself along the vista of his past years, and his thought was akin to Heine's:

> *Above the youth's inspired and flashing eyes*
> *I see the motley mocking fool's-cap rise.*

Fortunately he had not been allowed to bring his disappointment into his dear Sue's life by involving her in this collapse. And the painful details of his awakening to a sense of his limitations should now be spared her as far as possible. After all, she had only known a little part of the miserable struggle in which he had been engaged thus unequipped, poor, and unforeseeing.

He always remembered the appearance of the afternoon on which he awoke from his dream. Not quite knowing what to do with himself, he went up to an octagonal chamber in the lantern of a singularly built theatre that was set amidst this quaint and singular city.

It had windows all round, from which an outlook over the whole town and its edifices could be gained. Jude's eyes swept all the views in succession, meditatively, mournfully, yet sturdily. Those buildings and their associations and privileges were not for him. From the looming roof of the great library, into which he hardly ever had time to enter, his gaze travelled on to the varied spires, halls, gables, streets, chapels, gardens, quadrangles, which composed the *ensemble* of this unrivalled panorama. He saw that his destiny lay not with these, but among the manual toilers in the shabby purlieu which he himself occupied, unrecognised as part of the city at all by its visitors and panegyrists, yet without whose denizens the hard readers could not read nor the high thinkers live.

He looked over the town into the country beyond, to the trees which screened her whose presence had at first been the support of his heart, and whose loss was now a maddening torture. But for this blow he might have borne with his fate. With Sue as companion he could have renounced his ambitions with a smile. Without her it was inevitable that the reaction from the long strain to which he had subjected himself should affect him disastrously. Phillotson had no doubt passed through a similar intellectual disappointment to that which now enveloped him. But the schoolmaster had been since blest with the consolation of sweet Sue, while for him there was no consoler.

Descending to the streets, he went listlessly along till he arrived at an inn, and entered it. Here he drank several glasses of beer in rapid succession, and when he came out it was night. By the light of the flickering lamps he rambled home to supper, and had not long been sitting at table when his landlady brought up a letter that had just arrived for him. She laid it down as if impressed with a sense of its possible importance, and on looking at it Jude perceived that it bore the embossed stamp of one of the Colleges whose heads he had addressed. "*One*—at last!" cried Jude.

The communication was brief, and not exactly what he had expected; though it really was from the Master in person. It ran thus:

BIBLIOLL COLLEGE

SIR—I have read your letter with interest; and, judging from your description of yourself as a working-man, I venture to think that you will have a much better chance of success in life by remaining in your own sphere and sticking to your trade than by adopting any other course. That, therefore, is what I advise you to do. Yours faithfully,

T. TETUPHENAY

To Mr. J. FAWLEY, Stone-mason.

This terribly sensible advice exasperated Jude. He had known all that before. He knew it was true. Yet it seemed a hard slap after ten years of labour, and its effect upon him just now was to make him rise recklessly from the table, and, instead of reading as usual, to go downstairs and into the street. He stood at a bar and tossed off two or three glasses, then unconsciously sauntered along till he came to a spot called The Fourways in the middle of the city, gazing abstractedly at the groups of people like one in a trance, till, coming to himself, he began talking to the policeman fixed there.

That officer yawned, stretched out his elbows, elevated himself an inch and a half on the balls of his toes, smiled, and looking humorously at Jude, said, "You've had a wet, young man."

"No; I've only begun," he replied cynically.

Whatever his wetness, his brains were dry enough. He only heard in part the police-man's further remarks, having fallen into thought on what struggling people like himself had stood at that Crossway, whom nobody ever thought of now. It had more history than the oldest college in the city. It was literally teeming, stratified, with the shades of human groups, who had met there for tragedy, comedy, farce; real enactments of the intensest kind. At Fourways men had stood and talked of Napoleon, the loss of America, the exe-cution of King Charles, the burning of the Martyrs, the Crusades, the Norman Conquest, possibly of the arrival of Cæsar. Here the two sexes had met for loving, hating, coupling, parting; had waited, had suffered, for each other; had triumphed over each other; cursed each other in jealousy, blessed each other in forgiveness.

He began to see that the town life was a book of humanity infinitely more palpitating, varied, and compendious than the gown life. These struggling men and women before him were the reality of Christminster, though they knew little of Christ or Minster. That was one of the humours of things. The floating population of students and teachers, who did know both in a way, were not Christminster in a local sense at all.

He looked at his watch, and, in pursuit of this idea, he went on till he came to a pub-lic hall, where a promenade concert was in progress. Jude entered, and found the room full of shop youths and girls, soldiers, apprentices, boys of eleven smoking cigarettes, and light women of the more respectable and amateur class. He had tapped the real Christ-minster life. A band was playing, and the crowd walked about and jostled each other, and every now and then a man got upon a platform and sang a comic song.

The spirit of Sue seemed to hover round him and prevent his flirting and drinking with the frolicsome girls who made advances—wistful to gain a little joy. At ten o'clock he came away, choosing a circuitous route homeward to pass the gates of the College whose Head had just sent him the note.

The gates were shut, and, by an impulse, he took from his pocket the lump of chalk which as a workman he usually carried there, and wrote along the wall:

"I have understanding as well as you; I am not inferior to you: yea, who knoweth not such things as these?"—Job xii. 3.

VII

THE STROKE OF SCORN RELIEVED HIS MIND, AND THE NEXT MORNING HE LAUGHED AT his self-conceit. But the laugh was not a healthy one. He reread the letter from the Master, and the wisdom in its lines, which had at first exasperated him, chilled and de-pressed him now. He saw himself as a fool indeed.

Deprived of the objects of both intellect and emotion, he could not proceed to his work. Whenever he felt reconciled to his fate as a student, there came to disturb his calm his hopeless relations with Sue. That the one affined soul he had ever met was lost to him through his marriage returned upon him with cruel persistency, till, unable to bear it longer, he again rushed for distraction to the real Christminster life. He now sought it out in an obscure and low-ceiled tavern up a court which was well known to certain worthies of the place, and in brighter times would have interested him simply by its quaintness. Here he sat more or less all the day, convinced that he was at bottom a vicious character, of whom it was hopeless to expect anything.

In the evening the frequenters of the house dropped in one by one, Jude still retaining his seat in the corner, though his money was all spent, and he had not eaten anything the whole day except a biscuit. He surveyed his gathering companions with all the equanimity and philosophy of a man who has been drinking long and slowly, and made friends with several: to wit, Tinker Taylor, a decayed church-ironmonger who appeared to have been of a religious turn in earlier years, but was somewhat blasphemous now; also a red-nosed auctioneer; also two Gothic masons like himself, called Uncle Jim and Uncle Joe. There were present, too, some clerks, and a gown-and surplice-maker's assistant; two ladies who sported moral characters of various depths of shade, according to their company, nick-named "Bower o' Bliss" and "Freckles"; some horsey men "in the know" of betting circles; a travelling actor from the theatre, and two devil-may-care young men who proved to be gownless undergraduates; they had slipped in by stealth to meet a man about bull-pups, and stayed to drink and smoke short pipes with the racing gents aforesaid, looking at their watches every now and then.

The conversation waxed general. Christminster society was criticised, the Dons, magistrates, and other people in authority being sincerely pitied for their shortcomings, while opinions on how they ought to conduct themselves and their affairs to be properly respected, were exchanged in a large-minded and disinterested manner.

Jude Fawley, with the self-conceit, effrontery, and *aplomb* of a strong-brained fellow in liquor, threw in his remarks somewhat peremptorily; and his aims having been what they were for so many years, everything the others said turned upon his tongue, by a sort of mechanical craze, to the subject of scholarship and study, the extent of his own learning being dwelt upon with an insistence that would have appeared pitiable to himself in his sane hours.

"I don't care a damn," he was saying, "for any Provost, Warden, Principal, Fellow, or cursed Master of Arts in the University! What I know is that I'd lick 'em on their own ground if they'd give me a chance, and show 'em a few things they are not up to yet!"

"Hear, hear!" said the undergraduates from the corner, where they were talking privately about the pups.

"You always was fond o' books, I've heard," said Tinker Taylor, "and I don't doubt what you state. Now with me 'twas different. I always saw there was more to be learnt outside a book than in; and I took my steps accordingly, or I shouldn't have been the man I am."

"You aim at the Church, I believe?" said Uncle Joe. "If you are such a scholar as to pitch yer hopes so high as that, why not give us a specimen of your scholarship? Canst say the Creed in Latin, man? That was how they once put it to a chap down in my country."

"I should think so!" said Jude haughtily.

"Not he! Like his conceit!" screamed one of the ladies.

"Just you shut up, Bower o' Bliss!" said one of the undergraduates. "Silence!" He drank off the spirits in his tumbler, rapped with it on the counter, and announced, "The gentleman in the corner is going to rehearse the Articles of his Belief, in the Latin tongue, for the edification of the company."

"I won't!" said Jude.

"Yes—have a try!" said the surplice-maker.

"You can't!" said Uncle Joe.

"Yes, he can!" said Tinker Taylor.

"I'll swear I can!" said Jude. "Well, come now, stand me a small Scotch cold, and I'll do it straight off."

"That's a fair offer," said the undergraduate, throwing down the money for the whisky.

The barmaid concocted the mixture with the bearing of a person compelled to live amongst animals of an inferior species, and the glass was handed across to Jude, who, having drunk the contents, stood up and began rhetorically, without hesitation:

"Credo in unum Deum, Patrem omnipotentem, Factorem coeli et terrae, visibilium omnium et invisibilium."

"Good! Excellent Latin!" cried one of the undergraduates, who, however, had not the slightest conception of a single word.

A silence reigned among the rest in the bar, and the maid stood still, Jude's voice echoing sonorously into the inner parlour, where the landlord was dozing, and bringing him out to see what was going on. Jude had declaimed steadily ahead, and was continuing:

"Crucifixus etiam pro nobis: sub Pontio Pilato passus, et sepultus est. Et resurrexit tertia die, secundum Scripturas."

"That's the Nicene," sneered the second undergraduate. "And we wanted the Apostles'!"

"You didn't say so! And every fool knows, except you, that the Nicene is the only historic creed!"

"Let un go on, let un go on!" said the auctioneer.

But Jude's mind seemed to grow confused soon, and he could not get on. He put his hand to his forehead, and his face assumed an expression of pain.

"Give him another glass—then he'll fetch up and get through it," said Tinker Taylor.

Somebody threw down threepence, the glass was handed, Jude stretched out his arm for it without looking, and having swallowed the liquor, went on in a moment in a revived voice, continuing to the end with the manner of a priest leading a congregation:

"Et unam Catholicam et Apostolicam Ecclesiam.Confiteor unum Baptisma in remissionem peccatorum. Et expecto Resurrectionem mortuorum. Et vitam venturi saeculi. Amen."

"Well done!" said several, enjoying the last word, as being the first and only one they had recognised.

Then Jude seemed to shake the fumes from his brain, as he stared round upon them.

"You pack of fools!" he cried. "Which one of you knows whether I have said it or no? It might have been the Ratcatcher's Daughter in double Dutch for all that your besotted heads can tell! See what I have brought myself to—the crew I have come among!"

The landlord, who had already had his license endorsed for harbouring queer characters, feared a riot, and came outside the counter; but Jude, in his sudden flash of reason, had turned in disgust and left the scene, the door slamming with a dull thud behind him.

He hastened down the lane and round into the straight broad street, which he followed till it merged in the highway, and all sound of his late companions had been left behind.

Onward he still went, under the influence of a childlike yearning for the one being in the world to whom it seemed possible to fly—an unreasoning desire, whose ill judgment was not apparent to him now. In the course of an hour, when it was between ten and eleven o'clock, he entered the village of Lumsdon, and reaching the cottage, saw that a light was burning in a downstairs room, which he assumed, rightly as it happened, to be hers.

Jude stepped close to the wall, and tapped with his finger on the pane, saying impatiently, "Sue, Sue!"

She must have recognised his voice, for the light disappeared from the apartment, and in a second or two the door was unlocked and opened, and Sue appeared with a candle in her hand.

"Is it Jude? Yes, it is! My dear, dear cousin, what's the matter?"

"O, I am—I couldn't help coming, Sue!" said he, sinking down upon the door-step. "I am so wicked, Sue—my heart is nearly broken, and I could not bear my life as it was! So I have been drinking, and blaspheming, or next door to it, and saying holy things in disreputable quarters—repeating in idle bravado words which ought never to be uttered but reverently! O, do anything with me, Sue—kill me—I don't care! Only don't hate me and despise me like all the rest of the world!"

"You are ill, poor dear! No, I won't despise you; of course I won't! Come in and rest, and let me see what I can do for you. Now lean on me, and don't mind." With one hand holding the candle and the other supporting him, she led him indoors, and placed him in the only easy-chair the meagrely furnished house afforded, stretching his feet upon another, and pulling off his boots. Jude, now getting towards his sober senses, could only say, "Dear, dear Sue!" in a voice broken by grief and contrition.

She asked him if he wanted anything to eat, but he shook his head. Then telling him to go to sleep, and that she would come down early in the morning and get him some breakfast, she bade him good-night and ascended the stairs.

Almost immediately he fell into a heavy slumber, and did not wake till dawn. At first he did not know where he was, but by degrees his situation cleared to him, and he beheld it in all the ghastliness of a right mind. She knew the worst of him—the very worst. How could he face her now? She would soon be coming down to see about breakfast, as she had said, and there would he be in all his shame confronting her. He could not bear the thought, and softly drawing on his boots, and taking his hat from the nail on which she had hung it, he slipped noiselessly out of the house.

His fixed idea was to get away to some obscure spot and hide, and perhaps pray; and the only spot which occurred to him was Marygreen. He called at his lodging in Christminster, where he found awaiting him a note of dismissal from his employer; and having packed up, he turned his back upon the city that had been such a thorn in his side and struck southward into Wessex. He had no money left in his pocket, his small savings, deposited at one of the banks in Christminster, having fortunately been left untouched. To get to Marygreen, therefore, his only course was walking; and the distance being nearly twenty miles, he had ample time to complete on the way the sobering process begun in him.

At some hour of the evening he reached Alfredston. Here he pawned his waistcoat, and having gone out of the town a mile or two, slept under a rick that night. At dawn he rose, shook off the hayseeds and stems from his clothes, and started again, breasting the long white road up the hill to the downs, which had been visible to him a long way off, and passing the milestone at the top, whereon he had carved his hopes years ago.

He reached the ancient hamlet while the people were at breakfast. Weary and mud-bespattered, but quite possessed of his ordinary clearness of brain, he sat down by the well, thinking as he did so what a poor Christ he made. Seeing a trough of water near, he bathed his face, and went on to the cottage of his great-aunt, whom he found breakfasting in bed, attended by the woman who lived with her.

"What—out o' work?" asked his relative, regarding him through eyes sunken deep, under lids heavy as pot-covers, no other cause for his tumbled appearance suggesting itself to one whose whole life had been a struggle with material things.

"Yes," said Jude heavily. "I think I must have a little rest."

Refreshed by some breakfast, he went up to his old room and lay down in his shirt-sleeves, after the manner of the artizan. He fell asleep for a short while, and when he awoke it was as if he had awakened in hell. It *was* hell—"the hell of conscious failure," both in ambition and in love. He thought of that previous abyss into which he had fallen before leaving this part of the country; the deepest deep he had supposed it then; but it was not so deep as this. That had been the breaking in of the outer bulwarks of his hope: this was of his second line.

If he had been a woman he must have screamed under the nervous tension which he was now undergoing. But that relief being denied to his virility, he clenched his teeth in misery, bringing lines about his mouth like those in the Laocoon, and corrugations between his brows.

A mournful wind blew through the trees, and sounded in the chimney like the pedal notes of an organ. Each ivy leaf overgrowing the wall of the churchless churchyard hard by, now abandoned, pecked its neighbour smartly, and the vane on the new German-Gothic church in the new spot had already begun to creak. Yet apparently it was not always the outdoor wind that made the deep murmurs; it was a voice. He guessed its origin in a moment or two; the curate was praying with his aunt in the adjoining room. He remembered her speaking of him. Presently the sounds ceased, and a step seemed to cross the landing. Jude sat up, and shouted "Hoi!"

The step made for his door, which was open, and a man looked in. It was a young clergyman.

"I think you are Mr. Highridge," said Jude. "My aunt has mentioned you more than once. Well, here I am, just come home; a fellow gone to the bad; though I had the best intentions in the world at one time. Now I am melancholy mad, what with drinking and one thing and another."

Slowly Jude unfolded to the curate his late plans and movements, by an unconscious bias dwelling less upon the intellectual and ambitious side of his dream, and more upon the theological, though this had, up till now, been merely a portion of the general plan of advancement.

"Now I know I have been a fool, and that folly is with me," added Jude in conclusion. "And I don't regret the collapse of my University hopes one jot. I wouldn't begin again if I were sure to succeed. I don't care for social success any more at all. But I do feel I should like to do some good thing; and I bitterly regret the Church, and the loss of my chance of being her ordained minister."

The curate, who was a new man to this neighbourhood, had grown deeply interested, and at last he said: "If you feel a real call to the ministry, and I won't say from your conversation that you do not, for it is that of a thoughtful and educated man, you might enter the Church as a licentiate. Only you must make up your mind to avoid strong drink."

"I could avoid that easily enough, if I had any kind of hope to support me!"

PART THIRD

AT MELCHESTER

"For there was no other girl, O bridegroom, like her!"
—SAPPHO (H. T. WHARTON)

I

I T WAS A NEW IDEA—THE ECCLESIASTICAL AND ALTRUISTIC LIFE AS DISTINCT FROM THE intellectual and emulative life. A man could preach and do good to his fellow-creatures without taking double-firsts in the schools of Christminster, or having anything but ordinary knowledge. The old fancy which had led on to the culminating vision of the bishopric had not been an ethical or theological enthusiasm at all, but a mundane ambition masquerading in a surplice. He feared that his whole scheme had degenerated to, even though it might not have originated in, a social unrest which had no foundation in the nobler instincts; which was purely an artificial product of civilization. There were thousands of young men on the same self-seeking track at the present moment. The sensual hind who ate, drank, and lived carelessly with his wife through the days of his vanity was a more likable being than he.

But to enter the Church in such an unscholarly way that he could not in any probability rise to a higher grade through all his career than that of the humble curate wearing his life out in an obscure village or city slum—that might have a touch of goodness and greatness in it; that might be true religion, and a purgatorial course worthy of being followed by a remorseful man.

The favourable light in which this new thought showed itself by contrast with his foregone intentions cheered Jude, as he sat there, shabby and lonely; and it may be said to have given, during the next few days, the *coup de grâce* to his intellectual career—a career which had extended over the greater part of a dozen years. He did nothing, however, for some long stagnant time to advance his new desire, occupying himself with little local jobs in putting up and lettering head-stones about the neighbouring villages, and submitting to be regarded as a social failure, a returned purchase, by the half-dozen or so of farmers and other countrypeople who condescended to nod to him.

The human interest of the new intention—and a human interest is indispensable to the most spiritual and self-sacrificing—was created by a letter from Sue, bearing a fresh postmark. She evidently wrote with anxiety, and told very little about her own doings, more than that she had passed some sort of examination for a Queen's Scholarship, and was going to enter a Training College at Melchester to complete herself for the vocation she had chosen, partly by his influence. There was a Theological College at Melchester; Melchester was a quiet and soothing place, almost entirely ecclesiastical in its tone; a spot where worldly learning and intellectual smartness had no establishment; where the altruistic feeling that he did possess would perhaps be more highly estimated than a brilliancy which he did not.

As it would be necessary that he should continue for a time to work at his trade while reading up Divinity, which he had neglected at Christminster for the ordinary classical grind, what better course for him than to get employment at the further city, and pursue this plan of reading? That his excessive human interest in the new place was entirely of Sue's making, while at the same time Sue was to be regarded even less than formerly as proper to create it, had an ethical contradictoriness to which he was not blind. But that much he conceded to human frailty, and hoped to learn to love her only as a friend and kinswoman.

He considered that he might so mark out his coming years as to begin his ministry at the age of thirty—an age which much attracted him as being that of his exemplar when he first began to teach in Galilee. This would allow him plenty of time for deliberate study, and for acquiring capital by his trade to help his aftercourse of keeping the necessary terms at a Theological College.

Christmas had come and passed, and Sue had gone to the Melchester Normal School. The time was just the worst in the year for Jude to get into new employment, and he had written suggesting to her that he should postpone his arrival for a month or so, till the days had lengthened. She had acquiesced so readily that he wished he had not proposed it—she evidently did not much care about him, though she had never once reproached him for his strange conduct in coming to her that night, and his silent disappearance. Neither had she ever said a word about her relations with Mr. Phillotson.

Suddenly, however, quite a passionate letter arrived from Sue. She was quite lonely and miserable, she told him. She hated the place she was in; it was worse than the ecclesiastical designer's; worse than anywhere. She felt utterly friendless; could he come immediately?—though when he did come she would only be able to see him at limited times, the rules of the establishment she found herself in being strict to a degree. It was Mr. Phillotson who had advised her to come there, and she wished she had never listened to him.

Phillotson's suit was not exactly prospering, evidently; and Jude felt unreasonably glad. He packed up his things and went to Melchester with a lighter heart than he had known for months.

This being the turning over a new leaf he duly looked about for a temperance hotel, and found a little establishment of that description in the street leading from the station. When he had had something to eat he walked out into the dull winter light over the town bridge, and turned the corner towards the Close. The day was foggy, and standing under the walls of the most graceful architectural pile in England he paused and looked up. The lofty building was visible as far as the roof-ridge; above, the dwindling spire rose more and more remotely, till its apex was quite lost in the mist drifting across it.

The lamps now began to be lighted, and turning to the west front he walked round. He took it as a good omen that numerous blocks of stone were lying about, which signified that the cathedral was undergoing restoration or repair to a considerable extent. It seemed to him, full of the superstitions of his beliefs, that this was an exercise of forethought on the part of a ruling Power, that he might find plenty to do in the art he practised while waiting for a call to higher labours.

Then a wave of warmth came over him as he thought how near he now stood to the bright-eyed vivacious girl with the broad forehead and pile of dark hair above it; the girl with the kindling glance, daringly soft at times—something like that of the girls he had seen in engravings from paintings of the Spanish school. She was here—actually in this Close—in one of the houses confronting this very west *façade*.

He went down the broad gravel path towards the building. It was an ancient edifice of the fifteenth century, once a palace, now a Training-School, with mullioned and transomed windows, and a courtyard in front shut in from the road by a wall. Jude opened the gate and went up to the door through which, on inquiring for his cousin, he was gingerly admitted to a waiting-room, and in a few minutes she came.

Though she had been here such a short while, she was not as he had seen her last. All her bounding manner was gone; her curves of motion had become subdued lines. The screens and subtleties of convention had likewise disappeared. Yet neither was she quite the woman who had written the letter that summoned him. That had plainly been dashed off in an impulse which second thoughts had somewhat regretted; thoughts that were possibly of his recent self-disgrace. Jude was quite overcome with emotion.

"You don't—think me a demoralised wretch—for coming to you as I was—and going so shamefully, Sue?"

"O, I have tried not to! You said enough to let me know what had caused it. I hope I shall never have any doubt of your worthiness, my poor Jude! And I am glad you have come!"

She wore a murrey-coloured gown with a little lace collar. It was made quite plain, and hung about her slight figure with clinging gracefulness. Her hair, which formerly she had worn according to the custom of the day was now twisted up tightly, and she had altogether the air of a woman clipped and pruned by severe discipline, an under-brightness shining through from the depths which that discipline had not yet been able to reach.

She had come forward prettily; but Jude felt that she had hardly expected him to kiss her, as he was burning to do, under other colours than those of cousinship. He could not perceive the least sign that Sue regarded him as a lover, or ever would do so, now that she knew the worst of him, even if he had the right to behave as one; and this helped on his growing resolve to tell her of his matrimonial entanglement, which he had put off doing from time to time in sheer dread of losing the bliss of her company.

Sue came out into the town with him, and they walked and talked with tongues centred only on the passing moments. Jude said he would like to buy her a little present of some sort, and then she confessed, with something of shame, that she was dreadfully hungry. They were kept on very short allowances in the College, and a dinner, tea, and supper all in one was the present she most desired in the world. Jude thereupon took her to an inn and ordered whatever the house afforded, which was not much. The place, however, gave them a delightful opportunity for a *tête-à-tête*, nobody else being in the room, and they talked freely.

She told him about the school as it was at that date, and the rough living, and the mixed character of her fellow-students, gathered together from all parts of the diocese, and how she had to get up and work by gas-light in the early morning, with all the bitterness of a young person to whom restraint was new. To all this he listened; but it was not what he wanted especially to know—her relations with Phillotson. That was what she did not tell. When they had sat and eaten, Jude impulsively placed his hand upon hers; she looked up and smiled, and took his quite freely into her own little soft one, dividing his fingers and coolly examining them, as if they were the fingers of a glove she was purchasing.

"Your hands are rather rough, Jude, aren't they?" she said.

"Yes. So would yours be if they held a mallet and chisel all day."

"I don't dislike it, you know. I think it is noble to see a man's hands subdued to what he works in. . . . Well, I'm rather glad I came to this Training-School, after all. See how independent I shall be after the two years' training! I shall pass pretty high, I expect, and Mr. Phillotson will use his influence to get me a big school."

She had touched the subject at last. "I had a suspicion, a fear," said Jude, "that he—cared about you rather warmly, and perhaps wanted to marry you."

"Now don't be such a silly boy!"

"He has said something about it, I expect."

"If he had, what would it matter? An old man like him!"

"O, come, Sue; he's not so very old. And I know what I saw him doing——"

"Not kissing me—that I'm certain!"

"No. But putting his arm round your waist."

"Ah—I remember. But I didn't know he was going to."

"You are wriggling out if it, Sue, and it isn't quite kind!"

Her ever-sensitive lip began to quiver, and her eye to blink, at something this reproof was deciding her to say.

"I know you'll be angry if I tell you everything, and that's why I don't want to!"

"Very well, then, dear," he said soothingly. "I have no real right to ask you, and I don't wish to know."

"I shall tell you!" said she, with the perverseness that was part of her. "This is what I have done: I have promised—I have promised—that I will marry him when I come out of the Training-School two years hence, and have got my Certificate; his plan being that we shall then take a large double school in a great town—he the boys' and I the girls'—as married school-teachers often do, and make a good income between us."

"O, Sue! . . . But of course it is right—you couldn't have done better!"

He glanced at her and their eyes met, the reproach in his own belying his words. Then he drew his hand quite away from hers, and turned his face in estrangement from her to the window. Sue regarded him passively without moving.

"I knew you would be angry!" she said with an air of no emotion whatever. "Very well—I am wrong, I suppose! I ought not to have let you come to see me! We had better not meet again; and we'll only correspond at long intervals, on purely business matters!"

This was just the one thing he would not be able to bear, as she probably knew, and it brought him round at once. "O yes, we will," he said quickly. "Your being engaged can make no difference to me whatever. I have a perfect right to see you when I want to; and I shall!"

"Then don't let us talk of it any more. It is quite spoiling our evening together. What does it matter about what one is going to do two years hence!"

She was something of a riddle to him, and he let the subject drift away. "Shall we go and sit in the cathedral?" he asked, when their meal was finished.

"Cathedral? Yes. Though I think I'd rather sit in the railway-station," she answered, a remnant of vexation still in her voice. "That's the centre of the town life now. The Cathedral has had its day!"

"How modern you are!"

"So would you be if you had lived so much in the Middle Ages as I have done these last few years! The Cathedral was a very good place four or five centuries ago; but it is played out now . . . I am not modern, either. I am more ancient than medievalism, if you only knew."

Jude looked distressed.

"There—I won't say any more of that!" she cried. "Only you don't know how bad I am, from your point of view, or you wouldn't think so much of me, or care whether I was engaged or not. Now there's just time for us to walk round the Close, and then I must go in, or I shall be locked out for the night."

He took her to the gate and they parted. Jude had a conviction that his unhappy visit to her on that sad night had precipitated this marriage engagement, and it did anything but add to his happiness. Her reproach had taken that shape, then, and not the shape of words. However, next day he set about seeking employment, which it was not so easy to get as at Christminster, there being, as a rule, less stone-cutting in progress in this quiet city, and hands being mostly permanent. But he edged himself in by degrees. His first work was some carving at the cemetery on the hill; and ultimately he became engaged on the labour he most desired—the Cathedral repairs, which were very extensive, the whole interior fittings having been swept away, to be replaced by new.

It might be a labour of years to get it all done, and he had confidence enough in his own skill with the mallet and chisel to feel that it would be a matter of choice with himself how long he would stay.

The lodgings he took near the Close Gate would not have disgraced a curate, the rent representing a higher percentage on his wages than mechanics of any sort usually care to pay. His combined bed and sitting-room was furnished with framed photographs of the rectories and deaneries at which his landlady had lived as trusted servant in her time, and the parlour downstairs bore a clock on the mantelpiece inscribed to the effect that it was presented to the same serious-minded woman by her fellow-servants on the occasion of her marriage. Jude added to the furniture of his room by unpacking photographs of the ecclesiastical carvings and monuments that he had executed with his own hands; and he was deemed a satisfactory acquisition as tenant of the vacant apartment.

He found an ample supply of theological books in the city book-shops, and with these his studies were recommenced in a different spirit and direction from his former course. As a relaxation from the Fathers, and such stock works as Paley and Butler, he read Newman, Pusey, and many other modern lights. He hired a harmonium, set it up in his lodging, and practised chants thereon, single and double.

II

"TO-MORROW IS OUR GRAND DAY, YOU KNOW. WHERE SHALL WE GO?"

"I have leave from three till nine. Wherever we can get to and come back from in that time. Not ruins, Jude—I don't care for them."

"Well—Wardour Castle. And then we can do Fonthill if we like—all in the same afternoon."

"Wardour is Gothic ruins—and I hate Gothic!"

"No. Quite otherwise. It is a classic building—Corinthian, I think; with a lot of pictures."

"Ah—that will do. I like the sound of Corinthian. We'll go."

Their conversation had run thus some few weeks later, and next morning they prepared to start. Every detail of the outing was a facet reflecting a sparkle to Jude, and he did not venture to meditate on the life of inconsistency he was leading. His Sue's conduct was one lovely conundrum to him; he could say no more.

There duly came the charm of calling at the College door for her; her emergence in a nunlike simplicity of costume that was rather enforced than desired; the traipsing along to the station, the porters' "B'your leave!" the screaming of the trains—everything formed the basis of a beautiful crystallization. Nobody stared at Sue, because she was so plainly dressed, which comforted Jude in the thought that only himself knew the charms those habiliments subdued. A matter of ten pounds spent in a drapery-shop, which had no connection with her real life or her real self, would have set all Melchester staring. The guard of the train thought they were lovers, and put them into a compartment all by themselves.

"That's a good intention wasted!" said she.

Jude did not respond. He thought the remark unnecessarily cruel, and partly untrue.

They reached the Park and Castle and wandered through the picture-galleries, Jude stopping by preference in front of the devotional pictures by Del Sarto, Guido Reni, Spagnoletto, Sassoferrato, Carlo Dolci, and others. Sue paused patiently beside him, and stole critical looks into his face as, regarding the Virgins, Holy Families, and Saints, it grew reverent and abstracted. When she had thoroughly estimated him at this, she would move on and wait for him before a Lely or Reynolds. It was evident that her cousin deeply interested her, as one might be interested in a man puzzling out his way along a labyrinth from which one had one's self escaped.

When they came out a long time still remained to them and Jude proposed that as soon as they had had something to eat they should walk across the high country to the north of their present position, and intercept the train of another railway leading back to Melchester, at a station about seven miles off. Sue, who was inclined for any adventure that would intensify the sense of her day's freedom, readily agreed; and away they went, leaving the adjoining station behind them.

It was indeed open country, wide and high. They talked and bounded on, Jude cutting from a little covert a long walking-stick for Sue as tall as herself, with a great crook which made her look like a shepherdess. About half-way on their journey they crossed a main road running due east and west—the old road from London to Land's End. They paused, and looked up and down it for a moment, and remarked upon the desolation which had come over this once lively thoroughfare, while the wind dipped to earth and scooped straws and hay-stems from the ground.

They crossed the road and passed on, but during the next half-mile Sue seemed to grow tired, and Jude began to be distressed for her. They had walked a good distance altogether, and if they could not reach the other station it would be rather awkward. For a long time there was no cottage visible on the wide expanse of down and turnip-land; but presently they came to a sheepfold, and next to the shepherd, pitching hurdles. He told them that the only house near was his mother's and his, pointing to a little dip ahead from which a faint blue smoke arose, and recommended them to go on and rest there.

This they did, and entered the house, admitted by an old woman without a single tooth, to whom they were as civil as strangers can be when their only chance of rest and shelter lies in the favour of the householder.

"A nice little cottage," said Jude.

"O, I don't know about the niceness. I shall have to thatch it soon, and where the thatch is to come from I can't tell, for straw do get that dear, that 'twill soon be cheaper to cover your house wi' chainey plates than thatch."

They sat resting, and the shepherd came in. "Don't 'ee mind I," he said with a deprecating wave of the hand; "bide here as long as ye will. But mid you be thinking o' getting back to Melchester to-night by train? Because you'll never do it in this world, since you don't know the lie of the country. I don't mind going with ye some o' the ways, but even then the train mid be gone."

They started up.

"You can bide here, you know, over the night—can't 'em, mother? The place is welcome to ye. 'Tis hard lying, rather, but volk may do worse." He turned to Jude and asked privately: "Be you a married couple?"

"Hsh—no!" said Jude.

"O—I meant nothing ba'dy—not I! Well then, she can go into mother's room, and you and I can lie in the outer chimmer after they've gone through. I can call ye soon enough to catch the first train back. You've lost this one now."

On consideration they decided to close with this offer, and drew up and shared with the shepherd and his mother the boiled bacon and greens for supper.

"I rather like this," said Sue, while their entertainers were clearing away the dishes. "Outside all laws except gravitation and germination."

"You only think you like it; you don't: you are quite a product of civilization," said Jude, a recollection of her engagement reviving his soreness a little.

"Indeed I am not, Jude. I like reading and all that, but I crave to get back to the life of my infancy and its freedom."

"Do you remember it so well? You seem to me to have nothing unconventional at all about you."

"O, haven't I! You don't know what's inside me."

"What?"

"The Ishmaelite."

"An urban miss is what you are."

She looked severe disagreement, and turned away.

The shepherd aroused them the next morning, as he had said. It was bright and clear, and the four miles to the train were accomplished pleasantly. When they had reached Melchester, and walked to the Close, and the gables of the old building in which she was again to be immured rose before Sue's eyes, she looked a little scared. "I expect I shall catch it!" she murmured.

They rang the great bell and waited.

"O, I bought something for you, which I had nearly forgotten," she said quickly, searching her pocket. "It is a new little photograph of me. Would you like it?"

"*Would* I!" He took it gladly, and the porter came. There seemed to be an ominous glance on his face when he opened the gate. She passed in, looking back at Jude, and waving her hand.

III

THE SEVENTY YOUNG WOMEN, OF AGES VARYING IN THE MAIN FROM NINETEEN TO ONE-and-twenty, though several were older, who at this date filled the species of nunnery known as the Training-School at Melchester, formed a very mixed community, which included the daughters of mechanics, curates, surgeons, shopkeepers, farmers, dairymen, soldiers, sailors, and villagers. They sat in the large school-room of the establishment on the evening previously described, and word was passed round that Sue Bridehead had not come in at closing-time.

"She went out with her young man," said a second-year's student, who knew about young men. "And Miss Traceley saw her at the station with him. She'll have it hot when she does come."

"She said he was her cousin," observed a youthful new girl.

"That excuse has been made a little too often in this school to be effectual in saving our souls," said the head girl of the year, drily.

The fact was that, only twelve months before, there had occurred a lamentable seduction of one of the pupils, who had made the same statement in order to gain meetings with her lover. The affair had created a scandal, and the management had consequently been rough on cousins ever since.

At nine o'clock the names were called, Sue's being pronounced three times sonorously by Miss Traceley without eliciting an answer.

At a quarter past nine the seventy stood up to sing the "Evening Hymn," and then knelt down to prayers. After prayers they went in to supper, and every girl's thought was, Where is Sue Bridehead? Some of the students, who had seen Jude from the window, felt that they would not mind risking her punishment for the pleasure of being kissed by such a kindly-faced young man. Hardly one among them believed in the cousinship.

Half an hour later they all lay in their cubicles, their tender feminine faces upturned to the flaring gas-jets which at intervals stretched down the long dormitories, every face bearing the legend "The Weaker" upon it, as the penalty of the sex wherein they were moulded, which by no possible exertion of their willing hearts and abilities could be made strong while the inexorable laws of nature remain what they are. They formed a pretty, suggestive, pathetic sight, of whose pathos and beauty they were themselves unconscious, and would not discover till, amid the storms and strains of after-years, with their injustice, loneliness, child-bearing, and bereavement, their minds would revert to this experience as to something which had been allowed to slip past them insufficiently regarded.

One of the mistresses came in to turn out the lights, and before doing so gave a final glance at Sue's cot, which remained empty, and at her little dressing-table at the foot, which, like all the rest, was ornamented with various girlish trifles, framed photographs being not the least conspicuous among them. Sue's table had a moderate show, two men in their filigree and velvet frames standing together beside her looking-glass.

"Who are these men—did she ever say?" asked the mistress. "Strictly speaking, relations' portraits only are allowed on these tables, you know."

"One—the middle-aged man," said a student in the next bed—"is the schoolmaster she served under—Mr. Phillotson."

"And the other—this undergraduate in cap and gown—who is he?"

"He is a friend, or was. She has never told his name."

"Was it either of these two who came for her?"

"No."

"You are sure 'twas not the undergraduate?"

"Quite. He was a young man with a black beard."

The lights were promptly extinguished, and till they fell asleep the girls indulged in conjectures about Sue, and wondered what games she had carried on in London and at Christminster before she came here, some of the more restless ones getting out of bed and looking from the mullioned windows at the vast west front of the Cathedral opposite, and the spire rising behind it.

When they awoke the next morning they glanced into Sue's nook, to find it still without a tenant. After the early lessons by gas-light, in half-toilet, and when they had come up to dress for breakfast, the bell of the entrance gate was heard to ring loudly. The mistress of the dormitory went away, and presently came back to say that the Principal's orders were that nobody was to speak to Bridehead without permission.

When, accordingly, Sue came into the dormitory to hastily tidy herself, looking flushed and tired, she went to her cubicle in silence, none of them coming out to greet her or to make inquiry. When they had gone downstairs they found that she did not follow them into the dining-hall to breakfast, and they then learnt that she had been severely reprimanded, and ordered to a solitary room for a week, there to be confined, and take her meals, and do all her reading.

At this the seventy murmured, the sentence being, they thought, too severe. A round robin was prepared and sent in to the Principal, asking for a remission of Sue's punishment. No notice was taken. Towards evening, when the geography mistress began dictating her subject, the girls in the class sat with folded arms.

"You mean that you are not going to work?" said the mistress at last. "I may as well tell you that it has been ascertained that the young man Bridehead stayed out with was not her cousin, for the very good reason that she has no such relative. We have written to Christminster to ascertain."

"We are willing to take her word," said the head girl.

"This young man was discharged from his work at Christminster for drunkenness and blasphemy in public-houses, and he has come here to live, entirely to be near her."

However, they remained stolid and motionless, and the mistress left the room to enquire from her superiors what was to be done.

Presently, towards dusk, the pupils, as they sat, heard exclamations from the first-year's girls in an adjoining class-room, and one rushed in to say that Sue Bridehead had got out of the back-window of the room in which she had been confined, escaped in the dark across the lawn, and disappeared. How she had managed to get out of the garden nobody could tell, as it was bounded by the river at the bottom, and the side-door was locked.

They went and looked at the empty room, the casement between the middle mullions of which stood open. The lawn was again searched with a lantern, every bush and shrub being examined, but she was nowhere hidden. Then the porter of the front gate was interrogated, and on reflection he said that he remembered hearing a sort of splashing in the stream at the back, but he had taken no notice, thinking some ducks had come down the river from above.

"She must have walked through the river!" said a mistress.

"Or drounded herself," said the porter.

The mind of the matron was horrified—not so much at the possible death of Sue as at the possible half-column detailing that event in all the newspapers, which, added to the scandal of the year before, would give the College an unenviable notoriety for many months to come.

More lanterns were procured, and the river examined; and then, at last, on the opposite shore, which was open to the fields, some little boot-tracks were discerned in the mud, which left no doubt that the too excitable girl had waded through a depth of water reaching nearly to her shoulders—for this was the chief river of the county, and was mentioned in all the geography books with respect. As Sue had not brought disgrace upon the school by drowning herself, the matron began to speak superciliously of her, and to express gladness that she was gone.

On the self-same evening Jude sat in his lodgings by the Close Gate. Often at this hour after dusk he would enter the silent Close, and stand opposite the house that contained Sue, and watch the shadows of the girls' heads passing to and fro upon the blinds, and wish he had nothing else to do but to sit reading and learning all day what many of the thoughtless inmates despised. But to-night, having finished tea and brushed himself up, he was deep in the perusal of the Twenty-ninth Volume of Pusey's Library of the Fathers, a set of books which he had purchased of a second-hand dealer at a price that seemed to him to be one of miraculous cheapness for that invaluable work. He fancied he heard something rattle lightly against his window; then he heard it again. Certainly somebody had thrown gravel. He rose and gently lifted the sash.

"Jude!" (from below).

"Sue!"

"Yes—it is! Can I come up without being seen?"

"O yes!"

"Then don't come down. Shut the window."

Jude waited, knowing that she could enter easily enough, the front-door being opened merely by a knob which anybody could turn, as in most old country towns. He palpitated at the thought that she had fled to him in her trouble as he had fled to her in his. What counterparts they were! He unlatched the door of his room, heard a stealthy rustle on the dark stairs, and in a moment she appeared in the light of his lamp. He went up to seize her hand, and found she was clammy as a marine deity, and that her clothes clung to her like the robes upon the figures in the Parthenon frieze.

"I'm so cold!" she said through her chattering teeth. "Can I come by your fire, Jude?"

She crossed to his little grate and very little fire, but as the water dripped from her as she moved, the idea of drying herself was absurd. "Whatever have you done, darling?" he asked, with alarm, the tender epithet slipping out unawares.

"Walked through the largest river in the county—that's what I've done! They locked me up for being out with you; and it seemed so unjust that I couldn't bear it, so I got out of the window and escaped across the stream!" She had begun the explanation in her usual slightly independent tones, but before she had finished the thin pink lips trembled, and she could hardly refrain from crying.

"Dear Sue!" he said. "You must take off all your things! And let me see—you must borrow some from the landlady. I'll ask her."

"No, no! Don't let her know, for God's sake! We are so near the school that they'll come after me!"

"Then you must put on mine. You don't mind?"

"O no."

"My Sunday suit, you know. It is close here." In fact, everything was close and handy in Jude's single chamber, because there was not room for it to be otherwise. He opened a drawer, took out his best dark suit, and giving the garments a shake, said, "Now, how long shall I give you?"

"Ten minutes."

Jude left the room and went into the street, where he walked up and down. A clock struck half-past seven, and he returned. Sitting in his only arm-chair he saw a slim and fragile being masquerading as himself on a Sunday, so pathetic in her defencelessness that his heart felt big with the sense of it. On two other chairs before the fire were her wet garments. She blushed as he sat down beside her, but only for a moment.

"I suppose, Jude, it is odd that you should see me like this and all my things hanging there? Yet what nonsense! They are only a woman's clothes—sexless cloth and linen. . . . I wish I didn't feel so ill and sick! Will you dry my clothes now? Please do, Jude, and I'll get a lodging by and by. It is not late yet."

"No, you shan't, if you are ill. You must stay here. Dear, dear Sue, what can I get for you?"

"I don't know! I can't help shivering. I wish I could get warm." Jude put on her his great-coat in addition, and then ran out to the nearest public-house, whence he returned with a little bottle in his hand. "Here's six of best brandy," he said. "Now you drink it, dear; all of it."

"I can't out of the bottle, can I?" Jude fetched the glass from the dressing-table, and administered the spirit in some water. She gasped a little, but gulped it down, and lay back in the arm-chair.

She then began to relate circumstantially her experiences since they had parted; but in the middle of her story her voice faltered, her head nodded, and she ceased. She was in a sound sleep. Jude, dying of anxiety lest she should have caught a chill which might permanently injure her, was glad to hear the regular breathing. He softly went nearer to her, and observed that a warm flush now rosed her hitherto blue cheeks, and felt that her hanging hand was no longer cold. Then he stood with his back to the fire regarding her, and saw in her almost a divinity.

IV

Jude's reverie was interrupted by the creak of footsteps ascending the stairs. He whisked Sue's clothing from the chair where it was drying, thrust it under the bed, and sat down to his book. Somebody knocked and opened the door immediately. It was the landlady.

"O, I didn't know whether you was in or not, Mr. Fawley. I wanted to know if you would require supper. I see you've a young gentleman—"

"Yes, ma'am. But I think I won't come down to-night. Will you bring supper up on a tray, and I'll have a cup of tea as well."

It was Jude's custom to go downstairs to the kitchen, and eat his meals with the family, to save trouble. His landlady brought up the supper, however, on this occasion, and he took it from her at the door.

When she had descended he set the tea-pot on the hob, and drew out Sue's clothes anew; but they were far from dry. A thick woollen gown, he found, held a deal of water. So he hung them up again, and kept up his fire and mused as the steam from the garments went up the chimney.

Suddenly she said, "Jude!"

"Yes. All right. How do you feel now?"

"Better. Quite well. Why, I fell asleep, didn't I? What time is it? Not late surely?"

"It is past ten."

"Is it really? What *shall* I do!" she said, starting up.

"Stay where you are."

"Yes; that's what I want to do. But I don't know what they would say! And what will you do?"

"I am going to sit here by the fire all night, and read. To-morrow is Sunday, and I haven't to go out anywhere. Perhaps you will be saved a severe illness by resting there. Don't be frightened. I'm all right. Look here, what I have got for you. Some supper."

When she had sat upright she breathed plaintively and said, "I do feel rather weak still. I thought I was well; and I ought not to be here, ought I?" But the supper fortified her somewhat, and when she had had some tea and had lain back again she was bright and cheerful.

The tea must have been green, or too long drawn, for she seemed preternaturally wakeful afterwards, though Jude, who had not taken any, began to feel heavy; till her conversation fixed his attention.

"You called me a creature of civilization, or something, didn't you?" she said, breaking a silence. "It was very odd you should have done that."

"Why?"

"Well, because it is provokingly wrong. I am a sort of negation of it."

"You are very philosophical. 'A negation' is profound talking."

"Is it? Do I strike you as being learned?" she asked, with a touch of raillery.

"No—not learned. Only you don't talk quite like a girl—well, a girl who has had no advantages."

"I have had advantages. I don't know Latin and Greek, though I know the grammars of those tongues. But I know most of the Greek and Latin classics through translations, and other books too. I read Lemprière, Catullus, Martial, Juvenal, Lucian, Beaumont and Fletcher, Boccaccio, Scarron, De Brantôme, Sterne, De Foe, Smollett, Fielding, Shakespeare, the Bible, and other such; and found that all interest in the unwholesome part of those books ended with its mystery."

"You have read more than I," he said with a sigh. "How came you to read some of those queerer ones?"

"Well," she said thoughtfully, "it was by accident. My life has been entirely shaped by what people call a peculiarity in me. I have no fear of men, as such, nor of their books. I have mixed with them—one or two of them particularly—almost as one of their own sex. I mean I have not felt about them as most women are taught to feel—to be on their guard against attacks on their virtue; for no average man—no man short of a sensual savage—will molest a woman by day or night, at home or abroad, unless she invites him. Until she says by a look 'Come on' he is always afraid to, and if you never say it, or look it, he never comes. However, what I was going to say is that when I was eighteen I formed a friendly intimacy with an undergraduate at Christminster, and he taught me a great deal, and lent me books which I should never have got hold of otherwise."

"Is your friendship broken off?"

"Oh yes. He died, poor fellow, two or three years after he had taken his degree and left Christminster."

"You saw a good deal of him, I suppose?"

"Yes. We used to go about together—on walking tours, reading tours, and things of that sort—like two men almost. He asked me to live with him, and I agreed to by letter. But when I joined him in London I found he meant a different thing from what I meant. He wanted to be my lover, in fact, but I wasn't in love with him—and on my saying I should go away if he didn't agree to my plan, he did so. We shared a sitting-room for fifteen months; and he became a leader-writer for one of the great London dailies; till he was taken ill, and had to go abroad. He said I was breaking his heart by holding out against him so long at such close quarters; he could never have believed it of woman. I might play that game once too often, he said. He came home merely to die. His death caused a terrible remorse in me for my cruelty—though I hope he died of consumption and not of me entirely. I went down to Sandbourne to his funeral, and was his only mourner. He left me a little money—because I broke his heart, I suppose. That's how men are—so much better than women!"

"Good heavens!—what did you do then?"

"Ah—now you are angry with me!" she said, a contralto note of tragedy coming suddenly into her silvery voice. "I wouldn't have told you if I had known!"

"No, I am not. Tell me all."

"Well, I invested his money, poor fellow, in a bubble scheme, and lost it. I lived about London by myself for some time, and then I returned to Christminster, as my father—who was also in London, and had started as an art metal-worker near Long-Acre—wouldn't have me back; and I got that occupation in the artist-shop where you found me. . . . I said you didn't know how bad I was!"

Jude looked round upon the arm-chair and its occupant, as if to read more carefully the creature he had given shelter to. His voice trembled as he said: "However you have lived, Sue, I believe you are as innocent as you are unconventional!"

"I am not particularly innocent, as you see, now that I have

> 'twitched the robe
> From that blank lay-figure your fancy draped,' "

said she, with an ostensible sneer, though he could hear that she was brimming with tears. "But I have never yielded myself to any lover, if that's what you mean! I have remained as I began."

"I quite believe you. But some women would not have remained as they began."

"Pehaps not. Better women would not. People say I must be cold-natured—sexless—on account of it. But I won't have it! Some of the most passionately erotic poets have been the most self-contained in their daily lives."

"Have you told Mr. Phillotson about this University-scholar-friend?"

"Yes—long ago. I have never made any secret of it to anybody."

"What did he say?"

"He did not pass any criticism—only said I was everything to him, whatever I did; and things like that."

Jude felt much depressed; she seemed to get further and further away from him with her strange ways and curious unconsciousness of gender.

"Aren't you *really* vexed with me, dear Jude?" she suddenly asked, in a voice of such extraordinary tenderness that it hardly seemed to come from the same woman who had just told her story so lightly. "I would rather offend anybody in the world than you, I think!"

"I don't know whether I am vexed or not. I know I care very much about you!"

"I care as much for you as for anybody I ever met."

"You don't care *more!* There, I ought not to say that. Don't answer it!"

There was another long silence. He felt that she was treating him cruelly, though he could not quite say in what way. Her very helplessness seemed to make her so much stronger than he.

"I am awfully ignorant on general matters, although I have worked so hard," he said, to turn the subject. "I am absorbed in Theology, you know. And what do you think I should be doing just about now, if you weren't here? I should be saying my evening prayers. I suppose you wouldn't like—"

"O no, no," she answered, "I would rather not, if you don't mind. I should seem so—such a hypocrite."

"I thought you wouldn't join, so I didn't propose it. You must remember that I hope to be a useful minister some day."

"To be ordained, I think you said?"

"Yes."

"Then you haven't given up the idea?—I thought that perhaps you had by this time."

"Of course not. I fondly thought at first that you felt as I do about that, as you were so steeped in Christminster. And Mr. Phillotson—"

"I have no respect for Christminster whatever, except, in a qualified degree, on its intellectual side," said Sue Bridehead earnestly. "My friend I spoke of took that out of me. He was the most irreligious man I ever knew, and the most moral. And intellect at Christminster is new wine in old bottles. The medievalism of Christminster must go, be sloughed off, or Christminster itself will have to go. To be sure, at times one couldn't help having a sneaking liking for the traditions of the old faith, as preserved by a section of the thinkers there in touching and simple sincerity; but when I was in my saddest, rightest mind I always felt,

> 'O ghastly glories of saints, dead limbs of gibbeted Gods!' "...

"Sue, you are not a good friend of mine to talk like that!"

"Then I won't, dear Jude!" The emotional throat-note had come back, and she turned her face away.

"I still think Christminster has much that is glorious; though I was resentful because I couldn't get there." He spoke gently, and resisted his impulse to pique her on to tears.

"It is an ignorant place, except as to the townspeople, artizans, drunkards, and paupers," she said, hurt still at his differing from her. "*They* see life as it is, of course; but few of the people in the colleges do. You prove it in your own person. You are one of the very men Christminster was intended for when the colleges were founded; a man with a passion for learning, but no money, or opportunities, or friends. But you were elbowed off the pavement by the millionaires' sons."

"Well, I can do without what it confers. I care for something higher."

"And I for something broader, truer," she insisted. "At present intellect in Christminster is pushing one way, and religion the other; and so they stand stock-still, like two rams butting each other."

"What would Mr. Phillotson—"

"It is a place full of fetichists and ghost-seers!"

He noticed that whenever he tried to speak of the schoolmaster she turned the conversation to some generalizations about the offending University. Jude was extremely, morbidly, curious about her life as Phillotson's *protegée* and betrothed; yet she would not enlighten him.

"Well, that's just what I am, too," he said. "I am fearful of life, spectre-seeing always."

"But you are good and dear!" she murmured.

His heart bumped, and he made no reply.

"You are in the Tractarian stage just now, are you not?" she added, putting on flippancy to hide real feeling, a common trick with her. "Let me see—when was I there? In the year eighteen hundred and—"

"There's a sarcasm in that which is rather unpleasant to me, Sue. Now will you do what I want you to? At this time I read a chapter, and then say prayers, as I told you. Now will you concentrate your attention on any book of these you like, and sit with your back to me, and leave me to my custom? You are sure you won't join me?"

"I'll look at you."

"No. Don't tease, Sue!"

"Very well—I'll do just as you bid me, and I won't vex you, Jude," she replied, in the tone of a child who was going to be good forever after, turning her back upon him accordingly. A small Bible other than the one he used lay near her, and during his retreat she took it up, and turned over the leaves.

"Jude," she said brightly, when he had finished and come back to her; "will you let me make you a *new* New Testament, like the one I made for myself at Christminster?"

"O yes. How was that made?"

"I altered my old one by cutting up all the Epistles and Gospels into separate *brochures*, and rearranging them in chronological order as written, beginning the book with Thessalonians, following on with the Epistles, and putting the Gospels much further on. Then I had the volume rebound. My University friend Mr.—but never mind his name, poor boy—said it was an excellent idea. I know that reading it afterwards made it twice as interesting as before, and twice as understandable."

"H'm!" said Jude, with a sense of sacrilege.

"And what a literary enormity this is," she said, as she glanced into the pages of Solomon's Song. "I mean the synopsis at the head of each chapter, explaining away the real nature of that rhapsody. You needn't be alarmed: nobody claims inspiration for the chapter headings. Indeed, many divines treat them with contempt. It seems the drollest thing to think of the four-and-twenty elders, or bishops, or whatever number they were, sitting with long faces and writing down such stuff."

Jude looked pained. "You are quite Voltairean!" he murmured.

"Indeed? Then I won't say any more, except that people have no right to falsify the Bible! I *hate* such humbug as could attempt to plaster over with ecclesiastical abstractions such ecstatic, natural, human love as lies in that great and passionate song!" Her speech had grown spirited, and almost petulant at his rebuke, and her eyes moist. "I *wish* I had a friend here to support me; but nobody is ever on my side!"

"But, my dear Sue, my very dear Sue, I am not against you!" he said, taking her hand, and surprised at her introducing personal feeling into mere argument.

"Yes you are, yes you are!" she cried, turning away her face that he might not see her brimming eyes. "You are on the side of the people in the Training-School—at least you seem almost to be! What I insist on is, that to explain such verses as this: 'Whither is thy beloved gone, O thou fairest among women?' by the note: *'The Church professeth her faith,'* is supremely ridiculous!"

"Well then, let it be! You make such a personal matter of everything! I am—only too inclined just now to apply the words profanely. You know *you* are fairest among women to me, come to that!"

"But you are not to say it now!" Sue replied, her voice changing to its softest note of severity. Then their eyes met, and they shook hands like cronies in a tavern, and Jude saw the absurdity of quarrelling on such a hypothetical subject, and she the silliness of crying about what was written in an old book like the Bible.

"I won't disturb your convictions—I really won't!" she went on soothingly, for now he was rather more ruffled than she. "But I did want and long to ennoble some man to high aims; and when I saw you, and knew you wanted to be my comrade, I—shall I confess it?—thought that man might be you. But you take so much tradition on trust that I don't know what to say."

"Well, dear; I suppose one must take some things on trust. Life isn't long enough to work out everything in Euclid problems before you believe it. I take Christianity."

"Well, perhaps you might take something worse."

"Indeed I might. Perhaps I have done so!" He thought of Arabella.

"I won't ask what, because we are going to be *very* nice with each other, aren't we, and never, never, vex each other any more?" She looked up trustfully, and her voice seemed trying to nestle in his breast.

"I shall always care for you!" said Jude.

"And I for you. Because you are single-hearted, and forgiving to your faulty and tiresome little Sue!"

He looked away, for that epicene tenderness of hers was too harrowing. Was it that which had broken the heart of the poor leader-writer; and was he to be the next one? . . . But Sue was so dear! . . . If he could only get over the sense of her sex, as she seemed to be able to do so easily of his, what a comrade she would make; for their difference of opinion on conjectural subjects only drew them closer together on matters of daily human experience. She was nearer to him than any other woman he had ever met, and he could scarcely believe that time, creed, or absence, would ever divide him from her.

But his grief at her incredulities returned. They sat on till she fell asleep again, and he nodded in his chair likewise. Whenever he aroused himself he turned her things, and made up the fire anew. About six o'clock he awoke completely, and lighting a candle, found that her clothes were dry. Her chair being a far more comfortable one than his she still slept on, inside his great-coat, looking warm as a new bun and boyish as a Ganymede. Placing the garments by her and touching her on the shoulder he went downstairs, and washed himself by starlight in the yard.

V

W HEN HE RETURNED SHE WAS DRESSED AS USUAL.

"Now could I get out without anybody seeing me?" she asked. "The town is not yet astir."

"But you have had no breakfast."

"O, I don't want any! I fear I ought not to have run away from that school! Things seem so different in the cold light of morning, don't they? What Mr. Phillotson will say I don't know! It was quite by his wish that I went there. He is the only man in the world for whom I have any respect or fear. I hope he'll forgive me; but he'll scold me dreadfully, I expect!"

"I'll go to him and explain—" began Jude.

"O no, you shan't. I don't care for him! He may think what he likes—I shall do just as I choose!"

"But you just this moment said—"

"Well, if I did, I shall do as I like for all him! I have thought of what I shall do—go to the sister of one of my fellow-students in the Training-School, who has asked me to visit her. She has a school near Shaston, about eighteen miles from here—and I shall stay there till this has blown over, and I get back to the Training-School again."

At the last moment he persuaded her to let him make her a cup of coffee, in a portable apparatus he kept in his room for use on rising to go to his work everyday before the household was astir.

"Now a dew-bit to eat with it," he said; "and off we go. You can have a regular breakfast when you get there."

They went quietly out of the house, Jude accompanying her to the station. As they departed along the street a head was softly thrust out of an upper-window, and quickly withdrawn. Sue still seemed sorry for her rashness, and to wish she had not rebelled; telling him at parting that she would let him know as soon as she got readmitted to the Training-School. They stood rather miserably together on the platform; and it was apparent that he wanted to say more.

"I want to tell you something—two things," he said hurriedly as the train came up. "One is a warm one, the other a cold one!"

"Jude," she said. "I know one of them. And you mustn't!"

"What?"

"You mustn't love me. You are to like me—that's all!"

Jude's face became so full of complicated glooms that hers was agitated in sympathy as she bade him adieu through the carriage-window. And then the train moved on, and waving her pretty hand to him she vanished away.

Melchester was a dismal place enough for Jude that Sunday of her departure, and the Close so hateful that he did not go once to the Cathedral services. The next morning there came a letter from her, which, with her usual promptitude, she had written directly she had reached her friend's house. She told him of her safe arrival and comfortable quarters, and then added:—

What I really write about, dear Jude, is something I said to you at parting. You had been so very good and kind to me that when you were out of sight I felt what a cruel and ungrateful woman I was to say it, and it has reproached me ever since. *If you want to love me, Jude, you may:* I don't mind at all; and I'll never say again that you mustn't!

Now I won't write any more about that. You do forgive your thoughtless friend for her cruelty? and won't make her miserable by saying you don't?—Ever,

SUE

It would be superfluous to say what his answer was; and how he thought what he would have done had he been free, which should have rendered a long residence with a female friend quite unnecessary for Sue. He felt he might have been pretty sure of his own victory, if it had come to a conflict between Phillotson and himself for the possession of her.

Yet Jude was in danger of attaching more meaning to Sue's impulsive note than it really was intended to bear.

After the lapse of a few days he found himself hoping that she would write again. But he received no further communication; and in the intensity of his solicitude he sent another note, suggesting that he should pay her a visit some Sunday, the distance being under eighteen miles.

He expected a reply on the second morning after despatching his missive; but none came. The third morning arrived; the postman did not stop. This was Saturday, and in a feverish state of anxiety about her he sent off three brief lines stating that he was coming the following day, for he felt sure something had happened.

His first and natural thought had been that she was ill from her immersion; but it soon occurred to him that somebody would have written for her in such a case. Conjectures were put an end to by his arrival at the village school-house near Shaston on the bright morning of Sunday, between eleven and twelve o'clock, when the parish was as vacant as a desert, most of the inhabitants having gathered inside the church, whence their voices could occasionally be heard in unison.

A little girl opened the door. "Miss Bridehead is upstairs," she said. "And will you please walk up to her?"

"Is she ill?" asked Jude hastily.

"Only a little—not very."

Jude entered and ascended. On reaching the landing a voice told him which way to turn—the voice of Sue calling his name. He passed the doorway, and found her lying in a little bed in a room a dozen feet square.

"O Sue!" he cried, sitting down beside her and taking her hand. "How is this! You couldn't write?"

"No—it wasn't that!" she answered. "I did catch a bad cold—but I could have written. Only I wouldn't!"

"Why not?—frightening me like this!"

"Yes—that was what I was afraid of! But I had decided not to write to you any more. They won't have me back at the school—that's why I couldn't write. Not the fact, but the reason!"

"Well?"

"They not only won't have me, but they gave me a parting piece of advice—"

"What?"

She did not answer directly. "I vowed I never would tell you, Jude—it is so vulgar and distressing!"

"Is it about us?"

"Yes."

"But do tell me!"

"Well—somebody has sent them baseless reports about us, and they say you and I ought to marry as soon as possible, for the sake of my reputation! . . . There—now I have told you, and I wish I hadn't!"

"O poor Sue!"

"I don't think of you like that means! It did just *occur* to me to regard you in the way they think I do, but I hadn't begun to. I *have* recognised that the cousinship was merely nominal, since we met as total strangers. But my marrying you, dear Jude—why, of course, if I had reckoned upon marrying you I shouldn't have come to you so often! And I never supposed you thought of such a thing as marrying me till the other evening; when I began to fancy you did love me a little. Perhaps I ought not to have been so intimate with you. It is all my fault. Everything is my fault always!"

The speech seemed a little forced and unreal, and they regarded each other with a mutual distress.

"I was so blind at first!" she went on. "I didn't see what you felt at all. O you have been unkind to me—you have—to look upon me as a sweetheart without saying a word, and leaving me to discover it myself! Your attitude to me has become known; and naturally they think we've been doing wrong! I'll never trust you again!"

"Yes, Sue," he said simply; "I am to blame—more than you think. I was quite aware that you did not suspect till within the last meeting or two what I was feeling about you. I admit that our meeting as strangers prevented a sense of relationship, and that it was a sort of subterfuge to avail myself of it. But don't you think I deserve a little consideration for concealing my wrong, very wrong, sentiments, since I couldn't help having them?"

She turned her eyes doubtfully towards him, and then looked away as if afraid she might forgive him.

By every law of nature and sex a kiss was the only rejoinder that fitted the mood and the moment, under the suasion of which Sue's undemonstrative regard of him might not inconceivably have changed its temperature. Some men would have cast scruples to the winds, and ventured it, oblivious both of Sue's declaration of her neutral feelings, and of the pair of autographs in the vestry chest of Arabella's parish church. Jude did not. He had, in fact, come in part to tell his own fatal story. It was upon his lips; yet at the hour of this distress he could not disclose it. He preferred to dwell upon the recognised barriers between them.

"Of course—I know you don't—care about me in any particular way," he said huskily. "You ought not, and you are right. You belong to—Mr. Phillotson. I suppose he has been to see you?"

"Yes," she said shortly, her face changing a little. "Though I didn't ask him to come. You are glad, of course, that he has been! But I shouldn't care if he didn't come any more!"

It was very perplexing to her lover that she should be piqued at his honest acquiescence in his rival, if Jude's feelings of love were deprecated by her. He went on to something else.

"This will blow over, dear Sue," he said. "The Training-School authorities are not all the world. You can get to be a student in some other, no doubt."

"I'll ask Mr. Phillotson," she said decisively.

Sue's kind hostess now returned from church, and there was no more intimate conversation. Jude left in the afternoon, hopelessly unhappy. But he had seen her, and sat with her. Such intercourse as that would have to content him for the remainder of his life. The lesson of renunciation it was necessary and proper that he, as a parish priest, should learn.

But the next morning when he awoke he felt rather vexed with her, and decided that she was rather unreasonable, not to say capricious. Then, in illustration of what he had begun to discern as one of her redeeming characteristics there came promptly a note, which she must have written almost immediately he had gone from her:

Forgive me for my petulance yesterday! I was horrid to you; I know it, and I feel perfectly miserable at my horridness. It was so dear of you not to be angry! Jude, please still keep me as your friend and associate, with all my faults. I'll try not to be like it again.

I am coming to Melchester on Saturday, to get my things away from the T.S., &c. I could walk with you for half an hour, if you would like?—Your repentant

                                                                                SUE

Jude forgave her straightway, and asked her to call for him at the Cathedral works when she came.

VI

MEANWHILE A MIDDLE-AGED MAN WAS DREAMING A DREAM OF GREAT BEAUTY CONcerning the writer of the above letter. He was Richard Phillotson, who had recently removed from the mixed village school at Lumsdon near Christminster, to undertake a large boys' school in his native town of Shaston, which stood on a hill sixty miles to the south-west as the crow flies.

A glance at the place and its accessories was almost enough to reveal that the schoolmaster's plans and dreams so long indulged in had been abandoned for some new dream with which neither the Church nor literature had much in common. Essentially an unpractical man, he was now bent on making and saving money for a practical purpose—that of keeping a wife, who, if she chose, might conduct one of the girls' schools adjoining his own; for which purpose he had advised her to go into training, since she would not marry him offhand.

About the time that Jude was removing from Marygreen to Melchester, and entering on adventures at the latter place with Sue, the schoolmaster was settling down in the new school-house at Shaston. All the furniture being fixed, the books shelved, and the nails driven, he had begun to sit in his parlour during the dark winter nights and reattempt some of his old studies—one branch of which had included Roman-Britannic antiquities—an unremunerative labour for a National schoolmaster, but a subject that, after his abandonment of the University scheme, had interested him as being a comparatively unworked mine; practicable to those who, like himself, had lived in lonely spots where these remains were abundant, and were seen to compel inferences in startling contrast to accepted views on the civilization of that time.

A resumption of this investigation was the outward and apparent hobby of Phillotson at present—his ostensible reason for going alone into fields where causeways, dykes, and tumuli abounded, or shutting himself up in his house with a few urns, tiles, and mosaics he had collected, instead of calling round upon his new neighbours, who for their part had showed themselves willing enough to be friendly with him. But it was not the real, or the whole, reason, after all. Thus on a particular evening in the month, when it had grown quite late—to near midnight, indeed—and the light of his lamp, shining from his window at a salient angle of the hill-top town over infinite miles of valley westward, announced as by words a place and person given over to study, he was not exactly studying.

The interior of the room—the books, the furniture, the schoolmaster's loose coat, his attitude at the table, even the flickering of the fire, bespoke the same dignified tale of undistracted research—more than creditable to a man who had had no advantages beyond those of his own making. And yet the tale, true enough till latterly, was not true now. What he was regarding was not history. They were historic notes, written in a bold womanly hand at his dictation some months before, and it was the clerical rendering of word after word that absorbed him.

He presently took from a drawer a carefully tied bundle of letters, few, very few, as correspondence counts now-a-days. Each was in its envelope just as it had arrived, and the handwriting was of the same womanly character as the historic notes. He unfolded them one by one and read them musingly. At first sight there seemed in these small documents to be absolutely nothing to muse over. They were straightforward, frank letters, signed "Sue B——"; just such ones as would be written during short absences, with no other thought than their speedy destruction, and chiefly concerning books in reading and other experiences of a Training-School, forgotten doubtless by the writer with the passing of the day of their inditing. In one of them—quite a recent note—the young woman said that she had received his considerate letter, and that it was honourable and generous of him to say he would not come to see her oftener than she desired (the school being such an awkward place for callers, and because of her strong wish that her engagement to him should not be known, which it would infallibly be if he visited her often). Over these phrases the schoolmaster pored. What precise shade of satisfaction was to be gathered from a woman's gratitude that the man who loved her had not been often to see her? The problem occupied him, distracted him.

He opened another drawer, and found therein an envelope, from which he drew a photograph of Sue as a child, long before he had known her, standing under trellis-work with a little basket in her hand. There was another of her as a young woman, her dark eyes and hair making a very distinct and attractive picture of her, which just disclosed, too, the thoughtfulness that lay behind her lighter moods. It was a duplicate of the one she had given Jude, and would have given to any man. Phillotson brought it half-way to his lips, but withdrew it in doubt at her perplexing phrases: ultimately kissing the dead pasteboard with all the passionateness, and more than all the devotion, of a young man of eighteen.

The schoolmaster's was an unhealthy-looking, old-fashioned face, rendered more old-fashioned by his style of shaving. A certain gentlemanliness had been imparted to it by nature, suggesting an inherent wish to do rightly by all. His speech was a little slow, but his tones were sincere enough to make his hesitation no defect. His greying hair was curly, and radiated from a point in the middle of his crown. There were four lines across his forehead, and he only wore spectacles when reading at night. It was almost certainly a renunciation forced upon him by his academic purpose, rather than a distaste for women, which had hitherto kept him from closing with one of the sex in matrimony.

Such silent proceedings as those of this evening were repeated many and oft times when he was not under the eye of the boys, whose quick and penetrating regard would frequently become almost intolerable to the self-conscious master in his present anxious care for Sue, making him, in the grey hours of morning, dread to meet anew the gimlet glances, lest they should read what the dream within him was.

He had honourably acquiesced in Sue's announced wish that he was not often to visit her at the Training-School; but at length, his patience being sorely tried, he set out one Saturday afternoon to pay her an unexpected call. There the news of her departure—expulsion as it might almost have been considered—was flashed upon him without warning or mitigation as he stood at the door expecting in a few minutes to behold her face; and when he turned away he could hardly see the road before him.

Sue had, in fact, never written a line to her suitor on the subject, although it was fourteen days old. A short reflection told him that this proved nothing, a natural delicacy being as ample a reason for silence as any degree of blameworthiness.

They had informed him at the school where she was living, and having no immediate anxiety about her comfort his thoughts took the direction of a burning indignation against the Training-School Committee. In his bewilderment Phillotson entered the adjacent Cathedral, just now in a direly dismantled state by reason of the repairs. He sat down on a block of freestone, regardless of the dusty imprint it made on his breeches; and his listless eyes following the movements of the workmen he presently became aware that the reputed culprit, Sue's lover Jude, was one amongst them.

Jude had never spoken to his former hero since the meeting by the model of Jerusalem. Having inadvertently witnessed Phillotson's tentative courtship of Sue in the lane there had grown up in the younger man's mind a curious dislike to think of the elder, to meet him, to communicate in any way with him; and since Phillotson's success in obtaining at least her promise had become known to Jude, he had frankly recognised that he did not wish to see or hear of his senior any more, learn anything of his pursuits, or even imagine again what excellencies might appertain to his character. On this very day of the schoolmaster's visit Jude was expecting Sue, as she had promised; and when therefore he saw the schoolmaster in the nave of the building; saw, moreover, that he was coming to speak to him, he felt no little embarrassment; which Phillotson's own embarrassment prevented his observing.

Jude joined him, and they both withdrew from the other workmen to the spot where Phillotson had been sitting. Jude offered him a piece of sackcloth for a cushion, and told him it was dangerous to sit on the bare block.

"Yes; yes," said Phillotson abstractedly, as he reseated himself, his eyes resting on the ground as if he were trying to remember where he was. "I won't keep you long. It was merely that I have heard that you have seen my little friend Sue recently. It occurred to me to speak to you on that account. I merely want to ask—about her."

"I think I know what!" Jude hurriedly said. "About her escaping from the Training-School, and her coming to me?"

"Yes."

"Well"—Jude for a moment felt an unprincipled and fiendish wish to annihilate his rival at all cost. By the exercise of that treachery which love for the same woman renders possible to men the most honourable in every other relation of life, he could send off Phillotson in agony and defeat by saying that the scandal was true, and that Sue had irretrievably committed herself with him. But his action did not respond for a moment to his animal instinct; and what he said was, "I am glad of your kindness in coming to talk plainly to me about it. You know what they say?—that I ought to marry her."

"What!"

"And I wish with all my soul I could!"

Phillotson trembled, and his naturally pale face acquired a corpselike sharpness in its lines. "I had no idea that it was of this nature! God forbid!"

"No, no!" said Jude aghast. "I thought you understood? I mean that were I in a position to marry her, or someone, and settle down, instead of living in lodgings here and there, I should be glad!"

What he had really meant was simply that he loved her.

"But—since this painful matter has been opened up—what really happened?" asked Phillotson, with the firmness of a man who felt that a sharp smart now was better than a long agony of suspense hereafter. "Cases arise, and this is one, when even ungenerous questions must be put to make false assumptions impossible, and to kill scandal."

Jude explained readily; giving the whole series of adventures, including the night at the shepherd's, her wet arrival at his lodging, her indisposition from her immersion, their vigil of discussion, and his seeing her off next morning.

"Well now," said Phillotson at the conclusion, "I take it as your final word, and I know I can believe you, that the suspicion which led to her rustication is an absolutely baseless one?"

"It is," said Jude solemnly. "Absolutely. So help me God!"

The schoolmaster rose. Each of the twain felt that the interview could not comfortably merge in a friendly discussion of their recent experiences, after the manner of friends; and when Jude had taken him round, and shown him some features of the renovation which the old cathedral was undergoing, Phillotson bade the young man good-day and went away.

This visit took place about eleven o'clock in the morning; but no Sue appeared. When Jude went to his dinner at one he saw his beloved ahead of him in the street leading up from the North Gate, walking as if in no way looking for him. Speedily overtaking her he remarked that he had asked her to come to him at the Cathedral, and she had promised.

"I have been to get my things from the College," she said—an observation which he was expected to take as an answer, though it was not one. Finding her to be in this evasive mood he felt inclined to give her the information so long withheld.

"You have not seen Mr. Phillotson to-day?" he ventured to enquire.

"I have not. But I am not going to be cross-examined about him; and if you ask anything more I won't answer!"

"It is very odd that—" He stopped, regarding her.

"What?"

"That you are never so nice in your real presence as you are in your letters!"

"Does it really seem so to you?" said she, smiling with quick curiosity. "Well, that's strange; but I feel just the same about you, Jude. When you are gone away I seem such a cold-hearted—"

As she knew his sentiment towards her Jude saw that they were getting upon dangerous ground. It was now, he thought, that he must speak as an honest man.

But he did not speak, and she continued: "It was that which made me write and say—I didn't mind your loving me—if you wanted to, much!"

The exultation he might have felt at what that implied, or seemed to imply, was nullified by his intention, and he rested rigid till he began: "I have never told you—"

"Yes you have," murmured she.

"I mean, I have never told you my history—all of it."

"But I guess it. I know nearly."

Jude looked up. Could she possibly know of that morning performance of his with Arabella; which in a few months had ceased to be a marriage more completely than by death? He saw that she did not.

"I can't quite tell you here in the street," he went on with a gloomy tongue. "And you had better not come to my lodgings. Let us go in here."

The building by which they stood was the market-house, it was the only place available; and they entered, the market being over, and the stalls and areas empty. He would have preferred a more congenial spot, but, as usually happens, in place of a romantic field or solemn aisle for his tale, it was told while they walked up and down over a floor littered with rotten cabbage-leaves, and amid all the usual squalors of decayed vegetable matter and unsaleable refuse. He began and finished his brief narrative, which merely led up to the information that he had married a wife some years earlier, and that his wife was living still. Almost before her countenance had time to change she hurried out the words:

"Why didn't you tell me before!"

"I couldn't. It seemed so cruel to tell it."

"To yourself, Jude. So it was better to be cruel to me!"

"No, dear darling!" cried Jude passionately. He tried to take her hand, but she withdrew it. Their old relations of confidence seemed suddenly to have ended, and the antagonisms of sex to sex were left without any counterpoising predilections. She was his comrade, friend, unconscious sweetheart no longer; and her eyes regarded him in estranged silence.

"I was ashamed of the episode in my life which brought about the marriage," he continued. "I can't explain it precisely now. I could have done it if you had taken it differently!"

"But how can I?" she burst out. "Here I have been saying, or writing, that—that you might love me, or something of the sort!—just out of charity—and all the time—O it is perfectly damnable how things are!" she said, stamping her foot in a nervous quiver.

"You take me wrong, Sue! I never thought you cared for me at all, till quite lately; so I felt it did not matter! Do you care for me, Sue?—you know how I mean?—I don't like 'out of charity' at all!"

It was a question which in the circumstances Sue did not choose to answer.

"I suppose she—your wife—is—a very pretty woman, even if she's wicked?" she asked quickly.

"She's pretty enough, as far as that goes."

"Prettier than I am, no doubt!"

"You are not the least alike. And I have never seen her for years. . . . But she's sure to come back—they always do!"

"How strange of you to stay apart from her like this!" said Sue, her trembling lip and lumpy throat belying her irony. "You, such a religious man. How will the demi-gods in your Pantheon—I mean those legendary persons you call Saints—intercede for you after this? Now if I had done such a thing it would have been different, and not remarkable, for I at least don't regard marriage as a Sacrament. Your theories are not so advanced as your practice!"

"Sue, you are terribly cutting when you like to be—a perfect Voltaire! But you must treat me as you will!"

When she saw how wretched he was she softened, and trying to blink away her sympathetic tears said with all the winning reproachfulness of a heart-hurt woman: "Ah—you should have told me before you gave me that idea that you wanted to be allowed to love me! I had no feeling before that moment at the railway-station, except—" For once Sue was as miserable as he, in her attempts to keep herself free from emotion, and her less than half-success.

"Don't cry, dear!" he implored.

"I am—not crying—because I love you; but because of your want of—confidence!"

They were quite screened from the market-square without, and he could not help putting out his arm towards her waist. His momentary desire was the means of her rallying. "No, no!" she said, drawing back stringently, and wiping her eyes. "Of course not! It would be hypocrisy to pretend that it would be meant as from my cousin; and it can't be in any other way."

They moved on a dozen paces, and she showed herself recovered. It was distracting to Jude, and his heart would have ached less had she appeared anyhow but as she did appear; essentially large-minded and generous on reflection, despite a previous exercise of those narrow womanly humours on impulse that were necessary to give her sex.

"I don't blame you for what you couldn't help," she said smiling. "How should I be so foolish! I do blame you a little bit for not telling me before. But after all it doesn't matter. We should have had to keep apart, you see, even if this had not been in your life."

"No, we shouldn't, Sue! This is the only obstacle."

"You forget that I must have loved you, and wanted to be your wife, even if there had been no obstacle," said Sue, with a gentle seriousness which did not reveal her mind. "And then we are cousins, and it is bad for cousins to marry. And—I am engaged to somebody else. As to our going on together as we were going, in a sort of friendly way, the people round us would have made it unable to continue. Their views of the relations of man and woman are limited, as is proved by their expelling me from the school. Their philosophy only recognises relations based on animal desire. The wide field of strong attachment where desire plays, at least, only a secondary part, is ignored by them—the part of—who is it?—Venus Urania."

Her being able to talk learnedly showed that she was mistress of herself again; and before they parted she had almost regained her vivacious glance, her reciprocity of tone, her gay manner, and her second-thought attitude of critical largeness towards others of her age and sex.

He could speak more freely now. "There were several reasons against my telling you rashly. One was what I have said; another, that it was always impressed upon me that I ought not to marry—that I belonged to an odd and peculiar family—the wrong breed for marriage."

"Ah—who used to say that to you?"

"My great-aunt. She said it always ended badly with us Fawleys."

"That's strange. My father used to say the same to me!"

They stood possessed by the same thought, ugly enough, even as an assumption: that a union between them, had such been possible, would have meant a terrible intensification of unfitness—two bitters in one dish.

"O but there can't be anything in it!" she said with nervous lightness. "Our family have been unlucky of late years in choosing mates—that's all."

And then they pretended to persuade themselves that all that had happened was of no consequence, and that they could still be cousins and friends and warm correspondents, and have happy genial times when they met, even if they met less frequently than before. Their parting was in good friendship, and yet Jude's last look into her eyes was tinged with inquiry, for he felt that he did not even now quite know her mind.

VII

TIDINGS FROM SUE A DAY OR TWO AFTER PASSED ACROSS JUDE LIKE A WITHERING BLAST.
Before reading the letter he was led to suspect that its contents were of a somewhat serious kind by catching sight of the signature—which was in her full name, never used in her correspondence with him since her first note:

MY DEAR JUDE—I have something to tell you which perhaps you will not be surprised to hear, though certainly it may strike you as being accelerated (as the railway companies say of their trains). Mr. Phillotson and I are to be married quite soon—in three or four weeks. We had intended, as you know, to wait till I had gone through my course of training and obtained my certificate, so as to assist him, if necessary, in the teaching. But he generously says he does not see any object in waiting, now I am not at the Training-School. It is so good of him, because the awkwardness of my situation has really come about by my fault in getting expelled.

Wish me joy. Remember I say you are to, and you mustn't refuse!—Your affectionate cousin,

SUSANNA FLORENCE MARY BRIDEHEAD

Jude staggered under the news; could eat no breakfast; and kept on drinking tea because his mouth was so dry. Then presently he went back to his work and laughed the usual bitter laugh of a man so confronted. Everything seemed turning to satire. And yet, what could the poor girl do? he asked himself: and felt worse than shedding tears.

"O Susanna Florence Mary!" he said as he worked. "You don't know what marriage means!"

Could it be possible that his announcement of his own marriage had pricked her on to this, just as his visit to her when in liquor may have pricked her on to her engagement? To be sure, there seemed to exist these other and sufficient reasons, practical and social, for her decision; but Sue was not a very practical or calculating person; and he was compelled to think that a pique at having his secret sprung upon her had moved her to give way to Phillotson's probable representations, that the best course to prove how unfounded were the suspicions of the school authorities would be to marry him offhand, as in fulfilment of an ordinary engagement. Sue had, in fact, been placed in an awkward corner. Poor Sue!

He determined to play the Spartan; to make the best of it, and support her; but he could not write the requested good wishes for a day or two. Meanwhile there came another note from his impatient little dear:

Jude, will you give me away? I have nobody else who could do it so conveniently as you, being the only married relation I have here on the spot, even if my father were friendly enough to be willing, which he isn't. I hope you won't think it a trouble? I have been looking at the marriage service in the Prayer-book, and it seems to me very humiliating that a giver-away should be required at all. According to the ceremony as there printed, my bridegroom chooses me of his own will and pleasure; but I don't choose him. Somebody *gives* me to him, like a she-ass or she-goat, or any other domestic animal. Bless your exalted views of woman, O Churchman! But I forget: I am no longer privileged to tease you.—Ever,

SUSANNA FLORENCE MARY BRIDEHEAD

Jude screwed himself up to heroic key; and replied:

MY DEAR SUE—Of course I wish you joy! And also of course I will give you away. What I suggest is that, as you have no house of your own, you do not marry from your school friend's, but from mine. It would be more proper, I think, since I am, as you say, the person nearest related to you in this part of the world.

I don't see why you sign your letter in such a new and terribly formal way? Surely you care a bit about me still!—Ever your affectionate,

JUDE

What had jarred on him even more than the signature was a little sting he had been silent on—the phrase "married relation"—What an idiot it made him seem as her lover! If Sue had written that in satire, he could hardly forgive her; if in suffering—ah, that was another thing!

His offer of his lodging must have commended itself to Phillotson at any rate, for the schoolmaster sent him a line of warm thanks, accepting the convenience. Sue also thanked him. Jude immediately moved into more commodious quarters, as much to escape the espionage of the suspicious landlady who had been one cause of Sue's unpleasant experience as for the sake of room.

Then Sue wrote to tell him the day fixed for the wedding; and Jude decided, after inquiry, that she should come into residence on the following Saturday, which would allow of a ten days' stay in the city prior to the ceremony, sufficiently representing a nominal residence of fifteen.

She arrived by the ten o'clock train on the day aforesaid, Jude not going to meet her at the station, by her special request, that he should not lose a morning's work and pay, she said (if this were her true reason). But so well by this time did he know Sue that the remembrance of their mutual sensitiveness at emotional crises might, he thought, have weighed with her in this. When he came home to dinner she had taken possession of her apartment.

She lived in the same house with him, but on a different floor, and they saw each other little, an occasional supper being the only meal they took together, when Sue's manner was something like that of a scared child. What she felt he did not know; their conversation was mechanical, though she did not look pale or ill. Phillotson came frequently, but mostly when Jude was absent. On the morning of the wedding, when Jude had given himself a holiday, Sue and her cousin had breakfast together for the first and last time during this curious interval; in his room—the parlour—which he had hired for the period of Sue's residence. Seeing, as women do, how helpless he was in making the place comfortable, she bustled about.

"What's the matter, Jude?" she said suddenly.

He was leaning with his elbows on the table and his chin on his hands, looking into a futurity which seemed to be sketched out on the table cloth.

"O—nothing!"

"You are 'father,' you know. That's what they call the man who gives you away."

Jude could have said "Phillotson's age entitles him to be called that!" But he would not annoy her by such a cheap retort.

She talked incessantly, as if she dreaded his indulgence in reflection, and before the meal was over both he and she wished they had not put such confidence in their new view of things, and had taken breakfast apart. What oppressed Jude was the thought that, having done a wrong thing of this sort himself, he was aiding and abetting the woman he loved in doing a like wrong thing, instead of imploring and warning her against it. It was on his tongue to say, "You have quite made up your mind?"

After breakfast they went out on an errand together moved by a mutual thought that it was the last opportunity they would have of indulging in unceremonious companionship. By the irony of fate, and the curious trick in Sue's nature of tempting Providence at critical times, she took his arm as they walked through the muddy street—a thing she had never done before in her life—and on turning the corner they found themselves close to a grey Perpendicular church with a low-pitched roof—the church of St. Thomas.

"That's the church," said Jude.

"Where I am going to be married?"

"Yes."

"Indeed!" she exclaimed with curiosity. "How I should like to go in and see what the spot is like where I am so soon to kneel and do it."

Again he said to himself, "She does not realise what marriage means!"

He passively acquiesced in her wish to go in, and they entered by the western door. The only person inside the gloomy building was a charwoman cleaning. Sue still held Jude's arm, almost as if she loved him. Cruelly sweet, indeed, she had been to him that morning; but his thoughts of a penance in store for her were tempered by an ache:

> *. . . I can find no way*
> *How a blow should fall, such as falls on men,*
> *Nor prove too much for your womanhood!*

They strolled undemonstratively up the nave towards the altar railing, which they stood against in silence, turning then and walking down the nave again, her hand still on his arm, precisely like a couple just married. The too suggestive incident, entirely of her making, nearly broke down Jude.

"I like to do things like this," she said in the delicate voice of an epicure in emotions, which left no doubt that she spoke the truth.

"I know you do!" said Jude.

"They are interesting, because they have probably never been done before. I shall walk down the church like this with my husband in about two hours, shan't I!"

"No doubt you will!"

"Was it like this when you were married?"

"Good God, Sue—don't be so awfully merciless! . . . There, dear one, I didn't mean it!"

"Ah—you are vexed!" she said regretfully, as she blinked away an access of eye moisture. "And I promised never to vex you! . . . I suppose I ought not to have asked you to bring me in here. Oh, I oughtn't! I see it now. My curiosity to hunt up a new sensation always leads me into these scrapes. Forgive me! . . . You will, won't you, Jude?"

The appeal was so remorseful that Jude's eyes were even wetter than hers as he pressed her hand for Yes.

"Now we'll hurry away, and I won't do it any more!" she continued humbly; and they came out of the building, Sue intending to go on to the station to meet Phillotson. But the first person they encountered on entering the main street was the schoolmaster himself, whose train had arrived sooner than Sue expected. There was nothing really to demur to in her leaning on Jude's arm; but she withdrew her hand; and Jude thought that Phillotson had looked surprised.

"We have been doing such a funny thing!" said she, smiling candidly. "We've been to the church, rehearsing as it were. Haven't we, Jude?"

"How?" said Phillotson curiously.

Jude inwardly deplored what he thought to be unnecessary frankness; but she had gone too far not to explain all, which she accordingly did, telling him how they had marched up to the altar.

Seeing how puzzled Phillotson seemed, Jude said as cheerfully as he could, "I am going to buy her another little present. Will you both come to the shop with me?"

"No," said Sue, "I'll go on to the house with him"; and requesting her lover not to be a long time she departed with the schoolmaster.

Jude soon joined them at his rooms, and shortly after they prepared for the ceremony. Phillotson's hair was brushed to a painful extent, and his shirt collar appeared stiffer than it had been for the previous twenty years. Beyond this he looked dignified and thoughtful, and altogether a man of whom it was not unsafe to predicate that he would make a kind and considerate husband. That he adored Sue was obvious; and she could almost be seen to feel that she was undeserving his adoration.

Although the distance was so short he had hired a fly from the Red Lion, and six or seven women and children had gathered by the door when they came out. The schoolmaster and Sue were unknown, though Jude was getting to be recognised as a citizen; and the couple were judged to be some relations of his from a distance, nobody supposing Sue to have been a recent pupil at the Training-School.

In the carriage Jude took from his pocket his extra little wedding-present, which turned out to be two or three yards of white tulle, which he threw over her bonnet and all, as a veil.

"It looks so odd over a bonnet," she said. "I'll take the bonnet off."

"O no—let it stay," said Phillotson. And she obeyed.

When they had passed up the church and were standing in their places Jude found that the antecedent visit had certainly taken off the edge of this performance, but by the time they were half-way on with the service he wished from his heart that he had not undertaken the business of giving her away. How could Sue have had the temerity to ask him to do it—a cruelty possibly to herself as well as to him? Women were different from men in such matters. Was it that they were, instead of more sensitive, as reputed, more callous, and less romantic; or were they more heroic? Or was Sue simply so perverse that she wilfully gave herself and him pain for the odd and mournful luxury of practising long-suffering in her own person, and of being touched with tender pity for him at having made him practise it? He could perceive that her face was nervously set, and when they reached the trying ordeal of Jude giving her to Phillotson she could hardly command herself; rather, however, as it seemed, from her knowledge of what her cousin must feel, whom she need not have had there at all, than from self consideration. Possibly she would go on inflicting such pains again and again, and grieving for the sufferer again and again, in all her colossal inconsistency.

Phillotson seemed not to notice, to be surrounded by a mist which prevented his seeing the emotions of others. As soon as they had signed their names and come away, and the suspense was over, Jude felt relieved.

The meal at his lodging was a very simple affair, and at two o'clock they went off. In crossing the pavement to the fly she looked back; and there was a frightened light in her eyes. Could it be that Sue had acted with such unusual foolishness as to plunge into she knew not what for the sake of asserting her independence of him, of retaliating on him for his secrecy? Perhaps Sue was thus venturesome with men because she was childishly ignorant of that side of their natures which wore out women's hearts and lives.

When her foot was on the carriage-step she turned round, saying that she had forgotten something. Jude and the landlady offered to get it.

"No," she said, running back. "It is my handkerchief. I know where I left it."

Jude followed her back. She had found it, and came holding it in her hand. She looked into his eyes with her own tearful ones, and her lips suddenly parted as if she were going to say something. But she went on; and whatever she had meant to say remained unspoken.

VIII

JUDE WONDERED IF SHE HAD REALLY LEFT HER HANDKERCHIEF BEHIND; OR WHETHER IT were that she had miserably wished to tell him of a love that at the last moment she could not bring herself to express.

He could not stay in his silent lodging when they were gone, and fearing that he might be tempted to drown his misery in alcohol he went upstairs, changed his dark clothes for his white, his thin boots for his thick, and proceeded to his customary work for the afternoon.

But in the cathedral he seemed to hear a voice behind him, and to be possessed with an idea that she would come back. She could not possibly go home with Phillotson, he fancied. The feeling grew and stirred. The moment that the clock struck the last of his working hours he threw down his tools and rushed homeward. "Has anybody been for me?" he asked.

Nobody had been there.

As he could claim the downstairs sitting-room till twelve o'clock that night he sat in it all the evening; and even when the clock had struck eleven, and the family had retired, he could not shake off the feeling that she would come back and sleep in the little room adjoining his own, in which she had slept so many previous days. Her actions were always unpredictable: why should she not come? Gladly would he have compounded for the denial of her as a sweetheart and wife by having her live thus as a fellow-lodger and friend, even on the most distant terms. His supper still remained spread; and going to the front-door, and softly setting it open, he returned to the room and sat as watchers sit on Old-Midsummer eves, expecting the phantom of the Beloved. But she did not come.

Having indulged in this wild hope he went upstairs, and looked out of the window, and pictured her through the evening journey to London, whither she and Phillotson had gone for their holiday; their rattling along through the damp night to their hotel, under the same sky of ribbed cloud as that he beheld, through which the moon showed its position rather than its shape, and one or two of the larger stars made themselves visible as faint nebulae only. It was a new beginning of Sue's history. He projected his mind into the future, and saw her with children more or less in her own likeness around her. But the consolation of regarding them as a continuation of her identity was denied to him, as to all such dreamers, by the wilfulness of Nature in not allowing issue from one parent alone. Every desired renewal of an existence is debased by being half alloy. "If at the estrangement or death of my lost love, I could go and see her child—hers solely—there would be comfort in it!" said Jude. And then he again uneasily saw, as he had latterly seen with more and more frequency, the scorn of Nature for man's finer emotions, and her lack of interest in his aspirations.

The oppressive strength of his affection for Sue showed itself on the morrow and following days yet more clearly. He could no longer endure the light of the Melchester lamps; the sunshine was as drab paint; and the blue sky as zinc. Then he received news that his old aunt was dangerously ill at Marygreen, which intelligence almost coincided with a letter from his former employer at Christminster, who offered him permanent work of a good class if he would come back. The letters were almost a relief to him. He started to visit Aunt Drusilla, and resolved to go onward to Christminster to see what worth there might be in the builder's offer.

Jude found his aunt even worse than the communication from the Widow Edlin had led him to expect. There was every possibility of her lingering on for weeks or months, though little likelihood. He wrote to Sue informing her of the state of her aunt, and suggesting that she might like to see her aged relative alive. He would meet her at Alfredston Road, the following evening, Monday, on his way back from Christminster, if she could come by the up-train which crossed his down-train at that station. Next morning, accordingly, he went on to Christminster, intending to return to Alfredston soon enough to keep the suggested appointment with Sue.

The city of learning wore an estranged look, and he had lost all feeling for its associations. Yet as the sun made vivid lights and shades of the mullioned architecture of the façades, and drew patterns of the crinkled battlements on the young turf of the quadrangles, Jude thought he had never seen the place look more beautiful. He came to the street in which he had first beheld Sue. The chair she had occupied when, leaning over her ecclesiastical scrolls, a hog-hair brush in her hand, her girlish figure had arrested the gaze of his inquiring eyes, stood precisely in its former spot, empty. It was as if she were dead, and nobody had been found capable of succeeding her in that artistic pursuit. Hers was now the City phantom, while those of the intellectual and devotional worthies who had once moved him to emotion were no longer able to assert their presence there.

However, here he was; and in fulfilment of his intention he went on to his former lodging in "Beersheba," near the ceremonial church of St. Silas. The old landlady who opened the door seemed glad to see him again, and bringing some lunch informed him that the builder who had employed him had called to enquire his address.

Jude went on to the stone-yard where he had worked. But the old sheds and bankers were distasteful to him; he felt it impossible to engage himself to return and stay in this place of vanished dreams. He longed for the hour of the homeward train to Alfredston, where he might probably meet Sue.

Then, for one ghastly half-hour of depression caused by these scenes, there returned upon him that feeling which had been his undoing more than once—that he was not worth the trouble of being taken care of either by himself or others; and during this half-hour he met Tinker Taylor, the bankrupt ecclesiastical ironmonger, at Fourways, who proposed that they should adjourn to a bar and drink together. They walked along the street till they stood before one of the great palpitating centres of Christminster life, the inn wherein he formerly had responded to the challenge to rehearse the Creed in Latin—now a popular tavern with a spacious and inviting entrance, which gave admittance to a bar that had been entirely renovated and refitted in modern style since Jude's residence here.

Tinker Taylor drank off his glass and departed, saying it was too stylish a place now for him to feel at home in, unless he was drunker than he had money to be just then. Jude was longer finishing his, and stood abstractedly silent in the almost empty place. The bar had been gutted and newly arranged throughout, mahogany fixtures having taken the place of the old painted ones, while at the back of the standing-space there were stuffed sofa-benches. The room was divided into compartments in the approved manner, between which were screens of ground glass in mahogany framing, to prevent topers in one compartment being put to the blush by the recognitions of those in the next. On the inside of the counter two barmaids leant over the white-handled beer-engines, and the row of little silvered taps inside, dripping into a pewter trough.

Feeling tired, and having nothing more to do till the train left, Jude sat down on one of the sofas. At the back of the barmaids rose bevel-edged mirrors, with glass shelves running along their front, on which stood precious liquids that Jude did not know the name of, in bottles of topaz, sapphire, ruby and amethyst. The moment was enlivened by the entrance of some customers into the next compartment, and the starting of the mechanical tell-tale of monies received, which emitted a ting-ting every time a coin was put in.

The barmaid attending to this compartment was invisible to Jude's direct glance, though a reflection of her back in the glass behind her was occasionally caught by his eyes. He had only observed this listlessly, when she turned her face for a moment to the glass to set her hair tidy. Then he was amazed to discover that the face was Arabella's.

If she had come on to his compartment she would have seen him. But she did not, this being presided over by the maiden on the other side. Abby was in a black gown, with white linen cuffs and a broad white collar, and her figure, more developed than formerly, was accentuated by a bunch of daffodils that she wore on her left bosom. In the compartment she served stood an electro-plated fountain of water over a spirit-lamp, whose blue flame sent a steam from the top, all this being visible to him only in the mirror behind her; which also reflected the faces of the men she was attending to—one of them a handsome, dissipated young fellow, possibly an undergraduate, who had been relating to her an experience of some humorous sort.

"O, Mr. Cockman, now! How can you tell such a tale to me in my innocence!" she cried gaily. "Mr. Cockman, what do you use to make your moustache curl so beautiful?" As the young man was clean shaven the retort provoked a laugh at his expense.

"Come!" said he, "I'll have a Curaçoa; and a light, please."

She served the liqueur from one of the lovely bottles, and striking a match held it to his cigarette while he whiffed.

"Well, have you heard from your husband lately, my dear?" he asked.

"Not a sound," said she.

"Where is he?"

"I left him in Australia; and I suppose he's there still."

Jude's eyes grew rounder.

"What made you part from him?"

"Don't you ask questions, and you won't hear lies."

"Come then, give me my change, which you've been keeping from me for the last quarter of an hour; and I'll romantically vanish up the street of this picturesque city."

She handed the change over the counter, in taking which he caught her fingers and held them. There was a slight struggle and titter, and he bade her good-bye and left.

Jude had looked on with the eye of a dazed philosopher. It was extraordinary how far removed from his life Arabella now seemed to be. He could not realise their nominal closeness. And, this being the case, in his present frame of mind he was indifferent to the fact that Arabella was his wife indeed.

The compartment that she served emptied itself of visitors, and after a brief thought he entered it, and went forward to the counter. Arabella did not recognise him for a moment. Then their glances met. She started; till a humorous impudence sparkled in her eyes, and she spoke.

"Well, I'm blest! I thought you were underground years ago!"

"Oh!"

"I never heard anything of you, or I don't know that I should have come here. But never mind! What shall I treat you to this afternoon? A Scotch and soda? Come, anything that the house will afford, for old acquaintance' sake!"

"Thanks, Arabella," said Jude without a smile. "But I don't want anything more than I've had." The fact was that her unexpected presence there had destroyed at a stroke his momentary taste for strong liquor as completely as if it had whisked him back to his milk-fed infancy.

"That's a pity, now you could get it for nothing."

"How long have you been here?"

"About six weeks. I returned from Sydney three months ago. I always liked this business, you know."

"I wonder you came to this place!"

"Well, as I say, I thought you were gone to glory, and being in London I saw the situation in an advertisement. Nobody was likely to know me here, even if I had minded, for I was never in Christminster in my growing up."

"Why did you return from Australia?"

"Oh, I had my reasons. . . . Then you are not a Don yet?"

"No."

"Not even a Reverend?"

"No."

"Nor so much as a Rather Reverend dissenting gentleman?"

"I am as I was."

"True—you look so." She idly allowed her fingers to rest on the pull of the beer-engine as she inspected him critically. He observed that her hands were smaller and whiter than when he had lived with her, and that on the hand which pulled the engine she wore an ornamental ring set with what seemed to be a real sapphire—which it was, indeed, and was much admired as such by the young men who frequented the bar.

"So you pass as married," he continued.

"Yes. I thought it might be awkward if I called myself a widow, as I should have liked."

"True. I am known here a little."

"I didn't mean on that account—for as I said I didn't expect you. It was for other reasons."

"What were they?"

"I don't care to go into them," she replied evasively. "I make a very good living, and I don't know that I want your company."

Here a chappie with no chin, and a moustache like a lady's eyebrow, came and asked for a curiously compounded drink, and Arabella was obliged to go and attend to him. "We can't talk here," she said, stepping back a moment. "Can't you wait till nine? Say yes, and don't be a fool. I can get off duty two hours sooner than usual, if I ask. I am not living in the house at present."

He reflected and said gloomily, "I'll come back. I suppose we'd better arrange something."

"O bother arranging! I'm not going to arrange anything!"

"But I must know a thing or two; and, as you say, we can't talk here. Very well; I'll call for you."

Depositing his unemptied glass he went out and walked up and down the street. Here was a rude flounce into the pellucid sentimentality of his sad attachment to Sue. Though Arabella's word was absolutely untrustworthy, he thought there might be some truth in her implication that she had not wished to disturb him, and had really supposed him dead. However, there was only one thing now to be done, and that was to play a straightforward part, the law being the law, and the woman between whom and himself there was no more unity than between east and west being in the eye of the Church one person with him.

Having to meet Arabella here, it was impossible to meet Sue at Alfredston as he had promised. At every thought of this a pang had gone through him; but the conjuncture could not be helped. Arabella was perhaps an intended intervention to punish him for his unauthorised love. Passing the evening, therefore, in a desultory waiting about the town wherein he avoided the precincts of every Cloister and Hall, because he could not bear to behold them, he repaired to the tavern bar while the hundred and one strokes were resounding from the Great Bell of Cardinal College, a coincidence which seemed to him gratuitous irony. The inn was now brilliantly lighted up, and the scene was altogether more brisk and gay. The faces of the barmaidens had risen in colour, each having a pink flush on her cheek; their manners were still more vivacious than before—more abandoned, more excited, more sensuous, and they expressed their sentiments and desires less euphemistically, laughing in a lackadaisical tone, without reserve.

The bar had been crowded with men of all sorts during the previous hour, and he had heard from without the hubbub of their voices; but the customers were fewer just now. He nodded to Arabella, and told her that she would find him outside the door when she came away.

"But you must have something with me first," she said with great good-humour. "Just an early nightcap: I always do. Then you can go out and wait a minute, as it is best we should not be seen going together." She drew a couple of liqueur glasses of brandy; and though she had evidently, from her countenance, already taken in enough alcohol either by drinking or, more probably, from the atmosphere she had breathed for so many hours, she finished hers quickly. He also drank his, and went outside the house.

In a few minutes she came, in a thick jacket and a hat with a black feather. "I live quite near," she said, taking his arm, "and can let myself in by a latch-key at any time. What arrangement do you want to come to?"

"O—none in particular," he answered, thoroughly sick and tired, his thoughts again reverting to Alfredston, and the train he did not go by; the probable disappointment of Sue that he was not there when she arrived, and the missed pleasure of her company on the long and lonely climb by starlight up the hills to Marygreen. "I ought to have gone back really! My aunt is on her deathbed, I fear."

"I'll go over with you to-morrow morning. I think I could get a day off."

There was something particularly uncongenial in the idea of Arabella, who had no more sympathy than a tigress with his relations or him, coming to the bedside of his dying aunt, and meeting Sue. Yet he said, "Of course, if you'd like to, you can."

"Well, that we'll consider. . . . Now, until we have come to some agreement it is awkward our being together here—where you are known, and I am getting known, though without any suspicion that I have anything to do with you. As we are going towards the station suppose we take the nine-forty train to Aldbrickham? We shall be there in little more than half an hour, and nobody will know us for one night, and we shall be quite free to act as we choose till we have made up our minds whether we'll make anything public or not."

"As you like."

"Then wait till I get two or three things. This is my lodging. Sometimes when late I sleep at the hotel where I am engaged, so nobody will think anything of my staying out."

She speedily returned, and they went on to the railway, and made the half-hour's journey to Aldbrickham, where they entered a third-rate inn near the station in time for a late supper.

IX

ON THE MORROW BETWEEN NINE AND HALF-PAST THEY WERE JOURNEYING BACK TO Christminster, the only two occupants of a compartment in a third-class railway-carriage. Having, like Jude, made rather a hasty toilet to catch the train, Arabella looked a little frowsy, and her face was very far from possessing the animation which had characterised it at the bar the night before. When they came out of the station she found that she still had half an hour to spare before she was due at the bar. They walked in silence a little way out of the town in the direction of Alfredston. Jude looked up the far highway.

"Ah . . . poor feeble me!" he murmured at last.

"What?" said she.

"This is the very road by which I came into Christminster years ago full of plans!"

"Well, whatever the road is I think my time is nearly up, as I have to be in the bar by eleven o'clock. And as I said, I shan't ask for the day to go with you to see your aunt. So perhaps we had better part here. I'd sooner not walk up Chief Street with you, since we've come to no conclusion at all."

"Very well. But you said when we were getting up this morning that you had something you wished to tell me before I left?"

"So I had—two things—one in particular. But you wouldn't promise to keep it a secret. I'll tell you now if you promise? As an honest woman I wish you to know it. . . . It was what I began telling you in the night—about that gentleman who managed the Sydney hotel." Arabella spoke somewhat hurriedly for her. "You'll keep it close?"

"Yes—yes—I promise!" said Jude impatiently. "Of course I don't want to reveal your secrets."

"Whenever I met him out for a walk, he used to say that he was much taken with my looks, and he kept pressing me to marry him. I never thought of coming back to England again; and being out there in Australia, with no home of my own after leaving my father, I at last agreed, and did."

"What—marry him?"

"Yes."

"Regularly—legally—in church?"

"Yes. And lived with him till shortly before I left. It was stupid, I know; but I did! There, now I've told you. Don't round upon me! He talks of coming back to England, poor old chap. But if he does, he won't be likely to find me."

Jude stood pale and fixed.

"Why the devil didn't you tell me last night!" he said.

"Well—I didn't. . . . Won't you make it up with me, then?"

"I have nothing more to say!" replied Jude with sternness. "I have nothing at all to say about the—crime—you've confessed to!"

"Crime! Pooh. They don't think much of such as that over there! Lots of 'em do it. . . . Well, if you take it like that I shall go back to him! He was very fond of me, and we lived honourable enough, and as respectable as any married couple in the Colony! How did I know where you were?"

"I won't go blaming you. I could say a good deal; but perhaps it would be misplaced. What do you wish me to do?"

"Nothing. There was one thing more I wanted to tell you; but I fancy we've seen enough of one another for the present! I shall think over what you said about your circumstances, and let you know."

Thus they parted. Jude watched her disappear in the direction of the hotel, and entered the railway-station close by. Finding that it wanted three-quarters of an hour of the time at which he could get a train back to Alfredston, he strolled mechanically into the city as far as to the Fourways, where he stood as he had so often stood before, and surveyed

Chief Street stretching ahead, with its college after college, in picturesqueness unrivalled except by such Continental vistas as the Street of Palaces in Genoa; the lines of the buildings being as distinct in the morning air as in an architectural drawing. But Jude was far from seeing or criticizing these things; they were hidden by an indescribable consciousness of Arabella's midnight contiguity, a sense of degradation at his revived experiences with her, of her appearance as she lay asleep at dawn, which set upon his motionless face a look as of one accurst. If he could only have felt resentment towards her he would have been less unhappy; but he pitied while he contemned her.

Jude turned and retraced his steps. Drawing again towards the station he started at hearing his name pronounced—less at the name than at the voice. To his great surprise no other than Sue stood like a vision before him—her look bodeful and anxious as in a dream, her little mouth nervous, and her strained eyes speaking reproachful inquiry.

"O Jude—I am so glad—to meet you like this!" she said in quick, uneven accents not far from a sob. Then she flushed as she observed his thought that they had not met since her marriage.

They looked away from each other to hide their emotion, took each other's hand without further speech, and went on together a while, till she glanced at him with furtive solicitude. "I arrived at Alfredston station last night, as you asked me to, and there was nobody to meet me! But I reached Marygreen alone, and they told me Aunt was a trifle better. I sat up with her, and as you did not come all night I was frightened about you—I thought that perhaps, when you found yourself back in the old city, you were upset at—at thinking I was—married, and not there as I used to be; and that you had nobody to speak to; so you had tried to drown your gloom!—as you did at that former time when you were disappointed about entering as a student, and had forgotten your promise to me that you never would again. And this, I thought, was why you hadn't come to meet me!"

"And you came to hunt me up, and deliver me, like a good angel!"

"I thought I would come by the morning train and try to find you—in case—in case—"

"I did think of my promise to you, dear, continually! I shall never break out again as I did, I am sure. I may have been doing nothing better, but I was not doing that—I loath the thought of it."

"I am glad your staying had nothing to do with that. But," she said, the faintest pout entering into her tone, "you didn't come back last night and meet me, as you engaged to!"

"I didn't—I am sorry to say. I had an appointment at nine o'clock—too late for me to catch the train that would have met yours, or to get home at all."

Looking at his loved-one as she appeared to him now, in his tender thought the sweetest and most disinterested comrade that he had ever had, living largely in vivid imaginings, so ethereal a creature that her spirit could be seen trembling through her limbs, he felt heartily ashamed of his earthliness in spending the hours he had spent in Arabella's company. There was something rude and immoral in thrusting these recent facts of his life upon the mind of one who, to him, was so uncarnate as to seem at times impossible as a human wife to any average man. And yet she was Phillotson's. How she had become such, how she lived as such, passed his comprehension as he regarded her to-day.

"You'll go back with me?" he said. "There's a train just now. I wonder how my aunt is by this time. . . . And so, Sue, you really came on my account all this way! At what an early time you must have started, poor thing!"

"Yes. Sitting up watching alone made me all nerves for you, and instead of going to bed when it got light I started. And now you won't frighten me like this again about your morals for nothing?"

He was not so sure that she had been frightened about his morals for nothing. He released her hand till they had entered the train—it seemed the same carriage he had lately got out of with another—where they sat down side by side, Sue between him and the window. He regarded the delicate lines of her profile, and the small, tight, applelike curves of her bodice, so different from Arabella's amplitudes. Though she knew he was looking at her she did not turn to him, but kept her eyes forward, as if afraid that by meeting his own some troublous discussion would be initiated.

"Sue—you are married now, you know, like me; and yet we have been in such a hurry that we have not said a word about it!"

"There's no necessity," she quickly returned.

"O well—perhaps not. . . . But I wish"

"Jude—don't talk about *me*—I wish you wouldn't!" she entreated. "It distresses me, rather. Forgive my saying it! . . . Where did you stay last night?"

She had asked the question in perfect innocence, to change the topic. He knew that, and said merely, "At an inn," though it would have been a relief to tell her of his meeting with an unexpected one. But the latter's final announcement of her marriage in Australia bewildered him lest what he might say should do his ignorant wife an injury.

Their talk proceeded but awkwardly till they reached Alfredston. That Sue was not as she had been, but was labelled "Phillotson," paralyzed Jude whenever he wanted to commune with her as an individual. Yet she seemed unaltered—he could not say why. There remained the five-mile extra journey into the country, which it was just as easy to walk as to drive, the greater part of it being up-hill. Jude had never before in his life gone that road with Sue, though he had with another. It was now as if he carried a bright light which temporarily banished the shady associations of the earlier time.

Sue talked; but Jude noticed that she still kept the conversation from herself. At length he enquired if her husband were well.

"O yes," she said. "He is obliged to be in the school all the day, or he would have come with me. He is so good and kind that to accompany me he would have dismissed the school for a day, even against his principles—for he is strongly opposed to giving casual holidays—only I wouldn't let him. I felt it would be better to come alone. Aunt Drusilla, I knew, was so very eccentric; and his being almost a stranger to her now would have made it irksome to both. Since it turns out that she is hardly conscious I am glad I did not ask him."

Jude had walked moodily while this praise of Phillotson was being expressed. "Mr. Phillotson obliges you in everything, as he ought," he said.

"Of course."

"You ought to be a happy wife."

"And of course I am."

"Bride, I might almost have said, as yet. It is not so many weeks since I gave you to him, and—"

"Yes, I know! I know!" There was something in her face which belied her late assuring words, so strictly proper and so lifelessly spoken that they might have been taken from a list of model speeches in "The Wife's Guide to Conduct." Jude knew the quality of every vibration in Sue's voice, could read every symptom of her mental condition; and he was convinced that she was unhappy, although she had not been a month married. But her rushing away thus from home, to see the last of a relative whom she had hardly known in her life, proved nothing; for Sue naturally did such things as those.

"Well, you have my good wishes now as always, Mrs. Phillotson."

She reproached him by a glance.

"No, you are not Mrs. Phillotson," murmured Jude. "You are dear, free Sue Bride-head, only you don't know it! Wifedom has not yet squashed up and digested you in its vast maw as an atom which has no further individuality."

Sue put on a look of being offended, till she answered, "Nor has husbandom you, so far as I can see!"

"But it has!" he said, shaking his head sadly.

When they reached the lone cottage under the firs, between the Brown House and Marygreen, in which Jude and Arabella had lived and quarrelled, he turned to look at it. A squalid family lived there now. He could not help saying to Sue: "That's the house my wife and I occupied the whole of the time we lived together. I brought her home to that house."

She looked at it. "That to you was what the school-house at Shaston is to me."

"Yes; but I was not very happy there, as you are in yours."

She closed her lips in retortive silence, and they walked some way till she glanced at him to see how he was taking it. "Of course I may have exaggerated your happiness—one never knows," he continued blandly.

"Don't think that, Jude, for a moment, even though you may have said it to sting me! He's as good to me as a man can be, and gives me perfect liberty—which elderly husbands don't do in general. . . . If you think I am not happy because he's too old for me, you are wrong."

"I don't think anything against him—to you, dear."

"And you won't say things to distress me, will you?"

"I will not."

He said no more, but he knew that, from some cause or other, in taking Phillotson as a husband, Sue felt that she had done what she ought not to have done.

They plunged into the concave field on the other side of which rose the village—the field wherein Jude had received a thrashing from the farmer many years earlier. On ascending to the village and approaching the house they found Mrs. Edlin standing at the door, who at sight of them lifted her hands deprecatingly. "She's downstairs, if you'll believe me!" cried the widow. "Out o' bed she got, and nothing could turn her. What will come o't I do not know!"

On entering, there indeed by the fireplace sat the old woman, wrapped in blankets, and turning upon them a countenance like that of Sebastiano's Lazarus. They must have looked their amazement, for she said in a hollow voice:

"Ah—sceered ye, have I! I wasn't going to bide up there no longer, to please nobody! 'Tis more than flesh and blood can bear, to be ordered to do this and that by a feller that don't know half as well as you do yourself! . . . Ah—you'll rue this marrying as well as he!" she added, turning to Sue. "All our family do—and nearly all everybody else's. You should have done as I did, you simpleton! And Phillotson the schoolmaster, of all men! What made 'ee marry him?"

"What makes most women marry, aunt?"

"Ah! You mean to say you loved the man!"

"I don't meant to say anything definite."

"Do ye love un?"

"Don't ask me, aunt."

"I can mind the man very well. A very civil, honourable liver; but Lord!—I don't want to wownd your feelings, but—there be certain men here and there that no woman of any niceness can stomach. I should have said he was one. I don't say so *now*, since you must ha' known better than I—but that's what I *should* have said!"

Sue jumped up and went out. Jude followed her, and found her in the outhouse, crying.

"Don't cry, dear!" said Jude in distress. "She means well, but is very crusty and queer now, you know."

"O no—it isn't that!" said Sue, trying to dry her eyes. "I don't mind her roughness one bit."

"What is it, then?"

"It is that what she says is—is true!"

"God—what—you don't like him?" asked Jude.

"I don't mean that!" she said hastily. "That I ought—perhaps I ought not to have married!"

He wondered if she had really been going to say that at first. They went back, and the subject was smoothed over, and her aunt took rather kindly to Sue, telling her that not many young women newly married would have come so far to see a sick old crone like her. In the afternoon Sue prepared to depart, Jude hiring a neighbour to drive her to Alfredston.

"I'll go with you to the station, if you'd like?" he said.

She would not let him. The man came round with the trap, and Jude helped her into it, perhaps with unnecessary attention, for she looked at him prohibitively.

"I suppose—I may come to see you some day, when I am back again at Melchester?" he half-crossly observed.

She bent down and said softly: "No, dear—you are not to come yet. I don't think you are in a good mood."

"Very well," said Jude. "Good-bye!"

"Good-bye!" She waved her hand and was gone.

"She's right! I won't go!" he murmured.

He passed the evening and following days in mortifying by every possible means his wish to see her, nearly starving himself in attempts to extinguish by fasting his passionate tendency to love her. He read sermons on discipline; and hunted up passages in Church history that treated of the Ascetics of the second century. Before he had returned from Marygreen to Melchester there arrived a letter from Arabella. The sight of it revived a stronger feeling of self-condemnation for his brief return to her society than for his attachment to Sue.

The letter, he perceived, bore a London postmark instead of the Christminster one. Arabella informed him that a few days after their parting in the morning at Christminster, she had been surprised by an affectionate letter from her Australian husband, formerly manager of the hotel in Sydney. He had come to England on purpose to find her; and had taken a free, fully-licensed public, in Lambeth, where he wished her to join him in conducting the business, which was likely to be a very thriving one, the house being situated in an excellent, densely populated, gin-drinking neighbourhood, and already doing a trade of £200 a month, which could be easily doubled.

As he had said that he loved her very much still, and implored her to tell him where she was, and as they had only parted in a slight tiff, and as her engagement in Christminster was only temporary, she had just gone to join him as he urged. She could not help feeling that she belonged to him more than to Jude, since she had properly married him, and had lived with him much longer than with her first husband. In thus wishing Jude goodbye she bore him no ill-will, and trusted he would not turn upon her, a weak woman, and inform against her, and bring her to ruin now that she had a chance of improving her circumstances and leading a genteel life.

X

JUDE RETURNED TO MELCHESTER, WHICH HAD THE QUESTIONABLE RECOMMENDATION OF being only a dozen and a half miles from his Sue's now permanent residence. At first he felt that this nearness was a distinct reason for not going southward at all; but Christminster was too sad a place to bear, while the proximity of Shaston to Melchester might afford him the glory of worsting the Enemy in a close engagement, such as was deliberately sought by the priests and virgins of the early Church, who, disdaining an ignominious flight from temptation, became even chamber-partners with impunity. Jude did not pause to remember that, in the laconic words of the historian, "insulted Nature sometimes vindicated her rights" in such circumstances.

He now returned with feverish desperation to his study for the priesthood—in the recognition that the single-mindedness of his aims, and his fidelity to the cause, had been more than questionable of late. His passion for Sue troubled his soul; yet his abandonment to the society of Arabella for twelve hours seemed instinctively a worse thing—even though she had not told him of her Sydney husband till afterwards. He had, he verily believed, overcome all tendency to fly to liquor—which, indeed, he had never done from taste, but merely as an escape from intolerable misery of mind. Yet he perceived with despondency that, taken all round, he was a man of too many passions to make a good clergyman; the utmost he could hope for was that in a life of constant internal warfare between flesh and spirit the former might not always be victorious.

As a hobby, auxiliary to his readings in Divinity, he developed his slight skill in church-music and thorough-bass, till he could join in part-singing from notation with some accuracy. A mile or two from Melchester there was a restored village church, to which Jude had originally gone to fix the new columns and capitals. By this means he had become acquainted with the organist, and the ultimate result was that he joined the choir as a bass voice.

He walked out to this parish twice every Sunday, and sometimes in the week. One evening about Easter the choir met for practice, and a new hymn which Jude had heard of as being by a Wessex composer was to be tried and prepared for the following week. It turned out to be a strangely emotional composition. As they all sang it over and over again its harmonies grew upon Jude, and moved him exceedingly.

When they had finished he went round to the organist to make inquiries. The score was in manuscript, the name of the composer being at the head, together with the title of the hymn: "The Foot of the Cross."

"Yes," said the organist. "He is a local man. He is a professional musician at Kennetbridge—between here and Christminster. The vicar knows him. He was brought up and educated in Christminster traditions, which accounts for the quality of the piece. I think he plays in the large church there, and has a surpliced choir. He comes to Melchester sometimes, and once tried to get the Cathedral organ when the post was vacant. The hymn is getting about everywhere this Easter."

As he walked, humming the air, on his way home, Jude fell to musing on its composer, and the reasons why he composed it. What a man of sympathies he must be! Perplexed and harassed as he himself was about Sue, and Arabella, and troubled as was his conscience by the complication of his position, how he would like to know that man! "He of all men would understand my difficulties," said the impulsive Jude. If there were any person in the world to choose as a confidant, this composer would be the one, for he must have suffered, and throbbed, and yearned.

In brief, ill as he could afford the time and money for the journey, Fawley resolved, like the child that he was, to go to Kennetbridge the very next Sunday. He duly started, early in the morning, for it was only by a series of crooked railways that he could get to the town. About mid-day he reached it, and crossing the bridge into the quaint old borough he enquired for the house of the composer.

They told him it was a red brick building some little way further on. Also that the gentleman himself had just passed along the street not five minutes before.

"Which way?" asked Jude with alacrity.

"Straight along homeward from church."

Jude hastened on, and soon had the pleasure of observing a man in a black coat and a black slouched felt hat no considerable distance ahead. Stretching out his legs yet more widely he stalked after. "A hungry soul in pursuit of a full soul!" he said. "I must speak to that man!"

He could not, however, overtake the musician before he had entered his own house, and then arose the question if this were an expedient time to call. Whether or not he decided to do so there and then, now that he had got here, the distance home being too great for him to wait till late in the afternoon. This man of soul would understand scant ceremony, and might be quite a perfect adviser in a case in which an earthly and illegitimate passion had cunningly obtained entrance into his heart through the opening afforded for religion.

Jude accordingly rang the bell, and was admitted.

The musician came to him in a moment, and being respectably dressed, good-looking, and frank in manner, Jude obtained a favourable reception. He was nevertheless conscious that there would be a certain awkwardness in explaining his errand.

"I have been singing in the choir of a little church near Melchester," he said. "And we have this week practised 'The Foot of the Cross,' which I understand, sir, that you composed?"

"I did—a year or so ago."

"I—like it. I think it supremely beautiful!"

"Ah well—other people have said so too. Yes, there's money in it, if I could only see about getting it published. I have other compositions to go with it, too; I wish I could bring them out; for I haven't made a five-pound note out of any of them yet. These publishing people—they want the copyright of an obscure composer's work, such as mine is, for almost less than I should have to pay a person for making a fair manuscript copy of the score. The one you speak of I have lent to various friends about here and Melchester, and so it has got to be sung a little. But music is a poor staff to lean on—I am giving it up entirely. You must go into trade if you want to make money now-a-days. The wine business is what I am thinking of. This is my forthcoming list—it is not issued yet—but you can take one."

He handed Jude an advertisement list of several pages in booklet shape, ornamentally margined with a red line, in which were set forth the various clarets, champagnes, ports, sherries, and other wines with which he purposed to initiate his new venture. It took Jude rather by surprise that the man with the soul was thus and thus; and he felt that he could not open up his confidences.

They talked a little longer, but constrainedly, for when the musician found that Jude was a poor man his manner changed from what it had been while Jude's appearance and address deceived him as to his position and pursuits. Jude stammered out something about his feelings in wishing to congratulate the author on such an exalted composition, and took an embarrassed leave.

All the way home by the slow Sunday train, sitting in the fireless waiting-rooms on this cold spring day, he was depressed enough at his simplicity in taking such a journey. But no sooner did he reach his Melchester lodging than he found awaiting him a letter which had arrived that morning a few minutes after he had left the house. It was a contrite little note from Sue, in which she said, with sweet humility, that she felt she had been horrid in telling him he was not to come to see her; that she despised herself for having been so conventional; and that he was to be sure to come by the eleven-forty-five train that very Sunday, and have dinner with them at half-past one.

Jude almost tore his hair at having missed this letter till it was too late to act upon its contents; but he had chastened himself considerably of late, and at last his chimerical expedition to Kennetbridge really did seem to have been another special intervention of Providence to keep him away from temptation. But a growing impatience of faith, which he had noticed in himself more than once of late, made him pass over in ridicule the idea that God sent people on fools' errands. He longed to see her; he was angry at having missed her: and he wrote instantly, telling her what had happened, and saying he had not enough patience to wait till the following Sunday, but would come any day in the week that she liked to name.

Since he wrote a little over-ardently, Sue, as her manner was, delayed her reply till Thursday before Good Friday, when she said he might come that afternoon if he wished, this being the earliest day on which she could welcome him, for she was now assistant-teacher in her husband's school. Jude therefore got leave from the Cathedral works at the trifling expense of a stoppage of pay, and went.

PART FOURTH

AT SHASTON

"Whoso prefers either Matrimony or other Ordinance before the Good of Man and the plain Exigence of Charity, let him profess Papist, or Protestant, or what he will, he is no better than a Pharisee."

—J. MILTON

I

S HASTON, THE ANCIENT BRITISH PALLADOUR,

From whose foundation first such strange reports arise,

(as Drayton sang it), was, and is, in itself the city of a dream. Vague imaginings of its castle, its three mints, its magnificent apsidal Abbey, the chief glory of South Wessex, its twelve churches, its shrines, chantries, hospitals, its gabled freestone mansions—all now ruthlessly swept away—throw the visitor, even against his will, into a pensive melancholy, which the stimulating atmosphere and limitless landscape around him can scarcely dispel. The spot was the burial-place of a king and a queen, of abbots and abbesses, saints and bishops, knights and squires. The bones of King Edward "the Martyr," carefully removed hither for holy preservation, brought Shaston a renown which made it the resort of pilgrims from every part of Europe, and enabled it to maintain a reputation extending far beyond English shores. To this fair creation of the great Middle-Age the Dissolution was, as historians tell us, the death-knell. With the destruction of the enormous abbey the whole place collapsed in a general ruin: the Martyr's bones met with the fate of the sacred pile that held them, and not a stone is now left to tell where they lie.

The natural picturesqueness and singularity of the town still remain; but strange to say these qualities, which were noted by many writers in ages when scenic beauty is said to have been unappreciated, are passed over in this, and one of the queerest and quaintest spots in England stands virtually unvisited to-day.

It has a unique position on the summit of an almost perpendicular scarp, rising on the north, south, and west sides of the borough out of the deep alluvial Vale of Blackmoor, the view from the Castle Green over three counties of verdant pasture—South, Mid, and Nether Wessex—being as sudden a surprise to the unexpectant traveller's eyes as the medicinal air is to his lungs. Impossible to a railway, it can best be reached on foot, next best by light vehicles; and it is hardly accessible to these but by a sort of isthmus on the northeast, that connects it with the high chalk table-land on that side.

Such is, and such was, the now world-forgotten Shaston or Palladour. Its situation rendered water the great want of the town; and within living memory, horses, donkeys and men may have been seen toiling up the winding ways to the top of the steep, laden with tubs and barrels filled from the wells beneath the mountain, and hawkers retailing their contents at the price of a halfpenny a bucketful.

This difficulty in the water supply, together with two other odd facts, namely, that the chief graveyard slopes up as steeply as a roof behind the church, and that in former times the town passed through a curious period of corruption, conventual and domestic, gave rise to the saying that Shaston was remarkable for three consolations to man, such as the world afforded not elsewhere. It was a place where the churchyard lay nearer heaven than the church steeple, where beer was more plentiful than water, and where there were more wanton women than honest wives and maids. It is also said that after the middle ages the inhabitants were too poor to pay their priests, and hence were compelled to pull down their churches, and refrain altogether from the public worship of God; a necessity which they bemoaned over their cups in the settles of their inns on Sunday afternoons. In those days the Shastonians were apparently not without a sense of humour.

There was another peculiarity—this a modern one—which Shaston appeared to owe to its site. It was the resting-place and head-quarters of the proprietors of wandering vans, shows, shooting-galleries, and other itinerant concerns, whose business lay largely at fairs and markets. As strange wild birds are seen assembled on some lofty promontory, meditatively pausing for longer flights, or to return by the course they followed thither, so here, in this cliff-town, stood in stultified silence the yellow and green caravans bearing names not local, as if surprised by a change in the landscape so violent as to hinder their further progress; and here they usually remained all the winter till they turned to seek again their old tracks in the following spring.

It was to this breezy and whimsical spot that Jude ascended from the nearest station for the first time in his life about four o'clock one afternoon, and entering on the summit of the peak after a toilsome climb, passed the first houses of the aërial town; and drew towards the school-house. The hour was too early; the pupils were still in school, humming small, like a swarm of gnats; and he withdrew a few steps along Abbey Walk, whence he regarded the spot which fate had made the home of all he loved best in the world. In front of the schools, which were extensive and stone-built, grew two enormous beeches with smooth mouse-coloured trunks, as such trees will only grow on chalk uplands. Within the mullioned and transomed windows he could see the black, brown, and flaxen crowns of the scholars over the sills, and to pass the time away he walked down to the level terrace where the Abbey gardens once had spread, his heart throbbing in spite of him.

Unwilling to enter till the children were dismissed he remained here till young voices could be heard in the open air, and girls in white pinafores over red and blue frocks appeared dancing along the paths which the abbess, prioress, sub-prioress, and fifty nuns had demurely paced three centuries earlier. Retracing his steps he found that he had waited too long, and that Sue had gone out into the town at the heels of the last scholar, Mr. Phillotson having been absent all the afternoon at a teachers' meeting at Shottsford.

Jude went into the empty school-room and sat down, the girl who was sweeping the floor having informed him that Mrs. Phillotson would be back again in a few minutes. A piano stood near—actually the old piano that Phillotson had possessed at Marygreen—and though the dark afternoon almost prevented him seeing the notes Jude touched them in his humble way, and could not help modulating into the hymn which had so affected him in the previous week.

A figure moved behind him, and thinking it was still the girl with the broom Jude took no notice, till the person came close and laid her fingers lightly upon his bass hand. The imposed hand was a little one he seemed to know, and he turned.

"Don't stop," said Sue. "I like it. I learnt it before I left Melchester. They used to play it in the Training-School."

"I can't strum before you! Play it for me."

"O well—I don't mind."

Sue sat down, and her rendering of the piece, though not remarkable, seemed divine as compared with his own. She, like him, was evidently touched—to her own surprise—

by the recalled air; and when she had finished, and he moved his hand towards hers, it met his own half-way. Jude grasped it—just as he had done before her marriage.

"It is odd," she said, in a voice quite changed, "that I should care about that air; because—"

"Because what?"

"I am not that sort—quite."

"Not easily moved?"

"I didn't quite mean that."

"O, but you *are* one of that sort, for you are just like me at heart!"

"But not at head."

She played on, and suddenly turned round; and by an unpremeditated instinct each clasped the other's hand again.

She uttered a forced little laugh as she relinquished his quickly. "How funny!" she said. "I wonder what we both did that for?"

"I suppose because we are both alike, as I said before."

"Not in our thoughts! Perhaps a little in our feelings."

"And they rule thoughts. . . . Isn't it enough to make one blaspheme that the composer of that hymn is one of the most commonplace men I ever met!"

"What—you know him?"

"I went to see him."

"O you goose—to do just what I should have done! Why did you?"

"Because we are not alike," he said drily.

"Now we'll have some tea," said Sue. "Shall we have it here instead of in my house? It is no trouble to get the kettle and things brought in. We don't live at the school, you know, but in that ancient dwelling across the way called Old-Grove Place. It is so antique and dismal that it depresses me dreadfully. Such houses are very well to visit, but not to live in—I feel crushed into the earth by the weight of so many previous lives there spent. In a new place like these schools there is only your own life to support. Sit down, and I'll tell Ada to bring the tea-things across."

He waited in the light of the stove, the door of which she flung open before going out, and when she returned, followed by the maiden with tea, they sat down by the same light, assisted by the blue rays of a spirit-lamp under the brass kettle on the stand.

"This is one of your wedding-presents to me," she said, signifying the latter.

"Yes," said Jude.

The kettle of his gift sang with some satire in its note, to his mind; and to change the subject he said, "Do you know of any good readable edition of the uncanonical books of the New Testament? You don't read them in the school, I suppose?"

"O dear no!—'twould alarm the neighbourhood. . . . Yes, there is one. I am not familiar with it now, though I was interested in it when my former friend was alive. Cowper's *Apocryphal Gospels*."

"That sounds like what I want." His thoughts, however, reverted with a twinge to the "former friend"—by whom she meant, as he knew, the University comrade of her earlier days. He wondered if she talked of him to Phillotson.

"The Gospel of Nicodemus is very nice," she went on, to keep him from his jealous thoughts, which she read clearly, as she always did. Indeed when they talked on an indifferent subject, as now, there was ever a second silent conversation passing between their emotions, so perfect was the reciprocity between them. "It is quite like the genuine article. All cut up into verses, too; so that it is like one of the other evangelists read in a dream, when things are the same, yet not the same. But Jude, do you take an interest in those questions still? Are you getting up *Apologetica?*"

"Yes. I am reading Divinity harder than ever."

She regarded him curiously.

"Why do you look at me like that?" said Jude.

"Oh—why do you want to know?"

"I am sure you can tell me anything I may be ignorant of in that subject. You must have learnt a lot of everything from your dear dead friend!"

"We won't get on to that now!" she coaxed. "Will you be carving out at that church again next week, where you learnt the pretty hymn?"

"Yes, perhaps."

"That will be very nice. Shall I come and see you there? It is in this direction, and I could come any afternoon by train for half an hour?"

"No. Don't come!"

"What—aren't we going to be friends, then, any longer, as we used to be?"

"No."

"I didn't know that. I thought you were always going to be kind to me!"

"No, I am not."

"What have I done, then? I am sure I thought we two—" The *tremolo* in her voice caused her to break off.

"Sue, I sometimes think you are a flirt," said he abruptly.

There was a momentary pause, till she suddenly jumped up; and to his surprise he saw by the kettle-flame that her face was flushed.

"I can't talk to you any longer, Jude!" she said, the tragic contralto note having come back as of old. "It is getting too dark to stay together like this, after playing morbid Good Friday tunes that make one feel what one shouldn't! . . . We mustn't sit and talk in this way any more. Yes—you must go away, for you mistake me! I am very much the reverse of what you say so cruelly—O Jude, it *was* cruel to say that! Yet I can't tell you the truth—I should shock you by letting you know how I give way to my impulses, and how much I feel that I shouldn't have been provided with attractiveness unless it were meant to be exercised! Some women's love of being loved is insatiable; and so, often, is their love of loving; and in the last case they may find that they can't give it continuously to the chamber-officer appointed by the bishop's licence to receive it. But you are so straightforward, Jude, that you can't understand me! . . . Now you must go. I am sorry my husband is not at home."

"Are you?"

"I perceive I have said that in mere convention! Honestly I don't think I am sorry. It does not matter, either way, sad to say!"

As they had overdone the grasp of hands some time sooner, she touched his fingers but lightly when he went out now. He had hardly gone from the door when, with a dissatisfied look, she jumped on a form and opened the iron casement of a window beneath which he was passing in the path without. "When do you leave here to catch your train, Jude?" she asked.

He looked up in some surprise. "The coach that runs to meet it goes in three-quarters of an hour or so."

"What will you do with yourself for the time?"

"O—wander about, I suppose. Perhaps I shall go and sit in the old church."

"It does seem hard of me to pack you off so! You have thought enough of churches, Heaven knows, without going into one in the dark. Stay there."

"Where?"

"Where you are. I can talk to you better like this than when you were inside. . . . It was so kind and tender of you to give up half a day's work to come to see me! . . . You are Joseph the dreamer of dreams, dear Jude. And a tragic Don Quixote. And sometimes you are St. Stephen, who, while they were stoning him, could see Heaven opened. O my poor friend and comrade, you'll suffer yet!"

Now that the high window-sill was between them, so that he could not get at her, she seemed not to mind indulging in a frankness she had feared at close quarters. "I have been thinking," she continued, still in the tone of one brimful of feeling, "that the social moulds civilization fits us into have no more relation to our actual shapes than the conventional shapes of the constellations have to the real star-patterns. I am called Mrs. Richard Phillotson, living a calm wedded life with my counterpart of that name. But I am not really Mrs. Richard Phillotson, but a woman tossed about, all alone, with aberrant passions, and unaccountable antipathies. . . . Now you mustn't wait longer, or you will lose the coach. Come and see me again. You must come to the house then."

"Yes!" said Jude. "When shall it be?"

"To-morrow week. Good-bye—good-bye!" She stretched out her hand and stroked his forehead pitifully—just once. Jude said good-bye, and went away into the darkness.

Passing along Bimport Street he thought he heard the wheels of the coach departing, and, truly enough, when he reached the Duke's Arms in the market-place the coach had gone. It was impossible for him to get to the station on foot in time for this train, and he settled himself perforce to wait for the next—the last to Melchester that night.

He wandered about a while, obtained something to eat; and then, having another half-hour on his hands, his feet involuntarily took him through the venerable graveyard of Trinity Church, with its avenues of limes, in the direction of the schools again. They were entirely in darkness. She had said she lived over the way at Old-Grove's Place, a house which he soon discovered from her description of its antiquity.

A glimmering candle-light shone from a front-window, the shutters being yet unclosed. He could see the interior clearly—the floor sinking a couple of steps below the road without, which had become raised during the centuries since the house was built. Sue, evidently just come in, was standing with her hat on in this front parlour or sitting-room, whose walls were lined with wainscoting of panelled oak reaching from floor to ceiling, the latter being crossed by huge moulded beams only a little way above her head. The mantelpiece was of the same heavy description, carved with Jacobean pilasters and scroll-work. The centuries did, indeed, ponderously overhang a young wife who passed her time here.

She had opened a rosewood work-box, and was looking at a photograph. Having contemplated it a little while she pressed it against her bosom, and put it again in its place.

Then becoming aware that she had not obscured the windows she came forward to do so, candle in hand. It was too dark for her to see Jude without, but he could see her face distinctly, and there was an unmistakable tearfulness about the dark, long-lashed eyes.

She closed the shutters, and Jude turned away to pursue his solitary journey home. "Whose photograph was she looking at?" he said. He had once given her his; but she had others, he knew. Yet it was his, surely?

He knew he should go to see her again, according to her invitation. Those earnest men he read of, the saints, whom Sue, with gentle irreverence, called his demi-gods, would have shunned such encounters, if they doubted their own strength. But he could not. He might fast and pray during the whole interval, but the human was more powerful in him than the Divine.

II

HOWEVER, IF GOD DISPOSED NOT, WOMAN DID. THE NEXT MORNING BUT ONE BROUGHT him this note from her:

Don't come next week. On your own account don't! We were too free, under the influence of that morbid hymn and the twilight. Think no more than you can help of
SUSANNA FLORENCE MARY

The disappointment was keen. He knew her mood, the look of her face, when she subscribed herself at length thus. But whatever her mood he could not say she was wrong in her view. He replied:

I acquiesce. You are right. It is a lesson in renunciation which I suppose I ought to learn at this season.
JUDE

He despatched the note on Easter Eve, and there seemed a finality in their decisions. But other forces and laws than theirs were in operation. On Easter Monday morning he received a message from the Widow Edlin, whom he had directed to telegraph if anything serious happened:

Your aunt is sinking. Come at once.

He threw down his tools and went. Three and a half hours later he was crossing the downs about Marygreen, and presently plunged into the concave field across which the short cut was made to the village. As he ascended on the other side a labouring man, who had been watching his approach from a gate across the path, moved uneasily, and prepared to speak. "I can see in his face that she is dead," said Jude. "Poor Aunt Drusilla!"

It was as he had supposed, and Mrs. Edlin had sent out the man to break the news to him.

"She wouldn't have knowed 'ee. She lay like a doll wi' glass eyes; so it didn't matter that you wasn't here," said he.

Jude went on to the house, and in the afternoon, when everything was done, and the layers-out had finished their beer, and gone, he sat down alone in the silent place. It was absolutely necessary to communicate with Sue, though two or three days earlier they had agreed to mutual severance. He wrote in the briefest terms:

Aunt Drusilla is dead, having been taken almost suddenly. The funeral is on Friday afternoon.

He remained in and about Marygreen through the intervening days, went out on Friday morning to see that the grave was finished, and wondered if Sue would come. She had not written, and that seemed to signify rather that she would come than that she would not. Having timed her by her only possible train, he locked the door about mid-day, and crossed the hollow field to the verge of the upland by the Brown House, where he stood and looked over the vast prospect northwards, and over the nearer landscape in which Alfredston stood. Two miles behind it a jet of white steam was travelling from the left to the right of the picture.

There was a long time to wait, even now, till he would know if she had arrived. He did wait, however, and at last a small hired vehicle pulled up at the bottom of the hill, and a person alighted, the conveyance going back, while the passenger began ascending the hill. He knew her; and she looked so slender to-day that it seemed as if she might be crushed in the intensity of a too passionate embrace—such as it was not for him to give. Two-thirds of the way up her head suddenly took a solicitous poise, and he knew that she had at that moment recognised him. Her face soon began a pensive smile, which lasted till, having descended a little way, he met her.

"I thought," she began with nervous quickness, "that it would be so sad to let you attend the funeral alone! And so—at the last moment—I came."

"Dear faithful Sue!" murmured Jude.

With the elusiveness of her curious double nature, however, Sue did not stand still for any further greeting, though it wanted some time to the burial. A pathos so unusually compounded as that which attached to this hour was unlikely to repeat itself for years, if ever, and Jude would have paused, and meditated, and conversed. But Sue either saw it not at all, or, seeing it more than he, would not allow herself to feel it.

The sad and simple ceremony was soon over, their progress to the church being almost at a trot, the bustling undertaker having a more important funeral an hour later, three miles off. Drusilla was put into the new ground, quite away from her ancestors. Sue and Jude had gone side by side to the grave, and now sat down to tea in the familiar house; their lives united at least in this last attention to the dead.

"She was opposed to marriage, from first to last, you say?" murmured Sue.

"Yes. Particularly for members of our family."

Her eyes met his, and remained on him a while.

"We are rather a sad family, don't you think, Jude?"

"She said we made bad husbands and wives. Certainly we make unhappy ones. At all events, I do, for one!"

Sue was silent. "Is it wrong, Jude," she said with a tentative tremor, "for a husband or wife to tell a third person that they are unhappy in their marriage? If a marriage ceremony is a religious thing, it is possibly wrong; but if it is only a sordid contract, based on material convenience in householding, rating, and taxing, and the inheritance of land and money by children, making it necessary that the male parent should be known—which it seems to be—why surely a person may say, even proclaim upon the house-tops, that it hurts and grieves him or her?"

"I have said so, anyhow, to you."

Presently she went on: "Are there many couples, do you think, where one dislikes the other for no definite fault?"

"Yes, I suppose. If either cares for another person, for instance."

"But even apart from that? Wouldn't the woman, for example, be very bad-natured if she didn't like to live with her husband; merely"—her voice undulated, and he guessed things—"merely because she had a personal feeling against it—a physical objection—a fastidiousness, or whatever it may be called—although she might respect and be grateful to him? I am merely putting a case. Ought she to try to overcome her pruderies?"

Jude threw a troubled look at her. He said, looking away: "It would be just one of those cases in which my experiences go contrary to my dogmas. Speaking as an order-loving man—which I hope I am, though I fear I am not—I should say, yes. Speaking from experience and unbiased nature, I should say, no. . . . Sue, I believe you are not happy!"

"Yes I am!" said she excitedly. "How can a woman be unhappy who has only been married eight weeks to a man she chose freely?"

" 'Chose freely!' "

"Why do you repeat it? . . . But I have to go back by the six o'clock train. You will be staying on here, I suppose?"

"For a few days to wind up aunt's affairs. This house is gone now. Shall I go to the train with you?"

A little laugh of objection came from Sue. "I think not. You may come part of the way."

"But stop—you can't go to-night! That train won't take you to Shaston. You must stay and go back to-morrow. Mrs. Edlin has plenty of room, if you don't like to stay here?"

"Very well," she said dubiously. "I didn't tell him I would come for certain."

Jude went to the widow's house adjoining, to let her know; and returning in a few minutes sat down again.

"It is horrible how we are circumstanced, Sue—horrible!" he said abruptly, with his eyes bent to the floor.

"No! Why?"

"I can't tell you all my part of the gloom. Your part is that you ought not to have married him. I saw it before you had done it, but I thought I mustn't interfere. I was wrong. I ought to have!"

"But what makes you assume all this, dear?"

"Because—I can see you through your feathers my poor little bird!"

Her hand lay on the table, and Jude put his upon it. Sue drew hers away.

"That's absurd, Sue," cried he, "after what we've been talking about! I am more strict and formal than you, if it comes to that; and that you should object to such an innocent action shows that you are ridiculously inconsistent!"

"Perhaps it was too prudish," she said repentantly. "Only I have fancied it was a sort of trick of ours—too frequent perhaps. There, you may hold it as much as you like. Is that good of me?"

"Yes; very."

"But I must tell him."

"Who?"

"Richard."

"O—of course, if you think it necessary. But as it means nothing it may be bothering him needlessly."

"Well—are you sure you mean it only as my cousin?"

"Absolutely sure. I have no feelings of love left in me."

"That's news. How has it come to be?"

"I've seen Arabella."

She winced at the hit; then said curiously, "When did you see her?"

"When I was at Christminster."

"So she's come back; and you never told me! I suppose you will live with her now?"

"Of course—just as you live with your husband."

She looked at the window pots with the geraniums and cactuses, withered for want of attention, and through them at the outer distance, till her eyes began to grow moist. "What is it?" said Jude, in a softened tone.

"Why should you be so glad to go back to her if—if—what you used to say to me is still true—I mean if it were true then! Of course it is not now! How could your heart go back to Arabella so soon?"

"A special Providence, I suppose, helped it on its way."

"Ah—it isn't true!" she said with gentle resentment. "You are teasing me—that's all—because you think I am not happy!"

"I don't know. I don't wish to know."

"If I were unhappy it would be my fault, my wickedness; not that I should have a right to dislike him! He is considerate to me in everything; and he is very interesting, from the amount of general knowledge he has acquired by reading everything that comes in his way. . . . Do you think, Jude, that a man ought to marry a woman his own age, or one younger than himself—eighteen years—as I am than he?"

"It depends upon what they feel for each other."

He gave her no opportunity of self-satisfaction, and she had to go on unaided, which she did in a vanquished tone, verging on tears:

"I—I think I must be equally honest with you as you have been with me. Perhaps you have seen what it is I want to say?—that though I like Mr. Phillotson as a friend, I don't like him—it is a torture to me to—live with him as a husband!—There, now I have let it out—I couldn't help it, although I have been—pretending I am happy.—Now you'll have a contempt for me forever, I suppose!" She bent down her face upon her hands as they lay upon the cloth, and silently sobbed in little jerks that made the fragile three-legged table quiver.

"I have only been married a month or two!" she went on, still remaining bent upon the table, and talking into her hands. "And it is said that what a woman shrinks from—in the early days of her marriage—she shakes down to with comfortable indifference in half-a-dozen years. But that is much like saying that the amputation of a limb is no affliction, since a person gets comfortably accustomed to the use of a wooden leg or arm in the course of time!"

Jude could hardly speak, but he said, "I thought there was something wrong, Sue! O, I thought there was!"

"But it is not as you think!—there is nothing wrong except my own wickedness, I suppose you'd call it—a repugnance on my part, for a reason I cannot disclose, and what would not be admitted as one by the world in general! . . . What tortures me so much is the necessity of being responsive to this man whenever he wishes, good as he is morally!—the dreadful contract to feel in a particular way, in a matter whose essence is its voluntariness! . . . I wish he would beat me, or be faithless to me, or do some open thing that I could talk about as a justification for feeling as I do! But he does nothing, except that he has grown a little cold since he has found out how I feel. That's why he didn't come to the funeral. . . . O, I am very miserable—I don't know what to do! . . . Don't come near me, Jude, because you mustn't."

But he had jumped up and put his face against hers—or rather against her ear, her face being inaccessible.

"I told you not to, Jude!"

"I know you did—I only wish to—console you! It all arose through my being married before we met, didn't it? You would have been my wife, Sue, wouldn't you, if it hadn't been for that?"

Instead of replying she rose quickly, and saying she was going to walk to her aunt's grave in the churchyard to recover herself, went out of the house. Jude did not follow her. Twenty minutes later he saw her cross the village green towards Mrs. Edlin's, and soon she sent a little girl to fetch her bag, and tell him she was too tired to see him again that night.

In the lonely room of his aunt's house, Jude sat watching the cottage of the Widow Edlin as it disappeared behind the night shade. He knew that Sue was sitting within its walls equally lonely and disheartened; and again questioned his devotional motto that all was for the best.

He retired to rest early, but his sleep was fitful from the sense that Sue was so near at hand. At some time near two o'clock, when he was beginning to sleep more soundly, he was aroused by a shrill squeak that had been familiar enough to him when he lived regularly at Marygreen. It was the cry of a rabbit caught in a gin. As was the little creature's habit, it did not soon repeat its cry; and probably would not do so more than once or twice; but would remain bearing its torture till the morrow, when the trapper would come and knock it on the head.

He who in his childhood had saved the lives of the earthworms now began to picture the agonies of the rabbit from its lacerated leg. If it were a "bad catch" by the hind-leg, the animal would tug during the ensuing six hours till the iron teeth of the trap had stripped the leg-bone of its flesh, when, should a weak-springed instrument enable it to escape, it would die in the fields from the mortification of the limb. If it were a "good catch," namely, by the fore-leg, the bone would be broken and the limb nearly torn in two in attempts at an impossible escape.

Almost half an hour passed, and the rabbit repeated its cry. Jude could rest no longer till he had put it out of its pain, so dressing himself quickly he descended, and by the light of the moon went across the green in the direction of the sound. He reached the hedge bordering the widow's garden, when he stood still. The faint click of the trap as dragged about by the writhing animal guided him now, and reaching the spot he struck the rabbit on the back of the neck with the side of his palm, and it stretched itself out dead.

He was turning away when he saw a woman looking out of the open casement at a window on the ground floor of the adjacent cottage. "Jude!" said a voice timidly—Sue's voice. "It is you—is it not?"

"Yes, dear!"

"I haven't been able to sleep at all, and then I heard the rabbit, and couldn't help thinking of what it suffered, till I felt I must come down and kill it! But I am so glad you got there first. . . . They ought not to be allowed to set these steel traps, ought they!"

Jude had reached the window, which was quite a low one, so that she was visible down to her waist. She let go the casement-stay and put her hand upon his, her moonlit face regarding him wistfully.

"Did it keep you awake?" he said.

"No—I was awake."

"How was that?"

"O, you know—now! I know you, with your religious doctrines, think that a married woman in trouble of a kind like mine commits a mortal sin in making a man the confidant of it, as I did you. I wish I hadn't, now!"

"Don't wish it, dear," he said. "That may have *been* my view; but my doctrines and I begin to part company."

"I knew it—I knew it! And that's why I vowed I wouldn't disturb your beliefs. But— I am *so glad* to see you!—and, O, I didn't mean to see you again, now the last tie between us, Aunt Drusilla, is dead!"

Jude seized her hand and kissed it. "There is a stronger one left!" he said. "I'll never care about my doctrines or my religion any more! Let them go! Let me help you, even if I do love you, and even if you . . ."

"Don't say it!—I know what you mean; but I can't admit so much as that. There! Guess what you like, but don't press me to answer questions!"

"I wish you were happy, whatever I may be!"

"I *can't* be! So few could enter into my feeling—they would say 'twas my fanciful fastidiousness, or something of that sort, and condemn me. . . . It is none of the natural tragedies of love that's love's usual tragedy in civilised life, but a tragedy artificially manufactured for people who in a natural state would find relief in parting! . . . It would have been wrong, perhaps, for me to tell my distress to you, if I had been able to tell it to anybody else. But I have nobody. And I *must* tell somebody! Jude, before I married him I had never thought out fully what marriage meant, even though I knew. It was idiotic of me— there is no excuse. I was old enough, and I thought I was very experienced. So I rushed on, when I had got into that Training-School scrape, with all the cock-sureness of the fool that I was! . . . I am certain one ought to be allowed to undo what one has done so ignorantly! I daresay it happens to lots of women; only they submit, and I kick. . . . When people of a later age look back upon the barbarous customs and superstitions of the times that we have the unhappiness to live in, what *will* they say!"

"You are very bitter, darling Sue! How I wish—I wish—"

"You must go in now!"

In a moment of impulse she bent over the sill, and laid her face upon his hair, weeping, and then imprinting a scarcely perceptible little kiss upon the top of his head, withdrawing quickly, so that he could not put his arms round her, as he unquestionably would have otherwise done. She shut the casement, and he returned to his cottage.

III

S UE'S DISTRESSFUL CONFESSION RECURRED TO JUDE'S MIND ALL THE NIGHT AS BEING A sorrow indeed.

The morning after, when it was time for her to go, the neighbours saw her companion and herself disappearing on foot down the hill path which led into the lonely road to Alfredston. An hour passed before he returned along the same route, and in his face there was a look of exaltation not unmixed with recklessness. An incident had occurred.

They had stood parting in the silent highway, and their tense and passionate moods had led to bewildered inquiries of each other on how far their intimacy ought to go; till they had almost quarrelled, and she had said tearfully that it was hardly proper of him as a parson in embryo to think of such a thing as kissing her even in farewell, as he now wished to do. Then she had conceded that the fact of the kiss would be nothing: all would depend upon the spirit of it. If given in the spirit of a cousin and a friend she saw no objection: if in the spirit of a lover she could not permit it. "Will you swear that it will not be in that spirit?" she had said.

No: he would not. And then they had turned from each other in estrangement, and gone their several ways, till at a distance of twenty or thirty yards both had looked round simultaneously. That look behind was fatal to the reserve hitherto more or less maintained. They had quickly run back, and met, and embracing most unpremeditatedly, kissed each other. When they parted for good it was with flushed cheeks on her side, and a beating heart on his.

The kiss was a turning-point in Jude's career. Back again in the cottage, and left to reflection, he saw one thing: that though his kiss of that aërial being had seemed the purest moment of his faultful life, as long as he nourished this unlicensed tenderness it was glaringly inconsistent for him to pursue the idea of becoming the soldier and servant of a religion in which sexual love was regarded as at its best a frailty, and at its worst damnation. What Sue had said in warmth was really the cold truth. When to defend his affection tooth and nail, to persist with headlong force in impassioned attentions to her, was all he thought of, he was condemned *ipso facto* as a professor of the accepted school of morals. He was as unfit, obviously, by nature, as he had been by social position, to fill the part of a propounder of accredited dogma.

Strange that his first aspiration—towards academical proficiency—had been checked by a woman, and that his second aspiration—towards apostleship—had also been checked by a woman. "Is it," he said, "that the women are to blame; or is it the artificial system of things, under which the normal sex-impulses are turned into devilish domestic gins and springs to noose and hold back those who want to progress?"

It had been his standing desire to become a prophet, however humble, to his struggling fellow-creatures, without any thought of personal gain. Yet with a wife living away from him with another husband, and himself in love erratically, the loved-one's revolt against her state being possibly on his account, he had sunk to be barely respectable according to regulation views.

It was not for him to consider further: he had only to confront the obvious, which was that he had made himself quite an impostor as a law-abiding religious teacher.

At dusk that evening he went into the garden and dug a shallow hole, to which he brought out all the theological and ethical works that he possessed. He knew that, in this country of true believers, most of them were not saleable at a much higher price than waste-paper value, and preferred to get rid of them in his own way, even if he should sacrifice a little money to the sentiment of thus destroying them. Lighting some loose pamphlets to begin with, he cut the volumes into pieces as well as he could, and with a three-pronged fork shook them over the flames. They kindled, and lighted up the back of the house, the pigsty, and his own face, till they were more or less consumed.

Though he was almost a stranger here now, passing cottagers talked to him over the garden hedge.

"Burning up your awld aunt's rubbidge I suppose? Ay; a lot gets heaped up in nooks and corners when you've lived eighty years in one house."

It was nearly one o'clock in the morning before the leaves, covers, and binding of Jeremy Taylor, Butler, Doddridge, Paley, Pusey, Newman and the rest had gone to ashes; but the night was quiet, and as he turned and turned the paper shreds with the fork, the sense of being no longer a hypocrite to himself afforded a relief to his mind which gave him calm. He might go on believing as before, but he professed nothing, and no longer owned and exhibited engines of faith which, as their proprietor, he might naturally be supposed to exercise on himself first of all. In his passion for Sue he could not stand as an ordinary sinner, and not as a whited sepulchre.

Meanwhile Sue, after parting from him earlier in the day, had gone along to the station, with tears in her eyes for having run back and let him kiss her. Jude ought not to have pretended that he was not a lover, and made her give way to an impulse to act unconventionally, if not wrongly. She was inclined to call it the latter; for Sue's logic was extraordinarily compounded, and seemed to maintain that before a thing was done it might be right to do, but that being done it became wrong; or, in other words, that things which were right in theory were wrong in practice.

"I have been too weak I think!" she jerked out as she pranced on, shaking down teardrops now and then. "It was burning, like a lover's—O it was! And I won't write to him any more, or at least for a long time, to impress him with my dignity! And I hope it will hurt him very much—expecting a letter to-morrow morning, and the next, and the next, and no letter coming. He'll suffer then with suspense—won't he, that's all!—and I am very glad of it!"—Tears of pity for Jude's approaching sufferings at her hands mingled with those which had surged up in pity for herself.

Then the slim little wife of a husband whose person was disagreeable to her, the ethereal, fine-nerved, sensitive girl, quite unfitted by temperament and instinct to fulfil the conditions of the matrimonial relation with Phillotson, possibly with any man, walked fitfully along, and panted, and brought weariness into her eyes by gazing and worrying hopelessly.

Phillotson met her at the arrival station, and, seeing that she was troubled, thought it must be owing to the depressing effect of her aunt's death and funeral. He began telling her of his day's doings, and how his friend Gillingham, a neighbouring schoolmaster whom he had not seen for years, had called upon him. While ascending to the town, seated on the top of the omnibus beside him, she said suddenly and with an air of self-chastisement, regarding the white road and its bordering bushes of hazel:

"Richard—I let Mr. Fawley hold my hand. I don't know whether you think it wrong?"

He, waking apparently from thoughts of far different mould, said vaguely, "O, did you? What did you do that for?"

"I don't know. He wanted to, and I let him."

"I hope it pleased him. I should think it was hardly a novelty."

They lapsed into silence. Had this been a case in the court of an omniscient judge he might have entered on his notes the curious fact that Sue had placed the minor for the major indiscretion, and had not said a word about the kiss.

After tea that evening Phillotson sat balancing the school registers. She remained in an unusually silent, tense, and restless condition, and at last, saying she was tired, went to bed early. When Phillotson arrived upstairs, weary with the drudgery of the attendance-numbers, it was a quarter to twelve o'clock. Entering their chamber, which by day commanded a view of some thirty or forty miles over the Vale of Blackmoor, and even into Outer Wessex, he went to the window, and, pressing his face against the pane, gazed with hard-breathing fixity into the mysterious darkness which now covered the far-reaching scene. He was musing, "I think," he said at last, without turning his head, "that I must get the Committee to change the school-stationer. All the copybooks are sent wrong this time."

There was no reply. Thinking Sue was dozing he went on:

"And there must be a rearrangement of that ventilator in the class-room. The wind blows down upon my head unmercifully, and gives me the earache."

As the silence seemed more absolute than ordinarily he turned round. The heavy, gloomy oak wainscot, which extended over the walls upstairs and down in the dilapidated "Old-Grove's House," and the massive chimney-piece reaching to the ceiling, stood in odd contrast to the new and shining brass bedstead, and the new suite of birch furniture that he had bought for her, the two styles seeming to nod to each other across three centuries upon the shaking floor.

"Soo!" he said (this being the way in which he pronounced her name).

She was not in the bed, though she had apparently been there—the clothes on her side being flung back. Thinking she might have forgotten some kitchen detail and gone downstairs for a moment to see to it, he pulled off his coat and idled quietly enough for a few minutes, when, finding she did not come, he went out upon the landing, candle in hand, and said again "Soo!"

"Yes!" came back to him in her voice, from the distant kitchen quarter.

"What are you doing down there at midnight—tiring yourself out for nothing!"

"I am not sleepy; I am reading; and there is a larger fire here."

He went to bed. Some time in the night he awoke. She was not there, even now. Lighting a candle he hastily stepped out upon the landing, and again called her name.

She answered "Yes!" as before; but the tones were small and confined, and whence they came he could not at first understand. Under the staircase was a large clothes-closet, without a window; they seemed to come from it. The door was shut, but there was no lock or other fastening. Phillotson, alarmed, went towards it, wondering if she had suddenly become deranged.

"What are you doing in there?" he asked.

"Not to disturb you I came here, as it was so late."

"But there's no bed, is there? And no ventilation! Why, you'll be suffocated if you stay all night!"

"O no, I think not. Don't trouble about me."

"But—" Phillotson seized the knob and pulled at the door. She had fastened it inside with a piece of string, which broke at his pull. There being no bedstead she had flung down some rugs and made a little nest for herself in the very cramped quarters the closet afforded.

When he looked in upon her she sprang out of her lair, great-eyed and trembling.

"You ought not to have pulled open the door!" she cried excitedly. "It is not becoming in you! O, will you go away; please will you!"

She looked so pitiful and pleading in her white night-gown against the shadowy lumber-hole that he was quite worried. She continued to beseech him not to disturb her.

He said: "I've been kind to you, and given you every liberty; and it is monstrous that you should feel in this way!"

"Yes," said she, weeping. "I know that! It is wrong and wicked of me, I suppose! I am very sorry. But it is not I altogether that am to blame!"

"Who is then? Am I?"

"No—I don't know! The universe, I suppose—things in general, because they are so horrid and cruel!"

"Well, it is no use talking like that. Making a man's house so unseemly at this time o' night! Eliza will hear, if we don't mind." (He meant the servant.) "Just think if either of the parsons in this town was to see us now! I hate such eccentricities, Sue. There's no order or regularity in your sentiments! . . . But I won't intrude on you further; only I would advise you not to shut the door too tight, or I shall find you stifled to-morrow."

On rising the next morning he immediately looked into the closet, but Sue had already gone downstairs. There was a little nest where she had lain, and spiders' webs hung overhead. "What must a woman's aversion be when it is stronger than her fear of spiders!" he said bitterly.

He found her sitting at the breakfast-table, and the meal began almost in silence, the burghers walking past upon the pavement—or rather roadway, pavements being scarce here—which was two or three feet above the level of the parlour floor. They nodded down to the happy couple their morning greetings, as they went on.

"Richard," she said all at once; "would you mind my living away from you?"

"Away from me? Why, that's what you were doing when I married you. What then was the meaning of marrying at all?"

"You wouldn't like me any the better for telling you."

"I don't object to know."

"Because I thought I could do nothing else. You had got my promise a long time before that, remember. Then, as time went on, I regretted I had promised you, and was trying to see an honourable way to break it off. But as I couldn't I became rather reckless and careless about the conventions. Then you know what was said, and how I was turned out of the Training-School you had taken such time and trouble to prepare me for and get me into; and this frightened me, and it seemed then that the one thing I could do would be to let the engagement stand. Of course I, of all people, ought not to have cared what was said, for it was just what I fancied I never did care for. But I was a coward—as so many women are—and my theoretic unconventionality broke down. If that had not entered into the case it would have been better to have hurt your feelings once for all then, than to marry you and hurt them all my life after. . . . And you were so generous in never giving credit for a moment to the rumour."

"I am bound in honesty to tell you that I weighed its probability, and enquired of your cousin about it."

"Ah!" she said with pained surprise.

"I didn't doubt you."

"But you enquired!"

"I took his word."

Her eyes had filled. "*He* wouldn't have enquired!" she said. "But you haven't answered me. Will you let me go away? I know how irregular it is of me to ask it—"

"It is irregular."

"But I do ask it! Domestic laws should be made according to temperaments, which should be classified. If people are at all peculiar in character they have to suffer from the very rules that produce comfort in others! . . . Will you let me?"

"But we married—"

"What is the use of thinking of laws and ordinances," she burst out, "if they make you miserable when you know you are committing no sin?"

"But you are committing a sin in not liking me."

"I *do* like you! But I didn't reflect it would be—that it would be so much more than that. . . . For a man and woman to live on intimate terms when one feels as I do is adultery, in any circumstances, however legal. There—I've said it! . . . Will you let me, Richard?"

"You distress me, Susanna, by such importunity!"

"Why can't we agree to free each other? We made the compact, and surely we can cancel it—not legally, of course; but we can morally, especially as no new interests, in the shape of children, have arisen to be looked after. Then we might be friends, and meet without pain to either. O Richard, be my friend and have pity! We shall both be dead in a few years, and then what will it matter to anybody that you relieved me from constraint for a little while? I daresay you think me eccentric, or super-sensitive, or something absurd. Well—why should I suffer for what I was born to be, if it doesn't hurt other people?"

"But it does—it hurts *me!* And you vowed to love me."

"Yes—that's it! I am in the wrong. I always am! It is as culpable to bind yourself to love always as to believe a creed always, and as silly as to vow always to like a particular food or drink!"

"And do you mean, by living away from me, living by yourself?"

"Well, if you insisted, yes. But I meant living with Jude."

"As his wife?"

"As I choose."

Phillotson writhed.

Sue continued: "She, or he, 'who lets the world, or his own portion of it, choose his plan of life for him, has no need of any other faculty than the apelike one of imitation.' J. S. Mill's words, those are. Why can't you act upon them? I wish to, always."

"What do I care about J. S. Mill!" moaned he. "I only want to lead a quiet life! Do you mind my saying that I have guessed what never once occurred to me before our marriage—that you were in love, and are in love, with Jude Fawley!"

"You may go on guessing that I am, since you have begun. But do you suppose that if I had been I should have asked you to let me go and live with him?"

The ringing of the school bell saved Phillotson from the necessity of replying at present to what apparently did not strike him as being such a convincing *argumentum ad vere-cundiam* as she, in her loss of courage at the last moment, meant it to appear. She was beginning to be so puzzling and unstateable that he was ready to throw in with her other little peculiarities the extremest request which a wife could make.

They proceeded to the schools that morning as usual, Sue entering the class-room, where he could see the back of her head through the glass partition whenever he turned his eyes that way. As he went on giving and hearing lessons his forehead and eyebrows twitched from concentrated agitation of thought, till at length he tore a scrap from a sheet of scribbling paper and wrote:

Your request prevents my attending to work at all. I don't know what I am doing! Was it seri-ously made?

He folded the piece of paper very small, and gave it to a little boy to take to Sue. The child toddled off into the class-room. Phillotson saw his wife turn and take the note, and the bend of her pretty head as she read it, her lips slightly crisped, to prevent undue expression under fire of so many young eyes. He could not see her hands, but she changed her position, and soon the child returned, bringing nothing in reply. In a few minutes, however, one of Sue's class appeared, with a little note similar to his own. These words only were pencilled therein:

I am sincerely sorry to say that it was seriously made.

Phillotson looked more disturbed than before, and the meeting-place of his brows twitched again. In ten minutes he called up the child he had just sent to her, and despatched another missive:

God knows I don't want to thwart you in any reasonable way. My whole thought is to make you comfortable and happy. But I cannot agree to such a preposterous notion as your going to live with your lover. You would lose everybody's respect and regard; and so should I!

After an interval a similar part was enacted in the class-room, and an answer came:

I know you mean my good. But I don't want to be respectable! To produce "Human development in its richest diversity" (to quote your Humboldt) is to my mind far above respectability. No doubt my tastes are low—in your view—hopelessly low! If you won't let me go to him, will you grant me this one request—allow me to live in your house in a separate way?

To this he returned no answer.

She wrote again:

I know what you think. But cannot you have pity on me? I beg you to; I implore you to be merciful! I would not ask if I were not almost compelled by what I can't bear! No poor woman has ever wished more than I that Eve had not fallen, so that (as the primitive Christians believed) some harmless mode of vegetation might have peopled Paradise. But I won't trifle! Be kind to me—even though I have not been kind to you! I will go away, go abroad, anywhere, and never trouble you.

Nearly an hour passed, and then he returned an answer:

I do not wish to pain you. How well you know I don't! Give me a little time. I am disposed to agree to your last request.

One line from her:

Thank you from my heart, Richard. I do not deserve your kindness.

All day Phillotson bent a dazed regard upon her through the glazed partition; and he felt as lonely as when he had not known her.

But he was as good as his word, and consented to her living apart in the house. At first, when they met at meals, she had seemed more composed under the new arrangement; but the irksomeness of their position worked on her temperament, and the fibres of her nature seemed strained like harp-strings. She talked vaguely and indiscriminately to prevent his talking pertinently.

IV

PHILLOTSON WAS SITTING UP LATE, AS WAS OFTEN HIS CUSTOM, TRYING TO GET TOgether the materials for his long-neglected hobby of Roman antiquities. For the first time since reviving the subject he felt a return of his old interest in it. He forgot time and place, and when he remembered himself and ascended to rest it was nearly two o'clock.

His preoccupation was such that, though he now slept on the other side of the house, he mechanically went to the room that he and his wife had occupied when he first became a tenant of Old-Grove's Place, which since his differences with Sue had been hers exclusively. He entered, and unconsciously began to undress.

There was a cry from the bed, and a quick movement. Before the schoolmaster had realised where he was he perceived Sue starting up half-awake, staring wildly, and springing out upon the floor on the side away from him, which was towards the window. This was somewhat hidden by the canopy of the bedstead, and in a moment he heard her flinging up the sash. Before he had thought that she meant to do more than get air she had mounted upon the sill and leapt out. She disappeared in the darkness, and he heard her fall below.

Phillotson, horrified, ran downstairs, striking himself sharply against the newel in his haste. Opening the heavy door he ascended the two or three steps to the level of the ground, and there on the gravel before him lay a white heap. Phillotson seized it in his arms, and bringing Sue into the hall seated her on a chair, where he gazed at her by the flapping light of the candle which he had set down in the draught on the bottom stair.

She had certainly not broken her neck. She looked at him with eyes that seemed not to take him in; and though not particularly large in general they appeared so now. She pressed her side and rubbed her arm, as if conscious of pain; then stood up, averting her face, in evident distress at his gaze.

"Thank God—you are not killed! Though it's not for want of trying—not much hurt I hope?"

Her fall, in fact, had not been a serious one, probably owing to the lowness of the old rooms and to the high level of the ground outside. Beyond a scraped elbow and a blow in the side she had apparently incurred little harm.

"I was asleep, I think!" she began, her pale face still turned away from him. "And something frightened me—a terrible dream—I thought I saw you—" The actual circumstances seemed to come back to her, and she was silent.

Her cloak was hanging at the back of the door, and the wretched Phillotson flung it round her. "Shall I help you upstairs?" he asked drearily; for the significance of all this sickened him of himself and of everything.

"No thank you, Richard. I am very little hurt. I can walk."

"You ought to lock your door," he mechanically said, as if lecturing in school. "Then no one could intrude even by accident."

"I have tried—it won't lock. All the doors are out of order."

The aspect of things was not improved by her admission. She ascended the staircase slowly, the waving light of the candle shining on her. Phillotson did not approach her, or attempt to ascend himself till he heard her enter her room. Then he fastened up the front-door, and returning, sat down on the lower stairs, holding the newel with one hand, and bowing his face into the other. Thus he remained for a long long time—a pitiable object enough to one who had seen him; till, raising his head and sighing a sigh which seemed to say that the business of his life must be carried on, whether he had a wife or no, he took the candle and went upstairs to his lonely room on the other side of the landing.

No further incident touching the matter between them occurred till the following evening, when, immediately school was over, Phillotson walked out of Shaston, saying he required no tea, and not informing Sue where he was going. He descended from the town level by a steep road in a north-westerly direction, and continued to move downwards till the soil changed from its white dryness to a tough brown clay. He was now on the low alluvial beds

> *Where Duncliffe is the traveller's mark,*
> *And cloty Stour's a-rolling dark.*

More than once he looked back in the increasing obscurity of evening. Against the sky was Shaston, dimly visible

> On the grey-topp'd height
> Of Paladore, as pale day wore
> Away . . .[1]

The new-lit lights from its windows burnt with a steady shine as if watching him, one of which windows was his own. Above it he could just discern the pinnacled tower of Trinity Church. The air down here, tempered by the thick damp bed of tenacious clay, was not as it had been above, but soft and relaxing, so that when he had walked a mile or two he was obliged to wipe his face with his handkerchief.

Leaving Duncliffe Hill on the left he proceeded without hesitation through the shade, as a man goes on, night or day, in a district over which he has played as a boy. He had walked altogether about four and a half miles when he crossed a tributary of the Stour, and reached Leddenton—a little town of three or four thousand inhabitants—where he went on to the boys' school, and knocked at the door of the master's residence.

A boy pupil-teacher opened it, and to Phillotson's inquiry if Mr. Gillingham was at home replied that he was, going at once off to his own house, and leaving Phillotson to find his way in as he could. He discovered his friend putting away some books from which he had been giving evening lessons. The light of the paraffin lamp fell on Phillotson's face—pale and wretched by contrast with his friend's, who had a cool, practical look. They had been schoolmates in boyhood, and fellow-students at Wintoncester Training College, many years before this time.

"Glad to see you, Dick! But you don't look well? Nothing the matter?"

Phillotson advanced without replying, and Gillingham closed the cupboard and pulled up beside his visitor.

"Why you haven't been here—let me see—since you were married? I called, you know, but you were out; and upon my word it is such a climb after dark that I have been waiting till the days are longer before lumpering up again. I am glad you didn't wait, however."

Though well-trained and even proficient masters, they occasionally used a dialect-word of their boyhood to each other in private.

"I've come, George, to explain to you my reasons for taking a step that I am about to take, so that you, at least, will understand my motives if other people question them any-when—as they may, indeed certainly will. . . . But anything is better than the present condition of things. God forbid that you should ever have such an experience as mine!"

"Sit down. You don't mean—anything wrong between you and Mrs. Phillotson?"

"I do. . . . My wretched state is that I've a wife I love, who not only does not love me, but—but—Well, I won't say. I know her feeling! I should prefer hatred from her!"

"Ssh!"

"And the sad part of it is that she is not so much to blame as I. She was a pupil-teacher under me, as you know, and I took advantage of her inexperience, and toled her out for

1. William Barnes.

walks, and got her to agree to a long engagement before she well knew her own mind. Afterwards she saw somebody else, but she blindly fulfilled her engagement."

"Loving the other?"

"Yes; with a curious tender solicitude seemingly; though her exact feeling for him is a riddle to me—and to him too, I think—possibly to herself. She is one of the oddest creatures I ever met. However, I have been struck with these two facts; the extraordinary sympathy, or similarity, between the pair. (He is her cousin, which perhaps accounts for some of it. They seem to be one person split in two!) And with her unconquerable aversion to myself as a husband, even though she may like me as a friend, 'tis too much to bear longer. She has conscientiously struggled against it, but to no purpose. I cannot bear it—I cannot! I can't answer her arguments—she has read ten times as much as I. Her intellect sparkles like diamonds, while mine smoulders like brown paper. . . . She's one too many for me!"

"She'll get over it, good-now?"

"Never! It is—but I won't go into it—there are reasons why she never will. At last she calmly and firmly asked if she might leave me and go to him. The climax came last night, when, owing to my entering her room by accident, she jumped out of window—so strong was her dread of me! She pretended it was a dream, but that was to soothe me. Now when a woman jumps out of window without caring whether she breaks her neck or no, she's not to be mistaken; and this being the case I have come to a conclusion: that it is wrong to so torture a fellow-creature any longer; and I won't be the inhuman wretch to do it, cost what it may!"

"What—you'll let her go? And with her lover?"

"Whom with is her matter. I shall let her go; with him certainly, if she wishes. I know I may be wrong—I know I can't logically, or religiously, defend my concession to such a wish of hers; or harmonise it with the doctrines I was brought up in. Only I know one thing: something within me tells me I am doing wrong in refusing her. I, like other men, profess to hold that if a husband gets such a so-called preposterous request from his wife, the only course that can possibly be regarded as right and proper and honourable in him is to refuse it, and put her virtuously under lock and key, and murder her lover perhaps. But is that essentially right, and proper, and honourable, or is it contemptibly mean and selfish? I don't profess to decide. I simply am going to act by instinct, and let principles take care of themselves. If a person who has blindly walked into a quagmire cries for help, I am inclined to give it, if possible."

"But—you see, there's the question of neighbours and society—what will happen if everybody—"

"O, I am not going to be a philosopher any longer! I only see what's under my eyes."

"Well—I don't agree with your instinct, Dick!" said Gillingham gravely. "I am quite amazed, to tell the truth, that such a sedate, plodding fellow as you should have entertained such a craze for a moment. You said when I called that she was puzzling and peculiar: I think you are!"

"Have you ever stood before a woman whom you know to be intrinsically a good woman, while she has pleaded for release—been the man she has knelt to and implored indulgence of?"

"I am thankful to say I haven't."

"Then I don't think you are in a position to give an opinion. I have been that man, and it makes all the difference in the world, if one has any manliness or chivalry in him. I had not the remotest idea—living apart from women as I have done for so many years—that merely taking a woman to church and putting a ring upon her finger could by any possibility involve one in such a daily, continuous tragedy as that now shared by her and me!"

"Well, I could admit some excuse for letting her leave you, provided she kept to herself. But to go attended by a cavalier—that makes a difference."

"Not a bit. Suppose, as I believe, she would rather endure her present misery than be made to promise to keep apart from him? All that is a question for herself. It is not the same thing at all as the treachery of living on with a husband and playing him false. . . . However, she has not distinctly implied living with him as wife, though I think she means to. . . . And to the best of my understanding it is not an ignoble, merely animal, feeling between the two: that is the worst of it; because it makes me think their affection will be enduring. I did not mean to confess to you that in the first jealous weeks of my marriage, before I had come to my right mind, I hid myself in the school one evening when they were together there, and I heard what they said. I am ashamed of it now, though I suppose I was only exercising a legal right. I found from their manner that an extraordinary affinity, or sympathy, entered into their attachment, which somehow took away all flavour of grossness. Their supreme desire is to be together—to share each other's emotions, and fancies, and dreams."

"Platonic!"

"Well no. Shelleyan would be nearer to it. They remind me of Laon and Cythna. Also of Paul and Virginia a little. The more I reflect, the more *entirely* I am on their side!"

"But if people did as you want to do, there'd be a general domestic disintegration. The family would no longer be the social unit."

"Yes—I am all abroad, I suppose!" said Phillotson sadly. "I was never a very bright reasoner, you remember. . . . And yet, I don't see why the woman and the children should not be the unit without the man."

"By the Lord Harry!—Matriarchy! . . . Does *she* say all this too?"

"O no. She little thinks I have out-Sued Sue in this—all in the last twelve hours!"

"It will upset all received opinion hereabout. Good God—what will Shaston say!"

"I don't say that it won't. I don't know—I don't know! . . . As I say, I am only a feeler, not a reasoner."

"Now," said Gillingham, "let us take it quietly, and have something to drink over it." He went under the stairs, and produced a bottle of cider-wine, of which they drank a rummer each. "I think you are rafted, and not yourself," he continued. "Do go back and make up your mind to put up with a few whims. But keep her. I hear on all sides that she's a charming young thing."

"Ah yes! That's the bitterness of it! Well, I won't stay. I have a long walk before me."

Gillingham accompanied his friend a mile on his way, and at parting expressed his hope that this consultation, singular as its subject was, would be the renewal of their old comradeship. "Stick to her!" were his last words, flung into the darkness after Phillotson; from which his friend answered "Ay, ay!"

But when Phillotson was alone under the clouds of night, and no sound was audible but that of the purling tributaries of the Stour, he said, "So Gillingham, my friend, you had no stronger arguments against it than those!"

"I think she ought to be smacked, and brought to her senses—that's what I think!" murmured Gillingham, as he walked back alone.

The next morning came, and at breakfast Phillotson told Sue:

"You may go—with whom you will. I absolutely and unconditionally agree."

Having once come to this conclusion it seemed to Phillotson more and more indubitably the true one. His mild serenity at the sense that he was doing his duty by a woman who was at his mercy almost overpowered his grief at relinquishing her.

Some days passed, and the evening of their last meal together had come—a cloudy evening with wind—which indeed was very seldom absent in this elevated place. How permanently it was imprinted upon his vision; that look of her as she glided into the parlour to tea; a slim flexible figure; a face, strained from its roundness, and marked by the pallors of restless days and nights, suggesting tragic possibilities quite at variance with her times of buoyancy; a trying of this morsel and that, and an inability to eat either. Her nervous manner, begotten of a fear lest he should be injured by her course, might have been interpreted by a stranger as displeasure that Phillotson intruded his presence on her for the few brief minutes that remained.

"You had better have a slice of ham, or an egg, or something with your tea? You can't travel on a mouthful of bread-and-butter."

She took the slice he helped her to; and they discussed as they sat trivial questions of housekeeping, such as where he would find the key of this or that cupboard, what little bills were paid, and what not.

"I am a bachelor by nature, as you know, Sue," he said, in a heroic attempt to put her at her ease. "So that being without a wife will not really be irksome to me, as it might be to other men who have had one a little while. I have, too, this grand hobby in my head of writing 'The Roman Antiquities of Wessex,' which will occupy all my spare hours."

"If you will send me some of the manuscript to copy at any time, as you used to, I will do it with so much pleasure!" she said with amenable gentleness. "I should much like to be some help to you still—as a f-f-friend."

Phillotson mused, and said: "No, I think we ought to be really separate, if we are to be at all. And for this reason, that I don't wish to ask you any questions, and particularly wish you not to give me information as to your movements, or even your address. . . . Now, what money do you want? You must have some, you know."

"O, of course, Richard, I couldn't think of having any of *your* money to go away from you with! I don't want any either. I have enough of my own to last me for a long while, and Jude will let me have—"

"I would rather not know anything about him, if you don't mind. You are free, absolutely; and your course is your own."

"Very well. But I'll just say that I have packed only a change or two of my own personal clothing, and one or two little things besides that are my very own. I wish you would look into my trunk before it is closed. Besides that I have only a small parcel that will go into Jude's portmanteau."

"Of course I shall do no such thing as examine your luggage! I wish you would take three-quarters of the household furniture. I don't want to be bothered with it. I have a sort of affection for a little of it that belonged to my poor mother and father. But the rest you are welcome to whenever you like to send for it."

"That I shall never do."

"You go by the six-thirty train, don't you? It is now a quarter to six."

"You . . . You don't seem very sorry I am going, Richard!"

"O no—perhaps not."

"I like you much for how you have behaved. It is a curious thing that directly I have begun to regard you as not my husband, but as my old teacher, I like you. I won't be so affected as to say I love you, because you know I don't, except as a friend. But you do seem that to me!"

Sue was for a few moments a little tearful at these reflections, and then the station omnibus came round to take her up. Phillotson saw her things put on the top, handed her in, and was obliged to make an appearance of kissing her as he wished her good-bye, though she shrank even from that. From the cheerful manner in which they parted the omnibus-man had no other idea than that she was going for a short visit.

When Phillotson got back into the house he went upstairs and opened the window in the direction the omnibus had taken. Soon the noise of its wheels died away. He came down then, his face compressed like that of one bearing pain; he put on his hat and went out, following by the same route for nearly a mile. Suddenly turning round he came home.

He had no sooner entered than the voice of his friend Gillingham greeted him from the front-room.

"I could make nobody hear; so finding your door open I walked in, and made myself comfortable. I said I would call, you remember."

"Yes. I am much obliged to you, Gillingham, particularly for coming to-night."

"How is Mrs.—"

"She is quite well. She is gone—just gone. That's her tea-cup, that she drank out of only an hour ago. And that's the plate she—" Phillotson's throat got choked up, and he could not go on. He turned and pushed the tea-things aside.

"Have you had any tea, by the by?" he asked presently in a renewed voice.

"No—yes—never mind," said Gillingham, preoccupied. "Gone, you say she is?"

"Yes. . . . I would have died for her; but I wouldn't be cruel to her in the name of the law. She is, as I understand, gone to join her lover. What they are going to do I cannot say. Whatever it may be she has my full consent to."

There was a stability, a ballast, in Phillotson's pronouncement which restrained his friend's comment. "Shall I—leave you?" he asked.

"No, no. It is a mercy to me that you have come. I have some articles to arrange and clear away. Would you help me?"

Gillingham assented; and having gone to the upper-rooms the schoolmaster opened drawers, and began taking out all Sue's things that she had left behind, and laying them in a large box. "She wouldn't take all I wanted her to," he continued. "But when I made up my mind to her going to live in her own way I did make up my mind."

"Some men would have stopped at an agreement to separate."

"I've gone into all that, and don't wish to argue it. I was, and am, the most old-fashioned man in the world on the question of marriage—in fact I had never thought critically about its ethics at all. But certain facts stared me in the face, and I couldn't go against them."

They went on with the packing silently. When it was done Phillotson closed the box and turned the key.

"There," he said. "To adorn her in somebody's eyes; never again in mine!"

V

FOUR-AND-TWENTY HOURS BEFORE THIS TIME SUE HAD WRITTEN THE FOLLOWING NOTE to Jude:

It is as I told you; and I am leaving to-morrow evening. Richard and I thought it could be done with less obtrusiveness after dark. I feel rather frightened, and therefore ask you to be sure you are on the Melchester platform to meet me by the train arriving at a little to seven. I know you will, of course, dear Jude; but I feel so timid that I can't help begging you to be punctual. He has been so very kind to me through it all!

Now to our meeting!   S.

As she was carried by the omnibus further and further down from the mountain town—the single passenger that evening—she regarded the receding road with a sad face. But no hesitation was apparent therein.

The up-train by which she was departing stopped by signal only. To Sue it seemed strange that such a powerful organization as a railway-train should be brought to a standstill on purpose for her—a fugitive from her lawful home.

The twenty minutes' journey drew towards its close, and Sue began gathering her things together to alight. At the moment that the train came to a standstill by the Melchester platform a hand was laid on the door and she beheld Jude. He entered the compartment promptly. He had a black bag in his hand, and was dressed in the dark suit he wore on Sundays and in the evening after work. Altogether he looked a very handsome young fellow, his ardent affection for her burning in his eyes.

"O Jude!" She clasped his hand with both hers, and her tense state caused her to simmer over in a little succession of dry sobs. "I—I am so glad! I get out here?"

"No. I get in, dear one! I've packed. Besides this bag I've only a big box which is labelled."

"But don't I get out? Aren't we going to stay here?"

"We couldn't possibly, don't you see. We are known here—I, at any rate, am well known. I've booked for Aldbrickham; and here's your ticket for the same place, as you have only one to here."

"I thought we should have stayed here," she repeated.

"It wouldn't have done at all."

"Ah!—Perhaps not."

"There wasn't time for me to write and say the place I had decided on. Aldbrickham

is a much bigger town—sixty or seventy thousand inhabitants—and nobody knows anything about us there."

"And you have given up your Cathedral work here?"

"Yes. It was rather sudden—your message coming unexpectedly. Strictly, I might have
been made to finish out the week. But I pleaded urgency and I was let off. I would have deserted any day at your command, dear Sue. I have deserted more than that for you!"

"I fear I am doing you a lot of harm. Ruining your prospects of the Church; ruining
your progress in your trade; everything!"

"The Church is no more to me. Let it lie! *I* am not to be one of

> *The soldier-saints who, row on row,*
> *Burn upward each to his point of bliss,*

if any such there be! My point of bliss is not upward, but here."

"O I seem so bad—upsetting men's courses like this!" said she, taking up in her voice
the emotion that had begun in his. But she recovered her equanimity by the time they had
travelled a dozen miles.

"He has been so good in letting me go," she resumed. "And here's a note I found on
my dressing-table, addressed to you."

"Yes. He's not an unworthy fellow," said Jude, glancing at the note. "And I am
ashamed of myself for hating him because he married you."

"According to the rule of women's whims I suppose I ought to suddenly love him, because he has let me go so generously and unexpectedly," she answered smiling. "But I am
so cold, or devoid of gratitude, or so something, that even this generosity hasn't made me
love him, or repent, or want to stay with him as his wife; although I do feel I like his large-
mindedness, and respect him more than ever."

"It may not work so well for us as if he had been less kind, and you had run away
against his will," murmured Jude.

"That I *never* would have done."

Jude's eyes rested musingly on her face. Then he suddenly kissed her; and was going
to kiss her again. "No—only once now—please, Jude!"

"That's rather cruel," he answered; but acquiesced. "Such a strange thing has happened to me," Jude continued after a silence. "Arabella has actually written to ask me to
get a divorce from her—in kindness to her, she says. She wants to honestly and legally
marry that man she has already married virtually; and begs me to enable her to do it."

"What have you done?"

"I have agreed. I thought at first I couldn't do it without getting her into trouble about
that second marriage, and I don't want to injure her in any way. Perhaps she's no worse
than I am, after all! But nobody knows about it over here, and I find it will not be a difficult proceeding at all. If she wants to start afresh I have only too obvious reasons for not
hindering her."

"Then you'll be free?"

"Yes, I shall be free."

"Where are we booked for?" she asked, with the discontinuity that marked her to-
night.

"Aldbrickham, as I said."

"But it will be very late when we get there?"

"Yes. I thought of that, and I wired for a room for us at the Temperance Hotel there."

"One?"

"Yes—one."

She looked at him. "O Jude!" Sue bent her forehead against the corner of the compartment. "I thought you might do it; and that I was deceiving you. But I didn't mean that!"

In the pause which followed, Jude's eyes fixed themselves with a stultified expression on the opposite seat. "Well!" he said. . . . "Well!"

He remained in silence; and seeing how discomfited he was she put her face against his cheek, murmuring, "Don't be vexed, dear!"

"Oh—there's no harm done," he said. "But—I understood it like that. . . . Is this a sudden change of mind?"

"You have no right to ask me such a question; and I shan't answer!" she said, smiling.

"My dear one, your happiness is more to me than anything—although we seem to verge on quarrelling so often!—and your will is law to me. I am something more than a mere—selfish fellow, I hope. Have it as you wish!" On reflection his brow showed perplexity. "But perhaps it is that you don't love me—not that you have become conventional! Much as, under your teaching, I hate convention, I hope it *is* that, not the other terrible alternative!"

Even at this obvious moment for candour Sue could not be quite candid as to the state of that mystery, her heart. "Put it down to my timidity," she said with hurried evasiveness; "to a woman's natural timidity when the crisis comes. I *may* feel as well as you that I have a perfect right to live with you as you thought—from this moment. I *may* hold the opinion that, in a proper state of society, the father of a woman's child will be as much a private matter of hers as the cut of her under-linen, on whom nobody will have any right to conjecture. But partly, perhaps, because it is by his generosity that I am now free, I would rather not be other than a little rigid. If there had been a rope-ladder, and he had run after us with pistols, it would have seemed different, and I may have acted otherwise. But don't press me and criticise me, Jude! Assume that I haven't the courage of my opinions. I know I am a poor miserable creature. My nature is not so passionate as yours!"

He repeated simply: "I thought—what I naturally thought. But if we are not lovers, we are not. Phillotson thought so, I am sure. See, here is what he has written to me." He opened the letter she had brought, and read:

"I make only one condition—that you are tender and kind to her. I know you love her. But even love may be cruel at times. You are made for each other: it is obvious, palpable, to any unbiassed older person. You were all along 'the shadowy third' in my short life with her. I repeat, take care of Sue."

"He's a good fellow, isn't he!" she said with latent tears. On reconsideration she added, "He was very resigned to letting me go—too resigned almost! I never was so near being in love with him as when he made such thoughtful arrangements for my being comfortable on my journey, and offering to provide money. Yet I was not. If I loved him ever so little as a wife, I'd go back to him even now."

"But you don't, do you?"

"It is true—O so terribly true!—I don't."

"Nor me neither, I half-fear!" he said pettishly. "Nor anybody perhaps! Sue, sometimes, when I am vexed with you, I think you are incapable of real love."

"That's not good and loyal of you!" she said, and drawing away from him as far as she could, looked severely out into the darkness. She presently added, in hurt tones, turning round: "My liking for you is not as some women's perhaps. But it is a delight in being with you, of a supremely delicate kind, and I don't want to go further and risk it by—an attempt to intensify it! I quite realised that, as woman with man, it was a risk to come. But, as *me* with *you*, I resolved to trust you to set my wishes above your gratification. Don't discuss it further, dear Jude!"

"Of course, if it would make you reproach yourself . . . but you do like me very much, Sue? say you do! Say that you do a quarter, a tenth, as much as I do you; and I'll be content!"

"I've let you kiss me, and that tells enough."

"Just once or so!"

"Well—don't be a greedy boy."

He leant back, and did not look at her for a long time. That episode in her past history of which she had told him—of the poor Christminster graduate whom she had handled thus, returned to Jude's mind; and he saw himself as a possible second in such a torturing destiny.

"This is a queer elopement!" he murmured. "Perhaps you are making a cat's-paw of me with Phillotson all this time. Upon my word it almost seems so—to see you sitting up there so prim!"

"Now you mustn't be angry—I won't let you!" she coaxed, turning and moving nearer to him. "You did kiss me just now, you know; and I didn't dislike you to, very much, Jude. Only I don't want to let you do it again, just yet—considering how we are circumstanced, don't you see!"

He could never resist her when she pleaded (as she well knew). And they sat side by side with joined hands, till she aroused herself at some thought.

"I can't possibly go to that Temperance Inn, after your telegraphing that message!"

"Why not?"

"You can see well enough!"

"Very well; there'll be some other one open, no doubt. I have sometimes thought, since your marrying Phillotson because of a stupid scandal, that under the affectation of independent views you are as enslaved to the social code as any woman I know!"

"Not mentally. But I haven't the courage of my views, as I said before. I didn't marry him altogether because of the scandal. But sometimes a woman's *love of being loved* gets the better of her conscience, and though she is agonised at the thought of treating a man cruelly, she encourages him to love her while she doesn't love him at all. Then, when she sees him suffering, her remorse sets in, and she does what she can to repair the wrong."

"You simply mean that you flirted outrageously with him, poor old chap, and then repented, and to make reparation, married him, though you tortured yourself to death by doing it."

"Well—if you will put it brutally!—it was a little like that—that and the scandal together—and your concealing from me what you ought to have told me before!"

He could see that she was distressed and tearful at his criticisms, and soothed her, saying: "There, dear; don't mind! Crucify me, if you will! You know you are all the world to me, whatever you do!"

"I am very bad and unprincipled—I know you think that!" she said, trying to blink away her tears.

"I think and know you are my dear Sue, from whom neither length nor breadth, nor things present nor things to come, can divide me!"

Though so sophisticated in many things she was such a child in others that this satisfied her, and they reached the end of their journey on the best of terms. It was about ten o'clock when they arrived at Aldbrickham, the county town of North Wessex. As she would not go to the Temperance Hotel because of the form of his telegram, Jude enquired for another; and a youth who volunteered to find one wheeled their luggage to the George further on, which proved to be the inn at which Jude had stayed with Arabella on that one occasion of their meeting after their division for years.

Owing, however, to their now entering it by another door, and to his preoccupation, he did not at first recognise the place. When they had engaged their respective rooms they went down to a late supper. During Jude's temporary absence the waiting-maid spoke to Sue.

"I think, ma'am, I remember your relation, or friend, or whatever he is, coming here once before—late, just like this, with his wife—a lady, at any rate, that wasn't you by no manner of means—jest as med be with you now."

"O do you?" said Sue, with a certain sickness of heart. "Though I think you must be mistaken! How long ago was it?"

"About a month or two. A handsome, full-figured woman."

When Jude came back and sat down to supper Sue seemed moping and miserable. "Jude," she said to him plaintively, at their parting that night upon the landing, "it is not so nice and pleasant as it used to be with us! I don't like it here—I can't bear the place! And I don't like you so well as I did!"

"How fidgetted you seem, dear! Why do you change like this?"

"Because it was cruel to bring me here!"

"Why?"

"You were lately here with Arabella. There, now I have said it!"

"Dear me, why—" said Jude, looking round him. "Yes—it is the same! I really didn't know it, Sue. Well—it is not cruel, since we have come as we have—two relations staying together."

"How long ago was it you were here? Tell me, tell me!"

"The day before I met you in Christminster, when we went back to Marygreen together. I told you I had met her."

"Yes, you said you had met her, but you didn't tell me all. Your story was that you had met as estranged people, who were not husband and wife at all in Heaven's sight—not that you had made it up with her."

"We didn't make it up," he said sadly. "I can't explain, Sue."

"You've been false to me; you, my last hope! And I shall never forget it, never!"

"But by your own wish, dear Sue, we are only to be friends, not lovers! It is so very inconsistent of you to—"

"Friends can be jealous!"

"I don't see that. You concede nothing to me and I have to concede everything to you. After all, you were on good terms with your husband at that time."

"No, I wasn't, Jude. O how can you think so! And you have taken me in, even if you didn't intend to." She was so mortified that he was obliged to take her into her room and close the door lest the people should hear. "Was it this room? Yes it was—I see by your look it was! I won't have it for mine! O it was treacherous of you to have her again! *I* jumped out of the window!"

"But Sue, she was, after all, my legal wife, if not—"

Slipping down on her knees Sue buried her face in the bed and wept.

"I never knew such an unreasonable—such a dog-in-the-manger feeling," said Jude. "I am not to approach you, nor anybody else!"

"O don't you *understand* my feeling! *Why* don't you! Why are you so gross! *I* jumped out of the window!"

"Jumped out of window?"

"I can't explain!"

It was true that he did not understand her feeling very well. But he did a little; and began to love her none the less.

"I—I thought you cared for nobody—desired nobody in the world but me at that time—and ever since!" continued Sue.

"It is true. I did not, and don't now!" said Jude, as distressed as she.

"But you must have thought much of her! Or—"

"No—I need not—you don't understand me either—women never do! Why should you get into such a tantrum about nothing?"

Looking up from the quilt she replied provokingly: "If it hadn't been for that, perhaps I would have gone on to the Temperance Hotel, after all, as you proposed; for I was beginning to think I did belong to you!"

"O, it is of no consequence!" said Jude distantly.

"I thought, of course, that she had never been really your wife since she left you of her own accord years and years ago! My sense of it was, that a parting such as yours from her, and mine from him, ended the marriage."

"I can't say more without speaking against her, and I don't want to do that," said he. "Yet I must tell you one thing, which would settle the matter in any case. She has married another man—really married him! I knew nothing about it till after the visit we made here."

"Married another? . . . It is a crime—as the world treats it, but does not believe."

"There—now you are yourself again. Yes, it is a crime—as you don't hold, but would fearfully concede. But I shall never inform against her! and it is evidently a prick of conscience in her that has led her to urge me to get a divorce, that she may remarry this man legally. So you perceive I shall not be likely to see her again."

"And you didn't really know anything of this when you saw her?" said Sue more gently, as she rose.

"I did not. Considering all things, I don't think you ought to be angry, darling!"

"I am not. But I shan't go to the Temperance Hotel!"

He laughed. "Never mind!" he said. "So that I am near you, I am comparatively happy. It is more than this earthly wretch called Me deserves—you spirit, you disembodied creature, you dear, sweet, tantalizing phantom—hardly flesh at all; so that when I put my arms round you I almost expect them to pass through you as through air! Forgive me for being gross, as you call it! Remember that our calling cousins when really strangers was a snare. The enmity of our parents gave a piquancy to you in my eyes that was intenser even than the novelty of ordinary new acquaintance."

"Say those pretty lines, then, from Shelley's 'Epipsychidion' as if they meant me!" she solicited, slanting up closer to him as they stood. "Don't you know them?"

"I know hardly any poetry," he replied mournfully.

"Don't you? These are some of them:

> *There was a Being whom my spirit oft*
> *Met on its visioned wanderings far aloft.*
>
>   .   .   .   .
>
> *A seraph of Heaven, too gentle to be human,*
> *Veiling beneath that radiant form of woman. . . .*

O it is too flattering, so I won't go on! But say it's me!—say it's me!"

"It *is* you, dear; exactly like you!"

"Now I forgive you! And you shall kiss me just once there—not very long." She put the tip of her finger gingerly to her cheek; and he did as commanded. "You do care for me very much, don't you, in spite of my not—you know?"

"Yes, sweet!" he said with a sigh; and bade her good-night.

VI

IN RETURNING TO HIS NATIVE TOWN OF SHASTON AS SCHOOLMASTER PHILLOTSON HAD won the interest and awakened the memories of the inhabitants, who, though they did not honour him for his miscellaneous aquirements as he would have been honoured elsewhere, retained for him a sincere regard. When, shortly after his arrival, he brought home a pretty wife—awkwardly pretty for him, if he did not take care, they said—they were glad to have her settle among them.

For some time after her flight from that home Sue's absence did not excite comment. Her place as monitor in the school was taken by another young woman within a few days of her vacating it, which substitution also passed without remark, Sue's services having been of a provisional nature only. When, however, a month had passed, and Phillotson casually admitted to acquaintance that he did not know where his wife was staying, curiosity began to be aroused; till, jumping to conclusions, people ventured to affirm that Sue had played him false and run away from him. The schoolmaster's growing languor and listlessness over his work gave countenance to the idea.

Though Phillotson had held his tongue as long as he could, except to his friend Gillingham, his honesty and directness would not allow him to do so when misapprehensions as to Sue's conduct spread abroad. On a Monday morning the chairman of the

School Committee called, and after attending to the business of the school drew Phillotson aside out of earshot of the children.

"You'll excuse my asking, Phillotson, since everybody is talking of it: is this true as to your domestic affairs—that your wife's going away was on no visit, but a secret elopement with a lover? If so, I condole with you."

"Don't," said Phillotson. "There was no secret about it."

"She has gone to visit friends?"

"No."

"Then what has happened?"

"She has gone away under circumstances that usually call for condolence with the husband. But I gave my consent."

The chairman looked as if he had not apprehended the remark.

"What I say is quite true," Phillotson continued testily. "She asked leave to go away with her lover, and I let her. Why shouldn't I? A woman of full age, it was a question for her own conscience—not for me. I was not her gaoler. I can't explain any further. I don't wish to be questioned."

The children observed that much seriousness marked the faces of the two men, and went home and told their parents that something new had happened about Mrs. Phillotson. Then Phillotson's little maidservant, who was a schoolgirl just out of her standards, said that Mr. Phillotson had helped in his wife's packing, had offered her what money she required, and had written a friendly letter to her young man, telling him to take care of her. The chairman of committee thought the matter over, and talked to the other managers of the school, till a request came to Phillotson to meet them privately. The meeting lasted a long time, and at the end the schoolmaster came home, looking as usual pale and worn. Gillingham was sitting in his house awaiting him.

"Well; it is as you said," observed Phillotson, flinging himself down wearily in a chair. "They have requested me to send in my resignation on account of my scandalous conduct in giving my tortured wife her liberty—or, as they call it, condoning her adultery. But I shan't resign!"

"I think I would."

"I won't. It is no business of theirs. It doesn't affect me in my public capacity at all. They may expel me if they like."

"If you make a fuss it will get into the papers, and you'll never get appointed to another school. You see, they have to consider what you did as done by a teacher of youth—and its effects as such upon the morals of the town; and, to ordinary opinion, your position is indefensible. You must let me say that."

To this good advice, however, Phillotson would not listen.

"I don't care," he said. "I don't go unless I am turned out. And for this reason; that by resigning I acknowledge I have acted wrongly by her; when I am more and more convinced everyday that in the sight of Heaven and by all natural, straightforward humanity, I have acted rightly."

Gillingham saw that his rather headstrong friend would not be able to maintain such a position as this; but he said nothing further, and in due time—indeed, in a quarter of an hour—the formal letter of dismissal arrived, the managers having remained behind to write it after Phillotson's withdrawal. The latter replied that he should not accept dismissal; and called a public meeting, which he attended, although he looked so weak and ill that his friend implored him to stay at home. When he stood up to give his reasons for contesting the decision of the managers he advanced them firmly, as he had done to his friend, and contended, moreover, that the matter was a domestic theory which did not concern them. This they over-ruled, insisting that the private eccentricities of a teacher came quite within their sphere of control, as it touched the morals of those he taught. Phillotson replied that he did not see how an act of natural charity could injure morals.

All the respectable inhabitants and well-to-do fellow-natives of the town were against Phillotson to a man. But, somewhat to his surprise, some dozen or more champions rose up in his defence as from the ground.

It has been stated that Shaston was the anchorage of a curious and interesting group of itinerants, who frequented the numerous fairs and markets held up and down Wessex during the summer and autumn months. Although Phillotson had never spoken to one of these gentlemen they now nobly led the forlorn hope in his defence. The body included two cheap-jacks, a shooting-gallery proprietor and the ladies who loaded the guns, a pair of boxing-masters, a steam-roundabout manager, two travelling broom-makers, who called themselves widows, a gingerbread-stall keeper, a swing-boat owner, and a "test-your-strength" man.

This generous phalanx of supporters, and a few others of independent judgment, whose own domestic experiences had been not without vicissitude, came up and warmly shook hands with Phillotson; after which they expressed their thoughts so strongly to the meeting that issue was joined, the result being a general scuffle, wherein a blackboard was split, three panes of the school-windows were broken, an inkbottle was spilled over a town-councillor's shirt-front, and some black eyes and bleeding noses were given, one of which, to everybody's horror, was the venerable incumbent's, owing to the zeal of an emancipated chimney-sweep, who took the side of Phillotson's party. When Phillotson saw the blood running down the rector's face he deplored almost in groans the untoward and degrading circumstances, regretted that he had not resigned when called upon, and went home so ill that next morning he could not leave his bed.

The farcical yet melancholy event was the beginning of a serious illness for him; and he lay in his lonely bed in the pathetic state of mind of a middle-aged man who perceives at length that his life, intellectual and domestic, is tending to failure and gloom. Gillingham came to see him in the evenings, and on one occasion mentioned Sue's name.

"She doesn't care anything about me!" said Phillotson. "Why should she?"

"She doesn't know you are ill."

"So much the better for both of us."

"Where are her lover and she living?"

"At Melchester—I suppose; at least he was living there some time ago."

When Gillingham reached home he sat and reflected, and at last wrote an anonymous line to Sue, on the bare chance of its reaching her, the letter being enclosed in an envelope addressed to Jude at the diocesan capital. Arriving at that place it was forwarded to Marygreen in North Wessex, and thence to Aldbrickham by the only person who knew his present address—the widow who had nursed his aunt.

Three days later, in the evening, when the sun was going down in splendour over the lowlands of Blackmoor, and making the Shaston windows like tongues of fire to the eyes of the rustics in that Vale, the sick man fancied that he heard somebody come to the house, and a few minutes after there was a tap at the bedroom-door. Phillotson did not speak; the door was hesitatingly opened, and there entered—Sue.

She was in light spring clothing, and her advent seemed ghostly—like the flitting in of a moth. He turned his eyes upon her, and flushed; but appeared to check his primary impulse to speak.

"I have no business here," she said, bending her frightened face to him. "But I heard you were ill—very ill; and—and as I know that you recognise other feelings between man and woman than physical love, I have come."

"I am not very ill, my dear friend. Only unwell."

"I didn't know that; and I am afraid that only a severe illness would have justified my coming!"

"Yes . . . yes. And I almost wish you had not come! It is a little too soon—that's all I mean. Still, let us make the best of it. You haven't heard about the school, I suppose?"

"No—what about it?"

"Only that I am going away from here to another place. The managers and I don't agree, and we are going to part—that's all."

Sue did not for a moment, either now or later, suspect what troubles had resulted to him from letting her go; it never once seemed to cross her mind, and she had received no news whatever from Shaston. They talked on slight and ephemeral subjects, and when his tea was brought up he told the amazed little servant that a cup was to be set for Sue. That young person was much more interested in their history than they supposed, and as she descended the stairs she lifted her eyes and hands in grotesque amazement. While they sipped Sue went to the window and thoughtfully said, "It is such a beautiful sunset, Richard."

"They are mostly beautiful from here, owing to the rays crossing the mist of the Vale. But I lose them all, as they don't shine into this gloomy corner where I lie."

"Wouldn't you like to see this particular one? It is like heaven opened."

"Ah yes! But I can't."

"I'll help you to."

"No—the bedstead can't be shifted."

"But see how I mean."

She went to where a swing-glass stood, and taking it in her hands carried it to a spot by the window where it could catch the sunshine, moving the glass till the beams were reflected into Phillotson's face.

"There—you can see the great red sun now!" she said. "And I am sure it will cheer you—I do so hope it will!" She spoke with a childlike, repentant kindness, as if she could not do too much for him.

Phillotson smiled sadly. "You are an odd creature!" he murmured as the sun glowed in his eyes. "The idea of your coming to see me after what has passed!"

"Don't let us go back upon that!" she said quickly. "I have to catch the omnibus for the train, as Jude doesn't know I have come; he was out when I started; so I must return home almost directly. Richard, I am so very glad you are better. You don't hate me, do you? You have been such a kind friend to me!"

"I am glad to know you think so," said Phillotson huskily. "No. I don't hate you!"

It grew dusk quickly in the gloomy room during their intermittent chat, and when candles were brought and it was time to leave she put her hand in his—or rather allowed it to flit through his; for she was significantly light in touch. She had nearly closed the door when he said, "Sue!" He had noticed that, in turning away from him, tears were on her face and a quiver in her lip.

It was bad policy to recall her—he knew it while he pursued it. But he could not help it. She came back.

"Sue," he murmured, "do you wish to make it up, and stay? I'll forgive you and condone everything!"

"O you can't, you can't!" she said hastily. "You can't condone it now!"

"*He* is your husband now, in effect, you mean, of course?"

"You may assume it. He is obtaining a divorce from his wife Arabella."

"His wife! It is altogether news to me that he has a wife."

"It was a bad marriage."

"Like yours."

"Like mine. He is not doing it so much on his own account as on hers. She wrote and told him it would be a kindness to her, since then she could marry and live respectably. And Jude has agreed."

"A wife. . . . A kindness to her. Ah, yes; a kindness to her to release her altogether. . . . But I don't like the sound of it. *I* can forgive, Sue."

"No, no! You can't have me back now I have been so wicked—as to do what I have done!"

There had arisen in Sue's face that incipient fright which showed itself whenever he changed from friend to husband, and which made her adopt any line of defence against marital feeling in him. "I *must* go now. I'll come again—may I?"

"I don't ask you to go, even now. I ask you to stay."

"I thank you, Richard; but I must. As you are not so ill as I thought, I *cannot* stay!"

"She's his—his from lips to heel!" said Phillotson; but so faintly that in closing the door she did not hear it. The dread of a reactionary change in the schoolmaster's sentiments, coupled, perhaps, with a faint shamefacedness at letting even him know what a slipshod lack of thoroughness, from a man's point of view, characterised her transferred allegiance, prevented her telling him of her, thus far, incomplete relations with Jude; and Phillotson lay writhing like a man in hell as he pictured the prettily dressed, maddening compound of sympathy and averseness who bore his name, returning impatiently to the home of her lover.

Gillingham was so interested in Phillotson's affairs, and so seriously concerned about him, that he walked up the hillside to Shaston two or three times a week, although, there and back, it was a journey of nine miles, which had to be performed between tea and supper, after a hard day's work in school. When he called on the next occasion after Sue's visit his friend was downstairs, and Gillingham noticed that his restless mood had been supplanted by a more fixed and composed one.

"She's been here since you called last," said Phillotson.

"Not Mrs. Phillotson?"

"Yes."

"Ah! You have made it up?"

"No. . . . She just came, patted my pillow with her little white hand, played the thoughtful nurse for half an hour, and went away."

"Well—I'm hanged! A little hussy!"

"What do you say?"

"O—nothing!"

"What do you mean?"

"I mean, what a tantalizing, capricious little woman! If she were not your wife—"

"She is not; she's another man's except in name and law. And I have been thinking—it was suggested to me by a conversation I had with her—that, in kindness to her, I ought to dissolve the legal tie altogether; which, singularly enough, I think I can do, now she has been back, and refused my request to stay after I said I had forgiven her. I believe that fact would afford me opportunity of doing it, though I did not see it at the moment. What's the use of keeping her chained on to me if she doesn't belong to me? I know—I feel absolutely certain—that she would welcome my taking such a step as the greatest charity to her. For though as a fellow-creature she sympathises with, and pities me, and even weeps for me, as a husband she cannot endure me—she loaths me—there's no use in mincing words—she loaths me, and my only manly, and dignified, and merciful course is to complete what I have begun. . . . And for worldly reasons, too, it will be better for her to be independent. I have hopelessly ruined my prospects because of my decision as to what was best for us, though she does not know it; I see only dire poverty ahead from my feet to the grave; for I can be accepted as teacher no more. I shall probably have enough to do to make both ends meet during the remainder of my life, now my occupation's gone; and I shall be better able to bear it alone. I may as well tell you that what has suggested my letting her go is some news she brought me—the news that Fawley is doing the same."

"O—he had a spouse, too? A queer couple, these lovers!"

"Well—I don't want your opinion on that. What I was going to say is that my liberating her can do her no possible harm, and will open up a chance of happiness for her which she has never dreamt of hitherto. For then they'll be able to marry, as they ought to have done at first."

Gillingham did not hurry to reply. "I may disagree with your motive," he said gently, for he respected views he could not share. "But I think you are right in your determination—if you can carry it out. I doubt, however, if you can."

PART FIFTH

AT ALDBRICKHAM AND ELSEWHERE

"Thy aërial part, and all the fiery parts which are mingled in thee, though by nature they have an upward tendency, still in obedience to the disposition of the universe they are over-powered here in the compound mass the body."

M. ANTONINUS (LONG)

I

How Gillingham's doubts were disposed of will most quickly appear by passing over the series of dreary months and incidents that followed the events of the last chapter, and coming on to a Sunday in the February of the year following.

Sue and Jude were living in Aldbrickham, in precisely the same relations that they had established between themselves when she left Shaston to join him the year before. The proceedings in the Law-Courts had reached their consciousness but as a distant sound, and an occasional missive which they hardly understood.

They had met, as usual, to breakfast together in the little house with Jude's name on it, that he had taken at fifteen pounds a year, with three-pounds-ten extra for rates and taxes, and furnished with his aunt's ancient and lumbering goods, which had cost him about their full value to bring all the way from Marygreen. Sue kept house, and managed everything.

As he entered the room this morning Sue held up a letter she had just received.

"Well; and what is it about?" he said after kissing her.

"That the decree *nisi* in the case of Phillotson *versus* Phillotson and Fawley, pronounced six months ago, has just been made absolute."

"Ah," said Jude, as he sat down.

The same concluding incident in Jude's suit against Arabella had occurred about a month or two earlier. Both cases had been too insignificant to be reported in the papers, further than by name in a long list of other undefended cases.

"Now then, Sue, at any rate, you can do what you like!" He looked at his sweetheart curiously.

"Are we—you and I—just as free now as if we had never married at all?"

"Just as free—except, I believe, that a clergyman may object personally to remarry you, and hand the job on to somebody else."

"But I wonder—do you think it is really so with us? I know it is generally. But I have an uncomfortable feeling that my freedom has been obtained under false pretences!"

"How?"

"Well—if the truth about us had been known, the decree wouldn't have been pronounced. It is only, is it, because we have made no defence, and have led them into a false supposition? Therefore is my freedom lawful, however proper it may be?"

"Well—why did you let it be under false pretences? You have only yourself to blame," he said mischievously.

"Jude—don't! You ought not to be touchy about that still. You must take me as I am."

"Very well, darling: so I will. Perhaps you were right. As to your question, we were not obliged to prove anything. That was their business. Anyhow we are living together."

"Yes. Though not in their sense."

"One thing is certain, that however brought about, a marriage is dissolved when it is dissolved. There is this advantage in being poor obscure people like us—that these things are done for us in a rough and ready fashion. It was the same with me and Arabella. I was afraid her criminal second marriage would have been discovered, and she punished; but nobody took any interest in her—nobody enquired, nobody suspected it. If we'd been patented nobilities we should have had infinite trouble, and days and weeks would have been spent in investigations."

By degrees Sue acquired her lover's cheerfulness at the sense of freedom, and proposed that they should take a walk in the fields, even if they had to put up with a cold dinner on account of it. Jude agreed, and Sue went upstairs and prepared to start, putting on a joyful coloured gown in observance of her liberty; seeing which Jude put on a lighter tie.

"Now we'll strut arm in arm," he said, "like any other engaged couple. We've a legal right to."

They rambled out of the town, and along a path over the low-lying lands that bordered it, though these were frosty now, and the extensive seed-fields were bare of colour and produce. The pair, however, were so absorbed in their own situation that their surroundings were little in their consciousness.

"Well, my dearest, the result of all this is that we can marry after a decent interval."

"Yes; I suppose we can," said Sue, without enthusiasm.

"And aren't we going to?"

"I don't like to say no, dear Jude; but I feel just the same about it now as I have done all along. I have just the same dread lest an iron contract should extinguish your tenderness for me, and mine for you, as it did between our unfortunate parents."

"Still, what can we do? I do love you, as you know, Sue."

"I know it abundantly. But I think I would much rather go on living always as lovers, as we are living now, and only meeting by day. It is so much sweeter—for the woman at least, and when she is sure of the man. And henceforward we needn't be so particular as we have been about appearances."

"Our experiences of matrimony with others have not been encouraging, I own," said he with some gloom; "either owing to our own dissatisfied, unpractical natures, or by our misfortune. But we two—"

"Should be two dissatisfied ones linked together, which would be twice as bad as before. . . . I think I should begin to be afraid of you, Jude, the moment you had contracted to cherish me under a Government stamp, and I was licensed to be loved on the premises by you—Ugh, how horrible and sordid! Although, as you are, free, I trust you more than any other man in the world."

"No, no—don't say I should change!" he expostulated; yet there was misgiving in his own voice also.

"Apart from ourselves, and our unhappy peculiarities, it is foreign to a man's nature to go on loving a person when he is told that he must and shall be that person's lover. There would be a much likelier chance of his doing it if he were told not to love. If the marriage ceremony consisted in an oath and signed contract between the parties to cease loving from that day forward, in consideration of personal possession being given, and to avoid each other's society as much as possible in public, there would be more loving couples than there are now. Fancy the secret meetings between the perjuring husband and wife, the denials of having seen each other, the clambering in at bedroom-windows, and the hiding in closets! There'd be little cooling then."

"Yes; but admitting this, or something like it, to be true, you are not the only one in the world to see it, dear little Sue. People go on marrying because they can't resist natural forces, although many of them may know perfectly well that they are possibly buying a month's pleasure with a life's discomfort. No doubt my father and mother, and your father and mother, saw it, if they at all resembled us in habits of observation. But then they went and married just the same, because they had ordinary passions. But you, Sue, are such a phantasmal, bodiless creature, one who—if you'll allow me to say it—has so little animal passion in you, that you can act upon reason in the matter, when we poor unfortunate wretches of grosser substance can't."

"Well," she sighed, "you've owned that it would probably end in misery for us. And I am not so exceptional a woman as you think. Fewer women like marriage than you suppose, only they enter into it for the dignity it is assumed to confer, and the so-cial advantages it gains them sometimes—a dignity and an advantage that I am quite willing to do without."

Jude fell back upon his old complaint—that, intimate as they were, he had never once had from her an honest, candid declaration that she loved or could love him. "I really fear sometimes that you cannot," he said, with a dubiousness approaching anger. "And you are so reticent. I know that women are taught by other women that they must never admit the full truth to a man. But the highest form of affection is based on full sincerity on both sides. Not being men, these women don't know that in looking back on those he has had tender relations with, a man's heart returns closest to her who was the soul of truth in her con-duct. The better class of man, even if caught by airy affectations of dodging and parry-ing, is not retained by them. A Nemesis attends the woman who plays the game of elusiveness too often, in the utter contempt for her that, sooner or later, her old admirers feel; under which they allow her to go unlamented to her grave."

Sue, who was regarding the distance, had acquired a guilty look; and she suddenly replied in a tragic voice: "I don't think I like you to-day so well as I did, Jude!"

"Don't you? Why?"

"O, well—you are not nice—too sermony. Though I suppose I am so bad and worth-less that I deserve the utmost rigour of lecturing!"

"No, you are not bad. You are a dear. But as slippery as an eel when I want to get a confession from you."

"O yes I am bad, and obstinate, and all sorts! It is no use your pretending I am not! People who are good don't want scolding as I do. . . . But now that I have nobody but you, and nobody to defend me, it is *very* hard that I mustn't have my own way in deciding how I'll live with you, and whether I'll be married or no!"

"Sue, my own comrade and sweetheart, I don't want to force you either to marry or to do the other thing—of course I don't! It is too wicked of you to be so pettish! Now we won't say any more about it, and go on just the same as we have done; and during the rest of our walk we'll talk of the meadows only, and the floods, and the prospect of the farm-ers this coming year."

After this the subject of marriage was not mentioned by them for several days, though living as they were with only a landing between them it was constantly in their minds. Sue was assisting Jude very materially now: he had latterly occupied himself on his own ac-count in working and lettering head-stones, which he kept in a little yard at the back of his little house, where in the intervals of domestic duties she marked out the letters full size for him, and blacked them in after he had cut them. It was a lower class of handicraft than were his former performances as a cathedral mason, and his only patrons were the poor people who lived in his own neighbourhood, and knew what a cheap man this "Jude Fawley: Monumental Mason" (as he called himself on his front-door) was to employ for the simple memorials they required for their dead. But he seemed more independent than before, and it was the only arrangement under which Sue, who particularly wished to be no burden on him, could render any assistance.

II

IT WAS AN EVENING AT THE END OF THE MONTH, AND JUDE HAD JUST RETURNED HOME from hearing a lecture on ancient history in the public hall not far off. When he entered Sue, who had been keeping indoors during his absence, laid out supper for him. Contrary to custom she did not speak. Jude had taken up some illustrated paper, which he perused till, raising his eyes, he saw that her face was troubled.

"Are you depressed, Sue?" he said.

She paused a moment. "I have a message for you," she answered.

"Somebody has called?"

"Yes. A woman." Sue's voice quavered as she spoke, and she suddenly sat down from her preparations, laid her hands in her lap, and looked into the fire. "I don't know whether I did right or not!" she continued. "I said you were not at home, and when she said she would wait, I said I thought you might not be able to see her."

"Why did you say that, dear? I suppose she wanted a head-stone. Was she in mourning?"

"No. She wasn't in mourning, and she didn't want a head-stone; and I thought you wouldn't see her." Sue looked critically and imploringly at him.

"But who was she? Didn't she say?"

"No. She wouldn't give her name. But I know who she was—I think I do! It was Arabella!"

"Heaven save us! What should Arabella come for? What made you think it was she?"

"O, I can hardly tell. But I know it was! I feel perfectly certain it was—by the light in her eyes as she looked at me. She was a fleshy, coarse woman."

"Well—I should not have called Arabella coarse exactly, except in speech, though she may be getting so by this time under the duties of the public-house. She was rather handsome when I knew her."

"Handsome! But yes!—so she is!"

"I think I heard a quiver in your little mouth. Well, waiving that, as she is nothing to me, and virtuously married to another man, why should she come troubling us?"

"Are you sure she's married? Have you definite news of it?"

"No—not definite news. But that was why she asked me to release her. She and the man both wanted to lead a proper life, as I understood."

"O Jude—it was, it *was* Arabella!" cried Sue, covering her eyes with her hand. "And

I am so miserable! It seems such an ill-omen, whatever she may have come for. You could not possibly see her, could you?"

"I don't really think I could. It would be so very painful to talk to her now—for her as much as for me. However, she's gone. Did she say she would come again?"

"No. But she went away very reluctantly."

Sue, whom the least thing upset, could not eat any supper, and when Jude had finished his he prepared to go to bed. He had no sooner raked out the fire, fastened the doors, and got to the top of the stairs than there came a knock. Sue instantly emerged from her room, which she had but just entered.

"There she is again!" Sue whispered in appalled accents.

"How do you know?"

"She knocked like that last time."

They listened, and the knocking came again. No servant was kept in the house, and if the summons were to be responded to one of them would have to do it in person. "I'll open a window," said Jude. "Whoever it is cannot be expected to be let in at this time."

He accordingly went into his bedroom and lifted the sash. The obscure street of early retiring workpeople was empty from end to end save of one figure—that of a woman walking up and down by the lamp a few yards off.

"Who's there?" he asked.

"Is that Mr. Fawley?" came up from the woman, in a voice which was unmistakably Arabella's.

Jude replied that it was.

"Is it she?" asked Sue from the door, with lips apart.

"Yes, dear," said Jude. "What do you want, Arabella?" he enquired.

"I beg your pardon, Jude, for disturbing you," said Arabella humbly. "But I called earlier—I wanted particularly to see you to-night, if I could. I am in trouble, and have nobody to help me!"

"In trouble, are you?"

"Yes."

There was a silence. An inconvenient sympathy seemed to be rising in Jude's breast at the appeal. "But aren't you married?" he said.

Arabella hesitated. "No, Jude, I am not," she returned. "He wouldn't, after all. And I am in great difficulty. I hope to get another situation as barmaid soon. But it takes time, and I really am in great distress, because of a sudden responsibility that's been sprung upon me from Australia; or I wouldn't trouble you—believe me I wouldn't. I want to tell you about it."

Sue remained at gaze, in painful tension, hearing every word, but speaking none.

"You are not really in want of money, Arabella?" he asked, in a distinctly softened tone.

"I have enough to pay for the night's lodging I have obtained, but barely enough to take me back again."

"Where are you living?"

"In London still." She was about to give the address, but she said, "I am afraid somebody may hear, so I don't like to call out particulars of myself so loud. If you could come down and walk a little way with me towards the Prince Inn, where I am staying to-night, I would explain all. You may as well, for old time's sake!"

"Poor thing!—I must do her the kindness of hearing what's the matter, I suppose," said Jude in much perplexity. "As she's going back to-morrow it can't make much difference."

"But you can go and see her to-morrow, Jude! Don't go now, Jude!" came in plaintive accents from the doorway. "O, it is only to entrap you, I know it is, as she did before! Don't, don't go, dear! She is such a low-passioned woman—I can see it in her shape, and hear it in her voice!

"But I shall go," said Jude. "Don't attempt to detain me, Sue. God knows I love her little enough now, but I don't want to be cruel to her." He turned to the stairs.

"But she's not your wife!" cried Sue distractedly. "And I—"

"And you are not either, dear, yet," said Jude.

"O, but are you going to her? Don't! Stay at home! Please, please stay at home, Jude, and not go to her, now she's not your wife any more than I!"

"Well, she is, rather more than you, come to that," he said, taking his hat determinedly. "I've wanted you to be, and I've waited with the patience of Job, and I don't see that I've got anything by my self-denial. I shall certainly give her something, and hear what it is she is so anxious to tell me; no man could do less!"

There was that in his manner which she knew it would be futile to oppose. She said no more, but, turning to her room as meekly as a martyr, heard him go downstairs, unbolt the door, and close it behind him. With a woman's disregard of her dignity when in the presence of nobody but herself, she also trotted down, sobbing articulately as she went. She listened. She knew exactly how far it was to the inn that Arabella had named as her lodging. It would occupy about seven minutes to get there at an ordinary walking pace; seven to come back again. If he did not return in fourteen minutes he would have lingered. She looked at the clock. It was twenty-five minutes to eleven. He *might* enter the inn with Arabella, as they would reach it before closing time; she might get him to drink with her; and Heaven only knew what disasters would befall him then.

In a still suspense she waited on. It seemed as if the whole time had nearly elapsed when the door was opened again, and Jude appeared.

Sue gave a little ecstatic cry. "O, I knew I could trust you!—how good you are!"—she began.

"I can't find her anywhere in this street, and I went out in my slippers only. She has walked on, thinking I've been so hard-hearted as to refuse her requests entirely, poor woman. I've come back for my boots, as it is beginning to rain."

"O, but why should you take such trouble for a woman who has served you so badly!" said Sue in a jealous burst of disappointment.

"But, Sue, she's a woman, and I once cared for her; and one can't be a brute in such circumstances."

"She isn't your wife any longer!" exclaimed Sue, passionately excited. "You *mustn't* go out to find her! It isn't right! You *can't* join her, now she's a stranger to you. How can you forget such a thing, my dear, dear one!"

"She seems much the same as ever—an erring, careless, unreflecting fellow-creature," he said, continuing to pull on his boots. "What those legal fellows have been playing at in London makes no difference in my real relations to her. If she was my wife while she was away in Australia with another husband she's my wife now."

"But she wasn't! That's just what I hold! There's the absurdity!—Well—you'll come straight back, after a few minutes, won't you, dear? She is too low, too coarse for you to talk to long, Jude, and was always!"

"Perhaps I am coarse too, worse luck! I have the germs of every human infirmity in me, I verily believe—that was why I saw it was so preposterous of me to think of being a curate. I have cured myself of drunkenness I think; but I never know in what new form a suppressed vice will break out in me! I do love you, Sue, though I have danced attendance on you so long for such poor returns! All that's best and noblest in me loves you, and your freedom from everything that's gross has elevated me, and enabled me to do what I should never have dreamt myself capable of, or any man, a year or two ago. It is all very well to preach about self-control, and the wickedness of coercing a woman. But I should just like a few virtuous people who have condemned me in the past, about Arabella and other things, to have been in my tantalizing position with you through these late weeks!—they'd believe, I think, that I have exercised some little restraint in always giving in to your wishes—living here in one house, and not a soul between us."

"Yes, you have been good to me, Jude; I know you have, my dear protector."

"Well—Arabella appeals to me. I must go out and speak to her, Sue, at least!"

"I can't say any more!—O, if you must, you must!" she said, bursting out into sobs that seemed to tear her heart. "I have nobody but you, Jude, and you are deserting me! I didn't know you were like this—I can't bear it, I can't! If she were yours it would be different!"

"Or if you were."

"Very well then—if I must I must. Since you will have it so, I agree! I will be. Only I didn't mean to! And I didn't want to marry again, either! . . . But, yes—I agree, I agree! I do love you. I ought to have known that you would conquer in the long run, living like this!"

She ran across and flung her arms round his neck. "I am not a cold-natured, sexless creature, am I, for keeping you at such a distance? I am sure you don't think so! Wait and see! I do belong to you, don't I? I give in!"

"And I'll arrange for our marriage to-morrow, or as soon as ever you wish."

"Yes, Jude."

"Then I'll let her go," said he, embracing Sue softly. "I do feel that it would be unfair to you to see her, and perhaps unfair to her. She is not like you, my darling, and never was: it is only bare justice to say that. Don't cry any more. There; and there; and there!" He kissed her on one side, and on the other, and in the middle, and rebolted the front-door.

The next morning it was wet.

"Now, dear," said Jude gaily at breakfast; "as this is Saturday I mean to call about the banns at once, so as to get the first publishing done to-morrow, or we shall lose a week. Banns will do? We shall save a pound or two."

Sue absently agreed to banns. But her mind for the moment was running on something else. A glow had passed away from her, and depression sat upon her features.

"I feel I was wickedly selfish last night!" she murmured. "It was sheer unkindness in me—or worse—to treat Arabella as I did. I didn't care about her being in trouble, and what she wished to tell you! Perhaps it was really something she was justified in telling you. That's some more of my badness, I suppose! Love has its own dark morality when rivalry enters in—at least, mine has, if other people's hasn't. . . . I wonder how she got on? I hope she reached the inn all right, poor woman."

"O yes: she got on all right," said Jude placidly.

"I hope she wasn't shut out, and that she hadn't to walk the streets in the rain. Do you mind my putting on my waterproof and going to see if she got in? I've been thinking of her all the morning."

"Well—is it necessary? You haven't the least idea how Arabella is able to shift for herself. Still, darling, if you want to go and enquire you can."

There was no limit to the strange and unnecessary penances which Sue would meekly undertake when in a contrite mood; and this going to see all sorts of extraordinary persons whose relation to her was precisely of a kind that would have made other people shun them, was her instinct ever, so that the request did not surprise him.

"And when you come back," he added, "I'll be ready to go about the banns. You'll come with me?"

Sue agreed, and went off under cloak and umbrella, letting Jude kiss her freely, and returning his kisses in a way she had never done before. Times had decidedly changed. "The little bird is caught at last!" she said, a sadness showing in her smile.

"No—only nested," he assured her.

She walked along the muddy street till she reached the public-house mentioned by Arabella, which was not so very far off. She was informed that Arabella had not yet left, and in doubt how to announce herself so that her predecessor in Jude's affections would recognise her, she sent up word that a friend from Spring Street had called, naming the place of Jude's residence. She was asked to step upstairs, and on being shown into a room found that it was Arabella's bedroom, and that the latter had not yet risen. She halted on the turn of her toe till Arabella cried from the bed, "Come in and shut the door," which Sue accordingly did.

Arabella lay facing the window, and did not at once turn her head: and Sue was wicked enough, despite her penitence, to wish for a moment that Jude could behold her forerunner now, with the daylight full upon her. She may have seemed handsome enough in profile under the lamps, but a frowsiness was apparent this morning; and the sight of her own fresh charms in the looking-glass made Sue's manner bright, till she reflected what a meanly sexual emotion this was in her, and hated herself for it.

"I've just looked in to see if you got back comfortably last night, that's all," she said gently. "I was afraid afterwards that you might have met with any mishap?"

"O—how stupid this is! I thought my visitor was—your friend—your husband—Mrs. Fawley, as I suppose you call yourself?" said Arabella, flinging her head back upon the pillows with a disappointed toss, and ceasing to retain the dimple she had just taken the trouble to produce.

"Indeed I don't," said Sue.

"O, I thought you might have, even if he's not legally yours. Decency is decency, any hour of the twenty-four."

"I don't know what you mean," said Sue stiffly. "He is mine, if you come to that!"

"He wasn't yesterday."

Sue coloured roseate, and said "How do you know?"

"From your manner when you talked to me at the door. Well, my dear, you've been quick about it, and I expect my visit last night helped it on—ha-ha! But I don't want to get him away from you."

Sue looked out at the rain, and at the dirty toilet-cover, and at the detached tail of Arabella's hair hanging on the looking-glass, just as it had done in Jude's time; and wished she had not come. In the pause there was a knock at the door, and the chambermaid brought in a telegram for "Mrs. Cartlett."

Arabella opened it as she lay, and her ruffled look disappeared.

"I am much obliged to you for your anxiety about me," she said blandly when the maid had gone; "but it is not necessary you should feel it. My man finds he can't do without me after all, and agrees to stand by the promise to marry again over here that he has made me all along. See here! This is in answer to one from me." She held out the telegram for Sue to read, but Sue did not take it. "He asks me to come back. His little corner public in Lambeth would go to pieces without me, he says. But he isn't going to knock me about when he has had a drop, any more after we are spliced by English law than before! . . . As for you, I should coax Jude to take me before the parson straight off, and have done with it, if I were in your place. I say it as a friend, my dear."

"He's waiting to, any day," returned Sue with frigid pride.

"Then let him, in Heaven's name. Life with a man is more businesslike after it, and money matters work better. And then, you see, if you have rows, and he turns you out-of-doors, you can get the law to protect you, which you can't otherwise, unless he half runs you through with a knife, or cracks your noddle with a poker. And if he bolts away from you—I say it friendly, as woman to woman, for there's never any knowing what a man med do—you'll have the sticks o' furniture, and won't be looked upon as a thief. I shall marry my man over again, now he's willing, as there was a little flaw in the first ceremony. In my telegram last night which this is an answer to, I told him I had almost made it up with Jude; and that frightened him, I expect! Perhaps I should quite have done it if it hadn't been for you," she said laughing; "and then how different our histories might have been from to-day! Never such a tender fool as Jude is if a woman seems in trouble, and coaxes him a bit! Just as he used to be about birds and things. However, as it happens, it is just as well as if I had made it up, and I forgive you. And, as I say, I'd advise you to get the business legally done as soon as possible. You'll find it an awful bother later on if you don't."

"I have told you he is asking me to marry him—to make our natural marriage a legal one," said Sue, with yet more dignity. "It was quite by my wish that he didn't the moment I was free."

"Ah, yes—you are a oneyer too, like myself," said Arabella, eyeing her visitor with humorous criticism. "Bolted from your first, didn't you, like me?"

"Good-morning!—I must go," said Sue hastily.

"And I, too, must up and off!" replied the other, springing out of bed so suddenly that the soft parts of her person shook. Sue jumped aside in trepidation. "Lord, I am only a woman—not a six-foot sojer! . . . Just a moment, dear," she continued, putting her hand on Sue's arm. "I really did want to consult Jude on a little matter of business, as I told him. I came about that more than anything else. Would he run up to speak to me at the station as I am going? You think not. Well, I'll write to him about it. I didn't want to write it, but never mind—I will."

III

WHEN SUE REACHED HOME JUDE WAS AWAITING HER AT THE DOOR TO TAKE THE INI-tial step towards their marriage. She clasped his arm, and they went along silently together, as true comrades ofttimes do. He saw that she was preoccupied, and forbore to question her.

"O Jude—I've been talking to her," she said at last. "I wish I hadn't! And yet it is best to be reminded of things."

"I hope she was civil."

"Yes. I—I can't help liking her—just a little bit! She's not an ungenerous nature; and I am so glad her difficulties have all suddenly ended." She explained how Arabella had been summoned back, and would be enabled to retrieve her position. "I was referring to our old question. What Arabella has been saying to me has made me feel more than ever how hopelessly vulgar an institution legal marriage is—a sort of trap to catch a man—I can't bear to think of it. I wish I hadn't promised to let you put up the banns this morning!"

"O, don't mind me. Any time will do for me. I thought you might like to get it over quickly, now."

"Indeed, I don't feel any more anxious now than I did before. Perhaps with any other man I might be a little anxious; but among the very few virtues possessed by your family and mine, dear, I think I may set staunchness. So I am not a bit frightened about losing you, now I really am yours and you really are mine. In fact, I am easier in my mind than I was, for my conscience is clear about Richard, who now has a right to his freedom. I felt we were deceiving him before."

"Sue, you seem when you are like this to be one of the women of some grand old civ-ilization, whom I used to read about in my bygone, wasted, classical days, rather than a denizen of a mere Christian country. I almost expect you to say at these times that you have just been talking to some friend whom you met in the Via Sacra, about the latest news of Octavia or Livia; or have been listening to Aspasia's eloquence, or have been watching Praxiteles chiselling away at his latest Venus, while Phryne made complaint that she was tired of posing."

They had now reached the house of the parish-clerk. Sue stood back, while her lover went up to the door. His hand was raised to knock when she said: "Jude!"

He looked round.

"Wait a minute, would you mind?"

He came back to her.

"Just let us think," she said timidly. "I had such a horrid dream one night! . . . And Arabella—"

"What did Arabella say to you?" he asked

"O, she said that when people were tied up you could get the law of a man better if he beat you—and how when couples quarrelled. . . . Jude, do you think that when you *must* have me with you by law, we shall be so happy as we are now? The men and women of our family are very generous when everything depends upon their goodwill, but they always kick against compulsion. Don't you dread the attitude that insensibly arises out of legal obligation? Don't you think it is destructive to a passion whose essence is its gratuitousness?"

"Upon my word, love, you are beginning to frighten me, too, with all this foreboding! Well, let's go back and think it over."

Her face brightened. "Yes—so we will!" said she. And they turned from the clerk's door, Sue taking his arm and murmuring as they walked on homeward:

> Can you keep the bee from ranging,
> Or the ring-dove's neck from changing?
> No! Nor fetter'd love . . .

They thought it over, or postponed thinking. Certainly they postponed action, and seemed to live on in a dreamy paradise. At the end of a fortnight or three weeks matters remained unadvanced, and no banns were announced to the ears of any Aldbrickham congregation. ·

Whilst they were postponing and postponing thus a letter and a newspaper arrived before breakfast one morning from Arabella. Seeing the handwriting Jude went up to Sue's room and told her, and as soon as she was dressed she hastened down. Sue opened the newspaper; Jude the letter. After glancing at the paper she held across the first page to him with her finger on a paragraph; but he was so absorbed in his letter that he did not turn a while.

"Look!" said she.

He looked and read. The paper was one that circulated in South London only, and the marked advertisement was simply the announcement of a marriage at St. John's Church, Waterloo Road, under the names, "Cartlett—Donn"; the united pair being Arabella and the innkeeper.

"Well, it is satisfactory," said Sue complacently. "Though, after this, it seems rather low to do likewise, and I am glad.—However, she is provided for now in a way, I suppose, whatever her faults, poor thing. It is nicer that we are able to think that, than to be uneasy about her. I ought, too, to write to Richard and ask him how he is getting on, perhaps?"

But Jude's attention was still absorbed. Having merely glanced at the announcement he said in a disturbed voice: "Listen to this letter. What shall I say or do?"

THE THREE HORNS, LAMBETH

DEAR JUDE (I won't be so distant as to call you Mr. Fawley)—I send to-day a newspaper, from which useful document you will learn that I was married over again to Cartlett last Tuesday. So that business is settled right and tight at last. But what I write about more particular is that private affair I wanted to speak to you on when I came down to Aldbrickham. I couldn't very well tell it to your lady friend, and should much have liked to let you know it by word of mouth, as I could have explained better than by letter. The fact is, Jude, that, though I have never informed you before, there was a boy born of our marriage, eight months after I left you, when I was at Sydney, living with my father and mother. All that is easily provable. As I had separated from you before I thought such a thing was going to happen, and I was over there, and our quarrel had been sharp, I did not think it convenient to write about the birth. I was then looking out for a good situation, so my parents took the child, and he has been with them ever since. That was why I did not mention it when I met you in Christminster, nor at the law proceedings. He is now of an intelligent age, of course, and my mother and father have lately written to say that, as they have rather a hard struggle over there, and I am settled comfortably here, they don't see why they should be encumbered with the child any longer, his parents being alive. I would have him with me here in a moment, but he is not old enough to be of any use in the bar, nor will be for years and years, and naturally Cartlett might think him in the way. They have, however, packed him off to me in charge of some friends who happened to be coming home, and I must ask you to take him when he arrives, for I don't know what to do with him. He is lawfully yours, that I solemnly swear. If anybody says he isn't, call them brimstone liars, for my sake. Whatever I may have done before or afterwards, I was honest to you from the time we were married till I went away, and I remain, yours, &c.,

ARABELLA CARTLETT

Sue's look was one of dismay. "What will you do, dear?" she asked faintly.

Jude did not reply, and Sue watched him anxiously, with heavy breaths.

"It hits me hard!" said he in an under-voice. "It *may* be true! I can't make it out. Certainly, if his age is exactly what it ought to be. . . . I cannot think why she didn't tell me when I met her at Christminster, and came on here that evening with her! . . . Ah—I do remember now that she said something about having a thing on her mind that she would like me to know, if ever we lived together again."

"The poor child seems to be wanted by nobody!" Sue replied, and her eyes filled.

Jude had by this time come to himself. "What a view of life he must have, mine or not mine!" he said. "I must say that, if I were better off, I should not stop for a moment to think whose he might be. I would take him and bring him up. The beggarly question of parentage—what is it, after all? What does it matter, when you come to think of it, whether a child is yours by blood or not? All the little ones of our time are collectively the children of us adults of the time, and entitled to our general care. That excessive regard of parents for their own children, and their dislike of other people's, is, like class-feeling, patriotism, save-your-own-soul-ism, and other virtues, a mean exclusiveness at bottom."

Sue jumped up and kissed Jude with passionate devotion. "Yes—so it is, dearest! And we'll have him here! And if he isn't yours it makes it all the better. I do hope he isn't—though perhaps I ought not to feel quite that! If he isn't, I should like so much for us to have him as an adopted child!"

"Well, you must assume about him what is most pleasing to you, my curious little comrade!" he said. "I feel that, anyhow, I don't like to leave the unfortunate little fellow to neglect. Just think of his life in a Lambeth pothouse, and all its evil influences, with a parent who doesn't want him, and has, indeed, hardly seen him, and a stepfather who doesn't know him. 'Let the day perish wherein I was born, and the night in which it was said, There is a man child conceived!' That's what the boy—*my* boy, perhaps, will find himself saying before long!"

"O no!"

"As I was the petitioner, I am really entitled to his custody, I suppose."

"Whether or no, we must have him. I see that. I'll do the best I can to be a mother to him, and we can afford to keep him somehow. I'll work harder. I wonder when he'll arrive?"

"In the course of a few weeks, I suppose."

"I wish—When shall we have courage to marry, Jude?"

"Whenever you have it, I think I shall. It remains with you entirely, dear. Only say the word, and it's done."

"Before the boy comes?"

"Certainly."

"It would make a more natural home for him, perhaps," she murmured.

Jude thereupon wrote in purely formal terms to request that the boy should be sent on to them as soon as he arrived, making no remark whatever on the surprising nature of Arabella's information, nor vouchsafing a single word of opinion on the boy's paternity, nor on whether, had he known all this, his conduct towards her would have been quite the same.

In the down-train that was timed to reach Aldbrickham station about ten o'clock the next evening, a small, pale child's face could be seen in the gloom of a third-class carriage. He had large, frightened eyes, and wore a white woollen cravat, over which a key was suspended round his neck by a piece of common string: the key attracting attention by its occasional shine in the lamp-light. In the band of his hat his half-ticket was stuck. His eyes remained mostly fixed on the back of the seat opposite, and never turned to the window even when a station was reached and called. On the other seat were two or three passengers, one of them a working-woman who held a basket on her lap, in which was a tabby kitten. The woman opened the cover now and then, whereupon the kitten would put out its head, and indulge in playful antics. At these the fellow-passengers laughed, except the solitary boy bearing the key and ticket, who, regarding the kitten with his saucer eyes, seemed mutely to say: "All laughing comes from misapprehension. Rightly looked at there is no laughable thing under the sun."

Occasionally at a stoppage the guard would look into the compartment and say to the boy, "All right, my man. Your box is safe in the van." The boy would say, "Yes," without animation, would try to smile, and fail.

He was Age masquerading as Juvenility, and doing it so badly that his real self showed through crevices. A ground swell from ancient years of night seemed now and then to lift the child in this his morning-life, when his face took a back view over some great Atlantic of time, and appeared not to care about what it saw.

When the other travellers closed their eyes, which they did one by one—even the kitten curling itself up in the basket, weary of its too circumscribed play—the boy remained just as before. He then seemed to be doubly awake, like an enslaved and dwarfed Divinity, sitting passive and regarding his companions as if he saw their whole rounded lives rather than their immediate figures.

This was Arabella's boy. With her usual carelessness she had postponed writing to Jude about him till the eve of his landing, when she could absolutely postpone no longer, though she had known for weeks of his approaching arrival, and had, as she truly said, visited Aldbrickham mainly to reveal the boy's existence and his near home-coming to Jude. This very day on which she had received her former husband's answer at some time in the afternoon, the child reached the London Docks, and the family in whose charge he had come, having put him into a cab for Lambeth, and directed the cabman to his mother's house, bade him good-bye, and went their way.

On his arrival at the Three Horns, Arabella had looked him over with an expression that was as good as saying, "You are very much what I expected you to be," had given him a good meal, a little money, and, late as it was getting, despatched him to Jude by the next train, wishing her husband Cartlett, who was out, not to see him.

The train reached Aldbrickham, and the boy was deposited on the lonely platform beside his box. The collector took his ticket and, with a meditative sense of the unfitness of things, asked him where he was going by himself at that time of night.

"Going to Spring Street," said the little one impassively.

"Why, that's a long way from here; a'most out in the country; and the folks will be gone to bed."

"I've got to go there."

"You must have a fly for your box."

"No. I must walk."

"O well: you'd better leave your box here and send for it. There's a 'bus goes halfway, but you'll have to walk the rest."

"I am not afraid."

"Why didn't your friends come to meet 'ee?"

"I suppose they didn't know I was coming."

"Who is your friends?"

"Mother didn't wish me to say."

"All I can do, then, is to take charge of this. Now walk as fast as you can."

Saying nothing further the boy came out into the street, looking round to see that nobody followed or observed him. When he had walked some little distance he asked for the street of his destination. He was told to go straight on quite into the outskirts of the place.

The child fell into a steady mechanical creep which had in it an impersonal quality— the movement of the wave, or of the breeze, or of the cloud. He followed his directions literally, without an inquiring gaze at anything. It could have been seen that the boy's ideas of life were different from those of the local boys. Children begin with detail, and learn up to the general; they begin with the contiguous, and gradually comprehend the universal. The boy seemed to have begun with the generals of life, and never to have concerned himself with the particulars. To him the houses, the willows, the obscure fields beyond, were apparently regarded not as brick residences, pollards, meadows; but as human dwellings in the abstract, vegetation, and the wide dark world.

He found the way to the little lane, and knocked at the door of Jude's house. Jude had just retired to bed, and Sue was about to enter her chamber adjoining when she heard the knock and came down.

"Is this where father lives?" asked the child.

"Who?"

"Mr. Fawley, that's his name."

Sue ran up to Jude's room and told him, and he hurried down as soon as he could, though to her impatience he seemed long.

"What—is it he—so soon?" she asked as Jude came.

She scrutinised the child's features, and suddenly went away into the little sitting-room adjoining. Jude lifted the boy to a level with himself, keenly regarded him with gloomy tenderness, and telling him he would have been met if they had known of his coming so soon, set him provisionally in a chair whilst he went to look for Sue, whose super-sensitiveness was disturbed, as he knew. He found her in the dark, bending over an arm-chair. He enclosed her with his arm, and putting his face by hers, whispered, "What's the matter?"

"What Arabella says is true—true! I see you in him!"

"Well: that's one thing in my life as it should be, at any rate."

"But the other half of him is—*she!* And that's what I can't bear! But I ought to—I'll try to get used to it; yes, I ought!"

"Jealous little Sue! I withdraw all remarks about your sexlessness. Never mind! Time may right things. . . . And Sue, darling; I have an idea! We'll educate and train him with a view to the University. What I couldn't accomplish in my own person perhaps I can carry out through him? They are making it easier for poor students now, you know."

"O you dreamer!" said she, and holding his hand returned to the child with him. The boy looked at her as she had looked at him. "Is it you who's my *real* mother at last?" he enquired.

"Why? Do I look like your father's wife?"

"Well, yes; 'cept he seems fond of you, and you of him. Can I call you mother?"

Then a yearning look came over the child and he began to cry. Sue thereupon could not refrain from instantly doing likewise, being a harp which the least wind of emotion from another's heart could make to vibrate as readily as a radical stir in her own.

"You may call me mother, if you wish to, my poor dear!" she said, bending her cheek against his to hide her tears.

"What's this round your neck?" asked Jude with affected calmness.

"The key of my box that's at the station."

They bustled about and got him some supper, and made him up a temporary bed, where he soon fell asleep. Both went and looked at him as he lay.

"He called you mother two or three times before he dropped off," murmured Jude. "Wasn't it odd that he should have wanted to!"

"Well—it was significant," said Sue. "There's more for us to think about in that one little hungry heart than in all the stars of the sky. . . . I suppose, dear, we *must* pluck up courage, and get that ceremony over? It is no use struggling against the current, and I feel myself getting intertwined with my kind. O Jude, you'll love me dearly, won't you, afterwards! I do want to be kind to this child, and to be a mother to him; and our adding the legal form to our marriage might make it easier for me."

IV

THEIR NEXT AND SECOND ATTEMPT THEREAT WAS MORE DELIBERATELY MADE, THOUGH it was begun on the morning following the singular child's arrival at their home.

Him they found to be in the habit of sitting silent, his quaint and weird face set, and his eyes resting on things they did not see in the substantial world.

"His face is like the tragic mask of Melpomene," said Sue. "What is your name, dear? Did you tell us?"

"Little Father Time is what they always called me. It is a nick-name; because I look so aged, they say."

"And you talk so, too," said Sue tenderly. "It is strange, Jude, that these preternaturally old boys almost always come from new countries. But what were you christened?"

"I never was."

"Why was that?"

"Because, if I died in damnation, 'twould save the expense of a Christian funeral."

"O—your name is not Jude, then?" said his father with some disappointment.

The boy shook his head. "Never heerd on it."

"Of course not," said Sue quickly; "since she was hating you all the time!"

"We'll have him christened," said Jude; and privately to Sue: "The day we are married." Yet the advent of the child disturbed him.

Their position lent them shyness, and having an impression that a marriage at a Superintendent Registrar's office was more private than an ecclesiastical one, they decided to avoid a church this time. Both Sue and Jude together went to the office of the district to give notice: they had become such companions that they could hardly do anything of importance except in each other's company.

Jude Fawley signed the form of notice, Sue looking over his shoulder and watching his hand as it traced the words. As she read the four-square undertaking, never before seen by her, into which her own and Jude's names were inserted, and by which that very volatile essence, their love for each other, was supposed to be made permanent, her face seemed to grow painfully apprehensive. "Names and Surnames of the Parties"—(they were to be parties now, not lovers, she thought). "Condition"—(a horrid idea)—"Rank or Occupation"—"Age"—"Dwelling at"—"Length of Residence"—"Church or Building in which the Marriage is to be solemnised"—"District and County in which the Parties respectively dwell."

"It spoils the sentiment, doesn't it!" she said on their way home. "It seems making a more sordid business of it even than signing the contract in a vestry. There is a little poetry in a church. But we'll try to get through with it, dearest, now."

"We will. 'For what man is he that hath betrothed a wife and hath not taken her? Let him go and return unto his house, lest he die in the battle, and another man take her.' So said the Jewish law-giver."

"How you know the Scriptures, Jude! You really ought to have been a parson. I can only quote profane writers!"

During the interval before the issuing of the certificate Sue, in her housekeeping errands, sometimes walked past the office, and furtively glancing in saw affixed to the wall the notice of the purposed clinch to their union. She could not bear its aspect. Coming after her previous experience of matrimony, all the romance of their attachment seemed to be starved away by placing her present case in the same category. She was usually leading little Father Time by the hand, and fancied that people thought him hers, and regarded the intended ceremony as the patching up of an old error.

Meanwhile Jude decided to link his present with his past in some slight degree by inviting to the wedding the only person remaining on earth who was associated with his early life at Marygreen—the aged widow Mrs. Edlin, who had been his great-aunt's friend and nurse in her last illness. He hardly expected that she would come; but she did, bringing singular presents, in the form of apples, jam, brass snuffers, an ancient pewter dish, a warming-pan, and an enormous bag of goose feathers towards a bed. She was allotted the spare room in Jude's house, whither she retired early, and where they could hear her through the ceiling below, honestly saying the Lord's Prayer in a loud voice, as the Rubric directed.

As, however, she could not sleep, and discovered that Sue and Jude were still sitting up—it being in fact only ten o'clock—she dressed herself again, and came down; and they all sat by the fire till a late hour—Father Time included; though, as he never spoke, they were hardly conscious of him.

"Well, I bain't set against marrying as your great-aunt was," said the widow. "And I hope 'twill be a jocund wedding for ye in all respects this time. Nobody can hope it more, knowing what I do of your families, which is more, I suppose, than anybody else now living. For they have been unlucky that way, God knows."

Sue breathed uneasily.

"They was always good-hearted people, too—wouldn't kill a fly if they knowed it," continued the wedding guest. "But things happened to thwart 'em, and if everything wasn't vitty they were upset. No doubt that's how he that the tale is told of came to do what 'a did—if he *were* one of your family."

"What was that?" said Jude.

"Well—that tale, ye know; he that was gibbeted just on the brow of the hill by the Brown House—not far from the milestone between Marygreen and Alfredston, where the other road branches off. But Lord, 'twas in my grand-father's time; and it medn' have been one of your folk at all."

"I know where the gibbet is said to have stood, very well," murmured Jude. "But I never heard of this. What—did this man—my ancestor and Sue's—kill his wife?"

" 'Twer not that exactly. She ran away from him, with their child, to her friends; and while she was there the child died. He wanted the body, to bury it where his people lay, but she wouldn't give it up. Her husband then came in the night with a cart, and broke into the house to steal the coffin away; but he was catched, and being obstinate, wouldn't tell what he broke in for. They brought it in burglary, and that's why he was hanged and gibbeted on Brown House Hill. His wife went mad after he was dead. But it medn't be true that he belonged to ye more than to me."

A small slow voice rose from the shade of the fireside, as if out of the earth: "If I was you, mother, I wouldn't marry father!" It came from little Time, and they started, for they had forgotten him.

"O, it is only a tale," said Sue cheeringly.

After this exhilarating tradition from the widow on the eve of the solemnization they rose, and, wishing their guest good-night, retired.

The next morning Sue, whose nervousness intensified with the hours, took Jude privately into the sitting-room before starting. "Jude, I want you to kiss me, as a lover, incorporeally," she said, tremulously nestling up to him, with damp lashes. "It won't be ever like this any more, will it! I wish we hadn't begun the business. But I suppose we must go on. How horrid that story was last night! It spoilt my thoughts of to-day. It makes me feel as if a tragic doom overhung our family, as it did the house of Atreus."

"Or the house of Jeroboam," said the quondam theologian.

"Yes. And it seems awful temerity in us two to go marrying! I am going to vow to you in the same words I vowed in to my other husband, and you to me in the same as you used to your other wife; regardless of the deterrent lesson we were taught by those experiments!"

"If you are uneasy I am made unhappy," said he. "I had hoped you would feel quite joyful. But if you don't, you don't. It is no use pretending. It is a dismal business to you, and that makes it so to me!"

"It is unpleasantly like that other morning—that's all," she murmured. "Let us go on now."

They started arm in arm for the office aforesaid, no witness accompanying them except the Widow Edlin. The day was chilly and dull, and a clammy fog blew through the town from "Royal-tower'd Thame." On the steps of the office there were the muddy footmarks of people who had entered, and in the entry were damp umbrellas Within the office several persons were gathered, and our couple perceived that a marriage between a soldier and a young woman was just in progress. Sue, Jude, and the widow stood in the background while this was going on, Sue reading the notices of marriage on the wall. The room was a dreary place to two of their temperament, though to its usual frequenters it doubtless seemed ordinary enough. Law-books in musty calf covered one wall, and elsewhere were Post-Office Directories, and other books of reference. Papers in packets tied with red tape were pigeon-holed around, and some iron safes filled a recess, while the bare wood floor was, like the door-step, stained by previous visitors.

The soldier was sullen and reluctant: the bride sad and timid; she was soon, obviously, to become a mother, and she had a black eye. Their little business was soon done, and the twain and their friends straggled out, one of the witnesses saying casually to Jude and Sue in passing, as if he had known them before: "See the couple just come in? Ha, ha! That fellow is just out of gaol this morning. She met him at the gaol gates, and brought him straight here. She's paying for everything."

Sue turned her head and saw an ill-favoured man, closely cropped, with a broad-faced, pock-marked woman on his arm, ruddy with liquor and the satisfaction of being on the brink of a gratified desire. They jocosely saluted the outgoing couple, and went forward in front of Jude and Sue, whose diffidence was increasing. The latter drew back and turned to her lover, her mouth shaping itself like that of a child about to give way to grief:

"Jude—I don't like it here! I wish we hadn't come! The place gives me the horrors: it seems so unnatural as the climax of our love! I wish it had been at church, if it had to be at all. It is not so vulgar there!"

"Dear little girl," said Jude. "How troubled and pale you look!"

"It must be performed here now, I suppose?"

"No—perhaps not necessarily."

He spoke to the clerk, and came back. "No—we need not marry here or anywhere, unless we like, even now," he said. "We can be married in a church, if not with the same certificate with another he'll give us, I think. Anyhow, let us go out till you are calmer, dear, and I too, and talk it over."

They went out stealthily and guiltily, as if they had committed a misdemeanour, closing the door without noise, and telling the widow, who had remained in the entry, to go home and await them; that they would call in any casual passers as witnesses, if necessary.

When in the street they turned into an unfrequented side alley, where they walked up and down as they had done long ago in the market-house at Melchester.

"Now, darling, what shall we do? We are making a mess of it, it strikes me. Still, *anything* that pleases you will please me."

"But Jude, dearest, I am worrying you! You wanted it to be there, didn't you?"

"Well, to tell the truth, when I got inside I felt as if I didn't care much about it. The place depressed me almost as much as it did you—it was ugly. And then I thought of what you had said this morning as to whether we ought."

They walked on vaguely, till she paused, and her little voice began anew: "It seems so weak, too, to vacillate like this! And yet how much better than to act rashly a second time. . . . How terrible that scene was to me! The expression in that flabby woman's face, leading her on to give herself to that gaol-bird, not for a few hours, as she would, but for a lifetime, as she must. And the other poor soul—to escape a nominal shame which was owing to the weakness of her character, degrading herself to the real shame of bondage to a tyrant who scorned her—a man whom to avoid forever was her only chance of salvation. . . . This is our parish church, isn't it? This is where it would have to be, if we did it in the usual way? A service or something seems to be going on."

Jude went up and looked in at the door. "Why—it is a wedding here too," he said. "Everybody seems to be on our tack to-day."

Sue said she supposed it was because Lent was just over, when there was always a crowd of marriages. "Let us listen," she said, "and find how it feels to us when performed in a church."

They stepped in, and entered a back seat, and watched the proceedings at the altar. The contracting couple appeared to belong to the well-to-do middle class, and the wedding altogether was of ordinary prettiness and interest. They could see the flowers tremble in the bride's hand, even at that distance, and could hear her mechanical murmur of words whose meaning her brain seemed to gather not at all under the pressure of her self-consciousness. Sue and Jude listened, and severally saw themselves in time past going through the same form of self-committal.

"It is not the same to her, poor thing, as it would be to me doing it over again with my present knowledge," Sue whispered. "You see, they are fresh to it, and take the proceedings as a matter of course. But having been awakened to its awful solemnity as we have, or at least as I have, by experience, and to my own too squeamish feelings perhaps sometimes, it really does seem immoral in me to go and undertake the same thing again with open eyes. Coming in here and seeing this has frightened me from a church wedding as much as the other did from a registry one. . . . We are a weak, tremulous pair, Jude, and what others may feel confident in I feel doubts of—my being proof against the sordid conditions of a business contract again!"

Then they tried to laugh, and went on debating in whispers the object-lesson before them. And Jude said he also thought they were both too thin-skinned—that they ought never to have been born—much less have come together for the most preposterous of all joint ventures for *them*—matrimony.

His betrothed shuddered; and asked him earnestly if he indeed felt that they ought not to go in cold blood and sign that life-undertaking again? "It is awful if you think we have found ourselves not strong enough for it, and knowing this, are proposing to perjure ourselves," she said.

"I fancy I do think it—since you ask me," said Jude. "Remember I'll do it if you wish, own darling." While she hesitated he went on to confess that, though he thought they ought to be able to do it, he felt checked by the dread of incompetency just as she did—from their peculiarities, perhaps, because they were unlike other people. "We are horribly sensitive; that's really what's the matter with us, Sue!" he declared.

"I fancy more are like us than we think!"

"Well, I don't know. The intention of the contract is good, and right for many, no doubt; but in our case it may defeat its own ends because we are the queer sort of people we are—folk in whom domestic ties of a forced kind snuff out cordiality and spontaneousness."

Sue still held that there was not much queer or exceptional in it: that all were so. "Everybody is getting to feel as we do. We are a little beforehand, that's all. In fifty, a hundred, years the descendants of these two will act and feel worse than we. They will see weltering humanity still more vividly than we do now, as

Shapes like our own selves hideously multiplied,

and will be afraid to reproduce them."

"What a terrible line of poetry! . . . though I have felt it myself about my fellow-creatures, at morbid times."

Thus they murmured on, till Sue said more brightly:

"Well—the general question is not our business, and why should we plague ourselves about it? However different our reasons are we come to the same conclusion; that for us particular two, an irrevocable oath is risky. Then, Jude, let us go home without killing our dream! Yes? How good you are, my friend: you give way to all my whims!"

"They accord very much with my own."

He gave her a little kiss behind a pillar while the attention of everybody present was taken up in observing the bridal procession entering the vestry; and then they came outside the building. By the door they waited till two or three carriages, which had gone away for a while, returned, and the new husband and wife came into the open daylight. Sue sighed.

"The flowers in the bride's hand are sadly like the garland which decked the heifers of sacrifice in old times!"

"Still, Sue, it is no worse for the woman than for the man. That's what some women fail to see, and instead of protesting against the conditions they protest against the man, the other victim; just as a woman in a crowd will abuse the man who crushes against her, when he is only the helpless transmitter of the pressure put upon him."

"Yes—some are like that, instead of uniting with the man against the common enemy, coercion." The bride and bridegroom had by this time driven off, and the two moved away with the rest of the idlers. "No—don't let's do it," she continued. "At least just now."

They reached home, and passing the window arm in arm saw the widow looking out at them. "Well," cried their guest when they entered, "I said to myself when I zeed ye coming so loving up to the door, 'They made up their minds at last, then!' "

They briefly hinted that they had not.

"What—and ha'n't ye really done it? Chok' it all, that I should have lived to see a good old saying like 'marry in haste and repent at leisure' spoiled like this by you two! 'Tis time I got back again to Marygreen—sakes if tidden—if this is what the new notions be leading us to! Nobody thought o' being afeard o' matrimony in my time, nor of much else but a cannon-ball or empty cupboard! Why when I and my poor man were married we thought no more o't than of a game o' dibs!"

"Don't tell the child when he comes in," whispered Sue nervously. "He'll think it has all gone on right, and it will be better that he should not be surprised and puzzled. Of course it is only put off for reconsideration. If we are happy as we are, what does it matter to anybody?"

V

THE PURPOSE OF A CHRONICLER OF MOODS AND DEEDS DOES NOT REQUIRE HIM TO EXpress his personal views upon the grave controversy above given. That the twain were happy—between their times of sadness—was indubitable. And when the unexpected apparition of Jude's child in the house had shown itself to be no such disturbing event as it had looked, but one that brought into their lives a new and tender interest of an ennobling and unselfish kind, it rather helped than injured their happiness.

To be sure, with such pleasing anxious beings as they were, the boy's coming also brought with it much thought for the future, particularly as he seemed at present to be singularly deficient in all the usual hopes of childhood. But the pair tried to dismiss, for a while at least, a too strenuously forward view.

There is in Upper Wessex an old town of nine or ten thousand souls; the town may be called Stoke-Barehills. It stands with its gaunt, unattractive, ancient church, and its new red brick suburb, amid the open, chalk-soiled cornlands, near the middle of an imaginary triangle which has for its three corners the towns of Aldbrickham and Wintoncester, and the important military station of Quartershot. The great western highway from London passes through it, near a point where the road branches into two, merely to unite again some twenty miles further westward. Out of this bifurcation and reunion there used to arise among wheeled travellers, before railway days, endless questions of choice between the respective ways. But the question is now as dead as the scot-and-lot freeholder, the road waggoner, and the mail coachman who disputed it; and probably not a single inhabitant of Stoke-Barehills is now even aware that the two roads which part in his town ever meet again; for nobody now drives up and down the great western highway daily.

The most familiar object in Stoke-Barehills now-a-days is its cemetery, standing among some picturesque medieval ruins beside the railway; the modern chapels, modern tombs, and modern shrubs, having a look of intrusiveness amid the crumbling and ivy-covered decay of the ancient walls.

On a certain day, however, in the particular year which has now been reached by this narrative—the month being early June—the features of the town excite little interest, though many visitors arrive by the trains; some down-trains, in especial, nearly emptying themselves here. It is the week of the Great Wessex Agricultural Show, whose vast encampment spreads over the open outskirts of the town like the tents of an investing army. Rows of marquees, huts, booths, pavilions, arcades, porticoes—every kind of structure short of a permanent one—cover the green field for the space of a square half-mile, and the crowds of arrivals walk through the town in a mass, and make straight for the exhibition ground. The way thereto is lined with shows, stalls, and hawkers on foot, who make a market-place of the whole roadway to the show proper, and lead some of the improvident to lighten their pockets appreciably before they reach the gates of the exhibition they came expressly to see.

It is the popular day, the shilling day, and of the fast arriving excursion trains two from different directions enter the two contiguous railway-stations at almost the same minute. One, like several which have preceded it, comes from London: the other by a cross-line from Aldbrickham; and from the London train alights a couple; a short, rather bloated man, with a globular stomach and small legs, resembling a top on two pegs, accompanied by a woman of rather fine figure and rather red face, dressed in black material, and covered with beads from bonnet to skirt, that made her glisten as if clad in chain-mail.

They cast their eyes around. The man was about to hire a fly as some others had done, when the woman said, "Don't be in such a hurry, Cartlett. It isn't so very far to the showyard. Let us walk down the street into the place. Perhaps I can pick up a cheap bit of furniture or old china. It is years since I was here—never since I lived as a girl at Aldbrickham, and used to come across for a trip sometimes with my young man."

"You can't carry home furniture by excursion train," said, in a thick voice, her husband, the landlord of The Three Horns, Lambeth; for they had both come down from the tavern in that "excellent, densely populated, gin-drinking neighbourhood," which they had occupied ever since the advertisement in those words had attracted them thither. The configuration of the landlord showed that he, too, like his customers, was becoming affected by the liquors he retailed.

"Then I'll get it sent, if I see any worth having," said his wife.

They sauntered on, but had barely entered the town when her attention was attracted by a young couple leading a child, who had come out from the second platform, into which the train from Aldbrickham had steamed. They were walking just in front of the innkeepers.

"Sakes alive!" said Arabella.

"What's that?" said Cartlett.

"Who do you think that couple is? Don't you recognise the man?"

"No."

"Not from the photos I have showed you?"

"Is it Fawley?"

"Yes—of course."

"Oh, well. I suppose he was inclined for a little sight-seeing like the rest of us." Cartlett's interest in Jude, whatever it might have been when Arabella was new to him, had plainly flagged since her charms and her idiosyncrasies, her supernumerary hair-coils, and her optional dimples, were becoming as a tale that is told.

Arabella so regulated her pace and her husband's as to keep just in the rear of the other three, which it was easy to do without notice in such a stream of pedestrians. Her answers to Cartlett's remarks were vague and slight, for the group in front interested her more than all the rest of the spectacle.

"They are rather fond of one another and of their child, seemingly," continued the publican.

"*Their* child! 'Tisn't their child," said Arabella with a curious, sudden fierceness. "They haven't been married long enough for it to be theirs!"

But although the smouldering maternal instinct was strong enough in her to lead her to quash her husband's conjecture, she was not disposed on second thoughts to be more candid than necessary. Mr. Cartlett had no other idea than that his wife's child by her first husband was with his grandparents at the Antipodes.

"O I suppose not. She looks quite a girl."

"They are only lovers, or lately married, and have the child in charge, as anybody can see."

All continued to move ahead. The unwitting Sue and Jude, the couple in question, had determined to make this Agricultural Exhibition within twenty miles of their own town the occasion of a day's excursion which should combine exercise and amusement with instruction, at small expense. Not regardful of themselves alone, they had taken care to bring Father Time, to try every means of making him kindle and laugh like other boys, though he was to some extent a hindrance to the delightfully unreserved intercourse in their pilgrimages which they so much enjoyed. But they soon ceased to consider him an observer, and went along with that tender attention to each other which the shyest can scarcely disguise, and which these, among entire strangers as they imagined, took less trouble to disguise than they might have done at home. Sue, in her new summer clothes, flexible and light as a bird, her little thumb stuck up by the stem of her white cotton sunshade, went along as if she hardly touched ground, and as if a moderately strong puff of wind would float her over the hedge into the next field. Jude, in his light grey holiday-suit, was really proud of her companionship, not more for her external attractiveness than for her sympathetic words and ways. That complete mutual understanding, in which every glance and movement was as effectual as speech for conveying intelligence between them, made them almost the two parts of a single whole.

The pair with their charge passed through the turnstiles, Arabella and her husband not far behind them. When inside the enclosure the publican's wife could see that the two ahead began to take trouble with the youngster, pointing out and explaining the many objects of interest, alive and dead; and a passing sadness would touch their faces at their every failure to disturb his indifference.

"How she sticks to him!" said Arabella. "O no—I fancy they are not married, or they wouldn't be so much to one another as that. . . . I wonder!"

"But I thought you said he did marry her?"

"I heard he was going to—that's all, going to make another attempt, after putting it off once or twice. . . . As far as they themselves are concerned they are the only two in the show. I should be ashamed of making myself so silly if I were he!"

"I don't see as how there's anything remarkable in their behaviour. I should never have noticed their being in love, if you hadn't said so."

"You never see anything," she rejoined. Nevertheless Cartlett's view of the lovers' or married pair's conduct was undoubtedly that of the general crowd, whose attention seemed to be in no way attracted by what Arabella's sharpened vision discerned.

"He's charmed by her as if she were some fairy!" continued Arabella. "See how he looks round at her, and lets his eyes rest on her. I am inclined to think that she don't care for him quite so much as he does for her. She's not a particular warm-hearted creature to my thinking, though she cares for him pretty middling much—as much as she's able to; and he could make her heart ache a bit if he liked to try—which he's too simple to do. There—now they are going across to the cart-horse sheds. Come along."

"I don't want to see the cart-horses. It is no business of ours to follow these two. If we have come to see the show let us see it in our own way, as they do in theirs."

"Well—suppose we agree to meet somewhere in an hour's time—say at that refreshment tent over there, and go about independent? Then you can look at what you choose to, and so can I."

Cartlett was not loath to agree to this, and they parted—he proceeding to the shed where malting processes were being exhibited, and Arabella in the direction taken by Jude and Sue. Before, however, she had regained their wake a laughing face met her own, and she was confronted by Anny, the friend of her girlhood.

Anny had burst out in hearty laughter at the mere fact of the chance encounter. "I be still living down there," she said, as soon as she was composed. "I am soon going to be married, but my intended couldn't come up here to-day. But there's lots of us come by excursion, though I've lost the rest of 'em for the present."

"Have you met Jude and his young woman, or wife, or whatever she is? I saw 'em by now."

"No. Not a glimpse of un for years!"

"Well, they are close by here somewhere. Yes—there they are—by that grey horse!"

"O, that's his present young woman—wife did you say? Has he married again?"

"I don't know."

"She's pretty, isn't she!"

"Yes—nothing to complain of; or jump at. Not much to depend on, though; a slim, fidgetty-little thing like that."

"He's a nice-looking chap, too! You ought to ha' stuck to un, Arabella."

"I don't know but I ought," murmured she.

Anny laughed. "That's you, Arabella! Always wanting another man than your own."

"Well, and what woman don't I should like to know? As for that body with him—she don't know what love is—at least what I call love! I can see in her face she don't."

"And perhaps, Abby dear, you don't know what she calls love."

"I'm sure I don't wish to! . . . Ah—they are making for the Art Department. I should like to see some pictures myself. Suppose we go that way?—Why, if all Wessex isn't here, I verily believe! There's Dr. Vilbert. Haven't seen him for years and he's not looking a day older than when I used to know him. How do you do, Physician? I was just saying that you don't look a day older than when you knew me as a girl."

"Simply the result of taking my own pills regular, ma'am. Only two and threepence a box—warranted efficacious by the Government stamp. Now let me advise you to purchase the same immunity from the ravages of Time by following my example? Only two-and-three."

The physician had produced a box from his waistcoat pocket, and Arabella was induced to make the purchase.

"At the same time," continued he, when the pills were paid for, "you have the advantage of me, Mrs.—Surely not Mrs. Fawley, once Miss Donn, of the vicinity of Marygreen?"

"Yes. But Mrs. Cartlett now."

"Ah—you lost him, then? Promising young fellow! A pupil of mine, you know. I taught him the dead languages. And believe me, he soon knew nearly as much as I."

"I lost him; but not as you think," said Arabella drily. "The lawyers untied us. There he is, look, alive and lusty; along with that young woman, entering the Art Exhibition."

"Ah—dear me! Fond of her, apparently."

"They *say* they are cousins."

"Cousinship is a great convenience to their feelings, I should say?"

"Yes. So her husband thought, no doubt, when he divorced her. . . . Shall we look at the pictures, too?"

The trio followed across the green and entered. Jude and Sue, with the child, unaware of the interest they were exciting, had gone up to a model at one end of the building, which they regarded with considerable attention for a long while before they went on. Arabella and her friends came to it in due course, and the inscription it bore was: "Model of Cardinal College, Christminster; by J. Fawley and S. F. M. Bridehead."

"Admiring their own work," said Arabella. "How like Jude—always thinking of Colleges and Christminster, instead of attending to his business!"

They glanced cursorily at the pictures, and proceeded to the band-stand. When they had stood a little while listening to the music of the military performers, Jude, Sue, and the child came up on the other side. Arabella did not care if they should recognise her; but they were too deeply absorbed in their own lives, as translated into emotion by the military band, to perceive her under her beaded veil. She walked round the outside of the listening throng, passing behind the lovers, whose movements had an unexpected fascination for her to-day. Scrutinizing them narrowly from the rear she noticed that Jude's hand sought Sue's as they stood, the two standing close together so as to conceal, as they supposed, this tacit expression of their mutual responsiveness.

"Silly fools—like two children!" Arabella whispered to herself morosely, as she rejoined her companions, with whom she preserved a preoccupied silence.

Anny meanwhile had jokingly remarked to Vilbert on Arabella's hankering interest in her first husband.

"Now," said the physician to Arabella, apart; "do you want anything such as this, Mrs. Cartlett? It is not compounded out of my regular pharmacopoeia, but I am sometimes asked for such a thing." He produced a small phial of clear liquid. "A love-philtre, such as was used by the Ancients with great effect. I found it out by study of their writings, and have never known it to fail."

"What is it made of?" asked Arabella curiously.

"Well—a distillation of the juices of doves' hearts—otherwise pigeons'—is one of the ingredients. It took nearly a hundred hearts to produce that small bottle full."

"How do you get pigeons enough?"

"To tell a secret, I get a piece of rock-salt, of which pigeons are inordinately fond, and place it in a dovecot on my roof. In a few hours the birds come to it from all points of the compass—east, west, north and south—and thus I secure as many as I require. You use the liquid by contriving that the desired man shall take about ten drops of it in his drink. But remember, all this is told you because I gather from your questions that you mean to be a purchaser. You must keep faith with me?"

"Very well—I don't mind a bottle—to give some friend or other to try it on her young man." She produced five shillings, the price asked, and slipped the phial in her capacious bosom. Saying presently that she was due at an appointment with her husband she sauntered away towards the refreshment bar, Jude, his companion, and the child having gone on to the horticultural tent, where Arabella caught a glimpse of them standing before a group of roses in bloom.

She waited a few minutes observing them, and then proceeded to join her spouse with no very amiable sentiments. She found him seated on a stool by the bar, talking to one of the gaily dressed maids who had served him with spirits.

"I should think you had enough of this business at home!" Arabella remarked gloomily. "Surely you didn't come fifty miles from your own bar to go into another? Come, take me round the show, as other men do their wives! Dammy, one would think you were a young bachelor, with nobody to look after but yourself!"

"But we agreed to meet here; and what could I do but wait?"

"Well, now we have met, come along," she returned, ready to quarrel with the sun for shining on her. And they left the tent together, this pot-bellied man and florid woman, in the antipathetic, recriminatory mood of the average husband and wife of Christendom.

In the meantime the more exceptional couple and the boy still lingered in the pavilion of flowers—an enchanted palace to their appreciative taste—Sue's usually pale cheeks reflecting the pink of the tinted roses at which she gazed; for the gay sights, the air, the music, and the excitement of a day's outing with Jude, had quickened her blood and made her eyes sparkle with vivacity. She adored roses, and what Arabella had witnessed was Sue detaining Jude almost against his will while she learnt the names of this variety and that, and put her face within an inch of their blooms to smell them.

"I should like to push my face quite into them—the dears!" she had said. "But I suppose it is against the rules to touch them—isn't it, Jude?"

"Yes, you baby," said he: and then playfully gave her a little push, so that her nose went among the petals.

"The policeman will be down on us, and I shall say it was my husband's fault!"

Then she looked up at him, and smiled in a way that told so much to Arabella.

"Happy?" he murmured.

She nodded.

"Why? Because you have come to the great Wessex Agricultural Show—or because *we* have come?"

"You are always trying to make me confess to all sorts of absurdities. Because I am improving my mind, of course, by seeing all these steam-ploughs, and threshing-machines, and chaff-cutters, and cows, and pigs, and sheep."

Jude was quite content with a baffle from his ever evasive companion. But when he had forgotten that he had put the question, and because he no longer wished for an answer, she went on: "I feel that we have returned to Greek joyousness, and have blinded ourselves to sickness and sorrow, and have forgotten what twenty-five centuries have taught the race since their time, as one of your Christminster luminaries says. . . . There is one immediate shadow, however—only one." And she looked at the aged child, whom, though they had taken him to everything likely to attract a young intelligence, they had utterly failed to interest.

He knew what they were saying and thinking. "I am very, very sorry, father and mother," he said. "But please don't mind!—I can't help it. I should like the flowers very very much, if I didn't keep on thinking they'd be all withered in a few days!"

VI

THE UNNOTICED LIVES THAT THE PAIR HAD HITHERTO LED BEGAN, FROM THE DAY OF the suspended wedding onwards, to be observed and discussed by other persons than Arabella. The society of Spring Street and the neighbourhood generally did not understand, and probably could not have been made to understand, Sue and Jude's private minds, emotions, positions, and fears. The curious facts of a child coming to them unexpectedly, who called Jude father, and Sue mother, and a hitch in a marriage ceremony intended for quietness to be performed at a registrar's office, together with rumours of the undefended cases in the Law-Courts, bore only one translation to plain minds.

Little Time—for though he was formally turned into "Jude," the apt nick-name stuck to him—would come home from school in the evening, and repeat inquiries and remarks that had been made to him by the other boys; and cause Sue, and Jude when he heard them, a great deal of pain and sadness.

The result was that shortly after the attempt at the registrar's the pair went off—to London it was believed—for several days, hiring somebody to look to the boy. When they came back they let it be understood indirectly, and with total indifference and weariness of mien, that they were legally married at last. Sue, who had previously been called Mrs. Bridehead, now openly adopted the name of Mrs. Fawley. Her dull, cowed, and listless manner for days seemed to substantiate all this.

But the mistake (as it was called) of their going away so secretly to do the business, kept up much of the mystery of their lives; and they found that they made not such advances with their neighbours as they had expected to do thereby. A living mystery was not much less interesting than a dead scandal.

The baker's lad and the grocer's boy, who at first had used to lift their hats gallantly to Sue, when they came to execute their errands, in these days no longer took the trouble to render her that homage, and the neighbouring artizans' wives looked straight along the pavement when they encountered her.

Nobody molested them, it is true; but an oppressive atmosphere began to encircle their souls, particularly after their excursion to the Show, as if that visit had brought some evil influence to bear on them. And their temperaments were precisely of a kind to suffer from this atmosphere, and to be indisposed to lighten it by vigorous and open statements. Their apparent attempt at reparation had come too late to be effective.

The head-stone and epitaph orders fell off: and two or three months later, when autumn came, Jude perceived that he would have to return to journey-work again, a course all the more unfortunate just now, in that he had not as yet cleared off the debt he had unavoidably incurred in the payment of the law-costs of the previous year.

One evening he sat down to share the common meal with Sue and the child as usual. "I am thinking," he said to her, "that I'll hold on here no longer. The life suits us, certainly; but if we could get away to a place where we are unknown, we should be lighter hearted, and have a better chance. And so I am afraid we must break it up here, however awkward for you, poor dear!"

Sue was always much affected at a picture of herself as an object of pity, and a tear came at this.

"Well—I am not sorry," said she presently. "I am much depressed by the way they look at me here. And you have been keeping on this house and furniture entirely for me and the boy! You don't want it yourself, and the expense is unnecessary. But whatever we do, wherever we go, you won't take him away from me, Jude dear? I could not let him go now! The cloud upon his young mind makes him so pathetic to me; I do hope to lift it some day! And he loves me so. You won't take him away from me?"

"Certainly I won't, dear little girl! We'll get nice lodgings, wherever we go. I shall be moving about probably—getting a job here and a job there."

"I shall do something too, of course, till—till—Well, now I can't be useful in the lettering it behoves me to turn my hand to something else."

"Don't hurry about getting employment," he said regretfully. "I don't want you to do that. I wish you wouldn't, Sue. The boy and yourself are enough for you to attend to."

There was a knock at the door, and Jude answered it. Sue could hear the conversation:

"Is Mr. Fawley at home? . . . Biles and Willis the building contractors sent me to know if you'll undertake the relettering of the Ten Commandments in a little church they've been restoring lately in the country near here."

Jude reflected, and said he could undertake it.

"It is not a very artistic job," continued the messenger. "The clergyman is a very old-fashioned chap, and he has refused to let anything more be done to the church than cleaning and repairing."

"Excellent old man!" said Sue to herself, who was sentimentally opposed to the horrors of over-restoration.

"The Ten Commandments are fixed to the east end," the messenger went on, "and they want doing up with the rest of the wall there, since he won't have them carted off as old materials belonging to the contractor, in the usual way of the trade."

A bargain as to terms was struck, and Jude came indoors. "There, you see," he said cheerfully. "One more job yet, at any rate, and you can help in it—at least you can try. We shall have all the church to ourselves, as the rest of the work is finished."

Next day Jude went out to the church, which was only two miles off. He found that what the contractor's clerk had said was true. The tables of the Jewish law towered sternly over the utensils of Christian grace, as the chief ornament of the chancel end, in the fine dry style of the last century. And as their frame-work was constructed of ornamental plaster they could not be taken down for repair. A portion, crumbled by damp, required renewal; and when this had been done, and the whole cleansed, he began to renew the lettering. On the second morning Sue came to see what assistance she could render, and also because they liked to be together.

The silence and emptiness of the building gave her confidence, and, standing on a safe low platform erected by Jude, which she was nevertheless timid at mounting, she began painting in the letters of the first Table while he set about mending a portion of the second. She was quite pleased at her powers; she had acquired them in the days she painted illumined texts for the church-fitting shop at Christminster. Nobody seemed likely to disturb them; and the pleasant twitter of birds, and rustle of October leafage, came in through an open window, and mingled with their talk.

They were not, however, to be left thus snug and peaceful for long. About half-past twelve there came footsteps on the gravel without. The old vicar and his churchwarden entered, and, coming up to see what was being done, seemed surprised to discover that a young woman was assisting. They passed on into an aisle, at which time the door again opened, and another figure entered—a small one, that of little Time, who was crying. Sue had told him where he might find her between school-hours, if he wished. She came down from her perch, and said, "What's the matter, my dear?"

"I couldn't stay to eat my dinner in school, because they said—" He described how some boys had taunted him about his nominal mother, and Sue, grieved, expressed her indignation to Jude aloft. The child went into the churchyard, and Sue returned to her work. Meanwhile the door had opened again, and there shuffled in with a businesslike air the white-aproned woman who cleaned the church. Sue recognised her as one who had friends in Spring Street, whom she visited. The church-cleaner looked at Sue, gaped, and lifted her hands; she had evidently recognised Jude's companion as the latter had recognised her. Next came two ladies, and after talking to the charwoman they also moved forward, and as Sue stood reaching upward, watched her hand tracing the letters, and critically regarded her person in relief against the white wall, till she grew so nervous that she trembled visibly.

They went back to where the others were standing, talking in undertones: and one said—Sue could not hear which—"She's his wife, I suppose?"

"Some say Yes: some say No," was the reply from the charwoman.

"Not? Then she ought to be, or somebody's—that's very clear!"

"They've only been married a very few weeks, whether or no."

"A strange pair to be painting the Two Tables! I wonder Biles and Willis could think of such a thing as hiring those!"

The churchwarden supposed that Biles and Willis knew of nothing wrong, and then the other, who had been talking to the old woman, explained what she meant by calling them strange people.

The probable drift of the subdued conversation which followed was made plain by the churchwarden breaking into an anecdote, in a voice that everybody in the church could hear, though obviously suggested by the present situation:

"Well, now, it is a curious thing, but my grand-father told me a strange tale of a most immoral case that happened at the painting of the Commandments in a church out by Gaymead—which is quite within a walk of this one. In them days Commandments were mostly done in gilt letters on a black ground, and that's how they were out where I say, before the owld church was rebuilded. It must have been somewhere about a hundred years ago that them Commandments wanted doing up, just as ours do here, and they had to get men from Aldbrickham to do 'em. Now they wished to get the job finished by a particular Sunday, so the men had to work late Saturday night, against their will, for over-time was not paid then as 'tis now. There was no true religion in the country at that date, neither among pa'sons, clerks, nor people, and to keep the men up to their work the vicar had to let 'em have plenty of drink during the afternoon. As evening drawed on they sent for some more themselves; rum, by all account. It got later and later, and they got more and more fuddled, till at last they went a-putting their rum-bottle and rummers upon the Communion table, and drawed up a trestle or two, and sate round comfortable, and poured out again right hearty bumpers. No sooner had they tossed off their glasses than, so the story goes, they fell down senseless, one and all. How long they bode so they didn't know, but when they came to themselves there was a terrible thunder-storm a-raging, and they seemed to see in the gloom a dark figure with very thin legs and a curious voot, a-standing on the ladder, and finishing their work. When it got daylight they could see that the work was really finished, and couldn't at all mind finishing it themselves. They went home, and the next thing they heard was that a great scandal had been caused in the church that Sunday morning, for when the people came and service began, all saw that the Ten Commandments wez painted with the "Nots" left out. Decent people wouldn't attend service there for a long time, and the Bishop had to be sent for to reconsecrate the church. That's the tradition as I used to hear it as a child. You must take it for what it is wo'th, but this case to-day has reminded me o't, as I say."

The visitors gave one more glance, as if to see whether Jude and Sue had left the Nots out likewise, and then severally left the church, even the old woman at last. Sue and Jude, who had not stopped working, sent back the child to school, and remained without speaking; till, looking at her narrowly, he found she had been crying silently.

"Never mind, comrade!" he said. "I know what it is!"

"I can't *bear* that they, and everybody, should think people wicked because they may have chosen to live their own way! It is really these opinions that make the best intentioned people reckless, and actually become immoral!"

"Never be cast down! It was only a funny story."

"Ah, but we suggested it! I am afraid I have done you mischief, Jude, instead of helping you by coming!"

To have suggested such a story was certainly not very exhilarating, in a serious view of their position. However, in a few minutes Sue seemed to see that their position this morning had a ludicrous side, and wiping her eyes she laughed.

"It is droll, after all," she said, "that we two, of all people, with our queer history, should happen to be here doing this! You a reprobate, and I—in my condition. . . . O dear!" . . . And with her hand over her eyes she laughed again silently and intermittently, till she was quite weak.

"That's better," said Jude gaily. "Now we are right again, aren't we, little girl!"

"O but it is serious, all the same!" she sighed as she took up the brush and righted herself. "But do you see they don't think we are married? They *won't* believe it! It is extraordinary!"

"I don't care whether they think so or not," said Jude. "I shan't take any more trouble to make them."

They sat down to lunch—which they had brought with them not to hinder time—and having eaten it were about to set to work anew when a man entered the church, and Jude recognised in him the contractor Willis. He beckoned to Jude, and spoke to him apart.

"Here—I've just had a complaint about this," he said, with rather breathless awkwardness. "I don't wish to go into the matter—as of course I didn't know what was going on—but I am afraid I must ask you and her to leave off, and let somebody else finish this! It is best, to avoid all unpleasantness. I'll pay you for the week, all the same."

Jude was too independent to make any fuss; and the contractor paid him, and left. Jude picked up his tools, and Sue cleansed her brush. Then their eyes met.

"How could we—be so simple—as to suppose we might do this!" said she, dropping to her tragic note. "Of course we ought not—I ought not—to have come!"

"I had no idea that anybody was going to intrude into such a lonely place and see us!" Jude returned. "Well, it can't be helped, dear; and of course I wouldn't wish to injure Willis's trade-connection by staying." They sat down passively for a few minutes, proceeded out of the church, and overtaking the boy pursued their thoughtful way to Aldbrickham.

Fawley had still a pretty zeal in the cause of education, and, as was natural with his experiences, he was active in furthering "equality of opportunity" by any humble means open to him. He had joined an Artizans' Mutual Improvement Society established in the town about the time of his arrival there; its members being young men of all creeds and denominations, including Churchmen, Congregationalists, Baptists, Unitarians, Positivists, and others—Agnostics had scarcely been heard of at this time—their one common wish to enlarge their minds forming a sufficiently close bond of union. The subscription was small, and the room homely; and Jude's activity, uncustomary acquirements, and above all, singular intuition on what to read and how to set about it—begotten of his years of struggle against malignant stars—had led to his being placed on the committee.

A few evenings after his dismissal from the church repairs, and before he had obtained any more work to do, he went to attend a meeting of the aforesaid committee. It was late when he arrived: all the others had come, and as he entered they looked dubiously at him, and hardly uttered a word of greeting. He guessed that something bearing on himself had been either discussed or mooted. Some ordinary business was transacted, and it was disclosed that the number of subscriptions had shown a sudden falling off for that quarter. One member—a really well-meaning and upright man—began speaking in enigmas about certain possible causes: that it behoved them to look well into their constitution; for if the committee were not respected, and had not at least, in their differences, a common standard of *conduct*, they would bring the institution to the ground. Nothing further was said in Jude's presence, but he knew what this meant; and turning to the table wrote a note resigning his office there and then.

Thus the super-sensitive couple were more and more impelled to go away. And then bills were sent in, and the question arose, what could Jude do with his great-aunt's heavy old furniture, if he left the town to travel he knew not whither? This, and the necessity of ready money, compelled him to decide on an auction, much as he would have preferred to keep the venerable goods.

The day of the sale came on; and Sue for the last time cooked her own, the child's, and Jude's breakfast in the little house he had furnished. It chanced to be a wet day; moreover

Sue was unwell, and not wishing to desert her poor Jude in such gloomy circumstances, for he was compelled to stay a while, she acted on the suggestion of the auctioneer's man, and ensconced herself in an upper room, which could be emptied of its effects, and so kept closed to the bidders. Here Jude discovered her; and with the child, and their few trunks, baskets, and bundles, and two chairs and a table that were not in the sale, the two sat in meditative talk.

Footsteps began stamping up and down the bare stairs, the comers inspecting the goods, some of which were of so quaint and ancient a make as to acquire an adventitious value as art. Their door was tried once or twice, and to guard themselves against intrusion Jude wrote "Private" on a scrap of paper, and stuck it upon the panel.

They soon found that, instead of the furniture, their own personal histories and past conduct began to be discussed to an unexpected and intolerable extent by the intending bidders. It was not till now that they really discovered what a fools' paradise of supposed unrecognition they had been living in of late. Sue silently took her companion's hand, and with eyes on each other they heard these passing remarks—the quaint and mysterious personality of Father Time being a subject which formed a large ingredient in the hints and innuendoes. At length the auction began in the room below, whence they could hear each familiar article knocked down, the highly prized ones cheaply, the unconsidered at an unexpected price.

"People don't understand us," he sighed heavily. "I am glad we have decided to go."

"The question is, where to?"

"It ought to be to London. There one can live as one chooses."

"No—not London, dear! I know it well. We should be unhappy there."

"Why?"

"Can't you think?"

"Because Arabella is there?"

"That's the chief reason."

"But in the country I shall always be uneasy lest there should be some more of our late experience. And I don't care to lessen it by explaining, for one thing, all about the boy's history. To cut him off from his past I have determined to keep silence. I am sickened of ecclesiastical work now; and I shouldn't like to accept it, if offered me!"

"You ought to have learnt Classic. Gothic is barbaric art, after all. Pugin was wrong, and Wren was right. Remember the interior of Christminster Cathedral—almost the first place in which we looked in each other's faces. Under the picturesqueness of those Norman details one can see the grotesque childishness of uncouth people trying to imitate the vanished Roman forms, remembered by dim tradition only."

"Yes—you have half converted me to that view by what you have said before. But one can work, and despise what one does. I must do something, if not church-gothic."

"I wish we could both follow an occupation in which personal circumstances don't count," she said, smiling up wistfully. "I am as disqualified for teaching as you are for ecclesiastical art. You must fall back upon railway-stations, bridges, theatres, music-halls, hotels—everything that has no connection with conduct."

"I am not skilled in those. . . . I ought to take to bread-baking. I grew up in the baking business with aunt, you know. But even a baker must be conventional, to get customers."

"Unless he keeps a cake and gingerbread stall at markets and fairs, where people are gloriously indifferent to everything except the quality of the goods."

Their thoughts were diverted by the voice of the auctioneer: "Now this antique oak settle—a unique example of old English furniture, worthy the attention of all collectors!"

"That was my great-grand-father's," said Jude. "I wish we could have kept the poor old thing!"

One by one the articles went, and the afternoon passed away. Jude and the other two were getting tired and hungry, but after the conversation they had heard they were shy of going out while the purchasers were in their line of retreat. However, the later lots drew on, and it became necessary to emerge into the rain soon, to take on Sue's things to their temporary lodging.

"Now the next lot: two pairs of pigeons, all alive and plump—a nice pie for somebody for next Sunday's dinner!"

The impending sale of these birds had been the most trying suspense of the whole afternoon. They were Sue's pets, and when it was found that they could not possibly be kept, more sadness was caused than by parting from all the furniture. Sue tried to think away her tears as she heard the trifling sum that her dears were deemed to be worth advanced by small stages to the price at which they were finally knocked down. The purchaser was a neighbouring poulterer, and they were unquestionably doomed to die before the next market day.

Seeing her dissembled distress Jude kissed her, and said it was time to go and see if the lodgings were ready. He would go on with the boy, and fetch her soon.

When she was left alone she waited patiently, but Jude did not come back. At last she started, the coast being clear, and on passing the poulterer's shop, not far off, she saw her pigeons in a hamper by the door. An emotion at sight of them, assisted by the growing dusk of evening, caused her to act on impulse, and first looking around her quickly, she pulled out the peg which fastened down the cover, and went on. The cover was lifted from within, and the pigeons flew away with a clatter that brought the chagrined poulterer cursing and swearing to the door.

Sue reached the lodging trembling, and found Jude and the boy making it comfortable for her. "Do the buyers pay before they bring away the things?" she asked breathlessly.

"Yes, I think. Why?"

"Because, then, I've done such a wicked thing!" And she explained, in bitter contrition.

"I shall have to pay the poulterer for them, if he doesn't catch them," said Jude. "But never mind. Don't fret about it, dear."

"It was so foolish of me! O why should Nature's law be mutual butchery!"

"Is it so, mother?" asked the boy intently.

"Yes!" said Sue vehemently.

"Well, they must take their chance, now, poor things," said Jude. "As soon as the sale-account is wound up, and our bills paid, we go."

"Where do we go to?" asked Time, in suspense.

"We must sail under sealed orders, that nobody may trace us. . . . We mustn't go to Alfredston, or to Melchester, or to Shaston, or to Christminster. Apart from those we may go anywhere."

"Why mustn't we go there, father?"

"Because of a cloud that has gathered over us; though 'we have wronged no man, corrupted no man, defrauded no man!' Though perhaps we have 'done that which was right in our own eyes.' "

VII

FROM THAT WEEK JUDE FAWLEY AND SUE WALKED NO MORE IN THE TOWN OF ALDbrickham.

Whither they had gone nobody knew, chiefly because nobody cared to know. Anyone sufficiently curious to trace the steps of such an obscure pair might have discovered without great trouble that they had taken advantage of his adaptive craftsmanship to enter on a shifting, almost nomadic, life, which was not without its pleasantness for a time.

Wherever Jude heard of freestone work to be done, thither he went, choosing by preference places remote from his old haunts and Sue's. He laboured at a job, long or briefly, till it was finished; and then moved on.

Two whole years and a half passed thus. Sometimes he might have been found shaping the mullions of a country mansion, sometimes setting the parapet of a town-hall, sometimes ashlaring an hotel at Sandbourne, sometimes a museum at Casterbridge, sometimes as far down as Exonbury, sometimes at Stoke-Barehills. Later still he was at Kennetbridge, a thriving town not more than a dozen miles south of Marygreen, this being his nearest approach to the village where he was known; for he had a sensitive dread of being questioned as to his life and fortunes by those who had been acquainted with him during his ardent young manhood of study and promise, and his brief and unhappy married life at that time.

At some of these places he would be detained for months, at others only a few weeks. His curious and sudden antipathy to ecclesiastical work, both episcopal and noncomformist, which had risen in him when suffering under a smarting sense of misconception, remained with him in cold blood, less from any fear of renewed censure than from an ultra-conscientiousness which would not allow him to seek a living out of those who would disapprove of his ways; also, too, from a sense of inconsistency between his former dogmas and his present practice, hardly a shred of the beliefs with which he had first gone up to Christminster now remaining with him. He was mentally approaching the position which Sue had occupied when he first met her.

On a Saturday evening in May, nearly three years after Arabella's recognition of Sue and himself at the Agricultural Show, some of those who there encountered each other met again.

It was the spring fair at Kennetbridge, and, though this ancient trade-meeting had much dwindled from its dimensions of former times, the long straight street of the borough presented a lively scene about mid-day. At this hour a light trap, among other vehicles, was driven into the town by the north road, and up to the door of a temperance inn. There alighted two women, one the driver, an ordinary country person, the other a finely built figure in the deep mourning of a widow. Her sombre suit, of pronounced cut, caused her to appear a little out of place in the medley and bustle of a provincial fair.

"I will just find out where it is, Anny," said the widow-lady to her companion, when the horse and cart had been taken by a man who came forward: "and then I'll come back, and meet you here; and we'll go in and have something to eat and drink. I begin to feel quite a sinking."

"With all my heart," said the other. "Though I would sooner have put up at the Chequers or The Jack. You can't get much at these temperance houses."

"Now, don't you give way to gluttonous desires, my child," said the woman in weeds reprovingly. "This is the proper place. Very well: we'll meet in half an hour, unless you come with me to find out where the site of the new chapel is?"

"I don't care to. You can tell me."

The companions then went their several ways, the one in crape walking firmly along with a mien of disconnection from her miscellaneous surroundings. Making inquiries, she came to a hoarding, within which were excavations denoting the foundations of a building; and on the boards without one or two large posters announcing that the foundation-stone of the chapel about to be erected would be laid that afternoon at three o'clock by a London preacher of great popularity among his body.

Having ascertained thus much the immensely weeded widow retraced her steps, and gave herself leisure to observe the movements of the fair. By and by her attention was arrested by a little stall of cakes and gingerbreads, standing between the more pretentious erections of trestles and canvas. It was covered with an immaculate cloth, and tended by a young woman apparently unused to the business, she being accompanied by a boy with an octogenarian face, who assisted her.

"Upon my—senses!" murmured the widow to herself. "His wife Sue—if she is so!" She drew nearer to the stall. "How do you do, Mrs. Fawley?" she said blandly.

Sue changed colour and recognised Arabella through the crape veil.

"How are you, Mrs. Cartlett?" she said stiffly. And then perceiving Arabella's garb her voice grew sympathetic in spite of herself. "What?—you have lost—"

"My poor husband. Yes. He died suddenly, six weeks ago, leaving me none too well off, though he was a kind husband to me. But whatever profit there is in public-house keeping goes to them that brew the liquors, and not to them that retail 'em. . . . And you, my little old man! You don't know me, I expect?"

"Yes, I do. You be the woman I thought wer my mother for a bit, till I found you wasn't," replied Father Time, who had learned to use the Wessex tongue quite naturally by now.

"All right. Never mind. I am a friend."

"Juey," said Sue suddenly, "go down to the station platform with this tray—there's another train coming in, I think."

When he was gone Arabella continued: "He'll never be a beauty, will he, poor chap! Does he know I am his mother really?"

"No. He thinks there is some mystery about his parentage—that's all. Jude is going to tell him when he is a little older."

"But how do you come to be doing this? I am surprised."

"It is only a temporary occupation—a fancy of ours while we are in a difficulty."

"Then you are living with him still?"

"Yes."

"Married?"

"Of course."

"Any children?"

"Two."

"And another coming soon, I see."

Sue writhed under the hard and direct questioning, and her tender little mouth began to quiver.

"Lord—I mean goodness gracious—what is there to cry about? Some folks would be proud enough!"

"It is not that I am ashamed—not as you think! But it seems such a terribly tragic thing to bring beings into the world—so presumptuous—that I question my right to do it sometimes!"

"Take it easy, my dear. . . . But you don't tell me why you do such a thing as this? Jude used to be a proud sort of chap—above any business almost, leave alone keeping a standing."

"Perhaps my husband has altered a little since then. I am sure he is not proud now!" And Sue's lips quivered again. "I am doing this because he caught a chill early in the year while putting up some stonework of a music-hall, at Quartershot, which he had to do in the rain, the work having to be executed by a fixed day. He is better than he was; but it has been a long, weary time! We have had an old widow friend with us to help us through it; but she's leaving soon."

"Well, I am respectable too, thank God, and of a serious way of thinking since my loss. Why did you choose to sell gingerbreads?"

"That's a pure accident. He was brought up to the baking business, and it occurred to him to try his hand at these, which he can make without coming out-of-doors. We call them Christminster cakes. They are a great success."

"I never saw any like 'em. Why, they are windows and towers, and pinnacles! And upon my word they are very nice." She had helped herself, and was unceremoniously munching one of the cakes.

"Yes. They are reminiscences of the Christminster Colleges. Traceried windows, and cloisters, you see. It was a whim of his to do them in pastry."

"Still harping on Christminster—even in his cakes!" laughed Arabella. "Just like Jude. A ruling passion. What a queer fellow he is, and always will be!"

Sue sighed, and she looked her distress at hearing him criticised.

"Don't you think he is? Come now; you do, though you are so fond of him!"

"Of course Christminster is a sort of fixed vision with him, which I suppose he'll never be cured of believing in. He still thinks it a great centre of high and fearless thought, instead of what it is, a nest of commonplace schoolmasters whose characteristic is timid obsequiousness to tradition."

Arabella was quizzing Sue with more regard of how she was speaking than of what she was saying. "How odd to hear a woman selling cakes talk like that!" she said. "Why don't you go back to school-keeping?"

Sue shook her head. "They won't have me."

"Because of the divorce, I suppose?"

"That and other things. And there is no reason to wish it. We gave up all ambition, and were never so happy in our lives till his illness came."

"Where are you living?"

"I don't care to say."

"Here in Kennetbridge?"

Sue's manner showed Arabella that her random guess was right.

"Here comes the boy back again," continued Arabella. "My boy and Jude's!"

Sue's eyes darted a spark. "You needn't throw that in my face!" she cried.

"Very well—though I half feel as if I should like to have him with me! . . . But Lord, I don't want to take him from 'ee—ever I should sin to speak so profane—though I should think you must have enough of your own! He's in very good hands, that I know; and I am not the woman to find fault with what the Lord has ordained. I've reached a more resigned frame of mind."

"Indeed! I wish I had been able to do so."

"You should try," replied the widow, from the serene heights of a mind conscious not only of spiritual but of social superiority. "I make no boast of my awakening, but I'm not what I was. After Cartlett's death I was passing the chapel in the street next ours, and went into it for shelter from a shower of rain. I felt a need of some sort of support under my loss, and, as 'twas righter than gin, I took to going there regular, and found it a great comfort. But I've left London now, you know, and at present I am living at Alfredston, with my friend Anny, to be near my own old country. I'm not come here to the fair to-day. There's to be the foundation-stone of a new chapel laid this afternoon by a popular London preacher, and I drove over with Anny. Now I must go back to meet her."

Then Arabella wished Sue good-bye, and went on.

VIII

IN THE AFTERNOON SUE AND THE OTHER PEOPLE BUSTLING ABOUT KENNETBRIDGE FAIR could hear singing inside the placarded hoarding further down the street. Those who peeped through the opening saw a crowd of persons in broadcloth, with hymn-books in their hands, standing round the excavations for the new chapel-walls. Arabella Cartlett and her weeds stood among them. She had a clear, powerful voice, which could be distinctly heard with the rest, rising and falling to the tune, her inflated bosom being also seen doing likewise.

It was two hours later on the same day that Anny and Mrs. Cartlett, having had tea at the Temperance hotel, started on their return journey across the high and open country which stretches between Kennetbridge and Alfredston. Arabella was in a thoughtful mood; but her thoughts were not of the new chapel, as Anny at first surmised.

"No—it is something else," at last said Arabella sullenly. "I came here to-day never thinking of anybody but poor Cartlett, or of anything but spreading the Gospel by means of this new tabernacle they've begun this afternoon. But something has happened to turn my mind another way quite. Anny, I've heard of un again, and I've seen *her!*"

"Who?"

"I've heard of Jude, and I've seen his wife. And ever since, do what I will, and though I sung the hymns wi' all my strength, I have not been able to help thinking about 'n; which I've no right to do as a chapel member."

"Can't ye fix your mind upon what was said by the London preacher to-day, and try to get rid of your wandering fancies that way?"

"I do. But my wicked heart will ramble off in spite of myself!"

"Well—I know what it is to have a wanton mind o' my own, too! If you on'y knew what I do dream sometimes o' nights quite against my wishes, you'd say I had my struggles!" (Anny, too, had grown rather serious of late, her lover having jilted her.)

"What shall I do about it?" urged Arabella morbidly.

"You could take a lock of your late-lost husband's hair, and have it made into a mourning brooch, and look at it every hour of the day."

"I haven't a morsel!—and if I had 'twould be no good. . . . After all that's said about the comforts of this religion, I wish I had Jude back again!"

"You must fight valiant against the feeling, since he's another's. And I've heard that another good thing for it, when it afflicts volupshious widows, is to go to your husband's grave in the dusk of evening, and stand a long while a-bowed down."

"Pooh! I know as well as you what I must do; only I don't do it!"

They drove in silence along the straight road till they were within the horizon of Marygreen, which lay not far to the left of their route. They came to the junction of the highway and the cross-lane leading to that village, whose church-tower could be seen athwart the hollow. When they got yet further on, and were passing the lonely house in which Arabella and Jude had lived during the first months of their marriage, and where the pig-killing had taken place, she could control herself no longer.

"He's more mine than hers!" she burst out. "What right has she to him, I should like to know! I'd take him from her if I could!"

"Fie, Abby! And your husband only a month gone! Pray against it!"

"Be damned if I do! Feelings are feelings! I won't be a creeping hypocrite any longer—so there!"

Arabella had hastily drawn from her pocket a bundle of tracts which she had brought with her to distribute at the fair, and of which she had given away several. As she spoke she flung the whole remainder of the packet into the hedge "I've tried that sort o' physic and have failed wi' it. I must be as I was born!"

"Hush! You be excited, dear! Now you come along home quiet, and have a cup of tea, and don't let us talk about un no more. We won't come out this road again, as it leads to where he is, because it inflames 'ee so. You'll be all right again soon."

Arabella did calm herself down by degrees; and they crossed the Ridge-way. When they began to descend the long, straight hill, they saw plodding along in front of them an elderly man of spare stature and thoughtful gait. In his hand he carried a basket; and there was a touch of slovenliness in his attire, together with that indefinable something in his whole appearance which suggested one who was his own housekeeper, purveyor, confidant, and friend, through possessing nobody else at all in the world to act in those capacities for him. The remainder of the journey was down-hill, and guessing him to be going to Alfredston, they offered him a lift, which he accepted.

Arabella looked at him, and looked again, till at length she spoke. "If I don't mistake I am talking to Mr. Phillotson?"

The wayfarer faced round and regarded her in turn. "Yes; my name is Phillotson," he said. "But I don't recognise you, ma'am."

"I remember you well enough when you used to be schoolmaster out at Marygreen, and I one of your scholars. I used to walk up there from Cresscombe everyday, because we had only a mistress down at our place, and you taught better. But you wouldn't remember me as I should you?—Arabella Donn."

He shook his head. "No," he said politely, "I don't recall the name. And I should hardly recognise in your present portly self the slim schoolchild no doubt you were then."

"Well, I always had plenty of flesh on my bones. However, I am staying down here with some friends at present. You know, I suppose, who I married?"

"No."

"Jude Fawley—also a scholar of yours—at least a night scholar—for some little time I think? And known to you afterwards, if I am not mistaken."

"Dear me, dear me," said Phillotson, starting out of his stiffness. "*You* Fawley's wife? To be sure—he had a wife! And he—I understood—"

"Divorced her—as you did yours—perhaps for better reasons."

"Indeed?"

"Well—he med have been right in doing it—right for both; for I soon married again, and all went pretty straight till my husband died lately. But you—you were decidedly wrong!"

"No," said Phillotson, with sudden testiness. "I would rather not talk of this, but—I am convinced I did only what was right, and just, and moral. I have suffered for my act and opinions, but I hold to them; though her loss was a loss to me in more ways than one!"

"You lost your school and good income through her, did you not?"

"I don't care to talk of it. I have recently come back here—to Marygreen, I mean."

"You are keeping the school there again, just as formerly?"

The pressure of a sadness that would out unsealed him. "I am there," he replied. "Just as formerly, no. Merely on sufferance. It was a last resource—a small thing to return to after my move upwards, and my long indulged hopes—a returning to zero, with all its humiliations. But it is a refuge. I like the seclusion of the place, and the vicar having known me before my so-called eccentric conduct towards my wife had ruined my reputation as a schoolmaster, he accepted my services when all other schools were closed against me. However, although I take fifty pounds a year here after taking above two hundred elsewhere, I prefer it to running the risk of having my old domestic experiences raked up against me, as I should do if I tried to make a move."

"Right you are. A contented mind is a continual feast. She has done no better."

"She is not doing well, you mean?"

"I met her by accident at Kennetbridge this very day, and she is anything but thriving. Her husband is ill, and she anxious. You made a fool of a mistake about her, I tell 'ee again, and the harm you did yourself by dirting your own nest serves you right, excusing the liberty."

"How?"

"She was innocent."

"But nonsense! They did not even defend the case!"

"That was because they didn't care to. She was quite innocent of what obtained you your freedom, at the time you obtained it. I saw her just afterwards, and proved it to myself completely by talking to her."

Phillotson grasped the edge of the spring-cart, and appeared to be much stressed and worried by the information. "Still—she wanted to go," he said.

"Yes. But you shouldn't have let her. That's the only way with these fanciful women that chaw high—innocent or guilty. She'd have come round in time. We all do! Custom does it! it's all the same in the end! However, I think she's fond of her man still—whatever he med be of her. You were too quick about her. *I* shouldn't have let her go! I should have kept her chained on—her spirit for kicking would have been broke soon enough! There's nothing like bondage and a stone-deaf taskmaster for taming us women. Besides, you've got the laws on your side. Moses knew. Don't you call to mind what he says?"

"Not for the moment, ma'am, I regret to say."

"Call yourself a schoolmaster! I used to think o't when they read it in church, and I was carrying on a bit. 'Then shall the man be guiltless; but the woman shall bear her iniquity.' Damn rough on us women; but we must grin and put up wi' it! Haw haw! Well; she's got her deserts now."

"Yes," said Phillotson, with biting sadness. "Cruelty is the law pervading all nature and society; and we can't get out of it if we would!"

"Well—don't you forget to try it next time, old man."

"I cannot answer you, madam. I have never known much of womankind."

They had now reached the low levels bordering Alfredston, and passing through the outskirts approached a mill, to which Phillotson said his errand led him; whereupon they drew up, and he alighted, bidding them good-night in a preoccupied mood.

In the meantime Sue, though remarkably successful in her provisional business at Kennetbridge fair, had lost the temporary brightness which had begun to sit upon her sadness on account of that success. When all her "Christminster" cakes had been disposed of she took upon her arm the empty basket, and the cloth which had covered the standing she had hired, and giving the other things to the boy left the street with him. They followed a lane to a distance of half a mile, till they met an old woman carrying a child in short clothes, and leading a toddler in the other hand.

Sue kissed the children, and said, "How is he now?"

"Still better!" returned Mrs. Edlin cheerfully. "Before you are ill your husband will be well enough—don't 'ee trouble."

They turned, and came to some old, dun-tiled cottages with gardens and fruit-trees. Into one of these they entered by lifting the latch without knocking, and were at once in the general living-room. Here they greeted Jude, who was sitting in an arm-chair, the increased delicacy of his normally delicate features, and the childishly expectant look in his eyes, being alone sufficient to show that he had been passing through a severe illness.

"What—you have sold them all?" he said, a gleam of interest lighting up his face.

"Yes. Arcades, gables, east windows and all." She told him the pecuniary results, and then hesitated. At last, when they were left alone, she informed him of the unexpected meeting with Arabella, and the latter's widowhood.

Jude was discomposed. "What—is she living here?" he said.

"No; at Alfredston," said Sue.

Jude's countenance remained clouded. "I thought I had better tell you?" she continued, kissing him anxiously.

"Yes. . . . Dear me! Arabella not in the depths of London, but down here! It is only a little over a dozen miles across the country to Alfredston. What is she doing there?"

She told him all she knew. "She has taken to chapel-going," Sue added; "and talks accordingly."

"Well," said Jude, "perhaps it is for the best that we have almost decided to move on. I feel much better to-day, and shall be well enough to leave in a week or two. Then Mrs. Edlin can go home again—dear faithful old soul—the only friend we have in the world!"

"Where do you think to go to?" Sue asked, a tearfulness in her tones.

Then Jude confessed what was in his mind. He said it would surprise her, perhaps, after his having resolutely avoided all the old places for so long. But one thing and another had made him think a great deal of Christminster lately, and, if she didn't mind, he would like to go back there. Why should they care if they were known? It was over-sensitive of them to mind so much. They could go on selling cakes there, for that matter, if he couldn't work. He had no sense of shame at mere poverty; and perhaps he would be as strong as ever soon, and able to set up stone-cutting for himself there.

"Why should you care so much for Christminster?" she said pensively. "Christminster cares nothing for you, poor dear!"

"Well, I do, I can't help it. I love the place—although I know how it hates all men like me—the so-called Self-taught—how it scorns our laboured acquisitions, when it should be the first to respect them; how it sneers at our false quantities and mispronunciations, when it should say, I see you want help, my poor friend! . . . Nevertheless, it is the centre of the universe to me, because of my early dream: and nothing can alter it. Perhaps it will soon wake up, and be generous. I pray so! . . . I should like to go back to live there—perhaps to die there! In two or three weeks I might, I think. It will then be June, and I should like to be there by a particular day."

His hope that he was recovering proved so far well grounded that in three weeks they had arrived in the city of many memories; were actually treading its pavements, receiving the reflection of the sunshine from its wasting walls.

PART SIXTH

AT CHRISTMINSTER AGAIN

"... *And she humbled her body greatly, and all the places*
of her joy she filled with her torn hair."

—ESTHER (APOC.)

"*There are two who decline, a woman and I,*
And enjoy our death in the darkness here."

—R. BROWNING

I

O N THEIR ARRIVAL THE STATION WAS LIVELY WITH STRAW-HATTED YOUNG MEN, welcoming young girls who bore a remarkable family likeness to their welcomers, and who were dressed up in the brightest and lightest of raiment.

"The place seems gay," said Sue. "Why—it is Remembrance Day!—Jude—how sly of you—you came to-day on purpose!"

"Yes," said Jude quietly, as he took charge of the small child, and told Arabella's boy to keep close to them, Sue attending to their own eldest. "I thought we might as well come to-day as on any other."

"But I am afraid it will depress you!" she said looking anxiously at him, up and down.

"O, I mustn't let it interfere with our business; and we have a good deal to do before we shall be settled here. The first thing is lodgings."

Having left their luggage and his tools at the station they proceeded on foot up the familiar street, the holiday people all drifting in the same direction. Reaching the Fourways they were about to turn off to where accommodation was likely to be found when, looking at the clock and the hurrying crowd, Jude said: "Let us go and see the procession, and never mind the lodgings just now? We can get them afterwards."

"Oughtn't we to get a house over our heads first?" she asked.

But his soul seemed full of the anniversary, and together they went down Chief Street, their smallest child in Jude's arms, Sue leading her little girl, and Arabella's boy walking thoughtfully and silently beside them. Crowds of pretty sisters in airy costumes, and meekly ignorant parents, who had known no College in their youth, were under convoy in the same direction by brothers and sons bearing the opinion written large on them, that no properly qualified human beings had lived on earth till they came to grace it here and now.

"My failure is reflected on me by every one of those young fellows," said Jude. "A lesson on presumption is awaiting me to-day!—Humiliation Day for me! . . . If you, my dear darling, hadn't come to my rescue, I should have gone to the dogs with despair!"

She saw from his face that he was getting into one of his tempestuous, self-harrowing moods. "It would have been better if we had gone at once about our own affairs, dear," she answered. "I am sure this sight will awaken old sorrows in you, and do no good!"

"Well—we are near; we will see it now," said he.

They turned in on the left by the church with the Italian porch, whose helical columns were heavily draped with creepers, and pursued the lane till there arose on Jude's sight the circular theatre with that well-known lantern above it, which stood in his mind as the sad symbol of his abandoned hopes, for it was from that outlook that he had finally surveyed the City of Colleges on the afternoon of his great meditation, which convinced him at last of the futility of his attempt to be a son of the University.

To-day, in the open space stretching between this building and the nearest college, stood a crowd of expectant people. A passage was kept clear through their midst by two barriers of timber, extending from the door of the college to the door of the large building between it and the theatre.

"Here is the place—they are just going to pass!" cried Jude in sudden excitement. And pushing his way to the front he took up a position close to the barrier, still hugging the youngest child in his arms, while Sue and the others kept immediately behind him. The crowd filled in at their back, and fell to talking, joking, and laughing as carriage after carriage drew up at the lower door of the college, and solemn stately figures in blood-red robes began to alight. The sky had grown overcast and livid, and thunder rumbled now and then.

Father Time shuddered. "It do seem like the Judgment Day!" he whispered.

"They are only learned Doctors," said Sue.

While they waited big drops of rain fell on their heads and shoulders, and the delay grew tedious. Sue again wished not to stay.

"They won't be long now," said Jude, without turning his head.

But the procession did not come forth, and somebody in the crowd, to pass the time, looked at the *façade* of the nearest college, and said he wondered what was meant by the Latin inscription in its midst. Jude, who stood near the enquirer, explained it, and finding that the people all round him were listening with interest, went on to describe the carving of the frieze (which he had studied years before), and to criticise some details of masonry in other college fronts about the city.

The idle crowd, including the two policemen at the doors, stared like the Lycaonians at Paul, for Jude was apt to get too enthusiastic over any subject in hand, and they seemed to wonder how the stranger should know more about the buildings of their town than they themselves did; till one of them said: "Why, I know that man; he used to work here years ago—Jude Fawley, that's his name! Don't you mind he used to be nick-named Tutor of St. Slums, d'ye mind?—because he aimed at that line o' business? He's married, I suppose, then, and that's his child he's carrying. Taylor would know him, as he knows everybody."

The speaker was a man named Jack Stagg, with whom Jude had formerly worked in repairing the college masonries; Tinker Taylor was seen to be standing near. Having his attention called the latter cried across the barriers to Jude: "You've honoured us by coming back again, my friend!"

Jude nodded.

"An' you don't seem to have done any great things for yourself by going away?"

Jude assented to this also.

"Except found more mouths to fill!" This came in a new voice, and Jude recognised its owner to be Uncle Joe, another mason whom he had known.

Jude replied good-humouredly that he could not dispute it; and from remark to remark something like a general conversation arose between him and the crowd of idlers, during which Tinker Taylor asked Jude if he remembered the Apostles' Creed in Latin still, and the night of the challenge in the public-house.

"But Fortune didn't lie that way?" threw in Joe. "Yer powers wasn't enough to carry 'ee through?"

"Don't answer them any more!" entreated Sue.

"I don't think I like Christminster!" murmured little Time mournfully, as he stood submerged and invisible in the crowd.

But finding himself the centre of curiosity, quizzing, and comment, Jude was not inclined to shrink from open declarations of what he had no great reason to be ashamed of; and in a little while was stimulated to say in a loud voice to the listening throng generally:

"It is a difficult question, my friends, for any young man—that question I had to grapple with, and which thousands are weighing at the present moment in these uprising times—whether to follow uncritically the track he finds himself in, without considering his aptness for it, or to consider what his aptness or bent may be, and reshape his course accordingly. I tried to do the latter, and I failed. But I don't admit that my failure proved my view to be a wrong one, or that my success would have made it a right one; though that's how we appraise such attempts now-a-days—I mean, not by their essential soundness, but by their accidental outcomes. If I had ended by becoming like one of these gentlemen in red and black that we saw dropping in here by now, everybody would have said: 'See how wise that young man was, to follow the bent of his nature!' But having ended no better than I began they say: 'See what a fool that fellow was in following a freak of his fancy!'

"However it was my poverty and not my will that consented to be beaten. It takes two or three generations to do what I tried to do in one; and my impulses—affections—vices perhaps they should be called—were too strong not to hamper a man without advantages; who should be as cold-blooded as a fish and as selfish as a pig to have a really good chance of being one of his country's worthies. You may ridicule me—I am quite willing that you should—I am a fit subject, no doubt. But I think if you knew what I have gone through these last few years you would rather pity me. And if they knew"—he nodded towards the college at which the Dons were severally arriving—"it is just possible they would do the same."

"He do look ill and worn-out, it is true!" said a woman.

Sue's face grew more emotional; but though she stood close to Jude she was screened.

"I may do some good before I am dead—be a sort of success as a frightful example of what not to do; and so illustrate a moral story," continued Jude, beginning to grow bitter, though he had opened serenely enough. "I was, perhaps, after all, a paltry victim to the spirit of mental and social restlessness, that makes so many unhappy in these days!"

"Don't tell them that!" whispered Sue with tears, at perceiving Jude's state of mind. "You weren't that. You struggled nobly to acquire knowledge, and only the meanest souls in the world would blame you!"

Jude shifted the child into a more easy position on his arm, and concluded: "And what I appear, a sick and poor man, is not the worst of me. I am in a chaos of principles—groping in the dark—acting by instinct and not after example. Eight or nine years ago when I came here first, I had a neat stock of fixed opinions, but they dropped away one by one; and the further I get the less sure I am. I doubt if I have anything more for my present rule of life than following inclinations which do me and nobody else any harm, and actually give pleasure to those I love best. There, gentlemen, since you wanted to know how I was getting on, I have told you. Much good may it do you! I cannot explain further here. I perceive there is something wrong somewhere in our social formulas: what it is can only be discovered by men or women with greater insight than mine—if, indeed, they ever discover it—at least in our time. 'For who knoweth what is good for man in this life?—and who can tell a man what shall be after him under the sun?' "

"Hear, hear," said the populace.

"Well preached!" said Tinker Taylor. And privately to his neighbours: "Why, one of them jobbing pa'sons swarming about here, that takes the services when our head Reverends want a holiday, wouldn't ha' discoursed such doctrine for less than a guinea down? Hey? I'll take my oath not one o' 'em would! And then he must have had it wrote down for 'n. And this only a working-man!"

As a sort of objective commentary on Jude's remarks there drove up at this moment with a belated Doctor, robed and panting, a cab whose horse failed to stop at the exact point required for setting down the hirer, who jumped out and entered the door. The driver, alighting, began to kick the animal in the belly.

"If that can be done," said Jude, "at college gates in the most religious and educational city in the world, what shall we say as to how far we've got?"

"Order!" said one of the policemen, who had been engaged with a comrade in opening the large doors opposite the college. "Keep yer tongue quiet, my man, while the procession passes." The rain came on more heavily, and all who had umbrellas opened them. Jude was not one of these, and Sue only possessed a small one, half sunshade. She had grown pale, though Jude did not notice it then.

"Let us go on, dear," she whispered, endeavouring to shelter him. "We haven't any lodgings yet, remember, and all our things are at the station; and you are by no means well yet. I am afraid this wet will hurt you!"

"They are coming now. Just a moment, and I'll go!" said he.

A peal of six bells struck out, human faces began to crowd the windows around, and the procession of Heads of Houses and new Doctors emerged, their red and black gowned forms passing across the field of Jude's vision like inaccessible planets across an object glass.

As they went their names were called by knowing informants; and when they reached the old round theatre of Wren a cheer rose high.

"Let's go that way!" cried Jude, and though it now rained steadily he seemed not to know it, and took them round to the Theatre. Here they stood upon the straw that was laid to drown the discordant noise of wheels, where the quaint and frost-eaten stone busts encircling the building looked with pallid grimness on the proceedings, and in particular at the bedraggled Jude, Sue, and their children, as at ludicrous persons who had no business there.

"I wish I could get in!" he said to her fervidly. "Listen—I may catch a few words of the Latin speech by staying here; the windows are open."

However, beyond the peals of the organ, and the shouts and hurrahs between each piece of oratory, Jude's standing in the wet did not bring much Latin to his intelligence more than, now and then, a sonorous word in *um* or *ibus*.

"Well—I'm an outsider to the end of my days!" he sighed after a while. "Now I'll go, my patient Sue. How good of you to wait in the rain all this time—to gratify my infatuation! I'll never care any more about the infernal cursed place, upon my soul I won't! But what made you tremble so when we were at the barrier? And how pale you are, Sue!"

"I saw Richard amongst the people on the other side."

"Ah—did you!"

"He is evidently come up to Jerusalem to see the festival like the rest of us: and on that account is probably living not so very far away. He had the same hankering for the University that you had, in a milder form. I don't think he saw me, though he must have heard you speaking to the crowd. But he seemed not to notice."

"Well—suppose he did. Your mind is free from worries about him now, my Sue?"

"Yes, I suppose so. But I am weak. Although I know it is all right with our plans, I felt a curious dread of him; an awe, or terror, of conventions I don't believe in. It comes over me at times like a sort of creeping paralysis, and makes me so sad!"

"You are getting tired, Sue. O—I forgot, darling! Yes, we'll go on at once."

They started in quest of the lodging, and at last found something that seemed to promise well, in Mildew Lane—a spot which to Jude was irresistible—though to Sue it was not so fascinating—a narrow lane close to the back of a college, but having no communication with it. The little houses were darkened to gloom by the high collegiate buildings, within which life was so far removed from that of the people in the lane as if it had been on opposite sides of the globe; yet only a thickness of wall divided them. Two or three of the houses had notices of rooms to let, and the new-comers knocked at the door of one, which a woman opened.

"Ah—listen!" said Jude suddenly, instead of addressing her.

"What?"

"Why the bells—what church can that be? The tones are familiar."

Another peal of bells had begun to sound out at some distance off.

"I don't know!" said the landlady tartly. "Did you knock to ask that?"

"No; for lodgings," said Jude, coming to himself.

The householder scrutinised Sue a moment. "We haven't any to let," said she, shutting the door.

Jude looked discomfited, and the boy distressed. "Now, Jude," said Sue, "let me try. You don't know the way."

They found a second place hard by; but here the occupier, observing not only Sue, but the boy and the small children, said civilly, "I am sorry to say we don't let where there are children"; and also closed the door.

The small child squared its mouth and cried silently, with an instinct that trouble loomed. The boy sighed. "I don't like Christminster!" he said. "Are the great old houses gaols?"

"No; colleges," said Jude; "which perhaps you'll study in some day."

"I'd rather not!" the boy rejoined.

"Now we'll try again," said Sue. "I'll pull my cloak more round me. . . . Leaving Kennetbridge for this place is like coming from Caiaphas to Pilate! . . . How do I look now, dear?"

"Nobody would notice it now," said Jude.

There was one other house, and they tried a third time. The woman here was more amiable; but she had little room to spare, and could only agree to take in Sue and the children if her husband could go elsewhere. This arrangement they perforce adopted, in the stress from delaying their search till so late. They came to terms with her, though her price was rather high for their pockets. But they could not afford to be critical till Jude had time to get a more permanent abode; and in this house Sue took possession of a back room on the second floor with an inner closet-room for the children. Jude stayed and had a cup of tea; and was pleased to find that the window commanded the back of one of the colleges. Kissing all four he went to get a few necessaries and look for lodgings for himself.

When he was gone the landlady came up to talk a little with Sue, and gather something of the circumstances of the family she had taken in. Sue had not the art of prevarication, and, after admitting several facts as to their late difficulties and wanderings, she was startled by the landlady saying suddenly:

"Are you really a married woman?"

Sue hesitated; and then impulsively told the woman that her husband and herself had each been unhappy in their first marriages, after which, terrified at the thought of a second irrevocable union, and lest the conditions of the contract should kill their love, yet wishing to be together, they had literally not found the courage to repeat it, though they had attempted it two or three times. Therefore, though in her own sense of the words she was a married woman, in the landlady's sense she was not.

The housewife looked embarrassed, and went downstairs. Sue sat by the window in a reverie, watching the rain. Her quiet was broken by the noise of someone entering the house, and then the voices of a man and woman in conversation in the passage below. The landlady's husband had arrived, and she was explaining to him the incoming of the lodgers during his absence.

His voice rose in sudden anger. "Now who wants such a woman here? and perhaps a confinement! . . . Besides, didn't I say I wouldn't have children? The hall and stairs fresh painted, to be kicked about by them! You must have known all was not straight with 'em— coming like that. Taking in a family when I said a single man."

The wife expostulated, but, as it seemed, the husband insisted on his point; for presently a tap came to Sue's door, and the woman appeared.

"I am sorry to tell you, ma'am," she said, "that I can't let you have the room for the week after all. My husband objects; and therefore I must ask you to go. I don't mind your staying over to-night, as it is getting late in the afternoon; but I shall be glad if you can leave early in the morning."

Though she knew that she was entitled to the lodging for a week, Sue did not wish to create a disturbance between the wife and husband, and she said she would leave as requested. When the landlady had gone Sue looked out of the window again. Finding that the rain had ceased she proposed to the boy that, after putting the little ones to bed, they should go out and search about for another place, and bespeak it for the morrow, so as not to be so hard driven then as they had been that day.

Therefore, instead of unpacking her boxes, which had just been sent on from the station by Jude, they sallied out into the damp though not unpleasant, streets, Sue resolving not to disturb her husband with the news of her notice to quit while he was perhaps worried in obtaining a lodging for himself. In the company of the boy she wandered into this street and into that; but though she tried a dozen different houses she fared far worse alone than she had fared in Jude's company, and could get nobody to promise her a room for the following day. Every householder looked askance at such a woman and child inquiring for accommodation in the gloom.

"I ought not to be born, ought I?" said the boy with misgiving.

Thoroughly tired at last Sue returned to the place where she was not welcome, but where at least she had temporary shelter. In her absence Jude had left his address; but knowing how weak he still was she adhered to her determination not to disturb him till the next day.

II

S UE SAT LOOKING AT THE BARE FLOOR OF THE ROOM, THE HOUSE BEING LITTLE MORE than an old intramural cottage, and then she regarded the scene outside the uncurtained window. At some distance opposite, the outer walls of Sarcophagus College—silent, black, and windowless—threw their four centuries of gloom, bigotry, and decay into the little room she occupied, shutting out the moonlight by night and the sun by day. The outlines of Rubric College also were discernible beyond the other, and the tower of a third further off still. She thought of the strange operation of a simple-minded man's ruling passion, that it should have led Jude, who loved her and the children so tenderly, to place them here in this depressing purlieu, because he was still haunted by his dream. Even now he did not distinctly hear the freezing negative that those scholared walls had echoed to his desire.

The failure to find another lodging, and the lack of room in this house for his father, had made a deep impression on the boy;—a brooding undemonstrative horror seemed to have seized him. The silence was broken by his saying: "Mother, *what* shall we do to-morrow!"

"I don't know!" said Sue despondently. "I am afraid this will trouble your father."

"I wish father was quite well, and there had been room for him! Then it wouldn't matter so much! Poor father!"

"It wouldn't!"

"Can I do anything?"

"No! All is trouble, adversity and suffering!"

"Father went away to give us children room, didn't he?"

"Partly."

"It would be better to be out o' the world than in it, wouldn't it?"

"It would almost, dear."

" 'Tis because of us children, too, isn't it, that you can't get a good lodging?"

"Well—people do object to children sometimes."

"Then if children make so much trouble, why do people have 'em?"

"O—because it is a law of nature."

"But we don't ask to be born?"

"No indeed."

"And what makes it worse with me is that you are not my real mother, and you needn't have had me unless you liked. I oughtn't to have come to 'ee—that's the real truth! I troubled 'em in Australia, and I trouble folk here. I wish I hadn't been born!"

"You couldn't help it, my dear."

"I think that whenever children be born that are not wanted they should be killed directly, before their souls come to 'em, and not allowed to grow big and walk about!"

Sue did not reply. She was doubtfully pondering how to treat this too reflective child.

She at last concluded that, so far as circumstances permitted, she would be honest and candid with one who entered into her difficulties like an aged friend.

"There is going to be another in our family soon," she hesitatingly remarked.

"How?"

"There is going to be another baby."

"What!" The boy jumped up wildly. "O God, mother, you've never a-sent for another; and such trouble with what you've got!"

"Yes, I have, I am sorry to say!" murmured Sue, her eyes glistening with suspended tears.

The boy burst out weeping. "O you don't care, you don't care!" he cried in bitter reproach. "How *ever* could you, mother, be so wicked and cruel as this, when you needn't have done it till we was better off, and father well! To bring us all into *more* trouble! No room for us, and Father a-forced to go away, and we turned out to-morrow; and yet you be going to have another of us soon! . . . 'Tis done o' purpose!—'tis—'tis!" He walked up and down sobbing.

"Y-you must forgive me, little Jude!" she pleaded, her bosom heaving now as much as the boy's. "I can't explain—I will when you are older. It does seem—as if I had done it on purpose, now we are in these difficulties! I can't explain, dear! But it—is not quite on purpose—I can't help it!"

"Yes it is—it must be! For nobody would interfere with us, like that, unless you agreed! I won't forgive you, ever, ever! I'll never believe you care for me, or father, or any of us any more!"

He got up, and went away into the closet adjoining her room, in which a bed had been spread on the floor. There she heard him say: "If we children was gone there'd be no trouble at all!"

"Don't think that, dear," she cried, rather peremptorily. "But go to sleep!"

The following morning she awoke at a little past six, and decided to get up and run across before breakfast to the inn which Jude had informed her to be his quarters, to tell him what had happened before he went out. She arose softly, to avoid disturbing the children, who, as she knew, must be fatigued by their exertions of yesterday.

She found Jude at breakfast in the obscure tavern he had chosen as a counterpoise to the expense of her lodging: and she explained to him her homelessness. He had been so anxious about her all night, he said. Somehow, now it was morning, the request to leave the lodgings did not seem such a depressing incident as it had seemed the night before, nor did even her failure to find another place affect her so deeply as at first. Jude agreed with her that it would not be worthwhile to insist upon her right to stay a week, but to take immediate steps for removal.

"You must all come to this inn for a day or two," he said. "It is a rough place, and it will not be so nice for the children, but we shall have more time to look round. There are plenty of lodgings in the suburbs—in my old quarter of Beersheba. Have breakfast with me now you are here, my bird. You are sure you are well? There will be plenty of time to get back and prepare the children's meal before they wake. In fact, I'll go with you."

She joined Jude in a hasty meal, and in a quarter of an hour they started together, resolving to clear out from Sue's too respectable lodging immediately. On reaching the place and going upstairs she found that all was quiet in the children's room, and called to the landlady in timorous tones to please bring up the tea-kettle and something for their breakfast. This was perfunctorily done, and producing a couple of eggs which she had brought with her she put them into the boiling kettle, and summoned Jude to watch them for the youngsters, while she went to call them, it being now about half-past eight o'clock.

Jude stood bending over the kettle, with his watch in his hand, timing the eggs, so that his back was turned to the little inner chamber where the children lay. A shriek from Sue suddenly caused him to start round. He saw that the door of the room, or rather closet—which had seemed to go heavily upon its hinges as she pushed it back—was open, and that Sue had sunk to the floor just within it. Hastening forward to pick her up he turned his eyes to the little bed spread on the boards; no children were there. He looked in bewilderment round the room. At the back of the door were fixed two hooks for hanging garments, and from these the forms of the two youngest children were suspended, by a piece of box-cord round each of their necks, while from a nail a few yards off the body of little Jude was hanging in a similar manner. An overturned chair was near the elder boy, and his glazed eyes were staring into the room; but those of the girl and the baby boy were closed.

Half paralyzed by the strange and consummate horror of the scene, he let Sue lie, cut the cords with his pocket-knife and threw the three children on the bed; but the feel of their bodies in the momentary handling seemed to say that they were dead. He caught up Sue, who was in fainting fits, and put her on the bed in the other room, after which he breathlessly summoned the landlady and ran out for a doctor.

When he got back Sue had come to herself, and the two helpless women, bending over the children in wild efforts to restore them, and the triplet of little corpses, formed a scene which overthrew his self-command. The nearest surgeon came in, but, as Jude had inferred, his presence was superfluous. The children were past saving, for though their bodies were still barely cold it was conjectured that they had been hanging more than an hour. The probability held by the parents later on, when they were able to reason on the case, was that the elder boy, on waking, looked into the outer-room for Sue, and, finding her absent, was thrown into a fit of aggravated despondency that the events and information of the evening before had induced in his morbid temperament. Moreover a piece of paper was found upon the floor, on which was written, in the boy's hand, with the bit of lead pencil that he carried:

Done because we are too menny.

At sight of this Sue's nerves utterly gave way, an awful conviction that her discourse with the boy had been the main cause of the tragedy, throwing her into a convulsive agony which knew no abatement. They carried her away against her wish to a room on the lower floor; and there she lay, her slight figure shaken with her gasps, and her eyes staring at the ceiling, the woman of the house vainly trying to soothe her.

They could hear from this chamber the people moving about above, and she implored to be allowed to go back, and was only kept from doing so by the assurance that, if there were any hope, her presence might do harm, and the reminder that it was necessary to take care of herself lest she should endanger a coming life. Her inquiries were incessant, and at last Jude came down and told her there was no hope. As soon as she could speak she informed him what she had said to the boy, and how she thought herself the cause of this.

"No," said Jude. "It was in his nature to do it. The doctor says there are such boys springing up amongst us—boys of a sort unknown in the last generation—the outcome of new views of life. They seem to see all its terrors before they are old enough to have staying power to resist them. He says it is the beginning of the coming universal wish not to live. He's an advanced man, the doctor: but he can give no consolation to—"

Jude had kept back his own grief on account of her; but he now broke down; and this stimulated Sue to efforts of sympathy which in some degree distracted her from her poignant self-reproach. When everybody was gone, she was allowed to see the children.

The boy's face expressed the whole tale of their situation. On that little shape had converged all the inauspiciousness and shadow which had darkened the first union of Jude, and all the accidents, mistakes, fears, errors of the last. He was their nodal point, their focus, their expression in a single term. For the rashness of those parents he had groaned, for their ill assortment he had quaked, and for the misfortunes of these he had died.

When the house was silent, and they could do nothing but await the coroner's inquest, a subdued, large, low voice spread into the air of the room from behind the heavy walls at the back.

"What is it?" said Sue, her spasmodic breathing suspended.

"The organ of the College chapel. The organist practising I suppose. It's the anthem from the seventy-third Psalm; 'Truly God is loving unto Israel.' "

She sobbed again. "O my babies! They had done no harm! Why should they have been taken away, and not I!"

There was another stillness—broken at last by two persons in conversation somewhere without.

"They are talking about us, no doubt!" moaned Sue. " 'We are made a spectacle unto the world, and to angels, and to men!' "

Jude listened—"No—they are not talking of us," he said. "They are two clergymen of different views, arguing about the eastward position."

Then another silence, till she was seized with another uncontrollable fit of grief. "There is something external to us which says, 'You shan't!' First it said, 'You shan't learn!' Then it said, 'You shan't labour!' Now it says, 'You shan't love!' "

He tried to soothe her by saying, "That's bitter of you, darling."

"But it's true!"

Thus they waited, and she went back again to her room. The baby's frock, shoes, and socks, which had been lying on a chair at the time of his death, she would not now have removed, though Jude would fain have got them out of her sight. But whenever he touched them she implored him to let them lie, and burst out almost savagely at the woman of the house when she also attempted to put them away.

Jude dreaded her dull apathetic silences almost more than her paroxysms. "Why don't you speak to me, Jude?" she said, after one of these. "Don't turn away from me! I can't bear the loneliness of being out of your looks!"

"There, dear; here I am," he said, putting his face close to hers.

"Yes. . . . O my comrade, our perfect union—our two-in-oneness—is now stained with blood!"

"Shadowed by death—that's all."

"Ah; but it was I who incited him really, though I didn't know I was doing it! I talked to the child as one should only talk to people of mature age. I said the world was against us, that it was better to be out of life than in it at this price; and he took it literally. And I told him I was going to have another child. It upset him. O how bitterly he upbraided me!"

"Why did you do it, Sue?"

"I can't tell. It was that I wanted to be truthful. I couldn't bear deceiving him as to the

facts of life. And yet I wasn't truthful, for with a false delicacy I told him too obscurely.—
Why was I half wiser than my fellow-women? and not entirely wiser! Why didn't I tell
him pleasant untruths, instead of half realities? It was my want of self-control, so that I
could neither conceal things nor reveal them!"

"Your plan might have been a good one for the majority of cases; only in our peculiar
case it chanced to work badly perhaps. He must have known sooner or later."

"And I was just making my baby darling a new frock; and now I shall never see him
in it, and never talk to him any more! . . . My eyes are so swollen that I can scarcely see;
and yet little more than a year ago I called myself happy! We went about loving each other
too much—indulging ourselves to utter selfishness with each other! We said—do you
remember?—that we would make a virtue of joy. I said it was Nature's intention, Nature's
law and *raison d'être* that we should be joyful in what instincts she afforded us—instincts
which civilization had taken upon itself to thwart. What dreadful things I said! And now
Fate has given us this stab in the back for being such fools as to take Nature at her word!"

She sank into a quiet contemplation, till she said, "It is best, perhaps, that they should
be gone.—Yes—I see it is! Better that they should be plucked fresh than stay to wither
away miserably!"

"Yes," replied Jude. "Some say that the elders should rejoice when their children die
in infancy."

"But they don't know! . . . O my babies, my babies, could you be alive now! You may
say the boy wished to be out of life, or he wouldn't have done it. It was not unreasonable
for him to die: it was part of his incurably sad nature, poor little fellow! But then the others—
my *own* children and yours!"

Again Sue looked at the hanging little frock and at the socks and shoes; and her figure
quivered like a string. "I am a pitiable creature," she said, "good neither for earth nor
heaven any more! I am driven out of my mind by things! What ought to be done?" She
stared at Jude, and tightly held his hand.

"Nothing can be done," he replied. "Things are as they are, and will be brought to
their destined issue."

She paused. "Yes! Who said that?" she asked heavily.

"It comes in the chorus of the *Agamemnon*. It has been in my mind continually since
this happened."

"My poor Jude—how you've missed everything!—you more than I, for I did get you!
To think you should know that by your unassisted reading, and yet be in poverty and
despair!"

After such momentary diversions her grief would return in a wave.

The jury duly came and viewed the bodies, the inquest was held; and next arrived the
melancholy morning of the funeral. Accounts in the newspapers had brought to the spot
curious idlers, who stood apparently counting the window-panes and the stones of the
walls. Doubt of the real relations of the couple added zest to their curiosity. Sue had declared that she would follow the two little ones to the grave, but at the last moment she
gave way, and the coffins were quietly carried out of the house while she was lying down.
Jude got into the vehicle, and it drove away, much to the relief of the landlord, who now
had only Sue and her luggage remaining on his hands, which he hoped to be also clear of
later on in the day, and so to have freed his house from the exasperating notoriety it had

acquired during the week through his wife's unlucky admission of these strangers. In the afternoon he privately consulted with the owner of the house, and they agreed that if any objection to it arose from the tragedy which had occurred there they would try to get its number changed.

When Jude had seen the two little boxes—one containing little Jude, and the other the two smallest—deposited in the earth he hastened back to Sue, who was still in her room, and he therefore did not disturb her just then. Feeling anxious, however, he went again about four o'clock. The woman thought she was still lying down, but returned to him to say that she was not in her bedroom after all. Her hat and jacket, too, were missing: she had gone out. Jude hurried off to the public-house where he was sleeping. She had not been there. Then bethinking himself of possibilities he went along the road to the cemetery, which he entered, and crossed to where the interments had recently taken place. The idlers who had followed to the spot by reason of the tragedy were all gone now. A man with a shovel in his hands was attempting to earth in the common grave of the three children, but his arm was held back by an expostulating woman who stood in the half-filled hole. It was Sue, whose coloured clothing, which she had never thought of changing for the mourning he had bought, suggested to the eye a deeper grief than the conventional garb of bereavement could express.

"He's filling them in, and he shan't till I've seen my little ones again!" she cried wildly when she saw Jude. "I want to see them once more. O Jude—please Jude—I want to see them! I didn't know you would let them be taken away while I was asleep! You said perhaps I should see them once more before they were screwed down; and then you didn't, but took them away! O Jude, you are cruel to me too!"

"She's been wanting me to dig out the grave again, and let her get to the coffins," said the man with the spade. "She ought to be took home, by the look o' her. She is hardly responsible, poor thing, seemingly. Can't dig 'em up again now, ma'am. Do ye go home with your husband, and take it quiet, and thank God that there'll be another soon to swage yer grief."

But Sue kept asking: "Can't I see them once more—just once! Can't I? Only just one little minute, Jude? It would not take long! And I should be so glad, Jude! I will be so good, and not disobey you ever any more, Jude, if you will let me? I would go home quietly afterwards, and not want to see them any more! Can't I? Why can't I?"

Thus she went on. Jude was thrown into such acute sorrow that he almost felt he would try to get the man to accede. But it could do no good, and might make her still worse; and he saw that it was imperative to get her home at once. So he coaxed her, and whispered tenderly, and put his arm round her to support her; till she helplessly gave in, and was induced to leave the cemetery.

He wished to obtain a fly to take her back in, but economy being so imperative she deprecated his doing so, and they walked along slowly, Jude in black crape, she in brown and red clothing. They were to have gone to a new lodging that afternoon, but Jude saw that it was not practicable, and in course of time they entered the now hated house. Sue was at once got to bed, and the doctor sent for.

Jude waited all the evening downstairs. At a very late hour the intelligence was brought to him that a child had been prematurely born, and that it, like the others, was a corpse.

III

S UE WAS CONVALESCENT, THOUGH SHE HAD HOPED FOR DEATH, AND JUDE HAD AGAIN obtained work at his old trade. They were in other lodgings now, in the direction of Beersheba, and not far from the ceremonial Church of Saint Silas.

They would sit silent, more bodeful of the direct antagonism of things than of their insensate and stolid obstructiveness. Vague and quaint imaginings had haunted Sue, in the days when her intellect scintillated like a star, that the world resembled a stanza or melody composed in a dream; it was wonderfully excellent to the half-aroused intelligence, but hopelessly absurd at the full waking; that the First Cause worked automatically like a somnambulist, and not reflectively like a sage; that at the framing of the terrestrial conditions there seemed never to have been contemplated such a development of emotional perceptiveness among the creatures subject to those conditions as that reached by thinking and educated humanity. But affliction makes opposing forces loom anthropomorphous; and those ideas were now exchanged for a sense of Jude and herself fleeing from a persecutor.

"We must conform!" she said mournfully. "All the ancient wrath of the Power above us has been vented upon us. His poor creatures, and we must submit. There is no choice. We must. It is no use fighting against God!"

"It is only against man and senseless circumstance," said Jude.

"True!" she murmured. "What have I been thinking of! I am getting as superstitious as a savage! . . . But whoever or whatever our foe may be, I am cowed into submission. I have no more fighting strength left; no more enterprise. I am beaten, beaten! . . . 'We are made a spectacle unto the world, and to angels, and to men!' I am always saying that now."

"I feel the same!"

"What shall we do? You are in work now; but remember, it may only be because our history and relations are not absolutely known. . . . Possibly, if they knew our marriage had not been formalised they would turn you out of your job as they did at Aldbrickham!"

"I hardly know. Perhaps they would hardly do that. However, I think that we ought to make it legal now—as soon as you are able to go out."

"You think we ought?"

"Certainly."

And Jude fell into thought. "I have seemed to myself lately," he said, "to belong to that vast band of men shunned by the virtuous—the men called seducers. It amazes me when I think of it! I have not been conscious of it, or of any wrong-doing towards you, whom I love more than myself. Yet I *am* one of those men! I wonder if any other of them are the same purblind, simple creatures as I? . . . Yes, Sue—that's what I am. I seduced you. . . . You were a distinct type—a refined creature, intended by Nature to be left intact. But I couldn't leave you alone!"

"No, no, Jude!" she said quickly. "Don't reproach yourself with being what you are not. If anybody is to blame it is I."

"I supported you in your resolve to leave Phillotson; and without me perhaps you wouldn't have urged him to let you go."

"I should have, just the same. As to ourselves, the fact of our not having entered into a legal contract is the saving feature in our union. We have thereby avoided insulting, as it were, the solemnity of our first marriages."

"Solemnity?" Jude looked at her with some surprise, and grew conscious that she was not the Sue of their earlier time.

"Yes," she said, with a little quiver in her words, "I have had dreadful fears, a dreadful sense of my own insolence of action. I have thought—that I am still his wife!"

"Whose?"

"Richard's."

"Good God, dearest!—why?"

"O I can't explain! Only the thought comes to me."

"It is your weakness—a sick fancy, without reason or meaning! Don't let it trouble you."

Sue sighed uneasily.

As a set-off against such discussions as these there had come an improvement in their pecuniary position, which earlier in their experience would have made them cheerful. Jude had quite unexpectedly found good employment at his old trade almost directly he arrived, the summer weather suiting his fragile constitution; and outwardly his days went on with that monotonous uniformity which is in itself so grateful after vicissitude. People seemed to have forgotten that he had ever shown any awkward aberrancies: and he daily mounted to the parapets and copings of colleges he could never enter, and renewed the crumbling freestones of mullioned windows he would never look from, as if he had known no wish to do otherwise.

There was this change in him; that he did not often go to any service at the churches now. One thing troubled him more than any other; that Sue and himself had mentally travelled in opposite directions since the tragedy: events which had enlarged his own views of life, laws, customs, and dogmas, had not operated in the same manner on Sue's. She was no longer the same as in the independent days, when her intellect played like lambent lightning over conventions and formalities which he at that time respected, though he did not now.

On a particular Sunday evening he came in rather late. She was not at home, but she soon returned, when he found her silent and meditative.

"What are you thinking of, little woman?" he asked curiously.

"O I can't tell clearly! I have thought that we have been selfish, careless, even impious, in our courses, you and I. Our life has been a vain attempt at self-delight. But self-abnegation is the higher road. We should mortify the flesh—the terrible flesh—the curse of Adam!"

"Sue!" he murmured. "What has come over you?"

"We ought to be continually sacrificing ourselves on the altar of duty! But I have always striven to do what has pleased me. I well deserved the scourging I have got! I wish something would take the evil right out of me, and all my monstrous errors, and all my sinful ways!"

"Sue—my own too suffering dear!—there's no evil woman in you. Your natural instincts are perfectly healthy; not quite so impassioned, perhaps, as I could wish; but good, and dear, and pure. And as I have often said, you are absolutely the most ethereal, least sensual woman I ever knew to exist without inhuman sexlessness. Why do you talk in such a changed way? We have not been selfish, except when no one could profit by our being otherwise. You used to say that human nature was noble and long-suffering, not vile and corrupt, and at last I thought you spoke truly. And now you seem to take such a much lower view!"

"I want a humble heart; and a chastened mind; and I have never had them yet!"

"You have been fearless, both as a thinker and as a feeler, and you deserved more admiration than I gave. I was too full of narrow dogmas at that time to see it."

"Don't say that, Jude! I wish my every fearless word and thought could be rooted out of my history. Self-renunciation—that's everything! I cannot humiliate myself too much. I should like to prick myself all over with pins and bleed out the badness that's in me!"

"Hush!" he said, pressing her little face against his breast as if she were an infant. "It is bereavement that has brought you to this! Such remorse is not for you, my sensitive plant, but for the wicked ones of the earth—who never feel it!"

"I ought not to stay like this," she murmured, when she had remained in the position a long while.

"Why not?"

"It is indulgence."

"Still on the same tack! But is there anything better on earth than that we should love one another?"

"Yes. It depends on the sort of love; and yours—ours—is the wrong."

"I won't have it, Sue! Come, when do you wish our marriage to be signed in a vestry?"

She paused, and looked up uneasily. "Never," she whispered.

Not knowing the whole of her meaning he took the objection serenely, and said nothing. Several minutes elapsed, and he thought she had fallen asleep; but he spoke softly, and found that she was wide awake all the time. She sat upright and sighed.

"There is a strange, indescribable perfume or atmosphere about you to-night, Sue," he said. "I mean not only mentally, but about your clothes, also. A sort of vegetable scent, which I seem to know, yet cannot remember."

"It is incense."

"Incense?"

"I have been to the service at St. Silas', and I was in the fumes of it."

"Oh—St. Silas'."

"Yes. I go there sometimes."

"Indeed. You go there!"

"You see, Jude, it is lonely here in the week-day mornings, when you are at work, and I think and think of—of my—" She stopped till she could control the lumpiness of her throat. "And I have taken to go in there, as it is so near."

"O well—of course, I say nothing against it. Only it is odd, for you. They little think what sort of chiel is amang them!"

"What do you mean, Jude?"

"Well—a sceptic, to be plain."

"How can you pain me so, dear Jude, in my trouble! Yet I know you didn't mean it. But you ought not to say that."

"I won't. But I am much surprised!"

"Well—I want to tell you something else, Jude. You won't be angry, will you? I have thought of it a good deal since my babies died. I don't think I ought to be your wife—or as your wife—any longer."

"What? . . . But you *are!*"

"From your point of view; but—"

"Of course we were afraid of the ceremony, and a good many others would have been in our places, with such strong reasons for fears. But experience has proved how we mis-judged ourselves, and overrated our infirmities; and if you are beginning to respect rites and ceremonies, as you seem to be, I wonder you don't say it shall be carried out instantly? You certainly *are* my wife, Sue, in all but law. What do you mean by what you said?"

"I don't think I am!"

"Not? But suppose we *had* gone through the ceremony? Would you feel that you were then?"

"No. I should not feel even then that I was. I should feel worse than I do now."

"Why so—in the name of all that's perverse, my dear?"

"Because I am Richard's."

"Ah—you hinted that absurd fancy to me before!"

"It was only an impression with me then; I feel more and more convinced as time goes on that—I belong to him, or to nobody."

"My good heavens—how we are changing places!"

"Yes. Perhaps so."

Some few days later, in the dusk of the summer evening, they were sitting in the same small room downstairs, when a knock came to the front-door of the carpenter's house where they were lodging, and in a few moments there was a tap at the door of their room. Before they could open it the comer did so, and a woman's form appeared.

"Is Mr. Fawley here?"

Jude and Sue started as he mechanically replied in the affirmative, for the voice was Arabella's.

He formally requested her to come in, and she sat down in the window-bench, where they could distinctly see her outline against the light; but no characteristic that enabled them to estimate her general aspect and air. Yet something seemed to denote that she was not quite so comfortably circumstanced, nor so bouncingly attired, as she had been during Cartlett's lifetime.

The three attempted an awkward conversation about the tragedy, of which Jude had felt it to be his duty to inform her immediately, though she had never replied to his letter.

"I have just come from the cemetery," she said. "I enquired and found the child's grave. I couldn't come to the funeral—thank you for inviting me all the same. I read all about it in the papers, and I felt I wasn't wanted. . . . No—I couldn't come to the funeral," repeated Arabella, who, seeming utterly unable to reach the ideal of a catastrophic man-ner, fumbled with reiterations. "But I am glad I found the grave. As 'tis your trade, Jude, you'll be able to put up a handsome stone to 'em."

"I shall put up a head-stone," said Jude drearily.

"He was my child, and naturally I feel for him."

"I hope so. We all did."

"The others that weren't mine I didn't feel so much for, as was natural."

"Of course."

A sigh came from the dark corner where Sue sat.

"I had often wished I had mine with me," continued Mrs. Cartlett. "Perhaps 'twouldn't have happened then! But of course I didn't wish to take him away from your wife."

"I am not his wife," came from Sue.

The unexpectedness of her words struck Jude silent.

"O I beg your pardon, I'm sure," said Arabella. "I thought you were!"

Jude had known from the quality of Sue's tone that her new and transcendental views lurked in her words; but all except their obvious meaning was, naturally, missed by Arabella. The latter, after evincing that she was struck by Sue's avowal, recovered herself, and went on to talk with placid bluntness about "her" boy, for whom, though in his lifetime she had shown no care at all, she now exhibited a ceremonial mournfulness that was apparently sustaining to the conscience. She alluded to the past, and in making some remark appealed again to Sue. There was no answer: Sue had invisibly left the room.

"She said she was not your wife?" resumed Arabella in another voice. "Why should she do that?"

"I cannot inform you," said Jude shortly.

"She is, isn't she? She once told me so."

"I don't criticise what she says."

"Ah—I see! Well, my time is up. I am staying here to-night, and thought I could do no less than call, after our mutual affliction. I am sleeping at the place where I used to be barmaid, and to-morrow I go back to Alfredston. Father is come home again, and I am living with him."

"He has returned from Australia?" said Jude with languid curiosity.

"Yes. Couldn't get on there. Had a rough time of it. Mother died of dys—what do you call it—in the hot weather, and father and two of the young ones have just got back. He has got a cottage near the old place, and for the present I am keeping house for him."

Jude's former wife had maintained a stereotyped manner of strict good breeding even now that Sue was gone, and limited her stay to a number of minutes that should accord with the highest respectability. When she had departed Jude, much relieved, went to the stairs and called Sue—feeling anxious as to what had become of her.

There was no answer, and the carpenter who kept the lodgings said she had not come in. Jude was puzzled, and became quite alarmed at her absence, for the hour was growing late. The carpenter called his wife, who conjectured that Sue might have gone to St. Silas' church, as she often went there.

"Surely not at this time o' night?" said Jude. "It is shut."

"She knows somebody who keeps the key, and she has it whenever she wants it."

"How long has she been going on with this?"

"Oh, some few weeks, I think."

Jude went vaguely in the direction of the church, which he had never once approached since he lived out that way years before, when his young opinions were more mystical than they were now. The spot was deserted, but the door was certainly unfastened; he lifted the latch without noise, and pushing the door to behind him, stood absolutely still inside. The prevalent silence seemed to contain a faint sound, explicable as a breathing, or a sobbing, which came from the other end of the building. The floor-cloth deadened his footsteps as he moved in that direction through the obscurity, which was broken only by the faintest reflected night-light from without.

High overhead, above the chancel steps, Jude could discern a huge, solidly constructed Latin cross—as large, probably, as the original it was designed to commemorate. It seemed to be suspended in the air by invisible wires; it was set with large jewels, which faintly glimmered in some weak ray caught from outside, as the cross swayed to and fro in a silent and scarcely perceptible motion. Underneath, upon the floor, lay what appeared to be a heap of black clothes, and from this was repeated the sobbing that he had heard before. It was his Sue's form, prostrate on the paving.

"Sue!" he whispered.

Something white disclosed itself; she had turned up her face.

"What—do you want with me here, Jude?" she said. "You shouldn't come! I wanted to be alone! Why did you intrude here?"

"How can you ask!" he retorted in quick reproach, for his full heart was wounded to its centre at this attitude of hers towards him. "Why do I come? Who has a right to come, I should like to know, if I have not! I, who love you better than my own self—better—O far better—than you have loved me! What made you leave me to come here alone?"

"Don't criticise me, Jude—I can't bear it!—I have often told you so. You must take me as I am. I am a wretch—broken by my distractions! I couldn't *bear* it when Arabella came—I felt so utterly miserable I had to come away. She seems to be your wife still, and Richard to be my husband!"

"But they are nothing to us!"

"Yes, dear friend, they are. I see marriage differently now. My babies have been taken from me to show me this! Arabella's child killing mine was a judgment—the right slaying the wrong. What, *what* shall I do! I am such a vile creature—too worthless to mix with ordinary human beings!"

"This is terrible!" said Jude, almost in tears. "It is monstrous and unnatural for you to be so remorseful when you have done no wrong!"

"Ah—you don't know my badness!"

He returned vehemently: "I do! Every atom and dreg of it! You make me hate Christianity, or mysticism, or Sacerdotalism, or whatever it may be called, if it's that which has caused this deterioration in you. That a woman-poet, a woman-seer, a woman whose soul shone like a diamond—whom all the wise of the world would have been proud of, if they could have known you—should degrade herself like this! I am glad I had nothing to do with Divinity—damn glad—if it's going to ruin you in this way!"

"You are angry, Jude, and unkind to me, and don't see how things are."

"Then come along home with me, dearest, and perhaps I shall. I am over-burdened—and you, too, are unhinged just now." He put his arm round her and lifted her; but though she came, she preferred to walk without his support.

"I don't dislike you, Jude," she said in a sweet and imploring voice. "I love you as much as ever! Only—I ought not to love you—any more. O I must not any more!"

"I can't own it."

"But I have made up my mind that I am not your wife! I belong to him—I sacramentally joined myself to him for life. Nothing can alter it!"

"But surely we are man and wife, if ever two people were in this world? Nature's own marriage it is, unquestionably!"

"But not Heaven's. Another was made for me there, and ratified eternally in the church at Melchester."

"Sue, Sue—affliction has brought you to this unreasonable state! After converting me to your views on so many things, to find you suddenly turn to the right-about like this— for no reason whatever, confounding all you have formerly said through sentiment merely! You root out of me what little affection and reverence I had left in me for the Church as an old acquaintance. . . . What I can't understand in you is your extraordinary blindness now to your old logic. Is it peculiar to you, or is it common to woman? Is a woman a think-ing unit at all, or a fraction always wanting its integer? How you argued that marriage was only a clumsy contract—which it is—how you showed all the objections to it—all the ab-surdities! If two and two made four when we were happy together, surely they make four now? I can't understand it, I repeat!"

"Ah, dear Jude; that's because you are like a totally deaf man observing people listen-ing to music. You say 'What are they regarding? Nothing is there.' But something is."

"That is a hard saying from you; and not a true parallel! You threw off old husks of prejudices, and taught me to do it; and now you go back upon yourself. I confess I am ut-terly stultified in my estimate of you."

"Dear friend, my only friend, don't be hard with me! I can't help being as I am, and I am convinced I am right—that I see the light at last. But O, how to profit by it!"

They walked along a few more steps till they were outside the building, and she had returned the key. "Can this be the girl," said Jude when she came back, feeling a slight re-newal of elasticity now that he was in the open street; "can this be the girl who brought the Pagan deities into this most Christian city?—who mimicked Miss Fontover when she crushed them with her heel?—quoted Gibbon, and Shelley, and Mill? Where are dear Apollo, and dear Venus now!"

"O don't, don't be so cruel to me, Jude, and I so unhappy!" she sobbed. "I can't bear it! I was in error—I cannot reason with you. I was wrong—proud in my own conceit! Ara-bella's coming was the finish. Don't satirise me: it cuts like a knife!"

He flung his arms round her and kissed her passionately there in the silent street, be-fore she could hinder him. They went on till they came to a little coffee-house. "Jude," she said with suppressed tears, "would you mind getting a lodging here?"

"I will—if, if you really wish? But do you? Let me go to our door and understand you."

He went and conducted her in. She said she wanted no supper, and went in the dark upstairs and struck a light. Turning she found that Jude had followed her, and was stand-ing at the chamber-door. She went to him, put her hand in his, and said "Good-night."

"But Sue! Don't we live here?"

"You said you would do as I wished!"

"Yes. Very well! . . . Perhaps it was wrong of me to argue distastefully as I have done! Perhaps as we couldn't conscientiously marry at first in the old-fashioned way, we ought to have parted. Perhaps the world is not illuminated enough for such experiments as ours! Who were we, to think we could act as pioneers!"

"I am so glad you see that much, at any rate. I never deliberately meant to do as I did. I slipped into my false position through jealousy and agitation!"

"But surely through love—you loved me?"

"Yes. But I wanted to let it stop there, and go on always as mere lovers; until—"

"But people in love couldn't live forever like that!"

"Women could: men can't, because they—won't. An average woman is in this superior to an average man—that she never instigates, only responds. We ought to have lived in mental communion, and no more."

"I was the unhappy cause of the change, as I have said before! . . . Well, as you will! . . . But human nature can't help being itself."

"Oh yes—that's just what it has to learn—self-mastery."

"I repeat—if either were to blame it was not you but I."

"No—it was I. Your wickedness was only the natural man's desire to possess the woman. Mine was not the reciprocal wish till envy stimulated me to oust Arabella. I had thought I ought in charity to let you approach me—that it was damnably selfish to torture you as I did my other friend. But I shouldn't have given way if you hadn't broken me down by making me fear you would go back to her. . . . But don't let us say any more about it! Jude, will you leave me to myself now?"

"Yes. . . . But Sue—my wife, as you are!" he burst out; "my old reproach to you was, after all, a true one. You have never loved me as I love you—never—never! Yours is not a passionate heart—your heart does not burn in a flame! You are, upon the whole, cold— a sort of fay, or sprite—not a woman!"

"At first I did not love you, Jude; that I own. When I first knew you I merely wanted you to love me. I did not exactly flirt with you; but that inborn craving which undermines some women's morals almost more than unbridled passion—the craving to attract and captivate, regardless of the injury it may do the man—was in me; and when I found I had caught you, I was frightened. And then—I don't know how it was—I couldn't bear to let you go—possibly to Arabella again—and so I got to love you, Jude. But you see, however it ended, it began in the selfish and cruel wish to make your heart ache for me without letting mine ache for you."

"And now you add to your cruelty by leaving me!"

"Ah—yes! The further I flounder, the more harm I do!"

"O Sue!" said he with a sudden sense of his own danger. "Do not do an immoral thing for moral reasons! You have been my social salvation. Stay with me for humanity's sake! You know what a weak fellow I am. My two Arch Enemies you know—my weakness for women, and my impulse to strong liquor. Don't abandon me to them, Sue, to save your own soul only! They have been kept entirely at a distance since you became my guardian-angel! Since I have had you I have been able to go into any temptations of the sort, without risk. Isn't my safety worth a little sacrifice of dogmatic principle? I am in terror lest, if you leave me, it will be with me another case of the pig that was washed turning back to his wallowing in the mire!"

Sue burst out weeping. "O but you must not, Jude! You won't! I'll pray for you night and day!"

"Well—never mind; don't grieve," said Jude generously. "I did suffer, God knows, about you at that time; and now I suffer again. But perhaps not so much as you. The woman mostly gets the worst of it in the long run!"

"She does."

"Unless she is absolutely worthless and contemptible. And this one is not that, anyhow!"

Sue drew a nervous breath or two. "She is—I fear! . . . Now Jude—good-night—please!"

"I mustn't stay?—Not just once more? As it has been so many times—O Sue, my wife, why not!"

"No—no—not wife! . . . I am in your hands, Jude—don't tempt me back now I have advanced so far!"

"Very well. I do your bidding. I owe that to you, darling, in penance for how I over-ruled it at the first time. My God, how selfish I was! Perhaps—perhaps I spoilt one of the highest and purest loves that ever existed between man and woman! . . . Then let the veil of our temple be rent in two from this hour!"

He went to the bed, removed one of the pair of pillows thereon, and flung it to the floor.

Sue looked at him, and bending over the bed-rail wept silently. "You don't see that it is a matter of conscience with me, and not of dislike to you!" she brokenly murmured. "Dislike to you! But I can't say any more—it breaks my heart—it will be undoing all I have begun! Jude—good-night!"

"Good-night," he said, and turned to go.

"O but you shall kiss me!" said she, starting up. "I can't—bear—!"

He clasped her, and kissed her weeping face as he had scarcely ever done before, and they remained in silence till she said, "Good-bye, good-bye!" And then gently pressing him away she got free, trying to mitigate the sadness by saying: "We'll be dear friends just the same, Jude, won't we? And we'll see each other sometimes—Yes!—and forget all this, and try to be as we were long ago?"

Jude did not permit himself to speak, but turned and descended the stairs.

IV

THE MAN WHOM SUE, IN HER MENTAL VOLTE-FACE, WAS NOW REGARDING AS HER IN-separable husband, lived still at Marygreen.

On the day before the tragedy of the children, Phillotson had seen both her and Jude as they stood in the rain at Christminster watching the procession to the Theatre. But he had said nothing of it at the moment to his companion Gillingham, who, being an old friend, was staying with him at the village aforesaid, and had, indeed, suggested the day's trip to Christminster.

"What are you thinking of?" said Gillingham, as they went home. "The University degree you never obtained?"

"No, no," said Phillotson gruffly. "Of somebody I saw to-day." In a moment he added, "Susanna."

"I saw her, too."

"You said nothing."

"I didn't wish to draw your attention to her. But, as you did see her, you should have said: 'How d'ye do, my dear-that-was?' "

"Ah, well. I might have. But what do you think of this: I have good reason for supposing that she was innocent when I divorced her—that I was all wrong. Yes, indeed! Awkward, isn't it?"

"She has taken care to set you right since, anyhow, apparently."

"H'm. That's a cheap sneer. I ought to have waited, unquestionably."

At the end of the week, when Gillingham had gone back to his school near Shaston, Phillotson, as was his custom, went to Alfredston market; ruminating again on Arabella's intelligence as he walked down the long hill which he had known before Jude knew it, though his history had not beaten so intensely upon its incline. Arrived in the town he bought his usual weekly local paper; and when he had sat down in an inn to refresh himself for the five miles' walk back, he pulled the paper from his pocket and read a while. The account of the "Strange suicide of a stone-cutter's children" met his eye.

Unimpassioned as he was, it impressed him painfully, and puzzled him not a little, for he could not understand the age of the elder child being what it was stated to be. However, there was no doubt that the newspaper report was in some way true.

"Their cup of sorrow is now full!" he said: and thought and thought of Sue, and what she had gained by leaving him.

Arabella having made her home at Alfredston, and the schoolmaster coming to market there every Saturday, it was not wonderful that in a few weeks they met again—the precise time being just after her return from Christminster, where she had stayed much longer than she had at first intended, keeping an interested eye on Jude, though Jude had seen no more of her. Phillotson was on his way homeward when he encountered Arabella, and she was approaching the town.

"You like walking out this way, Mrs. Cartlett?" he said.

"I've just begun to again," she replied. "It is where I lived as maid and wife, and all the past things of my life that are interesting to my feelings are mixed up with this road. And they have been stirred up in me too, lately; for I've been visiting at Christminster. Yes; I've seen Jude."

"Ah! How do they bear their terrible affliction?"

"In a ve-ry strange way—ve-ry strange! She don't live with him any longer. I only heard of it as a certainty just before I left; though I had thought things were drifting that way from their manner when I called on them."

"Not live with her husband? Why, I should have thought 'twould have united them more."

"He's not her husband, after all. She has never really married him although they have passed as man and wife so long. And now, instead of this sad event making 'em hurry up, and get the thing done legally, she's took in a queer religious way, just as I was in my affliction at losing Cartlett, only hers is of a more 'sterical sort than mine. And she says, so I was told, that she's your wife in the eye of Heaven and the Church—yours only; and can't be anybody else's by any act of man."

"Ah—indeed? . . . Separated, have they!"

"You see, the eldest boy was mine—"

"O—yours!"

"Yes, poor little fellow—born in lawful wedlock, thank God. And perhaps she feels, over and above other things, that I ought to have been in her place. I can't say. However, as for me, I am soon off from here. I've got Father to look after now, and we can't live in such a humdrum place as this. I hope soon to be in a bar again at Christminster, or some other big town."

They parted. When Phillotson had ascended the hill a few steps he stopped, hastened back, and called her.

"What is, or was, their address?"

Arabella gave it.

"Thank you. Good afternoon."

Arabella smiled grimly as she resumed her way, and practised dimple-making all along the road, from where the pollard willows begin to the old almshouses in the first street of the town.

Meanwhile Phillotson ascended to Marygreen, and for the first time during a lengthened period he lived with a forward eye. On crossing under the large trees of the green to the humble school-house to which he had been reduced he stood a moment, and pictured Sue coming out of the door to meet him. No man had ever suffered more inconvenience from his own charity, Christian or heathen, than Phillotson had done in letting Sue go. He had been knocked about from pillar to post at the hands of the virtuous almost beyond endurance; he had been nearly starved, and was now dependent entirely upon the very small stipend from the school of this village (where the parson had got ill-spoken of for befriending him). He had often thought of Arabella's remarks that he should have been more severe with Sue, that her recalcitrant spirit would soon have been broken. Yet such was his obstinate and illogical disregard of opinion, and of the principles in which he had been trained, that his convictions on the rightness of his course with his wife had not been disturbed.

Principles which could be subverted by feeling in one direction were liable to the same catastrophe in another. The instincts which had allowed him to give Sue her liberty now enabled him to regard her as none the worse for her life with Jude. He wished for her still, in his curious way, if he did not love her, and, apart from policy, soon felt that he would be gratified to have her again as his, always provided that she came willingly.

But artifice was necessary, he had found, for stemming the cold and inhumane blast of the world's contempt. And here were the materials ready made. By getting Sue back and remarrying her on the respectable plea of having entertained erroneous views of her, and gained his divorce wrongfully, he might acquire some comfort, resume his old courses, perhaps return to the Shaston school, if not even to the Church itself as a licentiate.

He thought he would write to Gillingham to enquire his views, and what he thought of his, Phillotson's, sending a letter to her. Gillingham replied, naturally, that now she was gone it were best to let her be; and considered that if she were anybody's wife she was the wife of the man to whom she had borne three children and owed such tragical adventures. Probably, as his attachment to her seemed unusually strong, the singular pair would make their union legal in course of time, and all would be well, and decent, and in order.

"But they won't—Sue won't!" exclaimed Phillotson to himself. "Gillingham is so old-fashioned. She's affected by Christminster sentiment and teaching. I can see her views on the indissolubility of marriage well enough, and I know where she got them. They are not mine; but I shall make use of them to further mine."

He wrote a brief reply to Gillingham. "I know I am entirely wrong, but I don't agree with you. As to her having lived with and had three children by him, my feeling is (though I can advance no logical or moral defence of it, on the old lines) that it has done little more than finish her education. I shall write to her, and learn whether what that woman said is true or no."

As he had made up his mind to do this before he had written to his friend, there had not been much reason for writing to the latter at all. However, it was Phillotson's way to act thus.

He accordingly addressed a carefully considered epistle to Sue, and, knowing her emotional temperament, threw a Rhadamanthine strictness into it here and there, carefully hiding his heterodox feelings, not to frighten her. He stated that, it having come to his knowledge that her views had considerably changed, he felt compelled to say that his own, too, were largely modified by events subsequent to their parting. He would not conceal from her that passionate love had little to do with his communication. It arose from a wish to make their lives, if not a success, at least no such disastrous failure as they threatened to become, through his acting on what he had considered at the time a principle of justice, charity, and reason.

To indulge one's instinctive and uncontrolled sense of justice and right, was not, he had found, permitted with impunity in an old civilization like ours. It was necessary to act under an acquired and artificial sense of the same, if you wished to enjoy an average share of comfort and honour; and to let loving-kindness take care of itself.

He suggested that she should come to him there at Marygreen.

On second thoughts he took out the last paragraph but one; and having rewritten the letter he despatched it immediately, and in some excitement awaited the issue.

A few days after a figure moved through the white fog which enveloped the Beersheba suburb of Christminster, towards the quarter in which Jude Fawley had taken up his lodging since his division from Sue. A timid knock sounded upon the door of his abode.

It was evening—so he was at home; and by a species of divination he jumped up and rushed to the door himself.

"Will you come out with me? I would rather not come in. I want to—to talk with you—and to go with you to the cemetery."

It had been in the trembling accents of Sue that these words came. Jude put on his hat. "It is dreary for you to be out," he said. "But if you prefer not to come in, I don't mind."

"Yes—I do. I shall not keep you long."

Jude was too much affected to go on talking at first; she, too, was now such a mere cluster of nerves that all initiatory power seemed to have left her, and they proceeded through the fog like Acherontic shades for a long while, without sound or gesture.

"I want to tell you," she presently said, her voice now quick, now slow, "so that you may not hear of it by chance. I am going back to Richard. He has—so magnanimously— agreed to forgive all."

"Going back? How can you go—"

"He is going to marry me again. That is for form's sake, and to satisfy the world, which does not see things as they are. But of course I *am* his wife already. Nothing has changed that."

He turned upon her with an anguish that was well-nigh fierce.

"But you are *my* wife! Yes, you are. You know it. I have always regretted that feint of ours in going away and pretending to come back legally married, to save appearances. I loved you, and you loved me; and we closed with each other; and that made the marriage. We still love—you as well as I—I *know* it, Sue! Therefore our marriage is not cancelled."

"Yes; I know how you see it," she answered with despairing self-suppression. "But I am going to marry him again, as it would be called by you. Strictly speaking you, too—don't mind my saying it, Jude!—you should take back—Arabella."

"I should? Good God—what next! But how if you and I had married legally, as we were on the point of doing?"

"I should have felt just the same—that ours was not a marriage. And I would go back to Richard without repeating the sacrament, if he asked me. But 'the world and its ways have a certain worth' (I suppose): therefore I concede a repetition of the ceremony. . . . Don't crush all the life out of me by satire and argument, I implore you! I was strongest once, I know, and perhaps I treated you cruelly. But Jude, return good for evil! I am the weaker now. Don't retaliate upon me, but be kind. O be kind to me—a poor wicked woman who is trying to mend!"

He shook his head hopelessly, his eyes wet. The blow of her bereavement seemed to have destroyed her reasoning faculty. The once keen vision was dimmed. "All wrong, all wrong!" he said huskily. "Error—perversity! It drives me out of my senses. Do you care for him? Do you love him? You know you don't! It will be a fanatic prostitution—God forgive me, yes—that's what it will be!"

"I don't love him—I must, must, own it, in deepest remorse! But I shall try to learn to love him by obeying him."

Jude argued, urged, implored; but her conviction was proof against all. It seemed to be the one thing on earth on which she was firm, and that her firmness in this had left her tottering in every other impulse and wish she possessed.

"I have been considerate enough to let you know the whole truth, and to tell it you myself," she said in cut tones; "that you might not consider yourself slighted by hearing of it at second-hand. I have even owned the extreme fact that I do not love him. I did not think you would be so rough with me for doing so! I was going to ask you . . ."

"To give you away?"

"No. To send—my boxes to me—if you would. But I suppose you won't."

"Why, of course I will. What—isn't he coming to fetch you—to marry you from here? He won't condescend to do that?"

"No—I won't let him. I go to him voluntarily, just as I went away from him. We are to be married at his little church at Marygreen."

She was so sadly sweet in what he called her wrong-headedness that Jude could not help being moved to tears more than once for pity of her. "I never knew such a woman for doing impulsive penances as you, Sue! No sooner does one expect you to go straight on, as the one rational proceeding, than you double round the corner!"

"Ah, well; let that go! . . . Jude, I must say good-bye! But I wanted you to go to the cemetery with me. Let our farewell be there—beside the graves of those who died to bring home to me the error of my views."

They turned in the direction of the place, and the gate was opened to them on application. Sue had been there often, and she knew the way to the spot in the dark. They reached it, and stood still.

"It is here—I should like to part," said she.

"So be it!"

"Don't think me hard because I have acted on conviction. Your generous devotion to me is unparalleled, Jude! Your worldly failure, if you have failed, is to your credit rather than to your blame. Remember that the best and greatest among mankind are those who do themselves no worldly good. Every successful man is more or less a selfish man. The devoted fail. . . . 'Charity seeketh not her own.' "

"In that chapter we are at one, ever beloved darling, and on it we'll part friends. Its verses will stand fast when all the rest that you call religion has passed away!"

"Well—don't discuss it. Good-bye, Jude; my fellow-sinner, and kindest friend!"

"Good-bye, my mistaken wife. Good-bye!"

V

THE NEXT AFTERNOON THE FAMILIAR CHRISTMINSTER FOG STILL HUNG OVER ALL things. Sue's slim shape was only just discernible going towards the station.

Jude had no heart to go to his work that day. Neither could he go anywhere in the direction by which she would be likely to pass. He went in an opposite one, to a dreary, strange, flat scene, where boughs dripped, and coughs and consumption lurked, and where he had never been before.

"Sue's gone from me—gone!" he murmured miserably.

She in the meantime had left by the train, and reached Alfredston Road, where she entered the steam-tram and was conveyed into the town. It had been her request to Phillotson that he should not meet her. She wished, she said, to come to him voluntarily, to his very house and hearthstone.

It was Friday evening, which had been chosen because the schoolmaster was disengaged at four o'clock that day till the Monday morning following. The little car she hired at The Bear to drive her to Marygreen set her down at the end of the lane, half a mile from the village, by her desire, and preceded her to the school-house with such portion of her luggage as she had brought. On its return she encountered it, and asked the driver if he had found the master's house open. The man informed her that he had, and that her things had been taken in by the schoolmaster himself.

She could now enter Marygreen without exciting much observation. She crossed by the well and under the trees to the pretty new school on the other side, and lifted the latch of the dwelling without knocking. Phillotson stood in the middle of the room, awaiting her, as requested.

"I've come, Richard," said she, looking pale and shaken, and sinking into a chair. "I cannot believe—you forgive your—wife!"

"Everything, darling Susanna," said Phillotson.

She started at the endearment, though it had been spoken advisedly without fervour. Then she nerved herself again.

"My children—are dead—and it is right that they should be! I am glad—almost. They were sin-begotten. They were sacrificed to teach me how to live!—their death was the first stage of my purification. That's why they have not died in vain! . . . You will take me back?"

He was so stirred by her pitiful words and tone that he did more than he had meant to do. He bent and kissed her cheek.

Sue imperceptibly shrank away, her flesh quivering under the touch of his lips.

Phillotson's heart sank, for desire was renascent in him. "You still have an aversion to me!"

"O no, dear—I—have been driving through the damp, and I was chilly!" she said, with a hurried smile of apprehension. "When are we going to have the marriage? Soon?"

"To-morrow morning, early, I thought—if you really wish. I am sending round to the vicar to let him know you are come. I have told him all, and he highly approves—he says it will bring our lives to a triumphant and satisfactory issue. But—are you sure of yourself? It is not too late to refuse now if—you think you can't bring yourself to it, you know?"

"Yes, yes, I can! I want it done quick. Tell him, tell him at once! My strength is tried by the undertaking—I can't wait long!"

"Have something to eat and drink then, and go over to your room at Mrs. Edlin's. I'll tell the vicar half-past eight to-morrow, before anybody is about—if that's not too soon for you? My friend Gillingham is here to help us in the ceremony. He's been good enough to come all the way from Shaston at great inconvenience to himself."

Unlike a woman in ordinary, whose eye is so keen for material things, Sue seemed to see nothing of the room they were in, or any detail of her environment. But on moving across the parlour to put down her muff she uttered a little "O!" and grew paler than before. Her look was that of the condemned criminal who catches sight of his coffin.

"What?" said Phillotson.

The flap of the bureau chanced to be open, and in placing her muff upon it her eye had caught a document which lay there. "O—only a—funny surprise!" she said, trying to laugh away her cry as she came back to the table.

"Ah! Yes," said Phillotson. "The licence. . . . It has just come."

Gillingham now joined them from his room above, and Sue nervously made herself agreeable to him by talking on whatever she thought likely to interest him, except herself, though that interested him most of all. She obediently ate some supper, and prepared to leave for her lodging hard by. Phillotson crossed the green with her, bidding her goodnight at Mrs. Edlin's door.

The old woman accompanied Sue to her temporary quarters, and helped her to unpack. Among other things she laid out a night-gown tastefully embroidered.

"O—I didn't know *that* was put in!" said Sue quickly. "I didn't mean it to be. Here is a different one." She handed a new and absolutely plain garment, of coarse and unbleached calico.

"But this is the prettiest," said Mrs. Edlin. "That one is no better than very sackcloth o' Scripture!"

"Yes—I meant it to be. Give me the other."

She took it, and began rending it with all her might, the tears resounding through the house like a screech-owl.

"But my dear, dear!—whatever . . ."

"It is adulterous! It signifies what I don't feel—I bought it long ago—to please Jude. It must be destroyed!"

Mrs. Edlin lifted her hands, and Sue excitedly continued to tear the linen into strips, laying the pieces in the fire.

"You med ha' give it to me!" said the widow. "It do make my heart ache to see such pretty open-work as that a-burned by the flames—not that ornamental night-rails can be much use to a' ould 'ooman like I. My days for such be all past and gone!"

"It is an accursed thing—it reminds me of what I want to forget!" Sue repeated. "It is only fit for the fire."

"Lord, you be too strict! What do ye use such words for, and condemn to hell your dear little innocent children that's lost to 'ee! Upon my life I don't call that religion!"

Sue flung her face upon the bed, sobbing. "O, don't, don't! That kills me!" She remained shaken with her grief, and slipped down upon her knees.

"I'll tell 'ee what—you ought not to marry this man again!" said Mrs. Edlin indignantly. "You are in love wi' t' other still!"

"Yes I must—I am his already!"

"Pshoo! You be t' other man's. If you didn't like to commit yourselves to the binding vow again, just at first, 'twas all the more credit to your consciences, considering your reasons, and you med ha' lived on, and made it all right at last. After all, it concerned nobody but your own two selves."

"Richard says he'll have me back, and I'm bound to go! If he had refused, it might not have been so much my duty to—give up Jude. But—" She remained with her face in the bedclothes, and Mrs. Edlin left the room.

Phillotson in the interval had gone back to his friend Gillingham, who still sat over the supper-table. They soon rose, and walked out on the green to smoke a while. A light was burning in Sue's room, a shadow moving now and then across the blind.

Gillingham had evidently been impressed with the indefinable charm of Sue, and after a silence he said, "Well: you've all but got her again at last. She can't very well go a second time. The pear has dropped into your hand."

"Yes! . . . I suppose I am right in taking her at her word. I confess there seems a touch of selfishness in it. Apart from her being what she is, of course, a luxury for a fogey like me, it will set me right in the eyes of the clergy and orthodox laity, who have never forgiven me for letting her go. So I may get back in some degree into my old track."

"Well—if you've got any sound reason for marrying her again, do it now in God's name! I was always against your opening the cage-door and letting the bird go in such an obviously suicidal way. You might have been a school inspector by this time, or a reverend, if you hadn't been so weak about her."

"I did myself irreparable damage—I know it."

"Once you've got her housed again, stick to her."

Phillotson was more evasive to-night. He did not care to admit clearly that his taking Sue to him again had at bottom nothing to do with repentance of letting her go, but was, primarily, a human instinct flying in the face of custom and profession. He said, "Yes—I shall do that. I know woman better now. Whatever justice there was in releasing her, there was little logic, for one holding my views on other subjects."

Gillingham looked at him, and wondered whether it would ever happen that the reactionary spirit induced by the world's sneers and his own physical wishes would make Phillotson more orthodoxly cruel to her than he had erstwhile been informally and perversely kind.

"I perceive it won't do to give way to impulse," Phillotson resumed, feeling more and more every minute the necessity of acting up to his position. "I flew in the face of the Church's teaching; but I did it without malice prepense. Women are so strange in their influence, that they tempt you to misplaced kindness. However, I know myself better now. A little judicious severity, perhaps. . . ."

"Yes; but you must tighten the reins by degrees only. Don't be too strenuous at first. She'll come to any terms in time."

The caution was unnecessary, though Phillotson did not say so. "I remember what my vicar at Shaston said, when I left after the row that was made about my agreeing to her elopement. 'The only thing you can do to retrieve your position and hers is to admit your error in not restraining her with a wise and strong hand, and to get her back again if she'll come, and be firm in the future.' But I was so headstrong at that time that I paid no heed. And that after the divorce she should have thought of doing so I did not dream."

The gate of Mrs. Edlin's cottage clicked, and somebody began crossing in the direction of the school. Phillotson said "Good-night."

"Oh, is that Mr. Phillotson," said Mrs. Edlin. "I was going over to see 'ee. I've been upstairs with her, helping her to unpack her things; and upon my word, sir, I don't think this ought to be!"

"What—the wedding?"

"Yes. She's forcing herself to it, poor dear little thing; and you've no notion what she's suffering. I was never much for religion nor against it, but it can't be right to let her do this, and you ought to persuade her out of it. Of course everybody will say it was very good and forgiving of 'ee to take her to 'ee again. But for my part I don't."

"It's her wish, and I am willing," said Phillotson with grave reserve, opposition making him illogically tenacious now. "A great piece of laxity will be rectified."

"I don't believe it. She's his wife if anybody's. She's had three children by him, and he loves her dearly; and it's a wicked shame to egg her on to this, poor little quivering thing! She's got nobody on her side. The one man who'd be her friend the obstinate creature won't allow to come near her. What first put her into this mood o' mind, I wonder!"

"I can't tell. Not I certainly. It is all voluntary on her part. Now that's all I have to say." Phillotson spoke stiffly. "You've turned round, Mrs. Edlin. It is unseemly of you!"

"Well. I knowed you'd be affronted at what I had to say; but I don't mind that. The truth's the truth."

"I'm not affronted, Mrs. Edlin. You've been too kind a neighbour for that. But I must be allowed to know what's best for myself and Susanna. I suppose you won't go to church with us, then?"

"No. Be hanged if I can. . . . I don't know what the times be coming to! Matrimony have growed to be that serious in these days that one really do feel afeard to move in it at all. In my time we took it more careless; and I don't know that we was any the worse for it! When I and my poor man were jined in it we kept up the junketting all the week, and drunk the parish dry, and had to borrow half-a-crown to begin housekeeping!"

When Mrs. Edlin had gone back to her cottage Phillotson spoke moodily. "I don't know whether I ought to do it—at any rate quite so rapidly."

"Why?"

"If she is really compelling herself to this against her instincts—merely from this new sense of duty or religion—I ought perhaps to let her wait a bit."

"Now you've got so far you ought not to back out of it. That's my opinion."

"I can't very well put it off now; that's true. But I had a qualm when she gave that little cry at sight of the licence."

"Now, never you have qualms, old boy. I mean to give her away to-morrow morning, and you mean to take her. It has always been on my conscience that I didn't urge more objections to your letting her go, and now we've got to this stage I shan't be content if I don't help you to set the matter right."

Phillotson nodded, and seeing how staunch his friend was, became more frank. "No doubt when it gets known what I've done I shall be thought a soft fool by many. But they don't know Sue as I do. Hers is such a straight and open nature that I don't think she has ever done anything against her conscience. The fact of her having lived with Fawley goes for nothing. At the time she left me for him she thought she was quite within her right. Now she thinks otherwise."

The next morning came, and the self-sacrifice of the woman on the altar of what she was pleased to call her principles was acquiesced in by these two friends, each from his own point of view. Phillotson went across to the Widow Edlin's to fetch Sue a few minutes after eight o'clock. The fog of the previous day or two on the lowlands had travelled up here by now, and the trees on the green caught armfuls, and turned them into showers of big drops. The bride was waiting, ready; bonnet and all on. She had never in her life looked so much like the lily her name connoted as she did in that pallid morning light. Chastened, world-weary, remorseful, the strain on her nerves had preyed upon her flesh and bones, and she appeared smaller in outline than she had formerly done, though Sue had not been a large woman in her days of rudest health.

"Prompt," said the schoolmaster, magnanimously taking her hand. But he checked his impulse to kiss her, remembering her start of yesterday, which unpleasantly lingered in his mind.

Gillingham joined them, and they left the house, Widow Edlin continuing steadfast in her refusal to assist in the ceremony.

"Where is the church?" said Sue. She had not lived there for any length of time since the old church was pulled down, and in her preoccupation forgot the new one.

"Up here," said Phillotson; and presently the tower loomed large and solemn in the fog. The vicar had already crossed to the building, and when they entered he said pleasantly: "We almost want candles."

"You do—wish me to be yours, Richard?" gasped Sue in a whisper.

"Certainly, dear: above all things in the world."

Sue said no more; and for the second or third time he felt he was not quite following out the humane instinct which had induced him to let her go.

There they stood, five altogether: the parson, the clerk, the couple and Gillingham;

and the holy ordinance was resolemnised forthwith. In the nave of the edifice were two or three villagers, and when the clergyman came to the words, "What God hath joined," a woman's voice from among these was heard to utter audibly:

"God hath jined indeed!"

It was like a re-enactment by the ghosts of their former selves of the similar scene which had taken place at Melchester years before. When the books were signed the vicar congratulated the husband and wife on having performed a noble, and righteous, and mutually forgiving act. "All's well that ends well," he said smiling. "May you long be happy together, after thus having been 'saved as by fire.' "

They came down the nearly empty building, and crossed to the school-house. Gillingham wanted to get home that night, and left early. He, too, congratulated the couple. "Now," he said in parting from Phillotson, who walked out a little way, "I shall be able to tell the people in your native place a good round tale; and they'll all say 'Well done,' depend on it."

When the schoolmaster got back Sue was making a pretence of doing some housewifery as if she lived there. But she seemed timid at his approach.

"Of course, my dear, I shan't expect to intrude upon your personal privacy any more than I did before," he said gravely. "It is for our good socially to do this, and that's its justification, if it was not my reason."

Sue brightened a little.

VI

THE PLACE WAS THE DOOR OF JUDE'S LODGING IN THE OUTSKIRTS OF CHRISTMINSTER—far from the precincts of St. Silas' where he had formerly lived, which saddened him to sickness. The rain was coming down. A woman in shabby black stood on the door-step talking to Jude, who held the door in his hand.

"I am lonely, destitute, and houseless—that's what I am! Father has turned me out-of-doors after borrowing every penny I'd got, to put it into his business, and then accusing me of laziness when I was only waiting for a situation. I am at the mercy of the world! If you can't take me and help me, Jude, I must go to the workhouse, or to something worse. Only just now two undergraduates winked at me as I came along. 'Tis hard for a woman to keep virtuous where there's so many young men!"

The woman in the rain who spoke thus was Arabella, the evening being that of the day after Sue's remarriage with Phillotson.

"I am sorry for you, but I am only in lodgings," said Jude coldly.

"Then you turn me away?"

"I'll give you enough to get food and lodging for a few days."

"O, but can't you have the kindness to take me in? I cannot endure going to a public-house to lodge; and I am so lonely. Please, Jude, for old times' sake!"

"No, no," said Jude hastily. "I don't want to be reminded of those things; and if you talk about them I shall not help you."

"Then I suppose I must go!" said Arabella. She bent her head against the doorpost and began sobbing.

"The house is full," said Jude. "And I have only a little extra room to my own—not much more than a closet—where I keep my tools, and templates, and the few books I have left!"

"That would be a palace for me!"

"There is no bedstead in it."

"A bit of a bed could be made on the floor. It would be good enough for me."

Unable to be harsh with her, and not knowing what to do, Jude called the man who let the lodgings, and said this was an acquaintance of his in great distress for want of temporary shelter.

"You may remember me as barmaid at the Lamb and Flag formerly?" spoke up Arabella. "My father has insulted me this afternoon, and I've left him, though without a penny!"

The householder said he could not recall her features. "But still, if you are a friend of Mr. Fawley's we'll do what we can for a day or two—if he'll make himself answerable?"

"Yes, yes," said Jude. "She has really taken me quite unawares; but I should wish to help her out of her difficulty." And an arrangement was ultimately come to under which a bed was to be thrown down in Jude's lumber-room, to make it comfortable for Arabella till she could get out of the strait she was in—not by her own fault, as she declared—and return to her father's again.

While they were waiting for this to be done Arabella said: "You know the news, I suppose?"

"I guess what you mean; but I know nothing."

"I had a letter from Anny at Alfredston to-day. She had just heard that the wedding was to be yesterday: but she didn't know if it had come off."

"I don't wish to talk of it."

"No, no: of course you don't. Only it shows what kind of woman—"

"Don't speak of her I say! She's a fool!—And she's an angel, too, poor dear!"

"If it's done, he'll have a chance of getting back to his old position, by everybody's account, so Anny says. All his well-wishers will be pleased, including the bishop himself."

"Do spare me, Arabella."

Arabella was duly installed in the little attic, and at first she did not come near Jude at all. She went to and fro, about her own business, which, when they met for a moment on the stairs or in the passage, she informed him was that of obtaining another place in the occupation she understood best. When Jude suggested London as affording the most likely opening in the liquor trade, she shook her head. "No—the temptations are too many," she said. "Any humble tavern in the country before that for me."

On the Sunday morning following, when he breakfasted later than on other days, she meekly asked him if she might come in to breakfast with him, as she had broken her teapot, and could not replace it immediately, the shops being shut.

"Yes, if you like," he said indifferently.

While they sat without speaking she suddenly observed: "You seem all in a brood, old man. I'm sorry for you."

"I am all in a brood."

"It is about her, I know. It's no business of mine, but I could find out all about the wedding—if it really did take place—if you wanted to know."

"How could you?"

"I wanted to go to Alfredston to get a few things I left there. And I could see Anny, who'll be sure to have heard all about it, as she has friends at Marygreen."

Jude could not bear to acquiesce in this proposal; but his suspense pitted itself against his discretion, and won in the struggle. "You can ask about it if you like," he said. "I've not heard a sound from there. It must have been very private, if—they have married."

"I am afraid I haven't enough cash to take me there and back, or I should have gone before. I must wait till I have earned some."

"O—I can pay the journey for you," he said impatiently. And thus his suspense as to Sue's welfare, and the possible marriage, moved him to despatch for intelligence the last emissary he would have thought of choosing deliberately.

Arabella went, Jude requesting her to be home not later than by the seven o'clock train. When she had gone he said: "Why should I have charged her to be back by a particular time! She's nothing to me:—nor the other neither!"

But having finished work he could not help going to the station to meet Arabella, dragged thither by feverish haste to get the news she might bring, and know the worst. Arabella had made dimples most successfully all the way home, and when she stepped out of the railway-carriage she smiled. He merely said "Well?" with the very reverse of a smile.

"They are married."

"Yes—of course they are!" he returned. She observed, however, the hard strain upon his lip as he spoke.

"Anny says she has heard from Belinda, her relation out at Marygreen, that it was very sad, and curious!"

"How do you mean sad? She wanted to marry him again, didn't she?—and he her!"

"Yes—that was it. She wanted to in one sense, but not in the other. Mrs. Edlin was much upset by it all, and spoke out her mind at Phillotson. But Sue was that excited about it that she burnt her best embroidery, that she'd worn with you, to blot you out entirely. Well—if a woman feels like it, she ought to do it. I commend her for it, though others don't." Arabella sighed. "She felt he was her only husband, and that she belonged to nobody else in the sight of God A'mighty while he lived. Perhaps another woman feels the same about herself, too!" Arabella sighed again.

"I don't want any cant!" exclaimed Jude.

"It isn't cant," said Arabella. "I feel exactly the same as she!"

He closed that issue by remarking abruptly: "Well—now I know all I wanted to know. Many thanks for your information. I am not going back to my lodgings just yet." And he left her straightway.

In his misery and depression Jude walked to well-nigh every spot in the city that he had visited with Sue; thence he did not know whither, and then thought of going home to his usual evening meal. But having all the vices of his virtues, and some to spare, he turned into a public-house, for the first time during many months. Among the possible consequences of her marriage Sue had not dwelt on this.

Arabella, meanwhile, had gone back. The evening passed, and Jude did not return. At half-past nine Arabella herself went out, first proceeding to an outlying district near the river where her father lived, and had opened a small and precarious pork-shop lately.

"Well," she said to him, "for all your rowing me that night, I've come back, for I have something to tell you. I think I shall get married and settled again. Only you must help me: and you can do no less, after what I've stood 'ee."

"I'll do anything to get thee off my hands!"

"Very well. I am now going to look for my young man. He's on the loose I'm afraid, and I must get him home. All I want you to do to-night is not to fasten the door, in case I should want to sleep here, and should be late."

"I thought you'd soon get tired of giving yourself airs and keeping away!"

"Well—don't do the door. That's all I say."

She then sallied out again, and first hastening back to Jude's to make sure that he had not returned, began her search for him. A shrewd guess as to his probable course took her straight to the tavern which Jude had formerly frequented, and where she had been barmaid for a brief term. She had no sooner opened the door of the "Private Bar" than her eyes fell upon him—sitting in the shade at the back of the compartment, with his eyes fixed on the floor in a blank stare. He was drinking nothing stronger than ale just then. He did not observe her, and she entered and sat beside him.

Jude looked up, and said without surprise: "You've come to have something, Arabella? . . . I'm trying to forget her: that's all! But I can't; and I am going home." She saw that he was a little way on in liquor, but only a little as yet.

"I've come entirely to look for you, dear boy. You are not well. Now you must have something better than that." Arabella held up her finger to the barmaid. "You shall have a liqueur—that's better fit for a man of education than beer. You shall have maraschino, or curaçao dry or sweet, or cherry brandy. I'll treat you, poor chap!"

"I don't care which! Say cherry brandy. . . . Sue has served me badly, very badly. I didn't expect it of Sue! I stuck to her, and she ought to have stuck to me. I'd have sold my soul for her sake, but she wouldn't risk hers a jot for me. To save her own soul she lets mine go damn! . . . But it isn't her fault, poor little girl—I am sure it isn't!"

How Arabella had obtained money did not appear, but she ordered a liqueur each, and paid for them. When they had drunk these Arabella suggested another; and Jude had the pleasure of being, as it were, personally conducted through the varieties of spirituous delectation by one who knew the landmarks well. Arabella kept very considerably in the rear of Jude; but though she only sipped where he drank, she took as much as she could safely take without losing her head—which was not a little, as the crimson upon her countenance showed.

Her tone towards him to-night was uniformly soothing and cajoling; and whenever he said "I don't care what happens to me," a thing he did continually, she replied, "But I do very much!" The closing hour came, and they were compelled to turn out; whereupon Arabella put her arm round his waist, and guided his unsteady footsteps.

When they were in the streets she said: "I don't know what our landlord will say to my bringing you home in this state. I expect we are fastened out, so that he'll have to come down and let us in."

"I don't know—I don't know."

"That's the worst of not having a home of your own. I tell you, Jude, what we had best do. Come round to my father's—I made it up with him a bit to-day. I can let you in, and nobody will see you at all; and by to-morrow morning you'll be all right."

"Anything—anywhere," replied Jude. "What the devil does it matter to me?"

They went along together, like any other fuddling couple, her arm still round his waist, and his, at last, round hers; though with no amatory intent; but merely because he was weary, unstable, and in need of support.

"This—is th' Martyrs'—burning-place," he stammered as they dragged across a broad street. "I remember—in old Fuller's 'Holy State'—and I am reminded of it—by our passing by here—old Fuller in his 'Holy State' says, that at the burning of Ridley, Doctor Smith—preached sermon, and took as his text *'Though I give my body to be burned, and have not charity, it profiteth me nothing.'*—Often think of it as I pass here. Ridley was a—"

"Yes. Exactly. Very thoughtful of you, deary, even though it hasn't much to do with our present business."

"Why, yes it has! I'm giving my body to be burned! But—ah—you don't understand!—it wants Sue to understand such things! And I was her seducer—poor little girl! And she's gone—and I don't care about myself! Do what you like with me! . . . And yet she did it for conscience' sake, poor little Sue!"

"Hang her!—I mean, I think she was right," hiccupped Arabella. "I've my feelings too, like her; and I feel I belong to you in Heaven's eye, and to nobody else, till death us do part! It is—hic—never too late—hic—to mend!"

They had reached her father's house, and she softly unfastened the door, groping about for a light within.

The circumstances were not altogether unlike those of their entry into the cottage at Cresscombe, such a long time before. Nor were perhaps Arabella's motives. But Jude did not think of that, though she did.

"I can't find the matches, dear," she said when she had fastened up the door. "But never mind—this way. As quiet as you can, please."

"It is as dark as pitch," said Jude.

"Give me your hand, and I'll lead you. That's it. Just sit down here, and I'll pull off your boots. I don't want to wake him."

"Who?"

"Father. He'd make a row, perhaps."

She pulled off his boots. "Now," she whispered, "take hold of me—never mind your weight. Now—first stair, second stair—"

"But—are we out in our old house by Marygreen?" asked the stupefied Jude. "I haven't been inside it for years till now! Hey? And where are my books? That's what I want to know?"

"We are at my house, dear, where there's nobody to spy out how ill you are. Now—third stair, fourth stair—that's it. Now we shall get on."

VII

ARABELLA WAS PREPARING BREAKFAST IN THE DOWNSTAIRS ROOM OF THIS SMALL, RE-cently hired tenement of her father's. She put her head into the little pork-shop in front, and told Mr. Donn it was ready. Donn, endeavouring to look like a master pork-butcher, in a greasy blue blouse, and with a strap round his waist from which a steel dangled, came in promptly.

"You must mind the shop this morning," he said casually. "I've to go and get some inwards and half a pig from Lumsdon, and to call elsewhere. If you live here you must put your shoulder to the wheel, at least till I get the business started!"

"Well, for to-day I can't say." She looked deedily into his face. "I've got a prize upstairs."

"Oh?—What's that?"

"A husband—almost."

"No!"

"Yes. It's Jude. He's come back to me."

"Your old original one? Well, I'm damned!"

"Well, I always did like him, that I will say."

"But how does he come to be up there?" said Donn, humour-struck, and nodding to the ceiling.

"Don't ask inconvenient questions, father. What we've to do is to keep him here till he and I are—as we were."

"How was that?"

"Married."

"Ah. . . . Well it is the rummest thing I ever heard of—marrying an old husband again, and so much new blood in the world! He's no catch, to my thinking. I'd have had a new one while I was about it."

"It isn't rum for a woman to want her old husband back, for respectability, though for a man to want his old wife back—well, perhaps it is funny, rather!" And Arabella was suddenly seized with a fit of loud laughter, in which her father joined more moderately.

"Be civil to him, and I'll do the rest," she said when she had recovered seriousness. "He told me this morning that his head ached fit to burst, and he hardly seemed to know where he was. And no wonder, considering how he mixed his drink last night. We must keep him jolly and cheerful here for a day or two, and not let him go back to his lodging. Whatever you advance I'll pay back to you again. But I must go up and see how he is now, poor deary."

Arabella ascended the stairs, softly opened the door of the first bedroom, and peeped in. Finding that her shorn Samson was asleep she entered to the bedside and stood regarding him. The fevered flush on his face from the debauch of the previous evening lessened the fragility of his ordinary appearance, and his long lashes, dark brows, and curly back hair and beard against the white pillow, completed the physiognomy of one whom Arabella, as a woman of rank passions, still felt it worthwhile to recapture, highly important to recapture as a woman straitened both in means and in reputation. Her ardent gaze seemed to affect him; his quick breathing became suspended, and he opened his eyes.

"How are you now, dear?" said she. "It is I—Arabella."

"Ah!—where—O yes, I remember! You gave me shelter. . . . I am stranded—ill—de-moralised—damn bad! That's what I am!"

"Then do stay there. There's nobody in the house but father and me, and you can rest till you are thoroughly well. I'll tell them at the stone-works that you are knocked up."

"I wonder what they are thinking at the lodgings!"

"I'll go round and explain. Perhaps you had better let me pay up, or they'll think we've run away?"

"Yes. You'll find enough money in my pocket there."

Quite indifferent, and shutting his eyes because he could not bear the daylight in his throbbing eyeballs, Jude seemed to doze again. Arabella took his purse, softly left the room, and putting on her out-door things went off to the lodgings she and he had quitted the evening before.

Scarcely half an hour had elapsed ere she reappeared round the corner, walking be-side a lad wheeling a truck on which were piled all Jude's household possessions, and also the few of Arabella's things which she had taken to the lodging for her short sojourn there. Jude was in such physical pain from his unfortunate break-down of the previous night, and in such mental pain from the loss of Sue and from having yielded in his half-somnolent state to Arabella, that when he saw his few chattels unpacked and standing before his eyes in this strange bedroom, intermixed with woman's apparel, he scarcely considered how they had come there, or what their coming signalised.

"Now," said Arabella to her father downstairs, "we must keep plenty of good liquor going in the house these next few days. I know his nature, and if he once gets into that fear-fully low state that he does get into sometimes, he'll never do the honourable thing by me in this world, and I shall be left in the lurch. He must be kept cheerful. He has a little money in the savings bank, and he has given me his purse to pay for anything necessary. Well, that will be the licence; for I must have that ready at hand, to catch him the moment he's in the humour. You must pay for the liquor. A few friends, and a quiet convivial party would be the thing, if we could get it up. It would advertise the shop, and help me too."

"That can be got up easy enough by anybody who'll afford victuals and drink. . . . Well yes—it would advertise the shop—that's true."

Three days later, when Jude had recovered somewhat from the fearful throbbing of his eyes and brain, but was still considerably confused in his mind by what had been supplied to him by Arabella during the interval—to keep him jolly, as she expressed it—the quiet convivial gathering suggested by her, to wind Jude up to the striking point, took place.

Donn had only just opened his miserable little pork and sausage shop, which had as yet scarce any customers; nevertheless that party advertised it well, and the Donns ac-quired a real notoriety among a certain class in Christminster who knew not the colleges, nor their works, nor their ways. Jude was asked if he could suggest any guest in addition to those named by Arabella and her father, and in a saturnine humour of perfect reckless-ness mentioned Uncle Joe, and Stagg, and the decayed auctioneer, and others whom he re-membered as having been frequenters of the well-known tavern during his bout therein years before. He also suggested Freckles and Bower o' Bliss. Arabella took him at his word so far as the men went, but drew the line at the ladies.

Another man they knew, Tinker Taylor, though he lived in the same street, was not

invited; but as he went homeward from a late job on the evening of the party, he had occasion to call at the shop for trotters. There were none in, but he was promised some the
next morning. While making his inquiry Taylor glanced into the back-room, and saw the
guests sitting round, card-playing, and drinking, and otherwise enjoying themselves at
Donn's expense. He went home to bed, and on his way out next morning wondered how
the party went off. He thought it hardly worthwhile to call at the shop for his provisions
at that hour, Donn and his daughter being probably not up, if they caroused late the night
before. However, he found in passing that the door was open, and he could hear voices
within, though the shutters of the meat-stall were not down. He went and tapped at the
sitting-room door, and opened it.

"Well—to be sure!" he said, astonished.

Hosts and guests were sitting card-playing, smoking, and talking, precisely as he had
left them eleven hours earlier; the gas was burning and the curtains drawn, though it had
been broad daylight for two hours out-of-doors.

"Yes!" cried Arabella, laughing. "Here we are, just the same. We ought to be ashamed
of ourselves, oughtn't we! But it is a sort of housewarming, you see; and our friends are
in no hurry. Come in, Mr. Taylor, and sit down."

The tinker, or rather reduced ironmonger, was nothing loath, and entered and took
a seat. "I shall lose a quarter, but never mind," he said. "Well, really, I could hardly believe my eyes when I looked in! It seemed as if I was flung back again into last night, all
of a sudden."

"So you are. Pour out for Mr. Taylor."

He now perceived that she was sitting beside Jude, her arm being round his waist.
Jude, like the rest of the company, bore on his face the signs of how deeply he had been
indulging.

"Well, we've been waiting for certain legal hours to arrive, to tell the truth," she continued bashfully, and making her spirituous crimson look as much like a maiden blush as
possible. "Jude and I have decided to make up matters between us by tying the knot again,
as we find we can't do without one another after all. So, as a bright notion, we agreed to
sit on till it was late enough, and go and do it offhand."

Jude seemed to pay no great heed to what she was announcing, or indeed to anything
whatever. The entrance of Taylor infused fresh spirit into the company, and they remained
sitting, till Arabella whispered to her father: "Now we may as well go."

"But the parson don't know?"

"Yes, I told him last night that we might come between eight and nine, as there were
reasons of decency for doing it as early and quiet as possible; on account of it being our
second marriage, which might make people curious to look on if they knew. He highly
approved."

"O very well: I'm ready," said her father, getting up and shaking himself.

"Now, old darling," she said to Jude. "Come along, as you promised."

"When did I promise anything?" asked he, whom she had made so tipsy by her special knowledge of that line of business as almost to have made him sober again—or to
seem so to those who did not know him.

"Why!" said Arabella, affecting dismay. "You've promised to marry me several times
as we've sat here to-night. These gentlemen have heard you."

"I don't remember it," said Jude doggedly. "There's only one woman—but I won't mention her in this Capharnaum!"

Arabella looked towards her father. "Now, Mr. Fawley, be honourable," said Donn. "You and my daughter have been living here together these three or four days, quite on the understanding that you were going to marry her. Of course I shouldn't have had such goings on in my house if I hadn't understood that. As a point of honour you must do it now."

"Don't say anything against my honour!" enjoined Jude hotly, standing up. "I'd marry the W—— of Babylon rather than do anything dishonourable! No reflection on you, my dear. It is a mere rhetorical figure—what they call in the books, hyperbole."

"Keep your figures for your debts to friends who shelter you," said Donn.

"If I am bound in honour to marry her—as I suppose I am—though how I came to be here with her I know no more than a dead man—marry her I will, so help me God! I have never behaved dishonourably to a woman or to any living thing. I am not a man who wants to save himself at the expense of the weaker among us!"

"There—never mind him, deary," said she, putting her cheek against Jude's. "Come up and wash your face, and just put yourself tidy, and off we'll go. Make it up with father."

They shook hands. Jude went upstairs with her, and soon came down looking tidy and calm. Arabella, too, had hastily arranged herself, and accompanied by Donn away they went.

"Don't go," she said to the guests at parting. "I've told the little maid to get the breakfast while we are gone; and when we come back we'll all have some. A good strong cup of tea will set everybody right for going home."

When Arabella, Jude and Donn had disappeared on their matrimonial errand the assembled guests yawned themselves wider awake, and discussed the situation with great interest. Tinker Taylor, being the most sober, reasoned the most lucidly.

"I don't wish to speak against friends," he said. "But it do seem a rare curiosity for a couple to marry over again! If they couldn't get on the first time when their minds were limp, they won't the second, by my reckoning."

"Do you think he'll do it?"

"He's been put upon his honour by the woman, so he med."

"He'd hardly do it straight off like this. He's got no licence nor anything."

"She's got that, bless you. Didn't you hear her say so to her father?"

"Well," said Tinker Taylor, relighting his pipe at the gas-jet. "Take her all together, limb by limb, she's not such a bad-looking piece—particular by candle-light. To be sure, halfpence that have been in circulation can't be expected to look like new ones from the Mint. But for a woman that's been knocking about the four hemispheres for some time, she's passable enough. A little bit thick in the flitch perhaps: but I like a woman that a puff o' wind won't blow down."

Their eyes followed the movements of the little girl as she spread the breakfast cloth on the table they had been using, without wiping up the slops of the liquor. The curtains were undrawn, and the expression of the house made to look like morning. Some of the guests, however, fell asleep in their chairs. One or two went to the door, and gazed along the street more than once. Tinker Taylor was the chief of these, and after a time he came in with a leer on his face.

"By Gad, they are coming! I think the deed's done!"

"No," said Uncle Joe, following him in. "Take my word, he turned rusty at the last minute. They are walking in a very onusual way; and that's the meaning of it!"

They waited in silence till the wedding party could be heard entering the house. First into the room came Arabella boisterously; and her face was enough to show that her strategy had succeeded.

"Mrs. Fawley, I presume?" said Tinker Taylor with mock courtesy.

"Certainly. Mrs. Fawley again," replied Arabella blandly, pulling off her glove and holding out her left hand. "There's the padlock, see. . . . Well, he was a very nice, gentlemanly man indeed. I mean the clergyman. He said to me as gentle as a babe when all was done: 'Mrs. Fawley, I congratulate you heartily,' he says. 'For having heard your history, and that of your husband, I think you have both done the right and proper thing. And for your past errors as a wife, and his as a husband, I think you ought now to be forgiven by the world, as you have forgiven each other,' says he. Yes: he was a very, nice, gentlemanly man. 'The Church don't recognise divorce in her dogma, strictly speaking,' he says: 'and bear in mind the words of the Service in your goings out and your comings in: What God hath joined together let no man put asunder.' Yes: he was a very, nice, gentlemanly man. . . . But Jude, my dear, you were enough to make a cat laugh! You walked that straight, and held yourself that steady, that one would have thought you were going 'prentice to a judge; though I knew you were seeing double all the time, from the way you fumbled with my finger."

"I said I'd do anything to—save a woman's honour," muttered Jude. "And I've done it!"

"Well now, old deary, come along and have some breakfast."

"I want—some—more whisky," said Jude stolidly.

"Nonsense, dear. Not now! There's no more left. The tea will take the muddle out of our heads, and we shall be as fresh as larks."

"All right. I've—married you. She said I ought to marry you again, and I have straightway. It is true religion! Ha—ha—ha!"

VIII

MICHAELMAS CAME AND PASSED, AND JUDE AND HIS WIFE, WHO HAD LIVED BUT A SHORT time in her father's house after their remarriage, were in lodgings on the top floor of a house nearer to the centre of the city.

He had done a few days' work during the two or three months since the event, but his health had been indifferent, and it was now precarious. He was sitting in an arm-chair before the fire, and coughed a good deal.

"I've got a bargain for my trouble in marrying thee over again!" Arabella was saying to him. "I shall have to keep 'ee entirely—that's what 'twill come to! I shall have to make blackpot and sausages, and hawk 'em about the street, all to support an invalid husband I'd no business to be saddled with at all. Why didn't you keep your health, deceiving one like this? You were well enough when I married you!"

"Ah, yes!" said he, laughing acridly. "I have been thinking of my foolish feeling about the pig you and I killed during our first marriage. I feel now that the greatest mercy that could be vouchsafed to me would be that something should serve me as I served that animal."

This was the sort of discourse that went on between them everyday now. The landlord of the lodging, who had heard that they were a queer couple, had doubted if they were married at all, especially as he had seen Arabella kiss Jude one evening when she had taken a little cordial; and he was about to give them notice to quit, till by chance overhearing her one night haranguing Jude in rattling terms, and ultimately flinging a shoe at his head, he recognised the note of ordinary wedlock; and concluding that they must be respectable, said no more.

Jude did not get any better, and one day he requested Arabella, with considerable hesitation, to execute a commission for him. She asked him indifferently what it was.

"To write to Sue."

"What in the name—do you want me to write to her for?"

"To ask how she is, and if she'll come to see me, because I'm ill, and should like to see her—once again."

"It is like you to insult a lawful wife by asking such a thing!"

"It is just in order not to insult you that I ask you to do it. You know I love Sue. I don't wish to mince the matter—there stands the fact: I love her. I could find a dozen ways of sending a letter to her without your knowledge. But I wish to be quite above-board with you, and with her husband. A message through you asking her to come is at least free from any odour of intrigue. If she retains any of her old nature at all, she'll come."

"You've no respect for marriage whatever, or its rights and duties!"

"What *does* it matter what my opinions are—a wretch like me! Can it matter to anybody in the world who comes to see me for half an hour—here with one foot in the grave! . . . Come, please write, Arabella!" he pleaded. "Repay my candour by a little generosity!"

"I should think *not!*"

"Not just once?—O do!" He felt that his physical weakness had taken away all his dignity.

"What do you want *her* to know how you are for? She don't want to see 'ee. She's the rat that forsook the sinking ship!"

"Don't, don't!"

"And I stuck to un—the more fool I! Have that strumpet in the house indeed!"

Almost as soon as the words were spoken Jude sprang from the chair, and before Arabella knew where she was he had her on her back upon a little couch which stood there, he kneeling above her.

"Say another word of that sort," he whispered, "and I'll kill you—here and now! I've everything to gain by it—my own death not being the least part. So don't think there's no meaning in what I say!"

"What do you want me to do?" gasped Arabella.

"Promise never to speak of her."

"Very well. I do."

"I take your word," he said scornfully as he loosened her. "But what it is worth I can't say."

"You couldn't kill the pig, but you could kill me!"

"Ah—there you have me! No—I couldn't kill you—even in a passion. Taunt away!"

He then began coughing very much, and she estimated his life with an appraiser's eye as he sank back ghastly pale. "I'll send for her," Arabella murmured, "if you'll agree to my being in the room with you all the time she's here."

The softer side of his nature, the desire to see Sue, made him unable to resist the offer even now, provoked as he had been; and he replied breathlessly: "Yes, I agree. Only send for her!"

In the evening he enquired if she had written.

"Yes," she said; "I wrote a note telling her you were ill, and asking her to come to-morrow or the day after. I haven't posted it yet."

The next day Jude wondered if she really did post it, but would not ask her; and foolish Hope, that lives on a drop and a crumb, made him restless with expectation. He knew the times of the possible trains, and listened on each occasion for sounds of her.

She did not come; but Jude would not address Arabella again thereon. He hoped and expected all the next day; but no Sue appeared; neither was there any note of reply. Then Jude decided in the privacy of his mind that Arabella had never posted hers, although she had written it. There was something in her manner which told it. His physical weakness was such that he shed tears at the disappointment when she was not there to see. His suspicions were, in fact, well founded. Arabella, like other nurses, thought that your duty towards your invalid was to pacify him by any means short of really acting upon his fancies.

He never said another word to her about his wish or his conjecture. A silent, undiscerned resolve grew up in him, which gave him, if not strength, stability and calm. One midday when, after an absence of two hours, she came into the room, she beheld the chair empty.

Down she flopped on the bed, and sitting, meditated. "Now where the devil is my man gone to!" she said.

A driving rain from the north-east had been falling with more or less intermission all the morning, and looking from the window at the dripping spouts it seemed impossible to believe that any sick man would have ventured out to almost certain death. Yet a conviction possessed Arabella that he had gone out, and it became a certainty when she had searched the house. "If he's such a fool, let him be!" she said. "I can do no more."

Jude was at that moment in a railway-train that was drawing near to Alfredston, oddly swathed, pale as a monumental figure in alabaster, and much stared at by other passengers. An hour later his thin form, in the long great-coat and blanket he had come with, but without an umbrella, could have been seen walking along the five-mile road to Marygreen. On his face showed the determined purpose that alone sustained him, but to which has weakness afforded a sorry foundation. By the up-hill walk he was quite blown, but he pressed on; and at half-past three o'clock stood by the familiar well at Marygreen. The rain was keeping everybody indoors; Jude crossed the green to the church without observation, and found the building open. Here he stood, looking forth at the school, whence he could hear the usual sing-song tones of the little voices that had not learnt Creation's groan.

He waited till a small boy came from the school—one evidently allowed out before hours for some reason or other. Jude held up his hand, and the child came.

"Please call at the school-house and ask Mrs. Phillotson if she will be kind enough to come to the church for a few minutes."

The child departed, and Jude heard him knock at the door of the dwelling. He himself went further into the church. Everything was new, except a few pieces of carving preserved from the wrecked old fabric, now fixed against the new walls. He stood by these: they seemed akin to the perished people of that place who were his ancestors and Sue's.

A light footstep, which might have been accounted no more than an added drip to the rainfall, sounded in the porch, and he looked round.

"O—I didn't think it was you! I didn't—O Jude!" A hysterical catch in her breath ended in a succession of them. He advanced, but she quickly recovered and went back.

"Don't go—don't go!" he implored. "This is my last time! I thought it would be less intrusive than to enter your house. And I shall never come again. Don't then be unmerciful. Sue, Sue! we are acting by the letter; and 'the letter killeth!' "

"I'll stay—I won't be unkind!" she said, her mouth quivering and her tears flowing as she allowed him to come closer. "But why did you come, and do this wrong thing, after doing such a right thing as you have done?"

"What right thing?"

"Marrying Arabella again. It was in the Alfredston paper. She has never been other than yours, Jude—in a proper sense. And therefore you did so well—O so well!—in recognizing it—and taking her to you again."

"God above—and is that all I've come to hear? If there is anything more degrading, immoral, unnatural, than another in my life, it is this meretricious contract with Arabella which has been called doing the right thing! And you too—you call yourself Phillotson's wife! *His* wife! You are mine."

"Don't make me rush away from you—I can't bear much! But on this point I am decided."

"I cannot understand how you did it—how you think it—I cannot!"

"Never mind that. He is a kind husband to me—And I—I've wrestled and struggled, and fasted, and prayed. I have nearly brought my body into complete subjection. And you mustn't—will you—wake—"

"O you darling little fool; where is your reason? You seem to have suffered the loss of your faculties! I would argue with you if I didn't know that a woman in your state of feeling is quite beyond all appeals to her brains. Or is it that you are humbugging yourself, as so many women do about these things; and don't actually believe what you pretend to, and only are indulging in the luxury of the emotion raised by an affected belief?"

"Luxury! How can you be so cruel!"

"You dear, sad, soft, most melancholy wreck of a promising human intellect that it has ever been my lot to behold! Where is your scorn of convention gone? I *would* have died game!"

"You crush, almost insult me, Jude! Go away from me!" She turned off quickly.

"I will. I would never come to see you again, even if I had the strength to come, which I shall not have any more. Sue, Sue, you are not worth a man's love!"

Her bosom began to go up and down. "I can't endure you to say that!" she burst out, and her eye resting on him a moment, she turned back impulsively. "Don't, don't scorn me! Kiss me, O kiss me lots of times, and say I am not a coward and a contemptible humbug—I can't bear it!" She rushed up to him and, with her mouth on his, continued: "I must tell you—O I must—my darling Love! It has been—only a church marriage—an apparent marriage I mean! He suggested it at the very first!"

"How?"

"I mean it is a nominal marriage only. It hasn't been more than that at all since I came back to him!"

"Sue!" he said. Pressing her to him in his arms he bruised her lips with kisses: "If misery can know happiness, I have a moment's happiness now! Now, in the name of all you hold holy, tell me the truth, and no lie. You do love me still?"

"I do! You know it too well! . . . But I *mustn't* do this! I mustn't kiss you back as I would!"

"But do!"

"And yet you are so dear!—and you look so ill—"

"And so do you! There's one more, in memory of our dead little children—yours and mine!"

The words struck her like a blow, and she bent her head. "I *mustn't*—I *can't* go on with this!" she gasped presently. "But there, there, darling; I give you back your kisses; I do, I do! . . . And now I'll *hate* myself forever for my sin!"

"No—let me make my last appeal. Listen to this! We've both remarried out of our senses. I was made drunk to do it. You were the same. I was gin-drunk; you were creed-drunk. Either form of intoxication takes away the nobler vision. . . . Let us then shake off our mistakes, and run away together!"

"No; again no! . . . Why do you tempt me so far, Jude! It is too merciless! . . . But I've got over myself now. Don't follow me—don't look at me. Leave me, for pity's sake!"

She ran up the church to the east end, and Jude did as she requested. He did not turn his head, but took up his blanket, which she had not seen, and went straight out. As he passed the end of the church she heard his coughs mingling with the rain on the windows, and in a last instinct of human affection, even now unsubdued by her fetters, she sprang up as if to go and succour him. But she knelt down again, and stopped her ears with her hands till all possible sound of him had passed away.

He was by this time at the corner of the green, from which the path ran across the fields in which he had scared rooks as a boy. He turned and looked back, once, at the building which still contained Sue; and then went on, knowing that his eyes would light on that scene no more.

There are cold spots up and down Wessex in autumn and winter weather; but the coldest of all when a north or east wind is blowing is the crest of the down by the Brown House, where the road to Alfredston crosses the old Ridgeway. Here the first winter sleets and snows fall and lie, and here the spring frost lingers last unthawed. Here in the teeth of the north-east wind and rain Jude now pursued his way, wet through, the necessary slowness of his walk from lack of his former strength being insufficient to maintain his heat. He came to the milestone, and, raining as it was, spread his blanket and lay down there to rest. Before moving on he went and felt at the back of the stone for his own carving. It was still there; but nearly obliterated by moss. He passed the spot where the gibbet of his ancestor and Sue's had stood, and descended the hill.

It was dark when he reached Alfredston, where he had a cup of tea, the deadly chill that began to creep into his bones being too much for him to endure fasting. To get home he had to travel by a steam tram-car, and two branches of railway, with much waiting at a junction. He did not reach Christminster till ten o'clock.

IX

O N THE PLATFORM STOOD ARABELLA. SHE LOOKED HIM UP AND DOWN.
"You've been to see her?" she asked.

"I have," said Jude, literally tottering with cold and lassitude.

"Well, now you'd best march along home."

The water ran out of him as he went, and he was compelled to lean against the wall to support himself while coughing.

"You've done for yourself by this, young man," said she. "I don't know whether you know it."

"Of course I do. I meant to do for myself."

"What—to commit suicide?"

"Certainly."

"Well, I'm blest! Kill yourself for a woman."

"Listen to me, Arabella. You think you are the stronger; and so you are, in a physical sense, now. You could push me over like a ninepin. You did not send that letter the other day, and I could not resent your conduct. But I am not so weak in another way as you think. I made up my mind that a man confined to his room by inflammation of the lungs, a fellow who had only two wishes left in the world, to see a particular woman, and then to die, could neatly accomplish those two wishes at one stroke by taking this journey in the rain. That I've done. I have seen her for the last time, and I've finished myself—put an end to a feverish life which ought never to have been begun!"

"Lord—you do talk lofty! Won't you have something warm to drink?"

"No thank you. Let's get home."

They went along by the silent colleges, and Jude kept stopping.

"What are you looking at?"

"Stupid fancies. I see, in a way, those spirits of the dead again, on this my last walk, that I saw when I first came here!"

"What a curious chap you are!"

"I seem to see them, and almost hear them rustling. But I don't revere all of them as I did then. I don't believe in half of them. The theologians, the apologists, and their kin the metaphysicians, the high-handed statesmen, and others, no longer interest me. All that has been spoilt for me by the grind of stern reality!"

The expression of Jude's corpselike face in the watery lamplight was indeed as if he saw people where there was nobody. At moments he stood still by an archway, like one watching a figure walk out; then he would look at a window like one discerning a familiar face behind it. He seemed to hear voices, whose words he repeated as if to gather their meaning.

"They seem laughing at me!"

"Who?"

"O—I was talking to myself! The phantoms all about here, in the college archways, and windows. They used to look friendly in the old days, particularly Addison, and Gibbon, and Johnson, and Dr. Browne, and Bishop Ken—"

"Come along do! Phantoms! There's neither living nor dead hereabouts except a damn policeman! I never saw the streets emptier."

"Fancy! The Poet of Liberty used to walk here, and the great Dissector of Melancholy there!"

"I don't want to hear about 'em! They bore me."

"Walter Raleigh is beckoning to me from that lane—Wycliffe—Harvey—Hooker—Arnold—and a whole crowd of Tractarian Shades—"

"I *don't want* to know their names, I tell you! What do I care about folk dead and gone? Upon my soul you are more sober when you've been drinking than when you have not!"

"I must rest a moment," he said; and as he paused, holding to the railings, he measured with his eye the height of a college front. "This is old Rubric. And that Sarcophagus; and up that lane Crozier and Tudor: and all down there is Cardinal with its long front, and its windows with lifted eyebrows, representing the polite surprise of the University at the efforts of such as I."

"Come along, and I'll treat you!"

"Very well. It will help me home, for I feel the chilly fog from the meadows of Cardinal as if death-claws were grabbing me through and through. As Antigone said, I am neither a dweller among men nor ghosts. But, Arabella, when I am dead, you'll see my spirit flitting up and down here among these!"

"Pooh! You won't die. You are tough enough yet, old man."

It was night at Marygreen, and the rain of the afternoon showed no sign of abatement. About the time at which Jude and Arabella were walking the streets of Christminster homeward, the Widow Edlin crossed the green, and opened the back door of the schoolmaster's dwelling, which she often did now before bed-time, to assist Sue in putting things away.

Sue was muddling helplessly in the kitchen, for she was not a good housewife, though she tried to be, and grew impatient of domestic details.

"Lord love 'ee, what do ye do that yourself for, when I've come o' purpose! You knew I should come."

"O—I don't know—I forgot! No, I didn't forget. I did it to discipline myself. I have scrubbed the stairs since eight o'clock. I *must* practise myself in my household duties. I've shamefully neglected them!"

"Why should ye? He'll get a better school, perhaps be a parson, in time, and you'll keep two servants. 'Tis a pity to spoil them pretty hands."

"Don't talk of my pretty hands, Mrs. Edlin. This pretty body of mine has been the ruin of me already!"

"Pshoo—you've got no body to speak of! You put me more in mind of a sperrit. But there seems something wrong to-night, my dear. Husband cross?"

"No. He never is. He's gone to bed early."

"Then what is it?"

"I cannot tell you. I have done wrong to-day. And I want to eradicate it. . . . Well—I will tell you this—Jude has been here this afternoon, and I find I still love him—O, grossly! I cannot tell you more."

"Ah!" said the widow. "I told 'ee how 'twould be!"

"But it shan't be! I have not told my husband of his visit; it is not necessary to trou-

ble him about it, as I never mean to see Jude any more. But I am going to make my con
science right on my duty to Richard—by doing a penance—the ultimate thing. I must!"

"I wouldn't—since he agrees to it being otherwise, and it has gone on three month
very well as it is."

"Yes—he agrees to my living as I choose; but I feel it is an indulgence I ought not t
exact from him. It ought not to have been accepted by me. To reverse it will be terrible—
but I must be more just to him. O why was I so unheroic!"

"What is it you don't like in him?" asked Mrs. Edlin curiously.

"I cannot tell you. It is something . . . I cannot say. The mournful thing is, that no
body would admit it as a reason for feeling as I do; so that no excuse is left me."

"Did you ever tell Jude what it was?"

"Never."

"I've heard strange tales o' husbands in my time," observed the widow in a lowere
voice. "They say that when the saints were upon the earth devils used to take husbands
forms o' nights, and get poor women into all sorts of trouble. But I don't know why tha
should come into my head, for it is only a tale. . . . What a wind and rain it is to-night
Well—don't be in a hurry to alter things, my dear. Think it over."

"No, no! I've screwed my weak soul up to treating him more courteously—and i
must be now—at once—before I break down!"

"I don't think you ought to force your nature. No woman ought to be expected to."

"It is my duty. I will drink my cup to the dregs!"

Half an hour later when Mrs. Edlin put on her bonnet and shawl to leave, Sue seeme
to be seized with vague terror.

"No—no—don't go, Mrs. Edlin," she implored, her eyes enlarged, and with a quick
nervous look over her shoulder.

"But it is bed-time, child."

"Yes, but—there's the little spare room—my room that was. It is quite ready. Please
stay, Mrs. Edlin!—I shall want you in the morning."

"O well—I don't mind, if you wish. Nothing will happen to my four old walls.
whether I be there or no."

She then fastened up the doors, and they ascended the stairs together.

"Wait here, Mrs. Edlin," said Sue. "I'll go into my old room a moment by myself."

Leaving the widow on the landing Sue turned to the chamber which had been hers exclusively since her arrival at Marygreen, and pushing to the door knelt down by the bed
for a minute or two. She then arose, and taking her night-gown from the pillow undressed
and came out to Mrs. Edlin. A man could be heard snoring in the room opposite. She
wished Mrs. Edlin good-night, and the widow entered the room that Sue had just vacated.

Sue unlatched the other chamber-door, and, as if seized with faintness, sank down
outside it. Getting up again she half opened the door, and said "Richard." As the word
came out of her mouth she visibly shuddered.

The snoring had quite ceased for some time, but he did not reply. Sue seemed relieved,
and hurried back to Mrs. Edlin's chamber. "Are you in bed, Mrs. Edlin?" she asked.

"No, dear," said the widow, opening the door. "I be old and slow, and it takes me a
long while to un-ray. I han't unlaced my jumps yet."

"I—don't hear him! And perhaps—perhaps—"

"What, child?"

"Perhaps he's dead!" she gasped. "And then—I should be *free,* and I could go to
ude! . . . Ah—no—I forgot *her*—and God!"

"Let's go and hearken. No—he's snoring again. But the rain and the wind is so loud
hat you can hardly hear anything but between whiles."

Sue had dragged herself back. "Mrs. Edlin, good-night again! I am sorry I called you
out." The widow retreated a second time.

The strained, resigned look returned to Sue's face when she was alone. "I must do
t—I must! I must drink to the dregs!" she whispered. "Richard!" she said again.

"Hey—what? Is that you, Susanna?"

"Yes."

"What do you want? Anything the matter? Wait a moment." He pulled on some articles of clothing, and came to the door. "Yes?"

"When we were at Shaston I jumped out of the window rather than that you should
come near me. I have never reversed that treatment till now—when I have come to beg
your pardon for it, and ask you to let me in."

"Perhaps you only think you ought to do this? I don't wish you to come against your
impulses, as I have said."

"But I beg to be admitted." She waited a moment, and repeated, "I beg to be admitted! I have been in error—even to-day. I have exceeded my rights. I did not mean to tell
you, but perhaps I ought. I sinned against you this afternoon."

"How?"

"I met Jude! I didn't know he was coming. And—"

"Well?"

"I kissed him, and let him kiss me."

"O—the old story!"

"Richard, I didn't know we were going to kiss each other till we did!"

"How many times?"

"A good many. I don't know. I am horrified to look back on it, and the least I can do
after it is to come to you like this."

"Come—this is pretty bad, after what I've done! Anything else to confess?"

"No." She had been intending to say: "I called him my darling Love." But, as a contrite woman always keeps back a little, that portion of the scene remained untold. She went
on: "I am never going to see him any more. He spoke of some things of the past: and it
overcame me. He spoke of—the children.—But, as I have said, I am glad—almost glad I
mean—that they are dead, Richard. It blots out all that life of mine!"

"Well—about not seeing him again any more. Come—you really mean this?" There
was something in Phillotson's tone now which seemed to show that his three months of
remarriage with Sue had somehow not been so satisfactory as his magnanimity or amative
patience had anticipated.

"Yes, yes!"

"Perhaps you'll swear it on the New Testament?"

"I will."

He went back to the room and brought out a little brown Testament. "Now then: So
help you God!"

She swore.

"Very good!"

"Now I supplicate you, Richard, to whom I belong, and whom I wish to honour and obey, as I vowed, to let me in."

"Think it over well. You know what it means. Having you back in the house was one thing—this another. So think again."

"I have thought—I wish this!"

"That's a complaisant spirit—and perhaps you are right. With a lover hanging about a half-marriage should be completed. But I repeat my reminder this third and last time."

"It is my wish! . . . O God!"

"What did you say 'O God' for?"

"I don't know!"

"Yes you do! But . . ." He gloomily considered her thin and fragile form a moment longer as she crouched before him in her night-clothes. "Well, I thought it might end like this," he said presently. "I owe you nothing, after these signs; but I'll take you in at your word, and forgive you."

He put his arm round her to lift her up. Sue started back.

"What's the matter?" he asked, speaking for the first time sternly. "You shrink from me again?—just as formerly!"

"No, Richard—I—I—was not thinking—"

"You wish to come in here?"

"Yes."

"You still bear in mind what it means?"

"Yes. It is my duty!"

Placing the candlestick on the chest of drawers he led her through the doorway, and lifting her bodily, kissed her. A wild look of aversion passed over her face, but clenching her teeth she uttered no cry.

Mrs. Edlin had by this time undressed, and was about to get into bed when she said to herself: "Ah—perhaps I'd better go and see if the little thing is all right. How it do blow and rain!"

The widow went out on the landing, and saw that Sue had disappeared. "Ah! Poor soul! Weddings be funerals 'a b'lieve now-a-days. Fifty-five years ago, come Fall, since my man and I married! Times have changed since then!"

X

DESPITE HIMSELF, JUDE RECOVERED SOMEWHAT, AND WORKED AT HIS TRADE FOR SEV-eral weeks. After Christmas, however, he broke down again.

With the money he had earned he shifted his lodgings to a yet more central part of the town. But Arabella saw that he was not likely to do much work for a long while, and was cross enough at the turn affairs had taken since her remarriage to him. "I'm hanged if you haven't been clever in this last stroke!" she would say, "to get a nurse for nothing by marrying me!"

Jude was absolutely indifferent to what she said, and, indeed, often regarded her abuse
a humorous light. Sometimes his mood was more earnest, and as he lay he often ram-
ed on upon the defeat of his early aims.

"Every man has some little power in some one direction," he would say. "I was never
ally stout enough for the stone trade, particularly the fixing. Moving the blocks always
sed to strain me, and standing the trying draughts in buildings before the windows are in,
ways gave me colds, and I think that began the mischief inside. But I felt I could do one
ing if I had the opportunity. I could accumulate ideas, and impart them to others. I won-
er if the Founders had such as I in their minds—a fellow good for nothing else but that
articular thing? . . . I hear that soon there is going to be a better chance for such helpless
udents as I was. There are schemes afoot for making the University less exclusive, and
xtending its influence. I don't know much about it. And it is too late, too late for me!
h—and for how many worthier ones before me!"

"How you keep a-mumbling!" said Arabella. "I should have thought you'd have got
ver all that craze about books by this time. And so you would, if you'd had any sense to
egin with. You are as bad now as when we were first married."

On one occasion while soliloquizing thus he called her "Sue" unconsciously.

"I wish you'd mind who you are talking to!" said Arabella indignantly. "Calling a re-
ectable married woman by the name of that—" She remembered herself and he did not
atch the word.

But in the course of time, when she saw how things were going, and how very little
ie had to fear from Sue's rivalry, she had a fit of generosity. "I suppose you want to see
our—Sue?" she said. "Well, I don't mind her coming. You can have her here if you like."

"I don't wish to see her again."

"O—that's a change!"

"And don't tell her anything about me—that I'm ill, or anything. She has chosen her
ourse. Let her go!"

One day he received a surprise. Mrs. Edlin came to see him, quite on her own account.
ude's wife, whose feelings as to where his affections were centred had reached absolute
adifference by this time, went out, leaving the old woman alone with Jude. He impulsively
sked how Sue was, and then said bluntly, remembering what Sue had told him: "I suppose
iey are still only husband and wife in name?"

Mrs. Edlin hesitated. "Well, no—it's different now. She's begun it quite lately—all of
er own free will."

"When did she begin?" he asked quickly.

"The night after you came. But as a punishment to her poor self. He didn't wish it, but
he insisted."

"Sue, my Sue—you darling fool—this is almost more than I can endure! . . . Mrs.
dlin—don't be frightened at my rambling—I've got to talk to myself lying here so many
ours alone—she was once a woman whose intellect was to mine like a star to a benzoline
imp: who saw all *my* superstitions as cobwebs that she could brush away with a word.
hen bitter affliction came to us, and her intellect broke, and she veered round to darkness.
trange difference of sex, that time and circumstance, which enlarge the views of most
ien, narrow the views of women almost invariably. And now the ultimate horror has
ome—her giving herself like this to what she loaths, in her enslavement to forms!—she,

so sensitive, so shrinking, that the very wind seemed to blow on her with a touch of def erence. . . . As for Sue and me when we were at our own best, long ago—when our mind were clear, and our love of truth fearless—the time was not ripe for us! Our ideas were fifty years too soon to be any good to us. And so the resistance they met with brought re action in her, and recklessness and ruin on me! . . . There—this, Mrs. Edlin, is how I go on to myself continually, as I lie here. I must be boring you awfully."

"Not at all, my dear boy. I could hearken to 'ee all day."

As Jude reflected more and more on her news, and grew more restless, he began in his mental agony to use terribly profane language about social conventions, which started a fit of coughing. Presently there came a knock at the door downstairs. As nobody answered it Mrs. Edlin herself went down.

The visitor said blandly: "The doctor." The lanky form was that of Physician Vilbert who had been called in by Arabella.

"How is my patient at present?" asked the physician.

"O bad—very bad! Poor chap, he got excited, and do blaspeam terribly, since I let out some gossip by accident—the more to my blame. But there—you must excuse a man in suffering for what he says, and I hope God will forgive him."

"Ah. I'll go up and see him. Mrs. Fawley at home?"

"She's not in at present, but she'll be here soon."

Vilbert went; but though Jude had hitherto taken the medicines of that skilful practi tioner with the greatest indifference, whenever poured down his throat by Arabella, he was now so brought to bay by events that he vented his opinion of Vilbert in the physician's face, and so forcibly, and with such striking epithets, that Vilbert soon scurried downstairs again. At the door he met Arabella, Mrs. Edlin having left. Arabella enquired how he thought her husband was now, and seeing that the doctor looked ruffled, asked him to take something. He assented.

"I'll bring it to you here in the passage," she said. "There's nobody but me about the house to-day."

She brought him a bottle and a glass, and he drank. Arabella began shaking with sup pressed laughter. "What is this, my dear?" he asked, smacking his lips.

"O—a drop of wine—and something in it." Laughing again she said: "I poured your own love-philtre into it, that you sold me at the Agricultural Show, don't you remember?"

"I do, I do! Clever woman! But you must be prepared for the consequences." Putting his arm round her shoulders he kissed her there and then.

"Don't, don't," she whispered, laughing good-humouredly. "My man will hear."

She let him out of the house, and as she went back she said to herself: "Well! Weak women must provide for a rainy day. And if my poor fellow upstairs do go off—as I sup pose he will soon—it's well to keep chances open. And I can't pick and choose now as I could when I was younger. And one must take the old if one can't get the young."

XI

THE LAST PAGES TO WHICH THE CHRONICLER OF THESE LIVES WOULD ASK THE READER'S attention are concerned with the scene in and out of Jude's bedroom when leafy summer came round again.

His face was now so thin that his old friends would hardly have known him. It was afternoon, and Arabella was at the looking-glass curling her hair, which operation she performed by heating an umbrella-stay in the flame of a candle she had lighted, and using it upon the flowing lock. When she had finished this, practised a dimple, and put on her things, she cast her eyes round upon Jude. He seemed to be sleeping, though his position was an elevated one, his malady preventing him lying down.

Arabella, hatted, gloved, and ready, sat down and waited, as if expecting someone to come and take her place as nurse.

Certain sounds from without revealed that the town was in festivity, though little of the festival, whatever it might have been, could be seen here. Bells began to ring, and the notes came into the room through the open window, and travelled round Jude's head in a hum. They made her restless, and at last she said to herself: "Why ever doesn't father come!"

She looked again at Jude, critically gauged his ebbing life, as she had done so many times during the late months, and glancing at his watch, which was hung up by way of timepiece, rose impatiently. Still he slept, and coming to a resolution she slipped from the room, closed the door noiselessly, and descended the stairs. The house was empty. The attraction which moved Arabella to go abroad had evidently drawn away the other inmates long before.

It was a warm, cloudless, enticing day. She shut the front-door, and hastened round into Chief Street, and when near the Theatre could hear the notes of the organ, a rehearsal for a coming concert being in progress. She entered under the archway of Oldgate College, where men were putting up awnings round the quadrangle for a ball in the Hall that evening. People who had come up from the country for the day were picnicking on the grass, and Arabella walked along the gravel paths and under the aged limes. But finding this place rather dull she returned to the streets, and watched the carriages drawing up for the concert, numerous Dons and their wives, and undergraduates with gay female companions, crowding up likewise. When the doors were closed, and the concert began, she moved on.

The powerful notes of that concert rolled forth through the swinging yellow blinds of the open windows, over the house-tops, and into the still air of the lanes. They reached so far as to the room in which Jude lay; and it was about this time that his cough began again and awakened him.

As soon as he could speak he murmured, his eyes still closed: "A little water, please."

Nothing but the deserted room received his appeal, and he coughed to exhaustion again—saying still more feebly: "Water—some water—Sue—Arabella!"

The room remained still as before. Presently he gasped again: "Throat—water—Sue—darling—drop of water—please—O please!"

No water came, and the organ notes, faint as a bee's hum, rolled in as before.

While he remained, his face changing, shouts and hurrahs came from somewhere in the direction of the river.

"Ah—yes! The Remembrance games," he murmured. "And I here. And Sue defiled!"

The hurrahs were repeated, drowning the faint organ notes. Jude's face changed more: he whispered slowly, his lips scarcely moving:

"*Let the day perish wherein I was born, and the night in which it was said, There is a man child conceived.*"

("Hurrah!")

"*Let that day be darkness; let not God regard it from above, neither let the light shine upon it. Lo, let that night be solitary, let no joyful voice come therein.*"

("Hurrah!")

"*Why died I not from the womb? Why did I not give up the ghost when I came out of the belly? . . . For now should I have lain still and been quiet. I should have slept: then had I been at rest!*"

("Hurrah!")

"*There the prisoners rest together; they hear not the voice of the oppressor. . . . The small and the great are there; and the servant is free from his master. Wherefore is light given to him that is in misery, and life unto the bitter in soul?*"

Meanwhile Arabella, on her journey to discover what was going on, took a short cut down a narrow street and through an obscure nook into the quad of Cardinal. It was full of bustle, and brilliant in the sunlight with flowers and other preparations for a ball here also. A carpenter nodded to her, one who had formerly been a fellow-workman of Jude's. A corridor was in course of erection from the entrance to the Hall staircase, of gay red and buff bunting. Waggon-loads of boxes containing bright plants in full bloom were being placed about, and the great staircase was covered with red cloth. She nodded to one workman and another, and ascended to the Hall on the strength of their acquaintance, where they were putting down a new floor and decorating for the dance. The cathedral bell close at hand was sounding for five o'clock service.

"I should not mind having a spin there with a fellow's arm round my waist," she said to one of the men. "But Lord, I must be getting home again—there's a lot to do. No dancing for me!"

When she reached home she was met at the door by Stagg, and one or two other of Jude's fellow-stoneworkers. "We are just going down to the river," said the former, "to see the boat-bumping. But we've called round on our way to ask how your husband is."

"He's sleeping nicely, thank you," said Arabella.

"That's right. Well now, can't you give yourself half an hour's relaxation, Mrs. Fawley, and come along with us? 'Twould do you good."

"I should like to go," said she. "I've never seen the boat-racing, and I hear it is good fun."

"Come along!"

"How I *wish* I could!" She looked longingly down the street. "Wait a minute, then. I'll just run up and see how he is now. Father is with him, I believe; so I can most likely come."

They waited, and she entered. Downstairs the inmates were absent as before, having, in fact, gone in a body to the river where the procession of boats was to pass. When she reached the bedroom she found that her father had not even now come.

"Why couldn't he have been here!" she said impatiently. "He wants to see the boats imself—that's what it is!"

However, on looking round to the bed, she brightened, for she saw that Jude was apparently sleeping, though he was not in the usual half-elevated posture necessitated by his ough. He had slipped down, and lay flat. A second glance caused her to start, and she ent to the bed. His face was quite white, and gradually becoming rigid. She touched his ngers; they were cold, though his body was still warm. She listened at his chest. All was ill within. The bumping of near thirty years had ceased.

After her first appalled sense of what had happened the faint notes of a military or ther brass band from the river reached her ears; and in a provoked tone she exclaimed, To think he should die just now! Why did he die just now!" Then meditating another mo- ent or two she went to the door, softly closed it as before, and again descended the stairs.

"Here she is!" said one of the workmen. "We wondered if you were coming after all. Come along; we must be quick to get a good place. . . . Well, how is he? Sleeping well still? Of course, we don't want to drag 'ee away if—"

"O yes—sleeping quite sound. He won't wake yet," she said hurriedly.

They went with the crowd down Cardinal Street, where they presently reached the ridge, and the gay barges burst upon their view. Thence they passed by a narrow slit own to the riverside path—now dusty, hot, and thronged. Almost as soon as they had ar- ived the grand procession of boats began; the oars smacking with a loud kiss on the face f the stream, as they were lowered from the perpendicular.

"O, I say—how jolly! I'm glad I've come," said Arabella. "And—it can't hurt my usband—my being away."

On the opposite side of the river, on the crowded barges, were gorgeous nosegays of eminine beauty, fashionably arrayed in green, pink, blue, and white. The blue flag of the Boat Club denoted the centre of interest, beneath which a band in red uniform gave out he notes she had already heard in the death-chamber. Collegians of all sorts, in canoes with ladies, watching keenly for "our" boat, darted up and down. While she regarded the lively scene somebody touched Arabella in the ribs, and looking round she saw Vilbert.

"That philtre is operating, you know!" he said with a leer. "Shame on 'ee to wreck a heart so!"

"I shan't talk of love to-day."

"Why not? It is a general holiday."

She did not reply. Vilbert's arm stole round her waist, which act could be performed unobserved in the crowd. An arch expression overspread Arabella's face at the feel of the arm, but she kept her eyes on the river as if she did not know of the embrace.

The crowd surged, pushing Arabella and her friends sometimes nearly into the river, and she would have laughed heartily at the horse-play that succeeded, if the imprint on her mind's eye of a pale, statuesque countenance she had lately gazed upon had not sobered her a little.

The fun on the water reached the acme of excitement; there were immersions, there were shouts: the race was lost and won, the pink and blue and yellow ladies retired from the barges, and the people who had watched began to move.

"Well—it's been awfully good," cried Arabella. "But I think I must get back to my poor man. Father is there, so far as I know; but I had better get back."

"What's your hurry?"

"Well, I must go. . . . Dear, dear, this is awkward!"

At the narrow gangway where the people ascended from the riverside path to the bridge the crowd was literally jammed into one hot mass—Arabella and Vilbert with the rest; and here they remained motionless, Arabella exclaiming, "Dear, dear!" more and more impatiently; for it had just occurred to her mind that if Jude were discovered to have died alone an inquest might be deemed necessary.

"What a fidget you are, my love," said the physician, who, being pressed close against her by the throng, had no need of personal effort for contact. "Just as well have patience: there's no getting away yet!"

It was nearly ten minutes before the wedged multitude moved sufficiently to let them pass through. As soon as she got up into the street Arabella hastened on, forbidding the physician to accompany her further that day. She did not go straight to her house; but to the abode of a woman who performed the last necessary offices for the poorer dead; where she knocked.

"My husband has just gone, poor soul," she said. "Can you come and lay him out?"

Arabella waited a few minutes; and the two women went along, elbowing their way through the stream of fashionable people pouring out of Cardinal meadow, and being nearly knocked down by the carriages.

"I must call at the sexton's about the bell, too," said Arabella. "It is just round here, isn't it? I'll meet you at my door."

By ten o'clock that night Jude was lying on the bedstead at his lodging covered with a sheet, and straight as an arrow. Through the partly opened window the joyous throb of a waltz entered from the ball-room at Cardinal.

Two days later, when the sky was equally cloudless, and the air equally still, two persons stood beside Jude's open coffin in the same little bedroom. On one side was Arabella, on the other the Widow Edlin. They were both looking at Jude's face, the worn old eyelids of Mrs. Edlin being red.

"How beautiful he is!" said she.

"Yes. He's a 'andsome corpse," said Arabella.

The window was still open to ventilate the room, and it being about noontide the clear air was motionless and quiet without. From a distance came voices; and an apparent noise of persons stamping.

"What's that?" murmured the old woman.

"Oh, that's the doctors in the Theatre, conferring Honorary degrees on the Duke of Hamptonshire and a lot more illustrious gents of that sort. It's Remembrance Week, you know. The cheers come from the young men."

"Ay; young and strong-lunged! Not like our poor boy here."

An occasional word, as from someone making a speech, floated from the open windows of the Theatre across to this quiet corner, at which there seemed to be a smile of some sort upon the marble features of Jude; while the old, superseded, Delphin editions of Virgil and Homer, and the dog-eared Greek Testament on the neighbouring shelf, and the few other volumes of the sort that he had not parted with, roughened with stone-dust where he had been in the habit of catching them up for a few minutes between his labours,

eemed to pale to a sickly cast at the sounds. The bells struck out joyously; and their re-
erberations travelled round the bedroom.

Arabella's eyes removed from Jude to Mrs. Edlin. "D'ye think she will come?" she
sked.

"I could not say. She swore not to see him again."

"How is she looking?"

"Tired and miserable, poor heart. Years and years older than when you saw her last.
Quite a staid, worn woman now. 'Tis the man—she can't stomach un, even now!"

"If Jude had been alive to see her, he would hardly have cared for her any more,
perhaps."

"That's what we don't know. . . . Didn't he ever ask you to send for her, since he came
to see her in that strange way?"

"No. Quite the contrary. I offered to send, and he said I was not to let her know how
ill he was."

"Did he forgive her?"

"Not as I know."

"Well—poor little thing, 'tis to be believed she's found forgiveness somewhere! She
said she had found peace!"

"She may swear that on her knees to the holy cross upon her necklace till she's hoarse,
but it won't be true!" said Arabella. "She's never found peace since she left his arms, and
never will again till she's as he is now!"

THE END